THE DEADLIEST SIN SERIES

COMPLETE COLLECTION

GWYN McNAMEE

Finding Sin, Wrath, Envy, Lust, Pride, Sloth, Greed, Gluttony
© 2017, 2019, 2020,2021, 2022 Gwyn McNamee

To everyone who has sinned...and lived to tell the tale.

FINDING SIN

Some rise by sin, and some by virtue fall.

- William Shakespeare

PROLOGUE

REA

MY LIFE IS OVER.

Almost as if the sky understands what's happening, the black clouds above swirl and release a menacing rumble that shakes the car and rattles the very fiber of my being.

The moment we stop moving and Father opens the door, it's just fucking over.

All of it.

My hopes. My dreams. My freedom. Gone in the snap of his fingers and without a second thought.

If I believed, for one damn second, that I had any chance of succeeding, I would grab for the gun Father keeps at his hip and use it to end my inevitable suffering before it starts, before he turns me over to that man.

That monster.

My future husband.

But Father's watching me too closely for that. He knows me too well. Knows I'll do anything to escape this. Knows I'll fight.

Which is precisely why the bastard made sure I can't resist. His threat was clear. It isn't just the family business at stake. It's Mother's life, too.

He's cruel enough to terrorize her to get me to comply. He has no qualms about using me as a pawn in this sinister game. He doesn't give one fuck if I'm beaten or raped, or anything else happens to me, as long as he gets what he wants.

How can he call himself my father?

This isn't the man I remember as a child. That man was aloof and not around much, but he was never cruel to me. Maybe he was to others behind closed doors. I'm sure he was...now that I know who he is. But he always hid it, hid what he did, from me. Kept me insulated from the violence and deceptions that are part of his world.

Until he needed something only I could provide...

And now, there's no more time to consider what my future looks like. The tires squeal as the car turns the final corner, and we pull up in front of the looming house. The red brick and perfect black shutters look inconspicuous enough, but I know what hides inside. I know the terror that lurks within.

At least, I think I do.

Tarek Morina is ruthless. Cold. The type of killer you never want to cross, and now, he'll be my husband. The man who holds Philadelphia in his sinister hands will have mine in marriage—no matter how much I don't want it. No one fights back against the Albanian mob. Not if they want to survive.

Maybe I don't want to...

Not if it means this kind of life.

Father glances over from his seat next to me in the back of the car and places his hand over mine on my leg. "It will be okay, Rea."

I jerk my hand out from under his, swipe away the tears, and glare at him. If he's going to make me do this, I'm not going along with it without him knowing exactly what he's doing to me. He will *see* and *know* my pain. "How can you say that? How can you say that, knowing what you're sending me into?"

His face doesn't soften for even a second. The hard, craggy lines created by years of smoking and stress deepen, but only because he's angry at me for even voicing it. Not because he feels bad for what he's done.

"I've said it a hundred times, Rea, and this is the last time. You *will* go. You *will* walk up those steps. You *will* kiss your fiancé. You *will* do whatever the fuck he asks of you. You will be a *good* wife. You *will* give him children and whatever else he wants. You will make him happy *at any cost*. Because if you don't, we will *all* suffer the consequences." He leans closer, like it will make his words hit home harder. "I *need* this alliance with Tarek. I need the Morinas to secure our foothold and the future of the family. There are threats on every side now, and we need this. Do you understand me?"

"No." I shake my head, fighting back the sob that threatens to climb up my throat. It won't do any good, anyway. "I don't understand how you can call yourself a father when you're doing this to me—"

The car door next to me opens, and I jerk away and glance out it to find my worst nightmare staring down at me.

Tarek's hard amber eyes that almost darken to a black as he looks down at me match the ones I saw in the photographs of him, only they're even more soulless in real life. The corners of his mouth twist into a grin that sends a shiver down my spine unlike anything I've ever felt before—one that goes deep into my soul, into the very core of me.

I'll never survive this.

"Rea..." He holds out a hand for me, but it isn't a gentlemanly offer. It's more of a command.

I shrink away from him, but Father nudges me forward.

It's time.

I can't run from this.

I can't hide.

This is the end.

I reluctantly place my shaking hand in Tarek's, and he squeezes and pulls me roughly from the car, jerking me onto my feet on the wet pavement. The light rain falling chills my exposed skin in the lowcut, sleeveless dress Father insisted I wear, goosebumps spreading like wildfire. I stumble into Tarek's arms, and he wraps one around my waist and takes my chin in his hand, squeezing until it's almost painful.

"Your father was right. You are quite stunning. Like a little porcelain doll." He leans in and brushes his lips to my ear. "I can't wait to fucking break you."

I choke back a sob and push against his hard chest, trying to get away from him, but he only tightens his grip on my chin until his fingers dig into the sensitive flesh there.

"The more you fight me, the more I'll like it."

Tears well in my eyes, and this time, I can't brush them away. With my hands pinned between us, I'm completely at his mercy. Exactly how he wants it.

"Goodbye, Rea." Father's voice from behind makes me freeze.

Tarek drags his attention away from me and over my shoulder to look at him. "It's been a pleasure doing business with you."

"I look forward to working with you and the Morina *fis*."

My future husband inclines his head toward Father, and the car door slams behind me, sealing my fate.

A flash of movement behind Tarek draws my focus that way. Another set of hard eyes meet mine, on a face identical to my new fiancé's. Only, these are different. Not the endless sea of nothingness from a man with no soul.

These hold something in their depths, so deep you might miss it if you're not searching for it. A hint of humanity. A flicker of regret. Maybe compassion.

Though none of that could come from the man who must be Tarek's brother. I must be hallucinating. Just wishful thinking from a mind flooded with fear and searching for anything to hold on to.

The man offers me a tight, grim smile, almost like he knows what Tarek has planned for me. There's no way he couldn't.

We hold each other's gazes for a moment, and his eyes lighten with an almost golden hue before thunder rumbles overhead and straight through my body. It seems to shatter whatever moment passed between us, and he turns abruptly, walks to the car, pops the trunk, and grabs my bags, his tattoo-covered biceps bulging as he easily lifts them.

Tarek forces my attention back to him with his harsh grip. "Your old life is gone now. Your family. Your friends. All of it. You are mine. Do you understand me?"

My body shakes violently, a bone-deep chill that has nothing to do with the weather settling in.

He tightens his hold on my chin and jerks my head forward until his lips nearly brush mine, and I almost gag at the thought of him kissing me. "Answer me. Do. You. Understand?"

I incline my head a fraction of an inch, all that his hold will allow. "Ye-yes."

"Good."

He releases my chin but keeps his arm wrapped around me, then turns and guides me toward the house.

The other man waits at the top of the steps, just in front of the door of my new home, my bags in his hands, his strong, angular jaw set and locked. His shrewd gaze assesses every movement Tarek and I make, like he's analyzing each step to find the purpose behind it.

We reach the top, stepping onto the concrete porch, and Tarek motions toward him.

"This is Konstandin, my brother, my *kryetar,* and the person I trust most. He's in charge of security, and he will ensure no one can get to you except me." Tarek turns his head my way, that harsh gaze boring into me, almost daring me to question him or beg to leave. "And that you can't get the fuck out."

He waves up at the house almost absently, like he isn't pointing out the place that is to be my jail cell or that Konstandin isn't my new warden.

"This is your new life, Rea. Learn to accept it." Tarek leans in, his lips brushing my ear again. "Because while I like a fight, I'm only going to put up with so much. Do you understand me?"

I give him a sharp nod, and the world spirals around me, my vision going dark around the edges as the reality of my situation fully takes hold.

I was right.

My life is fucking over.

I should have reached for Father's gun.

ONE

Two Weeks After Arrival

REA

No AMOUNT of scalding-hot water pelting my body will wash away the filth on my flesh everywhere that man touched me or this sense of nothingness that has overtaken every fiber of my being.

I scrub at my already red, raw skin, harder and harder, trying to scrape away the remnants of *him* that are now permanently seared into me. All it does is create more soapy suds that rinse off immediately and trickle down the drain in the shower, but it can't remove any of what I'm trying desperately to rid myself of.

Maybe nothing will.

Despite the steam and heat in the bathroom, I can't stop shaking, can't stop feeling like a bucket of ice-cold water has been thrown over me, seeping deep into me, robbing me of any warmth.

It's the same way I felt for the last few weeks every time Tarek was in the same room, even knowing he's in the house. That man certainly lives up to his reputation. He has no qualms about taking what he believes is rightfully his—mainly me. He isn't deterred in the least by the fact that I want nothing to do with him, that I just want to go home.

But that isn't an option.

My fate was sealed the day Father took Tarek's money and made the alliance with him. One I don't understand. My entire life comes down to two men deciding their futures and using me like chattel in the business deal.

It doesn't matter what I want. Doesn't matter that we aren't even legally married yet. Father sold me to him—plain and simple—and now, I'm paying for it.

With my body and my sanity.

I shut off the water and step out of the shower, wrapping myself in the soft, luxuriousness of a plush towel, but even it can't help rid me of this chill. Nor can this beautiful room in this beautiful house, meant for comfort, meant to show off, meant to put its residents at ease, when it's really nothing more than a beautiful prison. A gilded cage in which to keep a bird Tarek doesn't want to fly away.

"This is Konstandin, my brother and the person I trust most. He's in charge of security, and he will ensure no one can get to you except me...and that you can't get the fuck out."

Yet the man who looks exactly like my tormentor has essentially disappeared since the day I arrived, handed off that responsibility to others. One of those lackeys is undoubtedly standing outside the bedroom door I now stare at, guarding the long hallway to nowhere that I can't even walk down without an escort. And even then, only to forced, awkward dinners sitting across the long table from the man determined to break me.

It's my only escape from this room. That and my sleep...

Though that isn't even safe.

I slowly lower myself to the bed and take a deep inhale. The last thing I need right now is to be reliving the nightmares that come more frequently than the good dreams, the ones that bear Tarek's face, his voice, his smell. The ones that encompass even my waking hours.

This is my new reality, and I have to learn to accept it. Because I'm not going anywhere. Tarek and Konstandin make sure of that even when they aren't here personally to tighten the noose around my neck.

At least I have a temporary break with the madman away on business for a few days. Hearing him say those words, telling me he would be gone for a while, sent a flood of relief through me unlike anything I've ever felt. The moment he left this room, I fled to the only safe space where I could try to wash away the memories.

Fruitless effort.

I muster up enough energy to rise from the bed and dress in the clothes Tarek filled the closet and drawers with, clothes he wants me to wear, ones he wants to see me in. Because other than Tarek and Konstandin's men, no one else ever lays eyes on me.

We aren't even married yet, and Tarek has already demonstrated his true colors. He has since the second I arrived. He doesn't want a wife; he wants a slave. He wants someone who will be at his beck and call. Someone who will do as they're told. Someone who will fulfill his needs without complaint.

And I can't complain. *I can't.* Not when Mother's safety is on the line.

How am I supposed to live like this? Forever the center of a madman's whims.

A tear slides down my cheek, but I brush it away as I approach the door.

Don't let them see you cry. Don't let them know you might break, that you're so damn close to it.

Even though he's gone, Tarek's men will keep him updated, feed him information on my every move. I don't have a single doubt in my mind about that. Anything they see, he knows. And I won't give them anything to report. Won't give *him* the satisfaction of seeing me weak.

I pause with my hand on the doorknob, suck in a deep, steadying breath, then twist it open. A new guard stands just outside in the hallway, gun visible at his hip, a very real reminder of why I can't run even if there weren't others in danger.

He turns toward me and opens his mouth to say something, then quickly snaps it closed when he sees me, almost as if he's struggling to find words. Finally, he clears his throat.

"Do you need something, ma'am? Your fiancé has already left."

My fiancé...

The word makes my stomach turn even more than it already was.

"I'm not feeling very well. Could I trouble the kitchen for some toast?"

I haven't had any appetite in weeks, mostly pushing my food around the plate while I avoid making eye contact with my captor. But now, the acid eats away at my stomach so badly that it feels like I'm being consumed alive from the inside out.

The man offers me a hard smile that isn't unkind. "I'm sure we can figure something out."

He inclines his head down the hall toward the central stairwell.

I raise a brow at him. "I can go myself?"

Maybe with Tarek gone, I'll have more freedom here to explore the house and grounds—the beautiful gardens outside my bedroom window.

He smirks, almost amused. "I'll be with you the entire time, and we're just going to the kitchen."

Of course, he will.

No one's going to leave me unattended, especially not with Tarek gone, likely off ruining someone else's life. Maybe even back home in Vlorë with Father, doing whatever it is that was so important that it required me to come here.

But it does beg the question...

Where is Konstandin?

Tarek said he would always be here, always be watching. Yet, I haven't seen him since he set my bags in this room and walked out without a glance back at me.

What is important enough to draw him away from what he's supposed to be doing?

Watching me.

TWO

KONSTANDIN

I THRUST the screwdriver into the man's thigh and twist it, burying the sharp instrument even deeper into his flesh and muscle, drawing out the pain as much as I can to ensure my point comes across crystal clear.

A scream rips from his lips and echoes throughout the warehouse, but none of his buddies will be coming to save him.

Doubt they would even if they weren't in their current state.

I glance around at my handiwork.

Blood pools under the bodies littering the dirty concrete. An hour after their deaths, the blood hasn't fully congealed yet. But without their hearts pumping to keep it flowing and warm, it will soon. It creates a ghastly mosaic—almost beautiful in a deadly, fucked-up sort of way.

Just how I like it.

My own unique, macabre art, spread out on another type of canvas, a poignant display of what happens when you cross the Morinas.

I yank the screwdriver from the man's thigh, blood flowing freely from the wound, and he sags forward against the restraints holding him to the chair, tightening around his already-abraded wrists and ankles. If not for those, he'd be flat on his face on the floor, unable to keep himself upright after the way I've already worked him over. And we're nowhere close to being done yet.

He deserves so much more...and so does the man he works for.

After weeks of digging, traveling, and hunting, I finally have my hands on someone who might actually be able to give me what I need to protect our *fis* and our territory.

I motion with the bloody instrument over my shoulder toward his friends. "Do you know why I killed them and not you?"

The man groans and slowly lifts his head, a trickle of blood pouring out of his mouth. "Because you're every bit the sadistic fuck everyone says you are."

I bark out a laugh and pat him on the back of the head. "Cute, and yes, I am. But there's another reason you're still breathing while your friends are not."

Examining the screwdriver under the harsh overhead florescent lights, the blood shimmers. I've never felt more at ease than with an enemy's blood on my hands, and even though lately, Tarek's behavior has added unusual stress, a grin still draws across my lips at the familiar sight.

I point it at the man I've chosen for this auspicious role. "Not necessarily my weapon of choice, but I'm always ready to use whatever's within reach." I squat in front of him and roll the handle of the Phillips-head between my palms. "I chose *you* because you seemed smart. You seemed like the one who would understand the situation and be most willing to do what needs to be done to save your own life."

The man releases a snort-laugh that makes him wince—no doubt the broken ribs I've already given him a harsh reminder not to do that again. "You're not going to let me live."

I let a cold grin spread across my face. "See"—I tap the side of the screwdriver against his head —"smart." Pushing to my feet, I step back, twirling the make-shift weapon in my fingers. "You're right. I won't. I can't after what you and your boss have done, but what I *can* do is offer you a release from this agony, or"—I spread out my hands—"I can search the warehouse for other fun things we can play with because the screwdriver just isn't cutting it."

In one swift motion, I jab into his opposite thigh. He jerks and cries out a second time, a litany of curses falling from his lips.

"What is it you had hoped to achieve here?" I motion behind me to the pile of crates. "Did you think we wouldn't find out what you were doing? That we wouldn't ensure that it stopped? Did you think the Morinas would just let you walk all over us and wave happily from the sidelines, wishing you luck in your endeavors?"

The man coughs up blood and spits it to the side. "Of course not." He locks hard black eyes with mine. "But we thought we were ready for you and could stand against anything Tarek could throw at us."

I grin at him and raise my eyebrows. "Bit of miscalculation on your part, isn't it?"

Chuckling, I wander back through the bodies on the floor. "One, two, three, four, five, six, seven men guarding one warehouse, and I managed to take out all of them and get you in this position without even breaking a sweat. *Giant* miscalculation on your part, so I think it's time for you to tell me what I need to know." I spin back to face him. "Unless you want to keep playing. "Which"—I twirl the screwdriver in my hand again—"I'm more than happy to do."

It gives me a much-needed break from being in that house, the dark cloud that always seems to hover over it, the one that has only gotten heavier over the years and especially over the last few months.

The information about what the Gashis were doing in our territory that brought me here tonight couldn't have come in at a better time for my sanity. Getting my hands dirty helps keep my mind from wandering to what's been happening.

Tarek's increasing brutality and secrecy, including what's going on with his mysterious new bride-to-be.

Even the blood on my hands and the two weeks that have passed doing Tarek's dirty work can't shake the surprise of him announcing she was coming or his refusal to explain why. Nor can I forget that look in her green eyes, the almost fear when he leaned in and whispered to her while her red hair darkened in the rain. Another woman throwing herself at Tarek, perhaps underestimating what he's capable of.

But something is going on between her father and Tarek, something he doesn't want me to know, and his keeping me in the dark makes my job even harder. This type of work usually gives me exactly the outlet I need. A way to work out the anger and frustration, to use my skill set to ensure this family remains on top, but that's getting harder and harder.

Still, it's what I have to do because it's my job. It's my role as his *kryetar* and as his brother.

I wander over to the workbench at the side of the warehouse where I originally found the screwdriver and examine the haphazard contents strewn across it. "Look here..." I grab a pair of bolt cutters and hold them up. "This—this is one of my absolute favorite toys. You would be amazed at what you can cut off with one of these things."

My victim's face pales even more, the blood still remaining in his body draining away as my words register. "I can't tell you because I don't know."

"I don't believe that. Saban trusts you more than he trusts anyone else. You're an integral piece of the Gashi organization. Don't tell me he wouldn't keep you in the loop about when his next shipment is coming in or inform you who his supplier is."

The man snarls at me, the remaining energy he has only coming from the adrenaline coursing through his veins, struggling desperately to keep him alive. "All I know is what happens here at the warehouse. The inventory comes in and I send it out when I'm supposed to. That's it. Anything else is above my paygrade."

"Again, I'm in a position where I don't believe you." I make my way back over to him slowly, opening and closing the bolt cutters. "Which means...we've come to an impasse."

I shrug slightly and stop in front of him.

"That's okay because I always get what I want eventually. No matter how hard it might be. Or how painful for anyone else..."

I'll get my answers from him, and I'll get my answers about what Tarek is keeping from me.

THREE

REA

FOOTSTEPS IN THE HALL, barely audible with the plush carpet absorbing them, tense my entire body. I hold my breath until my lungs burn, waiting for the knob to turn. It rattles slightly, and the sound vibrates in my chest. I shift back against the headboard, dragging up the covers like a shield against whatever or whoever is coming through that door.

Tarek said he would be gone for a few days, but I wouldn't put it past that man to come back early just to torture me more. To let me get a false sense of security for a few days just to rip it away by showing up unexpectedly while my guard is down.

All I want is to bury myself under the covers farther, but I can't close my eyes without reliving the horrors that have already occurred.

All I can do is wait...

The door swings open, and the familiar large frame and dark head of hair steps into the dimly lit room, and strong, wide shoulders tense, as if he's in a bad mood.

That's going to make this so much worse, so much harder.

Closing my eyes and pretending this isn't happening seems like a good idea, but something about the way he walks, the way he examines me on the bed, makes something flutter deep in my gut. And it isn't fear.

This isn't Tarek.

It's Konstandin.

It's there, just below the surface of his gaze. That tiny hint of something different I saw the day I arrived and haven't seen since.

He stops at the end of the bed and assesses me, his hard, dark eyes sweeping over my body covered in the comforter and zeroing in on my face with a frown. "Why are you awake?"

Why are you coming in if you thought I'd be asleep?

It's what I want to ask, but I don't dare. Not when I know the reputation this man holds proudly. Konstandin is an attack dog, an assassin, a killer who works at the whim of his brother. It didn't click initially when I arrived. I was too distracted by what awaited with Tarek to consider what his brother was capable of. But the Morina brothers didn't get to where they are without the kind of violence most people can't even fathom.

Swallowing thickly, the truth sits on the tip of my tongue, and I almost bite it back. But something about the way he's looking at me makes it tumble from my lips against my own better judgment. "I don't sleep anymore."

One of his dark brows rises slowly, like my answer is the last thing he expected to hear. "How come?"

I focus on the white bedspread, so pure that covers something so tainted, then lock eyes with him, trying to convey the truth without having to say the words. Instead, I squirm under the intensity there, like he's unraveling everything inside me and setting the truth free. I can't handle the force of it, and I relent.

"Because of what Tarek does when he comes."

It's only there for a split second—so brief, I could almost miss it. I probably would have if I hadn't been looking for it, searching for some sort of confirmation of the feeling I've had since I first saw him that day.

But it was there.

The tiniest flinch.

A wince.

A reaction to what I said his brother does.

And it sends a little flutter of hope through my chest, one I probably shouldn't have. Shouldn't allow myself. Because hope isn't what keeps people going in these situations. It's acceptance. It's finding a way to go on while living in a world designed to tear you apart and shatter your will.

Konstandin shifts uneasily, almost as if he can feel the same thing I do. A tension between unspoken words. "Well, he's gone now. You have a temporary reprieve."

"Temporary" being the key word.

Tarek will return, and with him...my living nightmare. But his brother is here now, not wherever Tarek is.

"Where have you been? I thought he said you were in charge of making sure I didn't get into any trouble."

He raises that dark eyebrow at me again—a hint of something I might even mistake as humor dancing in his dark eyes, made even darker by the room. "You're not going to cause any trouble." He squares his shoulders, making himself appear even larger as he looms over me. "Not when you know what it means if you do."

His reproach sends me shrinking back against the headboard again because he's right. It's what has kept me compliant this long—what Tarek would do to me and the threats Father made against Mother. What I know will happen to her if I don't make my fiancé happy.

Konstandin raises a hand and runs it through his hair. Dark-red splotches across his shirt sleeve, just barely visible in the lighting, catch my attention.

I shift forward slightly. "Oh, my God, are you bleeding?"

He freezes and looks at me, then glances at his arm and lowers it. "No. It's never *my* blood."

His words send the same icy chill through my veins that his brother's do. There may be something different about Konstandin, but he is every bit as dangerous as Tarek. Maybe even more so.

Because these tiny flickers, these infinitesimal hints that there might be something behind all the brutality, are likely all just part of a game to get me to do or say something Tarek can use against me.

It's brilliant, really. Use his brother as an olive branch of sorts, someone who might offer some glimmer of potential...something more than the terrors that happen in these walls, only to have him tell my tormentor every word I say and every move I make.

Konstandin's gaze roams over me, taking in everything exposed above the comforter. His jaw tenses, and a muscle there tics. He clenches and unclenches his fists at his sides, tension and anger controlling his body, making it seem even larger, harder, more oppressive. "Don't ever ask questions like that of my brother. I just gave you a pass, but you won't get another one from me. And you won't get *any* from him."

There it is.

The warning is clear. I'm here for one reason only. And if I try to involve myself in anything else, ask any questions about their business, things will get worse for me.

Even though it feels like that's not possible, it definitely is.

These men are notorious for their brutality and for torturing their enemies. Decimating anyone who stands in their way or dares to question them.

Being engaged to Tarek won't earn me any quarter from that.

His threat soundly delivered, Konstandin turns his back on me and stalks to the door without a glance over his shoulder, letting it slam behind him with a finality that seals my fate.

FOUR

Six Weeks After Arrival

KONSTANDIN

I STARE into the bottom of my empty drink glass, but no matter how long I keep my focus there, it doesn't miraculously refill itself, nor do the three—or maybe it's four—Scotches I've already drank do anything to quell the throbbing headache between my eyes as I listen to Ferid rambling on about the current situation with the Gashis in Chicago.

Squeezing the bridge of my nose, I let my eyes drift closed. "Just stop."

"They shot up..." he trails off. "Sir?"

I wait a few seconds and slowly open my eyes to find his brow furrowed.

He shifts restlessly on his feet in front of the desk. "Is, um, everything all right?"

Not even fucking close.

I wave a hand at him. "I know what you're telling me. Everything's going to shit."

It isn't anything I don't already know. I've been fighting the Gashis' encroachment for months while Tarek disappears for days or weeks at a time. The *fis* that was once our ally has become our enemy. Our fathers worked together to secure Albania all those years ago, to remove the Sylas and anyone else who stood in our way, and both the Morinas and Gashis reaped the rewards. Rewards that followed us to the States and allowed us to set up shop here and bring in even more profits.

Yet, it doesn't seem to be enough for the Gashis. Any alliance we had has long since disintegrated.

Ferid recoils slightly and clears his throat. "Um, not exactly. But the Gashis are definitely stepping up their game, probing at our borders to see how far they can extend before we fully retaliate."

Fully retaliate.

That would mean wiping out the family that controls Chicago and the entire surrounding area. It would mean disaster for us, given everything going on with Tarek and whatever he's doing back in Albania. We can't have our focus split right now, and stepping up to take over the void removing the Gashis would create would be spreading ourselves too thin.

I lean back in the leather chair in Tarek's office above the bakery and sigh. "We can't let them take a fucking inch."

He offers me a hard smile. "I know, sir. But..."

"But what?"

His furtive glance out the open door displays his unease. "But your brother. He's..."

"He's what?"

"Does he seem a little...different to you?"

Krishti.

If even Ferid has noticed, it definitely isn't a good sign. I thought maybe I was overreacting, that I was seeing things that weren't there because of how close we are, that I was making it out to be a bigger problem than it actually is. But it seems things have gone too far not to be noticed. Which means it's time to do a little damage control.

I fly from the chair and around the desk before Ferid can react, slamming him back against the wall, my hand at the base of his throat. He struggles slightly, his fingers tightening around my wrist, but I grab my gun with my free hand and force the barrel into his mouth.

"*Mbylle gojën!* Or I'll shut you up permanently!"

He tries to mumble something about the gun, but it comes out as indecipherable, slobbery gibberish.

"You don't question what Tarek does. *"A e kupton?"*"

Tarek is distracted by whatever he's doing back home in Albania and by his new "pet."

Even thinking about Rea in those terms brings a strange tightness to my chest, but I quickly brush away the foreign feeling. She isn't the first woman to garner Tarek's attention, not even the first he's promised to marry. But there's something different about her, the way he is around her. Something that is drawing him off his game. That could be deadly for a man in his position. Which is why he has *me* to watch his back and ensure his business is safe.

Even if it means taking out our own men who ask the wrong questions.

"My brother is well aware of what's going on and is committed to ensuring we maintain our stronghold here and reinforce our alliances back home."

Ferid nods slightly, mumbling around the barrel again, and I pull it from his mouth with a jerk.

He gasps, sucking in several deep breaths, never taking his eyes from mine.

I point the gun at him, not entirely convinced he knows to keep his mouth shut. "Tarek is doing what he needs to do. And I'm doing what I need to do in his absence."

"What do you want me to do about everything we discussed?"

I lower the gun and scrub a hand over my face. If Saban Gashi thinks he has enough power and men to handle all of the Chicago area and step in to clear a path all the way to Philadelphia to create some massive territory, he has another think coming.

Apparently, the message I left last month wasn't sufficient to get the point across. I spilled a lot of blood and killed a lot of his men. Left pieces of one scattered across the border we share. Yet, he still pushes and takes little jabs, attacking our shipments on the road and on the water, trying to hide who is behind it like we won't know it's him.

"I'm going to discuss this with Tarek, and we're going to decide our next move."

"But, sir, if we wait—"

I hold up my hand to stop him. "If we wait instead of lashing out in anger, we will come up with a well-reasoned, well-thought-out plan that can be executed perfectly without risk of rushing into something and having it backfire."

If my years in the Special Operations Battalion taught me anything, it's to be as prepared as possible before making a move but also be ready to act at any time because you never know what's coming for you. That seems especially wise given the fact that Tarek is keeping so much of his plan hidden from me.

Ferid sets his mouth in a grim line. "Yes, sir. And..."

"Was there something else?"

He rubs at the back of his neck and averts his eyes for a second. "About his fiancée..."

I cringe at the word, tightening my hand on the weapon still there. "Yeah? What about her?"

Other than the constant updates I've received from the men, I've steered clear of the house and her. The small bungalow I bought in the suburbs gives me the distance I need, a break from constantly being surrounded by the tension Tarek has created in what was once our shared home. But protecting Rea is my job, and it seems there's something I need to know.

"Well, sir, you know, Dalmat and Ermal have been primarily watching her since her arrival, along with Lorenc, who has filled in occasionally when his duties don't require him to be elsewhere."

"Yes."

Lorenc has spent a great deal of time assisting me in my missions against the Gashis, but he's also the one I trust most in my absence. If he knew whatever Ferid is dancing around, he would have told me.

"They're concerned."

"How come?"

"She never leaves her room, other than when Tarek forces her to come down to the dining room, but when she's there with him, she doesn't really eat. Not even when he's gone, except for an occasional small something from the kitchen. She's not eating enough, sir. And she's not looking...right."

Dreq!

The alliance with Rea's father is essential for our future. Even though Tarek is keeping me in the dark about *why*, he wouldn't have gone to such lengths to get her here or be spending as much time traveling back and forth to Albania if it weren't. This wasn't just about Tarek getting a wife or her father being desperate. It's a two-way deal. It has to be. Having her die before they can even get hitched would certainly throw a wrench into whatever plans Tarek has.

"I'll take care of it."

"Sir?"

"I said I'll fucking take care of it. Now go."

Ferid scurries toward the door.

"Anything we discussed doesn't leave this office."

His eyes dart down to the gun in my head, and he swallows thickly, rubbing at his throat absently. "Of course not, sir."

The last thing I need right now is for the men to be discussing how unhinged Tarek is becoming. An out-of-control leader with the type of power he has is more dangerous than just about anything.

Except maybe me.

The door slams shut behind Ferid, and I lean back against the desk and reach for my glass to down the rest of it.

As much as I would love to believe this will all pass, that Tarek will regain his senses and Rea will adjust to the new living situation, something stabbing at my gut tells me otherwise.

Hiding out up here while Tarek is away, shoring up our alliances, and making new ones isn't an option. The business has to keep running, and it's in my hands when he's out of reach.

I just don't want to deal with it right now.

FIVE

KONSTANDIN

THE FAMILIAR SCENT wafting up from the kitchen finally draws me out of the office and down the back stairs. Each step brings with it a memory I hoped would stay buried back in Albania when I came to start my new life here with Tarek, but some things are impossible to forget.

And scent can be such a powerful force.

My feet hit the tile on the ground floor, and I make my way toward the kitchen, avoiding the bakery and the chattering people inside it. My mouth waters the closer I get to the smell, and I step in and fight the grin on my face as I pull the old woman in the white apron into my arms from behind.

She yelps, jerking her head to the side to look over her shoulder. "*Djalosh!*" Pressing her hand over her chest, she sucks in a shaky breath. "You scared the crap out of me."

I lean down and press a kiss to her wrinkled cheek. "I'm sorry, *teto*. But I smelled you making *byrek*, and I couldn't resist coming down for one."

The same kind smile she's had since I was a child curls her lips, and she pats me on the arm. "I have a whole box of them over there for you to bring back to the house."

"Thank you, *teto*."

"I know how much your brother loves them."

I release her and grab the box from the counter to avoid responding to her comment. He's the last thing I want to dwell on right now.

With Tarek gone, it's a momentary break from the craziness that's been happening the last few months. It's no longer just about protecting our territory here in Philadelphia. Now, it's become a battle for more.

More power. More money. More men. More people who worship at Tarek's feet. More who fear him and what the Morinas can do.

More and more and more...

It's all he ever wants. It's all anyone ever wants.

Except me.

All I wanted was to get out, to get away from the hell I lived in, to get away from the history there, the war and the pain I had to endure and inflict, but here, all we're doing is creating new bloodstains, new enemies.

I won't discuss that with Drita. Her life is easy here, baking and living under our protection. She doesn't need to be dragged into the gritty, harsh realities of our lives outside what she sees. Not when she's finally secure and happy.

And baking some of my favorites.

I flip open the box and pull out a *byrek*. The soft pillow of dough gives slightly between my fingers, and I take a bite and let the familiar flavors of feta and spinach dance across my tongue. Warm memories of eating these in her kitchen as a child flood my mind, momentarily pushing away the concerns weighing so heavily on my shoulders.

"Perfection, as always."

Drita *tsks*. "Now, now, *djalosh*, don't go eating all of them. Bring some back for the boys. I know Lorenc loves them, too."

I wink at her. "Of course."

If Lorenc or the other men found out I had a whole box of *byrek* and didn't give them any, Tarek would come home to a mutiny. As it stands, it sounds like he may come back to a starved fiancée and men who think he's mentally unstable.

I press another kiss on Drita's cheek on my way out with the box in hand and head down the back hallway. Pushing out the rear door into the afternoon sunshine offers a bit of relief from the stifling, oppressive feel of being in Tarek's office all day, and I beeline to my car.

Usually, getting behind the wheel and flooring it on the drive to the house gives me a release from whatever stresses threaten to break me any given day, but today, the closer I get to home, the tighter my shoulders become, and a headache starts to form at the base of my skull.

I reach back and rub at it absently, trying not to think about the current predicament, but it's impossible not to.

Rea isn't the first—and surely won't be the last—woman who thought she could tame Tarek Morina, who imagined herself sitting at the right hand of one of the most powerful men in the country as his partner, only to realize he doesn't have one and never will. We shared a damn womb and the man still doesn't consider me one. He would never let a woman have any control over his empire, never let anyone in any more than he has me—and he keeps me at arm's length in so many ways.

Even now, when he's off "taking care of business," I'm not entirely sure *where* he is exactly or why. The deals he arranges, like securing the marriage to Rea, are increasingly happening behind closed doors. Ones I'm on the wrong side of.

He's becoming more and more secretive. And that makes everyone uneasy.

Especially me...

Still, I need to focus on the most imminent issue. The one I *do* have control over—Rea. She may just be another in a long line of women who have tried to be with Tarek, but none of them have ever done this. They've thrown themselves at him. They've sacrificed their freedom to gain the power and money he offers. They've bent over backward and done things they never thought they could to try to please him. They've endured his violence and his anger and his "games." But none of them have ever gone on a hunger strike, and if he comes back from his trip to find her sick or even worse, I'm going to be the one who pays for it.

Because she's *my* responsibility.

One I can't skirt any longer, even though the thought of her selling herself to a man like Tarek makes me want to let her languish in her own misery. She put herself in this position; she should have to deal with the consequences. But still, I don't want to face Tarek's wrath if he comes back to her any different than how he left her.

I pull through the gates, up the driveway, and park in front of the house. Lorenc opens the front door as I climb from the car and waits for me on the top step.

His focus darts immediately down to the box in my hands. "*Byrek?*"

I nod and flip it open for him. "Drita sent them just for you."

He snorts and takes a bite, scanning the front lawn of the house and the street for any threats—always vigilant even when enjoying a snack. "Good thing your brother isn't here. He'd be pissed two are missing."

"No shit."

I push past him to the door, and he follows me and locks it behind him. No one gets in or out of this house without Lorenc or me knowing, and the cameras all over the property ensure it's the same across all the acreage.

Tarek wanted a secure compound, and I've done my best to ensure he gets what he wants.

Keeping Tarek happy means, he's less volatile and less likely to make bad decisions. Which is why I head straight for the stairs to deal with the Rea situation before it deteriorates any more.

Lorenc's footsteps follow me across the foyer. "Where are you going?"

I pause at the bottom, my hand on the carved oak banister, and turn back toward him. "Ferid came and saw me today. Told me about the problem with Rea."

Lorenc winces slightly and shifts his focus away from me as he shoves the final bite of his *byrek* into his mouth. He swallows thickly and eventually returns his focus to me. "Everyone's noticed it, Konstandin, but everyone's afraid to speak up. You know what happened the last time anyone did."

"I sure as hell do."

I had to get a new pair of boots because I couldn't get the fucking bloodstains out of the ones I wore when I dealt with the man who questioned Tarek about how he was treating the last woman he had here.

That poor fucker ended up in fifteen pieces in the Delaware River, and I ended up missing what could have otherwise been a good night's sleep.

I tighten my hand on the banister. "I'll take care of it."

My foot doesn't even hit the next step before Lorenc calls out.

"Don't think you're safe just because he's your brother."

I glance over my shoulder at him. "Believe me, I'm not stupid or naïve enough to think that. I'm just protecting all our asses. If he comes back and sees her in bad shape, you know who's going to pay for that?"

Lorenc presses his lips together in a thin, firm line, his hands propped at his hips. He inclines his head to me in understanding and watches as I turn back to the steps and make my way to the top.

The long, bleak hallway to the bedroom lies in front of me, and I make my way down it slowly, toward the room where Rea has been locked since the day she arrived—the room where he locks all of them.

SIX

REA

THE WORDS on the page in front of me blur together, and I squeeze my eyes closed, trying to fight off the tears threatening to come again. I don't have the energy to cry anymore.

Even though Tarek has a chef here who will make me anything I want, everything tastes like dirt. My stomach won't stop churning—the acid eating away at the lining the way Tarek eats away at my will.

At least he's gone again. These brief respites from the terror of living with that man are the only thing keeping me going. Days and sometimes weeks where I don't have to see my tormentor. Don't need to be reminded of what Father did by giving me to a madman. But the more I think about him coming home this time, the worse it gets. That acid in my empty stomach burns up my throat, and I press my hand over my mouth and swallow it back.

My best efforts to lose myself in the book on my lap are failing. It's usually my one escape from this place, the only way I can free myself from this room and go to other worlds where the problems of fictional characters occupy my mind instead of my own.

Not today, though.

Sitting in the afternoon sunlight in the window seat hasn't even helped. Likely because he's been gone long enough that every creak of steps in the hallway makes me freeze, anticipating him walking through the door.

It hasn't been him, though, just the same goons who work to ensure I can't get away—or do anything else, for that matter. I can stare at the gardens all I want out of this prison window, but setting foot on the manicured lawn or pebbled walkways that wind through the flowers and topiaries can only happen in my dreams.

I try to return to my book, but murmured voices in the hallway reach me through the door and send ice through my veins.

Tarek is back...

Each time he leaves, I hope something will happen and he won't return, but I'm never that lucky.

Though, there seems to be *some* luck today because when the door opens, it isn't Tarek...

Konstandin enters slowly, cautiously, almost like he's afraid of what he'll find inside my room. His unease should put me more on edge. Especially since he's been absent since our last confrontation, letting his men continue to guard me rather than doing it himself. Only instead of dread settling over me, all the breath I've been holding in my lungs since I first heard the voices in the hall rushes out in one long whoosh of relief.

This man isn't any less dangerous than Tarek, but he won't lay a hand on me. His loyalty is to his brother, and that's who I belong to now. I'm Tarek's to do with what he will, and Konstandin is going to ensure he can continue to do just that.

His hard gaze immediately lands on me, but it holds none of that flicker of gold, that hint of humanity and understanding I thought I'd seen hiding there in the past.

They might look exactly the same. They might even be able to switch places and convince some people they are each other. But it's the eyes that give them away. Tarek's hold nothing but contempt and anger, but Konstandin's usually have something more. Not today, though.

This time, Konstandin is pissed, the look he gives me so much like the one Tarek often holds that I actually shift back farther onto the window seat to put even more distance between us.

His hand tightens around a pink bakery box as he approaches me slowly, his gaze darting down to the book on my lap then back up at me. "I brought you something."

He holds out the box toward me, and my stomach rumbles so hard that it's almost painful.

I swallow through my unease at having him so close, pressing my back against the molding of the window when I can't retreat anymore. "I'm not hungry."

Konstandin's lips twist into a sneer. "Bullshit." He motions over his shoulder toward the still-open door. "You think my men haven't been telling me what you've been doing? You think I don't know you haven't been eating?" He shakes his head, anger tightening the muscles in his neck and jaw. "I'm not going to let Tarek come home to find you fucking starved to death!"

"What does it matter?"

His free hand tightens into a fist at his side. "Believe me. It *fucking* matters."

The anger in his response rushes icy terror through me, but at the same time, a scent hits my nose. Something emanating from the box. Something familiar. Something that warms my chest in a way I haven't felt since I arrived here.

"What is that?"

"*Byrek.* My mother's cousin makes it at the bakery. I thought something familiar might help."

My mouth waters, and for a moment, it's almost like I'm back at home, sitting with Mother in the kitchen, helping make the dough and various fillings.

Konstandin takes a step closer and flips open the box. "Eat or I'll fucking make you."

I gape up at him. "You would do that? Force feed me?"

He leans over me, bracing his free hand on the wall above my head until his face is so close that I can see the gold in his eyes reflecting the sun streaming in the window. "If I have to, you bet your fucking ass, I will. It's *my* job to keep you safe, and part of that means keeping you *alive.*"

With a monster like this so close, the last thing I should do is offer a snide remark, but I can't bite it back. "So your brother can continue to terrorize me?"

Konstandin snorts and shakes his head, a little half grin that holds zero humor pulling at his lips. His eyes darken again, and he leans in even closer. "You *chose* this, *zemër.* You *chose* to come here. You're just one in a *very* long line of women who thought they would win Tarek's heart and sit beside him as he ruled his empire, who only wanted his money and the prestige that comes with being with him. You *had* to know that came with drawbacks and consequences. So, I don't want to hear you complain. You *chose* this life; now, you have to live it."

He shoves the box onto my lap on top of the book and whirls around to stalk toward the door while I sit stunned.

What?

I set the box on the window seat and rise to my feet. My legs shake under me, both because I've barely eaten in weeks and because my anger at this assumption about the situation has sent adrenaline coursing through me. "That's what you think? That I *chose* to come here?"

He freezes with his hand on the doorknob and turns his head slightly. "They all do. You're no different than any of them. You came from a family with power and money and sought a man who had more of it. A man who could spoil you rotten and give you what you thought you deserved. Accept the consequences and fucking *eat.*"

The sharp slam of the door behind him reverberates through the room and into my chest, sending me staggering back to drop onto the window seat again. Tears threaten to fall, but I blink them away and inhale a deep breath to try to calm my racing heart.

That familiar smell invades my nose and makes my stomach gurgle again. I turn slightly toward the pink box, and my hand moves almost of its own volition to pick one up. I lift it to my mouth and take a single bite. The flavors of my childhood flood my taste buds, igniting a thousand memories of a time when things were so different.

When I was in the dark about who and what Father was. When I hadn't become just something he could use to advance his own interests. When Mother wasn't being used as a hostage to ensure my compliance.

No matter how much I want to, I can't deny how good it tastes. How good it feels to eat something I love so much.

I chew slowly, savoring the bite for as long as it lasts, then swallow, the feeling foreign after barely eating for so long. My stomach rumbles—either in protest or excitement—and I can't stop myself from taking another bite, and another, until the *byrek* is gone and I'm left staring at my empty hand.

Konstandin Morina just got me to eat, something I never thought I'd be able to do again and actually enjoy it.

But the man despises me. He believes I'm only here for one thing, believes I deserve where I am and what I'm suffering because I *chose* it. He thinks I'm some gold-digging whore who wanted Tarek Morina and all that he controls. And he only came to see me to ensure his brother's investment stayed intact.

I can't let myself believe Konstandin Morina is any different than his brother. If I do, I might do or say something that will increase my anguish.

SEVEN

Two Months After Arrival

KONSTANDIN

A COLD, heavy rain falls from the dark, menacing sky, as oppressive as the weight that settles on my chest as I step out onto the front porch with Lorenc to watch Tarek's car pull up in front of the house.

He's back. Again.

Another mysterious trip. Another reappearance as if he hasn't just abandoned me here without telling me what the fuck is going on to deal with threats to our business and a fiancée who's balancing on the edge of breaking in a way that can't be repaired.

Lorenc rushes forward, but Tarek shoves open the door before Lorenc can get it for him and storms out of the car into the rain, his jaw locked tight and his eyes ablaze with a fury I haven't seen in a long time.

Ferr! I guess his meeting didn't go as planned.

We all know what that means. Tarek in a shit mood doesn't bode well for anyone. And the fact that he is keeping me in the dark about what he's doing means I can't protect us the way I need to.

I greet him at the top of the stairs with a hard smile. "Something we need to talk about?"

It's the same opening I give him each time he returns from a trip. The same request for him to fill me in, to let me do my fucking job with all the information available instead of the bits and pieces I've been able to scrounge together from the sources willing to give me anything.

He scowls at me, the rain soaking his thick, dark hair, trickling down the side of the face he shares with me. It's the same look he's always given me when he's pissed, the one that warns me to back off.

But I have no intention of doing that. Not anymore.

I lean toward him close enough that neither Lorenc, Noar, nor Manhar, who climb out of the car after Tarek, can hear me. "You know, it'd be a lot easier for me to help you if I went with you on these trips and knew exactly what the fuck was going on instead of getting stonewalled by you."

Tarek rears back slightly and narrows his eyes on me. "I can't have you with me when I need you protecting what's here while I'm gone, can I?"

Disdain drips off each of his words, and he isn't completely wrong about that. While I could leave Lorenc in charge here more permanently, it's ultimately my job to do whatever Tarek needs.

I never should have said anything, but something's going on. Something big. It eats away at me. Tickles every nerve. Ignites that sense of impending doom. That feeling something is coming. It's what kept me alive during the war, warned me when something was about to go down. It's the last thing I want to be feeling with regard to Tarek. Still, I can't ignore it.

The secret meetings. Disappearing for days, sometimes weeks at a time. Getting my usual sources to clam up about what he's been doing in Albania when he goes. Showing up more tense and angry. Becoming more aggressive with Rea and more volatile with the men and me. And I've only made things worse by saying something, especially out here with witnesses.

Tarek knows better than to lay into me in front of them, though. He may be the boss and demand loyalty from them, but I've *earned* it from them. If we ever came to blows, the chances of the men taking my side in the moment are high, even if they would suffer the ultimate consequences in the end for betraying Tarek.

I'll pay for it as soon as we're alone.

I follow him into the house and up the first few stairs but catch his arm before he can move up farther. Tightening my grip on his bicep, I incline my head toward the office. "We *need* to talk."

He jerks his arm from my hold and shakes his head, rolling his shoulders and fidgeting like he's uncomfortable in his own skin. Anxious doesn't make for a solid leader, yet that's exactly what he is now. "Not right now. I need to release a little tension..."

His eyes drift up the stairs.

Rea...

"That's part of what we need to talk about."

The longer Rea is here, the worse things get. I may have been able to get her to eat by bringing her some tastes of home from the bakery and having the chef prepare some of my favorites for her, but her mental state hasn't improved. Keeping her locked up in there and treating her the way he does is going to lead to a result neither of us will be happy with.

Tarek loves to break the women who come here for him but breaking them is different than burying them. If Rea means anything to a deal he has going on behind the scenes with her father, this could spell disaster.

He narrows his eyes on me. "Something wrong with her?"

"Office. *Now.*"

Talking to him like that isn't wise. Every one of us knows that. Even as a child, he would snap at me if I dared stand up to him. My only hope is that in this moment, he sees me as his brother, not his enemy, and listens.

He grinds his teeth together, fists his hands at his side, and pushes a finger into my chest. "Fine..." He leans in close. "But if you ever question me again in front of the men, you know the consequences."

Of course, I do. I'm usually the one getting my hands bloody executing anyone who stands in Tarek's way...

I turn away from him and move down the steps, with him hot on my heels, seething and only withholding his wrath long enough for him to make it into the office.

He steps past me at the threshold, and Lorenc offers me a sympathetic look where he stands near the front door before I seal myself into the room with a man about to blow.

Tarek stands with his back to me, fists flexing. "What's so important that it can't wait? That you had to *insult* me in front of the men?"

I wave my hands in front of me. "All of *this*! For months, you've been disappearing for days and weeks at a time, not giving me, your brother and your goddamn *kryetar,* any idea what the fuck is going on, what sort of deals you're making."

The day Rea arrived flashes through my head, the light rain falling, the look in her eyes before her father drove away and left her in Tarek's hands. The shudder that rolled through her body when Tarek leaned in and whispered something into her ear.

Pacing, I shove my hands back through my hair. "Then, Rea just *showed up* here one day, and all you tell me is that you have an agreement with her father. I assumed that meant you were marrying her in order to secure some sort of alliance. That she was here of her own volition, just another one of your women, moving from one family to another, trying to work her way up the power ladder." I point upstairs. "But that girl is fucking terrified. She has no idea why any of this is happening and acts like this is all some crazy new world to her."

He turns to face me slowly, his eyes darkening to almost black.

"Why are you making me keep her prisoner? I thought you wanted me to keep her safe from our enemies, but the longer she's here, the clearer it becomes to me that there's something else going on."

Tarek takes a half-step toward me. "She's my fucking fiancée, and I do with her as I please. And you, as my brother, do what I tell you to do, and as my *kryetar*, you do what I tell you to do."

"You're too hard on her, Tarek."

"Are you telling me what I should or should not do with my own fiancée?"

I shake my head. "I'm not, Tarek. But what you're doing to her has consequences. Dark ones I don't think you're going to like in the end. If she's at all important for some reason, if her father is to whatever you have planned, then shouldn't you be keeping her happy instead of slowly breaking her down?"

He raises a dark eyebrow at me. "Maybe leaving you here by yourself has given you the impression you're the one in charge. Let's make something clear. When we left Albania and came here, you knew your place. You knew what we were starting here, that I was going to need to rely on you. I can't rely on somebody who questions everything I do and thinks he knows better. So, tell me, do you think it's your fucking place to tell me what to do with my woman?"

I release a heavy sigh. I've never stepped in with any of the women he's had here, never interceded. Never *wanted* to. Remaining detached keeps you alive, and I have no intention of ever giving myself a weakness. "No, of course not. I just don't want to see you lose her if it could be avoidable. It wouldn't be the first time..."

That comment hangs in the air between us, thick with the words I'm not saying. But he knows exactly what I'm referring to—the many women who have come and gone. Some angry, others completely destroyed by him.

"If that girl does something to end her suffering, what do you think is going to happen with her father?" I raise an eyebrow at him. "Why don't you just fucking tell me why this alliance with him is so important? I don't get it. He's nobody. Nothing but a street-level thug who likes to pretend he's a big shot. What do you need from him so badly? We already control half the damn country and now Philadelphia. What does he offer that we don't already have?"

Tarek considers me for a moment, almost like he's contemplating how much to tell me. "Things back home have changed a lot since we left, Konstandin."

"You think I don't *know* that?"

It's been years since I've been home.

Running the business here allows Tarek to travel home often and take care of things there. Yet, things have shifted. Tensions have grown with the other families. People want more and are willing to do things to take it.

"It's my *job* to know what's happening, Tarek, but my sources have remained suspiciously quiet lately, unwilling or unable to give me what I need. And you've kept me busy here, ensuring I can't travel to find out personally. It makes me question what the fuck you've been up to. What kind of shit do you have us in the middle of, Tarek?"

"Things have been in flux for a while. The streets are unsettled in a way I've never seen them. Big changes are coming, ones that will affect us here. Ones that will potentially change everything —and not just for us. The Gashis in Chicago, too. All the Albanian families."

Another vague deflection that only tells me what I already know. "I know the Muratis and Delvinas have been instigating, trying to expand their territory. That isn't anything new." Ever since we expanded here, it's left us vulnerable there to other *fis* stepping up. "Tell me what I need to know to make sure we stay protected."

"Your top priority is keeping things secure and running here. Where do we stand with the Gashis since we last spoke?"

I sigh and scrub a hand over my face. His shift in topic was intentional, but pushing him doesn't seem to be getting me answers. "Basically, the same. He continues to deny involvement with anything happening inside of our territory. We know it is him. I've already taken out three of his men, and it hasn't been enough to stop him pushing into our business."

Tarek presses his lips together tightly. "I'll take care of it myself."

"What are you going to do, Tarek? We can't reason with him. We can't even frighten him. That man has the same ice in his veins that we do. Look at the family he comes from. Look at what his brother has done. What are you going to do that is going to change anything that I haven't already?"

I've spilled enough blood to paint all of Chicago red, yet it hasn't stopped Saban.

"I rely on you to get things done, Konstandin."

"Because I don't mind getting my hands bloody. Because I don't think twice about it. Because we insulate you from the things that could get you sent away to prison for the rest of your life. Not because you know better."

He steps up to me until we're almost chest to chest, fury emanating off him in waves. "We may have shared a womb, *vëlla*. We may share a face. But don't act like we share the same role here. You know yours, so stop overstepping, or I'll stop you and you'll end up in a body bag on the way back to Vlorë to be buried next to Mother and Father."

His threat doesn't faze me. I've always been the more lethal of the two of us. Always been the one who was willing to do whatever it took. Tarek has always let his emotions control him. Not having them allows me to be *in* control. And he could never hurt me. Not because he might not *want* to, but because he could never get close enough to do it without my knowing.

But it does make one thing clear—I have to find out what's happening back home. I need to know where he's going once he lands, who he's meeting with besides Rea's father, what they're saying in their meetings...and I have to do it without making anyone aware I don't know already. No one can suspect Tarek and I aren't on the same page, that he's keeping me in the dark.

"And as for my fiancée..." Tarek presses a finger into my chest again. "We'll be getting married in a few months. A very public affair that's very important to our future, so everyone who is anyone will be there. I've already picked a date and begun arrangements. You keep her here. You get her what she needs. And you do what you need to keep her safe. I don't want to hear another fucking word about it. She is important. Very. We need her for our end game, and I'm going to go make sure I get what I need from her now."

He slams his shoulder against mine intentionally on his way out the door, then storms up the stairs with heavy footsteps that echo through the foyer ominously.

Keeping Rea safe from the outside world is the easy part.

It's everything else I'm worried about.

EIGHT

Three Months After Arrival

KONSTANDIN

THE SHARP SUMMER sun finally breaks through the clouds that have seemed to linger the last few weeks like a harbinger of doom. Though, I can't simply blame the weather. Some of that feeling stemmed from my confrontation with Tarek when he returned from his last trip and the unsettled tension that has hung between us and over the entire organization since then.

My sources continue to stay tight-lipped about what Tarek has been doing when he isn't here. Tracking where he takes the jet isn't hard, but once he lands, he disappears like a ghost. Like we were both trained to do all those years ago. It's a skill set that served us well in wartime, but when I'm trying to keep tabs on him, it only leads to more frustration.

He's spending a lot of time back home in Vlorë, meeting with Rea's father behind closed doors, and whatever threats they've made to stop them from keeping me informed have worked. The men who usually get me what I need, who keep me apprised of what I need to know when I'm here, fear Tarek more than they fear me.

Which is why I end another useless call with a source, shove open the back door of the house, and step into the sunlight, hoping the warmth might relieve some of what's been building inside me over the last few months.

Things are changing. Shifting. The balance of power back home doesn't just affect things there. Every move someone makes in Albania has a ripple effect here in the States.

His words from our faceoff a few weeks ago still ring in my head.

Big changes are coming...

All I asked was to be let in on what was happening so I could do my fucking job. Yet, he couldn't do that. Couldn't give me what I needed. Instead, I've been doing my job silently—protecting *this* house, ensuring our territory isn't infiltrated by any rival groups, watching our borders for more bullshit from the Gashis. Tarek may have said he would deal with Saban, but I don't trust that man for one fucking minute. He has the balls to try to take from us, so he won't back down easily.

Which has left me standing here with my face turned up to the sky, absorbing the warmth and sunshine. I let my eyes drift closed and try, for one moment, to forget what a clusterfuck this all is. But as soon as I turn around to face the house again, a stunning reminder of all that I don't know stares down at me from a window on the second floor.

Rea...

Whatever is going on has something to do with her. Tarek has never been so concerned about any of the women he brings here—for their safety and security. He may believe he has a right to do whatever he wants to her, but he damn well made it clear no one else will touch her and nothing can ever threaten her.

She's important.

But why?

It's time I try to find out. If Tarek won't give me answers, she will.

I open the back door and make my way up to her room. Tarek may have everyone too afraid to talk to me, but Rea will. I'll make her.

The moment I open the door, she turns from where she still stands at the window, her brow furrowed in question.

"Come on."

One of her pale eyebrows rises. "Where are we going?"

Motioning back into the hallway, I step to the side of the doorjamb to allow her space to pass me. "Outside to the gardens."

Her mouth opens and closes a few times before she slowly she approaches me. "You're *allowed* to take me outside?"

Her confusion is to be expected. In all the time she's been here, she hasn't been allowed to set foot outside the house, and she's barely even left this room.

Still, I scowl at her choice of words. "I'm *allowed* to do anything I want. I'm in charge here—of the estate, of you—I'll do whatever the hell I want."

She recoils slightly, but when I sweep out my arm toward the open door, she squares her shoulders and slips past me into the hall. Despite having been cooped up in here for months, the light scent of something sugary floats off her through the air and fills my lungs.

Fresh. Sweet. Innocent.

All the things men like Tarek and me destroy. Yet, she hasn't broken. She hasn't been crushed under the weight of what Tarek is doing to her. There may be cracks. She may be holding on by a thread. But she still has a fire in her that hasn't been quenched. At least, not yet.

She pauses just outside her room and waits for direction from me. Her scent still lingering in my nose, I leave plenty of room as I move past her and head down the back stairs. Soft footsteps follow tentatively, and I open the back door and let her pass, holding my breath until she's well outside.

The deep inhale of fresh air I take helps clear my head, and I motion for her to head down the path to the left, toward the formal gardens. It's one of my favorite parts of the property and the thing I miss about now living in my own house—even though I desperately needed the separation from Tarek and his place.

I fall into step beside her down the pristine gravel, our feet crunching against it and filling the silent afternoon air. She chances a furtive glance at me, then returns her focus to the topiaries and flowers on either side of us. A rainbow of colors that belie the darkness that lives in the austere building to our left.

Unlike Tarek, who prefers to spend his time holed up in the den or office, the gardens are where I find myself when I need to think. Just like back home, growing up on Grandfather's land and exploring the wilderness surrounding it. Back before we knew what we were a part of. Before we understood who the Morinas really were or why people respected the family so much. We were just boys, chasing Agron and making her squeal with delight until Mother called us in for dinner. There was an innocence that we lost a long time ago. One Rea still manages to hold even with all she's been subjected to.

Now, Tarek and I are at each other's throats, and Agron has fully removed herself from the family business. She played her role and got out as soon as she could. She reinvented herself, became Adelina. Buried the role she played for Father and created a whole new life. Part of me envies her for that, but this was always my place. What I was born for. I just always thought Tarek and I were doing it together. He may be five minutes older and, therefore, the true *head* of the Morina family, but we've always been an unstoppable team, and now, it feels more like he sees me as an obstacle in his way to something I can't quite see.

Just like I can't figure out his situation with Rea. The abject horror in her words the last time we spoke still sticks in my chest like a knife that's been thrown into it.

"That's what you think? That I chose to come here?"

They all have. Every single woman who has ever been with Tarek has done so by choice. He doesn't need to force women to come here. They *want* to be close to him. Want to be *with* him. And they do things they never imagined to try to keep him happy before they leave. But Rea's different. So damn different.

She twists her hands together in front of her stomach as we wander down the path—silent except for the crunch of our shoes on the gravel. "Why did you bring me out here? I thought Tarek wanted me kept in the house."

I assess her out of the corner of my eye, unwilling to make direct eye contact with her when I have an ulterior motive. "It's the first beautiful day we've had in a long time, and you've been cooped up in there for far too long." I let out a deep sigh and finally glance at her to find her soft-green eyes watching me intently. "I know Tarek isn't...easy to deal with. You need to get out of that room."

A soft hand wraps around my forearm, and I freeze mid-step as her fingers tighten, just like the vise around my chest.

"Thank you."

Her soft words float through the air to me, and I squeeze my eyes shut and shake off her grip.

"Don't thank me." I turn my head to meet her gaze. "This is a temporary escape. One you won't get often. Tarek will be back from his trip soon, and he won't allow you out of the house while he's here."

"Are you going to get in trouble for letting me?"

I fully face her and take a step toward her, towering over her much smaller frame and making her crane her neck up to look at me with wide, terrified eyes. "I can handle my brother. My job is to keep you safe for him, and that includes making sure you *eat* and get fresh air when you need it. I'm just doing my *job*." The memory of her hand wrapped around my arm returns with an unexpected vengeance, warming my blood more than the high sun does my skin. "*Don't* make the mistake of thinking I'm doing this for any other reason."

She slowly raises an eyebrow at me, her arms crossed over her chest protectively. "Like because you're a *human being?*"

The growl rumbles low in my chest and makes her take a half-step back. "Don't mistake this for kindness or weakness, Rea. This is a necessity. I see what this is doing, and I don't want to have to deal with Tarek if anything happens to you. For some reason, you mean something to him in a way no other woman ever has."

And I know it has nothing to do with him *loving* her. Men like us are incapable of love, of even beginning to care about someone that deeply. Whatever his reason, it isn't genuine feelings for her. It's about control and something larger.

"What is your father doing for him that's so important? What makes *you* so important?"

I need answers. Ones only she can give.

Tell me, Rea. Tell me what I need to know.

Her pale-pink lips tremble slightly, but she doesn't look away, just holds my gaze as if letting go of it would make her float off into space. "Nothing. I'm not important at all."

Liar.

NINE

REA

KONSTANDIN SNARLS and takes another step closer to me until I can practically feel the anger rolling off him. "*Bullshit*. Tarek arranged this marriage to you to create some sort of alliance with your father, so there's something you or your father have offered him that he thinks he needs for his plans. Tell me what that is."

I throw up my hands and shake my head, his closeness making my legs quiver enough to make me feel unstable on the gravel walkway. "I don't *know!* Until a few months ago, I didn't even know what my father *did* for a living. He kept me in the dark, led me to believe he ran a bunch of different businesses, but I never knew he had any connections to..." I shift uneasily and dart my gaze away from Konstandin and toward a patch of beautiful white roses. "Well...you know..."

Organized crime.

That's what this is. The Morinas are one of the most powerful families in Albania. Everyone knows them and fears them, has heard the stories of what Konstandin and Tarek and their father and grandfather before them have done. And then they came here to stake their claim on Philadelphia and start an entirely new territory. I just never realized Father was involved, how deeply he was connected to this world.

Konstandin snorts and shakes his head, a sardonic grin tugging at his lips. "You didn't know? You expect me to believe that?" One of his dark eyebrows rises. "You aren't dumb, Rea, that much I can tell from the very little time I've spent with you. You really didn't know what your father was doing? How he was making his money? The blood he had on *his* hands?"

A shudder rolls through me despite the warm afternoon sun beating down on us out in the gardens. Even being surrounded by all this beauty, the dark reality of the lie my life had been before coming here and the terror it's been since arriving, sends ice rushing in my veins.

"I didn't know. I swear I didn't."

Memories of all the times Father came home late, in different clothes than the ones he left in. The fights with Mother they tried to keep quiet but always floated through the vents in the house. The lavish lifestyle we lived, expensive gifts and beautiful home that didn't quite match that of my peers. All of it should have triggered questions. I should have asked. I should have *wondered* where it all came from. But I didn't—I couldn't, and I didn't *want* to know.

"Maybe I was happy in my naiveté." I shake my head, trying to find the words that don't make me sound like the total idiot I feel like right now. "Maybe I was content to live the way we did without asking because I feared knowing the truth."

"Well, I need the truth *now*, Rea. I need to know what's going on, what Tarek isn't telling me."

I narrow my eyes on him. "Why isn't he telling you himself? Isn't that something you should know?"

"Fuck!" Konstandin takes a step away from me and shoves his hands through his hair, muttering under his breath. When he finally meets my gaze again, his eyes have darkened to almost pitch black. "Yes, I should know, but Tarek has some sort of plan he's keeping close to the chest."

"I could—"

"No!" he roars at me and grasps my upper arms so tightly it hurts. "You aren't going to do *anything.* Just tell me everything your father said to you about coming here, about Tarek."

"He-he said he had made some sort of deal. Something the family needed, and that part of it meant I had to marry Tarek. He said he would hurt my mother if I didn't go along with it."

Konstandin's hands tighten around me even more, and he drags me closer before casting a furtive glance around to ensure we aren't being watched. "I'm sorry you got dragged into whatever the hell Tarek's plan is, Rea, but what's done is done. I can't get you out of this any more than you can yourself. But I need you to *think.* Anything you might have overheard or seen. Something you might not have even realized was important at the time. I need to know everything to keep you and everyone else in this organization *safe.*"

I suck in a shaky breath, Konstandin's passion for his job and clear concern over what Tarek is doing ominous. "I-I, I'm thinking."

Squeezing my eyes shut, I bring myself back to that moment in the house when Father came into my room and told me he had something to tell me. That momentary flutter of excitement, thinking he had bought me a new car or something else I wanted. The stupid, greedy, naïve girl I was only a few months ago.

"He said...*'Just as the Morinas rose to power, so shall I, with their help.'*"

Konstandin releases me and steps away, motioning for me to follow him deeper into the gardens, farther away from the house. "So, he's making a move. A big one."

"I guess? I don't really know what it meant." Bits and pieces of our conversation that night float back to me, twisting my gut and causing acid to burn my throat. "He mentioned something about the *'changing face of Albania'* and about a *'power vacuum,'* but I have no idea what any of that means."

His strong jaw hardens, and he walks slowly down the path, his hands locked together behind his back. "It's nothing you need to understand or worry about. Whatever happens, you'll be protected."

"Do you know what it means? What my father and Tarek are doing?"

He pauses and looks back at the house. "I think I do. But I need confirmation."

I open my mouth, but he cuts me off with a look before I can say anything else.

"Don't ask questions, Rea. I've warned you once before. Questions get you killed around here. And despite how miserable you might be, I don't think you want to be six feet under."

I don't.

Maybe it's being outside in the sunshine, with all the beauty surrounding me, or the chirping birds darting between the trees. Maybe it's smelling fresh air and flowers for the first time in months. Or maybe it's the way Konstandin's hands felt wrapped around my arms.

Something is giving me hope.

But hope can be a dangerous thing.

Konstandin turns back toward the house and motions for me to follow him. "I don't have a lot of time. Tarek set a wedding date. Did he tell you that?"

That burning acid charges up my throat again at the thought of walking down the aisle with that man, of binding myself to him forever, of what he might do to me once I'm *truly,* legally *"his."*

I nod and swallow back the desire to hurl all over the manicured lawn. "Yes. Only a few months. But he wouldn't tell me anything else."

Part of me wants to beg, wants to plead with Konstandin to take me away from here, to save me from my fate, but he would never betray Tarek, never betray his *fis.*

Konstandin chances a glance at me before ushering me toward the house, almost as if he can read my mind and knows the words on the tip of my tongue. "Don't forget where you are and why, Rea. I never met your father personally, but if he's the kind of man who sells his daughter to a man like Tarek and threatens his wife in order to advance his own egotistical machinations, then you have nowhere to go even if you ever managed to find a way out of here. You can't go home. You can't go back to *him*. Tarek will be back again soon, and he has expectations of you. This life may be brutal, but it's your life now. Accept it." He pauses and leans closer, looming over me menacingly. "And stop asking fucking questions. This conversation never happened."

But it did.

His words still rattle through my bones, the warnings that are truer than I ever want to admit.

I don't have anywhere to go. Even if I managed to somehow escape this place and was assured Mother was safe, I can't go home, and I've never lived a day outside Father's house until I came to this Hell on Earth.

Konstandin is right. This is my life. And I need to learn to accept it and push away that glimmer of hope I had out in the garden.

It was nothing more than a fleeting fantasy. One I can't let myself latch onto. If I do, it will only make the reality hurt even more.

TEN

Four Months After Arrival

KONSTANDIN

BLOOD TRICKLES from Manhar's lips, dropping to the floor beneath him in little spots that are quickly starting to spread out beyond the chair where I have him seated.

He tries to lift his head, but I slam my fist against his jaw, snapping it back with a sickening crack that echoes slightly around us.

A low groan tumbles from his swollen mouth, the sound deep and anguished. It spurs me to continue my mission—to get to the bottom of what Tarek is up to.

As one of his trusted guards who goes everywhere with him, Manhar knows the truth, but his loyalty to Tarek has kept him silent. I may finally get my answers, the ones Tarek won't give me and Rea can't, but there will be a price to pay when he discovers what I've done.

I'm willing to pay it. If it's the only way to shake off the sense of impending doom that has settled over me since my walk in the gardens with Rea and get a true sense of what's happening, I'd pay it ten times over.

I grip Manhar's hair, forcing his face up. "Look at me."

His eyes flutter open slowly, unfocused. "*Pirdhu!.*"

"No, fuck you for keeping what Tarek has been doing hidden from me." I tighten my grip and tug until he winces again. "Tell me what you were doing in Vlorë."

Waiting on the tarmac under the guise of ensuring their safety when they landed made it easy to separate Manhar from Tarek. After a few drinks on the plane, Tarek was more than willing to head back to the house ahead of us, which gave me the chance to have this little conversation with Manhar in the hangar uninterrupted.

"If he wanted you to know, you would." He spits blood on my shoes and grins at me. "You trained me. Do you really think you can get me to break?"

Yes.

If I had the time, I could, but the longer I linger here, the more questions Tarek will have about Manhar's disappearance. I need to get him out of here and this place cleaned up before Tarek sobers up enough to ask.

I pull out my gun and push it into his chest. "You're lucky I don't have the time tonight."

One flick of my finger is all it takes to end his life, and I release his head and let him slump forward.

This didn't go as planned. It was rash, stupid, a move of desperation. Something I never do. But Tarek has left me no choice.

There's only one other thing I can think to do, one other person I trust who might be able to get to the bottom of it, to tell me the truth. I reholster my gun and dial the number I never thought I would again.

Each ring tightens a vise around my chest. As soon as she answers, everything will change.

"Hello?"

Hearing Agron's soft voice again after so long almost brings a tear to my eye, and I clear my throat to dislodge the unusual feeling there.

"Agron, it's me."

"Konstandin?" Something rustles into the phone, and footsteps tell me she's moving into another room—likely so Luan and the kids don't know she's talking to me. "Why are you calling me?"

"I'm sorry. But I need your help."

"You know I can't get involved with any of it. Not anymore. I paid my dues to the family. I'm not Agron anymore. I'm Adelina, and no one can ever know."

"I know. I hate to ask you this. I'm sorry I have to." I release a heavy sigh and examine my hand-iwork, proof of just how bad things have become. I'm taking out our own men to get answers. "But Tarek's up to something, and none of my sources are talking. Tarek has them scared shitless. I would come there and find out myself, but there are other things happening here that require my attention."

Like an enemy breathing down our necks from the west and a woman twisting at my gut back at the house.

"Tarek's *here?*"

The concern in her voice makes me tighten my hand on the phone. Even after all these years, the thought that she might get pulled back into this life terrifies her—and after what happened to her, I can't say I blame her for her unease.

"Yes, I know he's been there several times over the last few months, but I can't tell who he's been meeting with or where he's been going. I lose his trail after he deplanes. I've tried planting tracking devices on him and the men he takes, but they must be searching for them. I've contacted every single source I have, and they're all silent on what's happening. I need to know if you've heard anything, any rumblings or rumors."

Agron—*no, Adelina*—sighs heavily, the sound so much like Mother that for a split second, warmth actually floods my chest. "I heard he's getting married."

"Yes..."

"That's it, Konstandin. I don't know anything else. And I don't have any way of finding it out."

"*Gjepura!* You just don't want to."

She scoffs. "Do you blame me after what Father made me do?"

I squeeze my eyes closed and pinch the bridge of my nose to try to relieve the pressure building there. "I know. Which is why I wouldn't call you if it wasn't absolutely necessary. Tarek has cut me off completely. Whatever he's doing, he doesn't want me to know about it. Either because he thinks I'll stand against him publicly or because he thinks it might backfire. I'm more concerned about the latter. If that happens, the fallout could come back to you."

And everyone else, including Rea.

"But I'm *out.*"

"It doesn't matter, Ad. You *know* it doesn't matter. You never really get out. *No one* does."

"I don't need the reminder, Konstandin."

"Please see what you can find out. I've exhausted every other avenue except flying across the damn ocean myself and following him, but like I said, there are things happening here, and I can't leave."

She releases another heavy sigh. "I'll see what I can find out. I'm not making any promises, Konstandin. And this is the last time I can get involved. I can't risk the lives of my children. I know you don't understand because you're not a parent—"

"You're right. I don't."

I never could. And I never will. I would never bring a child into this world. I would never expose them to this kind of blood. This kind of violence. The constant state of being on edge, waiting for another attack or a new enemy to arise. Tarek and I can handle this life, but a child never could. Rea won't be able to, either.

That was made crystal clear that day in the garden. She's wholly unprepared to handle what being married to Tarek will entail. What it means for her future. She's only seen the tip of the iceberg when it comes to him and what both of us are capable of.

"I'm sorry, Ad. I promise it's the last time."

"It better be. I'll get back to you when I have something."

She ends the call, and I return my full attention to the body in front of me.

Voices trickle in from outside the closed hangar door—laughter. People who have no idea what just went on in here. Perhaps airport employees who wouldn't dare ask.

What I wouldn't give to be able to bury my head in the sand, ignore what is happening around me and behind my back, and concentrate on what I'm good at instead—spilling blood. But that isn't an option. If I don't figure out what's going on, I won't be able to protect what we've worked so hard for.

Ever since my talk with Rea in the gardens, my head won't stop spinning. Only one possibility seems to make sense. Her father has always been on the outside looking in, a low-level, small-town mobster under one of the larger *fis,* having to pay up the food chain.

But he's done with that. He and Tarek are going to be taking someone—or multiple someones— out there, creating a new regime. One Tarek is ensuring will remain friendly and cooperative with us here by marrying the man's daughter.

What Tarek said about it affecting everyone, including the Gashis in Chicago, falls right in line with that because any changes back home would shake up their business, too.

They need the cooperation of whoever is in charge there if they're going to continue to run their business here. The lines of communication, the access to weapons, drugs, and girls that they provide back home. The Gashis can't survive without that lifeline and continue to run their business here. And neither can we.

Tarek said he would deal with the Chicago threat since my warnings haven't stopped them, and now, it makes sense. If he succeeds, the Gashis won't be a threat anymore. They'll be on the outside looking in, having lost any connection they had to the families who control Albania.

As much as I hate to admit it, it's not a bad plan. It's a good one, actually—if it weren't so risky. The Muratis and the Delvinas are not going to just roll over and slink away with their tails tucked between their legs the way the Sylas did so many years ago.

They're not going to go quietly, and that means a war. One I'll be on the front lines of. One I'll be in charge of. Which is likely why Tarek hasn't said anything. He knows I would try to talk him out of this—at least, the way he's doing it. Because I know he won't do this delicately. He won't make his enemy disappear in a way that could be explained easily. He's going to send a message—a very public one—when he usually relies on me to do that. He'll use someone else this time, likely one of Rea's father's men, and that message is going to point directly back at us.

We won't be able to pretend we're neutral, not when Tarek is shoving his new alliance into everyone's faces by marrying Rea. Anyone loyal to the other controlling *fis* is going to set their sights on all of us, including his new wife.

And even the ocean won't keep them from reaching us.

ELEVEN

Five Months After Arrival

REA

ALL DAY, I've known something bad was coming. I've felt it deep in the marrow of my bones. A chill. Something off. Something alerting me to run even though I have nowhere to go and nowhere to hide.

Konstandin's warning from that day out in the gardens still rings in my ears. Because it's true. I don't have anywhere to go. Konstandin would never let me set foot off this property, and, even if, by some miracle, I do manage to get away, Father would only bring me right back, kicking and screaming this time. And Tarek would chain me to the damn bed before he ever let me escape again.

So even though I can't shake this sense of foreboding, there isn't anything I can do about it, either, except sit and wait for whatever—or whoever—might be coming.

Tarek's been gone a while this time—almost three weeks. The longest stretch he's left me alone. The most time I've ever had to take a deep breath and try to forget where I am for a while. But even though he's avoided me, I can't forget the way Konstandin looked at me, the way his hand felt against my skin, the passion that poured from him with every word he said, the way, for one brief moment, I felt almost safe from everything when I was out in that garden with him.

I know it's deadly to even consider it. For both of us. It doesn't stop my mind from going there, though. When I lie in bed at night, I can't prevent my body from heating, thinking about his touch.

It only takes one sound to rip that memory from me and bring me back to reality—Tarek's voice in the hallway, speaking with Lorenc, who's on duty outside my door again.

He's back.

I suck in a long, deep breath and prepare myself to face whatever mood he's in this time. And it's only gotten worse. The more time I spend locked in this room, the crueler he becomes. Whatever is going on outside this house, whatever he has himself tangled up in with Father, is eating away at him, making him take out his frustration on me. And there's nothing I can do about it.

Standing near the four-poster bed, my hands shake at my sides as the door flies open and Tarek stumbles in.

He's drunk.

Wherever he came from this time, he must have been enjoying a lot of alcohol on the way back. Something else that has noticeably increased as time has gone on. He's drowning himself to handle the stress, hoping he can escape whatever is hounding him the way I pray for escape from this.

His black gaze lands on me immediately, and a sly grin spreads across his lips. "There you are, *kafsha ime*. Did you miss me?"

It's the same game he plays every time he returns, the same question he always asks. And he expects the same answer.

"Of course, I did." It's a lie, but one I've learned to give to avoid any confrontation with him. I swallow thickly and force a fake smile. "How was your trip?"

The question leaves my lips before I can stop it, before I can consider the consequences of adding it to my usual greeting. He growls and launches himself across the room at me with speed I didn't know he possessed. His hands wrap around my throat so quickly I don't have time to attempt a retreat.

"Don't ask about my fucking business. Do you understand me?" Spittle flies from his twisted lips, the smell of smoky scotch on his breath. "You're here for one thing and one thing only—to please me. Your role is the dutiful fiancée, soon to be dutiful wife."

He brushes his thumb across my throat menacingly and presses it into the skin. I release a tiny little gasp of air and struggle to suck another one into my lungs. They burn already, desperate for the air he refuses to allow me.

I hadn't meant to set him off, and I know better than to ask. Konstandin warned me of the consequences. It just slipped out this time before I could bite it back, a natural question to ask someone who had just returned from a trip. But not with him.

Not here.

Here, questions mean death.

I kick out with my feet in a vain attempt to get him to release his deadly hold, but he keeps it there, his sneer twisting his lips.

"What have you been up to while I've been gone, Rea? I had hoped I would come back and you would be more agreeable, but it seems you haven't lost your attitude. Have you been a good girl, Rea? Have you behaved?"

I manage a nod—the only response I can offer with the pressure he's applying to my throat. The world starts to go dark around the edges of my vision while I struggle to take another breath.

Tarek leans in and brushes his lips to mine almost reverently while tightening his hands. "I've missed you, *kafsha ime*, and it seems I need to teach you a fucking lesson about your role..."

His words fade out with the rest of the room...

Indistinct sounds wrapped in dark gray, rushing toward an almost black...

I lean toward it, welcoming the embrace of something I should be afraid of...

A strange noise fills the room—a strangled grunt and something else...

Then I'm falling, tumbling to the mattress behind me. I slam down against it, gasping and sucking in breath after breath, trying to quell the burning of my lungs while I get my bearings.

I blink rapidly, trying to get them to focus on what's in front of me.

Someone with their arm around Tarek's neck, barely visible in the darkness. Tarek lashing out but unable to stop whoever has him in a headlock. Struggling until he finally relaxes and slumps in the arms restraining him.

The man behind him turns toward me enough for me to see his face.

Konstandin's gaze meets mine over his brother's shoulder. "He's not going to touch you tonight. Not like this."

His whispered words send a flood of relief through me, and I bite back a sob. I rub at my throat and continue to suck in sharp breaths. "But—"

Konstandin shakes his head and inclines it back toward the door in warning that the other men must still be out there, close enough that they can overhear anything we say.

He drags Tarek out of the room, and bits and pieces of the conversation in the hallway float toward me.

"Tarek passed out...really drunk...bringing him down to the other room where we can keep an eye on him...go watch him and make sure he's okay..."

I breathe deeply, trying to process what just happened with a brain still recovering from oxygen deprivation.

Konstandin reappears and shuts the door behind him. He shoves his hand angrily through his hair, approaching the bed. Konstandin pauses beside me and stares down, his eyes blazing with something I haven't seen there before—an anger that—for once—isn't directed at me.

He takes a deep breath, narrowing his eyes on me. "Are you all right?"

I swallow deeply and nod, even though I'm far from it. "Yes, I think so. But...you won't be when Tarek wakes up."

Konstandin's jaw hardens, and he lowers himself to the bed next to me and tilts my head to examine my neck. "He was going to kill you. He would have if I hadn't stopped him. He won't do anything to me. Not when I remind him why he needs you alive."

"Why *does* he need me alive?"

It's a question I've asked myself endlessly since that day in the garden. With Konstandin avoiding me since, I haven't been able to get the answer. Maybe he's been absent because he felt the same strange spark, or maybe he's been busy trying to get to the bottom of Tarek's plans. Either way, he's here now, and his timing couldn't have been more perfect.

He glances toward the door, then returns his focus to me, softly brushing his thumb across my neck that no doubt holds his brother's fingerprints. "I figured out enough. Enough to know that he does need you alive, healthy and cooperative because he needs your father."

His soft touch belies the brutality I know this man is capable of, yet I can't help but lean farther into it, farther into him, trying to absorb some of the warmth emanating from his hard body. He may look exactly like the man who haunts me day and night, but Konstandin is the one whose face heats my *other* dreams.

The closer I move to him, the more I lean into his touch, he stiffens, and finally, his hand stills against my neck. "What are you doing?"

I lock my gaze with the gold flashing in his. "I don't know. I just can't stop thinking about—"

"About how my brother's going to kill you?"

"No." I shake my head. "About how the only time I've felt safe since I've gotten here has been when I'm with you. How I know you'll never hurt me."

"Fuck, Rea." He tightens his grip on my neck, but not in the threatening way Tarek just did. It's almost possessive and protective at the same time. "Don't say stupid shit like that. It will get you killed."

I shake my head and shift closer, our lips only inches apart. "And what if you stop him?"

He issues a low growl of anger, frustration, something else. "It isn't that fucking simple, Rea. He's my *brother*."

"He's a *monster*..."

Konstandin's eyes flash darker. "The same type of monster I am."

"No." I shake my head and slide my hand onto his thigh. "That's not true."

A muscle in his tightened jaw tics. "It *is*, Rea."

This man may be a monster, but he's a different kind. A *far* different kind. One I can't stop myself from moving even closer to, one I *want* to touch me, to hold me, to *take* me.

Before I can even process what's happening, I press my lips to his, inhaling his surprise and the tiny little groan that rumbles from his chest against mine. His hand at my neck drags me even closer while the other circles my waist and pulls me to him fully. His tongue delves into my mouth, igniting a fire deep within me I never knew could burn again.

It sears through my blood and makes my head spin, briefly taking me away from where we are and why, but just as quickly as it sparked, he pulls back, dousing me with the icy coolness of his glare.

"No, Rea." His hold tightens on me. "We can't." He leaps from the bed and turns back to look at me. "You have no idea what you're doing. What you're asking..."

"Yes, I do." I shift toward the edge of the bed. "You just have to make the choice, too."

"It isn't a choice I *can* make. I know my role. Know yours."

He turns and stalks from the room, slamming the door behind him with a force that reverberates through me and makes me collapse back on the bed.

I raise my hand and press my fingers to my tingling lips.

Konstandin Morina is nothing like Tarek.

He may be cold and brutal, ruthless and cunning, but something else lurks beneath the surface. A tiny sliver of humanity. Something that prevented him from allowing Tarek to kill me tonight. He may say he was just protecting the deal Tarek is making, protecting their family, but that isn't what his kiss just told me.

It was so much more...

TWELVE

Six Months After Arrival

KONSTANDIN

I'M FUCKED.

Sitting here next to Tarek, staring down Rea's father over the massive desk that separates us from him, that reality slams into me harder than any bullet ever has.

It isn't just because things have been tense with Tarek since the night I knocked him the fuck out to protect Rea or because the man in front of us has far more ambition and drive than I imagined; it's because Rea's kiss made one thing abundantly clear to me, something that has only continued to solidify over the last few weeks despite actively avoiding her like my life depends on it.

Because it does.

Her lips pressed to mine left no doubt in my mind.

Zero.

Something snuck up on me over the course of the last six months since she stepped out of that car on that drizzly day as just another one of Tarek's women. She's become something so much more. She *is* something so much more.

Sweet. Innocent. Kind. Naïve in so many ways. But even after being thrown into the monster's lair, even after suffering at the hands of a man who has no qualms about doing whatever he wants, she hasn't let Tarek break her.

That will never happen. I saw it that night. How even after he almost killed her, she still managed to find hope. It might have been in the wrong place—I'm definitely not who she should be looking to—but she found it.

I can't let Tarek continue to move along this path with her. I can't let *this* continue—what we're here to discuss.

Their master plan.

When she marries Tarek, what he's done to her the past few months will pale in comparison. Not only will he *own* her, but what he and her father are doing will truly put a target on her back— as Tarek's wife and the daughter of the man who will become one of the most powerful people in the country. If they succeed, they'll control all of Albania and will be the target for anyone and everyone who wants a piece of it.

Yet, no matter how often I've voiced my concern since I confronted Tarek about his plans, no matter how many times I warn him what making such a public statement with violence will lead to, he stands his ground.

Just like now.

Insisting on coming with Tarek and Rea's father in person hasn't made any difference. It feels like I've been arguing with them for hours, trying to convince them of the dangers of what they propose. Even a well-coordinated strike against the Muratis and the Delvinas won't end things as easily as they think.

I release a heavy sigh filled with all the frustration that's been building inside me. "You two know how I feel on this matter."

Tarek casts an annoyed look at me. "I've heard your objections concerning how we're moving forward, but I am not about to cast aside everything we've been working for the last few months because you're a little fucking nervous."

"A little nervous?" I bark out a laugh and shake my head, focusing on Rea's father seated across from me. "A *lot* nervous, and you both should be, too. The Muratis and Delvinas aren't going to go down without a fight. And they have a lot of very powerful supporters—supporters who are going to come to their defense in this war." I turn toward Tarek. "A war we're going to be fighting on multiple fronts because as soon as we make a move here, Saban is going to take it as an opportunity to finish what he started back home, knowing we're distracted here and understanding what our success here will mean for him in the long run. We can't expect him not to act."

Tarek chuckles and shakes his head. "I don't. I expect him to do exactly what he agreed to."

What he agreed to?

I shift in my chair to fully face Tarek. "What do you mean?"

He pushes up from his seat and walks to the far side of the room to stare out the window at Vlorë—the place where this all began for us. The seat of our power. One I hope we can hold onto.

"I told you I would deal with him."

Weeks ago, back when I was still in the dark about Tarek's plans, Saban hadn't backed down. He had continued his activities against us, which was exactly what I had anticipated. I assumed Tarek had failed.

"When did you talk to him? What did he say? What did you promise him?"

The thought of making any sort of agreement with Saban, the man I've been fighting against for so long, makes my stomach tighten. He may be the lesser of the two evils in the Gashi family, but that isn't saying much. God knows no one wants to go head to head with The Dragon. I would pick Saban over him any day, and thankfully, his brother is locked away in a hole in some prison and won't be getting out in this lifetime. But it doesn't mean we can underestimate what Saban is capable of.

Rea's father grins at me. "You underestimated our ability to plan for all the possible scenarios. We have Saban on board."

"On board for what?"

Tarek turns back to me. "A truce—a real one. We will be in a position to ensure both us and the Gashis are taken care of."

Rea's father chuckles darkly. "Keep your enemies closer..."

A sardonic grin tilts Tarek's lips. "Something like that."

These two are far too calm about what they're about to attempt. "You really think that's going to work? You really think Gashi is going to just stop everything he's been doing, trying to encroach on our territory back home, trying to expand beyond the Midwest, simply because you asked him nicely and promised him you won't interfere with anything he has going on over here?"

Tarek shrugs. "I have no reason not to believe he's on board. As we all know, he has everything to lose when we succeed in this mission not to be our friend."

I scrub my hands over my face, then examine the two men in the room. This has clearly been a long time coming, something they've been working toward behind my back for at least a year, maybe more. I would have remained in the dark had Tarek not been forced to confirm his plan with me after that night with Rea.

He would have killed me when he finally came to had I not been waiting for it, not been ready to confront him about what he almost did to her and what I *knew* he'd been planning and hiding from me.

And while almost coming to blows with Tarek isn't high on my list of favorite activities, if it had come to that, I would have ended it and ended *this* right there in that room.

But now that he's admitted how important Rea is to his ultimate goals, he knows what he did was a massive mistake. That if he had harmed her or even worse, it would have meant the end to what he has going on with her father.

Still, that doesn't mean he has any intention of letting me in on all the details. He's keeping a lot of things close to the chest.

And that's what makes me nervous.

This information about the Gashis is something I should have known from the minute he decided to approach him. I've spent months fighting the man's advance, taking out his men, sending brutal and bloody messages to back off, yet Tarek invited him into the fold, told him of his plans, and added him to the list of those who will benefit.

I release a heavy sigh. "It sounds like you two are going to do whatever you want to no matter what I say." I throw up my hands. "As the one in charge of your security, the one who has done your dirty work for the last decade..." I glare at Tarek. "I'm telling you; this is a bad idea."

He shrugs nonchalantly, the same brush-off he's given me a hundred times when I've voiced concerns over his actions over the years. "It's a risk. That much is true. But if you don't take big risks, you will never have great rewards."

"That's one way to look at it."

His eyes widen slightly. "How else would you see it?"

"If you're greedy, you'll suffer the consequences."

He barks out a laugh, joined by his new partner across the desk, and shakes his head. "This isn't about greed, Konstandin. This is about finally succeeding and having everything we've ever wanted. After everything Father went through to secure our foothold here and all the work we did to secure Philadelphia, I'm not about to lose any of it. Expansion has always been the goal. And it will continue to be, whether you try to stand in the way or not."

"I'm not standing in the way of anything. Just trying to be the voice of reason, *vëlla i dashur*. Like I have been in the past..."

It's a subtle reminder of what happened with Rea, but I don't dare mention it in front of her father. Tarek is already on the verge of completely losing his patience with me, and I don't need to give him any further reason to do just that.

But what they're doing is insanity. Taking out the two other major families here and putting Rea's father in charge while Tarek splits his time between Philly and here...

Pure lunacy.

Rea's father clears his throat and shifts in his seat, rocking forward to rest his elbows on the desk. "We've been working on this for a long time, Konstandin. We're ready. We have the men in place to do what needs to be done. We've prepared for every scenario."

I chuckle and shake my head. "Famous last words."

Tarek leans against the desk, crossing his arms over his chest. "Trust me when I say we will come out of this on top and will have secured the future of our two families forever. Our successes will be their successes. Our greatness, our victories theirs. And in the end, when all is said and done, we'll be sitting at the top, looking down on people like the Gashis who will be forced, once and for all, to admit that we are the ones truly in control of this country, even if we don't live here anymore."

His words are meant to stir something in me, pull at some deep need inside me for more. More power. More money. More of everything.

But all that races through my blood is anger.

There's no stopping this train now.

Tarek and Rea's father are intent on going through with this, and that means only one thing—I have to get Rea out of there before the bullets start flying or there's a ring on her finger...

THIRTEEN

The Next Day...

KONSTANDIN

My hands haven't stopped shaking since the plane landed in Philly. It's a completely foreign feeling, like I'm a stranger in my own skin. Despite all the blood they've spilled, they've always been firm. Steady. Reliable. *I* have been always.

Not tonight.

Tonight, I can't be Tarek's *kryetar*. I can't be his brother. I have to betray him.

I place my hand on the banister to make my way up the stairs toward Rea's room, and I have to grip the wood tightly to stop my legs from quivering and giving out from under me.

It isn't fear that's doing it. I haven't feared anything a day in my life. It's knowing the consequences of my decision. It's knowing what I *have* to do.

Get Rea out.

Get her set up somewhere she'll be safe.

Then, I'll come back and deal with the fallout.

Try to fix whatever harm taking her causes.

I owe her that much.

I owe her a chance at a real life.

Away from Tarek. Away from all of this. Away from everything her father forced her into.

Each step up I take only cements that fact and what must happen deeper in my chest.

Lorenc stands outside her door tonight, and his eyes widen slightly at my approach. "You're back. Where's Tarek?"

"Still in Vlorë. He had some other things to take care of."

I needed the men focused on their mission here, keeping Rea safe and Saban Gashi at bay. It's why I haven't let them in on what Tarek has been doing. But I want to tell Lorenc everything. I want him to know what's about to come crashing down on this *fis*. What our family will soon be up against.

We brought him with us when we came to the States to offer him a new life, a chance to help us start our organization's footprint here, and he took it. He leaped at the chance to get away from the ruin his family had been left in, but now he's going to be facing the same kind of attack because of Tarek's decisions.

I want to warn him, but I can't.

Not yet.

Not until I get Rea out of here.

I glance at the closed door that contains the source of the tempest brewing inside me. "How is she doing?"

In the weeks since I saw her last, since she threw my world into a tailspin and unraveled all the things I thought I understood with one kiss, I've ensured I had valid reasons to stay away, to appear disinterested, when really, I hung on every word of every update the men offered me. I needed the validation that she was all right and not utterly destroyed the way I have been.

Lorenc glances at the door. "She's been quiet. Mostly reading."

"Take off for the rest of the night."

He raises an eyebrow at me. "What?"

"Tarek made me promise I would personally secure her when I returned. He wants *me* watching her now."

Lorenc tenses. "Is there a reason to be worried?"

I bite back the desire to tell him everything, to unburden myself and ensure he's prepared. Instead, I give my best friend a squeeze on the shoulder. "Not that I know of. At least, not yet."

It's as much of a warning as I can offer.

He narrows his eyes on me slightly. "Okay, *natën e mirë*."

I lean against the wall next to the door and watch Lorenc make his way down the hallway and disappear down the steps. Crossing one ankle over the other, I pause and rest my head, letting my eyes drift closed while I wait long enough to ensure he's long gone.

There can't be any witnesses to what's about to happen. I've cleared out the house. Shut off the cameras, ensured no one will see or hear anything they can pass along to Tarek when he learns what I've done.

We'll disappear into the night, and by the time he realizes it, she'll be safe and I'll be on my way back to face his wrath.

I try to relax. To let the necessary time pass. But knowing Rea's just on the other side of this piece of wood makes my heart thunder against my ribcage, and the memory of that kiss and the way her body felt pressed against mine stirs my body to life.

No.

I can't do this.

I can't...care about her. I'm not even sure what any of this means. I've never experienced anything like it. Never held it in my hands. Never wrapped my arms around it. Yet, that's what I want to do to her.

And it can never happen.

Just get her out of here and make sure she's safe. That's it.

I suck in a deep, fortifying breath so I won't have to inhale that scent of hers, and I open the door and step into the room, lit softly by the light from the bathroom.

It falls across the bed where Rea lies, an open book beside her, wide green eyes locked on me.

"You're back..."

I close the door behind me, but even the soft click echoes loudly in my ears. All my senses are heightened, my body primed for what I'm about to do.

She pushes herself up on one elbow and watches me approach slowly.

"I met your father..."

Her body tenses, and I slowly lower myself to the edge of the bed, rubbing at the stubble on my face.

"He and Tarek are planning something dangerous. Something that's going to happen very soon. And if you marry him, it's only going to put more of a target on your back."

"I don't have a choice—"

I hold up a hand to stop her. "You're right. You *don't* have a choice. I'm taking you away from here."

Her eyebrows fly up. "What?"

"I'm going to get you out of here, bring you somewhere safe. Set you up with money, a new identity, a new life. Make sure Tarek and your father, none of this will ever touch you again."

She shifts closer. "But what about you?"

"What about me?"

"Tarek and my father, they'll kill you when they find out."

"I can take care of myself, Rea."

She shakes her head, tears welling in her eyes. "No, you can't. Not against them, not against their men and all the power they hold. They'll kill you, and then they'll come find me."

I grip her chin, squeezing it between my fingers harder than I probably should. "I'm very good at my fucking job. And right now, my job is to protect you. This time, from Tarek. It's what I should have done from the beginning. I'm getting you out of here, and then, I'll come back to deal with the fallout." I release her chin and push up from the bed to stalk toward the door. "Start packing."

"Wait, Konstandin..." She leaps from the bed and rushes across the room toward me, plastering her back against the door to prevent me from leaving. "You can't! I'm not going to let you sacrifice yourself to protect me."

"Let me?" I step into her, glaring down at the woman who ignites every fire within me. Hatred. Longing. Lust. All of them centered on one beautiful redhead who can't just do what she's told. "We don't have any other choice, Rea. This is what has to happen."

She presses her small hands against my chest, the heat instantly seeping through my clothes and searing my skin. "No." She clutches my shirt, her fingers clinging to me with a desperation she hasn't even shown under Tarek's brutal hand. "Don't pretend you want to leave me somewhere and come back to this. Don't pretend this *life* is what you want. When I know *this* is."

Rea tugs at my shirt, dragging me a fraction of an inch closer to her. I press my hands flat on the door on either side of her and lean in until my lips almost brush hers.

"This isn't what you want, Rea. You just think it is because of what Tarek has done to you. Because you need something to hold onto. A lifeline. An anchor. You need something to want and to believe in."

"No..." She shakes her head, and a single tear rolls down her cheek. "That's not true, Konstandin. I want this." She tugs again. "I want *you*."

"The man who looks exactly like *him?*"

She shakes her head again. "Maybe no one else sees it, but I do. You two are different."

"No, we're not."

"Yes, you are." She lifts her hands to my neck, her warm palms setting my skin ablaze. "You don't look at me the way he does. He looks at me like he wants to possess me. You look at me like you want to consume me."

Her words cut to something deep in my core I didn't even know existed there. A longing for something real, something good, something men like me aren't supposed to have.

I accepted a long time ago that I would have to pay for my sins. The sins I committed in Father's name. The sins I committed when I wore the uniform and we were at war. The sins I committed in the name of the Morinas since we came here. The sins I've committed in Tarek's name...

Men with souls as black as mine don't get to have things as good as Rea. Not unless we take them the way Tarek did. But not freely offered. Not freely given. Not like this.

"Fuck, Rea. You don't mean that." I brush my lips against her forehead. "I'd give anything to consume you, to pull you inside me so that I could protect you from all the danger and violence and arrogance of this world. But it wouldn't work. Because I'm part of that world. I'm part of the problem."

"No." She pulls back and pushes up on her tiptoes to press her forehead against mine. "You're not. Don't lie to yourself and pretend you don't want this. Don't act like there isn't a way for this to work. Don't deny me this, Konstandin. Not after everything..."

FOURTEEN

REA

THIS MAN HAS BEEN SO strong. A rock. An unbreakable wall. Devoted to his brother and this violent and bloody world. Unwilling to bend an inch. Unyielding in his loyalty and dedicated to his role. Yet now, with my forehead pressed to his, his body brushing mine, my hands around his neck, he vibrates like the ground beneath us is quaking and may break apart and swallow him whole.

The way he's fighting this, he might actually prefer it. He may want to be able to disappear, to pretend none of this is happening. But there isn't any denying it.

Not for me.

Not for him, judging by the way he looks at me.

All it will take is for him to give in, to accept this pull. To close the distance between us. Between my *heart* and his.

All he has to do is take the leap...

It happens so fast that I don't even have a chance to take a breath. He crushes his lips to mine and presses me into the door, his hard body easily overtaking my much smaller one.

Somehow, despite everything that's happened, his kiss breathes life into me, pushing away the pain and the fear and everything else that has gripped me since the day I first arrived here.

Konstandin's hands move to my hips; he lifts me easily and pins me to the door with his massive frame. I wrap my legs around his waist, tugging up my nightshirt to align myself so his hard cock encased in jeans presses between my thighs in just the right spot.

He groans deeply, sweeping his tongue between my lips and tightening his grip on my hips. I cling to him, digging my heels into his lower back and twining my fingers in the hair at the nape of his neck. A heady scent I can only describe as lethal envelops me with each swipe of his tongue. Every roll of his hips winds me tighter, builds me higher, and I moan against his lips, wanting to plead with him but not willing to pull away from the kiss.

I don't know what I expected when I begged Konstandin to do this, but this man unleashed is like being in the crosshairs of a rabid animal. He warned me that he was just as much of a monster as Tarek, but somehow, the other man and all the awful things he stands for melt away in these arms. Under these lips. When breathing in *his* breath and scent.

He slides one hand down between us and brushes his fingers over the thin strip of fabric covering my core. "Damn, Rea. You're fucking soaked right now." He presses his forehead to mine, pinning me to the door with his body and his hard eyes. "You're sure you want this—"

"Yes!" My response comes out far more desperate than I intend, but if Konstandin stops now, it somehow feels like I might splinter apart and lose my ability to ever feel whole again.

To emphasize my point, I reach between us, undo the button on his jeans, and lower the zipper. The frantic tension building inside me makes my hands shake, and he shoves aside my thong and plunges a thick finger inside me, dragging a gasp from somewhere in my throat.

I drop my head back against the door and let my eyes drift closed as he pumps his digit into me, working me up even more, making my pussy clasp around it. But that isn't what I want. I want *him*. All of him. Everything he's willing or capable of giving me.

GWYN MCNAMEE

"We don't have time to play games, Rea. We need to leave. So, this is going to be quick and hard. Do you understand?"

A tiny mewl of consent slips from my lips, and I grasp his cock and stroke it hard, spreading the drop of precum over the head with my thumb, readying him as much as I am myself. He groans and nudges my hand away to grip his length and press between my legs.

He grits his teeth and drives into me, slamming me back against the door as he fills me in a way I never knew could exist. For the first time in my life, I truly feel complete with this man inside me, thrusting into me like his life depends on getting deeper. And it just might.

I told him he looked at me like he wants to consume me, and he's doing just that. He devours my mouth with frantic kisses that steal my breath and takes from my body, demanding I give him everything he's giving me.

Because as much as he may deny it, he won't be able to walk away any more than I can. Somehow, over the last few months, we've forged some kind of unbreakable bond, one that his loyalty to his brother and organization can't even top.

With each thrust of his hips, he cements our future and seals our fates.

He won't come back to this life. Not when I'm offering him a real one. Not when we can have *this*.

The head of his cock drags against that perfect spot inside of me, and I moan against his lips, sucking in quick breaths as heat spreads through my limbs and they begin to shake. I dig my nails into the flesh at the back of Konstandin's strong, tense neck, and he shifts his grip on me slightly, changing the angle of his cock and pelvis so it rubs against my clit.

It's all it takes to rip me from this world.

I hang amongst the stars, suspended in a haze of pleasure that ripples through and around me, that seizes hold of me and doesn't let go for what feels like an eternity. But Konstandin roaring my name brings me back to the here and now, and he buries his face against my neck and empties himself into me so deeply, I don't know if he'll ever be able to remove himself completely.

And I don't want him to.

I want to remain like this, in this moment, forever.

That's a dream, though.

Harsh reality comes the moment Konstandin drags his head back and locks dark eyes with mine. "We have to go. Now." There isn't an ounce of uncertainty in his words. "I'm an expert at disappearing, but I can't use any of the resources I normally would. That would make us too easy to find. We need to stop at my house so I can get some things we'll need. We'll leave from there. We'll have a head start, but not much. Once the men start coming in tomorrow morning, they'll realize the house is empty, and the hammer will fall."

Something new deepens his voice. Distress. This man is on the verge of losing everything he's worked for, everything he's ever cared about. He's going to lose his entire family, his twin brother, his job. He's going to lose everything...because of me.

"What about my mother? Once I'm gone, my father will—"

He captures my face in his palms, tilting it up to his. "I have someone taking care of that. She'll be safe, protected. But you can't ever see her or speak to her again. Any contact could expose you *and* her."

Tears trickle down my face, but I nod my understanding.

I came here innocent and naïve. I hated this world and the men in it. I longed for the peaceful, simple existence I once had, away from the violence and hate. But then I found sin in the arms of the man who was my jailer. The one charged with keeping me captive and helpless against his monster of a boss was the one who gave me hope.

I found sin.

And it may be what gets me killed.

What gets both of us killed.

Guilt churns my stomach, and he pulls out of me with a wince. Slowly, he lowers my feet to the floor, holding me until I can get steady on wobbly legs, watching me closely. Perhaps searching for regret on my part or fear.

But I'm not afraid of Konstandin. I never could be. He may be a monster, but he isn't like his brother. And once we leave here, we'll never look back.

We can't.

Looking back will get us killed as surely as what we just did will.

EPILOGUE

LATER...

KONSTANDIN

A TORRENT BATTERS THE CAR, the sky overhead pitch black except for the occasional flashes of lightning that highlight the billowing storm clouds above. The sound almost drowns out Rea's tears, but her sobs break through the deluge and tighten my grip on the wheel. Despite all she's been through, she's never broken this way. She's always been so strong. To see her fall apart tears at my chest and makes it hard to breathe.

And I can only imagine how things might get worse.

It didn't take long for us to get her small bag packed and race away from Tarek's house into the night and toward our next stop. I should have insisted we leave right away, keep moving, but having her in my home, in the one place where I found respite from the world I lived in, Tarek's world, made me want her even more.

The few hours we spent at my house, gathering the things I needed quickly gave way to losing ourselves in each other again. I shouldn't have let it happen, but we both knew it couldn't last. The memory of being together in my bed—and on or against just about every surface we could find— will have to get us through this trek toward the unknown.

We had to hit the road again, and the adrenaline coursing through her wore off and was quickly replaced by the sheer panic now consuming her.

I should comfort her, tell her everything will be okay, that *we'll* be okay. But that would be a lie. I don't know that. And more than likely, we won't be.

We'll never be okay. Things will never settle down. We'll never be able to stop running. Because Tarek will never stop coming for us, never stop looking, never stop seeking vengeance for the way we've betrayed him.

He will go to the ends of the Earth a thousand times over before he admits defeat and sulks back home empty-handed, before he forgets the treachery. Because this will cause a ripple effect through his plans. This isn't just personal; this is also business.

Another sob rips from between her lips, and I glance over at her, a vise tightening around my chest. I've never been good at the whole "emotion" thing. It's what has always made me good at my job—the best, really. It's what has earned me the reputation that has helped keep us in power all these years. It's what scares most grown men.

But it didn't scare her.

I didn't scare her.

Even though I share the name and face of her abuser.

I reach out and take her hand in mine, squeezing it gently. It's all I can offer her in this moment. All I might ever be able to offer her. I can't give her what she really needs, what she deserves. I can't be her white picket fence and two kids. I can't be *that* man.

It was always out of the realm of possibility—even more so now.

These hands are too dirty, too stained with the blood of all the men I've killed. I shouldn't have touched her with them, shouldn't have tainted her that way...

I pull my hand from hers, and her sobs increase until she's sucking in ragged breaths that don't seem to be helping.

Fuck.

We're still too close to Philly to be pulling over already, but we can't keep going like this—with her like *this*.

I pull the car over to the side of the road and throw it into park. She doesn't even move her hands away from her face. I open my door and step out into the rain, ignoring the cool sting of it against my exposed skin as the late fall chill in the air turns it almost to ice, and make my way around the car to her side.

Standing out here, soaked, looking through the glass at her, part of me wants to just walk away. To let her drive off alone and pray she makes it away from Tarek and from me. But I'm a selfish bastard, and I don't think I can let her go even if it might be what's best for her.

Instead, I jerk open her door, reach over to undo her seatbelt, and freeze. A sound. Something standing out against the rain and the sounds of the woods around us.

I turn my head to side to listen.

"What is it?" Her voice comes weak and shaky. "Why did we stop?"

"Shh…"

I motion for her to be quiet, and the sound comes again. Not the storm this time. Something else. Faint. A whining. From behind me, the ditch along the side of the tight two-lane county highway.

Instinctively, I reach for my gun at my waist, and I rise and turn toward the sound. In the darkness, almost nothing is visible except what the random flashes of lightning illuminate.

Whatever is making the sound, it's hiding well.

I approach slowly, ready for whatever threat may present itself out of the night, but the closer I move toward the sound, the more familiar it becomes until I re-holster my gun and squat in the thick, muddy, wet grass at the side of the road.

Dreq!

It's the last thing *I* need right now. Another mouth to feed. Another thing to have to watch over and take care of. But it might just be exactly what *Rea* needs.

I return to the car with the culprit and lean into her door.

She narrows her eyes at the wet blob in my arms. "What is that?"

Turning it toward her, the puppy raises its tiny head and lets out a pathetic whimper.

"Looks like we just got a traveling companion."

Her eyes widen, and a smile plays at her lips for the first time since I've known her. It lights up her entire face, bringing a brilliance I always knew was right there, just under the surface. "Oh, my God! The poor thing."

She reaches out and scoops it from my arms, pulling it close to her chest. I close the door and round the front of the car, keeping my eyes on the road as I do.

I'll never stop watching, never stop scanning for the threats I know are always lurking in the shadows.

I climb in and buckle my seatbelt, then throw the car into drive and hit the road again as fast as I dare with the violent weather. Rea's laughter and baby talk at the puppy warms me so much that the fact that I'm soaking the leather seat barely registers.

She's happy. For the moment.

I'd love to believe that will continue. That finding this stray as we flee from Tarek and Philadelphia is a sign of good things to come.

But I don't believe in signs, and I certainly don't believe I've earned anything good in this life.

I've committed far too many sins to get a glimpse of Heaven with Rea.

Tarek will come.

It's only a matter of how long we run before he finally catches up to us and we have to pay for our sins...

WRATH

"Of the Seven Deadly Sins, anger is possibly the most fun. To lick your wounds, to smack your lips over grievances long past, to roll over your tongue the prospect of bitter confrontations still to come, to savor to the last toothsome morsel both the pain you are given and the pain you are giving back--in many ways it is a feast fit for a king. The chief drawback is that what you are wolfing down is yourself. The skeleton at the feast is you."

- Frederick Buechner

PROLOGUE

GRIFFIN/KONSTANDIN

THE THING about having blood on my hands is, I don't want to wash it off.

Isn't that what you're supposed to want to do?

Yet, standing here, over the shredded, unrecognizable body of Tarek, my hands dripping with his blood, there is no regret. No remorse. No nagging conscience screaming at me. Nothing but an overwhelming sense of relief floods my body.

But it doesn't last. It can't.

Yelling and the *pop* of gunshots break my reverie and remind me where I am, and why.

This isn't over.

Not by a long shot.

ONE

Three Weeks Earlier

JADE'S CUNT WRAPPED around my cock is the greatest feeling in the world. It's better than any drug I've ever tried, any booze I've ever drank, and any high I've ever experienced from killing for a living.

I never thought I'd find solace in a woman.

Women were things that served a purpose. Holes to fill and places to get on and get off. But then, I saw Jade...

"Griffin!"

My name on her lips sends me into overdrive. Thrust after relentless thrust, I pound into her, racing toward a climax I know will steal my breath and vanquish any lingering ghosts from my head. My fingers tighten in her auburn hair, and I jerk her head back and to the side so I can sink my teeth into her neck.

The salty taste of her flesh is my undoing. I empty myself into her, wave after wave of pleasure coursing through my veins.

"JADE!" My roar of her name echoes in the sparse room in a voice that doesn't even sound like mine.

I collapse on top of her and roll to my side, bringing her with me. I press her back to my chest. My heart thuds against her warm, damp skin, and her heaving chest presses against my palms splayed across her breasts.

Absolute. Total. Bliss.

Something I never thought I'd find after everything I've done. You don't torture, maim, defile, and tear people apart and then get the kind of love Jade has given me. At least, you shouldn't.

Her hand slides up and around the back of my neck. "You okay, Griff?"

"Mmm..."

It's not much of a response, but it's really all I can manage at the moment. Between the explosive orgasm and the sudden rush of memories, I'm physically and mentally spent.

She pulls her arm back and turns to face me. The green eyes I've looked into for the last two years still hold the same reverence and love they did the first time we laid like this.

Who the fuck knows why?

Even at the beginning, she knew who I was, what I was, what I did. Yet, she gave herself over to me without question, without even the slightest hesitation.

She is my angel, and I am her demon.

Her fingers slip into my hair, and she scratches my scalp softly. A contented growl rumbles in my chest, and my eyes slip closed.

"Mmm...keep doing that."

Warm, wet lips find mine. Her tongue probes until I open for her and return the kiss.

My cock stirs between us, and I break away, putting some much-needed distance between her luscious body and my overly eager one.

"You need to stop if we're going to make it to the party on time."

GWYN MCNAMEE

The coy bat of her eyelashes should warn me of her intentions, but when her hand wraps around my hard flesh, my body jerks, and my heart races like the first time she ever touched me.

Her wicked tongue snakes out and across her lips. "We can be a few minutes late."

A few minutes? I should be insulted.

"When have you ever known me to only last a few minutes, *e dashur?*"

My love.

I capture her grin with my mouth before pushing away and slipping from the bed. If I don't put *considerable* distance between us, we won't make the party, and I know how important it is to her.

Jade gave up everything to be with me—money, power, authority, and, most of all, her safety. She knew it would mean changing our names and disappearing, leaving all her family and friends and the life she always knew. It meant giving up the promise of being royalty in our world, and it meant always running, always looking over her shoulder. But she did it anyway...for me. Because she somehow managed to see beyond what I did, who I was, to my core, to where what I was doing was beginning to eat away at me like a fucking cancer.

So, the fact she has finally found some friends, people she can truly be herself—or at least her new self—with, means everything to her...and me. I'm not going to let my throbbing cock and her tempting pussy derail us from making the party.

"You. Shower. Now. I'm going to let Bruiser out, then spray off, then we are out of here."

Her eyes glitter with mischief, and she shifts up onto her knees. "Are you going t—"

"No." I hold up my hand and take another step back from the bed. "I'm not going to join you in the shower, because we would never fucking leave." My finger directs her toward the bathroom. "Go get wet."

Her back stiffens, and a mock seriousness overtakes her face. She raises her hand to her forehead and salutes me. "Yes, sir."

Saucy wench.

I dive for her, but she scrambles off the bed and slams the bathroom door before I can grab her.

She's getting faster, or I'm slowing in my age. That needs to be remedied. The chase is only fun if I can still catch her.

My boxers somehow made their way across the room to dangle over the lampshade. A hazy memory of her tugging them off and tossing them over her shoulder last night surfaces, and I can't contain the grin.

That woman is voracious, especially the last month or so. It's like trying to keep a dog away from a bone. That's why we haven't managed to even get off the mattress all day.

Once my still-hard cock is covered, I open the bedroom door and am immediately thrown backward by the force of Bruiser slamming into me.

"Down, boy!"

His massive paws press against my chest, the nails scratching my bare skin. He tilts his head, almost as if considering whether to obey me or not.

"Down."

With a resigned whimper, he drops onto all fours and then sits at my feet.

Christ, this damn dog. He doesn't realize he's a fucking Newfoundland and weighs a hundred and fifty pounds. In his mind, he's still the tiny puppy we rescued from the side of the road as we were fleeing Philly. Why anyone would leave such a beautiful dog in a ditch is beyond me, but finding him seemed almost destined.

The fear permeated Jade so deeply at that point, she couldn't stop shaking. I only pulled over briefly to try to comfort her. That's when I spotted him.

As soon as that wet bundle of matted fur cuddled into her lap in the car, her quaking ceased. It was the first time I'd seen her eyes dry and her body still in almost eight hours.

70

I pat him on the head. "Come on, boy. Let's go."

We don't have much time before we need to head out, and I am far too tempted to break down that door and join Jade in the shower right now to do something about my aching dick.

TWO

IT SHOULD BE a sin to look that good in a dress.

I have to force myself to take my eyes off her and check out the rest of the room.

Old habits die hard. If my eyes aren't constantly scanning, surveilling the people around us and all the exits, I'm jittery as hell. The heavy weight of my Glock in the holster pressed against my side gives me a modicum of comfort, but I doubt any passage of time will ever eliminate the need to have it there at the ready.

"Griffin!" The slap between my shoulder blades makes me cringe and grit my teeth. "How you doin', man?"

Forcing a smile, I turn and examine the man standing next to me. Bobby isn't a bad guy. He just...tries too hard. He's one of those nerdy computer dudes who has zero social skills, but his wife is Jade's new best friend, so that makes me his, by default, I guess.

Time to muster up some small talk.

"I'm good, Bobby, and yourself?"

He shrugs and takes a swig of his beer. "Can't complain."

I wait for him to expand, but awkward silence fills the space between us instead. It's kind of his M.O.

Social interaction isn't really my thing. My job never necessitated me holding pleasant conversations with people. It was more get in, kill, get out. Or, get in, torture and taunt, maybe kill, get out, and then a little protection duty and helping with security mixed in. I was paid to be silent, not chitchat. But things are different now, and Bobby's social ineptness makes me uneasy.

So it's time to bail.

"I'm going to grab another beer. You need one?"

He holds up his bottle and grins. "Nope, I'm good."

Thank God. I don't need to come back.

A huge island in the center of Bobby and Janine's kitchen separates me from Jade. I wander around it, keeping an eye on her where she chats in the corner with a few of her new friends. She looks up, and her eyes meet mine. A megawatt smile spreads across her face and she mouths, "I'm sorry."

She knows how painful these types of things are for me. Crowds of people put me on edge. Too many unknowns. But after three cities in the last two years, she's finally found a group of women she really meshes with, and I can't deny her the opportunity to just be normal again.

I grab a beer from the fridge and pop the cap before taking a long swig. The cool, crisp, hoppy liquid slides down my throat and somewhat calms my nerves and quells my annoyance.

A brunette seated across from Jade bursts out laughing at something.

She must be new. I'd remember her if I had met her before. The hair, the golden eyes, the olive skin...she's a dead ringer for Adelina, and just about everyone else in my family.

I'll never see my sister again. I resigned myself to that when Jade and I decided to leave. Not that we had much choice. He didn't leave us one. It was either that, or we would both be dead.

If we were lucky.

Tarek Morina doesn't forgive betrayal. Nor does he believe in light retribution. It's how he's managed to establish the wide-reaching network that stretches across the Eastern states, and all the way home to Albania.

That network is why we've been steadily making our way west. There's no way we can leave the country without using our passports. That would be like putting a flashing red target on our backs. Not to mention, all my resources for getting a fake one would rat me out to Tarek in a heartbeat. Fake licenses were easy enough to locate on my own, but the forger was sketchy, and I didn't trust the crap he was offering for other documents.

The best bet was to change our names, lie low, and disappear into suburban life far away from anyone who could ever recognize us. It's worked for the last two years. I just hope we can stay here permanently.

Rockford made me antsy. Too many people and too close to Chicago and people who know us. Minneapolis gave me the creeps, though I couldn't put my finger on why. But Denver...it's felt like home almost from the beginning. The friendly, laid-back vibe has lulled us into a sense of security. I don't want to be the one to break that for Jade by being paranoid.

So, I'll tough out the party long enough to appease her, then drag her home and fuck her all night.

If not before...

The way she's eye-fucking me from across the room has my cock swelling painfully against my zipper. I reach down and adjust it, and those emerald orbs follow the movement, zoning in on my erection. Her tongue darts out and swipes over her bottom lip.

Fuck me.

I need to get the hell out of here.

She returns her attention to her friends while I drain my third beer. When her eyes meet mine again, it's clear we're on the same page. She mouths, "Outside" to me, then excuses herself and disappears down the hallway toward the front door.

Thank God...because Bobby is making his way toward me again, and I can't suffer through that without using my piece.

That would *definitely* draw some unwanted attention our way. We've managed to fly under the radar this long, I just need to keep my temper at bay for a bit.

Meeting Jade outside will help.

THREE

I KNOW exactly where to find her. Last time we were here, we discovered a small copse of trees toward the back of the property that create almost an archway of sorts and joked it was a great place to fuck without anyone ever seeing us.

That's where she's going to head as soon as she leaves the house. I'm confident of that.

But instead of chasing after her like the horny dog I am, I give her a couple of minutes so it's a little less conspicuous.

When I step out into the cool night air, I slowly scan the street, pretending to be enjoying the peaceful evening instead of just buying a little time.

All is quiet. The neighbors are a good mile away on either side, and it's a pretty low traffic area. After ensuring no one followed either of us out, I make my way around the house and along the edge of the property toward where I know Jade is waiting.

She practically launches herself at me the moment I set foot into the small clearing. Her legs wrap around my waist and squeeze like a vise.

"Jesus Christ, what took you so long?" Her warm breath floats through the cool air and over my lips.

I laugh and squeeze her ass. "Sorry, babe. I didn't want to be completely obvious."

There aren't any windows facing this area, and it's far enough back no one can see us. Still, I don't need my bare ass or my woman's pussy on display for anyone.

"Griff, stop worrying so much."

Her chastisement gives me pause. "Jade, you know I can't *not* worry."

The playful mood sobers for a moment before she reaches between us and grabs my hard cock, reminding me of the purpose of our little escape out to the wilderness.

"We better make this quick." Her whispered words feather across my lips.

I chuckle against the warm, wet heat of her mouth. "I feel like we had this conversation today already. I don't do quick, babe."

Her deft fingers slide down the zipper of my jeans. "Try."

I walk her back into a large oak and groan when she frees my cock from its tight confines. "Jesus, baby..." is all I manage to get out before her mouth descends on mine, stealing my breath and any other words I had.

The skirt of her dress is already hiked up around her waist, giving me easy access to slide my hand between her legs and pull her panties to the side, exposing her to me completely. The head of my cock presses against her scalding core.

She wriggles against me, urging me forward. I wait for a moment, taking in the wild look in her eyes and the way they blaze even in the dim light.

Christ, she really is the most fucking beautiful woman I've ever seen.

I slide in slowly, watching her eyes roll further and further back with every inch of cock I give her. The walls of her pussy clamp down around me, and I grit my teeth.

Holy shit. No matter how many times I've been inside of her, it still feels new every single fucking time. Being with her is well worth any risk we may have had to take. I pull my hips back and plunge into her again, hard enough to slam her back against the tree. She cries out, and I slant my mouth over hers, catching her moans and gasps, just in case anyone else is outside.

GWYN MCNAMEE

Dusk has already come and gone, and in the barely-there light, I can just make out the glint of satisfaction and lust in her eyes when she opens them again to meet mine.

"Yes...harder!"

Like I could ever deny Jade anything...

I slam into her...harder...faster...over and over, the bark of the tree no doubt abrading the exposed skin between her shoulder blades, but fuck if she cares. Neither do I. I'm inside of her, and that's the only place I ever want to be.

Her pants turn rhythmic in a telltale sign she's close to coming. The walls of her pussy ripple around my hard cock, and I slip my hand between us, pressing her harder against the tree so I can get to her clit. My fingers find it, like a heat-seeking missile finding a target. I swirl and press against her, and her pussy clenches around me, practically strangling my cock with her tight, hot, wet walls. She cries out my name—my real one—and it pushes me over the edge.

I roar and empty myself inside of her.

That's when I feel the familiar press of a cold muzzle against my temple and hear the *click* of a hammer being pulled back.

"Konstandin...I'm surprised. It's not like you to be caught with your guard, or your pants, down. How things have changed."

My blood freezes in my veins, and Jade stiffens. I don't bother to look at him. I keep my gaze locked on Jade, willing her to remain calm and not panic...yet.

A hand reaches under my jacket and removes my Glock from the holster.

I clench my teeth. "And it's not like you to do your own dirty work, Tarek."

He chuckles, a dark, disturbing sound that matches the ice in his heart. "Well, it's not every day your brother steals your fiancée. This called for my own hand."

# FOUR

Splitting pain in my head and darkness...

That's what greets me when I come to.

I don't even remember him hitting me, but the throbbing at my temple tells me it was likely with the butt of the gun.

Probably a Sig 226. It was always his weapon of choice.

The fact that Tarek hasn't killed me yet should be my first clue that things are about to get bad, really fucking quickly. But I don't even have time to consider it before a blow lands against my temple, knocking my head to the side and sending blood rushing down my cheek.

Motherfucker.

That woke me up.

I shift, and some sort of restraints bite into my wrists and ankles. The cool metal of a table presses against the exposed, naked skin of my back.

Where the fuck am I?

A blinding white light flips on above me.

"Fuck!"

I turn my head to the side and clench my eyes shut against the offensive bulb.

Familiar soft beeping noises fill my ears.

Medical equipment.

A hospital?

A blow to my stomach robs my lungs of air and removes any thought that I might be somewhere safe.

While I gasp for breath, heavy breathing echoes in the room from whoever is taking the shots at me.

A hand grabs my chin and turns my head back until the light shines through my lids. Something blocks it out, and I slowly open my eyes.

Emotionless dark eyes.

Surgical mask.

A doctor?

But where's Jade?

Any attempts to turn my head to search my surroundings are thwarted by the strong hand on my jaw.

"Well, Konstandin. It seems you've been a bad boy. You know what happens to bad boys? They get punished."

Another blow knocks away any ability to process his words. But not before I catch the slight accent. He's from the motherland.

Fuck.

Blood gushes into my mouth. I swallow it and choke. My gagging coughs ricochet around the room, and he laughs, a deep, sinister sound that sends chills over my already cold, exposed skin.

It's not Tarek. I would know his laugh anywhere.

This is someone new, someone he brought on after we fled. This is the new *me*. The enforcer. The bringer of pain.

This is the man who will eventually kill me, unless Tarek mans up and decides to do it himself.

Not yet, though.

Tarek won't make it that easy. He's going to drag this out, beating and torturing me for as long as he can, before I finally succumb and my body gives up.

And God only knows what he's doing to Jade.

Rage boils through me, breaking through the fog of pain, and I tug at the restraints. Leather bites into my skin.

Fuck.

I won't get anywhere. I know that. But I can't not try. I can't leave Jade in Tarek's hands, not even for a minute.

Blows rain down on my body until a dark haze overtakes me.

Any sense of time is lost.

All that remains is pain, fear for Jade, and rage.

I can handle just about anything. But her...

Christ, she's an innocent in all of this. It was a fucking arranged marriage to my brother, organized by her father who saw her as nothing more than a bargaining chip in his negotiations for territory. She didn't choose Tarek. She didn't choose his life...this life. She never wanted it.

And now she's alone with one of the most sadistic fuckers I've ever known.

A strike lands in my gut, forcing my breath from my lungs. My chest seizes, and I gasp for air through the agony.

Fuck!

"Better settle in and get comfy." It's a clear warning of things to come and only the second thing he's said to me since I awoke.

The silence is intentional, a tactic I've often used in these situations over the years. It makes people uneasy, desperate. I used it to get information, to get compliance, to get control. He is using it to try to break me, to make me panic.

But it won't work on me.

Whoever this motherfucker is, he clearly doesn't know who or what I am.

And that will be what gets him killed. It's only a matter of time before he makes a mistake. Everyone does.

Except me.

Until I got complacent...

I never should have let my guard down. Especially not in public. I don't know those people from the party...not really. Any one of them could have been working for Tarek or have made an offhand comment to someone who knows him and inadvertently outed us.

Now Jade's paying the price for my mistake.

Footsteps retreat—ten, twenty feet, maybe—and a door opens. The bright light above me remains on. I turn my head to the side, trying to survey my surroundings.

A metal door closes behind the man before I can catch a glimpse of him.

Click. Click. Click.

Three locks.

Footsteps on stairs.

Given the chill of the room, lack of any windows, and the stairs, I can tell I'm definitely underground.

Cocksucking motherfucker.

There's no way I'm getting out of here unless that door is open or I have the keys.

I don't know where I am or how long I was out.

I could be literally anywhere. Tarek would have had his plane waiting to take off as soon as he grabbed us. I could be back in Philly for all I know. Or we may have never even left Denver.

It doesn't matter. Wherever I am, I'm getting out. And then, I'm finding Jade, getting the fuck home to my dog, and ending this, once and for all.

FIVE

TIME HAS NO CLEAR MEANING. No definites.

With no windows, no phone, no contact with the outside world beyond my tormentor, all I can do is try to count the number of times he comes and goes.

Ten.

That door has opened and locked ten times since I arrived. At least since I woke up.

Ten opportunities to escape. Ten failures.

Because this guy is good. I didn't give him any credit that first day. I underestimated him.

He doesn't make mistakes.

I've never seen his face and haven't heard his voice since the first time he visited me here. The occasional wicked chuckle accompanies his sick, demented torture, usually when he breaks out some sort of implement designed to inflict maximum pain.

Blow torch.

Tire iron.

Vise grip.

The familiar tools I've used a hundred times have been turned on me.

With anyone else, I would have been out of here within twenty-four hours. Because most people are morons when it comes to keeping someone restrained and contained.

But not this fucker. He knows what he's doing, and he has medical training, that much is evident.

An IV keeps me hydrated, and he must be injecting some sort of nutrients or something to keep me alive this long, because he sure as shit isn't feeding me. He's also giving me some sort of drug I can only describe as diabolical. Whatever it is, it makes my limbs feel like lead, but allows me to experience the full pain of every single cut, burn, twist, and strike he inflicts.

It's the perfect drug, the ultimate in torture tech. I wish I'd had it when I was still working.

Instead, it renders me immobile while this asshole works me over.

And with every moment that passes, the rage inside me builds. At my brother, at this man, but mostly at myself for letting this happen.

I should have known I couldn't walk away from that life. Even if I hadn't fled with Jade, there's no way Tarek would have let me lead a regular life. He relied on me too much to keep everyone in line, to do his dirty work, to ensure his empire was protected from every conceivable threat. And I did it for him, time and time again, giving away a small piece of my soul with every limb I severed and each life I took. I did it because I loved him, because he was my flesh and blood, and because I had never known anything else, any other way of life.

It was a downward spiral into Hell. Until the day Jade was brought to him...to me. I never knew something so pure, so innocent, so beautiful existed in this world. It never had in *my* world, the world that was created the first time I took a life and then was nurtured and twisted further by my brother.

I tried to leave that world. That was my first mistake. The second was believing I could ever truly hide from him.

For the millionth time, I twist my wrists, digging the leather straps further into my irritated flesh. Blood trickles down and pools under my hands, spreading across the steel below me. Any skin under the restraints was ripped away days ago from me trying to free myself, but the ties won't budge.

No one is this good. No one except me.

He will make a mistake. Eventually. Even I did.

I just have to remain alert because not getting out isn't an option. I have to get to Jade.

If that fucker lays so much as a finger on her...

Blind fury overtakes every fiber of my being, as I imagine all the things that have been happening since I let her get taken.

I failed her.

But it won't happen again.

Footsteps descend the stairs, and a shadow blocks the thin line of light along the bottom of the door.

He's back.

Click. Click. Click.

The door pushes open, and he steps inside.

Click. Click. Click.

Once the door is secured, he makes his way across the bright room, casually, as if he's on a morning stroll instead of entering to rip me to shreds while my heart still beats.

I've been watching him. He's big and carries himself well. There's no doubt in my mind he doesn't need the medical tricks to inflict damage on me. I think he enjoys it, though. It's a game. A sick, twisted game, designed to prolong my agony.

Removing flesh.

Burning my body.

It would be hard to do without this setup. Much easier for the captive to escape.

This gives him time. As much as he wants to practice his craft.

He's a real sadistic fucker, and that's saying a lot, knowing what I've done to people.

The flash of a needle in the bright operating lights catches my attention. A mere moment after it's pushed into the IV in my arm, a heaviness descends on my limbs. I try to pull against the restraints, but my body is lethargic and useless.

He leans over me, and despite the mask, the smile is evident in his eyes. "Oh, what I have planned today..."

His head tips back with his laugh, and he reaches for a bolt cutter.

Shit.

This is gonna hurt.

SIX

HE DOESN'T EVEN REALIZE he's just made a huge mistake.

The agony in my hand and shooting up my arm barely registers over the thrill of knowing I'm getting out of here...soon.

Cutting off someone's finger is brutal and a staple of torture.

It's also *really* fucking stupid when you have them strapped down to something and are depending on the restraints to keep them compliant.

The leaden feeling in my limbs will wear off after a few hours. It always does.

Once that happens, I'll be able to slip my left hand free of the restraint, thanks to now being sans pinky.

The man who doesn't make mistakes has finally opened the door for his own demise.

It was only a matter of time, and now that it's happened, I can barely contain the excitement bubbling through me.

I study the back of the man who has sliced and diced me for almost two weeks. He has no idea that by this time tomorrow, he'll be dead.

What I wouldn't give to have a few days with him in this playroom, to inflict upon him tenfold what has been done to me.

He *will* get what's coming to him, but getting to Jade trumps my desire to exact the type of revenge that's burning in my brain and gut right now. She's the only thing that's mattered in my life since the moment she first smiled at me and that unfamiliar tug in my chest formed. My black, dead heart warmed with something I'd never experienced before.

And I won't fucking lose that.

"Are you done for the day?" My words come out more like a croak through my raw, scratchy throat.

It's stupid to engage him. I know that. I try to never give him any indication that anything he's done to me hurts, and that's a real motherfucking chore. I've gritted my teeth so much and so hard, at least two have cracked. But knowing I'll have the upper hand shortly has brought about a new bravado and desire to fuck with this cocksucker.

"Would you like more?" His turn back to me is slow and methodical, and dark eyes roam over my naked form. "Perhaps you wouldn't miss a rib or two?"

He stops at my cock. "Then again, the American serial killer...what was his name? Ah, yes... Dahmer...he may have had the right idea with keeping certain things as trophies. It would add a little something special to my collection. I can keep it next to your finger."

The mere mention of my missing digit causes a throbbing to erupt again in my hand. "Who needs a pinky anyway?"

The doc chuckles and returns his attention to my face. "That may be true, and you won't be needing *any* of your appendages anyway."

My balls shrink up into my body at his words. Maybe antagonizing him was a bad call. If he decides to continue working me over, there's nothing I can do to stop him.

He leans back and shakes his head. "But I won't take it tonight. You've lost enough blood as it is. I wouldn't want you to go into shock. Having to revive and stabilize you would ruin my dinner plans."

I don't think I've ever been so relieved by someone else's hunger.

"I'll see you bright and early tomorrow, Konstandin. We have a lot of work to do."

He's certainly right about that. I have a lot of work to do tomorrow. As soon as these drugs wear off, this fucker is mine.

His retreating footsteps and the clicks of the locks falling into place allow me to relax—as much as that's possible while strapped to a metal table, bleeding from an amputated finger, and about a million other cuts.

Jade's green eyes flash in my mind.

The pain means nothing.

Nothing means anything.

Not until Jade is safe and back in my arms.

Tarek won't kill her. No, in his own sick, twisted mind, he loves her. That's what terrifies me the most because Tarek's version of love isn't anything a normal person would recognize.

I didn't even know what it was until I met Jade. And even then, it took six months of watching her, guarding her, and seeing what a truly magnificent and innocent person she was to finally realize the tightness in my chest and the racing of my heart weren't caused by any ailment. I had fallen in love with my brother's fiancée. And for some reason only God knows, she loved me back. Even through the hard, bloody exterior, she saw into the depths of my black soul and found a sliver of light.

No one has ever meant anything to me. No one ever got close enough to touch my heart. But she didn't just touch it, she consumed it, and me.

I don't even care if she never forgives me, if she says she never wants to see me again after letting this happen. As long as she's okay, I can find a way to scrape and survive even without her. Even though she is the very air I breathe. I just need her to be safe.

# SEVEN

THE THUMP of his footsteps descending mirror the thudding of my heart.

But I'm not nervous. I don't get nervous.

I'm ready.

The agony of working my hand free from the restraint after the medication wore off took a while to ebb, but once it did, I was able to move from the table that has been my prison for almost two weeks and explore the room.

All the weapons of my torture were laid out for me like a fucking smorgasbord.

Fuck, I really wish I could spend some time with this asshole to give him what he really deserves.

I scrub my good hand over my face. I'm such a fucking hypocrite. He's not doing anything more than what I've spent the last fifteen years of my life doing. I guess it's different when you're on the other side of the fist, or crowbar, or bolt cutters...

Although, honestly, I'm not afraid of death, nor would I ever give my brother the satisfaction of knowing the torture got to me. But Jade changed everything.

I will fight to my last dying breath for that woman, no matter what it costs me.

My hand throbs. I managed to stitch up the worst of my wounds, but the pinky situation...there was no stitching that. A powdered clotting agent and a bandage was my only option. Luckily, this fucker also had antibiotics on hand, so I dosed myself with that too. There's no time to stop for medical care when I get out of here. I just have to pray infection doesn't set in before I can get to Jade.

Click. Click. Click.

It's music to my ears. One step closer to having Jade safe and back in my arms. One step closer to killing Tarek and ending this thing.

The second he's through the door, I strike.

One hand clamps over the mask covering his mouth, and the other arm circles his neck, pulling him back into a choke hold.

I kick the door shut with my foot to ensure anyone upstairs can't hear what's going on. Doc clutches at my arms and thrashes to free himself.

My arm tightens on his throat, and I walk him to the table. Dried blood and other things I don't want to think about cover the surface.

"Good morning, Doc. There's been a change of plans."

Once his struggles cease and I know he's out, I strap him to my former prison and set to work.

I need any information he has. As little as it may be, it could be essential to finding Jade and my asshole brother.

He stirs, and a sharp slap has his eyes flying open. They blink against the bright light overhead before finally focusing on me.

"What do you want?" His voice wavers so badly, I can barely make out the words.

Leaning over him, I grin. "Information, and for you to suffer as much as I have."

I have to give the guy credit. He doesn't even flinch at my words. But that mask has to go; I want to know who I'm really dealing with. I tear it off, and he has the balls to smirk at me.

Shit. I know that smirk.

Something niggles at the back of my mind...a very old memory...

"Recognize me, Konstandin? It's been a long, long time, *miku im*."

Old friend?

No.

It can't be...

A barrage of bullets twenty years ago made it impossible.

I shake my head and rack my brain for any way to explain it. "No, you're dead."

He grins. "No, not dead. Close to it. After you abandoned me, I managed to crawl to a blown-out building and perform basic triage until I was finally found by some locals who took me in and nursed me back to health."

Jesus.

We all thought he was dead. He didn't have a pulse, at least not one we could find in the two seconds we had to check. We didn't even have time to try to collect his body before we had to turn our attention to saving our own lives.

War is brutal. It's unforgiving and relentless. It makes men do things...things that can never be taken back or forgotten. It taught me how to kill and how to survive. It sent me down the path that led to this. To a place where one killer is facing down another. To a place where an old friend has to kill a ghost.

"Why didn't you contact me? Return to the unit?"

A low chuckle rumbles from his lips. "Because being dead gave me freedom. From debt. From servitude. From the life I had been living. I was born anew."

"Into a sick, twisted psychopath."

His eyebrows raise. "Look who is talking, *miku im*."

Ouch.

He's not wrong, but it's beside the point. Old friend or not, he's the enemy now, one who has something I desperately need.

"Armend, I need to know where Tarek took Jade. Tell me everything you know."

The firm set of his jaw assures me this won't go as easy as I had hoped. Perhaps he's forgotten what I was capable of even back then.

"Fine. We'll do it the hard way."

I grab a scalpel from the tray next to the table and cut away his clothing, exposing his skin. Scars riddle his torso from the rain of bullets that met him during the firefight so long ago. How could he think we abandoned him? He was my unit medic, and one of the closest friends I had.

Any other time, I may feel guilty about what happened. But not after what he's done, what he would have continued to do if I hadn't managed to free myself.

"I am sorry I have to do this, *miku im*."

The words are hollow, and he knows it. As the blade pierces his skin, his bellow of pain ricochets around the room and has my heart beating a rapid tattoo. Maybe I've missed this more than I thought. It feels like coming home.

"How about we start with the ribs?"

EIGHT

"*Ik pirdhu*, motherfucker."

Saying goodbye to Armend isn't bittersweet. It's just sweet. He'll linger here for days, as his body slowly succumbs to infection and blood loss. It's the only thing that could be done with so little time that would give him the full agonizing experience he deserves.

A quick death would have been too good for him.

I push the door open slowly, exposing a long ascending staircase. My legs shake violently, reminding me of the very real trauma my body has endured. The adrenaline of what just occurred is waning.

Fuck...I hope I can make it up there.

It looks like Mt. Everest from here, when, in reality, it's probably only fifteen steps. The door at the top of the stairs is closed, giving me a brief second to regain my breath and prepare myself.

With each step, searing pain radiates throughout every fiber of my being, but I can't acknowledge it. If I do, I'll stop, and there's no stopping from this point on.

The branding iron and crowbar are my only weapons. Anything else down there was too small and delicate or too heavy for what I have planned.

Knowing my brother, there's no way there aren't more men here. When I was working, he always ensured I wouldn't be interrupted by placing a handful of others in the building. I pause at the top of the stairs. Voices trickle through the crack at the bottom of the door.

I count three.

But there could be more.

It doesn't matter. I'm ready for anything. I just hope they've become complacent and aren't expecting me.

Why would they, though?

Doc Psychopath down there probably has them as convinced as he had himself that there was no way I could escape. Dumb fuckers.

I can barely make out their words.

Something about chicken?

How sweet, they're planning lunch. Too bad they've already had their last meals.

They have no idea what's about to be unleashed upon them.

One more brief pause to catch my breath and try to alleviate the spinning in my head is all I allow myself before I shove the door open. Three confused faces look up at me from where they play cards around a small table in the center of a kitchen.

"What the fu—"

The crowbar connects with the side of his head, and the question dies in his throat. Before the other two can even react, my hand is around the weapon that had been sitting on the table to his right, and I fire off two shots.

But I'm not quick enough. Searing pain laces through my side right as my two shots connect, dropping his buddies to the floor...at least momentarily. There's no time to assess the damage to me or acknowledge the pain.

A large Bowie knife sitting on the edge of the table catches my eye. The handle feels at home in my hand, and I step over to one of the wounded men. I press my bare heel against his chest where blood oozes from the entry wound.

His buddy sputters and moans next to him. My bullet hit him in the neck; it's only a matter of seconds before he bleeds out, so he's not a threat. I can focus my attention elsewhere.

Wide, scared eyes meet mine.

"I...I...I didn't...I don't—"

The tip of the blade presses into his jugular, and I smile down at him. "Don't waste your last words on bullshit excuses, my friend. If you just tell me where he took Jade, this will end much quicker for you."

He struggles underneath me, and I grind my heel into his chest harder. His scream rents the air.

"Fuck! Jesus...fuck...okay. I don't know. I don't know anything."

I don't believe that for one second. "Do you know who I am?"

The man nods, almost imperceptibly.

"Then you know that I'm going to get what I want, one way or the other. Tell me what I need to know, and I can end this quickly and relatively painlessly."

I have no intention of letting him get off lightly, but he doesn't need to know that. Most people will latch onto any thread of hope that they might not have to suffer. "Tell me where he took Jade."

His eyes narrow at me with defiance. Again with the tight lips. When will these assholes learn?

"All right, I guess you want to do this the hard way."

With a glee that should probably concern me, I press the knife into the base of his throat. Slowly. It doesn't take much for most people to crack, and the pressure of a blade against the skin usually does the trick.

He flails, scratching at my arms and my naked body, trying to free himself from underneath me. I don't relent, just press more firmly until it pierces the skin.

"No! Stop! Fucking stop!"

I pause but don't remove the blade.

"All I know is he left with her on his jet. That's all I know, though. I wasn't even there. I was here, and he told me to wait until you were brought here and the doc arrived."

"And where exactly is *here*?"

He sucks in a deep breath and coughs up blood. "Montana."

Christ, leave it to my brother to drop me in the middle of fucking nowhere. I don't think this guy knows anything about Jade. But his time on this planet is through.

I pull the knife from his throat, and he breathes a sigh of relief, then coughs again. Blood spews from his mouth. The bullet in his chest likely hit an organ. He's a dead man soon, but after what he's been part of, the least I can do is make it more painful, physically and mentally.

Before he can say anything else or react, I stab the knife into the middle of his gut and jerk it upward. The slice tears his shirt and flays him wide open.

Screams echo in the barren room, mingling with the gurgling sounds from his soon-to-be deceased friend.

I reach in and grab the first thing my hand finds. A quick jerk rips his intestines from his body, and I drop them onto his chest.

His eyes widen briefly, and he chokes on his own blood. Then the life slips from his body, far too quickly for my liking.

Fucker got off easy, and without giving me anything to go on. I need more information.

My crowbar victim is my next task. I wander over to where he lies next to the table where he fell when I struck him.

Shit...he's dead too.

My only solace is that he likely didn't have any more information than the other motherfucker did. These guys are just thugs. Mindless worker bees doing the dirty work while my brother controls the hive.

I'll just have to find Jade the old-fashioned way.

But first, I need some clothes.

I eye up the three men and determine Mr. Crowbar is pretty close to my size, and his clothes aren't bloody, yet. Once I don his T-shirt, jeans, and combat boots, I search their bodies and the house for any additional weapons, information, or useful supplies.

Loaded up with ammo, a few handguns, and the surprising amount of money I found stashed at the house, my confidence level about my chances has certainly increased.

Then, I open the front door to the vast nothingness outside, and my heart drops into my stomach.

NINE

EMPTY FIELDS SPAN as far as the eye can see. I don't even know if there are any neighboring houses. A mountain range looms to the south, and a gravel drive leads into the vast nothingness.

The first order of business when I step outside and survey the house, is locating a vehicle. The house itself is inconspicuous and looks like any other ranch home out here. You would never know the kind of depraved things that happened in that basement.

Which is likely why it was chosen.

No one to hear you scream.

No one to question your coming and going.

No one to watch you dig the fucking graves.

It wouldn't surprise me if Tarek had this place all set up just for when he found me. Or he may have been using it since I left for all I know.

A large building to the side of the house looks promising, and I make my way across the gravel driveway. The crunch of the stone under my borrowed boots reminds me a little too much of the sound the bolt cutter made going through my finger.

The two black SUVs parked inside the out building have keys in the ignitions.

Thank fuck.

The soft leather hugs my overly sensitive body. Everything fucking hurts. I managed to throw a few stitches into the wound on my right side. It looked like a through and through, but fuck, does it hurt. Coupled with the pinky situation, and all the other things done to me, I'm in rough shape.

When the engine roars to life, a wave of relief washes over me.

One more step closer.

A search of the GPS for my location has me slamming my good hand against the steering wheel.

Jesus fucking Christ...we have to be a hundred miles from anything even resembling a town.

The cell phone I took from one of the idiots in there doesn't even get service. Not that I'm sure who I would call at this point. I don't know who ratted us out to Tarek or who is on our side. The best course of action is to head toward the nearest city with an airport and start making my way east...

I eat up the miles racing across Montana toward Billings.

There's only one person I can think to go to for help who hates my brother maybe as much as I do. One person I can maybe, possibly, potentially, somewhat trust.

They always say the enemy of your enemy is your friend.

I hope that's true because, otherwise, I'm walking into a fucking lion's den while I'm weak and bleeding.

THE FLIGHT TO CHICAGO IS EXCRUCIATING. THERE WEREN'T ANY PAIN MEDS IN THE TORTURE chamber, and frankly, I probably wouldn't have taken them anyway. I need to have my wits about me when I talk to Saban.

There's a fifty-fifty chance his men will kill me as soon as they lay eyes on me. If I make it past his guards, and he actually listens to me, that chance may go from fifty-fifty to seventy-thirty, but it's still not great odds.

I don't have a choice, though. I don't have any resources, and almost all the money I got off the assholes back at the house was used to pay for this airplane ride. It was pure luck I even found someone with a plane willing to fly me halfway across the country at the drop of a hat. Cash talks, though, and I found a lot of it at the house. I probably paid his plane off for him. Plus, I think the pilot must have smelled my desperation and taken pity on me.

Seven hours, including a refueling stop in Minneapolis, later, we finally touch down in Chi-town. The old mechanic at the airport is kindhearted enough to loan me his vehicle in exchange for the last of my cash. It's not like I can rent a car with no I.D.

So now, it's time to beg, something I don't do.

Information...that's all I need. It doesn't seem like a lot to ask, but when we're talking about Saban Gashi, it might as well be asking for the world.

I just pray the tentative truce Tarek and Saban have had for the last few years was just smoke and mirrors, and Saban still wants to latch onto any opportunity he has to get rid of Tarek. It's really my only hope at this point.

As soon as I'm in my borrowed car, I hit the streets of Chicago and wind my way to the southwest side where Saban's headquarters are. It's been a long time since I've been here—at least five years—but it doesn't look like things have changed much.

Armed guards mill about outside Pasha, the restaurant they use as a front. Saban will be holed up in the back in his office, probably with at least two or three additional guards near him. If I can get in there without killing anyone, I'll be happy. I don't want to start a war with him and have to watch my back even after I get rid of my brother. Let's just hope he's receptive to visitors.

The car door slams behind me, and I slowly make my way across the street, my eyes never leaving the guards. When the big guy in front of the restaurant door finally notices me, he immediately goes for his weapon.

I raise my hands as I step onto the curb and stop a few feet from him.

"Stop right there." The barrel points directly to my chest. His voice is strong and steady. He's not afraid to use that gun if he needs to.

"I'm here to see Saban."

His eyebrow shoots up. "And who the fuck are you?"

I grin and snort. He must be new. "Konstandin Morina."

My name draws the full attention of the other two goons out front, and they immediately draw their weapons and point them in my direction. At least they've heard of me.

"I'm unarmed." I raise my shirt and turn, then I lift up my pant legs. "I just need to talk to him."

The guards are understandably skeptical at my request. They wouldn't be doing their jobs if they weren't. After a beat, the big guy lowers his weapon.

"I'll be right back, keep your guns on him." He disappears into the building, and I keep my hands raised. The neighborhood is quiet. No one reacts to the pulled weapons. Not even the patrons inside the restaurant, who can no doubt see what's happening through the front windows, seem to be paying any attention. My guess is, it's a common enough occurrence around here, people don't even give it a second thought anymore. Either that, or they are too afraid to acknowledge what's happening around them.

I send the guards a friendly grin. "Guys, this is really unnecessary."

They both chuckle, and one steps forward. "What kind of idiots do you think we are?"

I grin again. "You probably don't want me to answer that."

Before either of the geniuses can register my insult, the door opens and the big guy returns. "He says he'll see you."

Good. I'm able to at least get inside without any bloodshed. Let's just hope it stays that way. The last thing I need is more enemies.

TEN

"I WAS WONDERING if you were going to show up."

Saban leans back in his chair and grins smugly.

He's a smart man. Only someone with extreme intelligence would be able to establish the empire he has here. The same with my brother. The only difference is, at least from what I've seen, Saban seems to have a tiny bit of a conscience. Maybe.

I drop down into a chair opposite him. "You were expecting me?"

He chuckles and places his elbows on his desk. "I figured there was a pretty good chance you would eventually need my help when you screwed over your brother and then fucked his fiancée."

I had considered coming to Saban then, but I thought I had it under control and that he wouldn't want to become embroiled in such a mess.

Now, I'm starting to wonder whether Tarek knew where we were the whole time and was just waiting for his opportunity to swoop and ruin our bliss.

No...that's not like him. He wouldn't want me to have any form of love or contentment and especially not with the woman he loves. Whatever information led him to me, it came later. Maybe from Saban, maybe from someone else.

"What is it you want, Konstandin?"

Revenge. The word almost slips out. It's the most honest answer I can give. But if Saban has any heart at all—a proposition that's still very much up for debate—I need to appeal to it as well as to his desire for power.

"I need to know where he took Jade. Even though he probably assumes I'm dead by this point, I know he's not dumb enough to take her back to his place. At least, not for a while."

He chuckles and rubs a hand across his jaw. "First, what makes you think I have any idea where he took her? Second, what makes you think I'd help you and potentially piss off your brother? We're allies now, remember?"

Allies is a bit of a strong word for what they are. It's more like enemies who know they're both strong enough to destroy each other, so they don't bother. Talk about a fucking cold war.

"I have no doubt you've talked to Tarek."

He nods, and the corner of his mouth tips up. "I have. He called to tell me he found you in Denver and to thank me for the information I provided him."

My hands fist on the armrests of my chair. I'm not surprised. Saban always was a worm, but that doesn't stop the anger from making its way to the surface.

He waits for a response, and when he doesn't get one, he leans back in his chair again. "Come on, Konstandin, you had to have known I would know you were anywhere within a two hundred-mile radius of Chicago. I knew the moment you set foot in Rockford."

No wonder I was so damn uneasy. I should have fucking known we were too close to him and all his connections.

"So you're the reason my brother found us?"

Saban shrugs. "That was well over a year ago. I lost track of you for a while, although I did have my men looking. I knew it was only a matter of time before either they, or your brother, located you."

"Why did you help him?"

He raises his hands. "Why wouldn't I help him? From what I understand, he was the wronged party here, and as I mentioned, we made a truce. Telling him where he could find his fiancée, and his backstabbing brother, seemed like basic goodwill and something that may earn me some bonus points for future negotiations."

Blood roars through my veins like napalm. This asshole is the reason we got caught. Yes, my brother may have found us eventually, but I have no doubt in my mind the information Saban provided helped him along the way. More eyes. More ears. More opportunities to be caught.

"Tell me where Jade is. I could be an ally to you. We both know you've always wanted my brother gone. Why not join forces with me? We could end this together."

The smile he gives me is about as warm as dry ice. "I don't disagree with you on the fact that I want your brother gone, but there's something to be said for the status quo. I have a good thing going here. Taking on your brother's territory would stretch my capabilities to their limits. Controlling one city is hard enough. Controlling two, plus all the area between them, would be something else altogether."

I always knew Saban was a fucking ball-less pussy. It just would have been nice to have a friend with some power in all this. "Fine, but at least tell me where he took Jade."

I try to rein in my anger and not let it show in my words, but the quirk of his brow tells me I probably failed miserably at that.

"You aren't really in any position to be making demands, are you? You have no weapon, you're in foreign territory, and one call would have your brother's men here before the end of the day to take you to him."

All true, but Saban underestimates me. A mistake that usually doesn't end well for most people. I scan the room out of the corner of my eye.

"You're right." I stand and step slightly toward the desk. "I have no leverage. I have no way to force you to tell me anything, but I'm asking you nicely...please tell me where he took Jade."

Please is not a word that comes out of my mouth often. My throat burns from having even said it, but I'm making one last-ditch effort to get what I need without starting a *second* war.

He tucks his hands behind his head and gives me yet another grin. "He was heading back to Philly, that's all I know."

Whether he's being honest or lying is irrelevant at this point. He signed his death warrant the moment he admitted he helped my brother find me and Jade.

ELEVEN

THE *THWACK* the lamp makes connecting with Saban's skull sounds like a fucking heavenly chorus of angels. Blood splatters across the wall behind him, and he slumps down in his chair.

Shattered glass from the bulb crunches under my boots when I move to stand next to him.

A groan slips from his lips. I clamp my hand over his nose and mouth, silencing any protests or screams. I'll have to take care of this fast. As soon as the guys outside realize we aren't talking anymore, I'm toast. And if they heard the lamp break, I'm well and truly fucked.

His one working eye flies open and meets mine.

"I hope it was worth it...whatever benefit you received from betraying me to my brother."

He gurgles under my left hand while I yank open one of the drawers on his desk. The letter opener glints in the light.

Perfect.

My hand curls around it, and I bring it up so he can see it.

"I much prefer my own implements, but I'll make do."

The fear in his eyes warms my otherwise cold, dead heart. The heart that never felt anything before Jade walked into my life and has been slowly dying again since she was taken from me.

The blade of the opener slides into his ear easily with one hard shove. I muffle his scream with my hand and press down, watching him struggle for breath as I impale his brain. He jerks and spasms under me before finally going limp.

His one remaining eye stares back at me blindly as I step back and survey my handiwork. It was a far too easy and good of a death for him, but desperate times call for quick action.

Muffled voices outside the door draw my attention away from my latest kill, and I quickly rummage through the drawers on his desk, looking for anything useful.

Two handguns and a small pile of ammo later, I make my way to the corner where a safe hangs open. Stacks and stacks of cash line the inside.

"Thanks, Saban."

My mumbled words go unheard by the dead man in the chair as I grab bundles of bills and shove them into a duffel bag next to the safe on the floor.

This stash will certainly come in handy.

I press my ear against the door, listening for any signs of life in the hallway, but all is quiet. I'm not dumb enough to believe there isn't anyone out there, though. Saban always has at least two goons milling about in the back hallway, and they saw the big guy bring me back here.

Both weapons are loaded and ready to go.

So am I. I sling the bag over my shoulder and ready myself before I yank open the door and step out.

Three shots to the chest take out the guard to the right of the door and the suppressor on the weapon gives me enough time to maintain the element of surprise on his buddy down the hallway to the left. The asshole has a cell phone pressed to his ear, and when he turns and his eyes meet mine, they bulge just before two bullets enter his chest.

A few more pistols and some extra magazines join my friends in the bag, and I peer around the corner toward front of the restaurant. Clanking of dishes and silverware, and the light din of voices echo down the hallway toward me.

The back door down at the other end of the hallway is an option, but there are likely to be more guards that way than if I go through the restaurant. I know they congregate in a room back there. I just hope these assholes aren't dumb enough to shoot at me in such a public space.

I tuck my guns away and walk as casually as possible down the hallway, past the public bathrooms, and out into the restaurant. I'm just another guy. No one seems to be paying any attention to me until my hand curls around the handle on the front door. The big guy out front sees me through the windows. A brief moment of confusion flashes across his eyes before he draws his weapon.

It's all I need to see to know he never expected to see me again. Saban was going to kill me, or at least have someone come in and do the dirty work. Tarek may have wanted me back alive so he could personally finish the job, but Saban wanted me as a trophy.

The front door sticks slightly, losing me a precious second of time before I can fire at the large guard and empty the magazine into him. A burning flash of pain in my shoulder lets me know he managed to get at least one shot off before I took him down. His two buddies scramble and fire shots back at me. Another hits my left arm and a searing blaze of agony shoots through it.

I stumble momentarily but manage to fire a few more rounds before I dive into my car and hightail it away from the clusterfuck that was my Hail Mary.

Blood seeps into my shirt and trickles down my arm. Drops land on my leg and cover the steering wheel.

This one is bad. There's no way I can take care of this myself and stay standing for long.

I need help, and there's only once place I can think to go in Chicago.

I just hope he hasn't closed up shop since the last time we were here and needed his special brand of assistance.

TWELVE

Her tongue snakes out and trails along the underside of my cock. A shudder rolls through my body, and I tangle my hands into her hair and tug. She moans and wraps that wicked tongue of hers around the throbbing head, lapping up the bead of precum. A hum of approval vibrates around my engorged flesh as she sucks my entire length into her hot mouth.

My hips buck and roll, pushing me even further down her throat.

"FUCK! Rea!"

She hums, sending shockwaves of pleasure coursing through my body.

I won't last long. No way.

Not now that I finally have her exactly where I want her.

Not now that Rea has finally offered herself to me, body, mind, and heart.

Not now that Rea is finally mine.

Her sinful mouth suctions around my dick, and she starts a rhythm sure to having me blowing my load down her throat in ten seconds flat.

How can someone so sweet and innocent be so damn good at this?

The tingle in my balls warns me of my impending release. I grip her hair tighter, urging her head up and down faster, shoving even deeper.

Wave after wave of electrifying bliss shoots through my body as I come down her throat. She moans her approval and sucks me until I'm so sensitive, it almost hurts, and I have to yank my cock free from her warm depths.

I release her hair and cup her face, ensuring she's looking up at me and paying close attention. Her jade green eyes bore into mine with a love and compassion I've never seen from anyone in my life before. One I surely don't deserve.

"We can't go back, Rea. You are mine, and I am yours. But we must leave now. There's no other choice."

I jerk awake, the memory of my first time with Rea—and my last time with her *as* Rea before she became Jade—so crystal clear in my mind, my hard cock throbs between my legs. I shift on the bed.

Barking.

Chirping.

Scratching.

The unfamiliar sounds fill my ears and cause my swimming head to split with an agonizing headache.

Where the fuck am I?

I open my eyes to take stock of my surroundings. Blurry vision doesn't help the disorientation as I try to raise my head.

A hand presses against my chest and pushes me back down.

"Stay down."

I don't recognize the voice, and my first instinct is to lash out at him, but the floaty feeling in my head and limbs lulls me into a strange sense of security.

"I've given you propofol and isoflurane, so don't try to get up until it wears off completely."

What?

A memory stirs.

Gunshots.

Bleeding.

Driving across town.

The veterinary clinic.

Shit.

"Thanks." I manage the mumbled word before my world slips into a hazy black fog.

When I come to again, I push myself up slowly, using my right hand. My left arm throbs, reminding me of why I ended up here in the first place.

"I removed the bullet."

The voice makes me jump slightly, but I turn and find the doctor sitting in a chair across the room, a book open on his lap.

"It was fairly deep into the muscle, so it's going to hurt for a while. The other was just a flesh wound. A few stitches took care of that one."

I nod my understanding and scrub my hand over my face. Several weeks of not shaving have left a rough beard I'm not used to feeling on my jaw.

"Any chance you have somewhere I can clean up and shave before I take off?"

He raises an eyebrow and sets his book face down onto the counter next to him.

"You can't leave yet. Tomorrow morning at the earliest. I won't be able to hide you once my staff comes in, but you need to rest tonight."

I shake my head and swing my legs over the edge of the exam table. "No, I have to go."

An annoyed sigh fills the room. "I guess I can't stop you, can I? There's a bathroom with a shower down the hall on the left." He reaches into a cabinet and pulls out an electric razor. "And you can use this."

Just stretching out my right arm to try to take it from him makes me wobble and slide from the table. I grasp the edge with my good hand and grit my teeth against the pain in my left arm.

"I'll grab you some meds to take with you. Antibiotics and pain meds. You'll need both. That finger of yours, or what was left of it, was a mess. So was that stitch job you did on your side. Another bullet?"

I nod.

"It's a good thing you came in when you did, or infection would have likely taken that whole hand. I cleaned it up and gave you some IV antibiotics while you were out."

I mumble another thanks before righting myself on unsteady feet and grabbing the razor from his outstretched hand. "I won't be long."

"There are some clean clothes in my gym bag in the locker in the bathroom. You need them."

It hadn't even crossed my mind what I must look like at this point. I glance down. The pants I took from the guy at the ranch house are now splattered with both Saban's blood and my own. The shirt is in even worse condition. Barely anything remains after the doctor cut away the sleeve on the left side and what is there is drenched in blood.

"Thanks."

He nods and returns to his chair and book, leaving me to stagger down the hallway to the bathroom on my own. As soon as I'm cleaned up, I need to get heading east again.

Jade is out there with my monster of a brother. And now, I have not only his men after me, but also Saban's. Things just got a hell of a lot harder.

THIRTEEN

THE CLACKING of the rails threatens to lull me to sleep again, but I force my eyes open and stare out at the city flying by me.

Pittsburgh.

So fucking close to home. Yet somehow, I still feel a million miles away from Jade.

Every day, hour, and minute that passes only makes me more certain of what has to happen. Destroying Tarek isn't enough. His entire network needs to go up in flames.

But first...Jade.

The money in my bag, minus a few bundles that went to the vet, is going to be put to good use as soon as we stop in Philly. I managed a few hours of sleep between Chicago and here, enough time to somewhat recover from the backroom surgery I had last night.

And time to plan.

Tarek will be expecting me by now, so I can't storm in there, guns blazing, as much as I want to. My fingers are practically itching in anticipation of finally wrapping around my brother's throat and watching the life drain from his eyes.

He deserves nothing less than the worst of the worst. And I'll make sure he gets it...once Jade is safe.

Throbbing in my arm reminds me I'll be at somewhat of a disadvantage, but I've overcome worse. Seven years in the Special Operations Battalion in Albania exposed me to more death, destruction, and insane situations than most people could possibly imagine.

It also trained me to expect the unexpected and find a way to get the upper hand. Tarek may be anticipating my arrival, but there's no way he can understand or expect the type of blitzkrieg I plan on unleashing on him and his men.

The time it will take to make the arrangements will tick by slower than the miles on this train trip, but it's a necessary delay to ensure I can get her out safely.

I pull out the burner phone I bought in Chicago and make the call I pray I don't end up regretting.

A familiar gravelly voice answers. "Hello?"

The tightening in my chest is unexpected. I never thought I'd be so fucking happy to hear it.

"Lorenc...it's me."

Silence lingers over the line momentarily.

This could go one of two ways. Either he'll hang up on me and immediately tell Tarek I've contacted him...or he'll offer any assistance I need.

Obviously, the latter would make things a lot easier for me. Especially because I know I'll be coming face-to-face with him when I reach Philly. A friendly face and assistance are much-needed right now, but Lorenc has always been loyal to my brother, just as much as I was before I left.

"Fuck! Are you okay? Where the fuck are you?"

I sigh and look toward the passing city again. "Okayish. And on my way there."

"Shit. Do you have a fucking death wish?"

At one point in my life, I would have responded yes. When Rea came into our lives, I was nothing but a shell of a man. I'd done so many unspeakable things, I was certain there was no soul left to be saved. But one small smile from the green-eyed angel assured me there was still a heart beating in my chest and something alive deeper inside me.

Something that is clawing at my ribcage as I try to get to her now.

"No, but I have a plan."

A long, drawn-out sigh reaches me through the phone. "I was afraid you'd say that."

My chest burns. I rub it absently and immediately regret moving my left arm. "Are you gonna help me or not?"

We've been through a lot together. More than any one person should ever have to experience, both in the military at home and working for Tarek after we made it to the States. Lorenc has always been my friend and my confidant, and I know disappearing with Jade, without giving him any warning, was a real punch to the nuts. But I couldn't call him. I couldn't say a word to anyone because even a whisper of what we were about to do would've been a death sentence for everyone.

I'm counting on him hating my brother as much as I do even if he was always loyal. But it's been two years, and I've no idea what's been happening since I left. For all I know, they could be best buddies at this point.

"Of course, I'll help you. Your brother has turned into even more of a maniacal psychopath since you've been gone. Swear to God, that guy is unhinged."

Which is exactly what I've been worried about. "Have you seen Jade?"

"Who the fuck is Jade?"

"Oh shit, sorry, I mean Rea." I had to force myself to think of her by her new name. A slip of the tongue could have been enough to reveal our true identities. It's hard to think of her as anything *but* Jade now. She became Jade, and I became Griffin when we left Philly. Konstandin and Rea died the day we fled.

"No, he hasn't been back here after he grabbed her. He's keeping a low profile, but I have a few ideas where he might be. It's not like him not to have guards with him...just another reason I believe he's not thinking clearly anymore. Even after word got to us of what happened in Montana and in Chicago, he still won't tell us where he is to offer him protection. It's like he's become fucking paranoid that everyone is out to get him."

He should be paranoid, but paranoia is not going to be enough to stop me from reaching my goal—his head on a fucking stake.

FOURTEEN

THE DARK NIGHT sky is the perfect backdrop to the lit Philadelphia skyline. I never thought I'd be back here. I wish it were under completely different circumstances, like my brother's funeral, but that will come soon enough.

My love for this city runs deep. It's my second home and the place where I met *her*. But it's also my brother's city...one that's dark and deadly. One where people are waiting around every fucking corner to shoot me or slit my throat.

This isn't a pleasure trip, although finally ending my brother *will* bring me extraordinary pleasure. This is necessity now.

The car Lorenc secured is waiting when I climb off the train. The sleek black sedan is both ostentatious and inconspicuous in my brother's world. It's going to be a lot easier getting in and out of these places undetected if I blend in. The change of clothes he left in the backseat fits me perfectly, and as I walk out of the bathroom at the Amtrak station and make my way back toward the car, I can't help but feel like my old self.

My self before Jade.

My self before love.

My self before having anything to live for.

My self...the one who had absolutely everything he could ever want and also nothing.

A quick peek around the parking lot assures me I'm alone, and I pop the trunk to examine its contents. It's just as Lorenc promised. A duffel bag full of C-4, fuses, guns, ammo...everything I could possibly need to complete my plan.

Well, almost everything. I'm going to need a lot of luck and for things to go perfectly right to pull this off and still walk out alive.

But even if I don't make it, as long as Jade is safe and Tarek is dead, I'll have succeeded in my mission.

The engine rumbles and I peel away from the station toward the apartment Lorenc set up for me.

Tonight, I plan and I prepare. Tonight, I sleep in a bed alone for the first time in two years, or at least, attempt to.

Tomorrow, the shit is going to hit the fan, along with a whole fucking lot of blood hitting the floor.

BY THE TIME I'M DONE WITH MY PREPARATIONS, MY ARM THROBS SO BADLY, I'M FORCED TO down two of the tramadol the vet gave me.

I hate drugs and normally wouldn't leave myself so exposed and vulnerable in the middle of such a shit show, but I need to sleep—really fucking sleep—to be able to do what needs to be done tomorrow. The only way that's going to happen is with the help of some narcotics.

A warm, fuzzy haze descends on me.

But the euphoria filling me doesn't touch what it's like to be with Jade.

Her small, soft hands roaming over my body.

Stroking.

Caressing.

Scratching.

An unbidden moan slips from my mouth into the pillow.

Then I remember where she is now, who she's with, and my stomach roils.

Swallowing down the bile, I turn onto my side and try not to think about it, but it's useless. I race to the bathroom and heave over the toilet.

I can't even remember the last time I threw up. Maybe when I had the flu as a child? *Mami* would make soup and rock me on her lap while Tarek made attempt after attempt to steal her attention from me. Even back then, he was a fucking dick.

Where most people outgrow pettiness and jealousy, his lingered—he just learned to hide it better. I always knew it was there, festering just beneath the surface, but as we grew, we bonded over our shared experiences and struggles. And when he begged me to leave Albania with him, to come to America to start over and expand his newborn business, I jumped at the chance even if it meant being under his thumb at the time.

I can't say I regret the decision, because it brought me to her. But I would give anything to have met her in any other place, at any other time, in any other life.

Crawling back into the bed, I feel ten times weaker than I did only half an hour ago.

I need sleep. I'm useless to her without it.

So I let the fog envelop me again.

Vivid memories swirl through my head.

Stolen glances.

Soft touches.

Tangled limbs.

Sparring tongues.

Laughter.

Squealing tires.

Tears.

Warm wet flesh.

Green eyes looking up at me with love and adoration.

Whispered *I love yous*.

The echoed sound of her words is what finally drags me down into the dark abyss of sleep.

FIFTEEN

THE BUILDING IS INCONSPICUOUS ENOUGH. It's really nothing more than an old warehouse converted into a storefront business selling lawn care items.

A front for my brother's drug operation, just one of the many dirty rackets he has his hands in.

It's served him well for many years. Either the cops don't know or don't care about it, and the ones who do know are paid to stay away and keep their mouths shut. Money talks, and as much as people don't want to believe the men in blue can succumb to its siren's call...they're only human. They have bills, they have families, they have wants and dreams, and a little extra cash for turning a blind eye is something many are willing to accept.

Dawn is still two hours away, so all is dark and quiet for the time being.

It won't stay that way long.

Four of Tarek's men will arrive around six a.m., ready to spend the day sitting in the back office, bullshitting in between shipments while a clueless employee stands in the front, in case any customers actually show up. My brother is good at one thing—he's managed to keep a few people in the dark, so if things go to shit, they can't tell the cops anything if one he hasn't managed to pay off accidentally stumbles in. I'm sure the employees suspect something shady, but Tarek's men are scary enough to prevent questions.

I slip into the side entrance using the same passcode that's been in place for as long as Tarek has owned the building. The moron didn't even bother to change it after I left. Whoever is handling his security doesn't have a fucking clue.

Maneuvering through the dark, I make my way to the back offices and open yet another door that should have been secured. It's almost like he's begging me to do this.

Poker chips and cards lie scattered across the table, leftover from their last game, and empty beer bottles overflow from the trash bin.

The bomb goes in the most obvious place...smack dab in the middle of the underside of the table. The blast will take out his men but leave the innocents out front unharmed. No matter how much I hate my brother, I'll do what I can to avoid collateral damage. The blast will also draw the police to the warehouse, and any stock that isn't destroyed by the rest of the bombs will be confiscated.

If I were going to let him live, he'd be going away for the rest of his life. But Tarek will never see the inside of a jail cell. All he'll see is my face before his life ends.

Four more bombs placed in various locations around the main warehouse guarantee total annihilation of this location. Once assured everything is perfect, I head back out without leaving a trace. No one will know I was ever here until the whole place is up in smoke.

Tarek's empire is vast, but he centralizes most of his operations here in Philly. It makes taking off the head of the snake easier.

Three more warehouses. Twelve more bombs.

Then I make my way to the one place I had hoped to never return.

My brother's headquarters.

The bakery is a legitimate business run by one of our cousins who also came over from Albania. I hate that I have to do this to her. But Tarek set it up as a front almost immediately and took over the back portion and the upper floors of the building.

Lorenc already told me Tarek hasn't shown his face here with Jade, and I believe him. He has no reason to lie unless he's in bed with my brother, which I highly doubt given the amount of firepower and help he's provided since our telephone call.

He's also been staking out the other locations he suspected Tarek may be holed up, but the effort is futile. I know where my brother is. He's arrogant enough to think he's safe there. And it will be my next stop as soon as I get this place wired.

Getting in and out of here undetected is going to be a lot harder than at the warehouses. There's always someone here. The bakery runs twenty-four hours in order to keep up with the demand of the various specialty markets it provides baked goods for. Tarek would never leave the throne of his empire unprotected.

But he did leave it weak.

I make my way to the fire escape that runs along the side of the building. I begged him to have it removed a hundred times, or at least, have it wired with motion sensors, given how easily someone can get in and out undetected this way. Again, my brother thought he knew better and didn't take my advice, much to my benefit currently. The window to his office pops open easily from the old jamb, and I crawl in and take stock of the room I haven't set foot in for over two years.

The same large wooden desk dominates the space, and photographs of my brother and various friends and acquaintances of high-ranking stature line the walls. Tarek is always such a whore, kissing ass and licking the boots of anyone who can get him anywhere or anyone he would look good standing next to.

One picture in the room, in particular, draws my attention.

Jade...

It must have been from the first couple of days when she came to him all those years ago, though I've never seen it before. I doubt it was taken with her knowledge.

Her hair billows out behind her in the wind as she leans over the railing, staring out over the vastness of the ocean. A small smile tugs at the corner of her lip, but the sadness in her eyes is apparent even in the profile view. She knew what her father had done to her even then, and my brother was too big of an asshole to let her go even though it was the right thing to do.

Well, it's time she's free of him. She chose her monster, and it's me.

SIXTEEN

THE SMALL TWO-STORY bungalow sits on a quiet cul-de-sac in Trappe. I fell in love with it the moment I saw it five years ago, and I knew I had to have it, despite not really needing all that space just for myself.

It was more about the distance it put between me and Tarek, between me and that world. When I wasn't working, I needed the empty space. My head was already filled by the faces and voices and cries of those I've killed—I didn't need them crowding me in a one-bedroom apartment somewhere downtown too.

The curtains are drawn, and it's still early enough there's no movement at any of the neighbors' homes. My watch reads 6:30 a.m.

He'll be awake by now. He's never been able to break the habit of five a.m. wake-ups. Just like me, the military drilled it into him, and it's impossible to overcome the routine.

Before I can do anything, I make a necessary phone call.

"Hello?" The soft voice belies her dominant stature and overbearing presence.

My mother's cousin Drita is a force to be reckoned with, and I've missed her dearly since we left. She became a second mother to us and has always been there, no questions asked, for whatever we need from her. And she's not afraid to speak her mind even to me and my brother.

"Drita, *teto*, it's Konstandin."

Her audible gasp reaches through the line. "Konstandin, *djalosh*, where have you been? I've been worried sick about you. Your brother..." she trails off. The words don't need to be voiced. She knows what it means for me to be making contact with her. She knows there's only one reason I would be back.

"Drita, you and all the employees need to leave the building at precisely seven o'clock."

A brief silence descends as she contemplates my words.

"Okay, Konstandin. Whatever you need, dear."

"I'm sorry it has to end this way."

She sighs. I can practically picture her resting her chin in her hand, her gray hair piled atop her head in the ever-present bun.

"Your mother would be appalled at what your brother has become, Konstandin. You do whatever you need to do."

I didn't expect Drita's blessing, but it certainly sets my mind at ease with what I'm about to do to her business.

"There's a duffel bag full of cash in the third oven from the left. Take it with you when you leave." I managed to sneak it in there when one of the bakers stepped out for a smoke break.

"Are you never coming back after you get her?"

I sigh and scrub my hand over my face, my arm screaming at the movement. "I don't know, Drita. But I want you to be taken care of, no matter what happens, you and the rest of the family. Take care of Adelina."

Just thinking about my sister, at home with her husband and children, blissfully unaware of what's about to happen, makes my eyes burn.

"Have you spoken with her?"

"No. I can't put her in between me and Tarek. I'm sure he was hard enough on her when I left. I'll not tell her what I have planned."

Maybe it's a dick move, but my sister has managed to escape all the turmoil Tarek has created and made a real life for herself. I don't need to drag her into this mess now.

"*Shkoni me Perëndinë.*"

Her words have tears pricking in my eyes, the first since Jade told me she loved me. The same words my mother used to say haven't touched my ears in almost twenty years.

"So, take care of yourself, Konstandin."

The line goes dead.

It's done.

I can finally focus my attention on my real purpose. Getting my woman back and setting us free.

A haze of dawn touches the horizon when I slip from the car parked several blocks down the road. Branches and bushes pull and scratch at me as I make my way through backyards to the side of my house.

Even without any signs of life from inside, I'm confident he's here. It's just one more way for him to have what's mine, to show Jade he can, and will, take and possess whatever he wants.

Given the time, he will break her down until she's nothing but a shell of herself, someone even I can't recognize. But that won't happen. Rivers of blood will flood Philly before I ever let Tarek destroy her.

SEVENTEEN

THE MOMENT I open the back kitchen door, her scent invades my nostrils, and my cock stirs to life.

Cinnamon and sugar.

All things sweet and pure.

She's here.

There's not a doubt in my mind. Her presence wraps around me like a warm blanket, soothing my soul, and reinforcing my will to do what needs to be done.

Vivid memories of fucking her on the kitchen counter, against the hallway wall, and making love to her in my bed flood my mind. Fuck Tarek for tainting my home, my memories, by bringing her here.

My hand tightens around the grip of the M1911, and I move into the kitchen slowly, my eyes never leaving the doorway to the living room. When I reach the jamb, I take a deep breath and then peer around the corner.

No sounds.

No movement.

The hairs on the back of my neck stand on end.

Something's wrong.

Step by agonizingly slow step, I make my way down the hallway, passing the open bathroom door.

No steam on the mirror.

The door to the guest bedroom hangs open.

Rumpled sheets cover the bed, but no other signs of life permeate the air.

Where the fuck are they?

There's *no way* she isn't here. Jade and I only spent one night here together. The night before we left to start our new lives. There wasn't time for her scent and presence to invade the space the way they do now.

A half dozen steps bring me to the narrow stairs up to the master bedroom. It's the perfect place for an ambush. If Tarek is up there, there's a good chance I'll be under a hail of bullets the moment I set foot on the first step. But I don't have a choice.

My heart pulls me up the stairs as much as my need for revenge does.

When I reach the top, I know the house is empty.

No sounds or signs of life.

No barrage of bullets.

No Jade.

Where the *fuck* are they?

Rage boils in my gut as I approach the bed.

A single sheet of white paper lies in the center.

Konstandin –

Too late, brother. Knowing me as you do, I anticipated you coming here as soon as I learned of what you did to Armend and Saban. Don't worry, I'm taking excellent care of Rea.

While I'm impressed with your ability to make it this far, your days are numbered. There will be a reckoning, brother. Soon.

Tarek

The mattress sinks under my weight. My hand shakes, and I set my gun down next to me.

I'm too late.

They were here...

So fucking close.

My bellowed roar vibrates in my chest and bounces around the room. Something takes hold of me, wrapping around my chest and squeezing tightly. My vision blurs and before I even know I'm doing it, the mirror above the dresser is shattered into a thousand pieces, the mattress is flipped over against the wall, and angry tears are running down my face.

"No!" He can't win. I won't let him. I can't let that happen to her.

Fear is an unknown feeling for me. I've never truly loved anyone before. Even in the darkest and hardest days of my life, I never experienced the gut-clenching sensation that's overtaking my body now, because it is isn't fear for me or for my life—it's for her.

Only the ringing of my phone breaks me from the downward spiral of fear.

Lorenc's number flashes across the screen, and I notice the time.

Shit.

"Hello?"

"Everyone's in a mad scramble. Police are swarming over the warehouses and bakery. I sure as shit hope you have her and took care of Tarek already."

I scrub my hand over my face and survey the destruction in the room. "They aren't here."

"Shit."

"Yeah. I must have just missed them. And now I don't have a fucking clue where he may have taken her."

On top of destroying part of Tarek's vast network, the panic and disarray the bombs caused was supposed to be a distraction to keep both the police and the remaining members of Tarek's crew busy while I took care of him and got away.

I never thought for a second he wouldn't be here.

"Hold on."

The wait feels like hours.

"I may be able to help you with that."

Hope lightens the weight on my shoulders momentarily. "What do you know?"

"Enrik just sent me a text. He's meeting your brother at the Heritage Field airport in thirty minutes."

The motherfucker thinks he's getting away with my woman? Over my dead body.

Which begs the question...if he knew I would come here, why didn't he have an ambush waiting for me? Why not leave some of his men here to take me out the moment they set eyes on me?

Unease returns as I make my way down the stairs.

"Meet me at the airport in ten."

I'm not going into this alone. Not with so much at stake.

EIGHTEEN

A FEW SMALL planes litter the tarmac, but the parking lot outside the little building that houses the airport is empty.

"Where are they?"

I glance over at Lorenc. He shrugs while continuing to scan the area for signs of life.

"Probably on the way. I confirmed with Enrik that he was supposed to meet them here."

It could be a diversion so they can get out of the city some other way without me knowing, but that only makes sense if Tarek suspected Lorenc of assisting me.

I shove open the car door and step out into the cool morning air. It may be a diversion, or worse, a trap, but I can't take the chance of missing her.

Lorenc's footsteps on the pavement behind me break the silence of the early morning.

"You sure you want to just walk in there?"

I glance over my shoulder at him. "Yep."

No more sneaking around. No more stealth.

It's time for fucking shock and awe.

The glass in the door rattles with my quick jerk, and I storm into the lobby.

A vacant receptionist station sits in the center of the room.

These small airports tend to only have one or two staff members working at any one time inside the building, but there's no sign of anyone.

The eerie silence has every nerve in my body screaming to get out of here. But I ignore it and advance further into the building.

Bullets whiz by, and Lorenc and I dive down a small hallway to our left.

Lorenc falls beside me. "Fuck!"

"Are you hit?"

"No. You?"

I shake my head and peek out around the corner. Two shots fly past me and embed in the wall on the other side.

At least whoever is shooting at us has shit aim.

Lorenc points to a window at the end of the hall. "You circle around."

I nod my agreement and jog to the window. The old sash sticks, but it eventually wiggles free without too much noise. I drop onto the grass and circle the building toward the direction of the gunfire, checking each window as I come to it.

The first two are just empty offices, but on the third, I hit pay dirt.

Two guys dressed in black lean out the doorway, their guns raised and ready to fire. Their backs to me are the perfect targets. All I need to do is stop them long enough to unload a couple mags in them.

My left hand tightens around the grip of my second weapon. With both guns raised and aimed at them through the window, I take a deep breath. These assholes aren't gonna know what hit them.

Crack!

The window shatters almost at the same instant my bullets collide with the two gunmen. They jerk and twist back, firing off rounds wildly at the unknown shooter while I drop a mag into each of them. Their crumpled bodies lie just inside the door.

Lorenc appears in the doorway and examines my handiwork. "I see your aim hasn't gotten rusty over the last couple of years."

I climb through the now empty window frame. One man is clearly dead, but the other stares up at us, gasping and gurgling for breath through blood-soaked lips.

"He'll...never let...you...take...her."

Squatting down next to him, I pull my knife from my boot and examine it in the soft morning sunlight now filtering in the window. His eyes widen a fraction of a second before I bury the blade into his heart, up to the hilt.

"Why did you do that? He might've known where they are."

I stand and shake my head. "They'll be here."

He follows me out into the hallway. "How can you be so sure?"

"Because my brother believes he's invincible and that this ambush would be successful. That's why he was confident enough not to try to take me out at my house. He knew he wouldn't need to. He already had this planned."

Tarek set this up so he could kill Lorenc too. It's the only explanation. He knew Lorenc would betray him at the first opportunity, if I asked. I should have anticipated he would never fully trust him after I left.

But it's irrelevant now.

Now, all I have to do is sit and wait.

NINETEEN

Footsteps approach down the hallway and reach my ears through the cracked door.

We didn't have to wait long. It was just enough time to race out to the tarmac, plant the bomb on the airplane, and get repositioned inside.

Ten minutes after the ambush, car doors slammed outside and we were in position.

Despite the epic importance of the next few minutes, my heartbeat remains slow and steady. This is what I was built for. This is what I pushed away for the last two years, to try to create a new life for me and Jade. But what I am, what I *truly* am at my core, can never be changed.

I'm a killer.

And it's time to take lives.

The only concern is assuring Jade doesn't get caught in any crossfire.

A quick peek through the gap in the door tells me I'm dealing with two of Tarek's men. The first one I recognize. Emil has been with Tarek for at least half a decade. What he lacks in the brains department, he makes up for with reliability and willingness to do whatever he's asked, without question. He's the perfect employee for a twisted fuck like my brother.

The guy he's talking to as they make their way closer is new. At least to me.

"...radio...no answer..."

They've probably tried to get in touch with the two stone-cold losers on the floor next to me. Yet, they don't have their guns drawn.

Are they that fucking stupid?

More car doors slam and someone comments on the broken window on the front of the building.

Shit.

Just what I need...

"Tarek! Please! No."

Her voice cuts through everything else going on around me.

A dog barks.

Bruiser? That motherfucker took my woman *and* my dog?

My heart screams for me to run to the window...to see her...to take out Tarek right now. But my training tells me to wait. This only works if we can ensure she's safe, and Tarek and his men die. That only happens if I follow the plan.

And the plan starts with these two assholes strolling down the hall toward me without a fucking care in the world.

Two well-placed shots drop them both mid-step.

Lorenc rushes out and drags the bodies into one of the empty offices while I make my way down the hall toward the front entrance and duck into the first door before the reception area.

Waiting sucks.

But it isn't long before familiar voices enter the building.

Enrik's with him. So is Behar, his pilot.

These men I once called friends and my brother, are now the only thing standing between me and the woman I love.

"Go make sure the plane's ready. Load the bags. We'll be right out." My brother's order will be followed, leaving him and Jade unprotected. Hopefully.

This is our chance. I just hope Lorenc is ready too.

I step out into the hallway, exposing myself to Tarek and anyone else who may be lingering with a gun.

My eyes immediately find Jade's green, red-rimmed ones.

"Griffin!" She lunges toward me, only to be yanked back by Tarek. His nostrils flare, and his cheeks redden. The muscle in his jaw ticks.

Tears stream down Jade's face as his fingers tighten around her upper arm. I want nothing more than to shoot off those white knuckles to free her from his grip. But rash actions will get me nowhere.

I approach slowly.

A sneer curls the corner of Tarek's lips. "Well, brother, I'm impressed. You've managed to survive everything I've thrown at you. I'll admit, I never expected it to get this far. But it's irrelevant. You can't stop me."

I grin at him. "I already have."

An explosion rocks the tarmac, shattering the windows of the building and sending glass flying toward us. Tarek loosens his grip on Jade just enough for her to break free, but before she can move toward me, Lorenc steps out from his hiding place and grabs her.

I nod to them. "Go!"

She struggles with him, kicking and hitting him. "No! Griffin! Don't do this!" Her muffled cries dissipate as he drags her toward the entrance, and they disappear.

Tarek recovers from the shockwave of the blast and registers what just happened, taking in the carnage of what was once his plane. Only after seeing that does he look toward the entrance where Jade was just taken.

He turns his furious eyes on me...the same eyes I see every fucking day when I look in the mirror.

"You may have won this battle, but you will never win this war. All you've done is prolong the inevitable. Anywhere you go, anyone you try to become, I will find you. Rea is *mine*! And I will have her, no matter how long it takes."

I scoff and offer him a grin. "That's where you're wrong, brother. You've underestimated me from the very beginning. This ends now. You will never lay a finger on her again."

A vile sneer twists his mouth. "Oh, I've already laid much more than a finger on her..."

Rage turns my vision red, and I draw my weapons at the same time he reaches for his. He lunges for the open door of one of the offices as I send a stream of bullets toward him.

Fire sears my gut but doesn't stop me from advancing toward the door.

This ends now.

TWENTY

TAREK LIES in the middle of the room, his back to the desk, gun drawn and raised at me. His arm wavers.

Blood soaks the front of his pants and pools under him on the floor.

I must have hit an artery.

Bleeding out is too good a way for him to die.

Too easy.

Who would have thought it would end this way? Brother against brother. The same flesh and blood. The same DNA. Born only five minutes apart, we couldn't be more different. It wasn't always that way. At least, I don't think it was.

Our childhood flashes through my head in quick succession. Even then, I was his muscle, but I never reveled in it the way he did. It was just me helping my brother. My other half. I would have done anything for him back then, and thinking back on it now, I'm sure that's why I continued to work for him even when I began to question the rightness of my actions.

Tarek never worries about such trivial things as a conscience, though.

His gun centers on my chest.

Why hasn't he shot me yet?

His eyes meet mine, a sneer spreads across his lips, and he pulls the trigger. The empty *click* answers my question. He's out of ammo. The only reason I'm not dead right now is my brother's a piss poor-shot and doesn't have a backup mag.

How fucked up is that?

I squat down in front of him, the movement making me wince, and grab at my abdomen. Warm blood seeps onto my hand. This one's bad. I need to end this quickly if I'm gonna make it out of here alive and back to Jade.

Lorenc will take care of her, make sure she's okay. I have no doubt of that. But I can't leave this Earth without telling her I love her one more time, without kissing her lips or seeing her smile back at me.

"Looks like you lost this round, brother." The words fall from my lips like a prayer. I've been wanting this for so long.

Tarek laughs, which quickly dissolves into a coughing fit. "That's what you may think, but you will never walk away from this, Konstandin. You know that. I have too many friends in too many places. And I will always be with you. You will never be able to fuck Rea again without knowing I've been there too and that she loved it."

My hand lashes out before my mind can even register the movement, and the butt of my gun smashes into his temple. Tarek falls sideways but manages to catch himself and push himself back upright. Blood rushes down the side of his face but it doesn't stop the sinister laughter.

It doesn't matter though, I know the truth.

"Rea will always be mine, Tarek. No matter what you may have done to her, I will always be the one who has her heart. The rest...I can live with. As long as I have her."

Before he can offer another word, I drop the gun and unleash the fury of the past several weeks upon him.

Fists crunch bone.

Flesh tears.

Blood flows.

Tarek struggles only briefly before he's overwhelmed by my assault.

Time disintegrates, along with his face.

There's nothing but swinging fists, blood, and my unrelenting wrath.

Only the splitting pain of my knuckles breaking finally pauses the attack.

I stare down.

The thing about having blood on my hands is, I don't want to wash it off.

Isn't that what you're supposed to want to do?

Yet, standing here, over the shredded, unrecognizable body of Tarek, my hands dripping with his blood, there is no regret. No remorse. No nagging conscience screaming at me. Nothing but an overwhelming sense of relief floods my body.

But it doesn't last. It can't.

Yelling and the *pop* of gunshots break my reverie and remind me where I am, and why.

This isn't over.

Not by a long shot.

I turn away from the carnage before I try to push up onto my feet, but I stumble onto my palms. The room spins, blackening around the edges.

Shit.

The weakness crippling my body is total and complete. I register the pool of blood under me that's not all Tarek's.

As I sink down onto the floor, the tears in Jade's eyes when she saw me in the hallway are all I can see through the blackness enveloping me.

Those eyes are too beautiful to have tears, and now, she's going to lose me too.

AFTER
WRATH

WRATH...in its purest form, presents with self-destructiveness, violence, and hate that may provoke feuds...

- Author Unknown

PROLOGUE

ALEKSANDER

THE COOL DIRT sits heavy in my palm as I stare down at Saban's freshly dug grave. A cigarette dangles from my lips, slowly smoldering in the chilly air.

Scents of freshly churned earth, grass, and flowers fill my nose, mixed with the calming smell of nicotine.

A familiar collection of headstones surrounds his final resting place—each and every one representing a member of the Gashis who has gone before us.

Some were weak. Some were strong.

Saban...he was both.

How did we get here, vëlla i dashur?

Just two weeks ago, things were perfect, or at least, as perfect as anything can ever be in our dirty world.

Saban had iron-clad control over our territory in Chicago. He knew the game, and he played it well.

No one fucked with the Gashis. They knew the consequences.

That left me free to stay here to take care of Father after my release from that hellhole Albania calls a prison. Neither Saban nor I wanted him to die alone or in the hands of some random hospice worker. Family comes first. Saban wanted to be here too, but the business wouldn't allow for that. Family first, but business a close second.

No one could have anticipated the turn of events that brought Saban home to Albania in a coffin.

Krishti...why didn't you listen to me?

I warned Saban not to get involved with the Morina feud. Tarek and Konstandin were not the kind of people you wanted to mess with, and you certainly didn't want to get between them.

Especially when a woman was the reason for the animosity.

Those two were fire and ice, and when they came together, they burned hotter and froze deeper than any two men I've ever met. The only people who ever came close to what *I* am capable of.

They were absolutely, positively lethal.

He should have listened.

Instead...he paid the ultimate price for ignoring my warning.

Idiot.

I hate to think ill of the dead, but he was truly naïve or plain fucking stupid to believe Konstandin was just going to walk away after learning he helped Tarek track them down after they fled Philly.

He should have known.

I fucking told him.

I curl the fingers of my left hand around the dirt and take a drag on the cigarette before it burns too low.

This all could have been avoided.

So much bloodshed...over what?

Pussy.

Some fucking woman.

Man's downfall always seems to come back to the same thing every single time, since the moment time began...

You'd think we would learn by now.

It's not worth it.

They're not worth it.

Get in. Get off. Get out. Get gone.

Something the Morinas should have known.

Something Saban should have emphasized when he told Tarek he wouldn't help him find Rea and Konstandin.

Such a price to pay for a stupid mistake, vëllaçko.

Two long drags finish my cig. I drop it and crush it under my boot before I step up to the grave.

A cold wind whips down from the north, sending a shiver through my body despite my being bundled up in a sweater and long coat. The weather is just starting to turn. It shouldn't be this cold.

But maybe it isn't just the wind causing the chill. Maybe it's knowing what I have to do next.

I have to go to Chicago.

Konstandin is dead, but there are others who played a role in Saban's death. Others who need to pay. Rea and Lorenc are very much alive somewhere, and they don't deserve to be. Lorenc assisted Konstandin on his rampage, and Rea...she was the cause of it all.

The aggression cannot go unchecked.

It's only been weeks, but things are already starting to destabilize in Chicago because of what they did, because of Konstandin.

The Italians and the Serbians are moving in, staking their claims, and encroaching on our established territory and businesses. Because they see us as weak without Saban.

They think the Gashi family is done.

They couldn't be more mistaken.

They just woke a sleeping dragon.

The years I've spent in the background have come to an end. It's time to take my rightful place at the head of the family.

I release the dirt. It floats down and lands almost silently on the polished wood.

Goodbye, vëlla.

I step back from the grave and turn to the only other person to come out here with me to the desolate family graveyard.

Father looks up at me from his wheelchair with hate, not anguish, burning in his old, clouded eyes. He coughs and wheezes loudly before managing to gain enough breath to speak.

"You will fix this."

Four words.

A command. Not a question.

Saban was in control for one reason and one reason only—everyone feared what I would do if I took over. My forced vacation meant he had no choice but to step up, and Father's illness kept me from taking my place.

But now, the time has come.

I squeeze Father's frail, bony shoulder and give Saban's grave one last look before I motion to the two workers to begin filling it in.

Their shovels dig into the piles of dirt surrounding Saban's final resting place. Thick, dark soil pours down the hole. A deep *thunk* echoes up when the first pile hits the top of the casket.

"Don't worry, Father. I know what I need to do."
Even though it means leaving him here to die alone. I have to go.
Dragoni është lëshuar.
The dragon has been unleashed.

ONE

EIGHTEEN MONTHS LATER

"No, sir. Please don't!"

The man on the floor is supplicating to deaf ears.

I don't want to hear him beg. I don't want to hear him apologize. I don't want to hear his bullshit laundry list of excuses.

What I want is some goddamn information. Information he *should* have. But all I've gotten is verbal diarrhea and blabbering from him.

That ends now.

I reach down and wrap my hand around his throat. He gasps and grabs at my wrist, scratching and clawing in a useless attempt to loosen my grip. My fingers dig into his flesh, cutting off his air as I raise him from the floor and shove him against the wall.

"I've given you two months. Two fucking months. I asked for one simple thing—a location. And you can't give it to me?"

His nails tear at my wrist, and I release enough pressure to let him gasp in some air so he can reply.

"I'm sorry, Aleksander. I—"

I retighten my hold and shake my head. "No excuses. No apologies. I need results. Either you can get me what I need or you cannot."

He nods as much as my grip will allow. I release him, and he crumples to the floor, gasping for air and rubbing his throat.

Useless piece of shit.

A rattling cough fills the room, and he crawls toward me. I place my boot on his chest and push him back onto his ass.

"Talk."

"I... There's nothing, sir. I've scoured everywhere, talked to everyone. They just disappeared."

Fuck. Fuck. Fuck. Fuck.

This incompetence cannot continue. People don't just disappear. There's always a trail. There's always *something*.

"It's been two months, Andre. Two months, and you've brought me nothing. I've been more than patient."

His eyes widen, and he scrambles back until he hits the wall. He knows what I'm capable of... what's coming if he continues to fail me.

"I'm trying, sir. I checked flight records. I spoke with crew working at all the airports in and around Philly. No one knows anything or saw anything. I don't know how they left town."

It's the same answer I've now gotten from a dozen different men. All of them swore they could find Rea and Lorenc. All of them promised me a location within a week. All of them failed. All of them paid dearly for that failure.

The only reason Andre isn't dead already is familial obligation, but that only goes so far.

I *tsk* and shake my head as I squat down in front of him. The smell of piss permeates the room, and a dark stain spreads on his pants.

Mut!

"Cousin, the only reason you are still breathing is, I don't want to have to console your mother at your funeral. Get your shit together and get me some results, otherwise, I'll just skip the funeral and save myself that problem."

The implication is clear. He knows what will happen.

I rise to my feet and step back. He climbs up on shaking legs and bolts past me and out the back door of the club.

The frustration that's been building over the search for Rea and Lorenc has been threatening to explode for some time now. This latest failure shouldn't really come as a surprise, though. Lorenc is an expert at disappearing, just like Konstandin was. If he doesn't want to be found, he won't be—at least, not without making a mistake. And he will protect Rea at any cost.

With Konstantin gone, they are all that's left...my only chance to exact the vengeance owed to me. Saban deserved better than to be beaten to death in his office, and I've spent the last year and a half dreaming of all the things I'll do to Lorenc and Rea once they're found.

And they *will* be found. He may be an expert, but Rea isn't. She will make a mistake eventually —write or phone an old friend, accidentally use her real name, let something about her past slip to the wrong person—and when she does...

I flick open my blade and examine it in the light. The shiny surface reflects the smile spreading across my face.

It's important to find joy where you can in life—something I learned very early on growing up in Albania.

And it's time I got to enjoy myself.

The door opens behind me, and I whirl to find Erjon strolling in.

"Hey, boss."

I slip my blade back into my pocket and nod a greeting. "Where have you been?"

Erjon was supposed to be here an hour ago. Normally, tardiness would result in a loss of something very important to him, but he's one of my most reliable men, so there's probably a legitimate explanation.

He leans against the wall next to me and crosses his massive arms over his chest.

"I was meeting with a source. One who claimed to have information you would be very interested in."

Well, that's vague as fuck.

I raise an eyebrow and bite back the desire to beat an answer from him. The longer I wait to resolve the Lorenc and Rea issue, the shorter my temper has become. Since it wasn't very long to begin with, it's been creating a real issue with keeping employees.

"And?"

A sly grin plays at the corners of his mouth. "He says he knows a guy who knows a guy who knows a guy who used to fly a private jet for the Morinas."

Yes, finally!

"What does he know?"

Erjon shrugs. "Not much. But if we track down the pilot, we may hit pay dirt. The contact says he heard a plane may have flown the day Tarek and Konstandin died. Which would be difficult, since they were, you know, dead, and Konstandin blew up Tarek's plane."

I pull a cigarette from my pack and light it as I pace. This is certainly interesting information, and more than we've managed to find in all this time. Which makes me immediately suspect.

"Why is he coming forward now? Why not when I first came to Chicago? How do we know this isn't a setup?"

He pushes off the wall and lights his own stick. "I asked the same thing. Says the pilot is an old family friend of the friend of a friend and that he only just heard this information when he happened to mention to the friend that he knew someone who worked for you."

Tenuous. But plausible.

Everyone has been on edge since the Morinas and Saban died. Things in Philly are still a mess, with various factions warring over who will take over the family now that the twins are gone. And here, things aren't much better.

I came to find a house in disrepair. Saban did his job well, but the moment he died, his men fell apart. The Italians have worked their way into our territory, and the Serbians are doing their damnedest to acquire our primary businesses. With the ever-present cartel influence in the city pressing in on all sides, it's become impossible to breathe without another threat.

Rebuilding what we once had has been a major undertaking, especially when my concentration and heart are focused on finding Lorenc and Rea.

Slowly—far more so than I'm happy with—I've reestablished the Gashi name and taken back our territory one street at a time. I'm sure the Chicago cops aren't happy about the increased body count as of late, but one cannot do this job and maintain clean hands.

That was part of Saban's problem—he let his men do all the dirty work.

I revel in it. It makes doing this job a lot easier than I thought it would be. A release. A way to work out the anger and frustration.

I won't worry about the repercussions until absolutely necessary.

"Bring me the source, and find this pilot."

TWO

I STEEPLE my fingers in front of my mouth and lean back in my chair.

Arturo Marconi sits across from me with his ankle propped up on his knee, trying to look relaxed, but the tension in his shoulders gives him away.

He should be nervous.

What kind of asshole comes into my house expecting me to do favors after he's been encroaching on my territory for years?

I'll let him stew for a little bit.

Watching them squirm is almost as good as hearing them scream and smelling them burn.

Silence stretches between us, and he shifts and averts his eyes. It won't be much longer now. He's about to crack. They all do eventually.

He drops his foot to the floor and sits up straight. "So, Aleksander, what do you think?"

What I think is that you're an arrogant prick, even more so than your uncle.

Il Padrone and the Gashis have had our differences, but that man has done good for the Marconi family for years. Now, he's letting this little weasel inch his way into control, which has done a major disservice to the family name. At least *Il Padrone* knows how to show respect. This little prick thinks he owns the world and is entitled to everything he asks for, including assistance with this "little problem" he's having. One would think his uncle would have taught him how things work, but apparently not.

Still, it's an interesting proposition I'm not ready to dismiss outright.

I lean forward and lock eyes with him. "Why in the world would I want to get involved in this? I see no way this benefits me or this family. It sounds like more of a hassle than anything."

Arturo shifts forward to rest his elbows on his knees. "Because, if you take care of this for me, I will be of service when you need it."

Having the Marconi family at my beck and call with an owed favor would be like having a hidden ace up my sleeve. It's something to hold over Arturo's head in the future.

It's certainly a good thing to have tucked in my back pocket.

And really, what he's asking is huge. That means owing me a pretty damn big favor.

It's an opportunity too enticing to pass up.

"I'll take care of your problem for you. But you will owe me two favors, not one, in return. You will also move out of any remaining territory you stole from us when Saban was killed."

His dark eyes narrow on me, and his nostrils flare. He's not used to being told how things are going to work. He doesn't like not being in control one bit.

I can understand that feeling, but I'm surprised he's taking it this far.

He sits back, his mouth set in a firm line. "What's your timeline?"

The asshole probably wants it done ASAP, but I don't work on anyone else's timelines. Especially with something like this.

I raise an eyebrow at him and rest my elbows on the desk. "Whenever the time is right and an opportunity presents itself. Until then, we will have no further contact, and after, we will have no contact until I need my favor returned, understand?"

Sometimes even powerful men need to be treated like children.

It won't win me any goodwill, but I don't need goodwill. I have two favors.

GWYN MCNAMEE

He nods, rises to his feet, tugs his suit coat back into place, and extends his hand across the desk.

I leave him hanging there for a moment before I finally push up to my feet and clasp his hand in mine.

He just made a deal with the devil, and he doesn't even know it.

SHE MOVES LANGUIDLY, BUT NOT LIKE THE OTHER GIRLS WHO ARE CLEARLY ON SOMETHING THAT impairs their minds. Not her. Every twist of her hips, every thrust of her ass and chest...it's all deliberate and controlled. It's a slow act of seduction performed by a true artist.

What the fuck is a girl like this doing in this place?

Calling the club a dump would be a compliment. But the appearance is very calculated. I certainly have the money to set up wherever I want. Saban chose the restaurant, but I wanted something with better entertainment. I can always order in food.

And meeting at the club gives me security and the people who come to see me an explanation for being here. Rather they be seen as perverts than meeting with a crime boss.

I lean across the bar and nod to Valon. He wanders over to me and tosses a towel over his shoulder.

"Who is she?"

His eyes follow mine, and when I glance over at him, he gives me a knowing smirk.

I turn back the woman who's managed to captivate me in seconds.

Her long, dark hair flows down her smooth, pale back, and she wraps a leg around the pole and spins, sending it out into a halo around her. Large, high, round breasts bob with the movement, and my dick swells uncomfortably in my pants.

"Brynn. Dances as Kitty."

Kitty.

I chuckle and slide onto a stool where I can watch the rest of her dance. Meow is certainly right. She's slinky and mysterious, just like a cat on the prowl.

"Is she one of ours?"

He shakes his head.

The question doesn't need explanation. Valon knows we smuggle girls in from Albania to dance at the club and work at our various other businesses. It's almost impossible to get them into the country legally, and they jump at the chance to come to the States, despite the less-than-legal way they have to do it. Even the worst job here is better than what they had and what they had to do back home.

"No. But her mother is Albanian and has some family here in town. Grew up somewhere north of here. Milwaukee, maybe? She moved here with her mom when her father died a little while ago. Sounds like maybe some bad shit may have gone down up there that she wanted to get away from."

That's why I haven't seen her before.

She's new, and I haven't exactly been spending much time in club lately. Fixing what's broken requires more time in the office and out dealing with problems than sitting in here watching the girls.

I would most definitely remember her. A stunning woman with a talent like that? Hard to forget.

But I don't mess with our girls. It's bad for business. And I have enough things to worry about without throwing pussy into the mix.

My cock twitches. Doesn't mean I can't enjoy the show, though.

Unwinding doesn't happen much for me anymore, so when I can take a moment to sit back and watch something beautiful, I will.

The last notes of her song float out from the speakers, and her golden eyes find mine from across the room.

A pink flush spreads across her exposed alabaster skin.

My pants tighten even more, and I shift off the stool. Her eyes follow my hand as I adjust my very obvious erection, and she ducks her head and races from the stage into the back.

Running scared, pussycat? Good.

I'd love to stay and wait for her to reappear. Playing the cat-and-mouse game with her could be fun, even if nothing will ever come of it. But there are things to be done.

Big things.

And I need to take care of this throbbing situation south of the border.

"Valon, call Cecilia and get her over here. Send her back to my office when she arrives."

He nods his understanding, and I shove off the bar and make my way down the back hallway.

Soon enough, I'll have my dick buried deep down her throat or in her cunt, and everything else will momentarily fade away—including that look Kitty just gave me.

I don't need to pay for sex, but it certainly assures fewer complications that fucking one of my dancers would.

Cecilia is a real bitch, but the woman can suck like a damn Hoover vacuum, so I've managed to overlook her less appealing qualities.

By the time she gets here, I'll be ready to blow.

Then, it will be back to business.

THREE

THE SMALL, weaselly man seated in front of me shakes his head and cowers. "I swear, that's all I know. It came, like, third-or-fourth-hand, so I don't have details."

Of course. That would be too easy.

As far as sources go, though, I've had worse. Erjon did well finding this guy, or should I say, this guy did well in finding Erjon and getting this information to me.

It may be weak and seem insignificant, but it's the *only* real lead I've had since arriving in Chicago and starting this quest. All it takes is one tiny thread to unravel Lorenc's entire plan. Once I pull, everything will fall apart.

I will find them.

"But you're sure this pilot knows something?"

He nods vigorously. "I'm positive, sir. As soon as he heard that the information got back to you, he went into hiding. He wouldn't do that unless he knew something."

Absolutely right. He wouldn't.

We just need to find him, which will be a hell of a lot easier than finding Lorenc without this nugget of information.

"Thank you for coming to speak with me."

Like he had a choice.

I walk around the desk, and he rises to his feet.

"Erjon will make sure you get home safely and are compensated for your time and for the information."

The man grins, probably imaging a thick stack of bills coming his way, and turns to the door.

Erjon's dark eyes meet mine then flick to the informant. I give him a nod. He knows what needs to be done.

This is a dark and bloody business. But certain steps are necessary. We can't have word getting back to Lorenc or any of his supporters that we may be onto him. If the pilot went into hiding, it won't be long until they're on the run again.

I would handle it myself, but Cecilia's visit earlier has managed to calm the dragon for a while. This will be one of the very rare times I let him handle the dirty work.

With a nod, Erjon follows the informant out of my office and down the back hallway.

"Aleksander?"

Valon appears in the doorway just as I'm about to sit back down. His wild eyes and heavy breaths send ice racing through my veins.

"What is it?"

"I need you in the parking lot. One of the girls was attacked."

What the fuck?

I shoot around the desk and follow him down the back hallway. He shoves open the security door. Tires squeal as Erjon speeds away in his car with the informant in the back seat.

A single street lamp illuminates the parking lot, and in the shadowy area to the left near the dumpsters, several of the girls huddle around a hunched form.

My quick steps eat up the asphalt, and the girls back away when they see me and Valon approaching.

The quivering blonde I think goes by Layla turns to me. "She looks really bad, sir. Maybe we should call an ambulance."

I drop to my knees.

Fuck.

Blood roars in my ears as the girl on the ground turns her bloodied and bruised face a little, finally letting me see it.

Kitty.

"How the fuck did this happen?" My shouted words echo into the cool night air. Rage floods my veins, and I have to bite back the desire to tear into everyone standing around just looking at her.

Valon steps up behind me and leans down. "She told the girls she was running out to her car for something. None of the men knew she left."

Unfuckingacceptable.

Our girls *always* get escorted to their cars. *Always.* Things like this should *never* happen when the girls are under *our* care.

NEVER.

"Did anyone see who did this?" I drag my attention away from her for a second to scan the faces around us. Everyone shakes their heads. "No one?"

My low growl sends the observing girls scampering backward, and I lean down to the poor injured woman on the ground. I brush the bloody hair off the side of her face. My fingers come away sticky with blood.

"Can you hear me?"

A low moan is the only response I get. I clench my fists.

She's a wreck—busted lip, bruised eyes, gash on the side of her temple. Someone really worked her over.

Valon kneels next to me. "Should I call an ambulance, boss?"

I shake my head and slide my arms under her. "No. I'll take care of her."

It's the least I can do after negligence of my men caused this. She moans and cringes as I rise to my feet with her cradled against me.

She's light as a feather in my arms, but the weight of the situation sits heavy on my shoulders.

"Open my car. Call Doc and have him meet me at my place."

Valon nods, reaches into my pocket for my keys, and races ahead of me to where the Bentley is parked next to the building—where it's safe.

Fuck.

I did this. I chose this piece-of-shit club as a headquarters and did nothing to clean it up or make sure the parking lot was well-lit and safe for the girls. This is as much my fault as it is the guys for not walking her out.

Valon pulls the passenger door open, and I shake my head.

"No. You're driving. I'm riding in the back with her."

He hesitates momentarily before closing the door and tugging open the back one instead.

No one knows where I live except Doc. Not even my most trusted men, like Valon and Erjon.

After what happened to Saban, I don't trust anyone. I can't.

But this situation requires me to set aside my mistrust so I can help her.

I slide into the soft leather, cradling her against me, and settle her into place with her head resting on my shoulder.

Blood trickles from her split bottom lip and from one eyebrow, and her left eye is already swollen almost completely shut and is turning an ugly shade of purple.

The asshole brutalized her.

What kind of man lays a hand on an innocent woman like this?

Women like Rea, ones who betray and cause irreparable damage to others—they deserve whatever is coming to them, but I don't believe for a second this woman did anything to bring this upon herself.

The engine roars to life, and Valon turns his head to look back at me. "Where to?"

"Lincoln Park. I'll direct you when we get close."

He pauses and opens his mouth to say something before he thinks better of it and turns back to face forward. The tires squeal, and we race from the lot and out onto the street. He grabs his phone, and his mumbled words to Doc float to the back seat.

Kitty's shallow breathing assures me she's still with me, but I don't know what kind of damage the asshole may have done to her. Doc will fix her up. He's seen and handled much worse. But acid still crawls up my throat from looking at what's been done to her.

Her lovely pale skin, once so flawless, is now marred by the signs of her abuse.

I brush my thumb across her cheek, and she turns into me and wraps an arm around my neck with a whimper.

Whoever did this is going to fucking pay.

FOUR

Doc arrives at almost the same time we do, and he follows me into my bedroom and immediately goes to work examining Brynn. I hover at the edge of the room, not wanting to intrude in case there was anything intimate she needs to reveal to him.

That fucker better not have...

My nails bite into the skin on my palms as I wait for the exam to be done.

Her confused golden eyes—at least, the one that isn't swollen shut—shift over to me several times, but when Doc rises to leave, her entire attention moves to him, almost as if she's begging him to stay with a look.

She's scared of me.

After what she just went through, I can't blame her. She should be scared regardless of if she knows anything about the man she works for.

I walk Doc out to the front door, even though leaving her alone feels like a really shitty thing to do right now.

He pauses before he steps out. "She'll be okay. Lots of bruises and scrapes, but no broken bones or internal injuries as far as I can tell. No signs of sexual assault."

Thank God.

"Just have her take it easy for a few days and use ice packs."

He hands me a small orange pill bottle.

"Here's some Percocet. Give her five milligrams every eight hours as needed. If she doesn't need it, don't give it to her."

He doesn't have to expand on why. I've seen addiction to this shit, and it isn't pretty.

"Thanks, Doc."

The door falls closed behind him, and I turn the deadbolt and drop my forehead against the metal surface.

The first fucking time I bring a woman here, and it has to be like this?

A cynical laugh bubbles up my throat, and I shove away from the door and make my way back to the bedroom.

Her back is to me when I enter. The edge of the bed dips with my weight, and I settle against the headboard beside her.

She might be sleeping, or she may just want to pretend she is to avoid having to talk to me. Either way, I'll let her be.

"I'll be right outside if you need anything. Doc gave me some pain meds for you if you want them."

I pause for a moment, giving her time to answer, and just as I'm about to slide from the bed, she rolls onto her back and looks up at me.

"Why are you doing this?" Her words are nothing more than a whisper, barely audible even in the silence of the room. The busted bottom lip of her rosebud mouth quivers.

"Doing what?"

She sighs, and a single tear trickles from the corner of her eye down her temple to the black pillowcase beneath her head. "Taking care of me."

Krishti.

A strange tightness forms in the center of my chest from looking at her so broken and vulnerable.

Guilt.

It's a simple word, but it's far from a simple emotion.

I haven't felt it in a long time. Even with Saban's death. I warned him. He knew what he was doing. I won't feel responsible for the bad choices in his life. None of it was my doing. It was Konstandin, Lorenc, and Rea.

No, it wasn't my fault or a reason to feel guilt, but I can fix the situation by finding them and doling out the justice their actions demand.

And I can fix it for Brynn right now. She may be weak now, but the woman on that pole earlier was strong and confident. She'll get back there.

"Because you need it."

She releases an exasperated sigh and examines me. Unlike earlier, she meets my eyes and holds them, unblinking. "What do you expect in return?"

The tremble in her voice and the fear in the question has me shifting away from her on the bed.

She has the wrong idea entirely, and the last thing she needs right now is to worry about owing me anything.

"The only thing I want in return is the name of the man who did this to you."

A low whimper emanates from her before she rolls onto her side and gives me her back, ensuring I won't get the answer I'm looking for.

I clench my fists at my sides and take a deep breath. She doesn't need to be scared by me sounding like a crazed lunatic when I say this, but it needs to be said. She does need to understand the situation.

"Go to sleep, but tomorrow, you will tell me what I want to know."

The bedroom door clicks shut behind me, actively closing off the connection to Brynn. At least the physical one.

She needs rest and a little bit of time to get her head around what just happened before I probe her with questions. Besides, I may be able to get the answer elsewhere.

I shove the sliding glass door open and step out onto the balcony. The cool night air envelops me, and I suck in a deep, cleansing breath.

Chicago is beautiful this time of year, despite the honking horns and yells from the busy street below. It's so different from back home, and there's no telling when I'll get back. With Saban and now Father gone, all that's left for me are memories and a few random aunts and cousins.

This is the new world. My world.

I pull out a cigarette and light it. One long, slow drag sends nicotine coursing through my body and helps calm the tension in every fiber of my being.

Between searching for the opportunity for revenge, the favor I now have to do for Arturo, and the attack on Brynn, things are nearly out of control, and I don't *do* out of control.

A few more puffs relax me enough to pull out my phone and call Erjon.

"Boss?"

"Did you take care of it?"

"Yes. Valon told me that happened at the club. I figured it was best to get our friend gone before anyone in the parking lot saw him with me, otherwise I would have stayed. She okay?"

I glance back through the glass door toward the hallway that leads to my bedroom. She's probably fast asleep now, and hopefully won't be awoken by any nightmares over what happened.

"She will be. What did you and Valon find out?"

This fucker has already been breathing too long as it is.

"Not much. The piece-of-shit cameras at the back of the club either weren't working or weren't facing in the right direction to catch much. Just a glimpse of an old blue pickup barreling out of the parking lot about the time she was discovered."

Shit.

Another thing that should have been updated—damn security cameras.

"No license plate or driver were visible?"

"Asnjë. But we're still digging. We should have something for you tomorrow."

Fuck.

Frustration burns hot through my veins, and my fingers twitch with the need to destroy some-one, to set the world aflame with the fire of my reprisal.

I suck in a deep breath. It's not like I was going to leave her alone tonight anyway. Tomorrow will be soon enough.

Dial it back.

I light another cigarette and take a long drag.

She doesn't deserve this. There's no doubt in my mind she doesn't have a malicious bone in her body. Her simple, innocent reaction to me the other day at the club was all I needed to see to know that.

Most of these girls use their sex and their bodies like a prize to be won or a gift to be given.

Not her.

No. She's something else entirely. I just don't know what yet.

FIVE

MY PHONE BLARES TO LIFE, and I reach out to grab it off the nightstand in the guest bedroom with a groan.

The ache in my low back and stiffness in my entire body is testament to what an absolutely shit night of sleep I got last night.

Which is unusual.

You don't have trouble sleeping without worries or regrets. Neither of those are usually on my radar. There are things to accomplish, things I need to do, but worrying about something or regretting prior decisions serves no purpose.

Yet this girl has stirred up something I never even knew existed—a protective instinct and something...else.

It almost makes me understand why Konstandin did what he did.

Almost.

Nothing justifies that.

I clear my throat and swipe to answer. "Yeah?"

"Sorry to wake you, boss, but you need to get her to talk. The truck isn't enough to go on. Our friend at the DMV sent over a list of potential matches, but there are several hundred, and that's just in Illinois."

Figures.

Brynn is going to need to come clean, no matter how painful it may be. I should get up and check on her. She's had time to rest. Now, it's time to talk.

"I'll get her talking and call you."

"Got it. We'll keep at it."

"You better."

It's his damn job.

I end the call and drop back against the pillows with a sigh.

He shouldn't have called without any news. That's three wasted minutes he could have spent looking for this guy. Sometimes dealing with these people makes me wonder why they let just anyone procreate on this planet.

I relax back on the bed and take a deep breath. The aroma of coffee hits my nose.

What the hell?

I toss back the covers, tug my jeans on, and throw open the door. Rustling and the fridge door closing draw me to the kitchen.

Brynn stands at my stove in nothing but an old T-shirt and boxers I left in the room for her. Her silky black hair cascades down her shoulders and back, and her long, perfect legs seem to go on forever.

Mallkim!

"What the hell are you doing out of bed?" The question comes out a little more abrasively than I intended, but controlling my temper has never been one of my strong suits.

She jumps and whirls to face me with a spatula raised in her defense. Her wide, fear-laced golden eyes focus on me, and she relaxes slightly, curving in on herself and shaking with...

Fear.

"Shit. I'm sorry. I didn't mean to startle you."

I hold up my hands as I approach her, doing my best to appear nonthreatening. She takes a step back until she hits the cabinets and has nowhere left to retreat.

I guess I failed at that whole nonthreatening thing.

Can't say I blame her, though. I rushed out here in nothing but jeans, and I know what she sees. A monster.

The scars that crisscross my abdomen are nothing compared to the beast that covers my chest and wraps around my shoulders onto my back and then down my leg. The dragon took years to finish, but back then, all I had was time.

Albanian prison camps aren't exactly Club Med. You're lucky if you survive at all, let alone thrive. The only reason I got out of there with just some scars and a plethora of nasty memories is because of my family name and the fact that I made sure everybody knew exactly what I was when I got there.

I may have been something to fear before I went in, but I was the Dragon when I came out. And now, looking into the eyes of this bruised and battered girl, it's clear she sees it.

She sees what I am. She *knows* what I am. She's regretting letting me keep her here last night.

Those fear-filled eyes focus on the dragon's head over my heart.

"I promise I won't hurt you."

Her eyes snap back up to mine, and her shoulders relax slightly, but she maintains her defensive posture and clings to the counter behind her with both hands like it's the only thing holding her up.

"What are you doing out of bed?"

Her eyes dart to the stove before they return to me. "I woke up and couldn't fall back asleep. I thought I would make breakfast...to say thank you."

I take the final steps into the kitchen. A bowl of scrambled eggs and a pack of bacon sit on the counter next to the stove, and a fresh pot of coffee rests next to them in the machine.

The corner of my mouth quirks up into an uncharacteristic smile. It's so rare anyone does anything for me for any other reason than fear. "You didn't have to do that. Go back to bed."

She looks ready to argue with me for a second, then she presses her lips together and moves away from the counter. Her arm brushes against mine as she passes me on her way to the bedroom, and a little jolt of electricity shoots through my body and straight to my cock.

Damn.

Even after having the shit beaten out of her, this woman is beautiful. Part of the allure may be that she's in my kitchen, and I don't normally have women in my domain. It may be the vulnerability, or it may be the mile-long legs. Whatever it is, I need to ignore it.

There's no doubt where that path leads...straight toward ultimate destruction for both of us. Take care of her and send her on her way—that's all I should be doing.

But first, I'm going to make her breakfast.

SIX

HER HEAD SNAPS in my direction as I shove the door to the bedroom open. From her position reclined against the headboard of the king-size bed, she looks so tiny, so frail, so completely lost.

I'm not one to give anyone directions, but she needs my help, whether she wants it or not.

I approach and set the tray with bacon, eggs, toast, coffee, and juice on the bed next to her.

She looks down at my proffered breakfast and then back up at me. "What about you?"

So thoughtful, being concerned about me when she's the one beat to shit.

"I don't usually eat breakfast. All I need is a cup of coffee and a smoke in the morning."

"Oh." Dejection overtakes her face, and she drops her focus down to her bare legs.

Shit.

"But thank you for thinking of me."

That's what I should be saying, right?

I have no fucking clue how to comfort a woman. Women are for sex, nothing more. Having one here, crying in my bed, is the last thing I ever expected. Nor did I anticipate actually *caring* about her being so upset.

When she looks back up at me, something wet shines in her eyes.

Fuck. She's crying?

"Look, Brynn." I slide onto the bed beside her but keep the tray as a barrier between us. "I know you might not want to, but I need you to talk to me about what happened last night. I can't help you if I don't know what's going on."

Her black hair flies around her face as she shakes her head. "No, I can't. You don't understand."

"No. You don't understand." I point to the bruises on her face and the finger marks on her arms. "This is not okay. This is not something that can be ignored. This is not something that's acceptable to do to one of my women."

Her eyes widen, and she scoffs. "Your women? I'm not anybody's woman. That's exactly the problem."

She has some attitude hidden under all the distress. I'll give her that.

"Who is he?"

She shakes her head again, and tears trickle over her bruised face. "I can't. Please don't make me, sir."

I stiffen. "Don't call me sir."

It shouldn't bother me. Everyone calls me *sir* or *boss*, but from her lips, it just sounds...wrong. Like I'm her master and she's here to do my bidding.

"But—"

"No. You're in my house. In my bed. Call me Alek."

She hesitates before slowly nodding. "Okay, but I can't tell you, Alek. He's dangerous."

I don't mean to, but I bark out a sardonic laugh that echoes in the room. She recoils and shifts away from me on the bed.

Shit. I need to watch that.

"I'm sorry. I didn't mean to scare you, and I'm not laughing at you, it's just... You know who I am and you know what I do. Do you really think some shithead punk who thinks it's okay to do this to you would scare me?"

A pink blush spreads up her neck and over her cheeks. "Well, no…"

"You work for me. Which means you're my responsibility. I failed to keep you safe last night. That's my fault. I'm going to ensure that will not happen again to you or any other girl."

"You can't ensure every girl is safe at all times."

"Try me."

A long shudder rolls through her. Watching her react to me, to my presence, has my cock hardening, though I know how wrong it is in these circumstances and that it can never happen. The women I'm normally with are aggressive. They throw themselves at me like their lives depend on pleasing me, and maybe they do *actually* think that. This one…she has a natural shyness that's intoxicating.

"Now, tell me what I need to know. What the hell were you doing with an asshole who would lay a hand on you in the first place?"

She's too smart for that. Way too smart. There has to be more to the story. I don't believe she'd be with someone who treated her like shit.

The long sigh she releases is laced with pain and regret. "He wasn't always like that. Most of the time, he treated me really well. My mom had a stroke a few years ago, and after my dad died, he helped me take care of her. But it didn't take very long for things to change."

"Because your father wasn't around."

She nods. "Daddy was a little intimidating, so that could very well be. Whatever the case, he became more controlling—wanted to know where I was all the time and didn't want me going to school study groups. I caught him following me more than once. I ended things with him when my cousin Monica told me we could move down here and into their duplex."

This guy sounds like a real fucking piece of work, taking advantage of her when she was most vulnerable after the loss of her father.

My hands clench at my sides. "What were you in school for?"

A tiny smile plays on her split lips. "Nursing."

How the hell does a smart, beautiful woman go from nursing school to stripping at a shitty club for a mobster?

Something doesn't add up. Even with what she told me, she doesn't belong here.

"What are you doing dancing at my club?"

She shrugs and stares at her hands twisting on her lap. "Mom has a lot of medical bills, and I also have to pay my cousin rent, since we are occupying the other half of their duplex that was a rental property. Mom really can't take care of herself. My cousin helps out as much as she can, but Mom needs round-the-clock care. I do it when I'm there, but when I'm not, the burden falls on them, or I have to pay someone to come help. It all takes money I don't have."

"You don't have to worry about it anymore."

I'll never know what possessed me to say those words. They were out before I even knew I was going to say them.

A dark eyebrow rises. "What do you mean?"

"I'll take care of your mother's medical bills and pay for a healthcare worker to be there twenty-four seven so you can stop dancing and go back to school."

The disdain and anger she displays in her glare have me shifting back slightly.

What the hell is that for?

She scowls at me. "I don't want your money. I don't want anything from you. I'm going to work for every damn dime I get the rest of my life and never take a cent from a man again."

I want to be angry at her refusal, but I can't be. Her insistence on working and taking care of things on her own is so commendable, so brave, it makes me like her even more.

And that's dangerous.

I don't like anyone. I can't. That's a luxury not available to a man like me.

"We'll table that issue for the moment. Right now, you need to tell me who he is."

She shakes her head and shifts to face me. The real fear darkening her eyes goes straight to that part of me that wants to crush someone with my bare hands.

"He's part of the Devil Brothers MC. They'll kill you."

I laugh and lean in to press a kiss against her cheek in the only place it isn't bruised. Her soft skin against my lips hardens my cock.

Fuck. Why the hell did I do that?

She doesn't recoil, just eyes me with confusion as I pull back.

"You have nothing to worry about, sweetheart." I hand her my phone. "Call your cousin and tell her you won't be home for a few days and that someone is going to be coming over to take care of your mom."

Her brow furrows, and she sits up as I climb off the bed. "What do you mean I won't be home for a few days?"

I thought it would be obvious, but apparently, I'm going to have to spell it out for her.

"You're staying here until you're feeling better and I'm sure that man can't touch you again. You didn't really think I was going to let you walk out of here, did you?"

SEVEN

"His name is Terrance Duval."

Just saying the asshole's name has my blood thrumming through my veins and my fists flexing.

When I left to come back to the club, I was ready to drive up to Milwaukee to find him and take care of him myself. But going alone would be fucking stupid, even for me.

Brynn is doing okay, all things considered, but there's nothing keeping her at my place, really. Other than a deep-seated fear of what I might do if she does leave.

How the hell am I supposed to feel about that?

I don't want her to be afraid of me. She's already rightly terrified of one man. I just need her to understand why I'm doing this and why she needs to listen to me. It's all to protect her. To give me a chance to take care of the problem. To make sure it can *never* happen again.

There usually isn't any problem getting my point across. And I think I did it without scaring her even more, but I guess only time will tell. If she's there when I get home, then I wasn't as intimidating as I think.

Which could be a problem in and of itself.

Am I losing my edge?

This woman is certainly making me feel like I'm going soft—everywhere but between the legs.

Which is wholly unacceptable.

"The guy is some MC asshole out of Milwaukee. Find out where their clubhouse is and where he lives. Also, find me the best home healthcare workers here in town and hire one to go over to Brynn's place to care for her mom. Check her employment file for the address. Make sure it's clear they're not to pay a cent and to send all the bills here."

Erjon narrows his eyes but nods his understanding. "Do you really have time to be dealing with this, boss? I mean, with everything else that's going on?"

He's the only one who can ask me a question like that and not end up laid out on the floor. Sometimes, he's the important voice of reason when I get hotheaded. But not today.

"This is my top priority right now. You haven't found the pilot yet, have you?"

He rubs the back of his neck and shakes his head. "No. He definitely took off like the source said, but I don't think he'll be too hard to track down. A couple weeks, tops. We're not talking about some master of disguise."

The delay is still unacceptable, but understandable given the circumstances. We're starting from scratch tracking someone we know nothing about. It will take some time. But eventually, it will lead me to Lorenc and Rea.

"Until we have him, there's not a lot we can do, is there?"

"No, sir, but what about the Arturo situation?"

I sigh and shove to my feet. It must be handled delicately, with the utmost planning and care. If we rush into anything, it could spell doom for the Gashis.

We need to complete the task anonymously and make it look like someone else is at fault. The timing has to be perfect.

"It's not even a concern right now, Erjon. When the time's right, I will take care of it. I told Arturo timing is out of his hands, and if he thinks about pushing me on this, then we're done with him."

The last thing I need is that whiny bitch up my ass to get this done. He knows the stakes. Let's hope he also knows the repercussions of fucking with me. Just like Terrance is about to.

BY THE TIME WE REACH MILWAUKEE, THE FIRE OF RAGE BURNS SO HOT IN MY STOMACH, IT actually hurts. This kind of anger is still foreign. I haven't experienced the type of fury filling my veins since I learned what happened to Saban—not even when I was stabbed, not even when I was shot, not even when I was beaten within an inch of my life.

Because I don't care what happens to me.

I cared about Saban, and the fact that I do care what happens to *her* makes my eye twitch as we approach the MC compound.

It isn't hard to find. The two-story building sits just south of downtown, and the giant skull and crossbones with devil horns painted on the side isn't exactly inconspicuous.

"You sure you want to do this, boss?" The edge in Erjon's voice grates on my nerves.

I park across the street and glare at him. He's toeing a dangerous line with his questions lately. One he doesn't want to cross with me.

It's not about wanting. It's about needing.

Need for revenge.

Need for violence.

Need to let wrath consume me.

I slide out of the car and approach the gate of the compound with Erjon and two others in tow.

Our presence has not gone unnoticed. A line of beefy, tattooed bikers steps from the clubhouse and meets us on the other side of the barbed-wire fence.

I step up to the fence, and a man with a Grizzly Adams beard steps forward, puffing out his barreled chest. The word *President* on his cut above the name Otto tells me he's the man I need to deal with.

I hope he's not as big of a fucking moron as this Terrance guy.

He nods at me and crosses his arms over his chest. "Mr. Gashi, what are you doing this far north? You lost?"

I offer him a smile and wave my hand behind me in the general direction of the water a few miles east. "Beautiful day for a drive along Lake Michigan. I thought I would stop and say hello to my friends from Milwaukee."

Otto chuckles. "What do you want?"

Good. Let's cut the pleasantries.

"I'm here to remove some scum from the club. Someone you certainly don't want associated with your patch."

Dark eyes narrow on me, and he shifts his significant weight from one foot to the other. "Is that so? Why would that be?"

"Because he came into *my* territory and attacked one of *my* girls last night."

He huffs out an annoyed "huh," and glances back at the men surrounding him. "One of my men did this?"

Hopefully, this man is smarter than his friend Terrance and is willing to see the error of Terrance's ways.

I offer him a tight smile. "Yes. I hate to be the bearer of such bad tidings."

If one of my men did something like this, I would be fucking irate. If this man is any real type of leader, he won't allow this shit either.

Tension thickens the air as he considers me for a moment then nods at the gate. One of his men moves forward and slides it open.

A man in the back of the MC pack takes a step back, shaking his head slightly.

Terrance.

He wasn't expecting them to give him up so easily. The fucker clearly doesn't understand who he's dealing with.

"He's the man I'm looking for." I point toward Terrance, who retreats another step as his brothers turn and pierce him with accusatory stares.

Otto leans forward and extends his hand. "You know we prefer to keep these things within the club. But I don't want any trouble with the Gashis, so we're just gonna head inside. Close the gate behind you when you leave."

I shake Otto's hand as my men approach Terrance. He backs away and makes a break for a line of bikes to the side of the parking lot.

Cute. He thinks he can get away.

Erjon catches up to him with three large strides. He grabs Terrance's cut and yanks him backward. A girlish squeal rents the air.

Fucking pussy.

I wander over to them slowly as Erjon turns our captive to face me.

"Well, you must be Terrance. We have a few things to discuss."

EIGHT

THE DOOR SWINGS OPEN, and I step into the windowless room, letting the pitch black envelop me in its cool embrace.

I've always been at home in the dark.

It's where I live.

Where I thrive.

Where I am the Dragon.

I wait a moment, savoring what the delay is undoubtedly doing to my guest.

Time to think about why he's here. About what he's done. About the consequences of his actions.

I reach out and click the light switch. A single bulb buzzes to life above where Terrance sits lashed to a chair.

He jerks and blinks against the harsh light. "Please..."

It's the same chorus I've heard the last several hours.

"Don't bother, Terrance. You made your choices. Now it's time to live with the consequences for however long your life might be."

A low whimper slips from his quaking lips.

"You made a pretty bad fucking choice touching one of my girls. Does it make you feel like more of a man? To beat on someone smaller and weaker than you? To control her?"

He doesn't offer an answer, just whimpers again and shifts uncomfortably with his eyes locked on the floor in front of him.

The man can't even look at me.

"I hope it did feel good, because it's the last good memory you're going to have."

His head snaps up, and wide, terrified eyes meet mine. "Pl-please, don't kill me. I'm sorry. I didn't mean—"

"You didn't mean to drive to my place of business and physically assault one of my girls?"

He pauses his pleas as he watches me slide my suit coat off and hang it on the back of the other chair. I unbutton my shirt slowly and drop it off my shoulders.

His body stiffens, and he shakes his head. "Oh, God...please. No. Don't—"

I drop into a crouch in front of him. "Don't waste your last moments begging for something that will never happen, Terrance."

He presses his lips together in a firm line.

It won't last.

They all scream eventually.

I slide my knife from my boot. The perfectly honed blade made of the finest Damascus steel was specially designed to be razor sharp. It strips skin and flesh from bone as easily as my presence removes a smile from someone's face.

Perfect for my purposes.

The dragon-shaped handle built for my hand alone settles against my skin, and a smile spreads across my face.

"Now, Terrance, where shall I start?" I pause to give him a moment to consider my question. "Maybe the hands? Since that's what you used to bruise that beautiful girl."

A low whimper fills the room, and I bite back a chuckle as I set the blade down in front of him, where I know he can see it.

His eyes dart from the metal up to me.

The dragon head across my chest bunches and shifts, almost as if alive, with every movement of my body. Those terrified eyes follow as I toe off my boots and shove my slacks from my legs. I fold them and set them with my other clothes.

No need to destroy a perfectly nice suit.

The delay builds tension too. More fear to feed off.

I grab the blowtorch from beside the chair and turn back to face him. Then I step next to the blade, ensuring he'll look back in that direction.

When he drags his eyes back up to me and sees me fully naked, looming over him, there's no hiding his fear.

Piss pools under the chair, and he tugs against his restraints. "No! God no! Please! Don't hurt me!"

I *tsk* him as I close the distance and bend down to grab the knife. With it clenched in my right hand and the blowtorch in my left, I rise to my full height again.

With his hands tied behind his back, Terrance's struggles are for naught.

Erjon knows how I like them tied to give me the easiest access to the parts I want. He's done his job well and anticipated my every need.

I step behind Terrance, crouch, and light the torch. My cock throbs and grows between my legs as I stare at the flame.

"Are you ready to begin?"

I sure as hell am.

The flame hits his right hand and arm. The acrid smell of burning flesh fills my nostrils, and his strangled screams fill the room.

Music to my fucking ears.

My dick throbs, and I exchange the blowtorch for my knife.

Pressing the cool steel into his flesh is like coming home. The trickle of blood flowing onto the floor sticks under my bare feet.

He cries out and tugs, but the restraints hold him in place.

Fruitless effort, my friend.

I slowly rotate the blade around the entire wrist and then begin to peel the skin back with the razor-sharp edge slowly. The soundproof room holds in his screams as centimeter by centimeter, inch by inch, I peel the blistered skin off his hand and each finger.

Blood pools at my feet, and I hold the chunk of charred skin up to examine it better.

"This one came off pretty easy, Terrance, but there are other body parts that don't always cooperate and are a little bit tougher. We'll get to those. I always save the best for last."

His entire body vibrates. Probably a combination of fear and him going into shock.

I walk around and stop in front of him, holding up my prize.

Shit joins Terrance's piss and blood on the floor, and snot and tears cover his face.

It's not unusual to get one of my victims to last for hours like this, sometimes days if I don't get greedy or overzealous. But Terrace is a real fucking pussy. He's already this big of a mess, and we've only just begun to have fun.

I may have to give him some time. Unless I want this to end too quickly.

The man—if I can even call him that—doesn't deserve a quick death. So, I'll give him exactly what he has coming.

Part of me wishes I could bring Brynn here to witness what Terrance truly is, so she can see she doesn't need to be afraid of him anymore. But I don't want her to see me like this.

For some inexplicable reason, I care what that girl thinks, even though it's wrong. Even though I shouldn't care because when I'm done with him, I'll go tell her she's free and I'll never see her again.

She'll go back to her life, her *real* life—nursing school and a future. And I'll go back to mine—revenge, crime, and the darkness that comes with it.

NINE

ACID BURNS the back of my throat as I unlock the door and step into my condo.

Is she still here?

Ervin has been watching her, but I asked him to stay across the street. She isn't a prisoner here, as much as I want her to stay, and there's no need to scare her further by having an armed man sitting in the living room while she tries to recover from her ordeal. Then, I'd be no better than Terrance.

The muffled sound of the television in the bedroom has me breathing out a sigh of relief. She stayed.

Why does it matter?

That's a question I can't consider, or I'll find myself thinking about things that are impossible.

I look down at my bloodstained shirt and pants. No matter how hard I try, I never walk away completely clean.

Not in this life.

She can't see me like this.

Not when she's already terrified.

She doesn't need to see what I look like after I just flayed her ex-boyfriend alive. She can't know how doing it makes my heart race. How much I love it. How much I need it. How it made my cock rock fucking hard then, and how thinking about it now has it stirring to life again.

Hopefully she's asleep and just left the TV on. I need to get in the shower and cleaned up before she knows I'm back.

I step into the living room and glance down the hallway. My eyes meet her sleepy golden ones.

Fuck.

She looks like some sort of seductive goddamn angel with my white button-down shirt draped over her, barely brushing her thighs.

"Go back to bed, Brynn."

I can't be close to her right now. Not after that.

Soft footsteps carry her down the hallway toward me slowly. The heat of her eyes roaming over me goes straight to my already straining cock.

She rushes to close the distance between us.

"Oh, my God! Are you okay?"

What?

I glance down at myself again.

Shit. She thinks it's my blood.

"What happened?" She stops in front of me, and her eyes zero in on the stains on my shirt. "Are you hurt?"

I shake my head. "It's not my blood, honey."

A few seconds pass before she understands the implications of my statement. Her eyebrows rise slightly, and the split bottom lip that has just begun to start healing quivers slightly.

"Is someone else...hurt?"

Hurt?

Not quite. But it did hurt while he was still breathing.

I shove my hand back through my hair. "All you need to know is Terrance is no longer a threat."

Her brow furrows. "No longer a threat?"

A nod is the only response I give her. I refuse to tell her any details. She doesn't need to know how it happened, just that she's safe.

She takes a second to consider my words she just repeated. "What does that mean?"

"It means exactly what I just said, sweetheart. Get back to your life. Your real life. Now, I need to go shower."

I step around her, but she reaches out a small hand and wraps it around my bicep.

It takes every ounce of my self-control not to flinch or violently throw her hand off me. No one touches me. Not without me directing it.

"What are you doing?"

Soft eyes examine mine. I expected to see something like fear or hatred there, some sort of reaction to what I just told her. She has to know he's dead and that I did it, but none of that exists in the golden pools.

Instead, there's a calm. A sense of peace.

It's exactly what I hoped for, but I didn't anticipate the tightness it would cause in my chest.

There it is again.

"Thank you." Her words are barely more than a whisper, but they fill the entire space between us and hang heavy in the still air.

I can't remember the last time someone thanked me for anything. Usually, they're cursing me and begging me to stop. Now she's done it twice in the span of twenty-four hours.

"You don't need to thank me, sweetheart."

She drops her hand from my arm, and I force myself to walk away, into the bathroom. The door clicks shut, and I crank on the shower and turn to strip. My reflection catches my eye.

I went five years without seeing myself. Five years in the hole made of concrete and pain. So even now, looking at myself in a mirror still feels like seeing a stranger.

This is what she sees.

And she didn't run.

I pull off my shirt and toss it on the floor.

This is what she saw.

And she didn't run.

I take off my bloodstained boots and pants, and my hard cock juts out.

But if she saw all this...

Shit.

I can't even think about it.

If she knew doing *that* gets me harder than watching porn, harder than having my dick sucked, harder than being buried in hot, wet pussy...she would run.

And she should.

I slide open the glass door and step into the shower, letting the scalding water wash away the impurity of my wrath...of what I did.

The things I do are going to send me straight to hell on the day of my judgment. There's no question in my mind about that. But it won't stop me from doing them.

They have to be done. Someone has to do them. That someone is me.

With my eyes closed, I tip my head back and let the water beat down on my face and chest. I almost forget what I did for a second.

Almost.

The sound of the door opening has me swinging my head around. Through the wet and foggy glass, I can barely make out Brynn walking into the bathroom.

What the...

She reaches up and slowly undoes the buttons of the shirt then lets it slide off her shoulders, revealing her stunning naked form. High, round breasts, a trim, narrow waist, legs long enough to drive any man mad.

I've seen her naked at the club, but here, in my home, it's something else altogether.

I'm not big with words, but I can usually find the right ones when necessary. Right now, I might as well be mute.

This woman will be the end of me. I have no doubt.

My hard cock twitches, and she steps forward and pushes the glass door open.

Shit. Tell her to leave.

But I don't.

I can't.

I turn back into the spray. She steps in behind me.

Every muscle in my body tightens.

Delicate fingers trace down my spine, across the path of the dragon, to where it wraps around my hip and down my left leg.

Hot fucking damn.

I grit my teeth to keep from turning around and taking her with all the ferocity I used on Terrance tonight.

"What are you doing?" My words are more growled than spoken.

She leans in and presses soft lips against my shoulder blade. "I thought that would be obvious."

It's not. Not to me. Not in this fucked-up situation. Not when I'm still high off what I did.

"You don't have to do this. This isn't why I helped you."

Warm breath flutters across my wet neck. "I know. That's exactly why I *want* to do this. No one has ever helped me just because they could. No one's ever wanted to help me without anything in return."

I know that truth...all too well.

If I turn around, I'll give in to the soft, gentle caresses across my back. That only leads to one place, but after what I just did, my cock is so fucking hard, I don't have control over my body anymore.

I turn to face her, and she steps back slightly.

Out of fear?

No. Something else.

She has immense respect for me. She knows what I'm capable of, but I don't think she's actually afraid of me.

That's the biggest problem—she should be. Everyone should be.

I shove that unfortunate truth to the side.

Ignorance is bliss, especially when a beautiful woman is naked in your shower and offering herself to you.

She has no idea what she's asking for.

TEN

WATER BEATS down on my back, and I slide my rough hands over her smooth and delicate skin. I grip her trim hips and tug her against me, trapping my hard cock between our slick, wet bodies.

She moans, but before she can say anything, I press my lips to hers in a soul-searing, mind-bending kiss. One that leaves no question who's in control here. She may have initiated this, but I'm the one who's going to end it.

Her hands delve into my hair, and nails scratch the back of my neck as I plunge my tongue between her lips and groan into her mouth. She mewls and grinds her stomach against my dick.

This may be all sorts of wrong, but fuck, does it feel right in this moment.

This small, battered, and bruised woman has more strength in her than that stupid asshole boyfriend I just destroyed.

And it's so fucking sexy.

I lift her easily, and she wraps her legs around my waist. Two steps forward are all it takes to have her back to the tile wall. She gasps against my lips, and I reach between us to grab my cock and position it at her slick opening.

The heat of the water in the shower is nothing compared to the scalding of her pussy closing on the head of my cock.

Fucking perfect.

One hard thrust drives me deep inside her.

"Alek!"

My name echoes against the tile and glass of the bathroom and rings in my ears as I pull back and pound into her again. I grit my teeth and unleash everything still pent up inside me.

Her tight pussy grips me with every thrust and retreat. The drag of the head of my cock along the rippling walls of her cunt is absolute fucking heaven.

It's as close as I'll ever get to being there, and it's the only place I want to be right now.

Sharp nails score my shoulders while her heels dig into my back. Her hips meet every thrust of mine, driving us into a frenzied rhythm. The pounding of the water, the slapping of our skin, and the pants and groans of pleasure create a symphony only for our ears.

I capture her mouth again, working my tongue in time with my frantic thrusts. She twines hers with mine as we duel for control.

She won't win, of course. But her passion drives me closer and closer to release.

"Come for me." I dig my fingers even harder into her thighs and adjust the angle of her body slightly so her clit receives constant friction.

She drops her head back. "Oh...God...yes! Right there!"

Her pussy walls ripple along the length of my dick, and I drive into her deeper, harder. My impending orgasm already burns at the base of my spine.

Close. So close.

It won't take much to...

Fuck!

Her teeth in my shoulder and the muffled cry as she orgasms are my undoing.

Rolling waves of pleasure course through me as her clenching body rips my cum from me and I empty myself into her with a few hard thrusts.

She sags slightly, and I lean forward to press her harder against the tile to keep us both from falling over. Our harsh pants mingle with the sound of the running water.

My sex-fogged brain begins to clear.

Shit. What the hell did I just do?

Never mess with one of the girls—it's the first fucking rule.

And I just broke it.

The only consolation is that she's not going to work for me anymore. She's going back to school, not back to the pole.

But I shouldn't have touched her, not when she's vulnerable and hurt like this.

She didn't need to be fucked by a crazed monster who's high from skinning someone alive. She needed to be held by someone who loved her and treated with some compassion.

I really fucked this up.

Badly.

I need to fix it, as much as I can.

She needs to know this can't happen again. It was a slip. That's it.

I slowly lower her legs until her feet hit the tile. She clings to me, her arms wrapped around my neck for support.

Heavy-lidded eyes meet mine, and a small smile tugs up the corner of her kiss-swollen and split lips. "That was—"

I don't let her finish. I lean forward and kiss her gently—anything to silence her and the inevitable awkward questions and conversations that come after sex like that.

She wobbles a little, and I pull back, putting some distance between us. Once she's steady on her feet, I shift her into the spray.

A low moan sounds in her throat as she dips her head back into the hot water.

"God, that feels good."

Krishti.

That little noise she just made has my cock swelling again.

I need to get out of here.

There's no way to keep my shit together with her naked and moaning and wet in front of me. I'll have her back against that wall and on my cock in two seconds if I stay.

I slide the glass door open, and her head drops down. Her eyes meet mine.

"Enjoy your shower. I'm going to dry off."

Even the brief look of hurt on her face can't keep me from closing the door.

It's not safe to stay in there.

I grab my towel, wrap it around my waist, and get the fuck out the bathroom as fast as my feet will carry me.

The sun went down hours ago, and the bright lights of Chicago now create a warm glow through the sky. I light a cigarette and step out onto the balcony.

A long, deep inhale sends the much-needed calming nicotine into my system.

Fucking brilliant, Alek.

Ask me to organize an attack on an enemy.

No problem.

Ask me to kill someone in a completely brutal and inhumane way.

Done.

Ask me to run one of the most powerful crime families in the Midwest.

Absofuckinglutely.

Ask me to keep my hands off one woman for one damn night.

Utter, catastrophic failure.

The door slides open behind me, and I close my eyes and take another drag. Her small arms wrap around my waist, and she presses her face against my shoulder blade.

"Come to bed."

Her whispered words are almost lost in the din from the street below, but my cock sure hears them. It stirs to life under the towel, desperate for more of the sweet heat of her body.

I really am fucked.

ELEVEN

ONLY THE FAINTEST hint of morning light creeps in around the curtains. Brynn lies behind me, trailing those magical fingers up and down my spine and following the lines of my tattoo.

How long have we lain like this? Minutes? Hours?

My cock feels like it's ready to burst, but there's no time for that. There's no *room* for that in my life, especially with her.

Last night was a mistake. A slip—or three. A moment of weakness following my victory over Terrance.

I can't let it happen again, but I can't seem to drag myself away from her touch this morning, either.

Just as I couldn't resist taking her again and again in my bed. Driving my cock into her and feeling her respond to my every touch was too great a pleasure to deny myself. It was my reward for a job well done.

It's over, though.

She shifts closer and pushes the length of her body against me. Breasts press to my back. Her leg slips over mine. Her cheek hits my shoulder.

It's my cue to get the fuck up.

I toss back the covers and sit on the edge of the bed. The cold wood of the floor and the chilly air sharply contrast with the recent warmth of having her body wrapped around mine.

"What's wrong?"

Don't look back at her.

If I do, there's a good chance I'll cave.

I shove to my feet. "Nothing is wrong. I'm getting in the shower, and then I'm going. You will not be here when I get back."

She sucks in a gasp, and the sound of her shifting on the bed hits my ears as I walk toward the bathroom. "What...what do you mean? I thought..."

I pause at the door and resist the urge to peek back at her.

Don't.

Her dark hair will be sleep-tousled and sexy. Her bare breasts will be swaying with her movement. Her eyes will be asking questions I either can't or don't want to answer.

"I know what you thought. Last night didn't mean anything. I'll send someone to pick you up and bring you home."

Slamming the door is probably overkill, but I need to make sure she understands. She needs to know what happened was pure, hard-core fucking between two people who shared an attraction. Nothing more.

It's what she needed to move past what happened with Terrance, and what I needed to celebrate what I did.

We got it out of our systems. We go about our lives like it never happened.

I can focus on creating a plan for Arturo's little favor and on locating the damn pilot. She can get back to nursing school knowing she doesn't have to worry about her mother or her damn ex.

Everyone wins.

Except my cock.

It throbs and screams at me to go back and bury it in her wet heat.

Instead, I crank on the shower as cold as it will go and step under the freezing spray. Icy beads of water sting my skin and burn against my hard dick.

But I let them fall.

It's going to be a long fucking day. I'll somehow manage, but not if I don't do something about the situation throbbing between my legs.

I take my cock in my hand and squeeze as I glide down in one long stroke. Biting back a groan, I stroke again and remember what it felt like to be clasped inside her, driving into her. The sounds she made. Mewls. Groans. Gasps. Moans. The sting of her nails digging into my shoulders. The bite of her teeth into my flesh.

Mallkim!

It doesn't take long for an orgasm to roll through me. Jets of cum shoot onto the tile and drip to the floor. The falling water swirls it away down the drain.

Shit.

I've never felt dirty about anything I've done in my entire life—even the most disturbing and depraved things—but for some reason, doing that when I know I probably just broke her heart makes me feel lower than dirt.

What the fuck is that about?

My stomach roils as I quickly wash away the guilt and the feel of her hands all over me. I turn off the water and grab a towel without looking in the mirror. There's no way I can face my reflection today.

The bedroom is empty.

Where the hell did she go?

I tug on a pair of dark jeans and a black T-shirt and move out to the living room. The glass door on the balcony stands open, and Brynn leans against the railing, looking out at the city with the pink-orange hue of the rising sun as the perfect backdrop.

God, you're a jackass, Alek.

She's a beautiful, willing woman, but I'm doing what's best for both of us.

I'm out the door before she has a chance to turn around. There's a lot of work to be done. My phone rings just as I climb into my car. It better be good news, because I don't have the patience for anything else right now.

"Hello?"

"Hey, boss. We got him."

The words send my heart skittering. "The pilot?"

"Yeah. Should be arriving by noon."

Thank fucking God.

It's about time we got somewhere on this. It's been too long. Too much bullshit. Too many dead ends.

"I'll be at the club in ten. Come pick Brynn up and bring her back to her place. She won't need to come back here."

I'm so damn close to getting the information I need to find Lorenc and Rea. It's time they finally got what's coming to them, and a damn woman can't be distracting me right now.

No distractions. Only complete focus will get me what I crave the most—revenge for what was done to Saban.

He didn't deserve it. He would have faced his maker, the same as me, and answered for what he had done when his time came. But it was not his time.

Konstandin made that decision. Lorenc assisted. And Rea caused it all by betraying Tarek. All because she couldn't keep her legs closed for a man who was not her fiancé.

They will all pay.
You can only hide from the Dragon for so long.

TWELVE

THE MAN SEATED before me is absolutely nothing like what I anticipated when I walked into my office this morning.

Typically, the people dumb enough to think they can run and hide from me are nothing more than quivering masses by the time I show up. When they know they've been caught. When they know it's over.

But not this guy.

He sits ramrod straight and looks me right in the eye as I sit across from him.

We found him hiding up in Canada, of all places. I guess it was the easiest place to go, and the border really isn't that far from Philly. He wasn't hiding very well. Using his real name and staying in an easily accessible hotel. It was almost as if he weren't really hiding at all.

And he came easily. No fight.

That earns some respect in my book.

"Brandon, is it?"

He nods. With his massive frame, close-cropped sandy hair and stern, cold blue eyes, the man might be intimidating to someone else. It doesn't fool me, though. He may look tough as nails, but he still ran rather than coming to face me.

I clasp my hands together on the desk and examine him. He can't be more than forty. Steady eyes. Steady hands on the armrests. Not shaking like most would.

Interesting.

"Well, Brandon, I'm going to explain the situation, although I think you already have some idea what's going on, given the way you fled."

He gives me a small nod, but again, shows no signs of the fear I usually instill in people.

I relax back in my chair and light a cigarette. He watches me as I take my first drag and blow out a ring of smoke. "I'm looking for two people. I think you know where I can find them. Lorenc and Rea. She also goes by Jade. Where did you take them?"

The man shifts slightly in his seat. "Mr. Gashi, I want to make something clear before we start. I wasn't running from you, per se, I just really have no desire to be involved in any of this. I'm a pilot, not a mobster. No offense."

I chuckle and raise my hands. "None taken."

"I fly for a lot of people. One of them happened to be Tarek. He paid me well, and I didn't ask any questions, just filed the flight plans and took him wherever he wanted to go. I never anticipated there would be an issue like this."

While what he said makes sense, he knew what Tarek did when he took the job. Turning a blind eye to what you are doing and for whom doesn't excuse it. Anyone connected to this carries some level of guilt.

I nod for him to continue.

"The day it happened, I got a call from someone who told me to have the plane ready. I was at the tarmac and waiting for Tarek, only he didn't show. Lorenc did. And he had a woman and dog with him."

"Rea?"

He shakes his head and shrugs. "I can't be one hundred percent sure. She was never with Tarek when I flew him, and I never met her, only heard whispers about her from some of the other pilots and Tarek's men."

"He had other pilots?"

"Three pilots on rotation. Plus, he had two planes. The one I flew was smaller, and he rarely used it, so I didn't work for him as much as the others. I think it was designed to prevent any of us really knowing too much."

Smart.

For a guy with so much intelligence, Tarek really did make some pretty fucking bad decisions that put him in his grave. He should have just let Konstandin and Rea go. If there was anyone in this world as cold and fucked up as me, it's Konstandin. His brother should have known not to fuck with him or his woman, no matter how much he may have been pissed off at their betrayal. No matter how much they both deserved what he had planned for them.

"Tell me about Lorenc and Rea."

Silence hangs between us briefly before he shifts in his seat and clears his throat.

"Nothing seemed amiss, and I had no reason to suspect they had just had a hand in killing Tarek."

"Where did you take them?"

He doesn't even flinch. "Cuba."

"Cuba?"

He nods.

That's certainly an interesting choice. They would have had to fly through Pittsburgh first because of the travel restrictions, and also come up with a legitimate reason for the travel to get approval. It seems like a lot of work when they could have flown practically anywhere.

So, why Cuba?

"That's where you left them?"

"Yes, sir. I dropped them off, turned right back around, and came home. And I swear, that's all I know. I don't want to be in the middle of some war. That's not what I signed up for."

Going to work for one of the families means you're always going to be tied up in something. He can't be that naïve. Everyone who works for me is prepared to die for me. It's part of the job.

He holds up his hand. "Look, sir. I'm not stupid. I know I'm not walking out of here alive. I just don't see any reason for fighting and begging when it won't change anything. And I figured you'd make it less painful if I just cooperated."

I like this guy.

It's too bad he can't keep his mouth shut. I'd have a lot more respect for him if he hadn't told me everything right off the bat and maybe put up a bit of a fight. I respect loyalty, and I can always use a good pilot, but not someone who squeals like a fucking stuck pig.

He was in a no-win situation with me the moment he took the job flying for Tarek.

"I'm sorry it has to be this way, Brandon, but I do appreciate the information and that you made this easy for me."

I take another drag and wait for his reply.

Brandon presses his lips together in a tight line and nods. "Please make it easy for me in return."

I guess I owe him that. I nod at Erjon and give him a look that tells him it's time to take care of business. He nods his understanding and steps forward to place one large hand on Brandon's shoulder.

The man finally starts to shake. Perhaps reality has finally sunk in. He can say he knew what was coming, but having it standing behind him and laying a hand on him is something else altogether.

Sorry, my friend.

Erjon will dispose of him swiftly and discreetly.

I rise to my feet and wave them away. "We're done here."

When the door clicks behind them, I drop back into my chair and examine the ceiling while I finish my smoke.

Cuba? What are the chances there still there after all this time?

Almost two years.

I can't imagine Lorenc would want to stay in one place for that long, especially being so close the United States. Then again, it's probably one of the last places I would've looked for him.

There's only one way to find out.

THIRTEEN

THE DOOR OPENS, and Erjon gives me a look I can't quite decipher. Things have been relatively quiet the last several days as we've prepared to head to Cuba, but it's almost been like a calm before the storm.

I knew something was coming...

Jesus, what now?

I take a drag off my cigarette and nod. "What is it?"

He glances back over his shoulder toward the main club. "There's someone here to see you."

It must be important for him to interrupt me. If it wasn't, he would have handled it himself or sent the person packing.

"Who?"

A long, deep sigh slips from his lips, and he shrugs as if in apology. "Kitty."

Fuck.

"What is she doing here?"

I told her to go home and stay away. I don't think I stuttered or failed to make myself perfectly clear. After radio silence since I left her at the condo the other day, I was confident she got the message.

"She seems upset."

Shit.

Maybe something's wrong.

"Send her back."

He disappears, and a thousand terrible scenarios about why she might be here race through my head.

Did someone in the MC show up and threaten her? Is it her mom? Is she sick?

When she finally turns the corner and enters my office, my eyes meet hers.

My concern is quickly replaced with understanding.

Pure, unadulterated rage clouds her gaze, and her lips form a firm line across her hard face. Any softness I saw there the other night is gone.

She storms in carrying something under her arm and sets the new laptop I bought for her in the middle my desk.

"What the hell is this?" Her hands on her hips are probably meant to convey her annoyance and anger, but instead, they only draw attention to her tiny waist and make my fingers itch to wrap around her and squeeze her there.

I take another long, slow drag and blow the smoke out as I examine the laptop then glance back up at her. "I would think that would be obvious. It's a computer."

She growls and slams her palms on the desk. "That's not what I meant, and you know it! Why was this computer sent to my house?"

Anger looks good on her...

My cock stirs, and I raise one shoulder and let it fall slowly. "You are going back to school. You're going to need a computer, aren't you?"

It seems pretty self-explanatory to me.

"I have a computer."

I bark out a laugh, put out my cigarette in the ashtray on my desk, and lean back with my hands tucked behind my head.

"And how old is that?"

She scowls—a look that might be unattractive on anyone else, but on her, it's so damn cute.

"It gets the job done."

"This one will more than get the job done. You should just thank me and go."

Fury reddens her face, and she throws her hands up. "Thank you? *Thank* you? You're freaking insane."

A low chuckle rumbles in my chest. Many people have called me insane and much worse over the years, and most of them ended up at the wrong end of my blowtorch and knife. But from her, it's almost a compliment.

And her anger couldn't be sexier.

Hell.

The flush over her pale skin and the flashes of her heaving breasts every time she bends forward have me wanting to bend her over this desk and fuck that anger right out of her.

She's capable of coming in here like this, which means she's recovering from her ordeal nicely— what he did and what I did to her.

"I'm offering a life for you where you don't have to worry about money ever again. Your mother will be cared for. You can work in your chosen profession. And frankly, if you choose not to work at all, I'll still take care of you. So, what are you so angry with me about?"

Her eyes widen, and she shakes her head. "What? You can't be serious. Why would you pay for all this...do all of this for me? I don't understand. Are you trying to *pay* me for what happened the other night? I'm not a damn hooker."

I rise from my chair and stalk around the desk to stand in front of her. I want to grab her and shake some damn sense into her, but touching her would be a very bad idea.

"Because you deserve a better life than the one you're living. One where you don't have to live in fear. One where you don't have to worry about where money is coming from or if your mother is taken care of, because no one should have to live like that...especially you." I can't fight it anymore. I close the distance between us and reach out to grasp her chin and tilt her face up to me. "Let me take care of you."

Tears fill her eyes, and she shakes her head. "Why do you want to take care of somebody you don't even want to be with?"

Christ, she's a stubborn one.

And totally oblivious to what's happening here.

"You think I don't want to be with you?" I grab her hand and place it against my very hard cock currently struggling to make its way out of my pants. "I've been hard since the second you walked in this room. What I *want* and what's *possible* are two different things."

Her small hand squeezes me, and I bite back a groan. "Why is it not possible, Alek?"

A sardonic laugh comes from deep in my chest, and I toss my head back. "You know who I am. You know what I do, or at least, you think you have a suspicion about it. Believe me, you have no idea what the truth is."

It would fucking terrify her.

The Dragon would give her nightmares even during her waking hours.

"Being with me would mean being in danger every moment of your life. You would be making yourself and your family a target. If you think what Terrance did to you is bad, you can't even begin to fathom what my enemies would do to you if they found out you meant anything to me." I gesture between her and me. "This cannot happen."

She shifts closer and places her free hand flat against my chest, looking up at me with those warm, glowing eyes. "Why is that your decision to make for me? I want this." She squeezes my cock, and a groan rumbles from my lips. "I don't want your money."

So fucking stubborn.

Having her beside me, having her in my bed every night, is something I never even considered an option. Looking at her now, knowing that's exactly what she wants, has me considering a whole other world. One where my life and my work couldn't touch her. One where she'd be safe.

Yet it's not the real world. It's not possible.

But maybe some version of it is.

I take her face in my hands and turn her face up to me again. "This is what you want?"

She nods, and all my resolve cracks and crumbles away.

Her hand squeezes my cock again.

How the hell am I supposed to say no to her when she keeps doing that?

"There will be rules. Things you must do and things you can never do. Things you can never know and can never ask. I will never be like any man you've been with before. I will not be like the men your friends date. I am the Dragon."

She offers a slight whimper of reply. She doesn't truly understand what my words mean yet, what it will all entail, and instead of scaring her like I'd hoped, it almost appears my words have turned her on.

Total backfire.

"Are you sure that's what you want?"

There's no hesitation before she nods again.

It's all I need to know I'm doomed.

FOURTEEN

I HAVE her pushed against my desk in two seconds flat, and my mouth meets her with a greed I never knew I possessed.

It's only been a few days, but it feels like I haven't tasted her in years, decades, eons.

Her warm tongue slides along my lips before her teeth dig into the sensitive flesh there.

I growl and pull back from her. "Turn around."

She looks like she might argue for a second, but I grasp her hips and spin her before she can say a word.

The skirt she's wearing barely covers her luscious ass as it is. I slide my palm along her warm skin and shift it up to her hips. I smack her across one cheek hard enough to leave a handprint and watch her flesh jiggle.

"Ouch!" She whips her head around and glares at me, but there's no real anger there. No fight. Just lust. She loved it, just like I knew she would.

The other night, I took it easy on her.

She was healing.

She was fragile.

She hasn't seen anything yet.

If she really wants to be with me, she needs to see how it will be. How I am. All of me.

I smack her ass again, but this time, she drops her head down to the desk and releases a low moan of pleasure.

Damn right.

I slip my fingers under the barely-there lace of her thong and find her already soaked and ready for me. I free my aching cock from the confines of my pants and position it at her entrance.

She wiggles back against me, and it's an invitation I can't ignore. I shove into her hard, and she rocks across the desk with a mumbled curse. Her pussy clenches around me, and I dig my hands into the flesh of her hips as I pull back and then drive into her.

Every thrust of her hips. Every gasp and moan. Every single breath of hers is mine.

Mine!

I've never wanted anything as much as I want her. Except maybe my revenge for Saban. And that will come soon enough.

Right now, buried to the hilt in her hot, welcoming cunt is the only place I need to be.

"Alek! Please!" Her fingers wrap around the opposite edge of the desk, and she slams her hips backward harder to meet me on every single thrust.

The need. The violence. The roughness I'm showing her. None of it scares her. None of it gives her even a second's pause.

That only makes my cock harder and my need to mark her as mine even stronger. It roars through my blood and thrums in my ears.

A low growl rips from my chest, and I smack her gorgeous pink ass and redouble my efforts. I slide a hand around to her front and find her clit with my finger.

She jerks on my cock and starts grinding into my hand. "God...yes!"

Those strangled words have the low burn of my orgasm moving up my spine.

I grab her hair with my free hand and wrap it around my wrist. I jerk her head back sharply. She

GWYN MCNAMEE

yelps, but her eyes meet mine, and she comes apart all over me. My hand. My cock. Both are flooded with her release.

Her grasping and clenching pussy drags my orgasm free. Five hard thrusts and I collapse onto her.

I'll never see God, but this is pretty fucking close.

I release her hair and let it fall over her shoulder. Our heavy pants flutter it across the desk—jet-black hair against pale wood. The exposed skin on her neck is too much to resist. I press my lips there, and she moans softly beneath me.

"Alek."

"Hmm?"

"You're crushing me."

Shit.

Reveling in the moment momentarily made me forget what a big motherfucker I am and how tiny she is.

I pull back reluctantly and drag my dick from inside her slowly.

She moans, pushes herself up, and glances at me over her shoulder. I tug my pants up and slide the zipper in place as she rights her thong and skirt and turns to face me. Her pale skin glows pink in the aftermath of the very thorough fucking I just gave her. And something that feels an awful lot like pride swells in my heart.

This woman is mine. Whether or not it's smart. Whether or not it's right. Whether or not I want it to be true. She. Is. Mine.

Now I just need to figure out a way to ensure she's protected.

I capture her face between my hands and brush her hair off her cheeks. "You still sure this is what you want?"

She pulls her bottom lip—the one barely healed from her ordeal with Terrance—between her teeth and nods. "I'm sure, Alek."

Those words have my cock stirring back to life. But before we can take care of that, she needs to understand the rules.

It could be the deal-breaker.

Here goes nothing.

"You and your mother will move in with me."

Her mouth opens, but I silence her with a look.

"That's not negotiable. I need to know you're safe, and that's the best place to do that."

She nods and turns her head to kiss my palm. The soft brush of her lips against my rough skin sends a shiver down my spine.

When her eyes meet mine again, nothing but understanding shines there. "Okay. What else?"

"You will never set foot in the club or any other business I own. You won't ask me questions about my work. You won't question anything I tell you to do. This is all to keep you safe. Do you understand that?"

A light sigh slips from her lips, and she reaches up to twine her arms around my neck. "I understand. And I know why the rules are necessary."

Hell...

The ease with which she's willing to fall into this life, to risk her security, her mother's, is truly humbling.

I haven't been humbled much in my life. The things done to me while I was in that black hole of a prison were nothing compared to what she does to me with one fucking look.

These golden eyes will be my undoing, I know it.

But what a fucking way to go down.

FIFTEEN

IT WAS SO MUCH HARDER to leave Brynn than I thought it would be. It's only been a few days since I fucked her in my office and moved her into my place, yet already, I can't imagine not having her around.

But some things are more important right now, and at the top of that list is finding Lorenc and Rea.

Only one thing will cure the boiling rage in my soul, and that's unleashing what was done to Saban on them tenfold.

Brynn has quelled some of the aching in my chest when I think of him, but revenge is the best medicine...and that sweet release starts right now.

I step in front of the man strung from the ceiling. The man I've known for almost my entire life.

The one who betrayed us.

His black-as-night eyes burn into mine.

I couldn't figure out why Lorenc and Rea would come to Cuba. Imagine my surprise when we arrived and dug a little at the airport only to hear a familiar name.

"What are you doing in Cuba, Edon?"

He shakes his head and spits in my face. I wipe it away with a low chuckle.

"Are we really going to play these games, Edon? Are you really going to pretend you didn't help them? Tell me what you're doing in Cuba. Tell me where they are."

The man who once played in the same streets as Saban and me as a child growls and tugs at his restraints, but I know Erjon has him tied tightly. He's not going anywhere.

"Fuck you, Aleksander! You and your entire family can burn in fucking hell for all I care. The Morinas are gone, and it's only a matter of time before the Gashis go with them."

"Now, now, Edon, that's not very nice. What have I done to incur this wrath?"

He tosses his head back with a cynical laugh. "Are you kidding? Your brother decimated my Midwest business and then went after me. The only way I was able to escape with my life was because someone gave me a warning that he was coming."

So, my brother had a rat in his house...

That means little now. Konstandin eliminated most of Saban's men too, but it will make me take a closer look at those who remain with me.

"Why Cuba, Edon?"

He chuckles. "No extradition. Very little chance that you or anyone else will show up or look here. Lots of business opportunities for someone with my skill set."

It makes sense. The fact I didn't think of Cuba now seems as stupid as Saban thinking he could side with Tarek against Konstandin and live.

"Tell me what you know." I slowly undo the buttons on my shirt and slide it off my shoulders. After folding it, I place it on the small table behind me. My pants join it.

If he wants to do this the hard way, I'm more than happy to oblige.

The second my hands touch the blowtorch, my cock stiffens, and a rush of adrenaline surges through my veins.

I turn back to face him. Edon's eyes widen slightly at the sight of the blowtorch, but it doesn't loosen his lips.

He's tougher than I gave him credit for.

"You've chosen this path. Anything that happens is on you."

I step up to him and light the torch. He fights against the restraints, but the effort is futile.

If anyone knows what to anticipate from the Dragon, it's Edon. I would have expected him to be smarter than to betray the family by assisting Rea and Lorenc.

I point at his arm where his family crest is tattooed. "I'll start here."

When the flame hits the skin of his forearm, his scream echoes off the barren walls and into my ears. I tip my head back to watch the rising smoke, then return my attention to moving the flame up and down his arm, letting it blister the skin without completely charring it.

Erjon has done well finding a location that's isolated so I can complete my work without fear of discovery.

"You can scream all you want, Edon. No one is coming for you. Tell me what happened with Lorenc and Rea. Where are they?"

Edon gasps and tugs, gritting his teeth against the pain. It's a real art to work someone over without having them pass out or drop dead. An art I've perfected.

I pull the flame back to where the heat still licks at his skin but the flame itself isn't burning him any longer. If I want an answer, he needs to be able to speak.

"Tell me."

The silence that greets me is all the answer I'm going to get.

Fucker.

I place the tip of flame back against his skin.

"Okay! Okay!" He gasps, barely able to get the words out.

That's a start. I withdraw the flame.

"I didn't know they were coming. Lorenc contacted me when they got here. Said he needed help getting out of the country and new identities. They didn't have much time because they weren't sure how long it would take before you or Tarek's remaining crew came after them."

"Where did you send them?"

His dark eyes meet mine, and there's a momentary hesitation.

How dumb is this fucker?

I step to the side and place the flame against the unmarred skin there. He cries out again and struggles against the restraints so much, they bite into his wrists, sending blood trickling down over the burned flesh.

"Where did they go?"

The flames lick against his other arm, and my cock throbs as his screams echo around the room. Sweat and tears drip off his face, but my question remains unanswered. Obviously, the flames aren't enough to do the job here.

Excellent.

I grab my knife and return to face him. "You have one final chance."

The blade cuts through his burned skin like warm butter. One long slice down his forearm opens it for me, and I set to work peeling his skin back.

His screams are deafening. My cock twitches, and even though I don't want Brynn anywhere near this, I wish she were here for when I'm done with the job.

I've barely pulled an inch back before he cries out.

"Stop! Stop! I'll tell you. Just stop. I put them on a plane to Argentina."

I step back in front of him and pull his head up by his hair so he's forced to look at me.

"Where they went from there, I don't know."

"Argentina?"

What the hell are they doing in Argentina?

Tarek and Konstandin's family has ties all over Eastern Europe, but so do the Gashis, so I know they can't go back there. The UK has too many connections too.

I can't think of a single connection to anyone down in Argentina, though.

Maybe that's exactly the point.

"What names are they traveling under?"

He grunts and sways slightly against the ropes holding him up.

"Matthew and Isabella Michaelson."

"They're posing as a married couple?"

"Yes."

I let his head fall.

There's no telling what names they're using now. Lorenc is too smart to keep the same name once they landed in Argentina, especially if that was their final destination, but I have a feeling it wasn't.

Each tiny string is building a web, and every single one I find and pull helps it unravel. Eventually, I will find them.

They will meet the Dragon.

But until then, I have something to go home to.

Something I thought I would never have.

I'm not going to waste that.

I flash Edon a grin, one he doesn't even see with his head dropped down, but I know he's still conscious.

"Thank you for the information, Edon. Now, what do you say we finish what we've started?"

So I can get back to my girl.

EPILOGUE

REA/JADE

G OLDEN EYES SMILE up at me from under the mop of thick black hair. Those eyes hold everything in them—the past, the future, love, and hate.

Konstandin's been gone for two years, yet it feels like only yesterday Lorenc told me he didn't make it out.

He never got to meet his son. He never even got to know he existed.

I begged Lorenc to let me go back into the airport after him, but he refused. He promised Konstandin he would get me out and not look back, no matter what. Even telling Lorenc about the baby didn't deter him from throwing me over his shoulder and racing toward the car, leaving the love of my life to deal with his twisted brother. The only pause on our escape from the airport was to grab Bruiser out of Tarek's SUV and to fire off some shots at another car full of Tarek's men, who'd arrived late.

If only I'd realized I was pregnant before we ever went to that damn party...maybe things would have been different. His guard wouldn't have been down, and he would be here with me now.

But wondering about the past and *what-ifs* never got anyone anywhere good. It certainly hasn't served me well. The first few months were excruciating in a way I never knew possible. It was more painful, physically and mentally, than anything Tarek ever did to me.

It took a while for me to realize Konstandin isn't gone. Not really.

I will always have this piece of him. Despite Tarek's best efforts to destroy him, destroy *us*, he will live on through this beautiful boy.

"You ready to go?"

Lorenc's question draws my attention away from the toddler clinging to my leg and to the man on the steps up to the small plane on the tarmac.

I grin at him and nod. This trip has been a long time coming.

We deserve it. Even though we can never return to the States or Albania, my son deserves to see as much of the world as he can. The money Konstandin left for us will ensure we never have to worry about anything. And with Lorenc always at my back, I know I won't have to spend the rest of our lives looking over my shoulder.

Starting over—again—wasn't easy, but looking into the face of this angel every day makes all the gut-wrenching awful days manageable.

Lorenc steps down and grabs Pjeter, swinging him up into the air. The squeal of delight brings tears to my eyes. He will never know his father, but Lorenc has given him everything a child could ever need or ask for and has demanded nothing in return from me. He's a true friend, one who has sacrificed his own life to protect ours.

"You ready, big guy?"

Pjeter giggles and takes Lorenc's face between his tiny hands. "Yah, beach!"

A smile spreads across Lorenc's usually stoic face. "That's right, buddy. We're heading to the beach."

I worry about him, the weight on his shoulders of having to take care of us and ensure we aren't found by any of Konstandin's enemies. One thing that man was good at was pissing people off. But I always knew he would come for me, through Hell or high water, destroying anything and anyone in his path.

He may have become Griffin when we left Philly, but he never stopped being Konstandin at his core.

An animal.

A killer.

A mercenary.

A sinner.

I saw through all of it, though. From the first time our eyes met, I knew there was more, buried underneath that dark, dangerous surface. He was nothing like his brother, a man willing to force me into an unwanted marriage and worse.

Konstandin was loving, caring, misunderstood.

And I was right. He was someone who would, and did, move Heaven and Earth to ensure I was safe.

My prayer is that Pjeter will never know the violence and hate that permeated Konstandin's life.

But looking at him now, I know he is his father's son.

That may terrify someone else.

Not me.

This world needs more men like Konstandin.

GHOST

I'm dead.

That's for the best.

This is my life now.

Though it's not really a life, more of a morbid existence.

But it serves its purpose.

It keeps me safe. It keeps everyone safe.

It's necessary.

One of the cut-sluts I've seen at these parties once or twice before stumbles over to where I sit in the corner of the clubhouse and leans over me, exposing her massive, round fake breasts. Her platinum-blonde hair swings around her overly made-up face, and she flashes me a white smile surrounded by bright red lips.

I fight the desire to kick her away with my boot.

"Hey, handsome. How come you never party with us? You're always over here looking like someone killed your dog."

I growl.

The bitch should have never mentioned my dog.

Her alcohol-hazed eyes snap wide, and she scowls at me. "You're an asshole, Ghost." She turns and wobbles away, only to throw herself at Mack, who's leaning against the bar. She whispers something in his ear, and he glances over her shoulder at me and gives me a knowing grin.

I nod in his direction.

He can have her. I haven't touched a woman in two years, and I have no plans to.

Existence.

Breathing.

Eating.

Sleeping.

Riding my bike with these assholes.

Doing whatever I need to survive.

That's pretty much it right now.

And I'm okay with that.

I have to be. There's no other option.

Archer waves at me from behind the bar and holds up a beer. I nod, and he rounds the bar and ambles across the room toward me with two beers in hand. He gives me one and drops down in the chair next to me.

His eyes scan the room. The Rebel Chasers MC isn't large—a dozen members and a few prospects—but they're a tight-knit group of guys.

The only way I was able to work my way in with them so quickly was my role as a nomad, and because they saw what I was willing to do to help them. Having no qualms about taking a life—and worse—is a real asset in some circumstances. This is one of them.

Once they knew I had those skills and questionable—if any—morals, they stopped asking questions, at least openly.

There are always whispers. People wondering where I came from. Why all my tattoos are blacked out. Where all my scars came from. Where I learned to do what I do.

But no one voices those questions anymore.

They know better.

I tip my beer back and let the cool liquid calm my nerves. These parties always put me on edge. People in the clubhouse who shouldn't be. Eyes on me. Ones I don't know.

Archer leans forward and rests his elbows on his knees. "You okay, Ghost? You're even broodier than normal tonight."

I manage a low chuckle. Maybe I'm not as good at hiding my disdain for this shit as I thought. "I'm good. Just...ready for the night to be over. We have that run early tomorrow."

He nods and takes a swig of his beer. "I hear ya. We'll send everyone on their way soon if they don't clear out on their own."

Soon isn't *soon* enough for me.

I drain my beer and rise to my feet. "I'm calling it a night."

My nomad status means I can crash here whenever I want, but technically, I have no affiliation to any one regional club. It comes in handy when I need to get the fuck out and can go somewhere else. Time on the road alone helps me clear my head, but it can't make me forget.

Her.

Him.

The blood.

The pain.

"Goodnight, man!" Archer raises his beer, and I give him a nod before crossing the clubhouse main room toward the hallway leading to the bedrooms.

"Hey, Ghost!"

I turn toward whoever called my name. Butcher stands at the end of the bar and holds up his cell phone.

"What?"

He shakes it and holds it out toward me. "It's for you."

What?

That's impossible.

I don't have a phone. No one but the members of the Rebel Chasers even know me. And all they know is I'm nobody.

How would someone know to call his phone to get me?

I cross the room and snatch it from him. "Who is this?"

"Your friend and your girl are in trouble. The Dragon is on his way."

SURVIVING WRATH

WRATH is a sin.
However, it has dug our souls too deep, to allow us to let it go...
It burns us while holding onto it.
Yet, we are too consumed by it to leave it.

-Richa Dhingra

ONE

REA/JADE

THE COOL, early evening air washes over me through the open automatic doors, and I step out onto the dark parking lot. A few street lamps drop small halos of light on the asphalt and the few cars still here this close to closing. Sharp laughter draws my attention to a couple of teenage girls walking down the sidewalk in front of the store. Otherwise, it's quiet.

It should be calming. I should be comforted by the fact that nothing seems amiss. But it's times like this, nights like these, that always put me most on edge. Goose bumps pebble across my exposed skin.

It was a night like this when they came for Konstandin and me, when they took me and ended our bliss.

We were so naïve to think we could get away unscathed and that Tarek would let us escape with our lives and with each other. To believe we could hide forever in our little bubble and ignore the world we came from.

We both paid the price for that childish dream.

Konstandin with his life. Me with losing him and having to raise Pjeter without his father.

So, I can't let myself get complacent and believe I'm safe here just because things are quiet and have been for so long. A false sense of security is just as dangerous as the people still looking for us. Maybe even more so.

I tug my purse strap higher on my shoulder and set out across the lot toward the car. The plastic grocery bag in my hand crinkles as it swings from side to side with my movement, and aside from the wind blowing through the leaves in the trees lining the property, the night is eerily silent.

The usual unease of being out in the open crawls up my spine.

Keep moving. Everything's fine. Just get to the car.

In ten minutes, I'll be back home and cooking our late dinner. A few more steps and I'll be safely inside the car with the locks engaged and my foot on the gas pedal.

A sharp crack rings out, and something whizzes past my ear. I jerk away from it. Another crack, another, and another...

What the hell?

A second passes. Then the sounds of my former life come rushing back to me.

Gunfire.

A sharp pain slices through my arm, and the bag clatters to the pavement, the contents spilling out around my feet.

Shit!

Someone's shooting at me.

Crack. Crack. Crack. Crack. Crack.

A barrage of shots rattles out but from a different direction. I duck behind a car. Silence falls over the lot again.

What the hell just happened?

The roar of an engine fills my ears, and a motorcycle comes to a screeching halt six inches in front of me. A massive man in black leather, with a thick, dark beard and a helmet pulled low over his forehead reaches out and grabs me.

No!

I pound on his arms as he hauls me toward him.

"No! Let me go!"

Not again. They're not taking me again.

He growls and shoves me onto the seat in front of him. I shift to the opposite side to jump off, but strong arms wrap around me and hold me in place. It's like being pressed in a vise.

I'm trapped.

He revs the engine and flies out of the parking lot. Cold air stings my face, and we tear down Main Street with his massive chest pressed against my back.

My heart races, blood rushes in my ears, and warm tears stream down my chilled cheeks.

What the hell is going on? Who is he? One of Tarek's remaining men?

I won't let this happen. I won't let them take me away from Pjeter and Lorenc. I won't lose my life a second time.

Whatever it takes...I'm going home tonight.

I slam my elbow back into the gut of the man behind me. He grunts and growls, but when I try to do it again, my elbow meets nothing but a solid wall of flexed muscle. He's braced to absorb my blows now, and I might as well be banging against concrete.

Shit.

"Stop it." The command is dark, low, and barely audible over the roar of the bike and the road beneath us, but it still sends a chill through me.

The same words Tarek said to me so many times when I tried to fight him off, when I tried to stop what he was doing to me—the past I try not to think about.

Because if I do, it only takes away from the joy and light that Pjeter is in my life. Looking at him, I see Konstandin, but I also see the man who was my tormentor. Concentrating on what I had with Konstandin is the only way I can make it through the day. Even though I lost it, just knowing I had it once is enough to make the pain bearable.

This can't be happening again. I survived it once, but I won't survive it a second time. I have to end this before it's too late.

My kidnapper weaves in and out of traffic at breakneck speeds and blows through several traffic signals before heading out of town on one of the three tiny, two-lane highways that lead to this place.

Tears flow down my face in earnest now. The rush of the cold night air and rumble of the road fill my ears as we move deeper into the wilderness and farther from everyone I love.

Where did things go wrong?

We were safe. We've been safe for years.

Lorenc did everything he could to cover our trail. When we left Philly, we flew first to Pittsburgh then to Cuba then to Argentina. We might have stayed there forever, but Lorenc feared we stood out too much. We came here because Lorenc knew Canada would be the easiest place to blend in and probably the last place anyone would think to look for us. With my hair dyed black and posing as a couple with a young son, we are just another family living in a small town.

And things have been quiet and peaceful. We've built a life. Together. The three of us. This strange little family. So much shared love and loss, and now, it will all be gone again.

If I don't stop it.

Whoever this man is, he's not taking me.

As soon as we stop, I'll do whatever I can to prevent that, even if it means killing him with my bare hands.

I'm not going down without a fight.

TWO

THE SECONDS, the minutes, the hours tick by on the road as the stranger drives me farther and farther from Pjeter and Lorenc. Farther and farther from safety. Farther and farther from my ability to escape and get back to them in one piece.

My heart sinks into my ankles, and my body shakes violently in the chilly night air. The big man's massive body and arms wrapped around me provide some warmth, but I pull myself away from him as much as I can.

I don't want this stranger touching me.

Who knows what he'll do when we stop? Imagining the possibilities only turns my stomach, and I want as much peace as possible in the meantime.

The dark, desolate road stretches on in front of us.

After what feels like hours of not seeing another vehicle, he pulls down a narrow, gravel drive on the side of the road.

Oh, God, what is he doing?

There's nothing and no one around for probably a hundred miles. It's nothing but trees and wildlife out here. The perfect place to exact revenge...and anything else he has in mind.

This is it. I'm going to die.

Unless I stop this.

Bile rises in my throat, and I clench my fist and prepare myself to run as soon as he stops. The woods will provide a hundred different places to hide. I might freeze to death tonight, but it's my only option—my only chance to get away from my captor in one piece.

I don't have any weapons to fight him with, and he's twice my size.

If he's going to kill me, at least I'll make it more difficult for him by running. If he wants to do anything else...he's going to have to catch me first.

He pulls to a stop and kills the bike. I launch myself off the seat and fall onto all fours on the gravel. It bites into the skin on my palms, and I stumble to get to my feet and race toward the line of trees to our left.

"Stop it, *e dashur.*"

That voice. That name.

I freeze halfway to the tree line, my entire body shaking so violently, I can barely stay up on my legs.

No. It's impossible. It can't be him. He can't be...

I turn slowly to face my abductor.

The faint light from the bike's headlamp illuminates the right side of his face as he turns on the seat toward me, swings his leg over, and rises to his feet.

Familiar, dark eyes stare back at me through the night. Eyes I looked into every day for two glorious years before Tarek took him from me. Eyes now filled with a thousand different emotions I've never seen in them before.

I take a step toward him and shake my head. "Konstandin?"

"I haven't heard that name in over two years, *e dashur.*"

My heart screamed that name every second, every minute, of every hour, of every day since Lorenc dragged me away from Konstandin, kicking and screaming.

The beard does an excellent job of hiding his familiar jawline and high cheekbones, but it's there, just beneath the surface, the face of the man I love—Pjeter's father. The man who died two years ago takes a step forward, but instead of running to him, I instinctively step back.

"How can you be alive? How can this be happening?"

He raises a hand. "I'm sorry, *e dashur*, but it had to be this way. There was no choice."

No choice?

"You've been alive this whole time...and you never sent word...you never came for me?" I shake my head as countless agonizing days and nights run through my mind. Ones when I couldn't even get out of bed. Ones when I wanted to die, too, where the only thing that kept me alive was knowing I had his child growing inside me. "You bastard!"

He cringes and recoils slightly as he shakes his head and takes another step toward me, his black motorcycle boots crunching on the gravel beneath his feet.

I've dreamed of what it would be like to see Konstandin again. How it would feel to hold him in my arms, to tell him how much I love him. I imagined how I would introduce him to the son he never knew he had. All I wanted was to feel *his* arms wrapped around me, his lips pressed to mine... to experience his love again.

But right now, I don't want any of that because the only thing consuming my body is red-hot anger.

Anger at the man who could've been with me the last two years. Anger at the man who could've been here and been a father to Pjeter.

"How could you?"

He runs a shaky hand back through thick, long unruly hair so unlike how Konstandin wore it. He looks like a totally different person. And he must be because the Konstandin I knew would never have let me suffer like this.

How could he physically stay away?

If I had known he was alive, I would have moved Heaven and Earth to get to him. No matter what.

"I did it to protect you, Rea. When you and Lorenc left and I killed Tarek, I was in bad shape. I collapsed and almost died right there in that airport. I did die on the operating table. When I came back to, I was surrounded by FBI agents asking me thousands of questions. I kept my mouth shut and bided my time until I was strong enough to get out of there and escape their custody."

"FBI?"

He nods and takes another step toward me. "And they aren't the only ones after us, *e dashur*. Back there," he hitches a thumb over his shoulder, "those men shooting at you were Aleksander Gashi's men."

"The Gashis?"

I haven't thought about them in years. The rift between them and the Morinas, coupled with the distance between Chicago and Philly, kept them out of the picture.

"Yes. I killed Saban in Chicago on my way to get you back. His brother is not very happy about that."

I know what Konstandin went through to rescue me. Once we were safe, Lorenc filled me in on everything Konstandin had endured and everything he had to do. Lorenc was careful about making contact with anyone from our former lives, but everyone he did speak with told him Konstandin was dead. The FBI must've kept him hidden and faked his death to protect any case they were trying to build against the families involved.

A man like Konstandin in their pocket would have been a major coup for them. But I know this man—or at least, I used to—and they could never turn him.

He's not the kind of man to be told to do anything. And threats wouldn't have turned him against his people.

Which means, staying away was *his* choice.

"None of this explains why you didn't come for me. For us..."

He shakes his head and closes the distance between us so fast, I can't back away. His massive, rough palms tilt up my face. "You don't think I wanted that? You don't think that every fucking second of every day I didn't dream of having you back in my arms? *Krishti, e dashur*, I did it to protect you. To protect Lorenc. To give you a chance at a normal life where you weren't constantly looking over your shoulder and watching your back. I knew Lorenc could protect you and keep you safe. All the things you would never be as long as I was around. My being dead is what was best for everyone."

The wounds I've tried so hard to heal over the last few years are sliced open by his words. "You may think that, but it can't be further from the truth."

Tears trickle down my cheeks, and he brushes them away with his thumbs. "I'm so sorry, *e dashur*. I'll do everything in my power to make it up to you, but right now, we have to get out of here. I took care of the two back there, but there will be more. Aleksander found you, and if he learns I'm alive, things will get even messier. We have to leave now. We can get word to Lorenc, and he can join us."

"No. We can't leave."

His hands still. "Why not?"

Oh, hell...

He doesn't know. He doesn't know about Pjeter. I suck in a deep breath and look deep into the eyes of the only man I ever loved.

"Because I'm not leaving here without Lorenc."

THREE

He stiffens, and his dark eyes turn as black and cold as the night around us. "Lorenc can take care of himself."

Another tear rolls down my cheek, and this time, he lets it go and steps back from me. Anger radiates off him in hostile waves. He's slipped into the skin of the man he was before we were together. The man he became again when Tarek took me.

And I know why. I know what he's thinking.

Lorenc. Me.

The years we've spent together.

I could tell him about Pjeter, but this isn't the time or place to explain everything that's happened since we left him at that airport. I don't want him distracted by finding out he's a father. I need him focused. We can't risk making any mistakes. Not if we plan to get Lorenc and Pjeter out alive.

That's all that matters.

"We need to go get him. After everything he's done for me, I'm not leaving him behind."

Konstandin growls low and closes the distance between us. "I'm not risking you again to go back for him." He towers over me, his fists clenched at his sides.

Anyone else would cower or back away. Anyone else who knew him, who knew what he was capable of, would turn and run into the woods.

Not me.

I hold my ground, square my shoulders, and stare up at him. This man intimidates anyone he's near, but he will bend to me. He always has. I am his one weakness, and he knows it. Even after all this time, it's there in his eyes.

He still loves me.

"I'm not going with you...without him."

His scowl is barely visible through the growth of beard, but I know that look in his eyes and what lies under the hair. He's pissed, but there's also a resignation there. One that tells me some things haven't changed.

He will never deny me what I want...what I need.

I push past him toward the bike. "Let's go. Do you have a phone? I need to call Lorenc and warn him."

"Where is he now?"

"At our house."

"We can't go back there. When I got into town, it wasn't hard to find you and your house. You were just leaving on your way to the store when I arrived. There wasn't enough time to stop you. I was waiting to talk to you when you came out of the store, but Aleksander's men appeared out of nowhere, and I didn't have a choice but to take you. I left two bodies back there, and there are more men. I have no doubt of that."

"Oh, God, what if we're too late?"

The police are probably searching for us, and Aleksander's men are looking for the house if they aren't already there. The surveillance cameras likely caught everything outside the grocery store, including Konstandin gunning down two people.

He reaches into his pocket and hands me his phone. "Call Lorenc. Tell him to get out. Tell him they found you, but don't tell him I'm with you."

"What? Why not?"

Konstandin growls. "Because someone tipped off the Gashis about where to find you. And someone called me and told me where to pick up your trail in Argentina. Someone knew I was alive. I don't know who did any of this, and I don't know who I can trust."

Maybe he doesn't, but I do. Lorenc would never betray us. He's given up his entire life to protect me.

"You can trust Lorenc."

He growls and throws his leg over the bike. "That remains to be seen."

I can't blame him for being angry, but he wasn't here. He was dead. By his own choice. He can't hold a grudge for something that happened because we didn't know he was alive. He can't be mad at the man who helped him rescue me, then kept his son and me safe.

"I do trust him." With my life and Pjeter's.

I dial the number and slide onto the bike in front of Konstandin. His warm breath flutters against my neck, and a familiar shudder rolls through my body.

He might not answer an unknown number. Every ring tightens my throat a little bit more until he finally answers. "Hello?"

"Lorenc?"

"Rea? Where the hell are you? I've been trying to call you for hours."

I suck in a shaky breath. "Someone attacked me at the grocery store. I got away, but it's not safe for me to come home. You need to come to me."

"Attacked how? Are you okay?"

That's not the word I would use, but I'm alive.

"They shot at me, but I'm all right."

"How did you get away?"

I bite my lip and glance over my shoulder at the man who's supposed to be dead. I know why he's reluctant to trust anyone with everything he's been through, but I do trust Lorenc. "An old friend."

"*Krishti*. Where are you?"

Being taken by a hulking beast on a bike may have shaken me, but I never forgot what Konstandin and Lorenc taught me—pay attention. The entire ride, I've been keeping tabs on everything I could see that could help me find my way back.

"About a hundred and fifty miles south. Take Highway 15 north until you hit Highway 23, then head east. Be careful. They may be watching the house."

"Pjeter is fine, Rea. I won't let anything happen to him."

My chest tightens, and I fight through a sob threatening to escape my lips. "I know. Just come. Fast."

Konstandin leans forward and brushes his lips against my ear, and a shudder rolls through me. "There's a motel ten miles up the road. Tell him to meet us there."

"Meet me at the motel. You can reach me at this number if you need to. Be careful."

"I will. You, too."

I know he wants to ask me who I'm with since the number of people I would refer to as an *old friend* is basically zero, but he ends the call. With a shaky hand, I return the phone to Konstandin.

He fires up the bike and leans forward again, until his beard brushes against my exposed neck, and his breath flutters against my ear. "We have a couple of hours to kill. Any ideas?"

FOUR

THE DOOR CLICKS SHUT behind us, and I stare at the dark hotel room. A single queen-sized bed occupies the center, and the worn armchair in the corner of the room looks older than me. The low, long dresser running along the far wall is the only other piece of furniture, but I keep my gaze forward—anything not to look at Konstandin.

The whole ride here with his familiar body pressed against mine and the vibrations of the motorcycle between my legs was like one giant tease—to my body, to my heart...

But worry over Lorenc and Pjeter eats at my stomach. Too much for me to give in to my need for Konstandin. Once they're here and safe, I'll deal with these feelings, with what it means to have him alive and here.

His large hand falls on my shoulder, and he turns me to face him. He takes my face between his palms and tilts it up until I meet his eyes. The darkness and anger that were there when we left the clearing have been replaced with the love and passion I've always seen from him.

This is the Konstandin I fell in love with. This is Pjeter's father.

Yet, I can never forget Konstandin is so many things...

A cold killer. An assassin. A terrifying monster.

It was all those things that should have kept me away, but I saw more. I *saw* him, and making that choice cost both of us so damn much.

He brushes his thumb across my bottom lip. "I don't know what happened over the last two years to you, but I want to know. I want to know everything. Just not right now. Right now, I just want you."

A tear trickles down my cheek, and I close my eyes and shake my head. "I can't just pretend the last two years didn't happen. I can't just pretend you didn't choose to not come for me. Where have you been?"

Maybe he can push aside the uncertainty of the time lost to us and what happened during it, but I can't. I need to know.

He releases me and steps around me to drop down onto the edge of the bed. "When I slipped FBI custody, I went north...into Canada."

Here?

"You were here?"

He nods. "At first, I was toward the East Coast. It was easier to cross there near Philly, but I knew I had to hide. I had to reinvent myself." He runs his hands over his front and tugs on the beard. "So, I became this. I became Ghost."

"Ghost?"

A wry grin tilts up the side of his lip through his beard, and he twists to the side to show me the back of his leather jacket. The name GHOST sits above a skull with flames in the eyes and REBEL CHASERS MC along the bottom.

"I knew an MC would protect me. I knew my skill set wouldn't be questioned there, and that it would be prized. I knew it would be a good place to disappear. It took me a while to build up trust and create a believable backstory for myself, but eventually, they accepted me as a nomad, and the Rebel Chasers became my club."

I don't even want to *think* about what he had to do to prove himself to them. We worked so hard to put that life behind us, to become Griffin and Jade instead of Konstandin and Rea. But Tarek just couldn't let us go...

"You've been with them the whole time?"

He nods. "Mostly in Vancouver and Winnipeg, but I kind of moved around. I didn't want to stay in one place for too long. That just leads to people asking too many questions."

The only thing I know about MCs is they're usually bad news, and there are usually skanks running around, throwing themselves at the members.

Jealousy squeezes at my heart and turns my stomach.

Another woman touching him...kissing him...fucking him...

The blind heat of rage floods my blood.

He rises to his feet and approaches me. "I know what you're thinking, *e dashur*, but I haven't touched another woman since the first time you let me kiss you."

His palms capture my face again, and this time, he presses his lips to mine in a slow, sweet kiss.

The familiar taste that's all Konstandin—salty and sweet and bitter—rushes across my tongue. He pulls away and drops his forehead to mine.

"I could never be with anyone else, *e dashur*. I can't breathe without you. All I dreamed about for the last two years was this, having you in my arms again."

It's all I dreamed about, too. This man was my world. He was my everything, and I thought he was gone forever. But here he is, standing before me, offering me back everything we once had.

But Lorenc and Pjeter are still out there...

I glance away, toward the door, and Konstandin pulls my face back.

"There's nothing you can do for him now. He can take care of himself. He'll get here."

He's right. If there's anyone I trust to keep Pjeter safe, it's Lorenc.

And worrying doesn't do any good. I've done enough worrying in the last few years to last a lifetime...or longer. It only picks away at old wounds that have finally managed to scab over.

Don't reopen them. Trust in Lorenc and live in the moment now that you have it.

I shift up onto my toes and wrap my arms around his neck. This may not look like Konstandin, but I have never felt like this in the arms of any other man. I press my lips to his. He moans and drags me up against him fully.

His cock stirs to life between us and presses against my stomach. I whimper at the familiar feel of his body. His tongue lashes at mine, harsh and demanding. This isn't the same kiss he just gave me. This kiss is the start of something, something he plans to finish. And something I'm more than willing to give him.

FIVE

Familiar hands I've fantasized about for so long work their way down to the hem of my shirt. Konstandin tugs at it and breaks our kiss to pull the fabric up and over my head. My chest heaves, and my hands shake. I dig my nails into his sides, clinging to the comfort of the familiar to ground myself in this moment.

A soft groan slips from his lips.

God, I love that sound.

He unhooks my bra and frees my breasts. My nipples pebble and ache for his touch, for his lips, for everything. He drops to his knees in front of me. Warm breath flutters over my skin, spreading goose bumps in its wake.

Then he's there—laving, sucking, flicking...

Oh, Krishti!

I dig my fingers into his strong shoulders to keep from collapsing against him on wobbly legs. Everything he does sends lightning bolts of electricity straight to my core. It's been so long since I've felt his touch, experienced his unadulterated love and attention.

He works my pants and thong down, and I kick off my shoes and grab onto his shoulders as he tugs the last of my clothes off my feet and throws them to join the rest.

I'm naked in front of him, in front of anyone, for the first time in years. He stares up at me with the same eyes, but they hold so much more than they used to—the anguish of what he's missed in the last two years has changed them.

And he doesn't even know about Pjeter yet.

When he finally learns the truth, those eyes will never look at me the same way. He's going to flip. We always wanted children, but we held off because we wanted to ensure we were safe before bringing another life into this world. Only weeks before Tarek took me, we finally felt enough time had passed to try to start a family. We were so wrong. When he learns he left me while I was pregnant, he'll never forgive himself.

He leans forward and drags his tongue through my wetness. An appreciative groan rumbles against my heated flesh. I shudder and push him away.

"Konstandin, I need you. *You.*"

The only thing that will make me believe this is all real is having him inside me again, having that connection.

He ignores me and sticks his tongue back between my legs.

I moan and grasp his face to turn it back up. "Please, Konstandin."

When we were Griffin and Jade, he used to love to make me beg. It was a game we played, one we both enjoyed even though I pretended I didn't.

This isn't a game. This is a very real need.

Please don't play with me, Kon.

I can't handle that right now.

He growls and rises to his feet. The heat in his eyes makes my heart swell with hope. He throws off his jacket and pulls his T-shirt up and over his head. The same hard, lean lines and muscles are there, but so are new scars.

This is why I lost him.

I reach out and brush my fingers over them. He shudders and grabs my wrist to stop my hand.

"Not now." His voice is low and gravelly and shaking with need. "Later."

I nod, and he unzips his pants and kicks them off along with his boots. His hard cock springs free, and I clench my legs together against the throb there. He grabs me and lays me down on the bed.

In some shitty roadside motel in the middle-of-nowhere Canada, I'm finally going to have Konstandin back. It doesn't matter where we are. I'd take him anywhere and any way I can have him.

He sinks down on top of me, and his mouth finds mine again. Hard, demanding lips devour my breath, and the unfamiliar brush of the beard only heightens the intensity of his kiss.

This man may not look like Konstandin, but it's him. All him. The man who rescued me. The man who loved me. The man I've been mourning.

He reaches between us and grasps his cock, dragging it through my wetness. Then he positions himself at my core and pushes into me in one motion.

"Oh, God." I arch my back and open my legs more to take him even deeper.

Having him here, the press of his body against mine, his cock filling me, his breath mixing with my own...it feels like coming home when I haven't had a real one in years.

It doesn't matter where we are. It doesn't matter where we go. As long as I have this man, I know everything will be okay.

He pulls back and plunges into me, rolling his hips and setting a driving rhythm that says everything words can't.

I'm sorry.

I missed you.

I love you.

I'm never leaving you again.

Our bodies melt together like no time has passed. He pulls his head back and captures my face between his palms. "Rea, look at me."

I open my eyes to meet his gaze. Tears blur my vision, and he wipes away the ones that fall with his thumbs.

"Don't cry, *e dashur.*"

He kisses me again and slows his pace. I dig my heels into his lower back to urge him on.

I shake my head. "Don't stop."

"Never, *e dashur.*" He drives into me again, hard and deep, then reaches down to adjust my hips to a different angle.

My breath catches. The change starts a slow burn deep inside, one that promises an explosive orgasm. "Please!"

I'm so close to the release my body needs so badly.

He growls next to my ear and nips his way down my neck. His teeth dig into the flesh near my collarbone, and everything goes bright white.

The room disappears. The threat disappears—reality...gone.

All that exists are our two bodies entwined, the pleasure coursing through my veins, and Konstandin giving himself over to me completely.

Again.

SIX

THE DESOLATE HIGHWAY outside the motel sits dark and empty as I stare out through the dingy curtains.

They should've been here by now.

It's been over two hours. The way Lorenc drives, he should have been here a while ago. When I finally came out of the post-orgasmic haze, I was sure they'd be pulling in.

But there's been no sign. No word. Konstandin's phone sits silent. And the more time that passes, the more my nerves fray.

My heart squeezes, and I suck in a shaky breath, trying to fight the panic rising in my throat.

Konstandin's strong arms wrap around me from behind, and he pushes my hair to one side and buries his face against my neck. "He'll be here soon. Lorenc knows how to take care of himself, and we haven't heard anything from him. He would've called if there were trouble."

If he could call.

If Aleksander's men got to him, if anything happens to him or Pjeter, I don't think I can handle it.

Not again.

Not losing them.

Everything's a jumbled mess in my head right now. Konstandin's back from the dead and back in my heart, but we're right back where we started—with a madman chasing us.

And Aleksander Gashi makes Tarek look like a damn school girl. The Dragon isn't someone you mess with if you value your life. Even before Father sold me off to marry Tarek, I knew not to mess with the Gashis. Though back then, Aleksander was still in prison, and Saban had taken the reigns in Chicago.

Now, he's apparently out...and on the warpath. For us. Killing Saban will bring down wrath unlike anything any of us have ever seen, but Konstandin did it anyway...to get to me. He sacrificed *everything.*

He brushes his lips against my sensitive skin, and I shudder and lean back against him. This might be the only second of peace we have because once Lorenc does show up with Pjeter, I'm going to have a lot of explaining to do.

You did the right thing, not telling him right away.

He's not going to be very happy, but he has to understand why I did it. It was the only way to ensure he remained focused. If he knew, he may have gone off half-cocked and made things even worse.

I couldn't risk that. He'll understand.

He has to.

Headlights appear down the road, and I pull away from him and press up against the window to get a better view. An unfamiliar car turns into the motel lot and pulls up in front of our room.

The lack of lighting in the lot makes it impossible to see who's driving. Konstandin tenses behind me and moves for his gun. I reach back and grab his arm.

"Wait."

The driver side door opens, and Lorenc steps out, his face illuminated by the light of the full moon tonight. A rush of air slides from my lips, and I race to the door and throw it open before Konstandin can even try to stop me.

I practically launch myself at Lorenc, and he catches me and holds me tightly as he buries his face against my shoulder. Somehow, I manage to swallow through the sob crawling up my throat. "You're both okay?"

He nods and presses a kiss to my temple. "I'm okay, and he slept the entire ride, so he doesn't know what's going on."

I let out a deep, shaky breath and squeeze Lorenc hard before I release him. He lifts his head to look over my shoulder and freezes. "Who the hell is..."

The clothes, the hair, the beard...it's all so different. But if he really looks, Konstandin is there.

Only Konstandin doesn't give him a chance. He yanks me backward, and Konstandin's fist connects with Lorenc's jaw. The crack of bone on bone has me wincing. Lorenc throws a return punch, but Konstandin ducks and knocks him to the gravel next to the car.

"Stop it! Both of you!" I know better than to try to get between these two. If I do, I'm risking my life. They both have tunnel vision. Lorenc is defending his life, and Konstandin is determined to stake his claim.

Konstandin pulls his arm back to land another blow. Lorenc stares up at him, with blood dripping from the corner of his mouth, and his eyes widen.

"Konstandin?"

Konstandin stills, his arm still poised to unleash a torrent on Lorenc. He grunts in response, and even from several feet away, the anger rolling off him is palpable. But Konstandin's jealousy isn't important right now. The only important thing is Pjeter and making sure he's safe.

Forever.

"Are you two done?"

Konstandin glances over his shoulder at me and gives me a curt nod. He climbs to his feet and leaves Lorenc breathing heavily and bleeding on the gravel.

I push past Konstandin and to the back of the car. Pjeter's head rests against the side of his car seat. His chest rises and falls slowly and rhythmically.

So peacefully unaware of what's going on. Thank God.

I open the door slowly so he doesn't wake and lean in to unbuckle him. Lorenc and Konstandin's murmured words are unintelligible as I scoop Pjeter up into my arms.

His eyes flutter open. "Mama?"

I press a gentle kiss to his forehead. "Yeah, Bubba, I'm here."

He yawns and wraps his arms around my neck, snuggling close as I rise to my feet. The sweet scent of the baby shampoo I used in his hair earlier today invades my lungs and calms my racing heart slightly.

For a second.

Konstandin's eyes meet mine over the car, and then, they narrow on Pjeter.

His gaze flicks over to Lorenc and back at me. "You have a child?"

I don't answer, and neither does Lorenc. I push past both of them back into the motel room. I'm not having this conversation out on the sidewalk where we're exposed. I'm about to tell Konstandin he's a father. That's not something that gets done in public.

It's a risk leaving them out there alone, turning my back even for a second. If Konstandin thinks Pjeter is Lorenc's son, things will get really bad, really fast.

But I'm not giving in to their childish behavior.

They follow me and shut the door behind them. The tension in the room is practically suffocating as I lay Pjeter in the center of the bed and pull the covers up around him. He snuggles in and murmurs something I can't understand.

It's time to tell the truth—all of it.

Everything that's happened between Lorenc and me over the last two years. Everything he's become to Pjeter and me.

I suck in a deep breath and turn to face them.

This is going to hurt.

All of us.

SEVEN

THERE'S no easy way to say this.

Just do it.

I meet Konstandin's dark eyes and take a shaky breath. "I never got the chance to tell you. I already thought I might be pregnant when we went to the party, but I wasn't sure..."

For the prior week, I had been horny as hell and an emotional mess. I was going to buy a test the next day, but then Tarek took me...

"Krishti, e dashur."

Lorenc stiffens beside him and moves to sit in the raggedy chair in the corner. He steeples his fingers in front of his mouth and watches me with intense eyes.

He's been Pjeter's father for all intents and purposes since before he was even born. He was the one at my ultrasound appointments, the one holding my hand when we saw him for the first time on that fuzzy, black and white screen. Lorenc squeezed my hand when I was in agony during delivery, and he was the one who wrapped Pjeter in a blanket and held him with tears only moments after he was born. He's been there for every meltdown, every two-a.m. feeding, his first steps, his first words.

All of it.

And now, Konstandin is here, staring down at his son for the first time.

I shake my head and swipe at the tears. Konstandin still doesn't speak, just looks down at Pjeter.

"Now you understand why I needed you so badly the whole time you stayed away. It wasn't just about me. It's not just about me now. It's about Pjeter, too."

He turns his eyes on me and raises a dark eyebrow. "Pjeter? You named him after my grandfather?"

I nod and blink against my tear-blurred vision. "From everything you've told me, he seemed like a good man. Someone you were proud of, someone you looked up to, and someone who would be a perfect namesake for our son."

Konstandin moves over to the side of the bed and bends over Pjeter. His large hand shakes as he moves it over his son. He brushes Pjeter's dark hair off his forehead, then leans in to press a reverent kiss there.

I choke back a sob, and my heart practically bursts in my chest.

When he turns back, the tears shimmering in his usually hard eyes completely break me. The sob slips out, and the tears pour down in a deluge. He closes the distance between us and captures me in his strong embrace.

"I'm so sorry I wasn't here." His whispered words against my ear shatter my heart again. He means every word, yet it doesn't give us back that time, the time he *chose* to stay away. The days and nights my soul wept for him.

Lorenc rises to his feet. "But I was."

Oh, God.

The last thing we need right now is these two going at each other again.

I step back from Konstandin and shake my head. "Lorenc, please, don't..."

He scowls and shakes a hand at Konstandin. "Why not? He could have come and found us anytime. Was he even looking? Did he even bother? He let us believe he was dead. And we moved on. I'm the only father that boy knows."

I cringe at his words, but he's not wrong. Pjeter may not call him "dad," but he's been an amazing father figure to him since the second he came into this world, kicking and screaming.

He also loves me. I'd have to be blind not to see it—the way he looks at me, the way he touches me, the way he holds me just a little too long when we embrace...

Konstandin sees it, too, and he stands stock-still, his hands clenched at his sides. This is no time for a bloodbath. Violence will solve nothing here, but it's ingrained in both of them so deeply, there may not be any other way.

I move to step between them, and Konstandin pushes me back with his arm.

This is it. He's going to kill Lorenc.

Konstandin's eyes meet mine, and a calm washes over the almost-black irises. One I haven't ever seen there.

He shakes his head. "I've lost enough to anger. I'm not going to lose you or Pjeter now over Lorenc's jealousy." He takes a step toward the man who has been my best friend, my protector, and my rock for the last two years, and he embraces him. "Thank you for taking care of *my* family."

The inflection on the word "my" doesn't go unnoticed by Lorenc or me. Konstandin may not be ready for more bloodshed, but he is staking a claim.

He releases him and turns back to me. "Now, we need to figure out how Aleksander found us and come up with a plan."

Lorenc shoves a hand back through his hair. His frustration and unease seem to be growing with every passing second in Konstandin's presence, but he doesn't seem all that surprised to see him. He's not acting like a man who just found out his best friend is alive.

I wonder...

No.

Lorenc could never do that. Would never do that. There's no way he knew Konstandin was alive and kept it from me.

Is there?

"I think you should ask Lor how Aleksander might have found us." I stare at Lorenc, and he narrows his eyes on me. "I have a feeling he's been keeping some things from me."

"Shit." He paces the room and scrubs his hands over his face. "I've been in contact with a few people I trust. I needed to know where things stood. I hadn't spoken with anyone since we left Philly until we were in Argentina."

Konstandin growls. "Who did you talk to?"

"My brother, Michael."

"*Te qifsha*, Lorenc!"

Lorenc throws his hands up. "No, fuck you. He's my brother, Konstandin. I can trust him."

"Apparently not. If he's the only one you've spoken to, then he's the one who alerted Aleksander *and* me that you were in Argentina. He knew I was alive the whole time, which means, you knew I was alive since you were in Argentina."

Lorenc pauses for a moment.

He knew.

"How could you not tell me?"

His eyes lock with mine. "I didn't know for sure. When we were in Cuba, Edon said he had heard a rumor that Konstandin survived the airport, but that's all he knew. It was nothing more than speculation."

I stalk over to him and slap him across the face. My palm stings, but he barely flinches. "You asshole."

"I didn't want you to get your hopes up for what might be nothing. You were finally happy again, coming out of your shell. Things were good. And then, when I spoke with my brother, he confirmed it. But by then...Konstandin hadn't come for you, and I didn't want to break your heart."

Konstandin snorts. "I'm sure it was that altruistic."

I look between the two men—one my love, one my best friend—both who lied to me, then to Pjeter sleeping soundly in the bed. Arguing more about the situation solves nothing. "What do we do now?"

Lorenc locks eyes with Konstandin. "We prepare."

Konstandin nods. "Then, we end this."

EIGHT

I JERK awake and fumble for the gun I usually keep under my pillow. My hand comes out empty. A moment of panic seizes my heart, and I scramble up on my elbow with my breath caught in my throat.

Shit. The motel.

It takes a second for my eyes to adjust. The only light in the room comes from the partially cracked bathroom door. It's enough to illuminate Pjeter's serene face as he sleeps next to me. I scan the room.

My eyes meet Konstandin's where he sits in the old chair in the corner, watching Pjeter sleep. My heart squeezes in my chest. He's missed so much—his birth, his first steps, his first laugh, his first words. He missed being a father.

Yes, he made the choice to stay away, but would it have changed things had he known?

I hope so.

There's no sign of Lorenc. He must still be keeping watch outside. It's a huge relief to know we have someone to help watch our backs, even though I'm still angry at him for keeping what he knew from me. It could have saved us so much time, so much heartbreak.

But it's in the past now, and if I let it keep me angry, it could cloud the clarity I need to face The Dragon.

I slip from bed and pad over on bare feet to Konstandin. He opens his arms, and I climb onto the chair and straddle his lap. His hands come up and rub along my arms, the roughness sending goose bumps skittering across every inch of my skin.

"Did I wake you?"

I shake my head and brush a thumb over his bottom lip. "No. I never sleep well. Too anxious."

He moves one hand to cup my cheek. "You always slept well with me."

I sigh and drop my forehead against his. "I did, but I've been sleeping alone for a long time."

Far too long.

He freezes beneath me, and I pull back.

I guess he needs to hear the words. "I never slept with Lorenc. I know what you think, but it was never like that. At least, for me, it wasn't."

A tiny scowl tilts down his lips. "He's in love with you."

I nod. "I know. But I'm in love with you. It's always been you, since the moment you walked into that room and scowled at me. And even though Lorenc told me you were gone, and my head believed that, my heart never could."

"I'm so sorry, *e dashur*. For everything." He leans forward and pushes his lips to mine.

It's reverent, slow, and sweet. His tongue slides along my lips, begging for entrance. I open for him, and we tangle the way we always used to, giving each other everything we have and demanding everything in return.

His cock stirs to life between my legs, and I roll my hips and grind down against him. A low rumble vibrates in his chest. His hands shift down to my hips and fingers dig into my soft flesh.

It's only been a few hours, but I need him. I need everything only Konstandin can give me. The darkness and the light. All of it.

I fumble with the buckle on his belt but manage to free it so I can work at the zipper and button of his jeans. His hands move to the waistband of my pants and slide them down over my ass. Large palms caress the sensitive skin there, and he squeezes, eliciting a moan from my trembling lips.

God, I've missed this.

I reach between us and wrap my hand around his cock. He groans, dropping his head back against the chair.

Even after all this time, one touch can bring this man to his knees. I shift off him and to my feet long enough to free myself of my pants and for him to wiggle his jeans down to his knees before I climb back on top. I place the head of his cock at my core.

He reaches down and slides a finger through the wetness between my legs.

"*Krishti*. You're so ready for me."

"Always." I lower myself down his length slowly. "Oh, God."

I bite my lip to contain my scream as his cock stretches and fills me. He grunts and digs his fingers into my hips as he thrusts up, impaling himself all the way to the hilt.

I roll my hips and slide up, then lower myself back down. He braces his feet and pushes up to meet my movements.

The flawless symphony of give and take, push and pull, darkness and light, love and hate. The perfection that was always us.

He slides a hand down between us, and his thumb finds my clit. I groan, and he rolls it expertly under the pad of his finger as I continue to ride slowly, savoring every single second of having this man back with me.

Because this is far from over. And there are no guarantees of what tomorrow may bring.

This is life with Konstandin. A life on the run. A life on the edge. A life of uncertainty.

But it's the only life I ever want.

His lips press to my collarbone and make their way slowly up my neck to suck at that spot behind my ear that always drives me to the brink of insanity.

This man knows me, knows my body, knows everything I need and want. He growls low and thrusts harder. The head of his cock drags against my G-spot, and I clench around him. He grunts and pinches my clit between his fingers.

The room explodes with a flash of light before the whole world disappears and pleasure ripples through my body and out to my limbs. I lose my rhythm, but he continues to push into me, his fingers working my clit to drag my orgasm on for what feels like forever. His cock pulses, and then, he's coming, emptying himself into me.

"Rea..." My whispered name is a benediction. A promise.

He won't let me go again, and I won't let him.

NINE

PJETER STIRS in my arms and opens his big, dark eyes.

"Morning, baby."

I've never been so happy that he's a great sleeper and makes it through most nights without a peep.

"Hi, Mama." He sits up, rubs his eyes, and peers around the hotel room.

I'm sure he's wondering where we are and why...and who the dark man with the beard and permanent scowl is.

Konstandin stands at the window, watching us intently. I wave him over to the bed. He hesitates for a moment before closing the distance and coming to sit on the edge of the mattress.

I run my fingers back through Pjeter's sleep-tousled hair. "Pjeter, remember me telling you about your daddy and that he couldn't be with us?" Pjeter nods, and tears shimmer in Konstandin's eyes. "Well, this is your daddy. He's back."

Pjeter tilts his head and examines Konstandin. "He has a big beard."

A deep, rumbling chuckle comes from Konstandin's chest, and I laugh along with him. Children are always great at saying the obvious and breaking through tension.

Konstandin reaches up and runs a hand over his beard. "I do, buddy, but not for long. I'll get rid of it soon."

Pjeter nods but snuggles back against me. I can't expect him to understand who Konstandin is or what's happening. It will take some time for them to connect and build the kind of relationship he has with Lorenc.

Give it time.

The door flies open, and Lorenc storms in. The stern set of his mouth and darkness of his eyes announce what's happening even before his words do. "We've got company. Two black sedans are coming down the road. They don't belong here."

Konstandin nods and turns to me. "Take him into the bathroom. Stay there." He hands me a Glock, and I shove it into the back of my waistband. "Shoot anyone who isn't Lorenc or me."

No problem.

He presses a harsh kiss to my lips, then ushers us back toward the tiny bathroom.

"Mama?" Pjeter stares up at me with wide, terrified eyes.

I had hoped never to see that look, that he would never know fear the way I have for such a huge part of my life.

"It's okay, baby." I close the bathroom door behind us and turn the lock. "We're going to play a game. We're going to hide in here, and Daddy and Lor will try to find us. But they're not very good at this game, so it might take a little while."

His eyes brighten. "Hide and seek?"

I squeeze him tightly as I climb into the tub. "Yeah, hide and seek."

The first gunshots are nothing more than soft pops deadened by the silencers on Konstandin and Lorenc's weapons. But the crack of the return fire elicits a yelp from Pjeter. I cover his ears and huddle lower into the tub with him.

"It's okay, baby."

If anyone can get us out of this alive, it's Konstandin and Lorenc. No matter what animosity and bad feelings may exist between those two, they share a common goal—to protect Pjeter and me.

And there aren't many men on this planet deadlier than those two.

Wrath may have destroyed Konstandin, but it will be what helps him end this.

Another barrage of gunfire sends my heart racing and leaves my ears ringing. I hold my breath and strain to hear anything else.

Scuffling.

Slamming.

Breaking.

Grunting.

Shit.

I reach behind me and wrap my fingers around the grip of the Glock. My stomach roils, and Pjeter clings to me even tighter and whimpers.

My breath flutters his soft hair as I press a kiss to his head. "Shh, baby. It's okay."

The door rattles, and I hold my breath. Blood rushes in my ears, and all my focus narrows on that knob. If it moves, I have to fire.

"*E dashur*, it's me."

Oh, thank God.

I leave the gun in my waistband and set Pjeter into the tub. "Stay here. I need to talk to Daddy and Lor. Everything's okay."

He gives me a nod, but his bottom lip quivers.

I lean down and kiss his forehead. "I'll be right back. I promise."

I turn the lock and peek out the door. Konstandin stands just on the other side, blood splattered on his face.

"Oh, my God. Are you okay?" I open the door enough to slip out, then pull it closed behind me.

He wraps me in his arms. "It's not mine."

I glance over his shoulder.

Lorenc stands just inside the room. He nods at me and motions over his shoulder toward the parking lot. "The package is in the trunk. We need to get out of here before the cops show up."

"Package?"

Konstandin presses a kiss to my temple. "We'll explain later."

I open the door to the bathroom. Pjeter pops his head over the side of the tub. Tears trickle down his puffy cheeks. My chest tightens.

"It's okay, baby. Come here."

He climbs over the side and rushes to me. I catch him and pull him up as I rise to my feet.

My poor, sweet boy.

We've kept all this from him for the last two years. He has no idea what kind of life we all led before he came. The kind of life we escaped. The life we've tried to shelter him from.

And now...he's been thrust into the heart of it, in the most violent way possible.

I never wanted this for him. I thought it was over.

He whimpers and sniffles against my neck as I walk into the room.

I fight back my own tears. "Keep your head down, baby." I can't let him see the carnage that's likely strewn about outside this room.

Stay strong for him.

You can fall apart later.

Lorenc approaches and rubs Pjeter's back. "Pjeter, buddy. You okay?"

Pjeter turns and wraps his arms around Lorenc's neck. Lor pulls him from me and hugs him close, murmuring unintelligible words.

Konstandin freezes beside me, his eyes narrowing on them.

I can practically see the knife twisting in his heart. He turns back to the bed, grabs the bags, and pushes past me without a word.

Lorenc's eyes meet mine. An apology lies in their depths, but there's also a possessive glint. One that tells me this thing between him and Konstandin isn't over. Not by a long shot.

TEN

PJETER'S HEAD bobs to the side as we turn off the main highway and down a gravel road. The poor kid can barely keep his eyes open. Sleeping in a different bed and all the excitement has really worn him out. I wish I were capable of being so oblivious to what's happening around me. The innocence of childhood is so far in the past for me; I can't remember what it was like not to live in fear.

I lean forward between the front seats so Konstantin can hear me without disturbing Pjeter. "What is this place?"

Tall, thick forest surrounds us until it opens to what appears to be an old factory or warehouse of some sort. Overgrown trees arch over the large building, and other than this basic gravel drive, there are no signs of it from the road. It's completely hidden and forgotten—exactly the type of place we need.

Konstandin nods toward it. "I found this place when I was scouting the area on my way to get you. It's an old wood mill, but it looks like it's been abandoned for decades."

"What about our friend in the trunk?" I nod backward.

Once we got in the car at the motel, Konstandin explained they had taken one of Aleksander's men alive, subdued him, and tossed him in the trunk for questioning.

"*Questioning.*"

I know what that entails for Konstandin and Lorenc. It won't be pretty.

The last thing I want is Pjeter exposed to any of this, but I don't have much choice.

I peek out the back window at Lorenc following us on Konstandin's bike. Konstandin insisted he wasn't going to let Pjeter or me out of his sight, and he couldn't leave his bike there at the hotel with all the bullet holes and blood and bodies.

These small-town cops are probably freaking the hell out about what went down at the grocery store and motel and are, hopefully, totally clueless about who we are or why it happened. Lorenc did a thorough job of creating our new identities each time we moved, so the chances of them linking us to our real names are slim to none.

Konstandin parks on the backside of the building, shuts off the car, and then climbs out. I grab Konstandin's bag and follow with a glance back at Pjeter. His eyes don't even flutter.

Lorenc pulls up next to us and climbs off the bike.

I nod backward toward the car. "Let's find somewhere safe inside to get him down. He doesn't need to see what's about to happen."

The guys nod, and Lorenc moves toward the open back door to grab Pjeter. Konstandin snarls and steps in his way.

Can't say I blame him.

The two stare each other down, the heat of their gazes enough to combust into a raging inferno of jealousy and anger. It lasts longer than it should, but Konstandin breaks the eye-contact, leans in and unbuckles Pjeter, then lifts him onto his shoulder.

Tears sting my eyes as I see him hold his son for the first time. I always knew Konstandin would be a good father. One who would do anything for his child—just like he did for me—and now that he has the opportunity, he's not going to turn it over to Lorenc so easily.

A scowl curls Lorenc's lips as he walks toward the building. Konstandin closes the car door behind him, and we make our way inside.

Dust moats float through the sunlight streaming in from the mostly broken glass windows. Piles of wood and sawdust litter the space around massive machines that look like torture devices.

The corner of Konstandin's lip ticks up. He's probably thinking the same thing I am. It should bother me that it brings them so much joy to do the dirty work, but it's just part of who he is—part of the monster I fell in love with.

A row of doors along one wall seem to separate the main warehouse from some sort of offices, and a set of metal stairs leads up to a small room above the main warehouse, likely where the manager's office was when this place was active.

Lorenc takes off to explore the building, and Konstandin nods toward the row of doors. I follow him across sawdust-covered, concrete floors.

Creepy.

He kicks a partially ajar door the rest of the way open with his foot and carries Pjeter in. An old desk, some empty file cabinets, and random papers clutter the area under our feet.

I drop the bag and grab the blanket from inside to create a make-shift bed for Pjeter. Konstandin gently lowers Pjeter onto it and kisses his cheek. He shrugs out of his jacket and lays it over him.

He glances up at me. "How long do you think he'll be out?"

I shrug. "I don't know. It could be an hour, or it could be several. He's a good napper, and all this excitement has certainly exhausted him."

Konstandin rises and nods toward Pjeter. "Stay here with him."

"What? No. I want to know what he says." I point to the man Lorenc is dragging into the building.

If he thinks I'm going to hide back here while they talk to this guy, he's insane.

No fucking way.

Konstandin turns me to face him and rests his hands on my shoulders. "Rea, you don't want to see what we're going to do."

No. I don't *want* to see it.

But what I wanted disappeared a long time ago.

The night Tarek took me.

"I don't have any fantasies about who you are, Konstandin, or about who Lorenc is. I know exactly what you do and what you have done. I've always known, and you know that."

His dark eyes flash with concern. "Knowing and seeing it are two different things, *e dashur.*"

I look into his hard eyes and straighten my spine. "Then it's time that I see it."

ELEVEN

I STORM from the office and away from Konstandin. While his desire to shelter me from the bloody truth of what they will do to this man is heartwarming, I'm not some child who needs protecting.

After everything I've been through, he should know I'm strong enough to handle anything they can throw at me...or at him.

Lorenc drops the man into a chair he managed to find somewhere in the warehouse and sets to work securing him at the wrists and ankles with zip-ties.

Konstandin follows me out, his heavy footsteps echoing through the vast expanse of the space.

A sleeping Pjeter is still visible through the open door. As long as I can keep an eye on him from here, there's no way I'm missing a minute of this.

No matter how bad things might get, I won't glance away. I won't miss a second of what they're doing.

Lor looks up at me from where he squats next to our captive. "You shouldn't be out here."

"You don't start with me, too. I'm not moving. I can watch Pjeter from here."

He scowls but rises to his feet and walks around to join Konstandin and me in front of the bloody man tied to the chair. When they said they "subdued" him at the motel, they should have said they beat the shit out of him. The guy looks like he just went ten rounds with a heavyweight.

Konstandin steps up to our captive, grabs his thick, dark hair, and jerks his head back. The man stares at us through one badly swollen eye and spits blood on Konstandin's shoe.

Bad move.

The most dangerous man I know looks down at it and then back at the man who clearly has a death wish.

Konstandin moves so fast, I barely register he's swinging before his fist connects with the guy's face. The chair rocks backward, but Konstandin's hold on his hair keeps him upright.

He scowls at the man and watches fresh blood stream from the side of the man's eye. "*Mos u bë një kar.*"

I snort-laugh.

Don't be a dick.

Yeah, right.

Konstandin releases the man's hair and shoves his head back. "This will be a lot less painful for you if you tell us what we want to know."

A dark chuckle mixed with a wet cough bubbles from the man's lips as blood drips from the corner of his mouth. "He's going to kill you all."

Lorenc steps forward. "Who? Aleksander?"

Another bloody chuckle becomes a cough. "The Dragon. Once he's unleashed, there's no stopping him. Aleksander disappears. He's been looking for you for a long time." He tilts his head to look up at Konstandin. "And if you are who I think you are, he's going to have a very pleasant surprise. He thought he missed his opportunity with you."

Konstandin flashes a grin. One that says this man just made a big mistake. A chill climbs up my spine, and I wrap my arms around myself and peek over my shoulder. Pjeter hasn't moved.

He can't see what's about to happen.

I turn back as Konstandin reaches into his boot and flips open a knife.

Three lightning-fast slashes have the man's shirt falling off in shreds. A myriad of black, Cyrillic tattoos cover his chest and arms.

Konstandin squats down in front of him. "You act like you're the one in control here."

The man shakes his head. "I'm going to die anyway. If you don't kill me, he will."

Lorenc chuckles. "*If* we don't kill you? You're going to tell us what we want to know. How fast is going to determine how painful it gets. But you are dying today, one way or the other."

Konstandin rises to his feet. "Where is Aleksander?"

The man shakes his head. "Do what you will. I'm not telling you shit." He spits again. This time, the glob of blood lands on Konstandin's pants.

Konstandin snarls, and in one swift motion, embeds the knife deep into the man's stomach.

A roar of pain echoes through the warehouse.

I cringe and step back.

This is what's required. This is what needs to happen to keep us safe. I can't let myself be affected by it. This man is a killer. This man came to kill Lorenc and me, and he probably would've murdered Pjeter, too.

Don't confuse him with a human being.

He never would've treated us like one.

Konstandin slowly withdraws the blade, wiggling it back and forth, undoubtedly to increase the pain. The man screams and grits his teeth.

"Where is Aleksander?"

Blood seeps from the wound and from the corner of the man's mouth. Another slash of the blade rips open the man's chest. A river of blood flows down his abdomen.

"Where is Aleksander?" Konstandin steps behind the man and grabs one of his hands where it's tied behind him. "Tell us."

Oh, God, here we go.

He was just getting warmed up.

The sound of the blade cutting through the finger joint seems incredibly loud in the vast space. Metal on flesh. Metal on bone. It combines with the man's cries of agony to create a macabre symphony.

This is Konstandin. This is the monster I fell in love with. This is the monster who owns my heart.

I drag my eyes from the scene to find the corner of Lorenc's lips tilted up in a satisfied grin. They really do love this. They were built for it. Trained for it. They're mentally immune to the reality of what they're doing.

This is pure, unadulterated malevolence.

Pinky.

Ring finger.

Middle finger.

Pointer finger.

One by one, they dropped to the floor.

Konstandin's repeated question echoes with the man's screams. "Where is he? Where is he? Where is he?"

The man sucks in a shaky breath, coughs out blood, gasps, and meets my eyes. Evil lies in their dark depths. He grins. "Here. The Dragon is here."

TWELVE

"HERE?" Konstandin grabs him by the throat, lifting both him and the chair from the concrete floor, and shakes him violently. Blood pours down his chest from the wound there and out of his stomach and all the other places Konstandin worked him over. "What do you mean here? In Canada?"

The man coughs, gasps, and gurgles, struggling for breath as Konstandin tightens his fingers around his throat.

Lor growls. "He can't answer if you kill him."

Konstandin glares over his shoulder then lets the captive drop and takes a step back.

More wet coughs rattle from his mouth before the man manages to find his breath. "You are fools to think you could ever escape him. You're the walking dead."

A wet, sinister chuckle bubbles up from the man's chest. He laughs and coughs and sputters for a minute before Lorenc takes a step forward and jabs his knife straight through the man's throat.

Dark eyes widen, and a sick, gurgling sound fills the warehouse.

Then...

Nothing.

His head drops down, and his body slumps forward in the chair, held up only by the restraints. Blood drips down onto the concrete with a sickening *plop*. A chill cuts through the air.

Well, shit.

Lorenc removes the knife and wipes the blood on his pants before sticking the blade back into his boot. "He meant here." He turns to face Konstandin and me. "The Dragon is here. Local. Somewhere close. The nearest town is about twenty minutes west. It was one of the places I considered settling when we first moved."

Konstandin scowls at Lorenc. "What happened to not killing the guy?"

A simple shrug is the only reply he receives. Lorenc stares Konstandin down, almost challenging him without saying the words out loud. He's waiting for Konstandin to push him, to call him out on what he did, to throw a punch. Something.

The tension between these two is so thick, I could cut it with their damn knives. If they go at it again, I'll fucking lose my shit.

"Guys, what do we do?" I wrap my arms around myself and take another peek at Pjeter, who has somehow managed to remain sound asleep.

Pjeter's exhaustion has made things a lot easier for us today. A lot of questions I'm not ready to answer are going to come when he wakes up. Like why we can't go home. And things about Konstandin I may never be able to answer.

Konstandin approaches and wraps me in his arms. "We don't panic." He pulls away and tilts my face up until my eyes meet his. "I know you're terrified, and you have every right to be after everything that's happened. Lorenc and I...this is what we do. This is all we do. Trust that we will find a way to resolve this."

"Do we run?"

Lorenc stomps his foot. "No more running. We've seen what running does. It only lasts for so long. That's part of why I contacted my brother. I knew it was only a matter of time before we would have to move again. I just didn't want to break it to you yet. You were so happy, so content things were going well for all of us."

The unspoken words there make Konstandin tense in my arms. He growls and turns to Lorenc. "But you did call him...and that led The Dragon straight to you."

"No." Lor shakes his head. "I never told him where we were. If he found out, he figured it out on his own. Maybe he was tracing the call or something. I don't know, but I never told him where we were. I'm not that fucking stupid, Konstandin."

"Could've fooled me," he growls.

I step between them and hold up my hands toward the two men I love most in this world. "We're not doing this again. You two need to stop the bickering and work together."

Konstandin's chest vibrates with anger, but he takes a deep breath and drags his attention from Lorenc to meet my gaze. "You're right. We need to come up with a plan. We can't run. Running is only a temporary solution. We need to end this now. Then we start over."

Lorenc shoves a hand back through his hair and paces in front of the dead body. "If he's in town and sent the men after us, then he's probably still there. I'm sure he's monitoring police scanners and knows about the shootout at the motel. Even though it was miles from here, this is a desolate area. It will be big news."

My chest tightens. "So, he has confirmation we're here."

He nods and paces, with an occasional glance toward the room where Pjeter sleeps. "Basically, yeah. But he doesn't know where we are right now, or that we know he's here. Maybe we can use that to our advantage."

"How so?"

Konstandin nods toward Lorenc. "We draw him out."

"What?" I whirl to look at him. "What do you mean *draw him out?*"

Konstandine shrugs. "He's not going to find us here. He knew we were at the motel but not where we went after. And unless one of his men managed to make a phone call before we took them out—which I know didn't happen—then The Dragon doesn't know about me. We have the advantage here."

He's right. There's no way Aleksander could know Konstandin's alive.

And he's the ultimate weapon.

It's why Tarek valued him so much. Even if they hadn't been twins, even if they hadn't shared blood, Tarek needed Konstandin to do his dirty work.

Konstantin's unwavering gaze holds me in place. "The only way we're going to end this is if we draw him out into the open—somewhere that we can take him out."

Intentionally drawing The Dragon into the open...

I shudder. "How do we do that?"

A slow smile spreads across Konstandin's face. That same smile, hundreds of men have no doubt seen immediately before their very painful, very bloody deaths. "We use bait."

THIRTEEN

I CAN'T BELIEVE we're doing this.

I loop my arm through Lorenc's and let him lead me down the street with Pjeter's hand clenched tightly in my free one.

"Mama, look." He points across the street to a park with a giant playground.

Kids run around, screaming and chasing each other and climbing up the equipment. Adults linger on benches and around the outskirts, watching their children and chatting on their phones or with each other.

"Wow, buddy. That's pretty cool."

He stares up at me with Konstandin's dark eyes. "Go."

"No." I shake my head. "We can't go play right now. Another time."

His bottom lip quivers.

Shit. This isn't going to end well.

The poor kid got in a good nap this morning while we took care of business, and we ate a hearty meal at the diner down the street. But he's still tired and crabby, and denying him something like this is likely to result in a total meltdown.

Toddlers are almost as hard to handle as Lorenc and Konstandin.

Lorenc stops and bends down to him. "Hey, buddy. I know you want to play at the park, but we can't do that today. I promise you, we'll come back and go another time."

I bite back my desire to add "with your father."

But I'm not going to stir the pot right now. It's hard for Lorenc to have Konstandin back when he's played that role for so long, when he feels how he feels about me, but I'm also not going to let him push out Pjeter's real father.

Pjeter scowls and looks at the park but then nods slowly. He's still not one-hundred-percent sold on the offer.

I muss up his hair and bend down to him. "How about we try to find you some ice cream instead."

That brings a smile and a vigorous nod of agreement. "Ice cweam."

Lorenc scoops him up and plants a kiss on his forehead.

I suck in a deep breath and try my best to look casual as we continue down the street. Acting as bait seems like a pretty stupid idea to me, but I do trust them if they say this is the only way to try to draw Aleksander out.

Knowing Konstandin is somewhere nearby and watching us closely, waiting for his opportunity to strike makes things a little bit easier...but not much.

There are still too many ways this could go wrong. Too many variables they can't plan for. Too many people and too many spaces for someone to hide.

But we don't have much choice. We can't go on knowing Aleksander is here and waiting for him to make a move.

We walk down the street, passing by unsuspecting people just out enjoying a beautiful, crisp day utterly oblivious to the bloodshed that's gone on nearby and is about to go down again. This town is only fifteen miles from the motel. The same police working that crime scene are responsible for this area, and that means there aren't many out here today. They're tied up with the biggest crime scenes they've ever seen.

But even with the police absent, Konstandin can't do anything out in public like this. He can't draw attention to us by taking out Aleksander.

The simplest plan might've been lying in wait with a sniper rifle. That idea was immediately dismissed as too dangerous. Lorenc, Pjeter, and I might not be able to slip away in time before people saw us and started asking questions we don't have answers for and digging into pasts that are entirely fake.

A sign on a shop ahead boasts the city's best ice cream.

Lorenc grins and shakes Pjeter slightly. "Do you see that, buddy? Ice cream!"

Pjeter squeals with delight. A long line trails out the door, and there's no way Pjeter's going to cooperate while we wait.

Lorenc turns back and hands Pjeter off to me. "I'll stand in line. You stay close, but do what you need to do to keep him under control."

I nod and scan the crowd around us again. Nothing seems amiss. Just normal people on a normal day.

They have no damn idea.

We wander half a block further down the street to the corner. The park across the street really does look great. It's exactly the type of place I would bring Pjeter to play every day, if we lived here.

He struggles in my arms, and I set him down and clench his tiny hand in mine. "What's wrong?"

He scowls but doesn't answer. I rise to my feet and turn back to check on Lorenc. The line has barely moved. He shrugs his apology, then surreptitiously checks his surroundings.

It happens so fast.

His tiny hand slipping from mine...

His small body darting out across the road...

No!

A car horn blares as Pjeter dashes across the street toward the park. I lurch forward into traffic after him. A truck whizzes past me, barely missing me and blocking my view of Pjeter.

"Pjeter!"

My heart stops beating. The view to the other side of the street clears. I breathe again.

He's safe.

A tall, dark-haired man in a black suit scoops him into his arms. His eyes meet mine across the street, and he leans in to whisper something to Pjeter. Pjeter smiles and waves to me.

The man's lips curl up into a smile.

One I recognize.

One I've seen on Konstandin.

One that turns my blood to ice in my veins.

Aleksander.

"Pjeter!" Lorenc's cry floats in the afternoon air, and his pounding footsteps down the sidewalk rumble my ears.

A black SUV squeals to a stop in front of Aleksander and Pjeter. The Dragon nods at me and disappears inside. I dive forward, but a hand grabs my arm and jerks me backward just as a semi barrels past me, blaring its horn.

The second it's past, Lorenc releases me and takes off across the road.

No. No. No.

The SUV peels out and disappears around the corner before Lorenc can even reach the curb.

No. No. No.

This isn't happening.

My lungs won't take in air.
My heart stops beating.
My vision goes black.
The Dragon has my son.

FOURTEEN

Thunk. Thunk. Thunk. Thunk. Thunk. Thunk.

The road vibrating beneath the tires stirs me.

What? Where am...

The town. The park. Pjeter.

I bolt upright in the backseat of the car.

Lorenc glances over his shoulder at me from the driver's seat. "You okay?"

"Okay? How can you ask me that when he has Pjeter?"

That psycho has my baby. I am so *not* okay, and Lorenc shouldn't be either.

He grits his teeth and nods. "I know. But we're gonna get him back."

His words are strong. Assured. He doesn't exhibit any of the panic that courses through me, making breathing painful.

I shake my head and stare out the front windshield at the black forest around us. "How do you know that? You don't know what the fuck he's doing with him."

"He's not going to hurt him."

"How do you know that?"

He can't possibly know what's going through the head of The Dragon. The man burns and flays people alive. No sane person does that. And no one can predict what an *insane* man will do.

"Rea. Trust me. He's looking for revenge—"

"What better revenge than to kill mine and Konstandin's son?"

It's the ultimate win for a man like Aleksander. Taking the thing we care about the most and crushing it.

"Konstandin found a note tucked under a rock near where Aleksander was standing across the street. It was addressed to you."

Goose bumps spread across my skin, and I rub my hands over my arms. "What did it say?"

He shakes his head. "Nothing. Just a phone number."

But how could he have known?

"How could Aleksander know when we were going to be there and to leave the number?"

Lorenc scowls and shakes his head. "I don't think he did know. He must've been watching us from the moment we arrived in town. We spent a lot of time strolling up and down Main Street. He probably planned to show himself and leave the number. He never could've anticipated Pjeter would run right to him and give him all the leverage he needed."

"Oh, God..."

We handed him the single most important thing in the world.

I did. I let him get away. I let him get into that street. I let him run.

A sob rips from my chest and tears trickle down my cheeks. "What the hell are we going to do?"

"We're meeting Konstandin back at the warehouse. He tried to locate the vehicle but couldn't find it."

Krishti.

My breathing hitches, and Lorenc reaches back to place his hand against my shoulder. "Don't pass out on me again. I need you with me. Pjeter needs you."

I suck in several deep breathes. My thundering heart slows, and clarity about the situation starts to enter my brain finally.

He's right.

My hands shake, and I clasp them together. If I lose my shit, I may never see Pjeter again. "What's the plan?"

"Get back to the warehouse. Call him. See what he wants."

I snarl at him. "We know what he wants. All of us dead."

Lorenc shakes his head. "Yeah, but he doesn't know Konstandin is alive."

"That we know of."

"Until we hear differently, we assume he doesn't know. It's still to our advantage."

"Where was that advantage when he took Pjeter? Where the fuck was Konstandin?"

Anger floods my blood. His father was supposed to keep him safe, keep us *all* safe.

How the hell did this happen?

Lorenc growls, and his knuckles whiten on the wheel. "He was close but not close enough to stop it. It happened too fast. It wasn't his fault. No one could stop that. It was just bad fucking luck."

If I didn't have bad luck, I wouldn't have any at all.

Sold by Father to Tarek.

Abused and treated like property by Tarek.

Rescued by Konstandin.

Love.

Only to have it ripped away because of jealousy from a man I never cared about.

Then, when I finally thought things were calm and I was getting a life back, all of this happens.

"What did I ever do to deserve any of this?"

Lorenc releases a long sigh. "Nothing, Rea. None of this is your fault."

I hadn't even realized I had spoken those words aloud.

He turns onto the gravel drive to the warehouse. "You got sucked into this world without any regard for what you wanted. I'm so sorry, but I promise you, this will end. This will be the last time you ever have to worry about Pjeter or yourself again."

"You can't promise that."

He puts the car in park and turns to me. "I just did."

I wish I could believe his words.

But he said something very similar to me when we fled Philadelphia after they saved me from Tarek.

And look what happened.

There is no escaping this hate—this violence.

There's no living a normal life once wrath takes over.

Konstandin appears at the door to the warehouse, and I leap from the car and run to him. He envelops me in his arms, and I release a sob and let my tears fall. Lorenc follows us into the building, and Konstandin ushers me over to the office where Pjeter slept just this morning.

Konstandin walks me over to the desk and sits me on the edge of it.

I stare up at him through watery eyes. "What do we do?"

He looks at Lorenc. "We call him. We assume he doesn't know about me. You and Lorenc do all the talking. We find out what he wants."

"There's no question about what he wants. He wants us dead. He's not going to hand over Pjeter to us and let one of us walk away with him. It will never happen."

If it were anyone else, I would have some hope of negotiating.

But not The Dragon.

He never stops.

Lorenc steps forward. "We offer him a deal. He doesn't know about Konstandin, and you're an innocent in all that went down. Yes, you chose to leave with Konstandin, but Tarek treated you like fucking shit. It was an arranged marriage, and you never loved him." He sucks in a deep breath. "We try to convince Aleksander of that and to take me in exchange for Pjeter."

"No!" I jump to my feet and shake my head. "I'm not just handing you over to that madman."

Konstandin presses a hand to my chest, holding me back. "It's the only play we have right now. We have to make it work. When he gets in my sights, I'll take care of the rest."

FIFTEEN

EVERY RING through the phone waiting for Aleksander to answer drives a stake through my heart, but I fight back the sobs and the tears because they won't do any good. All we can do is wait for him to pick up. Wait to learn Pjeter's fate.

"Lorenc and Rea, I presume." The thick, dark voice comes through the speaker and chills my blood. "I've been having such a lovely time with your son, Pjeter. Or...is he Konstandin's son. Or Tarek's?"

Konstandin clenches his jaw, no doubt fighting the desire to leap through the phone to tear Aleksander to shreds.

Lorenc clears his throat and glances furtively between Konstandin and me. "What does it matter? We just want him back. What do you want?"

Aleksander's sinister chuckle floats across the line. It's so similar to Tarek's—the man who tried to destroy me—that my fists clench so hard, my nails dig into my palms. "What I've always wanted, Lorenc, to get justice for my brother."

I scoff and lean toward the phone. This man is insane. "Justice? Is that what you call this? Kidnapping an innocent child."

Konstandin drops a hand on my shoulder before I say anything else. It's a silent warning. I can't keep lashing out, especially at Aleksander. I could give something away or dig us into an even deeper hole.

The current situation seems to be about as bad as is possible, but I learned the hard way that things can always get worse. As soon as we feel safe and comfortable in anything, the rug gets pulled out from under us, and we're falling into a bottomless pit of despair. Right now, I'm dangling off that precipice, my nails biting into the loose earth, scrambling for purchase. It won't take much to send me careening over the edge.

Aleksander snarls into the phone, a sound more animal than human. "Your son may be innocent, but he's born of tainted blood—the blood of those who betrayed the truce between our families."

Lorenc grits his teeth. "Bullshit. Saban chose to help Tarek track down Konstandin and Rea. He knew what he was stepping into, and he knew what Konstandin would do if he ever found out. Your brother made a shitty choice, and he died for it. It has nothing to do with Rea or me. And definitely not Pjeter."

"I beg to differ. Rea's inability to keep her legs closed is what started this entire waterfall of blood. Konstandin chose to betray his brother and take what was rightfully his. You chose to help them both. That makes you all guilty in my book."

Rage blasts through my veins, and heat crawls across my skin.

Motherfucker. This asshole thinks this was my fault?

How can anyone possibly think that?

It was never about sex with Konstandin. It was about the way he treated me like a human being. The way he saw me and recognized how miserable I was with Tarek. Konstandin saw how close I was to taking my own life to end it all just to get away from Tarek.

Of course, there was always an attraction there, and it led to so much more, but that's never what it was about in the beginning. It was about finding a safe place in the storm of darkness and violence. Konstandin was that place, the light in the pitch-black night of my life, the warm arms in the chill of Tarek's wake.

And I have another chance with him, but it won't mean anything without Pjeter. Neither I nor Konstandin will survive that.

Lorenc looks to me and then Konstandin. He shakes his head. "She's innocent, Aleksander. Take me. I will gladly offer myself up in exchange for Pjeter, but let Rea leave with him. Leave her alone. Let her live her life. She's suffered enough."

Silence extends over the line. Every second feels like an eternity.

We all hold our collective breaths. The entire warehouse is as silent as death, a state we all know too well.

"It's an interesting proposition. One I had not yet considered, and one I probably never would have even remotely contemplated just a few months ago. But I find myself feeling generous."

Thank God.

The monster has a heart somewhere.

"We can make the exchange. I assume you two are hiding somewhere near the city."

Lorenc nods even though Aleksander can't see us. "Yes."

There's no way he's going to let us pick the meeting place. This needs to be on neutral ground, somewhere he feels safe or like he even has the advantage.

Aleksander clears his throat. "There's an abandoned sawmill fifteen miles outside town. There won't be anyone else there. Meet me in two hours."

The line goes dead, and we all turn to face each other.

Here.

The Dragon is coming here.

Of all the places he could have chosen, he picked *this* building. Maybe luck is on our side for once. Maybe it's karma paying us back for all the crap she's thrown at us over the last few years. Maybe it's the advantage we need to walk out of this alive.

A sinister smile spreads across Konstandin's lips. He's thinking the same thing. Giving Lorenc and Konstandin any advantage is like signing your own death warrant.

Lorenc grins back. "He'll come early to try to set up a trap."

Konstandin snarls. "Of course. He has no intention of making the exchange. The ultimate revenge for him would be to take both of you out and raise Pjeter as his own. To mold and shape and turn him into some vile little version of himself."

The thought churns my stomach. Bile climbs up my throat. I hadn't even considered that possibility.

No. Not my baby.

I shake my head as tears pour down my face. "He can't have my son. He can't."

Konstandin grabs my arms and shakes me. "I'm not going to let him have him. Never. He has no idea what he's walking into. The Dragon is about to be slayed."

SIXTEEN

THE PLACE that has been our safe haven is now a deathtrap...

Set for The Dragon.

He made a critical mistake in choosing this location. Konstandin and Lorenc know this place—every way in, every way out, every back corner, every machine, every damn window and light switch. And he's given us time to prepare for him.

The cool metal of the gun tucked into my waistband and pressed against my back gives me a modicum of peace. Knowing Konstantin is armed with a rifle and a half-dozen other weapons near the top of the metal staircase, hidden in the shadows of the office there, offers me even more.

And having Lorenc standing next to me, his hand clasped in mine while three different guns and two knives are tucked away on him makes it possible for me to breathe and not pass out, waiting for Aleksander.

The crunch of tires on the gravel outside has my stomach churning.

Maybe I'm not as confident as I thought it was.

But we're waiting for an attack.

Aleksander's agreement to the exchange was nothing more than a ruse to get us to meet him.

Konstandin was right—The Dragon will never let us go.

Never.

Lorenc and Konstandin are both capable of horrific things without batting an eyelash. But Aleksander...he's from a whole different world on an entirely different plane. When he wants something, he doesn't stop until he has it, toys with it, and destroys it.

What he did to those people back home...

I shudder.

When they locked him away in that prison, everyone thought it was safe. They never should've let him out. The only reason he even saw the light of day again was that his family finally found someone in the government stupid enough to be bought off. That same moron fell for their assurances that everything would be fine, that he would be controlled and never go on a rampage like that again.

But he will, and he'll do it here this time. He'll start with us, if he hasn't already slaughtered others getting here.

Who am I kidding? Of course, he has.

Lorenc squeezes my hand, and I glance up at him.

He can't give himself to Aleksander. Even if Aleksander were to actually consider the exchange—which we all know he won't—I could never let him take Lorenc and walk away.

I love him.

Not the same way I love Konstandin. I could never love anyone else like that. But Lorenc is my best friend, my confidant, and my protector. I can't lose him. I would give myself over to Aleksander if it meant he released Pjeter and I knew Lorenc and Konstandin would be with him. His two fathers. The men who love him more than anything.

I squeeze his hand back.

Don't lose your shit, Rea.

I have to be one-hundred-percent focused here. I can't be emotional—not with The Dragon involved and Pjeter's life at risk. *All* of our lives are at risk.

There's no room for emotions in this game. You have to be hard. Cold. Ruthless. All the things Lorenc and Konstandin are so naturally, and the things I've had to become since Tarek took me.

I suck in a deep breath.

Whatever walks through that door, I'm ready.

The door opens, and a big man in black fatigues enters, gun drawn. Lorenc drops my hand and raises his into the air. I do the same. The man lowers his weapon slightly and steps through the door. Another man enters, followed by...The Dragon...with a sleeping Pjeter cradled in his arms, his tiny face turned away from me.

My baby.

My chest tightens, and I fight back the sob threatening to claw its way up my throat.

Lorenc glances at me. "He's okay. He wouldn't hurt him."

I nod and watch as the man of everyone's nightmares marches toward us with a smug grin across his lips. The perfectly tailored black suit he wears shifts with every step he takes. His men continue to scan the warehouse, checking for threats.

They won't see Konstandin. The man is a master at blending in, and we made sure he was well-concealed in an area where he could still hopefully get a good shot.

Aleksander and his men stop ten feet in front of us. His dark, soulless eyes rake over me and then over Lorenc. "It's so nice to finally meet you. I've heard so many things." The corner was mouth tilts up. "Not all good, unfortunately."

Lorenc lowers his hands. "I could say the same about you, Aleksander."

A dark chuckle rumbles from The Dragon's chest, and he shifts Pjeter in his arms slightly. "Ouch, my feelings are hurt."

"You don't have feelings," I practically snarl at him.

His eyes flick over to mine. "Well, well, well, the woman who started the war. You must have a pussy of gold to have so many men willing to die for you."

A rage I didn't know was possible blisters my skin, and I lurch toward him, intent on strangling the life from him with my bare hands if necessary. Lorenc grabs my arm and pulls me back.

Aleksander tips back his head and laughs darkly, the sound echoing through the cavernous space.

Lorenc's lips brush my ear. "You okay?"

I nod, and he slowly releases his grip on my arm.

Maybe if Aleksander understood...

I never wanted to speak out loud what Tarek did to me. Saying the words makes it even more real, but I need to try. "Tarek was a monster. He treated me like a toy. Something to own, to possess, something to play with whenever and however he wanted. I was ready to die to escape him when Konstandin rescued me."

Aleksander narrows his eyes on me. "I don't want to hear your excuses. What you did killed my brother. That will not go unavenged."

Lorenc pushes me back slightly with one hand. "Let's just do what we came here for. Give Pjeter to Rea, and I'm all yours."

The eyes of the man who holds my entire world in his hands darken even more, to almost black. He flashes a deadly grin.

Ice floods my veins.

Oh shit.

There was no way this was going to end well. We all knew it would end with blood. But that look...that smile...

It's going to be worse than we ever imagined.

"There's been a slight change of plans." His right arm raises so fast, we don't have time to react.

Bang.

The blast from the gunshot rings in my ears, mixing with Lorenc's scream. Both echo through the warehouse and still my heart as Lorenc drops to the floor.

SEVENTEEN

"No!"

Bang.

Bang.

Bang.

My cry mixes with three quick shots in succession from above and behind me.

Aleksander's men drop one by one, and I throw myself to the floor where Lorenc lies. "Lorenc!"

Blood seeps from between his fingers pressed against the growing red spot on his chest.

No. No. No.

I press my hands over his and push down as I glare at Aleksander. "You bastard!"

But The Dragon isn't looking at me. His eyes are focused up and over my shoulder where he aims his gun—where the real threat is.

A low chuckle slips from his curled lips, and he shakes his head. "I should've known. What was done to my men at the motel...Lorenc would not have been able to do that himself, and Rea wouldn't have offered much help if she were protecting Pjeter. Who's out there? Michael?"

Michael? Lorenc's brother? Why would he think Michael is here?

Aleksander narrows his eyes, trying to see into the darkness. "Did you have a change of heart about coming on as my second-in-command? You should've thought of that before you told me they were here. Could've saved them a lot of pain."

Michael did *tell Aleksander.*

All because he wanted what the Gashi family could offer, something Lorenc and his family never had the ability to accomplish on their own.

Power.

"He did have second thoughts." Konstandin's ice-cold voice comes from the rafters. "Which is why he warned me that you were coming for them."

His heavy boots thud down the metal stairs, and he finally comes into view.

Aleksander's eyes widen as he shifts Pjeter again, struggling to hold him with one arm while pointing a gun at Konstandin with the other hand.

Shit.

That's why Konstandin hasn't taken him out yet. He can't while Aleksander is holding Pjeter. It's too much of a risk, which is precisely why the asshole is doing it. In case we set up something like this. In case there was anyone who was dumb enough to take a shot at him.

Smart. But no one ever said he wasn't intelligent.

Yet, he made a mistake when he chose to come after us because Konstandin is smarter, and now that he knows he has a son, he's not going to stop until he eliminates any threat.

Including The Dragon.

"Konstandin. My...this *is* a surprise. I was assured you died at that airport."

So was I.

Konstandin shrugs as he steps down the final stair onto the warehouse floor. "I did die, but I came back."

He certainly did.

The Dragon smirks. "But it's too little, too late. Anything you think you may have accomplished here is all for naught. Your friend," his eyes drift down to where I kneel with Lorenc, "will die. And so will you and your girl."

Konstandin chuckles.

This is dangerous.

Aleksander shifts again, the weight of holding a sleeping two-year-old starting to bother him.

I know that feeling.

He's going to have to put him down eventually, or he's going to have to lower his weapon. Either way, Konstandin will take advantage of any opening Aleksander gives us.

The man who holds my heart slowly makes his way across the warehouse floor toward us, gun still trained on Aleksander even though he can't shoot while he's holding Pjeter.

Lorenc coughs and groans.

I press against his wound harder. "Stay with me, Lor. You are not dying on me."

He shakes his head, and his eyelids flutter open. The eyes I stared into every day for the last two years are laced with pain, regret, and love. "I need you to tell Pjeter something for me."

"No." I shake my head as tears fall down my cheeks. "You're going to tell him yourself."

Lorenc coughs again, this time blood trickling from his lips. "No, I'm not. Please, Rea, I need you to tell him that I was his father in every way that mattered, blood or not, and that I love him more than anything on this planet, and I'm so sorry I had to leave him."

I choke back a sob.

Konstandin stops next to me, and I glance up at him. "How's he doing?"

I shake my head. "Not good."

Konstandin snarls toward Aleksander. "Do you really think I'm going to let you get out of here alive?"

"You can't touch me." Aleksander grins. "It would only take a second for me to end Pjeter's life. Your son?" He raises a dark eyebrow at Konstandin.

Konstandin growls low, and Aleksander chuckles, the sound of a man with a sinister plan and no soul.

"But I won't. I have plans for him, especially knowing he's your child. So many plans."

That motherfucker.

Konstandin closes the distance until only a few feet stand between them. Their raised guns point at each other.

But Aleksander has the upper hand here.

There may be two of us and only one of him, but he has Pjeter and therefore all the cards. Konstandin can't take a shot even that close with the risk that he might shift or Pjeter might move and get in the line of the bullet.

It's a no-win situation.

Konstandin and Aleksander stand with their guns pointed at each other, my son between them, and me desperately trying to keep the life in Lorenc.

Something's gotta give.

Unless...

I suck in a breath. "Pjeter!"

His name echoes in the space, and Konstandin and Aleksander's eyes both shift to me.

Konstandin glares. "What are you doing?"

Figure it out.

"Pjeter, wake up!"

I don't want him to see this. I don't want him to bear witness to any of the evil dealings here, but it's the only thing I can think of that might give us a shot right now.

My tiny man shifts and slowly lifts his head, rubbing and blinking his eyes.

Bang. Bang. Bang.

I jerk back, even though I was expecting the shots.

Pjeter cries out, and Konstandin lurches forward to catch him before he falls as Aleksander collapses, his gun clattering near his feet. A red stain blooms on the crisp white shirt covering his chest.

When my heart finally starts beating again, I look at Lorenc. The beautiful eyes that have been so kind and so important to me are staring into nothingness, the stony glaze of death settled over them.

No.

God no.

But there's no time to dwell on his passing.

I curl my fingers around the gun at my back and walk over to where Aleksander lies on the concrete floor.

Konstandin clutches Pjeter to him, keeping his face buried against his shoulder.

Please don't let him see Lorenc and what's about to happen...

The Dragon shifts backward, his left hand pressed against his chest. He laughs as he stares up at the barrel of my gun. "What are you going to do with that, Rea? Are you really going to shoot me? You don't have it in you. Either that or your story about Tarek is bullshit. Just an excuse to explain away your throwing yourself at Konstandin. Because if you had the balls to do what you're threatening right now, you would've killed Tarek and left him long ago."

He's right. Back then, I didn't have the balls. I didn't have anything. I was alone in the Morina household. Just a young girl in a shitty situation because Father wanted an alliance with the most powerful family he could find.

I had been sheltered from what Father was and from the people he was involved with, but I learned very quickly in Tarek's hands what man is capable of, especially men like the Morinas and Aleksander Gashi.

I don't know whether to laugh or cry as I stare down at the man who has hunted us since Konstandin killed Saban.

The Dragon.

The man everyone fears.

The man who was a fucking legend is right here right in front of me.

My hand doesn't waver as I step toward him and point the barrel down at his head.

"You might be right, Aleksander. Maybe I didn't have the balls back then, but I'm a completely different person now. I'm a fighter. I'm a lover. And I'm also a mother. And you threatened my child."

Aleksander will never stop. They were right. If we let him live, he will just come back for us, again, and again, and again.

Konstandin's wrath cost him years with us. Time he could have spent with me. Time he could have been a father to Pjeter. If he had just left with us, had just walked away and let Tarek bleed to death or, hell, even live to face the consequences of his actions in the courts instead of needing so badly to exact his revenge, things would've been so different.

Wrath cost him his life, and now, he holds a new life in his hands. I can't take the risk that Aleksander will try to take it again.

Aleksander's wrath brought him here, and even with the gun pointed at his head and bullets in his chest, he's incapable of letting it go. Incapable of giving us life, of letting us live, of forgiving whatever Konstandin did in the name of love.

So, what I've learned over the last two years is that wrath is a deadly sin. It will take your life. It will take your mind. It will take your heart, but sometimes...

The only way to survive wrath is to give into it. *Bang.*

NOTE FROM THE AUTHOR

Yes, Aleksander is really dead.

I know a lot of readers won't be happy about that because they fell in love with him in *After Wrath* even though he was the bad guy. And make no mistake, he *was* a bad guy. Ultimately, The Deadliest Sin Series Wrath trilogy is the love story of Konstandin and Rea/Griffin and Jade. It's about what the sin of wrath does to people, how it destroys their lives and costs them things that are important to them. If you missed them, check out the quotes before the start of each book. Each of these quotes accurately reflects the role and cost of wrath.

For Konstandin and Rea, Tarek's wrath after they left led to him taking her back and Konstandin's wrath over losing her led to him making a horrible decision to stay and finish off Tarek instead of leaving with Lorenc and Rea. Had he not given into that wrath, he wouldn't have "died" and lost those years with her and the son he didn't even know he had. It was Aleksander's wrath over Saban's death that blinded him from seeing the truth - that Tarek was in the wrong and so was Saban for helping him. Even the love of Brynn a.k.a. Kitty wasn't enough to soften him or let him see that Rea was an innocent victim in the entire situation. And finally, Rea's wrath over what Aleksander did and was willing to do to them and their son is what finally ended it. She will pay the price for her wrath, as everyone does in one way or another. For Rea, it will likely be living with the guilt of what she's done because it's not in her nature.

My goal with this trilogy was to explore the sin of wrath and what it does/can do to people and how it affects those around them. So, please, don't hate me if you loved Aleksander. I loved him, too, but it was the only way this trilogy could ever end.

However, this is not the end of The Deadliest Sin Series! Lorenc's brother Michael betrayed him. Want to know why and what price may be paid for it? Find out in the Envy trilogy, next!

- Gwyn

ENVY

Envy slays itself by its own arrows.

-Anonymous

PROLOGUE

THEN (A YEAR AGO)

Becoming Envy

MICHAEL

I END the call before the man on the other end of the line can ask any questions and take a long drag from my cigarette. Nicotine courses through my system, but even it can't still my shaking hand.

It's done.

He wouldn't get the answers he seeks anyway. Not from me. I gave him just enough to get him where he needs to go.

Things have been set in motion. A runaway train now barrels down on those who stand in my way. It's only a matter of time before the collision will occur, and there won't be any survivors of the carnage. Except me, watching at a safe distance from the sidelines, waiting in the wings to step up and take what's mine.

I've worked far too long to see this all come to fruition. To finally get what I *deserve*. It feels like it's been a lifetime. And it almost has been.

They say envy lives and breathes in your soul. That it eats away at you like a cancer, latching onto your vital organs. A disease you can't see or feel but one that will destroy you, nonetheless.

I've felt envy for longer than I can even remember.

For what everyone else has, for what *they* have—the Morenas, the Gashis, my own damn brother. But most of all, for what our family lost by trusting the wrong people—the power, the prestige, the wealth, the *fear*. We had all of it. Then it was taken away.

Well, *they're* the ones who trusted the wrong person this time. They trusted *me*.

Envy got me to where I am today, poised on the precipice of regaining what was so stupidly lost. And I'm not going to let anyone stand in my way now.

Not even my own blood.

ONE

NOW

THE GIRL with my cock down her throat tightens the suction around my hard flesh and moans, sending ripples of pleasure straight to my balls. I thread my fingers through her hair and shift my hips up, forcing myself farther down her throat.

My cell phone rings on the desk, and I glance at the screen to see who's calling.

Fuck.

I can't ignore this, as much as my cock and I would love to pretend it's not ringing. If it were anyone else, I might silence it and continue enjoying the moment. But that's not an option. I grab the phone with my free hand and swipe open the call. "Mr. Rose, to what do I owe the pleasure?"

The blonde pulls off my dick with wide eyes, and I force her back down with a firm hand.

"Did I tell you to fucking stop, bitch?"

Krishti, a man can't even get a good blow job anymore.

"Mr. Syla, it sounds like you're otherwise occupied. Would another time be better?" Rose's smooth, lightly accented voice grates on my nerves. He's always so damn smug.

The blonde sucks me back into the wet heat of her mouth and drags her tongue along the entire underside of my cock.

I grit my teeth and suck in a deep breath. "Now is fine, Rose."

"Excellent. Because we have something important to discuss."

"Oh, yeah? What the fuck is that?"

Rose and I aren't exactly chummy, and we haven't even spoken since the bombing, so I don't know what the hell he thinks we need to talk about so urgently. Whatever it is better be damn good to be taking attention away from this much-needed relaxation.

"Look, Mr. Syla, you and I are the new kids on the block, so to speak, and after what happened at the meeting—"

A strange mixture of pleasure and anger flares in my veins—one of the risks of getting blown while talking to an enemy. "A meeting which was set up in the first place to try to figure out a way to take me out, asshole. Let's not forget that."

I certainly never will.

Rose chuckles, and I can almost picture him shaking his head with his feet casually propped up on his desk, like he wasn't part of a combined effort of the families who run Chicago to get rid of me. Actually, Rose is too prim and proper to ever put his shoes on furniture. Probably wipes his ass with gold toilet paper and flushes with bottled water, too.

The man who leads one of the most powerful cartels in South America and seems intent on taking over Chi-town too laughs at my outburst. "Now, now, Michael, it was just a little get together amongst business acquaintances."

"That I wasn't invited to." So they could discuss ways to stop me from advancing my interests and encroaching on my territories.

"Which is exactly why you are the prime suspect in the bombing."

Oh, so this is why he's calling...

He's on a fishing expedition, hoping I'm going to open up to him and let something slip that will incriminate me. Give them the final straw they need to justify removing me permanently, just like I did my predecessor.

I push my hand through the blonde's hair as she tightens her fist around the base of my cock, adding a slight twisting motion every time her mouth retreats. "The way I see it, Rose, *you're* the prime suspect."

He chuckles again, a deeply arrogant sound that would get him shot between the eyes if we were in the same room. "Why is that, Michael?"

The girl swirls her tongue around the head of my dick, and I grit my teeth to bite back a groan. *Krishti, I wish I could be enjoying this more. Fucking Rose...*

If the man really needs *me* to explain why he's a suspect, then he's not as smart as everyone seems to think. "Because you moved in, guns blazing, and have been pushing against the boundaries of your deal with Valentina since basically day one. Everyone knows you're looking for an opportunity to snatch all of Chicago for yourself and taking out the heads of each of the major families would put you in that position."

A second of silence lingers on the line, giving me a brief moment to enjoy the deep suction on my dick.

"You're not wrong there, Mr. Syla. We may very well both be under suspicion, but I would venture to guess it weighs more heavily toward you. I was invited to that meeting, and not only was I there, but so was my sister. I don't think anyone who knows me at all would believe I would put both myself and her at risk."

The familiar tingle starts at the base of my spine as the girl bobs up and down on my cock. I'm not going to last long, and neither is this goddamn phone call. It has the irritation rising almost as fast as my orgasm. "That street moves two ways, Rose. If I'm the one who set the bomb, then why would I show up there myself? Why would I put myself in harm's way?"

"Maybe because you're incredibly intelligent and thought that it might pull suspicion away from you."

I'll give Rose credit; the man *is* smart. But about this...he's wrong. "It wasn't me, Rose."

He's silent for a moment. "It wasn't me, Syla."

"So, where does that leave us?" Besides me sitting on the brink of an orgasm that's only being held off by his annoying, accented voice in my ear.

"It leaves us both under suspicion. And I'm going to leave you with a warning. If I find definitive proof that it *was* you, that *you* are the reason my little sister ended up in the hospital and almost died, you better believe you'll pay for what you did."

The line goes dead, and I let the phone drop onto the desk so I can bury my other hand into blondie's hair and guide her even faster and my cock even deeper down her throat.

Fucking Rose. Fucking calling to threaten me. Who the fuck does he think he is?

Nobody ever would've called to threaten a Syla like that before Grandfather ruined everything back home and lost us any reputation and respect we once had. People knew not to fuck with us. They knew what Sylas were capable of. They revered us the same way they did the Gashis and the Morenas. There was *Besë*—a code of honor everyone respected. They took the oath and lived by it. That seems to have been long forgotten.

Well, Rose is about to learn a hard lesson. Nobody threatens Michael Syla and gets away with it. Nobody.

I thrust up into the woman's mouth hard. My cock hits the back of her throat, and she gags and swallows. The movement of her throat muscles against the head of my dick sends my orgasm slamming into me—a dark wave of pleasure mingling with the burning rage in my chest.

TWO

EVEN A GOOD NIGHT'S sleep hasn't released the tension coiled in my body. In the months since the bombing, it's almost like everyone is stuck in some sort of stalemate.

Valentina and the Italians have kept the status quo and have retained their tenuous relationship with the Roses, even though he's probably a suspect, too. The Irish and the Russians haven't retaliated, either. They've just gone about their business, albeit with their eyes slightly more open. And the few groups that hadn't received invitations to the meeting—the ones on their way out as opposed to their way up—just probably don't give a shit because they know they don't have the means to take on any of the bigger organizations—unless the bomb was them trying to make a statement.

I shouldn't put it past them. I've been making enemies left and right by killing off the street-level men and interrupting supply lines for several of the Mexican cartel groups and smaller gangs that control niches in the city. They were easy pickings compared to the people in that meeting. But ultimately, any one of them might've been responsible.

Yet I'm the fucking bad guy. Bad enough they had to call a fucking meeting in the first place to talk about me.

Motherfuckers.

The things I've done since I took over haven't been anything worse than what any of them have done to take and maintain their power. Nothing worse than anything my predecessors did. Hell, at least I wasn't skinning people alive. A double-tap is all it takes. There's no need for the extra blood and gore—just get the job done cleanly and efficiently.

Which is what I'm doing today. I'm sick of the men doing nothing. Every day, I wait for information about the bombing, about my rivals, about *anything* that could help advance my goals. And every damn day...nothing.

The stalemate has to end. It's going to end today.

I clench my fists as I climb from my car and storm toward the club. The light drizzle pelts my exposed skin but doesn't cool my temper. I woke with renewed vigor and determination to move things forward. Sitting around and making moves behind the scenes while constantly watching my back is getting fucking old.

Zamir and Genti struggle to keep up my pace. These two assholes are good for nothing. If I weren't worried someone would try to take a shot at me here walking to the club from my car, I wouldn't even bother with having them with me. But the bomb was too close a call to ignore. Until we have confirmation who set it and who the target was, everyone has to be careful—including me. I've made a lot of enemies, and it's only a matter of time before one of them succeeds where others have failed.

But not fucking today.

Chicago is a big city, but there are way too many fucking people who think they run it. It should be a one-man show. *Mine.* I fucking *earned* it. All my time spent back in Albania, taking care of what little we had left while Lorenc gallivanted around Philly, loyal to the Morenas. He was just a fucking lackey for Tarek and Konstandin. The man followed orders and obeyed like we don't come from one of the families that ran a massive portion of the entire country for almost a hundred years. But he did it for the prestige—the money and power it gave him to be part of that organization. And the respect. He craved it and got it. Everything I ever wanted but could never have because big brother did.

It's my time now. To rise to the top. To rule the Windy City like a king on his fucking throne.

I stride to the door, yank it open, and step into the club. Low, sultry bass vibrates through the floor and walls. Precious must be on stage. I'd know her song anywhere. Any other day, I might pause to enjoy the show and maybe drag her back into my office with me to relieve some of this tension, but fucking it out isn't going to cut it today.

Only blood will.

And as much as I hate making a mess where I work, some things are inevitable. If the men didn't see this day coming, then they're bigger idiots than I imagined them to be all this time.

My men at the bar jerk toward me and the open door and scramble off their stools when I stride in. Frenk knocks over his stool, struggling to get to his feet. He should be out talking to his sources, trying to gain new information on any of our *friends* at the meeting.

Lazy motherfuckers. All of them.

I grab a pint glass half full of beer from where Frenk had been sitting, toss the drink in his face, then smash the glass against the side of his head. "You piece of shit. Do you think I pay you to sit around on your ass, getting drunk, and watching the girls?"

Blood pours from the side of his head, and he scrambles back to his feet from where he ended up on the floor. "Sir, I—"

"Shut the fuck up!" I spin, taking in everyone in the club.

The music stops. An eerie quiet falls over the entire room. No patrons yet this early. Just the men, Precious on the pole, and one of the waitresses who has been with me since I took over. Another blonde.

Good. No witnesses who are stupid enough to talk.

"There's a reason nothing has advanced in months, and it isn't because of the damn bomb. It's because you fuckers are all lazy." I turn back to Zamir and Genti. "These fuckers who are supposed to be my bodyguards and keep me safe at all times couldn't *walk* fast enough to do any *guarding* on my way in here."

Wide eyes watch me from all around the club. Everyone is waiting to see where I go with this.

"This. Ends. Now." My voice booms around the place, but no one flinches. They know what that would mean. "The next time I see one of you sitting on your asses instead of doing your jobs, you won't be taking another breath."

I pull my gun and shoot Frenk between the eyes. He collapses at my feet with a thud. No one moves or says a word. I shove past two of the men and toward my office but pause just before I step into the hallway and turn back.

Altin stares at me from his spot behind the bar, a rag in his hand from when he paused midway through a wipe-down.

I motion toward the body and blood pooling all over the floor. "Clean up this fucking mess."

My gaze catches something, and I glance down at my thousand-dollar loafers.

Fucking blood splatter. Just what I fucking need.

I grab a napkin off the bar, wipe the blood from my shoe, and toss it on Frenk's body.

There's only one thing I want to do when I'm in a mood like this, and today's no fucking exception. I scan the bar. The waitress stands across from me, green eyes locked on mine. She doesn't flinch or look away, and she didn't react at all to what just happened in here.

Good.

"You," I point at her, "come with me."

Brandi? Candy?

I don't remember her name, and it doesn't matter. I've fucked her before, and she'll do in a pinch. She's a more than willing partner who doesn't expect anything like love or affection. None of that exists here.

She sets her tray on the bar and follows me back to my office, the *click, click, click* of her heels echoing down the hallway. I close the door behind her, grab her arm, and lead her over to the desk.

"Bend over."

The woman doesn't even look at me, just follows my command and lifts her skirt, exposing her bare ass underneath. No panties.

Thank fuck. That gets me inside her much faster.

THREE

THE HARDER I drive into the waitress bent over my desk, the angrier I get. Not because it doesn't feel great. Her hot, wet pussy clasping on my cock couldn't feel better. But the wrath doesn't subside like it usually does when I'm buried deep inside a willing woman.

I can't quite put my finger on why, though.

Rose? Frenk? The uncertainty of waiting for something to happen?

It could be anything. But with each thrust of my hips, the mix of envy and rage swirling inside me only gets darker, more sinister, rising closer to the surface. That bomb won't be the only thing to explode if things don't change soon. I didn't do what I did, I didn't *sacrifice* what I sacrificed, to sit in this office passively.

Passive just isn't my style. Life requires action if you want to accomplish anything. And I have a lot of plans.

The door to my office opens.

What the fuck?

I jerk up my head, but it isn't one of the men standing in the doorjamb. A dark-haired woman with hard, icy-blue eyes stares at me. Zamir stumbles behind her in the hallway, his gun drawn and pointed at her. She glances at him, seemingly unconcerned about the 1911 ready to take off her head, then returns her cool gaze to me.

Anyone else probably would've stopped fucking at this point, but I'm not letting whoever this bitch is ruin what's turned out to be a pretty decent lay, despite my wandering mind. I slam into the girl again. She gasps and clutches at the front of the desk for leverage against my brutal thrusts. Her pussy clenches around me.

Fuck.

The mystery woman's eyes never leave mine, but one corner of her mouth quirks up the tiniest bit—the only reaction she's given since she walked in on me.

My body tightens, and I grip the girl's hips and pound into her harder and faster. I force myself to keep my eyes open and locked on the dark-haired woman as I empty my load into the waitress with a grunt between gritted teeth.

I release her, pull out, and smack her ass. "Get the fuck out of here."

She pushes groggily onto her elbows and steps back on weak legs. My cum dribbles down her leg and drips onto the floor. She wobbles and grabs the desk for a second before she glances over her shoulder at me. I nod toward the door, and she slowly walks around the desk and past the mystery woman with nothing more than an inquisitive look her way.

Employees know not to ask questions, and she's a good one.

I stand, facing the woman, my still-hard cock hanging out of my pants, and raise an eyebrow at her. "Who the fuck are you?"

Her gaze drifts down to my cock for a second, then back up to meet mine. "Someone who's here to help you."

Help me? Well, isn't that presumptuous?

"Who the fuck said I needed help with anything?"

She smirks and takes two more steps in with Zamir following right behind her, gun trained at her head. "Well," she waves her hand behind her, "I managed to walk back here without being stopped, didn't I? That could lead some to call into question the competency of your security."

Fuck. She has a point there.

The slow curl of her red lips tells me she knows it, too. "But I'm thinking more long-term goals, big picture help."

I snort and shake my head while I push my cock back into my pants and zip them. "I don't know who you are, lady, but get the fuck out of my office before I have him shoot you."

Or I do it myself.

She smiles at me, but it doesn't hold any warmth. It's the same kind of cold, cruel smile I saw from the men who worked for Grandfather while I was growing up. The men who turned me into who and what I am today. It's almost like she thinks she knows me.

"You won't do that."

"Oh, yeah?" I raise an eyebrow at her again as I drop into my chair. "Why the fuck not?"

The apparently unflappable woman walks between the two chairs facing me on the other side of my desk then lowers herself into the plush leather of the one on the left. One long, pale leg crosses over the other, briefly exposing her bare pussy to me.

My cock stirs in my pants despite the fact that I just got off.

"Well, Mr. Syla, it's simple. Because you want to hear what I have to say. You would've already killed me if you didn't."

Who the fuck is this woman?

No one talks to me like that. And absolutely *no one* can read me that well. But she's right. I'm not going to shoot her—or have Zamir do it—because I want to know what's so damn important that she had the balls to walk in here like this.

I nod to Zamir, still standing behind her with his gun pointed. "Get out."

His mouth opens slightly, and he glances between us. "But, sir..."

I growl at him. "Are you fucking deaf? Get the fuck out!"

He raises his hands and steps back through the door. With one wary glance at me, he pulls it closed behind him, leaving me alone with the woman who managed to walk right back here past a room full of my men without so much as one of them blinking at her until she had already reached me.

Bunch of useless fucks.

I'll deal with that problem later. Right now, my focus needs to be on figuring out what the fuck this woman wants.

I grab my pack of cigarettes, light one, then lean forward in my chair and rest my elbow on the desk. "How about we start with your name?"

"My friends call me Kat."

A long, slow puff of smoke rolls from my mouth. "What makes you think we're friends?"

She smiles—this one more genuine than the last. "Because I have something you want, Mr. Syla."

This one has confidence. I'll give her that.

"What is it you think you have that I want?"

"Power. The power to have everything your heart has ever desired. The power to have it all."

FOUR

Whoever this woman is...she's clearly insane.

Too bad. She's hot as fuck.

"Look...Kat, is it?" I shift back into my chair. "I don't know how you got in here or what could possibly make you think you could give me anything I can't take for myself."

And already have plans to.

She smiles at me and nods toward my cigarettes in question. I push them and the lighter across the desk to her and watch her pull one out and light up. She sticks it between her red lips and takes a long pull. Her eyes briefly drift closed before they meet mine again.

A plume of smoke coils up from her mouth, and she grins at me. "You want Chicago. I can help you get it."

I snort and shake my head. "Yeah, and how are you gonna do that?"

Those beautiful, perfect red lips twist into a grin. "The way everyone gets power and control—sex."

My dick pushes against my pants, and I surreptitiously adjust it away from the zipper with one hand while taking a drag with the other.

She releases another puff of smoke and angles her head toward me. "I run a very profitable, upscale escort service. And with the connections you have and this place," she waves her hands to the side, "we could make a lot of money running the girls."

I lean back and watch her.

It isn't a bad idea, actually.

Although my predecessor felt kidnapping women and transporting them across the ocean to work as prostitutes was a good business plan, I believe employees willingly working for you are always better. More loyal. Less of a chance they'll go to the cops about anything that's happening versus somebody forced into it.

But the question is...how does she know about Erjon's operation?

"I'm not sure what you're talking about, Kat."

She smiles and uncrosses then re-crosses her legs again, flashing me those beautiful pink lips. "Let's not beat around the bush here, Mr. Syla. I know exactly the type of operation Erjon was running out of here, and I know you shut it down and eliminated everyone who was loyal to him here in the club. But you still have those connections. You still have ways to get people into the country—both legally and illegally. I'm not asking you to start trafficking again. I'm asking you to transport willing women from Albania and elsewhere in Eastern Europe into the US to work for us. I know how to run this business successfully and make you a lot of money."

I chuckle and shrug. "Money, I have."

"The more money you have, the more power you have, Mr. Syla, and there's something even more valuable than cash. The escort service could be a way to gather information on the organizations you're so intent on taking down."

Now that is an interesting idea.

If they feel safe coming to a location we ran, we might be able to use the girls to get insider information—information that could help me dismantle my rivals from the inside.

Kat holds up her hands, the cigarette dangling from her fingers. "I know you're hungry for it. You want it all, and I can help you get it."

Beautiful and smart. I don't fucking trust her.

The corner of her mouth tilts in that cold smile as she waits for my reaction.

"You've made an interesting proposal, Kat. But what makes you think I'm going to climb into bed with you—so to speak? You just walked in and handed me this idea. Why wouldn't I just do the same thing on my own?"

And the ultimate question: what do you get out of this deal?

She sits totally still, seemingly unfazed by my threat to steal her plan. Those cold, hard eyes bore into me, and she shifts forward slightly, exposing her breasts even more. "Because my place is already trusted. My girls already have established relationships with many members of your competitors' organizations. I have my foot in the door, so to speak."

Well, hell...

She came in here and saved the kicker for the very end.

"I'll have to consider your proposal."

And do a lot of digging.

There's no way she waltzed in here on her high heels to propose this partnership out of the goodness of her heart. She wants something. Otherwise, she wouldn't offer to help.

If life has taught me anything, it's that no one does anything selflessly. Especially in *this* business. She has an ulterior motive, and I need to find out what it is.

"Zamir!"

He shoves open the door and steps through.

"We're done here. Kat is ready to be shown out."

She rises to her feet slowly and inclines her head toward me. "It was a pleasure, Mr. Syla." She reaches over the desk and stubs out her cigarette in the ashtray in front of me before turning away.

Three steps bring her next to Zamir, and she pauses. Her hand flashes out. A split-second later, she has his gun in her grasp. I lunge for the one I keep in my top drawer, but she presses the barrel to his head and fires. The sound is deafening in the small room, and my hand finds the grip of my gun as she turns toward me.

Fuck.

This wasn't the way I imagined going out.

Only...she isn't pointing it at me.

She approaches with the gun dangling from her finger and sets it on my desk casually. "Your man let me walk right past him back here. Seems he thought I was a hooker you called to join your little party I interrupted. I could've been anyone with any kind of motive. You need better security."

With that, she turns and walks away without a glance back at me.

My heart hammers so hard, it hurts my ribs. My hard cock aches, and I scrub a hand over my face. I would have done the same thing to Zamir as soon as she left, but I don't think I've ever seen a member of the lesser sex so cold-blooded.

Who the fuck was that woman?

FIVE

ARDEN STANDS BEFORE ME, shifting nervously from foot to foot.

"Why don't you take a seat?" I motion toward one of the chairs facing my desk with one hand and take a drag off my cigarette.

He eyes me suspiciously but lowers himself slowly into one of them, shuffling the papers in his hand.

In the few days since my mysterious visitor, I've had him scouring for information on her, looking for any reason she would have to approach me with this deal. Given how nervous Arden is, my guess is it isn't good news.

"What have you been able to find?"

The small, timid man who has handled all my tech issues since taking over the territory here clears his throat and shifts the papers onto his lap. "Not a whole lot, Mr. Syla. Katherine Adair was born here in Chicago on December 3, 1992. She attended public school here, nothing special in terms of grades. I couldn't find any college records, so I don't think she went past high school. A few sporadic work records, but she didn't file taxes for many years." He glances up with dark-gray eyes.

"And?"

He offers a small shrug. "And that's about it, personally."

"What have you found out about her business?" I snuff out my cigarette and lean back.

"It's called Kat's Cradle."

I can't fight the smirk that brings.

Clever.

"She's only been set up in town here for a few months."

I raise an eyebrow. "Really?" And she's already managed to secure clients from some of the major organizations in town. "Where was she set up before that?"

"Well," he rubs the back of his neck, "that's where things get a little interesting."

"Interesting?"

His tongue darts out to lick his lips. He clears his throat and moves another paper to the top. "Prior to setting up Kat's Cradle, she was living in Europe. At least, apparently."

"Apparently?"

Not the word I want to hear when he's been researching someone for me. Likely why he's so damn nervous—even more so than normal.

"It's been a little difficult to track her. She doesn't have any credit cards in her name, so I can't use those to trace where she's traveled."

"So, what *have* you been able to find?"

It sounds like I shouldn't hold my breath waiting on a flood of information. Arden is *good.* Damn good. Or he wouldn't still be working for me or still be breathing. If she's a challenge for him, that means something is up.

"Her name popped up on a hotel register in Paris. One in Vienna. And then...she disappears for a while."

Something cold slithers across my skin. "What do you mean, disappears?"

He gives a slight shrug—a motion that's really starting to grate on my nerves. "I don't know how else to explain it, sir. There's just nothing for months until—"

"Until she reappears here in Chicago and sets up Kat's Cradle."

He nods. "Basically."

"Shit." I hate the unknown. The unknown is what gets you in trouble. It's what gets you killed. *Know your enemy, Michael.* Grandfather's words echo in my head even though I don't know *if* she is my enemy or not. It's smart to know your friends, too.

"Sir, there doesn't seem to be anything that jumps out. Nothing glaringly concerning."

"Nothing concerning? The woman waltzed in here, past my guards, who didn't even think to stop her or question her, then she makes me a business proposition and kills one of my men, and we can't find out anything about her. You don't think that's a little bit concerning?"

He nods sheepishly, his cheeks reddening. "I can see where you're going with this, sir."

"I would fucking hope so. Keep digging."

The papers in his hands shake. "Sir, there's nowhere else to dig."

I slam my palms against the desk, and he jumps out of his chair by a foot. "Then find somewhere else to fucking dig. There has to be something. If you have to fly to Vienna personally to pick up her fucking trail, then do it. I want to know every place she's eaten, slept, and fucked since she graduated from high school. Do you understand me?"

He nods slowly. "I-I do, sir. I'll do my best."

"I expect you to do your best all the time." Though maybe I haven't been making my expectations clear. The men are certainly acting like this is a fucking vacation instead of a time to be making big plans and making big moves.

His head bobs furiously. "Of course, of course, always."

Fucking Krishti.

I wave my hand to dismiss him, and he bolts out of his chair faster than I can take another breath. He can't get away from me quickly enough. And I can't say I blame him.

The thin edge I've been walking since I took my place here seems to be narrowing even more. Things are adding up. The bombing. The phone call with Rose the other day. The appearance of Kat. Too many uncomfortable unknowns. Too many things out of my control, and if there's one thing I hate, it's not being in control.

If Arden can't find anything else on Kat, I'm going to have to make this decision blind. Which isn't something I do often or lightly, if at all. It's a great way to end up in a body bag or even worse...disappear.

It's not like if that happens, there aren't those who wouldn't say I had it coming. I've certainly committed enough cardinal sins to more than justify anything anyone would do in taking my life and sending me to Hell, but it doesn't mean I have to offer myself up on a fucking platter.

I've been running around with increased security for months, trying to get a handle on who I can trust and who I can take out the easiest to eliminate my competition slowly. And so far, I have very little to show for it, except for two dead men and a whole lot of sexual frustration due to one very beautiful and very mysterious Kat.

She's gone to a lot of trouble to stay under the radar. But I've always loved a good game of cat and mouse. I just prefer to be the cat.

SIX

THE HARD RAIN falling on the Windy City can't wash away the taint that permeates everything. It's a stench. A dark stain. The sense that nothing is ever really settled or safe.

I've felt it since the moment I landed here and met with the Dragon. Partly because I came with my plan already set in motion. Despite the promises he made to me, it wasn't enough. It never could be. I wanted more, and now it's right there, just out of my reach, brushing my fingertips with no way to grasp it.

Short of setting up Valentine's Day Massacre type hits, no way to eliminate the competition has presented itself. At least, no way that wouldn't end with the rest of them coming after me right away. And Rose was right. I'm on everyone's radar and have been since the moment I started making moves. It's why they met to "discuss" me in the first place. Had that explosion not blown the meeting to kingdom come, I probably wouldn't be breathing right now. Especially with the shitty job my men have done keeping me protected.

But today officially ends the stagnation.

I pull my car into the harbor and dodge potholes all the way down to the pier, where the *Harbinger* sits bobbing in the water. The ship looks as dilapidated today as it did when I last saw her in the Port of Vlorë over a year ago, but looks can be deceiving.

It's handled more transports of cargo for me safely than any other has for the Gashis or the Morenas since they took power in Philly and Chicago over a hundred years ago. By staying under the radar and appearing to operate as a completely legitimate vessel flying a Maltese flag, neither the Coast Guard nor any other organization has ever managed to tie it to me.

A resource I need now more than ever, especially if I decide to move forward with Kat's offer. In the week since she paid me the unexpected visit, no new information on her has turned up, and the idea of having a way to acquire inside info on my enemies has become more and more appealing.

So much so that I would brave this deluge to come to talk to the man who could make it happen if I wanted to get into business with the dark-haired, cold-blooded woman.

Though it hasn't been getting into business with her that's been on my mind the most.

I park next to the dock and climb from the car into the pouring rain. The three SUVs trailing me, containing the useless men who are supposed to be my security, stop on either side of me and behind me, but I'm not waiting for these assholes to get out.

If anyone wants me dead bad enough to follow me out here on a night like this, then let them fucking kill me.

I jog up the ramp onto the *Harbinger* and duck into the wheelhouse to escape the downpour.

Esad waits in the captain's chair, his boots propped up on the control panel. He narrows his eyes on me and snorts. "You look like a drowned rat."

Ballsy motherfucker.

I shake off the excess water and glance around the wheelhouse. "You know...I've never actually been on board before."

He chuckles and lets his feet drop to the floorboards. "I know. I was surprised you wanted to meet here for that very reason."

The rain pummels the steel roof, the sound echoing in the tight space. I wave a hand toward the bow of the ship, where the storm rages so hard, I can barely see anything but a wall of black, falling water.

"I doubt anyone is watching the ship or me tonight."

He snorts and shakes his head as he approaches. Despite the fact that I'm soaked, he pulls me into his arms and embraces me tightly.

I slap him on the back and pull away from him. "It's good to see you, *miku im*."

"You, too, old friend. So, what is so important that you had to come out during this? I was surprised to get the message asking me to stay instead of leaving yesterday like I had originally planned."

The shipment of weapons that came in this week will be invaluable to my operation, but I couldn't let Esad leave without discussing other potentials in person. "I received an interesting offer last week."

His dark eyebrows rise, and he leans against the console. "From a friend?"

I shake my head. "That remains to be seen. And I wanted to talk to you before I committed to anything."

"About what?"

I wander to the chair he vacated and drop down into it. "You know Erjon was operating a human trafficking ring?"

He nods slowly. "Don't tell me you want to start it back up again."

"No," I hold up a hand, "at least, not exactly what he was doing." I made promises that have kept me alive and built a tentative trust with people who would be very angry if I started trafficking again. "This is a more…friendly version of the business."

"Friendly?" He smirks and shakes his head. "I don't know anyone who has ever called you friendly, Michael."

I chuckle and run a hand through my soaked hair. "True."

"So, what's the new version?"

I lock eyes with him. "Willing women coming into the country. Those we can get here legally, we will, but the vast majority will need to be smuggled in."

"For what purpose?"

"What else?"

"Sex?"

Kat was right about one thing; when it comes down to it, people get power through money and sex.

I nod at him and lean back in the chair. "Someone has offered me a partnership in a profitable escort service. We would need more girls to expand, clean up the club, and maybe open additional locations of both businesses."

There's no reason the girls would all have to operate out of Kat's Cradle. Having my competitors blind to my involvement there is essential, but we could make some serious money doing this on a larger scale, regardless of the information value.

Esad eyes me for a moment. "It wouldn't be any harder than it has been to get you guns, drugs, or anything else you've needed. The only real problem is the timing. It takes two months to get from Vlorë to Chicago and back if we don't get held up anywhere for inspections or any weather issues. With the Soo Locks closed January through March and the lake impassable, that means we can do three to four runs a year."

"Unless we add more ships."

He nods slowly, and a smile tilts his lips. "Ah, now I see why you wanted to meet in person. I know several captains I would trust to be involved in this operation."

"Are they as good as you? I can't afford to have one of the ships caught and what we're doing discovered." A federal indictment would end anything I've managed to accomplish here. And I have no desire to spend any time in prison. I've spent enough time in dank, dark, hopeless places to last a lifetime.

"Of course, *miku im*. Would I recommend anyone to you if I didn't know they were the best and completely loyal?"

No. He wouldn't, which is exactly why I came tonight.

"I'm still not one hundred percent sure I'm going to get involved in this, but I'll let you know one way or the other soon." I push to my feet and embrace him again. "It was good to see you, *miku im*."

He releases me and pulls back. "You, as well. Watch your back."

"I always do."

I know what happens when you don't.

SEVEN

THEN (25 years ago)

SOMETHING JERKS me from my sleep.

A sound.

Rustling.

Not the usual sounds that might wake us in the night—gunfire, explosions, screaming.

I push myself up and scan the dark room, wincing at the pain shooting through my ribs. A thin stream of moonlight filters in through the window, illuminating just enough to confirm I'm alone.

Something bumps in the hallway.

No one should be awake at this hour, not even Grandfather. *Gjyshi* hates the vulnerability of sleep, but he also knows he must stay rested to keep his wits about him. A mistake he won't repeat.

I climb from my bed, quickly make my way to the door, and ease it open. The creaking of the old hinges makes me cringe, and I freeze and listen. Another bump somewhere down the hall.

Lorenc's room.

He shouldn't be awake, either, not after what Grandfather put us through today.

My entire body aches from the beating. This one was the worst yet. Time hasn't softened the old man. Quite the opposite. His advancing age and the state we now find ourselves in, reduced to living in this shitty house instead of the grand family compound he's accustomed to, has only made him more vicious and cold.

The faint glow of light seeps through the crack below Lorenc's door. I push it open, and he whirls around where he stands at the bed to face me. "*Mbylle!* Close it!"

"What are you doing?" I make my way to the bed where a bag is laid open with his clothes and a few other items.

He avoids my gaze. "Leaving."

"Leaving? Where are you going?"

His hard, dark eyes finally meet mine, the bruise around the left one prominent and only darkening. "Away from here—to America."

America?

My heart thunders in my chest. "You can't leave. How will you get there? What will you do?"

He sighs and zips his bag. "Konstandin and Tarek made arrangements for me."

Anger heats my blood, and I grab his arm and squeeze. "You're going to the Morenas? *Gjyshi* will kill you when he finds out."

"He's going to kill me anyway if I stay." He shoves me off and grabs his bag. "You should leave, too. Find somewhere...anywhere."

Where would I go?

Panic tightens my lungs, making it impossible to take a deep breath. "Take me with you. You can't leave me here."

His eyes soften for a brief moment. "I can't bring you with me. I'm sorry. I'll send for you when I can...if I can."

"And what if Grandfather kills me before that?" Because he's right, the old man is unhinged. There's no telling when he might step over the line.

Lorenc turns his back on me and heads for the door. "I'm sorry. Just protect yourself any way you can, *vëllaçko*."

"You can't leave me!"

He opens the door and walks out without a glance back.

NOW

I bolt awake in a cold sweat, my heart thudding so hard, all I can hear is the rush of blood in my ears.

Fuck.

The cool air in my bedroom raises goosebumps across my damp, naked flesh, and I climb from the bed and scrub my hands over my face.

Fuck. Fuck. Fuck.

I haven't had a dream like that in a long time. So fucking long, I can't even remember the last one. Even after more than two decades, the memory is still so fresh, it felt like I was standing there watching him leave me in that place again.

My own brother. Stabbing me in the back. Escaping and running to the people who left the family in this state in the first place, who sent one of their own women to seduce Grandfather and open him up to the deal that destroyed us. Leaving me to spend years suffering at the hands of the monster who was our grandfather. The man who threw away all the power and wealth we had for a fucking woman. One who ended up being a plant by our rivals.

Ever since that moment, that night he walked away, I've made sure to close myself off from everyone. It's the only way to keep myself safe and to get what I've always wanted—*everything*.

These dreams are a burden. A dark, unhappy reminder I don't need. And the timing of their return couldn't be worse.

Bam. Bam. Bam.

The loud pounding on the door jerks me from the dark memory.

What the hell? I told them to leave me alone tonight.

Genti and Driton have one simple job. Guard the door. And these idiots can't even handle that.

I storm from my bedroom, across the loft, and yank open the door to the hallway. "What the fuck do you want?"

Familiar, cool-blue eyes assess me. Not the eyes of either of the terrified looking men flanking the doorway.

I narrow my gaze on my visitor, very aware I'm still naked and reeling from the dream. "Kat? What are you doing here?"

Genti and Driton's eyes widen. "Sir, we assumed you called her."

"You *assumed?*"

Fucking useless.

"We searched her, sir. She's clean."

She raises a thin, dark eyebrow at me, and that same cold smile she flashed me during our meeting crosses her lips. "Well, are you going to invite me in?"

EIGHT

INSTEAD OF WAITING FOR AN ANSWER, she brushes past me into my condo. The heady scent of something rich and sweet like cinnamon rolls in her wake. My cock stirs.

I scrub a hand over my face and look between Genti and Driton. "We'll talk about this later," I growl the words and slam the door in their faces before I turn back to her.

What the fuck is happening?

With my heart still beating a rapid tattoo and my limbs shaking after the nightmare, the last thing I want is to have a confrontation with anyone. And I'm definitely not in any shape for a showdown with a woman like her. She throws me off balance, and I don't even know why. Women don't affect me like this. *No one* does.

"What are you doing here?"

She shrugs nonchalantly and scans the condo like she's an interior decorator sizing up the space. "I was in the neighborhood."

Smooth.

And a total fucking lie. We both know it.

I approach her slowly, very aware of the way her breasts spill from the deeply cut black dress practically painted on her skin. "And how did you know what neighborhood I live in?"

The entire reason I chose this place was that it isn't residential. There are no prying eyes of neighbors. No neighbors period except a few factories that only have workers coming during early shifts. The converted loft space is perfect for what I require—a place to sleep and eat.

Nothing more.

No one comes here.

Before the bombing, not even my men.

I can fuck anywhere and never bring anyone back for a very specific reason—this is my personal space, not one to be invaded by all the bullshit the weaker sex brings with them. There's no way she was just "in the neighborhood" and happened to find my place.

Her perfectly red lips curl. "Lucky guess."

My hand is around her neck in a split second, and I pin her to the brick wall behind her so fast, all the air whooshes from her lungs. "Fucking bullshit. I don't know what kind of game you're playing, Kat. But it ends now."

She stares me down. No struggle despite the tight grip I have on her throat or the fact that she hasn't taken a breath since I knocked it out of her. Her snowy eyes burn into mine, never looking away.

Fuck.

I loosen my grip slightly, just enough for her to suck in a shaky breath. Her body relaxes against the wall, and her tongue slowly slips out and across her lower lip. Whether done intentionally to draw my attention to the plump, red flesh, or because I almost just strangled her to death, the move has an undeniable effect on me. My already interested cock stands at attention, so rock hard, it actually aches to be inside her.

There's absolutely no reason to trust this woman. *None.* She knows things she shouldn't, and her background is sketchy, at best. I should grab the gun from the drawer three feet to my left and end this. Or just tighten my grip on her throat again, steal the air from her until she suffocates—less mess that way.

But something in the crystal blue of her eyes prevents me from doing it. At least, for now.

Her small, warm hand curls around my hard cock, the long nails of her fingers brushing against my sensitive skin. "Remove your hand from my throat."

I tighten my grip, and she does the same.

Fuck.

The mix of pleasure and pain coursing through my body almost makes me shoot my load against the soft, silky fabric of her dress where it's pressed against the head of my dick.

I tighten my grip and force her chin up even farther. "Why the fuck would I do that?"

Those perfect, wet lips twist up into a knowing grin. "Because you'd much rather fuck me than kill me."

I lean into her, stopping with my lips a mere hair's breadth from hers. "You overestimate my desire to get my dick wet and underestimate my desire to end whatever this game is that you've been playing."

Her dark eyebrows rise. "Have I?"

She tightens her grip on my cock and strokes it slowly to the tip, sending a current straight to my balls. If she keeps that up, this will end before I get any sort of answers. That can't happen. I can't go into business with her without knowing what she wants and why, and I can't kill her for the same reason.

"Tell me how you found me."

A light chuckle spills from her lips. "You think I wouldn't do my research before coming to offer you a partnership? You may think this place is some big secret, but it wasn't hard to find if you know where to look. And just like you, I have people who can find just about anything."

Except any real information on you.

And that's frustrating as hell. It puts me at a major disadvantage—a position I hate and work very hard to avoid finding myself in.

She's probably right, though. Arden could have easily found this place if he were working for someone else, even though I did my best to hide my connection through various shell companies and straw purchases. Maybe I've underestimated her. She's smarter than I gave her credit for.

Another blow to the libido I obviously have no control over when it comes to this woman.

But everyone has a weakness. I just need to get close enough to discover hers. To get her to let down her guard so I can find out the truth.

The way she's been practically throwing herself at me since the moment she walked into my office...maybe *I'm* the one who has been underestimating how much she wants to fuck me. Maybe instead of trying to put out this attraction raging between us, I should be giving in to it, giving in to *her.*

Getting her in the most vulnerable position possible to get what I need.

Time for a change of tactic.

NINE

I BRUSH my thumb across her bottom lip while I dig the fingers of my other hand into her white throat. Instead of struggling or trying to pull away, she strokes my cock and nips at the pad of my thumb.

Game on, kotele.

Time to destroy her until she's forced to reveal everything to me—about herself and her motives.

I capture her mouth and steal her breath. She moans, and I drop my hand from her throat and grasp her thighs. Her tongue probes at my lips, demanding entrance as she twists her hand around my cock and pulls, brushing precum across the head with the pad of her thumb.

Any thought of stopping this insanity now flees when her tongue meets mine. We started this dance the moment she walked through my door. It's time to finish it. To finish her. To end this game.

I lift her from the floor, and she wraps her long legs around my waist and digs her heels into my back. The pressure there only urges me forward, and she directs my cock to the wet heat of her bare pussy and drags the head through it.

A groan slips from my mouth into hers as we wage a war for dominance. This isn't some meek, fragile woman who needs a man to validate that she's beautiful. She knows she is. She knows she's walking sex on a stick, and she's the type of woman willing to use her sexuality to get what she wants. I have no issue with that. I've used everything at my disposal to get what *I* want. And she's using everything at *hers* to get *me*.

Right now, for sex. But there's a bigger game plan here. One I plan to unravel as I tear her apart piece by piece.

Her free hand tangles in my hair, and she directs my cock inside her. The walls of her pussy clench around the sensitive head. I break off the kiss, grit my teeth, and shove into her in one long, hard thrust. She slams back against the wall and gasps. Her eyes roll back, and I pull my cock from inside her and drive back in.

Frantic hands claw at the back of my neck. Sweat dampens my skin. I hammer into her again and again. The head of my cock drags along her G-spot, and she clenches down around me. I shift one hand up to pull the top of her dress to the side and expose her breast. The pink flesh of her nipple is too much to resist. I bend down and bite it as I push into her.

She cries out. Her pussy ripples.

Kat likes a little pain mixed with her pleasure.

And now, she's close.

So close.

But so am I...to getting my fucking answers.

Two more thrusts. That's all Kat gets before I pull out and pin her to the wall with my hips. Her eyes fly open and meet mine.

"You want to come?" I raise an eyebrow at her, and she nods and shifts against me. "Too fucking bad, *kotele.*"

"What the hell are you doing, Michael?" For the first time since the woman walked into my office, there's a tiny waver in her voice. An undercurrent of *need*.

I grab her hands and pin them above her head. "I'm getting the fucking answers I need, Kat. What do you want with me?"

Her eyes widen. "I told you, you fucking bastard. I want to go into business with you."

"Why?" It's a simple question. One she can answer to end this once and for all.

"Why?" She practically spits the word at me. Those pale-blue eyes burn at me, hotter than any flame I've ever looked into. Her lips press into a thin line of determination. "Because I know what you *did*."

What I did?

Any number of deviant acts rush through my mind. I've done more to get to where I am today that will send me on a one-way trip directly to Hell than most people could even imagine.

"I need you to be a little more specific."

She snarls at me and tries to buck me off, but I keep her pinned.

Her lips curl. "Make me."

Fuck.

This woman seems to get off on the challenge. On the tension. On the danger.

She isn't the only one.

"Tell me how you know *anything, kotele*." Like where I live, let alone anything I've done.

A mirthless chuckle falls from her kiss-swollen lips. "I've learned a lot in the few months I've been operating, Michael. I have spies in every camp."

Every camp?

I return my hand to her throat and squeeze. "Have you been spying on *me*?" If she has, I'll kill everyone. It won't matter who the traitor is. Wiping them all out and starting with a clean slate will be the only way to move forward.

"No." She manages to get the word out on a gasped breath.

But I'm not convinced. This woman is a liar. I'm one hundred percent convinced of *that*. So, despite how amazing her pussy feels wrapped around my dick, I'm not getting off or letting her get off until I make myself very clear.

I press my thumb against her jugular, restricting the flow of blood just enough for her to feel it in her head. "If I find out you've been spying on me or have some ulterior motive, I'll make what Aleksander Gashi did to people look like child's play."

A flicker of fear breaks the surface of her glassy, blue eyes. A crack in her armor. Whatever she's hiding, it's big. And I'm going to fuck it out of her.

TEN

KAT STRUGGLES TO swallow against my hold, and I release my thumb from her jugular long enough to let her take a long breath and get some blood to her brain. "Tell me, Kat. Tell me what it is you really want from me."

She swallows thickly but never takes her eyes off mine. The fact that she continues to hold my gaze, looking me dead in the eye, is both unnerving and hot as fuck. It makes me want to drive my cock into this woman endlessly, but giving her what she wants right now would mean I might not get what I want.

"I want it all, Michael. I want the money. I want the control. I want the power. I want to see the fear in people's eyes the same way they feared the Dragon."

Another man's name falling from her lips makes me tighten my grip on her throat.

She stiffens but doesn't fight it. "You can give that to me, Michael. Because I know you're willing to do whatever it takes to get it all." A moment passes where she searches my face before she decides to continue. "I know you set that bomb. I know you were willing to take out all your rivals in one fell swoop. It was bold as hell to just waltz in there, knowing the bomb was about to go off and that you might get hurt."

I freeze but try not to show my surprise. If Kat wants to think I'm responsible for the bomb, let her. If she believes that makes me some sort of mob god, so be it. I've done worse things to get what I want, to get to where I am today. Things that would make a bomb look like nothing.

Those, I don't need to go into. Those are for me and me alone to know.

This woman already knows too much.

I lean in to her and brush my lips over her trembling ones. "You want all of that?"

She nods slowly.

"And what makes you think I'll share?"

With her or with anyone.

Her tongue darts out across her lips, and she gulps. "Because we're two of a kind, Michael. Both of us are willing to take risks and sacrifice to get what we want. We were meant for each other. Meant to be like this." Her nails dig into my shoulder blades. "Please. Give me what I want."

Everything she said is true...

Except for being responsible for the bombing.

But I would've done it. If I had known about the meeting early enough to have had enough time to plan it. Having to run in at the last minute wasn't ideal. And it almost got me killed. Still, Kat's right about us wanting the same things; I just never expected to find a woman built for this. Especially not one with eyes the color of liquid ice and the hottest, wettest cunt I've ever been inside of.

I cup her cheek with my free hand. "Women don't survive long in this world. It's not a safe place to be."

She reaches up and curls her hand around my wrist, my palm still wrapped around her thin neck. "I don't need safe, Michael. Squeeze harder."

Krishti fuck.

I almost blow my load all over her legs at her words, but I reach down and grab my cock, align it with her cunt, and shove into her, slamming her back against the wall again. She groans, the noise sending vibrations to my hand and down my arms, straight to my dick inside her.

GWYN MCNAMEE

This woman is a walking wet dream, and despite every reason not to, I can't seem to keep my hands off her or my cock out of her.

She tightens her legs around my hips and digs her heels into my lower back as I pound into her relentlessly. The frustration of this week and the nightmare of a memory I had just before she arrived, rush out of me with my orgasm and into her. She gasps and drops her head back. Her body jerks, and her pussy clenches and ripples around my cock. The color rising in her cheeks with her release makes me wish I could just keep coming.

With a groan, she goes limp against the wall, and I sag against her, pinning her in place, both of our heavy, panted breaths harsh and hot against each other. She drops her head to my shoulder and licks up my neck to my ear. The sharp bite of pain on my earlobe makes me jerk away from her, and she chuckles.

I tighten my hand on her throat and drag my head back to meet her gaze.

She grins at me and flexes her pussy around my still-hard cock inside her. "That was fun. Want to play again?"

This woman is fucking insane and intoxicating.

And she may like to play the game, but it's a deadly one. I just hope neither of us ends up paying the price for it.

I release her throat, wrap my arms around her, and walk to the bedroom with my dick still buried inside her. She kisses me deeply, and I reach the bed and lower her down onto her back, falling with her. I pull my hips back and drive into her again. She gasps and clutches at the mussed comforter that I kicked away in my nightmare.

Tonight definitely didn't end how I'd imagined it would—drunk and lost in dark, old memories.

This is a much better way to spend my time than wallowing in self-pity and anger.

I kiss my way up her neck to her ear. "If you want to play this game, *kotele,* just make sure you watch your fucking back. I know I'll be watching mine."

ELEVEN

THE DARK-HAIRED GODDESS I've managed to completely lose myself in takes a drag off her cigarette and blows it out in a ring of smoke that floats up from her red lips and hovers in front of her face for a second before it dissipates into the air.

I take a pull off mine and release it slowly, letting the nicotine burn through my blood.

There's nothing like a good smoke after a good fuck. And after spending another hour in the bedroom with Kat, it was time to come up for some air—or some poison for our lungs, I guess.

The brutal images from my nightmare are finally fading, and by the time this cigarette burns down, it will go back to being a distant memory.

Kat shifts her feet slightly where they're tucked to her side on my leather couch, and the white button-down shirt she grabbed off my floor and is wearing wide open rides up her thighs, exposing more of the creamy, white skin there. My cock twitches in the satin pants I pulled on. Knowing she's not wearing any underwear and that we haven't showered—so my cum is still up inside her despite her quick cleanup—makes me want to rush over there and fuck her again.

But other things need to happen here tonight, things that need to be decided. I can't let my attraction to Kat get in the way of business.

She takes another drag, blows out the smoke, and offers me a tiny grin. "So, does this mean we're going to work together?"

One of her dark eyebrows rises as she waits for my answer, dangling the cigarette between two of her fingers.

I take another long inhale and watch her for a moment, searching for any signs of weakness or deception. All I see is the woman who screamed my name and gave herself over to me completely. The one who managed to turn my night around after that dream.

"I think we can probably make this work." The need to qualify that response jumps out of my mouth faster than a bullet. "The business arrangement."

She flashes me a grin. "I knew what you were talking about."

"But, I need to see the operation first, before I commit to anything."

"Of course. I would never expect otherwise."

"Good. And if this ends up working out, I want to move rather quickly." I'm sick of waiting around for my time to come. Playing it safe never got anyone anywhere. I may have let the bomb knock me off course and delay my plans, but that's in the past. The woman in front of me has given me a new path to the future.

She nods slowly. "I agree. Now is the time to strike."

The smile she's giving me carries a sinister tilt.

I'm missing something here.

I lean forward, rest my elbow on my knee, and take another draw from my cig. "Strike at what?"

She pulls her legs down from the couch and crosses them, flashing me her pink, glistening pussy.

It was intentional. No question. The woman wields her sexuality like a sharp sword, and I reach down and adjust my cock before returning my focus to her golden eyes.

"The bombing left everyone in town shaken." She puffs and releases the smoke. "Many lost men or were injured. It's taken time for them to recover. To regain their strength and their balls to make any moves. Now that it's been months with nothing major happening, they're starting to let their guards down again. Their men have been spending more time in my place. Information is flowing like the liquor. And if you know how to use it properly, it could be the way to turn the tide."

I take another pull of my cigarette and lean back in my chair. She's right. It's the same thing I've been saying to my men for weeks. That we need to move. That we need to strike while the iron is hot, and yet, we haven't been doing anything but sitting around with our dicks in our hands because I haven't been able to get any information.

Now *is* the time to make my move. "I'll come to see the operation tomorrow, and we'll get the ball rolling."

She nods slowly, and her too red lips twist into a grin. "I had a feeling things would work out between us."

I raise my eyebrows at her. "Why is that?"

"Because we're the same, Michael. I already told you. We're both willing to do whatever it takes to get what we want."

And that's exactly what scares me about her. The cold, hard look in her eyes that says she'd be just as likely to kill me as fuck me.

I shift my semi in my pants and snuff out my cigarette in the ashtray on the side table. "What time tomorrow?"

"Do you want to sample the merchandise?"

I raise an eyebrow at her. "I thought I just did?"

She chuckles, and the sound goes straight to my cock, fully hardening it. "No," she shakes her head, "I'm not a hooker, Michael. I'm a madame. They are two entirely different things. I run the women, but I don't run myself. What happened here tonight had nothing to do with the business deal."

"Good," I grin at her, "I don't think I could afford your prices, anyway."

She drops her head back and laughs, the sound echoing around the lofted ceilings, then pushes up from the couch and walks over to me slowly. Each step deliberate—the swing of her hips against my shirt and her exposed breasts in the deep, unbuttoned *V* practically call out to me like a siren.

This woman is dangerous. The kind of dangerous that gets a man killed.

She's fucking perfect. And she straddles my legs and sinks down onto my lap, wrapping one arm around my neck as she puts the cigarette to her lips with the other hand to take a drag. She blows the smoke in my face and then kisses me, pushing her tongue between my lips and tangling it with mine.

The familiar taste of nicotine and the bourbon we've been drinking dances across my tongue. When Kat pulls back, my cock strains against her, and she rolls her hips, brushing the heat of her core directly over it.

"No, Michael, you most definitely can't afford me."

TWELVE

THE HOUSE my GPS leads me to on Lake Shore Drive is absolutely the last thing I expected to find today when I arranged to meet Kat to view her brothel location. She snuck out sometime during the night—or rather, early morning—though, I probably would have made her leave as soon as I woke up anyway and realized we had fallen asleep.

I don't do sleepovers. I don't do snuggling and cuddling and I love yous. And I sure as fuck don't leave myself completely vulnerable by letting down my guard and falling the hell to sleep.

Yet I did...with *her*.

But I don't *do* that shit. I'm not that kind of man, and Kat knows it. She's not that kind of woman, either. If she were, she wouldn't run a business like this, nor would she have been able to do what we did last night and again this morning.

The woman is full of surprises...and this is a huge one.

I climb out of my car and up the massive stone staircase to the opulent mansion. Set back from the road behind enormous iron gates, it really is the perfect location—right near the clientele she's trying to attract yet remain inconspicuous. It could belong to any Chicago socialite. Which is, no doubt, precisely why she chose this location.

It's hard to imagine what I know goes on inside these walls.

Debauchery.

Before I even make it to the doors, one swings open, and a huge man with shoulders twice as broad as mine and a nasty scar running down his left cheek steps out. "She's expecting you."

He ushers me in the door to a lavish foyer with a giant crystal chandelier hanging overhead and pristine white-and-gray marble floors. A parlor and a formal living room sit on either side of the entry, and a long hallway leads back to what I can only guess is the kitchen.

I want to explore, but I'm sure Kat will give me a tour later.

The man urges me past another guard at the bottom of a large staircase who doesn't even acknowledge me, and we make our way up. He pauses at a central landing where one set of stairs goes to the left, and another goes to the right and leads me over to the one veering left.

We reach a hallway, and at the second door on the right, he pauses and knocks.

"Enter." Kat's silky voice carries through the door, and my cock stirs at the memories it brings.

That woman's voice is pure velvet. It wraps around you, smooth and soft, and lulls you into a false sense of security—something I definitely need to watch out for.

My escort opens the door and waves me through before closing it behind me. I step into a spacious bedroom with a large, four-poster, canopied bed and a mammoth desk in one corner.

Kat rises from behind it, dressed in a low-cut, slinky red blouse and black linen pants that hang off her elegantly, a grin tilting her lips. With her hair pulled back into a tight bun at the back of her head, she looks every bit the CEO—and not of a brothel. This woman would be at home in any boardroom. Though, it's the bedroom I can't stop thinking about.

"I'm so glad you could make it." She meets me halfway across the room and kisses both my cheeks in a very nonchalant way, like we didn't just fuck each other's brains out only hours ago. "Shall I give you the tour?"

I was hoping you'd offer me something else...

My eyes travel down her long, pale neck and between her exposed breasts.

"My eyes are up here, Mr. Syla."

I drag my gaze up to meet hers. "Maybe it's not your eyes I'm interested in, *kotele*."

Her smile falters, and she pulls back. "This is a business meeting, Mr. Syla. I don't have time for games today."

The rejection and reproach send flames of anger licking over my skin. This woman should know who is in charge at all times, and it isn't her. But I do need her cooperation if I'm going to get access to the information her girls have gathered, which means biting back my rage and libido long enough for her to turn over all her secrets.

So, instead of pinning her against the desk and doing exactly what we spent so much of last night engaged in, I offer her my arm. "Yes, let's do a tour." And I can think of a few things we can do after. "I have to say," I glance around the room, from the colossal fireplace to the expensive furniture, "this wasn't what I was expecting."

She chuckles and motions around the room. "Well, if I were operating out of some fleabag on the Southside, do you really think I'd have the clientele I do?"

"Good point."

It seems she's thought of everything. Beautiful *and* intelligent—a lethal combination.

Kat leads me out of the bedroom and around the top of the stairwell to the other side of the house. "All the client rooms are on this wing. The other wing is my office and bedroom and the girls' private chambers."

"They live here?"

She nods and peeks over at me. "Most of them. Some of them do have their own places, but since I offer them room and board for free, most choose to stay here. The house has enough bedrooms that it's not a problem."

And having them here means they're available twenty-four/seven, and we can keep an eye on them more easily.

"How many girls are working here?"

"Right now?" She pauses to think then continues to lead me toward the rooms along the opposite wing of the house. "Twenty-two. Some part-time; some full-time."

"What do you consider full-time for a hooker?"

She freezes and presses her lips into a firm, hard line before continuing down the hall. "We don't use that word around here."

"Oh. Sorry. I didn't realize we were pretending this was something other than what it is."

A long, slow sigh slips from her red lips. She pauses outside a room with its door open. "It's more about making sure our clients are comfortable, and when they hear that word, it makes them uneasy."

It makes sense. An arrest for solicitation would embarrass anyone, but for the men she's targeting for this venture, it could end marriages and careers.

I nod slowly and peek into the room. A similar four-poster bed to the one in Kat's room occupies the center of the space, flanked by expensive-looking nightstands, a large armoire, and a rug that appears Persian.

"This is one of the client rooms." She points to a door on the far wall. "It has its own private bathroom for the clients, so they can shower and change if they want to." She leads me farther in and stops in front of the armoire. Her arm slips from mine, and she reaches into the pocket of her slim pencil pants and pulls out a key. "Each room comes equipped with an armoire like this that holds some of the toys our clients like to use."

With a tiny smirk, she opens it to reveal a collection of BDSM and other sex implements. Whips, floggers, handcuffs...

I step forward and pull out one of the drawers to reveal an array of vibrators and butt plugs. A thousand deviant activities float through my mind. Things I would love to do to Kat once this tour ends. I hold one of the butt plugs up and examine it. "Do the girls use these on the men, or do the men use these on the girls?"

She chuckles, takes it from me, places it back in its spot, and pushes the drawer closed. "Wouldn't you like to know."

"I would. That's why I asked."

Instead of answering, she just takes my hand and leads me from the room toward the staircase. "They're used in whatever way the client wants to use them. My girls aren't shy or nervous. But if there's anything they're uncomfortable with, all they have to do is say the word, and the client understands that it goes no further. If the client doesn't listen, they're escorted from the building."

I follow her down the stairs and glance at the two large men guarding the front doors. *Escorted from the building.* Likely in a body bag, at least, that's how it will be when I run this place. "Never to be heard from again?"

The tiniest grin tilts the corner of her lips, and she shrugs nonchalantly. "Maybe."

Krishti, that's hot.

She has the same ruthlessness I've built my entire life around. A cold heart. Even colder soul.

I squeeze her hand and pull her to a halt on the midway landing, then lean into her, crushing my lips against her ear. "Have I told you how much I like your style?"

She chuckles and pushes at my chest, playfully. "Now, now, this is a business meeting."

"What about after?"

"That's to be determined."

"By what?"

"By how you behave." She pulls away from me and makes it halfway down the final portion of stairs before I manage to catch up.

I grip her arm and pull her to a stop at the bottom of the stairs. The men at the door narrow their eyes on me, checking to make sure she's okay.

They're good at their jobs, unlike the useless fucks I have working for me.

I brush my lips against her ear again, so the two goons can't overhear me. "If you think I plan to behave, then I think you have the wrong idea about the type of man I am. And I don't think this arrangement is going to work."

She turns her head toward me and offers a coy smile while slowly peeling my hand off her arm. "If I thought you would follow any order I gave you, I wouldn't have asked you to be my partner in the first place."

Fuck, this woman is hot.

And does she ever have a set of balls on her.

She has more ambition and strength than most men in this industry.

Where the hell did she come from?

The mystery is still making me uneasy. I need to follow up with Arden to see if he's been able to find anything...

Like where she got the money to bankroll all this.

THIRTEEN

BY THE TIME she's done showing me the entire grounds, I'm itching to jump at the chance to partner with her...and to jump *her*. Every moment we spend together draws me deeper into her web of seduction. Which was probably her plan from the beginning.

From the moment she walked into my office, all sex and swagger, she knew what she was doing. And she knows she does it well.

The looks. The brush of her hand against me. The sinful smiles she tosses over her shoulder. It was all perfectly executed to have me vibrating by the time we end the tour.

She leads me back into her bedroom and to a door in the corner that I assume is a closet. "I haven't even shown you the best part."

"There's more?" I grab her hips and drag her back against me to kiss her neck. That warm, spicy scent wraps around me, and the taste of her skin in my mouth makes my cock stir against her leg.

"Much more." She shrugs me off and takes another key from her pocket, unlocks the door, and pushes it open.

I don't give a shit what's behind it. The only thing I care about is getting inside Kat right now. But she doesn't move toward me, just stands at the open door, waiting for me to examine whatever is inside.

Holy shit.

The wall of monitors shows every inch of the compound, including the bedrooms, in vivid color detail.

"Are you recording this?"

She leans against the small desk set up under the monitors and gives a sly smile. "I have blackmail material on several major local and state government officials. At least one high-ranking member of the Catholic church. Several married sports celebrities, and a ton of locals who definitely wouldn't want their country club wives finding out what they've been doing here."

I wander over to a row of filing cabinets and pull one open. Plastic boxes containing zip drives labeled with various names I recognize all too well fill it to the brim. I reach in and grab one.

"The governor?" I turn back to her with a raised eyebrow.

She just grins.

"How did you manage to get this type of clientele so quickly? I thought you said you've only been open for a few months?"

She turns back to examine one of the monitors where one of her girls has a heavyset, dark-haired man tied to the four posts of the bed and is working him over with a flogger. "Most of my clients can't get what they want at home and fear going anywhere else because they might be exposed. They feel safe here. Because of the location. The girls. The setting. Because I *make* them feel safe."

"But it's all a setup."

"Not really. It's a legitimate business, and I haven't used anything I've recorded yet. I haven't felt the need. It's really more of a rainy-day fund."

I approach her and push a stray strand of dark hair that's fallen from her tight bun at the back of her head behind her ear. "If we become partners, I'll have to be a silent one. There's no way these people will continue to come here if they know I have a hand in the business."

She nods slowly and rests her face against my palm. "I know. But it's not your face or name I'm after. I need your connections and additional capital to open more locations. This isn't exactly convenient for people on various sides of town, not to mention the suburbs we could be hitting."

The sheer scope of what we might be able to accomplish blows my mind. With cameras positioned carefully at every location, I'll have access to blackmail material on the people who can get me what I want—this fucking city. Government officials. Businessmen with pull and access to things I need and places I want to be. Information from members of every rival organization—the Italians, the Russians, the Irish, and the Colombians. They're ripe fruit prime for picking.

And my mind can't stop turning with the possibilities. "If I can bring in forty or fifty new girls every few months, would you have enough business to keep them busy?"

She barks out a laugh and waves toward the monitors. "Michael, I'm turning away business left and right every day because I can't draw too much attention to this location or my girls. If you give me the girls—*who want to be here*," she stresses the words as a reminder of our earlier understanding, "I'll make sure they're well taken care of. And I'll make us a lot of money and get you what you need to advance your interests."

I brush my thumb over her soft cheek. "I'll get them here."

"I have no doubt."

I glance at one of the screens behind her where a tall, thin man, who looks an awful lot like Senator Mason, fucks one girl while another sits on his face. My cock stirs—though not from watching the sexual escapades happening on the screens, from knowing what having these videos means for my future.

Everything I've ever wanted is within my grasp—all because of this woman.

One I fear as much as I crave.

I lean into her, pressing my erection against her leg. "Now, how about we end the business portion of this meeting."

She chuckles and shakes her head. "I don't do that here, Michael. I don't want people getting the wrong idea."

"But I already know I can't afford you. There will definitely be no wrong ideas."

Her hand at my chest pushes me away playfully. "It's not you I'm worried about. It's the girls and the guards. But I'll see you tomorrow night, I promise. I already have other plans this evening."

Other plans.

My gut tightens. I don't want to think about what or who Kat might be doing instead of spending the evening with me. It's not my business, and if I let feelings get in the way of this business arrangement, things could go south very fast. That's not something I'm willing to risk.

I quickly push away the envy for whoever gets to see her tonight and step back, adjusting my cock away from the zipper of my pants. I don't have any claim on Kat just as she has none on me. If she has a date or something this evening, I'm not going to show her I'm jealous. Sylas are strong. Sylas are merciless. Sylas don't get jealous or let women break them—at least, I won't. I can't fall into the same trap as Grandfather.

"Then, I guess we're done for the day, *kotele*. I look forward to doing business with you, Ms. Adair."

Her red lips curve into a sultry smile. "As do I, Mr. Syla."

FOURTEEN

"So, we're ready to proceed?" Esad doesn't sound convinced.

I lean back in my chair, kick my feet up onto my desk, and take a drag off my cigarette. "If you can get me the boats and the captains, I can make sure we have enough girls to fill them."

Esad's sigh echoes through the phone line. "Fifty per trip. That's a lot of girls to be bringing in."

I release the smoke from my lungs in a large puff. "It is, but it's necessary for what we're trying to do."

It's all about setting up the dominoes so that when one falls, they all do.

With what I'll be able to gather on video and through the men who come to the houses who work for the other families, I'll be able to strike hard, in a way that leaves no room to question who should control this city.

"You don't think the Dragushas or Berishas are going to have anything to say about this? You taking all these girls?"

It's a calculated risk, sending my connections in Albania out to recruit women who might otherwise work for the rival families, but if I'm going to secure my hold on Chicago, it's going to mean taking action back home, too. "If the women choose to come work for me, that's their decision. I'm not forcing anyone. If the Dragushas or Berishas have a problem with that, they know where to find me."

He chuckles low and deep. "Easy for you to say, *miku im*, when you're safely tucked away in America. I'm the one who is here and has to deal with them face to face. If anyone is going to stare down the barrel of an AK pointed at them, it will be me."

"That's true." There's a reason I haven't returned home, and it's not just because of the way the Syla name has been shit on there.

New families stepped into the void left when the Morinas and Gashis left, and the last thing they want to see is me stepping foot in their territory. Still, some things are necessary, including taking risks. "But it's not like I'm exactly safe here, either, Esad."

"Your men not doing their jobs?"

I snort, shake my head, and take another pull before snuffing out my cigarette in the ashtray. "They haven't been doing their jobs for a long time. If they had found out about that meeting before the last minute, I could have prepared instead of storming in there with almost no protection. The bombing wouldn't have blindsided me."

"But it's opened new doors for you, hasn't it?"

"Apparently so. Because Kat thinks I'm behind it." And I'm not about to correct her.

"You still don't know who was?"

I scrub a hand over my face and take a sip of my vodka. "No, and neither do the FBI, the Italians, the Russians, the Irish, or the Colombians. Everyone's in the dark as much as I am."

"It had to be one of them, though."

"It did. The truth will come out eventually. And when it does, someone's going to have a lot to answer for. But in the meantime, we move forward with this plan. You get me the boats and the captains, and I get you the girls."

"What about the docks?"

My hand tightens on the glass until my knuckles whiten. It's the only hiccup in my plan, the one thing I still need to smooth out. "I'm working on it."

Actually, avoiding what I know I have to do. But I will secure what we need.

Esad coughs, the years of smoking and hard living making him sound ancient. "With the frequency we'll be coming in, it will be hard to do it in secret. We'll need a new location. A dock that's less public, somewhere we can control."

I nod. "I have just the place in mind."

"Good."

"No. Not good. Valentina controls it."

"Shit. Are you going to be able to work something out with her?"

I shrug and stare at the clear liquid in my glass. "If I can't, I can just take her out."

Esad barks out a laugh, the line crackling slightly. "And start a war in the process."

"Yeah," I swirl the ice in my drink, "maybe a more diplomatic approach would be wise before I resort to that."

"I would recommend it, *miku im*. Keep me posted, and I'll get everything lined up on my end."

"You do that. I'll talk to you soon."

He hangs up, and I set down my phone on my desk and release a heavy sigh before I swallow the rest of my vodka.

Things are finally starting to come together, but I'm going to need Valentina's help if I'm going to get the girls in the country unscathed. I don't want her or her pirate crew thinking I'm starting up Erjon's trafficking business again, but I need their dock.

I haven't spoken with her since the bombing, and something tells me she's going to be less than receptive to this idea, but I don't have much choice. Sometimes, to get what you want, you need to bend a little. As long as I'm not the one who breaks, I don't care. I can play nice...

Sort of.

A knock sounds at the door, and I groan and drop my feet to the floor. "Come in."

Arden enters, his eyes darting around the room nervously. "You wanted to see me, sir?"

I motion for him to take a chair, and I recline back in mine. "We have a lot to talk about."

"We do?"

He can't be serious.

I'd really hate to have to kill him, but this playing dumb thing is starting to get on my nerves. The man is in Mensa. He shouldn't be this thick-headed.

"I asked you to get me more information on Kat. What have you found?"

He shifts in his seat and rubs the back of his neck. "Not much, sir. I think I may have to go over there, like you suggested."

I slam my palm against my desk and lean toward him. "Then why aren't you on a fucking plane?"

He winces and squeezes his eyes shut. "Because I thought I had a line on her, and then, it disappeared."

Who is this woman, fucking Houdini?

"Well, before you rush off to parts unknown to unravel the mystery that is Katherine Adair, I need you to help me with something else."

"Anything, sir."

"We're going to be bringing in a lot of girls."

His eyes widen. "Erjon's business? I thought you shut that down."

"I did. This is something else. We're going to need paperwork for every new girl coming in. IDs, Social Security cards, driver's licenses, complete fake backgrounds. Because there's no way we can give them all legitimate jobs at the club. They would never believe we need that many dancers. Plus, they'll be working from other locations, and I don't want it to be obvious that I'm connected to it."

He nods slowly and rubs the back of his neck. "I see, sir. I know a guy we can use for this."

"You trust him?"

"I've known him since I was five years old. We grew up on the same street. His parents are from the Vlorë. We can trust him."

While his parents being from the city the Sylas used to control offers some comfort, it doesn't mean he'll be loyal. People will do just about anything for the right price, and using someone new is always a risk.

"We better be able to because we can't afford any fuck ups right now. Not with the FBI still breathing down everyone's neck about the explosion and this new business venture taking off."

"I understand, sir."

"Well," I raise an eyebrow, "go fucking do it."

He leaps from his chair and rushes toward the door but pauses. "I'm going to need photos and basic information on all the girls before he can get to work."

"I'll make sure you have it before any of them get on the boat. That gives him plenty of time to produce everything we need while they're stuck on the ships."

"Good. Thank you, sir."

"And Arden..."

He freezes and turns around slowly to face me.

"I want you on that fucking plane to Vienna as soon as possible. I don't like not knowing who my enemies are, and I hate not knowing my friends even more."

He scurries away with his tail tucked between his legs.

Wherever Kat came from, she came prepared. She knows her business, knows what she wants, and apparently, knows how to get it. She would be a formidable enemy. Which makes me glad I'm on her side.

I wouldn't want to be on the receiving end if I were someone she didn't like.

FIFTEEN

KAT STEPS out the massive double doors and descends the front stairs of the mansion in sky-high heels, the slinky red dress that might as well be a second skin hugging every curve with each sway of her hips.

Each step down she takes makes my cock twitch.

One of her goons follows, holding an umbrella over her to protect her from the rain. She pauses outside my car for him to open the door for her, then slips into the passenger seat, and a sweet scent floats around me, making my mouth water. I lean across the center console and give her a quick kiss before I tear out down the long driveway to the damp road, tires squealing.

A light drizzle falls, making the night darker and murkier than it usually would be and the roads slick. It meets my mood. The one I've been stuck in since she blew me off for her "other plans" yesterday.

She watches me as I turn again and head toward the highway. "Are you in a bad mood tonight?"

Apparently, I'm not doing a very good job of hiding my annoyance from her. But all last night after my uncomfortable call with Valentina to set up our meeting—which was frustrating enough—I couldn't stop wondering where Kat was or who she was with. And climbing into bed alone at the end of a long day with that question still in my head meant I barely slept a fucking wink.

While it might not have been as bad as reliving my violent childhood through nightmares, I'm still feeling my lack of sleep today. I'm exhausted and angry at myself for even caring.

Kat is my business partner, who I enjoy fucking. That's all it is or ever will be.

Don't let this woman fuck with you, Michael.

She's not worth it. There are more important things to expend my energy on. If I learned anything from Grandfather's failures, it's that keeping women in their relegated places is the only way to ensure survival. That requires keeping Kat at arm's length—unless I'm using her as a warm hole to relieve stress.

I shrug and try to look like I don't care. "Not in a bad mood. Just tired."

"Busy night last night?"

I glance at her out of the corner of my eye and catch the playful smile on her red lips. "You're the one with the busy social calendar, not me."

She recoils slightly and chuckles. "Is that why you're all pissy? Because I couldn't spend the night with you? I didn't realize it was some sort of a requirement for us going into business with each other that I become your whore now."

I jerk my head in her direction and scowl at her. "I never said that."

"You didn't have to. You forget what business I'm in. I know how men think and how men like you work."

My hands tighten on the steering wheel, and I focus my attention on the wet road in front of us. "You don't know the first fucking thing about me."

Her hand inches across the center console to my thigh, and she squeezes gently. "I know more than you think."

My mind races back to all the things she knew about me before she even walked into my office, how she found my condo when no one should have been able to, the way she inserted herself into my life so damn easily. Unease creeps across my skin, raising my hair on end. "Are you ever going to tell me where you're getting all your information?"

The fact that she might have a spy in my camp still lingers in the back of my head, despite her assurance that she isn't spying on me.

She shakes her head and squeezes my thigh again, inching her fingers closer to my crotch. "No. What fun would that be?"

"Oh, this is supposed to be fun? Sure as hell doesn't feel fun."

Not when she plays these games and I'm left feeling like an ass. One who has been torn open and exposed.

"Damn," she grins, "you are in a bad mood tonight. Here I thought we were going to go out to dinner and have a nice time."

"We are. I arranged for us to have a very private dinner at a friend's restaurant so we won't be disturbed or seen together in any way that might affect our business plans."

She nods slowly. "So, this is a business dinner."

I clench my jaw and nod.

Her light laughter floats through the car and makes my cock stir. Her hand slips between my legs, and she squeezes the bulge in my pants. "Well, this looks like anything but business."

"You're right. Because, as you keep reminding me, you're not a prostitute."

"You're right. I'm not." She reaches over and deftly unbuttons and unzips my pants, then reaches her small, warm hand in to free my dick before I can stop her.

The car jerks to the side, and a semi in the left lane blares its horn. I maneuver us back into the right lane and grab her wrist. "What the fuck are you doing?"

She leans over the center console and grins at me, her hand tightening around my erection. "What does it look like I'm doing?"

"Trying to get us into a fucking car accident." I glance at the road then back down at her.

A sly smile curls her lips. "I trust you to keep us alive."

"Kat, don't—" The word barely leaves my mouth before she swallows my cock all the way to the back of her throat. "Jesus fucking Christ!"

Instinctively, my eyes close for a second, and I have to force them open and forward so I can stay in my lane. The traffic isn't too bad right now, but this isn't the place to get distracted.

"Shit, Kat. You're going to get us fucking killed."

She swirls her tongue around the head of my dick, and I grit my teeth and clench the wheel until my knuckles whiten. The woman is completely undeterred by the fact that we're hurtling down the highway at a hundred miles an hour. She bobs up and down and sucks my cock like she's parched and my cum is the only thing that can quench her thirst.

The exit signs fly past us, the road and the surrounding city rising on either side mere blurs, and she continues to suck, and lick, and flick her tongue until I can't take it anymore. I grab her hair with one hand and shove her farther down my dick until I hit the back of her throat and shoot my load straight down it. She moans and swallows, the motion of her throat rippling along my cock sending out even more spurts.

I glance up just in time to see our exit and swerve across a lane of traffic to make it as she slowly licks her lips and sits back in her seat.

"*Krishti*, Kat you almost killed us."

She glances over at me with an eyebrow raised in mock innocence. "Does that mean you're still in a shitty mood?"

Despite my heart racing at our near-death experience and the fact that I simultaneously want to strangle her and fuck her right now, I can't help but grin back at her. "No, I'm not in a shitty mood. At least, I won't be until we start talking about what I have to do tomorrow."

"And what's that?"

I tighten my hands on the wheel and peel off the exit ramp onto the road. "I have to meet with Valentina and her dog."

"Her dog?"

"Her boyfriend. Cutter Jackson." I glance over at her as I pull into the parking lot of the restaurant. "Trust me when I tell you, Valentina's dangerous, but Cutter is fucking lethal, so you don't want to cross him."

"Is that what you are planning to do? Cross him?"

That's a good fucking question. One I don't have the answer for yet.

SIXTEEN

This will be the least fun thing I have to do today. Having to make nice with one of your rivals is one of the most painful things in this job, and God knows the last thing I want to do is meet with the woman who might've set off the bomb. One of the people who want me dead. But sometimes in this business, you do things you don't want to in order to get what you need. And I *need* these girls brought in safely before I can make my next move.

So, driving down to the docks to meet with Valentina and Cutter is just an unpleasant necessity. One I take absolutely *zero* pleasure in.

I climb from my car and survey the surrounding darkness. The docks are deserted despite it only being early evening. It's precisely why this place is so perfect. Away from the hustle and bustle of the main port. Nowhere near prying eyes. The ideal location to smuggle in anything—or anyone.

It only made sense to meet here, the place I want to utilize, so I can get a feel of the layout and what it might take to convince her to agree to help me. If I tried to do this over the phone, it would've been so much harder to read her or gauge her reaction. Dealing with Valentina is never pleasant, and after the bombing, I assume she wants to slit my throat even more since I'm every-one's primary suspect.

Her boyfriend/guard/man who does all her dirty work stands just outside one of the enormous warehouse buildings to my left. He sneers at me, and even from behind the reflective aviator glasses he wears, I can feel the heat of hate in his gaze.

I approach him slowly, trying to keep my eyes on him and also everywhere else. Coming without my guards might end up being a bad call. It leaves me exposed, but that was the purpose. Alone, I assure Valentina I mean no harm and have no bad intentions. At least, in theory.

But in reality, it feels like walking in with a target painted on my back.

Cutter scowls when I stop in front of him and crosses his arms over his barrel chest. The shades he wears to cover his scars, even in the dark, look fucking ridiculous, but I doubt he cares.

I nod toward the door behind him. "Is she in there?"

He glances behind me toward my car. "Where is your security?"

The men who failed to stop Kat from walking in my office and then my fucking condo...

My lack of faith in them also played into my decision to come alone today. They haven't exactly inspired confidence recently. I've been protecting myself and watching my own back for most of my life, since the day Lorenc left me, so there's no reason I can't do it now.

I bite back a growl at him and shrug as nonchalantly as I can. Now he knows I'm exposed with no backup. It's the perfect time for someone like him to end me with one shot. The man could probably kill me before I even saw his hand move.

"I can take care of myself."

He chuckles and shrugs, the motion moving his mammoth chest out even more. "If you've got a death wish, who am I to stop you?"

I move to step past him into the warehouse, but he places a firm hand in the center of my ster-num. Heat rises in my blood, and every hair on my body stands on end. I have to physically fight the gut reaction to pull my piece and shoot him in the fucking head. "Get your hand off me if you don't want to lose it."

Cutter forces a saccharine-sweet smile, one that appears especially sinister when paired with the gnarly red scars covering the right side of his face. "No weapons inside."

He has to be fucking joking.

It's bad enough I'm here without backup, but walking in without any way to protect myself is ludicrous.

I chuckle and shake my head. "You expect me to walk in there unarmed when I know you're loaded to the teeth?"

He gives me the tiniest of grins and leans into me. "Kind of sucks when you need something from someone you hate so much, doesn't it? You have to play by their rules."

Every fiber of my being says to turn around and run the fuck away from this, that I can figure something else out that's better than having to deal with this asshole and his demands. But, the truth is, this is the best location, the one we're most likely to be able to use without any sort of interference from anyone, especially the police. I do need Valentina's cooperation, and Cutter knows it. Even though I didn't tell them what the meeting was about, they know I wouldn't be calling if it wasn't something important that I needed from them.

I'm not in control here, and I never wanted to be in this position again.

Old memories flood back without any way to stop them.

Grandfather.

The pit.

The darkness devouring me.

The days and weeks down there.

The "punishments" he assured me I had earned.

I reach into my waistband holster, pull out my Glock, and hand it to him. He takes it happily and then motions toward the door for me to proceed. The old, heavy metal creaks in protest as I pull it open and step in with Cutter hot on my heels.

Valentina stands toward the center of the massive space, armed guards on either side of her, looking every bit the mafia don she is. The blaze-red, skin-tight dress she wears sends a clear message—power. She has it and wants everyone to know. But it also reveals a secret she's managed to keep hidden since the bombing...

She's pregnant.

There's no mistaking the bulging belly or the way she lays her hand on it protectively. I'm sure she would have liked to keep this a secret longer, but it was bound to come out eventually. She can't hide forever. And this may make convincing her of my proposal even easier.

My footsteps echo up through the rafters with my approach.

She raises a hand to stop me a few feet away, and Cutter settles in just behind her on the right. "Let's dispense with the pleasantries, Mr. Syla. Tell me what you want."

I grin at her and avoid looking at Cutter. Very few people on this planet can unnerve me, but that man has ice in his veins in a way that should have frozen him solid years ago. It sends a chill through me to think what he might do if Valentina ever unleashed him, especially now that she's carrying his child. "I need use of these docks."

Cutter snorts and shakes his head. "And what the fuck makes you think she would let you use them?"

Of course, I anticipated she would never agree to help me without some sort of benefit to her organization, and I came armed with an offer. "I will, of course, pay for their use."

He leans over to her and whispers something in her ear, and she bats him away like a fly buzzing around her head. I fight the grin pulling at my lips. As much as I love dominating in this business and in the bedroom, I enjoy watching a strong woman who doesn't let a man take control. And Valentina never seems to let Cutter make her decisions for her. I may not like her or the fact that she stands in my way of taking over Chicago, but I can at least respect that.

She refocuses on me. "What is it you'll be bringing in, and how often?"

I glance from her to Cutter. "If you're wondering if I'm starting up Erjon's trafficking business again, I'm not. I made that agreement with you and am sticking by it. I'll be utilizing the docks for various purposes. None of which will affect any of your current business."

Cutter snorts, and Valentina tosses him a dirty look over her shoulder before turning back to me.

She crosses her arms over her chest, which only emphasizes her large breasts barely contained in the dress. "I have a hard time believing that you would do anything that benefits you that wouldn't hurt me in some way."

I shrug and try to appear unaffected by her response. If she knows how badly I need this, she'll use that to her advantage. "We don't have to have this animosity, Valentina. What have I ever done to you except make a deal with you and stick to it?"

Her red lips press together in a firm line. She can't deny that one. As far as they know, I haven't done anything to disrupt her business, and they'll never find out if I did. I shut down Erjon's trafficking business, as agreed, and kept my hands clean in that regard. It was part of our tentative truce when I took over, and she can't trace anything I've done since then back to me.

But between the bookies, gambling, extortion, prostitution, and other rackets she runs, more Kat's Cradle locations could end up ultimately competing with her. She doesn't need to know that, though. What's a little white lie between friends?

She glares at me, her hard, amber eyes blackening. "I'm not going to let you use the docks, Michael. Money, I have and don't need."

A response I anticipated, which is why I came prepared to offer her something even more significant. "What if I could offer you something else?"

One of her dark eyebrows wings up. "What do you have to give me?"

My eyes automatically drift to her belly, and Cutter growls behind her. This offer will be even sweeter to her, given her condition.

"What if I could get rid of the thorn in your side?" I don't have to elaborate for her to know who I'm talking about. Her relationship with Rose is tenuous, at best. From what I've learned, she only agreed to let him traffic in her area because of a personal issue with one of Cutter's friends. Something she got forced into to save a life rather than through a mutually beneficial negotiated deal. And now that he's expanding his domain and power center, he's unlikely to withdraw from her territory when they reach the end of their agreement without a very bloody fight. One I'm sure she wants to avoid—for herself and her child.

But instead of jumping at my offer, a sneer twists Valentina's lips. "What makes you think I can't remove the thorn myself if I wanted to?"

This time, I bark out a laugh that's so loud, it practically booms around the warehouse. "Because that thorn has been there and festering a long time, and you've had plenty of opportunities to remove it. You're afraid of what his family will do if anything happens to him. And my guess is the bombing turned your tenuous relationship even more fragile."

Cutter stiffens next to her, and his jaw tics. The man is like a coiled cobra ready to strike at any moment. And I'm his intended target.

I smile at them both. "Do we have a deal?"

Valentina studies me for a moment, her toe tapping in her stilettoes. "I'll think about it. That's the best I can do."

She walks past me without another word. Cutter hands my Glock to the man standing next to him, then takes off after Valentina, like a well-trained dog. Her other two goons watch me closely, and once she reaches the door and steps out, one hands me my gun, and they follow her, never taking their eyes off me.

I slip my piece back into the holster and examine the space more closely. The empty warehouse

GWYN MCNAMEE

is perfect for staging the unloading of the ships. We can usher the women off and in here before giving them their documents and getting them into vans for their various locations. This is precisely what I need, and I'll do anything to secure it.

She wants Rose gone as much as I do, and as an added bonus, it would also please the Russians and Irish to have him out of the picture. No one was thrilled when he started pushing his way into town, and one less competitor can only benefit everyone. Killing Rose helps us all. I just hope she realizes that and can set aside her pride to make a decision for the greater good...and for me.

SEVENTEEN

THUNDER RUMBLES ABOVE ME, shaking the metal roof and glass windows of the warehouse while I walk around and examine the various side rooms. This doesn't sound like it's just going to pass over with a quick drizzle.

Shit.

These storms have popped up most afternoons and evenings this week, and they make it cold, damp, and miserable to be outside. I'd much rather be indoors, naked, buried inside a warm body than out in this shit. But maybe if I hurry, I can make it back to the club before the rain hits.

It's time to set some plans in motion. Valentina will take me up on my offer to eliminate Rose. She may play coy and innocent about it; she may deny she wants to act, but everyone knows the truth. Valentina is stuck in a partnership she hates with a man she despises. Ending it for her is the perfect act of good faith, to demonstrate that I'm not a threat to her—at least, not yet.

I've had plenty of time to think about how to remove my competitors, and it will take patience. Especially now that I have access to the videos from Kat's Cradle plus any information the henchmen may have let slip to the girls. I may hate waiting and want to act, but running in guns blazing typically leads to negative consequences, which I can't afford right now.

Everything must go off without a hitch.

The first step is securing the docks and establishing more locations. The second is reviewing all the tapes Kat already has to see what I really have to work with. Then...I can finally start drawing blood until the city of Chicago is bathed in red.

My phone buzzes in my pocket as I make my way from a back office into the main warehouse.

Kat: Call me when you're done with the meeting. I have news.

I immediately call her and start for the door, but the sound of rain pelting the metal roof stops me in my tracks.

Dammit.

In my haste to make it to the meeting, I didn't bring a raincoat. Now I'll be annoyed *and* drenched.

Kat picks up on the third ring. "Hey, how was the meeting?"

I sigh and run a hand through my hair. "It happened. That's about all I can say."

Other than the fact that Cutter didn't kill me on sight, it's the best I could have hoped for, really. Valentina will cave. I have no doubt about that. It's just a show of power on her part not to jump at my offer. She doesn't want to admit she needs my help to keep her hands clean because that would mean she would owe me—something like the use of the docks.

"Does that mean it didn't go well?"

"Well, I'm walking out of here alive, so it went better than it could have, I guess."

She chuckles, and the sound goes straight to my dick. A round or two with her would help ease some of this tension. "Can you meet me?"

"That's why I wanted you to call. I want to go see a house in Forest Glen. It looks perfect from the photos, and if it is, I want to move fast and get an offer in on it before someone else snaps it up."

"How much is it?"

"One point five million."

285

"*Krishti*, Kat, you're going to cost me more than I thought." I scrub a hand over my face and sigh. It really isn't that much in the grand scheme of things. And any investment will be made back ten-fold once we're up and running with the prices Kat charges, not to mention the priceless nature of the blackmail material we'll have at our fingertips. "Okay, I'm still down at the docks right now, but I'll swing by and pick you up, then we can go check it out."

"No, it's okay. I'll text you the address and meet you there. I'm out and about already."

My phone dings with her incoming message, and I pull it back from my ear and glance at the address.

Shit.

I have to cross town at this hour. "I'll leave now, but with traffic, it could be an hour or more."

"No problem. I'm supervising something, and I'll wait if you're not there when I arrive."

I glance out of the small window on the metal door of the warehouse at the black clouds rolling in and the deluge coming down already. If it gets any worse, it could take me even longer to get there. People always drive like morons when it rains, and that's especially true on the Chicago expressway.

"Hey, Kat, bring me some dry clothes, if you can. I have a feeling I'll be drenched."

She laughs. "I'll see what I can do."

It would be just like Kat to bring me a pink shirt and skinny jeans or something else to completely embarrass me just because she can. Something tells me that woman's cold heart extends to humiliation if she has the power in her hands.

"I don't like the joy in your voice at that thought." I step out into the rain and jog to my car while I grab my keys with my free hand and hit unlock. My clothes are soaked almost immediately, and I jerk open the car door and slide in.

My leather seats are going to be fucked.

Kat jostles her phone slightly. "What are you doing after we're done at this house?"

"Hopefully you."

She chuckles again, but the beautiful sound disappears, replaced by squealing tires from behind me.

What the fuck?

No one should be out here at this time of night, but it sounds like someone is in a hurry. I turn to look out my open car door and find two black vans racing toward me across the wet parking lot.

"Oh, fuck!" My chest tightens, and I drop the phone onto the floorboard and reach for my gun.

The side doors of the vans open, and I grab my door handle with my free hand to yank it shut while I hit the ignition button just as automatic rifle fire slams into the car.

White-hot pain slices through my body before I can even get the car in gear.

Crimson blood flows in my narrowing vision.

Then...the whole world goes black.

BLEEDING ENVY

Jealousy is both reasonable and belongs to reasonable men, while envy is base and belongs to the base, for one makes himself get good things by jealous, while the other does not allow his neighbor to have them through envy.

-Aristotle

ONE

THIS IS the kind of darkness you can't understand unless you experience it yourself. One that swallows you whole and obliterates any ability even to remember what light looked like. The kind that eats away at your soul and decimates your sanity with every passing second.

And if the utter blackness isn't bad enough, the hard-packed earth under me doesn't yield, making it impossible to find a comfortable position to lie in. But I'm too weak to sit anymore or even to bother to try to stand. Getting up would be useless, anyway.

The pit is too deep to climb out, the rock walls purposely smoothed so there's no way to get a grip on anything, no way to scale out or seek relief from the despair the place brings.

Grandfather knew what he was doing. When he found it, he immediately recognized its usefulness, how he could twist it to his advantage. He understood what it would take to keep someone down here. The instinct to get out, to survive, makes people do wild things, and he knew what he would need to do to combat that.

Because no one is supposed to get out of here alive.

And Grandfather has thought nothing of throwing countless men down here to their deaths over the years.

Even at my young age, I understand the reality of my situation.

I'm never getting out of here.

At least, not alive.

Grandfather does have the decency to send someone down to get the bodies every once in a while, but I think that's mostly to control the stench that might otherwise waft up and permeate the property. So, eventually, someone will be lowered down this old, abandoned-well-turned-torture-chamber and will lift my corpse by rope into the light again to be dumped unceremoniously into one of the mass graves Grandfather has hidden all over the countryside.

It isn't an act of kindness on his part, more an act of necessity.

Just like breathing, though, I'm tired of even doing that. It's too painful, too laboring. I shift slightly, and pain shoots through my collarbone and down my left arm. I definitely broke it when I landed. And my bruised ribs from the beating the other day when Lorenc left make it difficult to breathe the dank, frigid air. When I do manage to inhale, it's so cold, my entire body shudders, only restarting the endless loop of agony.

It won't be long.

I'm too small. Too fragile to survive for any length of time.

One of the many reasons Grandfather hates me so much. He expects his grandsons to be strong and hard leaders. Ruthless—like him. He doesn't tolerate weakness, and it seems everything I do he sees as proof that that's exactly what I am.

Weak.

He's probably right.

I caved so easily when he asked where Lorenc was...

Another agonizing shiver rolls through my body, remembering the confrontation. It makes every broken bone in my body scream in protest, and I grit my teeth but can't fight back the tears.

I should have run. As soon as Lorenc walked out that door, I should have followed him, whether he wanted me to or not. I could have stowed away. I could have found something else to do to get away from Grandfather.

If I *had* run...

If Lorenc *hadn't* run...

I wouldn't be here.

"*Where is your brother?*"

"*I don't know.*"

"*Don't lie to me, djale i vogel. You know where he is.*"

I struggle against the hold he has on me, but he's too big, too strong for an eight-year-old boy to have any chance. "I don't know, Gjyshi. I don't."

"*You're lying." His blow knocks the wind from my lungs and sends pain so strong through my body that I vomit, which Grandfather only sees as another sign of weakness. He squeezes my jaw between his fingers so hard that his nails bite into the skin. "Where is your brother? The next time I ask and you don't answer, you're going down into the pit.*"

A shudder of revulsion rolls through me, more bile climbing my throat. "No. Please. Not that. Anything but that."

The blow to my face comes so fast that I don't have time to block it or brace myself. Agony slices through my jaw. Tears flow freely down my cheeks, now impossible to stop even if it might save me some additional pain.

"*America." The word comes out on the quivering gasp. The last bit of air I have left in my lungs. My defeat.*

Grandfather's eyes fly wide, his bushy eyebrows shooting high. "America? How?"

"*The Morinas.*"

His hold tightens, and he slams me back against the wall behind me. "The Morinas? Are you telling me he went to those fuckers for help?"

I nod slightly, his sneer visible even through the tears warping my vision.

"*You knew, and yet, you didn't wake me to stop him." His hand closes around my throat. "You're fucking weak. Just like your father was. And so, I'm going to do the same thing to you that I did to him."*

No!

I try to scream, but his hold prevents me from making any sound other than a strangled groan.

He easily lifts me and marches me over to the raised stones that mark the edge of the pit. I'd always suspected father's death wasn't at the hands of one of our rivals like we had been told, but I was too young to question it. Too afraid to confront the old man we knew had killed him to get the truth.

Now, I know...

And I'm going to die the same way.

He dangles me over the pit, a satisfied grin curling his lips, nothing but rage and hatred in his dark, menacing eyes. "Enjoy your stay in Hell, you useless piece of shit."

And then...he let's go.

The memory is so fresh, it's almost like it's happening again, even though it had to have been a week ago—maybe more.

It feels like falling forever. The rush of air around you while you're bracing yourself for the impact you know is coming. Barreling downward toward the hard ground hidden in the darkness. It's coming. Every second that ticks by brings you closer. But it still knocks the air out of your lungs and blindsides you no matter how much you try to prepare yourself.

I don't know how long I was unconscious.

And it doesn't really matter.

Time has no meaning here in the blackness.

But at least I'm not alone. Pain is my constant companion—a searing fire blazing over my skin and through my bones so deep that it threatens to burn me alive.

This must be Hell. Just like Grandfather said when he tossed me down here. This must be me paying for everything I've ever done in my life.

"Michael?"

My name floats to me on a whisper.

So far out of reach, the word is barely audible.

I try to turn my head toward the voice—a vaguely familiar one—but that only renews my agony.

"Don't move." The command is louder. Closer. Right near my head, though, the blackness surrounding me prevents me from seeing who it might be.

I want to fight against it.

I want to crawl my way out.

I want to know who it is and how they found me here...

But the darkness drags me under again.

TWO

THE PAIN finally forces a break in the darkness—a strange combination of bone-deep aches and constant throbbing marked with sharp stabs and twists to the left side of my body.

I groan and force open my eyes against the agony that begs me to keep them closed.

"Michael?" Kat's voice floats through the air, soft, almost lyrical.

Angelic.

But that woman is far from an angel. I stiffen immediately.

The darkness of the room isn't much different from the darkness I just came out of. I hadn't even known she was here.

Wherever here *is.*

I scan the room, but my eyes won't focus, especially without lights. A thick, gloomy fog bogs down everything; it seems impossible to break free.

Where the hell am I?

And why does it feel like a train has hit me?

I try to push myself up. The motion makes my stomach turn, and I swallow back the threat of vomit that will only make the pain worse.

A small, soft, warm hand presses gently against my chest, urging me to lie back down. "Don't try to sit up."

"What the fuck happened?" My voice comes out hoarse, barely audible, my throat so dry, it feels like I've been walking in the desert for weeks without water.

"That's what I want to know." Kat reaches to her side and produces a cup that she tips to my lips, letting me take a much-needed drink of cool water. "What do you remember?"

I reach up and scrub my right hand over my face, but the movement pulls at something attached to the top of it and at something painful on my left side. I wince. "Meeting with Valentina at the docks..."

Squealing tires. Gunshots.

Fuck.

Kat flips on the bedside lamp, illuminating my bedroom with dull, artificial light.

I blink away the spots in my vision and try to focus on her. "How the fuck did I get here?"

Her normally cold icy-blue eyes stare back at me with a softness I've never seen there before. "Our call was still connected when they started firing. Then you didn't answer, so I hung up and called the club and told the guys what happened. They were able to get down there before the police arrived and get you to Dr. Demiri. He worked on you for hours, pulling pieces of bullets and metal shrapnel from the door out of you and stitching you up. The one in your upper arm was a few millimeters from an artery. If it had hit it, you would've bled out before anyone got there."

"Fuck." I squeeze my eyes closed and try to take a full-body assessment.

It's too hard to tell. Everything hurts.

And the anger welling up from deep in my gut is only tensing my muscles and making things worse.

"Who the fuck did this?"

Kat leans forward in her chair, resting her arms on the side of the bed. "We were hoping you could tell us. Do you think it was Valentina?"

I suck in a deep breath and immediately regret it as my chest tightens painfully. "No. If they wanted me dead, I walked into that meeting without a weapon. Cutter or any one of her guys could've taken me out easily and ensured it was done properly. This was sloppy..."

The Russians? The Irish? Rose and the Colombians?

The fucking possibilities are endless. And I can't just lie in this fucking bed like a sitting duck, waiting for whoever it was to make another move.

Kat watches me, her dark eyebrows drawing up.

Kat...

We were talking...

I was on the phone with Kat...

Fuck!

I grit my teeth and push myself up into a sitting position with my right hand. The room spins, a murky haze fading into the edges of my vision. Kat's eyes widen as she reaches out for me, but I knock away her hand, ignoring the stab of pain that causes. I throw back the covers. Something tugs on my arm. An IV. I rip it out from my forearm, and blood spurts across the sheets. But I don't give a fuck. There's no time to worry about a little gore right now.

Whoever did this to me is going to fucking pay.

"Michael, stop!"

I grab the nightstand and push to my feet. My knees almost buckle under me. The world tilts obnoxiously, threatening to drag me down. Blood drips to the floor, now flowing freely from my arm. It strikes my bare foot, warm and wet. I squeeze my eyes closed, clench my jaw, and take a step.

"You lost a lot of blood. You need that IV. Get back into bed."

"Fuck you, Kat."

I stumble forward and grasp the wall to keep my body from collapsing in on itself. Everything that happened at the docks jumbles together in my head. Cutter's scowling threats. Valentina's disdain. The two huge men she had with her. The storm. Kat's text...

"How do I know it wasn't you?"

"What?" She jerks to her feet and rushes around the bed, but I'm already staggering toward the door, one hand against the wall for support.

The white bandages wrapped around my torso constrict my chest, and I can't move my left arm. But at least my legs seem to work, somewhat. Enough to let me get away from her—the very real potential threat in my fucking bedroom.

Where are my men? Genti and Driton? Anyone?

Kat's heels click across the floor behind me, the sound suddenly ominous and echoing in my head. "Michael, what's going on?"

I snarl at her, baring my teeth over my shoulder like a fucking wounded animal ready to attack. My head spins, images and sounds flooding together—the past and present merging violently. "I don't know that it wasn't you. You're the only person who knew where I was going."

She freezes behind me. "Fuck you, Michael. If I wanted you dead, you would be. I've had more than enough chances, and you know that."

I reach the bedroom door just as the world around me seems to twirl on some unknown axis. The fingers of my right hand clutching the jamb are the only things that keep me from falling over with the wave of nausea. Blood drips at my feet. "Not any chances that could've made it look like someone else did it. It was the perfect opportunity for you while I was meeting with one of my sworn enemies. Who wouldn't jump on that?"

Kat points to her chest, her other hand propped on her hip. "Me, Michael. I wouldn't take the opportunity. Why would I want to kill my business partner?"

"How the fuck should I know?" I roar the words at her, blinking my eyes to try to get them to focus so I can keep moving forward. Away from her. Away from the threat. "I don't know anything about you."

As much as I hate giving her my back and offering her the opportunity to finish what she potentially started, I have to get out of this fucking room. I stumble into the living room and grab the end table to prevent falling. My feet won't cooperate, won't move forward. Practically dragging them, I grip the back of the couch and use it to maneuver into the kitchen, where I crank on the cold water in the sink and splash some of it onto my face with my right hand—my left dangling at my side.

My legs wobble, and I grip the edge of the counter, drop my head, and try to regain control before I pass out. The room tilts, and the darkness threatens the edges of my vision again. I squeeze my eyes shut.

What the hell is happening?

Faces float against my eyelids. Images. Of all the people with reasons to want me dead.

Everyone in that room when the bomb went off...

Everyone I wronged back in Albania to get here...

So many, it feels like whirling on an amusement ride, trying to catch glimpses of those standing around it...

"Michael." My name comes soft but forceful. Directly behind me. "You have to get back into bed. You're not doing yourself any favors like this."

"No." I clench my fist on the countertop, still keeping my back to Kat.

The knife block sits to the right of the sink. If she comes at me in this state, I'm a sitting fucking duck, but at least I have a weapon nearby. One well-placed stab is all it would take if I need to defend myself.

I suck in a breath. "What I need is to figure out who the fuck did this to me." *And get the fuck away from you.* "I'm going to the club."

"No. You're not. You can barely stand up. The only place you're going is back to that fucking bed."

"I'm fine." The words sound like a weak lie even to my own ears, and when I glance over my shoulder at her, the whole world flips upside down.

My legs crumple.

Her small arms wrap around me and support as much of my weight as she can, my hand still on the counter, the only thing keeping me from hitting that cold tile floor.

She sighs. "Come on, let's get you back to bed."

Fuck.

THREE

KAT HELPS LOWER me onto the bed, and I can't bite back the strangled groan as I sink into the mattress. The discomfort doesn't subside with the new position, but at least the world isn't spinning anymore. If she hadn't grabbed me, I would have ended up face-first on the floor, and I'm confident I couldn't have gotten up.

She steps back and releases a heavy sigh, one hand propped on her hip while the other pushes through her thick, dark hair, which is free of its usual tight bun. "If you keep acting like this, you're going to make things worse."

Closing my eyes, I try to ignore her comment.

I don't need a fucking mother.

I've never had one, and it's never been a problem before. I definitely don't need one now. What I need is a fucking smoke and to get my bearings. I wave Kat off with a flick of my right hand. "Go."

"I'm not leaving you here alone."

"Yes," I grit my teeth and shift slightly, a lightning flash of pain stabbing at my side, "you are. Get the fuck out."

This woman is more infuriating than actually being shot.

"Michael, I'm not leaving you alone. Dr. Demiri will come back and check on you in a few hours, but I told him I would stay and call if there was a problem between now and then. I'm not leaving you by yourself, no matter how hard you try to get me out of here."

"Fuck." I growl and roll onto my back, every movement sending shards of glass through my body. "How many times was I shot? It feels like a million."

She sighs and lowers herself into a chair at the side of the bed, then grabs my arm and presses something against the spot where I ripped out the IV. "Four. And it could've been a lot worse. According to Genti and Driton, there were an awful lot of holes in that car."

Flashes of the day flit through my head. The sound of the tires on the wet pavement. The side doors of the van sliding open. Bullets striking the driver's side door.

"I was pulling it closed when they opened fire."

"Probably what saved your life. The shots shredded the metal like it was nothing. Most of the bullets grazed you—two in the arm and one in the shoulder. Then one went through your left side but didn't hit any bone or organs. Really...it was a miracle." She narrows her eyes on me. "But you don't remember anything that might help us identify who it was?"

I grit my teeth and shake my head. The van was dark and non-descript. And the faces of the men who opened the door were covered by black masks. "Nothing."

"It's time for you to take more pain medication."

"No." That will only make it harder to function. I need to be sharp right now...at least, as much as possible.

"Michael, please don't fight me on this. You were shot less than twelve hours ago and had major surgery to pull bullets and shrapnel out of your fucking body. You need pain medication, or you might go into shock."

I don't want anything that's going to dull my mind and senses. Nothing that will leave me even more vulnerable around anyone.

Even Kat.

Especially Kat.

Not when I don't know who just tried to fucking kill me. "I'm not taking it."

Even though the agony is starting to turn my stomach against me. Even when the darkness narcotics will bring is so damn inviting despite the memories that always come with it.

Kat pulls away whatever she has pressed against my arm, and I glance down at it. The bleeding seems to have stopped, which is probably a good thing. Losing more blood can't be beneficial.

She grabs something off the nightstand, shoves a pill into my hand, and holds up a cup of water. "Take it. You won't do yourself or anyone else any good if you wear yourself out or go into shock or something stupid that you could've prevented."

Shit. She's probably right.

It may be necessary now so I can get to work tomorrow on hunting down whoever was stupid enough to try to take me out without ensuring they actually succeeded. They've only poked the bear, who is already starving and rabid.

I pop the pill into my mouth and pull the cup to my lips long enough to swallow it down. Kat sets it onto the nightstand, and I relax back into the mattress, waiting for the blackness to take me again.

She grabs a pack of smokes off the nightstand and lights one, then puts it to her lips and takes a long, slow pull from it. The cigarette dangles from her fingers, looking so damn tempting.

"Lorenc is your brother, right?" Her question sounds hesitant, almost like she wasn't going to ask it but forced it out.

What the hell? Why would she be asking about him?

I freeze and let my gaze meet hers. "Yeah. Why?"

"You were mumbling his name. A few times before the doctor put you under and as you started coming around again. And something about your grandfather. It didn't sound too complimentary of either of them."

As if being stuck in bed with bullet holes littering my body isn't bad enough, now she wants to talk about family dynamics. I don't think so.

Her gaze darts down to her cigarette, and she takes another drag and sighs, the smoke puffing out from between her lips. "You know you can tell me things, Michael."

"Why would I want to do that?"

She snorts and shakes her head. "I don't know, maybe so I can get to know you?"

"That's not anything you want to know about. Trust me."

It's not anything *anyone* should hear. And certainly nothing I want to relive by rehashing every bloody and sordid detail with Kat.

"I wouldn't be asking if I didn't want to know, Michael."

I let my eyes drift closed, trying to remember back to whatever I may have been dreaming about while I was under.

Flashes of the familiar cool, dark place break through.

Watching Lorenc walk away...

The pain...

Only now, a soft, warm, fuzzy feeling floods my system.

Calming.

Peaceful.

My mouth opens almost of its own accord. I don't want to tell her, but something prevents me from holding up the dam that's always kept my secrets locked away.

"Lorenc and I were close growing up. Our grandfather helped raise us after our mother died giving birth to me. Our father died a few years later."

It feels like such a long time ago, yet at the same time, like it was only yesterday. Grandfather walking in and saying Father was gone but offering little more in the way of an explanation.

"We always suspected Grandfather had killed him. But I didn't get confirmation of that until the day Lorenc left."

"What do you mean *left?*"

The medication she practically forced down my throat melts away my inhibitions and tears open the oldest of wounds. "He left. In the middle of the night. Packed all his stuff in a duffel bag and came to America to work for the Morinas. He didn't even look back when he walked out on me."

My voice cracks slightly during that last sentence, but I won't acknowledge it. Won't look at her. I don't want to see the pity in her eyes. The pity for the small, naïve boy who wrongfully believed he was the most important thing to his brother.

"He didn't take you with him?"

I shake my head. "He said he couldn't. I begged him. I pleaded for him to take me and not to leave me with Grandfather. Because I knew what that meant. I knew what that man would do when he found out that Lorenc left."

Her warm hand presses against my side, grounding me back in the present. "What did he do?"

More like what didn't *he do…*

FOUR

I'VE NEVER TALKED to another living soul about what Grandfather did to me. The only one who knows is Esad because he witnessed it with his own eyes. Even after Lorenc reached out, years later, needing help and information, I didn't tell him what his selfishness had caused. It was in the past. It had already molded me and set me on my path. There was no use whining about it, especially to the person who let it happen.

"Saying my grandfather was a cold man would be the ultimate understatement. He may not have always been that way. I don't have any way of knowing that. But by the time we were growing up with him, things had started to go so bad that it had pushed him to a volatile tipping point."

"What do you mean, things went bad?"

Kat has always seemed to know things she shouldn't. She's always been one step ahead. It's odd she doesn't know the Syla history, given all the background information she's dug up on me. But with the drugs coursing through my blood and her soft hand gently stroking my sensitive skin, I can't question it now.

"Do you know anything about what happened to my family in Albania?" I drop my head to the side and open my eyes to meet her gaze.

Her lips twist, and she shakes her head as she snuffs out the cigarette in an ashtray. "Not really. Just that the family was once very powerful."

I nod slowly. "We were one of three families who pretty much ran the whole country. Our territory was the coast, headquartered in Vlorë. Grandfather and his father had established a reputation for being ruthless. He took over from his father and operated relatively easily with little pushback from rival operations for decades. The Morinas and the Gashis had their own territories and rackets. It was understood that they wouldn't cross a certain imaginary line."

"So, what happened?"

"The Morinas got greedy, wanted more, and they knew Grandfather had predilections for a certain type of woman. Young, beautiful, and naïve. Someone he could twist and mold and who wouldn't fight back. The moment my grandfather met Agron, Morina's oldest daughter, he knew he wanted her for himself. And once he set his sights on something, there was no denying him what he wanted. If you tried, you suffered an unspeakable fate."

One I was so close to myself. Because of Lorenc and the Morinas.

"When was this?"

I rub my eyes, memories assaulting my drug-fogged brain. "A few years before I was born, Morina used her like a Trojan horse. Sent her in to seduce a volatile, angry, obsessed old man so she could report back to him about the inner workings of the family business."

"Jesus...what happened?"

"Grandfather fell for it—hook, line, and sinker. He believed she had fallen in love with him. Never questioned it for a moment. And he let her in. Into our inner sanctum. He opened up and told her everything about our operation and helped build the arsenal that brought him down."

Which is precisely why I can't let this woman get under my skin. Even weak. Even drugged up and near passing out. This story should be a warning to her.

Not to fuck with the Sylas. Not to fuck with me.

She brushes her fingers over my hipbone, and despite all the anger and agony, my cock twitches. "How did it end?"

"The Morinas finally took him down with the help of the Gashis."

Her hand momentarily stills before she clears her throat and waits for me to continue. It's the second time she's reacted to the mention of the Gashi family. She clearly knows their reputation.

"They were powerful allies, and together, they had decided Albania wasn't enough. They expanded into the US—here and in Philly. And they agreed to split Albania once the Sylas were gone. Which is what they did, though the Dragushas and Berishas have essentially taken over since the Morinas and Gashis have been all but wiped out."

"Why didn't they kill your grandfather?"

I snort and sigh. "They would have if they had been able to get to him. He and Father tried to fight the coup. They took out many of the Morina and Gashi men before the smoke cleared. But it was too late. Our allies were gone. Our territory lost. Grandfather ran with his tail tucked between his legs and dragged us with him. And he was never the same."

The pain of his fist connecting with my ribs hits me so hard, I cringe away from her touch.

It's just a memory.

The drugs are playing tricks on you.

"Michael? Are you all right?"

It's time for her to understand who the Sylas really are. Who *I* really am.

"Grandfather became even more brutal. More driven. More of a monster. He struck without warning and killed without remorse. Even hidden away on the land he found in the middle of the countryside, he never let up being the boss his father raised him to be. His favorite torture device was something called the pit."

I swallow through a suddenly dry throat and shift farther away from where Kat sits. If she's going to hear this, the last thing I want is her feeling the need to comfort me over something that happened twenty years ago. I don't need or want her pity. I want her to understand.

"It was just an old well. One Grandfather modified for his own uses. He enjoyed throwing people down there to teach them a lesson. A permanent one."

Her sharp intake of breath assures me she understands what that means.

"I don't think anyone ever got out of there alive. Except me." My words hang in the air between us, heavy and thick with tension.

She wanted to know the truth. Well, this is all of it. Every dirty detail.

"I would have died down there. I was broken. Physically and mentally. On the verge of death. It had been over a week. The only reason I survived was it rained, and I drank dirty water from the ground. Then my friend, Esad, realized he hadn't seen me. He came looking in the one place he hoped *not* to find me. And he risked his own life to get me out."

When he called down to me in the pit, I thought it was a hallucination. An angel guiding me to Heaven or a demon playing a trick on me to drag me to Hell finally.

"He got me out and brought me to his home. Then Grandfather showed up. Only instead of killing me like I thought he would, he apparently saw my ability to survive all that as strength inside me that he hadn't known existed. So, instead of ending my life as he had intended, he trained me."

I turn my head and meet her gaze again. She needs to be looking me in the eye when I say these words. It's the only way for her to understand the lengths that I will go to. A final warning to her.

"When he tried to lay a hand on me again a few years later, I stabbed him in the gut twice and dropped him into the fucking pit."

FIVE

My phone rings on the nightstand, breaking through the foggy haze of drug-induced slumber. That warm, weightless feeling of deep sleep brought on by narcotics slowly lifts until I'm suddenly jolted into reality by the sound of the phone again.

When did I fall asleep?

The last thing I remember was the hard stare Kat gave me when I told her how I killed Grandfather.

Then...nothing.

No nightmares. No dark memories. Just sweet, peaceful, unbroken sleep. I can't even remember the last time that happened.

The shrill ring sounds again, and I grit my teeth and roll to the side to grab it. I open my eyes to a dark room again, with Kat nowhere in sight.

Hopefully, she got the message and decided to leave before she ended up on the same end of the knife Grandfather did. I turn the phone toward me and blink against the harsh light of the screen until my eyes can focus on the number.

Well, isn't this interesting.

I swipe to accept the call. "Valentina."

"Michael." My name comes cool and calm, without the usual edge of disdain it typically holds from her.

"To what do I owe the pleasure?"

Given what happened immediately after the last time we saw each other, I can only imagine what she believes I must be thinking and on the verge of doing.

She clears her throat—an odd move for the woman who so rarely shows a crack in her rock-hard demeanor. "I thought it best we talked as soon as possible."

"Oh, really," I grab the pack of cigarettes and lighter off the nightstand and lower myself onto the mattress again with a bitten-back groan, "why is that?"

I want to hear her say it.

"I wanted to make it clear to you that I had nothing to do with what happened."

I tuck the phone against my ear with my right shoulder, shove a cigarette into my mouth, and manage to get it lit with my right hand. My left arm still hurts too much to move. I take a long drag, letting the nicotine my body craves so much course through my blood before I respond. "Why should I believe you, Valentina? Your dog has made it clear how he feels about me, and only a few months ago, you were at a meeting with our competitors to form a plan about how to take me out. It seems only logical you finally took the opportunity to follow through on it."

"It *wasn't* me, Michael. If you had come into that meeting earlier, you would have seen and heard that I was trying to stay out of it while the rest of the families wanted blood."

I snort and squeeze my eyes shut against the twinge of pain it causes, then take another pull. "Stay out of it? No, let's be honest, Valentina. You were hoping somebody else would do the job so you could keep your hands clean. You were never *out* of it."

Valentina offers a moment of silence while considering my accusation. "I'm not going to play games with you. It's true. What you've been doing since you took over makes everyone nervous. And you don't seem to want to play nice."

"I played nice the other day, unlike someone else."

"It *wasn't* me, Michael." Anger hardens her voice, the force with which she throws the words at me almost physical. "You know that I had plenty of opportunities to do it in that warehouse without anyone seeing it or creating a scene like a drive-by shooting would. Don't you think I would've taken the opportunity when I had it if that's what I really wanted?"

It's a nice argument, but Valentina is smart enough not to kill someone on her territory, not when it could so easily be traced back to her by the police, the FBI, or anyone else who bothered to investigate it.

I take another drag off the cigarette and blow the smoke out in a long puff. I'm sure Kat and Doc would have a field day with my smoking right now, but I need it, regardless of whether or not it's good for me. "What *do* you really want, Valentina? Other than to protest your innocence, why are you calling?"

She releases a heavy sigh. "I've given your proposal some thought."

Now we're finally getting somewhere.

It isn't like Valentina to beat around the bush, so she obviously isn't one hundred percent confident with her decision. "And?"

"As a show of good faith to let you know once and for all that I had nothing to do with what happened, I'm willing to give you use of the docks."

A grin pulls at my lips, one I never would let her see if we were meeting in person, but here, in the privacy of my room, I can react to the news I so badly needed.

Whether she's doing it out of guilt because of her involvement—which I still heavily doubt—or whether she realizes what an asset I can be as an ally now doesn't really make a difference to me.

All that does matter is that I have what I need.

"Wonderful news, Valentina. And as for the offer I made to you in exchange?"

I won't say the words over the phone. Not when anyone could be listening despite the fact that we're careful about keeping our phones encrypted. I snuff out my cigarette and wait for her to say the words I've been anticipating.

She clears her throat. "There have been quite a few thorns in my side since taking over from Arturo. One in particular...I wouldn't mind if it got plucked."

Exactly as I anticipated—my offer to take out Rose was far too enticing for her to pass up.

"I can make sure that happens."

"Just make sure it's done cleanly, without any collateral damage."

Her warning is clear. Valentina can't have any of the other families knowing that she made that call, nor can anyone find out she gave me the use of the docks. She doesn't want anyone aware that she's been commiserating with the enemy. If any of her men ever leaked it, it could cause real trouble for her with the Russians and Irish, who have had a peaceful agreement in place for decades with the Italians.

"I'll get it taken care of, as discreetly as possible. It's been a pleasure doing business with you, Valentina, as always."

"I wish I could say the same." She ends the call.

I drop my phone onto the bed next to me. The conversation has only reinforced my belief that Valentina had nothing to do with the shooting. Which means I need to figure out who did. I can't stay in this bed indefinitely, waiting for answers to appear.

It's time to act.

I grab my cell and dial.

Genti answers on the third ring. "Boss?"

"Be at my place with Driton in the morning."

"Sir?"

No doubt Kat has informed the crew about the doctor's orders—I'm to remain in bed for at least a week. Taking it easy. Nothing that could aggravate my wounds or get me too worked up.

The man doesn't know me if he believes I'm going to abide by that—Kat, either. Though the fact that she felt comfortable enough to disappear suggests, she thinks I won't do anything stupid like try to leave myself.

But my plan doesn't work if I stay in this fucking bed.

"We're going to find out who was behind the shooting." And I already have a plan to do just that. "Listen to what I need for you and guys to do tonight."

SIX

"YOU REALLY SURE you're up for this, boss?"

I cast a glare at Genti and issue a low warning growl, blowing out smoke in his face. "If you intend to keep questioning me, then you can get the fuck out of here right now and pray I never see your face again."

He holds up his hands for a second and backs away a step, peeking at Driton, who is smart enough to keep his mouth shut. "Sorry, boss. It's just...it's only been two days."

Two long days of wondering who shot me and why. Though any number of people have very valid reasons to want me dead, the pool of who could have pulled it together and potentially discovered information about the meeting is small.

And I plan to have answers today.

I do my best not to stumble down the hallway, walking slowly and deliberately with my head held high and my shoulders back as far as they'll go, given the damage to my entire left side. But with the feeling in my wounded arm still coming and going with this strange burning and tingling, it's hard to stop myself from curling in slightly despite my best efforts to appear completely recovered.

I don't have any other choice but to be okay. For what I'm about to do, I can't show any weakness. I can't let them think there's any chance of getting one over on me. They have to know I'm just as lethal as always and willing to do what needs to be done—maybe even more so.

We pause outside our destination, and I take one final, fortifying drag off my cigarette before I nod to the men, drop the butt, and snuff it out under my shoe. Driton reaches for the knob, turns it, and pulls open the door to a room at the small warehouse I keep just for these occasions. Once I finish, they'll torch the place and eliminate any evidence we were ever here and of what we were doing. I step into the room with Genti and Driton at my back and scan the three men tied to the chairs in front of me.

Oleg Abramov—all-around asshole and Valerian Kamenev's right-hand man at the top of the Russian's Chicago empire. Padraig Byrne—enforcer for the Irish and cousin to Galen McGinnis, the man who calls all the shots in their organization. And finally, Santiago Parra—Rose's lackey and confidant.

It only took a few hours for my men to track them down and catch them in a position to take them—unlike Rose, these men aren't afraid to be seen in public and flaunt their power. But now that they're here and I'm strong enough to get out of bed without immediately passing out, my work can begin.

Oleg eyes me and struggles against his binding. "*Ty grebanyy mertvets.*"

I chuckle and shake my head. Moving isn't any less painful today than when I woke yesterday, but now I can fake it better than I did then. At least I can stand and move as if what happened to me didn't almost put me six feet under. "As you can see, Oleg. I'm *not* a fucking dead man. Far from it."

His threat—that I'm a fucking dead man—is meaningless, anyway. He's not in a position of power. He can't do anything but spit angry words. Even with four fucking bullet holes in me, I'm the one calling the shots here. He can thrash and threaten all he wants. It's only more entertaining for me. And the angrier he gets, the more likely he is to slip up and tell me what I want to know.

I take a step closer to him and rub my chin with my right hand. "But it's interesting you should say that. Because that's precisely what I'm here to talk to you about today."

Oleg sneers and spits at me.

"Like I'd tell you anything even if we did have something to do with it." Padraig's thick Irish accent grates in my ears.

I hadn't expected him to speak up, and I turn to him with a grin. "Oh, but you *will* talk. All three of you will. Because you don't have a choice."

One thing I learned from Grandfather was the art of getting what I want out of someone, by any means. I motion for Genti to come forward, and he steps up next to me and hands me the blade.

I turn it over in my hand, examining both sides as if I've never seen it before. Like it isn't the very weapon I used to kill Grandfather. "As you all know, my predecessor was quite fond of knives, and he liked to play with them to get the answers he needed." I grin at Santiago, who has yet to say anything. "But here's something I'll tell you about me. I can do things that would make Aleksander Gashi look like a fucking saint instead of The Dragon."

None of the men flinch, and I wouldn't expect them to. They've all been through this before. Maybe not tortured but certainly questioned or, at the very least, been put in a position where their lives were endangered.

But I can already tell they underestimate me and what I'm capable of. Even barely able to stand, with it taking every ounce of energy and willpower I have to stay vertical, I can still outsmart these pieces of shit.

"Now, let's talk about what happened to me. And let's not play any games and pretend you all don't know something. One of the organizations is responsible for the attempt on my life. I need to know which one and why."

Oleg snorts a laugh and shakes his head. "Why? You aren't that stupid, Syla. Everyone in this town wants you dead." He glances from Genti to Driton next to me. "Even your own men."

I try not to let my reaction to his statement show, but my body tenses, pulling at the destroyed muscle in my left shoulder and arm, and I clench my jaw to keep from letting out a noise that would reveal just how much pain I'm still in. "I'm well aware there are many in this town who might want me dead. But I trust my men implicitly."

It's a lie.

But I hope it's a good enough one to end this line of conversation.

They haven't exactly instilled a lot of confidence lately. And I'd be lying if I said I trust them any more than I trust Kat right now. But over the last two days, other than Doc coming to check on me, she's been the one making sure I'm alive.

Until I was finally strong enough to lock her the fuck out. As soon as I got off the phone with Genti last night and confirmed Kat was gone, I stumbled to the door and deadbolted that sucker.

There's only one way in, and until I sort all this out, I'm not letting that woman near me. But I need my men, and other than their lackluster work ethic, they've given me no reason to question their loyalty. They came over with me from Albania and assisted me in taking control from Erjon. There's no reason for them to turn against me.

I step in front of Oleg and grin down at him. "Am I to understand you don't wish to cooperate with my line of questioning?"

"Fuck you, Syla. I won't tell you a single fucking thi—"

Before he can even get the final word out, I drive my knife into his gut, twist it sideways, and drag it across his torso, letting his guts spill onto his lap and fall to the floor between his legs.

He gasps, and a choking sound emanates from his throat before blood starts to pour from his mouth.

"I can put you out of your misery now...if you answer my question. Or...I can let you sit here and bleed out or die from shock, whichever comes first."

"You're going to pay for this." Padraig watches the scene, his lips twisted into a snarl. "If you really think you can get away with killing the three of us without setting off a war, you're more insane than The Dragon."

I grin at him and wipe the blade against my leg to clean off the blood. "The difference between The Dragon and me is that I don't let passion and personal feelings get in the way of business. He was so intent on revenge for what happened to Saban that he lost sight of what was important. I won't do that. And I can't be killed easily, as I've already proven."

They're going to have to work a lot harder and smarter to bury me.

SEVEN

My statement is as much of a warning as these men will get.

But Padraig doesn't seem to take it as that. He smirks at me, like he knows something I don't and is completely ready to go to the grave with the information. "We'll see about that."

I glance back at Oleg and the blood pooling around him under his chair. His head lolls down, chin against his chest. I nod to Genti, who walks behind him and lifts his head so the man's half-dead eyes meet mine. "Tell me what I need to know."

I never expected this to be easy, but I had hoped a little display would loosen their tongues.

Oleg gurgles out more blood, then offers a red grin. "Never."

Maybe not his tongue.

Genti lets his head fall, and I move to stand in front of Padraig.

He sneers at me much the same way his Russian counterpart did. "I don't know anything about who tried to kill you. It wasn't us. If it had been, you wouldn't be here."

"You sound so certain of that, but your people can be very messy at times. And the way this attack was planned seemed very similar to some other incidents involving your organization. Galen is getting sloppy if this is what he calls a hit."

"If the gun were in my hand, you'd be missing your head right now."

I chuckle, but the motion jostles my side. I have to turn away from Padraig for a moment to hide my wince.

Khristi. I hope no one saw that.

This is the longest I've been on my feet in days and being out of bed is taking its toll quicker than I expected. If I don't get what I need fast, I may end up passing the fuck out in front of my captives.

I step over to my Colombian friend and stare down at him. His hard, dark eyes look back at me, but he doesn't say anything. "You've been awfully quiet. Nothing to say?" I raise an eyebrow at him, but he doesn't move or speak. "So stoic. So different from your gregarious boss, Mr. Rose."

That one will be hard to break. The Irishman is my best chance now.

I move back to Padraig and slice off his right ear.

"Fuck!" He screams and thrashes against his bindings while his appendage falls to the floor and into the blood of the Russian sitting next to him.

"I may have moved a little hastily with our Russian friend." Oleg's chest still moves, so I know he's alive and suffering, which gives me a bit of enjoyment, but he's going to be dead far quicker than I had hoped. "But you," I step closer to Padraig and point the bloody tip of the knife straight between his eyes, "you, I can toy with. My grandfather taught me well, and I have the skills you can't possibly comprehend. I would slice off your other ear, but you're going to need it to hear my questions. Instead, I'll take your eye."

Genti grabs his head and holds it back, fighting the struggling man, and I step forward and dig the point of the knife into Padraig's eye socket. Not deep enough to enter the brain, but just enough to flick out his eyeball and leave it hanging from the connected nerves.

He cries out something in Gaelic I don't understand and thrashes in his chair. "It wasn't us."

"Then, who the hell was it?"

"I don't know." He grits his teeth and shakes his head, blood dripping from where his ear once sat and down his cheek where his eye dangles. "It was sloppy. We aren't that, and neither are the Russians. And Rose is meticulous, so what does that tell you?"

I glance over at Rose's man, as stoic as ever, sitting stick-straight in the chair, not bothering to fight against his restraints.

He may be right.

The pain and the lingering drugs coursing through my system may be blinding me to the truth here.

Would any of them really have gone this route?

It only circles me back to the nagging feeling in the back of my brain.

The only one who knew where I was going to be.

Kat.

I step away from both men for a moment and take a deep breath. If she wanted me dead, she's had plenty of time to kill me. When I was at my weakest, most vulnerable state. And while everyone would've known it was her, since everyone wants me gone anyway, would she really have passed up the opportunity?

It doesn't make any sense.

And my brain, still foggy from everything that's happened and these pain meds, is making it harder and harder to keep my grasp on what's real and what's imagined. Standing here, wasting time isn't helping, either.

I turn back to the Irishman. "Tell me what you've heard."

He grits his teeth staring at me with his one good eye while the other dangles against his bloodied cheek. "I don't know. Like Oleg said, everyone wants you dead. Everyone has a motive. But I don't think it was any of us."

For some reason, I believe them. What he said rings true about the nature of the attack. But Rose is still at the top of my list. After the threatening phone call he made to me, it would be stupid for me to overlook him or dismiss him as a suspect.

I step in front of his man. "Was it your boss?"

He doesn't move, just stares straight ahead, not even making eye contact with me until I lower my head enough to force him to meet my gaze. "If you don't plan on speaking, then there's no reason to keep you alive."

I step forward and slit his throat before we waste any more time. Blood pours down his neck and over his chest, and his head drops forward.

Which only leaves my Irish friend here.

I tap the knife against my palm, considering my next move. While I could continue to torture the guy to get more information, I don't think he has any. And even if he does, the answers are unlikely to be accurate, anyway. "Since you have nothing to offer me by way of explanation, there's no reason to keep you around."

"Wait." He jerks against his bindings again. "You know if you kill me, Galen will come after you."

I shrug my one good shoulder and smile at him. "Like you and your friend here just said, everybody already wants me dead. So, what does it matter, anyway?"

With that, I jab the knife straight into his heart. His one good eye widens, and a strangled groan slips from his open mouth as I pull it from his flesh.

I glance down at my hands, covered in gore, at my blood-soaked clothing and shoes, and grit my teeth.

How did The Dragon do this without ending up all bloody? I guess I need more practice.

EIGHT

I SHOVE open the door to my condo and let it slam closed behind me. The moment it does, I lean back against it and wince. Squeezing my eyes closed, I grip the door handle to keep the spinning room from dragging me down to my knees. I pushed it too hard today. If I don't get into the bedroom and get horizontal, my ass will end up on the floor.

And it got me *nowhere*.

My fists clench at my sides, and I release a heavy sigh before sucking in a deep breath. Her scent hits me before I see or hear her—the same rich and sweet one that wraps around me when I'm buried inside her.

The familiar click of her heels on the hard floor comes from the kitchen, and she rounds the corner wearing her typical stilettoes and skin-tight dress, only this time, an apron I wasn't even aware I had in there covers her.

Her gaze rakes over the disheveled, bloody mess I must be, and she rushes toward me. "Oh, my God! Are you all right?"

I hold out a hand to stop her. "I'm fine."

The words barely make it out through gritted teeth, and I force myself to stand up straight and weave slowly to the bedroom to get out of these blood-soaked clothes. Only, my formerly white shirt poses a problem. Undoing buttons with only my right hand is more challenging than I could have anticipated. When I dressed this morning, I could still move my left arm enough to get the buttons through the tiny holes, but now that I can't even lift it without almost passing out, it's nearly impossible.

She follows me into the bedroom and stops behind me. "Let me help you."

I shoot a glance over my shoulder at her. "Don't touch me."

With more willpower than I thought I had left, I manage to raise my left hand, pain shooting through my arm and shoulder hard enough almost to drop me on the spot. Skipping my last dose of pain meds might not have been wise, but it was necessary to keep a clear head and to be able to function enough to do what was needed.

Every excruciating move I make, I can feel her eyes on me. The burn of her piercing assessment...and admonishment. If she had been here, I wouldn't have made it out that door this morning.

I somehow get my shirt unbuttoned and work it off my back, wiggling only my right shoulder until it pools at my feet. The room spins slightly, and I clench my eyes shut, still turned away from Kat.

"You're bleeding." Her anger-laced comment doesn't show an ounce of sympathy. She's pissed—perhaps rightfully so—and any concern she had when she saw me at the door seems to have fled as her anger rose.

"It's not my blood."

"Yes. It is." The click of her heels echoes in the room as she walks around to stand in front of me. "That is yours seeping through the bandage on your side."

Fuck.

I glance down at what is clearly spreading from my body and mingling with the older, drying blood of the men I just fucking killed.

"I'm going to call Doc—"

My hand snaps out and wraps around her wrist before she can move. She presses her lips into a thin, hard line and glares at me with icy eyes.

I scowl at her and narrow my gaze. "No, you aren't. I'm fine."

"Saying it over and over again doesn't make it true, Michael. You probably ripped open your stitches. You should never have gotten out of bed and left."

"Yeah?" I shift closer to her slightly, watching every hint of emotion in her eyes and on her face. "Well, where the fuck were you? And how the hell did you get back in here?"

"I do have a business to run, Michael. I was taking care of things that I couldn't put off." She motions down toward my blood-soaked clothes with her free hand. "If I had known you were going to be stupid, I never would have left."

I tighten my hand around her wrist until the flash of pain flickers in her eyes. "How the *fuck* did you get back in here?"

"I took your keys and had a key made when Doc told me someone needed to stay with you."

She had a fucking key made?

That takes some fucking balls. I thought Kat showing up here unannounced was gutsy, but she's taking things to a whole new level—one I am definitely *not* on board with.

"Who the fuck do you think you are? Who gave you the right to do that?"

One of her slim, dark eyebrows rises. "Who am I? The only one *here*, Michael. The only one who seems to give a fuck if you live or die."

My chest tightens slightly. Something I'm going to insist is only because I'm on the verge of passing out and *not* because her statement actually hurts. I left that kind of weakness down in the pit when Esad pulled me up. "That's not true."

"Isn't it?" She scoffs and tries to tug away her arm, but I only hold tighter. "Your men may have raced off to save your ass when I called, but why weren't they there to protect you in the first place?"

"Because I went alone. *Intentionally.* I wanted to show Valentina I meant no harm. If I had shown up armed to the teeth with a band of goons, there would've been even more tension there than there already was."

"So instead, you risked your life and almost lost it."

I drag her closer to me until I can feel her chest rising and falling against mine. "I risked my life for *you!* For this fucking business arrangement. To get the girls into the damn country for *you*. So, fuck you, Kat. Get the fuck out."

Blood rushes in my ears, a constant roar that drowns out almost everything else, but when I release her wrist and shove her away from me, her annoyed sigh makes it through.

"It's okay to admit you need help, Michael."

"I'm fucking fine."

She reaches back and unties the apron from around her waist, then pulls it over her head. "I'm not the best cook in the world, but there's a roasted chicken and potatoes in the oven." She tosses the apron onto the floor. "Listen for the timer. And have fun bending down to get it out of there."

With an annoyed huff, she storms past me, intentionally slamming her left shoulder into mine, sending knives of fire-burning pain through it.

Krishti, she's a cold bitch.

As soon as I hear the front door slam closed, I stumble to the bathroom and drop onto the closed toilet lid. My entire body sags with the relief, finally sitting down brings. I fumble on my side to locate the end of the gauze and pull it free, then start to unwrap the bandage.

"*Fuck!*"

There's no way I'm going to be able to do this without moving my left arm. And that's completely out of the question at this point. Not when I can barely keep the bile that's rising in my throat from ending up on the bathroom tile. I pull open the counter drawer and grab a pair of scissors from my grooming kit to cut away the bandages.

Doc usually does a pretty good job patching up the guys, but this looks like a vet school dropout stitched me up. Though, Kat did say Doc had to dig around for some of the shrapnel. And it appears like it's true.

It doesn't seem infected, though, so as long as I can get the bleeding under control, I'm sure I'll be fine. It trickles down my side freely, raising images of the blood flowing from my "friends" earlier today.

I drop my head and pause for a moment. It didn't go as planned at all.

But it doesn't mean it was a total loss.

The Russians and the Irish will redouble their efforts against me once they know what I've done, and Rose will undoubtedly take this as a full-on act of war. That might just make it easier to take him out.

People acting out of anger and fear often make bad and rash decisions. They leave themselves open to attack in ways they otherwise might not with clear heads. It's exactly what I've counted on to get where I am today and a mistake I try to avoid committing myself.

Knowing that steers my course forward.

It means there's only one thing I can do.

NINE

I NEVER THOUGHT I'd be so happy to see the piece of shit club Aleksander chose as a headquarters again. The place is far from where I would prefer to operate, but since The Dragon made this home base, it's become a location with enough history and ties to the organization that I can't really move from it.

For better or worse, it's home.

And finally walking back in, past the blonde on the pole and the whispers and stares of the men, down the back hallway, and into the office that was once his and is now mine feels like a supreme victory after the last few days where I've felt utterly defeated.

As much as I would have preferred to be here yesterday, I spent the vast majority of my time in bed, recovering from my escapades the day before that left me exhausted and bleeding—at least temporarily.

Now that the blood has stopped flowing and I've regained some of my strength and energy, it's time to set things in motion. Some things need to happen to ensure everything goes smoothly; otherwise, all of this will have been for nothing.

I slowly lower myself into my chair, light up a cigarette, stick it in my mouth, and dial Esad. Even though it's only been a few days since I last spoke with him about the status of lining up the ships and captains, now that I have confirmation from Valentina that we have unfettered access to the docks, I want to get things moving quickly.

After all, I took four fucking bullets to secure this deal.

He finally answers on the fourth ring, just as my annoyance is starting to get the better of me. "Michael, I was worried."

"How come?" I take a long, hard pull of smoke, letting it fill my lungs before slowly releasing it into the air.

"There were rumors of your early demise."

I tense and then lean back in my chair, my hand pressed against my side to keep from jostling the wound there. "How did you hear about that?"

Word of the shooting reaching home in Albania isn't that surprising. One of my men could easily have said something to a friend or family member, but Esad has done his best to live under the radar and not draw attention to himself or his connection to me. The only people who are aware of our long friendship are the ones who knew us as children, and there aren't many of those left.

So, who the hell told him?

"I heard a rumor at the Vlorë docks while I was working with a few of our captains to ready their ships."

"A rumor?"

"That someone tried to take you out and had succeeded."

I snort and sigh, then take another hit of nicotine. "Fortunately, not true, but I'm curious how the news got there and what's being said."

Esad jostles the phone for a moment. "It was some of Morina's former men who work for the Dragushas and Berishas now. Joking about how someone finally eliminated the last Syla after all these years."

"Bastards." After the Morinas lost Philly, their men scattered in the winds, some returning home, and others going to work for long-standing rivals. I would never allow any of their filth in my ranks, but the new men in power back home aren't always so careful about who they bring on board. "Did they say anything about who might have been responsible?"

"No, nothing like that."

Of course fucking not.

I lean forward with a groan as my body protests. "So, you don't have anything useful to tell me."

He chuckles. "Of course, I do, just not about who turned you into Swiss cheese."

"Ha ha. Very funny."

"Cheer up, *miku im*, I have four boats and captains lined up and ready as soon as you give the command."

For the first time in what feels like months, something is finally going my way. "I've secured the docks here, so we'll launch soon. I'll contact my man about the identifications and passengers and make the final arrangements."

"I'll see you soon, *miku im*."

I end the call, slide my phone back onto my desk, and eye the bottles sitting on the bar in the corner. No doubt, I shouldn't be drinking given the trauma I suffered and the drugs still lingering in my body. If Doc or Kat were here, they'd probably tear me a new one—between the smoking and drinking—but it's too tempting to pass up right now.

Thinking always seems easier with a drink in my hand, like it helps clear the cobwebs from my mind and relaxes me enough to help me focus on what I need to accomplish. And something huge is on the top of that list right now.

More accurately...*someone.*

I snuff out my cigarette, push myself to my feet, wander over to the bar, and pour myself a shot of vodka. But instead of sipping it, I take it back in a single shot, letting it burn down my throat and warm my chest.

It shouldn't feel like the weight of the world is on my shoulders right now. I should be thrilled. I managed to secure the use of the docks. Esad has what we need lined up back home. Things are falling into place to bring the plan to fruition—one that will get me even closer to taking what I want from the other families.

All it took was me almost dying.

I snort and shake my head. The hoops I've had to jump through the last few weeks to get everything in order better be worth it. Kat's files could be the single most important weapon in my arsenal, if I can get my hands on them.

After how things have gone down the last few days, it will be a miracle if she even lets me in the door again, but I have to move forward with the belief she'll allow me access to them. That kind of leverage, coupled with the money the brothels will bring in, will finally put me in a prime position to start dismantling the other families one by one.

The only loose end left is what to do with the girls once they get here. I pour another drink and return to my chair to dial Arden.

Unlike Esad, he's smart enough not to keep me waiting and answers on the second ring. "Boss, I-I wasn't expecting to hear from you."

"Why because you thought I was on my deathbed?"

"N-n-no."

"It's okay, Arden, I'm fine. What I need from you is a status update on where we are with the IDs."

"My guy has everything in the works. And your man in Vlorë has started providing him information on the girls he's already secured, so he'll make sure everything is ready to go as soon as they pull into the dock."

I release a sigh of relief and lean back in my chair, letting my eyes drift closed. At least everything seems to be going smoothly.

Arden clears his throat. "But...sir?"

"What?"

"On the other matter..."

I open my eyes and stare at the empty chair where Kat sat not so long ago and asked me to become her business partner. "Yeah, what about it?"

"Well, that's proving a little bit more difficult."

"Did you track her down in Vienna?"

"Yes, sir, and it seemed she was staying at hostels. Most of them keep physical records where people have to sign a logbook, so I've had to go to places to look manually. But so far, only one person has remembered her from her stay."

"What did they say?"

"Not much. She remembered a dark-haired American girl who didn't speak the language. Said she seemed to be interested in tourist locations and would disappear all day. Nothing suspicious."

"Keep digging."

"Sir? Can I ask why?"

I clench my fist around the glass and fight the urge to chuck it against the wall. "Because I fucking told you to, Arden. That's why."

The incompetence of everyone around me has me on the edge of letting loose some rounds and cleaning house.

I end the call and slam my phone onto the desk.

He needs to keep digging because what I'm about to do means I'm tying myself to Kat potentially forever, or, at the very least, for as long as this business relationship remains lucrative.

And I don't like surprises.

TEN

"THIS ISN'T GOING to be easy."

Genti nods and leans back in the chair across from my desk, resting his head in his hands. Though he's been with me longer than anyone—came over with me from Albania when I finally made my move—until now, he hasn't done much other than fail to live up to my expectations.

After he and Driton let Kat into my place so easily, I was on the verge of putting a bullet into his skull, but since the attempt on my life, he's proven he's capable of stepping up. He got to me and got me to Doc before I bled the fuck out, and he's managed to keep things running here while I've been laid up.

And if I'm going to take out Rose, I'm going to need men I can trust to do their jobs properly and cover their tracks—which is why it's essential we get to work on a plan now if we want the troublesome Colombian out of our hair for good.

Genti sighs. "It won't be easy at all. We're already getting blowback from what you did the other day."

Shit.

It's not that I didn't expect it. No one is going to let a rival organization pull their men off the street and kill them without some sort of massive repercussions—I had just hoped we might have a little bit more time before the shit hit the fan.

I rub at the tension in the back of my neck and eye the pack of cigarettes on my desk. The craving for another one makes my knee bounce, but I've been trying to avoid sucking them down the way I normally do—at least until I feel somewhat better. "What happened?"

He sighs and leans forward to rest his elbows on his knees. "Three of our guys were ambushed this morning when they went to pick up some payments."

"Shit." I scrub my hands over my face and then roll my left shoulder slightly to try to loosen the tightness there. "Did we lose them?"

He shakes his head. "Two only had minor wounds, but Driton was hit twice and is at Doc's now. Not sure what that outcome will be."

"Who did it?" I certainly know who my top three suspects are, but if this life has taught me anything, it's that if you think things are obvious, you're likely missing something important.

Genti shrugs slightly. "Dark SUV. No one got a good look, but if we think this is anything other than retaliation, we would be stupid."

"I know. And it's going to make it even harder to get to Rose."

His dark eyes hold mine, and his lips twist slightly. "I've been thinking about it ever since you went down, sir."

Nice of someone to actually do their job for once.

"And?" I raise an eyebrow at him.

"And we have a few options."

If they're the same ones I've been mulling over, none of them are very good. We still don't know where Rose's headquarters is. If we did, we could take it out in one fell swoop with a bomb or something just as cataclysmic. But Rose is too smart for that. He keeps the home base of his operations a secret like he's hiding the damn ark of the covenant there.

"We can't go after his home base."

Genti nods and shifts in his seat. "No, but we can go after him when he leaves it."

I throw my hands up. "How the hell are we supposed to do that when we can't watch him and don't know when he's leaving?"

"What if we knew where he was going?"

My ears perk up, and I lean forward and take a sip of my vodka. "He'll be watching and expecting that. If I try to arrange a meeting, he'll know it's a setup. He'll never come."

"Not if *you* invite him."

I raise an eyebrow at him. "What are you suggesting? That we have Valentina do it? Because she won't."

She doesn't want to have anything to do with what's about to go down. And Genti doesn't even know it was part of my agreement with her to take out Rose in order to get to use the docks. I'm the only person who will ever know it's not just for my own personal gain—well, Cutter and me. Having Rose out of the way will only benefit me, too, so there's no reason for anyone to question it.

It's one less person to compete with. One less risk. Once he's gone, the territories he stole from the smaller Hispanic gangs will be free for the taking again, and I'll swoop in before any smaller upstarts can even get their shit together.

Genti leans back in the chair and kicks out his feet, crossing them at the ankles. "I wasn't thinking Valentina."

"Then, who?"

He clears his throat and offers a slight shrug. "Kat."

"No." I slam my glass down against the desk. "She stays out of this."

One of his dark eyebrows wings up. "Isn't she already in it?"

He does have a point. She may not be personally involved in my business's day-to-day operations, but we are partners now—at least where the brothels are concerned.

I slowly nod as I consider the possibility. "She did say she had men from the other organizations coming to Kat's Cradle..."

"So, what if she managed to get one of his men to extend him an invitation there?"

It's not the worst idea in the world. Though I'm not thrilled with the thought of getting Kat involved in a hit on someone as dangerous as Rose, our options are certainly limited due to his ability to stay two steps ahead.

"I'll think about it and talk to her if I decide it's a viable option."

Genti holds up his hands and shrugs slightly. "It's just a suggestion. If you have a better idea I'm not thinking of, I'm all ears. Otherwise, it's just a waiting game for Rose to make a mistake or step out in public so that we can get him."

I'm sick of biding my time. "I want men at every location where you've ever seen him. I want them covering every potential place he could show up. Any opportunity we get, we take. But make sure it looks like one of the smaller gangs retaliating. This can't come back to us."

Having the Rose cartel out for blood would be very bad for all of us—very bad indeed. And I'm undoubtedly already on his hit list for what I did to Santiago. The attack on my men this morning could have been Rose just as easily as it could have been the Russians or the Irish.

With people coming at me from every side, it would be easy to give in to the instinct to hunker down and hide, but no one survives in this world by being a fucking pussy.

And I don't just want to survive.

I plan on thriving.

ELEVEN

THE BIG MAN at the door gives me a dirty look as I climb from my car and make my way up the stairs to Kat's house. He puffs out his barrel chest and peers at me over the rims of his dark sunglasses. "Is she expecting you today?"

I scowl at him. This isn't the day to fuck with me. I am so not in the mood. "Fuck you."

He moves in front of the door, his enormous frame blocking my path, making it very evident how much bigger than me he is. That, combined with my recent injuries, means there's no way I'm getting through that door unless he lets me.

Or unless I kill him, which, unfortunately, isn't an option since I need Kat cooperative and not *angrier* with me.

"No," I suck in a breath to keep from snapping and attempting something stupid—like slamming my fist into his smug face or pulling my gun, "she's not expecting me, but I need to see her."

"She's otherwise engaged at the moment."

What the fuck is that supposed to mean?

He grabs the radio from his side without taking his eyes off me. "Let me check to see when she'll be available."

I scowl at him and cross my arms over my chest, hopefully hiding the wince from the bite of pain in my arm.

His lips twist into a sneer. "She just finished her meeting. You can go in."

Something tells me there was no meeting and this was all designed to make me wait and feel like an insignificant asshole to prove a point. I'll give Kat props for that one. Here, I am at her mercy. This is her turf, her world.

I push past him through the door and slowly make my way up the steps to her room. I might as well be climbing Everest. The last time I felt this tired and worn out was when Esad dragged me up from the pit. But I'm not about to give anyone the satisfaction of seeing how much I'm suffering— especially Kat, given our last interaction.

The door to her room stands cracked, and I take a deep breath before pushing it open. If I show signs of weakness, she'll see them immediately and worm her way into the cracks to break them open. I need to be one hundred percent on.

She sits at her desk, watching the door with cold ambivalence, a cigarette dangling from her manicured fingertips. "Michael, I didn't expect to see you here today. Or ever again, really."

"Why's that?" I make my way through the room to her and gingerly lower myself into the chair across from her desk.

It's best to downplay what happened at my place the other night. If I make it seem like it wasn't a big deal, perhaps she'll be more amenable to the favor I need today.

She barely moves, her gaze fixed on me like she's trying to read something written all over my face but it's in a foreign language she doesn't understand. Then she brings the cigarette to her lips and slowly inhales. The smoke leaves her perfect lips in small circles, floating across the desk toward me. "I wasn't sure where you and I stand or if we're still moving forward with our partnership."

Shit.

This is precisely what I was worried about. Pissing Kat off the last few days is only going to make it harder to get her to agree to what I need now.

But I also don't apologize...*ever.* I didn't do anything wrong other than protecting myself, and I'm not about to drop to my knees to beg for her forgiveness.

And she needs to know that.

"I'm not going to apologize for what happened, Kat. You had no business getting a key made for my place or trying to mother me. As you can see, I'm perfectly capable of taking care of myself."

She snorts and shakes her head, humor pulling at her red lips. "This is taking care of yourself? Michael, you look like shit. Did you even get that chicken out of the oven?"

"Yes, I did."

She doesn't need to know that it was the next day after I had slept like the dead for fourteen hours and taken a lot of narcotic pain medication. Or that it ended up right in the trash.

"I don't know why you have to fight me on everything, Michael." She takes another pull from her cigarette then snuffs it out in the ashtray on her desk.

I scowl at her and lean forward, squaring my shoulders and readying myself for the battle that feels like it's coming my way. "I don't fight you on everything. You just need to learn that if we're going to continue to work together that I don't like decisions being made for me."

She nods slowly, her gaze never leaving mine. "That's fair enough. But you need to understand that if we are going to be business partners, you're not going to boss me around, either."

Not going to boss her around?

A smile I rarely use outside the bedroom spreads across my lips. "But I so love bossing you around."

Her armor finally cracks, and she chuckles and shakes her head. "That's not what I'm talking about, and you know it. So, if you didn't come to apologize, why are you here?" She raises a dark eyebrow and drums her long red nails on the top of the desk. "Because you need something, perhaps?"

Am I that transparent?

I certainly never thought so. I wouldn't have made it this far in this business if I were. "Valentina agreed to our use of the docks. And Esad has the ships and captains lined up and ready to go. The IDs are being prepared for the girls, so we're basically ready to launch."

"Good because I bought that house."

"What house?"

"The one we were supposed to go look at after you left the docks."

"How did you manage that?" There's no way she had the money for it. It was one of the reasons she came to me in the first place.

Her slim shoulders rise and fall. "I borrowed it from a friend."

Acid crawls up the back of my throat, and I swallow it down and narrow my eyes on her. "And who is this friend who has that kind of money?"

The corners of her mouth tug up into a little smug grin. "A very good client of one of my girls happens to be the head of Chicagoland Bank. He was more than willing to accommodate me with the loan when I mentioned his wife finding out about where he's been."

Clever girl...

I lean back into the chair and release a relieved sigh. The thought of what she might have done to get the money almost made me lose my shit. "So, you finally dug into the blackmail files, huh?"

Kat offers another nonchalant shrug. "I did what I had to do because I didn't know where we stood."

"What would you have done if I didn't want to continue in the business? You would've been stuck with a loan on that house with no way to get any more girls here."

One corner of her mouth curls up. "Girls are easy to find, Michael. I could get them on the street here if I really needed to. Or Milwaukee or Minneapolis. But those aren't the girls I want. Middle Eastern women are better workers. So, while it wouldn't have been ideal if you had bailed, I would've made it work."

She watches me for a moment, waiting for me to say something.

I tap my knuckles on the arm of the chair. "Seems like you have it all worked out."

With a sigh, she leans forward rests her arms on the desk. "Can I assume your being here means you still want to proceed?"

"There's only one more piece that needs to get taken care of."

"What's that?"

"I need to take care of Rose."

She rocks back in her chair slightly and runs a hand over her slicked-back hair. "And why is that my problem? I don't see how that has anything to do with this business venture."

"Our business will do a lot better without Rose around. Plus, if we don't get rid of him, we may lose Valentina's cooperation. And in order to get rid of him, I need your help."

"So," her dark eyebrows rise, "you did come because you need something from me."

I scowl at her and lean forward in my chair. "Yes, I need my *partner* to step up to secure the future of this business. To prove your loyalty to me in our endeavor."

TWELVE

KAT RECOILS SLIGHTLY AND SCOFFS, anger shading the pale skin of her cheeks pink. "Prove my loyalty? You have to be fucking kidding me. Keeping you alive wasn't enough?"

Somehow, I knew she would bring that up. She seems to think it gives her carte blanche to do and say whatever she wants without question, though. That's something that can't continue. "I don't trust anyone in this business, Kat. Not even you."

Especially you...

She considers me for a moment, the *click, click, click* of her nails still hitting the top of the desk rhythmically and also annoyingly. Finally, her hand stills, and her shoulders relax back, almost like she found some calm at the center of her storm of anger. "What do you need me to do?"

Now that some of the tension in the room has dissipated somewhat, I relax back in the chair and cross my ankle over my knee. "One of the biggest problems with Rose is that he's too smart. No one has been able to locate his headquarters or pin him down. Unless he's at the meeting and gives us a location, we never know where he's going to be. And after what just happened, there's no way he'll meet with me."

Her head bobs slowly, and her lips twist. "But you think he'll meet with me, someone he's never met and doesn't know?"

"You said that members of the other organizations had men coming here. I assume some of them are Colombians?"

She grabs a pen from her desktop and twirls it between her fingers. "Yes, we've had a few of his men in here."

"Well, I'm hoping we can use that to our advantage. Perhaps make an enticing offer to get him here."

Her eyes widen, and she freezes. "You want to kill him on my property? Are you fucking insane? You know how that would look. His men would know I was involved, and word would get out very quickly. There's no way you could keep that a secret."

"I never said we would take him out here. Treat him as a potential investor, or hell, even a customer if he seems interested. And then when the time comes, you alert me that he'll be here, and my men will be able to follow him and figure out a time and place to take him out that won't point any fingers back at you or me."

Kat snorts, shakes her head, and pushes to her feet to pace behind her desk. "You make it sound easy."

I let out a mirthless chuckle. "I know it won't be easy. But it will be far easier than our other option, which is to wait for Rose to show up. For all I know, it could be with the death squad to take me out."

She pauses behind her chair and rests her arms across the back. "Do you think it was him? How would he have found out about your meeting?"

Instead of answering her right away, I watch her, examining every line on her face, every twitch of her eyes, looking for any crack in her perfectly manicured armor that might tell me she had something to do with it. "That's exactly what I've been wondering."

"And you still don't trust me?"

That's the ultimate question.

A tiny piece of me still wants to scream *no*. The part that Grandfather nurtured and twisted into a cynical and untrusting dark shell of a person. The part I've always leaned toward. But looking at her and remembering the genuine concern in her eyes when she left my place the other day, I can't manage to voice that.

This hauntingly beautiful woman walked into my life on high heels, with attitude to spare and dropped this in my lap for no apparent reason. Anyone would be skeptical. Anyone *should* be, according to Grandfather.

It's precisely what brought the Syla family down in the first place. I won't fall for the same deception, and doing this would go a long way to her proving herself to me.

I flash her a grin, one I hope hides that reservation in the back of my mind. "Of course, I trust you. Would I be going into business with you if I didn't?"

She snorts and shakes her head. "I know you better than that, Michael. You don't trust me, but you need me. My guess is if it was Rose who tried to kill you, one of his men has probably been watching you and followed you there to the docks. Would that really have been so hard?"

I want to answer no because I watched for any tails and did my best to ensure nobody was following me to the docks, but I can't be one hundred percent certain. "No, I can't say for sure that I wasn't followed."

"And you've been on his radar for a long time."

"He told me as much when he called about the bombing. Said that if he found that I was involved, he would be sure to end me."

"His sister got injured badly, didn't she?"

I nod slowly. "Yes. She was hospitalized for a while, though I'm not certain of her injuries. It's my understanding that she's recovering now, but he still wants someone to blame. And while he may not have had evidence to nail me when we last spoke, he certainly does now that I've taken out one of his men. He'll take it as an excuse to act even if he didn't have the support of the other families."

"Which he will because you also fucked over the Irish and the Russians."

"For all I know, they were all involved. They finally got together and decided to do what they tried to do all those months ago. Only this time, they left Valentina out of it because they knew she was reluctant then."

She shrugs. "Definitely possible. You seem to have a lot of enemies, Michael."

"I do. And I hope you don't ever become one."

With a sigh, she walks around the desk to stand in front of me then leans back against it, her dress riding up precariously high on her creamy white thighs. "I'm not your enemy, Michael. Let's get that straight right now. And while I don't like you demanding that I prove my loyalty to you, I will help you with Rose. Because if we don't get rid of him, our new operations are constantly going to be at risk, and I need you to ensure they continue and run smoothly."

I drag my eyes off her exposed skin to meet her gaze. "So, you're helping me for the business."

"Of course." She grins and shifts, making the material rise even higher. "Like you told me repeatedly, this is a business arrangement."

Of course—a business arrangement.

THIRTEEN

Rose's black SUV pulls up in front of the house, and my entire body tenses. I clench my fists on the edge of the table in the surveillance room where I watch, my hands tied. All I want is to fly down those stairs and empty the entire magazine in my gun into him—end this *right* here, *right* now.

But letting my wrath take control would only put me at greater risk.

I may want what Rose has—what *all* the families have—but I also know enough to stay locked in this tiny room rather than act on my desires.

Kat places her small, warm hand against the back of my neck and squeezes gently, watching the same screens. "Relax. It will be fine."

She's been trying to reassure me since she got the call that he was coming, but whether it's my continued lack of strength or the stress of the week finally getting to me, I can't seem to quell the nervous energy surging through my body.

The only thing keeping me grounded is knowing my men are waiting outside the gates to follow Rose. We've had two days to plan this, and there's no way he's slipping past them. So, the end is in sight.

Two men in suits emerge from the front driver and passenger side doors and pull open one of the rear ones. Rose steps out, adjusting his perfectly tailored suit coat and looking like the cover of *GQ* magazine.

Fucking asshole.

He always looks so polished, so put together, like his entire world doesn't revolve around murder and mayhem. The man seems to breeze through life, oblivious to how the blood on his hands stains him and taints everything he touches.

I don't have the same lack of self-awareness. I'm not blind to the reality of Michael Syla. I know exactly who and what I am and make no qualms about trying to hide it behind a flashy, gregarious smile and pleasant demeanor. We're both ruthless killers who will do anything to get to the top. The only difference is, I admit it.

Rose approaches the steps outside, his two bodyguards on either side of him.

"Here we go." Kat's hand slips from my skin.

I immediately shiver at the loss of the warmth and connection to her.

Fuck, I hate that.

A woman shouldn't get to me like this. I shouldn't crave her near me, shouldn't *want* her touch. Yet, the past week with the constant tension between us has me wound up so tight, every brush of her skin against mine makes me want to slam her against a wall and fuck her the way I did that first night.

She opens the door and slips out of the surveillance room. I walk over and lock it behind her, ensuring there won't be any surprises. It's a risk even to be here while Rose is, but I wanted to witness this with my own eyes while my men wait for him to leave so they can follow him and hopefully gain some insight on his daily activities and potential locations for an ambush.

Rose climbs the stairs outside as Kat descends the ones inside. I would have loved to keep her out of this, to protect her from ever being in Rose's sights, but this was the best plan, the easiest way to remove the thorn from my side—and Valentina's.

I just fucking hate that man.

Taking control of the city would be so much easier without him here, without having him to compete against. But instead, he's one more enemy to constantly fight against to maintain my position and to step on to climb higher. And I plan on ending up on the top—exactly where the Sylas used to be before Grandfather ruined everything.

She reaches the bottom of the staircase, and the front door opens. A brilliant smile lights Rose's face as he takes in Kat and approaches her across the foyer. She returns his grin, and the two embrace and kiss each other on both cheeks.

What the fuck is going on?

I tense again, the ruined muscles of my body protesting. I never would've imagined how much seeing another man touch her would bother me, but the seemingly familiar way they look at each other and continue to hold each other's hands makes me slam my fists against the table.

They're looking awfully cozy...and a little too fucking friendly.

Kat motions behind her toward the staircase, probably offering to give him a tour of the house, and he nods and offers her his elbow. She slips her arm through it, smiling at him and batting her perfectly long lashes.

If I knew how this was going to go down, the comfortableness between them, the rage it would cause to bubble up through my body...I might have second-guessed this plan.

It's almost like...

I shake my head and squeeze my eyes shut for a moment to rid my mind of the thoughts darkening my vision before I return to watching them ascend the steps toward the client rooms. She leans in and whispers something to Rose, and he drops his head back and laughs.

Fuck. What if I was right? What if it was Rose all along and she's been working with him?

They walk along the top of the staircase and down toward the client rooms. She leads him inside one, her arm still locked with his, and he says something to her that makes her laugh in a way I've never seen her do when I've been with her.

What the fuck is happening?

She brings him over to the armoire full of toys and accessories—just like she did when she gave me a tour—pulls her arm from around his, removes a key, unlocks it, and opens the door. He steps forward and does the same thing I did—pulls open a drawer and takes out a butt plug.

Whatever he says to her makes her laugh and wave a hand at him playfully. The way she puffs her breasts out toward him causes me to dig my nails into my palms.

She's enjoying this little too fucking much.

And as soon as he leaves, she's going to tell me what the fuck has been going on with Rose.

FOURTEEN

THE SECOND THE bedroom door opens, I'm on her before she can even take a breath. I grab her around the waist and push her back against the wall. "What the fuck was that?"

Her brow furrows as she stares back at me. "What are you talking about?"

I point toward the door. "*That*. What the fuck did I just see between you and Rose?"

Her red lips twist into an indignant frown. "I don't know what the hell you're talking about, Michael."

Kat shifts on her heels to try to move around me.

"The fuck you don't." I press a hand against her chest, forcing her against the unyielding wall. "Your heart's racing harder than I've ever felt it. Why? Because you're nervous that I'm going to figure it out?"

"Figure what out?" She pushes her hands against my chest. "I don't know what the hell you're talking about."

"Bullshit!" I roar the word in her face, my rage making the edges of my vision darken and the room spin. "Fuck!"

I push away from Kat and the wall and run my hand through my hair, squeezing my eyes closed. When I open them again, she hasn't moved an inch.

"Don't try to deny it, Kat. I saw it with my own fucking eyes, or did you forget that this whole place is wired."

She takes a step toward me, then seems to think better of it and retreats. "I don't know what you think you saw, Michael, but—"

"No! Not what I *thought* I saw—what I *did* see. There's no fucking way that was the first time you met Rose. You were too familiar with each other." I watch her for a reaction, but she stands stock still. "Are you fucking him?"

"What?" Her eyebrows fly up, and she glances back toward the door, even though Rose is long gone.

"I saw the way you two touched each other, the way you laughed and whispered together. That's not two people meeting for the first fucking time."

She clenches her fists at her sides, and she steps up to me, getting directly in my face. "It is when one of them is a fucking madame and is trying to reel in a big-fish investor."

"Yeah, or a client for yourself."

Her hand lashes out so fast that I don't have a chance to stop it. It connects with my cheek, sending a sting across it and down into my jaw. I slowly raise my hand and rub where she connected with my tingling skin.

She watches me, her jaw tense, nostrils flaring, and breath heavy between her lips. "Fuck you, Michael. I'm not going to keep explaining to you how this works. If you're so jealous that all you see is betrayal when I'm trying to do you a fucking favor, then whatever the hell is going on between us is over."

Like hell, it is!

I close the distance between us and grab her arm, ignoring the sting of pain to my shoulder. "You think you get to decide when this is over?"

"Yeah, Michael. I do, but if you just stopped and thought for one fucking second instead of seeing everything through the green eyes of jealousy, you would know that I was doing what I had to in order to make Rose feel comfortable here." She stares me down, anger flashing like lightning across her blue eyes. "I know your guys followed him as soon as he left, but the only way he'll ever come back here if they don't manage to take him out between now and then is if he believes this is a safe place and is interested in partnering with me. Men like Rose need to have their egos stroked, and a beautiful woman flirting with them does exactly that."

I grit my teeth, digging my nails into her forearm and my own palm.

She slowly raises her hands to capture my face between them. "If Rose is what I wanted, I would've gone to him to become my partner. But I didn't. I came to you for a reason."

"Yeah, and I'm still not sure exactly what that is."

"Then, maybe I'll just have to show you." She rises onto her tiptoes and presses her lips against mine harshly, tightening her hold on my face.

I release her wrist, wrap my arms around her, and drag her up against my body, grunting at the sharp bite of discomfort the motion brings. But despite the pain I can't seem to shake, my cock responds to her touch instantly, hardening where it's pressed between our bodies.

Kat pushes her hips against mine, drags her head back, and licks her lips. "If I wanted to fuck Rose, I would have. And if I'd wanted to hurt you as much as you have hurt me the last couple of days, I would've done it on camera and made you watch. But I didn't."

I dig my fingers into her hips, harshly. "I would have fucking killed you and him if you had."

She brushes her fingers across my lips. "I know."

Even the slightest touch from her sends an electric charge surging through my body. I still don't trust her. I still don't trust that little spark I saw between them on the video, but my body can't seem to get on the same page as my head.

The last thing I should be doing right now is having sex with Kat. Not with all the uncertainty in my mind and my body still on the mend, but I need this. I need to prove she belongs to me even when I'm not sure of it myself or am even sure I want it.

I capture her lips in a demanding kiss and walk her backward toward the bed. Her knees hit the mattress, but I hold her steady, devouring her and preventing her from falling back.

She drags her mouth away with a pant, deftly unbuckles my belt, and lowers the zipper of my pants. Eager hands shove them down to the floor, and she wraps her palm around my hard cock.

Krishti...

Her tongue slides along mine, and she nips at my bottom lip. "Get on the fucking bed."

"I thought you didn't do this here. Ever." I allow her to turn me until my back is to the bed, then she presses against my chest until I drop with a groan.

"Yeah, then that should tell you all you need to know."

There's a good chance she's only doing this to get me to forget my concerns about Rose, but when my ass hits the mattress and she pulls up her dress to expose her bare pussy, I don't fucking care anymore.

I shift on the mattress until my back presses against the headboard, and she crawls across after me and straddles my hips. She grasps my cock in her right hand and drags the head of it through her wet cunt.

"Fuck." I grab her hips and dig into them.

She leans down and brushes her lips over mine. "Don't worry, Michael. I won't hurt you."

I growl and suck her bottom lip into my mouth, then bite down on it. "Bullshit."

A low chuckle vibrates in her chest pressed to mine, and she sinks onto my cock slowly, inch by agonizing inch, until she's fully impaled on me.

Kat rolls her hips and glides up until only the head sits inside of her. Then she leans down and slides her tongue across my lips as she lowers herself, starting a mind-bending rhythm—up and down, rotating her hips, and squeezing my dick like a vise.

Her tongue tangles with mine, thrusting and rolling, and I suck it into my mouth. She moans, and her pussy ripples along my shaft.

Every fiber of my being wants me to dig my heels into the mattress and thrust up to meet her, to drive myself even harder and deeper inside her hot cunt, but there's no way my body can handle that right now. I need to let her take control and giving that up might as well be giving up my life. Because that's what it feels like right now—like her pussy is trying to suck the goddamn life out of me.

And at this moment...I'm more than ready to let her.

For the first time in over a week, something other than pain is taking over my body. Adrenaline and testosterone and lust surge through my veins, finally making me feel alive again.

And it makes me more determined than ever on my mission.

Kat releases my mouth and leans back to brace her hands on my legs, changing the angle so that the head of my cock drags against her G-spot. She gasps and drops her head back, her mouth falling open, and exposing her long, elegant neck down to her perfect breasts spilling out of the V-neck of her dress.

I reach up and drag the stretchy material down to free her erect nipples. They call to me like beacons in a dark storm, and I lean forward, ignoring the sharp bite of pain in my side, to pull the right one between my teeth and bite down.

She gasps and jerks on my dick, and then, she's coming—her pussy rippling and clasping at my cock, dragging my orgasm from me, and sucking my load inside of her.

Along with a little piece of my soul.

FIFTEEN

KAT SAGS AGAINST ME, and I lean back against the headboard for a moment, both of our chests heaving and her pants of breath fluttering against my neck. I brush my hand slowly along her spine, and she shudders and clenches around my still-hard cock inside her.

I've had a lot of sex in my life, with a lot of different women. But there's something about Kat...

About the way we clash together—like two massive ships colliding in a storm. It should destroy us both, send us to the watery depths, but instead, it makes me feel stronger, more ready for what's to come.

This is probably what Grandfather felt like when the Morina bitch latched onto him. It's likely exactly what brought him down.

Kat slowly leans back and brushes her fingers across my cheek. "Don't ever be jealous like that again."

I nip at her lip and pull it between my teeth before releasing it with a *pop*. "Stop acting like I'm going to do anything you tell me to. We both know I won't."

A tiny smile turns the corner of her lips. "Unfortunately, I do know that."

"Let's just hope my men were able to stay on Rose and we figure out a way to take care of him and fast. The sooner he's gone, the sooner we can set the plan into motion."

She sighs and rolls off me, both of us releasing strangled groans as our bodies separate. She shifts her dress back down and turns onto her side, propping her head up on her hand. I don't have the energy to try to tuck my still-hard dick back in my pants, so I just recline against the headboard and let my eyes drift closed.

She reaches into my jacket pocket and pulls out my cigarettes and lighter, then lights one up. The familiar smell of smoke wafts up to me, and then she places the cigarette at my lips. "What exactly is the plan now? You wait for an opportunity to take out Rose, and then what?"

I reach up and take a pull from the cigarette—the rush of the nicotine mixing with the adrenaline and testosterone still filling my blood. "Then we move forward with everything we've been talking about. Esad will have the girls on their way here next week, and we need to get the new house ready and start looking for others." I turn my head to look at her. "And you need to give me access to the files so I can start figuring out what I can use."

She pulls the cigarette from my hand to take a hit. "What about the Russians and the Irish? They're going to keep coming at you after what you did."

I shrug slightly and close my eyes again. "With the information that I'm anticipating is in your files, I'll hopefully own the people who can make their businesses much harder to run, and eventually, we can crush them to the point that we can take over all their territory without much of a struggle."

It's much better than the alternative—an all-out bloody war that could cost me something I'm not willing to give.

"As much as I would love to move things along from the stand-still we seem to have been in for the last few months," I release a heavy sigh, "this is a long game. Rushing in with brute force to try to take them all out would leave me exposed and cost me a lot of men. And while I might not exactly be fond of several of them, I need people to protect me as much as I need them to fight for me."

"I think you're going to have a big fight on your hands soon."

"No doubt."

Perhaps taking the Russian, the Irishman, the Colombian wasn't the best plan. It seemed like it was at the time, but looking back on it, all I got from it was more questions and even angrier enemies.

She drags her fingertips across my thigh, sending a shiver through my body. "But, in the meantime, you're just going to dodge the bullets?"

I chuckle and wink at her. "That's the plan."

Her gaze travels to my side, even though she can't see the healing wounds through my shirt. "That didn't seem to go so well for you last time."

"No, I guess not. And we still don't know who the fuck it was."

She passes the cigarette back to me. "My money is on Rose."

I tense just hearing his name from her mouth again. "What did he say while he was here?"

She sighs and leans back against the headboard. "Not much. He said his men have been raving about the place, and just like you suspected, when I told them I might be looking for a partner, he jumped at the chance to come to see it."

"I knew that fucker would want in on this." I take another drag and let the smoke slowly trickle from my mouth. "He's smart enough to know a big money operation opportunity. And he's probably thinking he can get South American girls up here the same way I'm getting our girls."

"Through Valentina's docks?"

I nod slowly. "With the relationship already established with Rose running drugs in her territory, he probably thinks she'd be amenable to that."

Kat chuckles and shakes her head. "That wouldn't surprise me. He seems to think he has me eating out of the palm of his hand. I don't think he reads women very well."

"The fucker probably thinks they all worship at his feet."

"It wouldn't surprise me if they do."

I whip my head around to look at her.

She shrugs and takes the cigarette from me for one last hit before putting it out in the ashtray on the nightstand. "I can't lie and say he's not handsome and a little bit charming."

My jaw clenches, and my hands fist where they sit at my sides.

One of her warm hands finds my cheek before I can say anything. She brushes her thumb across my lips, preventing me from uttering the angry words on the tip of my tongue. "But that shit doesn't work on me."

I scoff and shake my head. "What handsome and charming?" I raise an eyebrow. "So, I'm neither?"

She grins at me, humor flashing in her eyes, and leans forward to press a kiss to my lips. "Scary and ruthless are much more my type."

SIXTEEN

"WHAT DO you mean you lost him?" I slam my fist against my desk and tighten my grip on my phone with the other hand.

This cannot be happening.

"I'm sorry, boss." Altin's voice wavers through the line as he tries to come up with an excuse that won't get him killed. "We had three cars on him and two hanging back in case he turned too fast for us to follow, but his SUV pulled into a parking garage near the Riverwalk, Millennium Park, and by the time we got in, we couldn't locate them. No one ever saw it come back out, either."

"Fuck. How is that fucking possible? Are you saying he just disappeared?"

He pauses for a moment before he finally manages to come up with an answer. "Yes."

"Or maybe you're just fucking idiots who can't do your fucking jobs. Fuck!" I end the call and chuck my phone across the room. It hits the wall and shatters, pieces scattering across the floor. I drop my head into my palms and tug at my hair. "Fuck! Fuck! Fuck!"

How the fuck did they lose him?

He's like fucking Houdini.

Always slipping through my fingers.

Though...maybe the location they lost him is a clue in and of itself. He can't have just disappeared. He had to go *somewhere.*

"Genti!"

He pushes open the door and pops his head into my office. "Yeah, boss?"

"Give me your phone."

His eyes drift down to the remains of mine on the floor, and he walks in and hands me his cell.

"I'll need this for a while."

He nods and retreats, closing the door behind him while I dial Arden.

I don't even care that it's two in the morning there. This can't wait.

He answers on the fifth ring with a yawn. "Boss? What's up?"

"I need you awake and functioning right now."

"Shit." He sucks in a breath, and the sound of sheets rustling in the background tells me he's getting up. "What's going on? Kat?"

"No. Rose. The guys followed him to a parking garage near Millennium Park and the Riverwalk. I need to know everything around there, anywhere he might've been going. Crosscheck everything we know about him and anywhere he's ever been seen. Also, see if you can hack into any surveillance cameras in the area and find the car when it leaves. I want to know where I can find this fucker."

Arden sighs. "Sir, I don't think we're going to find much. Whoever he has working for him on the IT side does an excellent job of covering his tracks. I've been trying to get something on him for a while, and—"

I slam my fist down again, and pain radiates up my left arm. "I don't fucking care. Be better. I need to locate him."

Kat may have agreed to work with me to locate him, but she can only prolong the charade of needing a partner for so long before she'll actually have to take some actions to convince him it's real.

And I don't even want to think about what kind of action he's going to want. Something tells me it isn't anything I'm going to be willing to let him do. Nor do I fully trust Kat to be alone with him again.

"Okay, boss." The click of keys comes through the line. "I'm on it."

He better be.

My razor-thin patience is on the verge of snapping—the stress of the events over the last few weeks finally taking its toll.

"I'll call you as soon as I have anything." He ends the call without another word.

I clutch Genti's phone in my hand and fight the urge to chuck it against the wall to join mine. Despite my desire to destroy something, this can't be it. I can't be unreachable, and there are people I need to talk to. Things that need to be done. So, instead of tossing it, I set it onto the desk and suck in a deep breath to try to control the anger raising my blood pressure before making the next call.

Kat needs to know what's happened because the only hope we have of salvaging the plan is for her to arrange another meeting with Rose. One where we might be able to attempt another way to ensure we don't lose him.

I grab the phone and dial Kat.

She's been waiting for an update, so she answers on the first ring. "Is it done?"

I pinch the bridge of my nose and squeeze my eyes shut. "I wish. But no. Rose managed to slip away."

"Shit."

"Yeah."

Shit.

The plan seemed fool-proof at the time we implemented it, but sometimes I forget, men are fools. Lately, especially my men. It seems they fuck up everything they touch. The only reliable one in the past few weeks has been Kat, the one I trust the least of my allies at the moment.

She releases a frustrated sigh, one that matches my own feelings about this new development. "So, what are you going to do? What's the plan?"

"I'm working on something. If Rose calls you, try to put off meeting with him again for a few days. Give me time to get what I need together."

A plan is starting to form in my head, one I wish I had thought of before we had Rose at our fingertips and lost him. If we can pull it off, it will ensure there's no way he can slip past us a second time.

But it will require a sacrificial lamb...

And I have just the one in mind.

"Genti!" My voice booms around the room, and I tap my fist on the desk while I wait for him.

He pushes open the door and sticks his head in. "Yeah?"

"I need you to—"

The blast hits so hard, Genti flies into the room on a ball of fire, and I'm thrown back in my chair to slam against the wall behind me. A conflagration of flames fills the office, and a massive beam drops from the ceiling into the middle of the room. Thick, black smoke billows around me, and scorching heat licks at my exposed skin.

Krishti...I've finally found Hell.

ENDURING ENVY

As iron is eaten by rust, so are the envious consumed by envy.

-Antisthenes

ONE

HEAT BLAZES around me and licks across my exposed skin. A sharp ringing fills my ears. I shake my head to try to clear it from the fog enveloping me after being thrown against the wall by the explosion. Familiar pain slices through my side, where my body is still desperately trying to recover from the shooting.

I open my eyes and push myself up to take in what used to be my office.

Flames billow through the door and climb up and across the ceiling. A beam hangs down in the middle of the office where Genti had been thrown by the blast.

Shit.

It was some sort of explosion.

The inferno hasn't reached me yet, but there's only one way out of this room—the door the flames surge through. A pretty shitty error in planning if you ask me. Aleksander likely thought it was safest that way—hard to ambush someone when you have to walk right in the door in front of his desk. He never could have anticipated being in a situation like this with no escape.

Smoke fills the air and chokes out the oxygen from the room. I cough and cover my mouth with my arm.

I need to get the fuck out of here.

But how?

It seems like a lost cause from where I crouch next to the back wall. I make my way around the desk, closer to the fire. Genti groans on the floor, the fallen beam lying next to him.

Fuck. It might have hit him.

I drop to my knees and crawl over to him, trying to avoid the smoke billowing in the air closer to the ceiling. "Genti." I shake him and roll him onto his back. "Wake up."

His eyes flicker open, though they seem lost and unfocused. Blood drips onto the floor from a nasty gash on his temple, but he otherwise looks unharmed.

"We need to get out of here." But with the raging inferno mere feet away, coming from the hallway and only exit, I'm not sure how.

I pull Genti into a seated position and slide my arm under his to help him to his feet. "You need to get up."

He grunts in response and shakes his head. I drag him up and toward the door, but the heat is so intense, I have to back away as it almost blisters my skin.

Fuck. Fuck. Fuck.

Why haven't the sprinklers kicked on?

I glance up at the ceiling and the ancient fire suppression sprinkler system embedded there. It's probably from the goddamn seventies and doesn't work anyway. But we either sit here and wait for the smoke and flames to overrun us, or we die trying to get out.

I'm not going to sit back and wait for my death to engulf me. It's not the Syla way. Even trapped at the bottom of that damn pit, I fought. Maybe not physically because there was nowhere to go, but I fought the encroaching darkness. I fought against the Grim Reaper trying to drag me down below. I fucking fought.

And I'm not about to give up now.

I jostled Genti to try to wake him more. "You need to walk. I can't carry you out."

He nods his understanding and tries to steady his feet more. I keep my arm around him and cover my mouth with my free arm. He does the same, but flames leap through the door at us.

SHIT!

The conflagration rages higher and thicker across the ceiling, over the old sprinkler system.

Come on, you motherfucker!

Almost as if in answer, cold water rains down on us.

Thank fuck.

Either God heard my plea and decided to forgive my many sins and indiscretions, or we just got damn fucking lucky.

My lungs instantly welcome the minor relief from the smoke, and the flames begin to dissipate slightly in both the office and the hallway. If we wait another minute, we might be able to get out without charring ourselves to a crisp.

"Michael?" Altin's voice carries down the hallway toward us.

I open my mouth to respond, but a fit of coughing steals my words.

Altin appears in the doorway, spraying the flames with the industrial fire extinguisher from behind the bar. "Let's get the fuck out of here."

Trying his best to keep the inferno around us at bay, Altin ushers us out into the engulfed hallway.

The heat batters my skin where my clothes don't cover it, but I keep my head down and help Genti toward the main club—or what's left of it. What was once the stage now resembles a pile of burning, charred rubble, and the bar to the right side of the room is practically obliterated—only the strong, solid wood main portion is still standing.

Charred bodies lie on the floor, surrounded by partially singed wood and debris.

"Jesus Christ." I scan the room and suck in a smoky breath. "What happened?"

Altin shakes his head as he leads us toward the front entrance. "Not sure. The whole place just fucking exploded. The only reason Agon and I survived is we were behind the bar. It absorbed the shock of the explosion."

The familiar blond hair of the waitress I had fucked in my office only a few weeks ago gives me pause, and I looked down at her body, already destroyed by the fire. If I had cared about her at all, even an ounce, I might be feeling something right now other than anger at having to find another waitress. But there's no time to dwell in any sort of sentiment—or lack thereof—now. We need to get the fuck out of here.

Water continues to stream down from the rest of the sprinklers in the club, and the sounds of sirens in the distance jerk my head up and draw me toward the front door and out of it into the fresh, cool night air.

I suck in several deep, cleansing breaths, and a rattling cough seizes my chest. Genti does the same, and I lower him down onto the street and turn back to look at the club.

Flames still billow from parts of the building, the ancient sprinklers unable to control the inferno.

"Jesus." I wipe my hands over my face to try to remove some of the soot and water. "Was it a bomb?"

Altin shakes his head and follows my gaze at the building. "I don't know. It sure felt like it."

"How the fuck did someone get it in?"

He shrugs. "I don't know, sir. Maybe it wasn't inside at all but outside?"

"Maybe?" I shake my head and step toward the blaze. "There doesn't appear to be much damage on the opposite side of the building."

I cough and drop my hands to my knees to take several deep breaths. This is the second time in two weeks somebody has tried to take me out. And whoever the fuck it is has stepped up their game and come at me in *my* house.

That takes some real fucking gall.

A fire engine roars around the corner, sirens blaring, followed closely by two police cars.

Fuck.

And now I'm going to have to deal with the cops.

At least when I was shot, the guys got me out of there before the cops could arrive and moved my car so there wasn't anything for them to examine. Here, I'll have the police crawling all over my actual headquarters. It's a good thing I don't keep anything incriminating here.

I turned to Altin and Genti. "Don't tell them anything more than needed to keep yourself out of custody. As far as we're concerned, we don't know what happened."

Because it's true. We don't.

All I do know is we're in some seriously deep shit.

TWO

I TAKE a long drag from the cigarette dangling from my lips and blow the smoke straight across the table and into the face of Detective Lopez. I have to give the man credit—he doesn't even flinch. His dark-brown eyes stay locked on mine in what feels like a never-ending stare-down deathmatch.

It has to have been at least an hour since he came in here and sat down without a word. Sixty minutes of looking at each other, sizing each other up, neither of us willing to break eye contact or be the first to speak.

Intimidation tactics like this won't work on me, though.

I could sit here all fucking day and play this game as long as I have a pack of smokes with me. It might be uncomfortable without them, but I could survive even with the lack of nicotine if I really had to.

Whatever it takes to break the man on the opposite side of the small, metal table.

I lean forward and stub out my cigarette in this shiny plastic ashtray in the center of the table, then recline back in the torturously uncomfortable hard plastic chair.

This could go on forever. And I would let it. But it doesn't really serve a purpose. Not when I know he has nothing on me and all I want to do is take a long, hot shower to get the stink of the fire off me and then sleep.

So, while I hate to lose this battle of wills, I'm willing to in order to get clean and horizontal. "How long do you plan on keeping me here, officer?"

The corner of his mouth quirks up. "Detective."

"Oh, yeah." I rap my knuckles on the table. "That's right. Recently promoted, as I hear it."

That stone-hard demeanor of his disappears for a split second before he throws it back up in place.

That's right, Detective Lopez, you may think you know a thing or two about me, but I know about you, too.

I make it my business to know about the officers in the organized crime division, the FBI, and anyone else who might be digging into what goes on in the underworld of Chicago. Knowing your enemy is important for many reasons, the least of which is that there may be something to use to twist their arm and get cooperation. Unfortunately, Lopez seems squeaky clean.

How annoying.

He offers me a cool, unfriendly smile—one I'm used to seeing from anyone in law enforcement unless they're on my payroll. "We're not here to talk about my job, Mr. Syla. We're here so I can find out who blew up your club."

I shrug nonchalantly, pull out another cigarette, light it, and take a drag. He watches every movement with keen interest, like it might tell him something I'm unwilling to.

Blowing out another cloud of smoke, I shift forward and rest my elbows on the table. "Did you think making me sit here for hours was going to somehow get you the answers you're looking for right away?"

After the ambulances arrived and the fire trucks managed to extinguish the blaze, Detective Lopez threw me in his squad car so fast, it almost gave me whiplash. A rush to get me here just to let me sit for hours, then another hour with him across from me in tense silence.

Assholes.

I take a drag off my cigarette and sigh, releasing the smoke into the tiny room. "I'm the victim here, Detective. Shouldn't you be looking for the people who did it instead of interrogating me?"

He snorts and shakes his head. "This isn't an interrogation, Mr. Syla, just a few simple questions that might help us do just that."

I inhale some much-needed nicotine and then blow out another ring of smoke toward him. A lesser man might be getting annoyed with being hit in the face with it by now, but Lopez remains cool and collected. It almost makes me like the guy. "Well, I'm sorry to break it to you, Detective, but I don't have a fucking clue what happened at the club today."

Though I wish I did.

Someone clearly wants me dead bad enough to try twice in quick succession. It's definitely a development I'm not pleased with.

He leans back in his chair and crosses his burly arms over his chest. His dark eyebrows rise. "So...that's the way we're gonna play it? You're going to pretend this had nothing to do with your business dealings, nothing to do with the bodies of three rival organization members who were found charred to a crisp in a warehouse ten blocks from your club only a few days ago? That this is nothing to do with the explosion some months back that almost killed the head of every organized crime group in the city and everyone seems to be fingering you for?"

I raise my hands and shrug. "I don't know anything about any of that." I lean forward and tap off my ash into the ashtray. "And if you want to go down that road of unfounded accusations, then I'm going to decline to continue to speak with you. I want my lawyer."

The magic words.

Lopez's lips twist into a sneer. He shoves back from the table and rises to his feet. "You're a real piece of work, Syla. You show up in town, immediately stirring up shit, and suddenly, the violence that's been relatively contained for the last couple of decades has exploded again."

I keep my eyes locked on his as I finish my cigarette and snuff it out in the ashtray. His rant doesn't intimidate me. I'm untouchable as far as the cops are concerned. Too careful to get caught. Too smart to say anything to ever implicate myself. A fact that has good old Detective Lopez hot around the collar.

And the blood was going to flow here one way or the other. No peace is ever permanent, and the world changes fast. That means expanding businesses and territories is inevitable—for everyone. Those both mean having to make sacrifices, like men.

I rise to my feet, adjust my smoke and ash stained suit coat, and button it. "I have noticed an alarming rise in violence lately. Sounds like you guys aren't doing your jobs very effectively."

He storms past me, opens the door, and then pauses before he steps through it. "You're free to leave. But if I find out you retaliated against whoever did this instead of letting us do it through legal means, you can bet your ass I'm gonna have you behind fucking bars."

I take a step toward him, then lean in until I'm too close for his comfort. "I'm positively quivering in fear."

A low growl emanates from deep in his barrel chest, but the man is smart enough not to lash out at me. If he did, he'd be looking at a lawsuit the department couldn't afford.

Instead, he snarls and storms out the door. I let him lead me through the police station, keenly aware of the inquisitive gazes of the officers and staff that follow each step I take.

Genti waits on a bench off to the side of the front entry. He jerks to his feet as I approach.

I lean into him while keeping my eye on the retreating Lopez. "Did they question you?"

He nods and rolls his eyes. "Sure fucking tried after the doctors cleared me at the hospital."

"What did you tell them?"

He shrugs and ushers me out of the police station and down the front steps. "The same thing you did—that I don't have a fucking clue what happened at the club."

It's the truth. No one can argue with that.

Or prove otherwise.

Which means there's no basis to keep us here. A fact Detective Lopez is no doubt lamenting at this very moment.

I glance around us as we make our way down the sidewalk toward a black SUV waiting at the curb. "What have you heard since I've been in there?"

Genti opens the rear passenger door for me, and I slide in. He closes it behind me then climbs into the front passenger seat—Altin at the wheel. Then he turns back to me as Altin tears away from the curb. "Three girls dead. Bernard and Gazmend dead. But as to the cause of the explosion? Nothing."

"Shit."

Altin glances at me in the rearview mirror. "You okay, boss?"

"I'm fucking fine. But the club isn't. We can't operate out of there until things get fixed. Any idea how long that's gonna take?"

He shrugs before he returns his focus to the traffic on the road. "The arson investigators were still there when I headed out here. Who knows when they'll release it to us. Could be days or weeks."

"Fuck." I slam my fist against the door.

Altin glances in the rearview again. "Where do you want to go, sir?"

Well, since the office is out of the question for the foreseeable future, that narrows my options. "Take me home. I'll figure it out from there."

Another wrench thrown into the fucking plan.

Another attempt on my life.

I don't know how many more I'll survive.

A cat may have nine lives, but a man can't have much more than three. I should've died at least three times in my life—twice in the last month alone.

I don't want to risk a fourth.

THREE

I PUSH open the door to my condo and slip inside the darkness, not even bothering with the light switch. After today, all I want to do is shower, sit in the dark, and have a smoke and drink...

A lot.

Then head to bed.

But the familiar smell of Kat's cigarettes mixed with her perfume hits me as the door clicks shut behind me. A flame blazes to life, illuminating her face where she sits on the couch. She lights her cigarette and extinguishes the lighter, leaving the only light in the room the glowing ember at the end of her Marlboro and a sliver of moonlight coming in from the window.

She takes a drag of her cigarette but doesn't say anything. The looming silence thickens the air worse than the smoke from the fire earlier today.

This isn't going to be pleasant.

I trudge over to the bar and pour myself a stiff drink, then lower myself into the chair facing her. She continues to sit stock straight as I take a sip and let the whiskey burn down my throat and into my gut.

"You couldn't have called to tell me you were alive?" Her question floats across the distance between us, laced with anger I can feel in my chest like a punch.

"Sorry, I was a little busy being harassed by the fucking cops."

She takes another long pull on her cigarette. "I had to find out about the explosion on the fucking news. And the only reason I knew you were okay is I managed to get a hold of Altin."

I groan and scrub a hand over my face, then pinch the bridge of my nose against the growing headache forming behind my eyes. "I don't need this right now, Kat. I've already been interrogated once today."

"How did that go?" The icy coolness of her question matches the vibe slamming into me even from across the coffee table separating us.

"It went as fine as it fucking could have, considering I don't know anything."

"No idea what caused the explosion?"

"No," I shake my head and take another drink, "but it seems whoever wants me gone is pretty intent on making it happen."

"It would seem so."

"I'm getting awfully sick of it."

She snorts and shakes her head before she snuffs out her cigarette in the ashtray. "You and me both."

"My men are looking for a clue that could point to who did this, but I'm doubtful about finding anything. Just like with the shooting, whoever did this made sure it wasn't traceable back to them. I'm certain of that."

"That should be a hint in and of itself."

"You're right." I set down my drink and pull a cigarette out of the pack in my jacket pocket. I light it and take the first hit, letting the nicotine course through my system, and I lean forward and rest my elbows on my knees. "The problem is the first attack was sloppy. But hitting me at my own headquarters is pretty calculated. Not something they would've just done at the drop of a hat or rushed into."

Kat shifts on the couch and uncrosses her legs, her creamy-white thigh practically glowing in the faint moonlight streaming in from the window to my left. "It does seem a little suspicious given the timing."

"What timing?"

"Of my meeting with Rose."

"The thought had crossed my mind, but I don't know how he would've known we're connected."

"The same way anyone knows anything. He watches you. He probably started watching me the moment I made contact with him. Maybe you're not as careful as you think you are."

I pull in a long drag and hold the smoke in my lungs, then blow it out on a mirthless laugh. Only hours ago, I was trying to escape the smoke, and now, I'm desperate to suck it into my lungs like it's the air I need to breathe.

"I don't have the answers, Kat. Not even fucking close. All I have is a whole lot of questions and an aching body that's screaming at me right now. And apparently, a woman who is, too." Even in the darkness of the room, the tension of her anger reaches me, tightening my skin and making me clench my free hand into a fist. "I don't know what you want from me, *kotele*."

She shoves up from her spot on the couch and makes her way over to the bar. The heavy crystal glass clinks against the decanter as she pours a drink then slams it back in one gulp. "I think you know exactly what I want, Michael. You're just not willing to give it to me."

I push to my feet, stub out my cig, and stalk over to her, grabbing her wrist to twist her around to face me. "Why don't you just fucking tell me instead of being cryptic all the fucking time."

Her red lips twist into a sneer. "I'm not cryptic, Michael. You're just dense and incapable of reading a woman at all."

I tighten my grip on her wrist and drag her up against me. Even in the dark, this close, she can't hide her response to me—the way her breath quickens, her heart racing where it presses against mine, the slight little moan she releases as I push my growing cock to her hips. "I can read you just fucking fine, *kotele*."

My free hand finds the hem of her dress and slips between her thighs. As per usual, she isn't wearing any panties, and my fingers find her hot and wet for me. I drag the tip of one through her arousal and up around her clit. She jerks and a tiny gasp slips from her mouth despite an obvious attempt to keep it in by biting her plump bottom lip.

"You want me, Kat. We both know that. And you've been willing to do anything you can to get me. That's the only reason I know it wasn't you who tried to kill me. If it were, then you deserve a goddamn Academy Award for your acting."

She presses her lips together in a thin line and stiffens in my hold. "You're an arrogant bastard; do you know that, Michael?"

I lean in and grin against her ear before I suck the lobe between my teeth and then bite down. "I know. And you fucking love me for it."

She doesn't acknowledge my words, but a soft mewl escapes her mouth, and she sags slightly against me, her free hand clutching at the front of my shirt.

My clothing still stinks like smoke from the fire, but she doesn't seem to care...and God knows I don't. After almost dying—*again*—I need something life-affirming. Something that reminds me that I'm alive and kicking despite some motherfucker's desire to send me six feet under.

And burying my dick inside Kat's warm heat right now will do just that.

FOUR

I CRASH my mouth down against hers in a brutal kiss. Kat's tongue glides against my lips, begging for entrance, and I open, allowing her access. She thrusts her hips against mine, trapping my hard cock between us as she claws at my shirt.

Her fingers fumble with the buttons, but I'm not worried about that at this moment. I don't need my shirt off to fuck her brains out.

And that's the only goal here. To remind Kat of why she's here with me. What it is she really *wants* from me even if she won't admit it out loud.

She wants me to love her. Something both of us are likely incapable of. But I'll get her and myself off as much as she wants. It's the only form of affection I can ever show her.

I dip my fingers into her hot cunt again and back her up against the bar. The glassware on it rattles. She gasps and fumbles with my zipper until she manages to lower it while tangling her greedy tongue with mine.

Her small warm hand slips into my pants and tightens around my cock. I groan into her mouth and shift my thumb up to press it against her clit. She bucks against my hand, tightening her pussy around my fingers, and I knock her hand away from my shaft and position the head at her core.

I lift her up onto the bar and push her ass back on it. She smacks into the glasses and bottles. They clink against each other, but she doesn't seem to notice, wrapping her legs around my back and pulling me toward her in a desperate move.

All it would take for me to bury myself inside her is one hard thrust, but I hold back, barely brushing my throbbing cock through her wetness.

"Please, Michael." Her whispered plea further heats my skin and redoubles my resolve.

"Tell me, *kotele*."

Her eyes widen. "Tell you what?"

"That you love that I'm an arrogant bastard."

She scowls at me, pulling again with her feet to try to get me inside her.

I wrap my right hand around her throat—images of our first night together against the wall just across the room flashing in my memory—and squeeze. "Tell me."

Defiance glints in her eyes, but when she opens her mouth, it isn't to argue. "Yes, I love it, you arrogant bastard!"

It's all I wanted. All I needed to hear to give her what she wants...and what *I* want.

One hand on her throat, the other digging into the flesh at her hip, I drive into her, rocking her back against the booze and sending a glass careening to shatter on the hard floor at our feet.

Neither of us even glance at it.

Her cunt clenches around my cock, drawing me even deeper, and I grit my teeth. She drops her head back, her mouth falling open, and I drag my dick out slowly, letting the head glide against her G-spot, eliciting an agonized moan from her.

I plunge back in, and she rolls her hips up to meet mine in one fluid motion.

Even after as many times as I've been inside Kat, each one seems more incredible than the last. The woman is pure fire. Burning and searing my skin more than the flames at the club ever could have. And just like that inferno, she doesn't care if she scorches me alive.

It's a mind-bending juxtaposition—how she can be so hot yet so frigid.

Cold and calculating, she's the type of woman I should never let anywhere near me, yet she's the one I can't stay away from. No matter the reservations I've had, they can't keep me from her.

From *this*.

She scrapes her nails against the back of my neck as I pull my hips back and drive into her again, pushing her against the glassware again. Another tumbler slides off the side and crashes to the floor, pieces ricocheting off the wood of the bar and the leg of my pants.

None of it matters. Nothing but being inside her.

Only hours ago, I thought my life was over. The flames were closing in, the smoke suffocating me. I thought whoever was behind the shooting had finally won. But *I'm* the one winning now.

Every time I withdraw and plunge back into her...I win.

Every time her lips brush over mine...I win.

Every time her nails score my skin...I win.

Over and over again...I win. I win.

I. Fucking. Win.

Each move brings me closer to a cataclysmic release, one that I'm confident will draw every last breath from me.

Her hips arch to meet mine. The glasses rattle, mingling with our gasps and moans to fill the air. It all finally culminates in a tightening at the base of my spine and a strangled cry from her as I bury myself deep inside her core while her cunt ripples and clenches me with her release.

She sags forward with a gasp and shudders against me as I drop my forehead to hers.

Neither of us is one for sentiment. Neither of us would ever be comfortable with that. But that was exactly what I needed.

Life-affirming and hard.

Nothing sweet, nothing romantic. Nothing but a reminder of what it feels like to sink inside a beautiful woman and to control her mind, body, and soul.

Kat may appear to be immune to feeling, immune to anything more than the physical connection between us, but when she opens her eyes and looks up at me, I see a flicker there. A flicker of something I never expected to see from her or any other woman, for that matter. She opens her mouth to say something but then bites it back.

I brush my thumb over her quivering lips and then lean down to press a kiss there. "What's wrong?"

She shakes her head and sighs. "Nothing. I was just thinking that I almost lost you today."

I grin at her and lean in to press a kiss to her lips. "You won't get rid of me that easily."

Even though I'm still not completely convinced that she hasn't tried.

She smiles and wiggles her eyebrows. "Good because finding someone else who could do *that*," she clenches around my cock, "so well would consume more time than I have right now."

I chuckle and wrap my hand around her throat, squeezing gently. "So, we're still going to pretend that's all this is, Kat? That it's all this will ever be?"

She lets her eyes drift closed, leaning into my touch. "Business partners, right?"

I snort and shake my head. "Sure, business partners."

FIVE

"Do you really think this is a good idea?" The uncertainty lacing Kat's question comes through as strong as the flavor of the hundred-day dry-aged ribeye on my plate.

I shrug, take a bite of my steak, and chew slowly while I watch her take a sip of her wine, where she sits across from me at our usual table in the backroom of *Sofra*. "I'm not sure what else we can do. Rose isn't going to just go away now that you've got him hooked on the idea of the partnership. You're going to have to meet with him again."

She shifts in her seat, the movement pushing her ample breasts up even higher. "But what if he knows? What if the explosion was him trying to take out my *current* partner? What if it had nothing to do with all your past history?"

I swallow and shake my head, even though I've contemplated that very question in the day since the explosion. Every potential possibility has gone through my mind, but none have been confirmed. "It would be naïve to think that. If it were Rose, we have a lot of bad blood built-up over the last few months that was plenty enough reason. If he really knew we were partners, he would have taken you out, too."

She taps her nails against the side of her wine glass and considers me for a moment. "I guess you're probably right, but his eagerness to meet again is somewhat concerning."

"Why?" I raise an eyebrow at her. "You have a lucrative business, and he's a businessman. The Russians and the Irish already run girls, while he's primarily kept his business to drugs. This could be a major opening for him. Why wouldn't he leap at the chance? Or do you think all men are just trying to get into your pants?"

She laughs and takes another sip of her wine. "Don't sound so jealous, Michael. It's not like I'm going to let him."

"How the fuck do I know that?"

She presses her lips together and sets her glass down with a little too much force. "Because I told you so, Michael. It was your idea to connect me with Rose in the first place, so don't give me shit now that you have. I was doing you a favor. And now you may have dragged me into the crossfire."

I set down my knife and fork, locking my gaze with hers. "I'm not going to let anything happen to you."

A mirthless chuckle slips from her mouth, and she shakes her head. "You really think you can protect me, Michael? First, I've been protecting myself for a long time. I had to learn how to do that. And second, I have reliable men to watch my back. I'm not the one who ended up with bullet holes in me or got blown up. That was you."

"Yeah, well," I flash her a grin, despite my annoyance at her pointing out the obvious, "I guess my personality just brings that out in people."

"Agreed." She scowls and drums her fingers on the table. "We need a game plan. A way to ensure we're both safe while you try to figure out a way to take out Rose."

My phone buzzes in my pocket, and I reach into my jacket and pull it out. Speaking of which... hopefully, this call will provide a way to do that. I hit *accept* and bring the phone to my ear. "Arden, what do you have for me?"

He clears his throat, and static zings through the line, his connection complete shit. "Hey, boss.

GWYN MCNAMEE

I scoured every camera in a ten-block radius of the parking structure where Rose disappeared. It took me forever to gain access, and there are some I can't get into. But I think I got good enough coverage that I would have seen them leave. They must've switched cars in the parking structure. It's the only explanation I have for why we can't find him. Why he never came out."

"Fuck." I slam my fist against the table, rattling the silverware, china, and wine glasses. Thankfully, we're in her usual private room; otherwise, Arvin might've been pissed that I made a scene in the restaurant. "So, you're telling me you have nothing?"

"Well…" he sucks in a breath. "Not nothing. I may have a lead on some information about Kat."

I shift in my chair, keeping my eyes on the woman in question. I can't give away anything to her, but my curiosity has been piqued. "What is it?"

"Remember how I told you the one hostel owner remembered her?"

"Yes."

"Well, she called me back. Said she found something that was left when Kat checked out."

"She left things there?" It doesn't make any sense unless it was accidental. That might mean she made a mistake that could actually give me something. "What do you have?"

"A travel guide for Eastern Europe and the Baltics…and a picture tucked inside."

"A picture of what?"

Kat watches me, sipping slowly at her wine, undoubtedly trying to unravel the other side of the conversation. I take a drink of my wine, doing my best to appear disinterested in what Arden is telling me.

"It's an interesting photo of a woman who looks like Kat with an older woman in a wheelchair."

"What's so interesting about that?"

"Well…if it is Kat…her eyes are a different color."

"What do you mean?"

"Katherine's license has her eye color listed as blue, and the woman in this picture's eyes appear more of an amber golden color."

I hold Kat's icy blue gaze. "Then it can't be her."

"I don't know, sir. It looks an awful lot like her."

"Maybe a relative?"

"I don't know, sir. I'm gonna keep digging."

"You do that." I don't want any stone unturned where Kat's concerned. Not when my involvement with her deepens every day.

"Oh, there's one more thing."

"What's that?"

"The photo was stuck into the chapter about Albania."

My blood runs cold. Nothing good could come from Kat or one of her relatives exploring Albania. *Nothing.* "I'll talk to you later."

I hang up and slip the phone back into my jacket's inside pocket, then reach for my wine and take a long, slow gulp.

One of Kat's thin dark eyebrows rises slowly. "Everything all right?"

I offer her a slow nod. "Yep. Just Esad checking in about one of the girls on the boat."

That seems like a legitimate excuse for my side of the conversation she overheard.

"Is everything on track?"

"Thankfully, yes." I spoke to Esad earlier today, and they were already underway. "We should have the girls here in only a matter of weeks."

A slow grin spreads across Kat's face, and she holds up her glass of wine toward me. "Then a toast is in order. To our new business venture."

I raise my glass and clink it against hers. "To our partnership."

However long it may last.

Kat takes a sip of her wine and smiles. "I know you've been anxious to get in and take a look at some of the surveillance videos. While your office is destroyed, it might be a good time to do that. We just have to make sure Rose doesn't make any unexpected visits while you're there."

"That's a good point. If he shows up and sees me, we're fucked."

"You'll have to view them at your place, just to be safe."

"Agreed."

"Let's start tomorrow."

It can't come soon enough for me. With Rose out there stirring up trouble and me with the target still on my back, the only thing I can do is start moving the pieces around in the background and prepare for what's about to come.

"Are you ready to take the next steps, Michael?"

I grin at her, Arden's news playing in the back of my mind. "As ready as I'll ever be. Are you?"

She leans forward, across the table, and presses a kiss to my lips. It's slow and sweet and sensual, the taste of the wine we're drinking swirling from her tongue to mine.

I've never been more ready for anything in my life.

SIX

TOTALLY FUCKED UP. There's no other way to describe it. The entire main area of the club, the back hallway, and my office are destroyed.

Even after a week—five days for the arson investigation squad to release the building back to us and another two working to get the smoke and water-damaged drywall out and replaced and the burned support beams back up—the place still looks like hell raged through here and smells like it.

I had hoped there would be enough progress that I could at least work today, but that seems unlikely. Reviewing the videos from Kat's at my place is getting tedious and uncomfortable, and I need a change of scenery.

So much for that.

I wave Altin over to where I stand, examining the place. "When will this place be functional?"

It isn't even about the money the club brings in. It's mostly locals and other Albanians in town who come here, anyway, but I need a base of operations. As much as I'd love to go work in luxury at Kat's house, I can't be seen there. Not with Rose breathing down her neck about the potential partnership. She's already blown off meeting with him again once, and I don't know how many more times she'll be able to. If he just showed up there unannounced and I were there, a whole lot of bullets would fly, which would ruin the plans Kat and I have.

My phone rings in my pocket, and I pull it out and glance at the number. The caller ID says *Chicago Police Department.*

Fucking wonderful. Just who I want to hear from.

I accept the call and put the phone to my ear. "Detective Lopez, I presume? To what do I owe this pleasure?"

"I was just calling to give you the results of our investigation."

I lean back against the smoke-stained bar and pinch the bridge of my nose against the headache the smell is giving me. "Any idea who did it?"

A moment of silence lingers on the line before he clears his throat. "Nobody."

I stand up straight and drop my hand. "What the hell is that supposed to mean?"

"It means that the fire department says it was an accident. A leak in the gas line on the side of the building and a spark from something, probably the electrical box, set it off."

Bull fucking shit.

"You don't really believe that, do you?"

"Of course, I don't believe it. It's too much of a coincidence. Somebody cut that damn gas line and lit the place up."

He and I both know it.

But whoever did it knew what they were doing and how not to leave any evidence. That means we're dealing with somebody who's a true professional. It certainly narrows down the suspect pool. Though not enough for me to point my finger at anyone.

At least, not yet.

"I appreciate the phone call, Officer...I mean Detective."

"I suggest you watch your back, Michael. I don't think I have to tell you that you have a lot of enemies out there, and I don't want the next call to be for me to come look at your body."

I chuckle and shake my head. "Come on, Detective, we both know that would be a dream for you."

"No, actually, Michael, it wouldn't. Because if you die, it's gonna set off a war that none of us want to deal with in the city. Your men will retaliate, and there'll be blood in the streets—more than there already is."

"Wow, Detective, I didn't know you cared so much."

"Don't let it go to your head."

I end the call and slide my phone back into my pocket.

Altin raises an eyebrow at me. "Detective Lopez?"

"Yeah." I rub my eyes, stinging from the smoke in the air, and sigh. "Says it was a gas leak. An accident."

Altin snorts and shakes his head.

Genti approaches from the back hallways and flicks his gaze between us. "What's so funny?"

I spread my arms wide at the carnage caused by the explosion. "Detective Lopez says it was an accident. Gas line leak."

He scowls and waves his arms around. "Does this look like a fucking accident?"

I don't have the heart to tell him that when gas lines explode, the damage is usually a lot worse than this. Whoever cut ours couldn't have let it go for very long. Only enough to let it build up to make that kind of explosion. My guess is they expected a lot more damage.

While the news from Lopez isn't all that surprising, it's still frustrating as fuck not to have any leads.

"And no one was able to gather any surveillance video from any surrounding buildings that might help see who did it?"

They shake their heads, and Altin motions toward the front of the building. "No. Nothing's pointed in this direction intentionally."

Nobody wants any evidence of anything that might drag them into any trouble. If the police knew they had cameras catching who was coming and going from here, they could end up in a really shitty position.

I slam my fists against the bar and drop my head down, squeezing my eyes shut.

Genti clears his throat. "Uh...so, where does this leave us, sir?"

"In the middle of a fucking quagmire."

Esad will be here with the shipment soon. Kat has already set to work furnishing the new house, and everything is lined up for the new girls with their new identification, money, and housing. And Kat has brought over a small portion of the videos from Kat's Cradle to start reviewing, but it's slow-going, and there are literally hundreds of hours of tapes to weed through. It has to be done carefully and meticulously. I don't want to miss any potential information that could help me or any blackmail material. That means it could take months to get what I really need.

And I'm not a patient man.

I push off the bar and make my way toward the front door.

Altin and Genti follow, hot on my heels.

I pause at the door and turn back to examine the construction.

Altin watches me closely. "You leaving?"

"Yeah, I'm leaving. Keep trying to find Rose. Arden has been doing his thing, so touch base with him, and tell him to call me about the other thing he's working on, too. In the meantime, we move ahead with everything as planned."

Genti raises his dark eyebrows. "When can we retaliate for this?"

I flashback to the three men sitting tied to the chairs, their bloody entrails and body parts on the floor. "Don't. I already lost men, and Driton is barely hanging on to life because I rushed into retaliation last time. This time, we wait and see. Once we have proof, we go to the other families."

"You think they'll care?"

"It might help stop a war if they know I'm not doing it just to be a fucking asshole."

Genti's lips twist into a scowl. "Isn't a war what we want, though?"

"Of course, it is, you fucking idiot, but I want a war I can win. I can't win if I have all four other families coming at me at once. And while Valentina and I may appear to be on the same side right now, I'm not stupid enough to believe that will last forever." I rub at the back of my neck, trying to release the tension building there. "Our priorities are Rose and repairing the club. We get those taken care of and then we'll deal with whoever the fucker is who wants me dead."

Genti steps toward me. "I should come with you, sir."

I throw up a hand to stop him. "If they can get me here, they can get me anywhere. It doesn't matter how many of you surround me walking to and from my car, or drive me anywhere, or try to watch my back. If they want me, they can come fucking get me." I tap where my gun sits in the holster at my side. "I'm ready for them."

SEVEN

I TAKE a bite of my *fërgesë me melçi,* letting the garlic and other flavors dance across my tongue, bringing more memories of home—some good, most bad. Slowly chewing, my gaze drifts around the restaurant. It's been a long time since I've eaten in the front room, where I can watch the people coming and going. Laughing. Talking. Enjoying each other's company.

But I'm sick of hiding.

I'm not going to let whoever the asshole is who's trying to take me out win by holing myself up somewhere and cowering in the dark. I've spent enough time there.

If they want me that badly, they can come get me here while I enjoy one of my favorite dishes.

Arvin approaches me with his brow furrowed and his lips twisting. "Michael? Several dark SUVs just pulled up in front of the restaurant."

I raise an eyebrow.

He glances over his shoulder toward the front. "I'm a little concerned about what may be walking in the door."

I wave him off. "Don't worry, Arvin, I assure you, no one is stupid enough to do anything while I'm in public like this."

The New York mob may have routinely taken out people publicly in the streets, but I don't think any of my counterparts here in Chicago are that brazen or stupid. Not with the way the police are going to be bearing down on us now after the explosion.

The front door opens, and Galen McGinnis walks in, followed closely by his Russian counterpart, Valerian Kamenev.

Well, well, well, isn't this interesting.

While the peace that was brokered in Chicago prior to my and Rose's arrival meant they weren't tearing at each other's throats anymore, they definitely make for strange bedfellows. And their being here together can only mean one thing—they're here to talk to me.

They spot me in the back-corner booth and approach cautiously, scanning their surroundings carefully. Genti and Altin step from their place just to the side of the booth to block the progress of the Irishman and Russian, but I wave them off and allow the heads of the other families to approach.

"Well, gentlemen, this is an unusual surprise." I motion toward the empty chairs on the opposite side of the table from the red leather bench where I sit.

They both scowl at me, the move twisting the fresh scar on the side of Galen's face that bisects his left eye—a little souvenir from the bombing everyone seems to think I'm responsible for.

I offer a grin. "If you wanted a meeting, you should've just called."

Galen pulls out a chair across from me and sits while Valerian continues to survey the restaurant for a minute before finally taking his seat, too. "You never would've agreed to meet with us if we had."

"Oh, you don't give me enough credit. I'm always open to seeing friends."

Galen snorts, then reaches forward and grabs my wine glass to down what's left of it.

I chuckle and wave a hand at it. "Do help yourself."

Arvin eyes me cautiously from the corner of the room, and I motion for him to bring another bottle of wine and some more glasses. He hurries off to do that while I lean back in the booth and push away my half-eaten plate.

"To what do I owe the honor of this audience?"

I haven't been in the same room with either of them since the bombing months ago at the meeting designed to plan my demise. I certainly never would've expected them to show up here and be seen with me voluntarily, especially after what I did to their men.

Valerian locks his hard blue gaze with mine. "We've heard about several attempts on your life. It seems you've made a few enemies since arriving in Chicago."

I chuckle and spread out my hands. "It's a good thing I have friends like you."

He grins at me and shakes his head. "We don't have an issue with you as long as you steer clear of us and our men...which you didn't." He lowers his voice and leans forward slightly. "You retaliated by taking out Oleg and Padraig without any evidence we were involved in the shooting—which we weren't."

I shrug and shift slightly to ensure I'm close enough that no one else will hear. They won't be getting an apology from me for what I did. "So, what, you're here to kill me? To retaliate for my actions?" I motion around the restaurant. "It wouldn't be wise to do it in such a public place."

They both lean back and examine the restaurant as Arvin brings a bottle of wine. He pops it open, pours three glasses, and backs away like his ass is on fire.

Galen watches him, and once he's gone, he returns his focus to me. "As much as we would love to do to you what you did to our men, we're here about something else."

Oh, well, this just got interesting.

"I'm shocked. Wasn't it only a few months ago you had your big meeting to try to figure out a way to get rid of me?"

They glance at each other and shrug.

Valerian inclines his head toward me. "Things change."

I raise an eyebrow. "What's changed so much recently?"

The huge Russian takes a sip of his wine and stares at the glass for a moment. "Have you heard anything about what Rose is up to?"

"Rose?" I reach for my wine and take a slow sip.

His question definitely piques my interest. I hadn't expected them to bring up our other *friend*. I had assumed this conversation was about me.

I shrug nonchalantly. "I hear he has his hands in a few things. Why?"

Valerian sips his wine and twirls the glass in his hand, watching the red liquid swirl. "I understand he may be looking into a new investment opportunity."

Shit. Kat...

I keep my expression neutral even though I sense where they're going with this. "Really? What's that?"

Galen offers a hard smile that doesn't reach his green eyes. "Girls."

I raise an eyebrow. "Girls? I'm not sure I understand what you mean."

He rests his elbows on the table, leaning toward me slightly. "There's a new player in the market. A woman named Katherine. And it seems she's looking for a partner—Rose."

EIGHT

HOW THE FUCK did they find out about that?

Concern tightens my gut, the wine churning there like acid. I force myself to take another sip anyway and watch the two men across from me. Kat has been careful, or so I thought. So if they know about her and her meeting with Rose, then there's a lot more talking going on somewhere that I'm not aware of. Either that or they've managed to follow Rose better than I have. "I don't understand what any of this has to do with me?"

Valerian leans forward and glances around to ensure no prying ears. "One thing you've always stayed out of our way with is our girls. This Katherine hasn't been too problematic because she only had one location and was running a very particular business model that didn't conflict with ours."

"Okay." I nod slowly, waiting for him to continue. "But..."

"But if Rose gets involved with her and begins backing an expansion, then we may see it eat into our business."

Ah, that's why they're here.

They're concerned their cheap street hookers and cat houses will be affected once she gets a large-scale operation up and running. I'm not so sure they have anything to worry about. Their clientele and Kat's aren't anywhere near the same league, but maybe some of her clients had been slumming it before she popped up.

"I'm not sure how I can be of any help in this situation, boys. It's not really my area of expertise."

Erjon may have been trafficking girls during his brief stint at the head of this organization before I took over, but it was never anything Saban or Aleksander were ever interested in or were historically involved with. And everyone knows I've made my agreement with Cutter and his crew to stop trafficking.

Valerian grins at me and glances around the restaurant again. "It's no secret Rose has it out for you. Hell...we all do. But if Rose were to disappear...it would certainly help the bottom line of all three of us."

I tilt my glass toward him. "What about our Italian friend? Her partnership with Rose could make your plan troublesome."

Galen grabs the wine in front of him and takes a sip, then twists his lips and sets the glass down. "This is shit." He motions for Arvin. "Bring me a Jameson." As Arvin scurries away, Galen returns his focus to me. "I have a feeling Valentina doesn't like Rose operating out of her area any more than we want him involved in ours. If he were to disappear...and if you were to assist with that...we might be willing to overlook some of the other things that have occurred recently."

I fight the grin pulling at my lips. It seems everyone in Chicago wants Rose gone, but no one has the balls to do it except me. The plan was already to take care of him for Valentina, so if I can let these assholes believe I'm doing it for them...all the better.

"I'll tell you what...if an opportunity were to arise for Rose to disappear, I would certainly be willing to take it in exchange for some goodwill and a mutual agreement of sorts regarding any business he may leave behind."

Both men nod slowly and glance at each other.

Valerian inclines his head toward me. "I don't think that would be a problem."

I offer them a grin. "Thank you for stopping by, gentlemen. This has certainly been an interesting afternoon."

They both push to their feet, and Arvin returns with Galen's whiskey. He grabs the glass and downs it in one gulp, then steps away from the table.

"Oh, boys."

They stop and turn back to me.

I pull my now-cold plate of food back in front of me. "Next time, just call. I don't like having my lunch interrupted."

Both men scowl at me before they make their way out of the restaurant.

The enemy of my enemy is my friend.

That's how the saying goes. Though I've never experienced it for myself. But now, things just got a whole lot easier while they also got a whole lot more complicated.

Taking out Rose will please everyone, but now, the brothels are on the radar of the other families, too. It means I can't go back there...ever. I can't risk anyone seeing me with her again, either.

Things can never be simple in this business.

Still, I wouldn't trade it for the world.

It just means we're going to have to be more careful, and once Rose is gone, perhaps strike some sort of deal with the Russians and Irish. We're far from friends, but after today's conversation, I have a feeling they might be amenable to some sort of an agreement that the door might not have been open to only hours ago. One that could hold them off until I can take them out one by one.

I take a bite of my cold food then push it away. Someone might normally get a bullet in their head for interrupting my lunch, but today, I can't even manage to get angry about it. Not with the opportunity that was just dropped in my lap.

Arvin rushes toward the table, a ball of nervous energy. The poor guy knew what I might bring into his restaurant with me when he began to allow me to come here and use the back room, but I doubt even he expected Galen and Valerian to waltz in and sit with me.

I motion toward my ruined lunch. "Bring me another plate. This one is cold now."

He nods, grabs the old plate, and moves off toward the kitchen. Genti and Altin approach and take the seats vacated by Galen and Valerian.

Genti peeks over his shoulder before focusing on me. "Everything okay, boss?"

I grin at him and take a drink of my wine. The sour feeling in my stomach has dissipated, replaced by warm contentment. "Things are definitely looking up."

If I can just get rid of that fucker Rose.

NINE

KAT MAKES her way through the door of my condo and lets it slam behind her. A flush touches her pale cheeks, and she storms across the room and tosses her purse down onto the coffee table.

I set my drink onto the table beside me and watch the tension vibrate through her body. "What's wrong?"

She makes her way straight over to the bar and pours herself a shot of vodka, which she tips back in one gulp before plopping down on the chair across from me. "I had a visitor today."

I raise an eyebrow and lean forward slightly to close the laptop in front of me where I've been viewing the videos from Kat's Cradle. "That's interesting...so did I."

Her eyebrows wing up, her brow furrowed. "Who came to see you? Rose?"

I shake my head and take a sip of my bourbon. "Galen and Valerian, while I was having lunch at *Sofra*."

The blue of her eyes darkens. "What? What did they want?"

I shrug and recline against the back of the couch. "What everyone wants—Rose gone."

"Shit."

"I'm guessing he was your visitor today."

She chews on her bottom lip and nods slowly. "Yeah. Showed up unannounced at the house."

"You had to expect it would happen eventually. You couldn't ignore his calls forever and put off meeting with him."

She nods and then pushes up from her seat to pace behind the chair.

"What did he say?"

It's not like her to look so nervous, which has my good mood from earlier dissipating as fast as my buzz from my drink.

Kat freezes, and her eyes lock with mine. "He wants to move forward right away. With our partnership."

"Personal or professional?" The green monster of jealousy floods my system again, tightening my skin and heating it until it feels like it can barely contain my body

She contemplates her answer.

The delay in her response tells me everything I need to know. I jerk to my feet and stalk over to her, stopping directly in front of her. "Did that fucker touch you?"

Her pause before answering makes my heart climb up my throat.

"What did he do?"

She sucks in a deep breath. "He made it very clear that he wants more than a professional relationship."

I grit my teeth and growl. "What did you say?"

She runs a hand over her slightly disheveled hair and shrugs, trying to make it look like whatever happened wasn't a big deal when she's already made it clear it was.

Oh, no. You are not blowing off this question!

I grab her shoulders and give her a shake. "Tell me what the fuck happened, so I'm not imagining you bent over your desk with Rose behind you."

She scowls at me, those perfect lips twisting down. "He said he would set up a joint account for us. He made it sound like it was for the business as well as...personal."

"He was trying to *pay* for you? Or he wants you to be his kept woman? I don't understand."

"I don't entirely, either. I told him what I've been telling you. That I work the girls, but that's the extent of my involvement in the business. All I know is he definitely does not want a professional-only relationship."

I tighten my grip on her shoulders. "That isn't going to fucking happen. You need to tell him no."

She chews her bottom lip again and averts her gaze.

The way she talks about Rose and after what I saw when they met, the idea that he's propositioning her is enough to make me drive around town tonight until I find Rose and can shoot him myself.

"I don't know, Michael. I'm not sure of what will happen if I try to put off this business agreement any longer."

"Then do what you have to on that front."

She whips her head around to meet my gaze again. "You want me to sleep with him?"

I step into her until her breasts press against my chest. "If Rose fucking touches you, I will tear him apart piece by piece, limb from limb."

"But I'm not sure how to keep him from doing that once were partners. He seems like the kind of man who always gets what he wants." The true uncertainty in her voice makes her words waver. "You need to get rid of him...and fast."

"No shit." I release her, taking a step back. "That's what the Irish and the Russians want, too."

"So, everyone's on the same page now? They've flipped their target to Rose instead of you."

I nod and shove my hands back through my hair. "It seems that way."

"But no one has fessed up to the shooting or the bombing yet."

"No," I shake my head, "they haven't. Which means it could've been any of them or none of them."

"So, what do we do now?"

That's the ultimate question. One I feel like I've been asking myself endlessly since the day I stepped into place as the head of the organization.

I step away from her and pour myself another shot. The warm burn hits my throat and slides down to my stomach, a welcome break from the fiery anger. "We keep Rose on the hook as long as possible. Get him to set up the bank account. If we can take him out and get access to a bunch of money, that's only a win for us."

"And in the meantime?"

I whirl back around to face her. "You stay the fuck away and never be alone in a room with him."

"That might be easier said than done, Michael."

"I don't give a fuck." My roared words echo around the high ceilings of the condo, but she doesn't even flinch. "That man is *never* touching you. Not while I'm alive and have anything to say about it. I'm going to post one of my newer men at the house, so if Rose shows up again, we can try to follow him. But it has to be someone who hasn't been with me long, someone Rose won't recognize."

She nods. "Okay."

I slam my fist into the wall, the pain radiating through it and up my arm, barely a blip on my radar. "It's all we have right now. Arden hasn't been able to find anything useful."

At least on the Rose front.

Kat approaches me, and I turn and stare down into her blue eyes. Arden's words echo in my head.

It looks an awful lot like her...
Her eyes are a different color.

I capture her face between my palms and tilt her chin up toward me. "I've been meaning to ask you. Do you have a sister?"

Her eyebrows fly up. "What? Where did that come from?"

"Humor me."

"No. I'm an only child."

Which is exactly what Arden said when he was giving me her background.

"Cousins? Other close family?" She doesn't answer, and I brush my thumb across her lips. "Our involvement will make them targets, too. I need to know who I need to protect, especially if I take out Rose and his crew retaliates."

"Oh." She swallows thickly, a hint of trepidation in her eyes as she avoids my gaze. "I have a cousin, but she doesn't live anywhere near here, so it won't be an issue."

She's lying.

And she's hiding something from me.

It's time for Arden to do more digging and find out what it is.

TEN

My vision begins to blur, and I squeeze my eyes shut and rub them to try to clear the ache and fuzziness. After days and days of sitting here and watching the videos from Kat's Cradle while I wait for the club to be back up and running, I'm starting to even see people fucking with my eyes closed. It's like a constant stream of pornography, only the men don't seem to know what they're doing.

I snort and open my eyes to watch as the governor fucks one of Kat's girls doggy style, with absolutely no rhythm. It's no wonder these guys go to Kat's for sex. Their wives probably want nothing to do with them if this is how they think they're getting them off at home.

Maybe Kat should be giving sex lessons to these guys instead of just letting them rut like animals...

I rise up from the couch and stretch, rolling my neck from side to side and trying to release the tension in my shoulders. This would be so much easier to do if I were at the office, but the repairs and rebuilding won't happen overnight and everything needs to be done properly.

So that leaves me here, on the couch, watching and keeping a log of everything I see. It's important. But I sometimes need to remind myself of that.

I make my way to the kitchen and grab a *sheqerpare* from the box on the counter. My mouth practically waters, and vivid memories of eating the pastry with Grandfather in the mornings growing up slams into my head.

The man may have been a monster, but he loved his sweets. And as long as I was in his good graces on any given day, he would allow me one.

Shaking off the things I'd rather forget, I toss it into my mouth and enjoy the sweet and buttery flavors before I swallow. I haven't been eating nearly enough since I dove into the video files. My focus has been narrowed on my goal, not taking care of myself. But after being shot and almost burned alive, I doubt eating shitty food and drinking is going to be what finally brings me down.

And at least all this effort is paying off. Hours spent watching the videos have given me exactly what I had hoped to find. More blackmail material than anyone ever imagined. Exactly what it will take to start maneuvering the pieces around in the final game in the bid for control of Chicago.

The other families may have thought they could get rid of me, but they're finding it isn't so easy to kill a Syla.

I head to the bar and pour myself a drink before lowering my sore body onto the couch again. I glance at the time in the corner of my computer screen and sigh.

This would be a lot easier if Kat were here to assist. But she's been tied up, working on the new house and keeping things running at the old one. Including ensuring our friends from the various organizations are well-taken care of with free-flowing booze and tight pussy designed to open their lips. A steady stream of videos like this, plus men who can't keep their mouths shut, will ensure this partnership gets me exactly what I want.

The phone buzzes on the coffee table next to my computer, and I freeze at the number that comes up.

Shit. Rose.

The man has been relentless in trying to nail down their new partnership. And I only have myself to blame for putting those two into each other's orbit, but the thought of them spending more time together and Kat's suggestion the other night that he might know what's happening between us has my stomach twisting into a knot.

He hasn't made a move that I can directly tie to him or contacted me since before the first attack on my life.

Why the hell would he be calling me now?

I'd be stupid not to answer it and find out. I accept the call and hit the speakerphone button before sitting back and taking a sip of my scotch. "Mr. Rose. It's been a while."

His deep chuckle rumbles through the phone to me, making me cringe.

Krishti, I hate the guy.

"It has been a while, Mr. Syla, and I see you've been very busy dodging bullets and flames."

I scowl and take another sip of my drink, the burn of the alcohol matching the searing rage I feel toward this man. "Yes, it would seem someone wants me dead. I can't imagine why."

He laughs, which makes my skin crawl.

"Is that why you're calling? To gloat?" I wouldn't put it past him. The man loves to push buttons.

"Me?" He feigns innocence. "No, I'm not the gloating type, Michael."

"Then, what do you want?"

"I've been hearing a lot of things on the street that give me reason for concern."

"Oh, really? Like what?"

Hopefully, nothing about Kat and me.

The fact that Valerian and Galen knew about Rose and her has made me even more concerned about watching our backs.

"Like you may have been at the docks the day you were shot to meet with Valentina."

It's no secret she controls those docks, so if he knows where the shooting happened, it's not a big leap for him to make that assumption. "So, what if I was?"

"Well, it would make things awkward if you and she had entered into some kind of agreement behind my back."

Where is he going with this? He must just be fishing.

There's no way he can know what happened or what was said. Valentina's men are loyal, especially Cutter. If anyone talked, they'd be floating in the Chicago River right now.

I take another drink and sigh. "You know there's no love lost between Valentina and me. And from what I hear, you two have a very tenuous relationship, too."

He chuckles. "You'd like to believe that, but I can assure you my agreement with Valentina is very friendly."

I bite back a snort.

If he only knew.

"What is it you want, Rose?"

"I want to make sure you're staying in your own lane, Mr. Syla. I'm still looking for what I need to confirm that you were behind the bombing that almost killed my sister. And I know you took and killed my man after you were shot. While I wait for a chance to end you, I don't want you interfering with my relationship and agreement with Valentina."

"What you and Valentina do is no business of mine. As long as it doesn't affect my business."

"You know I wouldn't set foot in your territory. Not unless I had to. I would've thought that was true about Valentina, yet there you were at her dock when you were fired upon."

I grin, even though he can't see me. "I was just taking in the view. Scoping out locations. You never know when things might change hands."

"If you think there's any chance that Valentina will ever give up those docks, then you're crazier than I thought."

I chuckle and take a sip of my drink. "I appreciate the call and the concern for my well-being, Rose. But at this point in time, I don't think we have anything left to say to each other."

He snorts. "Oh, I have plenty to say to you, Syla. But it can wait until we see each other again."

"Do we have a meeting or some plans I've forgotten about?"

"No. I just know I can't seem to escape you."

"You make that sound like a bad thing. Here I thought you really liked me." I end the call, shove the next thumb drive into the computer, and hit play on the video in front of me.

It's from the unlabeled box of videos Kat never had the opportunity to organize yet. With as busy as she is at Kat's Cradle, I can only imagine how much time it would take to get things in an easily searchable order.

This video features a man I haven't seen before join one of the girls in her room.

Dark hair.

Tan skin.

I freeze.

The way he enters.

The way he carries himself.

He moves like the man I just got off the phone with.

Strong.

Confident.

A swagger.

Fucking Rose.

From the camera angle showing him only from above and slightly in profile, I might think it was him, except this man doesn't dress like Rose, nor does Rose have any visible tattoos like the ones on this man's forearms.

Interesting.

Perhaps one of Rose's men? A relative?

Maybe Kat can identify the man.

If not, the redhead who comes out from the bathroom should be able to.

She approaches him cautiously, almost like she's afraid. Not at all the typical interaction between one of Kat's girls and one of the customers.

I'll definitely have to show this one to Kat.

The redhead glances up toward the camera and then says something to the man so low that it's not audible. The camera cuts out.

"What the hell?"

In all the videos I've watched...this never happens.

Could it be a pure coincidence?

I guess only Kat can tell me. But I haven't believed in coincidences in a very long time.

ELEVEN

"WHO'S THE REDHEAD?" My question cuts through the room to Kat the moment the door to the condo opens.

Kat freezes, lets the door shut behind her, and raises her eyebrows. "What redhead?"

I motion toward the image pulled up on my computer of the woman standing in front of the mystery man, looking absolutely terrified. The image I've been staring at for almost an hour, trying to figure out who he is and what is happening. "One of your girls."

She sets her purse onto the end table and settles next to me on the couch. "Oh, that's Rowan. She works as 'Red.' Why?"

"Watch this." I lean forward and press play. Rowan approaches the man, then glances at the camera...and the recording cuts out.

Kat's head jerks toward me. "What just happened?"

"I don't know. The video cuts out. Any idea who the guy is?" I raise an eyebrow at her. "He reminds me of someone we both know..."

"Play it again from the beginning."

I rewind it and press play, watching her eyes as they follow the man in and everything that happens until the recording cuts out. There are only a few minutes, but the picture quality is good enough to see the fear in her eyes when she sees him.

She sits back and turns to me. "He looks like Rose."

"I thought the same thing. Who is he? And what happened to the video?"

Her bottom lip disappears between her teeth, and she shakes her head. "I don't know who he is. I manage the girl's schedules, and I try to meet the clients when they arrive, but I can't be there twenty-four seven. When was this video dated?"

"The day I was shot."

"Shit." She pushes to her feet and makes her way around to the bar—now missing two glasses. "I was out taking care of some business and getting ready to meet you at the new house. He must have come in without an appointment. Otherwise, I would have seen a record of it after that."

I rise and wander over to meet her. "Any idea why the video cuts out?"

She shakes her head and pours a bourbon. "No, I've never seen that before."

"So, it sounds like we need to talk to Rowan."

Kat steps to the window and looks out as she downs her drink. "I would...except she's gone." She turns to face me. "She quit a few days later and left. I haven't heard from her since."

"Shit."

"Yeah." She nods slowly and wanders back to set her glass on the bar. "I'll check into the recording equipment in that room and ask around to see if any of the other girls or my security remember him."

"Who the hell could he be? Does Rose have a brother?"

She shakes her head. "Not that I know of, but it's not like he and I chat about our families."

I pour myself a drink and take a sip. "I'll have Arden and my guys try to track down Rowan. Give me whatever information you have on her."

Kat nods and approaches me slowly. "And I can see what I can get out of Rose, too?"

"No." It comes out more growl than I intended, but Kat remains unfazed, as always. "Don't ask him anything that might raise suspicions. We'll figure out what happened. In the meantime, we'll keep reviewing the tapes and wait for Esad to arrive in a few days."

"Have you heard from him?"

"No, but I wouldn't expect to unless there was an issue."

The man knows what he's doing and how important the cargo is. Once the girls are here, we'll double our opportunities for information like I've been reviewing. A goddamn goldmine.

I take another drink and flash her a grin. "I'm finding some really interesting stuff. I think I'll be paying a visit to a few of the friends of your girls in the next few days."

Her red lips curl into a devious grin. "You're ready to make your move?"

I set down my glass and drag her against me. "I'm more than ready. If I'm ever going to control this city, I need people in certain places to have my back."

"Like who?"

"Senator Mason."

Her dark eyebrows wing up. "Oh, aiming high right from the start. I like it."

I grin at her and brush my thumb over her lips. "Always. And I've heard some rumblings from some connections in Washington that have me a bit uneasy. I think I'll need the senator in my pocket sooner rather than later. Then I'll work on some of the other people I've found in the recordings."

"What about me?"

"What about you?"

"Well," she wraps her arms around my waist, "what am I going to be doing?"

I hadn't expected her to ask that. This has always been a one-man show. Working with a partner never crossed my mind, nor was it part of any plan. My goal has always been to take Chicago and to build an organization stronger and larger than Grandfather ever had back home, to rebuild the Syla name. A woman was never in the picture, and I can't let her get involved in anything besides what's happening already.

"You keep doing what you're doing. We keep our relationship secret."

"And Rose?"

That fucker.

My hands tighten on her waist. "I'll take care of Rose. There isn't any other option, especially now that he's on the hook for a partnership with you. We need him gone, sooner rather than later, or I'll have some very angry 'friends' in Valentina, Galen, and Valerian."

Those aren't the people you want mad at you. And I've given each and every one of them reasons to be. The fact that Galen and Valerian didn't shoot me on sight at the restaurant the other night only goes to show how unstable things really are here, mostly because of Rose coming in...but also because of me.

Once Rose is gone, the four families will settle into a new way of life.

And eventually...the four families will become three...then two...then one—me.

TWELVE

"It's a very interesting and entertaining video, isn't it?"

Senator Mason scowls at me and drags his eyes away from my phone currently playing a little excerpt from his greatest hits at Kat's place. This one involves three blondes, handcuffs, and some of the items I saw in the toy chest—being used on him. "How did you get this?"

I shrug nonchalantly, turn off the video, and offer him a smile.

He slams his fist against the desk between us. "Did that bitch Kat set me up?"

My hand tightens into a fist, but I manage to restrain myself from belting the old fucker. "It doesn't matter where I got it, Senator. What does matter is what it means for our relationship."

A low growl rumbles deep in his chest. "We don't have a relationship."

I smile at him. "We didn't. But now...we do."

"What makes you think I would ever help the likes of you?"

"This." I wave my phone. "Because you don't want your wife or your constituents seeing what you do with these blondes, or the brunettes, or the redheads, or the ones with equipment down below, not up above."

He freezes, his eyes widening as the color drains from his face.

I grin at him and push to my feet out of the chair. The man couldn't usher me into his office fast enough when I showed up unannounced and told his secretary it was regarding our mutual friend, Kat, and I know why. It's not just about being caught cheating; it's about who he was cheating with. I walk behind the chair and place my hands on the back. "Yes, Senator, I've seen those as well. It seems you have quite eclectic tastes."

His mouth opens, but I hold up my hand to stop him.

"I don't want to or need to hear your excuses or explanations, Senator. I'm not judging you, nor am I the one you need to explain yourself to. Your wife will be...when she sees all of this."

His lips twist into a scowl. "You're a real scumbag, Syla."

I chuckle and nod. "I've been called worse."

"I bet you have. It's criminals like you who have ruined this city. This country. Terrorizing innocent people—"

I hold up my hands. "Now, now, Senator. Let's not try to pass the blame here. You're the one who made this decision. You're the one who put yourself in this position. All I'm doing is taking advantage of something you created."

The man had to know what he was risking when he went to Kat's and stuck his dick into anything that moved. One word of any of it to anyone and he would be toast.

His thin, wrinkled lips press together. "What do you want from me?"

I spread my hands wide. "Friendship. An open relationship in which we help each other."

"I don't need your help."

"Oh, yes, you do. You need my help in keeping these from becoming public."

"And in return?" He raises an eyebrow.

"In return, I will require certain favors from you."

Someone with his kind of power in Washington is an immeasurable asset to the organization. With his contacts throughout the government at the federal and even the state and city level here, I'll have whatever I need within reach.

"I know who you are and what you do, Mr. Syla. So does everyone else. I can't help you."

"You may not be able to do so publicly. But we all know the really important stuff goes on behind closed doors. Money is exchanged. Deals are made. Your vote is for sale, and so is everyone else's. It's just a matter of the price."

And money isn't an object when it comes to accomplishing my goals. The more government officials in my back pocket, the easier it will be to expand into legitimate avenues of business without the cops or FBI breathing down my neck. The easier I can move weapons, money, drugs, and whatever else I may want to without worrying about busts. And now that Esad will be arriving with the girls tomorrow, it's time to make moves.

Senator Mason shakes his head. "I don't know what you think I can help you with."

"I'm sure things will come up the longer our relationship goes on, but right now, I can think of a few things."

He clenches his fists on his desk, his chest puffing with his hard, angered breaths. "Like?"

I shrug. "Like the new bill being introduced to revise the RICO statute."

A red flush spreads up his neck and across his cheeks. "I don't know what you're talking about."

"Really?" I raise an eyebrow.

He's a shitty liar. How he ever managed to remain in Congress for so long is beyond me.

"That's interesting because I had heard that you are on the committee spearheading the move."

His eyes widen. "How the hell do you know that?"

"I know a lot of things, Senator. A lot of things that could hurt you or things that I would be willing to keep private for a friend."

He considers my words for a moment, no doubt replaying the video I have on my phone in his head. Not to mention the dozens of others he now knows I also have access to and have reviewed.

"What is it exactly that you need?"

Bingo.

It was only a matter of time and a little push of persuasion before he realized it was useless to try to fight this. There's no way out for a man like him who has been caught in a scandal like this.

"I need you to torpedo the bill. It'll make my job a lot harder if it passes, and it will make it a lot easier for the people I work with to end up in some very uncomfortable places, like federal prison." I flash him a grin. "And since we're friends, that's the last place you would want me."

He scowls at me and shakes his head. "I can't do it. I just can't. My office drafted the damn bill. How would I explain a one-eighty to the other members of the committee, to my office staff?"

"Not my problem, Senator. You can, and you *will* make sure that bill never reaches a vote."

He watches me for a moment. I can almost see the wheels turning in his head. The way he's rushing through every objection and argument he wants to make. But he is undoubtedly coming to the same conclusion that I did the moment I saw what Kat had in that surveillance room—he won't be in any position to fight me on this.

No one who is on those videos will be.

Because this is the type of information that could destroy a man like him—publicly and personally.

And he's precisely the type of person willing to do whatever it takes to protect his snow-white reputation from being tarnished.

He shoves his hands back through his graying hair and pushes to his feet to pace behind his desk. For a few seconds, his eyes fall on the American flag standing behind him, on one side of the large window. When he turns back to face me, the stern set of his jaw gives his answer before he even speaks. "All right. Tell me what I need to do."

I grin at him and shrug. "Now, that wasn't so hard or painful, was it?"

THIRTEEN

THE DOOR to my office opens, and Kat saunters in on her high heels with a grin that promises all sorts of wonderfully dirty things. In the couple of days since I last saw her, I've been touching base with Arden about what he's been able to find on Kat and the mysterious Rowan or where to find Rose. But so far...nothing of any value has come to me. That's made me tense.

Seeing Kat and knowing where my dick will end up has some of that tension dissipating.

I motion for her to come over to me. "What's that look for?"

She makes her way around my desk and set her purse off to the side before she slides up onto it in front of me. Her skirt rides up her thighs, exposing her bare pussy only a foot in front of me. She widens her legs slightly so I can shift forward between them and wrap my arms around her waist. "I just got done at the new house."

I raise an eyebrow. "And?"

"All the girls have settled in well and seem eager to get to work. I anticipate being able to open within a week."

I grin at her and brush my thumbs up the inside of her thighs, making them quiver under my touch. "That is excellent news. And I have some of my own."

Her eyebrows wing up. "Oh, yeah? What's that?"

"I secured the cooperation of Senator Mason."

"Oh, really?" A slow smile curls her lips. "What did he agree to?"

I shrug nonchalantly and lean down to press a kiss against the top of her right thigh. "Whatever we need. With where he's been putting his cock, he's not really in any position to be denying us anything, now is he?"

She grins and shakes her head. "I guess not considering what we have him doing on tape."

The very things I want to do to her right now. My cock grows in my pants, pressing against the zipper. I shift forward between her legs, my hands gliding even closer to the apex of her thighs.

"With his assistance and the continued cooperation of the Italians, we should have no problem expanding into other areas of the city, maybe even the state."

She waves her hand around the office. "What about this place?"

I pull back slightly and look at the unfinished room. Bare drywall covers the walls, but at least I can work here while they finish it out. "What do you mean?"

"What do you plan on doing with it?"

I snort and shake my head. "Nothing. Other than the minor improvements being made during the cleanup, I don't plan on changing much here. There's no point. If we're going to keep our business relationship a secret, then making this place as upscale as the others wouldn't make any sense."

She nods slowly and runs her hands through my hair, dragging her nails against my scalp. I groan and lean into her touch.

Her lips press against my forehead. "True, but I think you might be missing out on a good opportunity here."

"Opportunity for what?"

"Expanding into strip clubs. There's a lot you could do with it."

I run my hands up her thighs again, and she shudders. "I don't want to talk about business right now. There's a lot of things I could do to you and want to right now."

She chuckles and digs her nails in the back of my neck, dragging me closer between her legs. "Oh yeah? What do you have in mind?"

I lick my lips and brush them against her thigh. "Well, for starters...I'm going to eat your fucking pussy until your legs shake so hard you can't move."

She grins at me and pinches my ear. "Promises, promises."

I dig my fingers into the flesh of her ass and drag her to the edge of the desk. "You know I always keep mine."

"Oh, I know you do, Michael. It's one of the reasons I got involved with you in the first place. I knew once you committed to this partnership, you would ensure we got everything established and ready to go flawlessly."

I reach forward and brush my fingers through her wet folds. "The most flawless thing here is this."

Her hips twitch at my touch, and I push up her skirt around her hips and lean forward to drag my tongue through her wetness. She groans and arches back, digging her nails into my neck and scraping them along my scalp.

Fuck yes!

The taste of her arousal coats my tongue, and I roll the tip of it around her clit while my cock twitches, begging to be released.

But not until I make her come first.

She deserves it.

Things are finally on track, and it's only because of her. Because she came into my life and opened up this whole new world to me. If not for Kat, I would have struggled to find ways to get to my competitors, to work around law enforcement and the government red tape here. Now, I'll have free rein.

I slip two fingers inside her and curl them up to find her G-spot. "You better hold on, *kotele*."

She digs her hands into me, and I set to work, fucking her with my mouth and fingers until her entire body quivers. She gasps and jerks against my hold, her hips rolling in time with my tongue. One of her hands disappears behind her to brace herself on the desk as her orgasm starts to mount.

With a strength I didn't know she possessed, she shoves my face against her harder, the pants falling from her lips coming faster. "Fuck, yes, Michael. I'm gonna come."

And as soon as she's done, I'm going to plunge inside this wet heat and fuck her until she can't walk.

Her orgasm slams into her, and her body jerks up and grinds against my face, wave after wave of pleasure coursing through. She releases a final gasp and sags slightly.

I give her pussy one final lick, pull my fingers out, and start to lean back when the familiar cold press of the barrel of the gun against my temple stops me.

FOURTEEN

KAT

DESPITE A GUN PRESSED to his temple, the corner of Michael's mouth quirks up, and he raises a dark, menacing eyebrow. "I'm all for some kinky play in the bedroom, *kotele,* but this goes a little beyond what I'm comfortable with."

I offer him a sardonic smile and press the barrel harder against his head. "I'm not playing, Michael. I'm done with games."

"A little late for that, isn't it? You've been playing one for a long fucking time, it seems."

It's not something I enjoy. Not in the least. I would much rather be direct and honest, but that isn't always possible, especially in this business with these kinds of people.

I shrug. "The situation necessitated it." As it so often has in the last couple of years. "I had to work with what was available to me."

It took so long to get here...I thought it might never happen.

But the heavy steel in my hand and the determination in my heart are unwavering. And I have to give Michael credit; he doesn't quiver or cower, even with the barrel of the gun pressed to his temple, staring down death for a third time just since I've come into his life—he doesn't even blink.

In fact, the corners of his mouth twitch up again. "It's not that I haven't expected this, Kat, but to do it now with my cock as hard as granite and the taste of your cunt still on my tongue is pretty cold...even for you."

I shift the gun, pushing the muzzle against his forehead, driving his head back until he's against the leather of his chair. "You have no idea how cold I can be, Michael."

He considers me for a moment, searching my eyes for something. "So, have you been working with Rose the whole time?"

I growl at him and shift to close my legs. "I don't give a fuck about Rose."

His shoulders rise and fall. "Then why? Why the ruse? Why wait so long when you've had plenty of chances?"

He motions around the room, and I keep my eyes on his hands. There's no way I'll allow him to reach for a weapon.

"The first time you were in this office, you had a gun in your hand and could've taken me out then. You killed one of my men without even blinking. Why not me?"

I flash him a grin. "What fun would that have been? Besides, I needed you, Michael. You served a very specific purpose, and now that the purpose is complete, I can do what I've wanted to do for so damn long. End. You."

His dark eyes assess me, scanning every millimeter of my face like he's seeing it for the first time. "Who are you?"

My lips curve into a genuine smile, the first I've given him since I first walked into his life as Kat. I've waited a long time to tell him this. It will hurt him more to know the truth before he dies. And even if he doesn't care, he needs to understand why. "When I worked here and danced on the pole out there, I was known as Kitty."

He narrows his eyes on me. "You danced here?"

"I did a hell of a lot more than that." These words have sat on the tip of my tongue for so long.

I've practiced them a hundred times. Yet, I have to speak despite a dry throat. "My real name is Brynn Katherine Walker. Or it *was*. Now, it's Brynn Katherine Gashi."

Recognition flashes in his gaze, and his body tenses.

"That's right." I swallow thickly against the emotion threatening to clog my throat. "Aleksander was my husband."

Not for long.

Not nearly long enough.

Because of the clash of *this* damn monster and Aleksander's own wrath.

"And you led him to his slaughter. You set up my husband and your brother to ensure total anni-hilation. All because you envied what they had because you wanted it for yourself. Well, I hope it was worth it. I hope all the bloodshed and the lies and the terrible things you've done to get here felt amazing while they lasted."

He shakes his head and lets out a mirthless chuckle. "I don't get it. What did you need from me so badly that you had to drag this out?"

"This." I wave my free hand around his office. "I want what belonged to Aleksander and right-fully now belongs to me. And I want all of Chicago." I lick my lips and issue a frustrated growl. "That bomb was supposed to take care of it. Was supposed to wipe out everyone in one fell swoop."

His eyebrows fly up. "You set the bomb at that meeting?"

"Well, not me personally...but you see, Aleksander still has a lot of friends. A lot of people who weren't very happy with what you did to him and your brother. When I traveled to Albania to bring Aleksander's body home, I met a few of them."

That trip served another purpose, too.

It helped me establish Kat's identity. She disappeared from the States—traveling and staying places that don't keep good records. Something a lot of young people do. Easily slipping between European countries.

I had to make my way to Albania without any red flags going up with the Dragushas or Berishas, the families now in control there. Who knows what they would have done if they had known The Dragon's wife had returned? I needed to make my way there in secret and contact Aleksander's remaining family to figure out how to proceed.

And it worked flawlessly.

I went from nursing school and being taken care of by Aleksander to plotting a way to step up and take over his business while making sure those who were responsible paid. It meant completely leaving my old life behind. But there wasn't much left of it anyway.

"Shit." The single word drops from his lips as the puzzle pieces all click together in his head.

"If only there hadn't been faulty wiring on the bomb, the city would be mine."

"You leaked the information about the meeting to my man to get me there."

I shrug slightly. "If you hadn't shown up, I would've taken you out another way. It was too good an opportunity to pass up to take out the Russians, Italians, Irish, and the Colombians all at once. But since it failed rather miserably, I had to come up with another plan."

"So...you created Kat."

I smile and nod slowly, the months of hard work coming back to me. "Fake identity. Fake back-ground. Eye surgery in Europe to insert colored contact lenses to change my appearance. All of it designed to reel you in, and you fell for it hook, line, and sinker."

"And then you tried to kill me. You *were* behind the shooting and the explosion here?"

"No." I shake my head and lean back slightly, never taking my eyes off him. "I wasn't ready for you to be dead yet. Those attacks were actually very problematic for me and my plan."

"Then who was it?"

A smile pulls at my lips. "Your new enemies in Albania, the Dragushas and the Berishas. They heard about our little endeavor and weren't too happy with the idea of us taking girls from them."

"Then why aren't they after you, too?"

"Because I'm smarter than you, Michael. Instead of making enemies, I made friends. It took longer than I had hoped, hence the second attack here. But once they learned who I really was and how determined I am to take back what was Aleksander's, I came to an agreement with them, one that will allow Esad and his crews to continue their work while the Dragushas and Berishas get a cut. It's not ideal. But it's a small price to pay for what I want."

"You could have had it months ago if you had just let them kill me."

I shake my head and sigh. "I wish it had been that easy."

But nothing has been easy for me for a long time. Not since Aleksander was taken from me.

"If I had simply walked in here and killed you, or if I'd let them take you out, no one would've taken me seriously. No one would've respected me or allowed me to stay sitting at the head of this family. Regardless of who I married."

I grin at the man who has managed to get me exactly where I need to be through his reputation for ruthlessness. Esad is bringing in girls. Senator Mason is at my disposal. And Michael's crew now know me and what I'm capable of.

"Now, you've given me legitimacy, Michael. By partnering with me. And your men know I'm lethal. They'll fall in line once you're gone. No one will oppose me because they want you gone as badly as I do."

Our Russian and Irish counterparts only went to Michael because they were desperate to protect their organizations from Rose. They won't care that Michael's gone, not when I promise my business won't interfere with theirs.

"I'll play nice with the Russians, and the Irish, and Rose and Valentina as long as I have to in order to consolidate my power, and then, I'll use your plan to take them all down one by one."

FIFTEEN

KAT

MICHAEL'S LIPS, the ones I've kissed so many times in the recent past, curl into a real smile. It's the last thing I expected from him. "I have to say I'm impressed."

"Why is that, Michael?"

He shrugs slightly, but I keep my eyes on him and where his hands are at all times. "What you did took a lot of balls. To walk in here and stare down the man you hate that badly, to fuck me repeatedly and pretend you enjoyed it." He raises an eyebrow. "But you weren't pretending, were you?"

I swallow thickly, my body heating at the memory of his mouth on me, his cock inside me...

"It's okay, *kotele*. You can admit it. You can admit that I'm not as bad as you thought I was and you actually enjoyed fucking me."

My physical response to him doesn't override the burn of hate in my blood. Powerful and ruthless men are like crack to me after being with Aleksander. A traitorous body won't save Michael now, though.

"It doesn't matter. The truth is, you killed Aleksander. You fed his hate and set him on a collision course with Lorenc that would take them both out. Your *own brother*."

He slams his hand on the chair. "A brother who abandoned me. A brother who didn't give two shits about what happened to me, who only cared about protecting himself. What kind of brother is that?"

"Sometimes, we have to do bad things to survive. You may have killed your grandfather for survival. But what you did to Lorenc and Aleksander was pure envy. There's a reason they call it one of the deadliest sins, you know."

He barks out a laugh and shakes his head. "Ironic, coming from you."

"Why is that?"

"Because you are making a living off lust. You danced on that pole like a whore. Probably ended up in bed with Aleksander to make more money—"

I smash the gun against his temple. His head splits open, blood pouring down the side of his cheek. He cries out and presses his hand to the wound.

Seeing his pain brings me more joy than it should. Watching him suffer after the shooting was one of the greatest thrills of my life. "Yeah, I prey on other people's sin, Michael, but it's not my own. And Aleksander *loved* me."

"Whatever you need to tell yourself, Kat. Your brain is clearly so twisted, you don't what's real and what isn't."

"What the hell is that supposed to mean?"

"Well, it seems to me you're taking this out on the wrong person."

"How do you figure?"

He points to himself with the hand not pressed to his bleeding head. "I'm not the one who killed Aleksander. I'm not even the one who killed Saban and started the war between the Gashis and the Morinas. You should be hunting Konstandin and Rea. Their betrayal of Tarek is what started all of this. They're the ones who killed Aleksander."

Anger tightens my chest and my hand around the grip of the gun. "Konstandin and Rea will have to answer for their sins, too. But don't act like you're innocent in all of this. You're far from it. You set things into motion, knowing what the end result would be. You wanted Aleksander's power, his territory. You wanted what was *his*. And you were willing to do anything to get it."

He grins at me. "You told me that's what you liked about me. You said that we were one and the same."

"We are. We just have very different goals. You wanted to possess this. You wanted to control. You wanted what your grandfather lost, and you were willing to get it at any price. You were willing to betray your brother. You were willing to betray Rea and Konstandin. And you were willing to betray my husband when he embraced you into his organization and brought you into his fold."

"What do you know about it?"

I smile at him. "My husband was many things. Cold. Calculating. Violent and brutal. But he also loved me fiercely. And by the time you came into the picture, he had accepted the fact that I was part of his world and that keeping me completely in the dark was never going to work. I knew all about his plan. About his offer to you. That if you gave him information about where Lorenc was, he planned to bring you here to Chicago and make you his right-hand man. And I know you saw it as your opportunity to take him out, and then you waltzed in here and removed Erjon like he never existed."

"You seem to know a lot."

"I do. Like I know you have zero remorse for any of the things that you've done."

He raises his eyebrows. "What would it matter if I did? Would it change your mind or your endgame if I wept over Lorenc's death, if I wept over my grandfather's despite what he did to me? If I begged for forgiveness from God and for Him to save my soul, would you spare me, *kotele*?" He snorts and shakes his head, but I keep the gun trained on him. "Let's not pretend here, Kat, or should I call you Brynn?"

I offer him a smile, one I don't feel, one tinged with sadness and regret. "Brynn died with Aleksander. The girl who danced out on that pole ceased to exist the moment his heart stopped beating. There's no room for the idealistic views she once had or for the love she once held in her heart."

"You don't love me, Kat?" He presses his hand over his heart. "I'm hurt."

"Fuck you, Michael. You don't even know what love is. And you never will."

"Would it matter if I told you I love *you*?"

His words should give me pause. They should hit me straight in the chest and make my hand shake. But they don't. They only steel my resolve. Because they're a lie.

"It's been fun, Michael. But now, it's over."

Before he can even flinch, I pull the trigger. The bullet hits him square between the eyes, and he sags in the chair almost instantly.

Jesus. It's finally over.

I sit on the desk, holding the gun in my hand. Though it doesn't shake, the adrenaline coursing through my body makes it feel like I can't breathe. I suck in a deep breath.

The sense of satisfaction I'd anticipated once all this was done, the feeling like I've finally won... it just doesn't come.

Because this is only the beginning.

Only the first step in what will be a very long process. It may take me years, even decades, but I will follow through on what Aleksander had planned.

Otherwise, all this was for nothing.

SIXTEEN

KAT

THE DOOR to the office flies open, and Genti storms in with Altin, Driton—who is still recovering from almost dying and probably shouldn't be rushing anywhere—and Agon behind them, guns drawn and pointed right at me. Their eyes quickly flick from where I still sit on the desk to Michael's body slumped in the chair, his blood and brain matter scattered against the wall behind him.

Genti's eyes widen, his wide shoulders tensing. "What the fuck is going on?"

He moves forward, his gun still trained on me. I'm not sure what keeps him from firing, but something holds him back. Hopefully, it's exactly what I just explained to Michael. I've established myself with him, and he wants to give me a chance to explain rather than taking off my head.

I set my weapon next to me on the desk, slide off, and turn to face him. All four men stare me down, hate and anger hardening their gazes. I motion toward Michael's body. "Michael is no longer the head of this organization."

Genti growls. "You fucking killed him!"

"Yes." I shove at Michael's body until it falls over with a thump onto the floor, then slowly lower myself into his chair, the same chair Aleksander once occupied. "I did. But I was only taking back what is rightfully mine."

"Yours?" Genti's eyebrows fly up, and he takes another step closer.

I offer him a smile. "Michael stole this territory from the Gashis. I'm just doing what my husband would've wanted."

"Your husband?"

I level my gaze on him. "Aleksander Gashi...The Dragon."

He sucks in a deep breath and glances back at the other men. Aleksander's reputation is enough to bring anyone to their knees. Even these men. Genti lowers his weapon and motions for the other guys to do the same. Reluctantly, their guns drop to their sides.

Genti swallows thickly, and his gaze shifts to Michael's body.

I glance at what's left of the man I've spent so much time with, without an ounce of regret in my soul. Had he shown even a hint of remorse for everything he did during the time we were together, I can't say it would have changed the outcome, but who knows.

Michael and Aleksander were too alike.

And they both paid for it with their lives.

If Aleksander had been able to see through the red of his wrath, if he would have stopped to listen to me when I told him to just let Konstandin and Rea go, he would have focused his attention on the future instead of the past. He never would've walked straight into the crosshairs of Michael's plot.

Similarly, if Michael hadn't coveted what wasn't his, hadn't been so intent on taking from Aleksander, he wouldn't be dead on the floor right now.

We all have to pay for our sins.

And one day, I will likely pay for mine.

But today, I'm going to relish this victory. It's been long and hard-fought and has taken more out of me than I could have ever imagined.

Genti clears his throat, and I drag my eyes away from Michael's body to meet his.

"Sit." I motion to the chair in front of me to the right and then point for Altin to take the other one.

They slowly lower themselves into them, and Michael's two other men move closer and stand behind them.

I cross my legs and settle my hands on my exposed knee. "I understand this is difficult for you. You were loyal to Michael. But loyalty has its limits. Michael took his organization from Aleksander. It's rightfully mine. If you don't believe that..." I rest my hand on my gun sitting on the desk, "you can leave, but if I ever see your face again or find out you're working with any of my competitors, I will kill you faster than I killed him." The men stare me down, unflinching at my threats. "Or...you can help me finish what Michael and I started."

Genti raises an eyebrow. "What's that?"

A smile spreads across my lips, and I incline my head toward him. "We're going to take complete control of Chicago. The entire city will be mine."

"How do you plan on doing that? Michael wasn't exactly making much headway in that endeavor."

I chuckle and lean back in the chair, spreading my hands in front of me. "That's easy. I have something that Michael doesn't."

"What's that?"

"Lust. With lust working on our side, I'll put a stranglehold on the other four families."

NOTE FROM THE AUTHOR

Dear Reader –

Don't hate me. You're probably thinking, *OMG that BITCH Gwyn killed Aleksander and Michael! THESE ARE NOT ROMANCES!* But if you read the note after *Surviving Wrath*, you'll know that Aleksander *had* to die. *Wrath* was Konstandin and Rea's love story, and Aleksander was the antagonist and the *true* force of unrestrained wrath in the trilogy.

Everyone in the *Wrath* books paid for their sin in some way. For Konstandin and Rea, Tarek's wrath after they left led to him taking her back and Konstandin's wrath over losing her led to him making a horrible decision to stay and finish off Tarek instead of leaving with Lorenc and Rea. Had he not given into that wrath, he wouldn't have "died" and lost those years with her and the son he didn't even know he had. It was Aleksander's wrath over Saban's death that blinded him from seeing the truth - that Tarek was in the wrong and so was Saban for helping him. Even the love of Brynn a.k.a. Kitty wasn't enough to soften him or let him see that Rea was an innocent victim in the entire situation. And finally, Rea's wrath over what Aleksander did and was willing to do to them and their son is what finally ended it. She will pay the price for her wrath, as everyone does in one way or another.

But I always knew I wanted Brynn a.k.a. Kitty a.k.a Kat to become a different person because of relationship with Aleksander. She's sweet and somewhat weak in the start of *After Wrath*, but by the end, she's standing toe-to-toe with Aleksander, one of the scariest men on the planet. It proved to me that she would be a force to be reckoned with if ever in control, and given Michael's betrayal of Lorenc and Aleksander, I knew she couldn't let it slide and let him off the hook.

She gave into her wrath, and he lost his life because of his envy. While she may have softened to Michael in those private moments, that was because of *LUST*, not love, something she recognized since it's her business. *Envy* is the vehicle to get Kat to her eventual happily ever after (as much as anyone in her business can ever have) through the next trilogy in the series *Lust*.

So, please, don't hate me...

The Chicago underworld is a dark, dangerous place, where people always have ulterior motives and long-term plans. I promise that the upcoming stories of the remaining sins will be just as bloody and dark, but that the people who deserve them will get their HEAs.

Gwyn

LUST

Sex is the consolation you have when you can't have love.

-**Gabriel Garcia Marquez**

ONE

KAT

I CAN'T BELIEVE it's taken this long.

It's been almost a week since I killed Michael in the very chair I'm sitting in, and I'm finally getting the visit I've been anticipating every minute of every hour of every day since I pulled the trigger—the visit that has my stomach twisted into a knot and my palms sweaty more than any of the other bullshit that happened since Aleksander's death. More than being left alone after finally finding the other half of my soul, more than having to "kill" Brynn and become Kat, more than having to bring Aleksander's ashes back to Albania and bury him beside his family, more than having to return to Chicago to get my revenge on Michael by getting biblically close to him.

The man who is about to walk through my office door could be my biggest enemy or my biggest ally. But I don't want him for either. As far as I'm concerned, Rose could disappear and it would make my life a lot easier.

Hell, it would make a lot of lives easier.

Any number of people want him gone—the Italians, the Russians, the Irish, the smaller Hispanic gangs Rose has been pushing out of the Windy City, plus I'm sure a whole slew of other cartels back in South America. But with Michael out of the picture and Rose now aware of who I really am and my real intent in taking over this empire, there's only one reason he can be here—to confront me about setting him up so Michael and I could try to kill him.

A plan that might have eventually played out exactly as we intended had it not been time to remove Michael from the picture.

The guys won't let Rose back here with anything that could hurt me, but that doesn't mean he's not dangerous.

He's the worst kind of danger.

Charming and handsome, smooth and polished, the type of man who strips women of their clothes as well as their inhibitions.

Even while he was a pawn in my game with Michael, I couldn't ignore the way my body reacted to the man. A flutter in my chest. A heat low in my belly. A burning need between my legs. So, knowing he is walking down the hallway and about to open that door means I need to steel myself against any unwanted reaction that might give him the upper hand here.

One thing I will not do is cower or show weakness in the face of any man—let alone Rose. Not with what I've managed to accomplish in taking back Aleksander's territory. His empire. What is rightfully mine.

Though I can't say with complete confidence that he would be happy with my sitting in this chair. He never wanted this life for me. I glance at the desk I sit behind and run my hand over the nicked and worn wood, unleashing a torrent of memories.

My argument with Aleksander when I discovered he had bought me a computer and tried to pay for me to have a new life. My anger at him for pushing me away after the time we spent together. His belief that I was too weak to be with a man like him, to live this kind of life.

He didn't win that argument. I didn't let him. I forced him to face what we had and accept that we were inevitable. We may not have had a lot of time together before he was ripped away from me, but what we did have was intense and incredible, something you only find once in a lifetime.

I squeeze my eyes closed, and it's almost as if I can feel his hands on my hips. His hot breath against my neck as he bent me over this very desk and fucked me hard from behind, finally claiming me as his—forever.

Even death can't change that.

My entire body heats at the memory, aching and desperate for that touch again. The doorknob turns, and I release a heavy, shaky breath. It's time to pull myself together and stop living in the past.

No weakness.

The door opens, and Rose enters, looking as immaculate as always in his custom-tailored suit that fits him like it was painted onto his lean, hard body. His dark eyes zero in on me, and a grin twitches at the edge of his lips. "Well, Kat..." He takes a step forward and pauses. "Or are you going by Brynn now? It seems you haven't been honest with me." His accent slips into his perfect English with each step he takes. He stops behind the chair, facing me, and wraps his hands around the back, squeezing until his knuckles whiten. "And if there's one thing I cannot abide...it's dishonesty."

He's angry.

Good.

If he's mad, he'll be less likely to turn on the charm and direct it at me. That's much safer because being the focus of that is like staring down a freight train barreling at you full speed and not being able to get out of the way.

What I told Michael was true—typically, handsome and charming don't really do anything for me. Scary and ruthless men are much more my type. Terrance was the first, though when I became the focus of all of that rage and aggression, it became a whole different situation.

And then Aleksander came into my life and heart.

My chest aches just thinking about the way he swooped in and saved me—both from Terrance and from myself. If the same situation were to happen now, I wouldn't need him. He taught me how to defend myself, how to take care of myself, and how to be cold and ruthless. It's what got me back this chair that was stolen from him by Michael's envy.

Though I could never be the Dragon.

I can never be what he and Michael became. The kind of tunnel vision that overwhelmed them led them to make the kind of mistakes that got them killed. And I won't allow that to happen to me. Which is why I can't let down my guard around a man like Rose.

A man my body reacts to. A man I need to keep hating.

I offer him a cool smile and motion toward the chair he stands behind. "It's Kat."

Now and forever.

His lips twitch as he moves around and slowly lowers his silk-encased frame into the chair.

My foot rocks unseen under the desk, the only outward sign I'll allow that might hint at my unease, one I know is hidden from him. "And I won't apologize for the deception. It was necessary."

Dark eyebrows rise slowly over haunting ebony eyes. "Necessary for your master plans?"

"Something like that."

He waves his hands and glances around the still unfinished office. When I killed Michael, all renovations on the club ceased at my command. I'm going to rebuild this place from the ground up. That means redesigning it my way, leaving the current office walls nothing more than sheetrock and tape.

Rose smirks, more a condescending tilt of the lips. "What a glorious empire you have."

I smile despite my best efforts to remain unaffected by him. For a man like him to find humor in our situation only makes him more appealing—the absolute last thing I want in this moment. "My predecessors weren't as concerned with appearances, but I take pride in the things that belong to me. I have no intention of running my territory out of a complete shithole."

"What about Kat's Cradle? Why not there?"

It's something I've considered at length, but ultimately, I need my headquarters to remain in the place where Aleksander once ruled.

"I can hire people to monitor the day-to-day operations there. I now have more pressing matters to keep an eye on." I narrow my gaze on him, making sure he knows I'm talking about any threat he poses.

He gives me an easy grin. "Going to take another crack at me since Michael's attempt to have me followed from Kat's Cradle failed so miserably?"

At least he's getting right down to business and isn't beating around the bush or playing coy about why he's here. Rose wants revenge—plain and simple. Calling me out on what Michael and I were up to brings it out into the open.

No more hiding behind pleasantries and fake smiles.

Now it's time to *really* talk.

TWO

I cross my legs to stop my foot from bouncing and lean forward slightly to rest an elbow on the edge of the desk. "I'm impressed you were able to give Michael's men the slip."

Our plan should have worked. With multiple cars following him, Rose shouldn't have been able to disappear so easily.

He smiles smugly and shrugs, his broad, muscular shoulders shifting the suit coat's expensive material. "I'm not an idiot, Kat. My eyes are always open, and I'm always paying attention to what's happening around me." A dark eyebrow rises. "Did you to really think my men nor I would notice we are being followed? That I wouldn't have contingency plans in place that would allow me to slip away in such an event?"

We had certainly hoped not.

Instead of answering him, I grab my cigarettes and lighter from the desk in front of me. Nicotine will calm my nerves and give me something to do with my hands when all they want to do is wrap around his neck and strangle him. I light one up and take a long, deep pull on it.

Rose watches me intently, almost like he's waiting for me to express my frustration at having lost him that day, but I refuse to give him the satisfaction.

I shrug as nonchalantly as possible while I inhale again. "It seems you thought of everything."

But he has secrets. Lots of them, no doubt. Like who the mystery tattooed lookalike was who showed up at Kat's Cradle and startled Rowan right before she quit and disappeared. The video Michael found of the incident still rattles around in the back of my brain. There's something there, something important I'm missing, but until I can find Rowan or Rose decides to open up to reveal all, it's a mystery I'm unlikely to solve. Doesn't mean I won't still try, though.

Rose chuckles at my observation and shakes his head. "I like to hope so. But it does leave one unanswered question."

"What's that?" I blow a plume of smoke toward him.

He motions between us slowly. "Where do *we* stand?"

I grin at him and knock off some ash in the glass tray on my desk. "I'm not sure I understand your question."

"It's pretty simple, Kat." He relaxes into his chair and rests his right ankle onto his left knee. The move exposes his crotch, a move that was no-doubt intentional. "Where do you and I stand? Are you still looking for a partner, or are you still looking for a way to kill me?"

A grin pulls at my lips, but I hope I manage to hide it behind my cigarette.

He waits for me to reply, then flicks a hand toward me. "Now that you've taken over Michael's territory and become head of this organization, do you plan to continue down the warpath Michael was on, or are you going to play nice?"

I lean back in my chair and examine him while I take a few hits off my cigarette. His dark, slicked-back hair matches his perfectly suave demeanor. The man doesn't get rattled. Sitting here with me, knowing I undoubtedly have several weapons within reach that could take him out in an instant, he doesn't flinch.

It's impressive.

And also terrifying.

"I'm not looking for a partner, Rose. You saw what happened to my last one."

Rose chuckles and shifts slightly, and his loafers shine perfectly under the harsh overhead fluorescent light. "Yes. It was a rather unfortunate turn of events for our friend, Michael, wasn't it? And I have no doubt that if given the opportunity, if I were dumb enough to give you my back, that you would stab a knife straight into it."

I take a drag off my cigarette and drop my head back against the leather of the chair I cleaned Michael's blood from only a week ago. "Then why even ask?"

He leans forward slightly and focuses his gaze on me intently. "Because what I told you when we met before Michael's untimely demise still rings true. We would be amazing partners, Kat—in business and life. Unstoppable, really."

I snort and shake my head. "You guys are so persistent. So intent on making something happen when you know it's not only bad for you but it's also potentially lethal."

He grins at me and shrugs. "What can I say? I am a glutton for punishment."

"I told you before, Rose, I'm not anyone's whore."

"I never said you were." He raises his hands defensively. "And if that's how you took my offer, then I deeply apologize. I want you to be my partner—in the brothels," he waves his hand, "this club and any others."

"And what about me?" I raise an eyebrow at him. "What do I get out of this deal? Besides having to give half my profits to someone who hasn't earned them."

He presses a hand over his chest and grins. "You get me and everything that comes along with me."

I bark out a laugh that echoes off the undecorated walls. "You say that like it's a benefit." I take another drag and blow the smoke across the desk at him. "All I see is someone who will try to interfere with my plan and direct things the wrong way. A man who is just as likely to stab me in the back and shoot me down the way I had intended to do you. For all I know, this is just another game on your part to get close to me and take me out the way Michael planned to take you out with my assistance."

He chuckles, a deep rumbling sound that reaches across the desk and goes straight to a place in my body that I definitely don't want it. "I guess you don't. I guess you have to trust me when I tell you that while I'm definitely not pleased with the little game you were playing with Michael, I do respect it. And you."

"Really?"

Respect is that last thing I thought I'd receive from Rose. Not after what we tried to do to him. Yet, I somehow know he's speaking the truth.

His head bobs slowly, and he steeples his fingers in front of his mouth, elbows propped on the armrests. "You're a strong woman, Kat. From what I've been able to piece together, you've been through an awful lot and come out on the other side the better for it." One corner of his mouth curls. "I find powerful women like you incredibly attractive."

I lean forward and snuff out my cigarette. "We're also dangerous. Michael could attest to that, if he were here."

This time, it's Rose who barks out a laugh and shakes his head as he pushes to his feet. "You're cold as ice, Kat. And absolutely intoxicating. Consider my offer. I'd much rather have you as an ally than an enemy." He holds out his hands. "But if you choose to keep coming after me, I'm only going to have one recourse. And we both know what that is."

He turns and walks out, closing the door behind him with a soft click.

I shift back in my chair and squeeze my eyes closed as I let our conversation sink in. Rose isn't someone to fuck with. He's proven that. And if he ever learns that I'm the one who set the bomb that almost killed him and his sister as well as the rest of the heads of the Chicago families—not

Michael, like he and everyone else suspects—any potential partnership we could have would disappear.

And I'd be number one on his hit list.

I've come too far on my own to partner with a man like Rose, even *if* he might be able to bring *something* to the table. The only thing more lethal than him is me, and I'm the only one I know who I can truly trust.

THREE

I sit in my chair at the desk in my room Kat's Cradle and examine the two empty ones facing me. The last time anyone was in this office with me, it was Michael, and we ended up *there*...

My eyes drift to the bed, the one I swore I would never use in this house. The one where I did far more than just fuck him—my enemy and my target. Every time Michael and I were together, things got more twisted, more convoluted inside me. Even now, after I've ended the game, my body heats at the memory at the same time a cold dread settles in the pit of my stomach. My time with Michael isn't what I want to be remembering.

Forget it, Kat. Forget HIM.

I squeeze my eyes closed and picture the almost black eyes of the man who will always hold my heart.

Aleksander.

He's the one I did all of this for. He is the driving force behind every action I've taken since the moment I learned of his death. He is my end-all, be-all. But he's also gone. And maybe my punishment for my sins, for what I did to Michael to seek revenge and unleash my wrath, is to constantly have my memories of Aleksander tarnished by the memories of my time with another man.

I will have to live continuously haunted by the fact that no matter how much I didn't want to enjoy it, my body yearned for him and his touch. How despite my best efforts to see him only as the monster he was, there were glimmers of a real person beneath his thick, hard exterior.

It wasn't enough to make me alter my course, but it was apparently just enough to weigh me down with guilt and follow me in a way I never anticipated. And now I have Rose breathing down my neck, heating my body in the same way, flirting with the danger Michael once did.

But this isn't that. I won't get involved with Rose despite what he said during our meetings. Even if I were to consider a potential relationship with him, it would be strictly professional and done to ensure he doesn't become a bigger threat.

And in order to know what I'm truly dealing with where it comes to him, I need to figure out who the mystery man with Rowan was.

It's the only reason I came back to Kat's Cradle tonight. I need to take another run at the girls try to find out what they know. No one seemed to have anything to offer the first time I questioned them, but that was weeks ago, before I killed Michael and demonstrated my ruthlessness. And now, perhaps with a little more incentive, they might be willing to tell me what I need to find Rowan.

And I do need to find Rowan because even if one of these girls knows who the man is, who looks so eerily like Rose, they don't know what Rowan knows. That look in her eyes when the man entered the room, the way she furtively glanced at the camera before it shut down inexplicably, it all means there's a story there. One I need to know regardless of whether Rose is an enemy or a friend.

Or preferably neither.

I lean forward and press the button on the phone to dial Driton downstairs. "I need you to bring me Amber."

"You got it." He ends the call.

I force myself to keep my eyes straight forward toward the door instead of drifting back to the bed I'll never use again. Those memories are dead. Gone forever. I just need to figure out a way to wrap all of Michael in that same box and lock it away somewhere it can disappear.

A sharp knock sounds before the door opens and Driton ushers in Amber. She smiles sheepishly and approaches to take a seat in front of the desk as Driton steps into the hall and closes the door behind him.

I offer Amber a reassuring smile. I don't want her to think she's in any trouble. That will only make her clam up more and make finding what I need that much harder. "Amber, thanks for coming to meet with me. I was hoping we could have a little chat."

She gives me an unsure smile. "Sure, about what?"

I clasp my hands in front of me on the desk and lean forward slightly. "About what we talked about previously—Rowan and the man who came to see her before she quit."

Amber shifts in her chair, averting her gaze. "I...um...I told you what I know. I've never seen him before, and she didn't tell me what she was doing or why she was quitting, just that she was done working here."

I fight the urge to scowl at her—or worse. It's not in any of these girls' natures to have loose lips...at least where client information is concerned. They've been trained to remain quiet. To protect our clients' identities and anything else they may overhear or learn like steel traps. Of course, she's not going to want to volunteer any information; that could get her fired.

It almost makes me proud as much as it annoys me. If she had volunteered everything she knew right off the bat, it might be a sign she isn't Kat's Cradle material in the first place.

I force what I hope is a sympathetic smile. "I understand you may be reluctant to share with me, but I need you to understand the situation I'm in."

She nods slowly.

"As you know, I've managed to make Kat's Cradle *the* premiere brothel in all of Chicago and the surrounding suburbs and have set up a second location that is already taking flight."

Her eyes widen. "And I really appreciate the job here."

"Of course, you do. I treat my girls well, and I make sure your clientele does, too. And I know you may feel like you're betraying some sort of confidence with this client or with Rowan if you give me the information I'm seeking, but I need to know if we have been compromised."

She stiffens in her chair, and some of the color leaves her face.

Good. You should be nervous...especially if you're hiding something from me that will bite me in the ass.

It's time to push her. "This man was not on anyone's schedule. The guards don't know who he is or how he got into the house. And Rowan appeared frightened of him, then suddenly quit. That could pose a very serious issue for me, for you, and the rest of the girls here, not to mention my greater business plans."

She pulls her bottom lip between her teeth and chews on it as she considers me.

I hold up my hands. "I'm not asking you to tell me anything personal that Rowan may have revealed. I just need to know if we are in any sort of danger."

Hopefully, that will open her up enough that I can pry what I really need from her.

She crosses and uncrosses her legs and shifts in her seat again. "I only saw him once. The day of the video you showed me."

"Where did you see him?"

Her pale-blue eyes dart down to her hands twisting in her lap and back up at me. "I let him in the back door and up the private rear stairs."

I tense and narrow my gaze on her. "Is that why security never saw him?"

There aren't any cameras in the back stairwell. Only the staff uses it. And he must have slipped in the door when the guards were making their rounds and on the other side of the property.

She nods, and her cheeks flush. "I'm so sorry, Kat. I didn't mean to do anything wrong, but I thought it would be okay, given the circumstances."

"What circumstances?"

"He asked for Rowan by name. Her *real* name *Rowan*, not Red like she goes by here. He said it was urgent that he speak with her and that he was afraid if he came to the front, she would get in trouble."

I release a sigh and sit back in my chair. "So, you believed you were protecting your friend."

She practically sags in relief. "Yes."

As much as I want to be angry about her disregarding the rules, I can't bring myself to tear into her. "Tell me about the man. Did he give you a name?"

She shakes her head. "No."

"What else can you tell me about him?"

One of her slim shoulders rises and falls. "He was handsome. Hispanic, with an accent I couldn't quite place. Maybe South American? Tattoos on his forearms that were visible in the T-shirt he was wearing."

"Did he appear nervous?"

She bites her lip again and shakes her head. "Not really. More like it was urgent that he see Rowan."

I nod slowly and lean back in my chair. "Did you take him up to her room?"

She nods again and clears her throat. "Yes. I let him in."

"Do you know what happened between them in there?"

Her eyes dart away again. This is when I imagine she will shut down. Having to reveal something personal that Rowan might have told her might be pushing too far.

"Amber, please, this is important."

She sighs and shakes her head. "All I know is that he was in there for fifteen or twenty minutes and then left out the back. And after, Rowan seemed agitated. She was distracted the rest of the day. Even one of her clients mentioned something to me about it when he was on his way out and asked if she was okay."

I clench my fists on the arms of my chair. That's the last thing I want to hear—that one of our clients was not happy with her services. It makes me want to find Rowan and the answers even more. "But she didn't tell you who he was or why he was here?"

"No, I'm sorry I can't help you more."

"Have you heard from her since she left?"

That same blush spreads across her cheeks again, but she shakes her head in the negative. Amber would be a shitty poker player.

"Be honest with me, Amber."

A heavy sigh slips from her lips, and she reaches into her pocket and pulls out her phone. "She texted me once. She asked me to grab a few of her things from her room that she forgot and to meet her with them."

"Where did you meet?"

"A small coffee shop near the Loop."

"Did you two talk?"

She shrugs. "Not really. She seemed nervous and distracted. I asked her if she needed anything, and she said she was fine and then left."

Shit. A dead end.

At least, for now. I narrow my eyes on the phone in her hands. "I want you to send a text to Rowan. Tell her that something has come up and you need to talk to her. That it's urgent."

Amber's eyebrows fly up. "What do I do if she replies?"

"You schedule a meeting."

"For when? Where?"

"As soon as possible. See if she'll meet you outdoors somewhere you could have a conversation and not be overheard, like a park."

Somewhere she won't be expecting *me*.

Amber watches me for a moment before nodding. "Okay."

"And then, let me know as soon as the meeting is set."

Her hand shakes as she slips her phone back into her pocket. "You're not going to hurt her, are you?"

I force my best smile, the one that I used to fool Michael so many times. The one I hope I can use against Rose and the rest of the heads of the families, too. "No, Amber, I would never do *anything* like that."

FOUR

I TIGHTEN my hands on the steering wheel and take my exit off the freeway, glancing behind me to ensure Genti and Driton are still following in their SUV. If they had their way, I would be tucked safely away in the backseat with them instead of driving myself, but I needed some alone time—some time to mentally process what's been happening and to have a little private call with the man I'm hoping will get me what I need so badly to hopefully help vanquish some of my demons.

But right now, that man doesn't seem to want to cooperate. "I don't like the reluctance I hear in your voice, Arden."

Silence greets me through the line as Michael's cousin and tech guru considers his response. He finally clears his throat. "I'm sorry...I'm just..."

"Reluctant to assist me because of your familial relationship with my predecessor. I can understand that." After all, I did shoot his cousin in the head after seducing him and working my way into his inner circle. "But I think there are some things you need to understand, too. I'm the head of this organization now. I call the shots. And if you aren't going to get on board the way Michael's other men have, I suggest you disappear before I *make* you disappear."

Coming from anyone else, it might be an empty threat, but from me, it is a promise. As much as I despise having to even say it, he knows too much. About Michael. About me. About this operation that I've inherited. About my plans for the future that were intricately aligned with Michael's.

If he were ever to go to one of my competitors, or God forbid, fall into the wrong hands *unwillingly*, it could be catastrophic. I won't let that happen.

"I-I-I understand, ma'am. I can assist you."

My lips pull into a smile, and I take the final turn to pull my car in at the end of the docks and throw it into park while Genti pulls up and parks behind me. "I'm so glad to hear that, Arden. I know Michael already had you looking into Rose and any information you could find on him or his base of operations. I assume he showed you the video from Kat's Cradle of the man in one of my girl's rooms?"

"Yes, I have a copy of it."

"Good. I want you to go to Kat's Cradle and figure out how the video feed got shut off. Then, I want you to find everything you can on Rowan. I'll leave what little information I have from her employment file for you. Also, talk to a girl named Amber. She has a phone number for Rowan, and we might be able to track her that way, though she's going to try to arrange a meet."

"Okay."

"Also..." I swallow back the bile rising in my throat at this request. I've known I needed to make a decision and move on this since the day Aleksander died, but it was Michael who reminded me of it and brought it to the forefront of my mind once again. I had pushed it to the back while I focused on him. But now, it's time to wrap up loose ends. "I need you to find Konstandin Morina."

Another silence greets me before Arden clears his throat. "Uh, ma'am, that's like asking me to find Jesus Christ. The man is a ghost—"

I slam my palms against the steering wheel and grit my teeth. "It isn't just him now. He has Rea with him. That makes it harder to hide and blend in anywhere. Start where Aleksander was killed and work from there. Track them. Find them."

"I'll do my best, ma'am."

"Your best better mean you'll find them. Failure isn't an option."

"Understood."

"Oh, and Arden?"

"Yes, ma'am?"

"Stop calling me *ma'am*. Call me Kat."

Ma'am always makes me think of my teachers in grade school—old and stuffy women. The last thing I want to be associated with.

"But..."

"Goodbye, Arden." I end the call and remove my seatbelt as I examine the warehouse in front of me.

This is where it happened—the attempt on Michael's life. Perpetrated by the Dragushas and Berishas from back home in Albania. They wanted to shut down our operation, stop us from taking girls from back home and bringing them over here, but now, I need to ramp it up and get it going even stronger. They're only going to leave me alone if I keep paying them to. That necessitates more girls. More houses. More everything.

And that means convincing Valentina to retain the agreement she made with Michael to let him use these docks.

The next ship of women should be here within two weeks, and though Esad was as reluctant as Arden to work for me, he and I came to an agreement. Michael's oldest friend will continue to ensure things move smoothly in Albania and across the water, and as quickly as possible, per the agreement he had with my predecessor.

As Michael's only true friend, Esad surely wants me dead, and it's likely he's only agreeing to this so he can get physically close to me at some point and hope I let down my guard. But I'm not stupid enough to fall for that. We may have come to an understanding, but I will never give that man my back.

Nor will I offer it to *anyone*. Especially Valentina or any of her crew during our meeting today. Not after the stories I've heard about her "pirates."

A black SUV pulls up to the side entrance of the warehouse. The back door opens, and the man who can only be Cutter Jackson, steps out. Wide, muscular shoulders pull at the T-shirt he wears, and nasty scars spiral up the side of his neck and across the right side of his face. The aviators he wears do little to hide the damage. All they do is make him seem even more imposing and lethal.

I can see why Michael called him Valentina's dog because he looks like someone who would tear you apart, limb from limb while foaming at the mouth for more blood if you got within a foot of her.

With his gaze locked on me where I wait in my car, he walks around to the other side of the SUV and opens the door. A small, delicate hand stretches out from inside. He takes it and helps out the head of the Marconi family.

Valentina is practically glowing in her pregnancy—her bump now impossible to hide. Cutter places a protective hand on her lower back and ushers her into the warehouse while keeping his sunglasses-covered eyes trained on me.

Smart man. Never takes his focus off the threat.

If Michael had been so vigilant, I never would've been able to succeed in my mission. But today is a different one. Today means playing nice with Valentina and pretending we aren't on opposite sides of a five-way war waiting to explode in this town.

I push open my door, grab my purse, and step from the car. Genti and Driton remain in the SUV parked behind me. They already know I'm going in alone—though they weren't happy about it. Valentina and Cutter will be much more likely to speak with me and negotiate if I make this as nonthreatening as possible. Given what they know I did to Michael, they're already going to be on guard. If I walked in with those two meatheads armed to the teeth, the tension might impede my ability to accomplish my goal today.

Cutter waits just outside the door of the warehouse as I approach. The two other men who arrived in the vehicle with them have already led Valentina inside. Cutter stands with his arms crossed over his barrel chest, his tattooed biceps threatening to burst the T-shirt barely containing them. He scowls at me.

"Mr. Jackson, I presume?" I smile at him—hoping it appears warm and genuine. Something I'm not very good at anymore. Not since losing Aleksander. It's different than the one I offer most men, mostly because I know Cutter won't fall for that one. "It's a pleasure to finally meet you."

He grunts and shakes his head, but the corner of his mouth twitches, almost like he's fighting a smile. "I suppose I should be thanking you for getting rid of Michael."

"But?" I raise an eyebrow at him.

"But I'm not naïve enough to think you're going to be any better."

I chuckle and grin. "I guess I'll take that as a compliment."

"You shouldn't."

FIVE

Unease creeps over me, entering the warehouse, and not just because of my little chat with Cutter outside and the unspoken threat he left hanging in the air. After what happened to Michael here, it certainly isn't anywhere I want to spend a great deal of time. But it's a necessity. So is dealing with the woman standing in front of me.

One of her hands rubs protectively over her swollen belly, and I offer another hopefully friendly smile. Cutter follows closely behind me, with my gun tucked into his waistband. There was no way he was going to let me in here with it, and I never expected him to.

He steps up next to Valentina and places a hand on her lower back, then leans in and whispers something to her. She nods almost imperceptibly, never taking her amber eyes off me.

I extend a hand. "Ms. Marconi. It's a pleasure to finally meet you."

She raises a perfect, thin, dark eyebrow at me. "I wish I could say the same. But after what you pulled with Michael, I don't plan on us getting very friendly."

Her beauty combined with the Italian accent lacing her perfect English make her seem so out of place here in this shitty warehouse. This woman belongs on a runway in Milan.

I chuckle and sigh, both sounding loud in the almost complete silence of the massive space. "I can understand that sentiment. But tell me, Valentina...what would you have done if he had killed Cutter?"

She stiffens, and the hand on her belly freezes. Cutter issues a low warning growl.

It doesn't faze me, though. "Aleksander was my everything...and Michael took him away. I deserved retribution for that."

Valentina offers a mirthless laugh. "Did you really have to string him along like that, though?"

I grin at her—this time, a genuine one. "Some of that was for fun. Some of it was a necessity. I got what I wanted. And I'm here today to make sure I continue to receive it."

Her eyes widen slightly. "If you think I have any intention of letting you use the docks, then you're more insane than your predecessor."

Definitely a possibility.

I wave a hand around at the object of our discussion. "All I'm asking is that you abide by the agreement you had with Michael."

She snorts and shakes her head. "*Neanche per idea*! Michael and I had an agreement based upon an understanding of something that he would do for me in return. And from what *I* understand, you're not in any position to make good on, nor do you have any intention of following through on that part of the agreement even if you could."

The woman isn't wrong there. At least, for now. If I took out Rose the way Michael had intended, it would make securing and maintaining my position even more difficult. His cartel would come down on me harder than anything I can even fathom.

"For now, he stays. Though I can't tell you what the future may hold in that regard. What I *can* tell you is that you're going to let me use the docks."

"Why the hell would I do that?"

"Because you're obligated to."

I had hoped I wouldn't need to take things this far because opening this can of worms could unleash something I'm not able to put back in.

She opens her mouth to object, but I hold up a hand to stop her.

"Not because of your agreement with Michael. But because of your predecessor's agreement with Aleksander."

Her cool amber gaze narrows on me. "What the hell is that supposed to mean? What agreement?"

Cutter shifts behind her, inching closer.

This is where the fact that I'm unarmed gets a little dicey. I knew I'd have to tell her eventually. It just would've been a lot more comfortable to do it over the telephone instead of standing in the vacant warehouse with her pit bull armed and ready to lash out at me.

"Prior to Aleksander's and Arturo's deaths, they came to an agreement. Arturo asked Aleksander for a favor. One Aleksander granted in return for two favors in the future."

Valentina's brow furrows. "What the hell are you talking about? When did this happen?"

I grin at her. "About two weeks before Aleksander had his men take out *Il Padrone*."

Her nostrils flare, and she makes a move to step toward me, but Cutter holds her back, anger flashing in his gaze, too.

"It was Aleksander?" Valentina's words are barely more than a whisper as she struggles to comprehend what she's just learned. "You killed my father."

I hold up my hands and shake my head. "I didn't do anything. At that point in time, I was nothing more than a stripper working at Aleksander's club. What happened between your cousin and him had absolutely nothing to do with me until I became the head of this family. Then, I made it my business. And I know you understand the importance of us being able to rely on agreements we make with each other."

Valentina's lips twist into a sneer. "You think I'm going to honor an agreement that got my father killed? *Sei pazza!*"

I glance at the man to her left, the father of her child, the one willing to do anything for her. My own reflection bounces back at me from his aviator shades, but that doesn't stop the heat of his gaze from searing me. "The way I understand it, Cutter and his crew would have taken care of it if we hadn't. Perhaps he should be thanking me."

This time, it's Cutter who takes a step toward me, but Valentina presses a hand against his chest to hold him back despite the fiery wrath she casts my way. She studies me for a long, hard moment, her eyes never leaving mine. "Perhaps you're right."

"What?" Cutter jerks his attention away from me and to her. "You can't be serious, *principessa*."

She glances at him and digs her nails into his chest. "She's right. If Arturo hadn't done it, you would have, *amore mio*."

A fact that I am confident has been a point of contention in their relationship before, given the look she's giving him right now. The tension in his shoulders eases slightly, but he continues to sneer at me.

I plaster on another smile. "So, I have your agreement to continue the arrangement you had with Michael?"

Valentina takes a step toward me, and Cutter stiffens again but doesn't move to follow her this time. She rests her hand against her belly and leans in slightly. "I will not honor the agreement I had with Michael, but I will grant the favor the Marconi family promised to the Gashis. You can continue to use the docks as long as your business doesn't interfere with mine."

I nod toward her and then Cutter. "It's been a pleasure doing business with you both."

Cutter storms around her and ushers me toward the door. When he reaches it, he shoves it open, reaches for my gun still tucked in his waistband, and holds it out to me.

I wrap my hand around the pistol, but instead of releasing it, he pulls me toward him and leans in, the scars on his face twisting with his rage.

"She's the boss, so she's the one who gets to make this decision, but just know that if it were up to me, you'd be dead right now for how you betrayed Michael. Someone like you can't be trusted. Don't even think about trying to move against her, or I'll end you faster than your next breath."

A slow smile curls my lips, and I pull the gun from his grasp. His passion for her is almost romantic. "I would expect nothing less."

SIX

THAT WENT ABOUT AS WELL AS CAN be expected, given the circumstances. Frankly, just walking out of there alive is a win, let alone getting her agreement. Revealing to Valentina who was behind her father's death was a calculated risk. But if I was going to get her cooperation, I needed to pull the favor card. And I'm glad I did. Because now, we won't have any issue continuing to bring in the girls, and I'll be able to expand exponentially.

I pull out of the docks and away from the lake with Genti and Driton in their SUV behind me. The club really needs some attention if I'm going to get it updated and up-classed from how it's always operated and into a true destination and location people *want* to be seen in. But first, I need to swing by the new house to make sure everything is still on track there and that the new house mother is doing her job, keeping the girls who arrived just before I took over this territory happy. Without happy girls, we won't have happy clients. And happy clients not only bring in the money, but they're also more likely to open their mouths and reveal things they shouldn't.

Building up my arsenal of information is always a top priority, and while it certainly will be harder now that everyone knows who I am and that I run the houses, there's one thing I can always count on—the ability of lust to overpower reason.

I've built my business and all my plans around that principle. And it hasn't failed me yet.

The stockpile of blackmail material and information I've gathered over the last six months is far greater than Michael even knew. He may have made the first major move by getting Senator Mason on board, but there are so many avenues available at this point, it's almost overwhelming.

So as much as I'd like to go racing into using my new power and make more moves to position myself to do even more, I can only take one step at a time. Rushing only opens the door to stumbles. And in this business, stumbling means weakness and death.

I turn the corner to head toward the freeway, and a dark SUV whizzes past me on the left and turns directly in front of my car.

"Shit!" I slam on my brakes to avoid hitting it. "What the fuck?"

The doors of the SUV fly open, and four huge men storm toward my car.

"Fuck..." I throw it into reverse and glance behind me only to find another dark SUV blocking my retreat.

Where the fuck are Genti and Driton?

They were supposed to be right behind me. I wasn't really paying attention to them after we left the docks, but they must've been cut off from me at some point.

I reach for my gun in my purse, but something smashes through my window, shattering it and sending glass flying. One of the men reaches in, pops the door lock, and grabs my bicep to drag me from the car.

"Get your fucking hands off me." I lash out with my arm that isn't restrained and scratch the man holding me across the side of his face.

He roars like a wounded animal and backhands me. The strike sends my head whipping back and makes stars dance in my vision. He manhandles me into the SUV with him and another man slams the door shut after us before he jumps into the front seat.

We peel away, leaving my car running and empty with the driver's door open in the middle of the road.

What the fuck is going on?

I kick and thrash against the man's hold, but the other goon in the backseat pulls his gun and points it right at my chest.

"I suggest you stop fighting this, Ms. Gashi, or it could get very ugly for you."

Fuck. Who would be stupid enough to pull me off the fucking street and think they will live?

Whoever these fuckers are will pay.

We weave through the streets of Chicago, avoiding major thoroughfares and traffic and heading toward the South Side. That really only leaves one possibility for where they're taking me.

The fucking Irish.

Leave it to them to pull a stunt like this in broad fucking daylight. They seem to lack basic common sense, even though Michael seemed to think Galen McGinnis was someone to watch carefully.

I turn to the man who struck me and examine the bloody scratches on the side of his cheek. "Your boss is a fucking dead man. Tell Galen he's going to regret this."

He smirks at me. "I doubt that very much. And you can tell him yourself."

We squeal to a stop outside the old brick building that houses the headquarters of the McGinnis family. Bright neon signs for Guinness, Jameson, and Bushmills flash in the windows. To call *Bottom O' the Well* a dive bar would be generous.

At this moment, it seems a fitting place for Galen McGinnis to be operating—sleazy, dirty, and lacking any class whatsoever. It's also quite ironic, considering how Michael almost died at the hands of his grandfather at the bottom of one and only survived to have me take him out. Galen may think he can hide in here, but he *will* pay for this the same way Michael did.

Galen's goon drags me out of the SUV and ushers me in through the main entrance of the bar. Apparently, they have no qualms about marching me in front of any patrons who may be drinking even this early in the day.

It's a wonder the McGinnises have managed to maintain their power for so long if this is how they handle things. Seven decades controlling the South Side of Chicago have taught them nothing, or Galen has decided to ignore anything his predecessors learned about maintaining the status quo and avoiding a war between the families.

A war may have been what Michael wanted, but I'm not as confident it's in my best interests. There's a lot to be said for maintaining things the way they've comfortably existed. The families have co-existed for decades without any major bloodshed. But that all changed with Rose and Michael. They both wanted the city—the *whole* city. I want it, too. I'm just willing to do it the right way to ensure I don't get shot in the back in the process. It may mean being patient, making smaller moves and positioning things more carefully—like playing chess instead of checkers. But I'm willing to do what it takes...within reason.

Something the Irish seem to lack. Snatching me off the streets was the wrong move because all Galen has done is unleash what I learned from Aleksander and have kept restrained for so long.

SEVEN

GALEN MCGINNIS SITS at his desk, his feet propped up on it, black boots rocking gently from side to side as I'm led into his office. He grins at me like he's not about to pay for what he's done with his fucking life, the move twisting the scar that cuts across his left eye—a gift I gave him in the bombing, though he thankfully isn't privy to that bit of information yet. He doesn't seem to know he's going to end up six feet under for taking me, either.

The man can't be that dumb—to expect that I wouldn't have a problem with this.

But his face doesn't reflect that he's aware of the danger he's put himself in. Everyone always warned me Galen doesn't play nice, but judging by the smile, he must want me to think he does. "Kat, *a thaisce*, it's so nice to finally meet you in person. It's been a long time coming, don't you think?" He raises an eyebrow at me.

I scowl at him, giving him my iciest look. "If you wanted to meet, Galen, all you had to do was call."

He holds out his hands, sweeping them around the office. "I extended you an invitation."

"Oh, is that what you call this? Being attacked on the street, dragged out of my car, and assaulted."

His green eyes darken, and he narrows them on me as he drops his feet to the floor and leans forward. "What do you mean *assaulted?*"

The man who struck me and is now standing next to me retreats a step, like he can run or hide from whatever's coming.

I glance over my shoulder at him and scowl. "Your man here backhanded me like I'm some common street trash."

Galen's lips twist into a sneer, and he slams his fist against the desk, rattling the glass of amber liquid on it violently. *"Cad a bhí tú ag smaoineamh? Is amadán tú!"*

I don't have the slightest fucking idea what he just said to him—Gaelic has never been a top priority when it comes to learning another language—but I got the gist of it. Something tells me his man is in for a whole lot of pain sometime soon because of what he did to me. At least I can respect that even if I don't appreciate the way Galen went about getting me here.

The man who controls South Side, Chicago, holds up his hands apologetically. "I offer my sincerest apologies for the way you were treated. I told them to extend you an invitation, not manhandle you. Please, take a seat."

He points to one of the chairs facing his desk and waits. With the two goons standing behind me and at least half a dozen others I saw as we walked in through the bar, there's no way I'm getting out of here unless Galen wants me to leave.

Why bother trying?

This may be an opportunity in disguise. If Galen wants the meeting, perhaps he's looking to come to some sort of agreement that will mutually benefit us. Given what was happening before I took out Michael, chess pieces were being moved around rapidly, and now, the game has changed entirely. They went from playing with a beginner to facing down a master.

I reluctantly lower myself into the chair, never taking my eyes from Galen's. From where he's seated and the way he's leaning forward, he can certainly see up my skirt. I fight the grin threatening to spread on my lips, then cross my legs, making sure to flash him my bare pussy. Sex and lust make men weak, and I believe in using every weapon in my arsenal.

His gaze follows the move, and he centers in on that spot at the apex of my thighs for a moment before he breaks his trance and raises one of his dark eyebrows slowly. "Can I offer you a drink?"

I glance at the glass on his desk. "What are you having?"

He holds it up and takes a sip. "Jameson."

Drinking with this man might not be wise—while I can handle my liquor, anything that lowers inhibitions around sexy and dangerous men who just kidnapped you doesn't seem like a good plan. Yet, I have a feeling I'll need alcohol to deal with whatever he's about to bring up. "I'll take one."

He motions to one of his men, and the guy walks over to a bar in the corner, pours a drink, and hands it to me.

I take it from him without looking at him and enjoy the burn of my first sip. "Tell me what it is you wanted to talk to me about, Galen, because I do have places to be today."

A slow grin spreads across his lips, lifting the scar bisecting his eye. "Well, Kat, I figured that since you've now been in power for several weeks and you haven't reached out to me that it was perhaps a bad sign for our future working relationship."

"We don't have a relationship."

He points at me, humor dancing in his gaze. "Exactly. And that leads me to the uneasy feeling that now that you're in control, you're going to be encroaching on some of my businesses, if not worse. Your predecessor had no qualms about taking out my cousin, Padraig, in a very unpleasant and bloody fashion, I might add."

It seems the actions of those in power before me will forever be held against me, but nothing he said is a surprise, really. His concern over my plans and businesses is the same one he and Valerian expressed to Michael about Rose if he were to team up with me. And he has every right to be pissed about Michael torturing his cousin. Especially when, in the end, it wasn't the Irish who tried to take out Michael, and that had been his reason for retaliating in the first place.

I nod slowly and take another drink. "I can assure you, Galen, that I have no intention of getting into the gun business."

We both know that's his primary concern. The Irish have been the major suppliers of weapons in Chicago for decades. Their only rivals have been the Russians, but it seems he and Valerian have come to some sort of an agreement on that front since they approached Michael together about Rose.

"What about the girls? You know Valerian and I control most of the streets, aside from what Valentina does, and your focus seems to be in that same vein."

I can't control the laugh that slips from my lips, and I shake my head. "Oh, that's rich."

Galen's lips droop into a frown, and he narrows his eyes on me. "What the hell is that supposed to mean?"

I swirl my drink in the glass and take a sip. "If you think what you and Valerian do with your street trash is anything compared to the type of operation I have at Kat's Cradle, then you are not as intelligent as I've been told."

One of his eyebrows rises slowly. "Oh, so you heard I'm intelligent?"

Of course, that would be what he takes from my comment.

"I don't have any intention of running girls on the street, Mr. McGinnis. It's not my business. I'm all about upscale clients and making big money, not turning over twenty tricks a day for hundred bucks each."

He snorts and then chuckles. "You think my girls are that cheap, huh?"

"I know they are."

Men like Galen and Valerian make their money off quantity, not quality. They're the Walmart of lust, whereas I'm the specialty shop on Rodeo Drive.

"And what do you plan on doing with all the girls you're bringing in?"

Of course, word of the second house would've gotten to them at this point. He has to know I'm going to be expanding.

He motions toward me. "Do you plan on partnering with Rose? I heard he paid you a little visit the other day."

It's his not-so-subtle way of telling me he's watching the club. After what Michael did to Padraig, that isn't surprising in the least.

I take a sip of my drink and nod slowly. "He did pay me a visit. But I can assure you, I'm not in business with Rose, nor do I have any plans to be in the future."

Galen offers me a slick grin.

I can see why women like him. The slight Irish accent that came from all the time he spends back home despite the fact that he was born here. The strong jawline. The quick, easy grin that softens the hardness in his midnight eyes. That sexy salt-and-pepper hair with the hint of red. He's a handsome man, if not a bit arrogant.

His eyebrows rise. "Does that mean you'll consider a partnership with me?"

He hasn't exactly been hiding his interest in me...as more than a business partner. His eyes undress me the way he wants to with his hands, and if things were different...if *I* were different, I might explore that more. But the reality is, my heart will always belong to Aleksander, and while I may need to satisfy a very real need every once in a while, I have no plans on diving head-long into *any* form of relationship with anyone right now. Maybe ever.

I down the rest of my drink. It warms my throat and settles in my stomach, cementing my resolve. "Absolutely not."

A deep chuckle rumbles from his chest. "So, I'll continue to run my business myself, and you'll do the same?"

I nod my agreement.

"While I appreciate your assurances regarding not competing with me, I'm not so sure Valerian will be so easily appeased."

Not surprising.

The Russian is known for being stubborn and brutal. It's one reason no one has messed with him for so long. He won't easily accept my promise to stay out of his way, not after what I did to Michael.

I set my empty glass on top of Galen's desk and rise to my feet. "I can handle Valerian."

He stands and crosses his arms over his chest with a chuckle. "Oh, I'm quite confident you can."

EIGHT

AT LEAST GALEN had the good sense to have my car returned to me. Seeing it sitting in front of my condo building is definitely unexpected, but he probably knew it would only dig him into a deeper hole if he left it in the middle of the road, running, with my purse in it. The police would have found it and set off an investigation that might have led them straight to me and potentially right back to the Irish. They certainly don't want the cops sniffing around any more than I do.

I open the door of the black SUV and cast one final look at Galen on the other side of the back seat.

All he does is grin at me while something devious dances in his eyes. "Sure I can't convince you to change your mind regarding a partnership?"

He's persistent. I can respect that. You have to be in this game.

I shake my head and step out onto the sidewalk. "I'm a solo operator. That's not going to change."

He shrugs and smirks at me. "I had to try."

"And I had to say no." I close the door before he can make any more attempts to sway me.

A sharp breeze flows down the street between the buildings on either side and whips around me, sending a shiver through my body. They don't call it the Windy City for nothing. The doorman opens the door for me to step into the lobby of the building. I almost walk right past him, but the fear in his wide eyes makes me pause.

Did he see Galen drop me off and recognize him? Is that why he's so uneasy? Or maybe he's finally learned who I am?

Even though Aleksander and I lived in this building when we were together, the condo was vacant during my time setting up Kat's background. This doorman was never around when Aleksander was still alive, so if he's just finding out that I'm the head of the Albanian mob here, his former friendly demeanor may be long gone.

I offer him what I hope is a believable and friendly smile and step through the door. The last thing I want is a doorman who is so afraid of me that he goes to the cops with anything he sees. Aleksander chose this location because of the promise of confidentiality—a building where people wouldn't ask questions. I can't have that changing.

I push the elevator button and ride up to my floor. Between the meeting with Valentina and the unexpected one with Galen, my day is certainly not turning out how I thought it would. Exhaustion seeps deep into my bones, and my body craves a drink and a smoke—or ten.

The elevator doors slide open, revealing the hallway with a single door at the end—home is within sight. Driton stands sentry outside, and his eyes widen when his gaze meets mine. He rushes down the hall toward me. "You're back."

"No shit, Sherlock. Thank you for that brilliant observation. What the hell happened to you and Genti?"

He falls into stride with me. "They cut us off. Fucking descended on us at gunpoint, and by the time they left, you were long gone. We suspected it was the Irish, but when we tried to track your car, it was already parked here."

I stop my progress and turn to face him. "You should have come for me."

His dark eyebrows fly up. "Guns blazing into their headquarters?"

He has a point.

That likely wouldn't have gotten us anywhere except for into an all-out bloodbath with the Irish. Though I'm furious about what happened, I can't really say that they should have done anything else but wait for word from me or from whoever took me.

"Where's Genti?" He's quickly become my right-hand man and the one I've come to depend on when I need things handled properly.

"He's at the club. He has every available man looking for you everywhere."

I push past him toward the door. "Well, you fucking found me."

"There's something you should know before you go in—"

I open the door and step inside before he can finish the sentence, letting it slam closed behind me.

I need a smoke. And a drink.

Something better than that Irish swill Galen gave me. But when my eyes finally focus in the dark room, something else takes priority—the man sitting on my couch.

Rose slowly rises to his feet and stalks across the living room in his immaculate dark suit and crisp white dress shirt until he's immediately in front of me. Almost black eyes bore into mine, digging deep into my soul and threatening to unravel me on the spot.

I swallow thickly. "What the hell are you doing here?"

And why the hell did Driton let him in?

Rose continues to advance on me, and I retreat until my back presses against the door—my only means of escape. He stops just inches from me, the heat radiating off him enough to make me notice the chilly air for the first time since coming in. "I heard someone took you. I was ready to burn down Chicago to find you."

"What? Why would you do that?"

A muscle in his clenched jaw tics. "Why the fuck do you think?" His accent drips off every word, somehow thicker than normal in his agitated state. His dark eyes search mine and rake over me, almost like he's examining every inch of my body for any injury or assault. He reaches up and captures my chin in his hand, forcing my head back and my gaze to lock with his. "I would do anything for you, Kat. Why can't you understand that?"

Nothing is simple in this world. There's no way it's that cut and dried. "I told you before, Rose, more than once, that I won't be part of this game."

His thumb brushes over my bottom lip. "It's not a game. I'm deadly serious."

The move and his words send a zinging current of electricity through my body and straight between my legs. In the times we've been in the same room in the past, I always had to keep up this professional wall—first because of my ruse with Michael to get Rose on as a partner, and then in my office to keep him from getting the wrong idea about what I wanted.

And as much as I might want to deny my attraction to Rose, want to reject the way my body responds to his proximity, it's been there since that first time he stepped into Kat's Cradle all those months ago.

Sexy. Powerful. And capable of even more violence and carnage than Michael. I'm quite confident about that. Which is exactly why I need to stay away from him. Just like I played Michael, Rose could be playing me.

Get away, Kat.

Feeling his touch for the first time, seeing this look in his eyes—hungry and feral—it's too much for me to bear. I press my hands against the crisp white shirt exposed under his open suit coat and try to shove him back, but he doesn't budge, an immovable force with his sights set on me.

"Why are you fighting me on this, Kat? I heard it was the Irish who took you. Is it because of Galen? Did that smooth Irish fuck manage to crumble that wall you have around yourself?" He pauses, and one of his eyebrows wings up. "Or maybe it's Valerian? Maybe your whole plan with

Michael came from some agreement with them that I'm not aware of." His free hand slides down my hip to cup between my legs. "Who controls you here, Kat?"

I shove him again, harder this time, digging my nails into his chest. Yet, at the same time that I try to fight his advance, my body flares to life, need coursing through me. Need for *more* from him. For him to be *closer*. So much closer.

No. Not this man. Not now. I can't.

And if I don't do something drastic, this is going to go down a road there's no coming back from. I open my mouth and dig my teeth into his thumb. He jerks it back from my bite, and a slow, satisfied grin spreads over his lips.

Leaning in closer, he brushes his lips over my ear. "I don't mind a little nip, Kat. A little pain makes this so much more interesting."

A low growl of frustration slips from my mouth. "No one controls me there. Especially not you."

Even though I've made no attempt to bat his hand away...

Even though I know I would feel the loss immediately...

He squeezes me between the legs tighter, then slides his fingers to the hem of my dress and slowly inches it up. Every fiber of my being trembles in anticipation of his touch, of the soft drag of warm flesh against my most sensitive area, but then...his fingers still before they reach me.

A strange mixture of anger and annoyance courses through my trembling body. I want to bat his hand away just as much as I want him to keep going—the ultimate war raging inside me.

This is exactly what got me in trouble with Michael. It would've been so much easier to betray him if I hadn't actually been attracted to him. If I hadn't found his ruthlessness intoxicating. If his touch hadn't made me quiver. And from what I know about Rose, he's more than Michael's equal.

Yet, for as much as I might know about his reputation, there's even more he's kept hidden...

"I don't even know your real name."

The Blood Rose Cartel has been a player for the last decade. Even before Rose showed up in Chicago, what they were doing in Colombia and beyond was no secret, according to several conversations I had with Aleksander before his death. Yet everyone involved in that organization has somehow managed to keep their real names private all this time. They've remained cloaked in secrecy and hidden behind dark veils of brutality and cold maneuvers. I've never heard anyone refer to him as anything other than Rose...because no one knows who the fuck he really is.

His ability to remain anonymous has kept him alive this long. But I'll make it my mission to solve the mystery.

That slow grin returns, and he leans in and stops just short of pressing his lips to mine, close enough that his warm breath mingles with my own—the spicy and sweet scent of bourbon, likely mine from the bar across the room, hitting my nose. "Why do you want to know it, Kat? So you can scream my name while I'm inside you?"

Despite my best efforts to remain unaffected by him, a shiver of need wracks my body and centers at that traitorous spot between my legs. But I *refuse* to submit to this man. Now or ever. "No. So I can tell my men and they can figure out a way to finally kill you."

His deep chuckle vibrates across the minuscule space between us. "I do love this game you seem to think we're playing, even if it has been one-sided. I was serious when I said we would form the most powerful partnership anyone can imagine. Far more powerful than either of us could ever be separately. We could bring Chicago to its knees."

"I plan on doing that on my own, thank you very much." It's been my plan from the beginning, since the moment I learned of Aleksander's death. I couldn't let what he built crumble under the control of the incompetent fucks who stole it from him. I refuse to let the Gashi family disappear into oblivion all because Michael envied what he couldn't have and decided to take it at any cost.

Rose's fingers finally slip up to find the aching, wet spot between my legs. There's no hiding my reaction to him now. He slides a fingertip through my arousal and up around my clit, making me jerk and dig my nails into his chest again.

Warm lips barely brush over mine. "Just think how great we could be together. Your icy-cool ruthlessness and my...uncanny ability to throw people off their game. If the other families thought Michael was dangerous and determined, they completely underestimated me."

I huff out a heavy breath full of my frustration. "The number of people who want you dead suggests otherwise."

All the families wanted him gone the moment he appeared. They all knew he was a threat, knew what he intended the moment he showed up here.

He offers me a snort of laughter and works his finger around my clit. "People have always wanted that, Kat. If they didn't want me dead, then I probably wouldn't be doing my job very well. Tell me you'll at least consider my offer."

I open my mouth to respond, but he steals my breath with a kiss before I can utter a single word. His lips move over mine, demanding control and taking what I'm not even sure I want to give him.

God...

I never really enjoyed kissing. It always seemed like something pointless that just delayed the main event. But with Rose...

That silver tongue of his that he wields so dangerously in business is just as capable of destroying my control. He pushes a finger inside of me and glides it in and out, in a torturously slow rhythm, one he knows will drive me absolutely insane. My legs shake, and I cling to his shirt to keep them from buckling. The weight of his body pressing into me forces me against the door even harder, almost like he can sense my weakness and need for some support.

Then just as quickly as he kissed me, he pulls back and withdraws his heated touch.

What the hell?

He brings his hand to his mouth and sucks his middle finger between his lips. A satisfied hum fills the room, and his eyes momentarily leave mine to dart down to where he just had his hand in my exposed pussy. He pulls his finger free and glides his tongue down and around it again, like he's trying to ensure every single last trace of my taste is gone. "You're just as fucking delicious as I anticipated."

A single step brings him back to me, but instead of touching me again, he reaches next to me and grasps the door handle. "We can be partners, or we can be enemies, Kat. Your decision."

He tugs at the door, and I stumble away from it enough for him to slip out without another word. It clicks to a close behind me, and I stagger to the couch and grab the back of it for support while jerking my dress back down into place.

What the hell just happened?

NINE

"I DON'T UNDERSTAND what I'm looking at." I shuffle through the stack of papers on my desk, scanning over the words on the pages. Copies of invoices, newspaper articles, and various other random slips of paper that don't seem to have any readily apparent meaning to me even after looking them over for several minutes.

Arden watches me anxiously from his chair on the other side of my desk. "That's everything I could find on Rose."

"What?" I glance down at the very small stack again. "How is that even possible? The man has to be in his early forties. How can there be absolutely nothing on him?"

Michael's cousin shrugs slightly and shifts forward in his chair to point at one of the pages on my desk. "You know Michael had me looking into him well before you ever asked."

I nod slowly. Michael had told me that if anyone could find Rose, it would be Arden. He had faith in his cousin's abilities...a faith I am certainly not sharing right now.

"Well, back when Michael was still in Albania, he knew Rose was becoming a player in Chicago and he wanted to know who his competitors were going to be if he succeeded in taking control here. I had a problem right from the beginning trying to locate anything substantial on Rose, and the more I tried to look into him, the more I suspected it was a lot bigger than just him being able to stay out of the spotlight."

"What do you mean?"

"I mean, I think he has someone...someone with really fucking good hacking abilities who's been able to remove any trace of him. The only reason I was even able to find this," he motions toward the papers, "is because of the shipment Valentina's men intercepted from him. I was able to trace that holding company back through several fronts, but I only made it past about seven layers before I hit another dead end."

"Jesus. What about our Rose look-alike and Rowan?"

He sits back in his chair and shakes his head. "I spoke to her friend at the club like you asked, and I tried to track Rowan's phone. She must not have it turned on. She hasn't responded to the text message Amber sent, and her phone location program I managed to hack into isn't working because the phone isn't turned on."

"Shit!" She really doesn't want to be found, which only makes me even more confident she knows something important.

"As for the mystery man...I've come up completely blank on him, too. I hacked into several neighborhood cameras around Kat's Cradle and caught him a couple places but then lost him behind a line of bushes and was never able to pick up his trail again."

"Goddammit." I slam my fist onto the desk, and my knee bounces, thankfully hidden underneath the massive piece of wood so Arden can't see how agitated this entire situation is making me.

Especially after what happened with Rose last night, I need to know everything about him...starting with who the fuck he is. And a man who looks that much like him showing up at my place of business isn't just a coincidence.

I shove the apparently useless papers back toward Arden. "You think someone has deliberately wiped information."

He shrugs again. "It's the only explanation that makes any sense to me. This man is the head of one of the most powerful cartels in Colombia, yet all I find in newspaper articles are references to the name 'Rose' or 'the Blood Rose Cartel,' no legal names even going back years. I have some feelers out in Columbia to try to locate some resources there. Perhaps try to track down someone who knew him before he went incognito."

"Fuck. Sounds like that may be the only way to get anything on him."

"Probably."

"Well, don't give up."

I motion toward the stack of papers. "Keep digging until you unearth every fucking thing he has buried. Follow any leads you can."

"I even tried to find him through his sister. Since we know she was injured in the explosion and that her first name is Sofia. But check this out...all the records at the hospital where all the victims were taken for whoever she is have disappeared from their database."

"You are fucking kidding me!"

He shakes his head. "Nope. I hacked in there and located the records for the date of the bombing, but it's like she was never there."

"How is that even possible? They must have physical records somewhere, printed copies."

"They might. But most hospitals are going digital now, and we wouldn't have any way to access the physical files."

"So, you think it's a hacker, someone who went in the same way you did."

"I think that's a reasonable explanation. Michael had me. Valentina has Preacher Davis. It only makes sense that someone as powerful as Rose would have someone good, too."

I sigh, squeeze my eyes closed, and rub at my temples against the headache starting to form there. "What about our other little game of cat and mouse? What have you been able to find on Konstandin and Rea?"

He tenses slightly in his chair and shifts. Michael always warned me that Arden was nervous and fidgety, but he seems even more agitated than the last time I spoke with him. Maybe it's because we're in the same room and he knows I have a gun sitting in my desk drawer that can be pointed right at him in a matter of seconds.

"I haven't been able to find them."

"So, they just poof...vanished into thin air again?"

Arden swallows thickly. "Basically...but it's not that unexpected."

"Why do you say that?"

"Do you know what Konstandin did before he came to the states?"

Michael had once told me in passing how hard it was to locate Konstandin initially, but I was never made privy to his full background. "I don't really know, just that Michael said he was hard to find."

"He was Albanian special forces. The man knows how to disappear, how to leave no trace. He's literally a ghost and probably will remain one as long as he wants to be."

"Then how the hell did Michael find him in the first place to send him after Lorenc and Rea, to send Aleksander on the collision course with them?"

Arden shifts uncomfortably and averts his eyes from mine again. "That was my doing."

"You found him then, now find them again." We already had this conversation, and I thought I'd made clear how important this was.

"It's not that simple. Konstandin knows how to not leave tracks—even with Rea in tow now."

Which had been my one hope that he might slip up. "Then how did you find him?"

He sighs and rubs the back of his neck. "Michael heard about Saban's death almost immediately. He had been biding his time in Albania, trying to find a way to rebuild their family empire. But the Dragushas and Berishas were making that impossible."

Just like they had to make things difficult for me here.

Arden leans back in his chair, crossing his arms over his chest. "When he learned of Saban's death and what happened with Tarek and Konstandin, he knew there would be an opening...in Philly and possibly Chicago. So, he had me track everything relating to the situation. After the shootout at the airport, the showdown between Tarek and Konstandin, the official word was Konstandin was dead. That he had died from his gunshot wounds. But I knew what to look for. I hacked the US Marshall's database, and sure enough, only a few days after the airport incident, someone new was listed in the witness protection program. Male in his late thirties, dark hair, blank eyes, with visible identifying tattoos that needed to be removed."

"Well, shit...that sure sounds like Konstandin."

"It did to me, too. Especially when this person disappeared as quickly as he appeared. He escaped from their custody. Went AWOL."

"But you tracked him somehow."

"I did, but I doubt I will again. Konstandin doesn't make mistakes. Ever. But there are some things in his nature he can't control."

"What do you mean?"

"Much like your late husband, Konstandin has a certain calling card, a way that he likes to toy with people before he kills them."

A shudder rolls through my body at the memory of Aleksander coming to his place that first night covered in Terrance's blood. It should have made me run. His warning should have been the final nail in the coffin, but instead, his sheer brutality, his drive to ensure the man paid for what he did to me, only drew me closer to him.

"Konstandin likes to torture his victims." Arden's voice cracks, his fear starting to get the best of him. "He never kills anyone quickly or easily. So, as soon as I saw that he escaped custody, I kept my eyes open and set up alerts for certain words appearing in the newspaper or on newscasts. Words like torture and mutilation."

"But how could you know for sure it was him?"

He shrugs slightly. "I guess I wasn't one hundred percent sure, but I knew he would have to find somewhere to blend in, somewhere he could use his skills as a means to make a living without attracting too much attention. I started seeing news reports out of Canada about several murders that involved some...excessive things being done to the bodies. There were rumors the murders had to do with the motorcycle gangs. I connected the dots, and the Rebel Chasers had a club in each city. I started doing some digging and found out there was a nomad named Ghost who had fairly recently joined them and had quite the reputation."

"Shit."

"That's how I found Konstandin."

"Do you think he'd go back there?"

Arden shakes his head. "Definitely not. He's too smart for that."

I drum my nails on the table and chew on my lip as I contemplate how to best approach this. "He might not go back there. But someone may know something they don't even realize they know. Konstandin might not make mistakes, he may think he knows how to disappear again, but I've always enjoyed ghost hunting."

TEN

The plane sits on the tarmac, waiting for me to board so we can take off and head to Winnipeg—the location of the Rebel Chasers MC's clubhouse where Arden initially located Konstandin.

We can't get into the air fast enough for me. I want this over, and this is the first step to closing the lid on the final coffin of revenge. It started with Michael, but it will end with the man who actually pulled the trigger.

Genti pulls the SUV up next to the lowered staircase and gets out to open my door for me. He leads me up the stairs toward where Bernardo waits with a tight smile.

"Good morning, Ms. Gashi." My usual attendant for my flights nods and inclines his head toward me, but something akin to uncertainty flickers in his gaze. The man never looks nervous, and unease slows my progress up the final step.

I finally make it inside the plane and freeze. A familiar set of onyx eyes stare back at me from my usual seat. Genti steps on board and immediately reaches for his gun, but I hold out a hand to stop him and slowly approach Rose. "What the hell are you doing here? How did you even know where I'd be?"

Rose raises his hands slowly and shrugs. "Did you think I would let you run away so easily, Kat?"

"Run away? What the hell are you talking about?"

He pushes to his feet and approaches me slowly. Genti shifts closer to me on my right, puffing out his already imposing chest against any threat Rose might pose.

Rose stops a foot in front of me and offers me a knowing grin. "Imagine my surprise when I learned you had booked an international flight only a day after I left your place. That sure seems like you're running to me."

I scowl at him and glance over his shoulder at his two men standing at the back of the plane. There isn't any way Genti and I are getting Rose or them out of here unless they *want* to leave. Which means I need to convince him to go of his own accord. "I'm leaving town on business."

One of his dark eyebrows rises. "What sort of business do you have in Winnipeg?"

"The *personal* kind."

The tiniest of grins pulls at his lips. "I see you lied."

"About what?"

"About who controls you, Kat. You're going to see a man."

A whole group of them, but it's none of his fucking business. "Get off my plane, Rose."

He turns and lowers himself slowly back into the seat he just vacated. "I think I'll tag along."

"Tag along?" Anger heats my blood, and I clench my fists at my sides. "Are you fucking insane? What in the world makes you think I would let you come with me?"

His dark eyes harden, and he narrows them on me. "What makes you think you have a choice?"

Bernardo seals the cabin door behind us and turns to share a look with Genti. He doesn't know what to do, either. I already halted Genti from shooting Rose and his men, mostly because I don't want a bloodbath like that on my plane. But now, we're left in a dubious situation—where I have something very personal to take care of, and if Rose insists on coming, he could greatly interfere with the proceedings.

"You're seriously going to hijack my plane before we've even taken off?"

Rose grins at me and pats the plush leather seat next to him. "Come, sit down, Kat. Now we have some private time to chat." He motions for Genti to head backward in the plane. "Why don't you go hang out in the back with my men? We'll be just fine up here."

Genti raises an eyebrow at me in question.

What are the options?

There really aren't many. Rose isn't going anywhere except apparently to Winnipeg with me. I tilt my head toward the back, giving Genti permission to go, and he glances down toward my purse. I give a slight nod to confirm that I have my weapon there if I need it. Genti trudges past where Rose sits toward the other two men, leaving me to deal with Rose on my own.

I slowly lower myself into the seat next to Rose and turn slightly to face him. "You're a real piece of work, you know that? "

He grins at me. "I do. Now, why don't you explain to me what prompted this little trip."

"I told you." I turn away from him and look out the window at the tarmac. "Personal business."

Bernardo approaches with an apologetic smile. "Can I get either of you something to drink before we take off?"

If I'm going to have to sit next to Rose this entire flight, I'm definitely going to need some alcohol. "Glenlivet Nadurra. Neat."

Rose offers Bernardo a charming grin. "Same."

Bernardo scampers off to get our drinks, and I focus my attention on our slow taxi toward the runway. Anything to avoid starting up an awkward conversation with Rose. The man is relentless, and it's only a matter of time before he discovers I'm the one who set the bomb. The bomb that almost killed him and his sister. The very one he had planned to retaliate against Michael for. Every minute I spend with him is one where he might uncover the truth.

Our drinks appear, and I accept mine from Bernardo and immediately take a big, warming sip.

The overhead speakers crackle to life, and one of the pilots comes on. "We've been cleared for takeoff. Buckle up."

I reach for my seatbelt, but Rose's hand finds it first. He pulls it across my waist, his fingers lingering a little too long there before he buckles it and shifts away, no doubt to stir my memories of two nights ago. And unfortunately, it fucking works. Heat floods between my legs, and I shift away from him and stare out the window as we make our way down the runway.

Rose takes a sip of his drink and swirls the liquid in the crystal glass. "It doesn't have to be like this, Kat. You're clearly distressed by whatever you're about to do. Why don't you try letting me in on what's really happening? If it's another man, you might as well tell me now rather than have me find out when we land and he embraces you."

The plane picks up speed, and we launch into the air. The force pushes me back in the seat and gives me a moment to consider how to approach telling Rose what's happening. As much as I may want to, I can't remain silent for a six-hour flight. I need to tell him something to appease his inquiry.

"I'm going to talk to some people to try to get some information on someone I'm looking for."

Rose raises a quizzical brow. "Who are you looking for?"

Revealing the truth to Rose means opening up old wounds—ones I don't want anyone, especially him, to see. But if his hacker is as good as Arden seems to think, maybe he can be of some use to me if I don't find what I'm looking for in Winnipeg. "Konstandin Morina."

Rose raises an eyebrow again. "You think you're going to find him in Winnipeg? From what I've heard, he and Rea aren't exactly living out in the open. No one has seen or heard from them since Aleksander's death."

I nod slowly. "Michael was looking for them, and now, so am I."

"And you really think that you'll find them there?"

"No." I'm not that stupid. "But it's where Konstandin was before he met up with Lorenc and Rea and ultimately Aleksander. So, there's a chance they'll know where he is or how to find him."

He takes a sip of his drink. "I see. It seems like a bit of a longshot, does it not? That anyone he was friends with would assist you now?"

"I have to try."

A sigh slips from his lips, and his gaze softens. "I can understand why you want—"

"No. You can't." My ability to hold back my tirade snaps. "No one can possibly understand how badly I need to find them. How much I need this. What it feels like to lose the other half of you. No one ever had what I had with Aleksander, so no one, least of all *you* could possibly understand."

Men like Rose don't know what love is. They know control. They know possession. They don't know giving yourself completely to someone. They don't know the soul-wrenching pain of losing them.

Though, maybe if I tell him. Maybe if he comprehends that no one can ever be to me what Aleksander was, just maybe, he'll back off—from pushing for a partnership, personally and professionally. And if that doesn't work, I'll tell him I set the bomb—that will either send him running, or he'll try to kill me. Either way, it would be an end to trying to run from his pursuit.

I suck in a deep, fortifying breath and take another sip of my scotch. "This isn't a story I like telling. And I won't ever discuss it again. But you need to hear it."

ELEVEN

ROSE'S GAZE SOFTENS, and if I didn't know what I already do about him, I might almost think there's sympathy there. I focus my gaze on the amber liquid in the glass clasped tightly between my hands instead of having to see what he really thinks of what I'm about to say.

Memories of better days flit through my head, but it's only a matter of time before they're going to twist and turn darker. "I grew up in Milwaukee. My father worked at a local foundry. He didn't make great money, but we didn't starve. Things were okay. Until I turned sixteen. My mother had a stroke. She couldn't take care of herself or even speak. And we didn't have the kind of money necessary to put her in a facility that could care for her."

My chest tightens at the memories—finding her on the floor, watching her struggle to move, her eyes trying to speak the words her lips no longer could.

The burn of tears pricks at my eyes, but I refuse to let them fall in front of Rose. I squeeze my lids closed and take a deep breath. "I went to school then worked at a local diner until the evenings when I would go home and take care of her while my father worked third shift. We managed, but just barely, and it was exhausting." Physically and emotionally. "Then, I met Terrance. He was a regular at the diner. Older. In his early twenties. And charming. In that rugged, dangerous way that always draws women to bad men."

I force myself to keep looking out the window because one of those men is sitting right next to me. But even with my eyes locked on the blue sky out there, the heat of Rose's gaze burns across my skin.

Terrance is a nightmare I wish I never had to experience, and discussing this, especially with Rose, seems wrong somehow. However, I know I need to tell him so he'll understand what I had with Aleksander. "He was a member of a motorcycle club. One with quite the reputation. But when I was around him, I felt safe. Like nothing could touch me. He made sure I always had money, which helped relieve some of the stress at home. And I was able to cut back on my hours a little bit. He even charmed my father. Dad thought I was with a man who could help take care of me. And, for a while, he did."

That time was the calm before the storm. I was so young. So damn naïve.

"I graduated and had plans to go to nursing school. Then, shortly after I turned eighteen, my father had a massive heart attack and died."

A warm hand wraps around mine and squeezes gently. Rose shifts closer to me, the heat of his body radiating toward mine. "I'm so sorry."

I jerk my hand out from under his. Having him touch me won't make this any easier. It only makes it harder—harder to breathe. Harder to ignore the pull toward him. "Terrance insisted he move in with us. He said it was to help take care of my mother. But he became incredibly controlling, didn't even want me going to school or talking to other students. Then," I take a deep breath, "it became physical."

The only other person I've ever told this to was Aleksander. I had hoped to never speak the words again. Rose reaches for my hand again, but I pull it away, out of his easy reach and avoid making eye contact with him.

"Anyway..." I blow out all the air from my lungs, "I knew I had to get away. My mother was born in Albania and still had some cousins and friends who had settled in Chicago. I decided we could go there. I called my cousin and made arrangements. Terrance was often going to parties at the club-house. I waited 'til he was gone one night, loaded Mother into the car, and left with nothing but two small suitcases I could pack quickly."

We literally fled in the middle of the night, like in some cheesy movie on television. I'd become a cliché. Looking back now, I can't believe how stupid I was.

"We got to my cousin's place—a duplex we were going to have one side of—and I was told we would have to pay rent and do our share. If I was going to ask them to care for Mom when I was at work, I needed to bring in some serious money. My cousin suggested a club nearby."

"Aleksander's?"

I finally turn my head to meet Rose's questioning gaze. "Albanians take care of our own. It's a small, tight-knit community, and as soon as I walked in there, I knew what it was and who Alek-sander was. Everyone knew about the Dragon. I thought I would be safe there, with men like that around me. I was wrong..."

Sympathy, or maybe pity, flickers in Rose's dark gaze, and I have to look away. I never wanted to see that from anyone again. I became Kat so I'd never have to see it. So I could be a different person, one who never lived through this. And as soon as I finish telling him, I'll never have to discuss it again.

I down the rest of my drink to find the courage to continue with this portion of my nightmare. "I was only there a few weeks before Terrance found me. I was leaving out the back one night, and he was waiting in the parking lot. He almost beat me to death and tried to drag me into his truck." Even now, I can still feel his blows. The sting of my lip splitting. The mind-numbing pain each time a strike hit me. "Some of the girls came out. If they hadn't, he probably would've taken me. They scared him off, and then...Aleksander came..."

I twist my hands in my lap and stare out the window, remembering what it felt like when he pulled me off the cold concrete and into his arms that night.

"He saved me. Brought me to his place and got a doctor."

"He took advantage of you." Rose's accusation comes out on a low growl, his accent heavy and full of anger.

I whip my head around to glare at him. "What? God, no." I shake my head. "The opposite. He was gentle and respectful and warned me more than once to stay away from him." I chuckle darkly and release a mirthless laugh. "But I couldn't. I never really understood that phrase like a moth to a flame until I experienced it myself."

Something flashes in his eyes, maybe a hint of understanding. Something in his own past he's unlikely to ever reveal. Something I probably don't even want to know.

I sigh and drop my head back against the headrest. "Once we got together, it was all-in for both of us. I don't think either of us was prepared for how strongly we would feel for each other. We got married secretly almost immediately. Aleksander wanted to make sure I'd be taken care of if anything ever happened to him, wanted to ensure everything would be in both our names. It was almost prophetic...and when Michael told him where to find Lorenc and Rea, I begged him not to go. I begged him to let the whole thing go, to let them live their lives, to concentrate on our happi-ness instead of what they did to Saban, but he couldn't let go of his wrath. Even his love for me wasn't strong enough to overcome that. And it led him to his death."

"So, that's why you're going after Konstandin and Rea, now? To make them pay for what they did?"

I turn my head away and stare back out the window. "It needs to be resolved."

Rose contemplates me for a moment. The wheels churn behind his dark eyes, the deep intelli-gence there clear. "Why didn't you go after Michael sooner? Why the game? Why drag it out?"

I was waiting to see if he got here, for him to process the story and have it lead him to this ques-tion. The one that will make me expose what I did. But it may be for the best, a way to finally end whatever this thing is that vibrates between us. He was ready to kill Michael over the bombing, so he'll surely end whatever this obsession is with me.

"It wasn't by choice." I watch his eyes narrow slowly. "My first attempt to take him out when I arrived back in town was unsuccessful. I played his game and led him to the slaughter...only...I failed that time."

His body goes rigid in his seat, and anything soft that had been present in his gaze, even for a fleeting second, disappears. "The bombing...it was you?"

Now, the fireworks begin.

TWELVE

I'M NOT sure what's worse: seeing a train wreck coming and not being able to stop it or not seeing it and being struck without warning.

Right now, sitting next to Rose in the back seat of this SUV with Genti behind the wheel and Rose's men stuffed in the far back behind us, the silence might as well be the sound of the train barreling down the track right at me.

I expected him to explode. I anticipated he would lose his temper in an epic fashion, to come undone, to take it out on me—all the anger he had pent up inside of him about the bombing. I expected him to unleash what he kept threatening to rain down on Michael upon me...

But all he did on the plane was turn his head away from mine, settle back into his seat, and sip his drink in silence the rest of the flight. The *entire* rest of the flight. The man hasn't said a single fucking word since I confirmed I was the one who set the bomb.

I don't like waiting for the inevitable. Not with a man like Rose, who has already proven to be so volatile and has had no problem spilling blood all over the city of Chicago to stake his claim.

It makes for a very tense drive.

We make our way through Winnipeg's streets on a direct course toward the Rebel Chasers' club-house. I haven't really planned this out well, haven't really thought about what I would say to them to get them to give me information on one of their own. I had intended to do that on the plane ride, but Rose's inserting himself into the trip sidetracked my ability to do that.

I probably should plan now, but the man sitting next to me continues to make it difficult to think about anything else but him and what he may do to me.

Finally, he twists his head toward me, and hard eyes meet mine for the first time since he turned away from me on the flight. "Are you going to kill Konstandin and Rea when you find them?"

"What?" I shake my head slightly, my mouth agape. That can't be all he has to say to me after what I revealed. "Are *you* going to kill me now that you know I was behind the bomb?"

The tiniest tic at the corner of his mouth reveals his fight to withhold a grin. Rose enjoys playing with people the same way Konstandin and Aleksander did, only I don't think Rose does it with a knife or torture devices. This man does it psychologically. He uses his handsome face and smooth charm to get into the heads of the people he wants to fuck with and lets them tear themselves apart, wondering what he's thinking and what he's going to do to them. It may not be as direct an approach as that taken by Konstandin and Aleksander, but damn, is it effective.

He allows himself a tiny smirk. "Something like that."

Something like that? What the hell does that even mean?

Genti glances at me from the driver's seat, checking to make sure I don't need him, but even with my gun in my purse and his good aim, we wouldn't stand a chance against Rose and his two men sitting behind me.

Rose releases a deep sigh. "Believe it or not, Kat, I understand your anger toward Michael, toward Konstandin and Rea. I sympathize with your desire for revenge. It can heat your blood to the point that you feel like your skin might melt right off. I felt the same way when that bomb almost killed my sister."

I tense in my seat. This is what I was waiting for. The explosion. The reaction from a man who definitely has some *strong* feelings about my role in the entire situation.

"Don't look so scared, Kat. Weakness doesn't suit you." He shifts in his seat, turning slightly toward me. "This might surprise you, but I actually respect what you did more than you could possibly know."

"You do?" Those are certainly not the words I expected to come out of that perfectly sinful mouth of his.

He regards me with a look I can't quite place, almost like he's trying to size me up, but we both know he did that a *long* time ago. "I knew you were ambitious the first moment I met you at Kat's Cradle. When you led me through the house, your zeal for your business and your desire to make it a premier place struck a chord with me. I knew you were the type of person who could recognize what needed to be done to succeed. It never crossed my mind at that time that you might want more, though, that you might want the same thing I want."

Rose is so damn smug. So sure he knows all. "What is it that you think I want."

All humor drains from his face, and he leans closer to me. "*Everything*."

A shiver rolls through me—and not just from his proximity.

His warm breath flutters over my cheek. "The power. The whole damn city. What the Dragon had...the ability to make people tremble at the mention of your name."

"I'd have to know your name to tremble at it."

He smirks and leans even closer. "I'll tell you my name when you finally admit what's happening between us."

"Nothing is happening between us. You're only here right now because you '*invited*' yourself onto my plane and along on my trip."

He smirks. "That may be, Kat, but since I *am* here, I will help you in any way I can to find the information you need."

"Why would you do that, especially after what you just learned? What's in it for you? Why help me?"

His lips brush my ear, sending another shudder rolling down my spine. "For the same reason I waited at your place the other night. For the same reason my cock still gets hard when I think about the taste of you on my tongue. I want you, Kat, and if you let me have you, I promise you won't regret it."

I will regret it.

There's no doubt about that. What Rose is asking for—no *demanding*—is something I can't give anyone, not even him. It's something that went with Aleksander and is buried six feet under in a cemetery in Albania.

I swallow thickly, trying to keep how he affects me out of my voice. "I've already told you, Rose, I don't belong to anyone."

He issues a low, deep chuckle that resonates in his chest. "You can keep saying that, Kat. You can keep trying to deny it. You can let this tension between us build until it tears you apart. But eventually, you won't be able to fight it anymore, and I'll be waiting when the time comes."

Smug bastard.

"What if that time never comes? Will you kill me then because of what I did?"

He retreats to his side of the backseat, a loss my body immediately feels, and rests his elbow against the door. "I'd be lying if I said I wasn't furious about the bombing. About the very serious damage that was done to my sister. But in all fairness, you had no way of knowing she would be there." He pauses and narrows his eyes on me. "Though I doubt it would've stopped you if you *had* known."

I'd love to tell him it would have mattered to know a complete innocent was there, but it wouldn't have stopped me, and we *both* know that. I knew I would only have one chance to take everyone out like that—the man who stole Aleksander from me as well as all my competition if I wanted to regain what Michael took and then some. It was the perfect setup...yet, I failed.

I clench my jaw and try to push back the anger that still heats my blood every time I think about it. "It wouldn't have mattered."

"If you had said it did, you wouldn't be the person I think you are."

It almost sounds like a compliment, but I sigh. "I still can't believe I failed. All because I entrusted the placement of the bomb to someone else. It's something I should've done myself."

His dark eyebrows arch up over his wide eyes. "Are you an expert in placing bombs?"

I snort and shake my head. "No, but I do know my World War II history—and Operation Valkyrie teaches an important lesson. I would have known not to place it under a heavy, thick wooden table. It absorbed the majority of the blast."

"You're right. It's probably what saved my sister's life, as well as mine. I'm impressed, Kat. I know I've used that word a lot around you, but it's the one that keeps coming to mind every time."

Impressed.

I don't want Rose to be impressed with me. I want him to leave me alone. But apparently, even trying to kill him and almost killing his sister isn't enough to accomplish that.

We finally pull up outside a low brick building with a row of Harleys parked out front. This is the place.

Rose leans forward and glances out the windshield at the building. "You have a plan of attack?"

"Not in so many words. But one thing I've learned is that a beautiful woman often gets further than a man who comes in spouting threats."

He grins. "I can agree with that."

"So, please remain in the car with your men so I can get what I need."

He narrows his eyes on me and appears like he wants to argue, but Genti opens his door and makes his way around to open mine. Without further argument, I climb from the SUV and let Genti close the door behind me.

Genti glances at me. "Are you ready for this?"

"I've been ready for this since the day Aleksander died."

THIRTEEN

I'M NOT EXACTLY sure what the protocol is for entering an MC clubhouse. When I make it to the door with Genti, there isn't any indication of what to do—no doorbell or sign asking you to knock.

Nothing.

Probably because they don't want anyone coming in at all.

Too fucking bad for them.

Genti shrugs and grabs the door handle to pull it open for us. He enters before me, blocking my view of the room until I step in and he moves to the side.

All the talking and laughing immediately cease. The whole place goes silent as the hard eyes of at least a dozen men rake over me and then narrow on Genti with distrust and hatred.

"Who the fuck are you?" A big man with an unruly black beard and wearing a cut that bears a "President" patch and the name "Butcher" right below it addresses the question to Genti, but I step forward and nod toward him.

"My name is Kat—Kat Gashi." I wait for any flicker of recognition at the last name, but Butcher simply raises a dark eyebrow at me and sneers.

"Is that supposed to fucking mean something to me?"

"Whoa, whoa, whoa..." A thin blond man pushes from his seat, stalks forward, and places a hand against the chest of the big man. "You might not want to talk to her like that, Prez."

Butcher turns and glares at the other man. "Why the fuck would I care?"

The blond man leans in and whispers something in the big man's ear, and his dark eyes widen and then sweep over me again.

"Fuck." He mumbles the word under his breath, but it's loud enough I can hear it. Then, he takes a step forward and raises his hands slowly. "My apologies, Ms. Gashi. I didn't know. But the question still stands...what the hell are you doing here? You're a long way from Chicago."

I offer a smile to the blond man who retreats back to his chair.

Since the big man with the beard appears to be the president, that means if I want to get anything done, I'm going to need him to cooperate. I examine the room, scanning for familiar faces, but I know Konstandin won't be here. Arden is right—that man is too smart to come back.

"I'm looking for someone, and I had hoped the Rebel Chasers Motorcycle Club could be of assistance."

Butcher raises a dark eyebrow. "What makes you think we would get ourselves involved in your business?"

"Because you already are." I survey each man in the room, making sure they're all paying attention before I continue. "A man who called himself Ghost was a member of your club."

Several men shift uneasily, and Genti's hand moves closer to his hip.

I offer the men a cool smile. "This can go one of two ways. Either you can tell me the information I need to locate him, or you can play dumb and pretend you don't know who I'm talking about. I suggest the former. For everyone's sake."

Butcher scans his crew before turning back to me. "Yeah, we know a guy who went by Ghost, but he's long gone. Haven't heard from him in over a year, maybe longer."

For some reason, I believe the guy. He doesn't seem the type to lie when that doesn't benefit him. Assisting me can open doors for them in the long run, so he'd be stupid not to help.

"Perhaps you haven't heard from him, but maybe one of the other members has? Or maybe he said something while he was here that would assist me in locating him. A hideaway? Someplace he always talked about that he wanted to go? Something mentioned in passing, even?"

Low rumbles filter through the men, but no one steps forward.

"I understand your desire to protect your own. Admirable, really, but your Ghost is the man who killed my husband, and I won't let anything stop me from locating him, even if I have to go through all of you."

It's not the best odds—over a dozen of them and only two of us. But I'm banking on their wanting to cooperate more than they want a firefight in their clubhouse.

A man steps forward, running his hand along the scruff on his chin. The patch on his cut indicates he's the VP and his name is Mack. "Ghost was a friend of mine. And while I haven't heard from him since he got that call and took off like a bat out of hell, he did mention a sister."

Shit. Of course.

The story Michael told me about his grandfather's downfall comes rushing back. It had been a Morina girl—the one they used to get in on his grandfather's operation. It had to have been Tarek and Konstandin's sister. I don't know why I didn't think of it. Although, it wouldn't surprise me if Arden is already trying to locate her.

"Did he tell you his sister's name?"

The man shakes his head. "No. Just that he hadn't seen her in a long time and always hoped that one day he might again. Sounded like he thought circumstances would never allow that, though."

Konstandin was probably right. If he would ever go to his sister, I wouldn't be the only one hearing about it. I have no doubt that the Dragushas and Berishas are keeping track of everyone over here. Not just me because of our new agreement. They may be content to remain in power in Albania and let us have the US, but the last thing they want is one of the families building power here and then coming back to try to take over.

So, while this man's information is interesting, it's unlikely to be helpful in any real way.

"Does anyone else have any information to offer?"

All the club members glance around nervously, and Genti shifts next to me, his arm brushing mine deliberately. I glance up at him, and he inclines his head toward a door at the back of the building, barely visible down a hallway behind several of the men standing. Just as my eyes land on it, it swings closed.

Someone slipped out. Maybe many someones.

Unease crackles through my nerves, tightening my ribs around my chest. Maybe they aren't as eager to cooperate as I hoped. Someone slipping out means someone's waiting for us on the outside with who knows what purpose. The only way home may be shooting our way out of here.

I step forward and offer my hand to the President. He looks down at it for a moment, then reaches out and grasps it with his much larger one.

The forced smile on my face is unlikely to be convincing, but I try anyway. "I appreciate your assistance in this matter. If you do hear from him, I expect to receive a phone call. I'm sure you know how to get in touch with me."

He nods slowly, his eyes darting to Genti. "I'm sure I do."

I release his hand, and Genti and I retreat toward the door, never giving these men our backs. If we do, we'll end up pumped through with more holes than I could even count. As it stands, we're likely walking into an ambush on the other side of this door. I inch my hand into my purse and wrap it around the grip of my gun as Genti slides his hand to his waist for his.

It looks as though we're about to have a bloodbath.

FOURTEEN

GENTI REACHES BACK with his free hand, twists the doorknob, and opens it. Almost immediately, the bullets start flying—from outside and in. Only the ones outside aren't coming toward us.

Rose's men crouch beside the open back door of the SUV, shooting at two men at the side of the building. One motions us toward the vehicle, giving us cover while the group from inside the clubhouse hammers holes in the door we just stepped through.

We dive into the SUV, both of us firing, and Rose's men follow us in, scrambling into the back seats as Rose leaps into the driver's seat—he must have been on the other side of the vehicle—and peels out of the parking lot at top speed. Bullets strike the SUV, the ping sounding almost deafening to my ears despite the ringing in them from the gunshots.

I sag back into my seat, huffing and trying to catch my breath.

Genti leans forward and examines me. "Were you hit?"

I shake my head. "No. You?"

He shakes his head and issues a low sigh of relief.

Rose glances at us in the rearview mirror. "I'm fine, too, for the record."

Asshole.

He returns his focus to the road. "I saw the two come around the side of the building and knew what was coming. I climbed out the left side of the vehicle and had the guys get out on the right so we had good cover for you."

I've never been so happy I ordered Rose to stay in the car. If he and his men had come with us, we would've been completely surrounded with no means of escape.

Rose takes a hard left, the tires squealing. "You can thank me for saving your life, *gatita*."

I scowl at him, but that only earns me a grin from him in the rearview. "Don't call me that."

The last thing I want this man calling me is *kitty*. Terms of endearment like that lead to other terms...ones that express some sort of attachment—like love. He doesn't love me. He wants me. He wants what combining our businesses and power can bring to him.

"Did you find what you needed?"

I shake my head. "I don't know. I'm still not completely sure if what they gave me is going to be of any help."

Common sense would suggest that Arden wouldn't overlook something like a sister and would have already gone down that road, but at the same time, I know from personal experience that family can be a major weakness. It certainly was for me. If Mom hadn't been so sick, if Dad hadn't died, my life would have gone in a much different direction.

Though I can't regret anything because it led me to Aleksander. He can't ever be replaced. What we *had* can't be replicated, and I wouldn't even want to try. Something Rose doesn't seem capable of comprehending.

Rose merges on the highway and heads toward the airport. Next to me, Genti swipes open his phone and calls the pilots to have them get the plane ready.

He hangs up the phone and turns to me. "They can have the plane ready in an hour. There was some sort of maintenance issue that's been taken care of."

"Maintenance issue? Jesus, that's all we need right now—a delay." I slam my fist against the door.

"Hopefully, the MC isn't stupid enough to come after us. Because the first place they'll probably check is the airport. And we'll be sitting ducks."

Rose glances at me in the rearview. "Should I drive around until then?"

"It might not be a bad idea."

He nods. "A moving target is a much harder one."

Which is why sitting still always makes me nervous. And Rose's comment also sparks something in the back of my mind.

"They're probably moving around."

Genti raises an eyebrow. "Who are?"

"Konstandin and Rea. They're probably not staying in one place for very long. Because Rose is right, a moving target is a much harder one."

"That's going to make finding them almost impossible."

I glare at Genti. "Thanks for stating the obvious."

He holds up his hands and shakes his head. "Sorry, Kat."

I wave him off. "It's not your fault we can't find them."

As much as I'd love to blame him, to have anybody to blame it on, I really can't. Just like Arden being unable to locate anything on Rose isn't really his fault, either. The man is clearly far more clever and devious than I ever imagined. The fact that Michael and his men could never nail down where he operates from in Chicago suggests he's taking his own advice and remains a moving target. He might not even *have* a headquarters. It certainly would explain a lot.

But not why he insists on pursuing me despite my efforts to dissuade him in every way short of shooting him—which isn't totally out of the question at this point. He may have just saved our lives, but it wasn't completely altruistic. If he had tried to leave us before the bullets started flying and I had managed to survive, he would have faced my wrath. And now, he's earned himself some good-will, and it wouldn't surprise me if he asks for a favor he now feels he's owed.

We lapse into an awkward silence. Rose's men haven't said a word behind us, and Genti—who swore to protect Michael, and is now my right-hand man—sends off texts beside me and watches the road while Rose casts furtive glances at me every so often in the rearview mirror but keeps his mouth shut.

The tension between us has reached a breaking point. Some sort of move is going to have to be made...some sort of decision. I'm not getting involved with Rose, but pushing him away doesn't seem to be working, either. The man now knows I'm responsible for the explosion that almost killed his sister, and he seems almost proud. For Michael, confirmation he was behind the bombing would have meant a death sentence. That makes things even more complicated.

Rose might be playing the same deadly game I did with Michael, putting off his end game until he gets whatever it is he wants from me. It's so much different being on this side of things. Not being the one in control.

I fucking hate it.

And not being able to locate Konstandin and Rea leaves that situation open-ended. Not being able to have a resolution, some sort of peace, will only make everything else I'm trying to accomplish more difficult.

The longer we aimlessly drive around town, the more tense I become, my shoulders tightening to the point that pain shoots up my neck and into the base of my skull. Rose finally turns us into the airport after almost forty-five minutes, and my plane sits, waiting on the tarmac near the executive terminal.

We pull up outside the terminal, and I turn to Genti. "Just leave the SUV here. We can repay the rental company whatever they need for any damage that may have been caused by the storm of bullets. Right now, I just want to get out of here fast."

Genti nods his understanding, and we all pile out of the vehicle and rush through the executive terminal and customs there. All eyes scan around us for any threats, but either the MC decided not to pursue us, or they're too stupid to know where to come.

Bernardo stands at the bottom of the plane's stairs, and he ushers us up. As soon as we're in our seats and buckled in, the pilots start taxiing down the runway.

I rest back in my chair and let out a long, deep breath.

Rose's hand settles on top of mine, and he squeezes. "We'll find him. If it's this important to you, I'll make sure of it."

My first inclination is to jerk my hand away, to brush off the contact and sentiment behind it. But after just being shot at, a warm, comforting grip doesn't feel as bad as I thought it would. So, I let it sit there, but I don't return the gentle squeeze Rose gives it. Instead, I stare out the window as we take off and settle back in my chair to wait for Bernardo to bring me a drink.

God knows I'll need a couple of them.

We fly in silence for a while until we reach cruising altitude, nothing but darkness outside the window. Silence descends over the cabin and settles for what feels like hours.

Rose leans forward slightly until I focus on his dark eyes. "Don't look so worried. No one ever truly disappears. You, of all people, should know that."

Funny coming from a man who has managed to completely erase his own identity and past.

Perhaps he isn't so confident in his ability to maintain his anonymity for much longer. That might be a good sign for me.

I try to smile at him, but I know I fail by the downward turn to his lips. "I know. It's just that they've had a lot of time to hide. It's going to make finding them so much more difficult. Plus, there are other concerns."

Rose raises an eyebrow at me. "What other concerns?"

I purse my lips and pull my hand out from under his. "Like men who don't take no for an answer."

He smirks. "Am I really that terrible?"

That's a loaded and difficult question. And he knows it.

If we had met in another life, under different circumstances, things might be a lot different. But we are who and what we are. And that complicates things.

I open my mouth to answer that question, but the plane suddenly jerks and shakes violently. Even with my seatbelt on, I'm practically thrown out of my chair. "What the fuck?

Rose reaches to undo his seatbelt, but I drop my hand over his. "Leave it on."

Almost immediately, one of the pilots comes on over the intercom. "We just lost both engines. I'm going to try to put her down."

Shit.

The plane jerks again, this time rocketing toward one side like it was hit by something.

Rose glances that way, his hands tightening on the armrests. "That was an explosion."

"An explosion? What the hell would cause that?"

"I don't know, but we're going down. *Fast.*"

EMBRACING LUST

Love begins with an image; lust with a sensation.

-**Mason Cooley**

ONE

KAT

The ground rushes up at us so fast that it's more like flying *into* the ground than falling. What starts out as tiny dots quickly becomes a vast forest of trees climbing skyward. And we're headed right into them.

We're going to die.

Our pilots can't seem to get control of our descent, and the howling of the wind battering the small plane reaches a deafening roar, a warning of the inevitable impact about to happen.

Rose clutches my hand in his and squeezes. This time, instead of pulling away from his touch, I squeeze back in a vice-like grip. Somehow, clinging to him like a lifeline seems like the right move in this situation despite all my reservations.

At least I'm not dying alone.

Though, this isn't the way I imagined it would end. I always figured it would be one of Aleksander's enemies or one of the new ones I created who would ultimately take me out in a hail of bullets. Not some stupid plane malfunction. Though, maybe it's my final judgment. A statement from the big man upstairs that he sees what I've been doing and it's time to pay for my sins.

It certainly would be warranted.

For both the man beside me and me.

I glance over at Rose. His dark eyes meet mine, and he opens his mouth to say something—

The impact comes so hard and so abruptly, it crushes the air from my lungs and sends a jolt of agony through my body so intense, it feels like I'm collapsing in on myself.

A cataclysm of sounds fill my ears—screeching metal, bangs, cries of anguish. And then...everything goes dark.

Darkness envelops me. So dark, it's not just black, it's a void of absolutely nothing— no light, no sound, no air. Just *nothing*.

It seems to go on forever, but then slowly, something returns. Faint at first, then it slams into me.

I groan and try to roll to my side, but pain shoots through every fiber of my being, and something restrains me, holding me back and keeping me prone. Clenching my teeth against the throbbing in my head and ache in my chest, I make another attempt to shift my body. A moan slips from between my lips.

"Kat?"

My name comes through the din, soft, almost caressing me like a warm touch. I try to inhale a breath, but thick, acrid smoke chokes me, and my cough violently rattles my already-damaged body. Something shifts over me, blocking whatever light was hitting my closed eyelids.

Who is it?

I force my eyes open to find twisted metal and flames. Everything distorts around me, like walking through the mirror room of the funhouse at the county fair. My head swims, blurring my vision, bile rising in my throat. I choke on it and turn my head to the side to retch, the motion only creating more stabbing discomfort.

What happened? Am I even on the plane anymore?

The last thing I remember was going down fast.

I try to focus on what's in front of me, and finally, a face comes into focus.

Michael...

He grins down at me, that same cocky tilt of the lips he always gave me before he shoved his dick inside me. The grin that says *I own you and your body and there's no denying it.*

"Michael? But...how..." I squeeze my eyes shut for a second and open them again, hoping the disturbing vision before me will be gone.

But the man who already haunts my waking hours and sleep still stands there. His strong hand wraps around my throat. The pressure of his palm pushing into my windpipe brings back memories of that first night in his condo—the night he tried to get me to come clean about my intentions. The night I gave myself over to him and truly started my plan.

He squeezes hard, his strong hand closing and tightening easily, and I choke and try to inhale, desperate to get any air into my lungs, even the smoke-tainted air around me. My fingers clawing at his do nothing. I try to scream his name, to beg him to stop even though he never did when I was ready to take his life, but all that comes out is a strangled groan that gets swallowed up by the sound of the carnage around me.

How did he get here?

Memories mix with nightmares. What's real and what's imagined meld together 'til they're inextricable—a tangled, sticky web of past sins and present consequences.

He's dead.

The feel of the gun in my hand as I held it to his head, pressed it into his temple, locked eyes with him, and fired isn't something I could ever forget. The sound of his brains splattering across the wall behind him, of his body hitting the floor when I pushed it out of the chair to take my seat, will ring in my ears forever...

No.

I shake my head and squeeze my eyes closed, struggling to take a breath against the force trying to wring it out of me.

It's not him. It can't be.

"Go back to Hell!" This time, I manage to find enough breath to get the words out, and his dark brow furrows as he leans in closer to me.

"Kat?"

I lash out and strike at him, my fist connecting with his jaw, and the hand around my throat loosens. "Get the hell away from me. You're dead. Stay that way."

Pain slices through my knuckles where I hit him, and a violent headache hammers at my skull. I squeeze my eyes shut, trying to fight the miserable torment wracking my body.

"Kat, look at me."

"No." I shake my head. "I can't. I won't. You're dead—"

"Look at me."

I swallow another smoky lungful of air and open my eyes. Only the ones staring back at me aren't Michael's.

Dark and almost black, this time, they're the eyes of the man who owns my heart.

Aleksander?

He presses a finger over my lips and leans down to gently kiss my forehead. "I have you, *zemra ime.* Come with me."

I struggle to suck in another breath and try to move toward him, but something holds me back.

"It's okay. I have you..."

A hot trail of tears trickles down my cheek. "Aleksander..." His name comes out more like a gasp, and I doubt he can even hear me.

A strong hand wraps around my wrist and tightens. "Kat..."

It isn't Aleksander's voice this time. I open my eyes, and Rose's familiar face appears before me, a cut over his right eye trailing blood down his temple.

Why am I being punished like this?

First, haunted by the two men who have changed the course of my life so completely. And now, faced with the man who can alter it one more time. In this position, I'm helpless to defend myself. I won't be able to stop him when he tries to take me out.

I try to shift away, but something keeps me prone. Rose reaches to his ankle and flips out a knife, then bends down toward me. Instinctively, I throw my hands up, though they don't offer much protection from the blade.

He's not going to take me out like this. Not without a fight on my part.

I try to lash out at him, but my arms feel heavy, my movements jerky and undirected.

He freezes for a moment, then easily brushes my hands out of the way. "I'm going to cut you out of your seatbelt."

Seatbelt? Shit.

I press a hand to my temple only to have it come back bloody. My eyes start to focus, and through the thick, choking haze of smoke, I can make out the mangled remains of the cabin and blue sky toward the front where the cockpit is...or was...

"The pilots?"

Rose cuts at my seatbelt and shakes his head. "Dead."

Mumbling from behind me and to my left draws my attention, and Rose glances over his shoulder in that direction, too.

"Looks like the men are okay." He finally manages to get my seatbelt released, and I tumble forward slightly with a wince, gritting my teeth.

Strong arms wrap around me and pull me up. The room spins, and I clench my eyes shut to suppress the urge to vomit. Another cough rattles my chest, the thick smoke attacking my lungs even more.

Rose coughs and clutches me tightly to his chest. "We need to get out of here...before that fire reaches the fuel tanks."

Shit.

At least someone is thinking clearly because I sure as hell am not. Everything in front of me blurs again. Darkness encroaches on the edges of my vision. I shake my head and try to fight it.

"Stay with me, Kat." Rose shakes me gently.

I groan and try to squeeze my arms around his neck to indicate I'm doing my best because I can't seem to form the words to tell him I'm okay. At least, I think I am.

"Kat..." He shakes me gently, and then, we're moving.

The motion sends my world tumbling. Metal creaks and glass shatters behind us as the fire ravages the remains of the plane.

I have you, zemra ime. Come with me.

Those words send soft warmth spreading through my chilled body, and I relax and give in to the pull of the void.

TWO

I JERK AWAKE, some distant buzzing noise rousing me.

A lawn mower?

I don't have time to analyze it further. A sharp pain stabs at my temple, and I groan and squeeze my eyes closed against it as I roll onto my back. The mattress under me creaks, that slight noise only increasing the agony banging against my skull. I settle and wait for the spinning sensation and torment to ebb, but they don't seem to want to abate.

Scents that shouldn't be here hit my nose.

Fresh-cut grass.

Lilacs.

Someone cooking...

This isn't right.

I shouldn't be waking up to any of those smells. I force open my lids and scan the unfamiliar room through blurry, wavering vision. "Where the hell am I?"

Rubbing at my eyes and trying to blink away the fuzziness doesn't help my ability to focus. It's like my entire body is bogged down in some sort of haze, and combined with the damn throbbing in my temple banging away like a bass drum, it's impossible to focus.

I push myself up on my elbows and try to take stock of the room. The large, comfortable bed I'm lying in, covered with a dark-gray duvet, sure as hell isn't mine, and the high ceilings with broad archways above the doors certainly don't look like anywhere I've ever been.

Fuck.

I struggle to claw back my memories.

We were on the plane...

Something happened...

We were going down...

Flashes of Michael's face, then Aleksander's flit through my head.

No.

I squeeze my eyes closed tightly and shake my head.

No.

It had to have been a dream or hallucination. Or maybe I was finally paying for my sins by having to face them. Then, another memory comes. A deep, accented, soothing voice...strong arms wrapping around me...moving.

Rose...

He must've gotten me out.

But where am I?

Almost as if in answer to my internal question, the door to the bedroom creaks open softly and the man who can give me the answer enters. His gaze lands on me, and his dark eyebrows wing up. "You're awake."

I pinch the bridge of my nose and shake my head, wincing at the movement. "Apparently. What happened? Where are we?"

He casually makes his way over to the bed and sits on the mattress next to me. In loose, dark linen pants and white dress shirt with sleeves rolled up to his elbows, he's the most casual I've ever seen him "The plane went down in the middle of nowhere in northern Minnesota. I managed to get you out before fire consumed the whole thing."

The view of the torn-open cockpit flashes before my eyes. "The pilots are dead?"

Rose offers a tiny nod. "The nose of the plane appeared to have taken the brunt of the landing. Genti and my men were fine. Minor injuries. But you smacked your head against something, the bulkhead perhaps, and were in and out of consciousness and not completely lucid for a long time."

That explains the splitting headache and blurry vision. "Where are we? How did we get here?"

He sighs and rubs at his jaw with one hand while propping himself up with the other. A small cut closed with a row of stitches over his right eye brings back the memory of the blood flowing from it. "I figured avoiding police involvement was probably pretty essential for both of us, especially after what happened in Winnipeg, so I called a contact in Minneapolis and had him send his helicopter and a doctor so you could be treated as soon as they arrived and we could get out of there before the authorities showed up."

"We're in Minneapolis?"

His lips curl slightly into a bemused grin, and he shakes his head. "No. I brought you home."

"Chicago?"

He nods.

"But this isn't my condo."

A low, deep chuckle rolls through him, shaking the mattress beneath us, and he leans toward me. "Very observant. This is my place."

I freeze and narrow my eyes on him. "*Your* place?"

This man has spent the last few years hiding his headquarters and where he lives. He has ensured he can disappear whenever he needs to in order to avoid being found. He's intentionally made it hard for anyone—Michael and myself included—to locate anything about him that might be useful in tracking him down.

But now, he's willing to bring me to his place?

That tiny grin returns to his mouth. "I wanted to keep an eye on you."

How the hell am I supposed to take that statement? "Keep an eye on you."

It could mean as his business rival because he doesn't trust me. Or it could mean because he has nefarious plans that he can't complete if I get in the way because I didn't die like I was supposed to in that crash. I don't even want to consider the third option...the one that suggests something even more dangerous.

Rose leans in even closer and brushes my hair back from my face. "I've never seen you with your hair down before, *muñeca*. I like it."

Despite my head telling me to pull away from his touch, my body seems to have other ideas. Even Rose calling me "doll" doesn't seem to give me the normal reaction a term of endearment like that would. Before I can stop myself, I lean into his palm held against my cheek, the warmth there spreading through my aching body.

"How are you feeling? Do you need any pain medication? I'm going to send for the doctor to check on you."

Before I can even answer his questions, he pushes to his feet, but I grab his wrist to stop him.

He glances over his shoulder, his dark eyes assessing me with concern. "What is it?"

"I..."

Shit.

This isn't easy for me to say to anyone, let alone the man who is not only my rival but also my pursuer. "Thank you."

A slow, lazy smile spreads across his lips. "You're welcome...but don't thank me yet."

He doesn't say it, but the gleam in his eye tells me there's something more he wants from me. Something that says he isn't going to let me walk away from here so easily. However, before I can argue with him, a wave of dizziness rolls through me, turning my stomach and making me release his arm and sag back into the bed.

One of his large hands falls over mine and squeezes. "You're going to have to stay here for a little while. With this concussion, you're likely to be disoriented and dizzy and have headaches for some time. You shouldn't be alone."

Rose rises and moves toward the door.

I *am* alone. More alone than I've felt in my entire life. And it isn't just that I lost Aleksander and so much else. It's that, for a brief, fleeting moment when I was toying with Michael, I let myself enjoy it. I let myself feel safe and content in the arms of the man I was waiting to destroy. And once I did it, it was like everything changed. Now another man who could destroy me just as badly is forcing me to remain when I'm at my most vulnerable.

"I need to go home, Rose. I can't stay here."

He turns when he reaches the door, any humor from his face gone in a split-second. "It wasn't an invitation, *muñeca*. You *will* stay."

Without another word, he opens the door, steps out, and closes it behind him. The sound of a key sliding into the lock and clicking it into place seems to vibrate through the room.

That motherfucker just locked me in here!

THREE

I PACE the length of the room for the hundredth time today alone, craning my neck from side to side to try to work out the pain and tension that has centered at the base of my skull and hasn't let go since I woke.

Rose wasn't kidding about the headaches, dizziness, and disorientation. I'm not even sure exactly how long I've been here. The doctor he sent in to see me that first morning assured me my injuries weren't serious or life-threatening, but he warned that the after-effects of both the whiplash and a concussion could linger for quite some time.

Just fucking perfect.

I need my wits about me to deal with this situation with Rose. Though, he's been suspiciously absent. Other than bringing me my meals for the last few days and stopping in to check on me occasionally, he's been MIA...which brings cold dread and suspicion to my stomach.

What the hell is he doing while I'm locked up in here? Where the hell is Genti? Rose said he survived the crash, so why isn't he trying to get me out of here? Does Rose have him locked up somewhere, too?

I've tried to ask him. Tried to find out what I could, but he always brushes off my questions with a charming smile and retreats from the room without giving any answers.

Every fiber of my being screams at me to get out of here, but pounding on the locked door does nothing but zap what little energy I do have. And it gets me nowhere other than exhausted with painful, bruised hands.

The longer this goes on, the more agitated I become, practically wearing a track in the expensive rug under my feet with my pacing. I glance at the clock on the nightstand. Rose should be coming with my lunch soon—like clockwork at noon every day.

I watch the clock turn from 11:58 to 11:59 and wait. Seconds tick by slowly, my options turning in my head the same way the hands move around the clock face.

There aren't many. I could try to fight him—hit him with the lamp on the nightstand or some other weapon. Perhaps wiggle loose the metal bar in the shower in my bathroom.

But what good would that do me?

He undoubtedly has a dozen or more guards wherever we are, and I'd likely be stopped before I got more than ten feet out that door. Just like when he ambushed me on the plane, he has the upper hand here. And I can't see a way to alter that.

I make another lap around the room and hear the key slide into the lock. Rose pushes open the door with one of his trademark smiles and a tray in his hands. "Hello, Kat. How are you feeling?"

"I'd be feeling a lot better if you let me out of here."

His smile doesn't falter as he sets down the tray on the small table next to the window that has offered me very little in terms of information about where we are. All I can see out of it during the day is a large, perfectly manicured lawn and garden, and at night, the glow of lights in the distance. Nothing to indicate our location except a massive, beautiful estate.

Rose motions to one of the chairs at the table, and I scowl at him but reluctantly take the seat. Not because I want to, but because I'm starting to feel dizzy again.

Once my ass hits the chair, the room stops spinning, and I suck in a deep breath. Rose takes his seat across from me and leans back casually, as if we're sitting down to a pleasant lunch instead of him sitting with his captive.

I steady my gaze on him. "Let me go."

He narrows his eyes on me, a hint of annoyance darkening them. "I can't do that."

"Why the hell not?"

"I'm keeping you here for your own safety."

My fists clench on top of the table. "I'm perfectly capable of keeping myself safe."

His lips twist into a sneer. "Someone just tried to kill us three days ago. The last thing I'm going to do is let you go back out there when you're in a weak and vulnerable state."

I open my mouth to issue a retort, but then, his words register. "What do you mean someone tried to kill us?"

He snorts. "Did you think it was just some random malfunction that caused the crash, *muñeca*?"

My brain tries to push through the fog of the constant headache to replay the events leading up to the crash, but everything jumbles into an incomprehensible web I can't untangle. "They said there was a maintenance issue." Honestly, I've been so bogged down in trying to recover and find a way out of here, I don't think I really even considered it. "I...I guess I thought maybe something broke that they thought they had fixed."

He shakes his head and *tsks*. "Very naïve of you, Kat. Or maybe your head injury is clouding your judgment. The plane went down because somebody wanted one or both of us gone. It was sabotage."

"How can you possibly know that already? There's no way the NTSB has completed their investigation." I don't know a lot about plane crashes and protocol, but I know that it would've ended up in the hands of the federal government despite Rose getting us out of there quickly.

"No, they haven't issued a formal report yet. But that doesn't mean I don't have sources who have provided me information from the moment they arrived on the scene. People who have run interference and helped keep us out of this altogether." He sighs and leans forward to rest his elbows on the table. "The plane was tampered with, Kat. In a way that would ensure we went down within hours of takeoff. Whoever it was clearly wanted us dead. The fact that we survived is likely pissing someone off greatly at the moment."

"Jesus." I drop my elbows onto the table and push my hands back through my hair. "If you hadn't been with me on the plane, I would think it was you."

Rose's chuckle fills my ears, and I lift my head to find him grinning at me. He inclines his head toward me. "I would've thought the same."

"But no one's trying to claim responsibility? No one has contacted you?"

Rose shakes his head. "I've been doing my best to find out any information that might help point a finger at whoever is responsible. But unfortunately, that is not such an easy task."

I stare at the food in front of me, now getting cold, but any appetite I might have had disappeared the moment Rose told me about the plane. "The list can't be very long. Whatever they did to the plane had to have happened while we were on the ground in Winnipeg."

He nods his agreement. "I didn't tell anyone I was coming with you, except for my sister. She is one hundred percent trustworthy."

I narrow my eyes on him. He seems so sure about that. "How can you be so confident? Even our own blood can betray us. Michael and Lorenc are proof of that."

He considers me for a moment, pressing his lips into a hard, thin line. It seems whatever I said struck a chord, though I don't know what or why. "It wasn't Sofia."

"Only Genti knew where I was going, and I trust him implicitly." There's no way he betrayed us, especially when he was on the plane himself.

"Well, it seems the information got out somehow. Perhaps finding out how will lead us to whoever was responsible."

I lower my face into my hands again and rub at the throbbing in my temples.

"Are you in pain?" The genuine concern in his voice with the question almost makes it possible to forget that he's keeping me here against my will.

"I'd feel a lot better if I were at home."

He pushes up from the table, rounds it to stand at my side, then leans down and presses a gentle kiss to my forehead. The fact that I don't instinctively shrink away from him makes my stomach churn.

"Trust me to know what is best in the situation, *muñeca*." His dark eyes plead with me while he uses his fingers against my chin to tip my head up.

"That's just it. I don't. Haven't we just proven that neither of us trusts the other?"

He runs a hand over my hair gently and retreats toward the door. "Trust can be overrated, Kat. It can leave you open to betrayal. I find it is often better not to put your faith in anyone. If you always have one eye open, no one can ever sneak up on you."

Rose opens the door and slips out, the key sliding into the lock and turning his final statement on the subject.

He asks me to trust him then immediately tells me not to trust anyone. I can't make heads or tails of this man or his intentions. The way my body reacts when he is near only complicates things further.

I need to get out of here. I need to find a way to get home so I can figure out who tried to kill us and why.

My suspicion would fall on the man I had been looking for; it would fall on Konstandin, but how could he have known where I would be, let alone be able to arrange what he did on short notice? My trip happened fast, planned only a day in advance. It seems to me there may be a rat in one of our organizations. And Rose's reaction to my accusation against Sofia raises an important question—*who doesn't he trust and why?*

FOUR

"*Hermano, detente. Nosotros necesitamos hablar!*" The woman's muffled voice in the hall saying, "Brother, stop. We need to talk," is faint, but standing this close to the door, it's enough to make me stop in my tracks.

My Spanish isn't great, but I know enough to recognize the words and the urgency in them. I glance at the clock. 4:59. Rose should be coming with my dinner. It must be Sofia speaking to him.

I press my ear to the door and wait, holding my breath.

"*I'm serious. We need to talk now.*"

"*Not right now.*" Rose's angry woods practically vibrate through the wood.

"*Why the hell not?*" His sister's tone comes harsh and annoyed.

"*Can't you see I'm busy?*"

"*She can wait. This can't.*"

"*What's wrong? Did you find something regarding the plane?*"

Mention of the plane makes me press even tighter to the door, straining to make sure I don't miss anything.

"*No. Felipe.*"

Who the hell is Felipe?

I haven't heard the name before. If I had, I would remember it.

Rose's low growl slips under the crack in the door and sends a shiver through my spine. "*What about him?*"

"*He's here.*"

"*What do you mean he is here?*"

"*He's in Chicago.*"

"*Are you sure?*"

"*Si.*"

"Fuck!"

"*What the hell is he doing here? It can't be anything good.*"

"*We'll talk more about this later.*"

Sofia's sigh is just barely audible. "*Why don't you let her go?*"

"*Stay out of my personal business, Sofia.*"

"*Not when your personal business interferes with our family one. Know your place.*"

"*My place? If it weren't for me, where the hell do you think you would be?*"

"*Don't push me, Sofia. You will not like the results.*"

The key in the lock is my cue to move away from the door, and I dash into the bathroom as fast as my still-unsteady legs will carry me.

"Kat?" Tension still laces Rose's voice, evidence that whoever this Felipe is, the source of the argument, is a major concern.

I stick my head out of the bathroom and try to force an innocent-looking smile. "Right here."

His eyes meet mine, harder than normal, like solid onyx. I may not have personally experienced Rose's wrath, but I know enough to understand I don't want to be on the receiving end of it. Whoever Felipe is, he's clearly someone Rose doesn't want anywhere near Chicago.

Rose sets my dinner tray onto the table and approaches me. "You look better. Did you get some rest?"

I nod. "I did.'

He takes my face between gentle palms, tilting my head up until my eyes meet his. "Good, we have much to discuss."

"Felipe?"

Rose freezes, and his lips curl into a sneer. One of his hands slips from my cheek down around my throat. "Were you eavesdropping, *muñeca*?"

I swallow thickly and shake my head. "I didn't need to. You were talking awfully loudly. Who is he, and should I be worried that he's in town?"

For all I know, this *Felipe* could be the person Rose seemed so concerned about when we discussed who might have betrayed us. He could be the man responsible for the plane crash.

Rose tightens his grip on my throat and brushes his thumb across my windpipe. Under other circumstances, it might be delicate and sensual, but the anger flaming in his eyes assures me one squeeze would be enough to steal my breath and kill me. The man undoubtedly has the strength to do just that if he wants to. And I'm far too weak in this state to stop him.

"You don't need to worry about him. It's a personal matter."

"Didn't you just tell me earlier today that trusting anyone would be a mistake? You clearly don't trust Felipe, or you wouldn't be so concerned about him being here."

This man is intelligent enough to have thought the same thing, but he doesn't want to admit it to me. "I told you I would keep you safe. And I will. From *any* threat."

I swallow thickly against my dry throat. "What if I think you're the biggest threat to me?"

It slips out before I can stop myself. Maybe I'm giving Rose too much by admitting it. Or maybe telling him will actually show him that I can be trusted.

The tiniest of smiles hits his lips, and he leans into me, his hold on my throat loosening slightly. He hovers his mouth over mine, the smell of sweet and spicy bourbon floating over me. "Oh, I definitely am a threat, *muñeca*. One that you don't stand a chance of saving yourself from."

My body heats. The memory of the way he touched me in my condo flaring to life all the nerves that have remained dormant since I killed Michael...except when I've been with this man, who literally holds my life in his hand.

He presses his thumb into my neck. "Are you ready to admit you want me?"

The word *yes* almost slips from my lips. It hovers there, right on the tip, ready to fall off my tongue, but I know better. Giving in to lust always leads to negative consequences. It's one of the things I've built my empire on. Knowing what men want and what they're willing to give up to get it. The secrets they've all offered up while at the houses with my girls have become my currency, and I'm not about to fall prey to the same trap I set for those weak men.

"No." Getting the word out is more of a struggle than I anticipate, but being with Aleksander taught me one thing...how to lie.

I was never good at it before. Mother and Father could always see right through me. So could Terrence. But with Aleksander, it became clear that I would have to learn in order to protect both of us. And now, I'm glad that cold, hard man turned me into what I am now. Because if I were just Brynn, if I were that young, naïve girl dancing on the pole, Rose would have already decimated me. I know that for a *fact*.

He leans in and brushes his lips over mine gently—not so much a kiss as a threat of one. "Okay, *muñeca*, perhaps you're not ready. But you will be soon. And don't tell me I didn't warn you."

The hand curled around my neck slips away. Rose steps back and walks over to the table, where he set down the tray and lifts the cloche that covers the food. "My chef made you *cazuela de mariscos* tonight. It's one of his specialties."

My stomach rumbles, and I take a few deep breaths to try to calm my traitorous body, but it only brings the smell of the delicious seafood to me. If I can't gather myself together, I might as well just throw myself at Rose's feet now.

He takes his seat across the table and motions toward my usual one. "Please. Let's eat."

I take a cautious step forward and eye him. "You're eating with me tonight?"

Rose grins, and his tongue slowly slips out across his lips. "Why, Kat, we are expecting someone else? A date, perhaps?"

I chuckle and sit. "No, but you tend to disappear a lot."

He shrugs nonchalantly. "I'm a very busy man."

"I see that. And meanwhile, my business is going to shit while I'm locked up here and cut off from my men."

His face softens slightly. "I will give you access to a phone so that you may contact Genti and whoever else you need to."

"Just let me go."

He shakes his head. "Not yet."

"How did you manage to get Genti to let you take me in the first place?"

A sly grin pulls at his lips. "I left him in the middle of nowhere Minnesota with the plane wreckage."

"You did what?"

He chuckles and leans forward, clearly pleased with himself and his devious act. "I left him to explain what happened to the authorities." He shrugs and rests his elbows on the table. "It is not the first time he's been questioned by the police. I'm sure he's fine now and back at the club, trying to locate you." He glances around casually. "But he'll never find this place. I made sure of that."

Rose seems to have planned this perfectly, but he underestimates me and my desire to be free. It doesn't matter how charming he is or how much I might actually like him—because let's face it, I do—I'm not going to let him get under my skin. I'm not going to let him be the one who breaks me.

FIVE

"ARE you sure you don't want me to come to get you?" Genti's voice holds all the concern I expected to hear when I called.

After seeing Rose whisk me away from the crash site and being left there to deal with the authorities alone, I'm frankly shocked he's not more pissed and ready to tear apart the city looking for me.

I sigh and rub at my eyes, resting my elbow on the table in my little in my prison room—though, as luxurious as it is, I can hardly call it a cell. "Could you find me even if I told you to?"

Genti mimics my sigh. "Well...we haven't had any luck so far..."

"I figured as much."

Rose said no one would ever find this place, which means he very carefully covered his tracks. Even if I told Genti everything I know, it's not much and wouldn't get him anywhere except being sent on a fruitless search.

"And I'm okay, Genti, really." Aside from the headaches and bouts of dizziness that still accompany my frustration with Rose. At least now that I know what's going on with my own businesses while I'm away, I can relax a little.

"I'm happy to hear that. Everything's fine here. I have three guys over at the new house, making sure the girls are taken care of, and Agon is at Kat's Cradle. Everything is running smoothly there as well."

"What about the next shipment and looking into the new locations?"

While I still have room for one or two more boats of girls at the two existing houses, the expansion is going to be swift elsewhere. I want to overrun this city and the suburbs with as many of my brothels as possible. Because sex *sells*. It's one of the largest moneymakers, which is why all the families somehow dabble in it. Aleksander, Saban, and the other men who came before them have already established the Albanians as the go-to for certain things—mostly smuggling, money laundering, murder for hire, and any other kind of skilled violence where needed. This will add to our repertoire and bring in a lot of money and a lot of blackmail material to help me cement us as the true family in control in Chicago.

"They should arrive in another week or so. I talked with Esad, and we're good there. I'll go out and start scouting locations so that as soon as it's safe and you're well enough, we can purchase."

"And the renovations on the club?"

"Coming along."

"Good." Rose's warning tickles at the back of my mind. *Trust can be overrated, Kat. It can leave you open to betrayal.* I rise from my seat and walk to the window to stare out at the immaculate lawn and gardens. "Did you tell anyone we were going to Winnipeg?"

Genti is silent for a moment. "No, I didn't even tell Driton or Agon where we were going. I just told them we be out of pocket for the day."

A warm sense of relief floods through me, even though I hadn't doubted him. "That's what I thought."

"What's going on, Kat?"

"Rose says the crash wasn't an accident. That someone sabotaged the plane."

Genti issues a low growl. "Then it had to be someone from his camp."

"I agree. There wasn't enough time for the Rebel Chasers to have gotten to the airport before us to do it. Which means it was someone who knew we were there."

"You want me to have Arden look into this?"

He's already busy enough with other things for me, but this is important, too. "Yes, but tell him not to drop the ball on everything else he's working on, either."

"Will do."

"I'll call you tomorrow for another update." I end the call and turn to sit back at the table, but motion in the garden draws my attention.

Rose and Sofia. The girl looks so small next to her brother. Even though he's not a particularly large man, she's tiny in a way that almost makes her look younger than she probably is.

They bicker, both of them wildly gesturing.

What is this about?

Given their prior argument and Rose's reaction to my questioning, my guess is the mysterious Felipe is at the center of this tiff.

I grab my phone again and call Genti.

"Hello?"

"When you talk to Arden, give him the name Felipe. Tell him it has to do with Rowan and the man at Kat's Cradle."

It's the only logical conclusion I can make at this point—that the man I've been searching for is the same one they don't want here. I end the call and slide the phone into my back pocket, never taking my eyes off Rose and Sofia. She yells something at him, points to the house, and storms away toward the far side of the gardens and a small building out there.

Workers' quarters? Maybe the pool house?

Rose scrubs his hands over his face and glances up toward the window where I stand. There's no point in trying to hide. He sees me. The burn of his heated gaze sizzles across my skin even from this distance.

That man is dangerous—in inescapable ways. Ways that leave me more vulnerable than any of the damage to my body from the crash. And he knows it. Which makes it even worse.

He finally looks away and storms back toward the house. I glance at the door, waiting for him to turn the lock and throw it open, but the knob never moves.

Where did he go?

Whatever happened between him and Sofia was pretty heated. He looked genuinely upset, not just angry, but almost *anguished*.

Something in my chest tightens—something I never thought I'd feel again.

You shouldn't care, Kat.

I *shouldn't* care. I shouldn't give a damn about whether he's upset or irritated or hurt. A man like Rose wouldn't care if anyone else was. But he's actually been kind to me since I've been here, despite keeping me locked up in this room like a prisoner—even if it is for my own good like he claims. With Michael, it was easy to turn off that all-too-human emotion of sympathy because of what he did—how his actions personally affected me and brought up the wrath from deep in my veins. But with Rose, it pulls at me, making me cross the room to the door to wrap my hand around the knob.

Every morning, I've woken up and tried it. And every single morning, it's been locked. It never budges, only increasing my frustration and anger. But I never checked it this morning...because I found the phone on my nightstand and immediately called Genti.

For the first time since I woke up in this room, I turn the handle and it twists easily. My heart thunders against my ribcage. Either Rose was so distracted after he slipped in to leave the phone that he forgot to relock the door, or he left it open intentionally. Rose isn't the type of man who would "forget" something like that, though, not when he's been so diligent before. Which can only mean he meant for me to leave this room.

I've never been one to shy away from walking into the unknown. Yet, with this door wide open, I'm not entirely sure what to do. All I know is that my heart is dragging me toward the west wing of the house where Rose went after his argument with his sister.

This is stupid.

Go BACK!

SIX

Despite the warning sounding in my head, I step out of the room and make my way down a long, wide hallway with closed doors along each side. Likely more bedrooms. The place is monstrous. Large enough that there's no way it's in the Chicago city limits. It wouldn't fit. Not a place like this, with these grounds. It would actually make a great brothel house, but there's no way Rose would allow that, even if I *did* agree to partner with him.

I find myself at the top of a grand staircase that curls down to an immaculately tiled foyer with rich carpets and a crystal chandelier hanging above it. Each step down I take, my stomach twists into a tighter knot, and I clutch the railing in case another wave of dizziness overtakes me. They've been getting better—fewer with longer periods between them—but the headaches seem to be a constant reminder of the crash that don't want to leave.

Since I refuse to even consider taking any sort of narcotics for them, I'm stuck suffering. But I won't put that shit in my body. It only clouds my mind and my judgment. Something I can't possibly have when I'm around this man. Not when he clouds it enough on his own.

I pause at the double front doors and peek out through the frosted glass, hoping to catch something that might give me any indication of where we are. But a heavy fog covers most of the front lawn, blocking the view of anything beyond it. Fog like that only rolls in around Lake Michigan—so at least I know we're close to the water.

One of Rose's men stands sentry outside the front door and glances back at me. He inclines his head in acknowledgment, then refocuses his attention to the front of the property. Rose must've told them it's okay for me to be out of the room; otherwise, I have no doubt the man would be dragging me back up there—kicking and screaming. Because I can't stay in that room now that I've tasted freedom, even if only for a moment.

I'm not meant to be caged. That Rose has managed to do it only demonstrates how truly weak I was after the crash, but now, I'm not going to let him keep me here. Not anymore.

I turn toward the direction I saw Rose go from outside and cautiously make my way down the hallway. His angry voice hits my ears long before I find him.

"What the hell is he doing here? You didn't think to stop him? You didn't think to warn me that he was here? *Eres un idiota!*"

I pause outside a cracked door and press my back against the wall. If he catches me eavesdropping again, I doubt it will end well for me.

"No, Sofia found out. What the hell do I pay you for?" He lets out a frustrated scream and slams something down.

Rose doesn't lose his temper—at least, that's the impression he's given everyone since he arrived on the scene here. He's always cool, calm, and collected, like nothing fazes him—not even killing people who get in his way. It's one of the traits that makes him so damn terrifying, so whatever is happening with this Felipe, it's big. *Really* big.

Maybe the kind of *big* I need to work my way under Rose's skin the way he has mine.

I wait for a moment, holding my breath for any further violence from him, then the sound of a chair scraping against wood hits my ears, followed by heavy, hard footsteps moving.

Shit.

If he finds me, I'm toast. Before he can catch me, I whirl toward the door and push it open without knocking.

Rose whips around where he stands over a small bar in the corner of the room behind the desk, a decanter of amber liquid in one hand and an empty glass in the other. Anger and frustration etch deep creases around his eyes and over his brow. "What are you doing here?"

He pours himself a drink with a shaking hand that's usually so steady and sets the decanter back down before he faces me again. His dark eyes meet mine for a fleeting second before he raises the glass to his lips and takes a long drink, almost draining it.

I take a step into his office. "I saw you and Sofia outside. I..."

One of his dark eyebrows rises, and he moves around the side of his desk. "You what? Wanted to see what you could find out? Well—"

"No. I..." The truth is so much harder to voice than if I just admitted I was spying on him. "I wanted to make sure you were okay."

He freezes on the way back to his chair and turns to face me slowly. His now-steady hand brings his drink to his lips again, and he drains the rest of it and sets down the empty glass on the edge of the desk. "You wanted to make sure I was okay, *muñeca?*"

I square my shoulders and straighten my spine, ready to go to war with Rose because now that I've said those words, he's coming for me. Every inch of my body anticipates it, vibrating and aching. I could take it back now, pretend I misspoke or tell him I was lying, but something tells me Rose would see through me in a millisecond. There isn't any point in lying now. "That's what I said, wasn't it?"

He takes a step forward. "You did, but I'm not so sure I believe you. You haven't seemed too interested in admitting any sort of feelings for me except hatred and distrust, so I'm a little surprised by your admission. It makes me question the veracity of your statement."

He's questioning the veracity of my statement while I'm questioning my sanity.

Three more steps bring him even closer to me, but instead of stopping in front of me, he moves around me, pushes the door closed, and flips the lock. The heat of his body hits my back before he presses his chest into me, his warm breath fluttering over my ear. His lips hit the sensitive place just behind there. He sucks gently, and I bite back a mewl that threatens to escape my mouth.

"Tell me why you really came, Kat. Tell me the *real* reason.""

I swallow thickly and try to straighten my shoulders. "I just did."

He kisses his way down my neck and across the exposed portion of my collarbone, and his fingers slip along the edge of my collar and pull it to the side to expose my shoulder so his mouth can keep making progress. "Tell me again."

My legs tremble, and I shift my weight back to gain some support from his strong, hard body behind me. "I wanted to see if you were okay."

"Because?"

I clench my jaw and squeeze my eyes closed against the sensations assaulting my body with every press of his lips. "Because I *do* care, dammit. As much as I fucking hate you and what you are doing to me, seeing you that shaken shook something in *me.*"

He freezes with his lips against my shoulder blade and slowly drags his head back. His left hand wraps around my throat and tilts my face until my eyes meet his—blazing with unrestrained lust. The same thing I've relied on in men to get my way since the day I stepped foot on Aleksander's stage.

I'm still confident this is a terrible idea, but I can no longer deny the attraction to this powerful and dangerous man. Maybe it's time to embrace lust. Even if it may spell both our dooms.

SEVEN

ONE OF HIS dark eyebrows rises slowly, and he tightens his grip on my throat, jerking my head back even farther. His other hand squeezes my shoulder, keeping me pulled fully to his body. His hard cock rubs against my lower back, and he pushes into me, ensuring I can feel every inch of him.

"Are you sure this is what you want, *muñeca*? Are you sure you're ready for what all this means?"

All this means...

It doesn't mean anything. It can't. I can't *let* it. It can be nothing more than giving in to the physical attraction. Scratching an itch. That's it.

That story I told him on the plane should've been enough to understand that my heart will always belong to a dead man. I will always belong to Aleksander. I don't ever want to even consider what it would be like to be that connected to someone else, to open myself to that kind of loss and heartbreak again. He has to understand that. And I really should open my mouth to make sure he does, but instead of those words coming out, all that does is a breathy "*yes*" before his lips crash down on mine.

He tugs on my arm to turn me to face him and crushes our mouths and chests together. The kiss is hot and hungry, and we war for control over it, neither one of us willing to give in to the other.

I let Michael take the reins when we were together because I needed him to trust me. Because I needed him to believe I wasn't a threat. Because it felt so good after having to be the one in control for so long ever since Aleksander died. Because it felt good to have someone else do it just for once.

But if I let Rose do that, if I let myself hand over full control, even just when it comes to sex, he will take that small opening and use it to rip me apart. I have no doubt about that. I haven't doubted that for a second, which is exactly why I've been fighting this pull so hard.

His hands move to the waistband of my pants, and he shoves them down my hips in one smooth motion. I groan into his mouth, and he returns a low growl that goes straight to my core. My hand cups his rigid cock, and he backs me up until my ass hits something hard and sturdy—his mouth never leaving mine for a moment. Every swipe of his tongue, every glide of his lips against mine, ratchets me tighter. His fingers slide between my legs and slip up inside me easily.

I gasp and jerk against his hold, and he curls his fingers up to find my G-spot and pump into me. His touch feels incredible, but I'm not about to come on this man's hand. It won't be enough. Definitely not enough.

And he's not going to leave me hanging like he did last time. Neither of us would be able to stop this runaway train at this point.

I fumble at his waist, trying to undo the button of his pants and finally managed to pop it free so I can tug the zipper down. He mumbles something unintelligible in Spanish, but my lust-fogged brain can't seem to process it, let alone make any attempts to translate it.

He drags his mouth from mine and drops onto his knees to push my pants to my ankles. I kick off my shoes and let him jerk the fabric from my feet.

With me now completely exposed in front of him, he looks up with that knowing gleam in his eye. "I can smell how much you want me from here, *muñeca*."

Before I can dig up some half-hearted protest at his words, he leans forward and delves his tongue between my legs. I gasp at the pleasure coursing through my veins like a tidal wave, the rush of heat over my skin, the tightening low in my belly, and he flicks his tongue over my clit in a way that sends little jolts that make every fiber of my being vibrate. He slides his fingers back into me, and I clench my pussy around them, desperately clasping, but it isn't enough.

Not nearly enough.

I twine my hands into his thick, dark hair and tug, trying to force him up from his knees, but he doesn't relent. He lashes at my clit while he pumps his fingers inside me, offering me no quarter. My hips roll in time with his movements, working me harder, building me up higher and winding me tighter, begging for release of what I've been holding inside me.

The anger.

The guilt.

The burden of everything that brought me to this point.

He sucks my clit between his teeth and bites down. All the tension in my body—everything that's been pent up inside me since the moment Rose came into my life—finally shatters apart under the weight of the orgasm. I claw at the back of his head and shove my hips against his face, but his mouth and fingers never stop moving. He offers no mercy, no break from the mind-bending, overwhelming sensations wracking me.

Not until I'm forced to shove him away using every ounce of strength I have left to escape.

Good God!

The grin Rose gives me only grows as he licks his lips and pushes to his feet, taking his hard cock in his hand. I grab the front of his white shirt and tug him against me, sealing my mouth to his. The taste of my release on his tongue and feeling him stroking himself, the head of his dick brushing against my clit with each motion, is enough to almost make me come again.

But I need more. So much more. "*Metemelo ya!*"

Somehow telling him to get inside me in Spanish turns him even more feral. He growls, grabs my left hip with one hand, and aligns his cock with the other. His eyes lock with mine and darken even more, to an almost midnight black, and shoves into me forcefully enough to steal my breath. The motion sends me back, but his strong fingers digging into my flesh prevent me from bucking completely off the desk.

The feeling of him being inside me, of his cock stretching me with every thrust, sends ripples of euphoria through me. Something I haven't felt in what seems like forever—complete freedom from the pressures of the world and what it requires of me. He drags back his hips and plunges into me again, hitting exactly the right spot to make me see stars against my closed eyelids. I drop my head forward and wrap my legs around him, digging my heels into his lower back to urge him on.

He presses hot, fervent kisses up my neck and across my cheek to my lips and probes his tongue into my mouth, thrusting in time with his cock.

This man talks a big game. He's made a lot of threats and a lot of promises, but now I have to admit...he wasn't bullshitting. At least where sex is concerned.

Sex with Rose is like that first hit, that euphoric high that floods your system and keeps you suspended in another world. The harder he pounds into me and digs his fingers into my skin, the more I want it to never end.

I scratch my nails against the back of his neck and bite down on his tongue. Even the coppery tang of blood doesn't stop him. He groans and fucks me even harder, my hips meeting his merciless rhythm.

For so long, I thought what I was doing with Michael was going to break me, that it would destroy me from the inside out and eviscerate any lingering parts of the real me that were there, but this with Rose, *this* is what is truly going to do me in. Because now that I've had a taste of it, I know I won't be able to walk away easily. He's bringing things to the surface I thought had been buried with Aleksander.

His death may not have killed me. But this will.

He hammers into me relentlessly, neither of us willing to give, both of us wanting to take without caring how selfish we are. Whatever it is Rose is searching for so badly, he seems to have found it, and I'm *this close* to finding what I need again...at least, what I need for now.

Unlike the first time, the slow build to a peak, this orgasm hits me hard and fast, blindsiding me and slamming into me harder than we struck the ground during the crash. Blinding lights flash against my lids, and I jerk on Rose's cock, only held in place by his strong hands.

He grasps my chin and forces my face down. "Open your eyes, *muñeca!*"

Such a huge part of me wants to deny his command just to keep the upper hand, but I'm helpless to. I open them and meet his granite gaze. He clenches his jaw and pushes into me relentlessly.

This man knows how to take what he wants. I was stupid to think I would ever escape him. And now that I've been caught, I don't know if there's any way to work my way out of the web.

His eyes never waver from mine, and with each thrust, he cements his claim on me even more. A few more violent drives of his hips are all it takes to finally bring him over the edge. He comes, his cock pulsing along with my still-spasming walls, and he buries his face against my neck and brings his lips to my ear as his hands find my breasts and his fingers pinch and twist my nipples painfully. "I told you it was only a matter of time, *mi cielo*. But now, you're mine."

EIGHT

YOU ARE MINE.

His words echo in my ears even now, a dozen hours and ten orgasms later with the morning light streaming in through the window onto the bed we shared last night.

Onto *his* bed.

There was no question about whether I was going to return to the room he had me locked in, once we were finally able to breathe after what happened in his office. No question, I would be sleeping in his room for however long he forces me to stay here with him.

And while he may think he got what he wanted, that he got me to admit my weakness by saying I cared about seeing him upset, that he *won* because I finally caved to this attraction between us, what he doesn't understand is that *I* got *him*.

This was my *win.*

Rose brought me to his *home*. He exposed himself to me at *his* weakest—at least, the weakest I've ever seen him. And I got him to find solace and contentment in my body when he could've gone to anyone and just paid for it. He needed *me* as much as I needed him. Probably even more so. The man called me *mi cielo...*my heaven. That certainly changes things.

I have now become Rose's biggest weakness. That makes me more powerful today than I've ever been in my life, even though giving in to him exposes me in a way I never wanted to be again. It's a catch-22, really, but sometimes, you have to give something to get something in return. Having this kind of power over a man like Rose is priceless and well worth the risk of opening myself in this way.

At least it wasn't bad. Quite the opposite.

I turn my head to look at the man in question sleeping peacefully next to me—his eyes closed, lips slightly parted, thick, dark hair unruly and disheveled from the many rounds we went last night. He's even sexier like this than when he's perfectly coifed and in control, which I didn't imagine was even possible.

Danger.

The warning signs have flashed before my eyes since the moment I first saw him, but they blare now, vibrating in my brain so hard it feels like they're battering my brain against my skull—though maybe that's just my injury playing tricks on me.

One thing I've always prided myself on has been following my gut. It told me Aleksander could be trusted, that despite his appearance and reputation, he would never hurt me. It told me what I had to do to leave Brynn behind and become Kat—things that were so painful, I can't even bring myself to think about them for fear they'll leave me in a quivering mass on the floor.

And now that Rose has exposed himself like this to me, has given me what I need to figure out where we are, I could easily relay the information to countless enemies—Valentina, Galen, Valerian, the heads of any number of gangs he's pissed off since arriving here. But my gut is telling me that maybe it's best to keep it close to the chest. Playing the long game is always smarter than trying to take smaller victories in the immediate.

Something I wish Aleksander would have considered when he was face to face with Lorenc and Konstandin.

I stretch my arms above my head and roll my back, trying to release some of the tension and soreness—a combination of the hard crashing to the ground and the hard night we had last night.

GWYN MCNAMEE

I'll be feeling him for hours—there's no doubt about that. All day, I'll sit with the memories of how he dominated me. The pleasure and the pain. The way his lips and hands and cock brought me to new heights over and over again.

It's tempting to go for another round, but one thing's for certain, I can't stay here anymore. Despite Genti telling me things are fine, I can't leave my entire business in the hands of someone else. Aleksander never did it, and I can't, either. Not when there's so much left to be done. Not with what I have planned. If I'm not the one overseeing things, mistakes can happen. And in this business, mistakes get you killed.

I throw back the covers on my side of the massive king-size bed and inch to the side, but Rose snakes his arm around my waist and drags me back against him. Warm, hot lips press to the back of my neck, and I groan and arch against him.

He grinds his hard cock against my ass and nips at my ear. "Where do you think you're going, *mi cielo*? I'm not done with you yet."

Maybe I need to rethink going another round. This could be *perfect*. Now that Rose is wrapped around my finger—or should I say, I have my cunt wrapped around him—it's time to start using it to my advantage.

I turn to face him and grasp his cock in my hand, tightening around the base. "Maybe *I'm* the one who's not done with you."

With a grin, I push against his chiseled chest until he rolls onto his back, then straddle him and align his cock with my pussy so I can sink down slowly onto him.

His eyes roll up to the back of his head, and he groans, exposing his long neck and tightening his hands on my rolling hips. I work myself up and down, leisurely riding him with intent. Last night was hot and hard, furious, ardent, and aggressive. This is a seduction. One I hope achieves my ultimate purpose.

I reach down and wrap my hand around his neck. Almost instantly, he tilts his head down, and his eyes, darkened and clouded by lust, meet mine, yet he makes no attempt to remove my fingers wrapped around his flesh in such a delicate area. I roll my hips and slide up until the head of his cock barely rests inside me and slowly inch my way back down, then repeat the process again, squeezing and releasing in a way I know will drive him mad.

A simple brush of my thumb over his Adam's apple elicits a low groan from somewhere deep in his chest.

"Are you trying to torture me, *mi cielo*?"

I lean over and suck his bottom lip between my teeth. The gentle nip earns me a hard smack on the ass, and I let his lip pop free. "No. Just enjoying the ride."

One of his dark eyebrows rises. "Are you now?"

There's no use denying it. My body would tell him I'm lying even if I managed to get the words out. Instead, I give him a simple nod, and with a low growl, he braces his feet and thrusts up into me, driving himself even deeper. My mouth falls open on a gasp, and I suck my bottom lip between my teeth to keep myself from crying out words that should never be spoken during a fuck that's supposed to mean nothing. That *does* mean nothing. That *has* to mean nothing.

Nothing. Nothing. Nothing.

We move together, me riding and him thrusting until his hands tighten on my hips and heat builds between my legs. He slides one hand between us to find my clit and pinches it, letting loose an orgasm that has me clenching around his cock like a damn vise. He pumps into me two more times and empties himself with a groan.

I collapse on top of him and allow myself a second to catch my breath as he runs a hand languidly up and down my spine. This is my chance. "I need to leave today."

He releases a heavy sigh and stills for a moment before he shifts slightly under me. "I should've known you were up to something."

My entire body tenses, waiting for his anger.

Instead, he presses a kiss to my forehead that's oddly sweet. "It's not safe for you to leave."

"I have a business I have to take care of. People I need to see in person. Genti and the other men will be with me."

Silence lingers between us for a few moments, but it isn't the tense, awkward one I've been anticipating. It's almost...*comfortable*.

He finally takes my face in his hand and turns it toward him. "You're taking two of my men, too. And you're coming straight back here. *Muy rapida.* I don't want you alone ever—with anyone."

I would love to argue with him, but given the circumstances, it's not a wholly unreasonable request. And if I don't come back, he'll find me and haul me back thrown over his shoulder. "What about you?"

That same eyebrow wings up again. "What about me?"

"It's not safe for you, either. Not until we figure out what's going on."

He brushes his thumb over my lips with the tiniest of grins pulling at his. "Kat, it almost sounds like you care."

I slip out from his arms and climb from the bed. "Don't get a big head, Mr. Rose."

Though...I think we're well past that point.

NINE

My phone buzzes with an incoming text message just as I pull up outside the club. I roll my eyes and pull it from my purse. It's probably Rose checking in to make sure I arrive safely even though I have two of his goons escorting me...in *his* car that probably has a GPS tracker he's watching like a psycho from his office in his house.

Only the text isn't from Rose. It's from Genti.

You have someone waiting for you as soon as you walk in the door.

Fuck. **Who is it?**

Your favorite Russian.

Valerian?

Shit. What the hell is he doing here?

Just one more thing to add to today that I don't want to have to deal with.

Rose's man climbs out from the driver's seat and walks around to open the rear passenger door for me. I step out onto the street with his other man climbing out behind me—both focused on our surroundings, scanning for any threats.

Genti would normally meet me outside in a situation like this, but given our visitor waiting inside, my guess is he's keeping an eye on him. Which he should be. Valerian Kamenev showing up unannounced usually means someone is about to die—in a very violent way. The head of the Russian mob in Chicago doesn't make social house calls.

One of Rose's men rushes forward to open the door for me, and I step out of the bright daylight and into the club's darker, moody lighting. Even though we're not open to the public yet because of the on-going renovations, Valerian sits at the bar on a stool with a beer in his hand like he's just some average guy here to enjoy a drink and turns to greet me with a hard stare.

I don't bother mustering up a fake smile. "Mr. Kamenev, to what do I owe this little visit?"

He takes a swig from his bottle, his eyes raking over me. Bright blue, they sparkle in the flashing neon lights reflecting off the pole. Despite the construction still happening, the girls are still working the stages, practicing routines, and trying to get ready for my revamped club to reopen—plus, my men tend to be happier and work harder with a little entertainment as an incentive.

Valerian inclines his bottle toward me. "I thought it was time we had a little chat."

I raise an eyebrow and slide onto the stool next to him while Rose's men hang back by the entry. Genti stands on the other side of the bar, close enough to hear our conversation...or to kill Valerian with his bare hands if he really has to. Though I doubt the Russian would be bold enough to walk in here so casually if that were in his intent.

He waits for me to say something, but when I simply glare, he snorts and shakes his head. "I've heard a lot of rumors."

"About what?"

He chuckles and waves a hand behind him in the direction of the new stage and continued renovations. "About your intentions with this club and with some other things."

This is like déjà vu. "Have you spoken with your friend Galen?"

Valerian snorts and shakes his head. "*Friend* is a strong term."

I cross my legs and fight a grin when his eyes follow the motion. If both of them are nervous enough about me to arrange these meetings independently, then I must be doing something right. "I did find it rather odd that you two were on the same side of all this."

"I wouldn't say we are."

I raise an eyebrow at him. "You two approached Michael together to express your concerns about me."

A scowl twists his lips, and he spins his bottle on the bar top. "So, Michael told you about that before you killed him, huh?"

The casual way he talks about my taking out Michael brings a genuine smile to my lips, and I nod at Genti to get me a drink. "Michael told me a lot of things."

"You're a cold woman, Kat."

"I appreciate your willingness to cut right to the chase even though this is our first meeting. Anyone else might've tried to kiss up or hit on me...but not you."

He grins and lets his eyes travel over me again. "You're a beautiful woman, Kat, but you're not my type."

"Your type? What *is* your type?"

Valerian leans in closer, and Genti shifts and narrows his eyes on him.

"I like my women submissive." The Russian winks. "And something tells me you don't have a submissive bone in your body."

He isn't wrong about that. Anything in me that was inclined to submit died with Aleksander. He was the only one who ever drove that need in me. When I've submitted since, it was nothing more than a necessary act when I was with Michael and even Rose. While I can't deny that little rush that flitted through me when it happened, it's not something I can ever live with consistently. I have to be in control—making the decisions, driving the actions, choosing the ending.

It seems Valerian Kamenev feels the same.

I offer him a knowing grin. "Perhaps one of my girls would be more to your liking."

He chuckles. "I have my own girls, Kat, many of them. Which is why I'm here to talk to you. Before you so unceremoniously ousted your predecessor, there was talk of you making a partnership with Rose."

"Yes." I offer a slow nod. "I heard something about that, as well."

"Is it true?"

I snort and shake my head. "Do I look like the type of woman to get in bed with the Colombian cartel?"

He takes a sip of his beer and watches me. "I don't know you well enough to make that assessment, Kat. I had you pegged as something completely different before you went and turned this entire organization on its head."

"I'll take that as a compliment."

"You should. There are very few women who can survive in this business, who can do it right and maintain control. Valentina has managed it with the help of Cutter and his crew, and it seems to me you might be moving in that direction, too."

Genti slides a drink across the bar to me, never taking his eyes off Valerian.

I take a sip and sigh. "While this little chat has been fun, what is it you want, Valerian?"

His blue eyes harden to ice. "Assurances that you won't interfere with my business. That you won't overstep the bounds of your territory. The same thing we expect from anyone in your role." The hand wrapped around his bottle tightens until his knuckles turn white. "Michael was a problem, and Rose is turning out to be one, too. He's moved in on the drug trade and inserted himself into Valentina's territory. I don't want to have to split my focus on multiple fronts if I don't have to."

It's a fair assessment, one any intelligent man in his position should have made.

"I don't think Rose is going to just go away. Certainly not anytime soon." I uncross and recross my legs. "I can assure you I don't have any plans on interfering with your business, Valerian. My clientele and yours are very different."

"You'd be surprised by the kind of clientele I get."

"As would you, Mr. Kamenev. I'm not about to expand my business in any way that will conflict with yours." At least that he will be aware of until it's too late.

He narrows his eyes on me. "And what about Rose?"

"What about him?"

"Are you two partnering together?"

I take another sip of my drink and shake my head. "I have no plans for that." With a sigh, I turn to watch the girl on the pole.

Her beautiful brunette hair dangles down her back, and the way she moves is almost hypnotic. It seems like decades ago when it was me on that pole and I first locked eyes with Aleksander. But so much has changed so fast.

"Lust and sex are powerful things, Valerian. There's plenty to go around."

"I don't want to see anything shady going on, Ms. Gashi. If I do, make no mistake, our next meeting won't be so friendly."

"I appreciate the warning."

He pushes to his feet and drains his beer. "Be careful who you get into bed with, Kat, figuratively and literally."

That statement hangs ominously in the air, and he brushes past me and out the front door.

I'm not quite sure what just happened, and I can't tell if I made another friend or another enemy. All I know is it's time to kick things into overdrive. I've waited long enough to act on the information I have. Michael made a nice head start when he spoke with the senator before he died and got him on board. But there's far more work to be done. Work I need to start now.

I turn to Genti and finish my drink. "Were you able to arrange the meetings I asked you to?"

He nods slowly. "Your first one is in an hour, the next right after."

"Excellent. Let's go back to my office so you can catch me up on where we are on everything before we have to leave."

He inclines his head toward Rose's goons at the door. "What about those two."

"They've been instructed to stay on me like fucking glue. And I don't think they're going to disobey that order. But as long as you're with me, they can remain outside my office."

"Good." He casts one last look in their direction. "There are some things we need to discuss that I don't think Rose needs to hear about from his lackeys."

TEN

THROUGH A TORRENT OF RAIN, the unmarked, dark sedan pulls into the driveway of the modest, two-story, brick home and shuts off. A moment later, the driver's side door swings open, and the man we've been waiting for steps out, holding a basically useless briefcase over his head to try to protect himself from the storm.

It does nothing to stop him from being soaked. The dark, dreary environment matches the somber mood that has settled over me tonight. With my ever-present headache throbbing against my temples, I want to get this done and over with as quickly as possible.

Having Rose's men in the SUV behind us only complicates things. I'd rather they not be privy to this meeting, but at least all they'll know is who I'm meeting with, not why. It's why I insisted they take their own vehicle instead of riding with Genti and me. If Rose got wind of what is going to happen behind these closed doors, it could complicate things even more between us. And the last thing I need is more complications where Rose is concerned.

Even now, with every breath I take, his scent invades my lungs. My body remembers each brush of his fingers, tingling and heating whenever the memories relentlessly batter my brain.

But I have to push that all away for this meeting. I've always prided myself on my ability to control the thing I use against others. Lust is meant to be wielded. If I let it overwhelm me, this meeting could go awry in ways I can't afford.

It could be deadly.

The man I'm here to see turns from his car, and Genti flashes the lights on our SUV. From where we're parked at the stop sign just across the street facing the house, the harsh high beams strike the driveway, and he jerks his head toward us and narrows his eyes.

Even through the heavy rain, it's easy to see his hand reaching into his jacket. It would have been more of a surprise if he didn't reach for his weapon. A man like him never goes unarmed. He'd be stupid to. He's made a lot of enemies over the years in his position.

Coming to his home for this meeting is risky. He's likely to be more defensive and on-guard here, with his wife and children just inside. But I knew I'd never be able to do this at his office, and doing it here ensures he understands I know where he lives and how to get to those people who are so important to him.

Leverage. You can never have too much of it.

Genti opens his door and steps out, then motions for our guest, who still stands on his driveway, getting drenched, to come to the vehicle. He glances back at his house and considers Genti for a moment before jogging over, abandoning any attempt to keep himself dry at this point but keeping one hand near his weapon.

My right-hand man opens the back door, and the soaked man glances inside and clenches his jaw. Genti holds out a hand, and my guest growls, grabs his gun, and drops it into Genti's open palm. Now that we know he's unarmed, Genti allows him to slide into the back seat on the opposite side of me.

I offer a tight smile. There isn't any point in pretending we're friends. We both know what this meeting is. "Superintendent Canon…"

His hard green eyes narrow on me, then flick up to Genti when he climbs back into the driver's seat and watches us in the rearview mirror. The man knows exactly who we are. Between Genti's arrest with Michael less than two months ago and my taking over the Albanian territory, he would have to be really bad at his job not to recognize us. "What the hell do you want?"

It's not that I expected the Superintendent of the Chicago Police to greet me with open arms, but the hostility isn't warranted. I haven't even done anything to him...yet.

This can be a pleasant chat if he lets it be.

"I think the right question here is what do I *have*?" I reach into my jacket pocket and pull out the tiny piece of technology that is about to give me all the power I need over this man. With a grin, I jiggle the flash drive in my hand. So much power in something so easy to hide. "And what I have is something you don't want anyone else to see."

His eyes widen slightly, then narrow on the drive. "What the hell are you talking about?"

I hand the drive to Genti, who flips open the laptop on the center console, plugs it in, and hits play. The screen blinks to life and shows one of the rooms at Kat's Cradle and the man sitting next to me enjoying the company of several women who are most definitely not the wife who is likely asleep in the house directly across the street.

Technology is so amazing.

Canon's free hand clenches into a fist on his thigh, and the briefcase tumbles to the floorboard from his other one. He turns to me with his jaw squeezed so tightly, a muscle there tics, anger flashing in his hard gaze. "I should have known you were up to no good the day I stepped foot in that house. Do you think you can blackmail me?"

I chuckle and motion to Genti to close the computer. "I don't *think* I can, Superintendent. I *know* I can." Otherwise, I wouldn't have gone to all this trouble. The thing about lust is that people want to keep it behind closed doors. Especially when they give in to it with people they shouldn't. "What would the people of this city think if they found out the head of its police department, which is already under intense scrutiny for corruption, ended up enjoying the services at a brothel he went to go try to shut down? I don't think they'd appreciate discovering Mr. Law and Order is actually Mr. Can I Order a Threesome?"

It was almost too easy with Canon.

The day he first showed up couldn't be more crystal clear in my head if it had happened only yesterday instead of months ago. I had only been open a few weeks at that time, but word had already spread in certain circles about the quality of the establishment and girls.

I knew Canon wasn't there on official business. The house is well outside the city limits of Chicago and therefore not his jurisdiction anyway, but he marched in with his chest puffed out, pretending anyway, making threats about having us shut down.

Until I caught the way he "appreciated" the girls who walked by. Once I offered to introduce him to one of them...his mood changed fast, and it became evident almost immediately that this wasn't his first time partaking at such an establishment. Like so many of the men I have on these recordings, he flew right into my trap. All I had to do was supply the honey.

Now faced with the video evidence of his debauchery and infidelity, Canon scowls at me and shakes his head. "I'll tell them the video is doctored. That it isn't me. You can't prove that it is."

Genti's laughter mingles with mine, filling the car and clearly annoying our *friend*.

But really, that's funny.

I shake my head and sigh. "Now, now, Superintendent Canon, do you really think it's just one video?" I raise an eyebrow. "I have dozens. Documenting every moment you've ever spent at Kat's Cradle, including audio of you speaking with one of my security personnel outside about concern your vehicle might be spotted and identified." I point through the windshield at the very same car parked on his driveway. "You surely remember that, asking him to move it around to the back so no one would see it?"

All the color drains from Canon's face, and his wide shoulders slump. He might be able to convince some people that a single video wasn't real, but that many videos coupled with audio that can be voice-matched is something different entirely. A fact he seems to have just accepted. "What do you want?"

The words come out through gritted teeth, harsh and bitter.

I can't blame the man. He gave in to lust and expected to come out on top—literally and figuratively. Instead, he's being buried under dirt of his own making. He probably thought he got away with it since it's been over six months since he started coming to Kat's Cradle, but really, he was a man with a guillotine already hanging over his head. He just didn't know it.

Now it's time to lower it. But not all the way. I need him too much to behead him at this point. Yet the sharp bite of a blade against his neck will act as a gentle urge to make the right decision with what I'm about to present to him. A reminder of who he now belongs to.

"Listen closely, Mr. Canon, because your response to my offer determines the future for both of us."

And I'm not willing to take no for an answer.

ELEVEN

"I PLAN on opening at least half a dozen more brothels in the city limits in the next few months. Expanding rapidly."

With the girls coming in basically monthly from Albania and the rest of Eastern Europe, I will have an almost endless supply of willing workers, and God knows there's already an endless supply of men lusting for them in this city. But selling sex isn't my only goal.

There will be so much more beneath the surface. Things I couldn't start when Michael was still sniffing around. But now that he's gone and I'm on my own, I can really move forward with steps that will help me eliminate my competition on every front.

"There will also be other things happening at these locations, things you don't need to concern yourself with unless *I* need to be concerned." He doesn't need to worry about the specifics. "The important thing here is that we come to an understanding about what the police will and won't be doing."

I shift to face him more fully, to ensure he understands that this isn't a request. One thing I've perfected since becoming Kat is the icy-cold look that can wither even the hardest of men. It hasn't failed me yet.

"There will not be any raids on any of the houses, and there will be no attempts made to arrest any of my girls for *any* reason. Your men will act like the houses do not exist in their districts. There will be no written reports mentioning them, no whispers about them in back rooms. For all intents and purposes, the houses won't exist to your force."

His eyebrows fly up, and his mouth falls open. "How the fuck am I supposed to make that happen? My men aren't blind and deaf. They see and hear things in the neighborhoods they work in. They know those streets and aren't going to just pretend things aren't happening right under their noses."

"How you accomplish the end result isn't my concern. That's your problem. If people need to be bought, I'll provide you with those resources. If people need to be silenced other ways, that's on you."

He swallows thickly and glances at Genti in the front seat. "You're serious?"

Genti snarls at him. "Deadly serious."

My entire plan for this city requires I have the cooperation of certain high-ranking individuals with power over the things that might interfere with my advancement.

Michael got the senator to agree to watch our backs in Congress over the organized crime bill they keep trying to get passed that will tighten things up and almost double penalties for anyone caught doing what we do, but on the local level, there's still a lot to do to secure my stranglehold. Having the superintendent of police commit murder of one of his own men to protect me would ensure he will remain under my thumb...indefinitely.

That kind of sin never washes away, no matter how hard the rain may fall or how desperately you try to scrub it off.

I cross my legs and offer him what I hope is a reassuring smile. "I've already had a chat with your friend the mayor, and he's assured me his cooperation in zoning and any other matters that might cross his desk. You're going to assure me yours when it comes to your men in blue."

He shakes his head and shoves his hands through his wet hair. "You can't honestly expect me to be able to pull this off."

"Oh, I do." I pull my gun from my purse and lay it across my lap with the barrel pointed right at him. "Or the revelation of how you've been spending your free time will be the least of your worries. Do I have your cooperation?"

Canon huffs and glares at me, his eyes hardening. "You're a cold bitch, Ms. Gashi. I guess I shouldn't be surprised, considering who you married. Or what you did to Michael Syla."

I can't stop the smile that pulls at my lips. "You shouldn't believe rumors, Mr. Canon."

One of his eyebrows rises. "It isn't really a rumor since you appear to be at the head of the family now and no one has seen Michael in weeks."

And no one ever will. Genti, Altin, Driton, and Agon made sure his body would never be found. He doesn't deserve to end up buried back home. That man is exactly where he belongs, at the bottom of Lake Michigan in pieces.

"I'm flattered you think so highly of me, Mr. Canon, but I'm just a businesswoman looking for some cooperation from the local men committed to protecting our community. We have the same goal."

He snorts and shakes his head. "I highly doubt that, Ms. Gashi."

"Oh, but we do." I smile at him and shrug. "I want what you want—what's best for the city of Chicago. And that's me controlling all of it."

"All of you are the same." He holds up two fingers. "First, it was Italians and the Irish." He adds three more fingers. "Then the Russians and the black and Hispanic gangs came in trying to take over. Every time someone pops up wanting more power, a new war erupts. These streets get bathed in blood that I have to clean up. I've seen it time and time again in my almost thirty years on the force. And I'm telling you, you will fail, just like everyone else has."

Oh, ye of little faith.

"I won't fail, Mr. Canon. Because I have something none of them ever did."

"Oh, yeah?" He sneers. "What's that?"

A single word floats through my head. The same one that's been there since the moment I learned Aleksander had been taken from me.

I spread my hands out, palms open and up. "*Nothing.* Unlike everyone else who has tried and failed to expand their territory and take all of the city, I have nothing to lose."

"What about your territory. Your life? You can easily lose those with one wrong step."

He's right about that, and it's happened countless times in the history of this city. But I'm not concerned about it. "I've already lost the only thing that ever mattered to me. When Aleksander died, I might as well have died with him."

"You really have nothing to live for? Nothing that brings you joy?"

Brief flashes of being in Rose's arms and in his bed flicker through my head but then jumble with memories I've tried so hard to push away. Things I can't remember or they'll make me crumble. The façade who is Kat will cease to exist and I'll be nothing more than broken Brynn—the girl I left behind what feels like lifetimes ago.

"Everything I had to live for or that gave me joy was taken from me." Or I had to give it away. "This city is all I have left. And I don't like sharing it. So, you'll help me, Mr. Canon. With whatever I need. I'll be in touch."

He snarls one last time and shoves open the door to step out into the downpour. Genti and I watch him run back toward his house and disappear inside with a final glance back at us.

This is the start of the next phase of the plan. The dominoes are lining up, and all it will take is one gentle push from me and the entire Chicago underworld will topple at my feet, leaving me the only one standing.

Some people would think it's too dangerous, too big a move—what I'm attempting to do under the cover of the brothels—but I never believed in taking the easy path when the harder one is more rewarding. Aleksander tried to push me away, tried to prevent me from becoming part of this life. I could have taken his money, the financial support he offered me with no strings, and I could have walked away. But I chose the path no one else would have. I chose The Dragon.

Genti peers back at me, his brow furrowed. "Are you sure you want to do this? You'll be putting even more of a target on your back."

"Only if they find out it's me doing it..."

TWELVE

By the time I walk into the office, the rain has finally stopped falling, and my entire body aches like I just ran a marathon barefoot. The throbbing at my temples has turned into a full-on thundering against my skull. And while the meeting with Canon went as well as could be expected and is one item I can check off my list, it still leaves me feeling like I haven't accomplished anything.

At least, for now.

Canon will need some follow-up to ensure that he's staying on track and keeping us in mind during his decision-making. But with him and the mayor both in my pocket, things are moving in the right direction.

I gingerly lower myself into my desk chair, drop my head back, and close my eyes. After almost a week at Rose's, recuperating from my injuries and then staying up all night in his bed, going all day today was probably a bad idea.

Definitely a bad idea.

All I want is to crawl into my own soft bed and sleep for days. But that will never happen. There's too much to do and a very determined man who isn't going to let me disappear even if I could.

My phone dings in my purse, and I release a frustrated groan. It's probably Rose calling to find out where I am and when I'm going to be back at his place.

His two men standing outside the office door, waiting for me, seem to be just as anxious to return to his mystery estate. And they'll probably blindfold me again in an attempt to keep the exact location a secret. They are good. I'll give them that. It took me literally slipping in here, slamming the door on their faces, and throwing the lock into place to get some time alone. They seem almost annoyed by this assignment, and I can't say I blame them. Following me around all day when I have my own men who are perfectly capable of protecting me seems like a real shitty assignment.

Yet Rose wanting to ensure my safety is almost endearing.

Almost.

The man surely is an enigma. But the last thing I want right now is to see him. I'd give anything to go home and crawl into my own bed for one night. To get a little distance from him, a little perspective...or a lot.

I dig out my phone from my purse and swipe open the message.

Unknown number?

St. Mary of the Angels. One hour. Come alone.

What the fuck?

It's definitely not from Rose. And mysterious messages asking you to meet places alone typically don't lead to good things.

But something inside me stirs.

I doubt it's Valerian or Galen or even Valentina. It seems we've resolved our issues, at least for the time being, plus any of them would have just come out and said who they were.

That means it's a true unknown. After the attempt on our lives, the unknown isn't necessarily a good thing.

I stare at my phone for a moment, tossing around the various options. Which aren't many. I could try texting back. But whoever it is won't reply with any other information. That much is clear. I either go, or I don't.

Regardless of the instructions, I'm not going alone. That would be potential suicide. Instead, I text Genti to meet me in the office, then push to my feet with a pained groan and make my way to the door to unlock it.

A minute later, Genti pushes open the door and slips inside with an annoyed glance over his shoulder at Rose's men. He closes the door behind him and turns to me. "What's going on?"

"We need to go."

His eyebrows fly up. "Go where? Back to Rose's?"

"No." I shake my head and grab my purse. "I'll tell you in the car. We just need to get out without Rose's men."

"Shit." Genti shoves a hand back through his hair. "And you think they're really going to let us just walk out of here?"

"Of course not." I stop and wait for him to catch my meaning.

He nods his understanding and pulls his gun before opening the door. The two shots ring out, sharp and loud in our confined space.

Rose is going to be pissed—probably more than pissed—but I'll deal with the consequences of this later. My priority right now is figuring out who the mystery texter is and what's so important that a cryptic text and clandestine meeting is necessary.

Genti motions me out into the hallway, and we make our way out the back door into the parking lot. "Where are we headed?"

"Church."

He narrows his eyes on me as we head to one of the SUVs parked along the left side of the lot. "Since when are you religious?"

I chuckle and climb in the back seat while he slides into the driver's seat. "I'm not."

"Then why are we going to church?"

"To meet someone."

His eyes meet mine in the rearview mirror. "That sounds ominous."

I twist my lips and drum my nails on the door. "It just might be. And I need to be going alone."

His head jerks up again. "Like hell you are."

"I know. You can wait outside. But whoever it was made my instructions very clear, and I don't want to fuck up what could be an important meeting."

"You don't even know who you're meeting with, do you?"

It didn't take him long to figure out why I wasn't telling him that important piece of info. Because I don't have it.

I sigh and keep my eyes on the city passing by. "No. I have a few ideas."

"The Mexicans?"

"I've considered that."

When Rose showed up, he took out the smaller gangs that controlled certain portions of Chicago in one fell swoop and inserted himself as the primary drug source for not only the entire city but the entire region. That had to piss off a lot of very dangerous people not only in Chicago but also our neighbors south of the border. Perhaps they're looking for an ally against him.

Genti turns, bringing us closer to our destination. "I can't believe you're going to do this after what happened to the plane. Are you armed?"

"Of course."

"Good. I'm not letting you out of my sight. I'll stand at the back of church if I have to, but I'm going *in* with you."

I don't bother arguing with him. He's just doing his job. The last time I insisted on being anywhere alone was driving to and from my meeting with Valentina. And *that* resulted in my getting kidnapped by the fucking Irish. So, I can understand his reluctance in this situation.

We ride in silence the rest of the way to the church, both of us scanning the streets for any signs of an ambush, but none comes. Then it appears. Dark, foreboding spires climb into the sky, capped by a bell tower. We pull up outside the church, and I stare up at the large wooden doors.

Surely, they have to be locked at this time of night.

But I doubt whoever wants this meeting would set it somewhere inaccessible. I climb from the car, and Genti emerges beside me. We both look up as the bell dings nine times.

It's getting late. Far too late to be having impromptu meetings.

Genti motions toward the building. "Do you think they wanted to meet here because it's neutral ground?"

"That's my thought."

He shrugs and scans the sidewalk and behind us. "Let's go."

With a hand on my lower back, he ushers me up the stairs to the doors. He tugs one open, and we step inside the dark entrance and search for any signs we aren't alone.

No one comes from the shadows, so we move cautiously down the aisle toward the middle of the church. No sign of life. The entire church is plunged into darkness except for the candles lit in front of the Virgin Mary off in an alcove to the left.

Something tugs at my heart, tightening my chest and pulling me in that direction. Genti wants to follow me, but I hold up a hand. "Stay by the door."

He scowls at me and clenches his jaw. A muscle there tics, but he inclines his head in agreement and steps back the way we came while I cross the church toward the statue.

I can't even remember the last time I was in church. Probably my baptism. Dad had been raised Catholic and insisted. Mom was never particularly religious, though, so once Dad had that "requirement" out of the way, neither brought me to church.

So, it isn't any minute familial connection that drew me over here. It was one far stronger, one that even death can't break.

THIRTEEN

THE MOMENT I stepped into this church, the only thing I could feel was the overwhelming need to pray and beg for Aleksander's soul. And maybe my own.

I don't care what happens to Michael. That man made his bed and has to lie in it. Even if that bed means he's in Hell.

But Aleksander...I don't know what happens to him. And that terrifies me. Because when it's my time to go, I don't want to spend eternity alone. I want the promise of spending it with the man I want to be with forever, the man who was taken from me so abruptly by sin.

The man was no saint. In fact, he was the most brutal person I've ever met. What he did to his enemies, to those who failed to back him...it was a torture you might find in Hell. Yet, even though Aleksander was The Dragon, this inhuman beast filled with rage, he was a different man with me. One who truly loved. And anyone capable of that can't be all bad.

At least, that's what I hope as I step forward, grab one of the matches, and strike it so I can light two candles—one for me and one for him.

It's likely too little, too late, but it's better than doing nothing and letting the fate of our souls hang in the balance. I reach into my purse, pull out a one-hundred-dollar bill, and shove it in the little box for donations.

A little bribery never hurts, either.

"Whose soul are you praying for?"

I jerk toward the voice, my hand automatically delving into my purse for my gun. My fingers close around the grip, and I squint into the darkness for the threat, ready to face it with violence even in the house of God.

A man steps from the shadows slowly, deliberately, with his hands raised. "I'm unarmed."

Even though we've never met and all I've seen are very old photos from when he still lived in Albania and was part of their special forces, I recognize him immediately. The beard covering his jaw might conceal part of his face, but it can't hide the blackness of his eyes or soul.

"Konstandin..."

When I considered all the potential people who might have arranged this meeting, he was never even a blip on my radar. Not when he's spent so much time and effort to stay hidden.

The man who killed Aleksander takes another step toward me, lowering his arms to his sides. Dressed in jeans and a black T-shirt, someone might think he's just another nobody if they saw him on the street, but if anyone looked into the depths of his hard gaze, they would see the monster lurking beneath the surface.

A monster whose lips tilt into a smirk. "I heard you've been looking for me. I figured it was better just to get this over with than for us to dance around each other for all of eternity."

I relax my hand from around the gun and glance to where Genti stands at the rear of the church. His eyes locked on us, it's clear he'll pull the trigger before Konstandin could ever get near me. Plus, if he really wanted me dead, he could have killed me barehanded instead of announcing his presence.

So despite how deadly the man in front of me is, I let myself relax slightly. "I'm surprised you have the balls to set foot in a house of God, given what you've done."

One of his dark eyebrows rises. "What *I've* done?" He barks out a laugh that echoes around the vast, empty space. "That's funny considering what you did to Michael and the fact that I bet you were just lighting those candles for a man who flayed people alive for sport."

My hands clench at my sides instinctively, preparing for a fight, but there's no point in arguing with the man standing in front of me. All I want is to end him and finally have some form of closure over what happened to Aleksander. "Did you come here just to make me want to kill you even more?"

He chuckles and steps closer, making my entire body tense. Konstandin is huge—at least twice my size. Even unarmed, all it would take is one well-placed strike to knock me out...or worse. And I know he's more than capable of that without even thinking about it.

I sneer at him. "You find that funny?"

He shakes his head and scans our surroundings quickly before his obsidian gaze returns to mine. One of his shoulders rises and falls in a nonchalant shrug. "I didn't think it was possible for you to want to kill me even more."

"You killed Aleksander. I have every right to want you buried six feet under with him."

Konstandin crosses his massive arms over his chest, only making all of him seem larger and more menacing. "Aleksander was never going to stop until he had killed Lorenc and Rea. If he had known I was still alive, he would have been hunting me, too. I couldn't let him hurt her after everything I went through to ensure she was safe from Tarek."

"You're the one who set this all in motion, Konstandin. You and Rea betrayed your brother. Then you killed Saban. You're not a stupid man. You had to know The Dragon would come for you once you did that."

He considers me for a moment, the silence of the church around us suddenly oppressive enough to weigh down my chest and make breathing a little harder. "If you loved Aleksander even half as much as I do Rea, you would understand why I had to do what I did."

Shit.

His words slam into me like a ton of bricks being dropped.

He's right.

If Aleksander and I had been in the position Rea and Konstandin found themselves—her forced into an arranged marriage with a man like Tarek, Konstandin assigned to protect her, and them then falling in love—I can't say I would have acted any differently. Aleksander would have done anything to save me, including taking me away and trying to disappear like Konstandin and Rea managed for a while. And if I had been taken back, Aleksander would have gone on the warpath, destroying everything in his way to save me...just like Konstandin did.

But still...Konstandin made *one* fatal error. "You didn't have to kill Saban. You could have destroyed Tarek and taken Rea back and disappeared to live the rest of your lives together in absolute bliss."

He scowls at me and twists his lips. "It was a mistake. I can admit that. I acted in the heat of the moment. I acted on my wrath for anyone associated with taking Rea from me, and Saban had assisted Tarek in locating us." He shrugs and glances up at the crucifix. "Maybe I should have walked away, let him live another day. Forgiven the act that led to the love of my life being whisked away by the man who raped and tormented her before I saved her from that future." He takes another step closer, his voice lowering into almost a growl. "But we *both* know his death was inevitable. Maybe not at my hand. He might have lived a few more months, or a few more years even, but Saban had a lot of other enemies, ones who would have killed him for no reason at all rather than for love."

For love.

Love started this downward spiral of violence and death—Saban, Tarek, Lorenc, Aleksander, *Brynn*...and Michael. I thought I could end it by finishing off Konstandin and Rea, by removing the very people who set things down this path.

And deep down, something inside me still wants me to grab the gun from my purse and empty it into the man only feet in front of me.

It's the thing that I can't seem to push away. Not knowing all that I've suffered and lost because of this series of events, because of *this* man. "Give me one good reason why I shouldn't shoot you and end this now. *One.*"

His eyes soften for a moment, almost making him appear human. He glances at the lit candles and scrubs a hand over his whiskered face before returning his focus to me. When he does, the strength of the determination in his gaze sends a chill through me. This is the Konstandin who tortured his victims. "Because Rea and I have a son. And I know where *yours* is."

SEIZING LUST

Lust is a pleasure bought with pain, a delight hatched with disquiet, a content passed with fear, and a sin finished with sorrow.

- DEMONAX

ONE

KAT

"Because Rea and I have a son, and I know where *yours* is."

The air instantly sucks out of the church around me, tightening my chest, and it takes me a moment to process his words.

I know where yours is.

They whirl around my head like a hurricane-force wind, and I try to break them down one by one.

When they fully register. When the truth of what they mean finally hits that part of my brain where I've hidden all my secrets, I try not to show any reaction. I swallow thickly. "I...I don't know what you're talking about."

Konstandin regards me with something akin to pity in his eyes. Certainly not something he would ever have given any of his victims. "Let's cut the bullshit, Kat, or should I call you Brynn? Because that's who I'm talking to right now. The woman who gave birth to Aleksander's child and named him Jeton. The woman who tried to ensure that he would never be found. The woman who left him with that family in Albania to try to save him from the world that you stepped into as Kat."

Blood thunders in my ears, and my chest constricts so badly, I can barely take a breath. My vision starts to waver in front of me.

No. This can't be happening.

Everything I went through. Everything I did to make it to this point. Everything I *sacrificed*. All of it was for nothing. The carefully constructed façade of Kat is gone. It's all crashing down.

The web of lies I created is now wrapping me up and keeping me here to be devoured like some stupid fucking fly by the vicious spider named Konstandin.

He takes a step closer to me. "Brynn, look at me."

I don't want to. I don't want to stare into the eyes of someone so evil, someone who would threaten an innocent child. I would do a lot of things to get what I want, but there's a line I would never cross. *This* line.

My hands fist at my sides. I want to lash out, to rail against him and what his words mean. But I need to know what he knows. I need to know what he's already done. So, I force myself to open my eyes and meet his dark ones. "How did you...how did you find him?"

It should have been impossible. I did everything right. I covered my tracks. Ensured there weren't any records. Secured promises from people I trusted.

Konstandin sighs and runs a hand back through his hair. He glances toward the front of the church, almost like he's checking to ensure we're still alone. "Aleksander wasn't the only one who still has connections back home. After he tried—and failed—to kill Rea and me, after he used *our son* as bait..." He pauses to let those words sink in. "I knew I needed some help. People I could trust. People who go way back with my family to before we ever came to the States."

"You went home?"

That seems like a pretty idiotic thing to do if you're him. Just like there are a lot of people in Albania who wanted Michael and me dead, there are just as many who want to see the end of the

Morinas. And Konstandin is the last one. Except for, apparently, this son he managed to keep hidden.

He shakes his head. "No, but I made sure I had ears open there. I wanted to keep an eye on what was happening after Aleksander's death, who else might come for us from his crew. I didn't anticipate *you* showing up."

"No one did." I take a deep breath and squeeze my shaking hands together so Konstandin doesn't see them. Outward signs of weakness are invitations for a man like him. "For weeks, I didn't know what to do after he died. He didn't even know I was pregnant. All I knew was I had to take him home. I had to bury him with his brother, father, and the rest of the family. He deserved that much. And as I made my plans to go back, as I thought about all the things Aleksander had planned, all the things he would have wanted, I realized what I had to do."

Konstandin raises one dark eyebrow. "Become Kat?"

I nod slowly and lay a hand across my flat stomach, remembering what it felt like to have Aleksander's child growing inside me. "I knew what it meant. What I would have to give up. But our son wouldn't have been safe if I had stayed Brynn Gashi."

"You don't know that." His response comes fast and with a conviction I can't share.

"Bullshit." I narrow my eyes at him. "Are you telling me you wouldn't have come after my son and me? That you wouldn't have blamed us for Lorenc's death? Are you going to stand here and tell me you haven't been gunning for me since that very day?"

His best friend died in the confrontation with Aleksander, and I imagine Konstandin has a lot of feelings about that. A lot of feelings I share about him and what he did.

I had dismissed the possibility that Konstandin could have been behind the sabotage of the plane, but now that I know he's here in the States and that he's been watching me so closely, it's definitely not impossible if he somehow managed to get the information about where we were traveling.

"I'm not so sure you haven't already made an attempt on my life. Maybe we're only having this meeting because you failed."

He shakes his head. "I heard you had a little...plane trouble...but it wasn't me. I didn't even know you were in Winnipeg until one of my old friends in the MC left me a frantic message on a line I leave open for urgent calls. It wasn't me."

I'm not so sure I believe him, but deep down, I understand how hard it would have been for anyone to arrange the plane's sabotage without immediate inside information either from my camp or Rose's, and something tells me Konstandin doesn't have *that*.

"Even if it wasn't you, that doesn't mean you don't still want me dead for what happened to your best friend."

"Lorenc died because Michael betrayed him. He died because he loved Rea and me. And because he loved our son. He raised him for the first few years. He was the only father-figure my son had." His voice breaks for a second, and he swallows thickly.

Konstandin isn't the type of man to show emotion, to show he's human, or that he has any weaknesses, but Lorenc and his relationship with him obviously was one.

He centers his gaze back on me with new resolve. "I'll admit that when I first heard that you showed up back home, I was concerned. I thought that perhaps you were going to pick up where Aleksander left off, stalking us and trying to take us out, especially since he was now dead and you would blame us."

Rightfully so.

"Then I heard about the baby, and I *knew* I was right. You wouldn't have gone through everything you went through—creating this background, becoming a new person, giving up your son—if your ultimate goal didn't require it. I had assumed that goal was to take me out." He offers me a halfhearted grin. "I never thought you would take out Michael for me. Thanks for that, by the way."

I release a sardonic laugh that echoes through the church. It's so wrong to be having this conversation in this place, for him to be thanking me for killing someone while we stand before the crucifix, the judgmental eyes of the man whose death was supposed to forgive all our sins. "You're welcome, I guess. But if you just came here to threaten me through my son, then you've greatly underestimated what I'm capable of, and what I did to Michael hasn't taught you anything."

He holds up his hands and takes half a step back. "I don't have any intention of harming your son, Kat. From what I can tell, the family you left him with loves him and takes good care of him. Maybe you've truly saved him from being part of this fucked-up world. I only brought him up because I had hoped, as one parent to another, that you would understand why this has to end."

When I don't say anything, he sighs and continues.

"My son needs me. Rea needs me. And I don't want to lose them over some stupid vendetta that both of us are holding onto."

Stupid vendetta? Is that what he really thinks this is?

"This isn't a stupid vendetta, Konstandin. It's so much more than that. It's *justice*."

And for him to be suggesting we just...walk away from it boggles my mind. This isn't the same Konstandin Morina who developed the reputation as a violent, heartless killer. The man who tortures his victims just for the thrill of it. This man seems to have softened. Either that or he has taken up acting and gotten very good at it. But I'm not naïve enough to believe he wouldn't snap right back into his old self if Rea or his son were threatened.

"Brynn, listen to me." He levels his dark, hard gaze on me. "I killed Aleksander because I didn't have any choice."

While he says those words, something crinkles at the corner of his eyes that tells me something different.

Holy shit.

It's written right there in the way he's looking at me. The truth.

"*You* didn't kill Aleksander, did you?"

His stony face offers no answer, but his eyes don't lie.

It *wasn't* Kondstandin at all. It was *Rea*.

She was the one who pulled the trigger. She's the one who ended Aleksander's life.

And I can almost understand why.

If what Konstandin says is true, that Aleksander took their son and used him as bait, then I can see how the mama bear in Rea would have forced her to do whatever was necessary to protect him.

I would've done the same thing if they had taken Jet.

But it doesn't change anything. It doesn't bring Aleksander back or give me my son—the two things I want more than anything in this world.

TWO

YET, regardless of who pulled the trigger, the reason they did is one I can't deny. They did it to protect their son. To ensure he would never be hunted and devoured by the Dragon. They did it because Aleksander never would have stopped, and his ultimate win would have been to kill them and take their child to warp him into exactly what they feared.

Raising your enemy's child would be the ultimate win—one I don't doubt Aleksander would have relished. So while I can understand why Rea pulled the trigger, it doesn't give Konstandin the right to stand here in front of me and threaten my child. "Did you really think coming here and threatening my son was going to get you anywhere but dead?"

Konstandin scowls at me and takes another step closer. "No, I was hoping that I could appeal to you as a mother. To end this madness now."

I scoff.

Like it's that simple.

He's insane if he thinks just giving up my wrath now is an option.

He raises a hand. "Just listen to me, Brynn. A lot of people made a lot of mistakes that brought us to this point. And we don't need to be making any more of them."

"And I'm just supposed to let you walk away then?"

"Yes." He nods slowly and shrugs. "We both walk away. We let what started between me and Tarek end with you and me. It keeps both of our sons safe."

"You really think you'll ever be safe?"

He sighs and runs a hand over his beard. "I hope so. I don't have any plans or desire to ever go back to the life I led before. Rea and I thought we had left it behind us when we fled from Tarek. We thought we were free. That's all we ever wanted."

I stand, staring at the man responsible for Aleksander's death, all the pain and resentment that's built up since his death still burning through me so hot that it sears my soul.

It doesn't matter if it was Rea who actually pulled the final trigger. This man, the one before me, turned her into a killer. And what he did turned *me* into one.

I was a different person when I met Aleksander. Young. Naïve. I had never harmed another soul in my life, and I had stupidly believed what people told me about the world—that people are inherently good. But I gave up that way of thinking when I chose Aleksander. He showed me how the world really is, the true nature of people. What they keep buried deep inside them and only unleash in the darkest of times. The thing that makes me confident in what I'm about to say to Konstandin.

"You will never be safe, Konstandin. That's why I left my son in the hands of someone who could never be traced back to me."

Or so I thought.

Because it doesn't matter how much power I hold, how much fear I strike into the hearts of people now that they know what I'm capable of. It only offers an illusion of protection. A veil of safety that's easily pierced.

"Bad men will always come for the likes of us, Konstandin. And there's no way around that. You and I will always be looking over our shoulders and watching our backs, and so will Rea and your son. Because you know the moment you stop is the moment you feel the bullet hit."

"You're right about that. But at least if we come to a truce, it's one less bullet we have to dodge.

You have your hands full here in Chicago. And all I want to do is disappear. We don't have to be at war if we don't want to be."

As much as I want to grab my gun and unload it into this man, I can't. And not just because it would undo any good my prayers for my soul just did. It's because what he says makes some sense. Things are tenuous here. And as I expand the brothels and venture into other avenues that are even more dangerous, I'm only going to make more enemies on the home front. With the Dragushas and Berishas in Albania chomping at the bit for any excuse to take me out, and with someone already making an attempt, do I really need another enemy? Especially one as lethal as Konstandin?

But he's already threatened Jet.

I swallow through the emotion clogging my throat. I gave up my son to protect him, and this might be the only way. Just like Konstandin's appealing to me as a mother, he's also given me his Achilles heel. His own son. He didn't have to admit that to me. He didn't have to offer me that information. And by doing so, he's exposed himself in a way that could completely backfire on him. He must have a lot more faith in me than I have in myself.

"You'll disappear? Leave me, my son, and my empire alone?"

He holds up his hands. "I'm gone. But it doesn't mean I won't be keeping an eye on you. As one does with friends."

I snort and shake my head. "Don't be mistaken, Konstandin. If I agree to this, it's not because we're friends. It's because my son's life means more to me than anything, even my own."

A tiny bit of sympathy flashes in the blacks of his eyes. "You and me both. So let's neither of us do anything stupid. You let me walk out of here and disappear into the night, and I do the same. We never have to see each other again."

I sigh and finally let some of the tension in my shoulders relax. "You have a deal, Mr. Morina. But if you are ever so much as a blip on my radar again, all bets are off."

"Understood. And as a final parting gift..."

I raise an eyebrow at him. "What?"

He inclines his head toward the rear of the church where the rectory stands, the same direction he looked earlier. "I think you might find a conversation with the parish priest interesting."

"The parish priest? Doubtful."

One corner of his mouth tips up into a knowing grin. "You're welcome."

With those final words still hanging in the air between us, he backs away into the darkness of the church the same way he came. Silently.

And while it feels like one giant weight has been lifted off my shoulders, another one has settled to replace it.

What would Aleksander say if he knew I let the man who killed him walk out of here alive? A man who knows where our son is?

He would probably call me weak. But it was Aleksander's own blinding wrath that caused his death in the first place. If only he had listened to me. If only he had been willing to let Konstandin and Rea go about their lives instead of needing revenge, he would still be alive.

And yet, if Konstandin hadn't shown up tonight, would I have taken my own advice? If I had found him, would I have let him and Rea go?

I honestly don't know. And that uncertainty only shows me the weakness that was part of Brynn still exists somewhere inside me. The weakness I can't afford to have if I'm going to move forward with my plan.

Footsteps echoing in the church draw my attention behind me, and Genti appears at my side. "Was that who I think it was?"

I nod as I return my attention to the dark archway Konstandin disappeared into. "It sure was."

"Are we getting out of here?"

I shake my head and turn to the entry to the rectory. "Not yet. I have to talk to the priest."

THREE

GENTI FOLLOWS BEHIND ME, his brow furrowed, but I'm not about to try to explain to him what I don't understand myself. I thought Konstandin chose this place to meet because it would be neutral ground, somewhere neither of us would dare to spill blood, but his comments suggest otherwise.

What could I possibly want from a priest?

Except maybe absolution.

The short, narrow hallway at the side of the church leads to a wooden door with a small sign that reads *RECTORY* attached to the center of it, but before I can even start to make my way down it, the door opens and a man steps out into the dim lighting.

Holy shit.

Genti immediately reaches for his gun, but I hold out my arm to stop him from taking any rash action.

"No." I shake my head. "That isn't him."

With his gaze narrowed on the approaching man, Genti relaxes slightly but keeps his hand hovering over his weapon.

Though, at first glance, the man may appear to be a carbon copy of Rose—the same dark, almost black eyes, the same perfectly cut and styled dark hair, mirrored face—this is certainly not the man whose bed I woke up in this morning. Dressed in the black garb and white collar of a priest, the only thing that gives away that he isn't just Rose undercover are the tattoos on his exposed forearms.

He moves toward us with a soft smile, far friendlier and more natural than that of Rose. "Since our mutual acquaintance has left, I think it's time you and I have a chat."

"I've been looking for you for a long time."

A low chuckle slips from his mouth, and he crosses his arms over his chest. The black shirt he wears stretches around his biceps and draws my attention to the ink there, though, in the low light from the candles, I can't quite make out any of the swirling patterns or words.

I follow them up to where they disappear into his sleeves, then meet his gaze and raise an eyebrow at the man I can only assume is Rose's brother. "You must be Felipe."

It makes perfect sense, really. Family so easily becomes the greatest source of strife, and when Sofia told Rose that Felipe was in town, it definitely shook something deep in him.

His eyes widen slightly, and he inclines his head toward me. "I'm surprised my brother told you."

I shake my head. "He didn't. I overheard him and Sofia arguing about you earlier."

His gaze softens, and a genuine smile lights his face. "Just how is my baby sister? Has she fully recovered from her injuries?"

So, he knows about the explosion...

Though I doubt he knows I'm responsible. It sounds as though Rose hasn't spoken with him in some time, and that means he hasn't revealed what I told him on the plane.

I shake my head. "I'm not totally sure. I haven't actually met her or spoken with her."

His eyebrows rise. "That's surprising. You're living with my brother, are you not?"

How the hell does he know that?

I press my lips into a hard line and look around the church. Its eerie silence is more welcome now that I understand why this was so important. If we were meeting somewhere bustling and busy, it might be difficult to have this conversation.

Although, I really don't know why I'm here, why this was arranged—by Konstandin or Felipe.

"I was staying with him while I recovered from an injury. I most certainly don't live with him."

He issues another low chuckle and nods. "We'll see what he has to say about that. When my brother sets his sights on something he wants, rarely does he not get it."

Christ. He sounds so much like Rose and seems to know him so well.

They both talk in such absolutes, with so much confidence. It's unsettling, to say the least.

"What is it you want, Felipe? If you wanted to know how your brother and sister are doing, I'm sure there are better ways than tracking me down."

He motions toward an empty pew behind us. "Let's talk."

I glance at Genti and incline my head to direct him to the other side of the church. If Felipe tells me anything Genti needs to know, I can inform him later. There are things I may need to keep private. If Konstandin were here with Felipe's knowledge, then it's more than possible Felipe also knows about Jet and other secrets that need to stay buried, even from Genti.

Genti reluctantly retreats to the far side of the church, where he can still maintain a direct line of sight on me. Even in the presence of a man of God, Genti isn't about to let down his guard. He learned that lesson the hard way with Michael and me.

I follow Felipe into the pew and lower myself onto its hard, unyielding surface. It's the last place I expected to find the two men I've spent so much time and energy searching for. "Is this your church?"

He nods and motions toward the altar. "For now, I'm helping here."

"And how long have you been in Chicago?"

He turns his head toward me, his lips curling into a grin. "What makes you think I'd tell you that?"

I return his grin. "I was just making conversation."

Trying to figure out what the fuck is going on...

He chuckles again and points at me. "I can see why my brother likes you so much. You're funny."

I bark out a laugh that echoes around the vast, cavernous space. "I don't think anyone's ever called me that before."

"Well, there's a first time for everything."

"That's certainly true." And I've had a lot of firsts since taking over as head of this family. It seems everything that can be thrown at me has been, including this mysterious meeting with Konstandin and now Felipe. And this may be my only chance to get some answers. "You know, I don't even know your brother's first name, or last, for that matter. I assume it's not Rose."

Felipe's expression hardens to a stone-cold look I would never expect to see from a priest staring back at me. "There's a reason you don't and probably never will."

An ominous statement from a man who apparently arranged this meeting for a reason.

"If anonymity is so important, why did you bring me here? Why expose yourself this way? Maybe you have something to tell me?" The video from Kat's Cradle of him speaking with Rowan flashes through my mind. "Perhaps about Rowan?"

He releases a sigh and turns his focus to the crucifix hanging above the altar. "No. This isn't about Rowan. Just know that she's safe, and you don't need to worry about her."

"And I'm just supposed to take your word for this? Knowing who you are."

Felipe releases a low chuckle and offers a bright smile that actually reaches his eyes. "I've been told I have a face people can trust."

I climb to my feet and narrow my eyes at him. "That might be true if you didn't share your face with your brother."

He grins at me. "Touché. But please, Kat, sit. I'm just a priest who has sworn to protect God's children in any way I can and do the Lord's work. That's what I'm trying to do tonight by brokering peace between you and Konstandin and by meeting with you."

The words sound good, but I'm not about to let down my guard around this man. Not when his brother is a cold, calculating killer. "How did you and your brother fall on such opposite sides of the tree?"

He runs a hand back through his hair and shakes his head. "That's a very long and complicated story and not one I intend to ever tell, nor do I think he will."

Of course not.

Rose will never open up to me and reveal anything of true worth, nothing about who he really is or what made him that way. And if his brother doesn't intend to, either, that leaves the reason for this meeting a mystery. One I intend on solving now...

FOUR

"WHAT DO YOU WANT, Felipe? How did you manage to arrange this meeting with Konstandin, and why?"

Felipe raises one shoulder and lets it fall nonchalantly, though this situation feels anything but. "This collar affords me a lot of power I might not otherwise have. People are much more willing to offer information and to speak with me when I wear this."

I snort and shake my head. "That doesn't surprise me at all. But it doesn't answer my questions."

"I wanted to broker a peace between you and Konstandin."

"Why? What's in it for you?"

He spreads his hands wide. "As I said, it's my job to protect God's children, and a war between you two puts innocents at risk."

It puts *everyone* at risk. He's right about that. Because if we went head to head, barrel to barrel, things would get very bloody. They still might. That remains to be seen since I don't fully trust anything Konstandin said to me tonight.

"But why have us meet here? I assume you offered this location to him for a reason."

His dark eyes meet mine, wide and determined. "Because I wanted to warn you."

"Warn me about what? The man who just walked out of here? Are you saying he's the one who sabotaged the plane?"

He shakes his head. "I don't know anything about that. Who lives and who dies is God's judgment. But I don't want to see my family hurt by becoming entwined with you and your organization. My brother is playing a dangerous game with you, one that I fear could get him killed."

"By me?" I raise an eyebrow at him, and he grins.

"You've certainly proven that isn't completely out of the question, haven't you?"

That's fair.

And I guess if I were in his shoes, in the same position, I might not believe me, either. Might not trust my motives. After what I did to Michael, it would be hard to. But truth be told, my motives have morphed and changed so many times since I became Kat that I'm not entirely sure I trust them myself.

"You don't have anything to worry about, Felipe. I have no intention of merging my business with your brother's."

"His business. What about merging with *him* personally?"

I shift on the suddenly uncomfortable seat. Of course, he would ask the one question I have no answer to. "I don't plan on that, either."

It's as honest I can be with him at this moment.

He nods slowly. "Good, because I already have enough on my plate praying for his soul and safety. If I have to watch his back to protect him from you, I might miss morning mass." He offers me a tentative smile and pushes to his feet. "I suggest you don't tell my brother about our little conversation."

"Why is that?"

"We don't have the best of relationships." He motions to his collar. "For obvious reasons, we have very differing views of the world and our places in it. I doubt very much he would appreciate my interference."

I chuckle and shake my head. "We can agree on that."

"It was wonderful to meet you, Kat. Any chance I'll see you at mass in the future?"

I peer up at the crucifix and the judgmental gaze of the man hanging from it. "I don't think I would be very welcome."

Felipe pauses at the end of the pew and turns back to me. "That's where you're wrong. God loves all his children, and all are welcome in his house."

"Even your brother?"

A glimpse of something hard flickers in his eyes—the first real outward sign that he and his brother might not be so different after all. "I have no doubt my brother knows where to find me. My sister is quite good with the computer."

His sister? Sofia is his hacker?

That certainly explains why she was with Valentina's crew when they arrived at the meeting before the bomb went off. She must've been working with Preacher on something. It ended up with her in the wrong place at the wrong time, but if she works for Rose, then she isn't the innocent everyone assumed she was, either.

"Is he welcome here, though?"

"By God."

"What about by you?"

"That's a much harder question, Ms. Gashi. One I'm in no position to answer this evening. I believe my brother's waiting for you."

No doubt he is, and after I killed his men to get here tonight, it's not going to be a very pleasant meeting.

Felipe motions toward the back door. "Leave whenever you're ready. I'll lock up later."

I don't have any intention of spending one minute longer than I have to in this place. I never quite understood it when people said they felt the presence of God in churches and other "holy" locations, that they feel at peace as soon as they step foot inside, but standing here tonight, I definitely feel something—and it isn't good.

Maybe it's God, or maybe it's my own conscience casting judgment. Either way, the feeling like bugs are crawling across my skin is too much for me to bear any longer.

With a shudder, I stand and turn toward where Genti leans against a column on the other side of the aisle. I incline my head toward the back of the church, and he follows me. With each step I take, my heels echo hauntingly. Genti pushes open the door for me, and we step out into the cool, crisp night.

The smell of rain still lingers in the air, and the damp pavement still holds the evidence of the most recent shower. I never thought I'd pray for more rain after the last few days, but the overwhelming need to cleanse myself and my skin tightens my chest.

Genti opens the back door of the SUV. "Where to?"

"Home."

"What about Rose?"

"I wouldn't know how to get to his place, anyway. But I have no doubt he'll find me."

FIVE

THE MOMENT the condo door closes behind me, I beeline for the bar, pour two fingers of whiskey, and toss it back like it's water. The sweet burn down my throat makes me wince slightly, but I pour another and lower myself into the leather chair across from the couch to light the cigarette I've needed for so long.

My body vibrates so badly that when I try to bring it to my mouth, it looks like an earthquake shaking it, and I have to pause and try to take several deep breaths before I can even bring it all the way to my mouth to fill my lungs with smoke and my body with nicotine.

Get a fucking grip.

I can't lose my shit right now. Not when a hurricane named Rose is going to come barreling through that door at any moment.

And he will.

After he's not able to get a hold of his men or me for a while, he'll come looking for me with all the force of a deadly storm. My only hope of surviving it is to keep my wits about me, maintain my cool, and stand my ground, but that's hard to do after my conversation with Konstandin and the warning from Felipe.

I take a deep inhale of my cigarette, letting the smoke fill my lungs and nicotine calm my nerves slightly.

Fuck, I needed that. And I need to get a fucking grip.

It's not just me who is in danger anymore.

Konstandin found Jet. That means other people might be able to. I have to figure out what to do to protect him, and I have to do it all without letting Rose in. If he finds out I have a son, it's going to change everything. It will give him all the leverage he'll ever need to take whatever he wants from me. And there are some things I'm just not willing to give him. *That* part of me is one of them.

That part of me belongs to the Dragon. Jet is all I have left of Aleksander, and I won't let him be corrupted by the world his father chose, the one that took his life, the same world that I chose in order to ensure his name was never forgotten, in order to seek revenge. But now, I let my opportunity for vengeance go. He walked right out the door so I could protect Jet.

Would Aleksander have understood my giving up our child and then letting Konstandin go?

I hope so. I want to believe he would see me putting our son's safety above all else for what it is —a necessity that tears me apart every second of every day. But there's still that part of me, the part that's been eating away like acid deep inside since the moment I left Albania, that tells me I did the wrong thing. A part that insists I could have protected and cared for Jet myself, that I can raise him and have that little piece of Aleksander with me forever, that I'm missing out on everything for nothing.

That regret may never go away, no matter what I decide to do. But having Konstandin seek me out, hearing my son's name from his lips, it all just proves my concern was warranted. I don't even want to consider how much more he would be targeted if everyone knew he existed. One man found him when I thought he was well hidden. If he were here, it would be like drawing a target on his back.

Which makes one thing crystal clear—I can't let Rose find out about him or that I met with

Felipe. Whatever happened between the two of them, their issues run deep. That much was evident from the few minutes I spent with Felipe and what I overheard and saw between Rose and Sofia. And that means there's something there that I might be able to use to my advantage. I just need to find out what it is before Rose finds out I've spoken with Felipe...or before he kills me for taking out his men in order to slip away from his watchful eye.

A very real possibility.

This may be the last cigarette and drink I ever have. I better enjoy them while I can.

I take another drag and then a sip of my drink. The combination of the two should be helping me relax, but I can't stop my knee from bouncing or my hand from shaking.

Get your shit together, Kat.

Rose isn't a man I want to be around when I'm not at one hundred percent. And right now, I'm running on fumes. Physically and emotionally spent. I can barely bring the cigarette to my mouth without ashes falling all over me because of my violent quaking.

What will happen when that storm of a man comes for me?

Under normal circumstances, I can handle Rose. After standing toe to toe with Aleksander and living that life, I can deal with anything. But as soon as Konstandin mentioned Jet, it was like I unraveled.

This is why I didn't want Jet here. Having a vulnerability that huge makes the target on my back that much bigger. And the last thing I need is to encourage people to take shots at me.

People like Rose.

I down the rest of my drink and take another drag off my cigarette.

Dealing with Rose is doable. But first, I have to survive him.

You've survived worse, Kat. You can do this.

My phone rings, and I answer it immediately when I see Genti's name. "He's here. He just killed Altin and left a hole in my fucking arm."

Shit!

Genti insisted on being the first line of defense outside, knowing that Rose would be coming for me since we killed his men. I had confidence he could handle anything Rose brought, and I assured him *I* can handle it, too. That may have been an overstatement.

The call only gives me a brief moment to prepare. Enough time to finish my cigarette and stamp it out before the door flings open and bangs against the wall violently. Agon must be dead in the hall, too, to have let Rose get this far.

Rose flies in, a tempest of fury. His wild, dark eyes sweep over the room frantically. One hand holds his gun; the other he fists, his knuckles white. His gaze finally finds me, and his lips twist into a sneer. He issues a low, deep growl that rumbles across the room to send a shiver through me.

It's the only warning I get before he comes for me.

SIX

I BRACE myself for what's coming, steel my body and wrap my soul in an extra layer of *don't give a fuck* protection so there's no chance Rose will get anything that happened tonight out of me. No chance I'll slip and come undone. No chance I'll let my biggest secret fall into the hands of this man.

Not even with fury and determination blazing in his eyes.

I will not cave.

When he reaches me, he wraps his strong hand around my throat and jerks me to my feet with enough power to force my breath from my lungs.

"Do you think this is a fucking joke, *mi cielo*?" His voice booms around the condo, reverberating off the high ceilings and hard floors. "Were you and Genti sitting here, laughing after you killed my men? After I trusted you and let you leave?"

Let me leave.

He sees nothing wrong with that statement when it's at the very heart of the matter. The way he thinks he can control me, claim me, bend me to his will. Rose has convinced himself he did it because he was trying to protect me from whoever sabotaged the plane, but in reality, he was doing it because he craves that power over me.

Maybe he *needs* it.

But I need to retain it more.

I swallow, and the pressure of his palm pushing against my windpipe sends a shudder through me. But it isn't from fear, and I don't blink or look away from him. You give this man an inch and he'll take a mile and stretch that into a thousand.

"It's not a joke, Rose. Far from it. And I'm not a woman you can control. If you think I am, then I have somehow managed to give you the wrong fucking impression."

He glares at me, rage setting his almost black eyes aflame. He tightens his grip and backs me up until my knees hit the chair, then leans over me, forcing my back to arch. "You killed my men."

"No. I ordered Genti to do it."

"Fucking semantics." He practically spits the words at me, the rage making his body shake more than mine was only moments ago. "I just took out two of yours as repayment, and I only left Genti alive as a warning. Don't play *this* game with me. I told you I wasn't playing any game with *you*, so why do you insist on doing it?"

I still don't believe for a second that Rose doesn't have *some* game. This man may claim to be a straight-shooter with no hidden agenda, but men like Rose don't play fair. If they did, they'd never get anywhere.

"No game, Rose." Truly. I didn't have Genti kill Rose's men as some sort of power play. It was just a necessity. "I wasn't going to let your men follow me around forever to appease your need to keep me on a fucking leash. Every man who has ever tried to control me is dead. That should be a lesson to you."

His dark eyebrows fly up. "Are we back to threatening each other, *mi cielo*? I thought we were past that."

"Yet you say that with your hand around my throat."

He squeezes tightly, restricting my ability to pull in a deep breath. His gaze locked on mine. We play a game of chicken. Neither of us willing to budge. Neither of us willing to break.

My head starts to spin from the lack of oxygen. Darkness starts to seep into the edges of my vision. He holds me here for a moment, allowing me just enough air that I don't pass out fully, keeping me hanging on that edge.

But I won't flinch away from him. I won't give him the satisfaction of clawing at his hand or begging him to release me.

He'll do it on his own when he realizes I'm never going to cave. Unless he really wants me dead...

Rose may call me his heaven. He may swear he's trying to protect me. He may swear none of this is about anything more than wanting to be together—personally and professionally. But it all could be one massive act with an endgame I can't see.

My lust for him, for his strength, his power...it may be my downfall. After everything I've done and been through to bring me to this point, it may be my traitorous body that does me in.

I never should have given in to my attraction to him in the first place. That's clear...even now, as my body heats with his threatening hand around my neck, even as it remembers the way it felt to have him inside me, even more so now.

This couldn't be more dangerous to my life or my heart. And as the world continues to darken around me, my biggest regret is not knowing if Jet will be safe.

But Rose slightly releases the pressure on my throat, just enough for me to draw in a tiny breath. Then another. And another. Until I can finally find my voice again.

"I don't know what it is you want from me, Rose. But if it's my submission, you're not going to get it. I will not have you or your men following me around and watching my every move. I will not follow your commands as if I'm a fucking dog and you're my master. You may have the upper hand with a lot of people, but with me, you're on a level playing field. And you'll have to accept that."

Rose shoves me back into the chair and drops a knee between my spread legs, lowering his face only inches above mine. He isn't just angry about the death of his men; he's angry that I'd fight him if he tries to push this any further. He's not used to being challenged, at least not in any way that really means anything, and anyone who ever has challenged him probably finds their way to the end of a bullet.

His warm breath tinged with the scent of strong liquor floats over my face as he brushes his lips gently over mine—a move that's more dangerous than his hand against my neck. "This is what you want? For us to be on opposite sides? For us to play a game? For us to go back to being enemies?" His brow furrows as if he's genuinely confused by what's happening between us. "Did nothing change in the last week? Was it all an act?"

Isn't everything?

My entire life has been an act since Aleksander died and I knew what I had to do. First, because I was a grieving widow with a secret. It wasn't hard to avoid contact with anyone. I locked myself away, not only to hide my fear of what might be coming for me because of what the Dragon did but also to hide my pregnancy. Then, by the time I made it to Europe and had my plan in mind, there was no one there who knew me, and it was easy for me to disappear to Albania and become someone else with the help of those Aleksander still trusted. I gave birth, handed over my son, and tried to pretend like it never happened. I changed my name, my background, even my damn eye color. I changed it all. Changed who and what I am.

All of it was an act—one that broke me little by little, day by day until I'm nothing left but these shattered pieces of a person I can never be again. The pieces of Brynn that I've tried to glue back together as Kat, that are hopefully stronger, braver, and more ready for a fight than that innocent girl on the pole who locked eyes with the Dragon ever was.

Now those precariously placed parts are threatening to shatter again because I feel more for this man than just hatred. My body longs for his. My heart aches, trying to force him out. But there's just something about Rose that keeps drawing me in. Something that makes me weak around him. Something that I can't let him see.

"I didn't make you any promises, Rose, and I never would. If that's what you're waiting for from me, Hell will freeze over before you get it."

He flinches at my words, almost as if I physically struck him. It's the last response I expect to see from him. He's shown more vulnerability to me in the last few days than he has to anyone in the years he's been embroiled in the underworld here.

Even before he came to Chicago, he was known as a steely, unmovable force—one who struck with brutality and wrath against anyone who dared stand in his path of becoming head of the most powerful cartel in South America.

Yet *my* words hurt him. Which means I'm further under his skin than I ever thought.

I slide out my tongue to wet my dry lips, and his eyes follow the movement.

He shifts his knee forward until it presses against my bare pussy, his hard cock pushed against my stomach. The hand with the gun comes up to press the muzzle to my temple. "I should kill you right here, right now, for what you did to my men. For lying to me."

It won't surprise me if he does.

Then a long, slow breath escapes him, a resignation. "But I'm not going to. Because for some insane reason, the fact that you defy me turns me the fuck on more than anything I've ever experienced in my entire life." He brushes his thumb over my windpipe. "You're a dangerous woman, Kat."

More fucking dangerous than he knows.

SEVEN

AT THIS POINT, I have everything to lose. That makes me the most dangerous I've ever been.

Konstandin threatened Jet, and I can't let the supposed truce allow me to believe the only person who matters to me anymore is truly safe.

Like Rea, when she killed Aleksander, Konstandin has unleashed a mother bear willing to do whatever it takes to protect her son. That includes making sure Rose isn't a threat to him.

That means not allowing Rose to get any closer. If he manages to weasel his way in deeper, I have to do whatever must be done. Even if it means starting a war with the cartel by dropping him the way I did Michael.

But the way he's looking at me now, he's only a moment away from making a decision that's he's been on the edge about.

I press my hands against his chest. "Kill me or fuck me. Either way, do it fast."

My words light a fire in Rose, one that blackens his gaze and singes me where his hand still wraps around my neck. "If that's the way you want it, *mi cielo*, I can make both happen." He drops his gun onto the side table and slips his hand between us to cup my wet pussy. "But I won't let you die without getting you off first like you did with Michael. I'm not that cruel."

Isn't he, though?

The man was after me for months, before he even knew who I was, and when he learned the truth of what I was capable of, he only pursued me harder. He inserted himself into my life and my business, he took care of me, and he held me hostage. That's the definition of cruelty. He just hasn't taken it as far as I did with Michael. Yet...it seems that's very much still on the table.

He releases his hold on me and frees his hard cock, taking it in his hand with determination, setting his lips into a hard line. This man doesn't know gentle. He doesn't know soft. He doesn't understand what it is to love someone else and have them love you in return. And that's okay. Because I don't want his love. Not now. Not ever.

I just want *him*. No...*need* him. To fill the void that feels like it's been ripped open inside me by Konstandin's threat. To make me forget for one damn moment that everything is falling apart. All my best-laid plans are crumbling. But he can hold me together for one damn night.

He leans over me, aligning his cock and angling me back so he can glide into me on one single drive of his hips. He bottoms out inside me, and I release a gasp he catches in his mouth.

Stealing my breath isn't his only goal, though. He's here to punish me, and the rhythm he sets ensures I'll be feeling him for days if he lets me live that long.

Every thrust of his cock seems to drive deeper inside me. Like he's searching for something there.

My fears.

My plans.

My dreams.

My soul.

And I don't care. Right now, I'm ready to give it all to him if he'll just take away my pain and the torture that's been making me shake.

He can have my body. He can pound into me. He can devastate me. As long as I get that one minute. That precious moment when I can hang in that sweet state of bliss before it all crashes down around me again.

There isn't a slow build. No buzz and heat growing within me over time. This isn't meant to be long, drawn-out torture. Quite the opposite. This is designed to show me what Rose can give me and what he can take quickly.

And it comes hard and fast.

Each press of his cock into me ratchets me so tight that my body shatters, my limbs shaking as I cling to him to keep from being blown away completely.

He comes inside me on a roar and digs his fingers into my thighs hard enough to leave bruises. Another way of marking me. Of showing me that he owns me.

Or at least, he thinks he does.

Rose drags his head back and captures my chin in his hand. "I'm not done with you yet. I'm taking you to the bedroom."

I catch my breath enough to form the words I need him to hear. "If you aren't going to kill me, then leave."

His dark brows drop low over his eyes menacingly. "Defying me again, *mi cielo?*"

Defiance.

That word meant something so different to me only a few years ago, before I truly understood violence and power. Before I comprehended what goes on in the dark underworld the rest of humanity likes to pretend doesn't exist.

In *this* world, defiance means death.

But to bend to him, to give in and let him twist me into what he desires would be the ultimate death of Kat. It would mean throwing away everything I've sacrificed.

And I refuse to do that.

Perhaps Felipe was right in what he said. Maybe I am a threat to Rose and Sofia. Not because I have actual plans to harm or kill them but because I am opening up a chink in Rose's armor. I am exposing a weakness he never had before or at least never let anyone see.

I *am* a danger to Rose, just not in the way he thinks. "You shouldn't expect it any other way, Rose. I will always defy you, and if you know what's good for you, you'll leave."

He pulls his cock from me and stands, leaving me splayed out on the chair, still panting with the evidence of our violent fuck dripping from me. "I'm not going anywhere, *mi cielo.*"

"Yes, you are." I reach onto the end table beside the chair and grab the gun Rose was stupid enough to leave there. "Get the fuck out of my place. And don't come back unless and until you're invited."

Which won't be anytime soon.

His lips tilt into a grin, and he tucks himself back into his pants with a chuckle. "I have to say, Kat. You always manage to keep things interesting. Though, I would much have preferred for us to climb into bed together tonight to finish what we just started, I'll respect your request and leave." He turns toward the door but pauses and looks back at me over his shoulder. "For now. But I'll be back, and we'll have another discussion about what you did to my men and why."

There isn't anything to discuss. I wasn't about to allow him to treat me like a petulant child, a pet, or something he owned. It was the quickest way for him to comprehend where *I* stand.

And now he knows.

He offers me one final look before slipping out the door as fast as he came. I sag back into the chair and drop the gun next to me so I can lower my head into my hands.

The smell of booze, cigarette smoke, and sex fills my nose, but there isn't any time to concern myself with the meaning of what just went down.

Not when so much is at stake.

There are things to be done. Important things.

EIGHT

"So, Konstandin Morina just showed up at the church?" Arden's wide eyes demonstrate his disbelief at what I've just told him and match how I still feel about the entire situation.

I nod slowly and lean back in my chair. "I wouldn't have believed it if I hadn't experienced it myself."

Konstandin never had to show his face again. He has the means and knowledge to disappear forever. He could have hidden from me until the day I died. Yet, he *chose* not to. He chose to take a chance that meeting with me could end the war.

Arden shakes his head. "After all this time hiding. Just wow."

"I know."

"If he was just in town last night, that should make him a lot easier to track."

Exactly.

Even after everything that went down with Rose last night after my run-in with Konstandin, I was still able to get my shit together enough to know Arden might be able to take the fact that Morina was here and use it to our advantage.

"That was my thought and the reason I wanted to meet with you right away today. Though we have agreed to a truce, that doesn't mean I don't want to keep an eye on him just like he is me. I want you to find him and Rea and anything you can about their son."

I'm not about to spill to Arden about Jet, but I need to get some leverage over Konstandin. If he knows where my son is—at least until I can figure out a way to move him somewhere else safely —I sure as *hell* plan on knowing where his kid is at all times, too.

And knowing family is often an Achilles heel reminds me to ask Arden about something that's been nagging at me. "Did you ever talk to Konstandin's sister?"

Arden nods. "She's always been on my radar since Michael had me start looking for Konstandin, but I'm pretty confident she hasn't had any contact with him in years. It looks like after the Morinas took down the Sylas, she changed her name and got married and had a family of her own— totally out of the Morina family business and disconnected from that world. I haven't found any indication that she had contact with Tarek or Konstandin after that."

I drum my nails on the desk and mull over the options. "I want someone on her."

He raises an eyebrow. "You're going to go after his sister?"

It's cold. I know that, but if he has eyes on Jet, then I need eyes on something that's just as important to him. And if I can't find where he's hiding with Rea and his son, his sister and her children will have to be the next best option.

Just in case this entire thing is some sort of act. Though...I doubt that.

Last night, Konstandin showed me something I doubt many other people have ever seen. He let me see that he's human.

It was the same way with Aleksander. To everyone else, he was the Dragon—a single-minded monster with no soul—but to me, he was the man who saved me and who filled my heart with more love and affection than I thought possible. He was certainly hard and brutal, and it wasn't hearts-and-flowers romance, but he took care of me the only way he knew how.

And now, I need to protect his son the only way I know how.

"Just stay on her. But tell them to remain inconspicuous and not to make any moves until they hear from me directly."

If Konstandin gets wind I have someone on her, any peace we may have managed to broker last night will be in the wind.

Arden nods his understanding. "Got it. What about Felipe?"

The second of the three men who rattled my night...

I lean forward and rest my elbows on the desk, but I'm too antsy to keep sitting. And I need a damn cigarette. I grab my pack, pull one out, light it, and bring it to my lips to inhale as I push to my feet to pace around my office.

Last night didn't just wring me out emotionally; my body still feels everything Rose did to me. A very real physical reminder that things are not as simple as they once were. My plan is diverging, and what is happening now is something I could never have anticipated because I never thought Rose would get under my skin...or weasel his way inside my heart. It makes things far more complicated and makes me want to unravel what he's hiding even more.

Starting with Felipe—his tattooed carbon copy.

"We know more now than we did. He's a priest. That means there has to be records of seminary and potentially where he came from before that."

Arden nods slowly and taps his fingers on the notebook on his lap. "I haven't been able to find anything on the name 'Felipe' as it connects to the Rose Cartel, but this definitely gives me another avenue to pursue."

I wouldn't have expected him to find anything. Felipe has been well-hidden for a long time and separated himself from what his brother does. He wouldn't want to be connected in any way, and Rose would have ensured he eliminated anything that could link them—or at least tried to.

My heels click on the floors, and I take another drag off my cigarette, then blow the smoke up in a ring toward the still unfinished ceiling. "I want to know everything." I cross my arms over my chest and tap my foot. "Where he was born. Where he grew up. Where he took his first shit. Where he went to school. How he ended up in the priesthood. Everything."

Arden inclines his head. "That shouldn't be too hard to find now that we have the church connection. It'll give us a last name, and that's at least somewhere to start."

"If he even used his real last name." I wouldn't put it past Rose to have ensured Felipe used a false one just in case he was ever discovered and connected to Rose. If anyone who had ever seen Rose saw Felipe, it would be immediately apparent they're twins, and if they had Felipe's real name, they would have Rose's—something he has bent over backward to protect for so damn long.

"We have to assume it wouldn't be real, not if he were worried about protecting his family from being linked to him. But I think I can backtrack him."

"I sure as hell hope so since that's what I pay you for."

And if he can't do it, I'll find someone else who can.

NINE

ARDEN HAS the intelligence to look properly chastised. After working for Michael and seeing what he was capable of and knowing how easily I shot his cousin in the head in this very room, he should be worried when he keeps failing to get me what I need.

He raises his hands. "I swear. I'm doing everything I can. Running down every damn lead."

I return to my desk to snuff out my cigarette. "On the topic of Felipe, we still have no word from Rowan?"

Arden shakes his head. "No. She hasn't responded to the text message from her friend at Kat's Cradle, and she hasn't turned on her phone, so I haven't been able to track it."

Shit.

I return to pacing around the office, turning over the complicated web I can't seem to unravel involving Rose, Felipe, and Rowan. "I know Felipe has her stashed somewhere, but the question is why."

What would a Catholic priest want with one of my women? Why come to the brothel and spook her like that? And why keep her hidden?

"Do you think she's okay?"

"Probably." But there isn't really any way of knowing for sure unless we can find her.

Felipe didn't strike me as the type who would hurt a woman. I don't know what purpose it would serve. Rowan is nobody. Just a girl I found who had been brought into the country by dubious means and who needed a job and help establishing herself here legally. I got her set up, and she was a good worker—one of my best, actually. And she seemed happy...until Felipe showed up.

Could it really be as simple as him wanting to appeal to some sort of worry for her eternal soul? A reproach of what she was doing to support herself?

I doubt it. If that were the case, he would've tried to talk to the other women, too, and convince them to leave. But he never approached anyone else. He never made a move to try to talk to anyone about leaving, even Amber, who he had direct contact with.

His focus was clear. On *one* woman. There's something about Rowan. Something special. Something I need to know.

"Keep looking for her, and the second you hear anything on any of these matters, literally *anything*, you let me know."

He clears his throat. "Um...about that..."

"Yes?"

He rubs the back of his neck and avoids eye contact. "Well, I'm just wondering where you're going to be?"

"What do you mean?"

"Um, well, where can I find you if I uncover something urgent? Are you going to be back here once they finish this construction, or at Kat's Cradle, or is this thing with you and Rose going to become something permanent?"

My first instinct is to grab my gun from the desk and shoot Arden in the fucking head for even asking. It's none of his business who I fuck or where I decide to spend my time or lay my head at night, let alone whether it will continue.

Yet, that's the ultimate question, isn't it?

It's one I've been asking myself for weeks, and that hasn't stopped rattling around in my brain since what happened last night. The last thing I wanted was to develop any sort of feelings for Rose other than hate, but it happened all the same. Slowly. Against my best efforts otherwise. It happened.

Somehow, I care. I enjoy the push and pull between us. The hate and lust that combine into such a violent collision every time we're together. He may be ruthless, cunning, and deadly, but he has shown me there's so much more there hidden beneath the perfectly polished rock-hard surface.

He believes he's protecting me. He believes he's offering me a partnership that will be beneficial for us both. He believes in what we can accomplish together. I no longer doubt that. It doesn't mean he doesn't still have some ulterior motive, too, but it's wrapped in sincerity.

It makes the entire thing impossible to sort through in my head. "I don't know, Arden. But it's none of your fucking concern. Get the fuck out."

Before I lose my cool and pull the trigger.

He scrambles to his feet and rushes out the door without looking back at me, but before I can close it, Genti steps in.

I sigh and rub my eyes. "What is it?"

I'm not sure I can deal with any more today. Mental and physical exertion are taking their toll on me. I'm reaching my breaking point. And judging by the look on Genti's face, it seems something else is about to be dropped on my shoulders.

"Esad called. He's going to be docking in a few days."

"Perfect."

Some good news for once. Actual progress. With the next shipment of girls arriving and an offer in on a third house, things are at least moving along smoothly on that front. It means taking the next step in my plan, the thing I've been waiting for. Biding my time has been pure torture, but this move will rattle Chicago enough that I'll be able to secure a stranglehold on the city.

I return to my chair and grab another cigarette from my pack. "And what about the other thing I asked you to do?"

Genti glances out the door to ensure no one's there, then closes it behind him. "It's doable, but it's going to be harder than we thought."

All I needed to hear was that it's doable. From this point forward, there's no going back. This is the time where I'll sink or swim.

I light up and take a drag, then nod at him before I release the smoke from my lungs. "Get whatever you need lined up. Expense means nothing. I want it done at the earliest possible opportunity."

A slow grin spreads across his lips. "I have some good news on that front. We won't have to wait long."

I match his smile and lean back in the chair. My body finally relaxes slightly—though whether it's from the nicotine now coursing through my system or the fact that things are falling into place isn't clear.

But I can't let the good news overshadow the bad. Jet is in danger, whether Konstandin abides by our truce or not. I need a way to protect him. One that will ensure I won't ever find myself in the position of having to back down again in order to keep him from harm. And right now, I can't come up with a solution that doesn't involve telling people about him who I don't want to know.

Something needs to present itself soon, or I won't be sleeping at night, thinking of all the possible ways things can go wrong. All the people who could get hurt because of the decisions I made that I thought would protect them.

With so many balls in the air, things are starting to get complicated, but I've learned to thrive under stress. It's become necessary. And I'll figure something out.

There isn't any other choice.

TEN

ANOTHER LIGHT DRIZZLE falls on the city of Chicago as I stand under the protective overhang of the warehouse, watching Esad's ship pull into the dock.

It always seems to be shit weather when I have to be outside like this. Almost as if God is judging me. Trying to send me a message He can't do in any other way. A reminder that my life is a storm of lies, deceit, and sin that can't be washed away no matter how hard he tries. As if the visions of Michael and Aleksander that haunt me—waking and asleep—aren't enough.

Yet, if I were able to stand inside that church with Konstandin and not be struck down right then and there by the mighty power of God, then the big man upstairs must have something else in mind for me.

Though perhaps He just enjoys torturing me, keeping me in a purgatory of my own making for as long as possible. Questioning all the things I've done. Wondering if I've made mistakes I can't correct.

Like leaving Jet...

He's safe—for the moment. But I can't assume he will stay that way. It means I'll have to bring someone in to help. Someone I can truly trust.

Too bad I don't have that.

But I can't go home and move him on my own. I'm not inconspicuous anymore. And if I bring him here, he's only going to get caught in the crossfire.

Maybe the rain is a reminder that my past may drown me. It may already be. A shudder rolls through my body. Since that night at the church, I can't seem to stay warm. An ominous chill has settled over me—made worse by the inclement weather—and it feels like I'm treading water, being dragged down, unable to take a deep breath.

Anxiety like this hasn't ruled me since Aleksander saved me from Terrance. Standing up to him and being with him gave me the strength to overcome my own weaknesses, yet they're all rearing their ugly heads at the same time now. Most of all...guilt.

There isn't any time for it.

Not now. Not when I'm on the precipice of taking a step that will finally set in motion things that have been coming since the day I set foot back in Chicago as Kat.

So, I need to ignore everything else going on and focus on what this boat arriving and what my men will be doing tonight mean. The *good* things they mean.

Keep it together, Kat. Just a little while longer...

An engine roars behind us, and Genti and I turn toward the sound, both of us ready to draw our weapons if needed. This is the place Michael was attacked—the perfect place to stage one, really. Secluded and desolate, especially this time of night in this type of storm. No one would find us until morning, long after any evidence of the perpetrators of any attack was washed away.

A black SUV pulls up alongside the two vans Driton and Agon wait in to take the girls to the house when they unload from the ship. Genti narrows his eyes on the vehicle as the back door opens and Cutter slips out. Despite the dark of night and the falling rain, those damn aviators still adorn his face, a mask he wears—though whether it's to protect others from seeing his injuries or to protect himself isn't clear.

If he's anything like me, it's a little of both.

What does he look like under them?

Considering what I have seen of the scars on his neck and face, it sure as hell isn't pretty. I can only imagine what must be hidden behind the shades besides an angry man with violent tendencies who is willing to do anything for the woman carrying his child.

What would Aleksander have been like as a father?

I've asked myself the question so many times since the moment I realized I was pregnant. I cried and worried about his reaction, debated how to tell him, put it off...until it was too late. He was gone so fast that I never got to know whether he would have responded with joy or fear, anger or elation. All I have is fantasies of seeing the Dragon hold his son. Those dangerous, volatile hands capable of such violence with a tiny, completely dependent person cradled in them.

My chest tightens, and I have to swallow through the lump in my throat to try to push away the emotion.

Cutter reaches into the car, pops open an umbrella, and helps Valentina climb out.

Just what I didn't need. Another unexpected meeting with a "friend."

Genti glances at me, his heavy brow furrowed with concern. "Were you expecting them?"

I shake my head and check the boat's progress. Normally, I wouldn't take my eyes off a potential threat, but something tells me they're here for another reason. "No. But if they were here with ill intent, we'd probably be dodging bullets right now."

"Good point."

They walk toward us through the rain, Valentina as elegant as ever in high heels despite her condition.

Those days weren't so long ago for me. I remember them well, despite my best efforts to shove all that into the darkest recesses of my mind. How uncomfortable I was. How miserable it was knowing that I would have to give up the baby. But I shake my head to clear away those memories. If I don't, I'm liable to get lost in them.

I raise an eyebrow as they approach. "You checking up on me?"

Valentina shakes her head and glances toward the boat inching its way toward the dock. "Checking up on *them*. I wanted to make sure what you said was true and that every single one of these girls is here of their own free will."

She and Cutter come to stand at my side under the overhang. He collapses the umbrella and leans back against the building, crossing his arms over his barrel chest but never taking his focus off Genti or me.

I fight the smirk pulling at my lips. "You don't trust me?"

Cutter snorts. "Not after what you did to the last guy."

Valentina chuckles, ignoring his comment, and rests a hand on her belly watching the ship. "You forced me into agreeing to this. It doesn't mean I have to like it. But it does mean that I'm going to keep a very close eye on you, just like I do with Rose."

Shit.

The way she says it has me turning my head toward her.

Could she know about us? Or is this just a fishing expedition since we're here on the dock?

She raises a perfectly shaped eyebrow at me but doesn't say anything else. The minuscule body movement is enough to get her point across. The woman knows something.

I do my best not to flinch under her assessment and stand my ground, never breaking eye contact. "Is there something I should know about Rose?"

"You tell me." She waves a hand in my direction. "I heard the two of you had an unexpected landing in the Northwoods."

Fuck.

I guess there was no way we could keep it a secret forever. Genti has had enough trouble dodging the authorities and NTSB investigation of the crash. It was only a matter of time before someone connected us to it and got wind of who was really on that plane.

Valentina offers me a cool smile. "I'm happy to see you in one piece."

Lie.

Though I don't blame her. I would feel the same way if the roles were reversed. Losing her in a tragic "accident" would help clear the way for me. The same is true if I had perished along with Rose. She would have lost two competitors. Two people who twisted her arm into partnerships she despises. It would have been a huge win for her.

Perhaps an opportunity she couldn't pass up.

ELEVEN

"WERE YOU RESPONSIBLE FOR THAT?" If she were watching Rose that closely, perhaps she figured out where we were and arranged for our "accident."

It would make sense. She's wanted Rose out of her territory from the moment she made her deal with him, and she definitely never wanted this agreement with me. But she would have had to have people in place in Winnipeg already or been able to get wheels up and people there *fast*.

Cutter snorts again and shakes his head. "If it had been us, I would've made sure no one walked away from the crash."

I don't doubt that. He doesn't seem like the kind of man who fails often. Especially when it comes to killing. It wasn't them who tried to kill us. Yet, Valentina's comment about Rose held an underlying question and subtle threat.

"What is it you want, Valentina?"

She shrugs nonchalantly and watches the ship finally dock while one of the men runs forward to help tie it up. "I want to know who I'm in bed with." Her head turns so her eyes bore into mine. "And who I'm in bed with is in bed with."

Cutter steps forward, placing himself between us. "What was Rose doing on your plane?"

I don't owe them any explanations, but if I want to keep things amicable between us, I need to quell any suspicions they may have. "It isn't what you think." *At least...it wasn't at that time.* "He barged his way on and insisted on coming with me."

Valentina glances at Genti. "And you just let him?"

Genti growls at my side—angered by the jab at his ability to do his job and keep me safe. "The fucker was already on the plane when we got there with two of his men. There wasn't much we could do."

Cutter chuckles and shrugs nonchalantly. "I would've killed those fuckers."

My second in command casts a dirty look at him. "I would have liked to see you try in those circumstances and walk away yourself. But don't worry, I did kill them. It just took a little bit longer than I wanted."

Genti savored the chance to off them after what they did, leaving him at the crash site. It was a small victory and chance to act on his wrath.

Valentina raises an eyebrow. "So, you're killing Rose's men now? He can't be too happy about that."

Our confrontation the other night flits through my head.

The anger.

The violence.

The scorching-hot sex.

I shift on my feet to help dissipate the throb between my legs that reminds me just how incredible it really was. "He wasn't. But I'm not about to let any man, especially one like Rose, dictate how I live my life or how I run my business."

Valentina offers a hint of a genuine smile. "I appreciate that about you. Though we are rivals and certainly have conflicting interests in a lot of matters, it's nice to have another woman in charge. One who doesn't take shit from anyone."

I might have agreed that was true a few days ago, but after my conversation with Konstandin,

I'm not so sure anymore. Not after what I did. I backed down from him, from my ultimate goal to avenge what was done to Aleksander.

What does that make me?

Weak.

The word echoes in my head, only it isn't my own voice saying it—it's Aleksander's. I used to pray and beg to hear him one more time, but not like this. Just another form of punishment, I guess. Something I'll have to learn to live with.

I incline my head toward Valentina. "I appreciate the compliment."

Her features harden. "Don't expect too many other ones."

"Fair enough."

Getting too friendly with your rivals only leads to crossing lines that should be drawn heavy and kept high. I've already crossed too many to make the mistake of toeing one with Valentina.

Genti motions toward the ship, and we all turn our attention to the reason we're here tonight. The gangway is lowered to the dock, and Esad steps off and trudges down it toward us. Genti rests his hand near his weapon—ready if Michael's best friend decides he's finally ready to end this partnership and seek retribution for what I did. But he ambles over to us and inclines his head toward Valentina and Cutter.

"Kat..." He reaches into his back pocket, pulls out a bundle of papers, and hands them to Genti. "Passport and identity information for each girl. No problems. Everyone is in good health."

I smile at the man who is helping one of my visions become a reality. "Thank you, Esad."

Without a word, he turns and walks back to the boat. I'll never expect that man to enjoy being in business with me—the woman who murdered his best friend in cold blood—but he isn't about to turn down the money I've offered him or ignore the fact that telling me no would move him right up to the top of my hitlist.

Valentina watches closely as the women gather together in the rain on the deck, ready to descend the ramp and to their new lives working for me in my brothel. Like the first group of women I brought over before getting involved with Michael, they all look lost, like they're searching for something, somewhere to belong. I'll give them that place. That purpose.

Others may frown upon what I do, on what *they* do, but these women provide a precious commodity. Taking advantage of others' lust doesn't make them bad people; it makes them *smart*.

"You don't have to worry, Valentina. They're here willingly. That was one thing I would never tolerate. Even Aleksander wouldn't have."

Cutter shakes his head and scoffs. "I find that hard to believe. That man was a monster."

Forcing women into sexual slavery is something that wouldn't have flown in Aleksander's empire. And it won't in mine. It was one of the assurances I asked my contacts in Albania to confirm before Esad ever brought the girls onto that ship.

I turn my head and ensure Cutter's looking me directly in the eye even though I can't see his behind the shades. "Even monsters have weaknesses, Cutter. You should remember that."

It's meant as a threat and a warning, and the way his scarred lip curls up ensures me he got the message loud and clear.

I motion toward the girls starting to file down the ramp. "If you want to speak with them individually, go ahead, but I don't want them spending time out in this weather. We'll have to step inside."

Valentina glances between them and me and shakes her head. "That won't be necessary. I just wanted to see everything with my own eyes."

"Are you satisfied?"

She doesn't answer, which is as much of one as if she'd said the words. Turning to Cutter, she motions for him to open the umbrella, and they walk away without a look back.

I understand her response and know exactly what she means. Because I feel the same way. She'll never be satisfied, just like I won't be satisfied until she's out of the picture. Until the Russians and the Irish are gone, too. Until I'm the one in complete control of the city.

But that leaves the question of Rose and what to do about the cartel. That's one I haven't allowed myself to explore too deeply, or I might not like the answer I find. Those lines I've crossed have made things fuzzy. Nothing is crystal clear like I once thought it was and always believed it would remain.

This business twists you and blinds you. It does it to everyone.

I incline my head toward the vans. "Make sure the girls get into the vans safely. I'll wait in the car, and we'll meet them at the new house."

Genti nods, and we make our way across the damp pavement in stoic silence.

One more step forward. A small one. But other things are happening tonight, things that have been a long time coming. And I am more than ready for them to reach my desired end.

TWELVE

Lying in bed alone with the sound of the rain outside pounding down on the roof filling the room, a cold shiver rolls through me, spreading goose bumps across my skin.

These are the kind of nights Aleksander would come home, slide into bed with me, and pull me tightly into his arms. Warm and secure in the arms of a man many believed to be the Devil himself.

I never asked where he'd been. I never questioned what he'd been doing or why. And I knew if he went to the shower before coming to the bedroom...it was a bad night.

Or a good one...depending on how one looked at it. Bad for whoever crossed him, but good for the man who held me. Because Aleksander *needed* that. He *needed* to be the Dragon.

Whatever it was inside him, whatever he was born with that made him crave maiming and destroying everyone in his path, was a hungry beast, barely constrained under the best of circumstances. And just like the dragons of old legends, if it weren't fed properly, he would unleash his wrath on those around him. On the unsuspecting townsfolk. His loyal employees. Anyone within arm's reach. But never, never, *never* on me.

He wouldn't. He *couldn't*.

The Dragon was my protector. My safety. My solace. And that makes these nights the loneliest. The hardest. The ones where the struggle and the desire to end it all and join him wherever he may be, call to me the most. The times I see his face and hear his voice and wonder how it all went so damn wrong.

But I don't let those thoughts or feelings overwhelm me. I can't. Because I made a promise to him over his grave. A vow to seek retribution. To set in motion what he always wanted. To hold in the palm of my hand the thing he craved—this entire city under Gashi control.

And I'm so close to achieving it. So close, yet so, so far away.

One big step was taken tonight. One giant bloody step. But there are others in the way, and there will be those who seek revenge. It's the way this game is played.

I'm not afraid, though. Because I've played well. A master level, really. My coup over Michael proves that.

What happened tonight will forge the way forward—one bloody step at a time.

My phone dings, and I roll onto my side to grab it from the nightstand and glance at my messages.

DONE.

One simple word but the only one I needed to hear.

Despite the emotions warring inside me right now, a smile pulls at my lips as a relieved sigh escapes them. I set down my phone and relax back on the empty bed—the one I refused to share with Rose only a few nights ago.

I never thought I'd have another man in Aleksander's bed, and the thought of bringing him in here felt like driving a stake through all the love I had for the man who once held me here. A huge part of me thinks I might never be able to share this bed again, not in this place, the home I shared with Aleksander.

Why should I have happiness and contentment and safety again when he's lying cold in the ground? Why should I get any of that when I handed over our son to strangers to raise and walked away without looking back?

I don't deserve any of those things—*could* never deserve them. So even if Rose is the man who might be able to ease some of my pain, who might tug at my heart and could hold the potential to help pull me out of the dark place I reside, even if it's his touch I yearn for, all of it is wrong.

So wrong.

I can't give myself over to a man I don't know, a man who insists on talking in riddles and closing doors on my attempts to get in.

Yet did I really know Aleksander?

I knew what he *did*. Had heard the stories and the rumors well before I accepted the job at the club. I witnessed him drenched in the evidence of his brutality.

But that's different than truly *knowing* someone.

He kept me in the dark about so much at the beginning, tried to keep me in the dark about him and his life, his business, but by the time he died, he had opened up in ways I never expected, ways I'm sure he never did, either. Because deep down, he needed it. An outlet. Someone to talk to. A confidant he had one hundred percent faith in.

I long for that again, to be able to rely on someone else to help ease the burdens that weigh me down in this life, but it feels wrong for it to be with another man. Especially one who keeps so much back from me.

We all have our secrets. I have a living, breathing one on top of a huge pile of others, but the ones Rose keeps from me mean I can't trust him.

Something as basic as his name...

That thought lingers in my mind as the sweet relief of sleep starts to drag me under. It may not be Aleksander's warm embrace, but maybe knowing the mission this evening was a success will keep the nightmares at bay tonight. Maybe I won't be haunted by the Dragon, Michael, or Rose...or the sounds of a baby crying for his mother.

I'll never be that lucky.

I'll accept the welcoming darkness with the hope anyway...

But the clicks of the door to the condo opening and then closing jerk me up from the mattress. I rub at my eyes and slide open my bedside table to grab my gun.

Altin was at the door when I came in tonight, and he wouldn't come in unless it was an emergency or let anyone else in unless he was dead. Not after the kidnapping, attempt on my life, and after what went down with Rose the other night.

The weight of the gun, so familiar in my hand, helps keep it steady when it otherwise might waver, waiting for whatever is coming. With the door to my bedroom easing open, I slip my finger even closer to the trigger. The only thing that keeps me from unloading the magazine into the door swinging toward me is that it might be one of the men.

Though why they wouldn't call or text me to let me know they were coming in makes me dismiss that possibility almost immediately.

A dark figure appears in the doorway, but even with the lights off and the heavy rainclouds killing any moonlight that might've come into the room from the uncovered window, I would know the blistering heat of those eyes anywhere. One look is all it takes to send a fire roaring across my skin.

Rose steps forward, his hands raised in the air, close enough that I can finally see the grin twisting his lips. "I thought you might like some company tonight, *mi cielo*." He inclines his head toward the gun. "But the barrel of your Glock pointed at me suggests otherwise. Why don't you put it down now that you know it's me?"

I raise it from his chest up to his head. One should always aim for center mass to ensure the target goes down, but this close, there's no way I'm missing him no matter where I aim. And shooting someone in the face sends a real message. "Maybe I shouldn't because it *is* you."

"*Muy gracioso*, Kat." He smiles at me and inclines his head slightly. "You know, I got an interesting call while I was on my way over here."

"Oh, really?"

He shrugs slightly and lets his hands fall to his sides—a motion I don't miss since it brings one closer to where he keeps his gun. "Apparently, a group of heavily armed and well-trained men attacked one of Valerian's underground casinos...at the exact same time someone stole a shipment of weapons from the Irish and took out four of Galen's crew."

The almost awe with which he says it makes the extraordinary nature of what we managed to accomplish even more evident.

I try to remain impassive, though. "Simultaneous attacks. Impressive."

Rose takes another step toward the bed. "It is. They apparently left quite a river of blood in both places—one that will no doubt bring very serious retaliation on whoever it might've been who ordered it." He pauses for a moment, leveling his gaze on me. "That person better watch their back."

The threat isn't even veiled, and the challenge in his dark contemplation of me heats my blood, bringing forth the fire I've been trying to tamp down and douse whenever I'm around him.

But it's still there.

Blazing.

Searing.

Ready to burn him if he dares to touch me.

THIRTEEN

WE CERTAINLY DIDN'T LEAVE things on good terms the other night, and now he's here, uninvited after I just took major action against two of the families competing for control. He's right, too. Valerian Kamenev and Galen McGinnis won't let this aggression go unchecked.

I fight the urge to pull the trigger that would end whatever this is between us and make things so much simpler, and instead, I smile at him and nod. "I would think whoever did it should be watching their back quite carefully indeed."

He returns my smile and motions to the gun I still have pointed at him. "Now, Kat, are we really going to keep up this charade when we both know it was you?" One of his dark eyebrows wings up. "You and I are the only ones with enough balls to do something like that, and I sure as hell didn't do it. I've had other concerns occupying my focus."

I have to fight my lips threatening to spread into a grin at his compliment. He isn't a man who offers them easily, but I don't want to admit to him what I've done. The more he knows about my actions, the more he'll be able to anticipate my plans for the future, and he's still my biggest competitor.

My lack of response seems to amuse him, and he chuckles darkly. "Someone is making new enemies, Kat. I would think *you* have enough of those."

That's certainly true. Though, hopefully one less after my recent meeting. I haven't told Rose about Konstandin, and I have no intention of doing so. Just like Aleksander, I'm not confident Rose would understand backing down and letting Morina walk away.

I'm not so sure I made the right decision myself. And since Arden hasn't been able to pick up his trail, I may have blown any chance I might ever have to take him out.

Rose surges ahead, taking my silence as the admission it is. "If it was you, Kat, you're going to need all the allies you can muster."

Allies are fiction in this world. One that allows some to gain a false sense of security when they should be keeping their eyes open and guns loaded. It's one reason I refuse to bring on a partner. That, and the fact that I never thought I'd find anyone with the same drive and goals after I lost Aleksander. Someone who understood what it takes and isn't sidetracked by things like sentiment and conscience.

I square my shoulders and stare him down, ensuring he'll hear every word clearly. "This family has always acted alone, and it always will, Rose."

He snorts and takes another step closer until his knees bump the edge of the bed. "And look how well that worked out for your predecessors. Saban was beaten to death with a fucking lamp. Aleksander was shot in the head by Konstandin Morina. Erjon was strangled to death by a vengeful member of Valentina's crew. And then Michael was killed so callously in the very chair you now occupy..." His eyes darken as he leans in. "By a very cold and calculating woman. That isn't a great track record for going solo. That should tell you something."

"What? That I should partner with you?"

"I've made you an offer, Kat. You can't deny how good we are together." He climbs onto the bed, shifting closer to me on his knees until the barrel of my gun presses against his chest. "If you don't agree, then pull the trigger."

Holy hell.

I shake my head. "You don't mean that."

"I do, *mi cielo*. Our combined power can crush Valentina, Galen, Valerian, and anyone else who dares to stand in our way. We could rule more than just Chicago, take over the entire Midwest, put a stranglehold on the center of this great country."

One thing I can't deny is that Rose has ambition and drive as well as the cold brutality that might lead him to seduce me in order to get what he wants, the same way I did with Michael Syla.

But Rose's endgame isn't clear.

I had one with Michael, but I can't see one with this man who is willing to push himself against the muzzle of my Glock. If he wanted to kill me, he's had plenty of opportunities. I'm still not one hundred percent convinced he didn't stage the crash just so I'd let down my guard around him. The man seems capable of it. He's managed to hide a lot of things, so concealing his true motivations should be easy for him.

The only way I'll learn anything that might help me unravel his web is to take him off-guard. And I know just how to accomplish that.

"Speaking of enemies, has Sofia been able to find out anything about who sabotaged the plane?"

His dark eyebrows rise. "I'm not sure what you mean."

How cute that's he's trying to play dumb.

"I have it on good authority that she's your hacker and how you've managed to essentially disappear for so long."

A sly grin spreads across his lips, and he leans even closer. "Well, well, well, somebody's been busy. And I'm trying to figure out where you came across this information since the only people who know are Valentina and her crew. It makes me wonder if their lips aren't as tight as I thought they were."

I shrug nonchalantly, pressing the gun even more forcefully into his chest. "It wasn't Valentina or her crew."

"I question that, considering the little friendship the two of you have developed as of late."

I snort and release a mirthless laugh. "We most certainly aren't friends. She lets me use the docks because I have leverage, just like she only lets you sell in her territory because *you* had some."

"You may not be friends, but it sure seems like you're positioning yourself to become partners with the other most powerful woman in the city. Especially with your little stunt tonight. You're making moves. Ones that will require a strong partner."

"I told you, Rose. I don't do partners."

"We will see soon enough, *mi cielo*."

Despite the addition of the nickname he insists on using, his words hold a clear message—he is making moves, too. Ones that may bring me into the crossfire, or hell, maybe even square at the middle of the crosshairs. He isn't about to let me do anything that might interfere with his plans. His bid to get me to partner has a lot more to do with protecting his future than it does any future *we* might have together. This man has priorities, and I am not one of them, no matter what he may *want* me to believe.

The small flashes of humanity and weakness I've seen from him are likely all part of some elaborate game designed to get me to lower my guard...and my gun.

"My brother is playing a dangerous game with you, one that I fear could get him killed."

Felipe's warning rings loud in my ears. A man of God is telling me to stay away from his brother because he knows the life I've chosen is already the most dangerous possible. That should mean something. I should take it to heart, yet, Rose is here, straddling me, pressing his chest into the barrel of my gun willingly.

That does mean something. Though I have no fucking clue what. I never seem to know with Rose.

And that's precisely the problem.

He reaches down and cups my cheek in his right hand. The brush of his thumb over my skin sends a shiver of anticipation through me. His hand drifts down slowly, almost reverently, until it rests against my neck. That damn thumb glides across it, sending heat blazing through my body and making my pussy clench.

His eyes glow with dubious intent, and he tightens his hand.

It's a challenge.

He poses a very real threat, but all I have to do is move my finger a millimeter and pull the trigger to blast a massive hole in his chest. He's practically begging me to do it. Offering himself up on a silver platter.

This is it. My chance to remove my biggest competitor and the man who could suffocate me with the flex of a hand. So many have longed for a moment like this. It's one that doesn't usually come along. One any of the other heads of the families would take in a heartbeat.

All I have to do is pull the trigger...

FOURTEEN

THE LACK of fear in Rose's eyes should worry me.

Cold. Hard. Brutally sharp. His gaze could cut glass.

It's certainly cutting through me right now. Through all the walls I've tried to keep up. Through all the bullshit. Through the façade of Kat. He cuts straight down to who I was back then. That hurt, scared girl who woke in *this* bed and saw Aleksander. The girl who knew she should have been even more terrified of who she was looking at but instead felt a sense of comfort wash over her.

The girl who fell for the monster.

Rose wraps his free hand around the barrel of the gun and tugs it from my hand easily. I don't have any fight left in me. At least, not tonight.

He reaches into his waistband and removes his gun, too, and with the two weapons now on the nightstand, Rose crushes his lips to mine in a bruising kiss designed to send a message.

He knows.

The man *knows* I won't deny him. That I can't. That everything that tells me to push him away also pulls me to him. That my mind and my body are at war, and my mind is losing.

I've used lust against men for so long that I never thought I'd be the one to fall prey to it. But there's no denying I have. I embraced it, and now, Rose is seizing that weakness and using it to bend me to his will.

My body bows up toward his until his hard cock presses against the place I want it most. He groans into my mouth, his tongue dueling with mine. The two of us will always war for control, to be on top, to be the one calling all the shots.

It's just one of so many reasons this is a bad idea.

Including what I did tonight...

It did put new targets on my back, even if no one can ever confirm who orchestrated the attacks. They'll suspect me. They'll suspect Rose. With only two real possibilities, being with him like this ties me to him in a way that can't so easily be brushed under the rug or washed away.

People already suspect something is going on between us, and the longer *this* goes on, the stronger that connection and bond become—whether I like it or not.

Rose wants a partner, and by giving into lust, that's what I've made myself. There's no way to separate what happens on the streets and what happens in the bedroom. No way to keep him at arm's length in one place while simultaneously wrapping my arms and legs around him in another to drag him even closer.

But it isn't close enough. Not tonight.

I reach between us to fumble for his zipper, and he pulls back and starts unbuttoning his shirt. Before he can get the second button out, I abandon his pants and grasp his shirt, ripping it open in one swift, jerking motion. Buttons fly across the mattress and bounce onto the floor.

Rose's deep chuckle fills the room, the sound low and sultry. It goes straight between my legs, and my clit throbs. He swiftly undoes his pants and shoves them down, but I don't want to wait for him to get them off.

Our power play has left me panting and wet. Needy in a way I fucking hate. The only thing that will satisfy the desire clawing at my chest is Rose inside of me—right now.

I flip onto my hands and knees, offering up my bare pussy to him like it's on a silver fucking platter.

He growls low and smacks my ass before dragging me back against him. His hot skin hits mine, his cock brushing over where I need him most. Then his hand closes around my neck, and he angles my head back until my gaze meets his. He enters me hard, in one cruel thrust that rocks me forward. The hand at my throat is the only thing that keeps me from crashing into the headboard.

It's violent. It's harsh. It's rough and vicious.

Rose drives into me over and over again. His hand tightens on my throat with each thrust. The room spins, and the edges of my vision start to darken. My entire body vibrates. My lungs scream for air. My limbs shake. My pussy clamps around his dick, trying to keep it inside with every retreat.

The head of his cock drags against just the right spot, and my eyes drift closed, bright lights flashing against my lids. But my orgasm doesn't come. It just builds and builds.

Tighter.

Higher.

Harder.

The rougher Rose gets, the more I want it.

All of it.

The pleasure *and* the pain.

It almost feels like punishment. For all that I've done. For all that I plan to do. Past, present, and future sins. A penance being taken out on my body while my soul rips itself apart.

He plunges into me again. "Open your eyes, *mi cielo*."

I struggle to follow his strangled command, and when I do, the searing look that meets mine ignites something deep inside me. A cataclysm. A ferocious upheaval of everything building for so damn long. What once boiled deep beneath the surface unleashes in one massive wave of pleasure and agony. An orgasm that tears me apart. The only things holding me together are Rose's arms around me and his cock inside me.

He pushes in again, groaning as my pussy clutches and ripples around him, and then he drops his chest against my back and bites down on my collarbone. The sharp sting of pain releases something I haven't let happen in so damn long that I almost forgot what it was like. Tears trail down my cheeks and fall to the sheets. But he keeps going. Dragging out my orgasm and searching for his own, pushing me to liberate everything I've held inside.

And I do.

All of it.

It pours out of me as he pours into me, finally finding his own release while mine destroys me.

Rose collapses on top of me, the weight of his body crushing me into the mattress. My head turned to the side, his warm breath flutters against my neck and the hand still around my throat squeezes lightly.

He presses a kiss to the heated skin at the top of my spine and groans. "Isn't it better to be partners rather than enemies, *mi cielo*?"

It's a simple question. One I should be able to answer easily. But I can't seem to form coherent words. Like the rest of my body, my tongue doesn't seem to want to move or function.

Rose pushes up onto his elbow and stares down at me. The very real fear that he will see the evidence of my tears tightens my chest. If he sees, he'll know. He will understand what a broken mess I really am, and he'll pick through the pieces until he finds the things I can't let him know or see.

He examines me in the dark, searching for weakness or something else he can seize in order to get further under my skin. "*Mi cielo?*" He brushes his fingers over my cheek lightly. "Tell me what's wrong."

Rose can't know the truth. I can't let him.

I suck in a deep breath and release it slowly. Give him enough to make him drop it. "I haven't been with anyone in this bed since Aleksander."

His hard black eyes soften, and he leans in and kisses my forehead. "*Lo siento, mi cielo.* I know this must be hard for you, but your past cannot rule your future. I learned that the hard way."

FIFTEEN

I LEARNED that the hard way...

It's as close to Rose offering me information about his past as he's ever come. But I know better. He won't give me anything else. He'll never open up and reveal anything *real*, nothing that will let me know who he is besides "Rose."

"Please, Kat, tell me what's wrong. You look like you're crumbling. Let me help you."

"Help me?"

The man has some fucking balls. I try to suck in a deep breath to help steady my racing heart, but all it does is bring his scent deeper into my lungs.

"You're destroying me, Rose. You're eating away at me and breaking me down. And now, you expect me to open up to you? To show you my deepest, darkest secrets when you won't even tell me your fucking name."

Rose releases a sigh and presses a slow, lingering kiss to my lips. I want to pull away and push him back, to tell him how annoyed I am by him and by myself, but being in his arms like this feels too good to let it end despite my frustration and anger.

He drags his head back and raises an eyebrow. "Is that all you want? My name? Is that really all?"

"Of course not. I want a hell of a lot more than that."

I want to feel safe the way Aleksander made me feel safe. The way I feel for the brief moments I'm with Rose before I remember he might want to kill me. I want control—not just of my life which has felt like a runaway train for so long, but of this entire damn city. I want my *son*. I want to be able to raise him and not fear he'll become a pawn in this violent game we all play.

So many things.

Things that will never happen.

Things no one, not even Rose, can give me.

But he can give me one thing. "Your name is a place to start."

Rose turns onto his back and releases a soul-deep sigh, the motion sending his chest heaving up and down almost violently. He scrubs his hands over his face. "I wish it were that easy. But it is not a simple request."

"What is your name? How is that not the most simple question in the world?"

Even for me, who has been so many different people—Brynn, Kitty, Kat...I could answer it.

He rolls his head to the side so our eyes meet again, the true turmoil my question has brought evident in the deepest part of his gaze. "It's a long and very complicated story."

Fuck this.

I was going to wait until Arden had something, until I figured out who the fuck these guys are, but I've reached the end of my rope. Now I want to slide it around Rose's throat and pull until he comes clean. It's time to pull the trigger—so to speak—and stop dancing around the truth. "Maybe I should go ask Felipe."

Rose freezes, his entire body going absolutely stock-still. Dark eyes harden to almost pitch black. "What the fuck did you say?"

"Maybe I should go ask Felipe." I repeat the words deliberately slowly, so each one will be like a bullet slamming into him.

His hands fist at his sides, and he shifts onto his side toward me. "I told you to stay out of things that aren't your business."

He wouldn't be getting so upset if there weren't something to hide. It only makes me want to know more.

"It wasn't *me* who found *him*. Felipe found me."

"*Carajo!*" Rose pushes up into a seated position and shoves his hands back through his hair. For the first time since he came into my life, Rose actually looks afraid. "You have no idea what this means."

"You're right. I don't. You won't tell me anything. I did find it rather interesting how strongly he urged me to stay away from you, though."

He snorts a sardonic laugh and shakes his head. "I bet he did."

Something happened between these brothers. Something serious enough to make the other feel a need to warn me. Something that drove them apart and onto opposite sides of sin.

I reach out and lay my hand on Rose's arm. "Tell me what's going on."

The solemn set of his jaw sends a zing of apprehension through me.

He releases a sigh and gulps down a breath. "Felipe is the single most dangerous person I know."

"Felipe? The priest?"

"Oh, there's so much you don't understand."

I push myself up so I'm sitting next to him. "So, *tell* me."

I'm starting to feel like a broken record here, but I can't stop pushing. He's on the verge of breaking open, of telling me something that might give me even the slightest hint of insight into who the man known as Rose really is.

He forces his eyes shut again and tugs at the hair on the back of his head. "If I do, you'll be in more danger than you can ever possibly imagine."

More danger than I can ever possibly imagine?

Rose must be joking. After everything I've seen and done, after being married to Aleksander Gashi. That's a bold statement he's done nothing to back up.

"Aren't I already?"

His head whips around, and he narrows his eyes. "What you have seen, what you've done, it isn't even the tip of the fucking iceberg."

I chuckle and shake my head. "You sound insane right now. There's no need to try to scare me, Rose. I lived in fear for a long time and have no desire to be there again."

Yet, it's where I've found myself since Konstantin told me he knows about Jet. It's impossible not to be afraid when someone as deadly as that could swoop in and take him at any moment for any nefarious purposes. That's a situation that still needs a resolution, but in this moment, all I can do is pry at the crack Rose is showing in his wall of silence.

Rose climbs to his feet to tower over me at the edge of the bed, his chest heaving. "I am not fucking with you, Kat. This is serious. Deadly serious."

I wait for him to continue, but he paces away from the bed and mumbles something to himself in Spanish. Shifting up against the headboard, I watch him fall apart.

Finally, he pauses at the end of the bed and faces me. "If you want the truth, I will tell you. You might not believe the story, but it's true."

SIXTEEN

ROSE

Telling her this, revealing the whole sordid truth, will not only be dangerous for us both, but it will also destroy my well-constructed pride. But if I ever want her to trust me, if I ever want *her*, she needs to know how much danger she's really in.

Her icy-blue eyes lock with mine, and I struggle to find the right words to explain why I can't just give her what she wants—my name.

Finally, I release a deep sigh and shake my head. "The reason I can't tell you my name is because I haven't known it for twenty years."

PRIDE

Through pride the devil became the devil. Pride leads to every vice; it's the complete anti-God state of mind.

-C.S. LEWIS

PROLOGUE

20 YEARS AGO

ROSE

VULTURES CIRCLE in the sky above the field, the dark, billowing clouds allowing only glimpses of bright blue through them. The slow, lazy glide of the birds remains unhurried and meticulous.

It can only mean one thing—death.

Something below them is either staring down the final darkness or has already succumbed to it.

I know death well and can recognize the signs long before I ever reach that spot. From miles down the road, I noticed the birds and knew what I might find. Likely one of the things I've seen before here on the farm.

Perhaps one of the heifers who died giving birth to her first calf out in this far field. A calf that didn't survive the sometimes-violent process. A cow that was sick or injured and therefore no match for the coyotes roaming around the grazing land, waiting for an opportunity to strike against the weakest prey.

None of those things would be unexpected. Death is just a part of life, especially out here.

By the sweat of your brow, you will eat your food until you return to the ground, since from it you were taken; for dust you are and to dust you will return.

As I push my way through the long grasses toward the spot the vultures' victim lies, I'm prepared for any of the possibilities. It no longer fazes me. Just one more thing I need to deal with today to help *Mama y Papa* before it's time to settle in for the night and the cycle starts all over again tomorrow.

But the blood stops me in my tracks before I even lay eyes on the carnage. It coats everything in the small area that's been trampled down around the bodies.

Nothing but flashes and puddles of red.

Crimson, really. Deep and dark, yet brightly reflecting what sun creeps in through the building storm clouds.

Too much for a simple accident.

Too much for anything to have survived.

I stand at the edge of the small clearing, staring at it for what feels like a long time, the shadows of the birds circling occasionally casting darkness over the blood, deepening its color even more, making it almost onyx.

Slowly, I allow my gaze to drift across the destroyed grass. A foot. A hand. Familiar dark eyes that used to hold such love now lifeless and staring back at me. Lips that spoke words of affection frozen in a scream of horror.

All the air rushes from my lungs. The world around me spins, and a dark haze encroaches on my vision, narrowing it on the macabre scene until total blackness takes over.

But even the welcoming darkness can't erase what I've seen. It can't undo what's been done. It can't bring them back. All it can do is embrace me into the place I'll soon live in permanently.

ONE

NOW

THE MEMORIES of that day tear at my brain. Acid crawls up my throat, threatening to make me wretch the same way I did on the bloody grass so long ago. I force myself to swallow it down because this isn't the time to give in to my weakness. Now that I've opened the floodgates to the truth, I need to let it all out. I need to tell Kat *every* gory detail if I want her to really comprehend what happened and what we are facing.

"They hadn't just been killed, Kat." I shake my head, sucking in a deep breath while trying to find the words to describe what no one should ever have to see. "It was a slaughter."

Unlike anything I had ever seen in my short fifteen years on Earth at that time. And unlike anything I would ever see again except what I did with my own hands. A brutality I didn't know existed, yet one I gave into myself because of what happened that day.

"There were so many bullet holes in their bodies, it was hard to tell they had once been human."

If I had come along any later, the vultures would have gotten to them and I may not have even known who I was looking at when I stumbled upon them.

Kat sits up in the bed, resting her back against the headboard. "What? Who?"

I suck in a deep breath. "My mother and father." I can barely say it without emotion threatening to choke my words. "We lived on a farm just outside Cali. We didn't have a lot of money, but my father had the land that had been in his family for generations. It was lush and beautiful; the perfect place to farm and raise children."

At least, they thought...

If they had known what it would bring. The destruction. The betrayal. The blood. If they even had an inkling, things would have been so different. We could have made different choices. Ones that would have been difficult but necessary. But they loved it there. I loved it there. There was no reason to suspect the danger that lurked so nearby.

"Outside the city, they thought we would be protected from all the bad things in the world. Our own little eutopia, but instead, those things came to find us."

As evil always does...

"What the fuck happened?" Kat's question breaks through the fog of pain surrounding my past to bring me back to the present. She grabs her cigarettes off the nightstand and lights up. "Something tells me I'm going to need one for this story."

I run a shaky hand back through my hair, the memories I tried to bury for so long racing to the surface faster than I can control them. "One of the cartels showed up at the farm one day, wanting to buy the land to use for their operations. Father wouldn't sell. Not even for the amount of money they were offering us—far more than the land was worth. Enough to make us rich even by American standards. The man who came in an expensive suit smiled at us on his way out..."

A shiver rolls through me, picturing it—sly and twisted, a warning not warmth. Back then, it wasn't anything I had ever experienced. Not wrapped in my cocoon of love and faith. Yet, its message was clear.

"Even at that age, I knew it wasn't what it appeared. A sense of foreboding settled over me. Oppressive. The kind of things the priest at the church warned us about. It was evil, of that, I was certain. For a long time, I worried about what would happen, what the cartel would do to us for daring to reject their offer. But then...things went back to normal."

I turn back to face Kat and lean against the wall for support. Talking about this after two decades of silence makes me feel physically weak for the first time since then. Like I can't even hold up my own weight.

It isn't how I want Kat to see me, but I don't have a choice. I have to surge ahead with the story, no matter how painful.

"Normal, for me, was the church. I attended a Jesuit school run by missionaries. They taught us English and never let us slack in our learning. They wanted to ensure we were given excellent educations, even if it only returned to the farm with us. But one of the priests sort of took me under his wing. I was an altar boy, and people often joked about me becoming a priest one day. I thought that was my future. It was my safe place."

Kat raises one of her dark eyebrows and blows out a plume of smoke. "And your brother?"

I snort and shake my head. "Quite the opposite. For as much as we may look alike, our paths diverged greatly years before I lost my parents. He started skipping school around age twelve, asking me to pretend to be him and cover for him so that he wasn't always the one in trouble. He would sneak into town and run around with some of the street gangs. Even then, he was making choices that would change our world forever."

Choices that made me who I am today—for better or for worse. Perhaps both.

"What happened that day?"

The urge to tell her it's none of her business, to end this conversation before it goes any further, strikes me so hard, if I weren't supported by the wall behind me, I might actually fall forward in an effort to run. Away from her. Away from the memories. Away from the *truth* that still haunts me even twenty years later.

But I started this with a purpose—to open Kat's eyes to the reality of where we are now. Stuck in Felipe's crosshairs and now with the Irish and Russians also breathing down our necks due to her actions earlier tonight. We're dangling over the precipice, about to tumble down into the abyss we created ourselves because we wanted it all and were willing to do anything to obtain it.

I push away from the wall and walk to the window to stare out at the driving rain, wishing it could wash away all the pain talking about this and even thinking about it has caused. "I had gone to morning mass to help Father Nolan and was on my way home when I saw the vultures circling the field."

Until that moment, I had never understood the fear of them or why people considered them bad omens. They were just a part of the natural way of things, a common sight on the farm. I respected them, knew they were necessary. Until that moment...

"I assumed it was a cow or some other animal from the farm, but when I made it to that point..." I squeeze my eyes closed and swallow through the emotion clogging my throat. "I knew what happened immediately. That kind of violence could only come from the cartel. They had waited months after they approached us before they finally struck. Let us believe everything was fine to ensure our guard was down. *Mama y Papa* never saw it coming."

Neither did I. I had ignored my initial unease, let myself believe things were actually safe, that they would actually let us continue on with our lives as if we hadn't committed a sin by denying their attempt to purchase the land they needed.

A long, heavy silence permeates the air in the room for what feels like forever before Kat's voice finally reaches me with the question I knew was coming. "What did you do?"

The hair on the back of my neck stands on end, and I rub at it absently, avoiding answering for as long as I can. That single moment changed my entire life, changed who I am. "I stared at the carnage for a long time, frozen in place. And then, I realized what it meant. I raced back to the house and found it in shambles, but there was no sign of Sofia."

"Oh, my God! How old was she?"

"Just a baby. Barely a year old." Despite the current topic of conversation, a smile pulls at my lips, picturing the tiny, sweet baby she was then. Her feistiness and desire to constantly argue with me only developed later in life. "She had been quite a surprise for my parents when she arrived fifteen years after we did."

A joyful one. She brought so much life and love into the house—the kind I haven't felt since then.

"What did you do when you couldn't find her?"

I turn and lock my gaze with hers, my hands fisting at my sides. "I went to get her back."

TWO

A FULL-BODY SHUDDER rolls through Kat where she sits against the headboard, watching me with a strange mix of fear and confusion in her cool-blue eyes. It's so unlike her to show any sort of reaction, to give anything away, but even hearing this tiny portion of the story, she's already shaken, the hand holding her burned-down cigarette vibrating uncontrollably.

Good. It's time she understood what we're really up against.

She reaches over to the nightstand and snubs out her cigarette. "Did your brother go with you?"

I shake my head and flex my hands, the rage and pain of that day heating my skin and tightening it to the point that it's practically suffocating me. "No. I didn't know where he was. He would disappear for days, sometimes a week at a time, off getting into trouble in the city. I can't even count the number of times my parents had to pick him up from a police station. If we weren't so young, he might've been in prison already. I knew I couldn't try to wait to find him. Not when I knew what they would do to Sofia. So, I went to the home of the man who had offered to buy our land. I didn't even know his name..." It floods back to me as if I were standing, looking at that house now instead of out at a wet, dark Chicago. "A beautiful home set up on a hill surrounded by half a dozen armed guards. But they let me walk right in. They knew me, had been watching us since the day they decided they wanted our land. They knew I wasn't someone to be threatened by."

Not back then.

"They had no idea the wrath burning through my soul after seeing my parents and what it was doing to me, what it was turning me into in almost an instant. I walked in, walked right up to the man who ordered the hit on my parents, and stabbed him in the jugular with a letter opener on his desk."

"Good God..."

I whirl back to face Kat again. "No." Shaking my head, I take a step toward her. "God wasn't there that day. Maybe *el Diablo,* but certainly not God. I don't even think I was human at that moment, just possessed by something straight from Hell. I kept stabbing, even as his life spurted out of the side of his neck and all over his desk. I stabbed so many times, I lost count. There was so much blood that it covered me practically head to toe."

And two decades later, the feel of it all over my skin still lingers—hot and sticky. The metallic scent still invades every breath I take. No amount of penance or water could ever wash it away, could ever cleanse my soul of what I did.

What I *continued* to do.

"And then, I took a knife and gun from his desk and I laid waste to his guards before they could even react...but not before I did the unthinkable."

Kat clutches the sheet against her naked breasts, but whether she can even fathom the true depths of my depravity remains to be seen. There are days I can't believe I did it even though my own hands still tingle with the memory of their actions. Even when I can still hear the screams.

"I heard a baby crying. Only when I followed the sound, Sofia wasn't alone. She was in the arms of the man's wife." I clench my fists at my side, the vivid image of the woman smiling down at Sofia as if she were her own still seared in my mind. "I had assumed the man would sell her to some *puto enfermo* who would abuse her, but the truth was even worse. He intended to raise her as his own. To use her to appease a wife who could not have her own children. When I realized the truth, I went into a frenzy."

A flashing silver blade.

Sprays of red.

Cries of pain and fear.

They overwhelm my senses, and I bury my face in my hands and grit my teeth. All these years of pushing the past into a dark recess of my mind have been undone in a single moment. Because of Kat. Because of what she means to me. Because it *had* to be done.

"What about Sofia?"

Her question makes me drag my head back up, but I can't meet her assessing gaze, instead choosing to return to the window, to the rain that chills the air as much as the memories do.

"The only reason Sofia wasn't harmed during the attack was the woman had the good sense to put her down as soon as she saw me covered in her husband's blood. But I didn't give her time to try to get away. I slit her throat open with the knife I had taken from him, probably a gift from the very woman I was killing with it."

Killing. The word seems so wrong for what happened. It was so much more than that. Something darker. More sinister.

"I left her unrecognizable as even human, repayment for what happened to my parents." I press my hand against the windowpane, but the chill permeating from it into my skin can't quell the heat of my anger even now. "When I was done with her, I took the guns I found and laid waste to his men before they knew anything was wrong. Then I went back upstairs and grabbed Sofia. She was screaming by that time, and now, being held against my chest, she was covered in the bloody evidence of what had just transpired. Where my presence had once soothed her, now it only made her wail louder."

Her frantic screams still echo in my ears, mixing with the deluge pounding the windows and roof outside to form a sound loud enough to make me wince.

"I started to leave the room and noticed a vase of fresh roses. The thought that this man could murder my parents, steal my sister, and go on with his life, buying his wife roses as if none of it happened..." I close my eyes and shake my head. "It was more than I could handle. I grabbed them, broke the petals free, and dropped them around his wife's body."

Kat shifts on the bed behind me, the creaking mattress giving away her unease despite her being unable or unwilling to respond verbally.

I force myself to turn back to her and lock eyes when I tell the rest. "Then I walked out the front door with my sister and ran right into our dear brother on his way back to his boss' house."

"No!" Kat's eyes fly wide as the pieces fall into place for her. The things I don't even want to believe myself even though I know they're true. "He didn't..."

I twist back to the window and smash my hand against the pane. It vibrates but doesn't break despite my best efforts to throw all my rage into it. All my hatred for him and his betrayal. Everything I felt in that instant, I saw him coming toward the house and *knew*.

"I hadn't known until that point. None of us had known. But as I stood there, holding Sofia, covered in their blood, I looked at the boy who shared my own eyes, and I knew. I knew he had done it. I knew he had killed them to garner favor with the man *I* had just killed. I knew he had nothing left in his soul that wasn't dark and depraved, that wasn't so twisted and black that it was dead to any form of light."

"But I don't understand. How did he end up a priest? How did you end up here, as the head of the cartel?"

And now, we've reached the crux of the story, the point where the truth will unravel everything she thought she knew.

Twisting back to her, I shake my head and run my hand over the scruff on my jaw. "That is the part you won't believe."

THREE

20 YEARS AGO

I stare into the same eyes I see in the mirror every day, only his are darkened with something sinister.

How can we look the same yet be so different?

It's a question I've asked myself often. One *Mama* struggled with almost daily. *Papa* worried, too, but he held his emotions close and rarely let them show. Not like the tears that fell from *Mama's* eyes every time he did something she couldn't understand. It's a question they died without answering. One I won't be able to, either, not in a million lifetimes.

Because looking at him now, I'm confident he's the epitome of evil. Everything I've been warned about and told to stay away from. Everything Father Nolan said we should turn from and watch out for. But he's also the other half of me. Staying away has been impossible, no matter how much his actions may have diverged from my own.

Though, now that I'm standing here covered in the blood of all the people I just slaughtered so easily, without thought, perhaps we aren't so different. If I'm capable of that, I'm really only one step away from becoming what he already has. Whatever it is inside him that allowed him to kill our parents so effortlessly also lives inside me, and now, it's come out to play a deadly game that has brought us here.

Standing in the middle of the road, dark, ominous clouds billowing in the sky above us, it feels like everything has been building to this moment—this showdown between us. When brothers must face each other and what we've done.

Sofia wails in my arms, kicking and fighting against my hold on her, no doubt terrified by what's been happening around her even if she doesn't understand it. And thank God she doesn't. If she were any older, the trauma of today's events might have left a lasting impression on her, one that might scar her forever and twist her into something our parents would never have wanted. As it stands now, no matter what happens, she will forever be tainted by the blood of our parents and these people, but at least she's young enough I can do something about it, try to ensure her path remains the right one, protect her from the other dangers in the world—even the ones masquerading as her loving brother.

"What have you done?" Our brother's gaze darts from Sofia, across me, then back to the mansion over my shoulder, panic written in his features as he pieces together what must have happened. "What have you *done?*"

"Me? What have *I* done?" My words come out more like a snarl, spittle flying to strike him in the face. "What have *you* done? You *killed Mama y Papa!*" They never stood a chance when the Devil was in their own home. "And for what?" I wave a blood-stained hand back toward the house. "To have a house like this? To have this kind of money and power? Is that all you care about?"

He steps closer, anger radiating off him in waves, that thing that has always burned just beneath his surface when he's with me finally rising to visibility. "I did this for *us* so that we could have a better life than *Mama y Papa* could give us! Why can't you see that?" He points to Sofia. "I did this for her! To give her a chance!"

The absolute sincerity in his words sends a shiver through me despite the warmth of the cloudy day.

"You killed our parents and offered our sister to a ruthless man to raise as his own and you really believe it was the right choice?" I shake my head, tears finally welling in my eyes for the first time and trickling down my cheeks. "They did the best they could for us. They *loved* us unconditionally, put a roof over our heads, fed and clothed us, made sure we got an education, and were taught God's love. Why was that not enough for you?"

The sneer that curls up his lip sends ice through my veins. "Don't spew your religious platitudes at me. The world outside those church walls you hide behind isn't an easy one. Hard choices need to be made. I made one. You apparently did, too. And *we* need to make one now."

He's lost his mind. It's the only explanation for what he's saying, for how cold he's being. He's gone past the point of return to sanity. Lost to any argument that might make him see the error of his ways.

I shake my head, lightly bouncing Sofia in my arms to try to stop her fussing, which has only escalated with the tension and yelling between her brothers. "The only thing that's going to happen now is we're both going to prison for the rest of our lives."

"No." He steps forward and wrenches her from my arms. "I'm not. No one who knows what I did is alive...save for you. But there will be no hiding what you've done. You're covered head to toe in the evidence. Everyone will believe you did it because he killed *Mama y Papa*. People will understand. But you will go, and I will stay and care for Sofia."

He's right...

There isn't any way out of this for me. I'll be locked up behind iron bars in mere hours. There isn't any escaping the consequences of this. "They'll eat me alive in there."

He reaches out and rests his hand on my shoulder, covered in the gore of what I've done. The gesture once soothed me, but now, it feels more like the hand of death. "Not if they think you're *me*."

I jerk my head up to meet his gaze. "What?"

"People know me. I've built a reputation. People fear me already."

That much is true. Despite what *Mama y Papa* tried to instill in us, it didn't seem to take with my other half. I have no doubt theirs weren't the first lives he's taken. He had to be working for the cartel for a while to have been entrusted with such a task, likely since the day they came to the farm, if not before. He saw a chance. And he took it.

He nods slowly. "You know they will believe *I* did something like this, that I'm capable of it. No one would believe you, a quiet, good altar boy, would kill this way, would seek such revenge. So..." One of his dark eyebrows rises. "You become me, and I become you. It will help you survive in there, and it will give me a way to protect Sofia out here in the church."

"No!" I shake my head and shove off his touch, pressing my palms against my temples and squeezing my eyes shut as if I can make the reality of the world I've just created disappear if I try hard enough. "I can't..."

"You *can*. And you *will*. You *must*."

No. No. No. No. No!

His hand forces my chin up, and I open my eyes to stare at him, into the same dark eyes. The resolve is there.

This plan will work.

Almost as if he can see my resignation, my acceptance of his faith, he nods and cradles Sofia, who has finally calmed, against his chest. "From this moment on, you are Andres, and I am Felipe. We tell no one."

I nod my understanding that my life as I know it is over, that all the hopes and dreams I have for my future have drifted away on the river of blood created by both our actions. "We tell no one."

FOUR

NOW

I REST my palms flat against the cool glass and drop my head, letting my neck stretch and trying to relive some of the tension building there, but the creak of the bed behind me tenses every muscle in my body in an instant. This is me at my weakest, my most vulnerable. This is what my enemies, the enemies of the Blood Rose Cartel—have been looking for for the past two decades. The perfect opportunity to strike. And despite how much I care for her, how much I *love* her and would do anything for her, I'm still not one hundred percent sure I can trust her.

She's holding something back from me. Something important. Something *more* than just her plans here in Chicago. I see it in her eyes every time I look at her, every time I'm inside her.

Opening myself up this way tonight was meant to serve two purposes. Now she knows everything—or at least, the basics. She knows how dangerous Felipe is and what he's capable of. What we might be facing. I also hope it shows her I mean what I say to her and I can be trusted. That I would never betray her. Perhaps now, she'll share whatever she's been keeping buried so deep.

Still, it's been a long time since I left myself so exposed. It's not a pleasant feeling for a man like me, one who has lived a lie for twenty years and embraced it so fully. That lie has now crumbled. The name *Rose* no longer protects me. Now she *knows*.

Kat's soft footsteps across the hard floor echo in my ears. I stiffen in anticipation of her arrival, but when she wraps her arms around me and presses her face against my bare back, I relax slightly into her touch.

This kind of warm embrace hasn't been offered to me in so long, I've forgotten what it feels like to have it without the other person expecting something in return—money, a favor, worse...

She kisses my spine softly and squeezes me. "So, you've pretended to be Andres all these years, running the family and becoming exactly what he was while he took to the straight and narrow path you had been on and joined the church."

I spin around to face her, my rapid movement throwing her back. Her wide eyes watch as I capture her upper arms in my hands and squeeze until it's no doubt painful for her. "Fuck, Kat. You don't get it all, do you?" My frustration boils over, heating my blood and flaring my temper.

How can she not understand?

"I became Andres to save my life in prison. Pretended to be the head of the cartel I just took out and took over. Let everyone believe I was the one calling the shots from behind bars. I lived on the reputation Andres had started on the streets as a youth and then built on it, creating an even stronger one for myself." I grasp her chin and jerk her head up, her wide eyes meeting mine. "Why do you think they call us the Blood Rose Cartel? Because of what I did before I walked out of that fucking house. I made everyone call me Rose because I couldn't answer to Andres. It felt wrong, and I knew if I hesitated for even a second, if I flinched, if I gave any indication that I might not be who and what I said I was, not only would I have been dead, but it would have put Sofia in danger again."

Despite everything I had to suffer after what I had done, I would do it all over again to protect her. She was the true innocent in all of this. Along with our parents, she suffered for the price of pride and envy—Andres thought he needed to do it to become what he wanted, to puff up his chest and be the one everyone bowed down to. But he wasn't the one who had to live with the conse-quences. It was me.

"I became Andres, Kat, but *he* became something so much worse. He's been running this family from day one. *He* is the one making all the decisions and calling all the shots. He's worse than a wolf in sheep's clothing; he's a goddamn wolf in shepherd's clothing leading his flock to the slaughter. *Literally*. He hides behind the fucking church and the fact that no one would ever suspect a priest of being the true evil incarnate vile monster he really is. My brother isn't just the head of the Blood Rose Cartel; he runs every major cartel in Colombia. He began gobbling them up and bringing them under his control years ago. He uses me as his puppet, his face, his scapegoat if the shit should ever hit the fan." I let out a mirthless laugh and shake my head, digging my fingers into the sensitive flesh of her chin. "I warned you he was far more dangerous than you could ever imagine, and that's why. Because even *you*, after all you've seen and been through, after you've enforced the wall you've erected around yourself to keep threats out, even after hearing that *story, you* never suspected him."

It's the true genius of his plan—the one we plotted that day. As Felipe, he's unquestionable. He's a man of faith. A good priest who does God's work. He's a man of the people, even marking his skin with tattoos so when he goes into gang territories to "preach," he will fit in and be accepted. Only I know the truth. What he's really doing there—recruiting and scouting so I can issue threats against anyone who might stand against us and take out anyone who doesn't fall in line.

My hands may be bloody, but his have been stained black over the last two decades with all the deaths he's ordered, the things he's made me and others do.

Kat's jaw opens and closes a few times, and tears well in her eyes. "Oh, God." Her entire body starts shaking, and the thin sheet she has wrapped around her falls to the floor, leaving her naked and shivering in my arms. "I-I have to go."

"What?"

Of all the reactions I had gone over in my head, all the ways she could respond to my story, running away had never entered my mind. At least, not like *this*. Not after what we just shared.

She jerks out of my hold and rushes to the nightstand to grab her phone. Her hands shake so violently as she tries to dial that she lets out a frustrated cry and sucks in a deep breath before she can try again.

I stalk over to her, grab the phone, and grasp her chin, forcing her to meet my gaze. "What the hell is going on?"

Her actions are extreme, even in light of the shock my story might bring. Something else is going on, and she isn't going to keep it from me any longer.

FIVE

TEARS FALL down her cheeks now, completely unbidden, and she shakes her head, her lower lip quivering uncharacteristically for the woman who is always so stone cold. "I didn't know. About Felipe...Andres...whoever the fuck he is. I didn't know, and now...you don't understand."

After everything I just revealed to her tonight, she's still holding back, still trying to keep me at arm's length. I've exposed myself more to her than I have anyone in my entire life, and she's keeping me frozen out. Something inside me snaps the same way it did that fateful day, only instead of the need to kill, every fiber of my being cries for me to get the truth. "*I* don't understand?" I raise an eyebrow at her and jerk her head up, straining her neck. "Then *make* me, Kat. Stop freezing me out. Fucking *tell* me."

She hesitates a second more before she physically crumbles in front of me, sagging into my hold. "The other night when I killed your men to get away...it was to go to a meeting, only I didn't know who with. All I knew was to meet at a church."

"Felipe?"

"No." She shakes her head. "Not Felipe. At least, not at first. Konstandin was there, waiting for me to talk."

"Konstandin?" I issue a low growl and drag her up against me. "Did that fucker hurt you?"

She shakes her head again. "No. He wanted a truce." Another moment of hesitation brings a lingering silence between us as she searches my eyes for something.

"Just fucking tell me, Kat. I can't protect you if I don't know what we're up against."

Kat swallows thickly, seemingly gathering the courage to say whatever is about to leave her lips next. "He knows about Aleksander's son. *My* son."

"Your *son?*"

In all the time I've known Kat, all the research I did trying to track her background and history, I never once saw anything about a child. Sofia is good. She can find almost anything, but somehow, Kat has managed to completely hide something so explosive. And it explains so much of what she's been holding back from me and why.

"Tell me *everything.*"

"There isn't time for that. Konstandin and I came to a truce. He isn't my immediate concern."

I snort and shake my head. "And you believe that?"

A scowl turns her lips, and she shakes her head. "Not really, but he has a son, too, and we agreed to leave each other alone for our children's sake. Only we were talking about it openly in the church...and Felipe was the one who *arranged* the meeting. He probably heard everything, which means—"

I tighten my hold on her as my understanding of her panic sets in. "Which means Felipe will go after your son even if Konstandin has sworn he never will."

She nods, more tears trailing down her flawless skin. "Unless I can get to him and keep him safe."

"Where is he?"

Surely, if the boy were here in Chicago or anywhere nearby, I would have had some indication. She would have gone to see him or somehow sent money Sofia could trace. But there hasn't been anything to even *hint* he existed. Whatever she did to hide him, she did it well.

"Albania. A farming family far away from anyone or anything that could hurt him. Or so I thought."

The irony of her statement in light of the story I just told her isn't lost on me. But she's right. If we don't get there soon, it might be too late. There's no knowing what Felipe may have planned with the knowledge he acquired during the meeting between Konstandin and Kat. No telling what his true intentions might be in setting it up in the first place. Felipe always plays five steps ahead, leaving everyone scrambling to keep up and almost always failing at it.

I hand her the phone I took from her and press my lips to hers in a forceful kiss, one intended to show her how much I care, how much I am *in* this—no matter what. "Make the call. We'll fly out as soon as the plane is ready."

Her dark eyebrows fly up. "We?"

"You think I'm letting you go alone? You think I'm letting you step foot on that plane without me after what happened last time you got on one?"

"Oh, my God. Was that your brother?"

It isn't the first time she suggested it was someone in my camp. When she woke in my house, it was one of the first accusations she made, probably because she could read me and saw how uneasy things were, how mistrustful I was of certain people—or a certain *someone*.

I press my lips together and issue a low growl. "I don't fucking know. But the timing of him arriving back in Chicago can't be a coincidence. I've been making some decisions lately, doing some things that he feels are oversteps. I've wanted to truly take control for a long time. And things have been...tense between us. I certainly wouldn't put it past him."

"But who would've told him about our plans? How would he have known when and where we were flying? Sofia?"

My chest tightens at the mention of her name and the suggestion she could have been involved. "No."

"Could she have chosen him over you? Seen what you were doing, trying to push him out and decided she wanted to support him?"

I shake my head and shove my hands back through my hair. "She doesn't *know*, Kat."

"What do you mean she doesn't know?"

"Sofia doesn't *know* we switched places and names. She has no idea that I am not really Andres or that the man she knows as Felipe isn't anything more than a well-loved and respected man of the cloth. If she did say anything to him, which I highly doubt, it wasn't with any malicious intent because she didn't *know* there was a danger. Why would there be from a priest? Our own *brother*? All she knows is things are tense between us, but she believes that's because of how I choose to live my life, because of the cartel, and how juxtaposed we are. She has no *inkling* of the truth, Kat. *None*."

We may never know who sabotaged the plane, but if we stand here arguing about it, Felipe will only have more time to carry out whatever his endgame may be.

I reach for my clothes on the floor. "Make the call. We need to move now."

She nods and presses a button on her phone, holding it to her ear as she rushes in her closet and drags out a suitcase.

It's so much worse than I could've imagined. Not only are we in danger, but so is an innocent child. The son of the Dragon. The man everyone feared even more than the cartel I supposedly run. That boy would be the perfect prize for Felipe. Just as the man I slaughtered two decades ago would have raised Sofia as his own, I have no doubt my brother would do the same to Kat's son. Twisting him into a dark, merciless killer, annihilating anything good and sweet and pure in that child.

He doesn't deserve that. No child does. Yet, Felipe will use anything he can find. Any tiny weakness. Any hint of an opening. Kat just gave him a massive one, and since it appears he knows of my feelings for her, I've given him one as well. He'll use them both to get to me—anyway he can.

If we don't move swiftly, we might lose everything.

SIX

THE TIRES of the SUV squeal as we pull onto the tarmac at the executive airport north of the city where my plane already waits for us, along with half a dozen of my men I called to meet us from my compound and a few of Kat's gathered around it in the rain. I'm not taking any chances this time. With Genti at the wheel, ensuring we make it to the plane and then watching our backs as we board and make our way across the country and ocean, we're as well-protected as we can be.

It's only been an hour since we arranged the flight, not enough time for anyone to have tampered with anything on the plane; plus, I ensured no one has been alone with it. The pilots arrived together and had strict instructions not to leave each other's sights. Same for my men and Kat's who met us here.

Take no chances.

From the moment of the explosion on the flight back from Canada, I suspected Felipe was involved, but after hearing more details of what happened between Konstandin and Kat and then Kat and Felipe, I'm more convinced than ever that he was behind it. He's playing some sort of reckless game, throwing Konstandin and Kat together, hoping they would implode. He undoubtedly used his white collar to lull Konstandin into a false sense of security to arrange the fated meeting, and he plans to use what they said there to destroy them both.

What happens to Konstandin isn't my concern. He can die and burn in Hell for eternity, for all I care, but what happens to Kat's child very much is my concern—more than I ever thought possible.

I never wanted children. From a young age, I imagined myself committing myself to God and serving the church rather than giving my heart to a woman. That meant the possibility of fathering children and having a family never really entered my mind. And once that fateful day occurred, after I had served my time in that hell-hole of a prison, after I had become Rose and bathed myself in blood, I never much saw myself as a father figure or anyone worthy of being a parent. It was bad enough Sofia was going to be exposed to my life. I never wanted to bring a child into this world that's so cold and brutal, and even if I had wanted to, no woman would want that.

I never met anyone who ever made me second-guess that decision...until Kat.

From the moment I walked into Kat's Cradle and laid eyes on her, I knew she was *it* for me. *Mi Cielo. My heaven.* A woman who had as much drive and ambition as me, someone ruthless and cunning and willing to do whatever it takes to succeed.

She's my perfect match.

My *true* equal.

The other half I thought I lost when Felipe betrayed me that day was replaced by the stunning woman with a cool heart and even colder eyes.

She's exactly the woman I need by my side if I'm ever going to win against Felipe, let alone the others competing for control of the Windy City. And when she told me she had a son, it was like a switch flipped and something inside me flickered to life. Some instinct to protect this boy, this child of the man who was my enemy, because he belongs to the woman I love.

Kat may still have her doubts about my true intentions with her. She may still believe I have some master plan that involves seducing her in order to take her out in the end the same way she did Michael, but after tonight, after everything I told her, after coming clean with the truth no one but Felipe and I know, she can't possibly question it anymore. She has to see that we have the same enemy—the same *enemies*. We have a common goal and share the same desire to see it finished.

I reach out and clasp her hand in mine as we pull to a stop in front of the plane. She glances over at me with shimmering, bloodshot eyes. Fear lives in her gaze—the same soul-crushing fear I felt when I realized Sofia was gone that day. While she may not be my child, she's my responsibility as if she were, so Kat's willingness to tear the world apart to protect Jet tugs at my heart in a way I truly understand.

"We're going to get him, Kat. He'll be safe. I promise."

She shakes her head, her lower lip quivering. "You can't make that promise. You said it yourself —your brother is a monster and unpredictable. He told me to stay away from you. Flat out threat- ened me—I just didn't see it that way because I was blinded by the white collar and the place we were in. I believed he was trying to protect you or me. I never even considered his ulterior motives. But now, I know he won't hesitate to harm Jet."

I squeeze her hand and lean forward to press a kiss to her forehead. "Stop panicking. While you're right about Felipe and what he's willing to do without hesitation, you aren't alone anymore. You have me. I'm the only one who understands *him*. He's my other half. I know how he thinks. I know how he operates. I'm the only one who's ever challenged him in any way or questioned the decisions he makes and the actions he takes." I release a sigh and tip up her chin to force her to meet my gaze. "Don't get me wrong, I am the monster you think I am. All the stories you've heard, all the wrongs I've done over the last decade since I got out, have been me. I was the one pulling the trigger, even if I wasn't the one making the decision to do it. But I'm sick of being his puppet, and he knows it. We both knew this was coming. It's likely why he wanted you to stay away from me in the first place. Not because of his concern for me but because he's gunning for me and didn't want you in the crossfire."

Her dark brows furrow. "Why would he not want me out of the way? Wouldn't me getting 'caught in the crossfire' actually help him?"

I don't want to say the words to her. The truth is worse than anything she's thinking. "Not if he has other plans for you. Ones that require you to be alive."

"Like leveraging Jet against me to get me to comply with whatever his plan may be."

"Perhaps. Or maybe he intended to kill you after all. But knowing my brother, that would be too easy. He likes to play the long game. Likes to weave intricate webs people can't escape from. Loves to twist people and bend them to their breaking points just to watch them suffer." Including me. "But he isn't the only spider, Kat. I've been weaving a web of my own since I got here. Building my own network and alliances. I'll make sure your son is safe."

The words barely leave my lips when gunfire erupts outside, lighting up the dark, quiet night with muzzle flashes and loud blasts.

SEVEN

"Fuck!"

I drop her hand, and we both duck into the footwells of the back seat and reach for our weapons as the barrage only increases, bullets pinging off the parts of the car able to handle it. A few shots slam into the side panels, tearing easily through the metal doors and shattering the window in the rear cargo area.

Genti lowers his window and starts firing at our unknown assailants while I try to see what's happening through the darkly-tinted windows.

"Who's shooting?" Kat whips her head from side to side, trying to get a view over the edge of the doors barely protecting us without exposing herself—an almost impossible feat in our position. "Are our men turning on each other?"

It wouldn't be out of the question. My men have been on-edge ever since Genti and Kat killed the two I sent to keep an eye on her. They want to retaliate. They dream of drawing blood from those who took the lives of their friends, but I've warned them, Genti, Kat, and her other men are off-limits. It's pushing their loyalty to me to the absolute limit. I might believe it had finally happened if I didn't catch a glimpse of both sets of men firing past our vehicle.

I shake my head and peek out the window just as four dark SUVs screech to a halt behind us, windows down and flashes of gunfire from their muzzles visible in the pitch-black night. "No." I duck back down and turn toward her. "Someone else. A bunch of them."

Her wide blue eyes meet mine. "The Russians or the Irish?"

Shaking my head, I pull out my spare magazine and set it on the seat I just vacated so it's in easy reach. Something tells me I'm going to need it. "I can't tell. It's too dark."

But it's a definite possibility. After what Kat did to them earlier today, they'll be out for revenge and to try to track down the guns she took from Galen and the Irish and the money she took from Valerian and the Russians. Even I don't know what she did with it, though. She's smart enough to have it somewhere no one will ever think to look for it; of that, I'm certain.

Panic overtakes Kat's face, and a single tear slips down her right cheek. She glances out her window toward the waiting plane. "Shit. It's too far. I won't get to the plane with them shooting at us."

I open my mouth to reassure her, but several bullets strike the SUV again, and a sharp stab of pain slices through my left shoulder. "Shit!"

Pressing my hand against the wound does nothing to stop the warm, thick blood from flowing through my fingers and over my gun, and the hail of bullets keeps hitting the SUV, with no end to the assault in sight.

My window shatters, sending glass shards flying across us where we crouch in the back. Kat shifts up and fires out my now open window, anger mixing with her panic. This attack could prevent her from getting to Jet. It could end any hope we have of thwarting Felipe's plans.

Unless...she goes alone. It's the last thing I want, but it's our only hope right now.

I shift up and peek over her shoulder at the plane waiting on the tarmac, the engines already fired up and spinning. "You can make it, Kat."

She drops back down, taking cover once again. "What?"

"*We* aren't going to make it to the plane. There's no way. But *you* can."

"What?" She fires again, and I turn and join her. The return barrage ceases for a moment, and we duck back down. She grabs my good shoulder and turns me toward her. "What the hell are you talking about? We're going to be overrun in minutes!"

"You can make it." I slam my elbow against the back of the driver's seat to get Genti's attention. "Get us as close to the stairs as you can so Kat can get aboard."

He fires off more shots and glances over the seat at us, dark brow winged up. "Alone?"

I know he wants to go with her—God knows I do, too. Sending her there alone is practically suicide, especially when the Dragushas and Berishas have taken over most of Albania and only have a tenuous peace with her. If she shows up unannounced, they may take it as an act of war rather than see it as the rescue mission it really is. But we don't have a choice but to send her by herself.

Genti is on the driver's side, and there's no way he's scrambling across the center console to get out on the passenger side while we're trying to hold off the enemy. I might be able to get out her side and get up, but she has a much better chance if they see I'm still here. They won't suspect she's sneaking out the other side until it's too late—if all goes well.

Kat shakes her head. "You can't be serious."

"We'll hold them off as long as we can, and hopefully, one of the men near the plane is still moving and can follow you up. But you don't wait to find out. As soon as you get to the top, you shut that fucking door and order the pilots to take off. I don't care if they have clearance or not. You get off the fucking ground."

She swipes away another tear and nods. "But what about you?"

Hell. She does care...

It's always so hard to tell with this woman. The push and pull we seem to be so good at is intoxicating, but it's often left me wondering if I'm imagining that she wants me anything but dead. Even after she admitted she cared in my office that day, finally gave in to what we both wanted, she's continued to push me away and keep me at arm's length. Yet, staring at her now, I can almost believe she loves me the way I do her.

I lean in and press a harsh kiss to her lips before pulling back and offering her a grin. "Don't worry about me. I've survived worse."

Not giving her any time to object further, I smack the back of the driver seat again to send Genti toward the plane. He guns the engine, sending us shooting forward while a hail of bullets still rains down on us. The tires squeal as he jerks the wheel to the left, skidding us to a stop perpendicular to the stairs, putting us straight into the line of fire but offering Kat some protection.

As soon as the vehicle stops, Genti and I both fire out our broken windows, but I can't risk looking back to see if Kat made it or not because the door in front of me jerks open and a man dressed in black points his weapon straight at my head. I reach for my extra magazine to reload, but he presses the muzzle against my forehead, stopping me instantly.

Fuck.

EIGHT

Even sitting tied to this chair, my jaw and cheek aching from the strikes our captors have rained down on us, I can do it without complaint or regret knowing it got Kat onto that plane. Our gamble paid off, buying her enough time to get up those stairs with that door closed before we were overrun. And watching the plane taxi away and take off before I got shoved into the back of an SUV with Genti gave me a sense of relief despite knowing what we were about to face.

And it's been exactly what I expected.

Brutal and unrelenting.

A true showing of wrath from a man who has every reason to be this angry—just not at me.

Valerian Kamenev isn't one to offer any sort of relief from the pain he's inflicting, not when he's on a mission. And he certainly is tonight. With Genti unconscious and tied to the chair next to me, I can only imagine Kat would've found herself in the same position had she not made it up those stairs with one of her men and closed that door as quickly as she did. The fact that she's a woman would have gained her no quarter from Valerian's rage.

Nothing could stop him or give him pause right now.

Another hard blow lands on my left cheek, snapping my head sideways and back. The salty, metallic tang of blood fills my mouth, and I slowly turn my head forward again to face my assailant.

The head of the Russian bratva in Chicago just offers me a dark grin, one that holds all the ire he has built up for me over the last few years. I smile in return, then lean forward as much as the ropes will allow and spit blood onto his shiny loafers.

He glances down at it, then slowly back up at me. "You owe me five hundred dollars."

I chuckle to myself. A drop in the bucket for me. I've bought bottles of scotch worth ten times that and drank them in less than a few days. Either Valerian's finances aren't as good as he would have everyone believe, or the man just has cheap taste in footwear.

One of his dark eyebrows rises. "You think that's funny? I'll just add it to the tab for what you stole from me last night."

"I didn't take anything from you last night." Though, him thinking it's me might buy more time for Kat and keep her off his radar.

"Bullshit." He stalks forward and grabs the armrests of the chair I'm in, menacing over me and trying to intimidate me with his massive frame. "You think for one fucking second I believe you didn't have a hand in what went down last night? No one could've orchestrated simultaneous attacks on me and the Irish alone. It was a joint effort between you and your fucking whore, Kat. Now tell me where she's going!"

Not a fucking chance, carechimba.

I had anticipated this, had seen it coming soon as I knew Kat had been behind it, had *warned* her she was making two very powerful enemies even more dangerous. She's a bold woman who made a bold choice that might get both of us killed now. But it doesn't mean I'm about to throw her under the bus. I would take a bullet for her before I ever let anything harm her. I'll die in this chair before I offer Valerian a word that would lead him to her or confirm she was responsible for the attacks.

Swallowing the blood pooling in my mouth, I shake my head slightly, and the motion sends the room spinning. That last blow did a real number on me, but there isn't any time to be weak. "It wasn't us." And it's time to redirect his suspicions to someone else. "Perhaps Galen staged the whole thing as a ruse. I know you two are buddies now, but maybe the whole thing was a way for him to attack you without you ever suspecting? Did you even consider that before you attacked us on the tarmac?"

Valerian shoves off the chair and paces the room in front of me. "Of course, I did. And I believe him when he says his loss was true. Galen has big things in the works and losing that shipment has really fucked him." He scowls at me and flexes the hand he just punched me with. "I had planned to grab you and Kat from her place tonight, but when I saw you two rush out with the suitcase, I knew I had to act fast and follow. Once I saw you were headed for the airport, there wasn't any time to lose. We had to stop you and make you pay before you could flee with what is ours."

"I see you're eager for blood, Valerian, and I believe in retribution once someone has wronged you and that everyone must pay for what they've done, in this life or after. But you have this all wrong. It wasn't us."

I've lied about so much for so long that it's natural for me now. I don't even have to think of the lie before it falls from my tongue, don't have to try to put on any sort of airs to make it sound believable, don't need to do anything other than say the words. And people believe it.

Felipe has the same gift. It allowed him to seamlessly slip into my life like he hadn't spent all of his up to that point fighting the very things he was now forced to accept as his reality. He did it so flawlessly that no one questioned it, not even the people still alive who knew us best.

Father Nolan was the only one who had an inkling something was wrong, and it wasn't too long before he died mysteriously in his sleep. I knew what my dearest brother had done though he never said the words to me. When word reached the prison that Father Nolan had died, it was just one more weight and burden for me to bear. More blood on my hands. More death because of what I did. What I did, what Felipe started, put a truly innocent man into the crosshairs of a sociopath who shares my face.

But I can't worry about Felipe right now. Not when I'm staring down a very volatile Russian. One who doesn't seem to be buying my attempt to deflect the focus off us.

Valerian circles the chairs Genti and I rest in, considering my words, then he grasps Genti's hair and jerks back his head. The motion wakes Genti, and he stutters and rapidly blinks his eyes, trying to focus on the room around him. When he finally locks his gaze on Valerian, he snarls and tries to lash out, but the bindings holding him to the chair keep him tethered.

With his grip firm on Genti's hair, Valerian jerks his head again. "What about you? Tell me where Kat went and where I can find all the money you stole from me and weapons you took from Galen."

"Fuck you." Genti spits out the words, sending phlegm and blood splattering on Valerian's face.

Valerian shoves his head forward harshly. "I should've known you wouldn't cooperate easily. But that's okay. I have other ways to get what I need." He walks back around in front of us and focuses his gaze on me. "How is your sister these days, Mr. Rose? Recovered from her injuries sustained in the bombing?"

I freeze and narrow my eyes at him, fear gripping my chest, making it almost impossible to pull in a breath.

With me here and most of my men likely dead on the ground at the airport, Sofia is exposed at the house. If Galen ever found it, found her, she would never be able to defend herself.

She may be a whizz at the computer techy stuff, but I have never seen that girl touch a firearm or weapon of any kind for that matter. For all the bad Felipe has done, the one thing he managed during the years he raised her alone was to keep her from all the death and violence of our world, to protect her under the veil of the church. He hid his true nature from her.

It was only once I got out of prison and insisted on taking her from him that she truly understood what it is I do, and I couldn't break her heart and tell her the man she grew up believing was Felipe was really Andres and was the one responsible for our parents' deaths.

So, I let her believe I was the only devil she knew and allowed Felipe to remain her angel, the one she saw only doing good. It's bad enough I exposed her to this life, but I wasn't about to leave her with *him*—not knowing what he's capable of.

I was the lesser of two evils, even if she doesn't know it. And I can't let her be harmed now because of me. Not again.

"You leave her out of this."

Valerian shakes his head and *tsks*. "Now, now, Mr. Rose, you brought her into this, into this life, and it won't be the first time she has gotten caught up in one of your messes. The FBI may have determined that Michael Syla was behind the explosion at our meeting with the five families, but I'm not so easily convinced you weren't involved."

"Leave her alone," I growl the words and tug at my bindings, but his fist connects with my jaw again, snapping back my head.

"I'll leave her alone when you admit what you did and tell me where to find Kat and what you stole. Then, and only then, will I consider taking only your life and not hers, too. Because make no mistake, you're not walking out of here."

I never thought I would. I'm not that naïve. Nor is Genti. From the day I became Andres, the day I became Rose, I knew it would mean I would die a violent death one day and suffer for eternity in the pits of Hell.

Woe to the wicked! It shall be ill with him, for what his hands have dealt out shall be done to him.

Father Nolan's sermons never left my head even after all I've been through. They've eaten away at me, reminding me of the beliefs I held so close to my heart, despite my best efforts to become someone else completely. But in all the years I've lived this way, all the time I've spent becoming a vicious killer, I somehow never imagined I would bring so many other people down in flames with me. Like Sofia.

Valerian slowly moves forward, determination set in his jaw, pistol in his hand. "You're going to tell me what I want to know, one way or another. I can be patient."

The threat might work on someone else. Someone who hasn't been through what I have. But I can take anything he can dish out without ever saying a word about where Kat went or that she was the one behind the attack on his business.

I aim a smile at him, one that is no doubt tinged with the red blood still filling my mouth. "Try me, *amigo*."

He raises the gun and points it at me, his arm unwavering, then mumbles something to himself under his breath in Russian and smacks it against the side of my head. Darkness envelops me quickly, taking me back to the place that has been my home for twenty years.

NINE

THE DARK ABYSS SEEMS NEVER-ENDING. A swirling, nasty monster that engulfed me years ago and continues to drag me back in every time I think I've finally escaped it.

And it's sucked me into its vortex one more time.

I float through it, harsh memories I forced myself to relive in order to give Kat the truth beating at my brain, pain enveloping every fiber of my being. But then, something breaches the pitch-black. Another memory. Not the same black ones I've been drowning in.

A memory of the first light to break through the darkness in almost twenty years...

A day only a few weeks ago...

My office...

The cold blue eyes of the woman who came to me when I was at my worst...

And the words I so badly wanted to hear and feared I never would shattering the darkness...

"I wanted to make sure you were okay."

Kat's words make me freeze on the way back to my desk chair. They ring in my ears, taunting me, toying with something long buried. Something I never thought would be breathed back to life. But I heard her right, and it makes my heart stall in my chest. It breaks through the darkness surrounding me, offering me a lifeline. A glimpse of a shining, beautiful light I've never had in my life.

I turn to face her slowly. My hand that shook so badly only a moment ago is steady as I bring my drink to my lips again and drain the rest of it. I need it to help steel my nerves for what's about to go down. I set the empty glass on the edge of the desk. "You wanted to make sure I was okay, muñeca?"

She squares her shoulders and straightens her spine, readying herself for what she just brought on. It's almost like she knows I'm coming for her now, that by saying those words, she's unleashing the beast that's been barely contained.

I've waited so long to hear her admit she cares. I've been pushing up against her, fighting against the thick, impenetrable wall she's erected around herself, fearing I would never break through. But those words mean I have at least cracked it. It might not have tumbled yet, may not have completely come down, but there's a tiny opening. One I intend to probe until it finally shatters.

And now, she's scared. Every inch of her body vibrates, and she shifts on her feet, like she's debating whether to turn and bolt, make a run for it from my office. But she has nowhere to hide. Not here in my home. I know every inch of this place like the back of my hand, and when I'm done with her tonight, I'll know every inch of her body the same way.

She sucks in a deep breath, a pink blush spreading over her cheeks. "That's what I said, wasn't it?"

I take a step forward, a smirk spreading across my lips. "You did, but I'm not so sure I believe you. You haven't seemed too interested in admitting any sort of feelings for me except hatred and distrust, so I'm a little surprised by your admission. It makes me question the veracity of your statement."

As much as I want to believe her words, want them to be true more than I've wanted anything in my life, I'm not sure I can trust her. It could all be a ruse, some part of her master plan to get close to me in order to betray me the way she did Michael.

Three more steps bring me even closer to her, but instead of stopping in front of her, I move around her, push the door closed, and flip the lock. This close, her warm, sweet scent invades every breath I take, and I close the distance between us, pressing my chest into her back and lowering my head to taste the sensitive skin just behind her ear. I suck gently, and her knees almost buckle. A low hum of approval slips from her lips, and my cock swells against her ass.

"Tell me why you really came, Kat. Tell me the real reason.""

She swallows thickly and straightens her shoulders. "I just did."

I kiss my way down the long, elegant column of her neck and across the exposed portion of her collarbone. I'd give anything to see it all, to rip these clothes from her body and ravage her, and I slip my fingers along the edge of her collar and pull it to the side to expose a shoulder so I can continue to explore her with my mouth. But before this goes any further, I need to hear the words again, to assess them and be able to ascertain their truth. "Tell me again."

Kat's legs tremble, and she shifts her weight back to gain some support against me. "I wanted to see if you were okay."

Even hearing it a second time, the words have the same effect as if they'd never left her lips before. My heart stops for a second, waiting for her to take them back. "Because?"

I'm going to push Kat. It's the only way we'll ever stop playing this game, one I never wanted to begin with. I've never been anything but direct with Kat about what I wanted from her, but she continues to dance around me and lead me down an endless path filled with mixed signals and moves designed to throw me off. That stops now.

She clenches her jaw and squeezes her eyes closed, stiffening when I press my lips to her shoulder again. "Because I do care, dammit. As much as I fucking hate you and what you are doing to me, seeing you that shaken shook something in me."

I freeze with my lips against her shoulder blade and slowly drag my head back. She saw me with Sofia arguing about Felipe. She saw my distress. She saw my weakness, and it brought out something in her I've been trying to get to for months. I wrap my left hand around her throat and tilt her face until her eyes meet mine.

The same lust I feel for her stares back at me.

This. This is what I've been waiting for.

But she needs to know what she's doing, what she's asking for.

I raise an eyebrow at her and tighten my grip on her throat, jerking her head back even farther. My other hand squeezes her shoulder, keeping her pinned back against my body, and I rub my cock against her lower back, pushing into her, ensuring she can feel all of me. "Are you sure this is what you want, muñeca? *Are you sure you're ready for what all this means?"*

Her body tenses even more, but she doesn't look away. I see it there, deep in her eyes, that trepidation to fully let herself go and give herself to me. It's understandable, given all she went through with Aleksander and Michael, but continuing to deny what's happening between us will only hurt us both in the end.

For a split second, I think she's going to say no, but instead, a breathy "yes" slips from her lips before I crash mine down on them in a punishing kiss meant to claim her the way I've wanted to since I first saw her.

TEN

I JERK on her arm to turn her to face me and crash our mouths and chests together. Even with every inch of our bodies pressing against each other, it's not enough. Not nearly close enough. All the pent-up aggression and tension that's built between us for months has finally released, and it's a runaway train that can't be stopped.

Not when I've waited this long. Not when she's everything I thought I couldn't have—a true equal. A partner. Someone who wants the same thing.

I reach for the waistband of her pants and shove them down her hips in one smooth motion. Kat groans into my mouth, and I return a low growl that rumbles in my chest. She cups my hard cock, and I back her up until her ass hits the desk—never taking my lips from hers, refusing to give away even a second now that I have her.

I slide my hand between her legs and slip my fingers into her wet heat easily.

Fuck.

She is so ready for me. Ready for this. For us.

A gasp slips from her mouth into mine, and she jerks against my hold. I curl my fingers up to find her G-spot and pump into her. The last time we were like this, I left her hanging to show her how much she wanted it. To try to force her to see what was happening if she didn't want to accept it.

But not tonight. Tonight, she's finally mine.

She fumbles at my waist, trying to undo the button of my pants, and finally manages to free my cock.

Ella me tragó!

My mouth waters just thinking about what her cunt tastes like, so as much as I want to keep feeling her hands on my cock, I drag my mouth from hers and drop to my knees to pull her pants to her ankles. She kicks off her shoes, and I jerk the fabric from her feet, letting it fall to the floor beside me.

Completely exposed to me, the scent of her arousal makes my cock twitch, and I lock eyes with her to find an unrelenting lust soaking her gaze. "I can smell how much you want me from here, muñeca."

Before she can try to deny what we both know to be true, I lean forward and shove my tongue between her legs and through her slit. She gasps and clings to the edge of the desk, her body tensing under me.

Sweet fuck, she tastes incredible. I flick my tongue over her clit in a way that makes her jerk and spasm under me, her entire body practically vibrating. But it isn't near enough. I want her totally mindless, out of control, desperate and begging for me.

I slide my fingers back inside her, and she clenches her cunt around them so hard, I can almost feel it in my aching cock.

Her hands twine through my hair, and she tugs, trying to force me up from my knees, but I won't relent. I won't offer her any quarter from the assault on her clit. I lash at it with my tongue while I pump my fingers inside her. Her hips roll in time with my ministrations, building her up and winding her tighter.

Toying with her is fun, but I want her to explode. I want to feel her contract around my fingers and thrash at me while she comes.

I suck her clit between my teeth and bite down. It's exactly what she needs. She shatters, clawing at the back of my neck and shoving her hips against my face. I offer no mercy, no break from the pleasure that must be wracking her system right now. My mouth and fingers never stop moving, never stop demanding more from her and her body.

When she finally manages to shove me away, I offer her a slow grin and lick my lips as I push to my feet, taking my cock in my hand. She grasps the front of my white shirt and tugs me against her, sealing her mouth to mine.

The taste of her release on my tongue seems to only turn her on more, or maybe it's me stroking my cock and rubbing the head against her engorged clit with each movement. Whatever it is, she can barely control herself, kissing and practically mauling me like an animal.

She pulls back slightly, locking her needy gaze with mine. "Metemelo ya!"

Get inside me.

Her words are my undoing, turning me from a man into a ruthless animal. I growl, grip her left hip with one hand, and align my cock with the other. Eyes locked on hers, I shove into her violently enough to force the breath from her lips. The motion sends her back across the desk, but my strong fingers digging into her soft flesh prevent her from bucking completely off.

Being inside Kat—the wet heat that welcomes every driving thrust—is truly finding home. A place I haven't had since that fateful day. It's light. It's freedom from the lies I still have to live, the ones I still have to keep from her, even if only for a few moments.

I drag back my hips and plunge into her again, allowing the head of my cock to drag against the perfect spot inside her to make her gasp and drop her head forward. She wraps her legs around my hips, digging her heels into my lower back to urge me to move harder.

And it's still not enough.

I press urgent kisses up her neck and across her cheek to her lips and probe my tongue into her mouth, thrusting in time with my cock.

This isn't just sex. This is a coming together of two powerful people who are finally willing to share a moment of weakness in order to strengthen ourselves and each other. This seals our future, the one I've always wanted with her. The harder I thrust into her, the more certain I become that she's the one who will keep the darkness at bay forever.

She scratches her nails against the back of my neck and bites down on my tongue. But even the coppery tang of blood can't stop me. I groan and fuck her even harder, her hips meeting my merciless rhythm.

The second orgasm hits her, and she sucks in a breath and tenses, her pussy clasping around my cock like a vise. I hold her steady while I plow into her again and again, drawing out her release and searching for my own.

I grasp her chin and force her face down. "Open your eyes, muñeca!"

Those icy-blue orbs stare at me, and I clench my jaw and push into her, taking what I need from the body she's willing to offer.

A few more violent thrusts cement my claim on her, and I finally come, my cock throbbing and releasing all my cum into her still-spasming cunt. I bury my face against her neck and bring my lips to her ear as I trail my hands to her breasts to pinch and twist her nipples. "I told you it was only a matter of time, mi cielo. But now, you're mine."

ELEVEN

"ROSE! ROSE! WAKE THE FUCK UP!" A harsh, angry voice breaks through the warm, welcoming memory I had been lost in. Kat floats away into the light that races forward to push away the black. "Rose!"

I jerk awake to find myself in the same cold room, tied to the same chair. Seems not much about my situation has improved, but at least now Genti is conscious. It isn't much, but for a while there, I thought he might be dead. So, I'll take it as one for the win column right now. A win we could certainly use when everything seems to be stacked against us.

There isn't much hope for the future. They've left us alone in the room, strapped to these chairs and weak from being assaulted, and we're at their mercy unless something presents itself. The memory of my first time with Kat reminds me of what we're fighting for, though. I have to get to her, ensure she and Jet are safe and remain that way.

Genti struggles against the bindings at his hands and feet, grunting in frustration. I don't bother telling him it's pointless and doing it will only dig the material into his skin, hurting him more. He wouldn't listen anyway. Not when his instinct is to fight against anything preventing him from getting to her.

I shake my head to clear the fog enveloping it, fully pulling myself out of the memory and back to reality. Unfortunately, it's a harsh one. I would have preferred to stay unconscious, lost with Kat and the time we spent together in that way. "What happened while I was out?"

"I don't know. It's been a couple minutes since I woke up." Blood trickles down the side of his face from an open wound at his temple.

From the feel of something warm and wet on my cheek, I'm sure my face looks the same after Valerian pistol-whipped me. "Have you seen anyone?"

He shakes his head. "No. They must've assumed we'd be unconscious longer."

Shit.

We need to get out of here—fast.

Genti glances at me out of the corner of his eye, suddenly looking uneasy. "Do you think Kat is okay?"

Acid churns in my stomach, and it isn't just because we don't know about Kat; it's the look Genti is giving me now and the way I've seen him look at Kat.

He's in love with her. It's so obvious; I'm not sure why I never noticed it before. Probably because I wasn't looking for it and assumed he was just her loyal right hand. But it's only natural he would fall for her. She's the perfect woman if you're in this life. It doesn't scare her. In fact, she might be more ruthless than any of our enemies. She's precisely the woman I've been looking for since the moment I left those prison walls, someone who can handle this life and embrace it.

Why wouldn't Genti fall for her? I did in an instant.

Whether Kat feels anything for him is another question. It might explain her reluctance to commit to me, to accept my offer of partnership—in business and life. But I can't worry about that now and won't allow myself to wonder if she's harboring something for the man who protects her and the Gashi business. There are greater things at stake right now—our lives.

"I fucking hope she's okay. As they shoved me into the back of the SUV, I saw the plane take off. So at least we know she got airborne."

Now whether they were able to get out of the country and to Albania is another question. No doubt, the gunfire at the airport attracted the attention of the authorities. If they suspected anyone on board that plane was involved in any way, they might have big trouble I can't help her get out of.

"What do you want to do?" Genti looks to me like I have all the answers when all I have is frustration and pain.

I tug at my restraints and scan the room for anything that might be of use. But it seems this room was designed to do exactly what it's doing—keeping captives contained. Only one door—one way in and out. A single fluorescent bulb overhead, barely lighting the empty space. No obvious way to free ourselves.

"I don't know."

"Fuck! Do you think Valerian is going to kill us?"

I grit my jaw. "It's a distinct possibility. He told me as much. But he also wants back what was taken from him, and it seems that his friendship with Galen, however tenuous we may think it is, is strong enough that he doesn't believe me when I say it could have been him. But I have another idea."

"What's that?"

"Offer to help him locate it."

"You want to actually help that fucker?"

I whip my head toward him. "Of course not. And he'll likely try to kill us as soon as we get his shit back for him. But if I offer Sofia's services and you offer Arden's, perhaps we can buy Kat some more time she desperately needs."

If she doesn't get to Albania and get her hands on her son, I don't even want to think about the possible consequences.

Genti snarls at me. "That doesn't sound like much of a plan."

I scowl at him. "Then give me a fucking better one. I'm all ears."

He glares at me, anger flashing deep in his eyes, though whether or not it's actually directed at me isn't clear. "I get your point."

"I don't like it any more than you do, Genti, but unless we can get out of these bindings, we don't have a fighting chance."

"Even if we do get free from these chairs, how are we going to fight our way unarmed out the single door that undoubtedly leads to a facility swarming with Russians?"

I snort. "I'll think of something. I always do."

It seems this has become my life now, scrambling to survive in a hostile environment against enemies at every turn. And here, I thought surviving prison was hard. But the memory of my first day there that has haunted me my entire life suddenly offers a new possibility.

I glance around the cold room with renewed focus and hope welling in my chest. This room isn't unlike another one I once found myself in—four walls, one way in and out. But it's also old and crumbling, and that could be our ticket out of here.

"What?" Genti looks around like he's missing something, trying to figure out what I'm doing.

I finally turn my focus to the floor between my feet and grin. "I think I have a way out of here. Or at least, a way out of these bindings."

Genti follows my gaze, his eyes narrowing. "You really think that's gonna work?"

God willing.

Too bad I turned my back on Him a long time ago.

I shake my head, my heart pounding against my rib cage. "No." I turn my head to meet his scrutinizing gaze. "I don't *think* it will. I'm *sure* it will. I've done it before."

# TWELVE

20 YEARS AGO

THE SOUL-CRUSHING pain wakes me before any noise can, but as soon as reality starts eating away at the edges of the pitch-black darkness that's enveloped me, the cacophony of sound can't be ignored any longer—a deafening roar of hundreds of angry, frantic voices mixing with the inmates thumping against hard concrete and banging against heavy metal bars.

This is the sound of my life for the next several decades, maybe forever. Back-to-back sentences for over half a dozen murders. A new reality I have to embrace...along with a new name.

Andres...

All the time I pretended to be him as a child so he wouldn't get in trouble should have prepared me for this, but nothing could. Not really. This is a life I never contemplated. But the pain wracking my body, making it nearly impossible for me to move even slightly without agony turning my stomach will be a part of my new reality, if I don't do something about it fast, if I don't embrace who I have to become and what I have to do.

For the few weeks I was in the local jail, I was somewhat insulated. Some of the police may have been on the payroll of the man I killed, but many are also the neighbors I grew up with and friends of *Mama y Papa*. So, while they had an obligation to arrest me and try me for my crimes, they also understood why I did what I did—or why "Andres" did it, rather.

They held no ill will toward him/me and also knew enough not to lay a hand on him, so I was "safe" for a short while, but I knew as soon as I was transferred, as soon as I was moved out of the protection of the local police, that things would change.

And they did the moment I set foot in this prison.

It seems my victim had a lot of friends here, people who didn't appreciate what I did to him, his men, and especially his wife. Even Andres' reputation couldn't protect me from their wrath. The moment I stepped off the transport van, I was hit before I even had a chance to protect or defend myself, and the blows didn't stop until I was unconscious.

They may not have even stopped then, for all I know. They may have taken the opportunity to do other things to me they wouldn't dare attempt when I was awake. Rolling onto my side, the places I'm feeling the pain suggest they likely did.

I wince and grit my teeth, clenching my fists at my side. The guards took advantage of my vulnerable position. But it *won't* happen again. It *can't* if I'm going to survive in this place. If this ruse is going to have any effect, I have to show my dominance immediately. Not just stand up for myself but demonstrate what happens if anyone messes with me.

Fracture for fracture, eye for eye, tooth for tooth; whatever injury he has given a person shall be given to him.

Those words Father Nolan read from the Bible so often heat my blood. Wrath begs for revenge, but it crashes against what I was always taught by both the old priest and *Mama y Papa*.

If anyone slaps you on the right cheek, turn to them the other cheek also.

The warring biblical teachings push against each other in my aching head while I slowly push myself up on one elbow and wipe away the sticky, drying blood from around my eyes so I can take in the room.

Four crumbling cinderblock walls. A broken tile floor. Two bent and rusted showerheads. This must be the shower room where they bring new prisoners to welcome them the way they did me.

Over the constant din of the other prisoners, a laugh hits my ears that makes me freeze. Despite the injuries I just sustained no doubt affecting my ability to think and process, the memory of that laugh makes my fist clench.

One of the men who attacked me. I'd remember that laugh anywhere. They're no doubt celebrating what they did to me, relishing in the fact that they were able to beat up the great "Andres."

I force myself to my feet, wavering as the room spins around me and grabbing the wall to keep myself from falling over. It would be easy to give up. To collapse back into a broken heap on the floor. To give up the plan Andres and I so carefully crafted. To let this place defeat me. But one thing I learned at a young age was mind over matter.

You can accomplish anything if you set your mind to it, mijo.

Of course, *Mama* had been talking about my schooling and about my desire to one day join the priesthood. I'm sure she hadn't contemplated this scenario. How could she have? I was the perfect son, the perfect child. I was her angel while Andres was the devil. The reckless one. The one always pushing the boundaries and railing against authority.

Only now I am *Andres*. I have to stop thinking of myself as Felipe and start becoming my brother.

Now.

I pause near the opening in the far wall—the only way in or out of the shower room—to listen to try to gauge how many men are outside. Two distinct voices reach me, their words garbled by the distance and the fact that my head is still not quite on straight. I squeeze my eyes closed and shake it to try to clear the remaining cobwebs from the beating and flex and clench my hands, releasing the stiffness there. The cracked knuckles tell me I must've at least attempted to fight back even if I have no memory of it. Just that laugh and blows and kicks landing on me from all sides. There had to have been five or six of them—not just these two.

But I have to start somewhere, with someone.

This is the first step to truly becoming Andres and establishing myself here so I'll be protected.

I take a deep, fortifying breath that I immediately regret when instead of a fresh shower scent, the odor of the hundreds of men who are locked up in here to rot away hits me. No one cares about the men here. Don't care if we don't bathe for a month or even a year. Don't care if we die here or kill each other for sport. But they will care about what I'm about to do. At least, I hope they will. It will send exactly the message I need it to—fast and clear—one I can't have fall on deaf ears.

Do not repay anyone evil for evil. Do not take revenge, my dear friends, but leave room for God's wrath, for it is written: "It is mine to avenge; I will repay," says the Lord.

The words of the Apostle John echo in my head, drilling at my brain. My palms sweat, and I shake them off and wipe them against the dirty and bloodied pants they left on me.

That life is gone. I no longer have the luxury of having a conscience. I can no longer question whether what I'm doing is morally right or wrong. As far as I'm concerned, the moral compass will always be pointing north, no matter what I'm doing.

It's the only way I'll survive this, and if nothing else, I have to survive for Sofia. To ensure that she has someone besides Andres...Felipe...to mold her into a true human being. Because if he's the only influence she has in her life, she's doomed. As doomed as I now am to this life.

I push away everything I've been raised to believe, the teachings Father Nolan gave during his daily sermons. I force them all to the far recesses of my mind and lock them away in a vault I know can never open. Then I suck in a deep breath again, throw back my shoulders, and step out into the small room outside the shower.

The two guards sit chatting and eating at a small table—the one with his back to me has no clue what's coming. His buddy catches me move out of the corner of his eye, but before he can open his mouth to warn his friend, I'm on him.

I move on instinct, violence and anger I never knew I possessed rising to the surface just like it did in that beautiful home I covered in blood.

The piece of broken tile in my hand slices through his neck like butter. Despite being a less than ideal weapon, it rips his jugular easily, and arterial spray splashes across the table and their lunches as his friend leaps back and reaches for his gun.

But whether it's fear, stupidity, or because he's so tired from the beating he gave me, his movements are slow and telegraphed, and I kick his hand before he gets anywhere near the weapon and launch myself at him, knocking him to the ground and slashing down with the shard of tile in one movement.

It misses my intended target zone at his throat and slices open his cheek instead, but the well of blood makes him reach up and press a hand over it rather than defending himself with both. "No. Don't."

That voice.

Flashes of what occurred to me before I fell unconscious rush back. This was the ringleader. This was the man in charge. *This* was the man who was the driving force behind my attack.

I lean over him, sneering down. "I hope you had a fucking good time because now you're going to pay for what you've done."

He tries to scramble away, but when he realizes my body weight is enough to keep him down, his lip quivers violently and he shakes his head. "You're the one who's going to pay."

I press the shard of tile against his throat and grin at him. "That's what you can't possibly understand—I already have."

THIRTEEN

THE DOOR FLIES open ten minutes later, whoever's entering clearly expecting to find two unconscious secured prisoners unwilling and unable to fight back. The two big Russians chuckle and joke with each other until one turns his focus to where I sit on my chair and then darts it over to the empty one beside me where Genti used to sit before I freed him from his bindings after tipping my chair and grabbing the lifeline from the floor.

"*Chyort voz'mi!*"

Surprise, assholes.

In that split second, Genti strikes, using the sharp piece of broken tile from the floor like a dagger and driving it straight into the man's jugular. Before the second henchman can react, Genti grabs the gun from his first victim and I fly off my chair, ignoring the pain in my shoulder from the bullet still lodged in it and from the beatings I took at Valerian's hands and distracting the remaining man long enough for Genti to put three quick bullets into him.

I never liked the Albanian. Not when he worked for Michael Syla, and certainly not when he started working for Kat. And now that I have confirmed his feelings for her, it gives me even more reason not to trust him. He could just as easily turn that gun on me the same way he just did and eliminate any competition he has for Kat's affections.

For a split second, I almost think he might. He keeps the gun raised rather than lowering it. It would only take a tiny movement for him to turn it on me.

Do it. I dare you, amigo.

He might kill me, but the result would be so catastrophic for him and likely Kat at the hands of my brother that he would wish the Russians had just killed him at that fucking airport. Because truth be told, despite my disagreements with Felipe, despite the fact that he likely has tried to kill me already with the plane tampering, despite the warnings he gave Kat to stay away from me, he would still destroy anyone who ever harmed me. If he wants me gone, he wants to do it at his own hand. An attack by anyone else is an attack on the Blood Rose Cartel, regardless of whether it serves his ultimate goal or not.

And Genti must know that, must understand the position it puts him in, because he lowers the weapon and motions toward the body for me to grab the gun from the other man. Genti presses his back against the wall to the side of the door, and I move into position next to him. Those shots are sure to bring someone else running, and with only one entry and exit point, we're screwed trying to get out as much as they are walking in here.

"You ready to do this?" Genti checks the magazine to see what he has left for bullets and frowns.

That can't be a good sign.

Nodding my agreement to move forward, I do the same. Neither man has extra magazines on him, probably because they never anticipated needing to use their weapons in here, let alone reloading. It's bad luck for us, considering any number of Valerian's goons might be waiting for us just outside this door.

What I wouldn't give for a cell phone and a stack of loaded magazines. I could get us out of here in no time flat. But we need to work with what we have, however little it might be. Just like being back in prison, stay alive by any means.

Footsteps and frantic yelling in Russian move toward us down the hall, alerted by the shots. It was a calculated risk to use the firearms. We could have tried to fight both men with our hands and broken tile, but given both of our weakened states and the fact that they were both armed, it was a battle we could have easily lost—and likely would have. Tipping my chair and freeing Gentry sucked any energy I had from me, and I'm moving on barely existent stores of adrenaline.

It won't last long. *I* won't last long before I collapse.

We wait until the first idiot is stupid enough take a step into the room. Genti puts one well-placed shot in the side of his head, dropping him instantly. His comrade cries out behind him in the hall and is smart enough to fire through the door rather than step through it and take his chances of ending up like his friend on the floor.

Shifting back a few feet, anticipating the assault through the door, we wait, but instead of anyone coming through, bullets tear straight through the drywall we're pressed up against. One strikes me in the back of the thigh while one hits Genti in the left shoulder.

"Fuck!" We both whirl and start firing through the wall at an assailant we can't see.

Someone cries out, and we hear a thump in the hallway. The bullets stop, and we cease firing. With a lack of ammo, we don't want to waste what little we have, even if there is still a chance someone is alive out there.

I glance over at Genti's left arm, hanging limply at his side and his Glock useless in his hand. It's empty. Given the number of shots he's used, he's out, and I only have a few left. But we don't have any time to plan what to do next.

"We have to move." I grit out the words and try to take a step, but my leg buckles from under me. I press my hand against the wound and glance down at the pooling blood on the floor where I've been standing. "Shit."

The adrenaline coursing through my system momentarily let me forget about being shot, but there's no ignoring the pain or the amount of red at my feet. If that bullet hit an artery, then I'll bleed out in minutes before we'll ever be able to get out of here. And Genti is in no position to help me walk out of here with the blood flowing from his own arm.

I pull off my belt and wrap it around my thigh, tightening it with gritted teeth. There isn't any time for weakness now. Pressing my bloody hand against the wall to stabilize myself, I nod toward the door. We need to move as fast as possible. Any time we stand around waiting, we lose more blood and give them more time to get to us before we can figure out a way to escape this place. "Go."

Genti inclines his head and peeks out around the corner. Our only hope is whoever we dropped out here in the hallway has enough ammo left to get us out of here alive. But we don't even know where the fuck *here* is.

All we can do is pray Kat made it to her destination because it doesn't look like we're going to make it to ours. And given my relationship with the big man upstairs, I doubt our prayers will be heard anyway.

We need to save ourselves. But it won't be the first time I've had to fight my way out of some-where meant to keep me contained.

FOURTEEN

1 CORINTHIANS 10:13: *No temptation has overtaken you that is not common to man. God is faithful, and he will not let you be tempted beyond your ability, but with the temptation he will also provide the way of escape, that you may be able to endure it.*

I read the highlighted Bible passage again and slowly close the book and set it onto the small rickety table in my small cell. The worn, leather binding bears the scratches and marks of years of use. Resting my hand on it, the weight of the words seeps through the surface and pushes heavily on my shoulders.

Slowly, I raise my head to meet the gaze of the man who brought it to me. "Where did this come from?"

Santiago arrived only moments ago with the book in hand. Even though I know what it means and who sent it, I still have to ask, still have to be certain that the words truly hold the meaning I know in my heart they do.

He inclines his head toward the book. "Sister Rachel brought it from the church when she came today."

Felipe's church.

The one that used to belong to Father Nolan. Where I spent the most peaceful, joyful times of my life outside our family home. The place I once felt an overwhelming sense of God's presence that's now been tainted by the Devil himself.

It's the same way he's been sending me orders and messages for the last decade. Under the guise of ministry to the prisoners, secret messages written in plain sight for anyone who bothered to look, through simple highlighted passages that wouldn't mean anything to anyone else.

And like those, this one is only for me. I just hadn't expected it so soon.

My sentence for the three murders amounted to essentially life—because in here, no one would survive long enough to serve them out and be released. That was likely the hope of my sentencing judge—that I would die at the hands of an attack by another inmate or from one of the diseases that often ravage us here.

But our plan has worked perfectly. My first day here, I sent a message that left no room for interpretation. That I wasn't to be touched; that I wasn't to be messed with; that I was the one to fear. Leaving ten bodies of guards decimated around the facility has that effect. When the warden returned that day and found what I had done, he knew what it meant. He was no longer in control.

I could have easily escaped that day, walked right out the front door over the bodies of the men I had killed. But I didn't. That was never part of the plan. If I had left, it would have made me a fugitive rather than giving my brother the ability to use me to conduct his business. Plus, I never could have left Sofia. Even just seeing her when she comes to visit gives me an opportunity to still play a role in her life. Felipe never would've let me take her if I had tried back then, but maybe now...maybe there's a chance. Maybe I can free her from the grasp of that man once I'm free.

Because this message means only one thing—it's time for me to leave this literal prison and step into a figurative one. One where I play a role in public while Felipe pulls the strings in private.

"Did she say anything else?"

Santiago shakes his head. "Just that I should ensure you got this."

I nod slowly and cast my gaze on the Bible again—one more way Felipe has corrupted what I once loved to advance his sinister goals. Goals I am forced to work for with him as the "head" of this cartel, even from behind bars. I was never quite sure if, when the time came, Felipe would somehow arrange for my release legally or whether I would have to fight my way out, but this message makes his intentions clear.

He wants to see me send one final message on my way into the world from the prison. A statement that will ensure no one touches me on the outside just like they haven't in here. He's building up the reputation of "Rose" so that we'll only have more power once I'm in a suit and looking the part instead of here in these rags in this dirty cell.

I push up from my chair and slowly make my way over to the barred window that overlooks the common courtyard teeming with inmates. They sit together in various groups, laughing, joking, exchanging goods. This place has its heartbeat. It's a city, and I am its mayor.

Only, they'll soon have to elect a new one.

I clasp my hands behind me and glance over my shoulder at Santiago. "Are you prepared?"

His dark eyebrows furrow. "For what, *jefe?*"

Armageddon.

I turn back to him because I need to see his reaction, need to know he's behind me one hundred percent. Because none of these men know the truth. They don't know that I've just been biding my time, waiting for this order. They don't know what awaits them on the outside. Many have been here for so long, they don't remember what life out there is like. I'm not one of them. I remember it well; it haunts me every night when I close my eyes and every day as I wake. But Santiago has been here so long, I often wonder if he remembers what it is like to live normally.

Yet, he's the one I trust the most, the one who has been at my side almost from the beginning. He will be the only one leaving with me. If we tried to get all my men out, we would undoubtedly fail. If they even wanted to leave.

"To leave this place or die trying." I walk over to Santiago and clasp his shoulder. "We're leaving tonight, *mi amigo.*"

"Leaving?" His eyebrow rises as he tries to process what I'm saying.

"Yes."

"Should I get the men ready?"

"No." I shake my head.

A massive assault from the entire prison would ensure our successful escape, but it isn't the message Felipe would want me to send. He wants whatever we have to do to get out to be my decision and my actions so that "Rose" can claim responsibility rather than saying simply that his men did his dirty work.

He wants more blood on my hands; it seems it's all he's wanted since that day he pushed me to take my first life.

"We won't be needing them, Santiago. It's just you and me." I walk over to the thin mattress where I've slept for the last decade and reach under it to retrieve two large knives. This won't be the first time I've used them to kill, nor will it be the last. "We have each other's backs at all times. No one survives."

He nods his understanding, accepts the weapon from my outstretched hand, and steps toward the door.

We pause there for a moment, and I look back at the room where I've lived as Andres and Rose. Our plan has worked so far, and now, it's time for the next step.

Now, it's just Santiago and me. Two men on a mission—only one truly understanding the consequences of it.

FIFTEEN

THE HALLWAY HOLDS evidence of the fact that Genti and I are either excellent shots or lucky as hell. Probably the latter, given the fact that neither of us is in prime condition right now. Yet, somehow, the few rounds we let loose through the wall hit their marks. Two men lie on the old linoleum, blood pooling under their lifeless bodies.

Immediately, I check the hallway to the right and Genti scans to the left for any coming threats. The place is eerily silent, though. Nothing imminent. So we make our way to the bodies and search them for weapons.

Genti manages to work the sling for an assault rifle off the shoulder of one of the men while I grab a Glock from the other.

I hold it out to Genti. "Here. You're probably better off with this with only one arm."

He nods and hands me the AR before we conduct a quick search of the bodies that reveals nothing else of use. No additional magazines. No radio or cell phone. Nothing that can assist us in getting out of this building.

I scan the hallway for cameras but don't find any. "No cameras. Depending on how big this facility is, these may have been the only people who heard the shots."

Genti snorts and shakes his head. "You really think we're that lucky?"

"I sure as hell hope so."

He glances back and forth down the hall. "Which way?"

It's a crapshoot. A fifty-fifty chance that one way will lead us to safety while the other will lead us straight to the lion's den. Other than dirty gray walls and crumbling plaster, there isn't much to give us any information about either direction.

"That way." I incline my head to the right. "It sounded like these men came from the left."

At least, in that room, it did. I could be completely wrong about that. It could've been the acoustics off the old tile or a trick of the ear. But it's all we have right now.

Genti nods his agreement, and I force myself to take a step forward on the leg that doesn't want to cooperate. Half dragging it behind me, I grit my teeth. A trail of blood continues to follow both of us down the hall, dribbling from Genti's left fingers and down my pants leg. I may have managed to staunch the major flow, but I'm still losing blood fast. If we don't get out of here soon, this will be my final resting place.

I haven't gotten this far, done what I've done, to die like this.

No fucking way.

We make it to end of the hall, where it branches off again to the left and the right. A familiar scent hits my nose, and I lift my head in each direction.

"This way." I point to the left.

"Why?"

"Because I smell garlic coming from that way. Maybe a kitchen or break area."

Genti nods his agreement and follows behind me, keeping his eye on our backs. The hallway seems to go on forever, closed doors on either side, any one of which might contain any number of our enemy. But we don't pause to check.

The farther we make our way down the hall, the tighter unease wraps around my spine. Wherever we are seems to be a vast endless maze of corridors that could be leading us anywhere. One of the doors on my left stands open, and I glance in and freeze. An old metal bed frame and dirty mattress sit against the far wall, along with ancient medical equipment.

"An old medical facility?" I incline my head toward the door for Genti to take a look.

His eyes open wide. "I think I know where we are. There's an old hospital in the East Village. We always suspected the Russians were using it for something, but they weren't exactly our top priority, so we never investigated it further."

The East Village?

That's a long way from anyone I know, or any place I can think of that would be safe for us to get to fast...if we even manage to get out of this hell hole.

"You have any idea the layout of the place?"

Genti shakes his head. "No. Other than I think it was several stories high."

We haven't seen any windows yet, so for all I know, we could be five floors up, making a window escape impossible. I'm not sure I could do stairs to make it to the ground floor even if we found them. The way my leg feels right now, it might as well be dead weight.

The blood loss starts to make me woozy, the hallway fading in and out of focus, but I keep pushing forward.

I can't give up. Not when Kat is out there alone with Felipe potentially after her.

Suck it up. Keep moving.

Aside from Sofia, I've never cared what happened to anyone else in my life until I set eyes on Kat. Now, it feels like her life is tied to mine. That if anything were to happen to her or her son, *I* would feel it as if it were happening to me.

It's insane. Stupid. Some hopeless romantic bullshit I have no desire or right to feel, yet, it's there all the same, sitting in the center of my chest and driving me forward when my body wants to give up.

Not an option.

I push on, Genti following slowly behind me, until the end of the hallway comes into view, along with a possible chance of escape. An ancient-looking elevator stands at the end. The call button only goes one way—up. We must be in a basement. It would make sense if this were a medical facility. The room they were holding us in was probably once part of a morgue or an operating room of some sort. It would explain the tile floors and lack of windows.

Please be working.

Genti points his gun at the elevator door. "You want to get *in* this thing?"

I glance up and down the hallway. An unlit exit sign hangs on a door at the far end. "I don't think I can make the stairs. I say we press the button and see what happens."

He scowls at me, his annoyance at me and the situation twisting his lips. "You really enjoy gambling with your life, don't you?"

"No. Really, I don't. It just seems to be the way my life is." I smash my hand against the button, and it lights up.

The elevator doors open slowly with a strangled screech of metal, and I wince. This really does feel like rolling the dice with my life stepping into this deathtrap, but death has become a friend as well as an almost continuous enemy. The threat of the Grim Reaper won't stop me now.

I limp inside it with Genti watching my back, and we both turn to face the open doors. One of Valerian's men turns the corner at the far end of the hallway and spots us, just as the doors slip closed.

"Shit."

SIXTEEN

GENTI GLANCES over at me the moment the doors fully close and slams the muzzle of his gun against the button on the elevator control panel on his side that will bring us to the first floor—and hopefully a way out of here. "They're going to be waiting for us as soon as those doors open."

I lean against the wall to keep from toppling over, fatigue and blood loss blurring my vision and making me feel as weak as a newborn, and nod. "Yep."

"We'll never get out of here alive."

A dark laugh slips from my lips, and I shrug, wincing at the pain in my shoulder where I took the bullet at the airport. "We might not live even if we do get out." I glance at the blood dripping from his fingers and down at the small pool forming under me from only seconds standing still. "Neither of us in ideal shape for a race for our lives, *amigo*."

He grunts his acknowledgment as the ancient elevator car jerks up, a grinding squeal rattling the metal walls. It doesn't instill much confidence.

I glance up at the ceiling and around the tight car. It has to be at least fifty years old, maybe even as much as a century. Long before Gentry or I were born, and likely not serviced since around that time, either. "This thing might kill us, too."

Genti chuckles mirthlessly and shakes his head. "What's our plan?"

"Same as before. Shoot our fucking way out and try to find a car. God knows I'm not getting out of here on foot." I cast him an accusatory look and scan his two working legs from the floor up to meet his gaze.

He raises a dark eyebrow at me and growls. "You think I'm going to leave you here and run away?"

"If you haven't lost so much blood that you can't, why wouldn't you?"

He snorts and shakes his head. "Because I'm too afraid of Kat to do that. She would fucking kill me if I left you here to die."

Now I'm the one to snort and shake my head. His statement is likely true, but he's glossing over the way it would help him immensely. "It would only open the door for you if I were out of the way..."

He opens his mouth like he's going to argue that point, but the elevator dings and the doors start to slide open. The moment they do, bullets come flying through the opening, and we jump forward to take cover against the front panels to either side.

They were definitely waiting for us—no doubt their friend downstairs called in an SOS after he saw us get into the elevator. There isn't any way of knowing how many of them there are, but whether it's two or twenty, we have no choice but to take them on.

One way in. One way out.

This is becoming a real recurring problem in my life.

I hold up a hand and count down. *Three. Two. One.*

We both turn toward the open doors and begin firing. My AR easily tears through the half dozen men in the hallway just outside. They clearly hadn't contemplated the fact that we might have stopped for their friends' weapons downstairs. Despite being hit, several of them keep firing, and a bullet grazes my shoulder that was hit at the airport. The stab of pain doesn't stop me from driving forward, forging a path through for me and Genti at my side.

I can't check to see if he's been hit again or not; I just have to rely on him to keep moving the same way I am. What he said about Kat killing him for leaving me behind is true for him as well. She'll expect me to do everything in my power to get him out of here alive with me, and I don't intend to let her down any more than I already have.

When the last man finally falls to the floor, I pause for a second to get my bearings. Loud yells in Russian come from the hallway to our left, and we're clearly in what used to be the reception area of the building. Dark, tinted windows and doors lie just ahead of us a few hundred feet—our ticket to escape even though once we're outside those doors, we'll be sitting ducks without a vehicle.

But we don't have much of a choice. If we stay here, we're dead for sure. I'll take my chances in the East Village, overrun with Valerian's lackies rather than stand here and wait to be shot.

I nudge Genti and incline my head toward the door, then move as fast as my dragging leg will allow. The pain and blood loss threaten to drag me down every second, but the look in Kat's eyes before she left that SUV at the airport keep me going.

She cares.

She loves me.

She just doesn't want to admit it yet.

After fighting for so long to have what I want, knowing the continued battle facing us against Felipe, I need to keep going—for myself and *her*. And now, her son, too.

Genti fires off several shots to the right, and I catch someone running toward us from the hallway on the left in time to issue a line of fire that holds anyone from advancing that way. When we hit the doors, the fresh, cool air of late-night Chicago invades my lungs. I suck it in and release a breath of relief that's short-lived.

Scanning the night and the area around the building and us, my heart sinks.

No vehicles. No easy way out except an old, cracked and buckling U-shaped driveway leading to the stairs we stand at the top of. Valerian's men must park in some kind of garage or around the back of the building so they're not as conspicuous. It's smart to not draw attention to the fact that they're here, but if anyone lives nearby and heard those shots, the police will be here before long despite their efforts to hide what they're doing here.

The pounding of feet and voices behind us is only getting louder. Shots shatter the glass behind us, and Genti and I glance back frantically, returning fire as I hobble down the steps to the driveway below.

Tires squeal far down it near the main road, and headlights flash, advancing toward us. I level my gun at it to return any on-coming fire, while Genti shoots back at our attackers still in the building. But no shots come toward us from the approaching vehicle. It advances rapidly, the dark, tinted windows and late night preventing me from seeing inside.

I motion for Genti to move toward it with me. There isn't any way to tell who the fuck that is, but they aren't firing at us at the moment, and that means they may be our way out.

The car squeals to a stop next to us, and the passenger side window rolls down. I duck my head slightly and freeze when my own face stares back at me.

Felipe grins at me, white collar standing out against his solid black shirt in the dim lighting. "Hello, brother, it looks like you could use a lift."

DEFENDING PRIDE

Pride is a spiritual cancer: it eats up the very possibility of love, or contentment, or even common sense.

-C.S. LEWIS

ONE

KAT

You have got to be kidding me.

The tension in my body that's been building since the moment Rose revealed to me the truth about Felipe doubles the instant the plane door opens and I see who stands outside.

I barely escape Chicago alive, then fly halfway across the world as covertly as possible with our transponder turned off to avoid anyone being able to easily track us. Then I call in some favors from my friends here in Albania to let me land without any problems—since I'm essentially trying to sneak into the country—and I find *these* two assholes waiting for me on the fucking tarmac.

One of the reasons we chose this airport was its remoteness. Less likely someone would see a private jet of this size landing and get curious. Easy to slip away and get Jet without anyone even knowing I'm here. But all my attempts to keep my visit under the radar appear to have failed.

Miserably.

The cool evening wind whips up the stairs of the plane and swirls around me, but Kreshnik Dragusha and Afrim Berisha appear unaffected by the shitty weather that's greeted my landing. They stand stock-still, hands at their sides, hard gazes never leaving me, looking almost exactly like they did the first time I saw them when I was here over a year ago.

Only then, I was observing them from the shadows, sneaking around to get Aleksander buried and give birth to Jet so I could get him somewhere safe before I returned to the States to take down Michael. Now, I'm their reluctant business partner, forced to cut them in on my brothel business in order to continue to permit Esad to use the docks in Vlorë. And I didn't tell them I was coming.

Shit.

Martin—one of Rose's men and the only one who managed to get onto the plane with me before I had to shut the door—stops behind me and leans in. "Should I shoot them?"

I clench my hand around my purse and angle my head toward him slightly to ensure he can hear me over the wind and the engines winding down. "Not until I see what they want."

Especially because there's no way they'd come here alone. Even if I can't see anyone else, there are undoubtedly men set up around the airport, some probably with sniper rifles or worse, waiting for a signal from them or for me to start a problem so they can end it...and me.

The last thing I need is for Rose's guy to have an itchy trigger finger and start an all-out gunfight we'll undoubtedly lose. But hopefully, he got my message on that loud and clear.

I plaster a fake smile on my face and slowly descend the stairs from the plane. The engines continue to wind down as I approach my business partners. They return my smile, though it doesn't reach the eyes of either man.

Kreshnik Dragusha, one of the most powerful men in the country—and one of the most ruthless—inclines his head toward me. "It's nice to see you in person."

I raise an eyebrow at him. "To what do I owe this warm reception?"

Both men chuckle and exchange a knowing look.

Afrim Berisha—Kreshnik's partner in crime who controls the other half of the country—shrugs slightly. "Imagine our surprise when we heard through the grapevine that you were coming to the motherland without notifying us. It made us feel quite neglected, almost as if you didn't want us to know you were here."

The way he says the final words sends a chill through my blood. This looks more than bad. It could be viewed as not only a slight on them but potentially a move against them, like I'm coming here under the cloak of secrecy to secure some backing to take over on this side of the world, even though that's the furthest thing from my mind.

"Is there a reason for that, Kat? You coming to our territory without telling us?"

They need an answer that will satisfy them, one that removes any question about my intentions toward them. There's only one I can think of.

I lock gazes with each of them, holding myself as still and steady as possible. "I came to see Aleksander."

Both men stiffen slightly and glance at each other, likely wondering if I've completely lost my mind and forgotten he's dead.

"To visit his grave. We are nearing the anniversary of his death, and I thought it only fitting."

The lie comes out easily because it's mostly true. If none of the drama were happening in Chicago, if I hadn't just boldly attacked two of my strongest competitors, and if I didn't have the threat of Felipe breathing down my neck, too, I might have come to Albania to talk to Aleksander. To tell him about Jet and about Rose, even confess what a mess I've made of everything and hope that by pressing my hand against the grass over his cremated remains that I might garner some sort of insight from the man who was so terrifyingly good at his job, so much better than me. It seems like all I've done since arriving back in Chicago as Kat is complicate things and fuck them up.

Kreshnik raises a bushy white eyebrow at me. "And you couldn't have informed us you were coming into town? So that we could greet you properly and sit down with our business partner?"

Anyone who wasn't blind could see where they're going with this. I hold up my free hand, the one not clutching my purse so that it can be close to my gun. "I can assure you it was not an intended insult, gentlemen. I just wanted some alone time with my late husband. I had every intention of alerting you I was here so we could sit down and discuss our future operations."

Afrim crosses his arms over his chest and offers me a scowl intended to display his displeasure. "I think it would be wise to have a conversation, Kat. Now."

I raise an eyebrow at them. "Why the rush? I'll call you when I'm finished with my affairs."

"No. Now."

"Why? You're no longer happy with our arrangement?"

They both chuckle, but there isn't any humor in their laughs. The only reason they agreed to our little deal where I bring women out through Albania from Europe to the States is that I'm paying them a large cut of what I bring in from the brothels. It's a financial loss I wish I didn't have to take, but it was a means to an end. A way of keeping the flow of women coming until power changes over here to someone more amenable. But I can see from the look in both of their eyes that neither of them is content.

Kreshnik shrugs nonchalantly, even though this confrontation is anything but. "An unexpected complication has developed from our deal. One that requires a renegotiation."

"What complication is that?"

"With you offering women such wonderful new lives in America, it is becoming harder and harder for us to find women willing to work for us here."

I'm fucking shocked.

Biting back the retort that wants to slip from my lips, instead, I offer a shrug. "I pay you handsomely to allow me to keep sending ships out of this port. I'll continue to do so because that was our agreement. There will be no renegotiation."

Dragusha's eyes darken to an almost black, and he takes a step toward me, his hands clenched. "That is not a decision you get to make."

Martin shifts from behind me to my side until I can see him in my peripheral vision. A question on his part about whether now is the time to take them out or not. I subtly shake my head and turn back. These men aren't going to let me leave here unless it's with them or unless we're in body bags. But if we try to shoot our way to freedom, we're as good as goners ourselves.

We've reached a standoff I don't see a way out of.

TWO

ROSE

¡Mierda!

Just when I thought things couldn't get any worse, I'm staring into the face of the devil himself —the face I share with him—and it suddenly has become my worst nightmare.

As if escaping from Valerian's goons hasn't been hard enough, now I have Felipe showing up instead of the rescue I had hoped the car coming up the drive would offer us. This may be worse than what the men chasing us would do.

Gunfire strikes the pavement just to my right, and Genti and I return fire as Felipe raises a dark eyebrow at me. "I suggest you get in before your friends' aim improves."

¡Ay hijueputa! Like I have a fucking choice.

If we don't get into this car, Valerian's men will be on us in seconds, and while I don't trust Felipe at all, in this moment and this moment only, getting into his car appears to be the only viable option. At least there's a *chance* of surviving with him, but Valerian is out for blood and revenge, and if he doesn't get what he wants from Genti or me, he *will* kill us as a statement to Kat.

So, it's into the car with the man who is my greatest weakness instead. I motion to the back door for Genti and climb into the passenger seat while I fire the last bullets from my gun at the men pouring out of the front of the building.

Before either of our doors even close, Felipe peels away, tires screeching in the still, dark night. Bullets slam into the car as we make our escape down the jagged, cracked driveway toward the tree-lined street. At least we know their vehicles are in the back of the old hospital where they were holding us, and that's going to buy us a little time before they can follow us.

Felipe makes the sharp right turn onto the main road and glances over at me. "What? No hello? No thank you?"

I press my lips together to force myself to fight back the stream of curses I want to unleash on him. Instead, I turn to peek over my shoulder at Genti. His eyes locked on Felipe, he trains his gun at him, even though it's likely out of bullets just like mine.

"You didn't mention you and your brother were identical twins."

Narrowing my eyes on Genti, I sneer. I can understand the question since when we rushed out of Kat's place and to the airport, we only gave the men the basics—that my brother was a threat and that Kat needed to get to Albania. He has no idea who or what Felipe really is, nor does he have any idea that Kat has a son waiting for her back home. It was need to know, and he didn't at the time. But I'm not about to get into anything with him *now*.

"I think we have more important things to worry about at the moment." My gaze drops to where blood drips down Genti's hanging arm and onto the tan upholstery. "Like the fact that we're both bleeding badly."

Fuck.

With the rush of adrenaline coursing through me as we fought our way out, I had momentarily forgotten I'm leaking blood like a fucking sieve, too.

I glance at my leg and find the same ominous signs on my seat. Pressing my palm against the wound, I turn toward Felipe. "I'll thank you when we make it out of this alive."

It seems the appropriate response given the circumstances. This could lead to any number of possibilities. He could drive around and let us bleed out. He could bring us to some hidden lair and torture us and make it even worse. He could use my current vulnerable position to finally get what he wants—complete control without a puppet named Rose doing all the work.

Of course, it would mean giving up his cloak of the church and the veil that protects him that has kept him from suspicion, in prison, or worse, all these years. But it will be the only option if he offs me. He'll have to become Rose and pick up where I left off. It isn't like Sofia will step up…

Felipe offers a low chuckle in response to my snide comment. "I got you out of there, didn't I?"

I scowl at him, even though his eyes remain locked on the road so he can't see it. "How'd you know where we were?"

He grins and glances at me as we speed through the mostly deserted streets. Though we're not out of the woods yet. Not by a longshot. Valerian and his crew control this area completely, and any of the locals would bend over backward to assist any of them. All they have to do is put out one call and block all of our escape routes in minutes.

"For all I know, you are working with Valerian and that's how you knew where and when to come to our rescue."

Felipe shakes his head and offers a *tsking* noise with his tongue. "Oh, ye of so little faith."

I snort and drop my head back, but the motion sends pain stabbing to my temples. "Don't mention *faith* to me, *desgraciado!*"

The fact that he can sit right next to me and act like everything is completely normal and we're friends is fucking ludicrous.

Even after not seeing him for almost two years, my ire toward him hasn't cooled. It's only grown, especially over the last few days since revealing the truth to Kat. Speaking those words out loud for the first time, letting her in on the greatest lie of all, has opened the floodgate of old pain and horrific memories. And they all center around the man to my left who drives like a bat out of Hell, turning onto seemingly random side streets to get us out of the sights and hands of the Russians.

Felipe might have already set things in motion on what Kat and I have feared. Just because he's here doesn't mean someone else isn't in Albania doing his bidding and going after Jeton. Even if Kat managed to land there safely, it doesn't mean Felipe can't get to him first. It wouldn't even surprise me if Konstandin were the one who did it and the entire meeting and suggested truce between him and Kat was all a giant ruse perpetrated by the man who always seems to be pulling the strings.

There are just so many possibilities. So many ways Felipe could have fucked us over and could in the future. And I have no way of knowing where Kat is.

I don't dare mention her name to him. And it's not like he's going to hand me his fucking cell phone to call to check on her.

Right now, we're bleeding and at the mercy of a madman.

I glance at the clock on the dashboard and do a double-take.

Has it really only been twenty hours since Valerian attacked us on the tarmac?

It seems like a lifetime has passed. But by now, even with stops for refueling, Kat should have landed. I just need to get the fuck away from him to ensure she made it safely.

And I need to stop both Genti and me from bleeding to death.

I press my hand harder to my thigh, though what it will do to help stop the bleeding is negligible at this point. The damage has already been done; the wounds have bled for hours and been exposed to all sorts of things that can cause infection. "We need a doctor."

Felipe glances down at the blood on the seat. "It would appear so. But you know what the book of Jeremiah says: 'I will restore you to health and heal your wounds,' declares the Lord."

We're so fucked.

Blackness starts to creep into the edges of my vision, and my entire body suddenly feels weighed down. I try to raise my arm to rub my eyes and clear them, but it doesn't want to cooperate.

A heavy fog envelops my head, and I shake it, but it doesn't help. The blood loss and exertion of the day have finally caught up with me.

And it seems, so has my dear brother...

THREE

KAT

I INCH my hand down the strap of my purse and closer to the side pocket that contains my gun as quickly as I dare—which is pretty damn slowly. These two didn't come into power here and take control over the entire country by being mindless thugs. They're smart. Smart enough to know I won't go with them willingly. They have to suspect I'm going to try something. I'd be stupid not to.

They watch us closely, but neither of their gazes seem to follow my hand movement toward my weapon. Instead, they appear to be waiting for Martin to do something rather than focusing on me. Perhaps they're distracted enough that they won't catch me grabbing it before it's too late.

Though, even if we managed to get off a few shots, there is no way we're going to make it out of here. With the car I ordered nowhere in sight, we have no means of escape. And even if we got back onto the plane, it would take time to restart the engines and take off. Plus, doing so without filing a flight plan could cause all sorts of issues that even my powerful friends here in Albania couldn't fully clear up for me.

But ultimately, I can't and won't just leave—not with Jet's safety hanging in the balance—not until I have him in my arms and out of harm's way.

It was my mistake to believe he would be safe here, anonymous, far away from the violence and betrayals of the world his father thrived in and I embraced. All I did was make him a target without protection.

That changes today, no matter what I have to do to get there.

Martin shifts next to me, inching closer, preparing himself to act as soon as I give him the order. Kreshnik and Afrim share a look. These two are like brothers and have no doubt already discussed what they would do if I wasn't amenable to the changes they wanted in our agreement. Likely just taking me out if given the opportunity—which I just gave them by landing here essentially unprotected.

They may lose all the money I've been sending them for their cut of my business when I'm gone, but if it's been eating into theirs here so badly, it will be a hit they're willing to take to improve their own plans.

But I have to make one last-ditch effort to resolve things without bloodshed. I clear my throat and offer a half-smile. "It seems we've come to an impasse. How do you suggest we resolve this? Because I need to get going." I raise an eyebrow. "Perhaps a meeting for dinner tomorrow evening?"

They scowl and shake their heads.

Kreshnik offers an incredulous look. "Like we're going to just let you leave—"

An engine revving cuts him off. A black sedan roars onto the tarmac and approaches, racing toward us fast enough to draw everyone's attention.

My two adversaries jerk toward it, reaching for their weapons.

One of theirs? Or the car I hired to pick me up when we stopped to refuel?

Either way, it doesn't matter. It offers me the opportunity Martin and I need with my business partners distracted. We both reach for weapons at the same time, but Kreshnik and Afrim whirl back to us with theirs pointed squarely on us.

Kreshnik shakes his head. "Don't even think about it."

The black car skids to a stop between them and us, providing me cover as both men open fire. The passenger door flies open.

"Get in, Kat." The unfamiliar voice's order jerks my attention in that direction and away from returning fire.

Who the hell is that?

At this point, it doesn't even matter. Any opportunity to get out of here is one I'll take.

I dive into the open passenger door, and the man behind the wheel guns it, pulling us away while Martin fires back at Dragusha and Berisha with nothing to protect him anymore. I jerk my door closed and lower the window to fire back in a fruitless attempt to help Martin before I run out of ammo.

Bullets ping off the car as we race across the short tarmac and toward freedom, while Martin crumples to the damp pavement under the assault he had to take on alone.

Shit.

Another man down. Now, I'm truly alone. I can't trust any of my contacts here enough to let them know about Jet. And I'm in a car with a complete stranger.

I twist my head to my left, toward the man driving the vehicle like a bat out of hell. In the darkness of the evening, I can only see his profile in the light from an occasional home we pass on the desolate streets.

"Who are you?" I shift my weapon to aim it toward him, even though it's empty.

"Does it matter?"

"Good point." But I don't relax in my seat.

This man's accent is clearly American, and no one here I know would ever use an American. Which means one of my local contacts did not send him.

My savior speeds through the night across the slick pavement, weaving around any vehicles out this time of night at breakneck speed. He extends his hand toward me, flat palm out, and even without saying it, I know what he's asking for.

Shit.

Something tells me even if I moved as fast as I can, I could never get my gun reloaded quickly enough to do anything with it before this guy could stop me. And he knows it, too, which is why he's been unconcerned about me pointing it at him.

I'm at the mystery man's mercy—at least for the time being.

I set my empty gun into his hand, then slowly and carefully, I reach into my purse and extract my extra magazines, placing them next to my only weapon and giving away my only chance at escaping from whoever this is. "Who sent you? Where are you taking me?"

He glances at me for a second before returning his focus to the road while he shifts my gun into the storage compartment on the driver's side door. "You aren't in any position to be asking me questions."

If Rose did manage to get away from the tarmac, he might have sent help. But there's no way this is one of Rose's guys. He would just tell me who sent him because there wouldn't be any reason not to. That means someone else is pulling the strings.

Felipe?

The thought makes my heart thunder against my chest. If he's here, if he got to Jet first, all of this was for nothing. I came clean to Rose, finally opened up and gave him the pieces of myself I've been holding back, and yet, it may have all been too little too late to stop the inevitable. Maybe there was never any way to truly protect Jet.

If Aleksander had lived, would his son have really been able to break free from this life?

I'd be stupid to think he wouldn't have become everything his father was. Attempting to hide him only delayed what was meant to happen. He will still be sucked into this world because Konstandin found him and therefore exposed him to Felipe.

And this man driving us through the barren streets outside Vlorë could be the right hand of the man trying to destroy us all.

A few minutes pass in silence before he pulls up to an old, rundown farmhouse that appears completely abandoned. I lean forward and stare out the windshield at the dilapidated building, then glance at the driver.

He throws the car into park, turns it off, and points toward the house. "Get inside."

I scowl at him but open my door and step out into the chilly night air. The same cool wind that struck me at the airport whips around me again, howling in the trees at the front of the house. Glancing at the side of the car and seeing the damage Dragusha and Berisha's bullets did makes my stomach turn.

We wouldn't have gotten out of there alive. So, even though I don't know who this man is or what he wants from me, I don't have much choice but to play along until I have an idea where I stand or find a way to escape and get to Jet.

The driver climbs from the car, my gun in hand, never taking his eyes off me, and motions for me to enter the house. My first step onto the drooping steps up to the porch garners a creak of protest from the old wood threatening to disintegrate under my foot. I take another step and wait, but I don't crash through to the ground, so I make my way across the porch to the front door.

I glance back at the man, and he inclines his head, ushering me forward. The doorknob turns easily under my hand, and I push open the door into a surprisingly clean living room.

Old, sagging furniture litters the space, and heavy footsteps follow me in. The door slams behind me, and my savior turned captor walks to a small table on the side of the room, sets my gun and magazines on it, then turns toward me and pulls out a phone.

He presses a couple buttons and brings it to his ear. A few seconds pass, during which he watches me with hard, cold eyes before he holds it out. "There's a call for you."

FOUR

ROSE

I JERK awake for what feels like the umpteenth time in my life with my entire body wracked with pain. It's a cycle I'd like to stop, but for now, it seems like I'm in an endless loop of this agony.

A groan slips from my lips, and I roll onto my side. The soft give of the mattress under me makes my eyes fly open.

What the fuck happened? Where am I?

Without any way to know how long I was out, I could be literally anywhere by now. The last thing I remember was being in the car with Felipe...and the dimly lit room doesn't offer much of an answer.

Fuck.

Struggling to push myself up into a seated position, I scan my surroundings through fuzzy vision and a pounding headache slamming against my temples. Genti lies on a bed across the room, the steady rise and fall of his chest a sign he's alive, at least for now. I release a sigh of relief.

Gracias a Dios.

If he didn't make it out of this alive and I went back to Kat without him, she might kill me herself. Though with the way I felt in the car with Felipe, I was on the verge of going that route without any assistance.

Which means, perhaps my dear brother found an ounce of decency left in his soul.

I glance down at the formerly bleeding hole in my arm to find it bandaged and throw back the white sheet over my legs to discover the same is true of my thigh wound. Someone patched us up, at least enough to stop the major bleeding.

But where the fuck are we?

The room comes more into focus now, and I rub my temples as my gaze lands on the crucifix hanging over the door.

"Shit. He brought us to his church?"

I always knew Felipe was crazy, but this...it truly takes the cake. Like it isn't bad enough that he's scamming the Catholic Church and his entire congregation into believing he's a pious man of God. Now he brings the head of the Blood Rose Cartel into his church for sanctuary after helping him escape a shootout with the Russian mob. That doesn't bode well for any sliver of a soul he might have remaining after everything he's done.

The door to the room opens, harsh light from the hallway blinding me momentarily. I raise a hand over my eyes and blink against the black spots clouding my vision until I can finally focus on an older woman in a black habit.

Flashes of a memory flicker back to me. This woman. Blood. A younger redheaded woman. Someone holding me down.

She pauses when she sees me. "Oh, you're awake. How are you feeling?"

I study her for a moment, hoping the rest of what happened after I passed out in the car would come back, before releasing a deep sigh when nothing else surfaces. "Alive."

A not unkind smile crosses her lips. "Progress, then."

I bite back a retort that would scandalize a woman like this and shift to the side of the bed to stand, but she rushes forward and holds out a hand.

"I don't suggest you attempt to move yet. You lost a lot of blood, and I had to dig around for some bullet fragments in your leg. You're going to be weak for some time."

Dig around for some bullet fragments? Who the hell is this woman?

Maybe this is all some weird hallucination.

I shake my head and squeeze my eyes closed. But when I reopen them, she still stands in front of me, concern wrinkling her brow. "Who are you? Who was the redhead helping you? And where the hell are we?"

She hesitates for a moment, then squares her shoulders. "I'm Sister Agnes. I was a surgical nurse in the army before being called to this life. The redhead is another sister who offered to assist. And you're somewhere safe."

A low growl rumbles in my chest before I can think to stop it, and she takes half a step back—likely not used to being shown aggression in a house of God. "Did my brother instruct you not to tell me anything?"

It would be just like Felipe to somehow convince this woman she was doing me a favor by not revealing any information.

She presses her lips together in a firm line and clasps her hands in front of her. The poor woman is probably praying for my soul. "Father Felipe offered you sanctuary, despite who you are and what you do. While I may not understand why he hasn't turned you over to the police, I will respect his wishes when he asks me not to give you any further information so he can speak with you himself."

Anger boils the remaining blood in my veins, though not at her. She's just another innocent who has been drawn into Felipe's web, wrapped up in his sticky lies and convinced he's everything he claims to be.

I fist my hands against the mattress and shove up from the bed. The infinitesimal movement is enough to make the room spin, but there isn't any time to let my body adjust to the rapid change. I take a tentative step, gritting my teeth against the pain in my thigh, but my leg gives out almost instantly and I grip the foot of the metal bed frame to keep from falling over.

Sister Agnes rushes forward to help me, but I bat away her hand.

"Get the fuck out of here."

She gasps and backs away slightly, her reproachful gaze sweeping over me slowly. Her lips twist into a scowl, and she rushes from the room in a flow of black polyester.

I probably just scared the fuck out of the old nun.

Based on what she said, she knows who I am and the bullet wounds suggest less than legal activities happening recently—something that wouldn't surprise her if she's familiar with the Blood Rose Cartel. But she clearly has no idea *who* Felipe *really* is or *what* he is. Though he can't hide being my brother anymore now that she's seen us together.

She was right about one thing, though. I'm not in any position to try to get out of here at this moment. But that doesn't mean I'm not going to try to get fucking answers from the good Father.

And I do need answers. Because I can't seem to grasp his end game. For the first time since that fateful, bloody day that I discovered who he really is, I have no idea what's happening in his head.

He didn't kill us. If he wanted Genti and me dead, all he had to do was keep us from medical treatment for a relatively short amount of time. If he wanted us out of the way, he could have brought us to a hospital where the employees would have been obligated to report our gunshot wounds to the authorities, who are undoubtedly looking for us after the shootout at the airport. But he did neither.

He brought us to a *church*. A house of God. A place of sanctuary, even for the dreges of society.

Back home, Father Nolan always emphasized the importance of accepting everyone into God's fold, even those society rejected or those who refused to conform to the norms—even rejecting the law. He thought there was a way to reach everyone, from the heads of the worst cartels on down the chain, including my wayward brother. All that got him was killed.

I refuse to suffer the same fate as *Mama y Papa,* Father Nolan, and countless others who fell into Felipe's clutches. I *won't* be lulled into a false sense of security because he brought us here instead of letting us die or get thrown into prison. He has a plan. One that requires us to be alive. One that includes Konstandin Morina and Kat, otherwise he never would have arranged their meeting here. He *always* has a plan. And I'm going to figure out what the fuck it is.

This isn't just a matter of my pride anymore. This is about defending what is *mine!* The cartel I've been the face of for twenty years. The woman who has become my world. The son she felt she had to hide to protect him from this life. I'll do whatever it takes. No matter how much it may hurt —physically or otherwise.

FIVE

KAT

"Kat…" Valentina's smoothly accented voice floats through the line, making my stomach clench and my hand tighten around the phone.

I turn my head to examine the man who picked me up. He leans casually against the door jamb with his arms crossed over his massive chest, looking about as nonchalant as Valentina's pit bull, Cutter, usually does—which is not at all.

If Valentina Marconi is behind my miraculous rescue, then this man is likely one of Cutter's and every bit as lethal as the man who is at her beck and call. He may have saved me from my less than happy business partners, but that doesn't mean he can't take me out just as easily—if not more so—at any moment he—or Valentina—chooses.

"Valentina, should I assume you're the one who sent this gentleman to pick me up?"

Valentina laughs. "Pick you up? That seems a gross understatement of what I just did for you. We should start with a thank you."

"For what?"

"For saving your life. The Dragushas and Berishas would have killed you, eventually. From what my contacts in the region tell me, they're getting pretty damn sick of you taking all the top-quality women they'd like to have for themselves."

I clench my free hand, digging my nails into my palm until it's painful to avoid snapping back with the retort I want to. "I could handle them myself."

She snorts. "Would you like me to have him take you back? That can be arranged."

This bitch.

She knows exactly the position she rescued me from and where she has me now. It's almost too convenient. "Just how *did* you know where I was and how to find me?"

"The little shootout you and Rose had with the Russians at the airport wasn't exactly under the radar. It wasn't hard for my contacts to find you, despite your efforts to hide your travels. Italy's only a quick jump across the Adriatic, and I have a lot of friends in the region. Friends who keep me abreast of anything happening that I might be interested in. It became pretty clear where your plane was headed because I didn't think you were going to pop over to my homeland to say hello to anyone there. So, it begs the question…what was so important that you had to get back to Albania and that Rose was willing to risk his life for you to get on that plane?"

Risk his life?

My chest tightens, and the ability to draw air into my lungs suddenly vanishes with my panic. I drop my hand to the arm of the dilapidated couch, the rough material barely registering. "Is he…dead?"

Valentina chuckles. "I'm not that lucky. From what I hear, Valerian snatched him right off the tarmac along with one of your men."

Shit. Genti.

And the damn Russians probably killed everyone else who was there without a second thought. Most of the men were down by the time I managed to get onto the plane, but there was a chance a few survived the initial gunfight. But not if Valerian Kamanev got to them. He isn't known for leaving behind witnesses.

"If I had to wager a guess, Valerian is now letting Rose know how displeased he is with what the two of you have been up to. Pretty ballsy of you to hit the Russians and the Irish in the same night."

I swallow thickly, trying to keep my voice level despite my rising concern for Rose, Genti, Jet, and myself. Another glance at the man on the other side of the room finds him in the same position, apparently disinterested but definitely just putting on an act to that effect. He's hearing every single word and noting them.

"I don't know what you're talking about."

No way in *hell* I'm about to admit to Valentina that I ordered the attacks on Galen's gun shipment and Valerian's underground casino. There isn't any way anyone can definitively prove my involvement, and I won't offer the ammunition to. It's best to let people speculate and believe whatever they want to believe.

Valentina scoffs, her disbelief apparent through the line all the way from the city I just fled. "Bullshit. Valerian and Galen have been under some sort of odd truce lately. I doubt they'd attack each other, and none of the smaller groups have the manpower or firepower, let alone the balls to do that. That leaves me, you, and Rose. I sure as hell didn't do it. So, whether you made the decision or he did or whether you did it together, you're responsible for it. And you're responsible for the fallout. So, I'll ask you again, what was so important that Rose was willing to risk his life to let you get away when you both should have been lying low after what you did?"

The man by the door offers a smirk, almost as if he can hear Valentina's words, even though I'm certain he can't. He's positioned himself perfectly to keep me from leaving until whatever Valentina's goal here is can be reached. "If I don't tell you?"

She chuckles again. "I don't think you're in any position not to cooperate, Kat. I could have Reaper return you to your friends on the runway at any time...or worse."

Or worse.

All the awful possibilities scroll through my head at the speed of light, each more soul-gutting than the last.

I can't let Jet fall into Felipe's hands. If what Rose said is true—and seeing his reaction to the story, I believe every single word—my son would be the ultimate bargaining chip. A way to twist me and force me to do whatever Felipe needs from me to fulfill his master plan. But I can't offer up Jet to Valentina, either, by revealing my real reason for being here. That would just be adding another arrow into the quiver of yet another enemy.

"What do you want, Valentina? You want my thanks?" I turn my back to the man by the door and instead focus on the dingy walls. "Fine. Thank you for rescuing me, but I don't believe for a second that you did it out of the goodness of your heart, if you even have one. So, what is it you *actually* want?"

She pauses for a moment before replying, though I have no doubt she already has the answer. "My predecessor made a deal with your late husband that left me indebted to you. It's the only reason you're using my docks to bring in your girls. So now, I would like a favor for what I did for you today. One I will ask for when the time is appropriate."

The woman might as well be asking me to sign over my soul. An unfettered "favor" means she will have a blank check, *carte blanche* to insist I do or *not* do something that may interfere with my own plans and needs.

But what choice do I have?

I can't let her return me to the Berishas and Dragushas. And I can't have any interference with what I really came to Albania to accomplish.

"You don't want this favor now?"

"No. Not now. I'm sure there will come a time in the near future when it will come in handy."

Exactly what I'm worried about...

I clear my throat and squeeze my eyes shut. Maybe I'm not giving Valentina enough credit. She's about to give birth any day now. While she may be cold and calculating, perhaps underneath that tough exterior, there's a mother who will understand what I'm doing and why and want to help without thinking of Jet as a pawn in a game she can play with me.

Or she could end up being even worse than what I'm trying to rescue him from in the first place.

It's a chance I have to take...

SIX

ROSE

A PILE of clothes sits at the end of my bed, and I shrug on the shirt, grunting through the searing pain in my arm. But I don't even bother trying with the pants I would have to drag over my legs. If anyone sees me wandering around the church in these boxers, so be it.

Fuck them.

They're in for a worse shock if the truth about their exalted leader ever sees the light of day. This is just a precursor if his ultimate plan is to take over. The shepherd will be exposed as the wolf. The wool won't be pulled over anyone's eyes anymore.

Not the way it was pulled over mine until that bloody day twenty years ago. But I can't let myself be dragged back to the past right now. Not when my entire future depends on discovering Felipe's plan and thwarting it.

After I regain a bit of my composure, I check on my companion on the other side of the room. Genti still hasn't moved an inch, even during my confrontation with Sister Agnes, so he'll be of no help right now. I have to go out into the unknown alone—weaponless and wholly unprepared for whatever Felipe may have in store for us out there.

I shuffle awkwardly to the door, trying to avoid putting too much weight on my bad leg. With my palm wrapped around the knob, I pause to try to locate enough strength to keep going.

Every fiber of my being screams for me to crawl back into that bed and sleep. Let the darkness I've intermittently fought and embraced my whole life drag me back under. But I don't have that luxury.

Too much time has already passed without me knowing where Kat is or whether she succeeded in her mission. Too much has happened for me to push it all out of my head and pretend the world around me doesn't exist anymore.

I twist the knob and find a dimly lit, narrow hallway that stretches out in either direction with a door at the end to the right. Photos of various priests, who likely ran this church before Felipe, line the wall across from me.

Singing echoes off the marble floors, coming from my left. It reverberates through my body, every bone, every muscle, every cell of my being, bringing me back to a different time. A different place. A different life. When I was just a naïve child and this was my entire world...

Voices raised in praise. True believers wanting to worship.

I stagger toward the sound, my hand on the wall to support me, basically dragging my leg behind me like dead weight. The louder the singing becomes, the more my body tenses, tightening damaged muscles and flesh and drawing a strangled gasp from deep in my lungs.

Familiar words bouncing off the marble floors and basic white walls bring vivid memories...

A song about finding God no matter where you might be and not fearing because he will always be at your side.

This was Father Nolan's favorite hymn. One I would often catch him singing alone in his office late in the evening after we cleaned up for the day. He was truly a pious man, one who bent over backward to give me an education and prepare me for the priesthood, to show me genuine friendship and give me direction. He was everything I wanted to be for so long...and in one instant, that all changed.

What would he think of me now?

I pause and squeeze my eyes closed against the last memory I have of him from that morning before I walked home and discovered my world had been bathed in blood, everything I knew devastated.

When I open my eyes again, my anger toward Felipe has only grown.

All of this, everything I've suffered the last two decades, happened because of *him*. Because of *his* choices. What he did forced *my* hand, turned *me* into something else. Something dark and hard when it should have been joy and light. And then he stole the life that was mine and used it for his own evil purposes.

Stumbling down the hallway toward what must be the main church, the choir's singing halts and a familiar voice rises in its place, offering a solo that makes my gut clench.

Hearing Felipe sing about standing before Satan at the gates of Hell and knowing God is at his side is enough to give me the strength to drive forward.

I step out from around the corner and shuffle forward until I can see him and the choir members in the choir box. A woman glances toward me, no doubt her attention drawn by the sudden motion, and a sharp gasp echoes through cathedral ceilings.

The almost empty church is a mixed blessing. Fewer people to witness the showdown that's about to occur, but it also means it will be easier for Felipe to smooth over and explain away whatever goes down between us. It's a lot easier to convince a small handful of people here for choir practice that they may not have seen what they think they did than an entire packed church here for Mass.

Part of me wishes the place was filled to the brim with devout worshippers. Letting members of his flock see who Felipe really is would be the ultimate fuck you to him. To ensure he can no longer hide behind his collar would push his hand, force him to take his next step, and perhaps throw him off his game.

As it stands, he only has a few people in the choir box. But all heads turn my way, confused gazes taking in my appearance. After the way Valerian worked me over, I'm confident it isn't a pretty sight. The ache in my jaw and tenderness on my face are sure signs of the bruising and swelling there.

Felipe turns slowly to face me, in no rush to address the source of the choir's reaction. He knows what they see. He knew I was awake and coming for him. Because just like I can sense him, *feel* him, he can do the same with me.

Though somehow, as a child, I missed what he was doing. For those years when I convinced myself he was just messing around and blowing off steam, living out childish desires to rebel against authority figures, I failed to sense his last turn into madness. Maybe I was blinded by love for my brother or by the beliefs I held so dear that everyone was inherently good. That everyone could be *saved*. Whatever the cause may have been then, it no longer taints my view.

I see him crystal clearly now. See the sinister tilt to the smile he offers. The hint of madness at the corners of his eyes crinkled by it. The evil darkening his soul where there should be joy and the love of God. The firm set of his shoulders, a statement he won't be moved or budged by anything or anyone—including me.

We'll fucking see about that, mi querido hermano.

SEVEN

ROSE

FELIPE TURNS back to the choir, which has been struck to silence by my sudden appearance in this holy place—certainly not what any of them is used to when they come for practice. "Please continue in my absence."

Soft, indecipherable mumbles of reply float across the vast space, and he offers them a slight little half-bow and then slowly descends the steps from the choir box and approaches me.

Each inch closer he moves ratchets up my anger another notch until I'm vibrating with the effort it takes to control it. I open and close my fists at my sides, equally wanting to deck him the moment he's close enough and afraid I'm going to fall over if I move even a fraction of a millimeter.

It takes the choir a minute or two to regain enough composure to continue their rehearsal, their voices finally filling the church and drowning out the sound of Felipe's approaching footsteps.

His familiar eyes sweep over me—eyes I see every damn time I look in a mirror—and a satisfied, arrogant grin tips the corners of his lips. "It's good to see you up and about, *hermano*."

"Cut the bullshit, Felipe." Using *my* name when addressing him still feels wrong even after two decades, and my words come out growled loudly despite my intention to keep my voice low for the sake of the parishioners. "What the hell do you want?"

He raises his dark eyebrows and spreads out his hands. "Only to shepherd my flock and teach them to embrace God's love."

I take a step toward him, fighting a wince by grinding my jaw. No fucking way I'll give him the satisfaction of knowing how much pain I'm in and how close I am to collapsing to this ancient marble under my bare feet. "Drop the fucking pretense, *Padre,* and tell me what you're doing here in Chicago."

That's the ultimate question that will answer anything else I could ever need to know. Felipe has always maintained his control over the cartel from Colombia. He feels safe there. Sheltered by the façade and persona he's created over the years as a faithful member of the clergy who preaches God's love and non-violence. No one suspects him there. No one questions how different he is from me, his vile brother known for brutality and heartlessness. For him to come to Chicago, to leave the protection home afforded him, means something drastic has changed.

Understanding that is like knowing a bullet is coming straight at you and being unable to stop it.

He crosses his arms over his chest, further exposing the ink covering his forearms—the only thing that sets us apart when we are otherwise identical in every way. "I'm tending to my flock, *Andres*." He glances over his shoulder before he leans in. "And *my fucking business*."

There it is.

That crack in the façade. A millisecond of truth. A glimpse of the real man he keeps hidden under that white collar and priestly robes. The genuine anger and violence he tries so damn hard to control.

I lean back into him, determined to show him I'm not intimidated by his presence, even if I'm physically weaker at the moment. "I've been handling *my business* more than fine on my own."

He barks out a laugh that draws the attention of the choir. Knowing they're watching us, he glances over his shoulder and offers them a friendly wave and smile, then motions for them to continue before he turns back to me. "Is that what you really think, *hermano*? That this is *your* business and that you've been handling things fine? If so, then you're worse off than I thought."

I open my mouth to retort, but he holds up a hand to stop me, stepping closer.

"You let a major shipment get stolen by the Italians, thus pissing off half of our major customers. Then you made a deal with Valentina that only gives us a brief window of opportunity to utilize their territory—a territory I sent you here to *take over* by now. You almost died in an attack, one you dragged our sister into and almost got her killed, too." He shakes his head and *tsks*. "I expected you to take care of business, but it seems you've lost focus because of a certain woman."

Fisting my hands at my sides to keep from lashing out at him, I close the distance between us until our chests almost touch. Despite how angry I am and what a fraud he is, the thought of striking him in the house of God still claws at what is left of my conscience. "I've done what I had to do, Felipe. Unexpected things came up, and I fucking dealt with them the best I could. Just like I always do. And our business has grown exponentially since I've been here. I'll deal with Valentina when necessary. I have a plan."

He snorts and shakes his head. "A plan that seems quite divergent from mine. From the one I outlined for you before I sent you here. The one we set in motion twenty years ago when we were both mere children playing at being men. But it seems I can no longer rely on you to carry out my orders. That leaves us in a difficult position, doesn't it, *Andres*?"

"Fuck you, *Felipe*."

I turn back toward the room where Genti still lies, but a strong hand grabs my arm directly where I was shot and squeezes. A cry of pain slips from my lips before I can stop it, echoing around the vestibule and out into the church.

Felipe steps into me, jerking me back against him until his hot breath pants in my ear. "Don't forget who's in charge here, *Rose*." He spits the nickname at me like venom. "Do what you're fucking told. Or I'll take matters into my own hands."

His threat sends a shiver through me, but not because I'm afraid of him.

Because I know what it means. What I'll have to do.

I manage to jerk out of his grip and take a step away from him before I turn back. "I'd like to see you fucking try."

My parting words echo behind me as I move down the hallway, but his voice stops me in my tracks.

"Where do you think you're going?"

I glance over my shoulder at him. "To get Genti and get the fuck out of here."

So I can find Kat.

I don't dare mention her to Felipe despite his reference to how she has interfered with his plans. I won't give him that opening, that way to get under my skin further.

"You're not leaving." The command comes harsh and clear. It might give anyone else pause, but I've had enough of taking orders from Felipe.

I snort and twist back to him, then motion with my good arm toward the choir. "We already have a captive audience, Felipe. There's no way you're going to physically stop me in front of members of your parish. After all, we have appearances to keep up, don't we?" I raise an eyebrow at him, then turn my back and hobble down the hallway as fast as I can. "That's what I fucking thought."

Felipe was right about one thing—my course has diverged from the one I was on when I came to Chicago at his behest. My new one is now forever aligned with Kat's, and that means I need to find her and ensure that she and her son are safe, regardless of what that decision means for things between Felipe and me.

Even if it means a civil war on top of the one we're already facing with the other families.

EIGHT

ROSE

"You want to tell me what the hell is going on?" Sofia glares at me from behind the wheel as I settle into the passenger seat with a groan and pull the door closed behind me.

I guess it's the obvious question given the fact that I disappeared and then called her out of the blue to pick me up here. But I don't have the energy to get into a long, detailed explanation right now. Instead, I offer a grunt.

"Really? That's it? You've been missing for *three days*."

Don't fucking remind me.

"After the little shootout you and Kat got into at the airport, I couldn't find you anywhere. Then I heard Valerian had you. I searched the whole goddamn internet and hacked into every database I could think of to locate where he was holding you...but nothing." She waves a frantic hand toward the church behind us. "Now, you call me out of the blue and ask me to pick you up at a fucking church." She points. "*Felipe's* fucking church! You have a lot of explaining to do."

She doesn't know the half of it.

But I am not about to open that can of worms while sitting here in front of Felipe's home base.

"Just drive." I motion toward the street in front of us while I glance back at the building, half-expecting Felipe to appear on the steps to try to stop us. I catch a glimpse of the car Genti called driving off in the opposite direction and return my focus to the front doors. But Felipe won't come.

After our confrontation, he isn't about to risk creating an even bigger scene in front of any parishioners. Especially after I staggered around looking for a phone and managed to terrify his secretary. The poor woman didn't know Genti and I were there. That much was evident based on her reaction to seeing us. She almost had a damn heart attack on the spot.

Felipe is already going to have to answer some uncomfortable questions. Rushing out and trying to drag me back or continuing our argument would only make things worse.

I just want to get home and find Kat. But the car hasn't moved, and I shift in my seat to glare at Sofia. "Drive!"

She scowls but peels away from the curb and speeds down the street.

"What do you know about Kat?"

She glances over at me, her mouth agape. "That's all you have to say? You're not going to tell me what the hell is going on? Just ask about the woman you're fucking?"

I jerk my head toward her and issue a low warning growl. "Don't talk about her like that. I need to know what happened to her after we got taken from the airport."

Thank God Sofia doesn't know Kat was behind the bombing. If she did, she'd be even more volatile toward her.

Sofia tightens her hands around the steering wheel until her knuckles whiten. "They got off the ground. I managed to track the plane to the East Coast where they stopped in New York to refuel. But I lost them over the Atlantic. They must've turned off their transponder."

"Smart."

"Yeah, until they show up on someone's radar and have to explain who the fuck they are." She holds up a hand to stop me from asking. "But I don't know what happened with that. All I could find was there was some kind of shootout at a small airport outside of Vlorë right around the time they would've landed."

"¡Hijueputa!"

"I tried to get more information, but so far, I haven't gotten any additional details."

I swallow the bile climbing up the back of my throat. "So, you don't know if she's okay or where she is?"

She shakes her head. "I've been monitoring everything since you called the other night to tell me where you were going and why. But I don't have magic powers, Andres. I can't track what isn't there to track."

I drop my head back against the headrest, squeezing my eyes shut. "I know."

"You want to tell me how you ended up at Felipe's church?"

I sigh and consider my answer. Sofia only knows bits and pieces of the puzzle. Kat and I were heading to Albania to get her son because she was worried he was in danger from Konstandin and the Irish and Russians after the action she took against them. It wasn't a lie, just not the full truth. I couldn't tell her about Felipe and his potential involvement. Not without exposing the whole dirty reality of our subterfuge.

"Valerian pulled Genti and me off the tarmac when Kat took off. He tortured us, tried to get us to tell him where Kat was keeping the money she stole from him and the guns she took from Galen. But even if I knew, I wasn't going to reveal it, and Genti sure as hell wasn't, either."

That man is loyal. Though I guess when you're in love with your boss, you're willing to do just about anything for her.

I shift in my seat, trying to relieve some of the pain in my thigh the position is causing. "We managed to get out. Only when we hit the street, our dear brother showed up in a vehicle to greet us."

Her eyebrows fly up, and she slams on the brakes at a red light, jerking us forward. "How the hell did Felipe know where you were?"

"That's a very good question." And one I can't even reason out with her or have her look into too thoroughly. Not when she doesn't have an inkling of the truth about him, about me, or about what is really going on.

All she knows is that Felipe doesn't appreciate my business. She believes all the tension stems from his pious nature compared to what I do for a living and the life I dragged her into. She thinks this is about judgment, not deceit.

If she only knew what was really going on, it would change so much and also destroy everything she has ever believed. This isn't the time to do that to her.

"So?" The light turns green, and she races through the intersection. "What did he say?"

"Not much. He brought us back to the church and got us patched up. Then I woke up and left before we could talk."

At least, that's the story I'm sticking to where Sofia is concerned. She'll learn the truth only when absolutely necessary. And until I understand more about his plans and where Kat is as it relates to them, I'm keeping Sofia in the dark as long as I can.

She drives us toward the estate, her hand tapping restlessly on the wheel. We've been so wrapped up in her asking what's been going on with me for the last few days that I haven't even had a chance to ask her about what happened there.

"Has everything been quiet at home?"

After Valerian's threat to her while he held me, my concern has been leaving Sofia out there with minimal protection as much as it has been for Kat's safety. Almost all my most trusted men were at the airport to ensure we got off the ground. That left only a few at the house with Sofia while I normally have every inch covered.

She shrugs. "Everything's been quiet. I'm fine. But you look like shit."

"I'm sure I do." I reach up to my cheek and wince at the pain only a light touch of my fingers brings. "Valerian really worked me over."

"I'll call right now and have the doctor meet us at the house."

I want to argue with her that I'm fine. That whatever Felipe had Sister Agnes do to us is sufficient. But I can barely get my eyes to open. "Just find Kat. Make sure she's okay. That's all that matters."

Sofia's string of curses is the last thing I hear before I let the familiar darkness take me under again.

NINE

ROSE

THE ROAR of a lawnmower starting up drags me from a sleep that felt so deep, I might've been dead. Maybe I would have been better off if I had died with the way I feel. Every muscle and joint aches, and pain ripples across most of my body.

How long have I been out?

Brief flashes of the ride home from the church start to return. My conversation with Sofia. A familiar male voice...Dr. Hart. More pain. Someone holding me down. They float around my head in jumbled chaos, refusing to fall into an understandable order. Any sense of time has been completely lost.

Shit. I was more fucked up than I thought.

I push myself up to a sitting position and wince at the stab of pain and throb in my shoulder. My thigh isn't much better. It appears Dr. Hart did a little further work in both places if the new bandages are any indication. The patch-up job Sister Agnes and the redhead did at the church likely didn't last long after I ignored her advice to stay in bed and confronted Felipe and then fled instead.

The way I'm feeling, maybe I should have stayed and taken my chances with him. It's worse than after the damn plane crash. Which I guess isn't surprising considering Valerian's size and strength. The man knows how to work someone over—plus, getting shot twice does a number on the human body.

I rub my burning eyes and squint at the clock on my nightstand until it finally comes into focus.

Eight o'clock.

Judging from the sound of the gardener and the bright daylight streaming into the window, it must be morning—which means it's now been four days since Kat took off on that plane. Four days of torture, not knowing if she's okay or if she got to Jet.

Despite having never met the child, despite him being Aleksander's son, the thought of something happening to him brings bile up my throat that I have to force down with a thick swallow.

A bottle of medication and a glass of water sit on the nightstand, and I grab it and read the label, then toss it back.

Nope. Not taking it.

I'm not putting anything into my system right now that might dull my senses. Not when Kat's life is still at risk. I need to be one hundred percent *on,* or things could go south very fast.

The door opens without a knock, and Sofia rushes in, carrying a cup in one hand and an open laptop in the other. "I thought I heard you moving around up here." She motions toward the window with the mug. "I told the gardeners to hold off on the mowing until later this morning, but it seems they don't give a shit."

I rub my temple and lean over the side of the bed. "How long have I been out?"

She shrugs and hands me the cup of steaming coffee. The aroma makes my stomach rumble, and I take a tentative sip.

"Doc left here around nine o'clock last night. So, about eleven hours."

Shit.

"Anything happen in the meantime?"

An array of possibilities flash through my head. Kat could be dead or worse. Valerian and Galen could have retaliated against one of her locations or even one of mine. Felipe could have shown up and made the big reveal to Sofia...

She settles on the end of the bed next to me and motions to the laptop screen. "Not much. Touched base with Genti and Kat's people, but they're still scrambling and clueless. However, I got a message from one of my contacts in Eastern Europe. Looks like Berisha and Dragusha are both in the hospital after whatever went down at the airport there. But no mention of a woman being brought in anywhere."

"That's good, isn't it?" If Kat were hurt or killed, surely, there would be *some* evidence of that.

One of her shoulders rises and falls, and she types something while I sip at my coffee. "Probably. But neither of them are talking for obvious reasons, so getting info is hard."

"There's nothing else you can do to find out what happened?" The question comes out more like a demand, clipped and harsh—not how I usually speak with Sofia.

She freezes and glares at me. "I'm doing the best I can."

I hold up a hand in apology. "I wasn't trying to suggest you weren't."

Even though she has no love for Kat, Sofia will do anything for me and always has been one hundred percent reliable. As one of the best hackers in the world, she'll find something if there's anything to find. It's what she does, what she excels at.

When I got out of prison, my plan had been to try to prevent her from ending up sucked into the life Felipe and I were part of, but she was already showing so much skill with hacking. I didn't think allowing her to continue behind the scenes would put her in any danger.

The explosion at that meeting of the five families last year proved otherwise. And the threat against her that Valerian just made only days ago was crystal clear. He considers her fair game, and maybe she is an easy target. I've made her that way by keeping her locked up here rather than training her how to protect and defend herself.

I swallow a gulp of the coffee, hoping the caffeine will work as a jolt to get my body and mind running again. "Maybe you could get Preacher to help you?"

She scoffs at my mention of Valentina's computer whizz, who she managed to hack and previously worked with when the Italian needed help. "Why? You think he's better than I am? Remember, he was the one who needed *my* help last year."

"I know; I know. But he has government access and connections that might be able to get some answers you can't."

Her lips press together in a firm line. "You really want to bring Valentina in on this? Wouldn't we be better off keeping this under wraps?"

"Of course, we would. I don't want to be indebted to Valentina or expose Kat's secrets to her. But I also need to find Kat and make sure she's okay. The longer we go without any contact from her, the more worried I'm getting."

She has a lot of enemies. Konstandin resurfaced at the same time Felipe made his presence known, and both know about Jet. I don't trust for one moment that Konstandin truly wants a truce with her, either. As far as I'm concerned, he's still as much of a threat as Felipe. And all of it couldn't have had worse timing with Kat's attack on the Irish and the Russians. She crossed a line we've all been carefully dancing along and put a target squarely on her back. We need all the help we can get, even if it means exposing a weakness to the Italians by admitting we need Preacher's skills.

Sofia releases a heavy sigh. "Shit." She shakes her head and releases a deep, exasperated sigh. "You're in love with her, aren't you?"

TEN

ROSE

You're in love with her, aren't you?

Sofia's question catches me off-guard enough that I actually flinch. I didn't anticipate needing to have to bare my soul to her today—or any day for that matter. She stays out of my personal life because I've demanded she stay out.

And there hasn't been much to talk about in that regard before Kat anyway. Mostly faceless, nameless women who served a purpose. Who gave me the release I needed. A few who stayed around long enough for me to realize they wanted to change me and could never live this life. Then, they were gone as fast as they appeared.

But Kat's different.

So much so...

And I knew it from the moment I first laid eyes on her at Kat's Cradle. I recognized a kindred spirit, someone who could truly be the queen of my kingdom.

I wrap my hands around the mug tightly. The words sit on the tip of my tongue, but for some reason, saying them to Sofia, admitting it, is far harder than I ever imagined. If talking about my feelings for Kat is this difficult, I can't even fathom how bad it will be when I eventually have to reveal everything that's happened during her life that she's been lied to about.

"I do." I force myself to turn my head to lock eyes with her even though it would be so much easier to say this without having to. "And I have every intention of protecting her and her son as if he were my own."

Sofia raises an eyebrow and laughs.

"What?" I sit up straighter, squaring my shoulders to prepare for whatever Sofia might throw at me. "Why is that funny?"

"*You*...as a father." She smirks. "Just not something I can really picture."

If I were being honest with her, neither have I. There was never any room for love, let alone considering bringing a child into this world. In fact, I always thought it was out of the realm of possibility once I became Rose, but the situation changed so fast, I really haven't had much time to process what it all means since Kat revealed Jet's existence. Still, she doesn't have to act so shocked, like my being a father is so crazy it's not even fathomable.

"I raised you, didn't I?"

She shrugs, brushing off everything I've done for her in twenty years in one single motion. "Felipe and the nuns did in the beginning. By the time you came back into the picture, I could practically take care of myself."

Now it's my turn to snort-laugh and nudge her shoulder with my good one. "Yeah, that's exactly what your ten-year-old little snotty ass thought."

Her mouth drops open in mock indignation. "I was not snotty."

"*Si*, you were. And you thought you were smarter than everyone else and always right."

"I *was* smarter than everyone else and always right."

I wave her off with my free hand. "That's beside the point. Just because you're smarter than everyone doesn't mean you know better. You were a child. You still are."

She snorts and shakes her head while typing away. "I'm almost twenty-one, Andres. I'm far from a child."

I don't even want to know.

Just like any parent does with their kid, I want to keep her that young, innocent baby I held in my arms before *Mama y Papa* died. The one who didn't know pain or violence and hadn't been baptized in blood. I don't want to think about what that day did to her or what *we* did to her in the two decades after with our lies.

Sofia hammers away at the keyboard then sits back. "There. I messaged Preacher and told him we're looking for Kat and what I already have."

I reach out and squeeze her shoulder. It wasn't easy for her to ask for help, and she never would have done it if I hadn't insisted. "You'll let me know as soon as you have anything?"

She inclines her head. "Of course. I don't need you stroking out up here because you're so worried. Doc says you need to take it easy because you lost a lot of blood and there's always a risk of infection. Though, he said whoever patched you up at the church did a fairly decent job."

I didn't have much of a chance to examine the work on my injuries, but whatever she did saved my life—and Genti's—I have no doubt of that. There were so many times while we were fighting our way out of that place that I thought it was over. The fact that I'm breathing now is a bit of a miracle. One I don't deserve.

Sofia pushes off the bed and averts her gaze awkwardly.

It always means she's holding something back. "What is it?"

Her lips twist as she stares out the window then finally turns to face me. "Felipe...did he...did he ask about me?"

My chest tightens, and I take a sip of my coffee to give myself time to consider how to respond. She thinks the rift between them and his silence toward her is purely because she's working for me now and he doesn't approve of this life. But the truth is so much more complicated than that.

I shake my head. "No, *mija*. He didn't."

She stalks toward the door with her laptop in her hand, hurt and anger rolling off her in waves. "I'll keep you updated."

"Sofia, wait."

Paused at the door, she looks over her shoulder at me.

How do I explain this to her without giving too much away?

I shove my hand through my hair and sigh. "Things with Felipe are complicated. Please don't—"

She holds up a hand to stop me. "I don't want to talk about it. He knows how to get a hold of me if he wants to. And he's chosen not to even though we're now in the same city. That says all it needs to."

It says he's afraid she's going to uncover our secret. That's why when I showed up, demanding he turn Sofia over to me ten years ago after I fought my way out of prison, instead of fighting me, he let me take her. Because he knew the longer she was there, the older she got, the smarter she became, the greater the chance Sofia would see through our charade to the sick, twisted truth, and he couldn't risk that. He still can't.

So, instead, he lets our sister believe he doesn't love her and doesn't care. That he's so disappointed in her choice of an immoral path working for me that he won't even speak with her.

It's for the best, but it doesn't mean it doesn't hurt to see the way it's affected her. I may be a ruthless piece of shit, but at least she knows I love her and always will. And I need her more than I could ever express. She isn't just my sister, the only person on the planet I trust implicitly and have been able to rely on for the last decade; she's also my only chance of finding Kat.

ELEVEN

ROSE

THE LONG, scalding shower does nothing to release the tension in my body like I had hoped it would. I'm more tightly wound than ever—on the razor-sharp edge of exploding and destroying everything around me the way the bomb Kat set off did.

Even dragging myself into the bathroom took all the energy I had managed to build up after my talk with Sofia.

Things might not seem so hopeless if I could tell Sofia what's really going on. If I could warn her about the true threat Felipe poses to more than just our moral compasses. But I can't destroy her like that. Not after everything she went through recovering from her injuries sustained in the explosion. I have to keep her in the dark for as long as possible, let her believe the only real focus here is the other families, and deal with the Felipe situation on my own. Because I can't put it off any longer.

Felipe's words at the church left me more convinced than ever that he's on the precipice of making a major change in the organization, perhaps stepping out of the shadows to take what he thinks is his "rightful" place. If that happens, he no longer needs me. I become a liability, a reminder that he never *was* in control. It would make more sense for him to just become Rose than to try to explain he's been pulling the strings from behind the scenes like some master puppeteer for so long.

If I'm right and he intends to take over, then it's only a matter of time before he pulls the trigger on his plans. He may just be biding his time, lining up all the pieces to finally fall into place when he's ready. And if that's the case, Kat and I have a guillotine hanging over our heads that's waiting to fall at any moment.

Unless we do something about it first. But we can't do that until I have her back—something that seems less and less likely with each passing hour.

I slam my fists against the marble counter in the bathroom and squeeze my eyes closed, frustration burning through my body as fast as the pain.

Being helpless isn't in my nature. Since that day I took my first life, first shed blood with my own two hands, I've done everything in my power to ensure things are always in my control—by setting myself up as someone not to be fucked with in prison then making sure once I was out people understood I was willing to do whatever it took to force loyalty and advance the Blood Rose Cartel's interests. Despite Felipe being the one calling the shots behind the scenes, I was the one in control of the day-to-day, the one pulling the trigger, the one who continued to get his hands bloody to solidify our power.

But ever since Kat walked into my life, all the carefully crafted plans have been thrown out the window, along with my resolve to spend my life alone. Doing this, facing Felipe for power, it's a daunting task to take on. Yet, with Kat by my side, it might just be possible.

It will be the culmination of everything I've done since setting foot in Chicago. It has all led to this moment in time, one I don't want to face without her. It doesn't matter how exhausted I am, how close to collapse.

Keep going...

I swipe my hand over the mirror to wipe away the fog that's formed on the glass and take in my reflection. Valerian did a number on me, that's for sure. Dark-blue and black bruises mar my jaw and cheek, creeping up around my left eye socket. But it's nothing I can't handle. Neither are the wounds on my arm and thigh.

Pain means nothing when I have a goal in sight. And I won't rest until I get Kat back in my arms.

The fact that she isn't here right now, that I haven't heard anything, and neither has Genti nor anyone else in her crew, tears at my chest until I can't stand looking at myself anymore. I lash out, slamming my fist against the mirror and shattering it across the counter and floor.

Blood drips down my knuckles, but it doesn't matter. I've become so used to seeing it, to feeling it there, that I don't even bother to wipe it off.

The sound of the bedroom door opening cuts through my anger.

Hopefully, Sofia has something for me. I doubt she would bother me unless she does. It would only frustrate me further. And I've already made the decision that if we don't find Kat before tonight, I'm flying out as soon as the sun goes down.

The simple act of showering has exhausted me so badly, all I want to do is settle back onto the bed even though there's no time for that. With the towel wrapped around my waist, I push away from the counter and hobble to the bedroom door.

Familiar blue eyes meet mine, and all the air rushes from my lungs in one exhale.

"Hi." Kat's voice hitting my ears is the sweetest sound I've ever heard.

She stands at the foot of my bed with a baby I can only assume is her son sleeping against her chest. I've never seen anything more beautiful in my entire life. Her dark hair, normally tightly contained in a bun at the back of head, flows around her face and down to her shoulders—loose and wild and so completely *not* Kat.

The woman she lets the world see would never let anyone see her like this. But what's happened over the last week has changed things. It has changed us.

Mi cielo...

I struggle to take a step toward her, but my leg threatens to give out and I grip the jamb of the door to keep myself upright. Relief mixes with anger, a volatile concoction that bubbles just beneath my skin. "Where the hell have you been? Are you all right?"

She holds up a hand to stop me from trying to advance and instead closes the distance until only a few inches separate us. Her eyes dart to my bloody hand on the jamb, then across to my bandaged shoulder, down to my leg, and then finally settle on my mangled face.

Silence lingers for a moment, long enough for my relief to momentarily win out over my fury at her just showing up and not contacting me. Without another word, I lean in and press my lips to hers as I reach out and drag her against me, wrapping my arms around her as tightly as I dare.

I need it to convince myself she's really here—no matter how mad I might be.

Her body shakes against mine, and she returns the kiss with a hunger that matches my own. When she pulls back, a tear trickles down her cheek and toward the baby in her arms.

I palm her cheek in my bloody hand and tilt it up. "You got to him okay? You're not hurt?"

She offers me a humorless little half-smile. "I got to him. That's all that matters. This is Jeton."

My hand shakes as I lower it to brush my palm over the dark head of soft hair on Kat's son. He shifts slightly and nuzzles tighter against his mother's collarbone, and the blood on my hand touching him suddenly registers, making me jerk it away. A reminder of how fucking pissed I was only minutes ago by her disappearance.

"What the fuck happened? Sofia couldn't find you."

Kat presses a finger across my lips, silencing me. "It's a long story. Sofia is setting up the room next door for him. I need to go put him down."

She moves to step back, but I wrap my hand around her wrist, pulling her back to me with as much force as I dare with Jet in her arms.

"I'm coming with you."

She presses her free hand against my chest, the warm touch against my skin sending a shiver through me. "Lie down. You look fucking exhausted. I promise I'll be right back as soon as he's down."

I tighten my grip around her wrist until I know it hurts and jerk her closer to me. "If you think I'm letting you out of my *fucking* sight again for one *damn* second, you're fucking crazy, *mi cielo*. I don't care if I have to crawl. I'm coming with you."

The corner of her mouth twitches slightly, like she's fighting a smile, but instead, she just inclines her head in agreement. This isn't the time to start a fight with me, not with her son in her arms.

I release my hand from around her, and Jet shifts and releases a strangled little cry. She bounces him softly until he settles again before we slowly make our way from my room and to the one next door.

Sofia has somehow managed to locate a Pack 'N Play and set it up as a temporary place for Jet. I'll have to thank her for that later when I figure out how the hell she got Kat here and curse her out for not telling me she was coming.

Kat kisses Jet, and then she lays him down. He stretches and rolls sideways before settling back into a slow, deep sleep. She motions for me to follow her into the hallway and pulls the door closed behind her, then leans back against it with her eyes closed.

She looks as exhausted as I feel, but the ire I had the moment I saw her in my room returns with a vengeance. I've been torturing myself for days *while* being tortured, agonizing over whether or not she was okay. And she just shows up, like it's any other day. Like I haven't been on the verge of burning down the fucking world to find her.

I press my body against hers and capture her face between my palms, jerking it up toward me. "What the hell happened, Kat?"

Her eyes fly open and meet mine. "We have a lot to talk about."

TWELVE

ROSE

"*Damn right we do.*" I wrap my hand around her throat, pushing her back against the door even harder.

She swallows thickly against my palm, her hands pressed into my chest.

"You owe me an explanation, *mi cielo*. For why you didn't contact me to let me know you got him and that you were all right." I tighten my grip even more. "Why did you wait? Why make me suffer? Are we back to playing some sort of game?"

This woman almost gave me a damn coronary thinking she was dead...or worse. Then she just shows up like nothing happened and everything is fine...

Instead of cowering under my wrath, Kat merely releases a sigh. "I'll explain everything. But not right now."

She wraps her arms around my neck and drags me down to her. Her lips find mine for a needy, frantic kiss. Despite how angry I am, how exhausted I am, how absolutely destroyed my body is, my cock hardens against her thigh, and I shift to push it into her while returning her desperate kiss.

Any other time, I might've scooped her up in my arms and banged her right against this damn door or carried her into the bedroom to do it properly, but since I can barely stand, there's no fucking way that's happening right now.

Kat seems to understand the complication my current state brings because she pulls her head away from mine, grabs my hand, and practically drags me to my bedroom.

The towel wrapped around my waist falls away easily on the way across the room, leaving my naked skin exposed to the chilly air. Stopping next to the edge of the bed, Kat pushes me backward until I'm sprawled out across the mattress, my aching cock hard and ready.

Her concerned gaze sweeps over my leg to the wound Doc patched up and up to meet mine. "Are you sure we—"

I push myself up, grab her wrist, and drag her down on top of me, ignoring the scream of pain from my leg and arm the motion creates. "If you don't sit down on my cock in the next ten seconds, you're going to see just how fucking serious I really am, *mi cielo*."

She offers a little mewl and grasps the hem of her dress to drag it up and off over her head. It floats to the floor without her even caring, leaving her completely naked and exposed in a way she never has been with me before. Because now, there are no secrets. Everything is out in the open. And no matter how angry I am, no matter how badly I want answers about where she's been, I need *this* moment more.

Kat straddles my waist, careful to avoid putting any pressure against my leg, and grips my dick with a firm grasp in her warm palm. I groan at her touch. Only a few hours ago, I wasn't sure I would ever feel it again. Now, I can't imagine ever living without it.

Her icy-blue eyes lock with mine as she lines up the head of my cock at her core and slowly sinks down.

"Fucking hell, Kat..." My hands find her soft hips, and I dig my fingers into the flesh there as she seats herself fully on me.

Heaven and Hell collide in an instant—a beautiful sense of peace mixing with the scorching heat of her cunt wrapped around my cock.

She groans and rolls her hips, taking me a fraction of an inch deeper than I even thought possible. I bite back the roar that threatens to slip out of my throat, afraid to wake Jet next door or that it might bring Sofia running to check on me and scar her for life more than she already has been.

I don't want anything to interrupt this moment with Kat. Finally having her back with me like this, being buried inside her after thinking I lost her forever, might be the closest to Heaven I'll ever get with what I've done in my life.

Kat places one hand flat against my chest, then pushes herself up until only the head of my dick sits inside her, then rocks forward, letting my entire length glide into her welcoming heat once again.

"Fuck, Kat."

Long nails dig into my pecs, the sharp sting tightening my balls and threatening to make me come. But I'm not ready for this to be over. Not after how long it feels like it's been since we were last together. Not after all we've been through to get here again.

For this brief moment, everything that's happened, everything that's gone wrong, all the threats looming in our future disappear. I can forget Felipe. I can forget Rose. I can forget that we have the Russians and the Irish breathing down our necks. I can just let myself enjoy the clench of her pussy around my hard flesh. Her moans echoing in the room. Her nails scoring my hot skin.

She presses her other hand to my chest to give herself more leverage and arches back, letting her head fall and eyes close. Every roll of her hips. Every clench of her hot walls on my cock. The way she rides me in a rhythm designed to drag us both over the same cliff of ecstasy we're dancing along the edge of. It's all too much and not enough at the same time.

With her head dropped back and her long, elegant neck exposed, the desire to bite into the perfect white flesh burns through me. To simultaneously mark her as mine and let her feel a fraction of the pain I've been in the last few days worrying about her.

I push myself up, wrap my hand around her neck, and sink my teeth into the spot where it meets her collarbone. Kat jerks and cries out, both from the pain and from the orgasm that ripples through her body. She bucks wildly, unable to maintain her steady rhythm, but I brace my foot the best I can and push up into her as I lick at the teeth marks on her otherwise flawless skin.

"You. Are. Mine." I brush my lips against her ear, every undulation of her body as she rides out her orgasm dragging me closer to mine. "The last time I told you, you didn't seem to believe that, but I'm not letting you go now. Not ever, *mi cielo*."

She squeezes down on me tighter with a strangled gasp, and I empty myself into her with one hard thrust. I release everything that's been pent up since the night she left. All the lies and frustration. The fear and the pain.

This is our real first time together now that we've both come clean and know each other's darkest truths. The first time I've ever really been with someone who truly understands who and what I am.

But as I collapse back onto the bed, bringing Kat with me, our pants the only sound in the room, one thought plays on repeat in my head.

This is too good to last. Something bad is coming. How long will we have until the guillotine drops?

THIRTEEN

ROSE

An unfamiliar sound wakes me.

What the hell is that?

It takes my sleep-fogged brain a moment to process it. Something I haven't heard in over twenty years.

A baby crying...

I bolt upright in bed and glance down at Kat lying beside me. Sprawled on her back, her exposed breasts rise and fall in the steady rhythm of deep sleep. Jet's wail doesn't wake her, but I can hear it easily even through the closed door and wall that separates our rooms. Whatever she went through over the last few days, it's taken as much out of her as my ordeal has me.

She needs to sleep...which leaves me to handle a baby who doesn't know me when I haven't touched an infant in two decades.

That thought settles heavily on my shoulders as I slip out of bed, tug on a pair of boxers, and stagger to the door on a very unhappy leg. While being with Kat like that was something we both needed, it definitely didn't do anything to help me in my recovery. Every step sends a jolt of agony through my leg, and reaching out to open the door makes my arm ache enough that I clench my jaw.

The moment I crack the door, the volume of Jet's cries jacks up another decibel, sending my heart racing. Flashes of another baby crying so many years ago.

But there isn't time to dwell on the past, though, not when Jet needs me.

The door to the room next to mine stands open, and Sofia paces back and forth, a very angry-looking baby in her arms and a bottle in one hand. She turns toward me, her eyebrows flying up. "Good." She rushes over and pushes him into my arms before I can protest. "I can't seem to get him to stop crying."

I stare down at the dark-haired little boy in my arms, his eyes squeezed shut with his wails. "What am I supposed to do?"

She shoves the bottle into my hand. "Give him this. Kat left a bag with some clothes, bottles, and formula. I made it according to the directions. I heard him when I came in to grab something from the kitchen." Holding her hands up, she backs out the door into the hallway. "That's all you now, *Padre*.

Padre...

The word means so many things in so many different contexts. It was what my parishioners would have called me had I gone to seminary as planned. It was what I became to Sofia. Now, I guess it is what I am to this child. Maybe. But I'm far from prepared for this right now.

"What? Don't leave."

But it's too late. Sofia's already rushing down the hall. She glances over her shoulder at me and shrugs unapologetically. "I have work to do! I'm sure you can handle it."

I'm sure you can handle it.

That's easy for her to say when she's running away. The last time I held a baby in my arms, it was

Sofia and she was covered in the blood of the people I had just killed. Even after twenty years, that pivotal moment when my life veered off its straight course still feels like yesterday.

The metallic smell of the carnage...

The stickiness of it all over my hands...

The way it looked against Sofia's baby-soft and flawless skin...

I'll never understand how something can happen so long ago and yet be so crystal clear and vivid in my mind. There isn't time to allow myself to be sucked back to that place, though, not with Kat's son hysterical in my arms.

I bring the bottle to Jet's open mouth, but he screams and refuses it, batting it away with his flailing arms.

Shit.

The last thing I want to do is wake Kat to take care of him, not when she so obviously needs the sleep. But it's been a long fucking time since I cared for an infant. I never minded helping with Sofia when she was born, but that was another lifetime. I'm not sure I remember how to do it properly anymore.

Bouncing him in my arms, I step back into the hall to make sure Kat didn't wake up, but the door to my room is still closed. I take a few steps one direction, then the other, my movements jerky and slow due to the very real possibility my leg may give out on me. "Come on, *mijo*. You need to eat."

His eyes flutter open, and his cries slow to a whimper as he examines me with wide, golden irises that undoubtedly match what his mother's looked like before she had to change her appearance and hide who she was. It's strange to think the cold, calculating blue eyes I've been looking into are fake and hers underneath are this warm color. The iciness fits her so much better, except the momentary flickers I've seen where Jet is concerned.

I take the temporary silence in his distress as a success and use the lull to slip the nipple of the bottle into his mouth. This time, he takes it with a gurgle and snuggles against me.

My chest tightens, and my legs wobble slightly—though whether it's from the lack of energy or the fact that this innocent child is relying on me in this moment isn't something I'm completely ready to examine. Everything has happened so fast. From telling Kat the truth to her coming clean about Jet, the shootout at the airport, escaping Valerian, escaping Felipe...

Has it really been less than a week?

Now, this tiny person is inextricably linked to my life, my business. Kat's son has become the biggest target of all for our enemies, not just because of her but because of *me*.

Just like Sofia was forever tainted by her bath in blood, this child will forever be marked by the fact that he's the son of the Dragon...and now...me.

Clenching my jaw, I ignore my protesting body and make my way back to my room, easing the door open and shutting it behind me as quietly as possible. Kat still sleeps soundly, and with as much finesse as I can manage, I settle onto the bed and shift to lean back against the headboard with Jeton cradled in my arms, happily sucking at the now half-empty bottle.

Only instead of being able to relish in this unusual peaceful moment with him and Kat safe in my bed, acid churns in my stomach, threatening to make its way up my throat just thinking about how vulnerable they are now, how exposed we *all* are now that Jet is no longer hidden away and Kat has poked a bear by moving against the Irish and the Russians. Coupled with the not-so-veiled threats Felipe made, it seems anywhere we turn, we'll have guns pointed at our chests and knives driven into our backs.

It isn't a new way of living for me. It's the reality of the life I chose the day I became Rose. Kat chose this life, too. She could have disappeared after Aleksander's death. Just melted away into a world far away from the death and violence of this city. She could have had her son and been someone else entirely. But she *chose* this for herself, and she chose a different life for him. One she thought would keep him safe.

This child doesn't deserve to be a target just because of who his parents are. He doesn't deserve to have to be looking over his shoulder every day for the rest of his life, but that's the reality of what his being *here* with *us* means.

I lower my head and press a kiss to the top of his ~~Jet's~~ soft, dark hair. "I will protect you, *mijo*."

With my life...

He may not be mine. He may never call me *Padre or Papa* or think of me as his, but for Kat, I will ensure he's safe. Always.

When I drag my head back up, Kat watches me from where she lies beside us, with wide blue eyes, her bottom lip trembling. She's never looked so exposed, so vulnerable. "You're really okay with this?"

Her question hurts more than getting struck with two bullets. More than Valerian pistol-whipping me. More than almost anything I've experienced in the last twenty years. Though, it shouldn't. It's a fair question, given the circumstances. Still, she shouldn't have to ask it.

"Okay with this? He's your *son*, Kat. Just like I would do anything for you, I'll do anything for him."

Kat shifts up onto her elbows, watching him with teary eyes. "But—"

"No." I reach out and lift her chin 'til her gaze meets mine. Tightening my hold, I ensure she can't look away. "This partnership has been sealed in the blood we've shed for each other—both our own and of our shared enemies. We fight one battle now, and we stop fighting each other."

It's what I've always wanted with her—a united front. Combining our forces to secure our place at the head of the Chicago underworld. It's what she's been fighting for since day one.

And her silence now heats my blood.

Something is still holding her back, preventing her from embracing what I'm offering her despite the fact that I literally hold her son in my arms and I took fucking bullets for her.

I squeeze her chin harder and drag her closer to me. "Do you want to leave, *mi cielo*?"

She considers me for a moment before shaking her head. "No, it's not that. I'm just terrified of what's coming..."

I release her, and she pushes herself up until she can lean in and place a kiss on Jet's head and then my lips.

This one is slow, almost reverent, and when she pulls away and snuggles into my side, I allow myself one second to enjoy the feeling before all hell breaks loose.

FOURTEEN

ROSE

KAT SHIFTING on the mattress beside me wakes me this time, and I roll over and reach out for her only to find her side of the bed empty. Light still streams in the window, so we can't have been asleep for too long after she brought Jet back to his room when he was done eating.

I push up and scan the room and find her standing at the end of the bed, her phone in her hand. "Kat? What's wrong?"

She jerks at the sound of my voice, and wide, cold eyes meet mine, shimmering in the moonlight. For a moment, she looks lost, scared, things I never would have thought she could be when we first met. It's what I imagine Aleksander must have seen in Brynn when he found her beaten and bloody in that parking lot after her ex attacked her. It's what she was before she became Kat.

But she quickly regains her composure and clears her throat, then makes her way over to where her purse sits on the table across the room in front of the window. She slips her phone back into her bag but keeps her back to me. "I never did get to tell you what happened over there."

With sleep still fogging the edges of my brain, I shake my head and sit up against the headboard. "Tell me now."

She releases a heavy sigh, and her shoulders sag slightly, but she stands, staring out the window. "Kreshnik Dragusha and Afrim Berisha were there, waiting when I landed."

I jerk up and narrow my eyes on her. "What?"

How the fuck did they know she was coming?

"They weren't too happy about my impromptu visit, either." She glances over her shoulder at me then returns her focus to the window. "I only had Martin with me, so I knew there was no way I would just walk away from them without some sort of showdown."

"How did you escape?"

Acid crawls up my throat. Those two are not people to fuck with, and Kat arriving in *their* territory would have been seen as a major intrusion, maybe even an act of war.

Did she make another deal with them? Something worse than what she already is committed to with them?

Even from here, I can see her throat work as she swallows thickly. "A car showed up."

"So, you climbed into a random car?"

She shakes her head. "I didn't have a choice...the shooting started. I dove in, and the driver pulled away before I could help Martin."

"Who was it?"

"A man who calls himself Reaper."

"Reaper? That doesn't sound too friendly. Who the hell is he?"

Her hand tightens on the top of her purse. "A friend of Cutter's."

"Shit. How did they know where you were?"

"Apparently, they tracked me as far as the transponder would allow before it was turned off, then it was just deductive reasoning on Valentina's part. But she knows the region, knows the people, so it wasn't hard for her to guess where I'd land. There's only one small airport outside of Vlorë I could use to try to avoid detection when I arrived. And their timing was just good."

"And this Reaper helped you get Jet?"

She nods slowly. "Things were quiet when I got there. The farm I left him at appeared normal, exactly the same as it was when I dropped him off there less than a year ago." Her voice cracks on her final words, and a tiny shudder rolls through her at the memory. "I explained the situation to the family who had been raising him, and Reaper ensured my back was protected and got me out of the country. Then I took one of Valentina's jets back here."

"And what did Valentina want in return for her generous help?"

Gunfire pops somewhere outside, and I jerk toward the sound and reach for the gun in my nightstand, but before I can grab it, Kat pulls hers from her purse and points it at me.

"She told me she would need a favor. I just didn't expect it would come so soon."

"Kat...what the hell are you doing?"

She steps toward me, the barrel of her gun trained on my chest. "I didn't know what the favor was going to be, but apparently, she would like to have you join her for a meeting to discuss your working relationship. She wasn't so sure you would go willingly."

"Fuck...Kat...you don't have to do this."

I inch my hand toward the nightstand, but she fires...the bullet striking the wood mere inches from my hand.

"I don't have a choice. Now she knows about Jet. And I gave her my word I would follow through on whatever she asked."

More gunfire erupts outside, breaking the silence.

"Those are her men coming now. I imagine they'll be here in a minute. I promised you would go easily."

¡Mierda!

Her bottom lip trembles for half a second before she squares her shoulders. "I am sorry, Felipe."

My chest tightens at her use of my real name. The name no one has called me in twenty years.

"If there was any other way—"

I growl and push up from the bed, ignoring the continued protests from the destroyed parts of my body. "There is another way. You and I fight this together like we fought everything and everyone else."

Kat shakes her head slightly but refuses to move the weapon pointed directly at me. "For what it's worth, I do hope you make it out of your meeting with your life. You know where to find me if you do."

She backs away slowly, and I move toward her, but she shakes her head. "Don't."

The door to the room bursts open, and four men dressed head to toe in black enter. With masks covering their faces, some sort of night vision goggles pulled over them, and semi-automatic weapons in their arms, they look like an attacking foreign force rather than the men of one of my rivals.

Fucking Kat. She led them right to me.

The man in the lead steps forward and shoves up his goggles to assess me with one blue eye and one milky, white dead one with a scar running across it.

Cutter. So that's what he's been hiding under those glasses all this time.

He glances at Kat and her gun but seems unconcerned—like he knows she wouldn't even *attempt* to use it against them. He knows she won't act out, that she'll choose to follow through with her promise to Valentina. Instead, he steps forward, grabs my arm, and drags me from the room.

Of course, I could try to fight him off. Make a grab for one of their guns. Try to keep them from taking me. But it wouldn't do any good. Not when I'm weak and hurt. Not when the person I thought was my partner is handing me over to one of our enemies.

So, I don't. I let Cutter lead me out into the hallway.

I glance over my shoulder in time to see Kat entering the room next door to get Jet before

Valentina's goons drag me down the front staircase, past the bodies of my men sprawled around, and into the waiting line of SUVs.

She betrayed me.

I guess it shouldn't really come as any surprise, given who and what we are, but it does mean one thing—Kat has just moved to the top of my enemy list.

COMMANDING PRIDE

We rise in glory as we sink in pride.

-Andrew Young

ONE

ROSE

WHAT THE FUCK JUST HAPPENED?

The whirlwind of the last few minutes has left my already sleep-fogged head spinning so fast, I can barely focus on what's happening around me.

One minute, I was sound asleep in bed with Kat cuddled up next to me, finally allowing myself a rare moment of peace, and the next, I'm in nothing but my boxers, bound at the wrists, and wedged between two goons in the back seat of this SUV with weapons pointed at me.

¡Mierda!

Anger burns through my veins like a raging inferno, threatening to burst from my skin and engulf everything around me. That look in Kat's cold blue eyes as she watched Cutter and his men lead me away flashes through my mind. I used to want to swim in them, but I never thought they would drown me—quite literally. The woman fucked me then turned me over in my fucking boxers without even blinking. Without hesitation. Like it was nothing. Like *I* was nothing.

The only thing worse would have been if Kat had betrayed me when I was stark fucking naked and had Cutter barge in while she was riding me. But this is pretty damn close to as bad as it can get. The woman I love, the one I opened myself up to, who I told my deepest, darkest secrets, the ones that leave me exposed and vulnerable to the people who would take advantage of it, treated me no better than any of her enemies.

She has made them promises, then stabbed them in the back, too. And now, she's created another one in the process.

How could I have so completely misjudged the situation? Her?

Somehow, I let the brief flashes beneath her frigid exterior lull me into a false sense of security. And I'm paying for it now.

I release a frustrated growl that my aching chest just can't contain, and Cutter's one working eye meets mine in the rearview mirror for a second before he returns his focus to the road. The goon to my left shifts slightly, and for a split second, I contemplate lashing out with my bound hands to grab for his weapon. But something tells me being partially blind won't stop Cutter from anticipating that very move, and if I made the attempt, I'd be dead before I ever got off a shot.

That's the problem with people who have been trained as well as Cutter Jackson—there's no way for me to compete with them. Not when I had to learn as I went and act on nothing more than instinct to survive. Not when my first kill came from pure rage instead of after being trained by the government and thrown into a war zone.

Cutter's too calculating to act on emotion, whereas I find myself falling prey to that more and more as time goes on here in Chicago. Things I promised myself I would never do, things that I never imagined would happen, have now become my reality.

Prime example: the woman who just betrayed me.

What the hell *was she thinking?*

She should have just told me. She should've woken me and warned me, and we could have escaped off the property before Valentina's crew ever showed. Instead, I'm on my way to God only knows where to face down a woman who was willing to use Kat's son as leverage. It doesn't bode well for me, nor for those I'm stupid enough to care about—like Sofia.

In all the rush and gunfire, there wasn't any way for me to check on her, to see if she was a victim of the gunfire, if she got out okay, or if she was snatched up by Cutter's crew as unceremoniously as I was. Only one of those possibilities is acceptable, as far as I'm concerned.

Swallowing through my anger, I stare straight into the rearview mirror, ensuring Valentina's right hand and the father of her unborn child will see in my gaze what will be coming for him if he or his men harmed Sofia in any way. "You better not have touched my sister."

Cutter glances at me again before he turns down a dimly lit street, huge lawns leading up to mansions set back far from the street on either side. A slight chuckle slips from him and to the backseat—an unusual sound given the circumstances. "Believe it or not, Rose, I actually like your sister. She was a big help to Preacher and us not so long ago. If I laid a fucking hand on her, I'm sure Preacher, amongst other people, would never let me hear the end of it."

It's nice to know she's safe—at least, from one of my enemies' camps, but Valerian has already made it clear she's fair game where he's concerned. His threat to her wasn't even veiled. And I can only assume Galen and the Irish feel the same way.

"What did you do with her?"

He peeks back again, and the man beside me on the other side shifts uncomfortably.

That's interesting...

Cutter returns his focus to the road. "She wasn't in the guesthouse."

"What?"

The guesthouse is Sofia's space. Where she has all her equipment and holes up for days or sometimes weeks at a time, delving deep into the dark web and hacking anything and everything that might help the organization and me. It's her safe haven. Her weird, digital world. One she has hidden even deeper under since the bombing and her lengthy recovery. She wouldn't leave without telling me unless she saw Cutter and his crew coming and didn't have time to warn me before she fled.

"She wasn't there. My men search the whole property, but it appears she managed to slip away at some point during our raid."

¡Gracias a Dios! Hopefully, she's smart enough to lay low until I can figure out a way out of this... and she doesn't do something stupid like go to Felipe looking for help. Even though they haven't been on speaking terms for a while, she also hasn't been without one of us taking care of her for her entire life. First, Felipe raised her under the roof of the church since she was an orphan. Then, once I escaped from prison, she became my ward. Now, she's alone, out there somewhere, with a target on her back at the very least from the Russians and likely the Irish, too.

God knows she won't go to Kat. If Sofia saw Cutter's men coming onto the property, she has to suspect the woman's betrayal. It's the only way Valentina could have found us—Sofia made sure of that. That property was so well-hidden, buried deep under dozens of layers of shadow corporations and fake names, no one could ever dig to the bottom. Until Kat led them right to me and handed me over on a silver fucking platter like a total chump instead of the head of one of the most powerful criminal organizations in the world—at least as far as anyone else is concerned.

I shift uncomfortably, the way my hands are bound in front of me putting a strain on my injured shoulder. "What is Valentina planning to do with me?"

Cutter issues another low chuckle and turns up a driveway that leads to a high metal gate with sharp, threatening spikes atop it. The house sits so far back off the road that it's barely visible through a small gap where the drive winds through a massive grove of oaks. He presses a button in the vehicle, and the gate swings open for us.

"Whatever the fuck she wants, Rose. You already know what I would tell her to do. But as much as I may hate it, she's the boss here, not me."

Somehow, despite Cutter's clear dominance in just about every aspect of life, they seem to make their relationship work even when Valentina is in charge.

What went wrong with Kat?

Here I thought we were equals. A partnership with neither of us taking a position of power over the other, both of us pushing and pulling equally. But Kat just shoved that notion into a giant pile of shit.

And the stench roils my stomach as we make our way up the dark drive and toward a well-lit mansion on top of a small hill. *Il Padrone* once ruled his empire from here before Arturo snatched it away from under him, but now, with Valentina at the reins, things have changed dramatically.

She's just as ruthless, if not more so, than *Il Padrone* ever was, but she is also smart in a way I don't think that man ever was. Smart enough to see the opportunity Kat opened up to her. Smart enough to use it to get me in this position.

I'm about to go up against a formidable opponent in my fucking underwear.

TWO

ROSE

CUTTER and his goons lead me out from the SUV, across gravel that bites into the bottom of my bare feet.

"Fuck." I wince, the jagged bits of rock slicing through my skin, adding to the pain already searing through my leg with the jerky steps I'm forced to take. "You couldn't have grabbed me some shoes?"

Ruthless fuckers.

The snort-laugh Cutter offers me as he pulls open the door to the mansion echoes in the still night air. He clearly has no sympathy for me—though, I never expected any from him. The man doesn't do emotions, especially ones that make him acknowledge that others are humans who love and hurt. It would make what he does impossible. And he's damn fucking good at his job.

He ushers me down a few dimly lit halls, the plush carpet runners a relief on my sore feet, past an elegant dining room and lavish living room with floor-to-ceiling windows flanking a massive fire-place, to an innocuous-looking closed door. Without knocking, he throws it open and motions me inside.

My bare feet slap against the cool hardwood, the momentary reprieve the carpet offered suddenly gone as I make my way across the small office to where Valentina sits behind a large desk —one her father no doubt once used while he was still in control and the location—rumor has it— where her cousin met his demise.

Her hard amber gaze assesses me, bouncing from my beaten face over my bare and bruised chest, settling on my zip-tied hands in front of me. She inclines her head toward Cutter. "You can take those off. Rose isn't going to be a problem." She raises a dark eyebrow. "Are you?"

I would fucking love to be.

But even if I did manage to get my hand on a gun, the likelihood of my being able to shoot my way out of here before Cutter or one of his guys kills me is about zero. That doesn't mean I wouldn't have taken the chance, though. Her words stop that desire and instinct instantly. Because the way she said them has something Kat uttered just before all hell broke loose coming to the fore-front of my brain.

I promised you would go easily.

What Valentina just said, repeating almost exactly the words Kat used, is a barely veiled threat, letting me know that the bargain isn't exactly fulfilled yet and that she still knows something that could be very harmful to Kat.

I would like to think the woman sitting before me with her hand resting on her enormous belly would have some compassion, some sort of heart buried deep beneath her cold exterior that would prevent her from harming a child. But I've also been in this business long enough to know there are other ways to hurt someone than just physically. There are any number of methods she can use Jet to her advantage if she got her hands on him.

That thought sends bile rising up my throat. So, instead of arguing with her, I swallow it down and incline my head in agreement that I'll cooperate. Cutter steps forward to slice the zip-ties from my wrists with a knife he pulls from his boot.

I rub at the red skin gently, my injured shoulder aching with the movement.

Valentina sweeps an arm toward one of the leather chairs facing her desk. "Please, Mr. Rose. Take a seat. We have a lot to discuss."

I step forward, the pain in my leg making me fight back a wince, but at least it isn't bleeding again. That's all I need, to be almost naked *and* bleeding at Valentina's mercy. Lowering myself down to the seat, I bite my tongue to hold in the grunt that threatens to slip out with the effort. "This couldn't have been done with a phone call?"

Since the day I kidnapped Everly and Valentina was forced to make the distribution agreement with me so she could get her friend back safely, this woman has been looking for a way to get rid of me, to force me out and end our forced partnership. I've never given her reason or a way to, though. I haven't stepped beyond our carefully delineated borders or pushed the issue beyond what we initially agreed to. I've kept to the status quo to ensure she didn't come after me, but we both know we're coming to the end of that agreement's timeline. That means the near future could end up very messy for us both.

She offers me a cool smile and shifts in her chair slightly, obviously uncomfortable in her state. "We are nearing the end of the agreement you forced me into, Mr. Rose. And now that you and Kat have joined forces—"

I open my mouth to argue, but she holds up a hand to stop me.

"Let's stop the bullshit, Rose. For all intents and purposes, you two are one and the same."

Snorting, I shake my head and glare at her. "I'm not so sure about that after tonight."

The anger I feel toward Kat over what she just did still burns through me like an inferno that threatens to fully consume me. After everything I've done for that woman, what I sacrificed, she so easily turned her back on me. It simultaneously makes me want to destroy her and everything around me and retreat into my own head where I can flagellate myself for being fucking stupid enough to believe I had found what I needed in her.

Valentina offers me an almost sympathetic look. "Don't be so hard on her. I had her backed into a corner."

"We most certainly could've shot our way out of that corner if I'd had some warning."

Cutter snorts where he stands beside my chair to the left, and I glance up. He has slipped his trademark shades back over his eyes, but amusement pulls up the scarred side of his lips that face me. He doesn't say anything, though; he just oozes arrogance and confidence in his ability to take us out even if I had been prepared for them. I could argue the point further, but I don't feel like getting into a dick-measuring competition with him, especially not after seeing how they decimated my men at the house.

Valentina just smiles knowingly. "It seems motherhood has made Kat a bit more careful in the way she conducts her business. It's made her soft. She doesn't want to take chances she may have before."

My eyes drift down to the bulge of her belly. "Seems you're about to be in the same position, Valentina. Perhaps you should have a bit of compassion."

Anger darkens her eyes to an almost black, and she leans forward slightly. "Compassion is the *only* reason you're not dead. That...and because I have a proposition for you."

"Again...if there were something you wanted from me, Valentina, we could have done it over the phone or hell, even a meeting I was invited to rather than getting dragged out of bed at four in the morning almost naked. It would have made me a lot more receptive to hearing anything you want to offer."

Her gaze rolls over me again. "I prefer to have the upper hand in negotiations, Mr. Rose, and your nakedness means there isn't anything you can conceal now. Literally and figuratively. As Kat has no doubt told you, I'm now in possession of certain knowledge that could make things very difficult for her...and you."

Jet.

That same unease settles in my chest.

"We're threatening children now?" I click my tongue and shake my head. "What would your father think? From what I understand, he was ruthless but had certain lines he wouldn't cross. And you seem to be crossing them an awful lot."

She leans forward and slams her palm against the desk. "You forced my hand on the drug issue, Rose, brought that *sporcizia* into my territory. That had nothing to do with any change in how this organization operates and everything to do with saving the life of a friend. Don't mistake the two." She relaxes back. "But it did teach me one thing."

I smirk at her. "That I'm a great partner?"

Otherwise, why would I be here?

She shakes her head. "No. That having friends means having weaknesses." Her gaze drops briefly to her stomach. "And as you noted, I'm about to have one very big weakness." She raises her head again, locking and holding my gaze. "And I don't trust you because you have nothing to lose. Nothing at risk when you make moves that put targets on your back. That makes you a very dangerous man."

Cutter steps forward and leans back against the edge of the desk, effectively putting a wall between himself and Valentina though he's far enough to the side that I can see her. Still, the move sends a clear message if I were about to make any threats to their unborn child. "I don't know, *principessa*. I think he does have a weakness. We just never realized how big it was before."

¡Mierda!

Valentina's guard dog crosses his arms over his barrel chest, the black shirt he wears tightening around his biceps, making him even more intimidating to somebody who actually gave a shit. "His sister."

I lurch to my feet, but he's in my face, shoving me back down to the chair faster than I can even react.

"Don't even fucking think about it, Rose."

Pain from the move mixes with the fury boiling in my blood. "My sister is off-limits."

Cutter grins over his shoulder at Valentina. "Told you."

She scowls. "I actually like his sister. Sofia proved quite useful when we needed help."

A sigh slips from Cutter's lips. "That's true. And I agree. I told him the same thing in the car." He shrugs slightly. "Still, she's a weak point."

Valentina leans forward again. "True. But since I have a bit of a soft spot for her, that leaves me at a bit of a disadvantage to Rose. That is unless I manage to find some other form of leverage."

I snort and shake my head. "Good luck. There's nothing to find. I came to Chicago for one reason and one reason only. Anything that doesn't advance that goal is of no consequence to me."

"Not even Kat's son?"

Fuck. She went there.

THREE

ROSE

THAT ANGER I've been barely containing toward Kat suddenly flips toward Valentina and Cutter. "So, you *are* threatening Jet? Pretty fucking low, even for you, Valentina."

She assesses me coolly. "I'm not threatening anyone, Rose. Just making an observation that tying yourself to Kat may strengthen you in many ways, but it also exposes you to a weakness you didn't have before. *Her* weakness becomes yours."

"That might have been true if she hadn't just stabbed me in the back. As far as I'm concerned, she's dead to me. Threats to her mean *nada*."

A tiny smile pulls at the corner of Valentina's lips, and she glances at Cutter, some unspoken words passing between them. "Whatever you say, Mr. Rose. But I think you'll want to hear my proposition either way."

Whatever will get me the hell out of here faster.

She inclines her head toward me. "Our deal ends shortly. And I have no doubt that you would've tried to find a way to extend it—by force if necessary. I'm telling you right now...that isn't going to happen. I have absolutely no desire to continue to permit you to sell drugs in my territory."

Almost as if to emphasize her statement, Cutter stands to his full height, towering over me.

"However..." Valentina sighs. "Keeping my territory clean means you'll have to go somewhere else."

"What are you suggesting?"

She shrugs slightly. "Well...you already have access to the Albanian territory through Kat. Perhaps that will appease you and we can agree not to push the subject further."

I bark out a laugh, then wince at the pain it radiates through my body. "That's your proposition? That I take something that's already mine, at least according to you, and lose what I get from you in the process?" I chuckle and lean back in the chair. "I don't think so. It doesn't sound like a very good deal for me, now does it?"

"It does if you consider the alternative."

"Which is what?"

She spreads out her hands. "All-out war with me. The major organizations that have existed in Chicago essentially since its founding have always managed to find a way to all remain. There have been fights. There have been slaughters. Blood has run through the city streets. That all is very true. But that only occurred once someone stepped out of line, pushed the boundaries of their territories. Got too greedy." A tiny sigh falls from her lips. "With the baby coming any day now...I am not in any position to want to start a war with you or anyone else. And you have a little one to think of now, too. So, it's not that I'm threatening Kat's son. I'm just pointing out the position we both find ourselves in, one Kat is very aware of."

I HATE THAT SHE'S RIGHT. THAT BEING WITH KAT NOT ONLY STRENGTHENS OUR FORCES BUT also means having a weakness. Because that's what Jet is, the weakness she mentioned earlier. And while I don't know that Valentina or Cutter could ever harm a child, if it came down to theirs or ours, I don't think they'd be pulling punches, either.

"Your girlfriend made a lot of angry enemies even angrier with what she did. You two are going to be dealing with Valerian and Galen's wrath for a while."

Not to mention Felipe, which she doesn't appear to know about yet. Thank God.

The last thing I need is her digging into my complicated family dynamics and realizing she might be negotiating with the wrong brother.

She raises a dark eyebrow at me. "Don't you think it's best you just walk away from what you have in my territory before you start a war on a third front?"

Fourth front. But who's counting?

"Your proposition is that I walk away from your territory, from my customers, the entire network I've established here and move it to Kat's territory?"

She shrugs nonchalantly, but what she's asking for isn't so simple.

"That will cost me millions, maybe more, in both time and product sales."

"Your problem, not mine. Cutter is more than happy to declare formal war against you if it needs to come to that."

He drops his head so I can see his eyes above the rim of his aviator glasses and winks with the one good one. "I'm still quite the marksman."

"WHY NOT JUST KILL ME NOW? WHY NOT KILL KAT WHEN YOU HAD HER IN ALBANIA? WHY not let Cutter take us all out if what you ultimately want is to take over the city?"

A smile pulls at her lips, again, this one full of genuine humor. "I never said that was my goal. I'm content to manage the territory my father built for us, the territory that's been part of our family and this legacy for so long. At least, for now. If you and Kat are gone, where do you think Valerian and Galen will turn their focus next?" She waves a hand around. "The three of us would fight over your territories even if I rightfully won them. The war would continue and only get bloodier."

"So...you want a truce with Kat and me?"

"Yes."

I look between her and Cutter and weigh the options. Not having to worry about Valentina would make it a lot easier to keep our focus on the anger Kat—and by association me—have created with the Russians and the Irish, but her territory loss would wreak havoc on my organization—something I can't afford when I'm about to go to war with Felipe for it.

Yet, the benefits could outweigh the losses...if I can get something from her that makes it worthwhile. "I ask a few things in return."

She scowls at me, her hands fisting on the armrests. "You're getting a truce in return."

"But you're getting a territory back."

"Which I would've gotten back, anyway."

I smirk at her. "That's what you think."

There was never any chance of my leaving the Marconi territory when our two years were up. I was simply waiting for the right time to make the moves to secure it permanently.

"What is it you want?"

That seems to be ever-changing, and after what Kat pulled this morning, I'm not entirely sure. But this is an opportunity I can't pass up, either. It isn't often one of your competitors wants something from you that you can leverage. "When the time comes that I need your backing, you will stand with me."

She raises an eyebrow. "Against whom? Valerian and Galen? I'm not about to go to war with them for you."

I shake my head. "I'm talking hypothetically. In the future, I want to know that not only do we have a truce but that there's an understanding that what benefits you also benefits me and vice versa."

"An interesting concept. A partnership without one?"

"If that's how you want to put it."

Her lips twist as she contemplates my request. "It's something to consider, Mr. Rose. In the meantime, I'll let Cutter show you to your accommodations."

"You're not letting me go?"

She snorts and shakes her head. "How stupid do you think I am, Mr. Rose? Until whatever this is gets settled, you're not going anywhere. Even almost naked, you're the type of man who would stab someone in the back just to watch them bleed and enjoy their pain. So, I think I'll wait and sit on this for a while."

The sadistic woman is relishing in this—having me at such a disadvantage. I never realized how much like Kat she really is. That woman I gave my heart to threw me to the wolves, not only without any weapons but with literally nothing protecting my wounded body.

Now, she's assaulted my pride. That was a huge mistake on her part. She better pray Valentina decides to kill me rather than accept my offer. Because once I'm out of here, I'm coming for Kat.

FOUR

ROSE

I TAKE stock of the tiny room, letting my gaze bounce from the small bed pushed against the wall to the rest of the barren, depressing space. It doesn't take long since it isn't even a bedroom, really, likely a closet someone shoved a bed and nothing else into at some point for a very specific reason. Since it's in the cold, unfinished basement of this mansion, it likely has been used for exactly this purpose—containing someone they don't want anyone else hearing or seeing.

It's a torture chamber, for lack of a better term. And while I don't see blood stains or other evidence of direct violence, I have no doubt it's occurred down here in the basement. Cutter's skills in that department are somewhat legendary. Any thought of escaping from here can go right out the proverbial window since there isn't a real one.

Not that I would have the energy or strength to do that if it were a possibility. Even taking the stairs down here left me hurting and breathing heavily. The last few days have utterly destroyed me in every way imaginable physically. Add in the emotional weight of what's happened, the way Kat's treachery decimated everything I thought I knew, and I'm dead on my cut, sore feet.

The frigid temperatures down here won't help me feel any better, either. It's a bit sadistic. But maybe the chilly air is part of the plan in this room—to leave its occupant shaking and cold to mentally break them down. It's a tried-and-true form of torture for many but not anything I've ever attempted before. I prefer things dirtier and more direct. Using my fists and anything else at my disposal to make whoever crossed me suffer to the utmost degree. If blood isn't spilled, I'm not doing my job. Apparently, Cutter and Valentina have a more varied approach, and I'd much rather be on the other side of determining whether this form works or not.

Raising an eyebrow, I turn back to Cutter, the chill of the room causing a shiver to run along my exposed spine. "Really? You're not even going to give me any clothes?"

Cutter's sunglass-covered gaze drifts over my bandaged arm, down to the wound on my leg, then briefly over my cock encased in my boxers. "Why? You cold?"

And I guess we're back to comparing dick sizes.

Under other circumstances, I would drop trou and prove to him that he has nothing to make fun of, but as it stands, I don't feel like exposing myself anymore to these people.

Instead, I cast a glare in Cutter's direction that demonstrates my annoyance with his comment and the entire situation. "In case you hadn't noticed, *amigo*, I kind of had the shit beaten out of me quite recently and was shot. If you're going to keep me here against my will, the least you can do for someone your partner is hoping to stay friends with is give me some fucking clothes so I don't freeze to death in this dungeon."

"Dungeon?" Cutter snorts and shakes his head but motions to somebody in the hall. He turns back and chucks a pile of clothing at me.

It hits the ground before I can catch it, my reflexes clearly affected far more by what's happened the last week than I realized. If I had tried to break free from my captors at any time during this nonsense, I likely wouldn't have gotten more than a few feet.

"There you go." Cutter plasters on a fake smile and sweeps out his arm. "Enjoy your stay."

Smug fucker.

Acting like this is The Four Seasons isn't doing anything to improve my mood or my opinion of him or Valentina. "How long are you planning to keep me here?"

He leans against the jamb and examines his cuticles, apparently unconcerned with the fact that he's about to lock me in this tomb. "However long it takes Valentina to decide what to do with you."

I bend over to grab the clothes from the ground and bite back a groan. This "feeling like shit" thing is getting old. "Well, tell her the longer I stay here, the less friendly I'm going to be."

As it stands, I haven't decided what I'll do with Valentina when I finally breathe fresh air again. Part of me sees the wisdom in her suggestion to establish a truce, but the bigger part wants to ensure I have solid ground to fight from when Felipe finally makes his move. I need the resources I can only pay for with the money being brought in from Valentina's territory. Weakening myself more, even to ostensibly gain her cooperation, goes against every instinct I have. And instincts are what have kept me alive for this long. Though, they've apparently failed me where Kat is concerned.

Cutter chuckles and pushes off the jamb. "I'll relay the message."

He closes the solid door, and the lock engages with a heavy, foreboding click that seems to reverberate around the tiny, windowless room.

I drop the clothes onto the bed and scrub my hands over my face, rubbing at my tired eyes.

Was it really only hours ago that Kat showed up in my room and fucked me like there was no tomorrow?

Maybe that was because she knew there wasn't one for us. Maybe she knew all along what Valentina would ask of her. Maybe Kat always planned to betray me regardless and this was just an opportunity for her to do now that she has Jet back while also appeasing Valentina and further cementing their relationship.

"Fuck!" The frustration building through me finally reaches the breaking point where I can no longer contain it, and I whirl and punch my fist into the wall. The drywall crumbles, and agony shoots through my hand and up my arm, but it doesn't even faze me at this point, not after everything that's happened. In fact, I almost welcome it, striking the wall again and again and again.

If I'm feeling pain, I'm still alive. And as long as I'm alive, there's an opportunity for revenge against those who hurt me the most.

How could I have been so stupid?

I let her in. Trusted her with literally everything—the ugly truth of who and what I am, the one that can destroy me now that it's in her hands.

I'm a fucking idiot.

The kind of idiot I promised myself I would never be over *una puta.* The kind I truly thought I never *could* be. Not until I met Kat and let her get under my skin, let her convince me she was truly my equal.

But that ends today. *Right. Now.*

I'm sure it didn't escape Valentina's notice that I asked for her to back me in the future—not *us,* as in Kat and me. As far as I'm concerned, there is no *us* anymore. Not when I gave her everything and she threw it back in my face without an ounce of regret.

I shake out my hand, grab the white T-shirt off the bed, and slide it on, gritting my teeth. Pulling on the sweatpants brings the same result. The pain in my shoulder every time I move it and my leg with each step I take are constant reminders of what I went through for her—for *them.* But what she did to me hurts far more than what Valerian did or ever could.

Our Lord and Savior may have said to turn the other cheek, but I was always far more drawn to the Old Testament ways during my time in the Church.

An eye for an eye...

That's a lot more my style. Though, I don't have any idea what could compare to what Kat did. She couldn't have done anything worse or driven the knife into my back any deeper—short of siding with Felipe.

And I wouldn't put even that past her.

FIVE

KAT

THE HEAVY, old wooden door creeks open ominously, and I step through it, my heels clicking against the marble underfoot. A shiver rolls through me, and a sense of dread settles on my shoulders the farther I move inside.

Was this place so menacing the last time I was here?

It certainly didn't seem so at the time. But things have changed so dramatically since then, even though not all that much time has passed. This time, my unease isn't caused by the unknown nature of my mysterious meeting or the watchful, judgmental eyes of Christ on the crucifix hanging above the altar. It's knowing what I have to do—the next step in my plan. The reason I came back to this place.

So many things have gone so damn wrong over the last few weeks. It almost seems as though God is finally punishing me for what I've done. Like He's setting me up to take the ultimate fall and atone for my sins. Perhaps I should have lit more candles the last time I set foot in this church. Maybe I should have taken the sense of foreboding I felt then as a sign of what was to come and tried to stop it. But it's too late to stop the runaway train barreling down on me now.

Things have been building to this since the day I set foot in Albania—pregnant, alone, scared. That's why leaving Jet at Kat's Cradle with the girls to come here was one the hardest things I've ever had to do. Almost harder than leaving him in Albania in the first place. Because at that point, I was resolved with the decision. I was prepared to leave him. He was going to have a better life. One free from this death and destruction. Away from the lies and backstabbing and deceit that rule this world. I knew then that it was the best thing for him. The only way. So, it was easier to walk away then than it was to drop him off today after I fled Rose's place.

Because now, that innocent baby is *here*, twisted up in this game we're all playing to establish our supremacy in a city that seems to want to fight me every step of the way. Now he's the target of both Valentina and Felipe, and I have no way of knowing what they might do if they get their hands on him or how else they will try to twist me to do their bidding and use him as leverage. Valentina has already used that power with a catastrophic effect.

It makes walking into this church feel like walking into the lion's den completely unarmed and unprepared. All I have is the resolve in my heart and mind to accomplish this necessary task.

I hope that's enough to survive this meeting...

The ominous, heavy silence of church midday weighs on me. I had anticipated someone being here—parishioners or maybe an employee or two. Instead, the sound of my heels echoes into the cavernous ceiling, following me deeper inside.

I cross in front of the altar, averting my gaze from the crucifix because I can't bear that kind of judgment right now on top of everything else. If I looked up and met those glazed, all-knowing eyes staring down at me, I might turn right around and head back out. That resolve I've been holding onto so tightly might not survive that.

Pushing ahead, I reach the hallway that leads back toward the door Felipe came from the night Genti and I were here.

Things were so different then. Jet was still hidden safely away with a loving family. My plans here were in motion and moving along nicely. I still had Rose at arm's length. Even though I had finally given in to my lust for the man, I had managed to keep up the wall behind which I kept all the pain and truth about Jet.

But that wall came crumbling down as soon as he revealed the truth about Felipe. And it left me with only one choice I could make. One thing I could do to protect Jet and ensure both of our futures. What I came today to do.

I suck in a deep breath and march toward my fate.

A door opens just ahead of me on the left, and a familiar redhead steps from it and turns back to lock it behind her. I personally interview and hire every girl who works for Kat's Cradle, so I would know Rowan anywhere. But this is the last place I would expect to find her hiding out. When Felipe said she was somewhere safe, I never thought that meant *here,* mere feet from where I sat with him on that bench during our first "chat," before I knew who and what he really was. If he's been keeping her *this* close, she must really be important. Though, any reason for that has remained elusive despite Arden's digging.

I freeze, halting my steps, unsure whether I should grab her so she can't run or approach carefully so she doesn't bolt. "Rowan?"

She jerks and whirls toward me, her green eyes wide. "Kat...wh-what are you doing here?"

The fear in her eyes has me narrowing mine. In the over six months Rowan worked for me, we always had a very good relationship—at least, as good as an employer can have with an employee. Her reaction now is far from the friendly one I used to get from her. Though she was always a bit quiet and unwilling to discuss much of anything personal, I never saw it as anything other than her trying to keep her professional life completely separate. That isn't something I could begrudge any of the girls. But now, it seems like I may have missed something major happening that created this change in her—that made her quit and run to Felipe.

"I came to see the good father." The words burn on my tongue, knowing what a lie they are. "What are you doing here? We've been looking for you."

Arden has been waiting for her to turn her phone back on to try to track her ever since she left Kat's Cradle with Felipe. And now that I've found her, I have questions that need answers.

"I know. I..." She glances toward the closed door at the end of the hallway. "I shouldn't be talking to you."

Shouldn't be talking to me?

"What?" I take a step toward her. "Why not?"

"I'm sorry. I have to go." She rushes past me down the hall toward the main portion of the church before I can make a move to stop her.

While a part of me longs to chase after her to try to find out how she got entangled in this mess with Felipe and what his interest in her really is, I have bigger things to worry about right now—like the man behind that door.

Whatever he wants with Rowan, the truth will surface soon enough. It always does, no matter how hard you try to hide it beneath layers of lies.

I reach the end of the hall and raise my hand to the door. It takes me a few seconds to build up enough courage to actually follow through. My knock bounces off the marble and high ceilings, heavy and dark.

"Come in." His voice sends another chill through me.

Exactly like his brother's...

Bile burns the back of my throat, but there isn't any time to think about Rose or what I've done. I have to leave that behind me and only look to the future. So, I swallow it down and release a deep sigh before I push open the door and step in to seal my fate.

SIX

KAT

"Well, well, well, look what the Kat dragged in." Felipe offers me a smooth, friendly smile and leans back in his chair behind his desk, his hands cradling his head. Unlike when his brother speaks, his words carry a genuine lightness and welcoming tone—one I can see working on anyone who might walk in off the street seeking solace or advice from the parish priest. He offers a tiny shrug. "Sorry about the pun, but I couldn't resist."

I scowl at him. There isn't any use hiding my annoyance at his little joke even though he appears open and non-threatening at the moment. Now that I know the truth, I can see the plastic fakeness in everything he says and every smile he offers. It's in his eyes—a warmth touched by ice. His lips— curled in a way that is almost *too* perfect. Too practiced.

How was I so blind to it before?

One of his dark eyebrows rises when I don't respond. "To what do I owe the pleasure, Ms. Gashi. I didn't expect to see you back here after our last conversation."

I close the door behind me and move to sit in one of the chairs facing him. "I thought it was time you and I have another little chat."

He grins at me, genuine amusement dancing in his eyes. It's easy to see why his parishioners love him and trust him to lead the flock. Years of practice mean the man has perfected his act. It even fooled me.

"Did you decide to take me up on my offer and come for confession?"

My eyes automatically drift to the white collar at his neck, which now seems to glow like a beacon of warning against the black shirt. "Something like that."

He leans forward and rests his forearms on his desk, the tattoos visible with the sleeves of his shirt rolled up. During our first meeting, I didn't pay much attention to them, but now, I can't seem to look away.

Depictions of the devil and an angel war on his opposing forearms, lightning strikes and flashes of ethereal power blazing around them. If he put them next to each other, it would appear the two were about to land blows. Moving up, other images and words blend into the sleeves. Some unfamiliar. But I linger on one word that stands out against the rest—*familia*.

Talk about ironic.

Family appears to be the least important thing to this man. How else could he kill his own parents? Doom his brother to a decade in prison and a lifetime under his thumb, living in this world he had no desire to be a part of?

I force myself to meet his inquisitive gaze and try to remain impassive, even knowing what I do about him. Those familiar eyes hold mine in silence for a moment longer than is perhaps polite. Each second they linger, the more positive I am he can see right through me.

Finally, he motions toward me with one hand. "I would ask if you heeded my advice from our last meeting and stayed away from my dear brother, but the rumor is, you two were involved in a little incident at the airport several days ago."

"A little incident?" I raise an eyebrow and release a humorless laugh. "Funny that a priest has so much inside information about what's happening in the Chicago underworld and is friends with Albanian mob assassins like Konstandin and hookers like Rowan."

He chuckles and spreads out his hands. "I told you before, Kat, this collar offers me many opportunities I couldn't have otherwise and opens doors closed to many. People feel it safe to speak to me and come to me with their problems. They seek safety and refuge under my roof."

"Is that how Rowan ended up here?"

He dodged my question about her the first time I was here and refused to give me anything to explain why he sought her out at Kat's Cradle or why he was keeping her hidden away. But after seeing Rowan and her reaction to me today, I'm even more curious what his interest in her might be. Because this man doesn't do anything that doesn't benefit *him* in some way, and I just can't see any way she can possibly give him anything more than her body. Yet, I also can't see him bringing a prostitute into this holy place for that purpose, either. Something tells me he wouldn't want the possibility of anyone seeing him associating with her in that way—if they even *are* involved sexually.

"I told you before, Kat, Rowan's safe, and that's all that matters."

"Safe because she's here with you?" I motion behind me. "I just saw her in the hall. She was terrified and ran away like there was a fire lit under her ass."

"Such foul language for the house of God..."

"I'm quite certain things that are far more foul than me using that word have occurred under this roof—and likely quite frequently."

He watches me for a moment, then barks out another laugh. "Really, Kat...what can I do for you? Or did you just stop by to say hello?"

He doesn't know. If he had any inkling that his brother told me the truth, he wouldn't be maintaining this façade any longer than he had to.

I cross and uncross my legs slowly, being sure to expose the bare flesh between them and watch his reaction. His eyes zone in on my most private area—a decidedly un-priest-like reaction. I bite back a grin. He may wear a priest's collar and spend his days preaching abstinence and piety to the masses, but this man is anything but holy. And something tells me the vows he took didn't mean a single fucking thing to him.

The game we're playing isn't doing either of us any good at this point. Progress can only happen when the wall of lies he holds up crumbles.

I offer him a half-smile and drum my nails on the armrest of my chair. A cigarette would be incredible to help calm me during the conversation we're about to have, but even I wouldn't light up in a church. "Let's cut the shit, Andres. I know who you are and why you're here."

His eyes widen slightly, and he sits back, rocked by my words. The genial demeanor with which he greeted me upon my arrival slips and is replaced by a stone-cold stare that could make even the strongest of women quiver in their heels. "It seems my brother has been running his mouth more than he should. That puts us in a very precarious situation, now doesn't it, Kat?"

Rose knew what he was doing when he told me the truth. He was preparing me for battle but also putting me even further in danger if Felipe ever knew I was now privy to their family secrets.

"That it does. But I have a proposal for you. One I think you're going to want to hear."

A smug grin tilts his lips. "I'm all ears, Kat."

SEVEN

ROSE

MY CELL DOOR swings open with the creak, and for a split second, I'm transported back to another cell during another time where that sound usually announced the arrival of a guard—often one who thought he was going to take some sort of stand against me or take some action to prove I wasn't the one in control. It never ended well for them. Because there, within the walls of the place that was supposed to be my punishment, I was king. I never had to look over my shoulder because I knew no one was stupid enough to ever stand against me. If they tried, they never breathed again.

Who the hell would've thought prison was the safest place I've ever lived?

I shake off the memory and push myself up from the hard, flimsy mattress to find Cutter leaning against the door jamb again. He's changed out of his black fatigues and now sports worn, ripped jeans and a white T-shirt that shows off the muscles he will undoubtedly use to kill me with his bare hands if he has to.

Rubbing at the stiffness in my neck, I raise an eyebrow. "You letting me go?"

Down here without any daylight or a watch, I've lost all sense of time.

He smirks at me. "Not yet. But Valentina would like you to join her for dinner. She figured you're hungry by now."

My stomach growls in response, not for the first time since I was brought down here. While I'd much rather say "fuck you and your food," there's a point where it's better to just accept what's being offered than try to make a statement about how fucking pissed off you really are. They know how mad I am, so there's no reason for me to starve myself to prove it.

I climb from the bed, the aches and pains in my body a thousand times worse than they were when I laid down. "This bed isn't fit for a dog, let alone a human being."

Cutter chuckles. "I know. My dog, Milo, won't even sleep on that thing."

"Fucking great." I move to push past him, but his hand shoots out and grabs me around my bad shoulder—which he's very aware of since he saw me basically naked, including the bandaged wound there. I grit my teeth as his grip tightens.

He leans in until I can see my own reflection in his glasses out of the corner of my eye. "Don't try anything stupid."

I turn to face him head-on, not intimidated in the least by his demonstration, and jerk my arm free of his hold. "Don't do anything stupid? If you or Valentina try to fuck me over, you're going to have a lot bigger problems, *amigo*."

He chuckles. "What? From the woman who handed you right over to us?"

I was thinking more along the lines of Felipe, but I'm not about to let this asshole know that my brother would wipe the entire Marconi organization off the face of the Earth if he knew what they did to me.

"Despite what you two may think, I have a lot of friends in the city, people who watch out for me."

Cutter spreads his arms wide. "Yet, here you are, staying at Château Marconi in our finest room."

"Fuck you."

He laughs and motions for me to walk in front of him. "I don't think you'd like that very much."

I climb the stairs as fast as my leg will allow, and Cutter directs me down the hallway to an elaborately set dining room. Candles burn across the center of the long table, and Valentina sits at the head, waiting for us.

Cutter motions to a chair at the other end of the table while he takes the seat next to her. A butler steps forward and lifts a cloche from the top of the plate in front of me. The smell of roasted meat and vegetables hits my nose, making my mouth water.

Valentina motions toward the plate. "I hope you enjoy a nice New York strip."

At this point, I'd eat just about anything.

I glance down at the beautifully plated dinner, but my eyes immediately drift to the glistening steak knife to the right of my plate. Now Cutter's words seem to make a little bit more sense...

Don't try anything stupid.

With a grin, I pick it up and turn it over, watching the light flicker off the sharp blade. Cutter's focus never leaves me until I lower it to my plate and begin cutting through the large steak.

"So...are you ready to release me from my confines, Valentina?" I pop a bite of steak into my mouth and let the fatty, delicious meat practically melt as I chew it.

Valentina takes a bite of hers and chews, making me wait for her response—no doubt deliberately. She finally swallows and takes a sip of water before setting down her glass. "I've given our situation some thought."

"And?"

"And I don't want partners. They only create"—she glances at Cutter—"complications."

"I understand that feeling." It's exactly what Kat said to me every time I approached her about joining forces with me—in business and life—until she finally gave in. Or, at least, I thought she had. Now I wonder if this was just one long game played by a woman who seems to be a true professional at it. "But I think our partnership has gone well?"

Valentina scoffs, her cheeks reddening. "What we had wasn't a partnership. It was blackmail. You would have killed Everly, and that would've destroyed Preacher, which in turn, would've hurt Cutter and me." She releases a sigh. "But it brings home a good point. One you raised during our earlier discussion. That perhaps we don't need to be partners to understand that what is good for one of us is good for us both."

She pauses to take another bite, and I take the opportunity to do the same. Cutter doesn't interrupt or interject any of his thoughts on the topic, though I'm sure he has many.

Valentina dabs her lips with her napkin and returns it to what's left of her lap. "I'm content with my business in my territory, but we all know you and Kat aren't. I don't want to be associated with any of the moves you're making against Valerian and Galen or any of the smaller groups. However... that doesn't mean that we can't come to some sort of an agreement."

I shrug while devouring more of the delicious steak, ensuring this time, she's the one waiting for my reply. "And what agreement is that?"

At this point, I don't care, as long as it gets me out here. I can always deal with anything I'm forced to agree to once I'm free.

"As in the past, when others like Michael Syla have made attempts to move in on the established territories, I'll remain quiet, a neutral party so to speak, siding neither with you or Kat nor the Russians or the Irish. At least, publicly."

I raise an eyebrow. "And privately?"

She purses her lips, clearly unhappy with having to say what she's about to. "And privately...I will provide you any assistance you may need. As long as it cannot, in any way, be traced back to me."

It's certainly not what I wanted. Having someone as powerful as Valentina back me *publicly* is priceless. Behind the scenes only loses some of the value of the deal, but it's more than I had thought she would be willing to give me when she threw me in that cold room downstairs.

I chew my steak in silence for a few moments, contemplating her offer. "You'll expect the same in return?"

"Naturally."

It seems the concept of mutually assured destruction has brought us to the point of ending this Cold War between us—at least between Valentina and me.

I take a sip of the red wine in the glass in front of me, letting the fruity, complex flavors dance across my tongue. "And what if I choose to end my ties with Kat? You two have an agreement of your own. Would that ruffle your feathers?"

She pauses with her knife raised over her steak for a moment. "Just as my working relationship with you was through force, so is mine with Kat. I owed her a favor, and I followed through on it by letting her use my docks. If you choose to alter your arrangement with her, as long as it doesn't affect me or my business, that's between the two of you. But...I will say this. I do think the two of you are stronger together than you are apart. You can watch each other's backs, double your power."

I nod and take another sip. "That all may be true. But as you've noted, aligning myself with her brings one great weakness."

Cutter shares a look with her, and she rests her free hand on her belly.

Her brow furrows before she picks up her fork and cuts her steak with the gleaming knife in her other hand. "Sometimes a weakness isn't a bad thing, Mr. Rose. It's what makes you human."

I chuckle and grin at them. "Who said I want to be human?"

EIGHT

KAT

"WHAT THE HELL WERE YOU THINKING?" Genti glares at me with eyes hard enough to cut diamonds from where he sits in the chair on the other side of my desk at Kat's Cradle.

It's not that this building ultimately offers any more protection than the strip club does. Almost my entire crew was wiped out on that tarmac while trying to get me on the plane so that leaves both locations barely covered until we can bring in more men who can be trusted. But after turning Rose over to Valentina, suddenly, the front gates and the long driveway seem like a better option than the building I so easily got to Michael in and that was so easily bombed. The place Aleksander once used to rule the same empire I'm fighting so hard for but still lost it. Somehow, it felt wrong to bring Jet there when I fled Rose's place. So, I brought him here, and after I left my meeting with Felipe, it's where I needed to come—for a lot of reasons.

Staring at Genti, his face bruised and beaten to shit, his arm in a sling, and the utter disbelief on his face, this suddenly feels less safe than it has since I arrived. For the first time ever, I shift uncomfortably under his scrutiny.

Since the day I killed Michael and took over this organization, Genti has always been my confidant, my right-hand man, the one I know I can count on when I need it. Yet, what I did to Rose has me questioning his absolute loyalty for the first time.

"I didn't have a choice, Genti. I made Valentina a promise that I would do whatever she asked, whenever she asked it. I couldn't just say 'no, sorry this doesn't work for me because I'm sleeping with him.'"

Genti shifts and winces. The injuries he suffered at the hands of the Russians will no doubt leave him sore for the foreseeable future. But at least he's not dead. I feared I would return to the States and find him and Rose had been killed. But instead, it's so much worse...

"Sleeping with him? Is that all he is to you?" He growls, pushing to his feet, and slams his good hand on the desk. "Fuck, Kat, that's cold, even for you."

"Since when do you care about what happens to Rose? Hell, I'm pretty sure even right before I got on that plane, you would have offed him without a second thought if I had made him fair game."

His eyes meet mine. "It's different now."

"Why is that?"

Genti shoves a hand back through his hair and paces. "The man saved my life, and I saved his. And I saw how he was Kat. How worried he was about you. How *distraught* that man was. He would've burned down the fucking world to get you back if you hadn't shown up. He loves you..." He looks like he wants to say something else, his gaze boring into me with a heat I've never seen there before.

Shit.

Part of me always suspected that Genti may have some feelings for me beyond those of his employer, but it's never been like that between us. And it never will be. He's like the brother I never had and never knew I needed until I stepped into this role.

And now, whatever went down while I was gone seems to have tied him to Rose in a way I've greatly underestimated. It's going to complicate things going forward. "I can see you care about Rose." I snort and shake my head, rubbing my eyes. "Christ, I can't believe I said those words. And I do, too, in a way. Whether you believe it or not." I hold up a hand to stop his interruption. "Don't let this one action paint your entire view of what happened here."

His eyebrows fly up. "What's happened here? You *betrayed* him. Literally turned the man over to the enemy."

He doesn't know the half of it since I haven't told him where I went after dropping Jet here.

"I'm not so sure she's the enemy, Genti. And it's not like I have a choice. If I hadn't, I would made myself a sitting duck and Jet, too, because she knows about him now. And the more people who know about my son, the more dangerous it becomes for him."

Genti's hand tightens on the back of the chair, and he scowls at me—hurt, and not just the physical kind, plastered across his features. "You could've told me, Kat. About Jet. What really happened when you disappeared to Albania after Aleksander's death. About what you've been hiding and why. I can't do my job and protect you, protect this fucking business, if you're hiding things that huge from me."

Of course, he's right.

I made his job ten times harder by not coming clean about Jeton from the beginning. Now, the first time Genti and I have been alone face to face since he found out, I have to deal with the reality of what my deception caused. It's his first real opportunity to express his true feelings about everything, and I can't say I blame him for being angry.

"I couldn't trust anyone, Genti. Not when I fled to Albania, alone and pregnant, grieving Aleksander. Certainly not when I came back and established myself as Kat. Not when I infiltrated your organization to take out Michael. And certainly not after I became the head of this family. Like I said...the more people who knew, the more risk to him."

"You didn't think I would protect you and Jet with my life?"

"It wasn't you I was worried about. I know you would never say anything or do anything to put Jet or me in harm's way. But—"

His entire body tenses, and his lip curls into a sneer. "But what?"

I wave a hand up and down him. "But *this*. What happened to you. They beat you half to death and probably would've kept going if you hadn't gotten out. I know you didn't say anything to Valerian about Jet or where I was going, but it doesn't mean you wouldn't have if they had pushed the right buttons."

He issues a low, menacing growl that might have actually scared me if I weren't so confident that he would never lay a hand on me. "You think I would ever talk?"

"Not willingly. But everybody has a price. Everybody has that one point of weakness—whether it be physical or emotional. And Valerian would have found yours."

Valentina found mine. She knows about Jet now...and so does Felipe. That means two of the very people we're up against for control of the city have him squarely in their sights. It made what I did today essential.

Genti sighs. "I will never let anything happen to him."

"Neither will I. Which is why I had no choice but to give Rose to Valentina." I suck in a deep breath. "And it's why I went to Felipe after."

He arches an eyebrow and narrows his eyes on me. "What the fuck, Kat? Why did you do that?"

"Because I have a plan."

He releases a deep sigh. "Why do I have a feeling I'm not going to like this plan?"

"Because you definitely won't. I'm not even sure I do. But I don't have a lot of options left."

NINE

ROSE

THE LAST TRICKLES of daylight disappear below the clouds building on the horizon as I step from the SUV onto the street corner.

Cutter glances out the still-open door at me, then at the street beyond—toward my destination. "You sure this is where you want me to drop you?"

I can't go back to the compound that is no doubt crawling with police after the firefight we had, and I'm not about to give Cutter any information about my other housing in the city.

"This is as good a place as any."

He shrugs. "Your fucking neck, not mine."

I slam the door before he speeds away from the curb, leaving me alone on the sidewalk while dusk settles over the city and rain threatens.

Two days.

Valentina kept me locked up down there for two fucking days. Anything could have happened in that time.

How many fates may have been sealed in deals done in back rooms during the time I was locked in a fucking basement?

"You know where to find me..."

I look up at the club and scrub a hand over my face. She had to have known I would come for her. That the moment I was released, this is the first place I would look. If she values her life at all, she won't be here. But still, I have to try.

Even from outside, the deep, rumbling bass from the music inside fills the night air. I step forward and pull open the door. The bass vibrates my feet through the shoes Cutter gave me and into my chest.

Seems the renovations have been completed because what was once a dirty, disgusting cesspool of sex and filth now feels almost classy. I have to hand it to Kat—the woman knows what she's doing.

The eyes of the man working the bar fly up, and as soon as he takes me in, he glances back at another guy standing by the door that leads down the hallway to Kat's office.

He locks eyes with me and approaches. Several patrons glance our way but seem to understand this isn't something they should be watching and quickly avert their eyes and at least pretend to focus on the girl on stage. She may be as naked as the day God made her, but I don't spare her a single glance. Only one woman occupies my entire focus right now, and it isn't her.

I close the distance between us and stop just short of him. "I need to see Kat."

He shakes his head. "She isn't here."

¡Ay hijueputa!

"Where is she?"

He scowls at me. "What the fuck makes you think I'm going to tell you that?"

After most of our men were wiped out at the airport, either this guy is brand-new, or he is so low on the totem pole that we have never met before. I would definitely remember this asshole.

"Do you know who the fuck I am?"

He nods. "Yep. I'm still not telling you where she is."

I fist my hands at my sides, fighting the urge to swing at him. Any other time, I would, but I'm unarmed, in borrowed clothes, and still weak from the events of the past week. "Then let me talk to Genti."

He'll know where she is, and he'll tell me.

The man shakes his head. "Not here, either."

Fuck. And of course, I don't have my phone, so I can't even call him.

"Call him and tell him I'm here, looking for her."

The man sneers at me but reaches into his pocket, pulls out a cell phone, and dials. He brings the phone to his ear, though how he thinks he'll hear over the music in here is beyond me. "Rose is at the club." His eyes never leave mine. "Uh-huh. Uh-huh. Got it."

He hands over the phone, and I press it to my ear and take a step away from him and toward a corner of the club I'm hoping is a little less noisy.

"Genti?"

"Yeah. It's nice to see Valentina didn't finish what Valerian started."

I snort and shake my head. "Well, it's nice to know someone gives a shit about what happened to me. Want to tell me where your boss is?"

Silence comes from the other end of the line, and Genti releases a deep sigh. "Look, I'm in a shitty position here, Rose. You know where my loyalties are."

"To the woman who treated me like dirt and tossed me to the wolves?"

He mumbles something that sounds like it must be a curse in Albanian. "It's worse than that."

"What the hell is that supposed to mean?"

"I can't say anything else. Just know I don't agree with everything she's doing right now."

Well, shit.

"I need to be watching my back?"

He chuckles low. "Shouldn't we always?"

"True."

"But seriously...I think you should be watching your front, too. Don't trust anyone...and I hope we both make it out of this alive."

The line goes dead.

FUCK!

I dial the number Sofia set up for emergencies and wait as it rings and rings and rings.

Come on, mija. Pick up.

Finally, a male voice answers. "Hello?"

"Who the fuck is this? Where's Sofia?"

"Mr. Rose?"

"Who the *fuck* is this?"

"Emmanuel."

One of the few men who didn't die at the airstrip and who I assumed was taken out by Cutter's crew at the house when they came for me. At least someone else survived that massacre.

"I need you to come to get me at Kat's club."

"I'll be there in twenty minutes."

I end the call and toss the phone back to her goon.

Twenty minutes...

Good. That gives me time for a few stiff drinks.

I march over to the bar, slide onto a stool, and wave over the bartender. "The twenty-five-year Macallan."

He raises his eyebrows at me and opens his mouth to argue.

"Yes, I know how expensive it is. Give me the whole bottle. I'll pay you when my ride gets here."

The bartender glances over my shoulder at the man I was just talking to, who inclines his head, granting him permission. Once he's sure it's okay, he goes to the back of the bar, grabs the bottle of scotch, and sticks it in front of me.

Before, this wouldn't have been the kind of place that would keep such expensive scotch for patrons. If it were in the building at all, it would have been hidden away in the office of whoever was in charge at the time, their own private stock. But Kat's renovation has upped their game—and greatly improved the alcohol selection.

Good thing, too, because I need the hard stuff. And a lot of it.

I pull out the stopper and lift the bottle to my lips, letting the harsh burn of the liquor that's almost as old as me make its way down my throat into my stomach.

There's only one other place Kat would be, only one other place she would go.

You can't hide from me, mi cielo. Not for long.

TEN

ROSE

THE LIGHT DRIZZLE falling makes the pitch-black of the night even more ominous as I make my way up the long, winding driveway to Kat's Cradle. There isn't any point in trying to hide my arrival or sneak onto the property. I want her to know I'm here, want her to see me coming. I want her quivering in her fucking heels, wondering what the hell I'm going to do to her.

Even the time I took to shower and change at one of my condos before coming here didn't quell the heat of my wrath. And it isn't just about her betraying me. Sofia is still out there somewhere—alone and probably terrified. Not knowing where she is or what happened to her has me even closer to completely losing control than the fact that Kat stabbed me in the back. I should have heard from Sofia by now. She should have figured out a way to get a message to me that she's safe and where I can find her. Yet, it's been radio silence.

That only angers me more. Because all of this...*all* of it...is Kat's fault.

I park at the base of the steps leading up to the main doors and pull my gun from the holster at my hip before climbing out. Not that I want to use it out here where it might draw unwanted attention from one of the nosy neighbors. But if anyone stands in my way of getting to Kat, I won't think twice about pulling the trigger as many times as I need to.

The two men she usually has at the front door are conspicuously absent—maybe victims of the airport ambush, too—but as I climb the steps, the door opens, and Genti stands silhouetted by the light from the chandelier hanging over the foyer behind him.

He crosses his one working arm over his chest, where the other hangs in a sling, blocking my way. "I can't let you in."

"Fuck you, Genti. How many times did I save your life in the last week alone?"

He shakes his head. "You know this has absolutely nothing to do with that."

"I had hoped you would let me in to avoid any more unnecessary pain."

A deep chuckle rumbles in his chest. "You going to shoot me? After everything we've been through together?"

"Why the hell not? Loyalty doesn't seem to mean anything to you guys, so why should it to me?"

He sighs and glances behind him. "I guess that's fair, considering what she did to you."

Something about the way he says it gives me pause. "What is it exactly that she did to me? Besides turn me over to Valentina?"

There's something more. Something he isn't saying.

He averts his gaze and runs his free hand through his hair. "That isn't for me to say. But heed my advice from earlier." He holds up a hand to keep me from stepping forward. "I'm still not letting you in."

I raise my gun and point it at him. "Don't make me shoot you, Genti."

Resignation drops his shoulders. He knows I'll fire before he can pull his weapon. He likely knew before I even arrived that he would eventually have to let me see her or suffer the consequences. "You're going to have to shoot me to get in here, Rose. But if you're intent on doing that, just promise me you won't hurt her."

"You know I can't make that promise. Not after what she did."

GWYN MCNAMEE

"Let him in." Her voice carries through the towering foyer and makes me freeze. There isn't any fear there, not even the tiniest bit of wavering. Whatever she's done, she is confident she's made the right choices and is ready to face the consequences.

Genti turns to peek up at her, but I still can't see her from where I stand just outside the front door. He nods at her and steps aside, giving me room to enter. I lower my gun to my side and take a step in, but his free hand lashes out and pushes against my chest.

At least the fucker didn't grab my bad arm.

"If you hurt her, you know you will answer to me."

I incline my head. "I hope it doesn't come to that."

His loyalty to Kat is commendable. She needs all the loyal men she can get right now. I'd hate for him to lose her. But it would be through her own choices. The future of her own making.

Genti moves his hand, and I step in from the cool drizzle that just started to the warm air and bright lights of Kat's Cradle. My gaze immediately lifts to find her standing behind the banister on the second floor, hands resting casually on it, staring down and waiting for me.

She offers me a tight smile. "I've been expecting you."

It's time to face the consequences of your sins, Kat. And I know you're running out of lives.

I ascend the stairs slowly, deliberately, and not just because each step sends a jolt of pain through my leg. Because the last time I climbed these stairs, it was with Kat on my arm, with her still pretending to want to partner while she was working over Michael to serve her ultimate plan. But it isn't just the memory that slows me. I also want her to suffer waiting.

Each step brings me closer to the confrontation she has to know is coming and must have prepared herself for. Though I doubt anyone could truly be ready for the true force of my wrath.

I may have told her the story of what I did, decimating those responsible for *Mama y Papa's* deaths, but really...she has no concept of the things I'm incapable of. She can't imagine the amount of blood, the force of the screams, the things I did to keep myself alive and the Rose Cartel in power over the last two decades.

But she's about to learn that fucking with me means paying the price.

I reach the top of the stairs, and she turns to face me—a few feet is all that separates us even though it feels like a giant chasm the size of the Grand Canyon has suddenly broken open between me and the woman I thought I was so close to. Who I thought I understood and could plan a future with.

How could I have been so wrong?

Moving toward her slowly, each step gives her a chance to change her mind, to turn and run, or call out for Genti's protection. Yet, she stands her ground, unwavering, not even a quiver in her lip or her body. Her bright-red heels hold solid against the white carpet, and her stark black dress remains perfectly pressed. Not a hair has fallen out of place from her tight signature bun. She's back to being Kat, the ruthless, cold woman I fell in love with. The one who doesn't let her weaknesses get in the way of absolute world domination.

But I know what lingers just under the surface. And she's about to know what I'm barely containing.

I reach out and brush my fingertips over her cheek, then cup it and tilt her face up to mine. The blue eyes I once swam in to find a few moments of peace now threaten to drag me under and drown me. "I hope you're ready, *mi cielo.*"

The corner of her lip twitches, and she leans in to my touch slightly. "Always."

ELEVEN

ROSE

SHE SAYS SHE'S READY, and I thought I was. But even knowing what she did, the desire to drag her against me, bend her over this railing, and fuck her until she begs for mercy wars with the desire to wrap my hands around her throat and squeeze until there's nothing left.

But not here.

Not while we have an audience.

I can feel Genti watching us from below, assessing whether he needs to come to her rescue or not. Even if he tried, he'd never make it up the stairs or get off a shot before I finish what I came here to do.

Because I won't let him—or anyone else—stop me.

Not now that I'm standing in front of her and literally have her in the palm of my hand.

I slide my hand down from her cheek, across the delicate skin of her neck, over her exposed collarbone, and down to her side. Squeezing sharply, I nudge her and nod toward the hallway to her bedroom office.

She casts a furtive glance at Genti before moving in that direction, my hand pressed firmly to her lower back.

"Where is Jet?"

"Here." Her steps don't falter, but her eyes dart up to meet mine for a moment. "The girls have him."

"You trust them?"

She pauses outside her closed door and turns to face me. "I trust them as much as I trust you."

That statement could be taken a dozen different ways, but instead of dwelling on its potential hidden meaning, I push open the door and usher her inside the room. She takes a few steps and turns to face me, her shoulders back and head held high.

I close the door and turn the lock. "You know why I'm here, *mi cielo?*"

She nods slowly. "I do, but you aren't going to get an apology from me. I did what I had to."

I tighten my grip on the gun still in my hand while my empty one flexes at my side. "What you had to?" Shaking my head, I take a step toward her. "No, *mi cielo,* you didn't *have* to do that. You could've warned me. We could've prepared. We could have run. There were a thousand ways things could have gone differently that didn't involve you giving me to Cutter and Valentina on a silver fucking platter."

"I knew she wouldn't hurt you."

"Bullshit—"

"You're too important. She knows what a mistake it would be to lose you as a potential partner."

"And what about *you?* Is she *your* partner now?"

Who knows what they discussed when Valentina put the screws to her? For all I know, Kat might have agreed to far more than just making sure I would go quietly.

Kat shakes her head. "No. Felipe is."

The whole world goes red as the warning Genti gave me flashes through my head.

"Watch your front... It's worse than that..."

GWYN MCNAMEE

Now I understand.

Three quick steps close the distance between us, and I wrap my free hand around her throat and push her until her back hits the wall behind her. "What the hell did you just say?"

Her icy blue gaze stays locked on mine. "I said Felipe is my new partner."

Hearing his name fall from her lips in that context sends a new fury roaring through me. "You went to my brother?"

She nods, never breaking eye contact, her nerves strong and in-tact despite how easily I could choke the life from her body in a matter of seconds.

I step into her until my heaving chest pushes against hers. "So that's it? That's what you want? *Him*? Or is it just that you're placing your bets on the horse you think will win this race?"

Her tongue darts out to lick her lips, and a familiar pink blush crawls up her neck and over the cheeks. She isn't scared. She's turned on.

"Is that why you want *me* right now? Because I look like *him*?" I pull my hand from her throat and shove it between her legs to find her cunt wet and ready for me. My cock twitches between us, and I easily shove two fingers inside her.

She groans, her eyes rolling back into her head as she exposes the delicate skin of her neck even more to me.

"Are you imagining *his* hand here? *His* touch?" I withdraw my fingers only to shove them back in harder.

Her pussy tenses around them, drawing them in even deeper, almost as if her body wants to consume that part of me.

"I already know you get off on the threat. The excitement of not knowing if you're going to live or die."

She's proven that over and over again since I met her. The rush she felt is what drew her into this life and kept her here through Aleksander, Michael, me...and apparently, now Felipe. "Is that what he gives you that I can't anymore? Because you know he's really the one in control and the most danger to you? Is it the knowledge that he can end you in a split-second that makes your cunt drip like this? Because if that's what you're after, I'm happy to give it to you."

I jerk my fingers free from her body and shove the gun between her legs, brushing the barrel along her bare thighs. My cock aches, straining against the confines of the hard zipper pressed against it, but that isn't what she wants—not really. She's had that over and over again, and it wasn't enough for her. She needs something *more*.

Her entire body vibrates, her hands clinging to the front of my shirt. Delicate fingers curl tightly into the crisp material, and pure, unadulterated lust sparks in her eyes.

Mi cielo isn't scared. The terror that should be present in the way she looks at me couldn't be further from the truth of what I see there.

I nudge her wet slit with the barrel of the gun. "This is what you want? This kind of danger?" I lean in and brush my lips across hers gently, catching her gasp in my mouth while I press my weapon firmly against her clit. "You want to know that it will only take one twitch of my finger for this gun to go off?"

Her head drops back, and she releases a strangled groan. But she doesn't ask me to stop. She doesn't exhibit even one hint of fear. This is getting her off, being this close to death, having me so close to wanting to pull the trigger. Dancing the thin edge.

She's far colder, more calculating, and more fucked up than I ever gave her credit for.

Brushing my lips against her ear, I inhale her scent. "Will you fuck me and pretend I'm my brother?"

Her entire body starts shaking, and I rub the barrel in circles around her most sensitive spot. She shifts slightly, clenching her legs together around my wrist and hand, then opening herself more, almost an invitation—one I'm more than willing to accept.

I slip the barrel inside her, and her eyes fly open to meet mine. Her whimper spurs me onward, and as I push it even deeper, I capture her gasp with a violent kiss. Her pussy clamping around the hard metal makes it twitch in my hand, and the feeling runs straight through me to my cock. I drag out the gun and push it back in again, never removing my finger from the trigger.

Kat likes playing games with life and death—her own, mine, Sofia's, even Valentina's and her unborn child's. But that's okay because this is one game I intend to win.

TWELVE

KAT

Heat spreads from my core out through all my shaking, tingling limbs. Clinging to the front of Rose's shirt is the only thing that keeps me grounded in this world and my legs from collapsing out from under me—thin, crisp fabric my only lifeline to reality.

The way he reads me. The way he's not afraid to give me exactly what I need and simultaneously fear the most. It's too much and not enough at the same time. My heart and head can't process the constant struggle. My body exists in a never-ending state of turmoil and bliss with this man. And tonight is the pinnacle. The ultimate reckoning.

I never knew this could exist. That it could be like this. Yet, here we are, toying with death and life and lust and love as if they're things that can be easily replaced.

He withdraws the cool, hard metal from inside me and pushes the whole barrel back in, sending another jolt of pleasure coursing through me and pulling me even closer to the brink of madness. The knuckles of the hand wrapped around the grip and trigger brush the inside of my thigh with each stroke, vividly reminding me of how close he is to ending me.

What he's doing would horrify anyone else. But not me. My heart thunders against my chest, threatening to explode the same way I would if he just twitched his damn finger. Dancing the line between love and hate, life and death, anger and lust, it's almost too much to bear.

A low, needy moan climbs up my throat and into Rose's mouth as his tongue lashes against mine with purpose.

Hungry.

Needy.

Fucking pissed off and on the edge of losing control.

He's right—one quick flinch of his hand would kill me. It would end everything in a split-second of gore I probably deserve. But I've never been more turned on my entire fucking life. Not even when Aleksander came home covered in Terrance's blood after he killed him for me.

The Dragon tried to protect me from the danger, keep me locked away and pristine while Rose pushes me toward something no other man ever has, forces me to face my own demons and desires head-on with my eyes wide open. Though there are those who would look at the two men and see them as the same, that couldn't be more wrong. One tried to keep me from his world; the other wants me to rule it with him.

I slide my shaky hands down between us to his belt and fumble with the buckle. It's too late to go back now, too late to stop what I've become or undo what I've done to him.

He has every right to be angry and want to hurt me. And I'll let him because even when it hurts, he gives me what I need. What I'm often not even capable of voicing. He can do what he will with me. I don't even care. I deserve it and so much more.

I finally manage to free Rose's cock and take it in my hand, giving the hard length a firm stroke. He groans and pulls the gun from inside my cunt, letting it clatter to the floor beside us so he can lift my legs to wrap them around his waist. Digging my heels into his lower back, I capture his mouth with mine, needing that exchange of power that always occurs when we battle for dominance during a kiss.

After what I did, I never imagined I'd be in his arms again, and whether it's the anger or the adrenaline or the lust coursing through him, the pain that plagued him the last time we were together seems to be long forgotten. Rather than wincing and being careful to ensure he doesn't hurt himself, his entire focus is on this moment and the blaze burning between us, threatening to fully engulf everything human about us and reduce us to ashes on the floor.

He reaches down, aligns his cock, and drives into me in one aggressive thrust, driving me harder against the wall. While his lips steal every exhale, his hand moves up to tighten around my throat.

"Open your eyes, *mi cielo!*" He drags back his hips and plunges into me again, so hard, it feels like he's cementing himself there permanently.

Maybe that's what he's trying to do—leave a permanent mark on me so I'm incapable of ever forgetting what we had together. As easily as I've managed to push what happened with Michael from my head, that can never happen with *this* man. He will haunt me until my dying day, which very well might be today. That isn't off the table by any means.

Anything might happen when this ends...a race where we're rapidly approaching the finish line.

His strokes reach a relentless pace, and he increases the pressure on my throat until a murky, dark warmth encroaches on the edges of my vision. He withdraws from me and slams in again, pushing me closer and closer to the point of no return. Hanging in this space between the harsh reality of what I've done and the beautiful possibility of what could have been. But reality in the form of my orgasm crashes over me so intensely, my heart stalls in my chest.

Rose mumbles something in Spanish while lights flash against my closed lids, but my brain isn't working well enough for me to translate it, nor do I care. He eliminates any ability to care about anything else when he drives into me harder than I ever knew possible, his hold on my neck so tight, I can't suck in a breath.

The strange mix of pleasure and pain drag out another orgasm that I didn't even know was possible. My entire body vibrates and jerks, hands clinging to the back of his neck, nails scoring his skin. He finally screams and empties himself into my pussy in short, hot bursts and collapses against me, pinning me to the wall just as the darkness starts to envelop me.

He lowers me slowly, brushing his lips up my neck, over my cheek, and across my mouth until I'm standing on wobbly legs. His warm breath that smells vaguely of scotch tickles my nose, making me hungry for his kiss again. But I don't lean forward to take what I want. Instead, we stand, staring at each other for what feels like forever. Until his eyes darken even more...

"*¡Mierda!*" He withdraws from inside me, his rage building again—if ever dissipated.

A feeling of emptiness and loss floods me, and he pushes away from the wall and leans down. The breath I just regained catches in my throat when I realize what he's doing. My legs wobble again, so violently I lean back against the wall to stop from falling over.

He grabs the gun from the floor before slowly rising to face me again, his hand curled firmly around it. That source of pleasure only moments ago will also be the vehicle of my demise. "It's time, *mi cielo.*"

THIRTEEN

KAT

His knuckles whiten where he tightly grips the gun at this side. The fury he felt when he walked in the door downstairs hasn't abated. In fact, it may have only enraged him more to have given in to me like that, to have shown his weakness for me and my body despite his wrath.

But clarity seems to be returning to his hard, dark gaze more and more with every passing second we stand in silence. The lust that fogged them over the last several minutes has been replaced with determination. He came here on a mission—one he intends to complete.

I won't stop him from doing whatever he feels needs to be done, but not before he knows everything. Not until I give him the chance to make the right decision. He can't be in the dark anymore. It's too painful for him...and for me.

It's time for the truth. "Before you do whatever it is you think you have to do, there's something you need to hear first."

His eyes narrow on me, and he takes a step forward, flexing his free hand at his side like he's restraining himself from lashing out—either with it or the gun in the other hand. "I don't want any empty apologies or platitudes, Kat. I don't want anything you have to give me."

I raise an eyebrow and tug my dress back down my thighs. "I wouldn't be so sure about that."

Rose could react to this in a number of ways. Using that gun in his hand for its intended purpose is just as likely as him being thrilled with what I'm about to reveal. If he sees this as the opening it could be, then I have a chance of not only getting out of this alive but also with my plan intact. But if he can't see past what I've done to the reasons that justify my actions, then this will all be for naught.

I move around him, prepared to have him lash out and stop me, but he lets me walk to where my phone sits on the top of my desk. This is it—the moment I find out if my gamble was worth it. Placing my bets on the winning horse wasn't too far off base. I just pray he understands.

Turning to face him, I hit play.

"Well, well, well, look what the Kat dragged in..." Felipe's voice floats through the room like a ghost, its presence heavy.

Rose's eyes widen, and he snarls and takes a step toward me. "What the fuck is that?"

I close the distance between us, holding out the phone toward him. "A recording of my entire conversation with your brother, including when I got him to drop the act and partner with me in my stand against you."

He snatches it from my hand and hits play, listening intently to every word Felipe and I shared during our clandestine meeting. His gaze jerks back to me several times, but he paces while he takes it all in—phone in one hand and gun in the other, fingers flexing and curling around it with each step.

"I look forward to our partnership, Kat."

"As do I, Father."

Felipe's low chuckle sends a chill through me now, just as it did when I was sitting across from him only a few days ago, making the deal that could either break everything or set us up for the ultimate victory in the future.

Rose turns back to me, shaking his head. "I don't understand. Why are you telling me this, letting me listen to it?"

"Because I need you to understand I didn't have any other choice. This is war, Rose. It has been since the day you and Michael set foot in Chicago. Intentional or not, you two started a conflict that is still raging now and is only going to get worse when you both sought to move in and expand here, regardless of who you took out in the process."

I run a shaky hand over my disheveled hair falling out of the tight bun that once contained it. Over the last few days, I've gone over what I would say to Rose when he showed up at least a thousand times. But this is so much harder than I ever imagined it would be.

"And my first priority was...*is* to protect Jeton. Valentina had me backed into a corner in Albania. I didn't have a choice if I wanted to get Jet out of there. I did what I had to do, and I'd do it again. But I *never* betrayed you. I never *could*. And I never intended to hurt your pride or make you question my loyalty. All this"—I wave at the phone—"going to Felipe...it was all part of my plan to convince Valentina and your brother that we weren't aligned any longer. I thought I might have a shot to get him to open up to me about his plans if I agreed to help him and he knew that I had given you to the Marconis. And you heard what's on that recording. What he intends to do..."

He glances down at the phone and shakes his head. "I still can't believe he thinks he'll succeed. That he thinks the other families are just going to let this happen."

I take a tentative step toward him and pull the phone from his hand. The tips of my fingers brush his palm, and a little jolt rolls through me and straight between my legs where the evidence of what we just did still lingers. "This isn't everything. It can't be. Your brother is too smart to tell me his entire plan and reveal any aces he has up his sleeve. He doesn't trust me. Even if he is pretending to. I think we both know that. But with time...he will. Or I'll find a way to get him to talk."

Rose is on me so fast, I don't have time to back away or prepare myself for what's coming. He grabs my wrist and drags me up against him. A low growl vibrates in his chest where we're pressed together. "He will not fucking *touch* you. Do you hear me, *mi cielo*? You do whatever you have to but not *that*. Never that. You are *mine*, Kat. *Mine*." His words rumble through me, falling from his lips with more passion than I've ever seen from him. "It will be hard enough staying away from you and Jet to keep up appearances without having to think about what you're doing with Felipe behind closed doors."

It takes me a moment to process his words. "You believe me? That I never meant to betray you?"

He releases my wrist and cups my cheek in his palm, harshly dragging my face up to his. "You *did* betray me, *mi cielo*. By not telling me what was going on, by not giving me any choice in the matter. But you have the rest your life to pay for your sins. We've only just started your penance."

FOURTEEN

KAT

I SHOULD'VE KNOWN Rose would make me pay in every way imaginable—with my mind, my body, and my soul. He ran me hard and left me weak and shaking. Worked me up and brought me crashing back down so many times in the last few hours that I lost track.

And he will do it all over again the second he has the chance.

If I didn't have to meet with Superintendent Canon, I think Rose would've kept me in my room indefinitely. But in order for this plan to work, in order for everyone to believe we've broken our partnership and stand on opposite sides, certain steps must be taken. Sacrifices must be made. Like staying away from each other to ensure no one suspects we are still one joined force.

Watching him leave this morning felt like witnessing a part of me walk away. Yet, after everything we've been through together, I know we can make it through anything as long as we have faith in each other. It may have wavered when I turned Rose over to Valentina. It put a kernel of doubt into his head. But I've regained the trust I broke by having faith in him. We're on more solid ground now after what happened last night than we ever have been.

Our future in Chicago may not be known, but one thing is certain—it will be with us together.

Eventually...

If Valentina believes Rose cut ties with me after what I did and Felipe believes I've chosen to align myself with him because he's most likely to win this brotherly battle, then that makes us even more powerful. No one will know what we're planning in secret or how determined we are to ensure our success.

Considering how angry the Russians and Irish are after the attack I orchestrated against them, it's only a matter of time before Valerian strikes again and Galen comes for vengeance, too. I'm not naïve enough to think the head of the Irish mob is just sitting around, twiddling his thumbs after I stole a massive gun shipment from him. He's planning something big, and I need to be ready for it.

But the shoot-out with Valerian at the airport and then what Cutter and Valentina's other men did at Rose's compound just left us in a precarious position where law enforcement is concerned.

My agreement with the superintendent of the City of Chicago Police Department to keep things that occur in my territory under wraps doesn't do me any good when he doesn't have jurisdiction over the airport or where Rose's mansion sits. And Arden's hacks on databases for both departments have proven fruitless. While it's clear they're looking for us for questioning, there's little, if any, information about what evidence they may have to actually charge us with anything.

Which is why this meeting today is so important. Regardless of whether it's his jurisdiction or not, Superintendent Canon can assist me in getting information no one else is privy to. He can prepare me—and Rose when I inform him—for what's coming if, or *when*, we get brought in.

But he appears none too pleased with having to attend this meeting today. He climbs into the back of the SUV next to me and scowls. "You're a wanted woman, Kat. I can't be seen with you."

I incline my head and offer him a tight smile. "I understand your precarious position, Superintendent Canon, but we need to talk in person. Too many open ears in your department."

He releases an annoyed sigh. "What do you want, Kat? I already helped cover up the fact that your men were seen fleeing the scene of the attack on Galen McGinnis' shipment. I don't know what else I can do."

His help has been invaluable in keeping us out of the slammer for what we did, but just like everything in my life lately, things keep piling up that need attention. "Your assistance in making what happened at the airport go away."

His eyes widen. "How the hell am I supposed to do that? Half a dozen security cameras caught what happened."

"Then you should know, we were only acting in self-defense. Besides, I'm quite confident the cameras weren't close enough to positively identify those involved. Am I right?"

His lips twist, and his knee bounces nervously. "Yeah, the footage is fuzzy, at best. They did get a few license plates, but of course, they were dead ends."

"None of us are stupid enough to use a car registered to anyone tied to us."

"I figured as much. But there aren't a lot of women around who can afford to fly out on a private jet like that who are likely to get shot at. It was pretty clear this was an attempted hit on you, and given what happened to the Russians and Irish, it wasn't a big leap to peg you as the woman in the videos. Not only do you need to deal with the local PD, but the FBI has been sniffing around."

"Shit." The feds are the last thing we need right now. They're likely gathering all sorts of evidence to use in a RICO case against anyone and everyone they can drag into it.

"Yeah. So, I can't just make it go away, Kat."

"Yes, you can. Talk to the district attorney. Explain that even if they could prove it's me—which you have your doubts about—that it's clearly self-defense and no jury would ever convict me for it. And have a friendly chat with your buddies in the FBI. See what they know."

He drops his head back and squeezes his eyes closed. "I'll poke around and see what I can do." His gaze meets mine again. "But I can't make any promises. Like I said, it isn't even my jurisdiction. And speaking of which...rumor has it there was another shootout at a pretty ritzy estate outside the city. You wouldn't know anything about that, would you?"

Cutter took Rose from the house before he or anyone on his team could have a chance to secure any documents or anything else that could be incriminating toward him. And Rose said Sofia is still missing, so who knows what, if any, of what she was doing for him out in the guest house was found by the cops. I would love to believe they're both smart enough to never allow anything to be found, but that very real possibility still hovers on the horizon, a constant threat.

I shift and glance at Genti in the driver's seat. He stares straight ahead, listening to every word while letting me handle the situation. I'm sure he'd much rather throw a punch or two to get Canon to cooperate, but that isn't the kind of threat that works on a man like this.

"I'm not sure what you're talking about."

He scoffs and shakes his head. "Yeah, sure. The bodies strewn all over the grounds of that mansion all came back as Colombian nationals. But I'm sure your friend, Rose, had nothing to do with it. It's just a coincidence."

I grin at him. "Exactly." I raise an eyebrow, hoping he'll provide a bit more information without any prompting. "Unless there is any evidence to suggest otherwise?"

"Not that I'm aware of. My understanding is they found some computer equipment that was fried, but they're trying to scrape some data off it."

Knowing Sofia, there isn't any way she'd let them find anything. So as long as she had enough time to get her failsafe into play, Rose can rest easy, at least in that regard. Still, it never hurts to remain on top of potential points of weakness.

"Perhaps you should keep your eye on that situation, just in case."

He nods his understanding. "If I were you, Kat, I would keep to the shadows until things quiet down."

I bark a laugh that comes out unreasonably loud in the confined space. "Quiet down? Don't get too comfortable, Superintendent Canon. Things are about to get a lot noisier."

His brow furrows. "Why's that?"

It's time to clue him in a bit on what the future holds. At least he can mentally prepare, even if there isn't any chance of him preventing it from happening.

"There's a new player in town. One who isn't afraid to cross the invisible line the other families have drawn to prevent an all-out war. Things are going to get bloody very soon."

"Shit."

My thoughts exactly.

And I'll be right in the thick of it, aligning myself with the Devil himself. Staying away from Rose when he holds my heart will hurt, but it will be worth it if our ruse allows us to prevent the destruction of everything he and I have worked and sacrificed so damn hard for.

War is inevitable. I just hope I've *truly* chosen the winning side. Because if Felipe succeeds with even a portion of the plan he laid out for me in his office the other day, Chicago won't survive what's coming.

FIFTEEN

FATHER FELIPE

With the sun long set, the glistening lights of Chicago at night spread out below me, as far as I can see. From up here, the entire city is laid out like an endless sea of humanity. Millions of people, going about their daily lives, completely unaware of the turmoil bubbling beneath the surface.

Thousands of streets filled with potential occupy my view.

And all of it will be mine soon.

After so many years, decades of deception, deceit, and dirty deeds, I can finally take my position at the head of it all—the position I earned, the one *he* has taken as his own. My dear brother may want to head the Rose Cartel and think he's been doing it well despite my pulling the strings from the shadows. But his arrogance will be his destruction.

Everything is falling into place. My plans are finally aligning perfectly—the way I always imagined they would.

All I have to do is nudge the first domino, and the rest will fall. Just as God sent a great flood to purge the world of sin, so shall I issue forth a river of blood that will wash away all who oppose me, until anyone who continues to stand in my way and survives the initial purge will be knocked down, stomped out, and decimated to nothing more than dust that will simply blow away in the wind this city is known for.

Almost as if on cue, a gust buffets the glass around me, sending a slight rattle through it. The Skydeck at Willis Tower feels almost like being on top of the world—a view fit for God alone. And me.

The Book of Revelation warns that the ultimate showdown between good and evil is coming. And one passage in particular that has been burned into my mind for decades makes my lips curl into a smile:

Those who are victorious will inherit all this, and I will be their God and they will be my children. Revelation 21:7

I will be victorious. I cannot fail. Not with God on my side...

SLOTH

Sloth, not ill-will, makes me unjust.

-**Mason Cooley**

ONE

FATHER FELIPE

"TRUE EVIL EXISTS WHEN 'GOOD' people fail to act."

I let my words hang in the air of the nave, settling heavily on the rapt parishioners, including Rowan, where she sits in her usual spot in the front pew, attention focused fully on me, her hands clasped on her lap.

My cock hardens, watching her twist them delicately there, sometimes tugging at the fabric of the pale-blue dress she's wearing, imagining what it would feel like to have those small, delicate, soft hands on me, expertly stroking me until she climbs on top, straddles my hips, and sinks down. Or perhaps wraps one around the base of my cock and greedily sucks my length down her hot, wet throat.

All focus remains on me, waiting with bated breath for me to continue my sermon while I fantasize about Rowan and surreptitiously reach down to adjust my hard cock underneath my vestments —protected from view by the pulpit.

But I wait.

Not because I expect anyone to act or the words I just spoke to have any sort of real effect on the members of my congregation, but because I *can*.

Because seeing them uncomfortable, shifting on the hard, unforgiving wooden pews that their asses have sat on for an hour now while they bask in the guilt being here usually brings gives my cold, black heart a little twinge of joy that I rarely experience anymore.

While I prefer to spend as little time as possible in this place, dragging out Sunday Mass as long as possible serves two purposes. It allows me to torture the people inside St. Mary of the Angels on the holiest day of the week, and it also gives me the opportunity to have Rowan see me as the kind, gentle, devout man she believes me to be.

Her faith in that hasn't wavered in the time she's been here with me since I pulled her from Kat's pussy trap with promises of redemption for her soul and safety—both from that which she was running and the unknown danger I warned her was to come. But the need to reinforce that belief in the stunning redheaded hooker is even stronger now that she's made the connection between my dear brother and me and Kat knows where she is.

It's a dangerous situation. One I hadn't anticipated until I was forced to bring Andres and Genti here to be patched up after their run-in with Valerian.

The reality of her having that knowledge will force my hand and move my timeline up, but it's unavoidable at this point. Just as God will ultimately destroy mankind in a conflagration of flames for their sin, so shall I destroy those who stand in the way of my plans for Chicago.

And it all starts with the beautiful redhead staring up at me from the front row with wide, green eyes so intent on listening to every word that falls from my lips. It's almost as if coming here flipped something inside the woman who used to sell her body. She's seeking something she seems to have found in this church, with me as her spiritual leader.

When she learns the truth, her new faith will come crumbling down around her, but I'll be there to pick up the pieces and use them to rebuild her into who she was always destined to be.

Mi palomita...

I spread out my hands and scan the crowd gathered for Mass—a sea of both familiar and unfamiliar faces. Hundreds of people searching for God in these four walls and through my words.

Though they know not what they do.

Like Rowan, they seek connection to something larger than themselves in this place, from a human man who supposedly has a direct conduit to Him. A man who is pious. A man who blesses them with the body and blood of their savior, Jesus Christ, and who listens to them confess their sins and absolves them of all the stains on their souls.

Little do they know...I'm the greatest sinner of them all.

"Many do not connect this notion of *inaction* with the cardinal sin of sloth, but at its very core, that is what the term means. Sloth isn't about being 'lazy' per se. In fact, the original monk who outlined the eight deadly sins—and yes"—I hold up my hands with eight fingers raised—"there *were* originally eight—referred to this idea as *acedia*. And it was not about a physical ailment, but rather, a spiritual one."

Giving a sermon on the dangers of sloth to the soul always brings with it a sense of accomplishment and pride. Another deadly sin—the original and most serious of the seven deadly sins, thought to be the source of all the others—washing over me because I've managed to pull off the great charade for the last two decades, convincing these people I'm exactly what they see instead of the monster lurking beneath these robes and white collar.

It makes my hard cock twitch again beneath the layers of heavy, adorned fabric I hide under. It's the kind of power that can't be bought. The kind of faith that must be *earned*.

And I've more than paid my dues. Lived as Father Felipe for more than half my life. Hidden behind "Andres" and the Rose name while he enjoys getting his hands dirty and reaps the benefits, living life with all the power and anything else he could ever want in the world.

It would be a lie to say I don't feel envy for what he can do. But it's the least of my sins.

"*Acedia*, and its successor *sloth*, in fact, are addressing *spiritual* apathy. The desire for ease, even at the expense of doing the known will of God. A lack of feeling about self or others. Whatever we do in life requires effort. Everything we do is to be a means of salvation. The slothful person is unwilling to do what God wants because of the effort it takes to do it. Sloth becomes a sin when it slows down and even brings to a halt the energy we must expend in using the means to salvation."

I step from behind the pulpit and clasp my hands together behind my back as I stare out at the congregation, the irony of the words I'm about to say almost making my lips curl into a truly inappropriate smile for the subject.

"So, what does that mean for you? For your daily life and activities? Well..."

The purposeful dramatic pause I insert leaves the entire church utterly silent, waiting for the wisdom I'm about to bestow on them.

An empty statement from a man devoid of faith. Devoid of anything good. A man who is merely a shell standing in front of them, spewing regurgitated drivel they base their lives around.

"It means that every action we take in life must be taken with the intent to move us further down the proper path. The one toward God and good. Any divergence from the said path, whether it be because another sin grips you in its mighty clutches or because you are simply too lazy or apathetic to care about what it is doing to your eternal soul, is a step toward eternal damnation."

A path I've been down since childhood.

And now it's time to steer them—and one person in particular—in the direction that most benefits my plan.

I let my attention drift over Rowan again, offering her a kind half-smile of reassurance because I know she's beating herself up yet again for the sin she was living in when I found her.

"But do not fear because these divergences, these moments of weakness and sin, do not mean your path can't be corrected. Because as we learned in the first book of John, chapter one, verse three: 'If we confess our sins, he is faithful and just to forgive us our sins and to cleanse us from all unrighteousness.' The correct path is never so far away that you cannot return to it, soul cleansed, spirit free to make the right choices. As long as you keep the proper path in mind, sloth shall not lead you astray and on the road to Hell. Rather, the moments of apathy, the wrong choices, must be seen as opportunities to seek His forgiveness and redirection to the right path, the one that leads to His open and waiting arms."

That is sure to send Rowan running straight to the confessional—where she's the most vulnerable and open. Where I can manipulate her to my advantage and toward my final goal. Because she's the key to it all. Without her, all is lost. I must maintain the charade and hope she can't see through the veil of lies I live behind to the sins I continue to commit.

For even Satan disguises himself as an angel of light.

TWO

FATHER FELIPE

"I<small>T</small>'s good to see you again, Mr. Rose. Everything is ready in your usual suite."

I incline my head at the night manager of the hotel in acknowledgment as I brush past him on my way to the waiting, open elevator doors. The last thing I want to do is linger in the lobby for any longer than I have to.

The fewer people who see me here, the better for everyone. If it got back to Andres that he was seen here and he appeared confused, that wouldn't do at all. It could reveal the deception we've been leading for decades.

Twenty years of hard work keeping our lives separate. Keeping his existence and our connection a secret as good as down the drain faster than my cum is going to go down the throat of the hooker waiting for me in my room.

I step into the elevator and press the button for the penthouse. As it shoots to the top floor, I examine myself in the mirrored wall panels, tugging at the tight neck of the crisp white dress shirt. Somehow, it feels more restrictive than the collar I wear every day. But it's also a necessity if I hope to continue masquerading as Rose.

The tattoos that cover my body served their purpose—buying me street cred and ways in on the street that have led to streams of information I never would have otherwise—but having to hide them while I'm doing this makes things a bit uncomfortable.

Once I take over as Rose, the first order of business will be to begin introducing the "new" skin to those who know him so no one suspects that I've stepped into the role that my clean-skinned brother has occupied for so long.

All in due time.

A sharp ding signals my arrival on the top floor, and the doors slide open, revealing the familiar space. I step out onto the lush carpet and pause, taking in what has become my "home away from home" since I arrived in Chicago—at least on Sunday nights.

"About time you got here." The sultry voice echoes out from the bedroom and through the small foyer where I stand, stirring my cock.

I step farther into the suite and lean against the doorframe to examine her in the moonlight streaming in from the small windows to the sides of the bed. Her long red hair falls to her shoulders, and the pale freckles across her nose and cheeks are just barely visible in the low light.

Despite my very specific demands, the service did a great job finding exactly what I wanted. While she's a poor substitute for Rowan, she serves her purpose and does it well.

I angle my head back toward the main living room area. "Come out here."

She shifts up to a sitting position, her hands behind her on the mattress, and raises a pale eyebrow at me. "Not in the bed tonight?"

I shake my head as visions of everything we've done in that bed flash through my mind—each time, Rowan's face and voice replacing that of this woman who was actually with me. "No. I have something else in mind."

I've been thinking about it ever since I visited the Willis Tower a few days ago and stood, looking down at all the flickering lights and people below. What will be my kingdom.

She slides seductively off the bed and walks over to me slowly, her shapely hips swaying with each movement, her beautiful breasts hanging free and taut stomach leading down to her shaved pussy.

My cock stands at full attention, straining against the black dress pants that can barely contain it. She pauses next to me, her sickly sweet scent filling the air around me—so unlike the light, almost ethereal floral one I associate with Rowan—and pushes up on her tiptoes to kiss me, slipping her tongue along my lips and demanding entry. I open my mouth for her while I grab her legs and lift her to wrap them around my waist.

Her thighs squeeze my hips as I walk us over to the wall of windows overlooking the Chicago River. She rubs her bare cunt against my fabric-encased erection and offers a little mewl. A smile plays on her too-plump, too-red lips while pressed against mine. "Somebody's happy to see me."

Anger flares through my blood almost instantly, and I grasp her hair in my hand and jerk her head back, eliciting a little painful yelp. "Don't forget your role here."

A warm, welcoming cunt. Nothing more.

The last thing I need is this stupid bitch getting any ideas about what this is just because she sees me every Sunday night when I so desperately need this release. It isn't anything more than that, and she needs to understand completely.

Her wide blue eyes meet mine, and she gives a quick nod of acknowledgment before she slides down my body and settles her feet on the carpet, reaching for my belt. She deftly frees my cock and takes it into her warm palm.

I bite back a grunt and pin her with a heated glare. It isn't her hands I want on me, nor her body I've been lusting after daily. But she'll do for now. "Turn around."

She complies with my command and turns to face the windows, placing her hands flat against the glass and arching her back, offering herself to me. I align my cock with her wet heat and drive up into her without any preamble. The hard, harsh motion shoves her flat against the glass in front of her, pushing the air from her lungs in a warm rush against the window, momentarily blocking my view of the city below with a fog.

Digging my fingers into her bare waist, I drag my hips back and slam into her again, driving myself even deeper than the first time.

A low groan slips from her open lips. "Oh, God! Rose!"

I pull back and plunge into her again, all while staring at the city laid out before me like the forbidden fruit ripe for the taking. And take it, I will. *After* I get done fucking this whore to try to rid myself of the need for Rowan constantly coiling in my body.

She moans and rolls her hips back to meet mine eagerly, and I twist her hair around my wrist and grip it, jerking her head back in what must be a painful motion for her.

"Shut the fuck up."

I don't want to hear her soft, placating, practiced moans, the one she uses with her other clients. It isn't her voice I want in my ears while I pound into her. Not her contented, breathy sighs I want fluttering over this glass. Not her pussy I want clamping down on my cock with each thrust.

It's another redhead I have in my sights. Another who occupies my dreams and fantasies since the first moment I saw her. But that isn't part of the plan and would only complicate things that are already incredibly complicated.

This pussy will have to do for now, and I rail into her until all that exists is the thrashing of our hips and our pants filling the room while I look at the twinkling lights below. Until who I was and who I became blend together seamlessly and I can no longer fight back my impending release and come inside her hard enough that tears stream down her face.

But she's fine. None of this is new to her or us. It's the same dog and pony show every Sunday, and it will continue to be until I take my rightful place on the throne as Rose.

And that day is coming far sooner than anyone even knows. All it will take is one tiny step in the right direction from Rowan, one I hope my sermon today accomplished.

THREE

FATHER FELIPE

"BLESS ME, Father, for I have sinned. It has been..." She pauses for a moment and draws in a heavy breath that reaches me through the metal mesh screen that separates us in the confessional booth and makes my hair stand on end in anticipation. "I've never confessed before. At least, I don't think I have."

The uncertainty in her statement would pull at my heart strings if I had any, but after almost twenty years of listening to confessions, I have yet to actually feel bad for any of the souls who come in seeking absolution.

In fact, their sniveling and whining only annoys me and enforces what I've believed since day one of this endeavor—that man cannot worry about what *might* happen in some potentially mythical afterlife. What matters is the here and now. Life on this big, blue planet of ours. What you do as it spins on its axis every day. The name you make for yourself. What you leave behind when you finally face down that final bullet. Your legacy.

And I'm fighting tooth and nail to ensure mine is written in stone and appreciated.

I've worked too hard. Sacrificed far too much not to achieve my final goal. To just sit by and let my brother take everything from me. For now, that means sitting in this box, in these vestments, listening to parishioners beg forgiveness for things rather than owning their actions like they should.

It's exhausting. Though the woman on the other side of the partition now may make the whole day worth it.

Slipping into the persona of Father Felipe has become so easy after all these years that sometimes, for a moment, I forget who I really am and why I'm really doing this. This is not one of those moments, though. I'm keenly aware of what's at stake if things go badly, so it's time to play my part.

"I'm glad you finally sought out the confession booth and what it can offer you. What is on your mind? What finally brought you here today?"

As if I don't know. As if it hasn't been part of my plan all along to draw her into my web even deeper. To get her to see me as her protector, confessor, and her friend. And eventually...more.

She shifts restlessly, the movement of her clothes loud in the silence the tight confines of the booth otherwise provides. The move sends a little of that honeysuckle smell she carries to me, reminding me of the fantasies I've lived out a hundred times in my head and acted out last night with her stand-in.

I hold up a hand, knowing she will be able to see the outline of it through the privacy screen. "Don't be nervous. There is no judgment in this place. Only hope and forgiveness."

And a very patient man who has waited a long time for this moment. Ever since I realized who she is and what that means for the future of my plans, I knew I would have to tread carefully. That I would need to take a slow, tactful approach to the woman who could be the key to securing everything I've ever wanted.

Today is no different. She needs to lead this conversation. Needs to feel like *she* is the one in control. That I'm not pressuring her in any way to reveal her secrets and expose her inner-most thoughts, desires, and regrets.

She clears her throat, a sound that, for some reason, goes straight between my legs to the most unholy of places. "Your sermon yesterday about sloth and spiritual apathy got me thinking a lot about how I've lived my life."

"You feel guilt over the things you've done?"

A light, mirthless laugh slips to me, heavy with confusion. "How could I not?" She sighs and is no doubt twisting her hands on her lap. "I did what I had to do to survive. I sold myself for money. I used the lust of men against them. I helped Kat, a woman who is cold and ruthless, a killer, gather blackmail material against men so that she could destroy them with it later. I don't know how else to think about that now except for with regret."

Exactly as I had hoped. The sermon spoke to what I've seen Rowan struggling with internally since the moment I brought her here. The very reason I was able to lure her away from Kat's Cradle and the life she had established there.

All the time she's stayed in the spare room at the rectory. All the days she sat in that front row at Mass to listen to my sermons. It's all finally starting to pay off.

But her statement leads to another question, one I have to ask to get to the heart of why she's really here. "Have you come seeking absolution for your sins? Or to justify them?"

Rowan shifts again, and the faintest whiff of a light floral scent hits my nose again, making *me* shift uncomfortably this time.

"Maybe both, Father? At the time, I didn't really question the morality of what I was doing; it seemed necessary. But now..."

"But now you seek to go down another path?"

"I don't know. That seems easier said than done." She swallows thickly. "Despite my best efforts to keep my mind and body clear from certain thoughts and actions...I can't control where my mind goes sometimes."

I don't bother to fight the smile her confession draws across my lips. Weeks of innocent touches, of offering platonic comfort and reassurances, may have garnered me exactly the result I hoped for and drawn out the attraction.

"Sorry, Father. I—"

"Please continue. You know anything said in the confessional shall remain here, as if only God himself has heard it."

"I...I have impure thoughts and have touched myself thinking them."

My cock twitches to life, the sudden mental image of Rowan with her head tossed back, her hand between her legs, lips opened by her whimpers of pleasure all I can see.

"These...impure thoughts...it is perfectly natural to have them. Perfectly human." I gear up to give the same speech I've given to many who have entered the booth with similar confessions. To explain that it isn't just the thoughts but the actions that ultimately decide the path of right-eousness.

"But these are about..."

I freeze, waiting for her to finish her sentence, for her to make the confession I'm hoping so much to hear.

She releases a long, shaky breath. "These are about someone I shouldn't have these types of feel-ings toward. Someone I shouldn't see in this way."

Grinning, I adjust my erection and prepare to lead her down the path to my ultimate goal. "As I've said, we're all human. We all sin. Do not punish yourself or beat yourself up over your impulses and actions. Simply reflect on them and determine why you're having them. Is your attraction to this person simply because of the lifestyle you have led and lingering mentality from that, or is it something more, something deeper? Is it perhaps God's way of showing you your path in His love in the world? Is this person maybe meant to be the one you finally find peace with?"

That should give her enough to think about until it's time to finally act. In the meantime, I need to go take care of the raging hard-on she's given me by finally admitting my plan has worked.

The finish line is in sight. All I need to do is get her across it.

FOUR

FATHER FELIPE

THE SHARP KNOCK on my office door makes me jerk up my head from the stack of papers and books I've been reviewing for hours, preparing for this Sunday's sermon. Just one of many tiresome tasks living as Father Felipe requires of me. But it's necessary for keeping up appearances. If I half-assed things or said what was really on my mind at every Mass, people would see through me, straight to my dark heart, in a split second.

I drop my pen onto the desk and rub at the tightened muscles in my neck. "Come in."

With the church grounds typically quiet at mid-afternoon—and Rowan avoiding me after the tension-filled confession a few days ago—I wasn't expecting to have my day interrupted by anyone other than perhaps Sister Agnes with church business.

That old woman is a true pain in my ass, but she helps keep this place running relatively smoothly and doesn't ask questions I know she has about why I'm housing a beautiful redhead in the rectory or about the fact that my twin brother is the head of the notorious Blood Rose Cartel. She patched up Genti and the man who shares my face without comment, and even though she's been casting odd looks at me since then, she has kept her mouth shut—a good thing for me.

She is no push-over, and if she decided to confront me about what is really going on, I'm not so confident she wouldn't finally see through the farce I've managed to convince the rest of the world is real.

Only it isn't my devoted and pious assistant who opens the door to my office. Kat steps through the jamb and offers me the cold, hard smile of hers that doesn't reach her icy-blue eyes.

Even with her cool demeanor that gives off the *I-could-stab-you-with-my-stiletto-and-not-even-blink* vibe, I can see why Rose liked her so much—enough that he risked everything for her and her son. She exudes confidence and determination—an unwavering kind of strength that can be a true aphrodisiac for a man looking to take control who also seeks a partner in crime, one just as ruthless and tenacious as himself.

I have no intention of sharing the throne with anyone, though.

Especially not with the strikingly sexy and capable woman who closes the door and walks toward me on pencil-thin heels. She lowers herself slowly into the chair on the other side of my desk and crosses her legs, making sure to flash me her bare pussy during the movement.

I fight the pull of a grin on my lips. This woman is always testing the limits with anyone she faces, hoping to break them. And it's no different with me. Someone else in my position might be offended by her attempt to play on my urges, but not me.

One thing I have to appreciate is that Kat knows how to work with what she has been given in life. She knows men's weaknesses and how to exploit them.

It started with her as Brynn, dancing as "Kitty" in Aleksander's club, twisting her naked body around a metal pole in order to convince men to throw cash her way, and then, when she reinvented herself as Kat, she returned to Chicago to start an empire built on pussy and man's animalistic need for it.

This woman can get under a man's skin and make his cock twitch without ever touching him.

She certainly did it with my brother. Wrapped her cunt around him and led him down the primrose path that had him believing they were true partners.

Then she turned him over to Valentina and Cutter like he was yesterday's trash, shattering what could have been a very dangerous partnership to stand against when the time finally came.

It's one of the reasons I warned her away from him during our first meeting in this church. She was either going to partner with him and make my job harder or get caught in the crossfire, which meant she would be useless to me in my endeavors.

I lean back in my chair and steeple my fingers in front of my mouth. "I wasn't expecting to see you today."

Or at all.

After our last meeting, I warned her to stay away and wait to hear from me. Things have to happen in a very specific order to ensure they work. I have to play this one carefully because I don't trust Kat any more than I believe that there really is a God. And since she's here, apparently, she doesn't take orders well. Not really a surprise.

Kat inclines her head toward me. "I got sick of waiting around for something to happen. Plus, I have some interesting news."

I raise an eyebrow at her. One perk this collar has always afforded me is that people are willing to talk to me. They're eager to open their doors and their mouths and tell me everything without hesitation. It has made keeping my ear open for information that might be useful to me far easier than it otherwise would be. If there were anything *interesting* to know, I would already know it.

"I highly doubt there's anything you could tell me that I don't already know, Kat."

The tiniest of smiles tugs at the corner of her bright red lips. "I wouldn't be so sure about that, Felipe. I have my secrets just like you do."

She might be smug now, but she has no idea the secrets I hold. What I really want from her. What I really have in store for the future. When she showed up here, offering her help after betraying my dear brother, it played right into my plan—though she'll never know the extent of it. I don't dare tell her—or anyone else, for that matter—everything.

I shift forward and rest my elbows on my desk. If she wants to believe she has the upper hand when it comes to information, so be it. "Well, don't leave me hanging. Do fill me in."

"Valentina is in labor and should be delivering the baby soon."

"Well, that *is* news."

News I should've received from my source within the Marconi camp instead of having to hear it from Kat. But I'll deal with that failure later—with appropriate action. Right now, I need to focus on why Kat's really here. Because it can't just be to tell me about the new arrival. She could have called me with that. But she wanted to sit face to face for whatever reason, which makes me suspect it's something far bigger than the tiny bundle.

I raise an eyebrow at her. "Congratulations to the new mother and father are in order, I suppose. I'm sure my brother will send them a bottle of something to celebrate with."

She chuckles and shakes her head, her dark hair pulled back into the tight bun not budging even a millimeter with the movement. "Somehow, I doubt Valentina would drink anything your brother gave her. She'd probably assume it's poison."

I chuckle and nod. "Likely so. Especially after what you and they did to him, I can only imagine those two are on shaky footing. But what about you?" I shift forward and sweep a hand out. "Obviously, since you have this information, things must be friendly between you and the Marconis."

That would certainly put an interesting tangle into the plan. Their relationship has always been tenuous and appeared to only exist for the mutual benefit of their businesses. But if Valentina is now sharing intimate details of her life with Kat, that changes things.

Kat watches me for a moment, considering her words carefully. "Is that what you think I can offer to this partnership? A way to get past Cutter and to Valentina? Perhaps to take her out?"

It's an obvious deduction to make, one I would likely make, too, if I were in her position.

I shrug nonchalantly—unwilling and unable to give her too much information about my future plans. "I'm quite confident I can get what I want easily, Ms. Gashi. But my question is...what do *you* want? At our last meeting, you walked in here and offered me your allegiance because you said you knew I would come out on top when my brother and I finally face each other for control over the cartel, but what is it you expect to get out of the deal?"

It's one of the questions that's been plaguing me since she showed up. One I didn't get a satisfactory answer to the last time Kat was here because Sister Agnes interrupted our meeting.

Kat pulls back her shoulders and uncrosses and recrosses her legs seductively. "When all is said and done, and the blood has flowed and the smoke clears, I want you to leave me and everyone I care about alone."

I bark out a laugh I can't contain, her words rattling around in my head. "Leave them alone, huh?" I click my tongue against the roof of my mouth and shake my head, locking my hard gaze with hers to ensure she feels the weight of my words. "Do you think you can just walk away from this, Kat? If you do, you are sorely mistaken."

And in for some major fucking disappointment.

FIVE

FATHER FELIPE

Kᴀᴛ ᴘᴜʀsᴇs ʜᴇʀ ʟɪᴘs ᴛᴏɢᴇᴛʜᴇʀ, considering my words and her response carefully. "Konstandin did. He walked away."

My dark laugh fills the room, making her shudder—the first real sign of weakness she's ever displayed with me.

I rap my knuckles on the desk. "Konstandin hasn't walked away from anything, Kat. If you really believe that man has ridden off into the sunset with his woman and his child and will never be heard from again, then you are far more naïve than you look or that I thought you could ever be given all you've seen and done."

Red-hot anger flares in her normally cool gaze, and she shifts forward on her seat as if she might come across the desk at me. "Then why did you arrange the meeting between us? If not to broker some sort of truce so we could both live in peace?"

I grin at her. "Perhaps I thought you two would take out each other and solve two of my problems in one fell swoop."

She grins at me, but there isn't any humor in it—only a stony, dark determination. "Perhaps. Or perhaps you did it so you could lurk in the shadows of the church while we spoke and eavesdrop to learn our deepest, darkest secrets."

I don't even hesitate with my response. "Like about your son?"

Kat goes stock still. It's the first time I've actually brought up Jeton with her, even though his existence has been an unspoken elephant in the room since that fateful meeting she had here with Konstandin.

It was one of the most useful pieces of information I have ever obtained about her, and knowing she has a son to protect means, she'll always have a weakness I can exploit.

She squares her shoulders and clutches her purse tightly in her hand, trying to control her anger but doing a pretty shitty job of it. "I want you to leave him alone. He didn't choose this life or who his mother and father are. When all this is over, I want to be able to send him away somewhere I know he'll be safe."

"And will you be going with him?"

She drums her long, red nails of the hand not clenching her purse on her creamy-white thigh near the hem of her short skirt. "That depends on you."

"Really?" I raise my brows and lean forward farther, clasping my hands together on the desktop. "How do you figure?"

"Well, the way I see it, there are three possibilities. One—you kill me along with the heads of all the other families so that you can control the entire city yourself."

I grin at her but let her continue her speculation without a response. At this point, I'm more interested in learning what she *thinks* I'll do than actually confirming anything for her.

Her icy study of me doesn't waver. "Two—I help you and you repay my assistance by letting me maintain my own territory."

"And three?"

She takes a steadying breath and considers her words for a moment longer than is comfortable for two people in this situation. "Three...I walk away."

Walk away?

I bark out another laugh and shake my head, reclining in my chair. "You can't do that. You can't just *cancel* Kat and return to life as single-mother Brynn as if nothing has happened. Not after the things you've seen and done."

Of anyone else on this planet, I understand what it takes to create a different life, to live as someone else. And Kat isn't Brynn anymore. She buried her a long time ago and can't simply dig her back up and step into her skin again.

"That may be true." She shrugs nonchalantly. "I just said it was a possibility, but if you won't tell me what your plan is or what you want from me, it makes it hard to see the endgame."

"Maybe that's intentional."

She laughs, a bit of humor returning to her stoic face. "Oh, I'm sure that it is. And I would expect nothing less from you if you're even half the man your brother is."

It's meant as a dig to me, but it brings a smile to my face, nevertheless. As infuriating and annoying as it has been having to fight Andres for the role of Rose when he should just step down, seeing him so comfortable and unwavering in his role as a leader also brings a hint of pride I never imagined I'd feel in this situation.

Clearly, Kat still respects him despite having thrown him to the wolves. "Have you heard from my dear brother?"

Her eyes harden, and she shakes her head, any hint of affection I may have caught earlier erased immediately. "No. After Valentina and Cutter released him, I haven't seen or heard from him. My guess is my name has moved to the top of his hit list."

"And I'm sure his isn't the only hit list you're at the top of, either."

She smiles again and shrugs. "Likely true. Galen and Valerian are still out for blood over what I did, and I still haven't figured out who tried to kill Rose and me on that plane, either." She narrows a glare on me. "And even though you claim you had nothing to do with it, I'll be honest and say I don't believe you."

I chuckle and tsk. "Oh, Kat...and here you want us to be partners but you don't trust me."

Her thin shoulders rise and fall. "You don't trust me, either. It's why you're keeping me in the dark about important things I should know."

"Like what?"

"Like why you have one of my girls hiding out here in your rectory." She raises a slim, dark eyebrow. "Why is Rowan so important that you would risk being exposed by coming to Kat's Cradle and get her before anyone knew you even existed?"

I shrug as nonchalantly as possible, not wanting to confirm for her just how essential Rowan is to my master plan. "All souls are important, Kat. Even those who belong to dregs of society who might be judged harshly by how they live their lives."

"Cut the crap, Felipe. If you aren't going to let me in on your plan, then why not just kill me? Why send me home and tell me to wait for word on what you want done instead of pulling the trigger when you could? Why even agree to any sort of partnership at all?"

"Because you can be useful with me, Kat. But that doesn't mean I trust you or am going to tell you everything. That will *never* happen." I lean forward and glare at her, ensuring she can *feel* the chill I hope she can also see in my eyes. "You will know what you need to know when you need to know it."

I push to my feet, an invitation for her to leave before she presses this hard enough to truly see my anger rise to the surface. At this point, I do need Kat, which means keeping her dangling from the string I have her on. But if she were to cut it, it could leave me in a very precarious position in the near future.

It's a fine balancing act dealing with a woman like this—one who is just as lethal and conniving as I am. She easily sucked my brother into her orbit, but I won't let the same thing happen to me.

She pushes to her feet and scowls at me. "Right now, I know nothing. Other than you saying that you'll contact me when the time is right."

"And I will. You have to learn patience." I smile and make my way around the desk. "It is one of the virtues, after all."

She snorts and shakes her head. "And in the meantime?"

"Just keep your eyes and ears open for anything that could be of value. And, there is one more thing..."

Pausing at the door, she turns back to me.

"If your man, Arden, could do a little searching around for my sister, I would appreciate it."

"You still haven't heard from Sofia?" The tiniest bit of what almost sounds like true concern tints her question.

I usher her out into the hallway, and her man, who's been standing just outside the office door, steps in front of us to lead the way out from the rectory and into the church.

"No." I cross my hands behind my back as we make our way down the hall. "After the raid on Rose's compound, no one has heard from her, and my sources are getting nowhere tracking her whereabouts. My hope is that while we can't seem to physically locate her, she may have left a digital footprint your man can find."

Sofia is too smart to be found if she doesn't want to be, but Kat and Valentina have access to talented hackers who might find a breadcrumb. And I'd much rather locate her before the Marconis can.

We make our way through the empty nave and out the heavy wooden doors into the late afternoon sunlight. Kat pauses at the top of the steps as her man hurries down to her car parked on the street just in front of the church.

She peers over her shoulder at me, and something that almost passes as sympathy flashes there. "I'll see what he can find."

I incline my head toward her. "Most appreciated."

While I have no intention of being indebted to Kat, this task will keep her occupied and give her a chance to feel useful to me. It will keep her from asking more questions or stepping out of line, with the bonus of actually potentially locating Sofia.

Kat turns toward her car and takes two steps down toward it. Her man turns over the engine, and an explosion tears through the calm afternoon air, knocking me off my feet in a cataclysm of sound and shrapnel.

SIX

FATHER FELIPE

THE WORLD around me moves in slow motion, sharp ringing the only sound. A scream pierces through it, and I stretch my jaw to try to clear my ears. Dozens of sounds hit me at once.

I blink away the bright spots in my vision, and the carnage before me comes into full focus.

What's left of Kat's vehicle lies in pieces scattered on the street and sidewalk, the carcass engulfed in flames that leap into the sky twenty feet above the scene.

¡Mierda!

What the hell happened?

I shake my head to try to clear the cobwebs further and survey the area. Kat lies sprawled in front of me across the steps she had just started to make her way down when the explosion tore through the air, eyes closed, blood seeping from a gash at her temple.

"Kat..." I crawl toward her as people rush toward the firebombed car from farther down the street. "Kat!"

I shake her gently, and she groans and rolls onto her side before she sits up, blinking rapidly until her gaze can take in the carnage.

Her lips quiver, and she raises a shaky hand to the bleeding wound on the side of her head. She winces and scans around us, her mouth hanging open, taking in the wreckage. "Shit."

"My thoughts exactly."

She turns and focuses on me. "It was meant for me."

I nod. "No doubt."

Her gaze goes from questioning to accusing in a split second. "*You?*"

I scowl at her and glance at the Good Samaritans on their cell phones, no doubt contacting the police and fire department. "Why the hell would I want to bring attention to the church and me? Especially with *you* here?"

She sighs and winces again. "Good point."

Excited chatter draws my attention to a group of onlookers coming our way. If they make it here before Kat can disappear, then we will both be in hot water. The police are still looking for her for the shootout at the airport, and if they find her here with me, it won't be a big leap for them to see why there is a connection.

I grab her arm and squeeze it tightly to get her full attention. "You better get out of here."

Cloudy, confused eyes meet mine. "What?"

I shake my head back toward the rear of the church. "Get out of here before the cops show up."

"Shit." She gapes, like she's finally coming out of the daze caused by being thrown around like a rag doll, and she struggles to her feet and snags her shoe from the steps beside her.

"Father, are you okay?" Someone rushes forward and grabs my arm, helping me to my feet.

I catch a glimpse of Kat out of the corner of my eye but try not to focus any attention that way in hopes the onlookers won't spot her.

"Ma'am?" another man calls out at Kat's retreating form.

I hold my breath and wait for him to go after her, but she disappears around the side of the building, leaving the chaotic scene behind her. Hopefully, she was gone quickly enough that no one will be able to identify her.

Barring any more unforeseen happenings, she should be able to get far enough away that one of her men can pick her up without anyone seeing her or suspecting she was in any way involved in this incident. Since she's smart, nothing in that car will tie it back to her in any way the cops can prove.

It will be like she was never here.

Sirens wail in the distance, a sign of the threat I was concerned about arriving, and a few moments later, a squad car pulls up and uniformed officers jump out, talking into their radios at their shoulders.

One rushes toward me, eyes wide and lips twisted in concern. "Father, are you all right? Do you need medical attention?"

Despite the ache in my side and hip from slamming back against the concrete, I shake my head. The last thing I need is a trip to the hospital where they'll poke and prod me. I climb to my feet and brush off my hands. "I'm fine."

He motions toward the fiery wreckage while his partner talks to one of the bystanders near the street. "Was anyone in the car?"

There isn't any point in lying about that. They'll find the body—or what is left of it—once the flames have been extinguished. Though, identification is another matter that will likely take time given the state of anything they manage to locate.

I nod and do the sign of the cross while staring at the wreckage. "I don't know his name. He was in the church, praying just before coming out."

One of the men standing near us, who came rushing over right after the explosion, turns to the cop. "There was a woman with the man in the car, but she left."

The cop raises an eyebrow at me. "Know anything about that?"

"No. I saw her approaching the car, but then she was gone when I got my bearings after the explosion."

Hopefully, none of the witnesses are able to contradict that statement, and if they do, I can simply blame my confusion on a head injury from being thrown by the blast.

Everyone will believe me. They always do.

Another car squeals to a stop in front of the church. This time an undercover vehicle with nothing but a red light slapped on the roof, and a heavyset man steps from the driver's side and slams his door before coming around and approaching us.

He inspects me from head to toe, skepticism and surprise impossible for him to hide. "Father?"

I extend a hand. "Father Felipe."

"Detective Lopez." He accepts my proffered hand and squeezes it harder than is appropriate. "You know, Father...I'm pretty sure I know your brother."

¡Ay hijueputa!

Exactly what I didn't want. Now, the police are aware of my presence in town and the fact that we're identical twins. This could complicate things.

I plaster on my most pious-looking smile and release his hand. "Quite sure you do, Detective. But I'm not associated with him or his business. I am not my brother's keeper."

He turns and glances over his shoulder at the carnage and chuckles before returning his attention to me. "Then...what the hell happened there?" One of his dark eyebrows rises in question. "Just a coincidence that a car explodes into flames in front of your church?"

Many men probably buckle under this man's formidable presence and penetrating glare, but he's far from the toughest opponent I've ever been up against.

I shrug, the motion pulling at muscles already getting sore. "I don't know, Detective. Perhaps it was an accident."

He nods slowly. "Perhaps." He glances over his shoulder at where the officers are trying to control the growing crowd and the wailing sirens of the approaching fire engine tear through the air. "And you don't know who was inside?"

I shake my head. "No. I stepped out for a breath of fresh air and saw one of the parishioners who exited the church climb into it and start it before it exploded. But unfortunately, he wasn't anyone I recognized or was immediately familiar with."

Detective Lopez offers another slow bob of his head. "There seems to be an awful lot of explosions in the city lately. Your brother and sister were involved in one not all that long ago, along with the heads of the other crime families. Then there was one at Michael Syla's club before he vanished." He waves a hand. "Not to mention all the other recent violence. A plane crash I believe your brother may have been involved in and a shoot-out more recently at the airport here. Then just a few weeks ago, an estate outside of town got shot to hell."

"Do you have a question, Detective? Because I didn't hear one. And I don't know anything about any of those events." I spread out my hands. "I'm just here to look after my flock, and as I said, I don't know anything about my brother's business, nor are we even on speaking terms."

"I'm supposed to believe that? That you just happened to be at a church in the same city where your brother is stirring up trouble?"

I shrug. "I don't control what you believe, but it's the truth."

Sister Agnes rushes out from inside the church, her hand covering her gaping mouth. "Oh my! Father, are you okay?"

I nod and motion toward Detective Lopez. "I'm fine, Sister. This is Detective Lopez. Please assist him with any information he may need."

He scowls at me, apparently unmoved by my act. But there's nothing I can do about that now. I knew once anyone saw me who knew Rose, they would question my allegiance. It's the very reason I've kept my connection to him hidden for so long and stayed under the radar at small village churches in South America until requesting the transfer here. Now, it seems my cover has been blown. It's only a matter of time before the rest of the families find out he has a twin brother, and that will make what I'm about to do all the more difficult—or at least raise questions that otherwise wouldn't have come up.

But at least for now, it's time to put on a show before I retreat inside to avoid too many prying eyes and ears.

I step past Detective Lopez, toward the burning remains of the vehicle, then pause and close my eyes, raising my hands to the sky now filled with acrid, black smoke. "Heavenly Father, please bless the soul of our departed brother and watch over him on his way to your Heavenly kingdom. Amen."

Sister Agnes steps up next to me and crosses herself. "Amen."

"Sister, please schedule a prayer service for later today for this individual." I turn back toward Detective Lopez, who watches me apathetically.

"I'll be talking to you again soon, Father." Detective Lopez inclines his head toward me.

"I have no doubt you will. I'll be inside in my office when it's time for someone to come take a formal statement."

His skeptical stare burns at the back of my head as I walk back inside, not bothering to glance back at him or the wreckage. My cover has been blown apart as badly as Kat's car just was.

But who did it and why?

I make my way through the nave and down the hall toward my office. This is going to take some damage control. And it will mean moving up my timeline significantly. Though, maybe it is time to finally bite the proverbial bullet. I've given Andres one too many chances to change his tune about my taking over, to step back and into *this* role he wanted so badly in his youth. If he isn't willing to accept that, then I should do what I must swiftly to avoid any further issues.

My entire body starts to ache as I make my way down the hallway, but it could be the pressure to act, tensing my muscles just as much as being knocked over by the blast. It's been a long time coming, but still, finally stepping up and becoming Rose means all the dominoes I've lined up will have to fall in *perfect* order. And there's a part of me that still wonders which way a few of them will fall.

A door on my left flies open, and one of those dominoes I'm relying on—yet I'm so unsure about—rushes out, red hair floating behind her.

Rowan's wide green eyes frantically search the hallway until they meet mine, and she races toward me. "Oh, my God! Are you all right?"

She throws her arms around me without hesitation and buries her face against my shoulder, apparently forgetting all the decorum she seemed so desperate to try to uphold between us only days ago when it comes to *us*.

I wrap my arms around her, taking a moment to relish the feeling of finally, after *all* this time, having her in my arms. Her soft, supple body presses against mine, her warm breath fluttering over my neck, sending a little spark of pleasure straight to my cock.

Tightening my hold on her, I brush my lips against her ear, inhaling her soft honeysuckle scent. "I'm fine, *mi palomita*."

My little dove, who is more important than she could possibly know...

I inhale again, letting everything that is Rowan invade my lungs since I don't know when we'll be like this again. "No need to worry. I'm not going anywhere."

And neither are you.

SEVEN

FATHER FELIPE

ROWAN CLINGS to me like if she relaxes her hold even slightly, I might float away and disappear into the ether, when really, I'm the one who truly feels that is a real possibility, especially once she learns the truth.

She could fly away and never want to see me again. In fact, that would probably be the wisest decision for her to make, in light of all the circumstances. Though it's one I hope she rejects in favor of all the things I can offer her if she gives me a chance.

And this isn't the way I want her in my arms. I want her naked. Needy and begging. Desperate for all of me the way I am for her.

But at least this display brings warmth to my chest, hope for the future I have envisioned in my head. Faith that all I have been doing isn't for naught and might actually have a chance of success. Because she *cares*. She sees me as something more than the priest who rescued her from the sinful life she was living and the unknown danger I warned her about. I've become *someone* to her.

Now I just need to become the *only* one.

She sobs, turning her face toward me, her shaking lips next to my ear. "I was so scared. I heard an explosion, and...I wanted to come out to see if you were okay, but you told me I need to stay inside, stay hidden..."

I nudge her head back, despite how incredible her warm, fluttered breaths against my skin felt, and cup her face in one hand. The smooth, pale skin there, covered in light freckles, pinkens slightly as I brush my thumb over it. "You did the right thing, *mi palomita*."

If she had come out, she would have ended up a recorded witness, and Detective Lopez would have had even more questions I didn't want to answer. Ones I *couldn't* answer without bringing even further scrutiny to a situation that needs to remain under wraps—at least for the immediate time being.

Brushing my thumb over her flawless, alabaster skin, again, I lean in slightly, dipping my head to meet her tear-soaked green gaze. "And I'm fine."

I offer her what I hope is a reassuring smile. Physically, I managed to walk away with only a few bumps and bruises, but there is no telling what damage this has done to my plans. Being seen by someone who can connect me to Rose changes my timeline and exposes me in a way I can't afford right now. I'm going to have to push her faster than I had hoped.

She stares up at me with so much trust and a flicker of the emotion I've been longing to confirm from her. "What happened? I know you were meeting with someone right before..."

There isn't any point in lying to her about it. She already knows I've met with Kat on at least one previous occasion and has questioned me about it. I've been able to divert her inquiry by telling her I'm doing my best to protect her, but that vague explanation will only go so far. "Someone blew up Kat's car."

Her eyes widen even more. "Kat was here? Was she looking for me?"

"I told you not to worry about Kat when she saw you the last time she was here. You're safe. As long as you stay in these four walls, nothing can harm you. I'll make sure of it."

A shudder rolls through her and vibrates into my palm pressed to her cheek.

I'll make sure of it...

Not exactly what a good priest would be saying. I should be comforting her and reaffirming that God would protect her in these walls, that He would look after her and ensure her safety from any and all enemies—to her body and her soul.

But He already knows I'm not a good priest. The vows meant nothing to me. Mere words that would get me to my end goal. A collar that would serve a purpose until it no longer did.

I won't feel any guilt over what I do in this building or in these clothes. I won't feel it while my throbbing cock is pressed between our bodies. I won't feel it because it doesn't exist in my head or in any portion of what remains of my heart. All that does is my need for Rowan and my desire to finally have what I've waited twenty years for—all the power in my *own* hands, not in those of a puppet who shares my face.

She shakes her head. "I still don't understand what Kat wanted from me or why you thought it was so dangerous for me to stay there. She was always good to all the girls, to me. She never did anything that made me feel unsafe, even if she did have us trying to gather blackmail information for her." She squeezes her eyes closed and presses her lips together in frustration before reopening them and staring me down. "Why can't you tell me the truth?"

I brush my thumb over her quivering lips and watch her as hunger flares deep in her green eyes, her reaction only fueling fire already raging through my veins. "I told you, all in due time. In order to protect you, I need to sort out some other things before I can tell you everything." I raise my other hand to cup her face between both of them. "Don't you trust me, *mi palomita?*"

She releases a sigh that invades my breath again and tightens her grip around my waist. "I do. It's just..." Her focus darts down to my lips, and her tongue slips out from between hers to wet them. "I—"

"I know this is a struggle for you. That you want certain things that you feel you can't have."

Things I want, too. More than anything.

Just at the right time, which isn't now.

Soon.

"But I promise you, *mi palomita,* when all is said and done, things will be exactly the way they were meant to be. Have faith."

She swallows thickly, the movement of her throat almost breaking the steely control I've managed to hold onto this long. "I do."

Her response comes on a soft exhale that makes my hard cock ache to be inside her. And she seems to either feel it pressing against her or senses the tension between us leading down a dangerous road because she shakes her head and quickly steps back, letting my hands drop from her cheeks and hers fall from my waist.

"I-I'm"—she casts a furtive glance up and down the hallway, ensuring we're still alone—"glad you're okay."

I hold out a hand for her. This is the closest I've ever been to having everything I want, and I'm not ready to let her go. "Don't run away from me, Rowan."

"I-I'm not..." She whirls away from me, her red hair flying out around her, and dashes back into her room, throwing the lock into place to keep me from going after her.

Running from me is exactly what she's doing. Like she's Little Red Riding Hood and I'm the big bad wolf threatening to eat her alive. But I can't say I really blame her. She thought she was leaving Kat's Cradle to enter the safety of a Catholic church to hide from an unknown evil I warned her about.

She had no idea I *am* the evil and that she's played right into my plans perfectly.

Exactly as I intended it.

This explosion and the resulting exposure is a bump in the road that will make me adjust things, but soon, Rowan shall know the truth, and it will change everything between us.

It will change all of Chicago.

EIGHT

FATHER FELIPE

THE NUMBER that pops up on my caller ID makes my lips tilt up into a grin even after the frustration my run-in with Rowan earlier left me with. Even jerking off in my office didn't release that tension, but this is the call I've been waiting for. One that was inevitable after the events earlier today. Frankly, I'm surprised it took this long.

I walk toward the front pew of the empty church. The late-night stragglers have long ago headed home. Between all the excitement of the explosion, giving the statement to the police, and the prayer service for the "poor soul" who expired in the blaze, my entire day was pretty much shot.

And it seems so is my body. I accept the call and lower myself to the bench slowly, my back and side screaming in protest with the movement. "*Hola, mi querido hermano*. To what do I owe the call?"

"Rumor has it somebody tried to kill your new partner today."

I chuckle and lean back to stare at the crucifix mounted above the altar, the ever-present judgmental gaze of Christ staring down at me, seeing right through me just like it always does. "Now, where did you hear that?"

"One of my men received a very unwelcome call."

"Oh, yeah?"

"Of course, he has no way to get in contact with me directly, but Detective Lopez is tenacious and managed to track down a number for one of my men. The good detective is suddenly very interested in your little church and your connection to me."

"I'm sure he is. It has brought a lot of unwanted attention my way that's bound to come back on you, as well."

"He said a car exploded right in front of the church and that a witness spotted an unidentified female who fled the scene and who may have some relevant information. Lopez wanted to know if I had any idea who it could have been since you said you didn't remember seeing anyone else outside at the time of the explosion. There's only one woman I can think of who would have been there and who someone might want dead enough to set a bomb in her car while she was inside."

Rose knows Rowan is here, too, but he wouldn't have any reason to suspect anyone would be after her. "Were you the one who tried to kill Kat?"

He offers an incredulous snort in response.

"Why is that so absurd to suggest? It would make sense. Get revenge on her and eliminate my anonymity in one fell swoop."

"Oh, believe me, I want that backstabbing bitch dead, but if I had been trying to kill her or you, I wouldn't have done it in a way that offered such a chance at failure."

"True, *hermano*. But you have had a lot of failures lately. Your track record hasn't been so good."

"When is this going to end, *hermano*? What's your endgame? If you wanted to simply take me out and take over at the head of the family, you've had many opportunities to do just that and let someone else do the dirty work, even though I know that isn't really your style. But you haven't. In fact, you've gone so far as to save my life. I don't understand what you're hoping to accomplish with this."

"Maybe you're not supposed to understand. The Lord works in mysterious ways, after all. You, of all people, should know that."

"Fuck you, *hermano*."

I chuckle and run a hand over my face. "Such foul language from a man who once had such a close relationship with the Lord."

"Yeah. Well, those days were long gone after you killed *Mama y Papa* in cold blood. It didn't leave me a lot of choices."

I still and bite back the response I've wanted to make so many times at his accusations regarding *Mama y Papa*. It doesn't matter what I say to him, anyway. He will continue to believe what he wants to believe about me and what happened that day.

The truth shall set you free doesn't apply to me or this situation, so there isn't any use in uttering the words I've swallowed down for twenty years.

Instead, I lean forward to rest my elbows on my knees and offer him the only answer I can. "You want to know why I'm here, *mi querido hermano*? When I realized how badly you were struggling to expand into the Midwest. How badly you were fucking up everything. My initial goal was merely to come to set you on the right path again. I had no intention of interfering with our continued charade, one that has worked so well for two decades. But you made it clear that you have no intention of taking orders from me anymore or letting me step into the Rose shoes physically. I had hoped to change your mind, to show you the error of your ways. But since it became clear to me that you have other plans, I had to change my strategy."

"I won't go down without a fight, *hermano*. I've worked too hard and gotten my hands too bloody to let you show up here and take over the business I've built."

I slam my open palm against the pew, the sound echoing through the vaulted ceilings of the church. "Don't forget your place, *mi querido hermano*. The name Rose may have come from what you did in that house that day, but I have been the one building this cartel into what it is. Making the decisions. Moving us forward. All you are is a pretty face."

He chuckles deep and low, a sound that has no doubt struck fear into the hearts of many over the years. But it could never scare me. Nothing he does ever could. "While you were playing priest, I've been the one making deals, making connections, moving the product—"

"You mean *losing* the product, having it stolen? Pissing off some of our biggest clients with your incompetence?"

"A minor blip. One that I remedied and came out on top of with Valentina, in the end."

"In a deal set to expire soon."

And once it does, we will be right back in the same place we were when that shipment was intercepted by Valentina's crew out in Lake Michigan. Without our own territory or use of the Italians'. My partnership with Kat will gain me entry into that of the Albanians, but it isn't enough. Not nearly enough.

He snorts again, his incredulity coming through loud and clear. "Is that what you're waiting for? An opportunity to move on Valentina because of what happened?"

"I'm not about to tell you my plan, but I will tell you this. This is your last warning, your last opportunity to do what is right and step aside."

He chuckles again, this time with real humor in it. "And what? I become Felipe again? Take over your position at the church as if I haven't spent the last two decades bathed in blood, doing the dirty work for the Blood Rose Cartel?"

"Perhaps it's time for our roles to finally be what God intended."

"It's not that simple."

"It is. As the good book says, 'for even Satan disguises himself as an angel of light.' I've disguised myself long enough. Step down or face a wrath you can't even comprehend."

"Do your worst, Father. But remember, 'God is not mocked, for whatever one sows, that will he also reap.'"

NINE

FATHER FELIPE

TIGHTENING my hands in her silky, red tresses, I drive my cock even deeper down her clasping throat. Hard enough and far enough that she gags slightly and swallows to try to regain her breath.

Typically, I wouldn't see my favorite redheaded whore during the week. I reserve this type of debauchery and pleasure for the Lord's Day after I've performed my duties at Sunday mass. But after the day I had, the only thing that was going to even put a dent in the frustration I'm feeling was to come down this slut's throat.

And that's just what I plan to do before I flip her over and drill her from behind. A sorry substitution for who I really want to be doing it to. Yet, one thing I've learned wearing this collar for twenty years is that it's full of sacrifices.

I drag back my hips and shove my cock in her throat again, trying to bury what I can't reveal publicly inside her. She moans around my flesh and squeezes my thighs as I just keep pushing the limits of what she can take. But she's paid well for this—for giving me the one thing I can't get anywhere else.

Release.

From this name. From the collar I have to wear every day. From the confines of that prison people call a church. From the charade I've been living for two decades.

It isn't too much to ask. A few moments of pleasure. What we all deserve as living, breathing human beings. Yet, I haven't been free to indulge in my vices. Not really. I've been bound by the decision we made that fateful day. Trapped in a life that was meant for my brother. Only able to satisfy my base needs on rare occasions...

Well, not tonight.

Tonight, I'm going to do what I would if we had never made that pact. If he had never killed those people. If we had never switched places. This is where I would be. My rightful place. Instead of pretending to be Rose, I *would be* the man people feared. The man everyone thinks controls one of the largest and most vicious cartels in the world.

The gall he has to think he can push me out and take over for himself makes me tug on the whore's hair even harder, push even deeper with more urgency, trying to fuck out my anger and annoyance at the man I shared a womb with. To dissipate the frustration I feel over not being able to do this to Rowan.

These auburn strands twisted in my fingers might pull from her head with the tight grip I'm maintaining and use to hold her still, but she takes it like the good girl she is. She knows why she's here—what her role is, especially after what happened last time. She won't make the mistake of thinking her time with me means anything more than a paycheck for her.

And the only thing that would make this better is if it was another redhead on her fucking knees in his hotel room, sucking my cock.

Just thinking about finally doing what I've wanted since the moment I saw Rowan starts a low tingle at the base of my spine, signaling the release I've been seeking.

I thrust into her mouth harder and faster, driving down her throat until my body jerks with the pleasure coursing through my veins and hot spurts of cum finally shoot from my cock. She swallows, the movement of the warm, wet, rippling muscles along my dick only dragging my orgasm on further.

For a few moments, the entire world disappears, and all that exists in the bliss of release and the feeling of floating on air I can only get like this. It's what I imagine a drug addict must feel like when they finally get that high they seek so badly. That high *we* provide to them. What someone who is truly religious must feel when they are in God's presence. Maybe standing before the Pearly Gates. But this is the only place I feel it. The only *way* I feel this kind of absolute ecstasy.

Truly paradise.

But I don't even have time to pull my cock from her mouth before the elevator dings and the doors to the penthouse slide open.

Fuck. Just what I didn't need today—another complication.

Valerian and Galen step from the elevator car, smug smiles on their lips and weapons aimed squarely at me where I stand near the windows in the main living area of the suite.

Any warmth or sense of calm I got from that brief moment disappears in a split second, replaced with a cold sense of dread.

No one should have been able to find me here. My deal with the manager assured me that no one would be in the lobby when I entered except him and that the penthouse would be listed under a false name. It has worked flawlessly since my arrival in Chicago. And the whore drives in from Milwaukee for all our meetings to ensure Kat could never get wind of what's going on here through the Chicago grapevine.

So, what the fuck happened?

They couldn't have followed "Rose" here when I came straight from the church and this late. I would have noticed someone tailing me even if they had gotten wind from Detective Lopez or elsewhere that there may be something of interest there.

That only leaves two other possibilities. Either the manager sold me out, or the whore with my dick still in her mouth did.

Valerian examines the woman on her knees in front of me and motions with his gun for me to pull out.

I release my death grip on her hair and grunt as I pull my cock free. She glances over her shoulder at the intruders. A flash of recognition there is all I need to confirm she's the one who told them where I would be and when.

Perhaps what I said to her when we saw each other on Sunday set the wrong tone. The bitch obviously thought I really cared about her. Enough for her to betray me this way.

Apparently, I haven't learned from my brother's mistake in trusting a woman on any level.

Valerian points his weapon at her, and before she can move or protest, he pulls the trigger and puts a bullet straight through her forehead. She crumples to the floor in front of me, naked, with my cum still dribbling out of her lips.

Shit. This day just keeps getting better and better.

I glance down at her and her red hair spread out like a burning halo around her face, now marred by a hole in the middle of the otherwise flawless skin of her forehead.

At least Valerian has saved me from having to do it myself later, for betraying me, but it's just one more mess to add to the long list lately. Still, I wouldn't have shot her in the head. Now, she can't even have an open casket.

Nos vemos en el infierno, cariño.

With all the sins we've committed, we're both sure to end up there.

TEN

FATHER FELIPE

I RETURN my attention to the two men standing in front of me and slowly tuck away my semi-hard cock into my pants before I zip and button them. "Gentlemen. To what do I owe this surprise visit?"

This bitch dead on the floor in front of me must have decided the only way to make me pay for breaking her heart was to hand me over on a silver platter to the two men looking for Rose.

She didn't know any better. Couldn't have understood what she was really doing when she betrayed me—signing both our death warrants. They never would have let her live, and neither would I.

¡Puta estúpida!

Valerian checks the rest of the suite and motions for me to take a seat in the armchair to my left while Galen keeps his gun trained on me. "A lot has changed since we last sat down together, Rose."

I raise a dark eyebrow at Valerian and smile smugly. "Yes, from what I understand, one of your casinos got raided and your *amigo* here lost a pretty big gun shipment."

In reality, I have no fucking clue what went down when Rose was in Valerian's clutches since my brother wasn't exactly cooperative when he awoke at the church and wasn't about to tell me everything that had happened. He was already so far off the deep end on his power trip that there was no way to get that information.

But Valerian took him after Kat made her move and because he believed Rose was the way to get to her and what was stolen. The only reason he even escaped Valerian's clutches was that he managed to shoot his way out with Genti. And they wouldn't have gotten very far shot up like they were unless I had shown up to rescue them.

Bad move on my part, but I had hoped to give him one more chance to come to my side. To make the right decision.

Instead, he's declared war and I'm left to balance between playing him and upholding my duties to the church until I'm ready to unleash everything I have planned on the Windy City.

Valerian issues a low growl and steps toward me. "And you and Kat's goon took out a fuckload of my men."

I issue a little half-shrug. "You should find more competent employees if you want to hold people captive, Valerian."

It was far too easy for me to locate where he was holding them. A few phone calls and questions in the right area of the city led me straight to the old hospital they were using as a torture location.

The angry Russian sneers at me and points the gun at the leg he shot on my brother that Sister Agnes patched up to save his life. If the dumbass had bothered to pay any attention when he burst in, he would have seen there was no healing scar there and known I wasn't the man he shot. "You want another bullet in you?"

I sigh and lean back in the chair. "I would prefer not." I point to the bottle of scotch on the small table next to me. "But I could use a drink. Mind if I pour myself one for this conversation?"

Galen bobs his head, granting me permission, and I casually pour two fingers and take a sip, letting the spicy, smokey liquid burn down my throat.

"Really, gentlemen, your timing could not have been worse. So, let's cut to the chase. What can I do for you?"

Valerian crosses his arms over his chest, gun still held tightly in his right hand. "You can help us get that bitch. Tell us where we can find Kat."

I swirl my drink in the glass and raise it to them. "Well, I don't know if you've heard, but she and I are no longer partners, which means I don't give a fuck what you do to her, and I have no way of helping you get to her."

Galen sneers at me, the move twisting up the scar on the side of his face from the bomb Kat set to try to take out every other family in Chicago. "And you expect us to believe that?"

"I barely got away from Valentina and Cutter with my life. Why would I protect the cunt who put me there?"

Valerian narrows his eyes on me. "How *did* you get away?"

That's a very good question I *don't* have the answer to. When Kat gave my dear brother to the Marconis, I had plans to go in after him. If Valentina let Cutter take him out, my entire plan to step in as Rose would be dead along with him. As much as I may hate him, I need my brother alive long enough for me to replace him and convince everyone nothing has happened. It does me no good to allow someone else to end his life before I'm ready.

"I have my secrets, boys." I take another sip and sigh. "Speaking of which, I hear Valentina may be giving birth as we speak." I raise my glass and tip it toward them. "So, my congratulations to the new mother and father, but as for Kat...You two can do whatever the fuck you want to her, but I'm not going to help you do it because she's mine to end." I tighten my hand on the glass hard enough to whiten my knuckles, ensuring these volatile men see physical evidence of my wrath. "I want to be the one who watches her die a slow, agonizing death."

Galen raises an eyebrow. "Are you responsible for one of her cars getting bombed today?"

Seems news spreads fast. I wonder what else they know...

I shake my head. "No, but I have heard something about it."

Valerian glances at Galen. "We did, too. We heard there was someone very interesting at the location."

Apparently, they know that.

There isn't any point in denying it. If what Detective Lopez discovered was told to anyone else in the precinct, the news would have spread like wildfire by now. "Yes...my brother. He is the priest there."

The two men exchange a look and wait for me to elaborate, which I have no intention of doing. I down the rest of my drink and grab the bottle to pour myself another. Another to drag this out and make them wait. Men like Valerian and Galen hate silence. It unnerves them.

I take a sip of the second one and relax back into my chair casually.

Finally, Galen sighs. "And just what was Kat doing meeting with your brother?"

I shrug. "How the fuck should I know? Probably trying to get information she can use against me, and since he and I aren't exactly on good terms, the bitch may have succeeded."

Valerian snorts. "Were you the one who set the bomb?"

I smirk at him. "No. Were you?"

He scowls. "I wish I could say I was. We've been trying to get to her ever since she came back from Albania, with no luck. She's staying well-hidden and away from her club, Kat's Cradle, and her other locations."

"Well, gentlemen..." I push to my feet and hold up my drink. "I hope your luck changes. And if it does and you get a gun to her head, you tell her it's from me too before you pull the trigger."

Galen holds up a hand. "Stop right there. Do you really think this is the end of this conversation?"

I raise one shoulder and let it fall nonchalantly. "It is for me. We're all in the same boat. All betrayed by that same snake. There isn't any point in us fighting each other *and* her."

Valerian issues a low, rumbling laugh. "I seem to remember her suggesting something similar during my last meeting with her. She told Galen and me that she wasn't working with you when she really was. That was a bald-faced lie, so why should we trust you now?"

I take another sip and roll the glass between my hands. "Kat may have fudged the truth a little bit back then to get you boys on her side. But I am *not* Kat, and things have changed since she took out Michael and took over the Albanian crew. Things that never would have happened before. Overstepping on her part. An alliance between our three families would be hard to stand against, especially for Kat. She doesn't have any allies. No friends."

My words hang in the room around us, but they don't speak, mulling over the idea I've planted loosely in their heads.

"I have something that will be of great interest to you boys." I set my empty glass on the table and nod toward Valerian, then make my way toward Galen. "Something I think *you* especially will find very interesting, *amigo*."

He watches me for a moment, his cool eyes assessing my vague statement. "I don't like you, Rose. Don't like the way you or your former girlfriend do business, trying to push your way into territories that were established long before either of you were even born."

I hold up my hands. "I don't blame you. But I'm not just going away, and neither is Kat. At least, not without a bullet to her head like Valerian did to her." I motion back toward the dead hooker on the floor. "I assume you'll clean that up since you made the mess." I glance at Valerian. "If I find Kat and can end things, I'll let you know, but until the time one of the three of us succeeds in ending our mutual problem, I suggest we keep things amicable. Deal with one enemy at a time while we at least consider the possibility of future alliances."

Valerian doesn't react, just watches me stoically, not giving away anything.

"What'll it be, *amigos*?" I wave a hand toward the elevator. "Are you going to shoot me in the back while I walk out of here?"

They exchange a look, and Galen turns toward me.

"We'll hear you out, Rose. Because we want Kat gone more than we want you gone, and if you can help rid us of her faster, that only benefits us. But make no mistake, if we find out you've been in the same fucking room as that cunt and didn't blow her head off, then you'll be right there with her when we do."

I flash them a classic Rose smile and incline my head. "Understood. I'll contact both of you soon with some important information. Information that will change everything." I wink. "And I'll keep an eye out for our lady friend."

The two men watch me walk toward the elevator, but I don't look back until the doors have slid open and I've stepped inside and have to turn to face them. They aren't happy about what just went down tonight. They anticipated spilling my blood or finding a way to Kat.

I guess I should thank her for betraying my brother and giving me a way to create a bridge between the Irish and the Russians.

While their little visit couldn't have come at a worse time, it's actually playing directly into my hands. Now, let's just hope everything else goes the same way and there aren't any more unexpected surprises.

ELEVEN

FATHERN FELIPE

I UNLOCK the back door of the rectory and slip inside as quietly as possible. Sister Agnes has better hearing than most women half her age, almost like she has some sixth sense for knowing when people are up to something they shouldn't be. The woman was born to be a nun and sniff out sinners, so it makes sense she gave up her nursing career after serving in the army to become a member of the clergy.

The last thing I need is for her to find me sneaking back in this late at night with the smell of the hooker on me and blood spray on my pants and shoes if she flips on the lights and looks close enough.

That would lead to a lot of questions I can't answer yet. And though the little visit from my Irish and Russian friends tonight was an unexpected surprise, it wasn't wholly unproductive.

It may actually help me achieve my goal quicker than I planned...

Valerian and Galen are out for blood, but at least it isn't mine anymore—or should I say Rose's. What Kat did to my brother by turning him over to Valentina and Cutter and betraying him creates the perfect alibi for me and the ideal excuse for them to trust me when they didn't only such a short time ago.

The only complication will be the *other* Rose and his refusal to step down. If they try to contact him, he will know I've been masquerading as Rose and making moves behind his back. I had hoped it wouldn't come to this, but if he's not willing to take over here at the church and step back into the role he was destined for before that fateful day, then he's dug his own grave.

Literally.

There can't be two of us anymore, not when we have divergent goals and don't trust each other. The status quo that has stood for the last two decades has to change before everything blows up in our faces.

While nothing was finalized tonight, the boys did let me leave and promised to take care of the mess they created in the suite. It's the very beginnings of an alliance that will only solidify in the future once I've revealed all to them. One where I reign over the Windy City and eventually the entirety of North America.

If I can get to my room and out of these clothes fast enough...

I make my way down the hallway toward my room, careful to tiptoe past Sister Agnes' door, but it's another one that swings open with a creak that seems to echo off the hard floors loud enough to wake the dead.

¡Mierda!

Rowan.

Even before I see her step out, the smell of honeysuckle floats from the open door and settles over me, stirring my cock. I freeze and press myself back against the wall, hoping she won't see me in the darkness, but she steps out and turns to face me like she knows exactly where I am.

Her green gaze zeroes in on what I'm wearing with laser focus. "Where are you coming from dressed like that?"

I glance toward Sister Agnes' door and step toward Rowan. "Keep your voice down."

She opens her mouth to say something else, but I step forward, grab her by the elbow, and push her back into her room, closing the door softly behind me.

No way in Hell we're having this conversation in the hall when Sister Agnes could come out any moment.

She pulls out of my hold and whirls to face me, her lips pressed together in a tight line. "What are you doing?"

I step closer to her and drop my head toward hers. "Trying to keep us from being caught by Sister Agnes. Keep your damn voice down."

Rowan inhales a sharp breath, her eyes wide. She's never heard me talk like that, and her shock shows across her soft features. "What is going on? Where were you?"

Waiting for my response, she assesses me in the faint moonlight streaming in through the window. If the lights were on in here, she'd likely be able to see the spots of blood glinting on my black shoes, but the darkness gives me a modicum of protection. And I won't give her what she's asking for. The answers to those questions aren't anything she should ever be privy to.

She reaches up and grabs at the collar of my white dress shirt. "Lipstick on your shirt. And you smell like—" She takes a little half step back. "Like sex. What the hell is going on, Father?"

¡Ay hijueputa!

It's always a risk going to the hotel and sneaking back in here dressed like Rose, but I can't exactly walk out of there in my priestly garb, either. Nor can I change in the car or anywhere else before coming back. Too much risk someone might see me enter as one person and leave as another. If caught, it might cause a scandal I can't afford right now.

But apparently, the stupid whore's lipstick just gave me away and exposed something I never intended for Rowan to know about.

I take another step toward her, and she doesn't retreat, standing her ground with her hands fisted at her sides. "What I was doing is none of your business, *mi palomita*."

"Don't try to blow this off. You need to tell me what is going on!" She shakes her head and motions wildly toward the hallway. "You show up at Kat's Cradle and tell me that my life is in danger being there, but you won't tell me why. Then, you bring me here and practically hold me hostage, telling me I can't leave. And then, you show up with your identical twin brother and one of Kat's men both shot up and tell me not to question it." She releases a heavy breath. "And *now*, you're dressed like *him* coming in here smelling like one of my clients."

Her outburst brings a heat of pink blush to her pale cheeks, one I often fantasize about watching spread over her entire body if I ever got my hands on her the way I want to.

I doubt this woman has ever had a man touch her who actually saw her as more than a whore, someone to pay to fulfill a need. Her clients were always worried about their own desires and urges.

With a man who is determined to see *her* reach the pinnacle of pleasure, it would be something completely new for her, something she has only ever fantasized about. And I intend to show her that.

I take another step closer to her until my chest brushes against her heaving breasts in a way that sends a visible shiver through her body. "We all succumb to sin at some point, *mi palomita*."

Those beautiful, plump lips of hers that tempt me every day open and close, but I don't know whether it's to issue some sort of reproach or to ask questions I won't answer. Before she can utter a word, I reach out and brush my thumb across her bottom lip.

She practically sags against me, her small body pressing to mine, her hands coming to my chest. "I don't understand what's going on."

The confusion and fear in her voice mingle with the waver brought on by the tension of standing so close, of touching each other in a way completely inappropriate but that somehow still feels so right. "I know you don't. And I can't tell you yet." I cup her chin and tilt up her head until her eyes meet mine. "When the time comes, *mi palomita,* you will see what I'm truly capable of."

I press a kiss to her lips before she can process my words or even consider responding, savoring the sweet taste that's all Rowan. The taste I've denied myself for what feels like an eternity but that is more than even I have ever dreamed of.

My hard cock presses against her belly in a way she has to notice, but before she can react, I step back, let my hand fall from her face, and duck out the door.

It clicks closed behind me, leaving her bewildered and alone in her room while I stand on shaky legs in the hallway.

That kiss shouldn't have happened. It's too soon to push her toward where I want her. Too fast. Especially when she doesn't know the truth. But I couldn't help myself. Not with her right there in my arms. Not with her scent invading every breath I took.

I can't keep what's really happening from her much longer. Not if I want to keep her on my side and get her in my bed. The truth will blow up everything she knows, but it always comes out no matter how hard we try to bury it.

I just hope the lie my dear brother and I created can maintain its integrity until I step into the role of Rose. Because if it crumbles before then, all Hell will break loose before I'm ready for it.

TWELVE

FATHER FELIPE

SCANNING the attentive faces of those gathered for early morning Mass, I raise my hands and force myself to offer a kind smile despite the tension and unease wracking my body. "The Lord be with you."

"And with your spirit." The congregation's response, said perfectly in sync, echoes through the space.

But it's missing one very important voice.

The only one I *want* to hear.

I glance at the empty space in the front pew, where Rowan typically sits, for the thousandth time during today's service, but of course, nothing has changed. She's still absent, but I can't dwell on the potential meaning for her skipping service at this exact moment. Not when I have dozens of people waiting for me to conclude and dismiss them.

"May almighty God bless you, the Father, and the Son, and the Holy Spirit."

Their reply comes back, practiced and automatic. "Amen."

"Go in peace, to love and serve the Lord."

"Thanks be to God."

While services during the week are never as packed as they are on Sundays, especially the early morning ones, I spot all my usuals. Mostly elderly, they come like clockwork, brought in by a sense of duty or obligation; though, I'm sure some of them actually do enjoy coming as an excuse to get out of their homes at least once a day.

It's the last place I want to be today, but still, I make my way down the aisle, nodding to the parishioners, and take up my position at the rear of the church at the top of the steps to shake hands and offer smiles or a few words of encouragement as everyone migrates toward their vehicles.

Slipping into the role of a caring and pious parish priest has become so rote, it isn't even a conscious shift for me anymore.

Smile. Shake. Nod. Bless.

Smile. Shake. Nod. Bless.

On and on and on.

It feels like it takes another hour before the last parishioner finally trickles out and down the steps slowly. Sister Agnes approaches with her old mouth twisted in a frown.

"Is that the last of them, Sister?"

She nods, her shrewd eyes assessing me like she can see right through my act, as they always do. But if she suspects the truth, she has yet to ever call me out on it. "Yes, Father."

I rub a hand over the stubble forming on my jaw. What happened last night with Rowan in her room shook me badly enough that I completely forgot to shave this morning. "And what about Rowan? Is she feeling any better?"

When Rowan didn't appear as usual for early Mass, I sent Sister Agnes to check on her. Though, I'm certain the "illness" keeping her in her room is complete bullshit. And I suspect Sister Agnes does, too.

Last night clearly shook Rowan as much as it did me, or maybe even more so. Perhaps I pushed it too far, pushed *her* too far. Without knowing the truth, I'm sure her seeing me that way made her question everything and lose trust in me—the one person she has followed blindly and believed in since I first showed up at Kat's Cradle.

But I hadn't anticipated her completely avoiding me to the point of missing service. Not when the one constant since she first arrived here has been her desire to seek some sort of connection to God. Whether she's seeking absolution for her life as an escort like she suggested in the confessional or for her attraction to me—or for something else completely—she's sought it here. Missing church just isn't like her.

Sister Agnes glances behind her even though she just confirmed for me that we are alone. "I just checked her room, and I found this."

She hands me a folded piece of paper, and I reach out slowly to take it, a chill of trepidation over what it may say already hardening my stance and sending my hair standing on end.

"Did you read it?"

The old nun shakes her head. It's addressed to you, Father."

Felipe is scrawled across the front of the folded page. It's impossible to overlook that the word "Father" is now missing from the woman who has only ever referred to me in that formal way.

Things have changed.

And I'm sure Sister Agnes noted the missing word, too. Her shrewd assessment seems to focus right on it even now.

"Thank you, Sister. That'll be all."

She huffs slightly at my dismissal, then retreats through the nave toward the rectory to complete the day's tasks while I make my way to the sacristy to change out of my vestments.

Once I've closed the door and locked it behind me, I lower myself into one of the chairs and finally flip open the note.

I couldn't stay. Not after last night.
Thank you for everything you've done for me.
- Rowan.

¡Mierda!

I crumple the letter in my hand and squeeze until my knuckles whiten before I slam my fist down on the arm of the chair.

The timing for this couldn't be worse. Just when I'm attempting to cement an alliance with the Russians and the Irish, I have to shift my focus to finding her...and fast. Before someone else realizes who she is and uses her for their own purposes.

I toss the note into the garbage can in the room, grab my cell phone from the drawer where I keep it during service, and dial.

Keeping the truth hidden for the last twenty years hasn't been easy. It has meant "Rose" making all the calls, so I either had to direct my brother what to do and say, or I had to do it and then keep him updated on what I had done so that he wasn't surprised when one of our men mentioned it to him later.

Our rift has only complicated things further. I've had to bring in new men who answer only to me, who will think I am Rose. But it's necessary to keep my hands clean for as long as possible and maintain the charade. I don't have the time or the freedom to handle things completely on my own, and I can't access the network my brother and I have built without alerting him to what I'm doing.

The line rings twice before someone finally answers. "Sir?"

"I need you to find someone. I'll text you the information I have on her. When you locate her, bring her to St. Mary of the Angels church."

"Sir?"

I growl low into the phone. "Don't question me. When you find her, bring her to the church. It's a safe place of refuge. Somewhere I can hide her."

"Yes, sir. Right away, sir."

I end the call and immediately text him a photo of Rowan from my phone along with all of her stats and anywhere I think she might've gone. But it won't be easy to find her.

Before she went to work at Kat's Cradle, she was living and working the streets in New York. She only ended up here because one of the other girls told her to come to Chicago. Rowan had no idea that fate was intervening, bringing her halfway across the country to play the starring role in my plan.

But she's smart. Smart enough to lay low if she needs to. Still, there's always a chance she'll reach out to one of her old friends from the brothel or make some other mistake. People always do.

I just have to hope that she does and that I can get my hands on her first; otherwise, everything I've done may be for nothing.

THIRTEEN

FATHER FELIPE

BAPTISMS ARE HORSESHIT.

Definitely my least favorite part of being Father Felipe. Not because I have to deal with parents or godparents, but because the symbology of the act seems so ludicrous no matter how I look at it.

The cleansing of original sin. The idea that blessing water and raining it over some baby's head somehow removes some unseen mark on them, some sin they didn't choose yet will prevent them from finding eternity. The whole thing is almost comical, given what's happened in my life.

I had two baptisms. One *Mama y Papa* had the parish priest perform in our church in Cali and one I did myself where I was bathed in their blood.

That day changed everything.

It wasn't the first time I had killed, nor would it be the last, but when I pulled the trigger, I sealed my own fate. I was accepted into a different kind of religion, one where death and destruction and sin were just ways of life.

Yet, here I stand now, in front of the baptismal font, with smiling parents and godparents and an innocent child before me asking me to save his soul from something that happened at the beginning of time—if you believe Genesis.

I never did. Even at a young age, I saw the hypocrisy of religion and hated the way everyone, including Felipe, was pulled so easily into it and convinced they needed to say certain prayers at certain times to feel the love of some deity no one has ever seen.

But after my crimson baptism, *I* became the god. The one who pulls the strings of other people's lives and strikes down those who sin against me without a second thought.

More like the Old Testament God than the one presented in the New Testament, but a god all the same.

I may not have physically been Rose, but I held all the power. Called all the shots and ensured we were respected and feared. It worked for two decades, yet now, that power is fractured, split between two who started out as one from the first moment our lives were created.

How could we have come so far together only to end this way?

It's a question I may never get an answer to. The only explanation I can fathom is that my dear brother finally succumbed to envy and pride and truly wants what he has pretended to have all these years.

The hands have been dealt, now. He wouldn't fold his cards, so that means it's time to remove him from the table altogether. It's the only way this works. And until I can accomplish that monumental task, I'll keep up the act, going through the motions, and as soon as Rowan is back in my grasp, I'll act.

No more delays.

No more hopes I might step up as Rose without drawing more familial blood.

All I need is *her*.

But she's been on the lamb for days. Days I've spent waiting for word about her and for the other shoe to drop now that at least *part* of my secret has been revealed by the attack here at the church.

Though Kat walked away relatively unscathed, the fact that the rest of the families now know Rose has a twin brother could make things quite complicated. Every day, I wait for the door to open, either Rowan coming home or one of the cartel's many enemies appearing to try to use Father Felipe for their own purposes.

It's what I would do if I were in their positions. A kidnapping to use as leverage against Rose. Someone who might offer insider information. There are any number of reasons Father Felipe might be useful to one of our enemies...yet none have appeared.

That can't last forever. But until I have Rowan back, I can't move. So until she's here, it's business as usual...

"I baptize you in the name of the Father..."

I cast a glance out at the congregation before I cup my hand and dip it into the baptismal font so I can pour Holy water onto the baby's forehead. It splashes against his smooth skin and elicits an angry cry from the newborn.

"...and of the Son..."

My focus drifts to the watching crowd again, seeking out a familiar redhead, and I give him another dousing.

"...and of the Holy Spirit."

After a final pour over the child, his father lifts him from over the font and cradles him close to try to stop his crying.

Who can blame the poor kid?

The shock of the noise of Sunday Mass coupled with having water poured over him can't be pleasant, especially when he doesn't understand what's happening. But it's one of my duties. One I must perform to keep up appearances and serve the people of St. Mary of the Angels until I can get the fuck out of these suffocating vestments for good.

And that day may be coming sooner than I had hoped.

If the text I got from my men who have been out looking for Rowan the last few days is correct and they managed to locate her, it will be the sign I need that it's time to move now.

But I still don't see her seated in any of the pews, and my frustration only grows as the baptism ceremony continues.

I clear my throat and offer a smile to the parents and Godparents standing in front of me near the font. "God the Father of our Lord Jesus Christ has freed you from sin, given you a new birth by water and the Holy Spirit, and welcomed you into his holy people. He now anoints you with the chrism of salvation. As Christ was anointed Priest, Prophet, and King, so may you live always as a member of his body, sharing everlasting life."

"Amen."

I take the bottle of sacred chrism and anoint the child on the crown of his head. His pale-blue eyes stare up at me in confusion, and he releases another wail of protest.

Right there with you, niño.

This is tortuous and tiresome. And it's the life *he* wanted so badly before that day. He actually *chose* this and looked forward to spending his time serving a rapt congregation.

Yet look at him now, after a taste of what it feels like to have the kind of power Rose does, he doesn't want to come back to this. He can't. It's hard to hold that against him, really, when I want out so badly. But it has been like two decades of penance for the sins of my youth, and now, it's time for him to pay. He may have sat in those prison walls for ten years, but there, he was a god. He had all the power and control, so it wasn't truly a prison. Not the way these clothes and this life is.

And now that I've seen the way out, that she might be on her way back here to me, I won't squander my chance any longer.

It's time to cleanse my own soul the way I am this child's. I need to tell her the truth, come clean about why she's here and what she means to the future of the Blood Rose Cartel.

There's no guarantee she won't try to run again. What I reveal may send her fleeing even faster. But deep down, I believe she'll stay. She's shown me her true colors—even if she wants to deny them. And once she's back in my arms, I'll show her mine.

FOURTEEN

FATHER FELIPE

THE DOORS to the church open, and I catch a flash of auburn out of the corner of my eye. My heart thunders against my rib cage.

They found her.

I don't even need to see her face because I would know her anywhere. Just like I can sense my brother, I can feel when she's close. As if she's the other part of me and whatever is left of my soul seeks out hers.

And even though my men usher her to the side, toward one of the rooms in the back of the church where I directed them to leave her if they found her, just knowing she's here pulls my lips into a smile that's finally genuine.

The final blessings roll off my tongue without thought, and as I move down the aisle toward the rear of the church, I fight the desire to race to Rowan. It's only years of practiced patience that keep me at the top of the steps, shaking hands and smiling as people slowly trickle out into the late morning sunlight.

When the last ones close their car doors and pull away from the curb, I turn back to the vestibule and the two men waiting for me off to the side, casting a quick glance to ensure Sister Agnes is otherwise occupied in the nave.

Aaron motions toward the closed door behind him. "She's in there."

"Where did you find her?"

If she went to Kat, or God forbid, found her way to somewhere even *more* dangerous, it could lead to a lot of very bad things even though she's back in my grasp. She could have exposed us in ways she can't even imagine.

"She was holed up at a hotel on the South Side." He motions to his buddy standing next to him —Emiliano, if I remember correctly. "We figured she didn't have any money or very little of it, and she is hard to forget. We tried every seedy hotel we could think of until we eventually located her."

"Good. Now get the fuck out of here."

He glances around at the church before refocusing his attention on me and scanning my attire, eyebrow raised. "What's up with this?"

I move on him so fast, he doesn't even have time to react before I tighten my hand around his throat. "I don't pay you to ask fucking questions."

Emiliano stands silent, watching the exchange, never lifting a finger to help his *compadre*.

The tighter I squeeze his throat, choking off his airway and cutting off oxygen to his brain, the harder he claws at my hand and wrist. His physical protest doesn't bring him any relief, though.

These men haven't worked for me long—only since I came to Chicago—so they haven't witnessed much in person in terms of what I'm capable of. Though Rose's reputation comes with built-in fear, it clearly isn't enough to keep them from stepping out of line.

But killing him with Sister Agnes lurking around wouldn't be wise. So, just as his eyes start to roll up in the back of his head, I release him to crumple on the ground.

There are more important tasks at hand than proving who is in control here.

I turn to Emiliano. "Get him the fuck out of here and wait for my call."

He inclines his head and rushes forward to drag the half-conscious man from the floor and out. Once the exterior doors have closed behind them, I make my way to the closed door, twist the knob, and push it open.

Rowan whirls around to face me, anger reddening her cheeks, hands fisted at her sides. "What the hell, Felipe?"

"Why did you leave?"

Her jaw drops. "You send two goons after me and drag me back here and then ask why *I* left? Seriously?"

I step toward her, shaking my head while holding her fiery gaze. "It's not safe. Who have you talked to since you left?"

"Who did I talk to?" She raises her pale eyebrows incredulously. "What the *hell* is going on? And who the hell are you really?"

Smart girl.

"You're asking the wrong question, *mi palomita*. You should be asking who *you* are."

Confusion clouds her gaze, and she narrows it on me. "What do you mean?"

I step farther into the room and remove my vestments, laying them on the chair to her left. She watches me silently, her chest rising and falling rapidly, pale skin pinkening with each piece of clothing I remove.

Fighting back a knowing grin takes every ounce of willpower I have. Finally, I slowly start to unbutton my shirt.

She gapes at me and takes a step back. "What the hell are you doing?"

"You wanted the truth, Rowan? Well, I'm about to give it to you. Every dirty inch of it." I reach the final button and pull my shirt fully open, exposing the myriad of tattoos across my chest and abdomen.

She sucks in a sharp breath, and something else flashes to the surface of her green eyes, the desire I've seen there before that she always tries so hard to deny herself. The same one I've always felt for her but denied myself because of the circumstances.

"I am not who or what you think I am, Rowan. Neither are you."

She shakes her head and averts her gaze. "I don't understand. You keep saying all these cryptic things, but I don't know what any of it means."

I close the distance between us quickly and capture her chin in my hand, squeezing tightly so she's forced to look at me and not move away. "I'll tell you everything, *mi palomita*. All the dirty, dangerous, ugly truths."

And then, I'll take Chicago.

ACCEPTING SLOTH

What is right is often forgotten by what is convenient.

-Bodie Then

ONE

ROWAN

"I AM NOT who or what you think I am, Rowan. Neither are you."

Felipe's words slam into me, one by one, hammering at the very thing I've been struggling with for so damn long—the uncertainty fogging my memories and past.

I shake my head, trying to dispel the confusion clouding my brain from this entire situation, from everything that's been happening with Felipe recently, a man I thought I knew and thought I understood. With him standing here like this, heat in his gaze and shirtless, all his hard muscles and the myriad of tattoos on display, I can't even look him in the eye.

These aren't the words or actions of a pious priest. The sexual energy oozing from the man in front of me is all wrong for someone who committed himself to God and the church. So are the words he's speaking.

All of this is so wrong.

"I don't understand, Felipe. You keep saying all these cryptic things, but I don't know what any of it means."

He closes the distance between us so quickly that I don't have time to back away or prepare myself and captures my chin in his hand, squeezing it tightly and forcing me to look up at him. "I'll tell you everything, *mi palomita*. All the dirty, dangerous, ugly truths."

Finally...

It's all I ever wanted since the day he showed up at Kat's Cradle and told me I had to come with him, warned me I was in danger and that I needed to get away from Kat to somewhere safe.

For some reason, on that day, I believed him despite all the reasons not to accept the word of a strange man arriving at the brothel, making wild statements.

Something about him put me at ease. The sincerity of his plea for me to come with him, his promise that I would be safe at the church. Kindness in his dark eyes I rarely saw from any man who came to me at Kat's place.

The vision that flashed in my head that day slams to the front of my brain again, standing here with Felipe in his own church.

A large crucifix hanging above an altar—though, it isn't the modern one just outside this door in the church where Felipe has kept me hidden.

This one is different. More rustic. Simpler. Older.

A sense of well-being and calm settles over me, and a voice rings out, steady and determined.

Only it isn't Felipe's voice, accented by his South American upbringing. This one is tinted with a lilting Irish brogue and holds a familiarity I can't place.

Someone hugs me to them tightly and presses a kiss on top of my head.

"Rowan..." Felipe's voice jerks me back to the here and now, standing in the small room at the back of St. Mary of the Angels. He had his goons drag me back here, away from the safety of the seedy hotel I managed to keep myself hidden at for the last week—safety from this man and all the feelings he's stirred up in me.

The confusion. The lust. The shame. The regret.

He narrows his eyes on me and brushes a thumb across my cheek. "Where did you just go?"

"I...I don't know." Tears burn my eyes, threatening to fall like they have so many times over the last few months. "I keep having these...I don't know what they are. Memories? Ever since you brought me here. They come at the strangest times, and I don't understand any of them."

He releases his grip on my chin and uses his hand to brush my wild red hair back behind my ear in a move that's tender and comforting—but not in the way it should be from a priest. The move is too familiar, too personal, too heavy in unspoken words and desires. "That's because you've been lied to your entire life, Rowan. You've been used by dangerous people who have a very particular purpose. People who didn't care what it did to you."

"I don't understand!" My chest tightens, making it difficult for me to suck any air into my lungs, and the room spins around me slightly.

I feel like a broken record, stuck on some endless loop, but my brain can't process any of what's happening. Too many things don't make sense. They don't add up. There are too many missing pieces and holes.

But Felipe seems to have the answers.

"What's your earliest memory, *mi palomita? Real* memory that you hold and can feel and know that it actually happened?"

Almost instantly, bile climbs up my throat, and I squeeze my eyes closed again and shake my head. "No. Please don't make me go there."

I buried those things so deep such a long time ago that I don't ever want to relive them. If I let myself get dragged back there, I might completely fall apart, and the idea of doing that in front of Felipe somehow feels so wrong when he's so sure, so strong.

"I understand you're scared, Rowan." He slips his fingers under my chin and gently tilts my face up. "You should be. But if you want to truly understand what's happening, we have to go back to the beginning."

"The beginning?" I open my eyes and meet his stormy dark ones that flicker with concern. "I don't even know how to."

"What is your earliest memory?"

The image slams into my brain so strong that I stagger back; the only reason I don't fall is because of Felipe's firm grip around me with his tattooed arm.

"A house. An old one. A dark room...other kids with me..."

The cries...

The sniffling...

The begging...

They all fill my ears as if I were hearing them today rather than over twenty years ago.

"A squeaky hinge on the door as it opens..."

My heart beats faster, slamming against my ribs, panic rushing adrenaline through my veins.

"It's a sound we all know. A sound we all dread." I suck in several short breaths. "He's here!"

Felipe tightens his hold on me, pulling me close against his bare chest. Heat from his body seeps through my dress and into me. "You're safe here. But you have to remember."

"We cower together in a corner, terrified we'll be the one he picks." I cling to Felipe's shoulders, trying to use him to keep me grounded in the present, not wanting to get pulled into the past. "His footsteps echo across the creaky old floor. He doesn't say anything. Just reaches down and grabs the small girl next to me."

A sob slips from my lips, but I can't tell if it's in the memory or now.

"The girl clings to me with every bit of energy she has left in her tiny, frail body...but it isn't enough. He lifts her easily from the floor and carries her to the door. Her eyes meet mine over his shoulder, and she cries out a name."

"What's the name, *mi palomita?*"

I squeeze my eyes closed tighter, searching the memory that always seems so vivid up until this very point every time it comes to me. Then it always goes dark, fuzzy, unclear. "I'm never able to hear the name, only see her mouth opening and closing, forming the letters..."

"You know the name, Rowan. Tell me what name she called out."

Pain throbs at my temples with the effort to unravel the hidden memory.

Her face over and over.

Her lips opening and closing, forming the letters.

"Nessa. She's saying Nessa."

"And?"

I open my eyes again and meet Felipe's. "She's talking to me."

His lips curl into a half-smile, like he's proud of what I've unraveled. "That's because it's the name your parents gave you before you were taken from them."

TWO

ROWAN

Taken from them?

His words ring in my ears, the smooth timbre of his Colombian accent finally dragging me fully from the memory and painfully dropping me back in the present.

"What do you mean *taken?*"

How? Why? From where? By whom?

Felipe's gaze softens, almost back to the way he always looked standing in front of his congregation. "I'm sorry you have to learn it this way—"

He grasps my right arm and runs a finger over the jagged, red scar that's been there for as long as I can remember, one I have no memory of receiving. It's one more thing from my past I've locked away to avoid having to relive the anguish of whatever happened in my childhood.

A psychiatrist would have a field day with me, but it has worked. I've been able to live my life, to be relatively happy, or at least content, especially since going to work for Kat. Until Felipe arrived and unraveled everything, I thought I knew and understood about myself and my past.

Something clatters outside the closed door, and Felipe jerks back from me, his eyes immediately narrowing on the potential threat. He holds up a finger to his lips to silence me and cautiously makes his way over to the door.

Without his vestments, the white collar, or the black shirt covering his tattoos, he looks nothing like the priest I thought I knew. This man is something, some*one* different.

A switch has been flipped somehow. The way he carries himself. The way he speaks. The sexual energy he puts out. All of it seems to come so naturally, seems to fit him somehow. But it's the polar opposite of what he was like and how I saw him only a few weeks ago.

Who is this man?

He moves to the door, listens, then motions for me to step back into the corner before he slowly opens it and looks around while reaching for something in his boot. The glint of a blade in his hand makes me stagger back until my shoulders hit the wall.

Why does he keep a knife in his boot?

None of this makes any sense. It all feels like some sort of terrible dream I can't wake up from— a true nightmare that's bringing back memories I pushed down so deeply.

Felipe takes one step out, then another, until he vanishes from my sight. I hold my breath, waiting for something, *anything*, to wake me from this.

His words replay in my head...

That's because it's the name your parents gave you before you were taken from them.

Another vision strikes me. A red-haired woman laughing, swinging me in her arms outside in a field. Warmth floods my chest, a sense of peace, contentment.

Who is she? My mother?

A loud thump sounds from the vestibule outside the door, dragging me from the memory, but I don't dare call out for Felipe.

I wait for what feels like forever—the only sound the blood rushing in my ears.

Felipe barrels back into the room, knife between his teeth, dragging an unconscious, bloody man behind him.

"Oh, my God. What...who?"

His dark eyes meet mine, and he drops the man unceremoniously onto the tile floor, then races over to me and grabs my hand in his blood-covered one. "We have to go. It's not safe here."

"Who is he?" I examine the stranger, searching for anything familiar, anything that might explain who he is or why he's here. "What did you do?"

Felipe growls low, a sound I never heard emanate from him when I thought he was a man of God. "Too many people have seen me now and know where I am, who I am. That explosion exposed that Rose's brother is here at the church. It's not safe for either of us here anymore. Others will come for me—for us."

He tugs on my hand, grabs his clothes from the pile on the chair, and drags me out of the small room, closing the door behind us.

I look back toward the solid piece of wood concealing the body of the man who may be dead for all I know. "But—"

"I'll have someone come take care of that little problem."

Little problem? An unconscious, bloody man is nothing more than a little problem to Felipe?

I open my mouth to object, to ask Felipe to explain what's happening, but he tugs on my hand, pulling me through the vestibule and up the main aisle of the nave.

His eyes dart around all the darkened corners of the church the same way Kat's men always watched for dangers at Kat's Cradle. As if it's something he's done every day of his life. Like threats might always be right around the corner.

Who the hell is he?

Definitely not what he appears. He isn't a pious priest. If he were, he couldn't have done what he just did. He wouldn't carry a knife. He wouldn't seem so unaffected by using it on someone. He wouldn't have men working for him who can hunt someone down the way they did me and "take care of" the person we just left bleeding out in that room.

His large warm hand wrapped around mine drags me deeper through the church, down the back hallway, and into his office in the rectory.

He slams the door behind us and throws the lock before dropping my hand and rushing over to his desk. His jaw clenched, he tugs open a drawer, pulls out something, and sets it on the desktop.

A gun?

"Wh-why the hell do you have a gun?" My focus zeros in on the dark metal sitting so innocuously on the wooden desk. I search for any explanation, *anything* that might explain what's happening. Only two people I know are connected to Felipe who come to mind—Kat and the man who shares Felipe's face. "Does this have anything to do with your brother?"

It's the only logical leap I can make, given who and what his brother is—perhaps someone is looking for Rose and hoping to use Felipe to get to him.

Felipe looks up at me, his jaw hard and something dark in his gaze I've never seen before. "This has *everything* to do with my brother. And you."

Me?

My entire body starts shaking, a cold sweat breaking out on my skin. The legs that have somehow managed to hold me up give out, and I stumble forward to grip the back of the chair facing his desk to steady myself while he continues to tear through his drawers, searching for something.

The room around me spins, the walls closing in on me until everything is a pinpoint of light blinding my vision. I dig my fingers into the leather of the chair, my nails biting into it so hard that they threaten to break.

"Rowan?" Felipe's voice comes low and harsh. "Rowan!" He calls out to me again, but this time it sounds distant, like someone calling for me from a mile away.

The bright light slowly shrinks into nothing and darkness takes over.

THREE

ROWAN

I RETURN to the world slowly.

A faint light around the edges of my foggy brain...

Heaviness in my limbs...

Something soft underneath me...

Where am I?

Panic grips my heart, stalling in my chest, and I jerk upright, trying to suck in air that won't seem to fill my lungs.

Strong, warm arms wrap around me, securing me in place against a hard chest. "You're okay, *mi palomita*. You're safe."

Felipe...

His smooth, accented voice sends a rush of calm through me, and his secure hold on me keeps me grounded.

"What happened? Where are we?" I blink away the remnants of the nightmare I was stuck in and scan the dark room, taking in the sleek modern furniture and high ceilings—definitely not the church or rectory.

"One of my safe houses."

"Safe house?" I shake my head, but that does nothing to clear away the confusion over everything happening. "Felipe, what the hell is going on?"

"I'm sorry that remembering and learning the truth is putting you through this, but it's the only way for you to understand." He cups my cheek and brushes his thumb across it softly, in a rhythm that soothes some of the anxiety threatening to steal my breath. "After the memory you told me about earlier—the house and the man—what do you remember? "

Nothing. I want to remember nothing...

Bits and pieces float around my head. Words. Sounds. Places. People. But all the specifics seem just out of reach.

"Not much until I was about fourteen."

"What happened then?"

I escaped.

It was when my life really began. When I started to understand what it really meant to live. Freedom to be my own person, make my own decisions.

"I just remember running. Running as fast and as hard as I could, and then I found some other teenagers on the street. Kids like me who had nowhere to go. We protected each other. Watched each other's backs."

The memories of *those* years bring a peaceful calm and put a smile on my lips. Unlike the ones I've always waged war against, these are mostly good, outweighing the bad.

"We were in New York. I stayed there for a long time, made enough to take care of myself and keep myself safe. But then I heard about the opportunity at Kat's Cradle from an old friend who had moved to Chicago. So, I hopped on a plane and flew here."

His dark eyes assess me, the intelligence there as clear as it was the first time we met. "You don't remember anything else about your childhood?"

"Bits and pieces. Flashes that I can't really tell if they are memories or dreams." I fist my hands in his shirt, my frustration tightening my fingers until it almost hurts. "Please tell me what you know. I need to know the truth."

"The reason I came for you at Kat's Cradle was that you're important, in so many ways. You are not who you think you are. My guess is you've repressed the memories so much that you can't recall it anymore."

"Can't remember *what?*" I hold my breath and wait for him to answer, the possibilities turning my stomach and making my hands tremble where they still cling to him.

"You were born in Ireland."

"I was?"

He searches my face as if his statement is going to suddenly bring back all of my memories from the last twenty-plus years.

The Irish brogue at the church fills my ears again...

"What happened to my parents?"

His jaw hard, Felipe unravels me from around him and pushes to his feet to pace near the end of the bed, almost like he's concerned about being so close to me when he reveals the entire story. "Your father was involved in the IRA."

"What?"

"He made a lot of enemies. A lot of people who would see harm done to him. Or his family..."

"Oh, my God."

"One of those who wished to harm your father, to make a statement, bombed the church where your family attended Mass, where your uncle was the priest."

"My uncle?"

That voice plays in my head again, the sound comforting, familiar. Because I *knew* him. He was my uncle. My family...

And likely why I was drawn to Felipe and the church in the first place. Why it's always felt so safe and like home.

"It injured dozens and killed nineteen people, including your parents and your uncle. But you survived."

"How?"

"They waited until you were clear of the building...outside in the church courtyard playing because your father's enemies had plans for you." He takes a long, deep inhale, his hands fisted at his sides so tightly his knuckles whiten. "They sold you, *mi palomita*. Used you as a way to fill their coffers."

"The man in the house..."

He nods slowly, his body tense with barely restrained anger. "I don't know who he was. Maybe the broker, a middleman, just a stop along the way. I know you eventually ended up in the States, in New York."

Flashes of a basement room and a locked door spring into my head. "I remember it..."

My entire body starts to vibrate again, and Felipe settles on the edge of the bed to pull me into his arms. It shouldn't feel so good being held by a priest like this, to be in the arms of a man who took vows and promised certain things. But somehow, it does. He strokes my hair gently, cradling my head against his neck, and I sink into his embrace, questions still bouncing around my brain at breakneck speed.

"I don't understand why that puts me in danger now, though..."

Felipe pulls back and cups my face between his palms. "Because, Rowan, your whole family didn't die in the church that day. You have a brother who survived and has spent years looking for you."

"A brother?"

He nods. "His name is Galen McGinnis."

That name stops me cold, and goosebumps break out over my skin. "*The* Galen McGinnis. The head of the Irish mob here in Chicago?"

Felipe inclines his head in confirmation. "Ever since he was old enough to understand what happened, he's been looking for you. It's why he came to the U.S. in the first place. Someone got a lead that suggested you'd been sent somewhere in the States. Since your family already had connections to those in control in Chicago at that time, he came over and worked his way to the top while he continued his search for you. Unsuccessfully."

I have a brother. A family. Someone who has been looking for me.

The new reality that Felipe has just thrust upon me chokes my breath. "But why didn't you just tell him? Tell *me*? He could've protected me from anyone who wanted to use me against him, right?"

He brushes hair from my face. "Oh, *mi palomita*, you are so naïve about so many things considering the life you've led and the things you've been subjected to. There's so much you don't understand about the way this world works. Or our roles in it."

Something about the cold way he delivers his words sends an icy chill flooding through my veins. This isn't the man who came to me at Kat's Cradle. This isn't the man who stood at the altar and preached the love of God and forgiveness. This man is someone darker, someone far more dangerous.

"Who the hell are you?"

"I go by a lot of different names—Felipe...Andres...Rose..."

I shift away from him, out of his reach, pressing my back to the headboard, as far from this stranger as I can be. "I don't understand. I met your brother, Andres...Rose, at the church when he was shot. How can you be all those people?"

"That's a rather long story, *mi palomita*, but it's one you need to hear."

FOUR

20 YEARS AGO

FELIPE

THE ROAR of an engine jerks me awake, and I blink away the lingering remnants of sleep as I push myself up on the mattress. Felipe's bed on the other side of the room sits empty, and given how high the sun has already risen, he's likely been at the church with Father Nolan for some time already.

At this time, *Mama y Papa* should be long gone, out in the fields working, feeding the animals, and taking care of everything else on the farm.

They didn't tell me they were expecting anyone today.

A car door slams outside, and I climb from bed and make my way toward the front of the house. The knock comes hard and heavy at the door, and a dark sense of foreboding settles over me, my stomach tightening in a way it hasn't before.

One thing I've learned from my time on the streets, trying to make a name for myself, is that you can't show any fear. Your adversary can sense it a mile away and any weaknesses you may have will be exploited.

I steel myself for what may be on the other side of the door and pull it open. Elonzo Medina stands outside, wearing a crisp off-white suit that looks every bit as expensive as it surely is. His right-hand man, who never leaves his side when he ventures away from his home, lingers beside him, arms crossed over his barrel chest.

Elonzo offers me a wide smile he's clearly practiced and perfected over the years—one designed to lull people into a false sense of security before he does whatever he has planned for them. "*Buenos días*." He glances behind me into the house. "Are your parents home?"

My stomach turns again, and I peek behind me even though I know they aren't here. "No. They're out in the fields."

He nods as if it's the answer he expected and flashes another grin at me. "May we come in?"

No.

The Medina cartel is the most powerful in Cali, and they've already made it very clear what they want from us—something *Papa* will never give them. But I can't say no to this request. They would just come in through force, anyway.

I step back from the door and allow them to enter. They scan the room and glance down the small hallway toward the bedrooms at the rear.

"You are Andres, are you not?"

The fact that Felipe and I share a face usually works in my favor. It makes it easier to pull off switching places when it benefits me. But I've also worked hard on the streets, to build a reputation, to try to establish myself, to be the type of man Elonzo Medina is, one who holds immense power and instills fear.

And he knows me.

It may be the opening I've been waiting for, an opportunity to join the ranks of the most powerful organization in our region. Maybe he isn't here for the land at all but he came for me.

"I am. Why?"

The grin he gives me holds a sinister tilt. "Because I have a proposition for you."

Crossing my arms over my chest, I stare down the man. I'm barely fifteen and have nothing to offer except what I've earned on the streets. "What do you want?"

He spreads out his arms wide. "This. And as you know, my last meeting with your parents was not as productive as I had hoped."

"No." I fist my hands at my sides. "This land has been in my father's family for generations."

"I know, *mijo*. They made that very clear the last time we were here." His smile falters, his face hardening into the pure darkness I would expect from this man. "This is why I came to speak with *you* directly. Because you have a reputation that suggests you will be able to see the situation clearly."

"What is it you think I can do? It isn't mine to sell."

His sly grin returns. "Not yet. You inherit this land should your parents die, do you not?"

I freeze, the implication of the statement slamming against my chest like the bullets they're sure to put into *Mama y Papa* as soon as they can find them. "Is that a threat?"

A low, deep chuckle slips from his mouth, and his minion next to him joins in his laughter.

"No, Andres, it's a promise of what is to come. With your parents out of the way, it would open a path for us to take this land we so badly need for our operations. And it would also open the door to you to join our organization." He crosses his hands behind his back and eyes me. "I've been watching you over the last year. I've seen how you operate on the streets. You may be a small-time crook now, but you have potential. You have the intelligence and foresight to become something so much more. And I can help mold you into what you want to be."

"What do you want me to do?"

He walks slowly around the room and examines the family photo on the wall. "Agree to sell us the land and join the organization as my protégé. All you have to do is prove your loyalty to me." He pulls a gun from inside his suit coat. "Do what it takes to advance the organization and cement your position within it."

"You want me to kill my parents?"

He steps forward and places the gun in my hand but doesn't remove his from it. "I want you to remove the obstacles to our advancement."

A cold sweat breaks out over my skin, and I clench my jaw to bite back the automatic retort sitting on my tongue that would likely get me killed.

I've had my differences with *Mama y Papa* over the years. Rebelled against their values, the strict religious beliefs, and what they wanted for me, but removing them from my life, from this world, never even crossed my mind.

I shake my head. "I can't. They're my parents."

Elonzo sneers, taking another step closer to me. "You're a grown man in a boy's body, Andres. You know what you want and how to get it."

"My brother and sister..."

He offers a little half-shrug. "It is my understanding that your brother already has his future mapped out with the church. And your sister will be well cared for. I promise you that she will have a life your parents never could have offered her, a life you could never offer her on your own."

All the dreams I've ever had for my future and those of Felipe and Sofia flash before my eyes—money, power, a beautiful home, anything else we could ever want. The things we will never have in this house. But *Mama y Papa's* faces quickly fill my vision.

"I can't." I try to tug my hand from under the weapon but he holds it firm.

"Then it will happen without you, and I will instruct my men to make it a painful, prolonged process. They defied me by denying my most generous offer. They should've known what they were doing and what was coming."

Images of all the brutal things the cartel has done to its enemies now flood my mind.

Dismemberment.

Burning people alive.

Forcing families to watch their loved ones dying in agony.

I can't let that happen to them.

No matter how hard what he's demanding might be, I have to do it to save them from something even worse.

I pull the gun from Elonzo's hand, and he offers a satisfied grin, knowing he's won.

"I thought you might see it our way. You made the right decision, Andres."

It feels more like I just sold my soul to *El Diablo*.

Sofia wails from the other room—awoken by the talking or maybe some sort of innate ability to know her own life is about to change.

Elonzo clasps my shoulder and squeezes gently. "See that it's done before your brother returns home...or there will be more bullets necessary."

I swallow the bile rising up my throat and give him a little half nod of agreement. He goes toward the rear of the house and *Mama y Papa's* room, where Sofia lies, crying in her cradle. I stand frozen, unable to move as he reappears in the room, cradling her as if she were his own child.

"My wife and I have always wanted a daughter. *Mijita* will be loved."

He steps around me, holding her, and I fight against the desire to raise the gun in my hand and fire it at him for taking my little sister. But it wouldn't do any good. His man would stop me before I ever got off a shot.

The two men exit the front door, and their car's engine roars to life. I stand dumbstruck in the house I've lived in my entire life, knowing what it is I have to do in order to save *Mama y Papa from* unimaginable pain and torture.

I have to be the one who kills them.

FIVE

ROWAN

"And from that day on, I have been Felipe and he has been Andres. He has been 'Rose,' but I have been the one calling all the shots. I am the *real* Rose, the real brains behind the Blood Rose Cartel, even if it got its name from what my brother did to Medina. He is nothing but a body, a stand-in, someone who could play the role while I remain faithfully hidden by the church. And it worked flawlessly. Until he got a taste of what this kind of power and influence really feels like and decided to challenge me."

Felipe's hands tighten into fists where they rest on the bed, his knuckles whitening. I knew things were tense with his brother when he was recuperating from his wounds at the church, but the kind of anger that Felipe holds for him borders on the wrath described in the book Felipe preaches from.

A book that clearly means absolutely nothing to him. It can't with what he's done, with how he's deceived the world and me. With all the blood he's spilled and been responsible for.

Throughout the entire story he just told, all the sordid and bloody details of who he is and what's led him to where he is today, I've felt like a noose has been slowly tightening around my throat.

Each revelation brought with it new questions and more uncertainty when I didn't even think that was possible after what he told me about myself.

I was so damn wrong.

The man in front of me is a stranger—not the one who came for me and told me he would protect me from the dangers that lurked in the dark.

He is *the darkness. He is the* epitome *of danger.*

I open and close my mouth, unable to find the words to respond to what he just revealed. It doesn't make any sense, yet, it explains so much. "You're not a priest..."

A slow grin spreads across his lips—one filled with heat and promise—and he catches my chin in his hand and squeezes. "I am, *mi palomita*. I went to seminary and took the vows just as my brother had planned. Only I knew that every single word I said was a lie and that I had no intention of fulfilling my promise to the Good Lord. It was all an act, all a show. One that I'm very good at."

A vise squeezes my chest. "Very." I stare into the hard, dark eyes of a complete stranger. "I don't know you at all."

"Yes, you do, Rowan. I'm the man who took you from being used by men who only wanted one thing from you and brought you to a place where there were no expectations of you. No one asked anything of you, and everything I said to you is the truth. Every word of it."

He leans in and brushes his lips against my trembling ones. My body and mind war—simultaneously wanting to push him away and drag him closer. He's far more dangerous than anyone else ever has been to me in my life—at least, what I can remember of it. Yet something about him pulls me in, makes me feel safe and protected. Even knowing the truth. Even knowing what he did to his parents. To his brother. To all the people the Blood Rose Cartel has destroyed. All of it.

I still can't deny the attraction I feel for him. The way my body trembles in his presence, the pull I feel toward him whenever we're in the room together. The way heat floods through my core when he's near.

Sitting here in his arms is no different. Every part of my brain tells me to run, to make another break for freedom, to put as much distance between myself and *Father* Felipe and as possible, yet I lean closer, crave the heat of his body and the feel of his touch against my skin.

"What do you want from me, Felipe? And don't say 'nothing' because after what you just told me, I know that wouldn't be true."

He grins, apparently amused by my calling him out rather than angered by it. "Do you know why I call you *mi palomita*—my little dove?"

I shake my head. This whole time, I had just assumed it was a pet name.

"It's because you will be the one to help end this war, Rowan. The peace offering to a man who wants nothing more than to locate his sister. I'm going to go to Galen McGinnis and tell him I found you. I'm going to forge a relationship with him that will not be easily broken. One in which our two families will work together to ensure the future of them both, with me in ultimate control."

"Is that all I am to you? A way to get to a man who would otherwise shoot you—not only in the back but also the front—the moment he lays eyes on you?"

"I told you, Rowan, every word I ever said to you is true. You might be the only thing in this world I want more than I want to control the city and to run the organization I built from the bottom up. With you by my side, I'll have everything I ever wanted."

"I wish I could believe you. I wish I could take the words coming out of your mouth to heart..." I take an unsteady breath, averting my gaze because looking him in the eye makes this ten times harder. "But how can I trust anything you say to me after all the lies you've told? When it's all based on the ultimate deception?"

He captures my face in his hands and jerks up my head aggressively, forcing me to meet his gaze. "I've told more lies in my life than I can count, but hear me now when I say, I would die before I let anyone touch you again. I want to give you everything you ever dreamed of, everything you never had. I want you to forget the fear that keeps you awake at night, the memories and nightmares that haunt you every day."

"And what if *you* are the nightmare?"

His jaw hardens, and a muscle there tics. "The only people who need to be afraid of me are those outside this room. I'll give you everything and more. But it will take a lot of blood being spilled to get there. Are you with me, *mi palomita*?"

I don't even have to think about my answer. He's saying all the right things, promising what I've longed for so many times—a safe place to land. A man who loves me and would burn down the world for me. An end to the terror in my mind. A way to forget the past and leave it where it belongs.

But only one word feels right.

Only one word sits on the tip of my tongue.

I square my shoulders and prepare to face the ramifications of what I'm about to say to this very dangerous man. "No."

SIX

ROWAN

Crack.

The sharp sound jolts me awake from the restless sleep I managed to fall into after I made Felipe—or Andres...or Rose...or whoever the hell he is—leave the room.

After his confession and even in spite of his promises, I couldn't handle being in here with him anymore. Not when I don't know what to think or who to trust, not when my attraction to him still rages on despite everything he told me.

Another crack rips through the night air, pulling a scream from somewhere deep in my chest.

Gunfire. Someone found us.

Heavy footsteps sound outside the bedroom door, and it flies open. I scramble back against the headboard, but the man who enters isn't a threat to anything but my body and soul.

Felipe rushes over to the side of the bed, his eyes wide and scanning the room and me. "You all right, *mi palomita?*"

Another loud crack sounds, but this time, I'm awake enough to process what it is.

Thunder.

The sound of driving rain slamming against the window panes and pelting the roof fills the room, and the next crack of thunder doesn't make me jump nearly as much.

I press my hand against my racing heart, trying to pull air into my lungs in quick pants. "The thunder...I thought it was gunfire."

Felipe climbs onto the bed and drags me into his arms, all hard, warm exposed skin. Somehow, all the reasons I shouldn't let him don't matter. Not when I need the comfort he can offer.

He pulls my head against his neck, and a familiar scent envelops me, one I haven't allowed myself to enjoy for fear of what that would mean for my eternal soul, which has already been tarnished so badly.

"Don't worry, *mi palomita.* No one will ever get close enough to you again to hurt you like that."

"What about you?"

He pulls back, and his hard gaze meets mine. "What about me?"

"You've lied to me since the moment we met. How am I supposed to ever believe anything you tell me again? How am I supposed to believe anything was real? That you won't hurt me."

"I'm sorry it had to be this way, but I lied to everyone. Even my own sister doesn't know the truth about what happened that day or that Felipe and I switched places. She was too young to know the difference, and we've bent over backward to keep her in the dark for the past twenty years."

"You didn't have to keep *me* in the dark. You could've told me the truth from the beginning."

Thunder crashes and rattles the windows and building, the storm now closer, hovering right above the safehouse—wherever we might be. Rain lashes against the window, the sound almost melodic. The tormented sky mimics the tempest inside me, swirling with anger and threatening to crack the world right open.

"No, I couldn't, Rowan. If I had, you would have run. Either straight into the arms of your brother or away from all of it where none of us could ever find you again."

He's probably right about that.

The truths have been too real, too volatile. And the more memories that come back, the more I want them to stay buried. Finally meeting my brother will mean facing all of it, something I'm not sure I'm ready for or ever will be.

"I can't trust you, Felipe. Or Andres, or Rose. I don't even know who you are."

"Yes, you do. I'm the man who is telling you that I will do anything I have to in order to protect you from all the evils of this world. I'll do anything to give you everything you've always wanted. A home. A man who loves you. Never having to worry about money or safety again."

"You've taken vows before. Vows you never meant."

"The only vow that matters to me is the one I make to you, Rowan. You will never want for anything in his life again as long as you are by my side."

"You want me to stay with you?"

"Of course, I do."

"As what?"

Captive. Friend. Lover?

I still don't understand what he wants from me. Everything is so jumbled in my head—all the lies and ulterior motives. All the possibilities.

"As whatever you want to be. But I'm telling you right now that I want you, Rowan. I've always wanted you."

He grinds his hard cock, restrained only by his boxer briefs, up against my ass, and I have to bite back a groan as my body responds.

His white collar flashes in my head again. A memory of him on the altar giving the sermon. Him in the confessional booth while I told him of the dirty fantasies I had about him. Him undressing in that room at the back of the church, walking toward me with determination and purpose.

"Tell me you don't want this, Rowan. Tell me you don't want me. Look into my eyes and do it." His hand slides up my inner thigh and stops just short of the place that yearns for his touch. "Come on, *mi palomita*, tell me."

I want to. I want to rail and scream and beat my hands against his bare chest until I can't anymore. I want to tell him no, tell him that I don't want him or this.

But there have already been so many lies. I don't want any more of them in my life.

"I can't do that—"

He crashes his lips down against mine, capturing the little gasp of pleasure I release, and his hand shifts up to cup my aching core. I groan into his mouth and shift on his lap to give him better access to where I want him.

His kiss is demanding, desperate, claiming, and I roll my hips and grind down against his cock, earning me a little growl from somewhere deep in his chest. The sound goes straight between my legs, making me clasp for something I don't have.

The needy mewl that slips from my lips to his makes him drag his head back and kiss his way down my neck and over to my ear.

"This is what I've dreamed of every night since I brought you home. What I fantasized about every waking moment of every day. Having you like this, in my arms, so I can show you how badly I want you. How badly I *need* you."

They're the words I've longed to hear—ones that sound so sincere, so absolute. They wash away the uncertainty weighing on my mind.

I move on his lap again, swinging a leg over so I'm straddling him, pressing my wet core against his hard cock in his boxer briefs. One tiny shred of fabric separates us the same way the white collar did before I learned the truth.

My head might be filled with a million different thoughts, might be twisting me in a thousand different directions, but one thing has never wavered. And that's my desire for this man. The man I thought I could never have. The man I thought God would punish me for wanting.

And now that he's touching me, now that his mouth is pressing to mine, all I can think about is how good it's going to feel to sin.

SEVEN

ROWAN

Each eager brush of his lips, every frantic touch of his hand, the press of his hard body to mine only wind me tighter and tighter, the building pressure enough to make it feel like I'll explode and shatter across the room if I don't get what I need soon.

And I need *him.*

Even if I don't want to. Even if a war still wages inside me. Even when everything is so uncertain.

A strange combination of exhilarating power and reckless abandon drive me on without any hope to slow down and consider the consequences of what we're doing.

My hips move of their own accord, grinding against him like some horny teenager dry-humping her boyfriend for the first time rather than a grown woman who has a sexual history that is sure to get me sent straight to Hell when my day finally comes.

I reach between us and slip my hand inside the waistband of his boxers to grasp his hard cock in my palm, brushing my thumb across the head and spreading the drop of pre-cum. He growls against my lips and kisses me harder and deeper, probing his tongue inside my mouth as his hips jerk to meet my strokes.

"*Te voy a destruir...*"

I have no idea what he just said, but I certainly understand the sentiment.

Thunder rumbles again, shaking the roof and rattling the windowpanes as I push down the offending fabric and guide the head of his cock to my pussy. I drag it through my arousal, and his grip tightens on my hips before one hand shifts up to my hair and tugs it harshly, pulling my mouth from his to lock our gazes.

"Now you know the truth, every bit of it. If we do this, you're mine. Do you understand that? Mine forever. There is no walking away from this, no escaping once I've had you."

His words should terrify me, especially given the memories that have resurfaced the last few days. The thought of being *owned* by someone, of never being able to leave, should still my heart and freeze my body. But instead, knowing I'll be *his,* that he'll use all his power to protect me and hold me close, sends a rush of heat and excitement through me that makes me shudder with anticipation of everything that is to come with this man.

"Answer me, *mi palomita.*" He fists my hair even tighter until the sharp bite of pain on my scalp makes me whimper. "Tell me you understand."

I take in a shaky breath and stare into the dark pools of desire and determination. There isn't any room for confusion here. He means every single word he says. It's a warning *and* a promise all in one statement. "I understand, *Andres.*"

Completely.

"Fuck..." He grips my hip with his free hand and drives up into me, impaling me on his hard length and stealing the air straight from my lungs in the process. "Rowan..."

"Oh, God." I squeeze my eyes shut against the intrusion, his dick stretching me and filling me the way no other man ever has.

It reaches places deep inside me I thought didn't exist anymore—the ones that crave this kind of connection, the ones that are so dangerous for a woman in my position.

But that was before...

Before Felipe...

Before the truth...

Before my life really began...

Because as I ride the man with three names, rising and sinking down on him in a steady, reckless rhythm, I know his warning is true. I do belong to him now. And I always will. He is the man who rescued me from a life that wasn't mine. One I never should have had. One forced upon me by bad men with bad intentions. He is the man who will ensure my future. One without pain. One without fear. *Our* future.

He releases my hair, digs his fingers into my hips, and braces his feet to drive up into me harder and faster, more desperate even than I am. To make his point. To stake his claim on me. To ensure I understand it fully.

And I do.

This isn't a man who does things lightly or accepts anything less than what he wants and thinks he deserves. He isn't someone who will walk away or let *me* walk away. This means I'm here forever —however long that may be.

He presses his mouth to mine, and it's almost sweet, his tongue gliding along my lips, begging for entrance and compliance even though he's already stolen my heart. There isn't anything else I can give him. He has it all now.

I may not know who this man really is. I may have my doubts about what he wants and what he has planned. But one thing I'm clear about is how he feels about me.

I've seen it in the way he looks at me. Felt it in his delicate touches over the months I've been with him, hiding at the church. Heard it in the words he said from the altar and in the confessional. Even though he couldn't act on it, I *felt* it, knew something was building between us. Something that would have ruined him and his place as the congregation's spiritual leader. Something that would have made him choose lust over his vows. Something that made me *run* rather than have it destroy his life. Something that's coming to fruition now that he's exposed the reality I never knew existed.

He reaches back and jerks my hair again, angling my head away so he can kiss along my neck and tug down the top of my dress, freeing my breasts. His dark eyes burn with lust as he lowers his head to suck one nipple into his mouth while I continue to meet the movements of his hips with mine, cresting together, each of us seeking the same release.

A release from the tension that's been building between us for weeks. A release of the lies that have stood between us. A release from the reality of what waits for us outside this room. A release of *everything*.

"Oh, God. Oh, God..."

The combination of him sucking and nipping at my breasts and grinding my clit against his pelvis with every thrust brings my orgasm barreling down on me so hard the entire room goes bright white before Felipe growls and thrusts deep, coming inside me and dragging me down on top of him while the whole world goes black again.

EIGHT

FATHER FELIPE

"*DISCÚLPAME*, I didn't mean to keep you waiting."

Galen climbs to his feet from the chair near the window of the hotel room, a scowl turning down his lips, making the scar along the left side of his face over his eye twist even more. That gift from Kat must be a constant reminder of how badly he wants her gone.

He crosses his arms over his chest and glares at me. "What do you want, Rose? This better be important because I have a lot of shit to do, and you're interrupting my day."

I'd much rather have stayed in bed with Rowan this morning, held her in my arms, and relished in the fact that I'm *this* close to having it all, but after what went down last night, I knew it was finally time to make my move, to set things in motion that will ultimately result in me on top of the food chain here in Chicago.

Rowan is mine now. The city will be next.

As long as I can get Galen on board.

I make my way over to the bar set up at the side of the hotel room I booked for this meeting and pour myself a drink. "You having anything?"

Galen shakes his head and continues to shoot daggers at me with his sharp green eyes. Though it's only been a few days since our confrontation in a similar room that left the whore with a hole in her head and me potential targets for Galen and Valerian, it seems his hostility toward me has only grown—his impatience evident. "What the hell do you want, Rose?"

Everything.

I take a sip of the bourbon and let the sweet, spicy liquid heat my throat. "I thought it was time we finished the conversation we started the other evening."

Rowan's brother snorts. "If you're going to offer me more cryptic bullshit, I have other places to be."

He takes a step toward the door, but I move in front of him and plant my hand firmly against his chest, halting his progress. Hard eyes look down at my hand, then slowly back up.

"I suggest you take your fucking hand off me if you don't want to lose it."

I bark out a laugh and withdraw it, then point at him. "I like you, Galen. Enough that I'm going to do you a big favor."

"Or so you keep telling me. But I don't have time for games. Unless you're about to tell me how I can find Kat, we don't have anything to discuss."

"I beg to differ." I take another pull off my drink and lean back against the paneled wall, crossing my ankles. "I'm about to offer you something better than getting to Kat."

He sneers. "There isn't anything more that I want than to pay Kat back for what she did to Valerian and me."

A feeling I understand all too well.

When she intercepted the shipment intended for Galen and hit one of Valerian's operations, she made enemies of the men she had kept a tentative peace with for the short time she's been in control of her late husband's empire. None of us are the kind of men to sit back and let a coordinated attack at the very heart of our businesses go unanswered. The fact that she's managed to slip away from them and stay hidden for so long must eat away at both men fiercely, but it's put me in a precarious position. Continuing to use her for my purposes means there's a chance they will take me out while trying to get to her.

I study Rowan's brother for a moment, really looking for the similarities between him and the woman waiting for me back at the safe house. While Rowan takes after her mother—with her soft red waves and pale, freckled skin, Galen favors their father—dark hair and stern brow. No one would ever suspect they were related. I could bring her into this room and he wouldn't know she's anything other than another redheaded whore, unless they looked closely at the eyes. The same green eyes they share.

Knowing I have something he wants gives me the upper hand today—and in the future. And he'll learn that soon enough.

"Forget Kat for the moment, Galen. The time will come for her to get what she deserves for what she's done. There's something you want more than to nail Kat. Something you've sought for far longer."

He narrows his hard gaze on me. "What the hell are you talking about, Rose?"

I take another sip of my drink and roll the tumbler between my palms. "It's something I'm sure by now you thought you would never find."

He freezes, his shoulders tensing as he takes a step toward me. "Again—what the fuck are you talking about?"

I offer him a slow, lazy grin. Either the man is good at playing stupid, or he's far less intelligent than I've given him credit for. "Think about it, Galen. I'm sure it will come to you."

His brow furrows, his hands fisting at his sides.

I drain my glass and raise an eyebrow. "Nothing? Really?" I set the empty tumbler on the bar and refill it. "Perhaps I overestimated how much this particular thing means to you." Glancing over my shoulder, I catch a flicker in his eye that tells me he's made the connection. "Ah, you're starting to catch on."

He watches me carefully as I turn back to face him and take a sip.

"Nessa," I utter the one word I expect to bowl him over. But I have to give the man credit...he barely flinches, barely acknowledges that I've just hit a massive soft spot and found his major weakness.

"I don't know what you're talking about, Rose."

Chuckling, I take another drink. "Playing dumb, are we? Then, I guess we have nothing to discuss."

I down the rest of the bourbon and slam the tumbler onto the counter before I make my way toward the door. This time, it's his hand on my chest that stops me, and Galen leans in.

"You better not be fucking with me, Rose." He pulls a knife and puts it to the center of my sternum. "I'll cut out your heart and eat it for dinner."

For some reason, I don't doubt that. Galen isn't known for his violence the way Valerian is or Aleksander was, but when it comes to his sister, this man might just snap.

"I found her."

His entire body starts to tremble so badly that I can feel the vibration through where his palm is pressed against my chest. He jerks away his hand and takes a half-step back. "No, you didn't."

"You don't believe me?" I lash out and grab his wrist, then snatch the knife from his grip and slash it across his exposed forearm before he has a chance to pull it away.

He jerks his injured limb back while the other reaches for his gun, but I hold up my free hand in surrender and the bloody knife in the other.

"I'll prove it to you. I should have the DNA test results within a week."

"And then what? You're going to keep her from me until I comply with whatever it is you want me to do?"

I chuckle as I examine the knife that contains the proof of everything I've been telling Rowan and now have revealed to Galen. "I told you the other night, Galen..." I look up and meet his gaze again. "We have a lot in common—you, me, and Valerian. And we're about to have even more. I'll fill you in, if and when, the time comes. But until then, sit tight, and tell your Russian friend to sit tight too and wait for my call."

He watches me closely as I walk to the elevator and press the call button. The ding fills the silence hanging between us, and the doors slide open. I step into the waiting car, then turn to face him.

Galen grips his injury tightly, disbelief and anger hardening his jaw. I offer him a smile as the doors close and lean back against the wall, satisfied.

Things have finally been set in motion. The only one who can fuck this up now for me is *mi querido hermano*.

And I don't have any plans to let him do that.

NINE

ROWAN

Y<small>AWNING AND STRETCHING</small>, the ache in certain parts of my body reminds me of exactly what Felipe and I did last night...and again this morning. I pause and wait for the guilt I should probably feel to overwhelm me.

For what we did.

For sleeping with the man who took a vow to the church to remain celibate.

For putting aside my own fears and reservations to give in to what my body wanted.

But it never comes.

Though I'm not sure whether that's because my soul is so tarnished that I can't feel it anymore or because the man who took those vows never meant them.

I roll to the side and stare at the empty place next to me in bed, the sheets cool under my touch. He's been gone for a while, but that's a good thing. I can't seem to think straight when he's close to me. Things get cloudy. The path I should take and the things I should worry about seem to float away with one look or touch from him.

It's how we ended up in this bed together in the first place. I never intended for things to go that far between us. Never anticipated that it was even a possibility. But somehow, my fantasy paled in comparison to the real thing.

Yet now, in the light of day, after the best night's sleep I've ever had, wrapped in the arms of a man who runs a brutal empire, knowing my brother is out there somewhere, drags me from the bed in search of more answers.

I was too exhausted to even move this morning when I felt him rise, let alone to question him about his plans for Galen and me. The uncertainty of what's coming replaces all the light, pleasant feelings lingering in my body as I slip on a T-shirt I find on top of the dresser.

My bare feet barely make a sound across beautiful hardwood floors to the door. I wrap my hand around the knob but pause and listen with my ear pressed against the wood—though, I don't know for what. Maybe something that will give me some insights into the man I can't seem to wrap my head around. The man who has warped from my pious savior to a violent, dangerous person full of secrets.

But all I hear is silence.

I ease open the door carefully and step out into a broad loft filled with sleek modern furniture. The pristine kitchen to the right looks like it's never been used. Whatever this place is, Felipe doesn't spend much time here. He called it a "safe house," but it doesn't seem to fit his style. At least, not what I've seen of it at the church and rectory.

Stop thinking of him that way. That isn't him.

Everything I thought I knew about Father Felipe was an act, one that was far better than I want to admit. I thought my years on the streets had developed my ability to seek out and spot people's bullshit and made me a good judge of situations. But he had me fooled. He has *everyone* fooled.

I make my way over to the massive windows and stare out at Lake Michigan far below.

This place must cost a fortune.

No doubt because he wants privacy. They won't ask questions at a place like this. Not about where his money comes from or what he's using it for. Neighbors don't bother each other here, staying locked in their own private oases.

Pressing my hands flat against the glass, I watch a boat on the water drifting aimlessly, the way I feel like I am at this moment. Like I have been my entire life.

Except for when I'm in Felipe's arms. Whether he was the noble priest leading his congregation and offering me safety or the man I was with last night didn't matter—I always felt safe with him, like I was at a home I never had before, like nothing could or would ever harm me. But he does harm people. He's killed people. Or, at the very least, ordered them killed in his name, in the name of the Blood Rose Cartel. Yet he says others are threats to me, that others might use me for their own purposes.

I can't believe Kat would do that. She can't be any more dangerous to me than that man, and my own brother wouldn't hurt me.

Would he?

There's so much I don't understand. So many questions still remaining.

I need to talk to Amber to find out what's been going on at Kat's Cradle. Maybe she can shed some light on Kat and her connection to Felipe. The woman has been at the church—multiple times, holding secret meetings with Father Felipe.

It suggests something more going on than he's telling me.

All the misgivings and concerns I've had since he told me who I am and who *he* is rush back as I make my way into the bedroom and throw on the clothes I wore yesterday since they're all I have.

Pulling my hair back into a ponytail, I beeline for the front door and turn the handle. The moment I pull it open, the two men who nabbed me from the motel turn from where they stand on either side of the door to block my exit.

The bigger of the two crosses his arms over his chest. "Mr. Rose has asked us to ensure you remain here for your own safety."

"What?"

It shouldn't surprise me after the way he flipped out when I left the church. He doesn't want me going anywhere. He was serious when he said I couldn't leave him once he had taken me.

At the time, it felt good to be claimed, to be protected by him. But now, it feels like a prison sentence.

I scowl at the two men. "Give me one of your phones. I need to make a call."

They exchange a look, and the bigger of the two shakes his head. "Can't do that, ma'am."

Dammit.

I square my shoulders and prepare myself for battle. "If you don't want anyone to come looking for me, you need to let me make a phone call. I was supposed to meet my friend today. If I don't, she'll stir up trouble and you'll have to tell Rose that the reason the police are looking for me is that you didn't let me make one little phone call."

It's a lie.

No one will be looking for me. Amber tried after I left, and I tried to dissuade her from continuing when I met with her the one time I was able to sneak away from the church. I assured her I was okay, that I was safe, but I know she's likely concerned with how much time has passed since we last spoke. Probably not enough to contact the police, but they don't know that.

I tap my foot and cross *my* arms over my chest, trying to look more confident than I really am that this will work.

Finally, the big man sighs, reaches into his pocket, and holds out his phone. "One call. Make it quick."

I grab his cell and go to close the door when he sticks his foot between it and the jamb, keeping it open, and steps inside.

"You make the call out here where I can see you and give the phone right back."

Asshole.

With him standing right in the room, trying to listen to every word I say, I'm going to have to be careful. I make my way back over to the windows and dial.

Thank God I remember Amber's number.

Waiting while it rings, I glance over my shoulder at my babysitter, who stands near the door, steely eyes locked on me.

Please answer. Please answer.

Coming from a number she doesn't know, there's a good chance she'll just let the call go to voicemail.

"Hello?"

Oh, thank God!

"Amber, it's me."

"Rowan? Oh, my God, are you okay? Where are you?"

I peek at Felipe's man standing by the door. "Safe."

"You have to tell me more than that." Rustling comes through the line like she's trying to move somewhere.

"Look, I can't really get into it." I lower my voice and lean as close to the window as I can to try to prevent him from hearing me. "I need you to tell me what's going on there."

"What? Here?"

"Yes. With Kat. Has she been acting...I don't know...weird? Anything unusual?"

"Jesus, Rowan, you've been gone for a while. A lot has happened. She has a son."

Goosebumps pebble across my skin, and I place my hand against the glass to keep from falling over at her words. "What?"

"She has a baby. She just showed up with him one night and asked us girls to look after him while she took care of something. Then she came back and grabbed him and has been MIA since then."

The question sits on the tip of my tongue, but it won't come out. I swallow and squeeze my eyes shut, then open them to stare at my own reflection in the glass. "Who's the father?"

All those times I saw her at the church and meeting with Felipe in his private office flicker through my head.

What was she doing there? If Felipe thinks she's so dangerous to me, why would he allow her in and have her keep coming back?

"We don't know. Her dead husband? Rose? I don't think anyone has any idea what's going on. She's looking for you, though. A lot."

An icy chill floods my veins, and I swallow thickly and glance at the goon again, who looks impatiently back at me. "Why?"

Every time I saw her at the church, I avoided any conversation and got away from her and to "safety" as fast as I could. I thought I needed to because Felipe had warned me I wasn't safe at Kat's Cradle. That I wasn't safe with *her.*

Was any of that even true?

"I don't know, Rowan. All I do know is that she's had this guy, Arden, trying to check your phone and locate you basically any way he can ever since you left. They even tried to get me to call you so they could trace it."

"I don't have my phone anymore."

Felipe took it from me for this very reason after the first time I snuck away to meet with her.

"Rowan? Are you sure you're okay?"

"Yes. I swear. I'm sorry I just disappeared. There are some things I'm working out, but I'll try to call you again soon. Please don't mention that I called to anyone."

"Of course not."

GWYN MCNAMEE

"Talk to you later."
I jab the *End* button with my heart in my throat.
Kat has a son.
It could be Rose's...
But which one?

TEN

FATHER FELIPE

BLOOD SPRAYS against the wall behind the man tied to the chair, spewing from his mouth along with a litany of curses.

I shake out my hand, the pain in my knuckles ebbing away slowly. Typically, this wouldn't be an option for me. Standing in front of a congregation with bruised and split knuckles would raise questions. But one good thing about my forced "sabbatical" is that I can finally get my hands dirty again.

¡Mierda! I've missed this...

Since arriving in Chicago, I've had to let most of the dirty work be handled by my men.

But not this.

It's too important to be left in the hands of those idiots.

The man's head drops forward, blood and drool dripping from his lips.

I grip his hair and jerk it up. "Do you want to reconsider your answer?"

He struggles to focus on me with his one good eye, the other swollen shut already. "I don't understand..." A labored inhale leads to more wheezing. "Tell me what you want me to say."

Fucking idiota.

I release his hair and adjust the watch on my wrist, casually walking behind him. He strains to look over his shoulder and follow my movements. If I were him, I would be concerned about having me at his back, too. It would only take a second for me to slip a garrote or my hands around his throat and strangle the life right out of him. But that wouldn't serve my purposes. Not at all.

This has to send a message. That can only happen by making my point slowly and painfully.

"Who sent you?"

I know the answer to the question, but still, if I'm going to do this, if I'm going to take this big a step and make this final determination, I need definitive confirmation.

"I don't..." The man shakes his head and winces. "I don't understand what you're asking."

"Still interested in playing games?"

"What?" He lifts his head and tries to turn enough to focus on me, his confusion twisting his mangled face.

I step around in front of him and reach into my pocket for my blade. "I enjoy playing games, too."

"Is that...is that what this is? A game?"

"Have you ever heard of a man named Aleksander Gashi?"

"The Dragon?"

"Oh, so you have heard of him." I flash him a grin. "Good. His reputation precedes him. Unfortunately, he's no longer with us. But I was able to learn some very important things from him based on how he ran his business and lived his life. The most important of which is that I must show no mercy. But you see..." I chuckle, the sound reverberating in the small, empty room. "That presents a bit of a conflict with the way I've vowed to live my life."

The man's confusion since the moment I walked in has only increased the longer we've been together in this room. "What the hell are you talking about?"

He had no idea what he was getting into when he took this job.

Squatting in front of him, I turn the knife over in my hand, watching the way the overhead light reflects off its shiny surface. "You poor, stupid man."

I jab the knife into the top of his thigh all the way to the hilt. His strangled cry shifts to almost soundless as blood and spit drip from his mouth.

"You see..." I push to my feet and pace in front of him. "I have a very important job. I play a very important role to a lot of true believers."

The man sucks in a ragged breath, his fluid and blood filling his lungs. "I don't know what the fuck you're talking about."

"Who fucking sent you?" I grasp the handle of the blade and yank it out fast, letting the serrated edge instill the most damage possible, then drive it into his other thigh with all my strength. "Who. Fucking. Sent. You?"

A gasp slips from his lips before he swallows back the blood and coughs. "You. *You* sent me!"

I smile at him and remove my jacket, draping it over the small table behind me so I can slowly roll up the sleeves on my dress shirt, exposing the tattoos covering my arms while blood drips down both his legs and pools on the floor.

"Who the fuck are you?" He shakes his head and coughs, wincing and tugging fruitlessly at the ropes restraining him. "Not Rose."

I grin at him and waggle my eyebrows. "Surprise."

"You're-you're the priest?"

Took him long enough.

The man who was sent to kill me took far too long to figure out what was actually happening in this room. My dear brother must not have informed his assassin that his target was his twin, only that he would have to take out the priest at St. Mary of the Angels.

"What did you think? That the man you were paid to take out would just sit back and let it happen?"

This *pendejo* would have killed me and likely Rowan in the process without ever knowing how invaluable she is. The money in his pocket would have gotten the person who sent him after me exactly what they wanted—me out of the way and no witnesses. Poor Sister Agnes would have returned to the church and found our bloodied bodies instead of the message from me that I had a family emergency and had to leave unexpectedly.

I yank the knife from his leg again and hold it up to the light. Blood drips from my blade, and I turn it over in my hand, examining the way the viscous liquid adds to the glimmer of the metal. "It's beautiful, isn't it?"

He offers a rattling cough in response, now struggling to take every breath. The wound I put in his chest at the church last night and the damage I've done since my men brought him here are finally, slowly taking the life from his body.

No one can survive this, but it isn't enough. I want to watch him die, hold his heart in my hand and feel it stop beating. Unleash the rage I've held inside since the first time my brother defied me. It has only grown the longer this dispute has gone on, and since I can't have him strapped to this chair, his minion will have to do.

I drive the knife into his stomach and slice down. A low gurgling joins the slosh of his entrails spilling out onto the floor.

It won't be long now.

I wanted my answer, and I got it. Even if it wasn't what I really wanted to hear. Despite his insistence the last time we spoke that he would never give up being Rose, a small part of me had hoped *mi querido hermano* would come to his senses, would see that the correct path isn't *through me* but *with* me.

Now I see it was a lost cause. A fool's errand. A prayer that would never be answered, certainly not for a man who has sinned as much as I have in my lifetime.

It's a lesson I learned at a very young age that has only been reaffirmed time and again. If I want to succeed in this life, if I want to hold the things I dream of in my hands, I need to attain them myself.

I set this all in motion on that fateful day, and then *he* ended it by destroying the man who was to be my guide. When Felipe killed Elonzo and I was forced to become him, it altered the path God set out for us both. But it's time to right those paths.

To end his and ensure mine goes in the proper direction.

ELEVEN

ROWAN

THE DOOR to the condo slowly opens, the light spilling in from the hallway, breaking the total darkness of the room. Felipe steps in, and almost instantly, all the hairs on my arms rise. But I don't move from where I stand at the window, staring out on evening settling over Chicago and the lake. I won't give him the satisfaction of acknowledging his presence or letting him know I've been waiting for him all day. Waiting for answers.

His heavy footsteps tread on the wood, closing in on me, each one ratcheting up the tension in my body more and more. I've spent hours waiting for him, running through every word he said to me since the moment he arrived at Kat's Cradle that night, trying to weed out what was the truth and what was some elaborate fiction he created to fit the game he was playing with me.

I'm not even sure if I succeeded. Perhaps I'm naïve for even considering that a possibility. A man like Felipe isn't one to offer up his secrets easily, and God knows he's keeping many, especially from me.

He slides a hand down my exposed arm and leans in to brush his lips against the back of my neck. A shudder rolls through me against my will, desire to sink back against him warring with what I know has to happen.

"What are you doing, *mi palomita?*"

Stewing.

Obsessing.

Letting my anger build and build until I can barely contain it.

Without turning toward him, I clear my throat. "Where have you been?"

"Trying to secure our futures."

Such a simple answer, one I know has so many layers to it that I would get lost trying to unravel them.

I tighten my arms wrapped around myself, trying to kill the chill that keeps sending little shivers through me, but I don't look away from the view. "How do you plan on doing that? With Kat's help?"

He issues a low, deep chuckle and leans to the side to nip at my earlobe. Heat spreads through my core while anger floods my veins. "Do I detect a hint of jealousy in that question?"

"Tell me about her son."

Felipe freezes behind me, then shifts to my side and turns me to face him, his dark brows drawn low over hard eyes, jaw tight. "How do you know about him?"

I raise an eyebrow at him. "Why didn't you tell me about him?"

"Why would I, *mi palomita?*"

"Stop calling me that."

The name used to be cute. Endearing. A sign that Felipe cared for me. But now that I know what it means and why he uses it, now that I have new questions about Kat and his plans, I don't want to hear it from him anymore.

Strong hands closing around my shoulders keep me from bolting away when all I want is to put as much distance between us as possible.

GWYN MCNAMEE

The question that has been plaguing me since I spoke with Amber rushes out before I can bite it back. "Is he yours?"

His eyes widen, and a slow, devious grin curls at his lips. "Is that what this is about? You think Kat and I share a son?"

"I don't know what to think. All I know is that she and 'Rose'"—I raise my hands and do air quotes—"had a thing, and now, all of a sudden, she has a son."

He raises a hand and cups my cheek, tilting up my head, forcing me to meet his heated gaze. "Oh, *mi palomita*. Jealousy doesn't look good on you. Though, I do appreciate it."

"You didn't answer my question."

"No. I didn't." He tightens his grip. "Because it's preposterous. Kat's son was fathered by Aleksander."

"But...Aleksander is dead."

"Very much so. And she gave birth to Jeton after his death and hid him with a family in Albania. She only brought him back here because she was finally forced to when Konstandin Morina and I learned of his existence and she wanted to protect him. That child is over a year old, *mi palomita*. I haven't even been in Chicago that long."

"No...but *Rose* has. And now, I don't know what was you and what was him. I don't know what's a lie and what's the truth. All I know is you've kept who I am from me for months while you took meetings with Kat in your office at the church and snuck off to do God only knows what. She obviously knew exactly who you were while I was still in the dark. How the hell am I supposed to react to that?"

"You're supposed to trust me."

"Trust is something that has to be earned, Felipe...Rose...*Andres*." I emphasize his true name and watch his jaw harden.

"No one can ever hear you calling me anything other than Felipe. Too many people have too many questions as it is."

"What about that man at the church?"

"My men took care of it before anyone found him. And I alerted the diocese that I had a family emergency and had to leave unexpectedly. No one will be looking for Father Felipe for a while."

I shake my head, and his hand on my cheek falls away. "I just don't understand what the endgame is here. What are we doing?"

Felipe grabs my face between his palms and holds it tightly. "I'm securing our future. One in which I will be able to give you anything you ever wanted. One in which the city will be mine."

The glint in his eye tells me he means it. He's absolutely convinced that whatever his plan is, it will work. He thinks he can somehow take out or control the other families.

"What about your brother? Kat? Valentina and Valerian? My...brother?"

None of them seem likely to go down without a fight.

He gently glides his thumb across my bottom lip, sending another shiver through me. "Don't worry about them, *mi palomita*. I sent a serious message tonight."

Goosebumps break out across my skin. "What kind of message?"

"A bloody one, and soon enough, they'll figure out that standing against me will cost them dearly." Lowering his head, he stops with his lips a mere hairsbreadth from mine. "There will be no indecision, no more questions."

His kiss comes swiftly, taking my breath and retort with it.

I want to tell him no. I want to push him away and demand he stop all the cryptic bullshit. I want to know more about what *he* knows. About my family, about me, about everything that's happened over the last twenty years that I've pushed down and suppressed.

But as his tongue meets mine, all hope of denying him, of denying this attraction, flees along with my reservations.

TWELVE

ROWAN

Felipe turns me slowly and walks me back until my shoulders press to the cool glass behind me. He dips his head, running his lips along my neck until I arch, pressing my hips against his growing cock. "I thought about you all day, *mi palomita*. Fantasized and remembered how good it felt to finally take you, to finally make you mine."

A tiny little mewl slips from my lips before I can catch it. It's embarrassing how easily this man can turn me to putty in his hands. Even the name I just told him I never wanted to hear again makes my pussy clench in anticipation.

He drifts one up between my bare legs, dragging his fingertips along my inner thigh, stopping just short of where I desperately want his touch. I shift slightly, trying to force his hand up, but he drifts it back down.

"Ah, ah, ah, *mi palomita*. There's something I've been thinking about all day." He kisses his way down my neck and across my exposed collarbone. His teeth catch one of the straps of my dress and pull it down my arm while his free hand does the same with the other. He lets the material fall to the floor, pooling at my feet. His eyes zero in on my bare pussy. "No other man will ever touch you, Rowan. Never again. Because you're mine."

Felipe lowers his hand between my legs, brushing his fingers through my wet slit, and I jerk, pushing back harder against the glass behind me for support. He slowly drops to his knees and presses his palms against my inner thighs, spreading my shaking legs even wider, exposing me to him even more.

Hard, lust-filled eyes meet mine as he dips his head and glides his tongue over my lips to my aching clit.

"Oh, God..." I bury my hands in his thick, dark hair, clinging to it as he probes me with his tongue.

Every lick makes me tighten my fingers. Every flick brings a roll of my hips. Every groan of pleasure he issues vibrates against my wet flesh. And when he slips a finger inside me, I gasp and drop my head against the glass.

All the men I've been with in my life, the ones who called me *baby*, the ones who paid for the privilege of my time and my body never did this. They never feasted on me like I was their last meal. Like they needed me to survive. But Felipe is a man obsessed. A man on a mission, driving his fingers in and out of me slowly as he laps up my arousal and grips my thigh tightly with the other hand, holding me steady.

That's what he's somehow become—an anchor in the stormy sea that is my life. Only this anchor also threatens to drag me under with it, down into the dark abyss full of monsters.

My head swims, and heat floats through my limbs, building slowly from a mere spark into a suddenly raging inferno that can only be put out by one thing. The orgasm crashes over me, almost drowning me in pleasure as my body clasps and rolls in time with Felipe's ministrations. He bites down on my clit and sucks it between his lips, starting the process all over again, dragging my release on and on, harder and harder, until I can't even suck in a breath anymore.

And he doesn't relent.

It's as if he's proving a point, trying to drive home the words he just said to me and the promises he made, by killing me with pleasure.

I push his head, desperate to seek relief from the hypersensitivity of my body, but he has other plans. He continues to lash at my clit and curls his fingers inside me, pumping into that perfect spot. I score my nails along his scalp, my gasps echoing through the high ceilings of the loft. Reaching, trying to find something just beyond my fingertips.

"Felipe...please...I...I need..."

I need *him*.

I need what he gave me last night.

An escape from the madness, no matter how brief, no matter how futile. Because the lies he told me will still exist when I come down from this orgasm, when I pull myself from his arms, but for a few fleeting moments, I can forget he's Father Felipe, I can forget he's Andres, I can forget he's Rose, and he can just be the man who worships my body like this and makes me feel pleasure I've never experienced in my life.

I grind my hips against his face seeking more. He slips another finger inside me, and I thrash my head from side to side.

It's not enough. Not enough.

"More. More."

"Fuck, *mi palomita*." Felipe drags his head back and pulls his fingers from inside so he can shove down his pants as he rises to his feet. He grips my hip, aligns his cock, and drives up into me in one hard thrust.

It rocks me back against the glass, pinning me between his hard, warm body and the cool, unyielding wall of windows behind me.

It's exactly what I need. The icing on top of his promises and reassurances. The feeling of being complete.

He grasps my thighs and lifts me to wrap my legs around his hips. I dig my heels into his lower back and pull him into me aggressively with every thrust.

One of his large hands presses against the glass next to my head, and the other grips my chin and drags my mouth to his for a demanding kiss, one that tastes like my release and everything I need in the future.

But I can't think about that potential future while I'm doing this. This incredible feeling will be marred by my doubts, by the uncertainty that he created. By all the dark things that linger in the hidden places of my psyche. And I don't want that now. Don't want to wonder about his motives or what he's not telling me.

I want to believe that every time his cock fills me, it's exactly where it's meant to be. That I am exactly where I'm meant to be. That all the pain of my past was simply to get me to this moment of freedom where I finally know the truth and can finally experience this with the man who wants me for more than just my body. A man who wants a future with me even though it isn't clear what that future looks like.

He made a lot of promises tonight, ones I hope are true, ones I hope he can follow through on. Because if he can't, I don't think I'll make it.

Despite everything I survived in my life, I don't know that I'll survive Felipe.

THIRTEEN

ROWAN

STEPPING out of the shower stall, the chilly air hits my wet skin. Even with the bathroom door closed and the steam accumulating, goosebumps break out over my body and a tiny shiver rolls through me. Though maybe it's less about the cold front that's taken over the city and more about the warring feelings plaguing me.

I grab the towel off the rack and wrap it around me, pulling it tight and still feeling everything Felipe and I did last night. My anger over his deception and continuing to keep me in the dark still battles with the way I naturally gravitate toward him. The comfort I find in his arms from the storm it seems he may have created.

It's no wonder his parishioners love him. There's just something about the man, even when he's not performing his Father Felipe act, that acts like a tractor beam, drawing people in to latch onto him like a lifeline. The passion he directed at me last night is the same he fakes toward his role in the church.

I wipe at the mirror and stare at the woman looking back at me.

Nessa.

I've been tossing around the name since he told me, waiting for more memories from before I was taken from my family to return. But I was so young. I couldn't have been more than two or three when I was abducted, when those happy, pleasant memories were replaced by the ones I've tried so hard to forget.

The vision of the red-haired woman spinning me around flashes in my head again, and I lean toward the mirror, searching for any sort of resemblance. Kind green eyes sparking with joy look at me in my memory, but the ones staring back at me are heavy and lost. Just like I am.

The only time I don't feel that way is when I'm in his arms. Yet, I can't help but continue to feel as though he's keeping something important from me. Something he's hiding the same way he hid my identity and me away at that church until coming forward would help his cause.

A cause I don't understand.

There isn't any way the other families are just going to roll over and let him take control. I haven't been in Chicago long, but I've been around enough to understand the way the city's underworld works. The tenuous peace that used to exist between the families is long gone. Agreements that may still exist could end with a simple knife to the back or the pull of a trigger.

And on top of all that, Felipe has his brother fighting him for the top spot.

They've both proven how cold and ruthless they can be, which only begs the question: how will anyone come out of this unscathed?

I don't think it's possible, but today, I'm demanding answers from Felipe. No more distractions. The man won't touch me again until I know *everything*. I *have* to know.

Staying in the dark isn't an option anymore. Not after I've spent my entire life in it.

I slowly step out of the bathroom and find a pile of women's clothes on the dresser—apparently brought by one of Felipe's men at some point this morning. As I change, the showdown I'm about to have with Felipe makes my hands shake uncontrollably.

How can I be so afraid of the man and need him so badly at the same time?

It's a dichotomy I'm not sure I'm ready to examine, but I may not be able to ignore it anymore.

I wrap my hand around the doorknob to head out into the loft and look for the man who has me so twisted up in knots when a loud knock on the outer condo door stops me.

Felipe said no one knows about this place, so there shouldn't be anyone knocking. His men would just come in.

Wouldn't they?

I press my ear to the door, and heavy footsteps crossing the wood floor echo in the living room.

"What is it?" Felipe's angry tone vibrates through the door.

My back stiffens. He's never spoken to me with that tone, but it's there all the same. That voice is Rose, not Felipe. And his men are likely still standing outside, and if they're interrupting him, it isn't a good sign.

"What the hell are you doing here?"

Who is he talking to?

"Did you really think no one would ever find you here?" The familiar voice makes me perk up.

Kat...

"How did you find me?"

She laughs, a sound that somehow seems colder than I remember it being before I learned so much, her heels clicking across the floor. If either of them knew I was here, this conversation wouldn't be happening. But Felipe probably thinks I'm still asleep or in the shower.

"I've had someone keeping an eye on the church since the explosion. I saw Rowan slip away from you, and I knew you left with her the other day. My man followed you here."

"If you've had someone sitting on me and you knew where I was, why didn't you come right away?"

"Because I wanted to know what you are up to, and since you'll never tell me, watching you yields better results."

"What do you want?"

"You met with the Irish and the Russians. Why?"

"None of your fucking business."

"Oh...but it is. When they're my enemies and want me dead and you're supposed to be my partner, it certainly is my business."

"Partners?" Felipe's low chuckle hits my ears, and I wince.

My confrontation with him last night flashes in my head. He denied that he and Kat were involved with each other—at least sexually—but after all the lies he told me in the past, it makes it hard to believe it's true. Especially when the woman arrives here, calling herself his *partner*. Maybe she's referencing something that happened between them in his office, something beyond discussing his aspirations for taking over this city.

"It *isn't* any of your business, Kat, and we *aren't* partners, *but* we've reached the point where it benefits me for you to know."

"Know what?"

Goosebumps prickle along my arms again, and I lean my ear closer to the crack, hoping I don't miss a single word. This may be my chance to learn what Felipe is keeping from me, what he doesn't want me to know or thinks I can't handle.

"It's time for you to know about Rowan and why she's so important."

FOURTEEN

FATHER FELIPE

KAT SITS FACING me in the leather armchair; her shoulders back and legs crossed, watching expectantly and waiting for me to continue. Her cool blue eyes give nothing away, offer nothing in terms of what she's thinking about what I might say.

While her appearance here was unexpected and could be quite problematic given that my safe house is no longer safe, it does give me the opportunity to read her in on the next step, the one I will need her assistance with.

"You've been asking me about Rowan...and she is far more important than you could ever imagine. She isn't just some woman who came to you from the streets, Kat."

"I suspected as much, given your interest in her."

I nod slowly and glance toward the closed door where Rowan still sleeps. Given how late we were up last night, she barely budged when I slid out of bed this morning; the toll of everything that's happened physically and all she's gone through mentally and emotionally has exhausted her.

Turning back to Kat, I cross my arms over my chest. "I always spend a great deal of time researching my enemies. Trying to discover ways to use their weaknesses to my advantage."

She tenses. "You've made that very clear."

Her desire to protect her son is commendable. The woman has no idea what I have planned for him if she doesn't comply.

"And during my travels as a seminarian, I discovered some information concerning the missing daughter of the head of a very important family."

Kat's eyebrows rise. "Who is she, Felipe?"

"She's Galen McGinnis' sister."

Her jaw drops slightly. "Well, I definitely wasn't expecting that. If she's so well connected, why was she working for me at Kat's Cradle?"

I run a hand over the stubble forming on my jaw and glance out at the dark clouds building over the city. Another storm is coming, one that will rival the one we had the other night. "She was trafficked, Kat. Sold away and used by men who only wanted one thing from her. When she managed to flee from captivity, she made her way to New York because she didn't have anywhere else to go. She had no memory of who she was. Of her name or that there were people out there who might be looking for her. She repressed all of her memories—good and bad—in order to save herself from reliving the horror she was subjected to."

Kat winces and presses her lips together into a hard line. "No matter what anyone might say about the business I run, I never force the girls to do anything. I never put them in positions where they feel obligated to. Kat's Cradle is about letting these women have control of their own lives, their own bodies. If I had known, I never would've let her come work for me."

"I know that. It's the only reason you aren't already dead."

My words hang in the air between us, adding to the tension of the story I'm telling her. If I thought for a moment that Kat had been abusing the girls or making them do anything they didn't want to, I would have killed the bitch the first chance I got and certainly wouldn't have let her set foot in here.

"I learned of her kidnapping while I was in Ireland, from an old friend of her uncle who was still in the church, and I began to use my resources to see how I could find her."

"Did Sofia do it? Have you located her yet?"

The question makes my chest tighten, and I shake my head. "No, and no. Has Arden found anything about her that could be useful in tracking her down?"

Kat shakes her head. "Not that I'm aware of. He said her username has been quiet in the normal places he would think she might pop up. He thinks she's in hiding."

"Shit." I rub at my eyes and sigh. "Anyway, I didn't use Sofia to try to find Rowan. She was still very young, though already clearly a computer prodigy, but I couldn't risk my brother finding out what I'd learned. I went to another source, a woman hacker I know in New York, and she was able to start with the name of the man they initially sold her to, information I might add, that was not easy for me to get without a little persuasion."

Her chuckle floats to me, genuine humor in it. "If your persuasive tactics are anything like your brother's, I don't think I want to know."

"She started with him and located another girl who got away from him a year or two after Rowan had. Becca was able to provide her with a new description, including a very unique scar Rowan had on her right arm from one of the incidents where she tried to escape and failed in the past. My source learned that the girls had always talked about New York, of looking for each other there if they ever got away. So, that's where she went looking. Searching hospital records and home-less shelters—anything she could. And eventually"—I shrug—"I struck gold. I found her. Right about the time you returned here as Kat to seek revenge for Aleksander."

She flinches at my mention of her late husband but doesn't say anything.

"Only by the time I sent someone to get her, she was already gone."

"She came here."

I nod slowly. "Someone from her past on the streets there told her what you were doing, and she wanted to be a part of it. Felt it would help her regain control. So, when I got here, I sent a man to Kat's Cradle to check for the scar and to confirm it was her. And then, I waited…"

"For what?"

I release a long sigh. "To see if my dear brother would continue with his insurrection. To see if he would continue to defy surrendering what is mine. If he had chosen the smarter path, my plan would have gone a lot differently. But he's forced my hand now."

"Forced you to do what?"

"Forced me to use Rowan for what she was intended. She's nothing more than a bargaining chip. Something I can use to get Galen McGinnis to support me and my actions, to give me access to his resources."

"How much does Rowan know?"

"Enough to keep her compliant. Just like you, she will only know what she needs to know for me to get what I want."

"What is it you want, Felipe? Because I can't see any way this ends with everyone still breathing."

I grin at her. "That's what I like about you, Kat. You have foresight. You can see where things are going and you're smart enough to get ahead of them. And you're right, there are going to be a lot of bodies when I'm done and I have what I want. As long as I have that redhead in there, I have the greatest bargaining chip in the world."

FIFTEEN

ROWAN

EVERY WORD he says is like a knife driving straight into my heart.

She's nothing more than a bargaining chip.

Something I can use to get Galen McGinnis to support me and my actions, to give me access to his resources...

Enough to keep her compliant...

She will only know what she needs to know for me to get what I want...

Stumbling back from the door, I swipe at the tears streaming down my face and brush my fingers over the scar on my arm.

I was right.

I was right not to trust him completely, right to believe there was more going on than what he's telling me, right to suspect something more happening with Kat.

Those two don't talk like enemies. They talk like friends...or more. For all I know, she's been sleeping with both men who call themselves Rose this entire time, completely aware of the duplicity and willing to be a part of it. Spying for Felipe and relaying what his brother's plans are.

I slap my hand over my mouth to prevent the sob from climbing up my throat and alerting them to my presence. If they knew I'd overheard all of this, it would mean very bad things for me.

What the hell do I do?

Here, I'm at his mercy, but I don't have anywhere else to go. Nowhere else to run. Plus, even if I did, I tried before, and Felipe found me in only a matter of days. I have almost zero chance of hiding from him on my own, and Amber can only offer so much help while she's being watched by Kat.

What do I do?

I rush across the room, back into the bathroom, and close the door behind me as quietly as possible, then sink down against it and finally let loose the tears and anguish over what I just overheard.

It was all a lie.

Not just everything I believe about my past but *everything*. He fooled everyone. All the people he's known his entire life. The church. Even his own sister. All of it. I'm just another one in a long line.

He said he's wanted me since the first day we met, but that wasn't the truth.

I have the greatest bargaining chip in the world...

His words echo in my head as I bite my lip until it feels as though my teeth might actually break the skin. At this point, I would welcome the physical pain. It might be enough to snap me out of whatever dream world I've been living in, believing a word that came out of that man's mouth.

He never wanted to protect me. He wanted to protect his *investment*. The thing that he needed to secure whatever fucked-up plan he has in mind. Not because he loves me or even cares at all. He *needs* me. It's the only reason he's kept me alive and done all this for me.

It has nothing to do with love and everything to do with his ambition and his sloth. His apathy toward that which is good. The man doesn't just have apathy for the church and his role in it; he has apathy for anyone who isn't him.

And I fell for it—hook, line, and sinker. I was right to think Felipe would drag me under like an anchor. Only he's brought me somewhere even I couldn't have imagined. A place where I'm a prisoner again, at the mercy of another madman—just one wearing a white collar and crooked grin. All because I *fell* for his bullshit.

Well, not anymore.

I swipe at my eyes again and drag myself off the floor and onto shaking legs. The door to the bedroom opening makes me freeze in front of the mirror. I crank on the faucet and splash cool water onto my face to try to mask the red puffiness of my eyes.

Felipe turns the knob on the bathroom door, and I hold my breath as it opens.

He scans me, head to toe, his brow furrowing slightly. "I didn't know you were awake. Is everything okay?"

I force a smile and nod. "Everything's fine."

"Did you sleep all right, *mi palomita?*"

I have to swallow back the bile threatening to make me retch because the answer is *yes.* "Yes."

Anger floods my veins with the single word. But there isn't any use in denying it. I did sleep all right. I have ever since he pulled me into his arms during that storm. Because he gave me a false sense of security that I now know is a lie, one that I can't allow to bring down my guard again.

It's a good thing I had to learn to be an excellent actress doing what I did to survive. Felipe isn't the only one who can fake his way through life.

His dark gaze dips to the outfit I'm wearing. "I see you found the clothes I put out."

Shit. He knows...

He watches me for a moment, and I glance down at the yoga pants and shirt I'm wearing and force another smile.

"I did just now."

Please believe me. Please believe me. Please...

He smiles, though it seems tight, practiced. Not like the ones that appeared so genuine when he was in his role as Father Felipe. "Good. I need to go out and take care of some things. I'm leaving my men at the door again. Please don't give them any shit today. And no more chats with your friend."

Shit. They told him what I did yesterday.

"You didn't tell your friend where you are, did you?"

I shake my head, clasping my hands together in front of me to stop them from shaking. "Of course not. You told me it wasn't safe."

And now, I know that's true.

This is probably the most dangerous place I could be.

"Good." Felipe takes the few steps between us and drops a kiss on my forehead. "I'll be back later."

He walks out of the bathroom and across the bedroom, out through the open door into the loft, and disappears into the hallway.

Determination settles over me.

I can't be his bargaining chip if I'm not here.

The best way to take back all the power is to ensure he can't use me for his plans anymore. Which means I need to get past those two assholes outside.

And I know just how to do it.

# SIXTEEN

ROWAN

I ALMOST FEEL bad for Felipe's men for how easily they were duped. Because when he finds out I'm gone, there's no way they'll survive the repercussions.

But it was necessary. And I knew it would work flawlessly.

Setting off the smoke detector triggered the building's fire alarm and sprinkler systems which, while it may have left me soaked by the time we got outside, allowed me to sneak away from Felipe's goons in the throngs of people gathering on the street.

Those two really aren't very good at their jobs. Even I know never to take your eyes off the prize. But they work for a madman, so I can't let the guilt of what will happen to them get to me. Not when I have an important task ahead.

I examine my reflection in the window of the building next to *Bottom O' the Well* one last time. The dress and purse I had Amber bring me look perfect—exposing my long legs and the swells of my breasts in a way that leaves no question about my intended purpose.

Please, God, let this work.

It feels wrong to be asking for His help after everything that's happened, after everything I've done and what's been done to me, after I ignored how *wrong* it was to be with Felipe and did it anyway, but this might be my only chance to get away from the fake priest's lies and really find out who I am.

I pull open the door to the dive, and several heads turn my way immediately. The bartender raises dark, bushy eyebrows and wipes his hands on a cloth as I approach, intentionally swaying my hips. I lean over the bartop, flashing him my cleavage, and offer a seductive grin.

"I'm here to see Galen. A gift from Patrick."

The head of the Irish mob in Chicago must know someone *named Patrick...*

The man eyes me suspiciously and crosses his arms over his chest. "Galen isn't here right now."

Shit.

"Oh, I know." I shift across the wooden surface a little farther. "But I also know he'll be back shortly. I was told to wait for him and ensure he got a proper welcome when he returns, if you know what I mean."

A blond female slinging drinks who looks to be about my age gives me a once-over from where she stands slightly down from us, her pale blue eyes narrowing. "He said he'd be back in ten minutes."

The male bartender scowls at her and points to an empty stool at the end of the bar. "You can wait there."

I don't exactly want to have this conversation with an audience, so I lean over even more and motion for him to come closer. He sighs and complies, leaning over the bar to meet me halfway.

Sliding my tongue out across my lips, I watch his eyes follow the movement. "I was paid to welcome him...in the nude. I would hate to ruin the surprise by having him see me here the moment he walks in."

God, this better work.

The bartender sighs again and motions toward a guy sitting near the back of the room.

He pushes to his feet and towers over me by at least a foot and a half. "What?"

My new friend, the bartender, points to me. "Take her back to Galen's office and stay with her until he gets back."

The big guy's chocolate-brown gaze drinks me in, from the heels on my feet, up my legs, over the skintight dress, and pauses on my breasts before it finally meets mine. "Galen is one lucky man."

I wink at him. "You can be one, too, when I'm done with your boss."

He chuckles and offers me his arm. "Maybe when I'm off tonight, sweetheart. What's your name?"

"Whatever you want it to be."

His bark of laughter gets swallowed by the live band in the corner, and he opens a door along the back wall that takes us down a short hallway to another closed door. He pushes it open for me, and I step into Galen McGinnis' office.

He motions toward one of the chairs facing the desk. "Take a seat. I'll wait with you until he gets here."

And, hopefully, get out of here before I have a very private talk with my brother.

Brother...

The word feels so foreign to even think, but suddenly, a memory tugs at the corner of my mind.

A small hand holding mine and squeezing it affectionately.

I shake it off and slowly lower myself into the chair, being sure to open my legs and flash his lackey my bare pussy when I cross them. "You don't think he'll be long?"

"Shouldn't be."

"Good." I let my eyes wander around the office, and my breath catches at a framed picture on the credenza behind the desk.

The man in the picture bears a striking resemblance to the photos I've seen of Galen, but it's the little girl and the woman in the image who truly draw my attention. Me as a toddler held in the arms of a woman who could be me now, we look so much alike.

Swallowing thickly, I incline my head toward it. "Galen's family?"

The big guy shrugs and steps out into the hallway, looking back toward the bar area. "Not sure."

"Hey, Aiden..." the voice floats toward us, bringing my babysitter another foot out of the room.

He takes another few steps down the hallway until he disappears completely, whoever called him taking precedence over supervising me.

My knee bounces up and down, and I can't seem to stop my hands from shaking violently. I clutch my purse to try to conceal my nerves. Bits and pieces of a conversation from out in the hallway make it to me, but the noise coming from the bar itself drowns out any specifics.

Finally, my curiosity and nerves get the better of me, and I push to my feet and make my way over to the photo. Up close, the resemblance I bear to the woman who must be my mother is even more striking.

My eyes start to burn with unshed tears. I squeeze them closed. My knees start to wobble.

No. Not again.

This isn't the time for weakness. I can't pass out now. I need to find the strength to speak with Galen about this. To figure out what's really happening around me instead of merely being a pawn in some demented man's game.

I grip the back of his chair and turn to face the desk and the door. Something peeks out from the partially open center drawer of the desk—a flash of familiar red hair. I reach forward and pull it out.

A photo of Galen as a child holding me in his arms, proud big brother. I tug open the drawer, searching for more pictures, and find a stack resting underneath a black gun.

My hand shakes as I lift the weapon to set it on top of the desk.

"Who the fuck are you?"

I jerk up, and the familiar green eyes I just saw in the photo meet mine before a loud crack fills the air and pain slices through my abdomen.

ABIDING SLOTH

Sloth, not ill-will, makes me unjust.

-Mason Cooley

ONE

ROWAN

PAIN SLICES through my body the same instant the deafening sharp crack of Galen's gun firing hits my ears. The weapon I found in his drawer that I had been just about to set down on top of his desk tumbles from my hand and slams into the solid wood with a definitive thud.

For a second, I stand frozen, unable to move, unable to accept or fully process what's just happened. The world seems to still around me, too. No noise. No motion. No reaction to the fact that Galen just shot me.

The blazing fire searing through the right side of my abdomen finally spurs me into action and brings clarity to the whole fucked-up situation. I press my hand against the wound, my mouth falling open on a silent cry.

Familiar green eyes lock with mine.

My vision wavers in and out, getting hazier and hazier, making it harder to see him clearly, and an old memory of those same eyes looking at me mingles with the present.

The memory that goes with the photo I just saw of him holding me as a child...

"*Dearthair*." The word tumbles from my lips, from somewhere deep in my subconscious, somewhere I don't know yet. There are so many things I don't understand about what happened, about my past, but it just feels right to say to him even as warm blood coats my hand.

His eyes widen, tugging at the scar running through the left one, and he takes a step into the room. My knees buckle, and I collapse against the desk, struggling to keep my eyes open while blood flows between my fingers and out across the surface of Galen's workspace.

"Nessa?" Galen's voice quivers with uncertainty and surprise. Yet, the familiarity of it somehow settles over me like a warm blanket despite the dire circumstances.

I offer a slight incline of my head and open my mouth to explain, but nothing comes out except a strangled moan. Doubled over the desk, scorching heat and bitter ice alternately flow through me. The room spins and fades.

This must be what it feels like to die...

Somehow, I thought it would be different. After listening to Felipe's sermons for weeks and weeks about God and Heaven and man's salvation, I had expected something bright and warm; a welcoming presence to lift me from the misery of life on Earth and into a beautiful eternity.

Perhaps this is my penance for choosing Felipe, for accepting his sloth and my own and embracing him when I should have seen his apathy for the church and those around him and known to run immediately.

Maybe this is what I deserve.

My vision fades in and out, and I slump farther down, unable to keep myself even partially upright any longer. Galen rushes forward and around the desk to catch me before I fully collapse. Strong arms wrap around my waist, and despite the pain wracking my body, a calm settles over me, a sense of comfort and security I've only experienced in one other man's arms.

A man who drove me to this place and time to meet my fate.

"Nessa, I'm so sorry." Galen's eyes shimmer with unshed tears while my own flow freely down my cheeks. "I didn't know...I just saw you with the gun, and it looked like you were raising it."

I shake my head and try to speak, try to stop him from apologizing—because for men like him, firing to protect themselves is second nature—but only a tiny gasp of air comes out, the agony threatening to make me retch.

Galen holds me close, his face buried in my hair while he tries to apply pressure against my wound. "You're going to be okay. I'll take care of you, *deirfiúr bheag*."

Heavy footsteps pound down the hallway, and through the blur of tears, I can make out the man who was supposed to be babysitting me rush through the door and skid to a stop. "What happened?"

I try to focus on him, force my tongue to attempt an answer, but darkness clouds the edges of my vision in a way that seems final, like something I should fight.

If you give into it, you will never escape its clutches.

But my eyes drift closed all the same.

Just like this may be the only way I'll ever escape Felipe...

Galen compresses his hand harder on top of mine over the wound to try to control the bleeding. "Get Doc here right away."

"You don't want to take her there?"

Tightening his hold on me, he shakes his head. "We shouldn't move her. Find out how long it'll take him."

I force my eyes open, laboring to stay awake and focused, and turn my head toward Galen. His face melts into the blurry white ceiling, and I lift my other hand into my line of vision and find it crimson and wet.

His man's frantic, indistinguishable words echo in my ears with his retreating footsteps.

That doesn't sound good...

Another set of footsteps approaches, softer, faster. Shoes squeak on the tile floor as someone comes to a stop in the open doorway.

Galen tenses under me. "Who the hell are you?"

"Nicki...your new bartender. Connor hired me. Today is my first day."

I twist my head to the side and squint at the blonde who was behind the bar when I came in. Her wide blue eyes take in the scene. Though, despite what must be a bloody mess, she appears relatively calm.

Galen shifts me slightly, applying even more pressure on the wound, enough to make me grind my teeth together to keep from crying out. "What the fuck are you doing back here?"

"I-I heard a gunshot and overheard Sean calling a doctor. I have some basic first-aid training. I thought I might help."

It takes a moment of tense silence before anyone moves or says anything. No doubt Galen would prefer to keep her out of and away from this clusterfuck as much as possible—both for *his* sake and hers—but he finally relents and lays me across the top of the desk, the hard wood a stark contrast to the warm, strong arms that once supported me.

"Get over here. We'll do what we can then move her once we can get her stabilized." A large, rough hand brushes hair away from my face. "I'm so sorry, Nessa. I'll take care of you. I promise. I won't let anything ever happened to you."

Safety.

That had been my hope in coming here—that I would find safety from everything going on around me, from Felipe's lies and machinations, from Kat's mysterious involvement, from everyone who wants something from me but pretends to have my best interests at heart. I came looking for my brother. For the one person who should protect me without question, without ulterior motives or expectations of anything in return.

I force my eyes open and turn my head toward him. "Thank you, *deartháir*."

It's the last word I get out before the excruciating pain finally drags me into a darkness so deep that I lose all sense of what's going on around me.

TWO

FELIPE

THE ELEVATOR DINGS, and the doors slide open slowly to an overly-bright hallway. I slip through them and out onto the busy hospital floor. Grasping the flowers in my hand, I glance up and down the hallway for any indication that there might be trouble waiting for me.

It isn't like there's any question there will be. Trouble follows wherever I turn these days, even at my own church, the place I've always found refuge and been able to live under the radar.

Those days are long over, and the ones of casually stepping into the role of Rose while Andres does the same will end soon. There can no longer be two of us. No partnership. Given how tenuous the situation is at the moment and his sudden boldness and willingness to take a shot at me, the time to act has finally come.

And none too soon.

A man dressed all in black stands outside a door to the left.

Exactly what I'm looking for.

No one else is going to have security outside their door. On this floor, patients welcome family members and friends with open arms.

Something tells me I won't get such a warm reception.

I casually make my way down the hall toward him, the crisp white dress shirt and black suit I wear to conceal my tattoos making me appear every bit the polished Rose everyone knows. As soon as he catches sight of me, he stiffens and gives a hard knock on the door beside him, never taking his eyes off me.

Pausing in front of him, I plaster on a wide smile. "Can I see her?"

I hold up the flowers, and he scowls at me with his hand hovering near his weapon.

"I think that's unlikely."

The door flies open, and Cutter steps from inside the room, the scarred side of his face twisting with his anger. Even with his eyes concealed behind the reflective aviator sunglasses he wears like Roman armor, the stare-down he's giving me would make a lesser man shiver. "You have a lot of balls showing up here, Rose."

Shrugging slightly, I motion toward the flowers. "I wanted to offer my congratulations on the little one."

Cutter offers me a sneer. "The last thing Valentina needs right now is to be discussing any sort of business with you."

I hold up my hands the best I can while wrangling the bouquet. "I swear, no business. This is a personal visit."

He scowls at me, appearing entirely unconvinced of my motives, but in the end, Cutter isn't the one in control of the Marconis. Valentina firmly holds that seat and isn't afraid to draw blood to keep it. She likely wouldn't take it too well that he sent away the head of another family who came to pay his respects.

A muscle in Cutter's clenched jaw tics as he stares me down from behind the shades. He doesn't appear likely to budge on this.

Shrugging nonchalantly, I tip the flowers toward him. "Fine, then please give these to her, along with my congratulations. To you, too, *padre*."

He stiffens at the word, almost like my reference to his recent fatherhood also reminded him of his role in the organization. "Two minutes, in and out."

"I promise."

I incline my head toward his man at the door and follow Cutter into the hospital room where Valentina reclines on the bed with their sleeping newborn curled against her chest.

She watches me with sharp amber eyes and a raised dark eyebrow. "Well, this is an unexpected visit."

Undoubtedly so, since she so recently took the other Rose against his will and held him captive. Without knowing what was said between the two of them during that time, I have to tread lightly. Saying the wrong thing could get me killed. And I'm not about to let Andres win over something as stupid as a slip of the tongue.

I extend the flowers, and she nods toward a table beside her bed where many other bouquets and cards sit. The Blood Rose Cartel isn't the only one to send congratulations. I set them down, then lower myself into the chair, careful to keep a watchful eye on a very twitchy looking Cutter.

Since they released my brother, they must have reached some sort of understanding—one I hope I can figure out during what little time I'm given with the mother and child.

"I wanted to offer my congratulations to you and Cutter."

The baby sleeping against her chest shifts slightly, and Valentina wraps her arms around it more tightly, ever the protective mother.

"Boy or girl?"

Valentina exchanges a look with Cutter, and she inclines her head, granting him permission to answer.

"Girl."

Ignoring his tone, I grin at Valentina. "How lovely for you. Helping to raise my sister was one of the greatest joys of my life. I don't suppose you have heard anything about Sofia?" I raise an eyebrow toward Valentina and twist to glare at Cutter. "I haven't been able to locate her."

His attack on my brother's estate sent Sofia underground in the first place. The lack of even a whisper from her since has been more than unsettling since she's never been on her own before, without either Andres or me. The thought of her out there all alone any longer, especially knowing what happens to young women on the streets, makes my hands clench into fists on my lap.

Cutter crosses his arms over his chest. "No. And like I told you, we never touched her. She was already gone from the pool house by the time we got there."

Information he must have given Andres when they "invited" him to their home. He might be several steps ahead of me in locating her, which could be catastrophic. When she learns the truth, which he will inevitably tell her, she will need to choose sides, and being the first one to explain the reality of the situation to her is essential. Andres will twist the past to fit his narrative, to attempt to sway her to his side of this family feud. But she's too important to the organization for me to lose her to him. Nor would I be able to live with myself if anything ever happened to her because of us and our not-so-civil war.

I force a smile at Cutter and Valentina. "Of course. Do let me know if you hear anything about her. I've been quite worried and busy searching for her." And even though I promised Cutter this visit wouldn't include any business talk, I can't wait any longer or pass up this opportunity to discuss the topic with Valentina uninterrupted. "How long do you anticipate being out of commission?"

Valentina narrows her eyes at me. "Not that it's any of your business, but I'm perfectly capable of running my organization. Having a child doesn't make me an invalid, *cretino*."

"*Discúlpame.* I didn't mean it as an insult or attack on your ability to control your people,

Valentina." I shrug as calmly as I can and recline slightly in the chair, to a less oppositional seating position. "I think it's time that we have another meeting of all the families, and I wanted to ensure you were up to attending."

Her eyebrows wing up. "Because the last one went so well?"

I bark out a laugh, thinking of the shitshow I missed out on. "That was Kat's doing, not mine, and you two have a truce now, do you not?"

She presses her lips together in a firm line but doesn't respond, eyeing me warily.

¡Mierda!

It's time to tread lightly and carefully. I do not know what Andres or Kat have said to Valentina or what sort of deals they made behind closed doors. If I ask too many questions I'm supposed to know the answers to, Cutter and Valentina may suspect something.

As it stands now, the way she eyes me would make me squirm if I weren't so used to it. She sighs, a long, annoyed sound. "Any deals or conversations that I have with Kat, or anyone else for that matter, are between us and us alone. What's so important that you feel we need to have a meeting of the families?"

"That's something that's best discussed when everyone is together."

There's no way I'm going to reveal myself until I have certain assurances from those most important to my plan. I had hoped Valentina would alert me to any sort of alliance she may have made with Andres, but it seems she doesn't want to get into any specifics. Typical Valentina, considering she has always toed the line and tried to remain neutral, even as bullets flew between other families.

She offers an incredulous look. "What makes you think anyone is going to agree to be in a room all together?"

I push to my feet and glance between the new parents. "Because a lot of things are changing in this city." I motion toward their daughter. "For you. For me. For Kat. Even for Galen and Valerian. If we don't do something soon, the entire city will explode. I don't want to get burned."

At least, not completely.

I want to ensure that, like a phoenix, I can rise from the ashes.

THREE

FELIPE

"*Repitan, por favor.* I must have misheard you."

Emiliano looks at me, his pupils dilating as he tries to figure out what to say, what might actually excuse their failure. "We lost her, sir."

Lost her?

Fury ignites my blood, searing through my body and tightening my skin.

"Explain to me how one loses a person when said person is in a locked apartment with one way in and one way out and you're standing outside the fucking door?"

He rubs a hand across the back of his neck and averts his gaze, rightfully embarrassed by the epic nature of their mistake. "She set off the fire alarm and the whole building had to be evacuated. I had my hand on her arm and led her down the stairwell, but as soon as we got outside and in the mass of people evacuating the building, she managed to slip free and take off into the crowd before I could follow."

"Managed to slip free? She's a one-hundred-and-twenty-pound woman, so how does she 'slip free' from a man twice her size?"

Emiliano swallows thickly, a flush darkening his cheeks. "She stomped on my foot, and when I let go of her arm, she ran."

¡Increíble!

I look from him to Aaron. "And what about you? What were you doing while she was slipping away from your *compadre?*"

He clears his throat and straightens his shoulders, as if that will somehow make his position more defensible. A last-ditch effort to save face. "I was monitoring our surroundings, sir. Making sure nobody snuck up on us."

¡Ay hijueputa!

Before today, I wasn't aware incompetence could reach this level. The cartel has always had solid men, ones who could be counted on to carry out any tasks, but this split between Andres and me has created a real problem in finding men who will be completely loyal to me and competent at their jobs.

Which these two clearly are not.

I raise my hands and clap slowly as I approach them in the living room of the condo. "Well fucking done. As if it wasn't bad enough that it took you so long to locate her when she left the church, now, you've lost her *again.*"

They both flinch at my words.

Aaron shifts under my scrutiny, his unease growing as we approach the point in this conversation where they pay the price for their failure. "We're sorry, sir. We'll find her right away."

"No. You won't." I pull out my gun and fire two shots into each of their chests before they can react or even attempt to pull their weapons and put up a defense.

Not that it would have done them any good. Either way, even if they had got off a few shots, I would still have killed them for their failure.

I refuse to even consider the possibility of losing, and they've now made my job all the harder.

They both crumple to the floor, and blood pools out onto my beautiful hardwood.

¡Mierda!

I shake my head and reach down to grab their weapons from their holsters. Not that either of them will live long enough to do anything with them. But one thing I apparently learned a long time ago, that they hadn't taken into consideration when guarding Rowan, was that it's smart to expect the unexpected and be prepared for anything. That means no leaving guns within their reach.

Watching the blood spread out beneath their bodies, my ire over the situation they've now created makes the muscles of my neck tense until it's almost painful.

This is just one more mess in a long line of them that I'll now have to waste my time cleaning up. Then, on top of having to hunt for Rowan again, I'll need to bring in more men I can trust. It was a mistake to hire these two. I can see that now. They didn't have what it took to work for a man like me. They were still green, inexperienced, nowhere near the level of men I've been used to working with in the organization.

That is one mistake I won't make again, not with what is coming.

I walk over to the bar, set all the guns on it, and pour myself a stiff drink.

Two hours...

I was only gone for *two* hours. Yet, in that time, these worthless pieces of shit lost the most important thing to me.

Why did she run?

Again...

We had things figured out. We were in a good place. She had committed herself to me, to the future I have planned for us—a future *together*.

So, what changed?

The events of the morning race through my head, each moment a vivid flash, as if it were happening now. Rowan was perhaps acting a little off when I found her in the bathroom before I left, but she offered no explanation, nor was there any reason for me to suspect anything major was amiss.

What could have upset her?

Nothing comes to mind immediately—at least, nothing besides the same issues we've been working through during our time together.

Unless...

I freeze with the drink halfway up to my lips, my hand tightening around the crystal hard enough to whiten my knuckles.

Could she have overheard anything I said to Kat?

Running through our earlier conversation word-for-word, I cringe and down half my drink. The burn in my throat mirrors that of the unease in my gut. If Rowan heard some of that, any of it really, it would certainly explain her abrupt departure.

I told Kat what she needed to hear, what I had to in order to convince that woman that Rowan means nothing to me personally and this is all business. To ensure that if Kat ever tries to make a move against me, Rowan won't be caught in the cross-fire. If Kat really knew, if she even remotely suspected how much I need that woman, it would give her quite the upper hand that I can't afford to lose. It would put us on an even playing field—my knowledge of Jeton and the unspoken threat to him vs. her knowledge of how important Rowan is to me.

But Rowan doesn't know any of that.

She can't possibly comprehend how tenuous this situation has become. Even after Andres sent someone after us in the house of God, she *still* can't grasp how serious things are—how *dangerous*—especially to anyone who means *anything* to me.

It makes the fact that Sofia is still missing almost a mixed blessing. At least if no one can find her, she can't be hurt or used against either of her brothers.

Rowan is here, though. Somewhere in this city.

Exposed.

Alone.

And she believes the worst when it comes to me. Maybe she should. I can't blame her after what's happened and what she's seen and experienced. I've lied to her before and withheld information, let her remain in the dark when I could have shed light on so much about her life. She has every reason to think what I told Kat was the truth, but I have to try to explain myself. I have to make her believe me.

I need to get her back, but where the fuck would she go?

Sipping at my drink, I let the burning liquid mingle with my seething rage over the epic failure on the part of my men to keep her here. There aren't many possibilities left on the list of places for her to hide. Rowan doesn't know many people in Chicago.

Kat...

The girls from Kat's Cradle...

She wouldn't go there, though. Not if she overheard my conversation with Kat and believes any of it's true. Not after her accusations last night that something is going on between me and that vile woman. She's the last person she would go to for help, and anyone associated with her would only put Rowan at risk of falling into Kat's hands.

I walk to the windows and stare out at the view beyond the smudged glass where only yesterday Rowan and I gave into our base needs for each other at this very spot. It's a stark reminder of how fast things can change, how quickly things can go south, especially when people don't know the whole truth.

That's going to change soon.

Andres has forced my hand, and the exposure of Father Felipe as Rose's brother means hiding there, as a man of the cloth, is no longer an option.

It's time to reveal myself and to take action against my brother and anyone else who dares to defy me. He was an idiot to send someone after me, to think that would work, that he would succeed, and he'll pay for his arrogance with his life.

Just as soon as I find Rowan...

FOUR

ROWAN

A SOFT, gentle hand touches my face, pushing hair back from my forehead, and I shrink away from it as reality and the pain in the side of my abdomen slap me awake with a jerk.

"Shh. It's okay. Relax."

The unfamiliar voice has me blinking open my eyes against a harsh light on the ceiling and turning my head toward it. It takes a moment for my vision to adjust and focus on the woman in front of me at the side of the bed and another for me to remember where I know her from.

"You're the bartender."

She nods, her blond hair swinging with the movement, and offers me a kind smile, and flashes of memory return—her rushing into Galen's office. Hurried, hushed voices. More pain.

I scan the unfamiliar bedroom—rough, old furniture, ratty drapes partially covering dirty windows that look out at the Chicago night sky. "Where am I?"

"The apartment above the bar. They brought you up here after..." She trails off and bites her lip nervously. "You know..."

I press my hand against the bandage at my side and grimace. "After Galen shot me."

She glances over her shoulder toward an open door. "I'm not so sure you should be saying that."

Probably not.

People don't survive being shot by men like Galen, let alone if they're dumb enough to be talking about it. Leaving witnesses is a liability. A potential for what he's done to come back to bite him in the ass.

But I'm not just anyone.

I squeeze my eyes closed and shift my position on the uncomfortable bed, wincing at the tiny needles of pain it sends through me.

The blonde continues to cast furtive looks toward the door. "I'm sure he'll be in here any minute if he overhears us and realizes you're awake."

I release a steadying breath, trying to ignore the discomfort in order to get my bearings and a better grasp on what's happening.

"He had a doctor come patch you up." She peeks over her shoulder again. "Though, I honestly don't know if he was a real doctor or a vet."

"A vet?"

She shrugs nonchalantly, like having someone trained to operate on animals dig a bullet out of a human is normal. "I guess they're doctors, too, and he did seem to know what he was doing. I helped where I could. I did some basic training when I thought I wanted to be an EMT, but then life kind of took me in another direction."

"What are you doing working for Galen?"

If this girl was training to be an EMT, then bartending at an Irish dive owned by the head of the damn mob is quite the leap.

She chuckles and releases a heavy sigh. "Actually, today's my first full day. I never even met the man until I came back into his office after I heard the gunshot."

"You heard a shot and ran toward it?" I raise an eyebrow at her. "That wouldn't be my first instinct."

Running a hand through her pale hair, she offers a slight shrug. "I used to hunt with my father and brother. Guns don't scare me, but I had no idea what I was getting into when I took this job or came back there to see if anyone needed help."

"And now, you're in even deeper as a witness to what happened and by assisting in covering up a shooting in a mob bar."

Blowing out a breath, she shakes her head. "You have no idea. My brother is going to kill me." She offers me a tight smile. "I'm Nicki, by the way."

I offer her all the smile I can manage. "Rowan."

Her blue eyes flash with confusion, and her brow furrows. "Rowan? Galen called you Nessa while you were unconscious."

"Yes, that's...my name, too." Though, it still feels foreign somehow, like too much has happened since I was that girl for me to ever go back to using it. "It's complicated."

To say the least.

And I am not about to explain the situation to Nicki when I haven't even had a conversation with Galen himself yet.

"Okay. Well, the doctor said he was able to get the bullet out and he couldn't see any internal damage. So, I guess you're pretty lucky."

"I guess."

Somehow, being *shot* by Galen doesn't *feel* lucky. More like another chance for fate or karma or God to complicate my life even more.

Nicki pushes to her feet and moves toward the door, where she pauses and looks back at me one last time. "Good luck, if I don't see you again."

I have a feeling she will. Unless she's smart enough to quit this job now that she realizes what she's tied up in.

I settle back into the mattress again and attempt to adjust my position, but only manage to send another pang through my side.

"Don't try to move."

Galen's voice stills my movement, and I turn to find his hard green eyes locked on me.

My gaze automatically drifts to the jagged scar over his left eye. He definitely didn't have that when we were children. At least, not from what I can remember. But it looks painful. Almost as painful as what he did to me.

"I'm sorry." His words come stilted and heavy with emotion, most of the Irish accent either gone or hidden. "I didn't know who you were." He steps farther into the room. "I just saw the gun and someone I didn't know in my office and—"

"Assumed I was sent by one of your competitors to take you out."

His eyebrow wings up, and the corner of his lip curls into a little half grin. "Something like that."

"I'm sorry I didn't let you know I was coming. It was kind of an unplanned visit, and I wasn't sure how you would react to me just showing up."

He closes the distance between us and lowers himself into the chair Nicki just vacated. "Well, I wouldn't have shot you."

I snort a laugh, the motion making me wince and press my hand against my side again. "I would hope not."

"Where were you? I've been searching for you forever. Ever since..." He trails off and reaches out to lay his hand over mine.

I shake my head. "I'm not totally sure. My memories are foggy, if they're even there. I'll tell you what I do remember some other time. Right now, we need to deal with a bigger problem."

His gaze hardens. "Whatever it is, I'll protect you."

If only I could actually believe that.

Galen will do his best—I have no doubt about that—but Felipe won't be stopped by anything. Or anyone. Even someone as lethal as Galen McGinnis.

"He's going to come for me, and it's only a matter of time until he figures out that I'm here."

Galen narrows his eyes on me. "Who? Rose? I can handle him."

I squeeze his hand and shake my head again. "No, not Rose. Felipe."

His brow furrows. "I don't understand. Is that Rose's real name?"

"There's so much I have to tell you..."

FIVE

ROWAN

As soon as I voice the words, regret settles heavy on my chest. I had planned to come clean, to arrive here and reveal my identity and tell Galen everything Felipe had confided in me. All his plans. The way he wanted to use me to manipulate Galen's compliance.

That had been the plan...

Galen's jaw tightens, and he jerks his hand away from mine. "So, *tell* me. Is that where you've been? Has he been holding you to play a game with me?" He sets his fists on the edge of the bed beside my leg. "Against your will?"

I bite my lip to keep myself from answering the question and making things even more complicated. If I unload and tell him everything, all the dirty, ugly, vile truths I've recently learned, it could create a firebomb worse than the one that killed our family.

And I almost did.

Everything Felipe confided in me about his past, his brother, his plans, sits on the tip of my tongue. Yet, I can't say it. No matter what happened between us or how angry I am at him, over how he's lied to me, the thought of exposing all his secrets, the things he's kept hidden for decades, his own personal pain and tragedy, makes bile climb up the back of my throat.

Swallowing it back, I continue to avert my gaze from Galen's penetrating one. Even though we haven't seen each other in twenty years, it feels like he can see right through me. Like he already knows the answer and suspects what has gone on between me and Felipe.

But that's impossible.

No one knows the convoluted reality of the twin brothers who control The Blood Rose Cartel—or how easy it is to lose your heart to one.

I take a deep breath and close my eyes. Rather than answering his question, one that would only bring more uncomfortable truths, avoidance seems like the better option. "I'm so tired."

"Are you in pain?"

"A bit."

This conversation can't go any further until I can clear my head enough to figure out what I'm going to say and do. To determine if there's any way out of this unwinnable situation I've found myself in. Because right now, I don't see one.

This man is my brother. My blood. But that doesn't necessarily mean I can trust him. Felipe and Andres are proof that even blood can betray you. And apparently, so can your heart.

After what Felipe did to me, I shouldn't feel this need to remain loyal to him. I shouldn't hold his secrets so close to my chest, but I saw the look in his eyes, felt him tremble beneath me when he told me what happened that day that changed the lives of both brothers. I witnessed his pain, the excruciating agony that still haunts him even now, over what he felt he had to do to his parents.

He may not be the pious priest everyone thinks he is, and he may act like he's cold and heartless toward everything and everyone...but that isn't true.

Felipe is human. A man with flaws. A man with a conscience. A man with regrets and nightmares about the trauma of his past. He's rejected God and the tenets of the church he works in because he can't accept that God could have allowed *that* to have happened.

I saw all of that the night he revealed himself to me. He may not have voiced all those words, but it was there, deep in his dark gaze. The hunger for something more, a connection he lost the day he betrayed his family, when he thought he was doing what was *right* in the unwinnable situation he found *himself* in.

And I can't betray that. I can't tell Galen all Felipe's secrets. No matter how much I may want to in order to help my own brother.

Galen shifts to his feet. "I'll get the doctor back here."

I open my eyes, grab his hand, and pull him back toward me. "No, I just need to sleep."

"Here." He tugs his palm from mine, grabs a bottle of pills from a nightstand and offers me one, along with a glass of water.

Even while living on the streets, I avoided any sort of narcotics or hard drugs because I saw what it did to so many of my friends, how it ruined their lives and forced them into situations even worse than what I was in. I kept myself clean, maintained at least *that* when everything else was so messy. But I accept it from him anyway because the level of pain I'm experiencing now is something unlike I ever have before—the combination of the gunshot wound and what Felipe did to me is enough to make me not want to face reality, at least for a little while.

"I'll let you get some rest." Galen squeezes my hand again. "But we need to talk when you're up for it."

"Just be careful, *deartháir*. He *will* come for me. And it won't be gentle."

He gives me a little half smile and leans down to press a kiss on my forehead. "It's all right, *deirfiúr*. I know men like Rose and can handle them."

I release a heavy sigh and relax back on the bed as the medication starts to take hold. "You have no idea who you're dealing with."

"What do you mean?"

Some would probably think Galen and Felipe are cut from the same cloth because of what each of them does, but they couldn't be more different.

Felipe lurks in the shadows and hides in plain sight at the same time, wearing a mask that has fooled everyone, while moving amongst those who should fear him as a harmless friend. Whereas Galen embraces the reality of who and what he is. He doesn't hide it, doesn't pretend to be someone or something else. You get what you see with him. At least, from what I can tell. He stands in his role as the head of the family here in Chicago with pride, and for that, I respect him. But it doesn't mean I can let my guard down around him. It doesn't mean I can open my heart and tell him everything.

I need to play this close to my chest if I want any hope of surviving being torn between these two men because I know Felipe will not let me go, and now that Galen has found me, neither will he.

I'll be stuck between two of the most powerful people in Chicago, maybe even the country— one blood, one who holds my heart in his hands and who has shown me great kindnesses. Even if he had ulterior motives.

Galen needs to know what's coming, but he doesn't get an answer to his question because the light floating feeling in my head fully takes over and I let it pull me back into Felipe's comforting arms, a place I'm not so sure I'll ever be again, or if I even want to be.

No matter, it's what I yearn for.

SIX

FELIPE

THE MAN STANDING JUST inside the door of the *Bottom O' the Well* doesn't even have time to look up before I put three bullets into his chest. The force of the blasts knocks him backward against the wall before he collapses to the grimy floor.

The same goes for the bartender, only he has time to reach under the bar top and grab a shotgun before my bullets slam into him and throw him against the row of bottles behind him.

I pause at the wide-eyed blonde girl taking in the scene from next to her co-worker's body and motion with my weapon for her to step out from behind the bar.

"Where is she?"

The girl nods upward. "She's upstairs." She motions toward a door that must be for the hallway to Galen's office. "Stairs are back there."

I advance swiftly. Even with a suppressor on my gun, the shots will have alerted someone by now. The blond bartender keeps her hands raised and her eyes on my weapon.

"I'm not going to shoot you, *muñeca*. Just get the hell out of here. You saw nothing."

She gives me one sharp, quick incline of her head in understanding, then rushes out the front, letting the door close behind her with a thud. Within a second, the door leading to the back of the building flies open, and I fire off two shots at one of Galen's men who comes out of it.

Sometimes shock and awe is the only way to succeed. I could have called Galen, tried to negotiate and reason with him, but it would have proved fruitless.

I step over the body and into the hallway, scanning for other members of Galen's crew.

Only three?

I expected more resistance than this from a man like Galen, especially if Rowan told him I would come. Perhaps he has his firepower upstairs protecting her, waiting for me to make my way up to ambush me.

It's what I would probably do. Set up a choke point where I would be sure to have a clean shot at anyone coming at me. And he *must* know I'm coming.

It didn't take much to figure out where she went. It's not like Rowan had a lot of options, and for some reason, people seem to think *blood* matters. That it will never betray you. It will never do you wrong. I'm walking proof that's bullshit, but knowing what I do about Rowan, about how badly she's wanted to find stability and a real home and family her entire life, going to her brother was the most logical decision.

If things were different between Andres and me, he would be the first person I would run to for help, too. Or Sofia, if I had a fucking clue where she was. Finding Sofia has been at the top of my priority list, but I have everyone I can think of trying to locate her, and I can only concentrate on one woman I care about right now. The one who left for the entirely wrong reason. One who needs to have things straightened out in her head before she makes a decision that could get us all killed.

She would have met Galen eventually, anyway. I would have brought her to him as a peace offering along with the DNA test results proving who she was. I would have used the newfound connection to forge a bond with him that would survive the war with Andres. One that would ensure I'd have the Irish *and* the Russians on my side.

But now that Rowan has come on her own, she could have told him anything. She could have told him *everything*. All the secrets I revealed only to her in twenty damn years. The things I entrusted to her because I believed she would choose me, choose to stay. The things that would expose my own weaknesses to my enemies.

If she has, that rips away any bargaining power I had over Galen McGinnis. She is his sister, but if he thinks he can keep her hidden above his bar, he is sorely mistaken.

I've spent too long planning this, too many years searching for her just in case Andres wouldn't step down when the day came. Too much of my soul has been put into her. Too many words have been spoken and promises made for me to let her simply walk away.

Never.

Even if I die trying, I have to get her to listen to me, to *hear* what I really mean and not just the words I said to Kat to lead her along like the stray puppy she is.

I pause outside a partially closed door, push it open with one hand, and press myself back against the hallway wall, waiting for the barrage of gunfire.

It doesn't come.

Cautiously, I turn into the room.

Galen's office. It has to be.

My gaze immediately drifts to the blood-stained desk, a photo of Rowan and Galen as children sitting in the sticky, viscous mess. The crimson fills my vision and a chill creeps down my spine, something I haven't felt since the day I opened the front door to find my fate on the other side.

Someone's been injured here.

Badly.

I turn and make my way farther down the hall, searching for stairs that will lead me up, listening for the approach of any more of Galen's men. After Kat's attack and theft of their gun shipment, the Irish have been on high-alert. That there aren't many of them here now leaves a foreboding that tightens my hand on the gun. It means they're either waiting to ambush me or out doing something even more important than protecting Galen's sister. Neither is good for me.

Footsteps pound toward me, coming down a staircase at the far end of the hallway. The moment they sound like they reach the bottom and he will appear, I unleash on the poor *pendejo*.

He drops to his knees, his weapon tumbling from his hand onto the old, worn floor, and I step over him and charge up the stairs. Someone fires down at me, the bullets slamming into the old wooden boards at my feet. One grazes my arm, but the pain can't stop me from ascending.

Each round I let loose seems to find a target—cries of dying men and the thuds of them crumpling to the floor filling the air. It would be easy to get complacent now, to let down my guard and drop my injured arm, but I'm too smart for that. There will be others. And I *will* be ready for them.

Galen can throw every man he has at me; it won't stop me from finding Rowan and bringing her home.

I reach a small landing from which I can see the open door at the top of the stairs. Pressing my back to the wall, I reload as heavy footsteps come toward me from above. The way these idiots keep setting themselves up to get blown away makes this almost like shooting fish in a barrel

I'll have to thank Galen for training his men so badly when I finally find him.

It only adds to my suspicion that he has men elsewhere—likely his *best* men—occupied with something he considers vital enough to leave himself protected by these guys who are clearly not his top guys.

The second the poor fool reaches the door jamb, I fire. He drops to the warped floorboards at the top of the stairs, and I continue my ascent. Each step I take makes the old boards creak, and I wince at the way they announce my presence. Yet, I don't hear any other telltale signs of the cavalry arriving to assist.

Where the fuck is Galen? And where the hell is Rowan?

That blonde downstairs wasn't lying. Years of hearing confession have given me the ability to see through someone's bullshit in an instant. Her fear was real, and when she told me Rowan was upstairs, she genuinely believed it. Which means I have to keep going, creeping up the last few steps before I make my final turn into what could be a damn ambush.

If I were Galen and *knew* I was coming, I would sit and wait. Throw the men I don't care about at the enemy but be prepared for him to make it through to where I can unleash Hell upon him.

Only he has no idea how familiar I already am with Hell. How it's become my home. How the flames only encourage me, warming my cold, icy heart in a way nothing else but Rowan does.

I peek my head around the jamb. An empty hall greets me, one open door at the far end with several closed ones between me and it.

She's there.

It's almost like I can feel her calling out to me, luring me to her like a damn siren singing her deadly song. I don't know why she left me this time, but it won't happen again. Not until I'm dead and in the ground.

I creep toward the open door, exposing myself at any moment for someone to come out from one of the closed ones and ambush me. Each step I'm not gunned down, my confidence grows that I'll find her there—no doubt with Galen. But I can't turn back now.

Instead, I step into the room, and the bullet whizzes past me and strikes the wood of the door jamb directly next to my head.

"I won't miss next time, Rose."

SEVEN

FELIPE

Galen McGinnis stands beside the bed in the small room, gun pointed directly at me, finger at the trigger, ready to fire again. "Don't move another fucking step. That shot was a warning, but the next one won't be."

A warning?

He isn't the type of man to issue any sort of *warning* before he ends a life. Though, neither am I, usually. I've dragged my feet where Andres is concerned.

Call it loyalty.

Call it affection.

Call it conscience.

Or call it weakness.

All are true.

He is the other part me. *Was* the other part of me. Until he chose not to be. He left a gaping hole, one I thought could never be filled. Until I finally held Rowan in my arms and felt complete for the first time.

I stare down Galen and offer a half-shrug. "I've already taken out the rest of your men." I emphasize my gun pointed at his chest. "What's to stop me from ending this now?"

"I will." Rowan's soft voice comes from behind Galen, and her hand slips out and pushes at his waist, nudging him sideways and giving me a full view of her.

Mi palomita...

Her already pale skin appears pure white, almost ghostly, where she lies in the bed. Dark circles rim her eyes. Pain lines her face. The blood sprayed out across the office downstairs flashes in my mind. A part of me knew then what I can see with my own eyes now—she's hurt.

"What the hell did you do to her, Galen?"

Galen shakes his head, never lowering his weapon. "I didn't know who she was. She was holding a gun from my desk and—"

"And you fucking shot her?" My question booms around the small room, making Rowan flinch and wince.

She holds up a hand, a motion that seems to cost her a lot of energy she doesn't have. "I'm all right, Felipe. Really. It was an accident. I'll be fine. He didn't know..."

He shot her.

Rage flares so red hot through my blood that my skin feels like it's on fire and the normally steady hand holding the gun on Galen wavers slightly.

"Felipe..." Rowan's stress-laced pleading pulls my attention away from the man I'm ready to destroy, despite how essential he will be to my plan, and to her on the bed.

She shifts slightly and winces again, which only tightens my grip on the gun and heightens my resolve to end the man who did this to her.

"You're not going to shoot him." Rowan reaches out and touches her brother's side again. "And *you're* not going to shoot *him*."

Galen glances back at her. "You came to me to escape this man, and now you want me to spare him?"

Her eyes shimmer with unshed tears, and she reaches up to swipe at them before they can fall. "I don't want you to hurt him. I..."

The words sit there on the tip of her tongue. The ones I've wanted to hear so badly from her. The ones I know she feels and is too afraid to say. The ones *no one* aside from Sofia has said to me in twenty years.

"I love him. Despite the fact that he betrayed me."

My chest tightens at her accusation. "Betrayed you? What are you talking about, *mi palomita?*"

She clenches her fists at her sides, her lip quivering. "I heard you this morning. Talking to your visitor."

¡Mierda!

Rowan *did* overhead me speaking with Kat. She heard the words that would have crushed her. Yet, she was careful not to use Kat's name in front of Galen, careful to say it in a way he wouldn't know who or what we were talking about. If she had already revealed all my secrets to her brother, she wouldn't have gone out of her way to conceal my meeting with Kat.

"I'm not sure what you heard, *mi palomita*, but know it was all for the benefit of someone else's ears. Certain people can't know how important you are to me. That would put you in greater danger than you already find yourself."

"The only one she's in danger from is you!" Galen snarls and takes a step forward. "You've been keeping her from me for how long? Weeks? Months? *Years?* Trying to warp and twist her mind so you can ultimately use her against me."

"I've done nothing but tell her the truth. Help her remember her past. Give her the promise of a future she always dreamt of."

He snorts. "A future with *you?*" Raising an eyebrow, he curls his lips into a sneer. "Over my dead fucking body will my sister ever be with you."

His words don't surprise me. I had anticipated there would be some conflict and objection once Galen discovered the nature of my relationship with Rowan, but I also can't believe Rowan wants anyone telling her what is or is not good for her. She certainly didn't like it when I did.

"I don't think that's your decision to make, Galen. Is it, *mi palomita?*"

Her gaze darts between us and the guns we still have pointed squarely at each other. "I don't know. I feel like I don't know anything anymore..."

The pain. The confusion. The torment in her words tugs at something deep inside me I thought had died over twenty years ago, when I pulled the trigger and killed the two people who loved me the most, despite my rebellion against them.

She needs reassurance, confirmation she's making the right choice.

"I love you, *mi palomita*. You mean the world to me. Without you, all of this is for nothing."

Tears trail down her pale cheeks. "I wish I could believe you."

After everything I've done to get here, to reach this point in my plan, after everything that's gone wrong, I can't let her slip away from me. But one thing being Father Felipe has taught me is how to set aside what I may *want* to do in order to do what *must* be done.

I withdraw my hand holding the gun and slide the weapon back into the holster concealed by my jacket. "How about now? Galen could kill me in a second, and there's nothing that I could do to stop him. But I don't care because none of this, none of everything I've been fighting for, would mean anything without you by my side."

Rowan shakes her head. "You had all this set in motion before you ever met me."

"That's true, *mi palomita*. I never anticipated what I would feel when I saw you for the first time, how a heart I thought was dead would beat again. How everything seemed to fall into place in a way that it never had before. How my future would be so certain when I looked into your eyes—"

"How very touching." Galen sneers at me and takes another step forward. "But it all means nothing. Valerian and I should have killed you when we had the opportunity, but I guess better late than never."

"No!" Rowan lunges toward him from the bed and the sharp crack of the gun going off fills the room.

EIGHT

ROWAN

I WARNED Galen that Felipe would come for me.

It was a given. An inevitable consequence of my decision to leave. A showdown that would have to happen because Felipe told me I would be his forever.

Now he stands here, the blood of Galen's men on his hands—figuratively and literally sprayed across his clothes—looking every bit as dangerous as he truly is, but saying all the right things and making me promises I want so badly to believe.

The very real possibility that one or both of them is going to end up dead today hits me as hard as Galen's bullet did. Neither of these men is the type to back down. Neither will admit defeat.

Yet, Felipe puts away his gun, exposing himself, making the ultimate gesture to show how serious he is about the words he's saying to me.

And my God, do I want to believe him.

But it won't matter, anyway. Galen is not the type of man you want to be standing in front of unarmed, especially after Felipe just blasted his way in here. His hard green eyes tell me what I already know—he won't let Felipe walk out of here alive.

Unless I do something...

"No!" I lunge for Galen's gun, trying to knock it from his hand and tumbling from the bed.

An almost deafening shot echoes around the room while the sharp stab of pain my last-ditch effort caused makes me retch.

"*Mi palomita!*" Felipe rushes forward and pulls me from the floor into his arms.

I wrap my hands around his neck and grit my teeth, forcing my eyes open. Galen's shot struck only inches from where Felipe stood, the hole in the floor evidence of just how close it came to hitting its mark.

Galen bends to grab his weapon from the floor, unwilling to remain unarmed even for a minute.

The man who has flipped my entire world on its head and changed everything I thought I knew about myself and love turns to face Galen, holding me tightly against his chest, seemingly unconcerned with the fact that he no longer holds his own weapon. "I'm taking her."

"Over my dead fucking body." Galen points the barrel of his gun directly at Felipe's forehead, his arm unwavering, determination set in his stance. "I just found her. I'm not losing her again."

Felipe looks down at me, his brow drawn down with concern. "Do you want to come with me or stay here with him?"

It's an impossible choice. One I don't know if I can make. Not when I feel like this, when my head is clouded by medication, new truths, and anguish over it all.

"I don't know."

They aren't the words either of them wants to hear, but they're the only ones that makes sense right now. The only way I can think to *not* choose sides in what is surely to become another front to the war Felipe is already waging.

Felipe presses a kiss to my temple and steps forward, bringing Galen's muzzle almost directly against his skin. "You know where she is now, Galen, and you know how to reach me. I'm taking her somewhere where she'll be safe. Where I can protect her from *anything* that might harm her. If you want to talk to her or see her, you do so through me."

Something about the way he says it, the way he stands, unshaken by the fact that one twitch of a finger could end him, only offers to confirm the promises he made. He will protect me with his life. If he only wanted me as a pawn in his game with Galen, he wouldn't be antagonizing the very man he hopes to bring over to his side.

My brother.

The term still feels foreign despite the trickles of memory of a small boy that seem to have wormed their way free from somewhere deep in my psyche. I don't want to leave the only family I still have, but being in Felipe's arms feels right.

Felipe shifts toward the door, and Galen's free hand shoots out and grabs my arm, his grip firm yet careful.

"Is this what you want, Nessa? To go with *him*?"

I swallow past the emotion clogging my throat. "Would it matter if I said yes? Will you hate me forever?"

He clenches his jaw and shakes his head. "No. I could never hate you. But I don't understand why you're going with him. I can protect you. I can keep you safe. We have so much to talk about."

"We do. But"—I look up at Felipe and release a heavy sigh, the weight of this decision heavy on my shoulders—"I want to go with him."

Felipe drops a kiss to my forehead, and I press my face against the warm skin of his neck, where the white collar once separated us.

He stops next to the door and turns back to Galen. "I found her, Galen, and I never meant to fall in love with her. But now that it's happened, I will not give her up easily. You and I will be bound together forever through her, whether you like it or not. Don't make her pick sides. It doesn't need to be that way."

"What other way can it be?"

"I'm organizing a meeting with all the families."

Galen's eyes widen, his shoulders stiffening. "Why? What possible reason could there be to put us all into one room together other than to stoke tensions?"

"You've been looking for Kat, to seek retribution for what she did to you and Valerian. This will be a chance for you to confront her and possibly get retribution and reparations in a way that avoids the type of violence that brings unwanted attention on us."

"You mean like blasting your way in here?"

Felipe offers him a smug grin. "Something big is coming, McGinnis. Something that will change the landscape here in Chicago, and you'll need to choose sides."

"Sides? I don't understand. What sides? This family has always operated autonomously. We might have occasional agreements with other families because our interests align, but that doesn't mean it's anything permanent."

"You'll understand after the meeting." Felipe glances down at me, determination in his hard gaze. "It's time everyone learned the truth."

He's going to reveal himself at the meeting. It's finally time.

I raise an eyebrow. "Really?"

Felipe nods. "Don't you think this has gone on long enough, *mi palomita*?"

"Yes."

Too many years. Too many lies. Too much backstabbing and bloodshed.

Galen takes a step toward us. "You're really going to go with him?"

Tears sting my eyes, but I don't fight them when they fall. "I am. Please let us go and don't come after us. Don't try to find me. I'll call you or come back here when I can. I promise. I do want to talk."

He presses his lips into a hard line and finally lowers the barrel of his gun away from Felipe. "I'm sorry you got hurt because of me."

Felipe turns away from him and stalks out of the room without another word. "Close your eyes, Rowan. There are things you don't need to see out here."

Too late.

My gaze drops to the blood pooling near the stairs, and my stomach turns again. I swallow back the bile as Felipe steps over a body.

"Do you really think Galen is going to let this go? You killed his men. You're taking me."

Felipe pauses before descending the stairs, and his almost black eyes connect with mine. "If he comes for you and tries to take you from me, I'll kill him."

"Don't say that. He's my brother. He's just trying to protect me."

"That's my job now, *mi palomita*. It always will be."

NINE

ROWAN

The car coming to a stop wakes me, and I blink until I can finally focus on the large iron gate in front of us. Felipe presses a button on the visor, and the metal monstrosity creaks open to a long drive up to a massive house looming in the darkness.

I lean forward slightly to get a better view and grit my teeth against the pang of discomfort in my side. The pain medication Galen gave me must have worn off during the ride to wherever the hell we are. "This isn't the condo."

Felipe continues onto the long drive and glances over at me with a little half-grin. "No, it isn't."

"Where are we?"

He doesn't answer immediately, just keeps his focus on the road and pulls up in front of what I can only call a mansion. Shutting off the engine, he releases a heavy sigh, like the weight of everything that happened today has finally hit him. "Our house."

"*Our* house?" I stare up at it again. "What are you talking about?"

Maybe I'm still foggy from the meds.

I don't get my answer. Felipe pushes open his door, steps out, and makes his way around to my side. He pulls open my door and holds out a hand to me.

What is going on?

So much has happened in such a short time. Things that could drive me mad if I let them—things that likely *should*—but I can't let myself be derailed by the unexpected. Not after everything I've been through in my life.

I place my hand in Felipe's and let him help me out of the car. He gently pulls me into his arms, my chest pressing into his, and lowers his lips to mine. The kiss is slow and oddly almost sweet, like it's an apology for what just happened, a plea for forgiveness for all the lies and deception.

When he finally pulls away, the look in his dark eyes makes my stomach flip. It's the *real* Felipe. Not the mask he wore for so many years and not the one he now dons when he becomes Rose.

He brushes my hair back behind my ear. "We aren't going back to the condo. That was a temporary situation. This"—he motions toward the house—"is our future."

"You bought a house?"

"I did. For you. For us."

"But..." I turn in his arms to look at it and have to crane my neck to see the top. This place rivals Kat's Cradle. The same opulence and privacy. The kind of house I never thought I'd set foot in, let alone ever could have imagined living in. "It's *huge*. And—"

"And nothing." He wraps his arms around me from behind, careful not to squeeze my side. "This will be our home. A sanctuary for us from the insanity of the world outside. Somewhere you can be safe. As long as you don't run away again."

Shit.

Guilt at everything that happened with Galen and what Felipe had to do to get me back claws at my chest. "I'm so sorry, Felipe." I twist back to face him, still caged in his embrace. "I-I shouldn't have left."

He brushes his thumb over my lips and cups my cheek. "You should have."

"What?"

I must be hallucinating...

"After what you overheard, I can't blame you for thinking I didn't care. For believing what I said to Kat was the truth. I wish you had more faith in me, but I can't fault you for not, *mi palomita*. Not when you've been lied to and abused and had your life twisted a thousand different ways."

The laugh slips out before I can swallow it down, the stress and turmoil and physical pain finally making me crack.

"What's so funny?"

I swipe away a tear and finally gain some semblance of control over myself. "You talking to me about faith."

A grin spreads across his lips. "The irony is not lost on me, *mi palomita*." He stares into my eyes for a moment, considering his words carefully, and releases a long sigh. "I know keeping you from your brother and hiding the truth from you for so long was unforgiveable, and I'm sorry for that. Sorry that it led to you getting hurt and sorry that it means you can't trust me."

His words shatter the resolve I had holding me together, and a sob breaks free from my lips as tears stream unrestrained down my cheeks. "I do trust you, Felipe. I shouldn't." I shake my head. "God knows I shouldn't." I fight back another sob, my body shaking with the release of everything I've pent up. "And maybe I'm naïve for believing this, but I do think you kept the truth from me because you thought you were protecting me. I'm not stupid enough to think you didn't have self-serving motives, too, but in my heart, I know you mean what you say about wanting me at your side."

"It isn't a matter of *want*, Rowan." He buries his hand in my hair and tilts my head back even farther, forcing me to meet his intense gaze. "It's a matter of *need*. What I'm trying to do here is going to require a lot of blood, sweat, and tears, and me doing some very bad things to get the end result. I need to know I can come home to you at night and you won't judge me or be afraid of what you've seen, what I've done."

What I've done...

Something tells me I don't know even a fraction of what Felipe has done or what he is capable of, but I can certainly speculate easily about what he's referring to based on the Blood Rose Cartel's reputation. Yet, even knowing his sins, deep in my heart, I'm confident it will never change how I feel about him.

He saved me when I didn't even know I needed saving. I thought I was happy, or at least *content*, at Kat's Cradle, but that wasn't my life. It wasn't what was intended for me. My path was inextricably altered the day my parents' lives were taken. The day *I* was taken. Now, I've been set back onto the right path.

I reach up and brush my hand across Felipe's cheek. "I'm not afraid of you. You wouldn't hurt me, but I can't lie and say that this thing with your brother doesn't make me uneasy."

He narrows his eyes on me slightly. "This was set in motion long before you came into the picture, *mi palomita*, and once it's over, things will calm down and return to a normalcy."

"When will that happen? When will it be over?"

"Soon, *mi palomita*." He brushes his lips to my forehead and holds me close. "Soon."

"So, what happens now?"

It feels like we're waiting for the other shoe to drop, like something big is lurking in the shadows just out of eyesight and it will lunge out at us when we least expect it.

Felipe's gaze softens. "I carry you inside and up the grand staircase to our bedroom and take care of you until what your brother did to you is a distant memory."

"You're not going to hurt him, are you?"

He brushes his fingertips over my cheek, silent just long enough to make me shift on my feet before he finally answers. "I'll do my best to keep the people who support me safe in all of this."

"But what if he doesn't support you? What if he sides with your brother?"

His jaw hardens, and his dark brows angle down over ominous, stormy eyes. In the light coming from the house, hitting one side of his face, I truly see the dichotomy of this man.

The light and the dark. The priest and lover. The caretaker and the killer rolled into one.

"We'll cross that bridge when it comes. For now, let's just worry about getting you better. I have my doctor coming to see you to make sure you're all right."

"I'm okay. Just tired."

"Then, let's get you to bed."

Felipe bends down and lifts me easily into his arms, cradling me like precious cargo. I bury my face against his neck and inhale. The typical scent I associate with Felipe mingles with the metallic tang of gunpowder. Evidence of what he did to get me back, of what lengths he will go to in order to protect me.

It's a scent I'm sure will become familiar to me in the next few weeks and months.

There will be blood, sweat, and tears. I just hope it isn't ours.

TEN

FELIPE

ROWAN'S CHEST rises and falls in a slow, steady rhythm. Just like it has for the last six hours since I first woke. Just like it has over the last two days since I brought her home from Galen's. Yet, I still find myself standing here, leaning against the door jamb, watching her to make sure she's still breathing, that she's still okay. Even though Doc assured me that she's going to be fine, that she was very lucky, that someone was "watching out for her."

There was a time in my life when his words might have meant something, when I might have actually considered the possibility that God had somehow protected her from Galen's gunshot. When I might have believed there was someone who brought her into my life for a reason—maybe more than one—but I no longer believe in fairytales. Not when I've seen white knights turn into monsters. Not when I saw my brother become a killer so easily and watched him morph into someone I don't recognize even though we share a face.

It's unfortunate, really, but the time has come for lines to be drawn in the proverbial sand, for sides to be chosen.

What went down with Rowan and Galen may make achieving his compliance more difficult. It certainly wasn't how I had planned it, by any means. But it is the reality now, and once he understands the situation, once he fully grasps how dangerous I am and how treacherous it will be for him if he aligns with Andres, he'll end up on the correct side.

All I need to do is send a message to him and the rest of the families before we have our meeting, something that unequivocally tells them I shouldn't be fucked with. And I know just what to do. Though, the thought of leaving Rowan to actually *do* it makes me reach up and rub the ache in my chest.

She doesn't have any protection here. The men I've brought to replace the idiots who lost her in the first place have been loyal to the cartel for years in various other locations, but I don't know how they'll react when they learn

THE TRUTH ABOUT WHO THEY'VE BEEN WORKING FOR OR WHERE THEY WILL COME DOWN ON MY feud with Andres.

I can't trust them yet, not even with the location of this house. Nor do I want anyone else here. She needs this time to decompress and heal without wondering who is lurking around.

She will be safe. No one knows about this home or could possibly trace us here. Still, the need to check on her—again and again and again—makes me push off the door jamb and move to the bed. I reach out and brush my fingertips through her soft red hair.

Despite repeatedly berating myself and telling myself not to, I can't help but worry after all she's been through. A weaker woman would have broken by now, would have crumbled and become a shadow of herself, but Rowan has held her own, has shown her strength and ability to defy me over and over again. If she were afraid of me the way I feared she would be, she wouldn't do that.

She rolls toward me slightly, and her eyes flutter open. "Hey, what are you doing?"

I smile at her. "Watching you sleep."

A light laugh slips from her lips, the first time in days she's done that without wincing. "Because that's not creepy at all."

Chuckling, I lean down and drop a kiss on her forehead. "You're going to have to get used to me doing things like that, *mi palomita*. I like watching you when you're sleeping so peacefully."

"Why?"

"Because it helps me believe that your nightmares are gone."

I hold my breath after that confession, the fear that it isn't true preventing me from moving or drawing in any more air.

Rowan sighs softly and leans into my touch. "For the most part, they are. But I still get these flashes of memories."

"Your parents? Galen?"

She nods, her pale brow furrowing. "I think so."

"Are they bad?"

Rowan shakes her head. "Not really. Just murky. I'm hoping my brother can fill in some of the gaps in my memory. Remind me of the good things I lost along with the bad ones."

"I'm sure he will."

She watches me for a moment, waiting for me to offer something else to her. "When can I talk to him again?"

Never.

I press my lips together to bite back my initial inclination to say something that would break her heart. The man did *shoot* her, but I know he wouldn't hurt her willingly, and telling her she can't see him would only drive a wedge between us. I have no intention of keeping her from Galen as long as I'm confident of his support. "Soon. I wanted you to regain your strength before you start delving into any more potentially painful memories."

"I'm okay, Felipe, I promise."

"Good, but it doesn't mean I'll stop worrying about you."

She yawns and stretches. "You know what sounds great?"

"What?"

"A shower."

"The doctor said that's fine as long as we used the adhesive film bandage to keep your wound dry. I'll go turn it on and let the water warm up."

"I can do it, Felipe."

She starts to push herself up, but I gently press her chest back down.

"I know you can, but let me take care of you."

For the first time in my life, someone else's well-being and happiness means more to me than my plan, more than what I *should* be out doing right now in order to take care of the Andres situation.

She scowls a bit. "I took care of myself for a long time."

"I know." I press a kiss to her lips. "But you don't have to anymore. You can enjoy life without all the things that have threatened you in the past always keeping you on edge."

"Now, I'll just worry about you."

"You don't have to worry about me."

Her lips twist into a frown, but she doesn't say anything else as I make my way to the bathroom and turn on the shower. Icy-cold water sprays in the massive glass-encased stall, and I crank it to the left to heat the water. After lying in that bed almost non-stop for two days, it will feel good for Rowan to get clean, to hopefully wash away the pain of what happened.

I step back out into the bedroom and find her sitting on the edge of the bed, like she's trying to gather up enough energy to push to her feet.

Guilt gnaws at my stomach. She got hurt because she didn't trust me. Because I hurt her with the deception I had to use with Kat. She watches me advance on her slowly, and I scoop her up into my arms.

A little yelp flies from her mouth. "I can walk, Felipe."

"I know. But I enjoy carrying you."

Her perfect pink lips curl into a grin. "My knight in shining armor."

I bark out a laugh. "I don't know if that's a fitting description."

One of her blond brows rises. "My knight in a white collar?"

Shaking my head, I snort. "Not anymore."

"What are you going to do about the church?"

"I've sent in my resignation letter. It isn't unusual for priests to leave the church. Especially now, when faith is being questioned more and more. They'll replace me and it'll be as if I was never there."

"That's not true. Your parishioners love you. They'll definitely miss you."

"They'll be fine. And I don't want to talk about that right now. Forget the past. I want to concentrate on you and what *you* need."

And how I can give it to her.

ELEVEN

FELIPE

STEAM from the running shower fills the bathroom and envelops us more and more with each step I take. I lower Rowan to the tile and hold her gently as she finds her balance. She squeezes my arms and offers me a little half-smile of appreciation.

I reach for the hem of my shirt she's been sleeping in to pull it up and over her head. Letting it drop to the floor, my focus falls on the way her perfect breasts hang, her nipples pebbling under my assessment despite the warm, humid air. My cock twitches to life, and I slip my fingers along the waistband of her panties and slowly drag them down her legs, exposing her fully to me.

This isn't the time to be reacting to her this way, but when it comes to Rowan, any control I had over my body's responses to her disappeared with the collar. It was like a white chastity belt, helping me tame the beast inside while I had to, but once it was unleashed, it refuses to be put back into that damn cage.

Now that I've had Rowan, I will never be able to get enough. Just not right now. Not when the evidence of her injury is staring me right in the face.

I brush my hand over the wound, but she doesn't flinch, doesn't react to my touch except to wrap her fingers around my wrist and hold me there, like having my palm against her marred skin will somehow help it heal.

With my free hand, I grab the protective bandage Doc left for showering. Rowan releases my wrist and allows me to carefully cover the injury before I open the shower and help her into the hot spray.

She steps under it, turning her face up to the water. My dick aches watching it sluice over her breasts and down her stomach, and I quickly undress and slide in behind her, the steam engulfing me.

Her green eyes meet mine over her shoulder. "You're joining me?"

I wrap my arms around her from behind and nuzzle the back of her neck. "I would never miss an opportunity to be naked with you."

She giggles softly and drops her head to lean back against me. "True."

Instinct wants me to grind my hard cock against her ass, but instead, I kiss her behind her ear and take a step back. This is about taking care of Rowan. About what she needs, even if she doesn't want to admit it.

Her reluctance to accept my help over the last few days has only grown, but I wouldn't expect anything else from a woman who has been through everything she's suffered during her life. She took care of herself for a long time and never wanted to rely on anyone—for good reason.

But it's different now, and she needs to learn that I won't stop caring for her or allow her to brush aside my efforts. Aside from Sofia, Rowan is the only person I've ever wanted to protect so badly, ever been so intent on securing their happiness. It's all I want for her. The only selfless and good thing I've ever wanted in my life, the only remaining sign that I'm even human most days.

I grab the shampoo bottle, squirt some onto my hand, and slowly lather it into her red tresses. She issues a little groan that makes my cock twitch again and drops her head back to my shoulder.

Her eyes drift closed. "Oh, that feels good."

The strands darken in the water, sliding through my fingers like silk, and I turn her around to rinse the suds from her hair. Water cascades over her exquisite form, down her neck, over her breasts, and her legs. The only thing that stops me from pushing her back against the wall and driving into her relentlessly is the wound at her side and the last remaining ounce of restraint I possess.

Instead, I slip my hand down her taut stomach and between her legs. She jerks, and her eyes fly open to meet mine. But she doesn't push me away, doesn't object. She just holds my gaze as I gently brush my fingertips through her folds.

"What are you doing?" her question comes breathy and barely audible over the sound of the running water and my own blood pounding in my ears.

"Making you feel better. You tell me at any time if this hurts."

I slip a finger inside her, and a gasp tumbles from her open lips. She wraps her arms around my neck, shifting her weight and opening her legs slightly to give me better access. My thumb finds her clit, and she drops her head back, letting the water course over her as I work her body up slowly, curling in to find that perfect spot deep inside her.

A low moan vibrates her chest, and her legs start to shake. I lean forward and capture her mouth in a kiss that almost makes me come on the spot. Her tongue tangles with mine, twisting and caressing my mouth the way I long to feel it against my skin.

Her hands drift down from my neck, and she wraps her palm around my cock, making me jerk back.

"Fuck, Rowan, you don't have to do that. This is about you."

She tightens her grip in response, apparently unmoved by my objection, and kisses me again. I roll my finger over her clit and probe her hot cunt. Our movements become more frantic, but if she is experiencing any pain, she isn't showing it now—her face a mask of pure pleasure rather than the anguish that's been there recently.

This is what I wanted. To give her the pleasure and relief she deserves rather than the pain and uncertainty I have given her so much of.

Rowan clings to me with one hand and brushes the pad of her thumb across the head of my cock, stroking me with the other. I groan into her mouth, slipping my tongue between her lips, desperate to taste her.

This isn't enough.

I pull my hand away from between her legs, and her eyes fly open. But before she can utter a single word, I lower myself to my knees and urge her thighs apart to truly get what I want, to taste her release.

The second her arousal hits my tongue, I groan and pull her even tighter against my face. She buries her hand in my hair, and I slip two fingers inside her while I stroke my aching cock with my other hand.

She tugs hard on my hair and I issue a low moan of approval against her wet flesh. The hot water trickles over us the faster we race toward release. Every flick of my tongue and pulse of my fingers seems to wind her tighter until she finally stiffens. I suck her clit in between my teeth and gently bite down.

"Fuck!" Her pussy tightens around my fingers and her body shakes. The orgasm rolls through her hard, dragging mine with it, and I shoot my cum across the shower tile as she soaks my mouth and tongue with her release.

She sags slightly against me, and when I finally stop seeing stars and pull my head back, I wrap my arm around her to keep her from tipping forward.

I press kisses up her body as I push to my feet until I finally find her lips and angle her head back with a tug on her wet hair. Nothing tastes better than Rowan on my tongue, and now she's tasting it, too.

Even at the end of eternity, I could never get enough of Rowan.

The fact that I'm going to have to leave her in the bed alone tonight, that I need to slip out as soon as she falls asleep, makes an ache form in the center of my chest.

But there's something I have to accomplish.

A message must be sent, an invitation handed out in a fashion that leaves no question about what's coming.

TWELVE

FELIPE

THE PALE FIRST light of the sun just starting to rise peeks over the horizon, marking the start of a new day, and the timing couldn't be more poignant. My final destination lies just ahead, and as I make my way through the sleepy neighborhoods of Galen's territory, a sense of peace I haven't felt in a long time—if ever—settles over me.

As hard as it was to leave Rowan sleeping peacefully in our bed, it was necessary to accomplish this task. The meeting of the families will happen, and they will know going into it which side they should end up on. These invitations will guarantee that.

Spending the entire night hunting down everyone I needed to in order to carry out my plan was well worth it in the end to send this kind of message, to assure compliance when the time comes and that they won't underestimate me simply because of the collar I've worn for the last two decades.

With the same bloody messages already sent to Valentina, Valerian, and Kat, only one of the major families remains—perhaps the most important one. The one I hinged all my plans on when I first learned about Rowan. The one that could make or break this for me.

I turn the van down the final street and stop in front of the *Bottom O' the Well*. The last time I was here, I decimated Galen's men and carried Rowan out in my arms, her body broken and inexcusably scarred.

Today, it's a different body I'll be carrying, and for a completely different reason. Nothing says "you're fucked" quite like waking up in the morning to find one of your men slaughtered on your doorstep.

I throw the van into park and quickly climb from the driver's seat. The buildings on this stretch of the street still block the early morning light, casting the sidewalk in almost total darkness.

Perfect for my plan.

Though, even if anyone did see me, they'd be foolish to intercede. It would be pointless, anyway. What's done is done. All that's left is to leave the gift and invitation for Rowan's brother.

I pull open the panel door, my eyes falling on the man. A grin tugs at my lips. Doing the dirty work myself has felt better than I ever imagined. Andres probably thought I wouldn't be up to it, that I wouldn't be able to stomach what he has done for the cartel for so many years, but he forgets who he's dealing with. He forgets what I'm capable of and what I did as a child while he was still spending his days and nights in that church, praying for my eternal soul.

Wearing the collar never changed who I am, and he needs to remember that. No one else will make the mistake he did by underestimating me again. Especially not Galen.

Certainly not if he wants any sort of relationship with his sister. If he tries to distance her from me, tries to get in between us in any way, I won't hesitate to pull the trigger the way he did.

If the roles had been reversed, I would have ended things before he ever touched Sofia, before he had a chance to leave with her. But he's shown his weakness where Rowan's concerned. He couldn't hurt me because he knew it would hurt her, that she would never forgive him for it.

I won't have that weakness.

Rowan will be angry if I have to act, if he doesn't fall in line and I need to take him out, but anger fades and forgiveness is the greatest virtue. Something I may not believe, but she certainly seems to give the Word more weight than I ever have. It may take a lifetime for her to forgive me, but she will when she sees it's all to protect her. If Galen were to side with Andres, he would be putting his own sister in the crossfire. Taking him out protects her as much as it assures the success of my end goals.

And that all starts with the meeting. It's time to deliver the final invite. The moment Andres sent that man into the church after me, he started the ball rolling, initiated a cataclysm that can't be stopped. Like putting a flame to gasoline, this inferno can't be quenched.

The time for regret and second-guessing has long since passed. I've given him every opportunity to step down, to do what is right. Now, it's time to do what I must.

I grab my cargo from the back of the van and drag it out onto the street in front of the bar, scanning my surroundings to ensure there aren't any witnesses. At this time of day, the neighborhood is quiet. People are asleep, nestled snugly in their beds, oblivious to what is happening on the street just outside.

Though many around here wouldn't even bat an eyelash if they saw me. After living with Galen in control for so long, they know better than to ask questions that might invite the scrutiny of Chicago's finest. A body on the sidewalk won't even draw a second look—except from the man it's intended for.

Blood streaks the sidewalk where I drag him across it, a crimson path of destruction that is only the beginning should Galen choose to side with Andres.

While my dear brother may have been the one who gave this organization its name, he doesn't have the callous heart to finish what he started. When it comes down to it, if we stood face to face, he wouldn't—*couldn't*—pull the trigger.

I'm counting on that.

I set the body directly in front of the door, turning the man's head to expose the slit throat. Sticky blood runs down his neck and soaks the front of his shirt where the other slashes of my knife easily sliced through the fabric and flesh. A simple gunshot wouldn't have been sufficient. This tells Galen and the others that I prefer things up close and personal, that I won't hang back in the shadows and shoot like some sniper picking them off one by one.

When I take them out, I'll do it face to face and mercilessly.

The body perfectly placed, I return to retrieve the final element of my invitation from the van and place it against his chest. The bloody rose with the simple piece of paper stating the time and location should be a crystal-clear message to Galen and the others for whom I've already done the same.

This is happening and their attendance is required. Otherwise, they can expect more of this— their men slaughtered.

I can get to any of them anytime. Now, they know.

And I know where I have to go.

Though there are a hundred other things I should be doing to prepare for the meeting and my next steps, my heart pulls me in a different direction than my head—straight back to Rowan before she wakes and realizes I was ever gone.

Andres started this war, but it's time for me to respond in a way that leaves no question in anyone's mind what and who they're up against.

Time for them to meet the *real* Rose.

THIRTEEN

FELIPE

T<small>HE LAST TIME</small> the Chicago controlling families gathered together in one place, all hell broke loose. People lost their lives. Galen and Sofia ended up with permanent reminders of the blast. The shock wave was felt for months. Of course, that was because of Kat, because of her desire for revenge against Michael for Aleksander's death. But frankly, something would have exploded anyway with Andres stirring up shit in defiance of me.

We had a plan. A long-term one for domination of the Midwest and beyond. His impatience and arrogance have forced me to speed it up far more than what I'm comfortable with. I have other chess pieces on the board that I haven't been able to move into position yet.

Rowan was only the beginning of what should have been a meticulous process of gaining support for my position, but tonight, I make my move. I find out whether all the work I've done and everything I've sacrificed will be for naught or if I'll get what I've always wanted despite the condensed timeline.

I climb from my car, out into the light drizzle falling, and turn my face up to it. I've never particularly enjoyed the rain, but tonight, it almost feels like a cleansing, like a rebirth, a third baptism. Like I'm washing away Father Felipe to truly, finally become Rose in every way that was originally intended when we made our pact and switched lives twenty years ago.

Yet, I can't regret anything that brought me to this point, not now that I've found Rowan and know that she'll be at my side whatever the future holds. And while walking in here alone to expose the truth and draw a line for the rest of the families is a calculated risk, it's one I need to make.

The point has come where I can't trust anyone anymore. I can no longer be certain they'll be able to accomplish the tasks I set out for them. My men have failed me over and over again, but even worse, Andres has betrayed me.

So, no bodyguards. No backup. The best protection I have is myself. Tonight, I'm going to use all the skills I learned preaching to a congregation in order to align the families on my side of the Blood Rose Cartel war.

I slowly make my way up to the building I chose for this little meeting and grin, staring up at its familiar facade.

St. Mary of the Angels has been my home since I arrived in Chicago. It's where I brought Rowan to keep her safe and end her having to work as a whore for Kat. It's where she fell in love with me and where I became confident I couldn't live without her.

By this time at night, the parishioners will be long gone, Sister Agnes will be asleep and locked away in her quarters, and any priest who is filling in for me will have returned to his home parish elsewhere in the diocese.

The church should be deserted. It's a place *everyone* can feel safe—neutral ground for what could turn into a bloodbath elsewhere.

I pull the key from my pocket and unlock the door to step inside a place I had hoped I would never have to enter again. If things had gone as planned, Andres would be here, *he* would be Father Felipe, and this entire meeting would be unnecessary. I could make my way across Chicago, eliminating my competition and expanding the Blood Rose Cartel territory to include the entire area and beyond. Instead, I'm forced to partner with my enemies against the one person who should be unwavering in his loyalty.

But dwelling on what *should* have been will only get in the way of what *will* be. What I will ensure will happen at this meeting tonight. Because failure isn't an option. It never has been.

Moving through the vestibule where I once greeted members of the congregation after mass, I push those memories of living a life that wasn't mine aside. The moment Andres sent a man after me in my own church, he committed the ultimate sin of pride in the house of God by trying to take me out so he could be the sole Rose.

Once in the nave, the candles burning in front of the statue of the Virgin Mary draw me toward them, the only light in the space aside from a few dim overhead bulbs Sister Agnes leaves on.

The namesake of the church stares down at me from beneath her pale plaster veil, her arms open, hands extended, almost as if offering a hug to anyone standing before her.

How ironic.

The last time I stood here, the vestments and white collar hid who and what I really was, but now, in only a few minutes, I'll come clean, confess my sins and my identity to the most dangerous people in Chicago. No amount of praying to the Virgin Mother or falling into her sympathetic arms will cleanse any of the souls here tonight.

Turning my back to her, I make my way up the steps to the altar and move behind the lectern to await the rest of the attendees. Some people might be nervous standing here with the uncertainty about to walk through the doors, but I've waited so long for this that it's more anticipation than anything.

Mi tiempo ha llegado.

So has Valerian. He steps through the front doors of the church, his wide shoulders stiff, with one of his men on either side of him.

Raising my hands, I offer him a smile. "Valerian, thank you for coming." As he slowly approaches, I motion toward one of the pews. "I would ask that your men wait either outside or in the vestibule at the rear of church, as the conversations we are going to have are not for their ears."

Decisions will be made tonight. Secrets revealed. It's bad enough that it's necessary to do it for the heads of the other families, I have no intention of letting their underlings in on the deep workings of the cartel.

Valerian holds his hard glare on me for a moment before he motions backward and his men slowly slink away, but the head of the Bratva in Chicago doesn't accept my invitation to sit. Instead, he stands in the middle of the central aisle and crosses his arms over his chest. "Galen told me what you did."

"And how thankful he was that I located his sister?"

"Thankful isn't the word that I would use to describe it. That's pretty low, even for you, Rose, to use her as a way to get to Galen."

"Like you wouldn't have done the same thing?" I raise an eyebrow at him.

His stony facade cracks slightly, but he remains stoically silent.

"Let's not pretend that any one of us wouldn't have done the same thing. Because we all know that would be a lie. If any of you got your hands on my sister, wouldn't you try to use her as a bargaining chip?"

It's exactly the worry I've had since she disappeared. Not only is Sofia out there alone after having Andres' and my protection her entire life, but she's also a tremendous source of information on the organization should anyone locate her.

Valerian offers a sardonic laugh. "Fair enough. Why did you want this meeting?"

I spread out my hands. "Let's wait until all parties arrive before we get down to business."

This isn't something I want to repeat, and the Good Lord knows that tempers may flare when the secrets we've been holding are revealed.

The rear door opens again, and Galen enters with a very annoyed looking Cutter Jackson hot on his heels.

"Gentlemen, welcome! Is Miss Marconi joining us this evening?"

Cutter clenches his jaw and stops midway up the aisle, the aviators still covering his eyes despite the darkness in the church. "I speak for the Marconis."

It certainly isn't ideal having him here instead of Valentina, but Cutter knows her positions as well as anyone, and he also knows his place. If she has given him any instructions about this meeting, then he's likely to comply with them.

Galen steps up beside Valerian and scowls at me. "You didn't bring my sister as a hostage tonight?"

I chuckle and shake my head, crossing my hands behind my back. "You think so little of me. Do you really believe your sister would be with me if I was so horrible?"

He twists his lips and sinks himself into one of the pews, exchanging a look with Valerian. "Where's Kat? The only reason I'm here is because you said she would be, and I have a bone to pick with her." He motions toward his Russian counterpart. "We both do."

I hold up my hands. "There will be no violence tonight. Not in this space, not the house of God."

Cutter barks out a laugh that echoes around the place ominously as he approaches the altar. "What do you care about what happens in a church, aside from your brother having to clean up the mess tomorrow? This is his parish, isn't it?"

I can't stop the grin from spreading across my face. Even with the knowledge that Rose has a brother who is a priest, no one suspects the truth. No one can conceive of the fact that things are not what they appear.

"He doesn't care. Don't think that he does."

FOURTEEN

FELIPE

KAT MAKES her way down the aisle, her stilettoes clicking against the marble with each determined step she takes, her statement still reverberating through the high rafters. Genti stands near the doors, his jaw set hard, obviously perturbed by the fact that she left him there.

She offers me a cool smile and pauses when she reaches the front of the church. The woman issued a violent attack on both the Irish and Russians only weeks ago, but she seems indifferent to the fact that the two men she stands next to want her dead.

Cutter remains silent and lowers himself into a pew, almost like he's settling back to watch a movie instead of real life unfold in front of him.

"Kat..." I smile at her, unconcerned with her comment or the implications of it. Soon, everyone will know the truth, anyway. "How good of you to join us."

Valerian and Galen glare at her, their ire stiffening their shoulders, but they're both smart enough not to lash out at her here. If they do, they will never get back what she stole from them and might not walk out alive.

She sweeps her hand out and smirks. "Oh, I wouldn't miss this for the world." Her gaze locks with those of the other three men. "The man standing in front of you doesn't give a shit about what happens to this church, or the people in it. The only thing he cares about is getting what he wants."

"Which is?" Valerian returns his attention to me. "Now that we're all here, why don't you tell us what the hell this is all about?"

"Gladly." I hold out my hands, motioning to the surrounding building. "I've spent two decades working for this day, and now that it has finally come, it almost feels...surreal."

Galen sneers. "What day is that?"

"The one where I take what is rightfully mine."

Cutter pushes to his feet. "What the hell do you think that is? Chicago?" He snorts and shakes his head. "This city has belonged to the Irish, the Russians, and the Italians almost since its founding." He motions toward Kat. "When the Albanians showed up, they pushed out smaller groups and made a name for themselves, and as long as they didn't interfere with our game, we let them have what they could take. Now the cartels are coming in and expecting us to just bow to them. It isn't going to happen, Rose."

I grin. "It already has, Mr. Jackson. I've seized control of most of the drug market for the Midwest by slowly eliminating my smaller competitors from Mexico and other regions. My ships move easily through the Great Lakes uninspected. Unlike my competitors, I didn't have to try to sneak my product across the border in drug mules or small vehicles. The sheer quantity of high-quality product I have at my disposal is beyond what you could possibly fathom."

"Controlling the drug market doesn't mean you have power over any of us, Rose." Cutter crosses his arms over his chest and lets the heat of his shaded glare fall on me. "We've never been involved in the drug trade, and now that the deal you made with Valentina is over, we don't care what you do as long as you stay out of our territory and it doesn't affect any of our business."

"Valentina never made a deal with *him*." Andres' assertion booms through the church, bringing an icy chill with it.

Everyone turns to look at him as he makes his way down the aisle. Confused eyes dart between the two of us as mumbled, "what the hells?" slip from my counterparts' mouths.

Valerian's brow furrows. "What the hell kind of game is this?"

Andres stops at the end of the aisle just before the steps leading up to the pulpit and altar, Kat at his left, Valerian, Galen, and Cutter to his right. "I feel slighted by the lack of invite to this meeting, *hermano*."

His appearance here doesn't surprise me, even though I never sent him an invitation. I knew Kat would tell him, just like she's been informing him of everything else I said to her or have done since she waltzed into my office and pretended things were done between them.

She may be an excellent liar, but I know my brother, and like me, he wouldn't let her walk away so easily. Even after she betrayed him to Valentina and Cutter. I'm certain he made her pay the price for that, but it never ended their relationship.

Any idiot could see the game she was playing. And I am no idiot.

"The invitation must have gotten lost in the mail, *mi querido hermano*."

He barks out a laugh and turns toward the three men looking at him with raised brows. "I'm the man you've known as Rose for the past two years. This is my brother. Some of you might know him as Father Felipe of St. Mary of the Angels."

"Though"—I incline my head toward them—"I've met with you all as Rose in more recent times."

Cutter shakes his head. "I knew something was off the other day."

I give him a little half-grin. "You see, my brother and I once shared a vision for the Blood Rose Cartel. We worked together to ensure its prosperity and that we would have a legacy to pass on to many generations to come. We did this by creating Rose and by keeping me hidden somewhere no one would ever expect while I called the shots." I turn toward Andres, locking gazes with the man who shares my face. "But my brother has forgotten his place and has made attempts to take full control by force. Attempts that have failed, and it's time for all of you to pick sides in the coming war, knowing that one will lose."

Cutter steps out into the aisle and exchanges a look with Andres that raises the old concern about what may have been said between them when he was being held by the Marconis. "The Marconis won't pick sides. This isn't our war, and we don't want any part of it. If you two want to destroy each other over what you built, so be it. Just don't let it touch us or our business, or I'll take all you fuckers out."

Precisely what I had expected from the Italian delegation.

Valentina has done her best to at least *appear* to remain neutral whenever the families have conflict, but something tells me more happens behind the scenes than she allows anyone but Cutter to know. Now that they have a child, she's bound to become even more concerned with protecting herself and her turf at any cost. That could be invaluable to me if Andres insists on pushing her about extending their former arrangement, or it could bite me in the ass if some sort of deal was made when they held him captive.

I hold out my hands toward Cutter. "Even if that is the case, you should stay. There are things that need to be discussed, decisions to be made—"

Andres steps toward me and pulls a gun from his jacket, leveling the barrel directly at my chest. "The only decision to make is where to put the bullets."

FIFTEEN

FELIPE

"No! Stop!"

My attention immediately shifts from the gun Andres holds on me to the back of the church where Rowan stands, her green eyes wild with fear.

I step out from behind the pulpit. "Rowan, what are you doing here?"

She was passed out cold when I left only a few hours ago, and considering how weak she's been the last few days, coupled with what we did in the shower earlier, I thought she'd end up sleeping through the night and wouldn't even realize I had left at all.

The last thing I wanted to do was upset her by telling her I was going to a meeting with the other families. There wasn't any reason to make her worry when I had no expectation of any violence happening tonight.

These people may be at each other's throats, but even they have respect for the house of God.

All except Andres, apparently.

He glances over his shoulder at her, and everyone watches her walk steadily down the aisle, apparently unaffected by what happened to her only days ago, or at least able to push it to the back of her mind long enough to somehow get here from our house and confront a madman with a gun.

Her hands fisted at her sides, she walks straight up to Andres, still holding the barrel of his weapon at my chest. "What the hell are you doing?"

He scowls at her. "This is none of your business. Don't put yourself in the middle of it."

Galen pushes Valerian out of the way and approaches Rowan. "He's right. You shouldn't be here. This doesn't concern you."

"But it does." She glances over at me. "The two of you are *both* acting like idiots. You're brothers. You two shared the goddamn womb. You built up this business together."

Back off, Rowan.

She's walking a very dangerous path right now, trying to intervene, and even though appreciation swells in my chest for her attempts to mend what's broken between Andres and me, all her efforts will be futile.

This can't be fixed. Even in this place, where *mi querido hermano* intended to spend his life preaching about forgiveness and love, he can't find them within himself. And I can't blame him after what he went through. After what he did to me, I can't find them, either.

Andres sneers at her, shaking his head. "You don't have any idea what you're talking about."

Cutter clears his throat. "Does someone want to tell me what the fuck is going on and who the hell *she* is?"

Galen turns toward him. "She's my sister, and his"—he points a finger at me—"girlfriend...or...I don't know what."

Kat offers Rowan an almost kind smile. "And she used to work for me, before she knew who she was."

"Wow." Cutter snort-laughs. "Valentina is missing out on a real-life soap opera, but I still don't understand what's happening here."

Andres returns his focus to me. "Rowan doesn't have anything to do with this. It's between my brother and me. What's rightfully mine that he's trying to take from me. What I have *earned*."

Rowan whirls to face him again. "This *is* my business, Andres. I *do* understand. Felipe told me *everything*."

One of Andres' dark eyebrows rises, and he tightens his hand around the gun, his knuckles whitening. "Everything? Did he tell you how he killed our parents in cold fucking blood, without any remorse, without caring about it at all?"

"That's what you really think? That he did it for the joy of it? Because he wanted money and power more than he cared about them?" She shakes her head, and the tears finally escape her eyes and trickle down her cheeks—though I can't tell whether they're for him, me, or herself. "You couldn't be more wrong. You don't know what you're talking about."

I step forward to grab her, to pull her to me and tell her to stop, to get the hell out of here before Andres finally completely loses it and lets loose with that gun he's clutching so tightly. But my little dove is on a mission, one she intends to succeed in.

She was always meant to be the peace offering to the Irish, a way to seal a relationship with Galen, an olive branch, but tonight, it seems she's trying to broker a peace between two brothers instead.

Stepping up to Andres, she places herself directly between me and the barrel of his weapon. "You're the one who is wrong. Wrong about your brother, wrong about what happened and why. I've seen it in his eyes when he told me the story. The regret. The anguish over what he did. He pulled that trigger so that Medina wouldn't torture your parents. So they wouldn't die in a much more painful and dehumanizing way." She turns her tear-soaked gaze to me where I stand frozen in place by her words and insight. "And it destroyed him every day knowing that he's the one who had to do it, knowing that he pulled the trigger."

Andres' clenched jaw tics, and he releases a sardonic laugh that Kat matches. "If you really believe that, then my brother has succeeded in the greatest deception of all."

His words hurt me more than I thought any ever could. Probably because he knows so little and *thinks* so little of me. I've always known it, always knew he blamed me for everything and assumed the worst, but hearing him say it so callously to the woman I love, and in front of our counterparts from the other families, is another matter.

Even though I know it will fall on deaf ears, the need to explain, to make one *final* attempt to convince him of the truth he's denied for twenty years is too strong to push away.

I step forward, moving closer to him. "It's true, *hermano*. And I've tried to tell you over the years, but you never wanted to hear it. You never believed a word I said or thought that there was any possible way that it could be true. You wanted to believe the worst of me. And then you let yourself become angrier and angrier at me for doing what I had to in order to protect them. Because you know you could not have done the same. They would have suffered even more had I not done it and you know it. You know what Medina and his men were capable of."

He shakes his head, ready to argue whatever point he's intent on making, likely ways the tragedy could have been prevented, but it's too late to take things back now. Too late to change his mind about something that happened so long ago and the belief he's held in his heart so tightly since.

Rowan holds up a hand to him. "You two need to stop this before it goes any further. Can't you see what you're doing?" She looks to Kat. "Can't you, Kat? You've spent time with them both, seen them both operate. You've put yourself and those you love in danger because of this war between them."

Kat shifts uncomfortably under the scrutiny, but Rowan charges ahead, pointing her finger squarely at Andres.

"You spent twenty years secretly hating each other while you built this empire, and now you both want it all and are willing to destroy each other to get it." She takes the three steps up to stand beside me near the pulpit and turns her sad gaze on me for a moment before focusing it back at him. "You're *both* going to lose it."

SIXTEEN

FELIPE

ROWAN'S STATEMENT carries a heavy truth. One I've tried to ignore. Like Cain and Abel, envy and pride will destroy two brothers. As with them, sin will be our downfall—his of pride and mine of sloth.

We can't both succeed. One of us will fail, and that failure will be in the most final of ways. My little dove, the sweet girl who has been living the wrong life, sees that truth clearly. She's found the strength to speak it out loud, to confront two deadly men with how childish they are and call them out on their sins.

She glances between us again and shakes her head. "But it doesn't have to go this way."

I reach out and take her hand, pulling her closer to me. "I think it does, *mi palomita*. My brother has made his intentions clear and the bell cannot be unrung."

"Bullshit." She pulls her hand from mine and props it on her hip. "How many times have I heard you from this very pulpit preaching about forgiveness and second chances and brotherhood, the importance of family?"

"Empty words spoken because I had to."

"No." She shakes her head, her chest heaving with her tears. "They're not empty words. And I don't think that deep down you believe they are either." Turning her focus back to where Andres stands near Kat, his weapon at the ready, she holds out her hands. "If you two worked together, if you worked as one, the way you have for twenty years, you would be more powerful than all the other families combined."

Cutter barks out a laugh. "If they don't kill each other in the meantime. But if you think that any of us will let the cartel swoop in and take over anything that's ours, then you're right, a war is brewing, and not just between the two of them."

Rowan turns to him. "You don't know me, and this isn't my world. I don't know all the intricacies and the ins and outs. I don't know what sort of backdoor deals you've done with each other or what your expectations are. Who controls what territory, who wants who dead, any of it. None of it matters to me. All that does is seeing that these two"—she points at me and Andres—"don't destroy each other over something that happened twenty years ago."

She sucks in a shaky breath, letting her gaze drift over a stoic and silent Valerian, who has been taking in everything with great interest, and to her brother, whose hard stance indicates he's ready to grab her and make a run for it at any moment.

Where does she find the strength?

The woman doesn't appear the least bit intimated by those in this room or the fact that Andres could easily turn his gun on her. She won't back down. Not now. Not ever.

Her harsh glare lands on my brother. "You need to get over your pride." She turns back to me. "Both of you. And this apathy for what happens to each other, to remember that you're brothers—first and foremost. Look what you've accomplished together. Don't destroy it by pulling that trigger."

Her words shake my faith in my plan more than I ever thought would be possible, as memories of a childhood filled with laughter and love and my brother at my side fill my head. His hand holding the gun wavers slightly, and Kat leans into him and whispers something that makes him flinch.

He locks his gaze on mine, and for a flicker of a moment, they're the eyes of the fifteen-year-old boy I saw before our lives went to shit instead of the blood-covered one he became later that day. "I don't know if it's possible to undo the harm that's been done over the last two decades." He takes a deep breath, considering his words carefully. "But if there's any chance of us ending this without destroying each other, then I'm willing to at least *discuss* the possibility."

A true miracle.

Over the last two years, Andres hasn't given any indication whatsoever that he would even *consider* the possibility of the two of us working together. It's always been all or nothing for him. And therefore, it became all or nothing for me because his continued failures hurt the bottom line.

The idea of us working together as one unit again, truly, out in the open, squashing anyone who stands in our way and dominating the way only "Rose" can, has a certain appeal. But the other families aren't going to just stand by and let us take control, and without expanding into the Irish, Russian, and Italian territories, the Blood Rose Cartel will only be one of five when we should be one of one.

Almost as if he can read my mind, Valerian steps forward, laughing without any humor. "Let you two team up against the rest of us until you control the entire city? Is that what's happening when we leave here?"

I flash him my most genial smile. "The future isn't as clear as I thought it was when I walked in here tonight. When we leave here, I cannot guarantee there won't be conflicts that come naturally when these types of situations arise."

Truth be told, I don't know *what* will happen between Andres and me when we leave this church tonight. He says he's willing to *discuss* a truce, that he doesn't want this war to kill either of us. Yet, twenty years of pent up resentment and anger won't just disappear overnight, no matter how badly Rowan may want them to.

It will be a long, hard road, but it is one I'm willing to walk with him. We spent our early years attached at the hip, finishing each other's sentences and thoughts. Perhaps there's a way to get back to that place again.

Galen sneers and sidles up beside his Russian counterpart. "And you expect me to what? Fall in line with you because you're fucking my sister?"

Anger flashes hot through my blood, tightening my fists at my sides. I wrap my arm around Rowan and press a kiss against her temple. "I'm marrying your sister."

She stiffens next to me and glances up. Her perfect lips, the ones that have spoken so much truth tonight, and potentially forged a truce I never thought could happen, open and close a few times before she finally manages to speak. "You are?"

"Of course, *mi palomita*. I told you that once I made you mine, it was forever, and I meant it." I kiss her again before facing down her brother. "You can choose to accept that or create another enemy and drive a wedge in your relationship with her. That's up to you."

Galen fumes and lunges toward me from where he stands just behind the first row of pews. "You motherfucker—"

The fusillade of gunfire tears through the church, slamming into the pulpit, into the wooden pews, and the people who wrongfully assumed it would be safe here, killing any arguments from any sides, ending the meeting in a bath of blood.

GREED

Greed makes man blind and foolish, and makes him easy prey for death.

- **Rumi**

ONE

GALEN

GUNFIRE TEARS through the church and everyone in it, the sharp cracks of the bullets coming from automatic weapons echoing across the vaulted ceilings and all the marble and wood. The place was meant to be a safe meeting ground for the five families, neutral territory, a house of God, now bathed in blood.

Instinctively, I dive into the closest pew, but the sharp bite of pain in my left arm proves I'm not fast enough. I slam against the hard, cold floor with a grunt.

Fuck.

The barrage of shots continues from the rear of the church, where several of us had left some of our men, which means they were either taken out or are involved in a fight for their own lives back there. Even if they're alive, they won't be any help to us now.

What the hell is going on?

Everyone is here—the heads of all five families are in this damn church at the same time.

So, who the fuck is shooting?

I press my hand against the wound on my upper arm. Blood trickles off my elbow to plop in tiny little droplets on the white marble.

"Galen!" Valerian's deep voice comes from the pew to my right.

At least he's not dead...yet. But given the way the bullets continue to rip through the church, the shooters are firing relentlessly and without apparent care who or what they hit. That doesn't bode well for us getting out of here alive.

"Here."

"You hit?"

"I'm okay." As long as I can get out of here quickly, at least. "You?"

He mutters something under his breath in Russian. "Yes, who the hell is firing?"

The shots continue—the wood of the pew splintering just above my head.

Fuck.

I remove my hand from the wound, pull out my gun, aim over the top of the back of the pew, and return fire at the unknown assailants while trying to stay tucked behind the only protection I have. Which doesn't seem like very much at all.

More splinters fly past my face, falling to the floor to mix with my blood dripping there. More shots sound from my right—someone else firing back at the assailants. Others have survived. So far.

Dropping back down, I scan across the center aisle, trying to find Rowan and make sure she's okay.

After everything I went through to find her. All the sacrifices. All the promises I made to God... I can't lose her now.

But down here on the floor, tucked into a pew, my view is limited to what is directly across the middle aisle, where Kat huddles next to Rose.

Or whatever the hell his name is—the one not fucking my sister.

Blood splatter mars the side of Kat's pale face; though, it's impossible to tell whose blood it is from my vantage point.

I hope it's hers.

That woman has caused Valerian and me nothing but trouble since the minute she set foot in this city as Kat. Our tentative truce with Michael had paved the way for us to make big moves, then she shot him in the fucking head and ended any potential future we might have had with the Albanians as allies. Kat firmly cemented where we stood after she lied to my face and told me she had no intention of interfering with my business and then hit my gun shipment in the same fucking breath on the same night she hit Valerian.

But where is Rowan?

I drop slightly and lean down to try to scan under the pews on that side of the church, but the continued fusillade of bullets from the rear of the church prevents me from moving any more.

Who the fuck is back there?

None of the families would be stupid enough to fire on *all of us* in a church, putting themselves in danger. I guess, in this moment, it doesn't really matter *who* it is. Blood continues to ooze between my fingers and over my gun, where I press my hand against my wound. The real concern here is getting the fuck *out*.

"There *has* to be a side door to this place," I call out loudly enough for Valerian to hear over the shots, hoping he might know the layout of the place, but he doesn't respond.

Fuck.

Sliding down farther, I peek down to look under the pew and make sure he's not passed out or dead on the fucking floor...but he isn't there.

"Shit."

Apparently, it's every man—or woman—for himself when you're stuck in a damn firefight.

I glance behind me toward the dark outer walls of the church. There has to be another door out of this fucking place, and there's no way I can go out the way I came in. Despite leaking like a damn sieve, I don't have any choice but to move and keep moving until I can get the fuck out.

Inching backward in a squat, I fire off a few more rounds over the top of the pew, conscious of the fact that I only have a few left in this magazine and only one spare magazine. The opposing gunfire continues to rip through the place of worship—pinging off the marble and shattering wood pews like they're made of fucking toothpicks.

Whoever's pumping this kind of lead into us means business. You don't pull out automatic weapons unless you intend to cause serious carnage without care. And they've done exactly that, from what I can tell.

I grit my teeth against the agony in my arm and make it to the end of the pew closest to the outer side of the church. Three feet separate me from the marble wall. One of the Stations of the Cross hangs directly in front of me.

Jesus is condemned to death...

Flashes of my childhood in the church back home in Ireland flit through my head. Memories full of joy and happiness before it all went to hell.

Hopefully, it's not an omen of my future.

Though it's darker along the outer edges of the church than under the center where the lights are on, if I stand, whoever is shooting will definitely see me. But I'm out of options. I have to make a break for it, or I'll die here just waiting for them to advance down the aisle.

Fuck!

I clench my jaw and try to peek over the other side of the pew toward the altar, the last place I saw Rowan and Felipe. The last twenty years of my life were consumed with trying to find her, and now that I have, this isn't the way I'm going to lose her.

A bullet whizzes past my face, close enough to make me tumble backward onto the marble floor.

Fuck.

If they're alive, they're down on the floor or hiding behind something like the rest of us. There isn't any way I'll get to them, but I can take some minor comfort in knowing Felipe will take care of her. He didn't shoot up my entire fucking place and take her out of there to let her die like this.

I have to believe that.

Shifting to get my feet under me, my back pressed to the pew behind me, I grimace at the pain burning through my arm and the trail of blood I've left down the once-white marble.

There isn't any time to worry about anyone else. I need to get the fuck out of here if I want to survive this. Then I'll deal with the fallout.

I push to my feet and fire behind me as I race toward the wall, keeping my back to it. Four men in all black fatigues stand at the rear of the church, unleashing a hailstorm of bullets from AK-74s, the empty casings falling to the marble floor faster than water from a faucet.

But I don't have any time to try to analyze who the fuck they are or why they're doing this. Only one thing takes precedent now.

Running.

I move as fast as I can, shooting back. Another bullet slams into my left shoulder, knocking me forward and off my feet. I slam against the unyielding stone, and my gun tumbles from my hand and slides across the floor in front of me.

Fuck!

Pain sears through my arm and upper body, but I grit my teeth, push back to my feet and run, scooping up my gun on the way. I fire off the last three bullets and finally hit a hallway that leads back from the main church.

Though empty, drops of blood shine on the marble floor. Someone else came this way and hopefully found a fucking way out that I can use.

Reloading my gun, I follow the trail like Hansel and Gretel, hoping it will lead me to escape instead of to some vile witch's lair or to someone who can finally succeed in what those firing at the back of the church came here to achieve.

Total and utter destruction of the five Chicago families.

TWO

GALEN

THE ROAD in front of me shifts in and out of focus. Dark pavement and white lines fade into moments of gray and then total blackness.

I force my eyes open every time they drift closed. If I let myself succumb to the desire for sleep, I'll never make it. Of that, I am totally confident.

This isn't the first time I've been shot—and it likely won't be the last, as long as I survive this one. Which is still very much not a given. I've lost too much blood. Even with my belt cinched tightly around my arm as a tourniquet, the warm trickle down to my fingers continues relentlessly.

Fuck! I hope Luke was able to get a hold of Doc.

I would have gone straight to his place, but I won't be able to make it across town. Not like this. As it is, I'm barely going to make it back to *Bottom O' the Well*.

If it were any farther from the church, I'd likely pass out on the side of the damn road. Even being this close, I still might.

I turn onto the familiar street and release a breath of relief when the bar comes into view. After all these years, I never thought I'd be so happy to see such a shithole, but for better or worse, it's home. Even after Felipe came in and shot up the fucking place, there isn't anywhere else I'd rather be right now.

The future...that's another story. But my big plans will have to be put on hold until I deal with the current crimson situation.

I turn into the lot and pull behind the bar. Even the simple act of shutting off the car and reaching for the handle with my good arm makes me wince and the world whirl around me.

This is bad craic. Really fucking bad craic. I stagger from the car and kick the door closed behind me, gripping the front of the hood with my good hand to steady myself. My head spins, the world around me disintegrates into a dull gray, but I shake it off and continue to the back entrance of the bar to yank it open. At least Luke followed my instructions to leave it unlocked for me after I called.

When I left the church, I had to warn him. I had to make sure he knew someone may be coming for us, and I needed him to get Doc and have him ready and waiting for me.

Another wave of dizziness hits me, and I squeeze my eyes closed and push forward down the short hallway and into my office, letting the outer door slam closed behind me.

Luke appears almost instantly, just as I collapse into my chair. "Sir?"

My eyes drift shut. "Did you get Doc here?"

"I can't reach him, sir. I've tried every number we have."

Forcing my eyes open again, I lock a hard gaze on him. "Then fucking go get him." I grit out the words through a wave of dizziness that threatens to make me pass out completely. "Now!"

He flinches. "Sir, I already sent Shane and Colin over there, and they say the place is deserted. Doc isn't there."

"What about his house?"

"He isn't there, either."

"Fuck." It isn't like Doc not to be reachable.

"Maybe he's out of town?"

"How the fuck would I know?" I press my hand against the wound on my arm harder, even though it seems like a lost cause. Blood continues to leak through my fingers and trickle down my back from the shoulder shot.

"Is there someone else I can call?"

"Who the fuck else would you call?" I practically roar at him, the agony starting to make my stomach turn. "Doc is always the one. He's the only one we can trust to patch us up."

"But, sir..." Luke swallows thickly and takes a step forward. "You don't look so good."

"You think I don't fucking know that? Try to think of any other alternatives."

While Doc may be trained for surgery on animals, he gets the job done on humans just fine when needed, like he did for Nessa...Rowan. He's the reason she survived after I made such a horrible mistake. Him and one other person...

"I know who to get."

Luke raises an eyebrow. "Who?"

"The girl."

"What girl?"

I squeeze my eyes closed and try to remember. "I can't think of her name...the new bartender."

He shakes his head. "The blonde? I never met her. I was already out taking care of our situation when she arrived."

Our situation...

If my best men hadn't already been dealing with other things, Felipe never would have made it in here so far. Never would have gotten to Nessa and gotten her out of here. It could have changed everything, but I didn't have much of a choice but to face Felipe with younger, less experienced guys. A decision that proved deadly for them and costly for me.

Luke moves farther into my office and stops just in front of my desk.

The girl witnessed a lot that night. A lot that could cause all sorts of problems for us. But she was gone by the time Felipe left with Nessa, likely fled when he came in shooting. "Have we heard anything from her since then?"

He shakes his head. "No. We had intended to get in contact with her to make sure she understood her obligation with regard to what she saw, but then, we were busy cleaning up what Felipe did and handling our other situation. Then you got the *invitation* from him to the meeting..."

Fuck!

I was so caught up with Felipe taking Nessa that I somehow overlooked the fact that a brand-new employee I didn't even know witnessed a whole lot of bad shit. "Find her. Bring her here."

He raises a dark brow again. "The blonde, sir?"

"She has medical training. Get her here now."

"What if she doesn't want to come?"

"I don't give a fuck if you have to drag her out of her place kicking and screaming. Get her here."

"Yes, sir." He slowly takes a step back.

"Now! It seems you're not quite understanding the gravity of the situation here." I motion to my arm. "I've lost a lot of fucking blood."

"Yes, sir. Shane is on his way back from Doc's now with Colin. She left her purse downstairs the other night, so I'll get her address and send them over there. Right away."

I grit my teeth and lean back against the chair with my eyes closed. "Good."

"Sir?"

"*What?*"

"You might want to stay awake."

I drag my eyes open to glare at him. "I'm trying. You might want to try to get her here sooner rather than later."

"I'm going, sir. I've never seen you so pale."

Just fucking great.

I'm going to die in here.

Alone.

Shot up.

After I've finally made a move that will help secure my place in Chicago and ensure the future of the family, all hell breaks loose. All because of the fucking Colombians. That fucking cartel is going to be the death of me—maybe literally.

"Fuck." I grit out the word and try to keep my eyes open, but this time, they don't respond, and I sink back into that familiar darkness that's been beckoning me ever since I fled the church.

Fuck.

THREE

NICKI

I POP the cap off another beer and take a long pull of the cold, hoppy liquid. Two didn't do the trick, but maybe three will. Maybe, just maybe, it will be enough to wash away the memory of what happened to all those men in that bar.

Flashes of that night flood my vision, just like they have every moment since I ran out of there.

The ringing sound of the shots. Blood all over the bar after that man came through the door and just started the carnage.

I should have left the second I came downstairs from talking with Rowan that night. I should have grabbed my purse and fucking ran as fast as my feet would carry me, but that man didn't even give me time to do that. I barely had time to take a breath before he showed up, firing. And I have no doubt that when he made it upstairs, he did the same thing there. The other men were merely obstacles as he fired indiscriminately, taking out everyone in his path. Except me.

Why did he let me go?

It doesn't make any sense. I saw him. I *saw* him kill the men in the bar area. I was a witness.

Why did he let me live when he killed everyone else?

The same question has been rattling around my head endlessly.

But it doesn't matter why, just that I'm breathing. That's what I've been telling myself for days while I've stayed locked in here in the apartment, trying to wrap my head around that day.

Around *everything*.

I inhale deeply and let it out slowly, hoping to calm my thundering heart, but it races and skips a beat every time I think about what happened.

You can't go back, Nicki. You. Can't. Go. Back.

I've been repeating those words to myself since the moment I realized I left my purse under the bar, tucked away and hidden, with my cell phone, my ID, my cash and credit cards—everything important. All the things I *need*.

Hours and hours, I've paced this small apartment, considering the conflicting realities, battling with myself over what I have to do and the fact that no options are good ones.

I need what's in my purse. I need to go back and get it at some point. They probably don't even know it's there. Showing up would mean putting myself directly in the line of fire for Galen. After all, I know he *shot* Rowan and then I witnessed a massacre on his property. While Galen hasn't sent anyone for me yet, that doesn't mean he won't. That man who came in could have killed him, for all I know, or he's just been too busy to come to find me and deal with what I saw. But walking in there would give him—or his men—the opportunity.

Fuck.

I take another long drink of my beer and plop down onto my couch to find something mindless on television to try to keep my brain occupied with anything other than this.

"They found the body buried down three feet in the backyard..."

"Oh, hell no."

I grab the remote and flip the channel until I land on a cheesy romantic comedy. I'd rather be depressed about my love life, or lack thereof, than be reminded of all the violence I just witnessed by watching the true crime shows I used to enjoy.

Sagging back into the cushions, I take another swig of my beer, willing my body to relax.

You made it out. You're alive. You're okay—for the time being.

But I still need a job. I'll never be able to stay in Chicago unless I find one fast, which means I have to get over my constantly shaking hands and legs and get my shit together so I can start applying and going to interviews. Otherwise, I'm going to have to move back home, and that's the last thing I want to do.

That's a problem that can wait until tomorrow, though. Tonight, it's beer and romcoms.

Not gunshots and blood...

I finally manage to get my heartrate under control and melt into the cushions, losing myself in the antics of the crazy suitor in the movie.

It's the first time I've felt relaxed in what feels like days—the alcohol and the cheesy film having the desired effect. My eyes start to drift closed, but the apartment door bursts inward with a massive crash, ripping the lock right out of the apparently useless wood frame.

I jerk back. "What the fuck?"

Two big men enter, their hard eyes scanning the room until they land on me. My beer tumbles from my hand, the glass shattering on the wood floor, and I scramble over the back of the couch, away from them.

But it's no use. There isn't anywhere to go.

One of them advances around the couch, and strong hands wrap around my waist as a meaty hand clamps over my mouth. The smell of sweat and death clings to the palm. "You're coming with us."

I try to scream, but it's muffled by the damp flesh against my lips. Everything I've ever been taught about self-defense races through my head. All the things I was told growing up about protecting myself if someone ever tried something like this.

Back then, people were worried about some creeper rolling through the neighborhood, snatching kids off the street, not big killer goons breaking into apartments. But either way, the truth rings the same in both situations.

Don't let them take you!

I open my mouth as wide as his hold will allow, still kicking back at his shins, and bite down as hard as I can. He jerks away his hand immediately and curses, giving me the opportunity I need.

"Help! Someone, *help!*" My cries echo around the small, shitty apartment and out through the open door into the hallway.

Someone must have heard that.

But no help comes. No sounds of doors opening or rushed footsteps coming toward my apartment.

Nothing.

I don't know why I bothered. In this building, in this part of town, no one's going to come to rescue me. Nobody wants to get involved. No one runs toward screams for help. They turn a blind eye. They keep to themselves and keep their heads down. They see nothing. They know nothing.

Which means...I'm on my own.

I struggle against the man's tight hold on my waist. The brute clamps his hand over my mouth again in a way that barely allows me to breathe, let alone open my lips wide enough to bite him again.

He rushes toward the door with me kicking wildly, trying to get out of his hold long enough to hit him where it really hurts. His partner waits by the door, hand near a gun on his hip, watching for anyone approaching down the hallway.

My foot connects with the second guy's crotch and sends him a staggering back a few steps, but he just glares at me and keeps coming, falling in behind us as we leave my apartment.

They rush down the stairs and out to black SUV waiting on the street.

No amount of fighting or kicking is going to do any good. Not when these men are twice my size and clearly trained for this type of thing.

This is it.

This is how it ends for me...

FOUR

NICKI

THE SOUND of the road beneath the vehicle mingles with the occasional exchanges between the two goons who snatched me in some unfamiliar language. With a blindfold covering my eyes, everything seems so much louder, more intense.

I don't know what they're saying, but it probably isn't anything good for me. After all, they have me in an SUV, going God only knows where, to do God only knows what with me. I could scream for help. Not that it would matter, anyway. One of the goons sits beside me in the backseat, his thick, warm thigh pressed against the side of mine—a constant reminder that I won't get anywhere no matter how hard I fight him and his partner.

The gun in his hand, pointing in my direction, firmly secures that threat. He made *sure* I saw it before he wrapped the blindfold over my eyes. They may not want me to see where we're going, but he sure was making a statement with that gun before he darkened my vision.

He's right there. It's *right there.* One twitch of his finger would end whatever this is. It would end *me.*

Trying to escape from a moving vehicle with two armed and capable men watching me and ready to secure me would be stupid. And one thing I am *not* is stupid.

I pride myself on my ability to remain clearheaded about most things, and in almost every situation in my life, I've kept my cool. But this is different. Life or death.

I've already let them take me from my apartment. The longer they have me, the farther away they take me, the more likely it is that I won't make it out of this still breathing. So, maybe I am stupid because I inch to the left, toward where a door must be. A means of escape that can't be more than a foot away.

A thick hand grabs my right arm and drags me back across the leather bench seat. "Where do you think you're going?"

His low voice sends a chill through me and raises goosebumps on my arms, and I go stock-still.

They haven't killed me yet.

That could be a good sign or a bad one. Either they need somewhere more private to do what they're going to do—like blow off my damn head—or they need me alive for something even worse.

Visions of all the violent possibilities flash through my head. All the horrific things done to women when they're kidnapped.

A single tear rolls from my eye to be absorbed by the blindfold.

How the hell did I get myself into this?

All I wanted was a clean start, somewhere I could disappear and leave behind the life that had become so hard to struggle through. Then I went and helped a mob boss and witnessed a mass murder.

What the actual fuck happened?

Life took a hard turn I wasn't expecting, and now the man driving the SUV takes a hard left and finally comes to an abrupt stop.

I turn my head to the side to listen for anything that might tell me where we are, but all I hear is the heavy breathing of the two men and my own heart thundering in my ears.

"Let's go, blondie."

The sound of the door popping open makes me jump, and he tugs on my arm and drags me from the vehicle. I stumble forward. His harsh grip barely keeps me upright. My knee strikes the harsh pavement. The thin material of my pajama pants tears, and I cry out at the sharp bite of pain. But he just pulls me to my feet and keeps leading me forward, dragging me toward my uncertain fate.

Where the hell are we?

We step into a building, the soft sounds of the night and light breeze replaced by stagnant warm air. The lighting changes, darkening even more, and a door slams behind us. Our footsteps echo slightly down what sounds like a hallway, each one sending a shiver of dread down my spine.

The goon leads me to the right, digging his fingers into my arm more harshly than he needs to. There isn't anywhere for me to go. Nowhere for me to run. But he's making a point again. Because he *can*.

He pulls off the blindfold and shoves me forward slightly. I blink against the harsh light, disoriented after total darkness and being thrown around like a ragdoll, and blindly lash out at him, but he catches my hand before I can make contact.

"Nice try, blondie."

A push at my back rocks me forward until my legs bump into something in front of me. It takes my eyes a few seconds to adjust, but the moment they do, I easily recognize the room.

The office of Galen Fucking McGinnis.

"Here she is, boss."

Galen sits in the leather chair behind his desk, where I helped him control the bleeding he caused by shooting Rowan only a few days ago. His head of disheveled salt-and-pepper hair with hints of red is tipped toward me, and he slowly lifts it. Hazy, unfocused green eyes meet mine, the left one slashed through with a nasty scar.

I clench my fists at my sides. "You motherfucker! How dare you—"

He holds up his right hand to stop me—covered in crimson blood that stands out against his pale skin. ""Calm the fuck down, woman. Spare me the indignation and just get your arse over here and look at this."

The tiniest hints of an Irish accent slip through his words, and with a wince, Galen moves his left arm forward so I really get a good view of the carnage. The whole left sleeve of his shirt is soaked in blood, a belt wrapped around his arm like a tourniquet.

My stomach turns, worry replacing my initial fear. "What the fuck happened?"

"That's irrelevant. I need you to get the bleeding to stop."

"What?" I take a step back, but a hard body behind me stops my retreat. I shake my head and hold up my hands, palms out. "No, no. *Hell* no! I'm not a fucking doctor."

And I'm not getting involved in *more* of Galen McGinnis' illegal activities.

He grits his teeth, hard gaze locked on me. "I'm well fucking aware of that fact."

"Then *call* one. Go to one. The guy who helped you with Rowan...or Nessa...whatever the hell her name is."

His lips twist down in a scowl. "We can't find him."

"Then go to a fucking hospital."

This isn't rocket science. Galen clearly needs medical attention. *Serious* medical attention.

He sneers at me. "Not an option, for obvious reasons."

"Well, I'm not an option, either." I fist my hands at my sides to keep myself from lashing out again since the big goon still hovers behind me. "How dare you drag me out of my apartment after I was almost killed by that psycho who came in here looking for Rowan! What makes you think I'd help you after all that anyway?"

His cool gaze sends a shiver over my skin, putting a damper on my fiery resistance like water being thrown on a flame. "Because you don't seem like the type to sit back and watch somebody die."

Fuck...

I grit my teeth and dig my nails into my palms.

He isn't wrong about that. The entire reason I wanted to be a paramedic in the first place was to help people, to do whatever I could, however small it might be, to give them a fighting chance before they got to the hospital. His words call to that part of me deep down that I pushed aside and made excuses for, that part I have ignored ever since I walked out of the paramedic classes.

"I'm *not* a doctor."

"So you've said."

"I don't know what I can do."

"We have some supplies here. Stuff Doc left last time. Just do what you can."

Just do what you can?

Like it's that simple...

"And what happens if you still bleed to death?" I glance back at the goon standing guard behind me. "You're going to kill me for not saving him?"

Galen snorts. "The longer you stand there instead of fucking helping me, the more likely it is you're going to find out."

Shit. Shit. Shit.

This can't be happening. This can't be happening...

I squeeze my eyes closed in the hopes that when I reopen them, I'll be somewhere else. Maybe asleep in my bed. This having just been some horrific nightmare brought on by the trauma I experienced in this very building. But when I reopen my eyes, I'm still standing in the office at *Bottom O' the Well*. Still staring into the unwavering gaze of a man who looks near death. A man who has likely caused so much of it himself.

And I can't say no.

Fuck.

"If I do this, Galen, you'll let me go. Let me walk away?"

Galen considers me for a moment. "Deal."

He inclines his head toward his man, ensuring he heard the order, then tries to push to his feet but stumbles backward into the chair. "Fuck. You better move fast."

FIVE

NICKI

"Nessa…"

Galen's strangled moan brings me to his bedside again, for what feels like the hundredth time over the last few hours.

"No. Galen, it's Nicki."

He shifts slightly, trying to get comfortable, but the meds I gave him will keep him out for a while and hopefully relieve the majority of his pain.

"Is he okay?"

I glance over my shoulder at his man—the one whose hand I bit—and scowl at him. "I can't answer that. Like I've told him and told you half a dozen times, I'm not a damn doctor. I'm not even a nurse, for Christ's sake. I got the damn bullet fragments out of his shoulder and stopped most of the bleeding, but I have no way of knowing if there's any internal damage."

The goon just sneers at me.

"Were you able to get ahold of the doctor—the vet? Whatever the fuck he is?"

At this point, I'm desperate for a way out, and Galen said I could leave if Doc shows up.

He shakes his head. "No, he's either out of town or otherwise indisposed."

Fucking perfect.

That's all I need—Galen dying on my watch. I already have a target on my back after what I witnessed the other night, and now, he's lying here, pale as a ghost after losing a hell of a lot of blood. My future isn't looking so bright—not that there was much to look forward to, anyway.

Galen's man shifts on his feet and glances at his boss anxiously. "There anything else you can do for him?"

I return my focus to my annoying patient again and shake my head. "Not really. Unless you want to get him to a medical facility."

His man sets his lips in a firm line. "You know why we can't do that."

I hold up my hands. "I don't *know* anything. I didn't *see* anything. I want out of this whole situation." I motion toward the door behind him. "I left my purse downstairs the other day, and I just want to grab it and pretend none of this ever happened."

It's all some bad dream I can hopefully forget.

I move for the door, but he steps into my path and crosses his big arms across his chest, puffing it out even more. "You're not going anywhere."

"What? Why not? I did what you asked. I did everything I could for him with what you had available here. I gave him the meds Doc left here when he came and saw Rowan. Some pain meds, some antibiotics." I point to the pill bottles on the nightstand next to the same bed she lay in less than a week ago. "It's all right there. Just follow the directions on the bottle. There's nothing else I can do. I'm out of this now."

He snorts and shakes his head. "That's not your decision to make."

"Then whose is it?"

With a smug grin on his lips, he inclines his head toward the unconscious Galen. "His. So, we're going to wait 'til he wakes up, and then, he'll decide what to do with you."

"What to do with me?"

You've got to be kidding me.

"Can I at least go downstairs and get my purse?"

He raises an eyebrow at me. "With your cell phone in it?"

Shit.

When I don't respond, he smirks. "Nice try. But you're not calling the cops."

"I wasn't going to call the cops."

"Yeah, sure you weren't..."

"Really, I wasn't. I was going to call my brother." At this point, I need help. Someone who might be able to get me out of this whole damn situation.

He snorts. "Is *he* a cop?"

The thought makes me bark out a laugh—the first real humor I've felt since I was dragged out of my apartment. "Far from it, but if he doesn't hear from me, he's going to worry."

I hope I said that with enough believability to make this guy fall for it.

No one's looking for me. No one's expecting to hear from me. No one would know if I fell off the face of the Earth—or if some Irish thugs shot me and dumped me in the middle of Lake Michigan.

I cut myself off from almost everyone when I moved here. That's how I wanted things. But now, it could come back to bite me in the ass.

He motions toward the chair beside Galen's bed. "We already got your purse. It's safe, and you don't need anything from it."

With that definitive statement, he steps into the hall and says something indistinguishable to his partner. The man I kicked in the balls steps into the doorway, blocking my avenue of escape and offering me a sneer.

Hope your balls still ache, fucker!

I turn back to Galen and drop into the chair next to the bed. "I guess I'm stuck here—with you."

He shifts toward my voice slightly. "Nessa...Rowan, I'm so sorry."

"I'm not Rowan. I'm Nicki. The bartender."

He shakes his head side to side slightly. "It's all my fault they took you..."

Is he talking about the guy who came in here guns blazing? Did he take her?

I lean in closer toward him.

"You were only a wean. All of it. My fault. Just a baby."

What the hell is he talking about?

Rowan's words from only a few days ago come back to me. Two names. Her saying, *"It's complicated."*

"You're my sister...was supposed to protect you. And I didn't. My fault."

Sister...

I had wondered what their connection was that day, why he was so distraught over having shot her. He said it was an accident. And it sounds like they were separated as children, which means he wouldn't have recognized her when she came to the bar.

That sure explains a lot.

Why he shot her.

Why he felt so bad about it.

The two names.

But it doesn't explain who that man was who came in here after her.

Galen's face scrunches up again—whether because he's in physical pain or because of some memory that's attacking him in his sleep, I can't be sure. He shifts restlessly in the bed, gritting his teeth.

I reach out to lay my hand on his arm to settle him down. If he gets going too much, he could rip his stitches right out, and we would be back to square one—the last thing I need.

"Galen, calm down."

He continues his unsettled movements, squeezing his eyes closed. "You're not taking her, Felipe. You're not taking her."

Felipe...

Shifting even closer to Galen, I swallow through my reluctance. I shouldn't ask. I should stay the hell out of it...but curiosity has the better of me. And the more I find out is either going to get me killed or be the key to getting out of here alive. "Who is Felipe?"

"Rose...Rose Cartel...one of the twins. I—" He rolls his head toward me, his lips twisting. "I can't get her back. Gone now. Gone. What if she's hurt?"

My chest tightens at his words.

Was she with him when this *happened?*

"Galen. How did you get shot? Was Rowan with you?"

"The church..."

"What's he saying?"

I jerk back from the bed and twist toward the door where his man with the sore balls stands, hard eyes locked on his boss and me.

He raises an eyebrow at me. "He was just talking. What's he saying?"

Shit. I need to play dumb.

"I'm not sure. It's all just gibberish. He's not making any sense." I motion toward the pill bottles on the nightstand. "The drugs."

I shrug nonchalantly as if that explanation should be easily accepted, and the man nods and turns back toward the hallway. He keeps his wide, hard back to the door, keeping me locked in with the delirious man who seems to have loose lips while he's unconscious.

Galen is telling me things he shouldn't, stuff he never would if he were awake, but it might be the only way I learn anything that might be useful. Something that might *keep* me alive.

I lean toward the bed more, dragging the chair slightly closer, and rest my hand on his good shoulder. "Galen, tell me more about Rowan and Felipe and the church."

SIX

GALEN

REALITY SLAPS me in the face with a stab of agony, and I jerk awake and grit my teeth against the pain in my left shoulder and arm.

"Fuck." I blink against the bright light streaming in from the hallway and turn my head away from it and toward the other side of the room.

"Good, you're alive." Nicki sits in a chair in the dark corner, only the pale blond of her hair really visible, but she pushes up and steps over to me, annoyance flashing in her blue gaze, sharp enough to cut through me like a knife made of ice. "Can I go now?"

"What?"

She huffs out a sigh and crosses her arms over her ample chest, pressing her already high, perfect breasts even higher in the low V-neck tank top. "I was told I couldn't leave until we were sure you were going to survive. Well, there you go." She waves a hand toward me. "You're alive, so"—she points to the door—"am I free to go? Or are you going to have your goons physically restrain me...again?"

I scowl at her and turn my head back to stare at the ceiling. "Fuck." I run my good hand over my face and pinch at the ache forming between my eyes. "Can you give me five fucking seconds to wake up?"

Nicki lets out a huff but doesn't say anything else. Even through the silence, her annoyance rolls off her in waves.

"What time is it?" It feels like I've been asleep for days, the heavy fog of painkillers still lingering in my brain.

She gives me another long sigh and huffs again, like she isn't going to respond. I open my eyes and turn my head to look at her. That seems to be a motivation because she glances at her watch.

"Four o'clock in the morning."

"Shit. I was out a long time, huh?"

"Yeah, a while, but that was probably a good thing."

The memory of her digging in my shoulder to look for that fucking bullet makes my stomach churn. No amount of narcotics could completely numb that, but it was necessary.

"I don't remember what happened after you finished..."

"You passed the fuck out after I dug the bullet out of your shoulder."

"What about the shot in my arm?"

"That one went through."

"That's good, right?"

"Yes. Now, will you answer my question?"

Irritation tightens my chest. I was just fucking shot and don't need to be dealing with this shit the second I wake up. "No, you can't fucking leave."

Bits and pieces of a conversation start to tickle at the back of my mind. Words. Phrases. Enough to make unease settle over me.

Rowan...

Felipe...

The church...

Eyeing her, I lick my dry lips and try to get comfortable. "Did I say anything to you while I was out?"

She shifts on her feet and averts her gaze to her feet, clad in pink slippers I hadn't noticed before. "What do you mean?"

I grit my teeth and push myself up into a sitting position with a little more effort than I care to admit. If I stay lying down, I'm liable to fall asleep again, and I can't afford to do that right now. "I mean, I need to know what I fucking told you while I was unconscious and drugged up. You already saw too much the other night."

"Shit." She mutters it under her breath, but it's still loud enough that I can hear her. "Look..." She returns her gaze to mine, her blue eyes pleading. "I'm not going to say anything about any of this, okay? I just want to go back to my simple life before I ever set foot in this goddamn place."

That's a sentiment I can understand. Things were so simple before the explosion, before that bomb ripped my family apart. Before Nessa was ripped away from *me*.

"How did you end up here, anyway, Nicki?"

I had asked Connor to find a new bartender, but I didn't have any say in the hiring. That's what I pay people for. But if I had seen Nicki, I would have told him no fucking way. The girl just looks like trouble—the kind that comes in a blond-haired, blue-eyed, girl-next-door-looking package. He likely only hired her because he wanted some eye candy behind the bar with him...and look where that fucking got us.

Nicki glares at me, her hands propped on her hips now. "I must have royally pissed off God or karma or something. A friend of mine lives not far from here. She said it was a decent neighborhood bar where I could make some money and that she heard you were looking to hire somebody. I just moved to town, and I needed a job, so...of course, I'd have to pick a fucking bar owned by the mob."

I snort out a laugh, then wince at the anguish it sends through my body, pressing my good hand over my injured arm that's strapped to my chest by a make-shift sling made from a belt.

"But I don't want any trouble." She holds up her hands, palms out, doing her best to look innocent and unthreatening. "Please, just let me go. I won't say a fucking word. You'll never see me or hear from me again."

Her plea might as well be falling on deaf ears. It isn't that simple, and she doesn't strike me as being naïve or dumb, so she has to know that.

"I can't do that."

"Why the hell not? We made a deal. You said I could *go* once I helped you."

"Because I need to know what you know."

"I don't know *anything. Nothing.*"

Against my better judgment and my ability to fight it, a smile tugs at my lips. "I get your point, but I know I said something—"

"Really, you didn't say anything—"

Luke steps into the door. "You're awake."

"Sure fucking looks like it."

The goon points a finger at me. "And she's full of shit. You were muttering and talking the entire time you were out."

I turn back to her and glower. "Really? Did you hear what I said, Luke?"

Luke shakes his head. "No, I was mostly keeping a watch out here."

Perfect. Fucking perfect.

My eyelids get heavy again, and every muscle in my body screams for me to let them close. But I force myself to look at Nicki to try to convey how serious this really is. "You and I are going to have a little chat, and only when I'm comfortable will I even *consider* letting you go home."

Her beautiful pale-pink lips part incredulously. "So, I save your life, and now, you're holding me hostage?"

"I didn't say it was forever."

"Yeah, fucking brilliant." She flails her arms as she turns away and throws herself back onto the chair in the corner with enough force to send it skidding with a thud against the wall behind her.

I let my eyes drift closed and drop my head against the headboard.

Well, that went well.

"Fuck you, Galen McGinnis!"

Her words linger in the air, heavy with her wrath and tainted with something else I can't quite place.

Forcing my eyes open again, I meet her heated gaze. "Get out of here. I need to talk with him."

She scowls. "Where the hell am I supposed to go?"

"The kitchen just down the hall."

No way I'm letting this woman out of the sight of my men.

She shoves herself off the chair and storms away from it, with fury blazing in the blue eyes she keeps locked on me until she disappears out the door.

Luke steps into the room. "What do you need, boss?"

"I need you to tell me what the fuck happened. Who shot up the church? Is Rowan okay? Who got hit? Who's dead, and who's alive? Where the fuck do we stand?"

What the hell is going on?

That's the main question, the one I can't seem to get a handle on because everything happened so fast.

Luke sighs and glances over his shoulder, likely to ensure our female visitor isn't within earshot. "We've been trying to figure out what we can, boss. Grady never made it back from the church. So, we have to assume he's dead."

"Shit." Not that it's unexpected.

He was waiting at the rear of the church for me, and that's where the assailants entered from. They likely took out everyone standing there on their way in.

"What about everyone else? The rest of the five families. Injuries? Did anyone die? I need to know about my sister."

"We're not sure, sir. The shooting made the news, and the cops are swarming that place, but there hasn't been any information yet about casualties that we've seen."

Fuck.

The thought that Rowan might not have made it out of there makes bile climb up my throat. I swallow it back and try to get my head to focus on the numerous threats we need to be watching out for.

"What about the *other* situation? We stirred up a lot of shit."

He glances over his shoulder into the hallway again and takes another step in. "That is a little tenuous, as well. Definitely made us targets."

"Who *isn't* trying to fucking kill us?"

"They've been scrambling ever since we hit them the other night."

The very reason I was left here basically alone to defend against Felipe when he came for Rowan. Any other night, my best men would have helped me defend this place, defend her, ensure he couldn't have gotten in here or left with her. But it had to be *that* night. The night I made my big move, earned another enemy, and left myself exposed.

"Well, keep your eyes and ears open. I don't want to be surprised the way I was tonight."

"We've got eyes on them, boss. It wasn't them at the church."

"Good. Did you ever locate Doc?"

He shakes his head. "No."

"Shit."

"Do you think it's possible someone else got to him?"

I hadn't considered that possibility. He's been working for this family since before I was even part of it. The chances of him going to another group can't be very good...but still, it's a possibility.

"It's possible. If we figure out who got hit, we may find him. See what you can find out about Rowan, Felipe, Rose, Kat, and Cutter. And bring me my phone. I'm calling Valerian."

Luke's brow furrows. "You said Felipe *and* Rose. I thought Felipe *was* Rose?"

Shit.

With all that happened and the shape I was in, I haven't even been able to explain the big reveal that happened last night with the twins.

"That's complicated. Twins. Rose is with Kat; Felipe is with Rowan." I hold up my good hand before he can even ask. "Don't ask more right now. Just find out how everyone came out of that and where they are."

Considering the carnage at that church, I need to know who got hit and where things stand because this could mean an all-out fucking war on all five fronts.

SEVEN

NICKI

I scan the dingy, old kitchen in the tiny apartment above *Bottom O' the Well* for the hundredth time and release a heavy sigh, dropping my head into my hands. My knee bounces violently under the ragged, chipped table no matter how much I try to keep it still.

Being sent away felt like I was a child again being scolded. Not that I wanted to stay in there and potentially hear even more that would give him reason not to let me go, but sitting here, just doing nothing except considering all the horrible things that man could decide to do with me, is making me antsy.

Not to mention the fact that I haven't slept or eaten since those goons dragged me out of my place yesterday. Almost as if in response, my stomach rumbles and acid churns.

What are the chances they actually have any food in here?

I shove to my feet and walk over to the ancient fridge that looks older than me. My hand sticks to something on the handle, and I cringe as I tug it open.

Shit. Empty.

It seems no one actually uses the apartment up here.

Other than when someone gets shot and needs to get patched up...

I roll my eyes and slam the fridge door shut, then lean back against the counter and stare at the door to the hallway.

Come on, Galen. Come tell me I can leave...

It's a pipe dream. I'm not naïve enough to believe that infuriating man is going to let me walk away now. He may have promised I could leave before I started digging in his damn arm, but if he has any inkling of what he told me while he was delirious, there's no way I'm getting out of here alive.

I've been around the block enough to know that. But he'll also know I'm lying if I try to claim he didn't tell me anything.

I chew on my bottom lip and contemplate the possibilities. None of the options seem even remotely good. I need to find a line to walk—one that lies safely between revealing too much—enough that I'll put another target on my back—or too little that will *ensure* he knows I know too much.

Good God. How the hell did I get into this?

My exasperated sigh fills the small kitchen, and I return to my seat, drumming my nails on the table.

One of his men walks past, then stops and comes back, eyebrow raised. "What are you doing sitting in here?"

"Galen told me to come in here while he talked to that other guy."

He glances around. "So, you're just sitting here unsupervised?"

I smirk at him. "Why? You worried I'm gonna bite you again?" I snap my teeth. "Come over and try me."

He scowls at me and points his finger. "You're trouble. I'm going to make sure Galen knows that."

Oh, hell. There goes my big mouth again.

Shaking out his hand as if he can still feel the sting of my bite, he wanders away, mumbling under his breath. Likely some unkind words about me.

I continue to drum my nails on the table for what feels like an hour until my stomach hurts so much and I'm too fidgety to sit any longer. "Fuck this. If Galen is going to kill me, he better do it now instead of keeping me waiting."

My temper has gotten me into trouble before, but this may take the cake.

I shove away from the table, stomp out into the hallway, and back toward Galen's room. The man I bit stands in the doorway, his back to the hall, and I shove him to the side so I can enter.

His jaw drops open. "Whoa, where the hell do you think you're going?"

"The shipment—" Galen stops mid-sentence and raises an eyebrow in my direction. "What?"

I wave a hand back. "I can't just sit in there forever. You know, I've been awake for almost twenty hours. I haven't eaten. I'm fucking exhausted, and I just want to go home and go to bed. For the love of God, can I please just leave?"

Galen presses his lips together in a thin line, his annoyance mixing with the pain he's undoubtedly in to put him in a mood where it likely isn't wise to cross him. "No, we need to have our talk first." He looks to his men. "You guys know what to do."

They both incline their heads toward him and walk past me, casting dirty looks in my direction as they step out into the hall again.

"Shut the door."

I glance at it, then back at Galen. "Really?"

He wants to be alone with me?

There was a time in my life when being alone in a bedroom with a man as handsome as Galen McGinnis would make my heart race for a whole different reason than it is now.

He nods, and I reach back and close it, then slowly walk over to the bed, twisting my hands in front of me.

Galen watches me with cool green eyes, the one on the left bisected by that nasty scar I've tried so hard not to stare at. He motions toward the chair.

"I've been sitting for hours. I'll stand, thank you very much."

He snorts and shakes his head, his lips twitching with humor. "Christ, you're difficult."

"Only with people who kidnap me."

"I didn't kidnap you."

"Oh, really? Your men broke into my apartment, dragged me from it in the middle of the night in my pajamas, blindfolded me, and basically told me they were going to kill me if I didn't cooperate. What does that sound like to you other than kidnapping?"

Galen tenses, a flash of something almost resembling sympathy in his gaze. "My apologies. I didn't think they'd be that rough."

"Well, they *were*."

"They lack some social graces, but they get the job done."

I wave a hand at his prone form on the bed and his arm in the sling I managed to form using one of his men's belts after I dug the bullet fragments out of him. "Oh, yeah, it looks like they did a bang-up job protecting you."

He motions toward his injured arm and shoulder. "This was beyond their control." He narrows his eyes, making the scar look even more sinister. "Which I think you know. I remember enough to know I told you some things you shouldn't have heard. Like where I was when I got shot and who I was with."

I press my lips together and attempt to look unaffected by the fact that I'm in a no-win situation.

"You're better off just coming clean with me, Nicki. Once I know what you know, I can decide where we go from here."

"Yeah, where's that?" I huff. "Me out of here in a body bag?"

He snorts and shakes his head. "What makes you think we use body bags?"

I glare at him, my arms crossed defensively over my chest. "Oh, you think this is funny? The fact that you kill people is *funny?*"

"No." He shakes his head, his face sobering. "It isn't funny. It's just...you remind me of someone."

"Your sister?"

He stills, his hand fisting on his lap. "What do you know about that?"

This is it. This is where I walk that fine line.

Choose your words carefully, Nick.

"I know she was kidnapped as a child and you feel responsible for it, and that when she came here the other day, it was the first time you'd seen each other in twenty years. And you *shot* her."

He winces, though it clearly has nothing to do with the pain he's in physically. "That was an accident. A case of mistaken identity."

"I would fucking hope so. But really, that's all you said. I was curious because I had met Rowan, or Nessa, whatever you want to call her." I hold up my hands. "But that's it. I swear."

The scar over his left eye twitches. "So...I didn't tell you where I was last night?"

Come on, Nicki. Poker face.

"Nope."

He narrows his gaze on me again, like he's trying to see through the thin veil of lies I'm hiding behind. "Why are you in Chicago?"

"What? Why?"

"You said you had just moved here and that you needed a job. Where did you move from? And why are you in Chicago?"

"It's a very long, very complicated story I do not want to get into right now."

"If you want me to make the decision that's going to let you walk out of here, then I need to know *everything*. I need to know I can trust you not to reveal anything you saw here or anything I said last night. I need to know who you are and what you're doing here before you do anything else."

Shit. Well, that isn't happening.

If I truly want any chance of surviving Galen McGinnis, I need to tell him as little as possible.

I hold my gaze to his, knowing if I look away, he'll surely know I'm holding something important back. "Uh, I'm from Wisconsin, and I just needed a fresh start in a big city where I could lose myself."

He considers me for a moment, his lips twisting slightly. "Are you running from something?"

The hint of concern in his eyes actually starts to chip away at the wall of anger I've built up toward him. Apparently, the man isn't completely heartless—despite the current situation.

"Not in the way you mean it. No. Just a lot of history there. A lot of people who make my life more complicated."

He nods slowly as if he might actually understand, even though no one possibly could. "And none of these people are going to come looking for you?"

I don't have time to form a response before the sound of gunfire erupts below us in the bar.

Whirling toward the closed door, I press my hand over my racing heart. "Oh, my God! Is that someone shooting?"

Memories of the night Felipe stormed in here, guns blazing, and decimated the men in his way flash before my eyes, and my stomach tightens, all the hunger I felt replaced by a queasiness at the thought of the death and destruction. I turn back toward Galen in time to see his green eyes darken and his entire demeanor switch to a cold, ruthless presence I've only felt around one other person.

"Shit..." Galen throws back the bedspread with a wince and pushes to his feet, wobbling unsteadily. His hand lands on the nightstand to steady himself. "We need to go."

"What? Go where?"

"Not here."

"You can't be out of bed. You lost a lot of blood. You're weak. You can't—"

He opens the drawer of the nightstand and grabs a gun that he places into the hand of his injured arm. There's no way he'll have the strength to pull the trigger with that hand, though. He can barely even hold it—something he's struggling to conceal and isn't doing a very good job at.

His hard gaze locks with mine, and he rounds the bed toward me and grips my arm with this good hand. "If we stay here, we're as good as fucking dead."

"Just let me go."

"No, you're coming with me."

"Excuse me?"

He drags me toward the door and opens it slowly to scan up and down the hall. Gunfire comes from below us again, and he glances over at me. "I said, you're coming with me. All this movement could undo all the good you did for me. Plus, if the place was being watched when my men brought you here, then you're in danger, too, because they would have seen you get walked in."

"Shit." I hadn't even thought about that—the possibility that someone might see me here and think I'm somehow important to Galen and therefore useful to them. But it's irrelevant. "I'll be fine. I have somewhere I can go. I'll be safe."

"You will be"—he tightens his grip on my arm and sneers at me, and this close, the viciousness of the scar stops my retort—"because you're coming with me."

Fuck.

He drags me out into the hallway with a quick look back at where the man he called Luke stands near the top of a stairwell, firing down.

"Where are we going?"

As far as I know, that stairwell is the only way out of this upstairs apartment.

Galen inclines his head toward a window at the end of the hallway and ushers me toward it. "Out that window."

"Are you fucking insane?" I try to fight his hold, but even injured and weak, the man far outpowers me. "We can't climb out a second-floor window."

"There's a roof just outside it that we can slide down and only have to jump about ten feet to the ground."

"Ten feet?"

He forces me down the hallway toward the window, the shots coming steadily from below and behind us.

"Are you crazy? In your condition?"

There is *no* way he's making it to the ground in one piece.

Galen stops next to the window and tightens his grip on my arm enough to make me wince and bite my lip to keep from crying out and drawing any unwanted attention to us. "If I get hurt, you'll just have to fix me."

You've got to be fucking kidding me.

EIGHT

GALEN

"You're fucking crazy. Has anyone ever told you that?"

I cast a glare at Nicki from the driver's seat, my one working hand clenched around the steering wheel with white knuckles that stand out against the dried blood still smeared over it from my flight from the church. "No, actually. No one has the balls to."

She huffs and crosses her arms over her chest aggressively. "Well, maybe someone should because the last thing you should be doing right now is driving after you were just shot *twice*, climbed from a second-story fucking window, and jumped off a roof. Not to mention the fact that you are still on narcotics."

Like I need a reminder from her about how fucked up the last few hours have been...

The pain climbing through that window and jumping caused was more than enough of one.

"I haven't taken anything since I woke up."

"Beside the point."

The road in front of me blurs again, the oncoming bright headlights melding together to blind me and make me squeeze my eyes closed for a second.

"Maybe I shouldn't be driving, but there's no way in hell I was going to let you get behind the wheel."

She snorts a sardonic laugh. "Oh, yeah. Why is that? What the hell am I gonna do?"

"Oh, I don't know...drive us straight to the police station. Drive us into a fucking wall. Jump out of the vehicle while it's moving and leave me to die in a fiery crash."

She stares at me for a moment, her gaze heating my skin even while I try to keep my focus on the road. "You have a very vivid and violent imagination."

"Are you saying you wouldn't have tried any of those things?"

Her only reply is silence.

"I rest my case." We turn off the busy street and make our way deeper into the sleepy, quiet neighborhood. "We don't have to go much farther."

"Where are we going, anyway?"

"Somewhere safe."

I hope.

Given everything that's happened in the last few weeks, that may be a pipe dream.

"Safe?" She raises an eyebrow at me and leans forward enough that I can see her in my peripheral vision. "You're joking, right. Since I started working for you, you shot your sister, I survived a massacre, you got shot, I was kidnapped by you, and then some unknown assailants just attacked your bar...again. You really think there's anywhere safe with you? Because I sure as hell don't."

I snort. This girl is frustrating as hell, but she isn't wrong. "You might have a point there. We're going somewhere I *think* is safe."

"Gee, that makes me feel so much better." She huffs and motions absently behind us. "Any idea who was trying to kill you back there?"

I grit my teeth, both against the pain terrorizing my body and the annoyance that I don't have

GWYN MCNAMEE

an answer to her question. "I'm not sure. There are a couple people who are pretty high on my list of suspects."

"You care to enlighten me since you think I could now be in danger because of my association with you?"

I cast another glare at her and turn left, a wave of dizziness and nausea washing over me with the movement. Driving with one arm is no fucking joke. And having Nicki criticizing me and questioning me incessantly doesn't help. "Like I'm going to tell you that."

"What does it matter at this point?" Nicki shrugs exaggeratedly. "You said it yourself. I've already seen and know too much. That means you have to off me, right, or whatever it is you guys call it."

Despite the impossible situation, the fact that I'm only half-conscious and have at least one person trying to kill me—likely more than that—and that I can barely keep my eyes open, I bark out a laugh and wince. "You're funny."

"Yeah, real funny. About as funny as a coffin is going to be when my brother puts me in a fucking hole because I took a job with the wrong guy."

"You certainly didn't do your homework."

She gasps. "Oh, so this is *my* fault. *My* fault that people are trying to kill you and that you kidnapped me? You're crazy *and* delusional."

"Most people do a little background on potential future employers, you know."

"And what was I supposed to do? Google 'Bottom O' the Well...is it an Irish mob headquarters?'"

I fight the second snort-laugh that threatens to come out. This woman has to be the most difficult and infuriating female I've ever met. But something about her fuck-you attitude keeps making me crack a smile despite my best efforts not to.

She really is a lot like Rowan, or how I remember her from childhood. Even as a toddler, she was sassy and didn't back down from anyone.

"I don't know, Nicki... You could have like asked somebody, maybe your friend who recommended you apply. It isn't exactly a secret. But with two shootings in such a short span of time, I think it's likely I'm going to have to find a new base of operations for a while. The police will be all over this."

"Gee, thank you for your concern about my well-being instead of just minding your own damn business."

"Wow, you really love sarcasm, don't you?"

She throws up her hands incredulously. "I'm not exactly sure what else to do in this situation, Galen. Either I laugh about it, I cry, or I use sarcasm as a fucking crutch. I'm going to choose sarcasm because I feel like if I laugh, you'll shoot me."

Her words make me wince again, though this time, it has nothing to do with the two holes in my body.

Causing fear and bringing people to their knees in front of me is usually my goal, but Nicki believing I'm going to shoot her makes me suddenly uncomfortable in a way I never have been.

"I'm not going to shoot you."

"Really? Because that seemed to be exactly what you and your minions were threatening earlier. If you're not going to kill me, what are you going to do with me? Just hold me forever to make sure I stay quiet? I guess I'm not seeing what the other options are here."

I really haven't had time to think it through. But I'm not about to tell her that. Not when the edges of my vision are darkening again, it feels like someone is hammering at my skull with a sledgehammer, and we still have two miles to go to make it to the safe house.

"Look, do me a favor, Nicki."

"Yeah, what's that?"

"Just be quiet."

"Excuse me?"

"All your whingeing and blethering is giving me a headache."

She scowls and huffs again. "No, the blood loss is giving you a headache. The fact that you were shot and not resting is giving you a headache. Not my talking."

"I beg to differ."

Nicki *is* the most maddening woman I've ever met. I'm walking the tightrope between wanting to kill her and wanting to kiss her just to make her stop.

She snorts a sardonic laugh. "Well, you better get fucking used to it and deal because I plan to talk non-stop as long as you plan to hold me against my will."

I glance over at her. "I'm not holding you against your will."

Her blond eyebrows rise, her blue eyes flashing wide. "You're not? So, I'm free to leave?" She throws up her hands. "Oh, what great news. Why don't you just pull over here, and I'll get out and find my way home."

"Cute."

"I'm serious, Galen. If you're going to hold me captive, you might as well stop acting like it's something that it's not. You kidnapped me—twice. Plain and simple."

"Well, if that's what we're calling it, I'm at least going to argue with you on the number here. I *had* you kidnapped *once* and then simply moved your location. It's all *one* kidnapping."

She glowers at me, her icy gaze searing into the side of my head as I finally turn onto the street of the safe house and pull into the alley behind it. "Where are we?"

"I told you...somewhere we should be safe."

"And if we're not?"

I shut off the car and turn toward her. "Then we move again."

"Unless we're dead."

"What?"

"We move again *unless we're dead*. If we're not safe here, we won't be alive to move. Right?"

"God, you really are a negative person, you know that?"

She vehemently shakes her head, sending loose strands of her blond hair flying around her face. "No, I'm not negative. I'm a *realist*. I've gone through a lot of shit in my life and have seen the people I love do the same. Way too much for me to be perky and act like everything's hunky-dory all the time. I call it like I see it."

"Oh, yeah. And what do you see?"

Her cool gaze assesses me, scanning me from my head down over my torso where my left arm is still strung up in a make-shift sling, over the gun resting on my left thigh, and pauses a little too long on my crotch. "I think you have a Napoleon Complex."

"Excuse me?"

"You're a little man who bosses people around and throws around his weight in order to feel more important than he really is."

Holy shit.

I shake my head and reach across my body to open my door, biting back a little moan at the agony the movement causes. "First of all, I'm six-two, not four-ten or whatever the hell Napoleon was. Second"—I turn back to her—"I have more power than you could possibly fathom."

She snorts and shakes her head. "You would say that. But look what we're doing now." She spreads out her hands. "We're running. If you were so powerful, you wouldn't have to."

On that note, she throws open her door, steps out, and slams it hard enough to make the car rock.

Something tells me this isn't going to be easy—whatever this is or however long it lasts.

Hopefully not long at all.

But I need to figure out what to do with this woman...besides duct tape her fucking mouth shut or find something else to shove in there to silence her.

NINE

NICKI

"So, you're just going to leave me locked up in here?" I turn to face the door, where Galen stands, watching me closely with hard emerald eyes.

He scans the room, which is not luxurious by any means, but it's certainly nicer than most of the places I've lived in my life. "I'm going to be right outside. Not going anywhere. But I need to wait for my men to get in touch with me to let me know what happened and where we stand before we do anything else."

"I think we know where you stand—someone or multiple someones want you dead."

"God, you're a smartass."

I grin at him. "Thank you."

His lips twist into a scowl. "That wasn't a compliment."

"I know. But I took it as one."

He motions toward the bed behind me. "You're going to stay in this room until I figure out what's going on and make a decision."

"A decision about what? Whether to keep me locked up forever or kill me?" I raise an eyebrow and cross my arms over my chest. All it seems to do is draw his attention to that area, which is far more exposed than I'd like in the flimsy tank top I usually sleep in. "Because those are the two options, aren't they? Or trust me...there's the third option."

He doesn't utter the words, but the sharp edge to his glare says enough.

This is not a man you want to mess with, and I've been doing nothing *but* since pretty much the moment his goons dragged me into his office. I should keep my mouth shut for once in my life. There's just something about the scarred man that gets me going, that seems to drag the smartass right out of me when I know I should shut the hell up.

Galen rubs his hand over his face and returns his focus to me with eyes that long to be closed. "For your sanity and mine, just be quiet."

I shouldn't do it. I shouldn't push him further. I shouldn't poke the wounded wolf, but I can't seem to stop myself. "We've already had this discussion, haven't we?"

He scowls, reaches for the door handle, and starts to close it without another word.

"How's the arm feeling?"

His entire body tenses, and he glances back at me.

"I have to imagine after all the excitement, you're probably in a lot of pain." Getting up from bed after what he went through alone would have caused it but climbing through a window and jumping from the roof only to drive all the way over here must have left him in all-out agony. "I should probably recheck your wounds. Make sure you didn't rip anything open."

"I'm grand." He grits it out through clenched teeth and drags the door shut behind him with a finality that doesn't allow me to say anything else even though I so badly want to.

So badly need *to.*

That man pushes every button I have. He reminds me so much of someone else in my life. Someone who left me by the wayside and moved on so easily, like I meant nothing to him.

And Galen's threat just now was clear—he *hasn't* made a decision about what will happen to me. And killing me is definitely on the table despite his saying he won't shoot me.

The last thing I should be doing is antagonizing him.

That's not going to get him to trust me or make him believe I'll stay silent. Which I will. After I leave here, I have no intention of stirring up any unnecessary shit for Galen McGinnis. What he does on his own time in his own world has no bearing on me. Or at least, it didn't until I was stupid enough to end up like this—locked in a bedroom in some townhouse somewhere in Chicago.

I don't even know the city well enough to have any idea where we are. All I know is I'm stuck here.

Trapped.

It's why I left home. To escape that suffocating feeling of never being able to escape the past, but now, I'm *literally* trapped here, held captive by a man as ruthless as he is good-looking.

I lower myself to the king-sized bed and drop backward with a sigh to stare at the black ceiling.

Who paints a ceiling black?

Apparently, Galen fucking McGinnis. That's who.

Not only is the man intolerable, with terrible decorating taste. He's also insanely handsome, which only makes arguing with him feel more and more like foreplay to something that's never going to happen.

That man is never going to touch me. Not like that. Not *any* way again. Unless it's to shake my hand as he sends me on my way. And even then, I might have to stop to think about allowing it.

But I better get used to the black ceiling because something tells me I'm going to be here a long time while Galen "figures out where he stands."

First, someone shot up a meeting of the five families. Someone who has a lot of balls and no self-preservation instinct at all. Maybe a member of one of their organizations, trying to make a move, trying to take out the person at the top so they can step in. It's the only explanation that makes sense. Because while I may not know much about organized crime in Chicago—or anywhere else, for that matter—I *do* know that these types of people don't get to the heads of the families without at least some level of intelligence and cunning. Enough that they're not going to send people to shoot up a meeting they're attending if they hope to walk away unscathed.

There's too much possibility for stray bullets. Too much risk.

So...who was the target?

It's the question I'm sure Galen has been asking himself since he left that church. And now, someone's come after him at the bar, too. Though, it doesn't mean it's the same person.

He said it himself—there are any number of people who could want him dead and out of the way. Multiple directions the shots could be coming from. That means I'll probably be here a lot longer than either of us wants me to be.

Just fucking great.

Finally, the adrenaline brought on by the excitement of the day starts to wear off, and a wave of bone-deep exhaustion hits me so hard that I practically melt away into the mattress.

God, how long have I been awake?

I glance at my watch—the one *he* gave me for my sixteenth birthday—and fight back the tears starting to form in my eyes.

Twenty-two hours.

I can't remember the last time I was awake for this many consecutive hours . Maybe back in school, before I dropped out when I was studying for exams.

It feels like such a long time ago, yet patching up Galen has brought back that rush I once felt at the thought of being a paramedic, of saving lives.

I release a yawn and let the sweet oblivion of sleep start to pull me under. It's probably stupid. I shouldn't let down my guard. I shouldn't fall asleep and leave myself exposed to a man like Galen McGinnis. But I don't have much of a choice at this point.

If I don't get some sleep, I'll be useless. No energy or mental stamina to continue verbally sparring with that man.

Even injured, Galen is a force to be reckoned with.

And he is right. He is no Napoleon.

He's tall, and while he's not overly muscular, the lean, hard muscles I saw when I was patching him up show his true strength that he keeps hidden behind suits and a smile.

Well, that false smile isn't going to work on me.

I yawn again and shift up on the bed until my head hits the pillows.

Galen McGinnis' asshole-ish nature will win out over his minor charms, and I have to let him believe I'm compliant. Otherwise, I'll never get out of here. It means having to play nice with him a little bit. That's never really been in my nature, but I'll have to at least try.

My life may be a giant clusterfuck of uncertainty, but I'm not ready to let it go just yet. So, I'll do whatever it takes to make it out of here alive. Whatever it takes.

Complete the mission—that's what he always said.

TEN

GALEN

"WHAT?" Valerian answers my call, his deep voice floating through the line to me, short and clipped. Annoyed.

I know the fucking feeling.

"What the fuck is going on?"

"Galen, I'm happy to hear your voice."

"You almost didn't after you left me in that fucking church to die."

He chuckles darkly. "What was I to do? I saw an opening to get out and took it."

"Yeah, well, I made it back to *Bottom O' the Well* and barely had time to breathe before we were hit there, too."

"What?"

"Yeah. So, what the hell is going on? Have you heard from anyone else? Anything about Rowan?"

I turn on the TV and flip through the channels until I find the local news. Not knowing what happened to her has made it impossible for me to concentrate on anything else, like the fact that I'm damn near collapsing.

Finding her has been my focus for so long, the only thing I cared about aside from expanding my empire. Now, I've lost her to Felipe, maybe lost her forever if she didn't survive the church, and my organization is in shambles.

Perhaps it's God's way of punishing me for my greed. For breaking my promise to him that as soon as I found Nessa, I would stop. Instead, I found her and kept going, kept demonstrating my power and seeking more of it by sending out my best men with a message.

Valerian clears his throat. "No, I haven't heard from anyone else, but on my way out, I saw Rowan and Felipe hiding behind the pulpit. She was okay...as far as I could tell, but who knows?"

"Shit." I pinch the bridge of my nose against the headache forming there. "Who was shooting? All I saw were four guys in black."

"That's about all I saw, too. Other than they had AK-74s."

"Huh..." I almost forgot about that, but it raises a problematic question of where they got them. I've controlled the gun trade in Chicago and the entire Midwest for years. The only competitor who dared compete with me was sent a clear message to stop. But the guns had to come from somewhere.

"What?"

"Interesting that they have Soviet weapons. Are you sure you didn't have anything to do with this?"

"Fuck you, Galen, for even suggesting it. After Kat attacked us both, we came to an understanding that's been mutually beneficial to us. Why would I try to fuck that up when there's already so much going on?"

"I don't know, just making an observation."

One anyone in my position would. Anyone could have been responsible for the shooting at the church, and the AKs point a finger squarely toward Valerian.

"Yeah, well, fuck your observation—"

The image on the TV screen changes to a pan of the front of St. Mary of the Angels.

"Valerian, hold up."

"What?"

"I have the news on, and they're showing the church."

"What are they saying?"

"Shut the fuck up so I can hear."

"A massacre at a Catholic church brought Chicago PD's best detectives out to try to sort through the carnage in the second shockingly violent event in only a matter of weeks at this normally quiet center for prayer in this sleepy neighborhood..."

Detective Lopez appears on screen, his mouth set in a grim line.

The reporter shoves a microphone in his face. *"Detective, can you tell us what happened here last night?"*

"We aren't exactly sure, as the investigation is ongoing."

"Does this have anything to do with the car explosion here recently?"

He pauses for a moment and considers his words. *"We can't comment on that."*

"Should parishioners be concerned?"

His hard eyes soften slightly, and he shakes his head. *"We do not believe members of the general public are in any danger. Right now, it appears to have been some sort of organized crime-related activity."*

"Can you tell us if anyone was injured or killed?"

He shakes his head. *"Not at this time. We need to continue our investigation and notify next of kin before anything can be made public."*

I sigh and slowly lower myself onto the couch. "They aren't saying much."

"Detective, we also heard there was a shooting at Bottom O' the Well, a known hangout for the McGinnis crime family. Are these two incidents connected?"

To his credit, Lopez barely reacts to the pointed question. *"I can't say at this time."*

"Can you tell us anything?"

He looks directly at the camera. *"Things have been tense in this city the last few years. What peace once existed between the organized crime factions seems to have been broken. Whatever happened here is likely to stir up a lot of further unrest. Stay vigilant. Keep your eyes and ears open and stay off the streets, if you can. This could get bloody."*

Shit.

I squeeze my eyes closed, and when I reopen them, they've moved on to another story.

"Well, what did they say?"

"Nothing of consequence. Except they already know *Bottom O' the Well* was hit, too." Even though Lopez didn't say it, that much was clear in his words. "Considering they were just out there less than a week ago when Felipe came in guns blazing, and I had to deal with Detective Lopez then, he's going to be up my ass even harder now. There's only so many times I can tell him I don't know who attacked us or why before they start sitting someone on me twenty-four-seven, if they haven't already."

"Where are you?"

I snort. "Like I'm going to tell you that. Somewhere safe."

"I sure hope so. And you're all right?"

I grimace at the pain shooting through my shoulder, just like it has been non-stop since we climbed out that fucking window. "I think I'll live."

"I'm going to do some digging. Have my men scope out the Marconis and see what's going on there."

"What about the Rose brothers and Rowan? Do we even know where they are these days now that there's two of them?"

He snorts. "That was quite a surprise, wasn't it?"

"I don't know." I rub at the base of my neck and think about my recent interactions with the man who called himself *Rose*. "I always felt something was off that night when we found Rose with the redheaded hooker. He seemed different somehow. Now, I know it was Felipe when we had been used to dealing with his brother."

"Yeah. I know what you mean. But still...two of them." He groans. "Just what we fucking need... more enemies."

"No shit."

"Do you think whoever hit the church came after you to finish the job at *Bottom O' the Well*?"

"I guess it's possible. But we need more information, and with the cops crawling around the church and my place, we're not going to get any either place."

Something blocking us at every turn.

"I'll see what I can find out, and you do the same. Keep in touch."

"I will. And Valerian, watch your back."

"I always do, comrade. But it sounds like you're the one who needs to."

ELEVEN

NICKI

BRIGHT LIGHT HITTING my eyes jerks me awake, and I blink against it and shake my head, trying to get my bearings. A figure stands in the open door, watching me, light from behind him streaming in. It takes me a second to process where I am and what's going on.

Galen...

The townhouse...

I push myself up from the bed with a groan. "What time is it?"

"Late."

"How long was I asleep?"

"A while."

Galen's clipped responses make me narrow my eyes at him. Not that he was ever overly friendly or talkative, but he seems agitated. On edge even more than before when we were literally running for our lives.

"Come eat."

My stomach growls. I haven't eaten since well before Galen's goons grabbed me. It's long past time, even though I'd love nothing more than to tell him to shove the food up his smug ass.

I inhale, and the smell of something garlicky hits my nose, making my mouth water as I climb to my feet. "Damn. What smells so good?"

Galen watches me climb from the bed and make my way toward him. "Dinner."

"You cook?"

He offers me a little half-smirk. "Why is that so surprising?"

I shrug as I stop next to him. "I don't know. You just don't seem the type."

One of his eyebrows wings up. "The type who likes to eat?"

I snort. "No. The type who cooks. I figured you had somebody who cooked for you or that your men brought you take-out all the time."

His jaw hardens. "That's a pretty bold assumption about someone you don't know."

"I know enough."

He sneers at me and inclines his head back toward the living room. "Well, I'm going to eat, but if you're not hungry..."

I brush past him and his annoyed glare, and he keeps his eyes locked on me while I step into the living room. When we arrived earlier, I didn't really have time to explore the house. I just got ushered into this room quickly, but now that I have the opportunity to really see it, it almost takes my breath away.

Exposed brick. Metal and iron railings on a staircase that leads up to a second floor. An original brick fireplace along the far wall. Old, wide plank wood floors.

"This place is beautiful. Is it yours?"

He scowls at me as he makes his way over to the kitchen. "It's somewhere safe. That's all you need to know."

I walk toward the windows along the front wall, but Galen steps to block my path so quickly that my face almost slams into his wide chest. Staggering back a step, I glower at him.

Those hard eyes of his bore into me. "If you happen to be able to figure out where we are, it's only going to put both of us in more danger."

"You expect me not to try to look?"

He snorts. "Of course not. There's a window in the bedroom you can look out of at any time, and you were in the damn car driving over here. I'm just giving you a warning that sometimes curiosity kills the cat." He pauses, waiting for me to flinch or respond, but when I don't, he motions toward the kitchen. "Now, let's eat."

The immaculate and sleek, modern space and the takeout containers on the counter make me grin. "You didn't cook." I motion toward them. "This is kind of a dead giveaway."

He grumbles something under his breath in a language I don't recognize, grabs one of them with his good hand, and turns toward the table. "I know. I just didn't like that you assumed I couldn't."

"Can you?"

"That's irrelevant."

His too-fast response is all the proof I need that he can't cook a damn thing, and I bark out a laugh despite the fact that I really want to be mad at him.

The man had me kidnapped and got me shot at—twice—and yet, I can't seem to stop my natural reactions around him. As frustrating as he may be, he's equally charming, and his need to prove something to me when we're in this fucked-up situation only makes the absurdity of it laughable.

He's the type of man who would have gotten me in a lot of trouble of a different kind if I had stayed working there instead of almost dying on my first day and having to run for my life.

I grab the second takeout container and join him at the table. "What did you order?"

He shrugs, then winces, squeezing his eyes closed for one epically long moment before reopening them. "I had one of my men pick up something, then I sent him out to get us some clothes and other basics."

"Clothes?" I raise an eyebrow and flip open the container. "Why would I need clothes?"

His hand tightens on the plastic fork. "Because I don't know how long we're going to be here. You can't wear *that* forever."

He inclines his head toward me, and I look down at myself. This time, I'm the one who winces. *Shit.*

My baggy pajama pants and low-cut tank top were perfect for lounging around the house and sleeping in over the last few days when I did nothing but drink and contemplate what I had witnessed, but now that I look at them and realize Galen and his men have been staring at me looking like *this* all this time, it makes me want to crawl into a hole and never come out of it.

"Pajamas."

A corner of his mouth quirks up. "I figured."

I take my fork and stab it into what appears to be chicken parmesan a little aggressively. "Yeah, well, someone broke into my apartment and dragged me out of there." I offer him a fake smile. "I didn't exactly have time to dress for the occasion."

He freezes and sets down his fork as he clears his throat, his sharp emerald eyes softening slightly. "I'm sorry about that. Really. I was in bad shape and may have told them to do whatever it took to get you to come help."

"Oh, is that the way it works? You just do whatever you want, then apologize for it later and it's cool?"

His jaw tightens. "No. These were extenuating circumstances."

"Oh, you mean you don't get shot a lot?"

If I had access to a weapon, God knows I would have taken my finger to the trigger pretty damn easily at least a dozen times against this man.

I take a bite and moan at the flavors dancing on my tongue. "Oh God, this is good."

He glances down at his untouched food and takes a bite. "It is. I'll have to ask Luke where he got it."

A heavy, uncomfortable silence lingers between us as I continue to slowly eat. More than once, I consider pushing him harder, digging my claws in to irritate him until he finally snaps, but something holds me back. The paleness of his skin. The way he sits so still and barely touches his food.

He shifts uncomfortably on the chair a few times.

"Not hungry?"

Galen shakes his head. "No."

"You seem..."

He lifts his head and locks his gaze with mine. "I seem what?"

I shrug. "I don't know. Agitated?" I push my remaining food around in the Styrofoam. I shouldn't ask it, but I can't seem to stop the question. "Did something else happen while I was asleep?"

"Other than you apparently trying to die because you keep asking questions you shouldn't?" His harsh, clipped tone is meant to intimidate me, but instead, it only convinces me of something I've suspected but didn't dare hope for since I was first brought to his place.

"You won't hurt me."

"What makes you think that?"

There isn't any need to consider my answer, but I'm slow to voice it all the same. "Because you would have already."

He tosses his plastic fork onto the uneaten food and scowls. His continued silence tells me I can push however hard I need to. This man may be ruthless with his enemies. He may kill whoever gets in his way, but if he was going to hurt me, it would have been done a long time ago.

Something has shaken him since we last spoke. Something has him on edge. "Did you find out who is trying to kill you? "

"Who said anyone is trying to kill me?"

I bark out a laugh. "Someone shot you, and then someone came to your place of business and tried to do it again. To me, that kind of screams that somebody wants you dead."

He narrows his eyes on me. "Just what did I say to you back there?"

I shove another bite of my food into my mouth and chew slowly as a way to try to buy some time for my answer.

"I'm serious, Nicki. I need you to tell me. First, because I need to know what you know. But second, because I might have said something then that I don't remember now. It could be important."

He's right, of course.

People often say things when they're unconscious or semi-conscious that they don't remember afterward, and closer to the event, his memory was likely to be better about details that could help him now.

But do I really want to help him?

Shit.

"You were mumbling about a church, about Felipe and Rowan. You said a few other names. I got the impression there was some sort of meeting of important crime families that was attacked."

He nods slowly. "Yes. What else did I say?"

I shrug. "Not a whole lot. Something about Felipe and someone named Rose. I didn't quite follow all of it. But it sounded like whatever was going on before you got shot was important."

"Did I say anything else?" He tenses while he waits for my answer. "Please, Nicki, tell me."

Please.

That's one word I never expected to hear coming from his mouth.

"No."

It's a lie. One I hope he's going to buy.

He presses his mouth into a firm line. "I guess it isn't as bad as I thought."

I set down my fork and turn to face him fully. "I'm not going to say anything to anyone. Really. I swear to God, I'm not. The last thing I want is to get pulled into some sort of mob war."

"Who said anything about a mob war?"

All I can do is offer another shrug. "It seems pretty obvious, given your profession, that this has something to do with your business dealings."

"You should stay out of it. You're better off not knowing anything."

"I don't know anything. Remember?" I wink at him.

The tiniest of smiles twitches at the corner of his lips. "Right, but even if you *don't* know anything, that doesn't mean other people know that or will think that. If anyone's spotted you with me, if anyone saw my men take you, you could be a target."

"And what if they didn't? I'm supposed to live forever in hiding because someone may or may not have connected me to you? A connection that *doesn't* really exist."

A muscle in his jaw tics as he contemplates my question, but a sharp knock on the door draws his attention that way. "That should be Luke with our clothes and a few other things. Stay here."

He points to the table, and I hold up my hands.

"Where the fuck else am I going to go?"

Mumbling something to himself again, he pushes away from the table slowly and his face tightens, apparently pained by the simple action.

"You're sure you're okay?"

He grits his teeth. "I'm grand."

Something tells me he's anything but.

# TWELVE

GALEN

THE ROOM SPINS AROUND ME, dipping and rolling like I'm on some horrific carnival ride and can't get off. But I refuse to let Nicki see me any more off my game than she already has. She's the type of woman who will walk all over a weak man, who would take advantage of a situation. The only reason she didn't try to get away when we fled the bar or from here is because she knows I have a gun and that I'd just send my men after her again and drag her back here with even less care than before.

I force myself to keep walking forward on unsteady feet.

Don't stumble, don't stumble.

A sigh of relief slips from between my lips when I finally place my hand on the door, giving myself something to lean against for a brief moment I hope Nicki doesn't catch. I unlock and open the door for Luke, who steps in, carrying handfuls of bags.

"I grabbed a bunch of stuff for you and for her, and I can always go back out if you need something else." Luke glances toward the kitchen table, where Nicki stares us down intently.

She doesn't even bother to look away. Doesn't bother to pretend she's not trying to hear every single word we exchange.

He leans into me. "You and I need to talk in private."

I incline my head toward him and point to her. "Give her the bags with her shit."

He nods and walks over to the table, and I fall behind slowly. If I try to move at his pace, I'll end up flat on these beautiful wood floors.

Nicki looks at me with a furrowed brow.

"Your clothes are in the bag." I point toward the bedroom off the living room, the only bedroom on this floor and where I put her so I can keep an eye on her. "Go get changed and stay in there until I tell you to come out."

Her jaw drops, and she points to her half-eaten food. "I'm not done."

"Yes, you are."

She pops to her feet, hands at her hips. "I was definitely right about the Napoleon Complex."

With that, she snatches the bag from Luke's hand aggressively and stomps back to the room like a petulant child. I release a heavy sigh and slowly lower myself down into the chair in front of my uneaten meal.

The door slams, assuring me that we're alone. I release a heavy sigh and lean back as far as I dare. "What do you have for me?"

He slides into the chair she just vacated, setting the rest of the bags on the table. "Colin and Shane didn't make it out of the bar."

"Shit."

"Yeah. I took out two of the guys who came in, though, and I was able to snap a few photographs before I left out the window after you guys. I would have gotten more but didn't want to stay around for when the police got there."

"I don't fucking blame you."

He pulls out his phone and flips it toward me with a photo on it. "Guy number one." He scrolls to the side. "Guy number two."

"You recognize either of them?"

He shakes his head. "No, but check out the tattoo." He zooms in on the neck of one of the two men, the familiar symbol tightening a knot in my empty stomach.

I drop back in the chair. "Fuck."

"Yep."

"So, they know it was us who hit them the other night."

"Apparently..." He offers a half shrug and slides his phone back into his pocket. "Considering how they were muscling in on our gun sales, it shouldn't have been hard for them to figure it the fuck out."

"Do you think they're the ones who hit the church, too?"

It's possible they were watching the bar and followed me to the meet, but if I was the target, it doesn't make any sense that they wouldn't have just taken me out on the drive over there or when I got out of the car and walked into the church.

"I don't know, sir."

I motion toward the television. "I saw them interview Lopez, and he was pretty tight-lipped about everything. I'm not so sure we're going to find out much that route."

"Did you talk to Valerian?"

"Yes. And he didn't have much, either. Said he was going to have his guys do some digging. There's no word from the cartel or Cutter?"

He shakes his head. "No."

"Shit. It's bad enough we have one very well-armed group gunning for us, but now there's also another mystery one that hit the church."

"You don't think it was them?"

As much as I wish I could say I did, I shake my head. "The guys at the church were using AK-74s. Old Soviet stock that isn't exactly our other friends' typical weapon."

He nods slowly. "You're right. They're much more into ARS or pistols. They hit the bar with nothing but handguns."

"Exactly."

"You said Soviet stock...Valerian?"

I squeeze my fist on the top of the table. "The thought had crossed my mind, but when I brought it up to him, he was adamant that he wasn't involved."

"Do you believe him?"

"I don't have much of a choice at this point. He's the only ally I have."

"What about Felipe?"

"What about him?"

"Well, he's with your sister, isn't he?"

"Yeah."

"So, does that make him an ally or not?"

I pinch my eyes and try to force the room to stop spinning. "The fuck if I know. Rowan seemed to have diffused the situation between Felipe and his brother, and it sounded like they were going to try to work together, but that doesn't clarify anything as far as my relationship with the Blood Rose Cartel goes. As far as I'm concerned, everyone is an enemy right now. You got it?"

"Got it, sir."

"You keep digging. See what you can find out. I need to know who made it out of that church alive, what the damage was, and any information on the shooters. Got it?"

"I got it."

He pushes to his feet as the door to the bedroom opens, and Nicki strolls out wearing a pair of jeans that are practically painted on her hourglass frame and a T-shirt pulled tightly across her breasts.

"Didn't I tell you to stay in there?"

She scowls at me, and Luke looks at me with a raised eyebrow.

"Want me to secure her in there?"

Shit.

With anyone else, the answer would have been hell, yes, but with her, trying to physically restrain her is only going to make matters worse.

I wave him off. "No, it's grand. Go."

He nods and makes his way out the front door, letting it close behind him with a sharp click. I use my good hand to push up from the table and slowly walk over to the front door to slide the lock into place.

"Are you all right?" Nicki's question floats toward me from across the room, her words laced with something other than venom for the first time.

I turn back to face her. "I'm grand. Are you gonna keep asking me that?"

She raises a blond brow. "I will as long as you're white as a fucking sheet. You look like you're about to pass out."

"Fuck..." I glance down at the button-down black shirt someone managed to put on me while I was unconscious earlier. "I need to change."

I make my way over to the table and pull open one of the bags until I find the one with men's clothes. Nicki hovers on the other edge of the table, watching me intently.

This woman's gaze is unnerving, like an X-ray straight to your soul, aimed at you all the time. She doesn't accept anything I say at face value. She questions everything and argues about anything she can.

I slowly start unbuttoning my shirt, which is a lot more difficult with only one hand than I possibly could have imagined.

The two sides of the material finally fall open, and Nicki gasps.

"Oh, my God, Galen. Why didn't you tell me?"

THIRTEEN

NICKI

BLOOD COVERS his left side and trickles down his torso, bright red and angry.

How long has he been bleeding?

Likely since we made our escape from the bar, which means hours and hours.

I glance at the chair he was sitting in, and from this angle, I can see the smears of something wet against the back, even on the black surface of the wood.

Hell...

I rush around the table, pull off the sling, and push the shirt off his shoulders. He flinches with the movement of his bad arm, but it's a necessary evil.

"I'm grand. Just a couple of loose stitches."

Grand?

The man truly *is* insane. This is *anything* but *grand*. He's a complete mess.

I step around to his back to find almost all of the sutures I put in back at the bar have been ripped open.

"Oh, yeah, sure, it's nothing," I growl at him. "Look, Galen. I don't even know what the fuck I'm doing. I'm not a nurse. I never learned how to do stitches properly. I can take someone's pulse. I can do CPR. I can start an IV. I can do basic things to stop bleeding until I get somebody to the hospital. But this"—I wave a hand over his back and his arm—"this was all me just working on a wing and a fucking prayer. You need to see a doctor. A real one. Or at the very least, the vet."

"We still can't get a hold of him. You're it, *a chuisle*." He offers me a smirk. "Whether you like it or not."

"Don't call me that." I don't even know what he said, but I know I don't like the way it makes my entire body vibrate with anticipation.

His eyes darken to an almost forest green, and he takes a step closer to me. "Oh, yeah. Why? Because you like it?"

I scowl at him and try my best not to fidget under his assessing gaze. "No, I definitely don't like it."

He snorts and shakes his head. "Yeah, okay."

"Come on." I motion toward one of the kitchen chairs. "Sit."

Surprisingly, he moves without comment and slowly lowers himself into the chair. He points toward the sink. "There's a first-aid kit under the sink somewhere. Or at least there should be."

"You need a hell of a lot more than a first-aid kit. You need a fucking brain replacement. Because you're insane."

"You keep saying that..."

I squat under the sink and pull open the cabinet. Miscellaneous boxes and containers crowd the small space, and I shove them around until I find a plastic box that looks like medical supplies.

It will have to do unless we want to wait for one of his minions to run out and grab us what I would really need. But that would mean more time locked up in this space with a shirtless Galen McGinnis. Which would be *very* dangerous for us both.

I push to my feet. "I know men like you, Galen." I slowly approach him, keeping my gaze leveled on him. "Men who think they're invincible. Who think nothing can ever touch them. Who are so arrogant that the mere suggestion or thought that something could happen to them sends them into a tirade and drives them away from you."

Tears swell at the memory, and I blink them away rapidly, refusing to let this man see *my* weakness even when I'm staring at his blood smeared all over his arm and torso.

"And do you know what always happens to those people?"

He swallows slowly, never looking away, the tension between us so thick, I can barely breathe without choking on it. "What?"

"They all end up having to face their own humanity at some point, to accept the fact that they're mortal. That having a big set of balls doesn't mean you can escape death."

He raises an eyebrow at me, a smirk on his lips. "You think I have big balls?"

Of course, that's what he would focus on.

"I wouldn't know."

"You didn't look while I was unconscious?"

"Haha, very funny." But I'm being serious now, trying to warn the man who will likely take that warning and throw it right out the window along with any morals. "But you know what I'm trying to say, don't you?"

He nods slowly. "I do. But this is the business. This is the life. I've been shot before. I probably will be again. All I can do is keep moving forward each time."

I lower myself to my knees in front of him, box of supplies in hand. "If there is a next time."

He spreads his legs wide for me to shift between them so I can work on his arm, and the bulge in his pants draws my eyes straight toward it. Heat rushes up my neck and across my cheeks. I force myself to look away and at his left arm and swallow through my dry throat.

"I'm going to clean this up and re-suture it, then take a look at your shoulder. It seems like most of the blood is coming from here, though. The bullet may have nicked an artery, Galen." I take the rubbing alcohol onto a cotton pad and clean the blood from all around the wound. "If it did, it doesn't matter how well I stitched you up. You could still be bleeding internally."

"Nicki..." The deep, gravelly sound of his voice draws my attention away from his arm and up to his face, which is only a few inches away from mine.

"What?"

"Do you think I didn't see that?" He leans a fraction of an inch closer. "Did you think your blethering would make me forget?"

Now it's my turn to swallow thickly. "See what?"

He reaches out with his good hand and tucks a strand of my hair back behind my ear. "See the way you were checking out my crotch?"

"Medical interest only. Checking to see if my big balls assessment was correct."

He snorts and shakes his head, humor dancing in his eyes. For a man with such a hard and brutal job, he truly does seem to have a sense of humor.

I reach into the medical kit and pull out the sutures and needle. My hands shake violently as I try to thread it.

Dammit, Nicki, get your shit together.

Letting a man affect me like this—especially a man like Galen in a situation like *this*—is the absolute *last* thing I need when I'm trying to start a new life here. I just need to get him stitched up and figure out a way to convince him to let me go.

Easier said than done.

I suck in a deep breath, but all it does is draw Galen's scent into my lungs—whiskey, a light hint of smoke, and something else deeply masculine that makes something tighten low in my belly and between my legs.

Shit.

He leans in until his lips practically brush my ear. "And?"

I clear my throat. "And what?"

"And did they meet your assessment?"

I turn my head until I'm directly facing him, our lips mere inches from each other. His warm breath flutters over my face, the scent of whiskey there that he must have drunk while I was in that room earlier.

"Actually, I was unimpressed."

Something flashes in his eyes for a split second—anger, frustration, a combination of the two.

Oh, shit.

I just insulted the head of the fucking Irish mob, when my life is literally in his hands.

Shit, shit, shit, SHIT.

FOURTEEN

GALEN

THIS CLOSE, her scent envelops, soft and warm and sweet, like freshly baked cookies and laundry all mixed together. And with it comes a memory of her soft, gentle hands on me in the place where it hurt the most, her patching me up and reassuring me she was doing everything she could, even though my men had kidnapped her and dragged her to me against her will.

She may not have wanted to help me, but she did it all the same. With a whole lot of attitude that hasn't seemed to dissipate during our time together.

"You think you're cute, don't you, *a chuisle?*"

Her tongue darts out across her pink lips, but to her credit, she holds her ground, not even backing away from me remotely.

"I don't *think* I am." She moves a fraction of an inch closer. "I *know* I am. And I'm not about to let you bully me."

"You think I'm a bully?" I reach out and tug at a strand of the long, blond hair that's fallen from behind her ear again.

Her blue eyes burn, a flame threatening to scald me. "What are you doing?"

"Pulling your hair. Isn't that what bullies are supposed to do?"

"Maybe when you're five, but when you're a grown-ass adult and you still think you can control other people's lives...*ruin* other people's lives, that makes you a bully."

"I'm not ruining your life, Nicki. I'm protecting it."

"From whoever shot at *you*. Great. Perfect. But you still haven't told me what's going to happen when all this is over." She keeps her gaze locked on me, not giving me a single moment of reprieve from the accusation swimming in her eyes. "With what I know, what else I might find out while you and I are here together, are you really going to let me go?"

I capture her face in my palm and drag it toward me until her lips stop just short of mine. "I'm not so sure I'm ever letting you go."

It's the stupidest decision I've ever made. More stupid than starting a war over who controls the gun business in Chicago when I was already on edge with the other four families. More stupid than letting Felipe take Rowan after I spent so damn long looking for her. More stupid than going to that meeting and actually expecting to walk away from it unscathed. More stupid than all of that combined.

But...I do it, anyway.

I crash my lips against hers, hard and demanding, expecting her to pull away with every ounce of strength she has—which is a hell of a lot more than I have at the moment. But instead of fighting me, instead of telling me to go fuck myself and digging her small fingers into the wound on my arm to ensure I release her, she issues a little groan and kisses me back, pressing her lips to mine and gliding her tongue along the seam, requesting entry.

Opening for her, our tongues duel for supremacy, neither of us wanting to admit defeat or accept what's happening, both of us letting it go on like the verbal battles we've had almost since the moment we met.

Right now, neither one of us is willing to surrender. Neither one of us willing to give even an inch. Both of us determined to come out on top of whatever the hell this is.

It rages on for what feels like an eternity, yet, somehow, it isn't nearly long enough.

Her hand flattens against my chest, over my racing heart, and she jerks her head back and away from mine, almost like she's forcing herself to stop when she wants to keep going. Her breath comes out from between her kiss-swollen lips in heavy pants.

Panic fills her gaze. "We can't do this."

"Why the hell not?"

She squeezes her eyes closed and shakes her head, sucking in a few deep breaths to try to calm whatever's going on in her body. Likely the same thing that's going on between my legs.

"We can't...you don't understand how dangerous this is."

"I think I do, Nicki." I wrap my hand around her arm and drag her closer. "I think I have a pretty good fucking idea how dangerous this is. You're literally sewing up a fucking gunshot wound."

"That's not what I mean." She yanks her arm free of my grip, pushes to her feet, and takes a step back from me, running her empty hand through her hair while the other one still holds the needle and shakes violently at her side. "Oh, God...there's...there's something I have to tell you."

Cold dread forms like a rock in my stomach. "You didn't say anything to anyone, did you? After the other night with Rowan and Felipe? What you saw?"

She shakes her head. "No. God, no. Not that. It's..." Terrified blue eyes meet mine, the first actual *fear* I've seen in them despite the entire fucked-up situation. "You don't know who I am."

I raise an eyebrow at her. "I'm not sure what you mean."

"Fuck!" She screams the word through clenched teeth. "This is hard." She holds up her free hand, almost like it might form some sort of shield against my response to what she's about to tell me. "I didn't know before. I swear to God. I didn't know."

"You didn't know what?"

"Who you were. What *Bottom O' the Well* was when I took the job. I swear to *God* I didn't know. I never would have taken the job if I had known."

"Jesus, Nicki, you're scaring the shit out of me here. Just fucking come out and say it."

"When my brother finds out what you've done, he's going to kill you."

"Excuse me?"

"My brother. It doesn't matter what I say. He's...he's going to kill you."

Her concern for my well-being, given everything, almost warms my heart, but the fact that she's actually worried about what her brother could do to me makes me laugh.

"I can handle a disgruntled sibling, Nicki. You don't understand the power I have. I'm not worried about it."

"Well, I fucking am. You don't understand who my brother is. What he's capable of."

Something about the way she says the word sobers me immediately. "Then why don't you tell me, *a chuisle?*"

That same true fear darkens her gaze. "I'm sure you know him. You said his name. When you were delirious, when you were talking about the church."

"What?" I push to my feet and grimace. "What the fuck are you blethering about, Nicki?"

She runs that hand back through her hair again and takes a little half step away from me, like she's finally afraid of what I might do, all her bravado and sass gone in an instant. The way she's talking, maybe she does have reason to be afraid.

I take a step toward her, and she tenses, her entire body going on alert, ready to react to however I may come at her.

"My brother...he's Cutter Jackson."

CAPTURING GREED

Greed is a bottomless pit which exhausts the person in an endless effort to satisfy the need without ever reaching satisfaction.

- Erich Fromm

ONE

NICKI

GALEN TENSES, every muscle in his exposed chest rock hard, his shoulders squared, his jaw clenched so tightly he might crack his teeth. His hands fist at his sides, his knuckles white with his rage, and he takes a step closer to me. "What the fuck did you just say?"

Shit.

I run my hands through my hair and squeeze my eyes closed. Maybe if I wish hard enough, I can go back to two weeks ago, before I took that damn job at the bar and make all this go away. Maybe I can pretend I'm still in Sheboygan, working at Smitty's and the worst thing I had to deal with was drunk patrons and seeing people I would rather forget existed.

"Nicki, open your fucking eyes and look at me."

Everything in me wants to fight his command, wants to *not* give in the way I just did when his lips touched mine. But I can *feel* him watching me. His hot glare practically sears my skin until I can't take the burn anymore.

My eyes fly open and meet his hard gaze.

A muscle in his jaw tics, and he takes a half-step closer to me. "What. Did. You. Just. Fucking. Say?"

Something that probably just sealed my fate...

Still, I can't hide it anymore. It's already out there, hanging in the air between us. The truth. The thing that I *knew* would be a problem as soon as I realized who I was working for but I had hoped would remain a secret only I would know.

The truth I can't keep in the dark any longer.

"That my brother is Cutter Jackson."

"As in *the* Cutter Jackson, the one at the right hand of Valentina Marconi, the head of the goddamn Italian Mafia here in Chicago?"

I wince and nod.

Galen flies at me so fast—despite the fact that he's literally bleeding and has likely been for hours—that I don't have time to back away. The fact that he should be weak and unsteady doesn't seem to interfere with his plans for me one bit.

Not when he's this full of wrath.

I scramble a retreat until my back hits the wall, and his hand shoots out and curls around my throat. He presses his body against mine, until I can feel his heart beating rapidly with my own and the heat from his hot skin reaches mine through my thin shirt.

He sneers at me, and up this close, the gnarly scar that splits his left eye from top to bottom makes him look every bit as sinister and deadly as he seems right now. All it would take is one squeeze of his hand to cut off my air supply and end me. "What are you playing at, *a chuisle*? Is this some fucking game?" His eyebrow wings up menacingly. "A ploy to try to get a spy into my organization? Was the church just some fucking setup?"

"The church?" It takes a moment for my brain to register that he thinks I'm involved in what happened there. "No." I shake my head and shift to relieve the pressure on my throat. "No. No."

He loosens his hold slightly, and I inhale a breath full of his rage.

"I swear to God, Galen..." I gasp and try to find the words to make him understand. "I didn't know what the bar was, that you owned it, when I took the job. I swear I didn't."

Nothing changes in his hard eyes. The green only darkens more.

"What have you told your brother?"

"Nothing." I shake my head again, his hold on my neck preventing me from moving it too much. "I haven't even spoken to him since I took the job there. He doesn't know anything."

He leans in, his snarled lips millimeters from mine. "I don't fucking believe you. It's too much of a coincidence for you to end up at my place with your connection to him, and I don't believe in coincidences."

I swallow thickly against his palm and angle my head up to give myself more room. He isn't choking me, not restricting my breathing like he so easily could. But he *could*. And that's all that matters. He keeps his hand there, present as a reminder that all it would take would be for him to tighten it and my life would be sucked away while he watched.

Payment for a betrayal he considers unforgiveable.

I should have told him from the beginning. Before I ever let it get this far...

He seethes, taking short, harsh breaths while he stares into my eyes, looking for the lie, waiting for me to crack and reveal the truth. "You have no idea what you've done, Nicki. That man is dangerous and volatile, especially now that they have the baby."

I freeze. "Baby?"

Galen narrows his eyes on me. "You didn't know Valentina just gave birth?"

What the hell?

I open and close my mouth, trying to find an excuse for why my own brother wouldn't have told me that I became an aunt. If Galen knows we barely speak to each other, it might convince him I'm telling the truth, but it would also eliminate any threat of Cutter coming for me that I might use to actually get him to release me.

With this man, there's no telling what path is the better one to take for my own safety.

And that of my damn heart.

I swallow again, trying to choose between two impossibly unclear avenues. "I haven't talked to him in a while. Like I said, I was in the middle of moving. He probably had other things on his mind, but if he doesn't hear from me for much longer, he's going to come looking for me." It's a lie. Cutter won't notice I'm gone until whoever he has keeping tabs on me back home realizes I've been missing for a while. "You can't keep me here like this, locked away while you decide what to do with me."

The green of his eyes darkens even more, to an almost black—so dark, not a hint of humanity shines in them any longer. "Fucking watch me."

He brushes his thumb over my throat, a caress that's both sensual and threatening, and he closes his eyes for a moment. When he reopens them, they blaze with something completely different than what was there when he pressed his lips to mine only moments ago.

The twist of his lips deepens. "I can't trust a single word that comes out of your fucking mouth."

"No." I shake my head. "That's not true. I haven't lied to you about anything—"

The tension. The spark. The kiss...it was all real.

Everything was, as much as I wish it weren't. As much as I wish I could pretend it didn't happen or it was all some act to get me out of this.

It was real.

And fucking stupid.

"Shut up. Just *shut up*." His gaze narrows in on my lips, like he's debating whether to kiss me or tape my fucking mouth shut. "This changes everything—"

"I know. I—"

His grip tightens. "I don't want to hear it. I don't want to hear whatever excuse you come up with. Get back in that fucking room and don't come out. I don't want to hear a damn word out of your lying mouth. I need to figure out what to do."

My chest tightens, my breaths coming shorter. "Galen, I'm sorry."

He steps back and presses the hand that was around my throat over the wound on his arm I never got around to stitching closed. His hard gaze remains locked on me, and he inclines his head back toward the room. "Go."

The single word comes through gritted teeth but says all it needs to.

I know better than to try to challenge him again.

This was a mistake. This was all one huge mistake.

I stumble away from the wall on unsteady legs, my entire body vibrating so badly I can barely walk. He watches me with cold eyes as I make my way across the room and to my "cell," then slowly follows after me.

Each step he takes echoes off the wood floors, the sound somehow threatening, like being stalked by someone intent on doing me harm.

Maybe I had him all wrong.

Galen slams the door behind me, making me jump, sealing me in the room that has become my prison. I stagger forward and collapse onto the bed.

What the hell did I just do?

I just *kissed* Galen McGinnis, then revealed that my goddamn brother is the partner of one of his enemies. One of the people potentially responsible for everything that's happened to him in the last few days.

He's going to kill me.

That man is going to kill me now.

He doesn't have any other option. I may have been able to convince him to let me go before, may have found some way to get him to trust that I would not reveal anything, that I could keep my mouth shut and pretend nothing I saw ever happened. But now that he knows who I am, who Cutter is to me, it would be naïve to believe I'm simply walking away from this.

I bury my face in the nearest pillow to release a pent-up scream.

That man out there hasn't earned my loyalty. He hasn't said or done *anything* to suggest I should trust him—except maybe not kill me on the spot. But Cutter isn't much better.

My own brother didn't even tell me Valentina was pregnant, let alone that she had given birth...

Maybe I shouldn't be surprised given the tension between us since he joined War's crew, but after what I did for him, for *them*, I would have thought things would get better between us.

Yet, I didn't even know I was an aunt.

Tears burn my eyes, but I roll onto my back, refusing to let them fall. I can't cry over my shit relationship with Cutter or my predicament with Galen. I need to figure a way *out* of it all—with my life *and* sanity intact.

That may not be easy with that Irish blowhard out there, though.

The man pushes every button, even ones I didn't know I had. He's managed to twist me up in five hundred different directions in only the span of a damn day.

If he keeps me here any longer, I can't be held responsible for what I do.

TWO

GALEN

LUKE TIES off the suture and snips the remaining thread on the final stitch on my arm. "All set, boss."

"Thanks." I push up from the chair and grab a shirt from one of the bags on the table, trying not to let him see how uncomfortable I am after letting him do that without numbing me.

Pain meds were out of the question after what Nicki revealed. The last thing I need is my brain fogged right now, not when the shit has literally hit the fan on more than one front.

Besides, I need the pain. It reminds me not to trust that woman behind the closed door across the room. Not to give in to whateverthefuck this attraction is between us.

She will only cause me *more* pain in the end. Or worse.

If Cutter finds out everything that's happened since she came to work for me, I'll be six feet under before I can take another breath.

I slide my bad arm and shoulder into the sleeve, sucking in several deep breaths to keep myself from passing out. The room spins slightly, and I squeeze my eyes closed, insert the other arm, and slowly do up the buttons.

Luke watches me carefully the entire time, his dark brows drawn low over concerned eyes. "Sir?"

"What?"

He inclines his head toward the medical supplies spread out on the table. "Why wasn't Nicki doing that?"

I clench my jaw, glance at the door concealing the very big blond problem twisting me up right now, and turn back to him. "Because I told *you* to, you *fuckin'* wanker."

Fuck.

My words came out far angrier than I'd intended them, my accent dripping off them with my rage. It always seems to surface more when I lose my cool. And this entire situation just went from fucked to *beyond* fucked.

How in the fucking world did Cutter Fucking Jackson's sister end up working for me?

I walk over to the bar and pour myself a stiff whiskey, tossing it back in one gulp and gritting my teeth against the burn that slides down my throat. It's nothing compared to the heat that sizzled between that woman and me only minutes ago. Nothing compared to the inferno that will engulf me soon if I don't figure out what the fuck to do with her and about the apparent line of people out in this city who want me dead.

It would be easier to count those who don't.

A knock at the front door has both Luke and me tensing, and he inclines his head toward it to indicate he'll answer. He checks the peep hole, then opens the door and steps back to allow someone to enter. Considering only a handful of people know about this place, and I trust them all with my life, it must be one of the men coming with news—hopefully good.

I sure as shit could use some.

Jamie strolls in and nods at me, his pale red hair shifting over his forehead with the motion. "Sir."

"Have anything for me?"

He approaches and leans against the couch while I pour another drink. "My source at Chicago PD says six dead at the church, including one of the shooters in black. No ID on him yet."

"Any idea who are the other casualties?"

"Looks like two of Rose's guys, one of Kat's, one of ours, and one of Valerian's who were all out front of the church or in the back when they came in shooting."

And I would have been added to that list if I hadn't been able to sneak out that side fucking door and get to the car while they were occupied firing on everyone else.

Luke shifts, glancing at the door to the room where I have Nicki stashed. "I've been waiting for further confirmation, but from what I've been able to gather, Cutter was hit, so was Kat."

"Good." I snarl, tightening my hand on my glass. "The fucking bitch deserves it."

All of this started the day she set foot in Chicago. She set that bomb and tried to take out all the families in one fell swoop. She took out Michael Syla and pushed her way into Rose's business and Valentina's territory. She attacked Valerian and me, going right to the hearts of our businesses after promising not to. And I wouldn't put it past her to be somehow involved in what happened at the church, too.

If anyone deserved to take a bullet tonight, it was her.

Luke sighs at my comment. "But neither have life-threatening injuries."

"Shit. And here I thought I finally had some good luck."

Kat out of the picture would solve a lot of problems, and if Cutter had been hurt badly enough, it might resolve the issue of the feisty, beautiful, infuriating blond in the other room.

"You let me know as soon as *anyone* hears *anything*. We need to know what went down at the church and who was behind it. We can't fight an enemy we don't know." I take a sip of the whiskey in my glass, the familiar flavor dancing on my tongue the same way Nicki's did. "What about our problem from south of the border?"

Jamie glances at Luke before he speaks, almost as if he doesn't want to be the one to answer me. "Well, no word from them after they hit the bar. But we're keeping an eye out for any future problems."

And there will *undoubtedly* be future problems with them.

They're not going to let what we did that night go unchecked. The attack on the bar was only the beginning of their retaliation. If the man running their organization is anything like me, he won't stop until we're all wiped out.

But we didn't have a choice. We *had* to hit their shipment. We had to send a message. This family has been moving the majority of the guns through Chicago and the Midwest for decades, and now, these wee bastards think they're gonna step in and take over parts of my territory.

Over my dead fucking body. Literally.

Until these fuckers finally manage to stop me from breathing, I'll fight tooth and nail to keep what I've earned. I may have made a promise that I would stop once I found Nessa, that I would let this world go once my sister was safe, but I can't stop now. Not when I've come this far and fought this hard.

"We have to do whatever it takes to protect our territory and our most lucrative businesses." I tip my drink toward the men I rely on the most. "Things are getting messy and will likely continue to get worse. We can't let it stop us."

If we lose any of our clients to an upstart from Mexico thinking they can come in and sell weapons—likely at a cheaper price to sway them over—we're going to lose our power soon after. It's a slippery slope I have no intention of falling down.

Luke and Jamie nod their understanding.

Jamie steps toward the door and pauses. "We're on it, sir. No one will touch you again."

Hell, the only one I want touching me right now is the one I absolutely can't have.

I down the rest of my drink as the ring of my phone breaks the momentary silence of the condo. With a grimace, I set down my empty glass and grab the offending device from my pocket.

Valerian's number flashes across the screen, and despite my reservations about his motives at the church and potential involvement, he's the only "friend" I have right now.

"I need to take this."

Luke inclines his head toward me and disappears out into the hallway after Jamie.

The door clicks closed behind him, and I turn to one of the windows facing the street and peer out while I answer. "Hello?"

"How are you feeling, *comrade?*"

The slight humor in his question makes my clench my fingers around the phone. "Fucking grand." Besides the fucking holes in my arm and no clue who fucking shot me. "Just got an update from my men."

"Me, too. That's why I was calling."

"Do you have any info on the I.D. of the shooter?"

It's the ultimate question, the answer to which will affect everything going forward. Not being able to trust anyone is like being stuck alone on an island surrounded by hungry sharks, all of them snapping at me every time I try to enter the water.

Valerian sighs. "Not yet. But those Eastern European weapons and your *accusation* earlier have gotten me thinking..."

"Yeah?"

"Maybe somebody *wanted* everyone to believe it was me."

"Maybe?"

Or maybe it was you.

The entire "truce" between us over the last couple of years might be part of some long game Valerian is playing, one I've been an unwilling pawn in. He could be scrambling now that his plan backfired and he wasn't able to take out anyone who mattered.

No. That's just my paranoia talking.

Valerian and I have had this mutually beneficial relationship for a while. There's no reason for him to fuck it up. Not when there are other, bigger threats out there like the Rose twins and Kat. Valentina and Cutter will stay in their own lanes, but the others...they'll never be content with what they have.

And neither will I.

Some may call it greed, some may call it pride, but I call it doing what's necessary, no matter the price to be paid in the end.

"Perhaps someone is trying to break apart our alliance by putting doubt into your head, Galen?"

"It's definitely possible." I watch a dark sedan drive slowly down the street and step back from the window, unease coiling around my spine. "We need to find out who has been bringing in AK-74s. Have you?"

"We only bring in what we need for our men. I don't touch your business in that respect, but I haven't brought in any AK-74s."

"See what you can dig up on that." My arm throbs, and I slowly roll my shoulder, trying to relieve some of it. All I manage to do is send an even sharper pain through my bicep. "I heard Kat and Cutter both got hit but are doing okay."

"That's what I heard, too. Too bad, huh? It would have been nice to get rid of them both."

I chuckle despite every reason not to in this moment. At least Valerian and I are on the same page there, but if he had any idea how bad things could get with our Italian friends soon, he would have a few choice words for me. "Speaking of our old friend Cutter..." I swallow thickly, glancing over my shoulder at the closed door. "Did you know he has a sister?"

Silence lingers through the line for a moment, like Valerian is trying to process my words. "What? No. How the hell did you find that out?"

By shoving my damn tongue down her throat...

"A source."

"You better not be thinking what I think you're thinking, Galen, because if you are, then you're hammering the final nail in your own coffin."

"Don't I fucking know it."

THREE

NICKI

THIS TIME, when the door to the room opens and I lift my head and blink against the light, Galen stands in the door wearing a clean shirt, looking every bit as angry as he did when he threw me in here. The hours he's left me in here haven't done anything to quell his rage, and maybe that's a good thing.

If he's mad, there's no risk of anything else happening between us again...short of him shooting me.

He presses his lips together in a firm line and glares at me. "Get up."

"Why?"

"Because there's something you need to do."

An icy blast rockets through my veins, sending goosebumps skittering across my skin. I shift up from the mattress and over the side of the bed, rubbing my arms slowly to try to dissipate the chill.

It doesn't work, and as I walk on shaky legs toward him, my entire body begins to vibrate—both from fear and because getting close to this man is dangerous on so many levels.

"What's going on?"

Whatever happened between us before I made the big reveal seems like ancient history. The only fire in his gaze is one of wrath, not the lust that sizzled there when I knelt between his legs and he slammed his lips to mine.

"You're going to call Cutter."

"What?" I stop in front of him. "Why the hell would you want me to call him?"

It seems counterintuitive. If I call, Galen is opening the door for me to tip off Cutter about where I am and why. That wouldn't end well for either of us.

Galen scowls at me, his jaw set hard. "I need to know what they know. I need to know if the Italians were behind the shooting at the church or if they know who was. Nobody else seems to be able to find out anything right now, and I know Cutter has someone on his team who can hack anything and may have found out information that might help us."

That's certainly true. Preacher is an absolute god when it comes to finding information, but it's still a risk. A huge one. Especially considering my relationship status with big brother.

"And what makes you think he's going to tell me anything?"

Galen takes a step toward me, but in the jamb of the door, there's no room for me to retreat. "Because you're his sister. You're going to call him, tell him that you saw about the shooting on TV, and that you wanted to make sure he was okay."

"Shit." I scrub my hands over my face and lean against the doorjamb. "Do I have a choice?"

"Of course not." He hands me my phone someone must have dug out of my purse. "I'm going to be standing right next to you, listening to every fucking word. Don't try anything stupid."

Yeah, right. Like kissing you...

We went from kidnapping, to running for our lives, to bickering, to smashing our damn lips together. All in the span of a day. The insanity of the whole situation is not lost on me.

Why do I always choose the wrong men?

I hold his slicing green gaze and dial Cutter's number, putting it on speaker so Galen can hear. Each ring tightens the vise around my chest more and more until he finally answers, and my breath rushes out of my lungs in one big whoosh.

"Nick, what's wrong?"

Of course, he would assume something's wrong. Why else would I be calling him?

My annoyance at his assumption is tempered by a sudden rush of hope at hearing his familiar voice. No matter what happened between us, no matter how much he pushed me away and cut me out of his life, he's still my brother. You can't change blood.

Galen watches me closely, staying within reach so he can grab the phone from my hand if he needs to.

I clear my throat, trying to clear the emotion clogging it. "Um, I just heard about a shooting at a church here in Chicago. They said something about the five families being there. I wanted to make sure you were okay."

A moment of dead silence lingers through the line before Cutter issues a deep sigh. "Jesus, Nicki, I can't talk to you about this on the fucking phone."

"Just tell me you're okay."

He mutters an indecipherable curse under his breath. "I'm okay."

Galen nods toward the phone in my hand, encouraging me to push forward. "Do you know who did the shooting? The news says—"

"I told you I can't fucking talk about this. All you need to know is that I'm okay. This really isn't a good time, Nick. I have to go—"

"Wait, Cutter..."

"What?"

Galen's large hand falls to my shoulder, and he squeezes it in warning. I swallow back everything I had intended to say. The apology for not pushing harder to bridge the gap between us. The request for help escaping from this quagmire of a situation. Instead, the only three words I can think of tumble from my mouth. Ones I haven't said to him or anyone else in so damn long, they feel foreign on my lips.

"I-I love you."

The words reverberate through the air, heavy with a hundred other things I should have said. And this time, the silence I get in response lingers long enough to make even Galen shift uncomfortably. He knows something is wrong, something is *off* between Cutter and me. It has been for so long that I've become accustomed to it, but Galen had no idea how bad it really was until this exact moment.

He snatches the phone from my hand and hits the end button before Cutter can either do the same or issue some half-assed mumbled response.

I run my shaking hands through my hair, trying not to quiver violently under the death glare Galen is casting at me. "I told you he wasn't going to tell me anything. He has no reason to."

Galen shoves my phone into his pocket and paces out into the living room, rubbing at the back of his neck with his good hand, his other tucked against his side protectively. The tension and lack of sleep are mixing with his building frustration to form something volatile and combustible. He's on the edge of blowing, and I'm the only one in the path of the shrapnel.

His heavy footsteps smack against the hard wood. Back and forth. Back and forth. While I stand frozen, watching him, waiting for him to erupt.

"This has all turned into a fucking shit show." His mumbled words are loud enough for me to hear, but whether they were said for my benefit or meant to be for himself, I'm not entirely sure.

Understatement much?

This isn't the confident man everyone says he is. Not the confident man I've seen him be in flashes during the short time I've known him. This isn't the man who has led the Irish family in Chicago for so many years and earned a reputation as an unflappable leader.

He's off-kilter. Drifting. Lost. *Human.*

That can be very dangerous for a man in his position.

And for me.

FOUR

NICKI

GALEN NARROWS his shrewd gaze on me as I lower myself into one of the chairs in the living room to stop my legs from shaking. "He might not have told you anything about the shooting, but he told me a lot about what's going on with you."

"What?"

He walks over to stand in front of me, staring down with a heat that makes me shift uncomfortably. "Your brother didn't seem too happy to be hearing from you. Why is that?"

Shit. Was is that obvious how strained our relationship is these days?

The fact that I'm pretty much on the outs with Cutter could help me or hurt me right now, and I have no fucking idea which. If we were close, Galen might be concerned enough about what Cutter will do to just let me go, but if we aren't, he might let me go because I don't pose a threat.

When in doubt, it's best to just play dumb.

"I'm not sure what you mean."

He slowly squats down in front of me, somehow maintaining his balance despite how weak he must be. "That was one of the most strained conversations I've ever heard between siblings, Nicki. And it was impossible to miss that awkward silence when you told him you loved him at the end of the call."

No shit.

My chest tightens even more, threatening to restrict my breathing. "Cutter and I have a very... complicated relationship."

"Explain."

I'm not about to delve into my personal relationship with Cutter with this man, not when he already seems to see right through me and makes me do things I know I shouldn't. Like patch him up. Help him. *Kiss* him. Want to kiss him *again*.

I squeeze my eyes closed and shake my head. "Just complicated. Can we leave it at that?"

He reaches out and squeezes the top of my knee. "No, we can't. I need to know what's going on between you and your brother so that I can figure out what the hell to do about this entire situation."

"What 'situation'?" I throw up air quotes. "The fact that you're holding me hostage here or that you *kissed* me?"

His lips press into a hard line, but he doesn't respond, just continues to watch me with eyes that blaze like a fire across an evergreen forest.

I guess that's the only answer I'm going to get...

I sigh and run a hand back to my hair, trying to avoid looking at the man who has me more twisted up than Cutter, the one who changed the entire course of my life.

This can't get any worse, but maybe if Galen knows why I left Wisconsin, he will understand why Cutter isn't going to give me any information, why *complicated* doesn't even begin to describe what's happened between us.

"Cutter and I grew up in a very small town in Wisconsin. Farm country but near the lake. We weren't exactly close as kids, but I wouldn't say things were ever bad or strained. He was protective. Then, I met Warwick..."

Galen's hand tightens on my knee, and something else green flashes in his eyes. An envy I never thought I'd see from a man who can have whatever he wants whenever he wants it. "Who is Warwick?" His jaw tightens. "Your boyfriend?"

"Ex. We were high-school sweethearts, and he was around a lot. Cutter and War really hit it off and became close friends, even though Cutter was a few years older than us. Then Cutter enlisted and left, and when Warwick was set to go off to college, he broke up with me, pretty much out of the blue." I take a shaky breath, trying not to let the pain of the past affect me now. "We had planned to get married after he finished school. I was going to the community college to become an EMT, and he went off to university to get a business degree so that he could run the family fishing business."

Galen stiffens, his brow furrowing, tugging at that scar over his eye. "Part of Valentina's crew?"

I bob my head and try to breathe through the years of heavy memories. "There's a whole hell of a lot more to it, but basically, after he was discharged, Cutter joined Warwick's crew and that pissed me the fuck off for obvious reasons. I felt like he had betrayed me, and it caused a lot of tension between us that we haven't exactly sorted out yet."

Galen nods slowly. "And Warwick is the reason you left Wisconsin."

Shit.

That makes me sound like some sort of lovesick, jaded woman when really I just wanted a fresh start.

I grimace. "Sort of. Yes. Warwick still lives in the same area with his girlfriend and baby."

Galen's eyes widen slightly, and a muscle in his jaw tics. "You still love him?"

The hint of jealousy in his voice makes my chest ache in a whole different way for a whole different reason. "God no. I haven't loved him for a long time. But that doesn't mean I want to see him constantly. See the way that he looks at her. The way he looks at that baby."

The hard green of Galen's gaze softens slightly. "How does he look at her?"

I release a little wistful sigh—one that I hate. "Like she means the fucking world to him."

Tears prick my eyes, and I swipe them away, suddenly very aware of Galen's hand on my knee and how close we are. How stupid it is to be in this position with him again.

"He used to look at *me* like that. *Need* me like that. *Want* me like that."

Strong fingers slide up my thigh and grip it tightly, and I drag my focus from it to meet Galen's gaze again. Something burns deeply there. A fire that has nothing to do with his anger at me hiding my connection to Cutter or what I know that could do him in.

His voice deepens. "You're afraid you'll never have that again."

"I don't know." The words barely come out, and I swallow back the emotion threatening to clog my throat. "I guess I just couldn't stay up there anymore. Couldn't handle seeing that plus all of Cutter's friends all the time. My relationship with him is just...too complicated."

Galen snorts and squeezes my thigh again, leaning toward me slightly. "You don't have to explain complicated relationships with siblings to me. I shot my sister, remember?"

I offer a chuckle and shake my head. "How could I forget?"

It's what started this disaster. If Rowan had never come looking for him, if Luke and I hadn't sent her back to Galen's office to wait for him...none of this ever would have happened. I would have figured out who and what Galen was after a few days of working there, and I would have left before I got pulled into that world.

Now, I'm smack dab in the middle of it without a way out that I can see.

I look over to Galen's arm, the wounds now concealed by the clean shirt. "Did you get that taken care of?"

It shouldn't bother me that I never finished stitching him up before all hell broke loose with my confession, but the thought that he might still be bleeding or in pain makes my gut churn uncomfortably.

"I did. I'm grand."

"You're sure?"

"Do you have to question me about everything?" He leans a little closer, hovering just above me even in his squatting position, his wide, lean shoulders keeping my legs spread and me from moving.

"Apparently..."

The corner of his lips twitches. "I think you just like arguing with me."

"Normally, I don't like arguing with anyone."

I don't like confrontation. Which is exactly why I wanted to get the hell out of dodge and away from potential run-ins with people who are going to set me off and make me act in a way I'm not proud of.

Yet, here I am, with a man who's dangerous and volatile. A man who's so much like Cutter, who pushes my buttons and messes with my head in a way I never thought I would let someone do again. And all I want him to do is close the distance and press his lips to mine again.

I dart my tongue out to wet them, and his gaze drops to my lips for a moment before it flickers back up to mine.

"I'm a very dangerous man, Nicki. You've seen what's gone on just in the last week. You *must* understand this world, knowing who your brother is."

"I *don't*." I shake my head. "I don't understand this world at all. Or you. But I know you're dangerous." I lean in even more. "I know *this* is dangerous."

"Then why are you looking at me that way, *a chuisle?*"

A tiny thrill shoots through me, tingling every nerve in my body. "What way?"

He inches closer. "Like you want me to fucking kiss you. Like you want me to take you back into that room and slip my cock inside your cunt."

My pussy clenches, and I bite back a tiny little moan that I know would only further encourage him. "You know who I am now. You know how dangerous this is for you, too."

"I fucking know." He brushes his lips over mine briefly, so softly, it almost isn't there. Nothing more than a whispered promise of something explosive. "And that's what makes it so much worse."

"Makes *what* so much worse?"

"The fact that I'm not gonna fucking stop."

FIVE

GALEN

Fuck.

This is such a bad idea.

I slam my mouth against hers anyway.

She could have ratted me out to Cutter at any time during that call. Could have told him where we are, what I had done to her, and let him come after me with all the violent force he has at his disposal. She could have offered me to Cutter Jackson on a silver fucking platter and given him every reason in the world to take me out, a move that would benefit Valentina and her organization greatly.

But she didn't, and for this moment, I'm going to believe it's because she actually gives a shit and doesn't want to see me dead. Even if that isn't true. Even if there's some ulterior motive I can't quite see yet. Because now that I've tasted her, I'm not going to fucking pull away until a bullet stops me permanently.

The two she already pulled from me aren't enough to slow me down now.

My cock strains against my pants, begging for release, desperate to be buried inside this exasperating and intoxicating woman. She grips the back of my head, holding herself steady, shifting closer to me on the chair and spreading her legs even wider to let me settle between them and push my hard length against the apex of her thighs.

Fuck...

I'd give anything to be able to lift her up against the wall and drive into her right now, but even the thought of that strain on my left arm sends a wave of pain through me. I have to push it away to concentrate on Nicki, on the need coursing through my veins, the desire making me do something we both know is wrong.

Neither of us seems to care about the consequences of what we're doing. All the outside forces working against us float away on a cloud of lust we can't ignore.

I glide my tongue across her lips, and she inhales my breath with her kiss, just as frantic as I am, her nails scoring the back of my neck, urging me even closer. Her heart slamming against her ribcage vibrates through my chest and goes straight to my throbbing cock.

She opens her mouth, whimpering softly and tangling her tongue with my own. Her hips roll up, seeking something that I'm more than willing to give her any way I can. I may not be running at one hundred percent—not even close—but that won't stop me now.

Nothing will.

I shift my hand from the top of her thigh over to the waistband of her yoga pants and slip it beneath the stretchy fabric to find her slick core ready for me. Devouring her eager mouth, I slip a finger inside her.

Her pussy clasps around me, and she pulls her head back and gasps. "Oh, God..."

Leaning forward, I brush my lips against her ear. "Do you have any idea how badly I want it to be my cock inside you right now, Nicki?"

She moans and clenches around me greedily, her nails digging into my skin. My cock twitches in response, and I push another finger into her and curl them both slightly to find her G-spot.

GWYN MCNAMEE

"How badly I want to hear you scream my name as I fuck you so hard that you can't walk tomorrow."

"Oh, God..."

Her legs start to quiver against my waist, and I shift my position slightly so I can find her clit with my thumb. The second I touch it, her hips buck up and she rolls them against my hand, eager and seeking. Hooded blue eyes meet mine, swimming with desire. They pull me in, bottomless pools I want to drown in forever.

"I'm going to make you come, Nicki. And then, you're going to suck my fucking cock until I come down your pretty throat."

She nods vigorously, pressing her face against my neck and issuing another whimper. "God, yes."

Just the thought of sliding my dick between her lips and feeling them wrap tightly around me makes it twitch in my pants. If I had less self-control, I might come right now with her cunt wrapped around my fingers and her warm breath fluttering against my skin.

Fuck.

I curl my fingers into her, probing her and rolling my thumb against her clit in a hurried circular motion. Her hips jerk, and I take her mouth again and capture her final gasp as her orgasm slams into her. She bucks against my hand, her cry of release echoing through the room.

Her body stiffens. She clings to the back of my neck, her nails digging into my flesh, and finally, she sags back against the chair, releasing the iron grip her pussy has on my fingers.

Sweet fuck.

I pull back, dragging my hand away from her body, and raising my fingers to my mouth. She watches me lazily as I suck her release from my skin, making my body ache to be inside her.

"Fuck, *a chuisle,* you taste good."

She reaches for my waistband and fumbles to free my cock while the flavor of her orgasm slides over my tongue and down my throat. Her small, warm hand wraps around the base of my hard flesh, and I groan, my eyes rolling back in my head. I shift closer, into a better position to drive my cock between her pink lips, into that hot, wet mouth where her greedy tongue will lap me until I blow my fucking load straight down her throat.

But the shrill ring of my phone in my pocket makes me freeze.

Fuck. Whoever it is can just fuck right off.

Nicki strokes her hand along my length, and my hips buck to shove me deeper into her grip. But the damn ringing doesn't stop. And as much as I'd like to push away everything that's going on right now, it would be stupid to ignore what could be an important call just to get my dick sucked.

No matter how good it would undoubtedly be.

I pull the offending phone from my pocket and stare down at Nicki who looks up at me expectantly, her kiss-swollen lips ready for me to slip between them. Her hot breath flutters over the head of my cock, making pre-cum bead there in anticipation. All it would take is her pulling me between her lips for me to explode, but instead of doing what we both want, I put the phone to my ear.

"What?"

"Galen..."

"Rowan?" She's the last person I expected to hear from, and the distress in her voice makes any thoughts of what I was just about to do to Nicki flee immediately. "Rowan, what's wrong? Are you hurt?"

Nicki releases her hold on my cock and frowns slightly, shifting back on the chair and watching me carefully.

Rowan takes a sharp inhale. "I-I need to see you." Her plea comes on a whisper, almost like she's trying to conceal that she's making this call. "Please..."

I tighten my hand around the phone. "What's wrong? Tell me."

"I-I can't. Not right now. We need to talk in person. Alone. I'll text you the address."

She ends the call before I can question her any further, and my throat tightens.

Fuck.

SIX

GALEN

I BACK AWAY FROM the chair and the woman who has—yet again—somehow managed to wipe away any semblance of sanity I once held. Her blue eyes widen at my retreat, and her lips dip into a deeper frown. She watches me take another step away from her, then another.

"I have to go."

Nicki's mouth falls open, her pale cheeks pink, her breathing still heavy. "Seriously? Right now?"

Fuck. Fuck. Fuck.

I shove my still-hard cock back into my pants and secure again rather than answering her. There isn't any explanation I can offer that justifies walking away from what we just started.

Instead, I stalk to the front door, unlock it, and yank it open. "Luke, get in here."

He steps in and closes the door behind him. "What's up?"

"I have to go see Rowan."

Luke tilts his head to the side. "Now?"

My fucking thought exactly.

"This isn't ideal. Believe me, I know." But she didn't sound right. Something's wrong. And after what went down at the church and at the bar, I have to be sure she's safe. "She said she needed to see me in person. So, I have to go."

"Sir..." He glances toward Nicki, then steps closer to me, even though she'll still be able to hear us. "It could be a trap. You said you didn't trust the Rose brothers."

"I fucking *don't*. But she's my sister, and she says she needs me. I have to go and find out what's happening."

If she's hurt or in trouble...I don't think I could handle losing her again. Not when I just found her. Not when I haven't even had a chance to rebuild my relationship with her because Felipe snatched her away again.

I cast a quick glance at Nicki, whose confusion seems to have morphed into a fiery anger. "*Coinnigh súil uirthi.*"

Luke is the only one who can keep an eye on her while I'm trying to figure out what's going on with Rowan.

Nicki pushes to her feet, swaying slightly with the quick motion. "What did you just say to him?" She takes a step toward us, hands on her hips, eyes narrowed on me. "I hope you don't think you're leaving without me."

I scowl at her, all the sexual frustration turning my balls blue now mixing with the familiar frustration this woman causes in all aspects of my life. "You are *not* coming with me. The situation is already complicated enough without me showing up with you and people asking questions."

Her eyebrows rise and she throws up her hands. "I'll stay in the car."

Shaking my head, I snort incredulously. "You are *not* coming with me."

She steps up to me, getting more in my face than any of my men dare to. "I'm not staying here. If you leave me with him"—she points to Luke—"I'm going to do everything I can to get out. He'll be so busy trying to keep me from escaping that he won't be able to do whatever else it is you have your minions off doing all day."

927

GWYN MCNAMEE

I scowl at her again and grit my teeth, my cock twitching against my zipper—her defiance both the biggest turn on and the most infuriating thing I've ever experienced in my life. The last thing I want is her tagging along out in the open or having to explain to Rowan and Felipe why she's with me. But I also know her well enough to understand she's serious in her threat. She won't make this easy on Luke if he's left to watch her. At least if she's with me, I can *attempt* to control her.

"Fine." I bite out the word between my clenched teeth. "At least if you're with me, I'll know you're safe and not fucking something else up for me. Since she already knows you, we'll tell Rowan you came to help stitch me up and that's why you're with me, that you came along in case she needed help." I lean into her, so close our lips almost touch, and grip her biceps hard enough to make her flinch. "But don't mention a fucking *word* about your brother. Got it?"

Nicki offers me a little smug half-smirk and nods. "Sounds good to me."

She tugs out of my hold and brushes past Luke, whose jaw falls open as he watches us.

His gaze darts from me to her and back to me. "What the hell is going on with you two?"

I scrub my right hand over my face. "Don't fucking ask. Keep your eyes and ears open. Let me know if there's any movement from anyone. I'll get back here as soon as I can."

Nicki opens the door and raises an eyebrow. "You coming?"

Fucking should be...

I should be emptying my load straight down her throat. Instead, I'm bringing this woman out into a war zone with my cock still hard enough to pound fucking nails.

But I'm not going unarmed. I grab my gun from the drawer in the end table and slide it into the holster at my waist. Luke offers me another look that screams *what the fuck is going on* as I let Nicki walk out in front of me. She rushes down the steps toward the car, while I scan up and down the street, alert for any threats that might present themselves.

She wanders over to the driver's side and holds out her hand. "Give me the keys?"

I shake my head and approach her. "No fucking way are we going to have this argument again."

Her gaze darts down to my arm for a second before returning to meet mine. "I saw how much blood you lost last night and earlier today when you opened those wounds back up."

"Luke stitched me up, and I feel fucking grand."

Her narrowed eyes tell me she doesn't buy it, but she lets me push her out of the way and open the door. Maybe because my hand is so damn close to my gun.

She rounds the car with a huff and climbs into the passenger seat. "Where are we going?"

I start up the car, check the text Rowan sent with the address, and back out. "To see Rowan."

And hopefully not walk into a fucking trap.

Nicki raises an eyebrow. "Is she with Felipe?"

"I assume so."

"So...Luke says it could be a setup."

I tighten my hand around the wheel and shift under her assessing gaze coming at me from the side. "Maybe, but I trust her."

"What if she doesn't know it's a setup and they're just using her to get you there?"

Fucking hell.

Gritting my teeth, I focus on the road ahead, the last of the setting sun casting long shadows over the city. It's only been two days since I drove to the church and walked into an ambush.

Am I about to do the same again?

I glance over at my companion, who sits with her arms crossed over her chest. "The thought had crossed my mind which is why I didn't want you to come with me. Didn't want you to be in the line of fire. If anything happens..."

For some reason, the words I'm searching for fail me. They seem to do that with Nicki around. But I can't let her distract me. I turn onto the main road and let that sentence hang unfinished in the thick air between us.

She huffs again and shakes her head. "You really don't think I can take care of myself, do you?"

I bark out a sardonic laugh. "You got kidnapped...*twice*...because of me, have been almost shot *twice*...because of me, yet you're now willingly coming with me somewhere unknown and potentially dangerous when you could have just stayed back at the condo and been completely safe. That doesn't sound like taking care of yourself."

Nicki turns her head to face me, and I peek over at her before returning my attention to the road. "Maybe you haven't picked up on this yet, Galen, but I don't always do what's safe."

The heated look in her eyes when she dragged my cock out only a few moments ago flashes in my head and makes it twitch for her touch again.

"Believe me...I fucking noticed."

And apparently, neither do I.

If I did what was safe, we wouldn't be in this mess. I would have followed through on my promise to God to leave this life as soon as I found Rowan. I would have put it all behind me the moment she appeared in my office and I discovered who she was.

Instead, I kept pushing. Kept taking and wanting. I needed more. I still do.

We stop at a red light, and she turns toward me to say something—likely another smartass comment about how I choose to live my life and run my business—but a sharp crack and the rear window shattering inward breaks the silence before she can.

SEVEN

GALEN

GLASS FLIES INTO THE CAR, stinging against the right side of my face. "Fuck!"

We both jerk forward, away from the sound and flying shards, then whirl to look over our shoulders at the damage.

What the hell?

Nicki clutches her chest, her eyes darting around the car and out the space where the window once was. "What the hell was that?"

A second crack shatters the night—this one, instantly familiar.

I'd know that sound anywhere, especially after recent events.

It sends a chill down my spine and eliminates any hope it was just a rock or something else accidentally hitting the vehicle.

I scan our surroundings the best I can while trying to keep myself protected behind the seat. "Someone's shooting at us."

An every damn fucking day occurrence lately...

Nicki scrambles, surveying what she can see in the dimming light of early evening. "From where?"

"I don't fucking know."

My heart thunders against my ribcage, as I frantically search both ways down the cross street. Rush hour traffic flies both directions—cars, trucks, vans—everyone anxious to get home as quickly as possible while all I want to do is get away from the threat.

The light stays red, trapping us in place, making us sitting ducks for whoever might be pulling the trigger. A car to our right blocks me from being able to turn down the side street, its occupants also twisting and searching for the source of the sounds that just rend the night air.

There's only one way to go—forward.

I slam my foot to the gas pedal. The engine roars, and we shoot across the intersection, through bustling traffic barreling down on us. Horns blare. Cars slam on screeching brakes. Metal crunches with metal as people try to dodge us and the other vehicles that have stopped to try to avoid hitting us.

But I can't worry about what happens to anyone else. Not when someone is fucking shooting at us. My track record with flying bullets recently doesn't incline me to take any chances. Especially with Nicki right next to me.

Nicki clutches the armrest. "Holy shit. You're trying to get us killed."

Settling my hand over hers, I squeeze it quickly—the only way I have to comfort and assure her —then return it to the wheel. "We either risk it with the fucking traffic or wait to get shot. Do either of those options seem particularly good to you?"

She sits back in silence as we barrel down the road without a back window. Honking horns and tires on the pavement fill my ears. Far better than the alternative of more gunshots.

Maybe we lost them at the intersection.

Hope blooms in my chest, until I check the rearview mirror and see two cars swerving around the accidents we caused in the intersection. They go up onto the sidewalk in order to advance and give chase.

"Fuck." I jerk my gaze between the rearview mirror and the road. "We're being followed."

Nicki turns around to check behind us again. "By whom?"

"Get down!"

Whoever is after us isn't going to care where their bullets end up. Whether it's in me or in her, they win either way. If anything happens to Nicki because of me...

Stop.

I can't let myself think about that. The only chance we have of making it out of this alive is to keep my focus on the road and getting somewhere safe.

Rather than questioning my order, Nicki ducks and slouches slightly in her seat.

"Whoever is chasing us is likely whoever shot at us."

Though I don't have a fucking clue who it could be...

All I know is we need to keep moving, and traffic slows in front of me to a standstill. Instead of slamming on the brakes and allowing the people following us to catch up, I weave around the cars stopped in front of us and into oncoming traffic.

Headlights almost blind me, and someone lays on a horn as I swerve to narrowly avoid a head-on collision.

"Jesus Christ, Galen." Nicki grips the handle on the door. "You're going to get us killed."

"We have a better chance of surviving *this* than we do if whoever's back there gets a hold of us."

I'll take my chances with reckless driving over more bullets.

The light up ahead changes from green to yellow to red. It might as well be a damn guillotine because if we stop for it, we're fucking dead.

"Shit." I jerk the wheel to the right, sliding across another lane of traffic and down a side street, lined with small bungalows in what is otherwise a sleepy area of Chicago.

Tires squeal behind us, easily heard through the opening now missing a window, and I glance in the rearview mirror and see that we haven't lost our friends.

I slam my fist against the steering wheel. "They're still back there."

Nicki peeks over the back of her seat again, then slinks back down. "What do I do?"

"Christ, I can't believe I'm going to say this." I chance a glance at her and see fear mixed with the usual determination in her eyes.

"What? Galen, what can I do?"

"Grab my gun."

She shifts up in the seat. "What?"

"Grab my fucking gun."

"Where is it?"

I incline my head toward the holster at my waist. "Holster."

She throws up her hands. "What the hell am I supposed to do with it?"

"Do you know how to shoot?"

She snorts, undoes her seatbelt, and leans across my lap to the left side of my pants to my gun. Her head only inches from where it was before we were so rudely interrupted makes my cock stir to life, even when we're literally running for our lives.

I bite back a groan, and she settles back in her seat with a smug smile and the gun in her hand.

"Cutter and my father used to hunt a lot. I learned how to shoot at a very young age, though it was rifles and it's been a few years."

That isn't reassuring at all, but I can barely move my left arm, let alone drive and try to shoot to defend ourselves, if need be.

Another peek in the rearview mirror makes me wince. They're still back there, but a car entering the road slows them down slightly as they try to weave around it. "Hopefully, you won't have to use it."

She glances behind us. "Unfortunately, I don't think that's going to be an option."

"Why?"

"Because a third car just pulled behind them and joined the chase...and they're gaining on us."

"Shit."

I floor it again, and the car jumps to almost seventy miles an hour, tearing down the quiet suburban street. People out enjoying the pleasant weather before night fully falls watch us fly past them.

Nicki settles back in her seat and straps on her seatbelt. "What are we going to do?"

"Try to lose them." I jerk the wheel to the left, turning us back toward the main road and flow of traffic where we may be able to find some cover.

Tires squeal again, and a peek in the rearview makes me tighten my hands on the wheel. They're getting closer, and I'll have to slow down to make the next turn.

"Galen, watch out!"

I shift my focus to the road in time to see the red ball bounce across the road and a small child race out in front of us from behind a parked car.

"Fuck!"

I slam on the brakes and jerk the wheel to the left to avoid him, but there's no way to dodge the massive oak tree or our collision with it.

EIGHT

NICKI

SOMEONE YANKS back the white curtain, jerking me up from where I recline on the uncomfortable hospital bed. I blink against the lights streaming down on me and finally focus on a stocky man in slacks and a white button-down shirt who flashes me a badge.

"Hello, Miss..."—his dark-brown eyes drop to a small notepad in his hand—"Jackson, is it?"

He waits for me to respond, but I sit silently, chewing on my bottom lip. I've been waiting for someone to show up. There isn't any way a man like Galen McGinnis gets shot at, gets in a high-speed chase, slams into a tree, and it doesn't draw the attention of the kind of people he wants to avoid.

Like the fucking cops.

"I'm Detective Lopez..."

I rub at the throb in my temple and stare at the man, refusing to give him what he's here for. The tension in my neck builds the longer he holds my gaze, but I simply roll my head side to side to crack it without looking away.

The corner of his mouth quirks up slightly into a little grin that someone might almost mistake as friendly if they didn't know better—like I do. "And I have some questions for you."

"I already told the other officers at the scene everything."

He nods slowly, watching me carefully. "I know what you told them, but now, you're talking to me."

I release a heavy sigh and shift back on the bed to sit against the raised back, relaxing my head to the uncomfortable mattress. Something tells me if I don't at least *attempt* to answer his questions, I could end up being brought down to the station, which is the last thing I want. "Fine."

"Well, let's start with what happened."

Raising my eyebrows at him, I try my best to appear confused. "What do you mean what happened?"

"Well, you were a passenger in a car that was shot at, sped through city streets recklessly, and slammed into a tree. When police officers got there, they found several gunmen shooting at your vehicle. Following an exchange of fire, the officers found you passed out in the car with the driver."

I nod slowly, the memory of coming to after the crash and discovering police swarming the scene and bodies on the road coming back clear as day. "That about sums it up."

One of his dark eyebrows rises. "You don't have anything else to add to that?"

"Nope. That's it."

There isn't any reason to volunteer additional information to the police. It will only make a shitty, unsettled situation even worse.

"And how do you know Galen McGinnis?"

He had his hand down my pants and tongue in my mouth a couple of hours ago...

I clear my throat. "He's an acquaintance."

That eyebrow wings up again incredulously. "An acquaintance?"

"Yup."

"An acquaintance who just happens to be recovering from what appears to be gunshot wounds."

I shrug as nonchalantly as I can. "I don't know anything about that. And I don't understand why I am the one being interrogated here. I'm a victim. A stranger shot at me and then chased me through the streets."

"Yes..." He nods slowly. "And I don't suppose that has anything to do with who you were in the car with?"

An exasperated sigh slips from my lips. Detective Lopez might just be doing his job, but with this pounding headache and after everything that has happened, all I want is some peace and quiet. "I wouldn't have any way of knowing that. Am I under arrest or something?"

He shakes his head, examining something in his notebook. "No. Just trying to figure out what's really happening here."

"Good." I close my eyes and drop my head back, my body aching from the force of the impact and the airbag deploying. "We're done, then."

"Miss Jackson?"

I release an exasperated sigh. "What?"

"I think you need to think long and hard about who you're spending your time with. Galen McGinnis is dangerous. What happened today proved it. If you didn't already know, you know it now."

"I'll consider your advice."

"Good. I don't want the next time I see you to be in a body bag."

The sound of the curtain swinging open again makes me open my eyes, and the man himself stands on the other side, glaring at Detective Lopez with cool green eyes. "Detective Lopez, I see after you finished interrogating me, you moved on to her. Did you think she'd be easier to harass?"

Detective Lopez sighs, flips his notebook closed, and turns toward Galen. "I'm just trying to get a handle on the situation here, McGinnis. You not cooperating isn't making this any easier. I should arrest you right now for recklessly endangering safety for the way you were speeding through the streets. Maybe some time behind bars would make you more cooperative."

Galen's jaw tightens. "I was being *shot at*. Do you think any jury in the world would convict me?"

Lopez snarls. "If they knew who you were, they would."

The insult doesn't seem to have the desired effect on Galen. He just offers the detective a smug grin. "I'll take my fucking chances. Either charge me now or we're leaving."

Hard dark eyes drift over both of us, and Lopez tenses. "I don't know what sort of shit got stirred up the other night with the five families, Galen, but the men shooting at you today look like they were part of the Luna Cartel. They've been moving into Chicago, trafficking drugs and guns. If there's some war going on between the existing powers here, that we don't know about, this could be the least of your worries."

"Thanks for the warning." Galen's lips curl into a hard, cool smile. "I have it covered."

Lopez snorts and shakes his head. "Yeah, sure. Fucking looks like it." He moves to step away from the bed, then pauses and places his hand against Galen's chest. "Don't think you're out of the woods yet. Just because I'm letting you go now doesn't mean I'm not going to nail your ass to a fucking wall when I have more evidence."

Galen chuckles. "Good fucking luck with that."

The cop leaves in a huff, shaking his head, and Galen shifts to the side of the bed, looking down at me with concern darkening his gaze.

"Are you okay?"

I squeeze my eyes closed for a moment to take stock, then force them open to look up at him. A small cut above the scar slicing through his left eye has already been stitched closed, and minor red burns from the airbag deployment cross parts of his cheek.

Reaching up, I brush my fingers over his marred skin. "Do I look as bad as you?"

He gives me a little half-grin. "No, you look beautiful."

I wave him off and shove a hand through my hair to get it away from my face. "Shut up."

There isn't any way I look beautiful. I haven't showered since I was snatched from my apartment two days ago and I have barely slept except for a few hours here and there when I gave into exhaustion.

Galen glances toward the curtain. "What did you tell Lopez?"

"Nothing, since there's nothing to tell."

He leans in and brushes his lips against my ear. "Why didn't you tell him I was holding you against your will?"

His warm breath flutters across my skin, and a shudder rolls through my body. With him this close, a scent that's all Galen—power, money, rage, and lust—fills my veins and makes my head spin.

I turn my head toward him, until my lips brush his ear. "I don't know."

Galen rises slowly, pulling back from me as he considers my answer. "The doctor says I'm free to go and that you are, too. They're getting the final discharge paperwork ready. And Lopez won't arrest us. He knows I'd be out in ten minutes and he'd never get a conviction on anything."

That's likely true, plus Galen undoubtedly has people on his payroll who would ensure it would never happen even if the District Attorney or U.S. Attorney ever tried.

"What are we doing when we leave here?" I glance toward the open end of the curtain again. "Our original destination?"

He shakes his head. "No, it isn't safe. We're going back to the house."

"What about—"

He presses his lips together and shakes his head to stop me from finishing that sentence. "We'll deal with that when we're in the car. Right now, it seems the streets aren't safe, no matter where we go, and now the Luna Cartel has seen you with me."

Shit.

"The police officers who picked up the chase took out a few of the ones who were shooting at our car after we crashed, but two other cars got away. And there are more members of the cartel out there."

"And they're gunning for you."

His jaw hardens and he nods. "And you..."

NINE

GALEN

I LET the door slam closed behind us, leaving Luke outside to watch the place that doesn't feel as safe as it once used to.

Nicki wanders into the living room, and even from here, I can see how her body is practically vibrating. Her hands shake at her sides as she stands almost motionless, staring at nothing, just like she did the entire ride home.

Even while I was on the phone with Rowan, explaining why we wouldn't be there, Nicki sat stock still, watching the city pass us. Even while dealing with Rowan's distress at learning what happened. Even when I was trying to get her to reveal what she needed to tell me that was so important. Even when she refused to do it over the phone and hung up abruptly...

Through *all* of it...Nicki did nothing. She didn't say a word. Didn't react to my frustration. She completely shut down, and now, she's spiraling in front of my eyes.

I pause a few feet from her, observing her closely. "Nicki, are you all right?"

"Hmm?" She tilts her head toward me slightly but keeps her focus on the bare wall as if it's the most interesting thing she's ever seen.

"Shit." I take a few steps toward her and press my chest against her back gently, just enough to let her know I'm there. "Are you all right?"

She shivers slightly but nods. "Yeah. Sure."

"Are you in pain? We hit that tree hard."

The airbags did their jobs and prevented any serious injury, but a blow like that is still too much to just shake off. We both suffered mild concussions, not serious enough to put us in any danger, but enough to leave us both off kilter. Though, I don't think that's the problem.

"No." She shakes her head. "I'm okay."

Lie.

Even though we've only known each other a few tumultuous days, I can already read her well enough to know she's lying. She's far from okay. And frankly, so am I.

I wrap my arm around her waist and drag her all the way back against me, brushing my lips against the back of her ear. "You just got shot at again and almost killed."

"Uh huh." She nods slightly, shifting her weight to settle it against me. "I know."

"You have every right to be upset, scared, uneasy." I flatten my hand against her stomach, holding her to me. "This isn't your life. This isn't what you wanted. Yet, you've stumbled into it, and you could have gotten out. You could have told Detective Lopez exactly what was going on. You could have exposed me, exposed everything I told you..."

Nicki nods slightly. "You're right. I could have."

The entire time we were separated in the hospital, I imagined all the things that could have been happening to her. She could have been revealing everything. All my secrets. But she didn't. She protected me.

I know why I *want* to believe she did it. But asking the question tightens my chest. "Why didn't you?"

She turns her head to the side so she can look at me. "Because it felt right."

Fuck.

Those words shouldn't sound so sweet. It *shouldn't* feel so *right*. None of it should...

But all I want in this moment is her.

"What about this?" I slide my hand down to cup between her legs, gliding my thumb over her clit and absorbing the shudder that rolls through her. "Does this feel right?"

She squeezes her eyes closed but doesn't say a word—though, I can practically hear the debate raging in her head.

We *both* want this.

And we both know how *stupid* and *dangerous* it is.

She turns in my hold to face me fully and presses her hands flat against my chest. "More right than anything has in a long fucking time."

"Dammit, Nicki." I take her face between my palms, ignoring the twinge in my left arm. "I almost got you killed, on *three* separate occasions."

Her bottom lip quivers slightly, and she shakes her head. "I know, and I'm scared, utterly terrified of what doing this will mean, but I'm more scared of what will happen if you tell me to leave, if you let me go...because I don't know if I can walk away."

"Shit..." I brush my thumb across her soft, pale cheek. "You're making it very hard to say no to you, Nicki, but I need to know this isn't just all the adrenaline rushing through your body. That this isn't just some need to get back at your brother by fucking his enemy."

Trust is earned, not given. That's one thing I've learned the hard way in this business over the years, but Nicki has proven time and again that I can trust her, that her motives are good, intentions pure. Still, I have to ask. I need to hear her say it, *confirm* it.

"It's not, Galen." Her pale blue eyes bore into mine. "It's about the fact that arguing with you is the hottest foreplay I've ever experienced in my fucking life." She shakes her head slightly. "It's about the fact that when we were about to hit that goddamn tree, my life flashed before my eyes and I realized I hadn't truly felt *alive* for years, until you had me dragged into your office—"

I don't let her finish. Her words erased any restraint I had been hanging onto by a damn thread. I press my lips to hers, stealing her breath and whatever she was about to say, and lower my hand around her waist to drag her against me.

My cocks swells between us, pressing into her waist, and a tiny gasp slips from her lips and into mine. I groan and shift my grip to her ass, then slowly walk her backward through the open door to the bedroom.

I could take her to the bedroom upstairs for more privacy, but I don't have the energy or the patience to wait that long. It feels like we've been hurtling toward this result since the moment we first met, a collision neither of us could avoid.

Her hands cup the back of my neck, and she angles her mouth under mine, getting me exactly where she wants me, so her tongue can probe at mine and tangle in the endless dance for supremacy.

One I intend to win.

Because I *always* win. And I always intend to.

This woman has me wound so tight that it feels like my body might snap in half if I don't do something about it. That, combined with the tension and stress of the last few weeks, is enough to make me let all the reasons this is so dangerous fall away the closer we get to the bed.

I back her up until her knees hit the mattress, and she drags her head away and drops her hands to the waistband of my pants. She frees my cock and takes it in her small, warm hand again. Deft fingers stroke my length and glide over the head, spreading a bead of pre-cum there.

My eyes drift closed, and I release a strangled groan. "Fuuuuck..."

Her lips find mine, and I thrust into her hand, my hips moving of their own accord while our tongues mimic what our bodies so badly want to do.

I'm about to take the sister of my enemy to bed. I'm about to do things to her that will surely seal my fate. But in this moment, I can't care about paying for my sins.

That can wait.

TEN

NICKI

GALEN GRASPS my face between his palms and pulls back, his eyes searching mine. "Are you sure, *a chuisle?*"

I nod and struggle to find the breath to get out the one word I need to. "*Yes.*"

It's a lie.

I'm not sure about anything anymore.

Not about who I am or what I want or why I'm even here.

All I know is that, despite all the reasons I shouldn't—the fact that this man has gotten shot at so many goddamn times and almost got me killed, the fact that he's Cutter's enemy, the fact that he's a *bad* man who does *very bad* things—I feel safe with him.

Protected.

He wouldn't hurt *me*, and in this moment, that's enough. To be in his arms. To touch him. To feel...complete. To know I want him and he wants *me*. To feel whole and secure. That's enough.

His hard cock juts out in front of him, and I stroke it slowly, tightening my grip as I roll my thumb over the head in a way that has Galen clenching his jaw and securing his grip on me.

"Fuck, Nicki."

I pull out of his hold, and his eyes flutter open to watch me lower myself to the bed. Leaning forward, I flick my gaze up to meet his. He stares down at me, his eyes darkening as I slowly suck his entire length into my mouth and down my throat.

His right hand slips into my hair and tightens, his hold keeping me in place. I swallow, letting the head of his cock drag against the back of my throat, and glide my tongue along the hard flesh again.

"Fuck!"

It seems to be the only word he can muster right now. Knowing that makes warmth flood through my body, centering between my legs. I suction around him, pull back slowly, then slide it back inside my mouth, swirling my tongue as I go.

His hold on my hair tightens into a fist. "You're playing with fire, *a chuisle.*"

There's no doubt about it. Galen McGinnis is a raging inferno of wrong. A bad man who does bad things—no doubt sometimes to good people. But even knowing that doesn't stop me right now.

I pull back, letting his wet flesh slip from between my lips, squeezing my fingers around it hard and locking eyes with him. "Maybe I like the heat."

Before he can respond, I suck his dick into my mouth again, and his hips buck forward, driving him down my throat almost to the point of making me gag.

I breathe through my nose and swallow, starting a rhythm, letting him slip in and out of my lips while twisting my hand along the slick flesh until his hips are rolling forward violently, until he's on the brink of losing control fucking my mouth.

Yes.

Causing this man to lose control would be the ultimate win against him after everything that's happened.

But he stops abruptly and jerks on my hair, pulling his cock from my mouth harshly and forcing me to look up at him.

His normally green eyes appear almost black, swimming with a dark desire that sends a shiver down my spine. "Stop, *a chuisle*. As much as I want to come down your fucking throat—and believe me, I will—I want to be inside you the first time."

Fuck, why is that so hot?

It shouldn't be. The vulgar statements, the way he's making demands of me, physically taking control. I should hate it. I should tell him no. But instead, I grab his pants and shove them the rest of the way down his legs, then help him step out of them.

Knowing how sore he must be, how much it must still hurt for him to move his arm, I slowly unbutton his shirt while he watches me with a heated gaze and his hard cock brushing against my belly.

I thought Galen McGinnis was good looking before—with his sharp emerald eyes and salt and pepper hair with just a hint of the red it once was—but now that I see him naked and standing before me in all his badass glory, it steals my breath.

Scars litter his pale skin, but the lean, rippling muscles everywhere make my mouth water to lick and my fingers itch to explore every inch of them.

He steps forward, closing the distance between us and pressing his hard body against my still clothed one. Heat radiates from him into me, warming me in a way I didn't even know I needed. He tangles his fingers on his right hand in my hair again and drags my mouth to his, practically devouring me with a ferocity that makes my blood rush in my ears.

"You have far too many clothes on, *a chuisle*. Get naked and get on the fucking bed."

I've never wanted a man to tell me what to do and have fought against this very thing for so long. Yet with Galen, I want to comply. I want to do what he asks. I want him to know I will.

His gaze follows as I push down the waistband of the yoga pants, sliding them and my underwear over my hips and kicking them free. A tiny grin plays at the corner of his lips, and he climbs on the bed carefully and sits back against the headboard, laser focus on me.

I grab the hem of my shirt and tug it up and over my head, letting it fall to the floor to join the rest of our clothes in an unceremonious pile.

Knowing he's watching, waiting for me to join him, I take my time, slowly reaching back to the clasp of my bra and freeing my breasts, letting the straps roll down my arms until I'm fully exposed to him.

His cock twitches where it juts up between his legs, and he holds out his hand to me and curls his fingers, ordering me to him. "Climb on my cock, *a chuisle*."

I can't resist the pull any longer and crawl across the bed to him. With his eyes locked on mine, I straddle his legs, pushing his dick down flat against my already wet pussy and gliding along it, coating his length in my arousal.

"Fuck." His hands find my hips and dig into the flesh there, and he issues a low groan—one filled with a need and desperation I'm feeling as well. He lifts his hand on my cheek and grips my chin. "Are you going to toy with me, Nicki? Or are you going to give me what I need?"

I can't stop the little grin from pulling at my lips. "I'm just showing you what it's like to not be in control, Galen. How do you like it?"

He drags my face to his and flutters his lips against mine in a soft brush that holds a vicious threat. "I don't like it, *a chuisle*. And you'll fucking pay for it later."

The threat sends a shiver trickling down my spine and goosebumps spreading across my skin.

I reach between us and grasp his now slick cock, angling it up to brush the head along my wet slit. His breath catches slightly, and I press my lips to his as I slowly sink down on him.

A tiny gasp slips from my lips and into his mouth as his cock spreads me open, stretching me to my limits, filling me when I didn't even realize I was empty.

I spread my hands against his chest, careful to avoid putting unnecessary pressure against his left side, and squeeze around him. He groans and drops his hand to my hip again, urging me to move, to give him what he wants, but I hold still for another moment, relishing the feeling of being the one in control, because something tells me it isn't something Galen gives up easily, if at all.

And it's something I might not experience with him again.

But finally, it's too much. My entire body screams for friction, for me to move, for me to do *something*.

I lift up until only the head of his cock is still inside me, then squeeze as I come down on him again, grinding my pelvis against his and rubbing my clit in a way that is sure to set me off.

Everything that's built to this moment has been a giant tease, and I'm so close that I dig my nails into his chest to try to ground myself and force myself to hold off a bit.

But it's no use.

He braces his feet on the bed and shoves up into me, matching my rhythm and driving himself even deeper.

"Fuck..." This time, the word tumbles from my lips and into his, and he slams them against mine in another brutal kiss. One that says that I may be on top but he's the one still in control.

He grits his teeth and picks up speed. My eyes drift closed at the sensations wracking my body.

I never wanted this. Never wanted *any* of it. But now that I have it, I'm going to enjoy every fucking second of it until it's inevitably over and reality comes crashing down on us.

Galen shifts his hand down to where our bodies connect, and his thumb finds my clit. He rolls it there in time with our movements, and that's all it takes for me to explode.

The orgasm hits me as hard as we did that fucking tree, barreling down on me and knocking me free from all the troublesome realities weighing down on us. Free from the violence. Free from the very real threat what we're doing is going to create. Free from all of it.

My body spasms as he thrusts up, my hips bucking in a wild frenzy, losing any rhythm I once had. Heat floods my limbs, a blissful weightlessness pulling me from myself for a brief moment. Galen digs harder into my hip and drives up harshly, a wild man seeking the most base need.

"*Tá mé ag dul go hifreann, ach is fiú é.*"

I don't have a fucking clue what he just said, but he stills under me, grits his teeth, and comes on a roar that fills the room and my ears as his cum spurts deep inside me—all while his wild gaze locks with mine.

This was stupid. This was reckless.

This was exactly what I fucking needed.

ELEVEN

GALEN

NICKI SAGS on top of me, burying her face against my neck. Her heavy breaths flutter against my sweat-soaked skin. I let my body sag back and eyes drift closed as the tiny aftershocks of my orgasm make every muscle in my body twitch.

Fuck.

It really is the only word I'm able to come up with in this moment. It's the only one that has seemed relevant since I met her.

I turn my head to the side and press a kiss to her temple. She moans slightly, then lifts her head, her blond hair wild and disheveled, her lips swollen and beautiful from me fucking her mouth and kissing her senseless.

A stray strand of hair falls against her cheek, and I brush it back from her face and tuck it behind her ear, letting my fingers linger against her warm skin.

Something flickers across her orgasm-fogged gaze.

Fear?

Confusion?

A combination of both?

The last thing you want to see in a woman's eyes after you just fuck like that.

I frown and narrow my eyes on her. "What's wrong?"

"Shit." She shoves her hands through her hair and climbs off me. "Shit..."

My cock slips free from inside her welcoming heat, and a deep groan leaves my chest. The cool air of the bedroom slaps my body, shocking away any lingering effects of my release and bringing back the reality I tried to ignore.

She settles on her back next to me, her hands pressed over her face. "Shit. What did we just do?"

I reach out and drag her against my side, tilting her still-covered face up. "What we both wanted."

"Yes, but..."

"But what?"

The woman who has both saved my life and complicated it more than I thought anything could lowers her hands and looks at me. "But my brother..."

I clench my jaw until it hurts, trying to fight back the natural inclination to lash out at her. "You're an adult. You can do whatever the fuck you want. What your brother thinks or wants doesn't matter. Your brother doesn't matter, Nicki."

She blows out a puff of air. "I know that, but...what if he finds out about *this* or about how I ended up at the bar after the shooting at the church?"

"Do you really think it matters? You said your relationship with him was strained."

Shifting into a sitting position, she releases a deep sigh. "It is, but he's still my brother and I still love him. And I know him, Galen. This"—she motions between us—"is *not* going to be okay. Ever."

"Why would you let him have any say in your life? What the hell happened between you two? There has to be more to it than just him being friends with your ex."

She presses her lips together, like she's sealing the vault of information and I won't ever be able to break into it. This isn't a woman who is used to opening up to anyone, and I understand the desire to keep things locked away. To hide necessary secrets and try to forget old pain. I do it all the time. So, I know she isn't going to answer me. She's going to keep me in the dark when her relationship with him could mean life or death for me.

I take her chin in my hand and force her to look at me again. "I need to know, *a chuisle*. If I'm going to figure this out..."

Being with Nicki complicates things in an already fucked up situation. After what happened at the church, everyone suspects everyone else, and what was merely tension and little jabs here and there will move to full-scale war. Plus, I have the Luna Cartel out for revenge. The last thing I need is a pissed off Cutter.

She hesitates again, worrying her bottom lip between her teeth, and I lean forward and brush a kiss over her mouth.

"Please, *a chuisle*. Tell me."

A heavy sigh finally fills the space between us, and her shoulders sag slightly, like she's giving into something she knew was inevitable. "I told you when he got discharged that he eventually took a job with Warwick, but there's a lot more to it. After Warwick broke up with me, I was devastated. I tried to bury myself in my work at school toward becoming an EMT. Tried to pretend I wasn't utterly destroyed. But then Cutter was hurt in an explosion..."

The gnarly red and white scars that twist over the side of Cutter's face, neck, and arm flash through my head. "Is that what happened to him?"

I nod. "Their caravan was ambushed, and he got scarred like that helping to lift a Humvee off one of his friends to save his life."

"Christ"—I shake my head—"almost makes me respect the motherfucker."

A little half smile pulls at her lips. "Yeah. Well, one thing Cutter always has been is loyal to his friends. But he came back a different person than he had been when he left. Angrier, more volatile. He didn't want anyone to visit him at the hospital. Didn't want anyone's help. Didn't want anyone to see him like that."

She swallows thickly and glances at me, like she's contemplating her next words. Despite wanting to urge her to continue, I bite it back. I don't want to say or do anything that will stop her from telling me what could be important to securing our safety.

"He closed everyone out. Everyone. My parents weren't even on speaking terms with him when they died. And no matter how much I reached out to him, no matter what I tried to do to get through to him, he continued to push me away, cut me out of his life. He was really bad. Angry. Violent. Suicidal even. But somehow, Warwick got through to him. Got him to see what he was doing to himself, that he was throwing away his life." She shrugs slightly. "And I felt like a failure. I was going to school to be an EMT. I wanted to help people, and I couldn't even help my own brother. It made me feel like everything I was doing would be pointless anyway. It changed everything for me." A heavy sigh slips from her quivering lips, one that holds all the anguish she's feeling reliving this story. "And we've barely spoken since then."

"When was the last time you spoke before I made you call him?"

She glances at me. "A little less than a year ago. I discovered something important. Something that I thought could hurt him and his friends."

I narrow my eyes on her. "What was it?"

Her blue eyes consider me for a moment. "One of his friends, Rion, he was dating a woman I bartended with, and I discovered that she was actually an undercover FBI agent."

"Fuck."

"And then there was a bomb..."

I freeze, my hand tightening next to me on the bed. The sounds. The smells. The pain. All of it comes rushing back to me. "How do you think I got this fucking scar?"

Her eyes widen, zeroing in on my old injury. "Shit. Really?"

I reach up and run my fingers along the scar over my eye. "I'm sure you know, the five families were all there at the meeting."

She nods slowly. "Yeah, it was all over the news, but they never said anything about who did it."

I glance over at her. "I can't tell you that."

She holds up her hands. "I wasn't asking."

The mood between us suddenly shifts like ice being thrown over us. Our few moments of bliss have been replaced by the reality neither of us wants to address but that can't be ignored any longer.

Her eyes drop to her lap, and she lowers her hands and twists her fingers together. "What are we going to do?"

I drop my head against the headboard and release a long, heavy sigh, staring at the ceiling like it's going to offer me the answer we both seek. "Take a shower."

"What?"

Tipping my head to the side, I meet her confused gaze. "We're gonna go take a shower. Get cleaned up, eat something, and then figure it the fuck out."

She shakes her head. "Like it's that fucking easy."

It isn't. Not by a fucking longshot.

I don't respond, just shift off the bed and make my way to the bathroom, pausing at the door and turning back to her. "You coming?"

Those blue eyes I could drown in assess me—from my head, down my body, and across my still hard cock that aches to be inside her again.

"Yeah." She climbs off the bed, her perfect breasts swaying slightly in time with her hips.

I wait for her, watching every move her body makes, searing it into my memory in case we're never like this again and it's all I have to remember her by.

She reaches the door to slip past me, and I wrap my arm around her to stop her.

"Whatever happens, you need to know something."

Her eyes open slightly wider. "What?"

"This never would have happened if I didn't let it. If I didn't know exactly what the fuck I was doing and made the decision to let it happen. This was real for me, too. I don't know how, but we'll figure it the fuck out. I promise."

Maybe it's a promise I can't keep, but it's one I damn sure am going to try to.

TWELVE

NICKI

How can he make that promise?

None of this is okay. None of this is *going to be* okay. Even if Cutter never finds out that Galen had me kidnapped, how all this started, he's still never going to allow me to be with him. He will chain me to a fucking wall in Valentina's basement before he lets that happen. Before he lets me get sucked into this world any more than I already am.

When he finds out, all hell is going to break loose.

Yet, Galen looks at me with such calm intensity when he says the words, like he truly believes them and will burn the world down to make sure it happens.

The man is fucking delusional.

"Yeah"—I force a smile on my face even as a vise tightens around my chest with a force that makes it impossible to suck in a breath—"everything will be fine."

I push up on my tiptoes and press a kiss to his lips, then slip from his loose hold and step into the bathroom.

Distance.

That's what I need. A little damn space between me and that man who seems to make me forget *who* I am with one damn look. Who makes me forget *where* I am and *why* with one touch.

I should have stayed in bed. Let him walk away and close himself off in here while I had a fucking meltdown alone. Instead, I followed him, like he's some damn tractor beam drawing me to him when it's so much safer to run away.

Years of being angry with Warwick and Cutter and at myself brought me here. To running away to Chicago to get away from the reminders and them. But it didn't prepare me for *this*—for wanting a man I *should* be angry with.

What the hell do I do?

I reach in the shower and crank on the water, and Galen sidles up behind me and slips his arm around my waist, pulling me back against him. His hard cock presses against my lower back.

He nuzzles my neck and nips there, the sharp sting sending goosebumps across my skin. "I had intended to get clean in the shower. But now, I'm just thinking about how badly I want to fuck you against the tile."

A shiver rolls through me and my pussy clenches, still wet and full of the evidence of what we just did.

He wants control. He wants to take it back after I just had it. I can understand why. It seems like he's lost it recently—in so many ways. He's struggling to get it back in any aspect of his life.

Steam starts to thicken and warm the air around us, and I step in under the spray with Galen hot on my heels. Scalding water hits my back, and Galen steps toward me, taking his cock in his hand and stroking it.

As badly as my body wants him again, I want something else even more. I press my hand against his chest to stop his advance and slowly lower myself to my knees onto the slick tile. "I want to taste us together on your cock."

His eyes widen slightly. "Fuck." He drops his hand from his hard flesh, and I take it in mine. "That's the hottest fucking thing anyone's ever said to me."

I lean forward and suck his cock into my mouth, the salty flavor of his cum and my release mingling along the hard ridges dances across my tongue, and I groan, my cunt spasming and clenching for what it wants.

Galen buries his hands in my hair as water pelts my back while I work him clean. His grip in my hair tightens. "Fuck, Nicki—"

I grasp his balls in my other hand, squeezing them tightly. He groans and shoves down my throat, coming in a hot rush that I have to swallow quickly before I choke on it.

My clit aches for his touch, and my body vibrates in anticipation of what he's going to do next. I swallow again and lick his cock, and as soon as he's done, he jerks himself free and pulls me to my feet by my hair, the sharp sting on my head barely registering.

He brushes his lips against mine, sliding his tongue inside and moaning before pulling away abruptly. "Turn the fuck around."

I do as he asks and turn to face the spray. He presses his body against mine, his cock still hard, and wraps his hand around my throat from behind, dragging my head back until he can press his lips on my neck up to my ear.

"When we get out of the shower, I'm going to fucking devour you. I'm going to eat you like you're my last fucking meal. I'm going to make you come so many damn times that you can't even walk. Do you understand?"

My pussy throbs and clenches, and I squirm in his hold, wanting him to do it, not just say the words.

"But right now, I'm going to fuck you. Hard. Do you understand?"

I nod, and he shoves me forward until I'm pressed against the tile and he's under the spray. He releases my throat so he can drag my hips back and up and positions himself perfectly, then thrusts into me hard enough that my bones rattle when they slam into the tile.

"Fuck!" I press my cheek against the cool, smooth surface—so different than the hot, wet flesh at my back.

He drags his hips back and plunges into me hard.

"Oh, God...Galen. Fuck."

Again and again.

Harder and faster.

He pounds into me like his life depends on it. Like fucking me gives him the oxygen he needs to breathe.

The slap of our skin against each other echoes off the tile, mingling with the groans and gasps that tumble from both our lips.

He returns one hand to my throat and drags my head back and to the side so he can kiss me hard as he pushes into me, reaching a part I didn't know was possible.

Tears well in my eyes as he drives me to the brink of something I know I'm not ready for, a release that will top the one he just gave me in that bed. My head spins, and any ability to think washes away down the drain with the water falling around us.

He drags his mouth back and increases his pace, barreling me toward another orgasm. I open my eyes to watch him. A muscle in his jaw tics and the veins in his neck throb.

His hand squeezes against my throat, tighter and tighter, until my vision goes slightly fuzzy around the edges, a floating sensation overtaking me. It mingles with the overwhelming tingling and pleasure rolling through my body.

The slight shift of his hips makes the head of his cock drag against that perfect spot inside me. It's all it takes to send me over the edge I've been dangling off. My pussy spasms and clenches around him as he pumps into me relentlessly, driving away all my concerns and worries, forcing away the real world for one fucking second until a little gasp falls from his lips and he empties himself inside of me again.

"Fuck, Nicki." He drops his lips to my shoulder and sags against me on the wall, panting heavily. His hand presses over mine, interlocking our fingers. "You need to know..."

"What?"

My orgasm-fogged brain can't process what he just said.

He nudges my face toward him. "Open your eyes."

I open them and glance back at him.

"There are some things you need to know. You're too deep into this. *I'm* too deep into you for you to just walk away, which means you need to know certain things so you can make a fucking choice."

"What are you saying?"

His jaw hardens, the green of his eyes flashing with hints of gold. "I'm saying I want you, *mo chuisle*. Not just now because we were forced into this situation and needed to fuck out the tension between us. I want you to fucking stay."

I try to respond, try to make words, but my mouth has suddenly gone as dry as the fucking Sahara. "You-you know how complicated that's going to be..."

"I know...which is why you need to know."

Shit.

THIRTEEN

NICKI

I CURL up in the corner of the couch, glass of some sort of expensive liquor—what I imagine is Irish whiskey based on the smell of it—in my hand. The liquid vibrates, and I take a deep breath to try to stop myself from shaking.

It doesn't work.

The intensity of what happened with Galen over the last few days, and more specifically, over the last few hours, has finally broken down the strength I've used to try to keep my shit together.

"You need to know..."

What does that even mean?

Galen pours himself a drink and turns back to me when he's finished, leaning against the bar in the dark jeans and button-up shirt I helped him into when we finally came up for air after our shower and a few more hours in bed. The minimal sleep we eventually got was anything but restorative, though. Nightmares plagued me, and Galen tossed and turned beside me, his heart racing against my back when he pulled me against his body.

I'm not the only one completely unsettled over the situation. Knowing that makes it even worse. If Galen's nervous, it means it's really bad. Maybe even worse than I imagined.

He takes a sip of his drink and stares into it, like it might hold all the answers he's looking for. "We're at war, Nicki."

"Who is?"

His fingers tighten on the glass, his knuckles whitening. He raises his head, locking his eyes with mine before he responds. "Everyone."

The word hangs in the air between us along with all the things we don't dare say, heavy with meaning and the unknown.

He closes his eyes for a second and shakes his head. "There are things I can never tell you. Things you can't ever know—for your safety *and* mine. But it's important you understand what you're getting into if I'm going to ask you to stay."

I nod my understanding, though in reality, I have no fucking idea what he's about to tell me or how knowing it could change everything.

Galen shifts his weight restlessly, staring into his glass again. "Things used to be...not easy. Nothing's ever easy. But they were...*easier*."

Given what little I know about the dealings of the families from what's been made public through the news, I can't imagine anything would ever be easy. They're all notoriously cruel and violent—including the family now controlled by the woman Cutter is attached to.

Including *this* man.

I take a sip of my drink to hopefully find the courage to ask what I need to and wince at the burn. "How so?"

"Valerian, *Il Padrone*, Saban Gashi, and I had an understanding of sorts. We didn't fuck with each other. Dare I say, we even respected each other. We stayed out of each other's ways. Prevented all-out war in the city for a decade." He takes a drink and sighs, rolling his injured shoulder slightly like he's trying to release some tension in it. "But then Saban, the head of the Albanian organization, was killed by a man named Konstandin Morina, whose family controlled Philadelphia. It was over a personal issue, something with his brother's fiancée, but it started a chain of events no one could have seen coming."

Galen shakes his head and offers me a sad grin.

"What's so funny?"

He tips his glass toward me. "It always comes down to a woman."

Though not funny at all, I can't fight the pull of the slight smile at my lips.

"Aleksander Gashi stepped in for his brother, and even then, things were okay for a while. Aleksander was harsh. They called him The Dragon, and you don't even want to know what he did to some people, but he understood what a war would cost all of us, so he maintained the status quo amongst the families. Arturo Marconi, on the other hand, didn't like living in his uncle's shadow in the Italian organization and had *Il Padrone* killed. Then Valentina took *him* out and stepped up as head of the family since she was *Il Padrone's* daughter. That would have been right around the time she met Cutter."

I nod slowly, trying to take in all the names and history. "I wasn't speaking with him then. It had been a while…"

All of this is news to me. I never really paid much attention to what was going on in Chicago unless I happened to catch some of it on the Milwaukee news. I had no reason to care. It never affected me…until it did.

Galen takes a drink and stares off toward the front window. "Shortly thereafter, Aleksander was also killed by Konstandin Morina, and a man named Erjon stepped in briefly as head of the Albanians, though that didn't last long. He was trafficking women, and that didn't sit well with your brother and his friends. One of Warwick's crew killed him, and a man named Michael Syla took over."

"I know that name…"

It's familiar, something tickling at the back of my mind, but I can't quite place how I know it.

"Probably because people thought he was responsible for the bombing of the meeting of the families. There was more tension after Valentina and Michael took over, people feeling out what the change would mean and mistrusting everyone else. There was also another new player. Someone who had been bringing in a hell of a lot of drugs. A lot more than we had previously seen in the city. Higher quality shit, too. We initially figured it was one of the Mexican cartels."

"The ones who shot at us? Luna Cartel?"

"No." He shakes his head and takes a sip, reminding me that I still have my drink clenched in my hand. I bring the glass to my lips and let the harsh liquid pour down my throat, coughing slightly.

Galen chuckles. "That's the good shit."

"Yeah." I cough again. "Real good."

A grin plays on his lips. "You get used to it." He stares into his own drink. "Anyway, the crew your brother was on was working for Valentina's cousin and uncle at the time, and they intercepted a shipment that belonged to the Blood Rose Cartel out of Colombia."

I narrow my eyes. "Felipe?"

He nods. "Felipe and his identical twin brother, who we all knew as just Rose. Turns out, they'd been running the business together the entire time as one person, with Felipe pretending to be a good Catholic priest in order to keep himself and what he was doing hidden."

"Jesus…talk about going to fucking hell."

Galen snorts and shakes his head. "I was raised in a very religious family. My uncle was a priest back in Ireland, and even though it was a long fucking time ago, I still remember what it felt like to sit in the church and listen to his sermons." He tightens his hand on the glass again. "But that's a story for another day. Anyway, they hit the shipment, and it sent Rose and the cartel on a bit of a hunting expedition. They eventually came to an agreement with Valentina to sell in her territory, which didn't sit well with anyone. Any sort of concession to someone new moving in like that opens the door for them to take even more from other people. And then...Kat showed up." He locks his gaze with mine, like he's waiting to drop a bomb. "She's Aleksander Gashi's widow."

"Shit."

"Yeah. Though, no one knew that at the time. We all believed she was just opening brothels in the city. We thought she was teaming up with Rose and were skeptical of her because of that, but in the end, she partnered up with Michael. Got him to trust her and..."

"And what?"

Galen pauses for a moment, upping the tension in the room even more. "And then she shot him in the fucking head while he was going down on her."

FOURTEEN

NICKI

"What?"

I must have misheard him.

These people are vicious, but that seems extreme, even for what I know about these people and this world.

Galen nods slowly, pushes off the bar, and makes his way over to me. "Yep." He settles in the chair across from me, wincing slightly, likely hoping I won't notice. "It was a huge clusterfuck, and it only got worse from there. Not only were we dealing with Rose, but now, we had this new woman as the head of the Albanian family, a woman who felt her husband had been murdered and that it was her job to pick up the pieces and expand his empire."

I can already see where this is going. "A woman scorned..."

Galen offers me a tight smile. "Exactly. She started with the brothels, but it was clear she wanted to branch out into other areas despite promising both me and Valerian that she wouldn't. She already had an agreement with Valentina to use her docks to bring in girls, but then she took it a step further and hit Valerian and me where it hurt, likely because she thought we were the two easiest to attack."

"How?"

He shakes his head. "I can't get into details of my business with you. It's better if you don't know the details, just the big picture."

His rebuke shouldn't hurt as much. Frankly, I don't *want* to know all the bloody details, but at the same time, knowing he's keeping things from me makes the whiskey in my stomach churn.

Valerian and Galen are two people I would *not* want to cross. Kat must have some serious balls to be going up against them.

Galen relaxes back in the chair slightly. "Kat's been at the top of our hit list for a while because of that."

"I can understand why. But if there's all this tension, everybody's trying to kill each other and expand their territories, then why would you all get together for a meeting?"

He sighs and scrubs his hand over his cheek. "It wasn't like we had much of a choice. Felipe went all over town and killed one man from each of us—tortured them actually and then left them as a very bloody invitation to the meeting. We knew what he wanted. He wanted us to fear him and know that if we didn't show up, something even worse would happen. So, we met at the church, somewhere we all thought would be neutral ground."

Images of his bloody wounds and pale face when he had me brought into his office flash before my eyes. "But it wasn't."

He snorts and shakes his head. "No, it wasn't, not even fucking close. We discovered the Rose twins were fighting over their territory and business and wanted us to pick sides, but Rowan somehow managed to convince them to work out their differences. The rest of us were trying to figure out what the fuck that meant for us...when someone came in shooting."

"Why would one of the other families do that? If the head of their family was there, wouldn't they be putting themselves at risk?"

Galen points a finger at me. "That's exactly the problem. It doesn't make any sense. None of them would be that stupid."

"Do you think it was the Luna Cartel that Detective Lopez said came after us?"

"No." He shakes his head and takes a sip of his drink. "That night Felipe came for Rowan..."

My stomach churns, the drink I just took souring. "Yeah..."

The night that started all of this.

If I hadn't been there, I wouldn't be *here* now. I wouldn't be entangled with a man who is willing to do anything to get what he wants and has his sights set on me.

"A lot of my most experienced men weren't there."

"Why not?"

His eyes harden, flashes of the man I should probably fear coming through now. "Because I had them taking care of another problem."

He pauses for a moment, almost as if he's considering whether or not to reveal more. It might be dangerous to know everything, but at this point, I have to know. I have to know what I'm getting into.

"Look at what you've already told me, Galen. What can you possibly say now that's going to shock me or put me in any more danger than I already am?" I raise an eyebrow at him. "Really."

"Mmm." He considers my words for a moment, swirling his drink. "Good point." He takes another pull from it. "The Luna Cartel from Mexico. You've been intimately introduced to them already. They've been bringing in drugs for a while, but we left that issue to the other groups handling the majority of the drug trade. I didn't give a fuck if Rose's business was affected by them. The problem is, they've since expanded to guns and other weapons. The Irish have controlled the gun trade in the Midwest for a long time. I let the other families move a little bit here and there for their own needs, but this is our primary business. So, when we got word that the cartel was bringing in shit, we had to make a move."

I swirl my drink in the glass and then down the rest of it. Something tells me I may need the liquid support for what he's about to tell me.

"I made a decisive blow against them, took out an entire warehouse where they had been housing their guns and drugs...after we took out all the men there first."

"Shit. So...why can't it be them who came for you at the church? It seems like retaliation for something."

"It can't be them because we wiped out almost the entire crew in town. They would have had to bring people in from Mexico, and that would take time. Whoever hit us at the church was thorough. Experienced. Coordinated. The Luna Cartel seems to act rather than plan."

"That's who came into the bar?"

"Yes, we were able to confirm it from their tattoos."

"And they were who came after us in the car?"

"That's what Detective Lopez confirmed."

I glance around the "safehouse" as a shiver rolls through me. "How did they find us, find the car?"

"I don't know. May have been luck. They may have someone giving them information."

"Luke?"

His jaw hardens. "Fuck no. The only person I trusted more in this world than Luke was my cousin Padraig, but Michael Syla killed him."

"Jesus, I'm sorry."

His hand flies up to silence me. "I don't want your sympathy. I need you to understand how volatile the situation is. We don't know who shot up the church, but I do know the Luna Cartel wants me dead. That alone should be bad enough, but when you don't know who your enemy is, it makes it a hundred times worse. Getting involved with me is probably the most dangerous fucking thing you could ever do..."

No shit.

He takes a deep breath, watching me and waiting for me to say or do something, to somehow react. But honestly, I have no idea what to do or say.

"And now that you know that, *mo chuisle,* I need to know if you're in this or not." He swallows thickly, holding my gaze with an intensity that heats my skin and brings a flood of memories of what we just did in that bedroom. "Because even if you aren't, even if I never see you again, you're still in danger. I've put you there, and for that, I'm sorry. But I'll protect you. I'll send you wherever you want to go. Help you start a new life. Buy you a house and give you money to live on...whatever the fuck you want. Whatever you could possibly ever need, as long as you're safe. I just need to know—"

The front door flies open, and Luke rushes in, cutting off Galen. "Sorry, sir."

He glances at me and shifts uneasily.

Galen glares at him. *"WHAT?"*

Luke flinches slightly but takes another step forward. "The warehouse in Morgan Park was just hit."

"Fuck!"

Galen jerks up from the chair and chucks his tumbler against the wall. Glass shatters across the room, and a darkness settles over him that obliterates all the things I thought I saw in him and confirms all the things he's warning me about.

This is the Galen I've been waiting for.

The one I should fear.

FIFTEEN

GALEN

I STARE at the shards of glass strewn across the wood floors and waver on my feet slightly. Maybe my activities with Nicki were a little beyond what I should be doing right now given my physical condition, but now, I apparently have bigger things to worry about than whether I'm fit enough to fuck.

Luke's focus darts over to her again, reluctant to say anything more with her present, not wanting to enrage me any further.

"Don't worry about her." I motion toward Nicki dismissively. "Tell me what the fuck is going on."

"I'm not totally sure. I just got a call from Killian over at the warehouse, and he said the whole place is basically gone."

"What do you mean *gone?*"

Luke holds out his hands, empty palms up. "Fucking gone. We lost three men who were inside when the whole place exploded. Killian is the only one who survived and only because he had been patrolling the perimeter and was far enough away that they didn't see him."

Fuck. Fuck. Fucking HELL!

"What the hell is going on?" I pay my men to protect our product and ensure these kinds of things can't happen to us. "Did Killian see anything that could help us figure out who the fuck it was?"

"Not that I know of."

"Get him on the fucking phone and find out. Was the place left unattended at any time?"

He shakes his head. "No, we have people there twenty-four-seven."

"Then how the fuck did explosives get in?"

"I don't know."

FUCK!

I shove my hand through my still damp hair and rub at the back of my neck where the tension is starting to knot. "Increase security at every location and pull any camera footage from any businesses around to see what the fuck we might be able to make out. Go make the fucking calls *now.* I'm going to make some calls myself to see if anyone else was hit or if it was just us."

Luke rushes out the door, casting another furtive glance at Nicki on his way out, and I grab my phone out of my pocket and dial Valerian first. If someone is coming after all of us, then he needs a warning if he hasn't been hit yet.

He answers on the third ring, likely busy getting his dick sucked by one of the whores who hangs out at his underground clubs. "*Comrade—*"

"One of my warehouses was just hit."

"What?" The phone jostles loudly.

"Explosives of some sort."

"Shit."

"What about you?

"As far as I know, everything's fine here."

Fucking brilliant.

That means it's possible *I* am the only target.

"Double your security, just in case. I don't know if this is related to what happened at the church or something else."

"Of course."

I end the call and dial Felipe next. With Rowan's life in his bloody hands, I don't trust that she'll remain unscathed. Especially when I still don't know what she needed to tell me that was so important.

It was something she didn't want to say over the phone, likely because she didn't want Felipe to overhear it.

Shit. Could she have been trying to warn me about this?

The phone rings again, and I almost hang up before Felipe can answer, but his smooth, accented voice floats through the line.

"Galen, why are you—"

"Someone just hit one of our warehouses."

"Hell...and before you ask, I had nothing to do with it." He mumbles something to someone else, then the phone jostles. "Rowan's here. She wants to talk to you."

Hell.

The last thing I want is to scare her even more by telling her what's going on. She seemed off before. Clearly upset about something urgent enough to need to see me in person when we were all hiding out after the church.

Her breathy voice floats through the line. "Galen? What happened?"

"Somebody hit one of our warehouses, but I'm fine."

"Oh, my God..."

"Are you okay? Were you trying to—"

"I'm fine."

She cut me off.

Rowan doesn't want Felipe to know she spoke with me earlier. Maybe he had no idea I was going to meet with her at all. I'm not going to say or do anything that could put her in danger with that man. All I can do is play along and try to protect her even from here.

"Don't worry, Nessa. Put Felipe back on the line."

Something rustles through the phone, and Felipe clears his throat. "I'll let you know if I hear anything."

I won't hold my breath.

He isn't a man I can trust, especially not with all this weirdness with Rowan. None of the relationships between the families are the same anymore. Everything changed in that church. But there are two people who always seem to be at the center of the problems arising here in Chicago recently.

"What about your brother and Kat?"

Felipe releases a heavy sigh. "I spoke with them after they got out of church. They went right to get Kat's son and lie low. It wasn't them. I can guarantee you that."

"Can you?" I tighten my hand around the phone and glance at Nicki, who sits stock still, watching and listening intently. "You really know what the hell your brother and that bitch are up to?"

"You're upset, Galen, but I'm telling you, this wasn't them. From what I understand, you pissed off the Luna Cartel, and they've already come after you more than once. Perhaps it's them again."

"It's possible, but these attacks are too coordinated."

"All you can do right now is keep yourself alive."

"That's my plan."

Nicki shifts in her chair under my assessment, and I end the call, my frustration starting to boil over. My hand tightens even more around the phone, images of the last few weeks flooding my head.

Felipe tearing apart the bar and decimating my men.

Taking Rowan after I had just gotten my sister back.

Being shot at the church.

The cartel coming into the bar and taking out even *more* of my guys.

Those assholes chasing us and now hitting the damn warehouse.

When will it end?

How can I fucking end it?

"FUCK!" My scream echoes around the high ceilings, and I hurl my phone against the wall and watch it shatter into a million pieces, joining the broken tumbler.

Nicki winces, and I stalk over to the door and jerk it open, holding my hand out to one of my only remaining reliable men.

"Give me your phone." I let my focus drift over my shoulder to Nicki. "There's someone else I need to call."

Her eyes widen slightly as she watches me take the phone from Luke's hand. She knows exactly who I'm calling...and why. Besides Rose and Kat, Cutter and Valentina are the only ones I haven't spoken with since the church. He might be the last person I want to talk to after what just happened with Nicki, but I have to do it. I have to know if it was them.

The phone rings twice, and I flip it to speaker phone as Cutter answers abruptly. "You're still alive?"

I growl. "How did you know who it was?"

He snorts. "I had a feeling I'd hear from you after what went down. I heard you got chased through the streets and had to visit with Detective Lopez."

"Yeah, it wasn't the best day of my life."

"You've gotten in deep at this point."

Visions of drilling into his sister in a shower flash in my head, and my cock stirs against my zipper. I clear my throat to dislodge the lump forming there. "Yeah, you could say that. Someone just hit one of my warehouses."

Cutter chuckles darkly. "You really *are* having a shit day. Was it Luna?"

"No."

"Are you sure?"

"Yes."

"Why?"

"Because of how organized this all seems. The men at the church were trained mercenaries, the type of men *you* work with."

"Are you accusing me of something, McGinnis?"

"It wouldn't be the first time you went after one of us. It wasn't so long ago you had Rose locked up in that house of yours..."

Cutter growls a low warning. "If it had been me, you'd be dead on that marble floor."

Fuck.

He's right. Cutter and his crew move with precision. So many people wouldn't have escaped the church if it had been them. These men were trained and organized, but not the way Cutter is.

"If you hear anything on any of these fronts, Cutter, I would appreciate a call."

Cutter barks out a laugh with no humor, and I can almost picture his trademark sneer twisting his scarred lips. "You would appreciate a call? You're not my concern, Galen."

"I may not be, but there are *other* considerations."

"Like what?"

I hold Nicki's gaze. She won't like this, and even though my gut twists thinking about it, I have to say it.

"Like that new baby of yours..."

A gasp slips from Nicki's lips, and she jumps from the chair and rushes toward me. "Galen! No!"

Shit.

I wince.

Cutter growls low. "What the fuck was that? Nicki?"

Fuck.

She winces and retreats a step.

"Nicki?" Cutter's voice practically vibrates through the phone. "What the fuck are you doing with my sister, Galen? Is that what the fuck this is? Did you call to threaten me? To threaten my *child* and to let me know you have Nicki and try to use it as some sort of leverage now that you seem to have the whole fucking city after you?"

Nicki shifts toward me, staying far enough back that she's out of reach. "Cutter, it's me." She holds my gaze, fear darkening hers. "I'm okay—"

"You sure as fuck better be. Galen...when I get my fucking hands on you, you're dead. Do you understand me? Fucking dead."

The line goes dead, along with any chance we had of ever approaching this situation delicately.

I end the call and slip Luke's phone into my pocket slowly, never looking away from the woman who just turned my world on its head.

She opens and closes her mouth a few times, her pretty pink lips that were wrapped around my cock not so long ago parting in a way that brings visions of things I shouldn't be thinking about right now.

"I'm so sorry, Galen. I didn't mean to. I just heard you threatening the baby, and I—"

"You just signed our fucking death warrants."

AMASSING GREED

Greed is a fat demon with a small mouth and whatever you feed it is never enough.

- Janwillem van de Wetering

ONE

NICKI

"YOU JUST SIGNED OUR DEATH WARRANTS." Galen's dark, definitive tone sends goosebumps skittering across my arms.

"No!" I step toward him, daring to close the distance between us, even when he's practically vibrating with rage. If we leave things like this, then Galen is right. Cutter will come for me, and he'll destroy anything and anyone in his path—including Galen. "Call him back."

Maybe I can reason with him. Make him listen.

Galen slams his palm against the table that runs along the back of the couch and glares at me with green eyes hard enough to feel like they're physically cutting me. "It doesn't matter, Nicki. There's absolutely nothing either of us could say to him right now that will change what's going to happen."

"You don't know that."

"I *do*." He squares his shoulders, his injury either no longer causing him pain, or he's become so accustomed to it that he doesn't even care or react to it anymore. "I know your brother. I know what kind of man he is. Maybe you've been sheltered from the truth because of the distance between the two of you, but your brother is a cold-blooded killer. An assassin who works for a woman who will do whatever it takes to survive and thrive. I know these people; these are *my* people, *my* world, and I *know* Cutter."

Galen may *think* he knows Cutter. No doubt things have happened that have proven how lethal Cutter really is, but I know the boy he once was still exists somewhere deep inside him. My *brother* still exists somewhere in there. And he's a completely different person from the one Galen is so afraid of. He was always protective of me, always watched over me and had my back, but he wasn't irrational. He wasn't a mindless machine.

What he saw and experienced and suffered during his time on Delta Force may have hardened him, may have made him push me away and shut him down emotionally, but he still cares. Enough that we can still do something about this to prevent bloodshed.

"We *make* him listen, Galen. Give me the phone."

Galen grits his teeth together. "No."

"Fine. Then I'll go find wherever you stashed my phone myself."

I turn away from him and make it half a step toward the bedroom before he grasps my wrist and stops me dead in my tracks. He tugs at me, whirling me around to face him and tightening his grip hard enough to hurt.

"You are *not* calling him back. Even if I believed you could reason with him, he's going to try to trace the call and figure out where we are.""

"He'll figure it out anyway, and I'm not going to sit here and wait for bullets to fly. We have to do something. Have to explain."

"Explain what?" He drags me closer until his warm breath that carries the sweet smell of whiskey flutters over my face. "That I kidnapped you? That you've witnessed multiple shootings because of me? That I fucked you mercilessly multiple times and made you come so many times we lost count? Just *what* are you going to explain to him?"

969

The pure anger vibrating through his touch makes me swallow thickly. I know it isn't really directed at me but at the situation we find ourselves in. And he's already proven he'll never hurt me —at least, physically.

"I'll make him see reason. I'll make him *understand*."

He barks a sardonic laugh and shakes his head. "Do you really think it will matter?"

It's a valid question given Cutter's reputation and the fact that he'll be in protective big brother mode on top of how volatile he normally is.

"Maybe not but sitting here and doing nothing while we wait for the world to explode around us isn't a very fucking good plan, either. Is it?" I raise an eyebrow defiantly, waiting for him to snap, to lose the control he's barely clinging to. "He would never hurt me. You're the only one in danger here, so I'll go see him alone."

His grip tightens on my wrist. "Like hell, you will. You're not going anywhere."

"You told me I could leave. That you would make sure I was safe. Set me up somewhere. Ensure I was protected. Even if we weren't together..."

His grip loosens slightly, his face softening for a split second, showing the man I *know* is in there somewhere. "Is that what you want?"

"I don't know, Galen, but if you stop me from leaving now, prevent me from going to my brother to try to stop him before he does something rash, I won't believe anything you've said to me. I can't believe it if you won't even let me go do this."

He releases my wrist, takes a step back, and shoves his hands through his hair, locking his gaze with mine. We stare at each other for what feels like an eternity. A battle of wills neither one of us wants to lose. One neither of us can afford to.

Galen's right. Cutter is going to destroy us. Destroy *him*. He's going to come for me. We're sitting ducks waiting for a trained hunter to flush us out from where we're hiding in the reeds. It won't take long for Preacher to find this place. No matter how good Galen thinks he is at hiding the location of the safehouse, Preacher is better. He can hack anything, *find* anything and anyone, and Cutter will use everything at his disposal to hunt down the man standing in front of me and pry me from his hold.

But Galen also isn't going to just let me walk out of here and go to Cutter. He can't, despite what he promised. It would be a concession, an admission that I have power over him, and he isn't a man who gives up power. His fight with the Luna Cartel and the other families has proven that.

Still, the longer we have this staredown, the more I question every decision I've made since leaving Wisconsin.

Galen sighs, then stalks over to the bar and pours himself a hefty tumbler full of whiskey. He downs it quickly, hissing at the burn, but keeps his back to me, staring out the window at the front of the condo onto the quiet street below—one that won't be so quiet once Cutter finds us.

Finally, after what feels like hours, Galen turns to face me. "Luke!"

His call echoes through the high ceilings, and he leans back against the bar and waits for his minion to enter.

The door swings open, and Luke sticks in his head. "Sir?"

Galen stands stock still for a moment, then considers me again. The silence settling over the room makes me shift on my feet under his scrutiny.

Why isn't he saying anything?

The dark energy radiating off him is so much worse than if he were ranting and raving and throwing a tantrum. The barely restrained rage is far more terrifying.

Ultimately, he releases me from his spell and returns his focus to Luke. "We're going to the Marconi estate."

Luke's eyes widen as he steps fully into the room. "What?"

Yeah...what?

"Nicki and I are going in to talk to Cutter and Valentina. You gather as many men as you can and follow us. Wait just outside the gates, and if we don't come out within an hour"—he locks eyes with me again—"come the fuck in after us."

It goes without saying that if it comes to that, a whole hell of a lot of people will be hurt—or worse. He's giving me the opportunity to prove what I can do with Cutter, that I can get this resolved. If I can't, the shit will truly hit the fan.

Luke glances toward me and swallows thickly, his adam's apple bobbing. "Understood, sir."

He steps back into the hall to call the rest of Galen's surviving men. The door closes with a click behind him, the sound almost deafening in the silence hanging between us.

Finally, Galen returns his hard green gaze to me. "I hope you know what you're doing, Nicki, because if you don't, I'm not walking out of there alive."

TWO

GALEN

THE CLOSER WE get to the Marconi compound, the thicker the tension builds in the narrow space between me and where Nicki sits in the passenger seat. I glance at her out of the corner of my eye, the last light of day fading away slowly. She shifts restlessly, twisting her hands on her lap and biting her lip in a way that has me imagining all sorts of wholly inappropriate things given the current circumstances.

There's a very good chance I won't walk out of Valentina's mansion alive, and it's because this woman refuses to back down to anything or anyone—including me.

But that doesn't mean I can't give it one more go...

Maybe try to save my fucking life...

I pull up in front of the massive metal gates—the only break in the high red brick walls surrounding the historic Marconi estate. "Are you sure you want to do this, *a chuisle*?"

She stares up at the cameras mounted on either side of the gate. "It's too late to turn back, anyway. He knows we're here."

Almost as if in response to her statement, the gates slowly swing open, allowing us to pass onto the grounds that've been the home of the Marconi crime family for generations, while my men wait just outside and down the street.

Il Padrone used it as his seat of power, requiring anyone who wanted to meet with him to make this same long drive up. Until Arturo stole it from him. Now Valentina has returned it to its prior use. Ruling from here with the same brutality as her father but with a slight reservation that can only be attributed to her prior profession as a police officer. She's smart and ruthless but also holds a respect for precedent and history, and Cutter only adds to the volatility of the situation.

The fact that I kidnapped and fucked his sister assures my destruction—at the hands of one or both of them. They won't care how this happened. Whether she tells them about the kidnapping or not is irrelevant. All that will matter is that she's with their enemy.

We pull through the massive oak trees and expansive lawn and park in front of the steps leading to the massive double doors that loom above. Cutter already waits just outside them, gun drawn and pointed at us before we even stop, sunglasses covering his damaged face even though night is quickly descending.

I glance at him and sigh, though it isn't unexpected. "I see we have a welcome party."

Nicki doesn't respond, just stares at her brother like she's never seen the man before. And even though his eyes are covered by the reflective aviators he never removes, the slight tilt of his head in her direction acknowledges her in a less-than-loving-brother way.

This'll be some craic.

I throw the car into park, shut it off, and inhale deeply, what might be my final chance to breathe air as a free man again, if I breathe again at all. Slipping the keys into my pocket, I open my door and slide from the driver's seat, raising my hands while trying not to wince at the twinge the motion brings to my arm. Ignoring the pain only works for so long.

Cutter takes a step down from the concrete porch toward the vehicle as I knock my door closed with my hip. He stops a few feet in front of me, gun trained squarely at my chest.

"Give me one reason I shouldn't unload this entire fucking magazine into you right now."

Nicki's door slams to my right, and she rounds the front of the car and shoves a hand into Cutter's chest. "Because I would do the same to you, asshole."

Cutter's jaw hardens like steel, and he glances down toward his sister for a split second before returning his focus to me.

There are those balls she's so fond of swinging around.

No one talks to Cutter like that and survives. At least, no one I know. Apparently, baby sisters can get away with just about anything. God knows I would let Rowan get away with anything now that I have her back in my life.

After all the years of praying, begging, making promises to God that I would give up this life and repent if I ever found her, she's finally back, and here I am, with a gun pointed at my heart by a master marksman and the only thing stopping him from firing is a five-foot, one-hundred-twenty-pound blonde firecracker who might not even want to be with me when all is said and done.

Fuck. How did it come to this?

I got greedy. I wanted it *all*—Rowan, Nicki, Chicago...

Cutter steps back slightly from his sister's hand at his chest, shoulders tense and body ready for a fight, but he finally inclines his head toward the house. "Inside. Now."

He's right, of course. This isn't the place to be having such a delicate conversation, nor would he want to spill blood on the cobblestones out here. It would be pretty damn hard to get them clean. The Marconis are too smart for that. They would never do their dirty work where there might be prying eyes from outsiders, and you never know who might be watching from a neighboring home or even from above.

I move past him and head for the front door, where two of his men wait on either side. Nicki shifts to step behind me, but Cutter grabs her bicep, snapping her to a stop. Anger flares deep in my chest at the way he manhandles her, and I turn toward him to say something, then think better of it when his gun remains squarely trained on me.

He sneers at Nicki, tightening his hold on her arm. "You stay with them." He motions toward the two at the door with his chin. "While I take care of Galen."

Her blue eyes widen, her lips twisting into a scowl. "Don't you dare hurt him, Cutter Samuel Jackson. I swear to fucking God, if you—"

"I don't want to hear it, Nicki." He pushes her toward one of his men. "You don't get to decide what happens right now."

She gasps incredulously before Cutter steps forward and grabs my left arm around the bicep.

Fuck!

His fingers dig into the stitches there, threatening to break through them and tear open the still-fresh wound. I wince and suck in a deep breath to fight against the nausea and dizziness making my head swim.

He leans forward slightly and examines me. "Oh, shit? Are you hurt?" He leans even closer until his hot breath hits me like a warning flame. "Good, I hope you're in agony. It's what you deserve for thinking you can touch my sister."

Fair enough.

It's the same way I felt when I realized Felipe had been with Rowan, that he was using her as a way to get to me. I can't blame the man for seeing red. I sure as hell did, and the only reason Felipe isn't already dead is that Rowan would never forgive me for it—and I can't lose her again.

He shoves me forward with a tight grip and leads me through a large foyer, past a huge staircase, and down an immaculately decorated hallway to a door at the rear of the house. We pause outside it, and he motions toward it with the gun he hasn't put away since the moment we arrived.

"Open it."

I'm not in any position to say no at this point. I pull it open to find a set of stairs leading down into utter darkness. He elbows me forward, and I flip on a light switch to our right to illuminate our descent.

If Nicki weren't here, if Cutter were holding me like this under any other circumstances, I would have made a hundred moves to disarm him and end this properly. But I can't risk that with her here. Not when so much is at stake. Not just my future with her, but my future *period*.

I can't create any more enmity with Cutter and Valentina than already exists.

We make our way down steps to a basement I'm sure has many stories to tell. This is the type of place you do your dirty work undetected.

Cutter digs his fingers into the wound on my arm again. "To your left."

Biting back the instinct to lash out at him with my free hand, I follow his direction and approach a door. I glance at him out of the corner of my eye. "You don't have to do this, you know. I never—"

The blow knocks me forward, and pain radiates from the back of my head through every cell of my brain and out into my limbs. I stagger forward on rubbery legs and manage to catch myself against the doorframe before I completely fall flat on my face.

"I don't want to hear a word you have to say, Galen. As if the situation here isn't bad enough, you drag my sister into this somehow. If you really think you're getting out of here alive, you're far stupider than I thought."

While I'm off-balance, Cutter shoves me easily into the room and slams the door behind me. A series of locks slide into place, each one echoing ominously in the small room clearly meant to be my cell.

The stars flashing in my vision start to clear, and I shake my head slightly, trying to focus on the space around me. Other than a small bed against one wall, it's completely empty.

This must be where they kept Rose…

Their own prison cell in the basement of an opulent mansion meant to lull visitors into a welcoming sense of security, make them forget who it belongs to and what the family has done to afford a place like this.

Yet Rose found a way out of his captivity—no doubt by making some sort of deal with Valentina and Cutter.

What could Nicki possibly say to that man that is going to get me out of here? Nothing.

My only hope is that Luke and the guys come in here in an hour with enough firepower to free me, but realistically, that's a pipe dream. Cutter has this place locked down tighter than Fort Knox. My men won't even get close enough to breathe on Cutter or his men before they're taken out.

This place is impenetrable.

And I'm fucked.

THREE

NICKI

ONE OF CUTTER's goons forces me into a room that would actually be cozy and comfortable if it weren't for the fact that I'm about to have to tear my own brother a new asshole.

A massive fireplace occupies one wall with overstuffed leather furniture placed precisely around it, welcoming visitors to sit and enjoy the warmth emanating from the leaping flames.

Instead, it feels more like I'm about to be burned by them. I had expected a cool reception, but gunpoint was a bit extreme, even for Cutter.

His man stops at the door. "Wait here."

I turn back toward him fully, about to voice my objection, but he steps aside and Cutter appears, my own reflection looking back at me from his sunglasses.

He steps into the room and slams the door behind him, his half-scarred lips twisting menacingly. It's a good thing his gun has been re-holstered because the way he's looking at me now, I'm not so confident he wouldn't use it against me. Especially after the way I confronted him outside in front of Galen and his men.

"What did you do with Galen?"

"Why the fuck do you care?" One of his eyebrows rises above the top of the glasses. "Who the fuck is *he* to *you*? What are you doing with him?"

"Take off those fucking sunglasses so I can see your face. You can't hide behind those, Cutter, no matter how much you might want to." I take a step toward him, not frightened in the least by his attitude.

It's an act, a mask he wears to protect himself from having to relive bad memories and experience the pain again.

"I've seen you at your worst, or have you already forgotten?"

I never could. I never will.

The charred skin.

The smell of burned flesh.

The way his body was almost unrecognizable.

Burned so severely that the doctors said he might not survive.

I sat there at his bedside. Held his good hand. Told him I wouldn't leave. That I would be there for *anything* he could need. And I didn't leave...until he finally *made* me. Until he made it *impossible* for me to stay.

He snarls and rips off the glasses, glaring at me with his one good eye and the dead white milky one. The scars covering the entire right side of his face and neck twist with his anger. They make the scar crossing Galen's eye look like a mild scratch.

"Tell me Galen is okay."

"He's alive...for now." His hand tightens around his glasses, his knuckles whitening. "Tell me what the fuck is going on. Did he kidnap you? Was he trying to use you to get to me? Or does he want to—"

I hold up a hand to silence him. "Just stop and let me fucking talk."

If I let him keep going on, thinking the worst of the worst, he'll get himself so worked up that I won't be able to ever talk him down.

He sucks in a deep breath, his wide chest heaving hard, and shoves his free hand through his hair. "What are you doing here, anyway? In Chicago. Why aren't you back home?"

I release a heavy sigh, walk over to one of the chairs, and lower myself into it. It was inevitable that I would have to tell him at some point. Even if none of this had ever happened with Galen, Cutter would have eventually checked in on me and found I had left. He would have hunted me down and asked the same question. I just thought I'd have more time to prepare my answer.

Somehow, telling Galen—a man who is practically a stranger, a man I *should* hate and fear—was so much easier than telling Cutter, the one who should love me unconditionally, the one I *do* love, no matter how volatile he is.

"I couldn't stay there anymore, Cutter. There were too many memories. Too many people who brought them up. I needed a fresh start."

"So, you came here and didn't even tell me you were in town?"

I look up at him. "Would it have mattered if I had?"

He flinches, a chink in the armor he wears so proudly and never lets anyone see him without.

"Seriously, would it? You've ignored my calls and texts since that day I came to see you at the warehouse to warn you about Gabby. I saved you and your friends, and then you treated me like fucking dirt. Left me to go back to what? A life alone where my brother doesn't even give a fuck about me?"

His shoulders tense. "I give a fuck, Nicki."

"You sure have a shitty way of showing it."

He mumbles a curse under his breath and shifts his solid frame uneasily. "It's complicated. I didn't want you dragged into any of *this*. But it seems you were, anyway. How long have you been here?"

"Just a couple of weeks. A friend of mine from high school...you remember Bridget? Anyway, she lives here and knew I wanted to move. She told me about a job bartending."

He crosses his arms over his chest. "You wanted a fresh start and just went back to bartending?"

"What the hell else was I supposed to do? It's one of the very few things I'm qualified for."

"You can finish school, become an EMT like you—"

"Don't even get me started on that, Cutter. You don't want to get into that with me right now." If we dig any more into our tenuous relationship and all the shit between us, we'll never get anywhere with the Galen situation. "Anyway, I got to town and went in to ask about this job, and I got it." I suck in a deep breath, steadying myself for the reaction I know is coming. "At *Bottom O' the Well*."

He winces. "Jesus, Nicki, of all the fucking bars in Chicago, it had to be there? Didn't you know who it belonged to? What the fuck it was?"

I push to my feet, fisting my hands at my sides. "How was I supposed to know that, Cutter? Tell me how I was I supposed to know it was run by the damn Irish mob?"

He throws up his hands, his glasses still fisted in one. "I don't fucking know. *Ask* someone. It's not like it was a fucking secret. They've operated out of there for a long fucking time."

"It wasn't exactly a concern at the forefront of my mind. In my world, you don't have to *ask* if someone is connected with organized crime when accepting a job."

"Why didn't you just call me? I would have given you any money you needed. I could have found you a job."

"Because I wanted to do this on my *own*. Coming here wasn't about *you*."

He scowls. "So, that's it?" He narrows his eyes on me, stripping away any hope I might have had of trying to conceal the reality of the situation. "You just *work* for Galen?"

I close the distance between us, coming to stand in front of him. If I'm going to say this, I'm going to do it on as level a playing field as I can, looking him right in the eyes without flinching. Still, he towers over me. He got all of Dad's height while I got Mom's petite frame.

"I do more than *work* for Galen." It's all I dare say.

Even expanding one single word will make him totally blow his gasket.

His jaw tenses. A muscle there tics rapidly. He clenches and unclenches his fist. "He's a fucking dead man. You have no idea what you've gotten yourself into, Nicki. No *fucking* clue."

I take a deep breath. "Yes, I do..."

This is stupid. I shouldn't be telling him. But he needs to know I understand.

"After the church attack, I'm the one who patched up Galen."

His eyes widen. "What? Jesus Christ, Nicki, are you insane? Do you have any idea what you've exposed yourself to?"

"Yes, but it was my choice. My life, Cutter. Not yours. And I don't have any intention of apologizing."

He takes a step toward me. "You have no idea what you've done, Nicki. We're at fucking war with the other families, with enemies we can't even identify, and you're *fucking* Galen McGinnis. Are you insane?"

I might be, but I'm not going to voice any of my doubts about my situation with the Irishman to Cutter. Not going to give him any reason to reinforce what he already thinks. Not if I want to get Galen out of here alive.

"Whatever happens between Galen and me is between Galen and me." I shove my hand against his chest, but he doesn't budge even an inch. "If you lay one fucking finger on him, so help me God, you will pay for it, Cutter Samuel Jackson."

He narrows his eyes on me, a menace twisting his lips again.

I give him another little shove. "You don't get to have any say in my life anymore. Not after what you did. After you had a damn baby and didn't even tell me I was an aunt."

He freezes and stiffens, his face softening slightly. "Galen told you..."

"Of course, he did. And that's why I spoke up when he mentioned the baby on that phone call. I'm not about to let him threaten you or Valentina or my niece or nephew any more than I'm going to let *you* threaten *Galen*."

"It's not that simple, Nicki."

"*Make it* that simple."

"I—"

The not-so-distant sharp pops of rapid gunfire end his retort...

FOUR

NICKI

CUTTER INSTANTLY CHANGES in front of me, from a concerned brother to the deadly operative the government trained him to be. He wraps his arm around me and pulls me toward him, putting himself between me and the direction of the sound.

Part of me wants to fight him, but I'm unarmed and have no fucking clue what's going on. "That sounds like gunfire."

He nods, weapon somehow in his free hand already while he shoves his glasses into his pocket with the other. "Galen's men?"

I shake my head. "No, he..." *Shit, I probably shouldn't be telling him this, but right now, we have everything to lose.* "He told them to wait and not come in unless we weren't out in an hour. We've only been here for like twenty minutes, tops."

"Fuck." He rushes me toward the door, hand tightening on his raised gun, and reaches for the doorknob just as one of his men opens the door. "What's happening?"

The man who shoved me in here only minutes ago glances over his shoulder, keeping an eye on the hall where gunfire continues to echo. "Four assault teams, heading in from all sides. They tore straight through the front gate and must have scaled the fence on the other sides after disconnecting the video cameras. We noticed the cameras were down but hadn't even had time to get out there to check them before they attacked."

"Where are Valentina and the baby?"

"I already got them out of the house with Milo, though the dog definitely didn't want to leave without you and made it known. They'll wait in the SUV for you to leave."

"Go. Take them. Get them the fuck out of here." Cutter shoves me toward his man. "And take my sister with you."

"What? No!" I jerk out of his goon's hold and whirl to face Cutter. "I'm not going anywhere without Galen."

Cutter grips my arm in his free hand, digging his fingers into my delicate skin. "This is not the fucking time for this, Nicki."

His goon steps into the room and scans the length of windows on the far wall, keeping an eye on whatever might be happening outside while Cutter and I have another showdown in here.

Cutter suddenly raises his gun, and I duck slightly—for a split second, believing he might actually shoot *me*. He fires over my shoulder; the noise so close to my head it makes my ears ring and actually hurt. A man collapses in the hall, just outside the door, blood pooling under him.

"Oh, my God." My heart thunders against my ribcage, but the sharp ringing in my ear overtakes my ability to hear anything else.

He grips my shoulder and lowers his face until our eyes meet. "You need to *go*, Nick. You'll be safe where they're taking Valentina."

His words are choppy in my right ear and battle with the ringing in my left, but I manage to make them out.

Anger rising in my chest, I plant my feet, setting my shoulders despite the fear coursing through me at the near-miss with the dead man in the hall. "I'm not going."

"Fuck." Cutter knows me well enough to know I'm not going to budge on this. He motions to his man. "Go. Get Valentina, the baby, and Milo out of here. I'll take care of the rest."

The man nods his understanding and rushes off to do as he's told.

Unlike me.

Cutter scans the hall and steps out. "Stay with me. Close."

"Where is Galen?"

He moves down the hallway toward some unknown part of the house while the sound of shots continues from all directions. Some far too close for comfort.

A quick glance at me reveals his annoyance. "Really? That's your concern right now? Galen?"

I grab his shoulder and try to pull him to a stop, but he keeps moving forward slowly, unaffected by the action. "Yes, it is. Where is he?"

It's clear Cutter has no intention of freeing Galen from wherever he's being held. His concern is this house, his men, and ensuring nothing important falls into the hands of the enemy. He doesn't give a shit about the man he almost killed once already today.

I plant my feet again and cross my arms over my chest. He jerks to a halt next to me and glances my way while maintaining a ready posture for anyone who may come at us from either direction.

"Seriously, Cutter, I'm not moving from this fucking spot until you tell me where he is. So, either you throw me over your shoulder and have to carry me with you, or you tell me and make this easier on both of us."

He grinds his teeth together, any patience he may have had for the situation and me long gone. "The basement."

"See, was that so hard?" I raise my eyebrows. "And how do I access the basement?"

He motions toward a door at the end of the hall, back the way we came. "That door, but you're not—"

"Thank you." I move to brush past him, but he grips my upper arm again, stopping me as gunshots ring out, even closer to us, just down the hall in the foyer.

"You're not letting him out."

I growl at him, low, the way he always does to people when he's trying to make a point. "Look, you can either fight whoever it is attacking your home by yourself or with two additional armed shooters." I hold out my hand. "Give me a gun."

He scoffs. "You haven't shot a gun in years."

Squaring my shoulders, I lean into him. "How would you fucking know?"

It's a low blow, but one I'm happy to see lands. He winces, then slowly hands me his gun and reaches down to pull another one from his ankle holster.

"You only have seventeen shots left in there."

"Hopefully, I won't need to use them."

I rush off toward the basement door before he can say anything else. Pausing with my hand on the knob, I glance back to find an empty hall. Cutter has headed for his destination, leaving me to free his prisoner on my own.

He would likely love to see Galen perish at the hands of whoever is attacking the house, but no matter how unsettled things may be between Galen and me, I can't leave him to die here.

I yank open the door to the basement and rush down the dark steps as fast as my feet will carry me. I don't have time to examine the dark, dungeon-like atmosphere. The shots continue above, and they don't seem to be letting up. Whatever is happening isn't going to stop. We need to get out of here now, or we won't walk away from this.

Loud banging draws me toward a closed door to my left.

"Let me out, you fucking wanker!" Galen's accent deepens, coming through even stronger with his anger as he slams against the door. "I swear to Christ, Cutter, I'm going to fucking kill you—"

I unlock the half-dozen deadbolts as fast as my fingers will move and pull open the door, then point my gun directly at the man who dragged me into this entire mess.

FIVE

GALEN

GUNFIRE CONTINUES above me and outside, muffled by the insulation of the basement, and I pound on the door again, the thick wood barely budging no matter how hard I rail on it. "Let me out, you fucking wanker. I swear to Christ, Cutter, I'm gonna fucking kill you—"

The locks click, and it swings open, only it isn't Cutter Jackson waiting with a gun trained me. It's the woman I'm doing all of this for.

"Nicki? What the hell is going on up there? I hear gunfire."

She stares at me for a moment, her blue eyes flashing with a million emotions, yet the gun doesn't waver. "Someone's attacking the house."

What the hell?

"My men?"

They were supposed to stay outside the estate to give us time to try to resolve things peacefully, and the sounds coming from upstairs are anything but peaceful.

Nicki shakes her head. "No, someone else."

A dozen different potential assailants flit through my head—Felipe, Rose and Kat, Valerian, our mystery men from the church. Any of them could be behind this, but I have no desire to wait around to find out.

"Let's get out of here." I take a step toward her and hold out my hand. "Give me the gun."

I need to be able to protect her if we're going to try to shoot our way out of here, and though she's unlikely to admit it, she knows I'm far more proficient with a firearm than she is. But instead of lowering the barrel and handing it to me, Nicki keeps it pointed squarely at my chest, her hand still steady even though her gaze holds uncertainty.

Raising an eyebrow at her, I take another step closer. "What are you doing, *a chuisle?*"

Nicki swallows thickly, like there's something lodged in her throat she can't manage to get down. "It looks like I'm pointing a gun at you, Galen."

Such a little smartass...

"That you are. But why, *a chuisle?*"

What could possibly have happened between our arrival and now that would make her turn the gun on me?

Since I had my men grab her, she's had more than enough opportunities to shoot me and flee if that's what she wanted.

"Because I don't trust you not to take it from me and use it on Cutter."

Ah. There we go.

No matter what may have happened between them, the bad blood and distance, she's still protecting him—even from me.

I close the short distance between us, stepping forward until the barrel of the gun presses directly in the center of my chest and drag her body flush with mine. "After all this, *a chuisle*, you still don't trust me? After I peacefully turned myself over to your brother for *you?* Still?"

The slightest hint of hesitation flashes through her gaze, but it's gone just as fast as it appeared. "I don't trust anyone anymore, Galen. It's nothing personal."

It shouldn't bother me that she said she doesn't trust me. And it certainly shouldn't make me feel like something deep inside my chest is trying to claw its way out.

No one truly trusts anyone in this game, nor *should* they. It's what gets you full of bullet holes or six feet under. I learned that long time ago when the church exploded and took everything from me, when I realized Nessa was gone, too. Yet, apparently, somehow, I either forgot it or got complacent, or I never would have been in Felipe's damn church in the first place.

But I *want* Nicki to trust me. I *need* her to trust me if I have any hope of keeping her, of getting her to stay with me despite all the reasons not to. If she doesn't trust me, I've already lost and there's no point to any of this.

"Oh, it's deeply personal, *a chuisle*—"

Gunfire at the top of the stairs behind her jerks us apart, and she whirls toward it, gun poised. Footsteps carry across the basement to us, and a set of shined black shoes finally appears.

Definitely not Cutter.

"Galen?" Luke's voice makes Nicki let out a breath in a long whoosh.

"Aye! Over here."

He finishes descending, and I reach out and push Nicki's arm down so she doesn't get trigger happy with one of my only reliable men left.

Luke comes to a stop at the bottom of the steps and narrows his eyes on us. "You all right?"

I nod. "Grand. What's going on out there?"

"We saw a bunch of black SUVs barrel through the gates, and then all hell broke loose."

All hell broke loose.

That seems about right for how things have been going the last few months. It's been one mess after another, and now, we're stuck in a shootout in enemy territory without knowing who the hell is even shooting.

Luke glances at the scene in front of him, with Nicki holding the gun when it would normally be me. "We figured you could use a little backup."

I smirk at him. It's a good thing he didn't see Nicki with that gun pressed to my chest. If he had, he might have fired on her before she ever had a chance to realize what a mistake she was making.

"A little backup would be most welcome." Leaning in toward Nicki, I brush my lips against her ear. "You better learn to trust me, *a chuisle*. Your life may depend on it."

The tiny shiver that rolls through her draws my lips into a grin, and I brush past her and approach Luke, motioning toward his gun. He quickly hands it over, and I glance back at Nicki, who just glares at me.

"I guess we're on an even playing field now, *a chuisle*."

She huffs and blows hair off her forehead. "Hardly..."

I head toward the stairs with Luke hot on my heels. "What did you see on your way in?"

He follows me up the stairs slowly, Nicki close behind. "A fucking bloodbath. At least half a dozen of Cutter's men are down out front and likely dead from trying to stop them from getting in. A few more between the door and here."

I glance back at him, ascending slowly toward the sound of gunfire. "How did you know where I was?"

Luke shakes his head. "I didn't. I fought my way in and saw Nicki heading this way, so I broke off from the rest of the guys and followed."

Pausing near the open door at the top of the steps, I turn back to look at Nicki where she stands behind Luke. "Where's your brother?"

She offers a shrug. "I don't know. I left him to come to find you. But I know he sent Valentina and the baby away. His man said whoever is attacking has the house surrounded, so there must be some way out of here we don't know about."

"Well, we better fucking find it..."

Fuck.

A quick flash of movement at the end of the hall draws my attention, and I fire off a few rounds, then duck back down the steps just as a barrage of bullets slams into the door jamb where I just stood.

I reach out and fire off a few rounds, then retreat again. "We're pinned here."

Luke mutters a curse under his breath, and Nicki takes a sharp inhale, her eyes widening slightly. This isn't a good position to be in—there's only one way out of here, and it's down the hall where someone is shooting at us. We can't go back down to the basement. We'd never make it out.

"Fuck." I check my magazine—and we're also low on bullets. "Fuck. Fuck. Fuck."

"Galen?" Cutter's voice floats down the hall toward us instead of another fusillade of bullets.

Fuck. Just what I need...

It's too bad none of my shots hit him, or if they did, they didn't do enough damage to drop him.

Nicki pushes past Luke and wedges herself between us, closer to the door. "We're here, Cutter."

"Motherfucking son of a fucking bitch."

Cutter's heavy curse matches his footsteps as he thunders down the hall toward the basement door. I take a step up and turn toward his approach, stepping right into the sights of his Glock and setting him directly in mine.

SIX

GALEN

WE STARE EACH OTHER DOWN, each of us knowing it would only take a single twitch of a finger to end the other. Even with only one working eye, the look Cutter gives me assures he won't miss or hold any regrets.

Nicki steps up behind me, followed closely by Luke. She pushes her way to my side, her gaze narrowing on our weapons while she holds hers at her side. Luke wisely doesn't get in the middle of the showdown between the two most important men in her life. He seems to understand that it would only result in him becoming a victim of the animosity boiling between us.

Cutter's focus shifts slightly to his sister. "Are you all right?"

She nods. "Yes."

I wave my free hand. "I'm just grand, too. Thanks for asking. I appreciate your concern."

Cutter snarls and steps toward me, but Luke muscles his way between us and points his weapon straight at him. He may have been willing to stand aside and let Nicki and us handle the situation, but he's not about to back down from a direct threat to me.

Still, I don't need him antagonizing Cutter any more than he already is.

I squeeze Luke's shoulder and nudge him out of the way. "Now, now, you two...let's play nice, shall we? It seems we have a common enemy right now. There's no need for us to fight, too."

The trademark snarl curls Cutter's scarred lips. "Don't, for one second, think that just because I'm not shooting you now doesn't mean I won't do it later."

I chuckle and nod. It's the same way I feel about Felipe. I may have let him walk out with Rowan that day, but it doesn't mean he's safe if he ever crosses me again. "Duly noted. Any idea who is out there slaughtering your men and mine?"

Cutter shakes his head. "No, and we need to get the fuck out of here. The place is overrun. I just checked out my security room, and they have us surrounded and most of the estate covered. It doesn't look like many, if any, of either of our men survived."

Nicki shifts uneasily, glancing toward the sound of the gunfire coming from the front of the house. "How did you get Valentina out?"

Cutter cuts his gaze to me for a second and mumbles something under his breath. "Fucking hell...There's a tunnel that leads out and comes up under the back wall in a wooded area. We always have a vehicle or two waiting there for emergencies."

A secret he never wanted to reveal to one of his competitors.

I approach Cutter and pause beside him. "Well, this certainly seems like a fucking emergency. How do we get to the tunnel?"

He glares at me with that dead white eye and one icy-blue one. "Follow me."

It's the last place I want to be—relying on Cutter Jackson to ensure my safety—but there aren't many good options. If what he says is true and the estate is overrun and surrounded, then we need his help. Help he no doubt is only offering because Nicki is with me. He would have been all too happy to leave me locked up in that basement, just waiting for whoever is leading this assault to find me and use me in whatever way best advances their plans.

Too fucking bad.

I'm not the kind of man to go down without a fight.

Not now.

Not ever.

I motion for Nicki to follow Cutter, then fall in behind them, with Luke bringing up the rear. Cutter will feel better having his sister at his back instead of me, and I can keep an eye on both of them from here.

The spurts of gunfire taper off as we approach the end of the hallway that opens up into the huge foyer at the front of the house.

Hell.

It isn't a good sign. Just like Cutter said, it means the resistance is failing, that most of Cutter and Valentina's men have succumbed to the attack—along with mine who came in for me—which means we're on our own.

Wherever Cutter is leading us, it's our only chance right now.

We came here, hoping Nicki could talk some sense into him and prevent his wrath, but instead, we've ended up at the center of an assault by an unknown entity—one apparently intent on taking out anyone who gets in their way.

My mind immediately goes to the shooters at the church. They fired indiscriminately, not caring who was hit. It's the same MO. Likely the same damn group.

But who the fuck are they?

We reach a corner, and Cutter motions toward the grand staircase. He takes one step out and automatic weapons fire tears through the wall just in front of us from somewhere above. Cutter jerks back and returns fire, crouching low, while I open fire high in the direction the bullets came from—likely the balcony of the second floor.

Several cries and grunts follow quickly, and two men on the stairs crumple and tumble down them. Cutter peaks around the corner and motions for us to move. We race toward the staircase and clamber over the two men sprawled on the steps, blood already flowing beneath them, marring the beautiful plush carpet runner.

Cutter and Luke reach down to snag their weapons on our way up, and our ragtag group hurries along a hallway toward the rear of the house. A set of double doors stands at the end, and Cutter pushes it open without even pausing. We funnel into a large office with oversized furniture and a brick fireplace along one wall.

I stop and scan the room. Photos of *Il Padrone* and other former heads of the family line the far wall. All except Arturo, though, I wouldn't expect Valentina to put her cousin up given what he did. "This isn't Valentina's office. I've met with her downstairs."

Cutter shakes his head and beelines for a bookshelf to the left. He puts his hand on a book on the second shelf and turns to look at me. "This is a private one."

I take a step closer and examine the bookshelf. "*Dante's Inferno?* Brilliant."

The irony isn't lost on me. It feels like I've been stuck in the nine circles of hell myself lately—perhaps punishment for my many sins.

He scowls and tilts the book toward him. A clicking noise fills the room, and the bookcase slides open, revealing a small elevator car.

"Let's move." Cutter ushers everyone in, scanning behind us toward the door. "We're taking it down under the house to the tunnel."

I step in, followed closely by Luke and a silent Nicki. She turns to put her back to me, and I lean in toward her as Cutter enters and presses the button to close the door behind us.

Her entire body shakes, the adrenaline and fear coursing through her, making her unsteady on her feet. I brush my hand along the back of her arm, and she almost collapses in my arms.

"Don't worry, *a chuisle*. I'll make sure nothing happens to you unless I'm the one doing it."

SEVEN

NICKI

THE ELEVATOR DOORS SLIDE OPEN, and heavy, musty, stale air that stinks of wet dirt greets us. It isn't anything anyone would want to breathe, but I still suck in greedy breaths, trying to stop my heart from racing and my hands from shaking.

I would have thought, after everything that's happened over the last few weeks, that nothing could faze me anymore.

Murders. Kidnappings. Gunshots. Threats and promises.

All of it has happened in what feels like a split second of my life, and my body doesn't seem to be on board with continuing to pretend everything's fine.

It hit me the moment we stepped into the small elevator. Crammed in between Cutter, Galen, and Luke—three criminals. Three killers. People who stand between life or death.

My feet don't want to budge, and my vision darkens around the edges. A hazy, fuzzy grayness threatens to overtake everything. I gasp in the dank air, struggling to take another breath, but a vise tightens around my chest so tightly it's painful.

Cutter's face appears in my line of vision. "Nick? Are you okay?"

A warm arm wraps around my waist, then lips brush against my ear. Galen's familiar scent envelops me, overtaking the one that permeates the tunnel. "I've got you, *a chuisle*."

Galen...

I sag into him, my body needing his support, his guidance in this moment of weakness, even though he's the last one I want to see me like this. I've somehow managed to be strong around him, to fight back and give him as good as he gives me. I've stood my ground with him and made demands that could have gotten other people killed, and somehow, I survived it. Being weak in front of him almost feels like I lost the battle we've been fighting.

He leads me down the narrow tunnel, the low ceiling buzzing with sporadically placed fluorescent lights on a string. The bizarre lighting and the jostling movement make my stomach churn, and I swallow back the bile threatening to come up.

Cutter moves ahead of us, ever vigilant, while Luke brings up the rear, carefully watching our backs in case anyone manages to come after us.

On and on.

It feels like we stumble down the tunnel forever, an endless path of narrow dirt walls and uneven earth under foot. I stumble several times, my feet unwilling to cooperate with what I'm telling them to do, but Galen's hard arm around me keeps me upright, just as mine did for him not so long ago.

This man is so strong, so resilient. You'd never know he was shot and almost bled to death less than a week ago.

Has it really only been a week?

With all that's going on, I've completely lost my ability to keep track of time.

It feels like forever ago that Galen's men snatched me from my apartment and dragged me kicking and screaming to his bloody side. Now, being at his side is the only thing keeping me upright.

How quickly things can change.

It's true in life and especially true when you're entangled with the mob.

Cutter glances back at us, narrowing his eyes at Galen's arm wrapped around me. "There's another SUV parked just outside the tunnel. We will take it to one of our safe houses where Valentina is with the baby."

"No." Galen's response echoes in the tunnel, loud and forceful.

Cutter's steps falter, and he pauses and turns back, everyone stopping behind him. "What do you mean *no?*"

Galen shakes his head. "We're not going with you."

A muscle in Cutter's jaw tics, and he takes a hard step toward us in the tight space. "Why the hell not? We need to go somewhere to regroup. Try to figure out what's going on."

"That's what I'm trying to do..." Galen glances down at me, then over his shoulder at Luke. "Which means I need to go see Felipe and my sister."

What?

I shake my head, his words finally shocking me out of the trance I seem to have been in since entering the tunnel. "Wait...what?" I turn toward him, his good arm still around my waist. "What do you mean? The last time we tried to go see them, we almost got killed."

Galen squeezes my waist. "Yes, and we almost got killed in Valentina and Cutter's home, a place that should have been safe. Whatever Rowan wanted to tell me, it was important, important enough to draw me out of my safe house and into the line of fire. And it was something that she didn't want Felipe to know about. Maybe she discovered he's behind all this..."

Cutter comes to stand directly in front of us now, narrowing his eyes on Galen. "What are you talking about?"

"My sister called me and said she needed to talk in person. I was on my way there when the Luna Cartel tried to take me out. Then when I got in touch with her again, she clearly couldn't talk in front of Felipe, which begs the question...why?"

"Hmm." Cutter scowls. "Something's definitely up."

"That's why I can't go with you. Until I have more information, I can't just sit around and wait for whoever's behind all this to present themselves. If they're the same people who hit the church and our warehouse, then someone's after more than just me, and the timing with a church meeting is beyond a little suspect. If there is any chance Rowan knows something, I need to find out what it is. Fast."

Cutter stalks away without responding toward a massive steel door at the end of the tunnel. When he gets there, he turns back toward us, his typical sneer on his lips. "Everyone be prepared just in case they found the vehicle."

Everyone nods and readies their weapons, and Cutter takes the short earthen steps up, then pushes open the door and steps out in the crisp, welcome fresh air. Galen urges me forward with a hand on my lower back. I slowly climb the short set of steps and out into the night. Cutter darts toward a black SUV that sits tucked near high bushes that almost completely conceal it. The tall wall of the rear of the estate looms a few hundred yards behind where we just popped up out of the ground.

Eerie silence lingers around us, nothing but the light wind rustling the leaves in the trees above us. Goosebumps break out over my skin, and I shudder.

Cutter stands beside the vehicle and motions for us. "Let's move."

We all scan the surrounding area, waiting and watching for anything amiss. Cutter unlocks the SUV and opens his door, eyes never stopping their survey. Luke climbs into the passenger seat, and Galen helps me into the back.

I barely have time to settle into the leather seat before Cutter turns over the engine and glances back at us.

"Where to?"

Galen pulls out his phone and shoots off a text message. "I'm finding out if they're still at the address I had earlier." His phone dings, and he shows it to Cutter. "Just drop us off there, then go wherever you need to go."

Cutter shakes his head. "No. I'm coming with you."

"What?"

"If you're right and Rowan somehow knows something about what's going on, then I need to know what she knows just as much as you do."

I lean forward and grab his arm, digging my fingers into his skin. "But what about Valentina and the baby?"

His jaw tenses, but something flashes in his gaze I haven't seen there before, something I thought he lost back in Iraq. "They're safe where they are. And the only way to ensure they stay that way is for me to go with you and figure out how to stop whatever the fuck is happening here."

Holy shit.

He loves her. He really, truly loves her. And that baby.

All the times I tried so damn hard to reach him, to convince him I loved him and his life was worth living even if he couldn't be a solider anymore, all the times I failed miserably at it. Warwick succeeded and gave him a reason to keep going. *She* succeeded. The brutal, ruthless woman succeeded where I failed. But I'm happy for him, despite my failures.

I turn back to Galen. "Let him come."

Galen looks ready for an arguement, but instead of starting one, he just leans forward and presses a kiss to my temple, one that makes Cutter's hand tighten on the wheel until his knuckles whiten. "Let's go."

EIGHT

GALEN

THE CLOSER WE get to arriving at the address Rowan sent me, the more tense Nicki becomes beside me. Her words from earlier echo through my head, beating around in my brain like a broken record designed to slice away at any hope I had that this might actually work even if we survive it.

I don't trust you...

And that's what it ultimately comes down to.

Trust.

In *this*.

In *me*.

That I'll do the right thing. That I'll do what she asks. That I'll do what I promised.

I told her she could walk away from this life and from me and that I'd let her do it, that I would help her do it, but the thought of her actually making that choice tightens my chest and makes it nearly impossible to take a breath.

She deserves to have a life free from the violence, free from all this she got involved in because of me. She doesn't deserve it, having to fear for her life. Having to *run* for it. Seeing her meltdown back in that tunnel only drove that truth home.

The woman is strong, resilient. She's stood up to me more times than I can count in the short time we've known each other. She stood toe to toe with me and didn't back down. Yet it finally caught up with—the danger and the death.

I shouldn't be selfish. I should be encouraging her to leave. To take my offer and run rather than sitting here next to her, praying to a God that I've lied to far too many times that she'll choose to stay.

Instead, I twine my fingers with hers on the seat between us and squeeze. She glances over at me, her eyes brighter and more focused than they were in the tunnel. Whatever hit her when we were down there seems to have passed, but whether that's because we're back above ground, away from whoever attacked the estate safely, or because she's only one step away from freeing herself from me completely, remains to be seen.

Cutter looks up at us in the rearview, his body stiff with the tension in the air. While he's remained silent during the drive, his discontent over the situation between Nicki and me has been palpable. What happened only cemented for him that she can't be with me, regardless of the fact that she would have been in the line of fire even if she had just been visiting him to meet his new baby.

None of that matters to him.

No amount of rationale will ease his worry.

And I can't really blame him.

Not when I feel the same way about Rowan.

Finally, we pull to a stop outside a tall condo complex in a bustling, trendy area of the city, the type of place young professionals live—not exactly somewhere you imagine the head of one of one the most successful and ruthless cartels in South America would hide out.

Cutter leans forward and stares up at it through the windshield. "You sure this is the right address?"

I glance at the numbers on the front of the building. "Yes. This is the address Rowan gave me."

Though, I can see why he's dubious. If there ever were going to be a trap, it would be set at a place like this—just like at the church—where we'd least expect it. In the middle of the city, surrounded by so many prying eyes.

The tall, glass front doors of the building open, and two of Felipe's men step out and nod in our direction. Definitely the right place, even if it doesn't look like it.

Perhaps that's the entire point.

If he's here and anyone tries anything, they'll leave a lot of witnesses. Witnesses create problems. That makes a very public place a very *bad* place to try to take anyone out.

Smart...

I holster the gun I've been gripping tightly in my hand the entire ride and offer Nicki's hand one final squeeze before I push open the door and step out. The blustery wind off Lake Michigan strikes me, sending a chill through my blood, and I reach back and offer my hand to Nicki to assist her out of the SUV.

She clutches it like it's her lifeline, like if she lets go, she'll drop immediately to the concrete under our feet. I squeeze back reassuringly as we follow Felipe's goons into a large, opulent foyer.

Luke casts a look my way, almost as if asking *are we really going to do this?*

It's insane.

We're voluntarily walking into Felipe's domain, but we don't have a choice. I need to find out what Rowan knows—good or bad.

Felipe's men stop at the elevator and hold out their hands expectantly. We weren't naïve enough to think we would be able to walk in here armed, but Cutter still growls low as he hands over his Glock. Luke gives Felipe's men a dirty look but also complies.

I take mine and Nicki's and hold them out. One of his men reaches to grab them, but I pull them away an inch. "Just because I'm giving you these doesn't mean I can't still kill you with my bare hands. If you or Felipe tries anything in there, you can count on it."

He jerks back slightly, then squares his big shoulders and snatches the guns from me. His friend presses the button to call the elevator, and the doors slide open with an ominous ding.

Nicki glances over at me, her bottom lip pulled between her teeth. The fear in her gaze matches the unease in my gut.

Something big is happening.

It has been for some time. The Luna Cartel coming in was only the start of the most recent wave. The church and the attacks since perhaps the culmination of something larger that's been going on behind the scenes longer than we know...

Nicki should be nervous.

Everyone should be.

I sure as hell am.

We cram into the elevator, with one of Felipe's goons in the front and one in the back, sandwiching the four of us between them, and the car shoots up to the fifteenth floor effortlessly.

The doors ding and slide open, and they usher us out into a short hallway leading to a single door labeled "penthouse."

I wouldn't expect any less from Felipe.

After years of living the life of a priest, he would only want the best now that he's free from the robes and the lie.

I turn to Luke and grab his arm when he tries to follow one of Felipe's men inside. "Wait out here."

"Sir?" He raises an eyebrow.

"Wait out here. I will bring you in if there's anything you need to know." I lean closer to ensure no one else can hear me. "Right now, I want you to have eyes and ears on everything that happens out here. I can take care of things in there."

"Yes, sir." Luke inclines his head in my direction and remains in the hall with one of Felipe's men while I follow Nicki and Cutter into the condo to meet the unknown.

NINE

GALEN

THE VAST OPEN space with polished concrete floors is about as welcoming as I'd expect from Felipe. Unlike Valentina, who likes things warm and comforting, Felipe is hard and cold.

He rises from a leather armchair, dressed in black trousers and a crisp white shirt rolled up at the sleeves, showing off an impressive display of tattoos he somehow managed to keep hidden when he was parading around as Rose instead of his brother. It certainly would have given away the fact that something was amiss if anyone had seen those since Andres, whom we'd always known as Rose, has tattoo-free skin.

Felipe offers a cool smile to Cutter and me. "Gentlemen..." He inclines his head toward Nicki, and his lips twist into a real smile. "Ma'am, so we meet again..."

She shudders next to me, and I wrap my arm around her protectively. The last time she saw Felipe, he came into *Bottom O' the Well* guns blazing and took out all my men—not exactly the best first impression, even if it is a valid and truthful one.

He assesses her with an amused grin, and I offer him a sneer, making it very clear he better keep his hands off. Cutter notices, too, and issues a low warning growl from her other side.

I smirk at Felipe's confused, furrowed brow. He has no idea who she is, except someone who worked at the bar.

"This is Nicki, Cutter's sister."

Felipe's smile falters, and his dark eyes widen slowly as they shift between Cutter and Nicki. "Well, well...wow." A new grin takes its place. "Isn't this an interesting twist to the story?"

Glaring at him, I shake my head. "We're not here to talk about my personal life or anyone else's."

"No, I imagine you aren't."

Cutter steps forward, his arms crossed over his chest. "Someone just hit our house."

Felipe nods and returns to his chair, casually motioning for us to take a seat on the couch and in the other spots around the room as if the last time we were all in a room together that we weren't all almost killed.

I usher Nicki over to a chair and let her sit, but neither Cutter nor I do. "Where's Rowan?"

Felipe's eyebrows rise. "And here I thought you were coming to see me."

This is a fine line to walk. Rowan obviously doesn't want him to know whatever it is she's going to tell me, but there isn't any time to waste in finding out what knowledge she might have.

I force what I hope is a believable smile. "I did, but I want to make sure my dear sister is all right first. I haven't seen her since the church."

His gaze hardens. "I assure you, she's fine. I got dinged up during the little incident at the church, but I'm happy to let you know I'll live."

Nicki clears her throat and shifts uneasily. "I do have some medical training if you want me to take a look at it."

He offers her a not unkind smile. "I'm fine but thank you." Then he shifts his glare to me and motions to the top of the metal staircase. "Rowan is upstairs in the bedroom." He pushes to his feet. "But don't do anything to upset her. She's been through enough."

I scowl at him and glance at Nicki and Cutter. "We all have…"

And he's now ensured Rowan will be tied to this life, to him, forever.

It twists my gut to walk away from Nicki and leave her sitting here with a man like Felipe, but Cutter will protect her with his life, just as I will. I slowly make my way up the stairs and pause at the top to stare down at the unlikely group below me before I knock once at the door and push it open.

Rowan paces along the side of the bed, but as soon as her eyes meet mine, she rushes toward me and throws her arms around me. "Galen!"

I push the door closed behind me and wrap her in my arms, relishing the feeling of having her here like this. There was a time not so long ago when I never thought this could happen. I never thought I'd have my baby sister in my arms safe—relatively speaking—and sound, and the last few days have only reminded me how easy it would be to lose her again.

How painfully easy it would be.

I pull back and take her face between my palms. "What's so important that we needed to speak alone?"

She glances toward the closed door behind me, hesitating slightly.

I force her eyes back to mine. "I don't know how much time we'll have before Felipe comes up to check on us."

Her lips twist in a grimace, and she pulls out of my hold and returns to pacing, running her hands back through her red hair. "I heard something…"

"What?" I step toward her, glancing toward the closed door again. "Felipe? Did he admit to something, to being behind the attack on the church or—"

She holds up a hand to silence me. "No." She shakes her head. "I-I don't want to say anything that's going to make things worse."

"I don't think things could get worse than they are right now. Whoever hit the church hit one of my warehouses and just hit Valentina and Cutter an hour ago."

Her soft green eyes widen, and she brings her hand to her mouth. "Oh, no. Are they okay? The baby?"

I nod. "They're all fine, but whoever this is seems pretty intent on wiping out everybody."

"Shit."

"Rowan…" I grasp her arm and turn her toward me. "Tell me what the hell is going on."

She releases a shaky breath and runs her hands back through her hair again. "At the church… between all the gunfire…"

"Yes?"

"I heard someone say something. One of the men in the black fatigues…"

"Okay…"

What is she getting at? Why can't she tell this to Felipe?

She locks her gaze with mine, her lips quivering. "I could have sworn it was Albanian."

Ice slowly spreads through my veins as the implications race through my head. "Albanian? Are you sure?"

Russian sounds an awful lot like Albanian to the untrained ear, and Valerian is the only one who has seemed to remain safe from this clusterfuck. It would make more sense than what she's suggesting.

Rowan nods, her wide eyes full of confidence. "I'm pretty sure. I heard Kat speaking it with Genti and her other men when I worked at Kat's Cradle. But this is why I didn't say anything to Felipe. If it was, and if it's somehow connected to Kat, if she's behind it, that could drive a wedge between Felipe and Andres when the peace I managed to attain between them is tenuous at best. We can't afford to have those two at war unless I'm one hundred percent positive."

"Shit…"

I can see why she didn't tell him and wanted to talk to me alone. The only reason Andres and Felipe didn't tear each other apart at the church was that she stepped in to broker a truce between them. She somehow managed to talk sense into the brothers once, but if it turns out that Andres/Rose was backing Kat in this coup attempt, it would shatter everything. It would put us all back to war again.

"What do I do, Galen? What do *we* do? I don't know if I should tell him or if—"

I hold up a hand. "No. Don't say anything to Felipe. I'm going to do a little digging and see what I can come up with to confirm this. If I can, then we'll go to Felipe. But if I can't..."

"Then what?"

"Then we'll have to figure that out when we get to that point."

Because I don't have a fucking clue.

Her entire body vibrates, and she wraps her slender arms around her thin frame. "I'm scared, Galen."

"I know." I pull her into my arms and hold her tightly. After everything she's been through in her life, she finally thought she was safe with Father Felipe, and then she had the rug pulled out from under her with the reality of who and what he is. Now all this. "But I promise, I won't let anything happen to you. Not again. I can't lose you again. I'll protect you from anyone and anything, even Felipe, if I have to."

She pulls back slightly. "He would never hurt me, Galen."

Just like I would never intentionally hurt Nicki, but the truth is, this life isn't the place for any of these women—except maybe Kat because she's just as merciless, if not more so, than the rest of us.

But Nicki and Rowan, they're innocents in this. They don't deserve to be dragged into the line of fire or worse. And it feels like *worse* is coming.

TEN

NICKI

FELIPE GLARES over his shoulder toward the closed door at the top of the stairs. They have been in there for a while, and he's getting restless, shifting slightly in his chair and checking his watch every few minutes.

I can't say I blame him.

Since Galen ascended those stairs, I haven't been able to stop my hands from shaking or my knee from bouncing. Whatever Rowan wanted to tell him was important, and the longer they're up there, the greater the chance of Felipe going up to see what's happening and finding out something he maybe shouldn't.

Cutter has done what he can to buy Galen some time, going into great detail about what happened during the attack on Valentina's house and our escape, but Felipe is only getting more and more annoyed the longer Cutter talks.

If Rowan and Galen don't come out soon, this isn't going to end well.

Almost as if on cue, Felipe pushes to his feet, fisting his hands at his sides. "I'm going to go check on them."

I lurch to my feet and hold up my hand. "I'll go." I force a smile and try to calm my breaths so he can't hear my heart thundering against my ribs, as it rings in my own ears. "She may need to have a little 'girl talk.'"

He eyes me for a moment, searching me for signs of deception or ulterior motives, but I don't offer him any. This man let me go once when he could have killed me with all of Galen's men, but he didn't. He trusted it was okay to set me free, that it wouldn't come back to bite him in the ass. And I need him to do it again.

Smiling, I hustle across the room before Felipe can object. "I'll be right back."

Cutter knows what I'm doing, and he isn't about to try to stop me. He's done everything he can to try to drag out our conversation while Galen is up there with her. Hopefully, he can continue to appease Felipe while I figure out what is holding them up.

I turn the knob and push open the door to find Galen and Rowan in an embrace, tears streaming down her face.

She jerks back from him, her eyes wide until they focus on me. "Oh, Nicki."

Galen raises an eyebrow at me. "Is everything okay?"

I close the door quickly behind me and shake my head. "Felipe is getting restless down there. He doesn't like that you two have been up here alone for so long. What's going on?"

They exchange a look, and Rowan takes a deep breath.

"I'll go down and stop him from worrying." She hustles past me, offering me a soft smile, and slips out the door, shutting it behind her.

I turn to Galen, and the tension rolling off him makes me tense. "What's going on? What did she have to tell you?"

He looks around the room and zeroes in on the open bathroom door off to the right. "Go in there where we have a little bit more privacy."

Privacy...

The word shouldn't send warmth rushing through me. It shouldn't make me rub my thighs together. But the last time Galen and I had *privacy*, he did things with his tongue that my brain still can't process.

He urges me toward the bathroom with a firm hand on my back and closes the door behind us. I lean back against the counter, and he stands in front of me, his shoulders tense.

Whatever she said has shaken him.

Badly.

"Rowan thought she heard one of the shooters at the church speaking Albanian."

Albanian?

"Kat?"

Though I've never met the woman, her reputation certainly precedes her. Galen certainly has no love for her, and if it was her behind the church attack and the subsequent ones, it would just be one more nail in the coffin he already has plans to put her in.

He shakes his head and runs a hand through his hair nervously. "I don't know. Some of her men were hit, too, at the back of the church. I can't fathom why she'd risk losing them and getting hit herself, but I can't just dismiss what Rowan says she heard."

My hands start to shake, and I turn to lay them flat against the counter and stare at myself in the mirror. This isn't a person I recognize. Not anymore. Everything that's happening is breaking me down, changing everything...

"How the hell did I end up here?"

The words tumble from my mouth before I can stop them. Regret immediately tightens my chest. Voicing my unease, my concerns, isn't anything I had ever planned to do with Galen. Especially not when I have to look at the man. He doesn't need to hear this right now, not with everything else he has to worry about.

He steps up to me and presses his chest against my back, then wraps his arms around me, flattening his hands over mine on the countertop. His warm breath flutters against my ear, and our eyes meet in the mirror. "I'm sorry, *a chuisle*, that you got pulled into all of this because of me. Truly, I am..."

Releasing a soft sigh, he drops his head and presses a kiss to the back of my neck. A shiver runs through me, one that makes me press back against him. Needing to feel even more of him. All of him. Needing his heat. His support. All of it.

Galen leaves his lips pressed to my skin and pushes himself against me harder, his cock swelling against my ass. "If you've made the decision that you want to leave, I'll help. I'll do it as soon as it's safe for us to get out of here."

It's the right thing to do. The *sane* thing to do. Yet, the thought of leaving Galen and never seeing him again, never feeling like *this* again, turns my stomach and makes tears sting my eyes. "I don't know."

I lift my head and let my eyes meet his in the mirror. A strange softness and sympathy reflect back in their green depths, the last thing anyone would expect to see from a man like Galen McGinnis.

But it doesn't surprise me.

Because I know it's there.

Under all the bravado, the hostility, and anger, lies a man who had his family destroyed, who spent the majority of his life searching for his sister and fighting to avenge what happened to her.

A man who does *feel*.

A man who *can* love.

"I want to stay. I want you, but—" I don't get to finish what I'm about to say because I can't bring myself to say the words.

He squeezes me tightly and places his hand flat against my stomach, raising goosebumps across my skin and sending a little shudder through me. "You cold, *a chuisle?*"

I shake my head, squeezing my eyes closed, but it does nothing to help clear my head. "Yes. I mean, no...shit. I don't know. I can't seem to stop shaking."

Warm lips brush against my ear. "Then let me warm you up, *a chuisle.*"

He slides his hand down my stomach and under the waistband of my pants, straight to where I need him the most. His fingers brush over my clit, and my body jerks at the friction. He nips at my ear while his skilled hand slips even lower to find my wet slit. He pushes one finger inside me, and a tiny gasp falls from my lips as I force my eyes open to meet his in the mirror again.

"Yes, keep your eyes open. I want you to see how beautiful you are when you come. I want you to see what I see. What I want to *keep* seeing." He strokes me softly, working me up gently, slowly, almost feather-light brushes that make my entire body crave more. So unlike the rough, desperate touches we've shared before, and heat spreads out from my core through my limbs. "I want you to stay, *a chuisle*, but I would understand if you can't."

I sag slightly against him, but he keeps me standing, keeps working me over with his deft fingers moving fluidly in my wet heat. His thumb glides across my clit, and I groan and clench around his digits, my lips fluttering closed with the sensation.

"That's it, *a chuisle.*" He nips at my ear again. "Come for me, but remember...eyes open."

I forced my eyes open again and watch my face contort as his ministrations finally have their desired effect. A slow-building orgasm starts deep in my belly. A rippling tide of pleasure. A growing thing that almost seems to be alive. Undulating and surging. A feeling that seems to contradict our situation but feels so right at the same time.

God, yes...

I gasp and struggle to keep my eyes open, to keep them locked with his—the emerald flashing under the fluorescent lights. They burn with something far deeper than lust. With something I've never seen when any man has looked at me before.

It's the kind of look that makes me want to stay when there are so many reasons not to, but I push them away to enjoy the soft, warm glow floating through my body.

My orgasm finally starts to ebb, and I sag back against him and watch him pull his fingers from me and slip them into his mouth. He slowly licks them clean, groaning softly, then presses his lips to mine.

The taste of my release coating his tongue wraps around mine, and he pulls away and takes my cheek in his palm. "I'll remember your taste forever. Even if you choose to leave. I need you to know that. That I'll think about you every day for the rest of my life no matter how things end, but I'll be content knowing you're safe and away from all this."

"Galen..."

He presses his lips to mine again to silence me, and I reach down and grasp his hard cock through his pants. A low groan rumbles in his chest, vibrating through my own and straight to my heart.

I need him now. More than I ever thought possible. More than I even want to admit or acknowledge.

This may be the last time we're together, and I'm not going to waste that worrying about what's happening outside this room.

Galen turns me fully to face him, grinding his cock into my hand as I fumble to free him from the confines of his pants. His hot flesh finally in my hand, he grips my hips and lifts me to set me on the edge of the counter. I release him long enough to shove down my leggings and kick them off, letting them fall unceremoniously to the tile floor. He steps between my legs and aligns himself, then drives into me in one hard thrust that rocks me backward and gives me everything I didn't know I needed.

He drags his hips back and plunges into me again, pulling my face to his to kiss me like it will be our last. And maybe it will be.

I wrap my arms around his neck and hook my feet together behind his back, urging him forward, driving him harder and deeper into me with each desperate motion.

Our frantic movements only grow more reckless, any tenderness that may have existed in the moment lost to the need for something more.

I clench around his cock with each retreat of his hips, my body not wanting to let it—*him*—go. He growls against my lips and bites down on my lower one. The sharp sting only makes me squeeze him tighter, dig my nails into the warm flesh of his neck, suck his tongue into my mouth, and groan.

He grips my hips and shifts me back on the cool granite countertop, altering the angle to let the head of his cock drag against just the right spot to steal my breath.

"Fuck, *a chuisle*..."

It's the only thing he's said. The only thing that *needs* to be said.

What we can't put into words, we're expressing through our bodies. Our connection. Our understanding that not only is nothing guaranteed, but we're more than likely parting ways soon.

The orgasm comes out of nowhere, washing over me like a tsunami, cascading from my core out through my limbs. I jerk against Galen's hold while he continues to plunge into me, seeking his own release and perhaps his own absolution.

He finds one on a strangled curse, but the other may not be possible for either of us.

ELEVEN

GALEN

THE MOMENT we step out of the room and onto the small landing that overlooks the living room, the change in the atmosphere is palpable. Felipe stands at one side of the room with four of his men, two on either side of him, weapons pointed at Cutter, who hasn't budged from where he stood when I came upstairs.

Rowan sits stock still on the couch, tears streaming down her face, frantically looking from Felipe to us and back again.

I squeeze Nicki's hand and slowly lead her down the stairs, meeting Luke's concerned gaze where he stands just inside the door, one of Felipe's men on either side. They must have insisted he come in—likely at gunpoint—while we were otherwise occupied upstairs.

If Felipe forced him in and felt the need to bring out weapons, then some really serious shit is going down.

Scanning the room, nothing else seems to have changed besides our host's attitude. "What's going on, everyone?"

Things weren't exactly *friendly* when we arrived, but this is something else. Something major has changed.

Felipe turns fully toward me and offers a fake smile he probably used with his parishioners while he was still pretending to be the good father. "After learning what Rowan overheard, I can't let you leave here with that information. I can't allow you to go after Kat and potentially catch my brother in the crossfire."

We reach the bottom of the stairs, and I scowl at him. "How did you know?"

Judging by the way Rowan is shaking, there's no way she told him. She knew what it could mean, and she held onto the information for days, staying silent until she could get me alone to tell me when she thought it would be safe. The last thing she would do was tell him the moment she walked out of that room.

Felipe chuckles and spreads his hands wide. "Do you really think I don't have every corner of this house monitored?" He raises an eyebrow and smirks at Nicki knowingly. "I'm glad you two got a little *alone time.*"

Shit. He had the damn bathroom wired.

Who the fuck does that?

Only a sick fuck like Felipe would bug a *bathroom.*

"Why does it matter?" I move away from the stairs a step, then stop, not willing to give his men any reason to shoot by approaching him too closely. "Why are you protecting your brother? He made his bed with Kat and should have to lie in it. Besides, how do you know he wasn't in on it from the beginning? That his little agreed truce that Rowan brokered at the church was only to buy time until their assassins arrived?"

It would explain why Rowan so easily convinced him to make amends with Felipe. The brothers have been at war with each other for a long time, and Andres pulled a gun on Felipe in the church. The speed with which he was willing to put it away when Rowan made her plea should have made everyone uneasy.

Hindsight is always twenty-twenty.

Our gracious host shakes his head. "I don't know that he wasn't involved. But one thing my little dove has taught me is that I should hear him out and look into the situation before I act rashly." He walks behind the couch where Rowan sits and stands behind her, squeezing her shoulder affectionately. "If we knew where Sofia was, I would have her dig into the situation to see what she could find to confirm what Rowan suspects, but we haven't been able to find her since Cutter raided my brother's home and took him."

Felipe casts a glare in Cutter's direction. It likely slices through other people like a razor blade, but Cutter doesn't even flinch, doesn't react at all, just stands with his arms crossed over his chest, looking seriously pissed at the insinuation Felipe is making.

After an uncomfortable moment, Cutter finally shakes his head, keeping his scarred gaze locked on Felipe. "I don't know where your sister is. She was gone by the time we got into her room. But I have my own sources. One of the best hackers in the world. He's worked with Sofia in the past and is just as concerned about her disappearance. I've had him looking for her ever since she vanished from your brother's compound. If anyone can find anything—on Sofia or about the potential connection between these attacks and Kat—it'll be him."

"Splendid." Felipe grins and motions toward the couch and chairs. "Then you should call him, and until we get some clarity on this issue, you're going to be my guests."

Fuck. Definitely not the invitation I was looking for. Or one I want to accept.

I wrap my arm around Nicki and force a cordial smile. "As charming as your offer is, Nicki and I will have to decline. I'll certainly call if any of my sources find anything."

We turn toward the door, and one of the men there with Luke steps forward, blocking our path. He holds his gun across his chest, making it visible in a way that can't be ignored.

It was a long shot. One that never would have succeeded, but I had to try before we get locked down in here with this unlikely group of "friends."

Felipe chuckles and shakes his head. "I think it best we all stay together until this is resolved. And I do so enjoy being your host."

I fucking bet you do.

We're all at his mercy now. Without weapons. Without any means of escape. All we can do is sit and wait, hoping Cutter's friend can somehow gather the information we need—one way or another.

If it turns out Kat is behind everything that's been happening...it'll be like the end of the IRA ceasefire—we'll all be fucked. No one will believe Rose—Andres—wasn't involved. Those two have been inseparable, working in unison. Two peas in the proverbial pod. She wouldn't keep him in the dark about anything that big. Which poses a very real problem for Felipe. And us...because we're here.

Felipe squeezes Rowan's shoulders again, then turns to Cutter. "Call your man. Until we clear up this issue, no one's going anywhere. It's about to get very cozy in here." He flashes a dark grin. "I guess it's time we settle in."

Cutter scowls at Felipe, then reaches into his pocket and pulls out his phone. He presses something on the screen and brings it to his ear, his gaze darting around the room while he waits. "Preacher. I need you to do some digging..."

He better dig fast. If he doesn't find something quickly, this "friendly get-together" is going to go downhill very fast.

Felipe motions to his men to put away their weapons, and they comply. But I see it for what it really is—a reminder that they *have* them and we don't.

We're completely at the mercy of a man who convinced the entire world he was a pious priest while he was secretly running one of the biggest and most dangerous cartels in the world.

And we can't trust a single word he says.

The chances of getting out of here alive have just plummeted, but that seems to be par for the course recently.

TWELVE

NICKI

I've been to some awkward parties before, but this takes it to a whole new level. Felipe and his men watch us like hawks while I sit with Galen and Rowan on the couch, trying not to lose my damn mind. I fear Rowan is already close to that. The poor woman hasn't said a word since Galen and I came down and Felipe insisted we all stay. I thought I was having a nightmare of a day, but hers might actually be worse, knowing Felipe is going to confront her about keeping this information from him once they're alone.

This entire day has been a living nightmare—save for the few moments of bliss Galen and I managed to find. Ones that were apparently witnessed by Felipe. I should have known that fucker was monitoring everything. The man who so casually walked into *Bottom O' the Well* and shot Galen's men in front of me wouldn't think twice about invading someone's privacy by recording what goes on in that space.

My skin crawls, thinking about what he saw. That intimate moment Galen and I needed—to release the tension, to express what we couldn't say in words, to say a potential goodbye...

I shiver and shift uneasily on the otherwise comfortable couch. Galen squeezes my shoulder from where he stands behind me, phone to his ear. Unfamiliar words float through the air. He's smart enough to know that if he speaks to his men in Irish, no one in the room is going to be able to understand him—including me.

But the reassuring touch settles me somewhat. Neither he nor Cutter will let Felipe do anything to hurt me. They may have been disarmed when we came in, but that doesn't mean they aren't still lethal.

Cutter is simply biding his time, taking in everything around him, creating a plan. Even with his aviators back in place, it's impossible to miss the way he scans the room and always knows where everyone is and what they're doing, even though he likely put them back in place to conceal just that along with his violent scars.

The phone in his hand rings, and he glances down at the screen and answers. "Preacher. Tell me you have something..."

Though it's only been three hours since Felipe gave us this "invitation" we couldn't refuse, Cutter seems pretty convinced Preacher has already found what we need. I know Preacher is good, but I never knew he was *that* good.

Please let him find something that helps us.

Please. Please. Please.

Galen ends his call with whoever he was speaking with—one of his very few men besides Luke left alive—and everyone in the tense room turns their attention to the man who might hold the key to getting us out of this elegant prison.

Cutter rubs his jaw while listening intently, his expression somewhat neutral despite the weight of the topic and the fact that what Preacher is saying could turn the tide. "Uh-huh. Uh-huh."

Rowan nudges me with her elbow. "Any idea what they're saying?"

Even though I'm closest to Cutter, I can't hear anything Preacher is telling him, and Cutter's grunts don't offer much of a clue, either.

"Cutter?" Felipe's heavy voice fills the room, and he raises a dark eyebrow in anxious anticipation. He's a man who doesn't like to be kept waiting, and that's all we've been doing—waiting to determine his brother's fate...and our own. "What did he find?"

Cutter holds up a hand to him. "Uh-huh. Uh-huh. Okay, I'm gonna put you on speakerphone, and you can repeat all that." He holds out the phone and hits a button. "Everyone, this is Preacher. Preacher, you're on with...well, everyone. Tell them what you just told me."

"Hey, everyone." The clicking of keys fills the line. "So, I'm still digging, but with the information that there might be an Albania connection to the attack on the church, I was able to combine the information I had already gathered and take a new approach. I searched all flight records for the two weeks prior to the attack out of Albania to Chicago. There was nothing. Whoever these guys are, they're too smart for that. But I kept digging, searching the names of all of Kat's men, contacts, anyone else I could think of connected to organized crime in Albania at all...and I found something."

We hold our collective breaths, and Rowan reaches out and squeezes my hand so hard it actually hurts.

"Twenty men flew from Albania into Toronto, rented cars, and drove down to Chicago."

Galen leans over the back of the couch, his lips twisting into a scowl. "Shit. Kat's men?"

"Not necessarily. All I know is they boarded in Vlorë originally. That could certainly be Kat, but there are other families there as well. Sometimes it's hard to tell where people are allied or who they're working for. I need more time to confirm those connections."

Cutter casts a furtive glance toward Galen and me. "Any way to track where they went once they arrived here?"

Fingers flying over a keyboard fills the line again. "I can go back and pull the old data to confirm where they've been, but I'd be more worried about where they are now. The rental cars have GPS. I was able to hack into them, and they're not too far from where Cutter's phone is pinging now."

Cutter's back goes ramrod straight. "Fuck."

Everyone looks to Felipe, who holds up his hands, seemingly unconcerned with this development. "We're safe here. No one knows about this place."

Galen snorts and spreads out his arms. "Except all of us. What about your brother and Kat?"

Felipe's jaw tenses, his hands fisting at his sides. A long silence lingers before he finally answers. "I called them as soon as I knew what Rowan overheard. They're on their way here."

"What?" Galen rounds the couch and advances toward Felipe. "Are you a fucking lunatic?"

Two of Felipe's men step between them before Galen can reach him.

Galen jerks to a stop, the anger radiating off him matching that of Cutter. "Why would you invite them here and tell them where we are when they're the prime fucking suspects in all this?"

It's the same question I have—one I'm sure we all share. Felipe is putting far too much trust in a man who might be responsible for all of the horrible things that have happened lately. Felipe isn't stupid. He had to know that inviting them here posed a threat and put us at risk. Yet, he did it anyway. He had to have a good reason.

Felipe's nostrils flare, his shoulders tensing. He doesn't like to have his actions questioned, and Galen is poking the damn bear by calling him out. "Because he's my brother, and I'm going to look him in the eye when I confront him about this. Because I can tell when he's lying. I know him almost better than I know myself."

Galen shakes his head and sneers. "Yeah, sure fucking seems like it. He and his woman have betrayed you, betrayed all of us. And you're going to let them do it again."

One of Felipe's men grabs a phone from his pocket, glances at the screen, then leans in and whispers something to his employer.

Felipe holds out his hands and offers a shrug. "Kat and my brother have just arrived outside. I guess we'll soon see."

THIRTEEN

GALEN

"ARE YOU INSANE?" I glance from Felipe toward the door we're about to let Kat and Rose—and likely an entire hit squad—in through. "You're bringing them right to us. They're following Kat and Rose. Why would you give them the benefit of the doubt? You heard what Rowan said, Felipe."

"I did, and one thing I have learned is that things are often not what they appear."

I snort and offer a sardonic grin. "Ironic coming from you."

The man who led his life as someone else, as something else, in full sight, hiding such a massive undertaking and secret. Ordering deaths. Bringing in more drugs than most people can even fathom.

He's far too trusting of his brother...and it's what will get us all killed.

Rowan watches our interaction, pain etched on her otherwise beautiful face. I hate having to do this, arguing with the man she loves and pointing out his very real flaws, the danger he's putting her in.

But it's too late to do anything about it now. One of Felipe's men opens the door, and I move to stand next to where Nicki sits as Kat and Andres, the man we all knew as Rose, enter the condo.

I need to be close to her for when this goes to shit.

And it will.

It's only a matter of *when*.

Kat looks as cool as ever despite the fact that she was apparently injured in the church shooting. She strides in on red sky-high heels, a black dress perfectly hugging her shapely frame. Long sleeves cover any damage a bullet may have done, but I watch her carefully, searching for points of weakness should I need that information.

Rose follows closely behind, scanning the room with a gaze hard enough to cut diamonds. This is the man we've spent years dealing with, the one we *thought* was running the Blood Rose Cartel the entire time, completely unaware that Felipe had been pulling the strings.

There hasn't been much time to process that information, to try to make sense of what all it might mean. If the world would stop trying to kill me for more than five minutes, I might actually have a chance to do that and create a plan for how to handle the brothers.

Felipe offers a broad smile and sweeps out his arms. "*Hermano*, Kat, thank you so much for joining us, but I fear we might have to cut our discussion a wee bit short."

Rose raises an eyebrow at his carbon copy, still searching the room for any potential threats the same way we all keep doing. "*Cómo?*"

Cutter growls low, phone still at his ear. "Because the fuckers who shot up the church, Galen's warehouse, and Valentina's place *today* are right behind *you* on their way *here*."

"What?" Kat's cool blue eyes widen, and she turns to Cutter with eyebrows high to her dark hairline. "What do you mean?"

Nice fucking acting.

Cutter takes another step toward her. "What I mean is, Rowan heard the shooters at the church talking in Albanian, and now, you've just led the hit squad right to all of us."

"No." She shakes her head and takes a little half-step back. "It wasn't me."

I snort and grab Nicki's hand to pull her from the couch. "You've betrayed everyone in this room, and we're supposed to believe you weren't behind it? That it's just a coincidence that it's an Albanian hit squad?"

She presses her bright-red lips together in a thin line and glances at everyone around the room. "I know how bad it looks, but it wasn't me. Why would I shoot up a meeting I would be at?"

Cutter snarls, rage twisting his scarred face even more. "To cover your own ass."

"No." She shakes her head again. "It has to be someone else."

Rose, who has remained silent and let his woman defend herself, finally enters the fray. "It wasn't her. Wasn't *us*."

Kat paces slightly, as if she's struggling to wrap her head around this new information. But her apparent confusion doesn't convince me of her innocence.

She's a great actress. She sat in my office and lied to my face, telling me she would remain out of my business and had no intention of expanding hers. She did the same to Valerian.

Kat Gashi is a liar—plain and simple.

She pauses her pacing and looks at Rose. "The Dragushas and Berishas. They tried to take me out when I landed in Albania to get my son. They weren't happy that I've been taking women from back home and Eastern Europe and bringing them here. They weren't content with how I cut them in on the deal. Maybe they developed the balls to try to come hit me here when they failed there."

Cutter steps forward, still on the phone with Preacher. "We don't have time to debate this. They'll be pulling up outside any minute. We need to get the fuck out of here."

Now.

It doesn't matter if it is Kat or if it's her enemies back home; either way, they're coming in here and not for a friendly chat. Staying would be suicide.

I turn to Felipe. "Is there another way out?"

Felipe nods, shifting in front of the couch to grab Rowan's hand and tug her to her feet. "Do you really think I would stay at a safe house that doesn't have more than one way out?"

Cutter ends the call and slides his phone into his pocket. "They're here. Give us our weapons back."

We might have to fight our way out of here, and right now, Felipe holds all the firepower.

He considers everyone in the room for a brief moment, then motions to his men. One disappears into another room off to the side of the living room and returns with a box. He opens it and hands me my gun. I check the ammo and ensure there's one in the chamber before holstering it. Nicki accepts the gun she used at Valentina's home and stuffs it into the waistband of her pants. He hands Cutter his Glock and Luke his, who each do the same.

But before we can make any progress on actually getting the fuck out of here, Rose pulls his gun and points it at us. "You think everyone is just going to walk out of here when you think Kat is guilty and you're ready to take her out? When you think *we* might be behind this?"

Felipe releases Rowan's hand and slowly approaches his brother. "*Hermano,* there is no way this can get resolved now. If you want to get out of here alive, we either go our separate ways to figure the fuck out where we stand, or we stay here and fight together."

I glance at the front door, waiting for any signs that our mutual enemies may be on their way up. "If those are the only two options, frankly, I've been shot at enough recently and would prefer option A."

Cutter nods. "I need to get back to Valentina and the baby. As much as I'd love to take these fuckers out and end this once and for all, this isn't the place or time."

Felipe shrugs slightly. "It seems you are outnumbered here, *hermano*." He takes his gun from one of his men and motions toward the rear of the condo, wrapping his free arm around Rowan's waist to lead her. "If you feel the need, shoot us. Go ahead and do it in our backs. I'm leaving, and anyone who wants to come with me can use my additional vehicles."

I grab Nicki with my free hand and drag her after Felipe. "We're getting the hell out of here."

Cutter shifts into our path and steps up to me until his chest almost brushes mine. "Like hell you are. You're not taking my sister. She's coming with me."

Nicki glances between us, her mouth slightly agape. Cutter reaches out for her, and I drag her closer to me, putting my entire body between them. I don't want to have to pull my gun on him—again—but I will if I have to.

"She's not going with you, Cutter."

He whips off his glasses, looking at his sister with his mismatched eyes. "Do you really want to go with him, Nicki? Is this the kind of life you want? To constantly be running and dodging bullets? Because that's what you'll have if you stay with him."

She shivers beside me, the same reaction she had earlier when she considered having to make this choice. Uncertainty taints her gaze, and she hesitates to offer an answer.

I shake my head. "We don't have time for this argument. She's coming with me. She knows how to get a hold of you if she needs to. And if she asks, then I promise I'll bring her to you."

It's all I can offer at this point. We can't argue about what's best for Nicki when staying here is the furthest thing from it.

Cutter snarls, about to argue again, when Felipe pushes open a door at the rear of the kitchen that opens to the living room. "This way."

I shove past Cutter, dragging Nicki behind me. He follows us—no doubt on the verge of physically preventing her from leaving with me. Rose and Kat exchange a look, then he lowers his gun, and they hustle across the kitchen to cram into the small elevator designed to look like a pantry door.

Felipe moves to the side with the control panel, with Rowan clutched to his side, her face pale and gaunt. He presses the down button as we all stand, crushed together, weapons within mere inches of each other.

I lean down and brush my lips against Nicki's ear. "Well, this is cozy."

She barks out a laugh that makes everyone jump and glare at her—the sound loud and foreign in the situation we find ourselves in. I drag her back against me, wrapping my arm around her waist to give her the physical and emotional support I know she must need.

Asking her to choose between leaving with me and leaving with Cutter isn't fair. None of this is. But I'm a selfish bastard and want her to choose me. To believe that *this* is worth the risk.

The elevator comes to a jolting stop, and the doors slide open to reveal an underground parking garage. We file out quickly, some of Felipe's men already waiting in a running SUV.

Felipe motions to three dark sedans. "Cutter, Galen, Andres, you take those. Keys are inside." He steps up to the SUV, opens the rear door, helps Rowan inside, then pauses to look back at us as we dart toward the sedans. "I have no doubt everyone will do their own investigation into the situation. I'm sure we'll be in touch."

He slips inside and closes the door with a finality that makes Nicki wince. We dart to a black Mercedes, and I slide into the driver's seat. She opens the passenger door but pauses, her gaze locked on Cutter climbing into the car next to ours.

Cutter holds open his door. "Last chance. You sure, Nick? You can still come with me."

I hold my breath, waiting for her response. It would be so easy for her to close that door and get in with him. He would protect her. Ensure none of this ever touches her again. He could make sure she finds true happiness somewhere far away from the gunfire and threats and blood.

She hesitates for only a moment before she shakes her head and slides into the passenger seat beside me, but that millisecond feels like a fucking eternity. I release my breath, grab the keys from the glovebox, and start up the car with a satisfying roar off the concrete surrounding us.

Nicki grabs her seatbelt and secures it before she looks over at me. "We haven't had the best of luck in car chases."

"Hopefully, there won't be one."

One of her eyebrows rises slowly. "Where are we going?"

I throw the car into gear. "Anywhere but here."

FOURTEEN

NICKI

GALEN TEARS out of the rear entrance to the subterranean parking garage, following the line of cars containing Felipe and Rowan, Cutter, Rose and Kat, and the rest of Felipe's men just as gunshots ring out from the front of the garage. The hit squad—whether sent by Kat or someone else—missed us by only seconds, thanks to Preacher's warning.

Thank God...

I release the breath I was holding, pull the gun from my waistband, set it on my lap, and sag back into the plush leather seat as the city whizzes by us.

Galen reaches over and twines his fingers with mine on my thigh. "I meant what I said to Cutter. If you want out of this with me, you can go at any time. I'm quite confident your brother can secure your safety, and I'll bring you to him. He'll make sure none of this is anything you ever have to deal with again."

I glance down at the gun in my lap, the one I took from Cutter and pointed at Galen only hours ago, ready to use it to protect my brother if I had to. "I just don't understand what's happening." I pull my hand out from under his, his touch making it hard to think, impossible to process all the feelings consuming me. "So much has happened. So much I don't understand. Why are these men suddenly here and after everyone?"

He shakes his head, taking a turn that brings us onto the highway heading north. "I don't know. And I can't guarantee you it won't happen again." He releases an exasperated sound and returns his hand to the steering wheel. "I just can't, *a chuisle*."

"What does that mean?"

"What does what mean?"

"*A chuisle?*" I just slaughtered that pronunciation, but I've been wondering since the first time he called me it what feels like ages ago.

A grin twitches the corner of his lips. "The literal translation is 'my pulse.' It basically means, 'what I live for.'"

Damn. That's pretty fucking romantic.

And I have absolutely no response to something like that. Instead, I watch the city out the window. "Where are we going?"

Galen stares at the road. "Out of the city. I need to put you somewhere where you'll be safe while I take care of something."

I swallow through the sudden lump in my throat. *Take care of something...* "You're going to leave me?"

He glances over at me, the scar on his face twisting as he offers an apology in his gaze. "Only for a short time. But it's necessary."

"Where are you going?"

His hands tighten on the steering wheel as he takes time to consider his answer. "I need time to figure out what's going on with the Albanians, to get that situation sorted out so we'll be safe. But there's one thing that I can deal with *now*. One threat I can eliminate so we're not looking over both shoulders in two different directions."

It doesn't take a massive leap to see where he is going with this. "The Luna Cartel?"

"Yes. Going back and forth with them almost got you killed. I'm not going to leave any stone unturned until they're all gone. Every last one of them—along with any potential threat to you."

That promise is all well and good, but the reality of the situation is something else entirely. That's a truth that's become abundantly clear in the time we've spent together.

"But how can you possibly do that, Galen? How can you know you got them all, that you completely eliminated the threat?"

He releases a heavy sigh. "Luke told me he has a lead on their headquarters. If he's right, I can cut the head off the snake and hope the rest of them scatter."

"Do you know who the head is?"

"We aren't entirely sure. They call him Luna, and he rose to power quite quickly and immediately moved in from Mexico to Chicago. It seemed to be his primary target right from the beginning of building his organization, so one would think he'd be here personally."

"You weren't at your warehouse when *your* guys were hit."

He offers me a little half-smirk. "True, but he's lost a lot of men to me recently—and to the police. Their numbers are dwindling. He'd be spread too thin at multiple locations and have likely consolidated to one defensible location. So, we think we can take them out there."

"But...you barely have any men left." Those he did have were lost at Valentina and Cutter's place.

"I know. Very few. Which is exactly why I'm going to call Valerian and ask him to help."

The Russian...

"You trust him?"

His shoulders rise and fall slowly like he's considering the answer and isn't wholly committed to it. "I don't have a choice. I can't go to any of the other families. It's my problem, and they have enough of their own and no reason to help me."

I stare out the window at the dark sky, considering everything that's happened over the last few weeks. "Can't we just..." I don't look at him when I say the words because I can't stand to see his reaction. "...I don't know...walk away from it all?"

His silence is all the answer I need, but still, my heart pulls at me and makes me turn to look at him.

"You told me you made a promise to God that once you had found your sister, you would leave all this behind, that you would have to let it go. That you'd become the good man I see glimpses of. Why can't you just do that now? Just let everything go and walk away."

It would make things so much simpler.

It would solve all our problems.

He reaches out and slides his hand over mine again, squeezing it gently. "I was just a kid when I made that promise. A young, naïve child who didn't understand the way the world works. This isn't a life you walk away from. You can't; it would follow us anywhere we went. We would never be safe. At least here, doing this, I know my enemies. Well...until recently. I know what battles I have to fight, and anywhere else, it would be starting over and never knowing if a friendly neighbor next door was really a hitman sent for payback against me for something I did in my past."

He's right.

Deep down, I know it, no matter how much I might want to deny it.

This isn't a life you can walk away from.

"Do you want to leave, Nicki? I asked you before, and we were interrupted before you could give me your answer. But now, I need to know before I drop you off. Before I meet up with Valerian, I need to know what I'm coming back to. Will you be there? Or should I have Cutter come pick you up?"

Acid burns up my throat, and I swallow it back along with a sob. This is the hardest decision

I've ever made in my life. Harder than giving up on Cutter all those years ago. Harder than quitting school. Harder than leaving home to come here.

I just hope it's one I can live with.

"If I leave, and Cutter does what you promise—sets me up with a new identity, a new home, a new life—there's no guarantee your enemies won't find me, is there?"

His jaw tightens, and he shakes his head. "No, there isn't. We would do everything we could, but there's never any guarantee."

"So, I'd be alone and miserable. Living a life that isn't mine. Without you, and it could all be for nothing."

He swallows thickly and glances at me. "It would be the only way to potentially keep you safe. The only shot we have."

"Or, I can stay here and have the same threats, but also...have you. Have *this*."

He squeezes my hand again. "*A chuisle*, I want that more than I want anything else in this world. Because I'm a greedy bastard, and I want it all. But I can't force you to do it. I can't ask you to, either. I won't."

"You don't have to. I've made my decision. I'll be there when you get back, when you get done taking care of whatever you need to do. I'll be waiting. I'm not going anywhere. Ever."

FIFTEEN

GALEN

A DARK SUV pulls up next to me, and Valerian slips from the back seat of it and opens the door to climb into the front seat of mine.

He closes the door and tosses me a look that holds a million questions in it. "Are you sure you want to do this, *comrade?*"

I stare at the building in front of us, the one that holds what's left of the Luna Cartel.

At least, I hope it does.

"If my intel is correct, I don't have a choice."

Now that I know everything I do about the shooting at the church, Kat's potential involvement, the hit squad that almost got us at Felipe's, and the promise I made to Nicki, I can't have one enemy breathing down my neck when we're still trying to confirm who the other one is.

Valerian relaxes back in the seat as if we're not about to go in and light the place up. "If you don't get all of them, they'll only come back for you again and again."

I turn toward the only ally I have and slam my palm against the steering wheel, gritting my teeth against the sharp stab of pain that runs through my arm—the pain I've been pushing away and trying not to think about through all of these last few days. "You think I don't know that?"

Only an idiot would believe anything is ever *truly* over with an enemy like the cartel. They have roots in Mexico, people there who will come seeking revenge. I can keep taking them out when they show, but there may never be an end to it. The only chance of that happening is by cutting the head off the snake like I explained to Nicki.

I grab my gun, eject the magazine to ensure it's full, then pop it back in and rack one into the chamber. "How many men did you bring?"

Valerian glances out the window at several vehicles that have pulled up next to us. "About twenty."

"I only have four reliable men left. The rest either got taken out by the cartel or are too green to be depended on."

The Russian grunts. "I don't envy your position."

"No, I imagine you don't. You've managed to remain relatively unscathed through all of this."

It's more an accusation than an observation, but I know how Valerian will take it.

He barks out a laugh and shakes his head. "Have you forgotten that Kat fucked me just as badly as she fucked you? I had to shut down two of my clubs because I can no longer bring in the girls I need. They all want to come work for *her*. And the shipment of weapons she stole from me means my men are stuck using antiquated equipment rather than the good stuff I paid for."

"Well, you seem to be doing just fine with whatever it is you have for the time being. But whether it's Kat who's after us, or her enemies in Albania, or the cartel, luck will only hold for so long. No one's does forever. That's why we're going in."

The speech is as much for me as it is for him. A reminder of why taking this risk is worth it. Securing a future with Nicki is worth it.

He inclines his head in agreement to proceed, and we both step from the vehicle and out into the fall Chicago air. His men climb from the vehicles dressed in dark fatigues and masks, ready for whatever might come our way and whoever we might find inside.

I stand in front of the group, addressing the men quietly. "I don't have any idea how many men are left or what we might be looking at, but we can't leave any survivors."

They all nod their understanding, and we make our way toward the entrance, where security guards sit at a desk just inside the door. They look through the glass at the movement outside, but it's too late. The rounds shatter the glass and go right into them before they can react and alert anyone in warning.

But our shots have just given away that we're here regardless of whether they sent up an alert or not. We enter and fan out, heading down the various hallways, and almost immediately, resistance gunfire echoes in my ears.

A man steps from a room to my left, and I pop two bullets into his chest before he can even pull his gun. Angry yells in Spanish fill the night, mixing with the various sounds of gunfire and cries of pain.

Valerian and I move with precision. Even though we've never worked together like this before, we both know what has to be done.

We shoot our way through any obstacle that appears and dodge the shots that come our way the best we can. A bullet grazes Valerian's shoulder, and he barks out a curse but continues pushing forward until we reach a massive warehouse filled with crates likely holding the weapons and drugs they've been bringing in.

The clank of the rear door to the warehouse rising draws me toward it. Valerian follows close behind.

An engine roars to life from the same direction.

"Fuck, someone's getting away."

We break into a sprint and turn around a row of boxes just in time to see a dark blue BMW tear out through the still-opening door with barely an inch to spare above the roof.

"Fuck!"

We both unload our magazines at the vehicle, trying to stop it, but it's no use. Return fire comes from up above and behind us, and I dive to the left behind a crate and reload a new magazine as Valerian dives to the right and does the same.

There isn't any time to worry about who might have just escaped, not when we're pinned down here. We look at each other across the opening between us, and I motion to go on the count of three.

One...

Two...

Three...

We both turn and begin firing up in the direction of the bullets. Two men on a catwalk return fire, but Valerian and I are good shots. They both tumble off it—their bodies and weapons clattering to the concrete below.

An office stands at the end of the catwalk, lit and potentially holding the man we're looking for. If this were my base of operations, that's where I would work from—where I could keep an eye on everything happening in the warehouse.

I motion toward it. "Let's go clear it."

Valerian nods his understanding, and we race up the steps and into the office. I scan it for anything useful, but it's nearly empty except for a wooden box sitting in the center of the desk.

Whoever left did so in a hurry, potentially leaving behind something invaluable. I take a step toward it and lift the lid slowly.

A strange beeping fills the room.

Sweet fucking Christ...

Valerian steps up next to me and stares down at it. "Is that what I think it is?"

I nod as I stare at the bomb and the numbers ticking down on the digital display.

10...

9...

8...

GLUTTONY

In love, as in gluttony, pleasure is a matter of the utmost importance.

- Italo Calvino

ONE

VALERIAN

7...

Galen's gaze darts up from the timer on the bomb to me. "What the fuck do we do?"

5...

"How the fuck should I know?" I examine the device in the box on the desk. Given its size, there's no way we have time to run to get far enough away to survive the blast. "Aren't you Irish supposed to be good with explosives?"

3...

"I don't fucking know. Maybe we can—"

1...

I jerk on the black wire as hard as I can, yanking it free from where it connects to the clock counting down to our demise, and wait for the pain to hit before I'm obliterated and go to meet my maker.

Only the world doesn't explode around Galen and me.

The clock stays on *1,* and absolutely nothing happens.

"Bloody hell, Valerian." Galen's relieved gaze zeroes in on the wire in my hand. "How the fuck did you know what wire to pull?"

I smile at him and shrug, trying not to show how truly shaken I am to have come so close to death. "I guessed."

"You bloody *guessed?*" His eyes widen, the scar over the left one twisting ominously, and he sneers. "Are you bloody *insane*? What if that had set off the bomb?"

"It was going to go off, anyway." I release the tiny black wire that somehow saved our lives and return to scanning the office for anything that might assist us in locating the head of the Luna Cartel, who seems so intent on destroying the one ally I have in this war for Chicago. "I figured red is dead, so black is safe."

"Un-fucking-believable." Galen shakes his head and releases a sardonic laugh. "We survived because red rhymes with dead. *Is abhlóir thu!*"

I scowl at him, my annoyance tightening my fists at my sides. "You're welcome, by the way. For saving your fucking ass. *Neblagodarnyy mudak!*"

Galen continues muttering to himself in Irish as he helps me search the office, but it's empty save for the now-defunct bomb. Whoever was here and who fled in that BMW took any answers with them—and left a dark cloud hanging over my Irish friend. One that he seems intent on wrapping me up in.

Shaking my head, I turn back to him. "There is nothing of import left. Let's get out of here."

He glances at the bomb on the desk. "Do you think this was a setup?"

Given how cleanly the head of the Luna Cartel got away, I can understand why Galen might suspect this was all some elaborate trap set to draw him here and destroy him once and for all with the bomb. But scanning the office again, I shake my head. "No, if they knew we were coming, even if they suspected it was just you, they would have been better prepared. They wouldn't have risked losing so many of their men. We wouldn't have been able to take them out so easily."

He considers me for a moment, his green eyes darkening. "Unless they *wanted* me to get in here to let the bomb take care of it and were willing to sacrifice the lives of the men out there to ensure I went down and stayed down."

"*Blyad!*"

I don't know enough about this Luna Cartel to ascertain if it's possible the man in charge is capable of something so heartless and cold, but I can't rule it out, either. Not with what I've seen over the years. Not with what I know the players in Chicago are willing to do to win.

"Either way, *comrade*, we should go."

I walk over to the desk and pick up the box containing the bomb.

Galen raises an eyebrow. "What the hell are you doing?"

I scowl at him. "What does it look like?"

"Trying to blow yourself up. Why?"

"Do I really need to explain it to you?" I tuck it under my arm. "All bomb makers have a signature. We may be able to trace who built this, and it may lead us back to where we need to be to finally find the head of the snake."

Galen nods slowly. "Good thinking."

"I'm smarter than I look."

"Doubtful." Galen mutters the word under his breath, and if it were anyone else, I'd put a bullet right between his eyes. But with everything my Irish friend has been through the last few weeks, I'll let this one slide.

"Everyone likes to joke about how dumb Russians are, but I'm not the one who picked a fight with a cartel."

Galen is in deep and has been ever since Luna showed up, pushing in on his gun sales, and on top of that, we have a roving death squad from Albania out trying to peg off *someone*—maybe *everyone*—and we have no proof of who is behind it.

He chuckles at my words. "Maybe not. But that hasn't stopped you from being a target for those men at Felipe's church."

I sneer at him. "We are *all* targets."

Just one more reason to help keep the pesky Irishman alive. If someone sent that group of assassins to Chicago to take out a single target or all of us, I'm leaving them one more person to focus on before they can get to me.

With the box under my arm, I lead Galen out of the office and down the stairs to the main warehouse. Several of my men linger nearby, examining the bodies strewn across the concrete with pools of blood spreading out under them.

I pause at the first body and incline my head for Galen to check him to see if there's anything useful. Galen squats and rifles through the man's pockets, eventually pulling out a cell phone.

"Take it. We may be able to use it and backtrace calls."

He pockets the phone, then slides back one of the man's sleeves, exposing a cartel tattoo. "At least we know we're in the right place."

"This could have ended very badly for you, *comrade*. You probably would have pulled the red wire."

"Fuck you, Valerian."

"I don't think you would like that very much." I grin at him. "Besides, I have someone else in mind."

Like burying my cock in a warm, willing cunt at the club tonight. Several of my favorite girls will be working, so maybe I'll enjoy multiple warm, willing cunts. After everything that's happened, a night lost in a beautiful woman's body—or three or four—sounds like exactly what I need to unwind.

We make our way across the cement floor of the warehouse and toward the rest of my men waiting near the entrance. Those checking the various bodies inside wander over to join us as we step outside.

"*Po mashinam ee pognali.*" I carefully hand off the bomb. "*Ostorozhno.*"

With our luck recently, it's likely to blow. If they aren't careful, we'll end up dead before we even get out of here.

I turn back to Galen. "I'm heading for the club. You're welcome to join me."

Galen considers the offer for a moment and shakes his head. "No, I'm going home to Nicki."

My laugh echoes into the night, and I shake my head. "Only you would be stupid enough to shack up with Cutter Jackson's sister."

"In my defense, I didn't know who she was."

I raise an eyebrow at him. "Maybe not in the beginning, *comrade,* but I very distinctly remember a conversation with you where you brought up the fact that he had a sister, so you knew by then and continued to pursue things with her. Let's not pretend you are some sort of innocent in this."

He chuckles. "No one has ever called me an innocent."

"I imagine not."

A seriousness hardens his features, and Galen inclines his head toward me. "Thank you for your assistance tonight."

"You're welcome." I poke a finger into his chest. "You know you're going to owe me for this."

He smirks. "I have no doubt you'll make me pay handsomely at some point."

I climb into my SUV as he does the same. We need to get out of here before anyone discovers the massacre inside.

Dmitri starts the ignition and glances toward me. "Home?"

I shake my head and release a heavy sigh. "The club. Bring the bomb to my office through the back entrance. We can't risk any potential prying eyes."

He nods his understanding and peels away from the bloodbath we just instigated on the Luna Cartel. The man at the head of this up-and-coming group got away tonight, but this fight isn't over for Galen. He'll keep looking, keep pushing to end the threat.

It isn't my fight, and getting involved will likely only bring more heat down on me. Yet Galen is the only one I can even remotely trust. So, if he needs my help, I'll give it to him. One day, I may be in his position and need an ally—even one who doesn't fully trust me.

"*Interesting that they have Soviet weapons. Are you sure you didn't have anything to do with this?*"

His accusation about my potentially being behind the Albanian hit squad coming after us at the church still rings in my ears, and the annoyance tightens my shoulders. I've never given him any reason not to trust me. We banded together against a common enemy in Kat when she fucked over both of us, and our tenuous alliance has benefitted everyone. Still, we can never *truly* trust each other. No one can in this business. If they do, they end up with a bullet in their back or head.

The city is ready to combust as it is, the five families at each other's throats, each pursuing their ultimate goals and willing to take out anyone in their way.

Any potential peace that may have been brokered during that church meeting vanished the instant the bullets started flying, and we may never reach that point again.

That means keeping any potential allies even closer, especially when we *all* have an unknown enemy to deal with. The group of men who attacked the church and Felipe's condo could be Kat's doing—or it could be *literally* anyone else trying to set up the most obvious target. Whoever it is has moved to the top of all our hit lists—but that doesn't mean the heads of the other families aren't all still in the top ten.

TWO

JULIA

THE DRIPS from the blood-red word spraypainted on the old, industrial, metal door in the alley should be a warning to turn back.

It should scream *this is a terrible idea*—one I should know is only going to end in disaster—but instead of doing that, instead of turning around and devising a different plan, one that doesn't require me to step into Valerian Kamenev's lair of sin, I take the two small steps down toward the door and knock three times on the metal.

A tiny window near the top slides open, and a dark, hard set of eyes meets mine. "*Da?*"

He assesses me coolly, almost immediately dismissing me and starting to close the window.

Speak. This is your only chance.

I clear my throat and offer the man a cool smile that matches the look he's giving me. "I've heard gluttony kills."

One of his dark eyebrows wings up, apparently surprised I know the password to the club. For someone else, it might have been hard—nearly impossible—to get, but all it took was a few minutes for me to find what I needed to gain entry to *Gluttony*.

The doorman closes the window, and the click of the massive door being unlocked reverberates off the brick down the alley. I glance in either direction to ensure no one's watching me—though dressed like this and with my hair dyed, anyone who knew me likely wouldn't recognize me anyway. The door swings open, allowing me entry, and I step in, my high heels clicking on the old concrete beneath my feet.

"You don't look like you belong here, *kukolka*."

His imposing frame towers over me even in four-inch stilettos, but I brush aside any unease and move past him down the long, dimly lit hall toward the low, thumping bass, trying to ignore his comment.

If I don't look like I belong here, even dressed in this tight leather dress, with my hair dyed white-blond, and wearing more makeup than I ever have in my entire life, then I don't know what else I *can* do not to stick out like a sore thumb in *Gluttony*.

The last thing I want to do is draw attention to myself.

That's the kind of thing that will get me killed.

A tall brunette in stilettos even higher than mine assesses me from head to toe from where she stands at the end of the hallway in front of the shiny black double doors, wrapped in a silky red dress that barely covers her perfect curves.

I approach her cautiously, keenly aware that she holds the keys to the kingdom. She's the gate-keeper, far more so than the big man behind me. This is the woman who decides who gets in and who doesn't.

Her green eyes sweep over me again, as if she'll see something different this time, and her lips press into a firm line as I come to a stop in front of her.

"Are you a member?"

I shake my head and force a tight smile. "Visitor."

Hopefully.

Her lips twist. "You can't participate tonight."

"I know."

As secretive as this place is, I've been able to learn enough to know what I'm getting myself into and at least attempt to prepare myself for what I'm about to see.

She continues to watch me, narrowing her eyes like she's searching for something. "How old are you?"

I swallow thickly. "Old enough."

"Over twenty-one?"

Nodding, I try to keep the nerves from shaking my hands as I reach into the purse slung over my shoulder. "I have my ID if you need to see it."

It's a good fake, but this girl likely sees enough of them to know the difference. Sweat beads on my forehead, and I pull the ID from my wallet.

She shakes her head. "That won't be necessary. The bar will card you if you want a drink." Apparently convinced I'm of age and that I know what I'm getting myself into, she reaches under a small table beside her and pulls out a sheet of paper. "You'll need to have these tests run and your results back to us before you are allowed to engage in any activities."

It makes sense. They want to protect their clientele from any diseases a participant might carry. By forcing everyone to get tested and reveal their results, at least they cover their asses on that.

That doesn't mean there aren't *other* dangers that lurk behind those heavy doors. A club run by the Russian bratva literally teems with sinister and ruthless men who no doubt have very depraved thoughts and plans.

She grabs another sheet. "And this one is a waiver of liability for any injuries sustained once you're engaged in any sort of activities."

My throat suddenly goes dry, and I struggle to swallow through it as I take the paper, fold it up with the other one, and slip them into the small bag slung across my shoulder. "Okay."

"Give me your wrist."

I hold it out, and she slips a red plastic bracelet around it.

"This tells everyone that you can't play tonight. Once you're approved, your color will change to green unless you don't want to play. Then you'll be a yellow, which means you're approved but choose not to participate."

So many rules.

It's what my life has always been—restricted by what others thought was best for me, controlled and restrained, both physically and otherwise. I've tried so hard to escape that, and this is just one more step toward the ultimate goal.

I nod my understanding, and she offers me a practiced smile, a hint of annoyance underneath it.

"Enjoy indulging in gluttony."

I return her tight smile and step past her, taking a long, deep inhale before I push through the double doors.

Here goes nothing. ¡Mantenerse fuerte!

The doors open into a scene of pure debauchery, the entire atmosphere only enhanced by the thumping bass coming from hidden speakers around the dimly lit, black-painted room.

On a couch immediately to my right, a redheaded woman rides a dark-haired man and moans around the cock of another buried down her throat. They undulate, moving together fluidly, like they've clearly done this before. My eyes travel over their naked bodies and to the green bands on their wrists—approved members, likely regulars. As are most of the people here, according to my research, which means a stranger stands out.

The last thing I want.

I move past the threesome and deeper inside the club, the sultry music making my chest thud in time with it. On the far side of the vast space, a woman strung up in some sort of intricate rope ties hangs from the ceiling while a man fucks her anally.

Heat flames between my legs, and I force myself to look away and scan the rest of the couples engaged in various sexual activities, searching past them for where to get a drink. If I'm going to be here, I'm going to need some liquid courage.

I make my way over to an open stool at the end of the bar, and a man built like a linebacker approaches from the other side. His bourbon-hued gaze darts down to my wrist.

"Just observing tonight?"

"First time."

"So, you're a virgin?" The tiniest twitch of a smile hits his lips. "At *Gluttony*, I mean."

Hell.

That heat spreads from between my legs through my body and over my cheeks. "Um. Yes, my first time...at *Gluttony*."

He grins. "At least you can indulge in one of my many brilliant concoctions, assuming you're twenty-one." His gaze narrows on me. "You certainly look young."

Apparently, all the makeup does nothing to hide that from anyone.

"I'm twenty-one."

"I'll have to see your ID. The boss would have my head if I served someone underage."

Shit.

I force a smile and pull the ID from my purse, flipping it over to him with a shaking hand. He accepts it slowly and brings it closer to his face since it's hard to see in the dim lighting.

"Julia Diaz..." He looks from the photo on the ID to me. "I like you as a blonde. It suits you."

The air I've been holding in my lungs whooshes out as he hands it back to me. I glance at the photo on the ID, with my natural dark hair and lacking makeup. There wasn't any time to get a new photo done after the dye job, and I couldn't wait any longer to come to *Gluttony*. I've waited long enough, spent too many years behind the scenes, moving pieces on the massive chess board that is the criminal underworld in the Windy City.

"What would you like to drink, Julia?"

I shake my head. "Corralejo Reposado—neat, please."

His brows fly up. "You still need to be able to walk out of here, *milaya*. You might want to go a little easier on the hard stuff."

I grin at him. "Don't worry about that. Pour me a double."

He sets a tumbler on the bar, pours the tequila, and scans the club, straightening suddenly. I follow his gaze and freeze. The familiar large frame fills the entire door frame, the broad shoulders almost brushing the wood on either side. His icy-blue gaze rakes over me, heating me from the inside out—somehow raising goosebumps over my skin as my pussy warms and clenches under his assessment.

It's the same reaction I had the first time I saw the man, what seems like so long ago. So much has happened since then. Everything has changed. That day altered the future for so many people. Set us all on a collision course with each other. This is an all-new world, one I have to navigate carefully.

Maybe the blond hair wasn't the way to remain inconspicuous.

The bartender makes his way to Valerian and whispers something to him, glancing over his shoulder at me briefly.

I raise the glass to my lips and down it in one gulp. I'm not going to heed his advice and take it easy tonight. I've never particularly liked things just handed to me. I'd much rather earn something the hard way. And something tells me Valerian Kamenev won't make things easy.

THREE

JULIA

¡Mierda!

Valerian approaches the bar slowly, his eyes locked on me the entire time, the bartender trailing behind him with his jaw tight and an apology in his gaze.

Oh, hell.

If Valerian recognizes me, it's all over. I'll never walk out of here alive. Despite my entire body tensing the closer he comes, it isn't only from fear. Just being in this man's presence is enough to light a flame I didn't know could burn so hot—it did that first time I saw him the same way it does now.

Valerian stops across from me and leans slightly on the bar toward me, the white sleeves of his dress shirt rolled up to expose strong, muscular forearms covered in ink. "I'm told you're a virgin."

I squirm at the word and low vibrating timber of his voice and nod. "Yes, it's my first time at *Gluttony.*"

"What brings you?"

Revenge.

I fight back the word and instead smile at him. "Curiosity."

He issues a low chuckle that sends a new wave of goosebumps skittering across my skin. "You know what they say about curiosity...it killed the cat."

I raise an eyebrow at him. "Then it's a good thing cats have nine lives."

Valerian barks out a laugh, his azure eyes twinkling with amusement. "Touché. Do you have a name?"

"I do."

He waits for a second and smiles. "Are you going to give it to me, *kotyonok?*"

I shake my head, fighting a grin. "Why would I do something like that?"

It's a dangerous game to play—flirting with Valerian—but it feels natural, like banter between old lovers rather than two people who have just spoken for the first time.

He pushes off the bar and walks toward the end of it, every step he moves farther away tightening my chest a little bit more.

Where the hell is he going?

So many possibilities float through my head...

To get security...

To get a gun...

Who am I kidding? He definitely already has one somewhere on him.

Valerian moves around the bar and approaches, sidling up behind me, the heat of his large body radiating against the skin exposed by my backless dress. "Come with me, *kotyonok.*"

¡Mierda!

I peek over my shoulder at him. "Where?"

He narrows his gaze on me. "Does it matter?"

I guess not at this point.

Whatever he intends to do to me, it likely wouldn't matter if we stayed out here or went somewhere else. No one here will talk about what they see. No one would dare cross the head of the most powerful Russian bratva in the Midwest.

I turn on the stool and slide off it, my breasts almost brushing his chest. He offers me his large, calloused hand, and I slide mine into it, a crackle of electricity buzzing from the connection and through my arm.

He dips his head, his warm breath fluttering against my cheek. "Let's go somewhere more private."

Those words send another tingle through me—a charge of satisfaction mixing with fear.

"After you..." I raise an eyebrow, waiting for him to give me his name since he expected me to give him mine.

Valerian chuckles. "If you don't know who I am, then you're in the wrong place."

"I know who you are, Mr. Kamenev. I just didn't expect to see you here."

I had hoped to be able to observe the club and Valerian's men, get a feel for how to make my approach, and perhaps glean some information that would assist in attaining my ultimate goal.

"Why not? It's my club."

"Yes, but I didn't know you..."—I scan everything going on around us—"partook in any of this."

He leans even closer, feathering his lips against my ear. "One of the perks of the job is doing just that. Now, *come*."

The single word is enough to make my pussy spasm. He tugs my hand and leads me toward the door he entered from only a few minutes ago.

As we move slowly through the club, Valerian releases my hand to slide his to my lower back. We pass a woman in black latex whipping a man strapped to a contraption resembling a pommel horse, and I squeeze my legs together against the throb there, watching the scene unfold.

Valerian peeks at me out of the corner of his eye, almost like he's observing my reaction to what's going on around us, gauging my interest, and when we reach the door at the far side of the room, he stops and grabs my wrist, leaning in until his heady masculine scent envelops me. "If you want to leave, this would be the time to do it, *kotyonok*."

Fucking hell.

He recognizes me.

He's giving me a way out.

He's telling me this is my only chance to escape from here alive.

But I can't just walk away because I'm scared of this man or what he's capable of. I don't have the luxury of being able to do that.

Not now, maybe not ever.

I square my shoulders with more bravado than I actually feel. "I'm not afraid of anything."

He issues a low, dark chuckle and shakes his head. "That's a very dangerous thing to tell a man like me, *kotyonok*."

I swallow thickly at the promise in his voice—of something dark and dirty and forbidden.

He opens the door and ushers me into the hall illuminated by dim red light. We pass several closed doors, each likely hiding one form of debauchery or another behind it.

The private playrooms...

They have their own kind of venerated status amongst the regulars, though the club itself remains below ground—literally and figuratively—word gets around about where to come to play. Of all Valerian's clubs, this is the most important, and anything that's important to Valerian Kamanev is important to me, too.

My body tenses imagining what's behind each door we pass. It isn't why I came. Isn't my grand purpose here. Yet if Valerian wants me, given my body's reaction, I'm not so sure I'll be able to resist and say no.

He pauses outside a closed door at the end of the hall, and I suck in a sharp breath, waiting for him to reveal what lies behind it. His large hand wraps around the knob, and he turns it, pushing it open, and urging me to step into the room with a firm nudge at my back.

A soft, warm glow surrounds me—unlike the harsher red-hued lighting in the hallway, in here, it's almost romantic. Something I never thought I'd be saying about the man with me.

The massive black wooden desk that dominates the center of this space matches the man at my back—hard, strong, elegant, yet somehow appearing dangerous.

Valerian motions toward a red leather couch along the far wall. "This is my private office. Not many people get to come back here."

I offer him a tight smile. "Should I be thanking you, then?"

He considers me for a moment before barking out a laugh. "You're feisty, *kotyonok*. I'll give you that. I would not have thought that just looking at you."

Because no matter how much makeup I wear, no matter what color I make my hair, I always look like an innocent child despite having turned twenty-one over two months ago.

I slowly lower myself onto the couch and give him my best demure smile. "Just because something looks sweet doesn't mean it doesn't have bite."

He issues another chuckle and walks over to a small bar next to his desk. "Unfortunately, I've learned the truth of those words on a personal level. So, are you going to tell me your name now?"

"Julia."

The lie comes out easily. Choosing my middle name for my alias was my attempt to ensure I wouldn't forget it when questioned.

He eyes me over his shoulder. "And what are you doing at my club, Julia?"

A question I'm not entirely certain I'm ready to answer. I thought I knew why I was here. Why I came. The reason I stood outside that door and risked my very life by setting foot inside. But being with him now, in here, I'm not so sure anymore.

"I'm looking for a way to let loose, to unwind, I guess."

He nods slowly as he pours two drinks—one tequila and one vodka. "You've definitely found the right place for that."

"Then why did you bring me here if not to tell me I have to leave?"

Valerian stops in front of me and connects his gaze with mine. "Is that what you thought? That I brought you back here because you are in trouble?"

He raises a dark brow at me, and I shrug.

"I wasn't sure what to think. I hadn't expected anyone to pay attention to my coming here just to observe."

In fact, I had counted on it.

"You're not the type of woman anyone can ignore."

¡Mierda!

He means it as a compliment, yet his words send an icy chill through me. If he realizes that we've met before, if he somehow recognizes me, this friendly banter is going to turn bad very quickly.

"Are you all right, Julia?"

I force a smile. "Yes. Why?"

"You've gotten awfully pale."

I snort and shake my head, clapping my hand over my mouth at the unladylike sound, but he just chuckles at me.

Dropping my hand, I assess him. "What's so funny?"

He grins. "You. You should see the way your cheeks flame so easily at every word I say, *kotyonok*."

I smile tightly. "My strict Catholic upbringing is hard to overcome."

Valerian slowly lowers himself onto the couch next to me and passes me the drink. "That certainly explains what a sweet girl like you is doing in a place like this."

"I don't follow..."

He takes a sip of his vodka, and I do the same from my tequila when all I want to do is down it in one gulp again. But considering I already did that with a double, I also don't want to be flat on my ass or let down my guard around this man.

"Do you know why I started this club?"

I shake my head. "Because you wanted to have a lot of raunchy sex?"

He barks out a laugh and drops his head back, the sound going straight between my legs. He winks at me. "You aren't wrong in that assessment, but that isn't why I started it."

"Then why?"

"To allow people to live out their fantasies somewhere safe, somewhere they won't be judged for their desires, for their wants, for their needs. Somewhere completely free." His gaze takes on an almost sympathetic softness. "I know many like you were brought up to believe sex was something dirty that you didn't talk about, that you are taught to pretend didn't exist."

"That was my upbringing to a T."

He nods slowly. "I believe the opposite. I believe this type of place, this type of freedom, is precisely what allows people to break from the confines of unreasonable expectations, and for me, nothing is more important than that."

"Nothing?"

The question comes out before I can bite it back, and regret instantly tightens my chest.

He narrows his eyes on me slightly and shifts closer to me on the couch until his thick, muscular thigh presses to mine. "No, Julia, nothing."

I stare him down, his icy eyes threatening to light a flame in one instant. "Don't you have other businesses, other interests? Other things that should be far more important than seeing the people of Chicago have somewhere to come to fuck?"

His gaze never leaves mine as he downs half his drink and sets the glass on the small table to his side. He leans in and brushes his thumb across my lips. "Such foul language from such a pretty, innocent-looking girl. We do more than fuck here, Julia. We allow our clientele to live out a fantasy, to indulge their heart's desire as much as they want to, hence the name *Gluttony*." A sly grin splits his lips. "No limitations. No expectations. No reason to stop when you see something you want."

FOUR

VALERIAN

JULIA SHIFTS NERVOUSLY NEXT to me on the couch, crossing and uncrossing her legs, the smooth tan skin begging for my touch. A strange mix of nervousness and anticipation rolls off her, like she can't quite decide how she should feel or act.

I rest my hand on her warm thigh. She doesn't flinch at the touch, doesn't pull away, but her dark bourbon eyes meet mine.

"Tell me what you're *really* doing here, Julia. You seem uncomfortable with what goes on inside these walls. Like this is the last place you want to be."

She shakes her head almost immediately, the blond locks floating around her face. "It's not that. Not that at all. I came to release some tension."

"Tension, hmm?" I reach for my tumbler and take a sip. "That's something I am familiar with."

Julia swallows slowly, and I slip my hand slightly higher up her thigh, closer to the hem of her short leather skirt.

"Since you're wearing the red wristband, and this is your first time, that's going to severely limit your options in terms of...*tension* release."

I watch her over the edge of my glass as I take another drink, and her eyes dart down to my throat as I swallow.

She gulps in a heavy breath and presses her legs together, pinning my fingers between her warm fleshy thighs. "What are my options?"

I grin at her and set my drink on the side table again. "Well..." I nudge her legs open with my hand, and she complies, never breaking eye contact. "I would love to help you relieve that tension, unless you saw someone out there you're more interested in."

Julia's cheeks pinken again, and she shakes her head quickly. "No. You're the only one in this place of any interest to me."

Right answer, kotyonok.

I glide my hand farther up until I can feel the heat of her cunt against my skin. She takes a heavy breath as the flush darkens her cheeks even more.

Pausing my hand, I raise a brow at her. "Are you nervous?"

She shakes her head, and her tongue darts out across her lips. "No, why would I be nervous?"

Julia isn't a very good liar. Whatever she's doing here has her rattled, and I intend to rattle her even further.

I encourage her legs open even more, bunching up the hem of the leather skirt around her waist, exposing the apex of her thighs, completely bare from any sort of fabric impediments. "I see you came prepared tonight. A pity we can't play more."

Her breath comes in short, hot pants. Her right hand tightens on the arm of the couch as her left fists at her side between us. I gently glide my middle finger between her wet pussy lips, and she bites her lip, issuing a little mewl.

It's just a brush, barely a whisper, but every one of her muscles tenses at the contact.

I shift my body toward her, giving me a better angle of attack, and slip the finger inside her fully.

Her wet heat clasps around me, making my already semi-hard cock swell painfully against my zipper. "I understand what it's like to need to release tension, Julia."

"Do you?" Her words come out breathy, as if she's struggling to speak.

I slowly withdraw my finger and then plunge it back in. Her thighs tighten around my hand again, but not enough to impede my play.

"I do. My job is very stressful, Julia." I continue to probe her, relishing in the heat radiating from her body, searing my flesh where it touches hers. "A lot of people rely on me for things—money, safety—a lot of lives rest in my hands."

Julia offers a sharp nod in response, and I move closer to her, finally letting my thumb graze over her clit. She bucks on my hand, forcing my finger deeper inside while she clenches around me tighter.

"Tell me, *kotyonok*. What are your fantasies?"

She opens her mouth to say something, then quickly glances at me and shakes her head. "No, I can't..."

"You can." I slip another finger inside her, spreading her wider and rolling my thumb over her most sensitive spot. "You can..."

Julia gasps and drops her head back, her mouth falling open. All I want to do is ram my cock down her throat, fuck her mouth, come hard, and watch her swallow it down greedily.

But I hold myself back, waiting for her answer.

I still my fingers.

Her eyes drift open to meet mine again.

"Tell me."

The bourbon color in her gaze shifts, darkened by something I can't quite place. "I want freedom, like you said. To do whatever I want."

"You don't have that?"

She shakes her head. "No."

"A pity anyone would try to restrict a woman like you."

I alter the position of my fingers and probe even deeper inside her, curling up to hit her G-spot. Another gasp tumbles from her pink parted lips, and her left hand clutches my forearm, her nails digging into the exposed skin just below my rolled-up sleeve.

Leaning in, I flutter my lips against her ear. "Tell me more, Julia. About what you want."

"This..."

"This what?"

"This. The club, the freedom, the lifestyle, the rush. This..."

My cock jerks in my pants, straining painfully, begging to be released after the night I've had. Almost dying with Galen put me on edge, one I was balancing on precariously before I ever entered the club and set my sights on this woman. But I was drawn to her like a moth to a flame. "You don't know what you're saying, *kotyonok*."

She looks at me again, releasing a breathy moan. "I do."

I continue to thrust into her, rolling my thumb at the apex of her thighs in time with my ministrations and winding her up tighter and tighter.

"I know what I want, Valerian."

"That's a very good quality to have, Julia. But knowing isn't the hard part, is it? It's *getting* it."

I pinch her clit between my fingers of my other hand, and her mouth falls open on a silent moan before she comes, her cunt squeezing around my fingers, clutching at them desperately, trying to take them deeper. I keep pumping into her, dragging out the sensation, watching pleasure contort her beautiful features with ecstasy.

She finally sags back, her death grip on my forearm loosening slightly, and her eyes flutter open, a determination in her gaze that hadn't been present at any other time during our conversation. "I will get what I want. Eventually. I promise you that."

"A very bold statement. A very confident one."

Her lips curl into a tiny grin. "Maybe it is."

I drag my hand from between her legs and pull my glistening fingers up to my mouth. She watches me suck them between my lips. The taste of her arousal coats my tongue in a way that makes my cock weep and my body ache with a hunger I haven't felt in a long time.

"I do wish you the best of luck, *kotyonok*. I have a feeling you have big plans, and you're going to need it."

"You have no idea."

She pushes to her feet and wobbles a little, unsteady at first on the stilettos, and walks to the door. Without a look back, she opens it and disappears down the hallway. I sit on the couch, my hard cock pressing painfully against my zipper, and reach down to adjust it. Here I thought I would get some relief tonight, have a way to dispel the pressure and tension that built through my body during our mission at the warehouse.

But Julia has only made it worse.

Far worse...

FIVE

VALERIAN

"What do you have for me?"

It better be something...

Days of waiting around for more information to surface, for the answers about the group attacking everyone to become clear, have left me back on the edge of violence.

Dmitri settles into the chair on the other side of my desk and shakes his head. "Nothing good, *pakhan*. We've scoured the entire city, looking for any signs of the men who came to the church and then to Felipe's condo, but they've vanished again."

"*Blyad!*"

The only thing worse than knowing you have a target on your back is not knowing who is shooting or from where. This death squad that appeared at the church and then tracked us to Felipe's poses a major threat—to me and everyone else. We don't know who their real target is—it could be all five families. But even if they aren't after me, taking out one of the heads of the other families would have catastrophic effects in Chicago. It's the only reason I never moved against Kat when she stole from me and slapped me in the face by lying to me about her intent, all while looking me right in the eye.

That woman is the kind of threat I always feared in this business—deathly beautiful and a brilliant manipulator. She may have sworn she had nothing to do with the group of men after us, but none of us trust her word. We can't. Not when we've all been burned by it and her before.

"What about the way Cutter's guy was tracking them before—the rental car?"

"Somebody must have gotten wise to what happened when they arrived at the condo and everyone was gone. They ditched it and set it on fire on the Southside."

"*Blyad!* So, we don't have anything?"

He shrugs slightly. "We have something..."

"What's that?"

"Surveillance video from the condo building of them coming into the lobby. Felipe sent it to everyone this morning to see if anyone had any sources who could use it in a helpful way."

"Could you ID any of them and track them that way?"

"I don't have the technology to run that through facial recognition software, but Cutter's guy is doing it. He said the names they flew under from Albania are likely aliases, anyway, so he's trying to track down who they really are to see if it gives any clue as to who sent them."

I tighten my hand into a fist and slam it against the desk. "*Eto blyad' khuinya*. Why can't we find anyone who knows what the fuck they're doing? I don't want to have to rely on Valentina and Cutter, or anyone else for that matter, to get information for us about our enemies."

It puts us in a weak position, one I refuse to let us fall into. There's already too much conflict and uncertainty. I won't give my belly to one of my enemies by calling them for help.

We need our own resource on this, someone who can do a deep dive, but I've never been able to find anyone with the skills of Cutter's friend.

"I want you to find somebody who can do this, who can track down these fuckers and figure out who hired them and who their target really is—whether it's all of us or just one of us and we all happened to get caught in the crossfire. And see what you can get from any of Kat's men. Until then, we stay on high alert. Keep the club locked down to members only and double the protection on all the girls when you send them out on calls."

He inclines his head and pushes to his feet. "Will do, *pakhan*. You really think this wasn't Kat?"

I drum my fingers on the desk and lean back in my chair. "I honestly don't know, Dmitri. They came from Albania—Vlorë. She's fucking Albanian, and the city was the center of her late husband's empire. We know she's had her sights set on getting rid of all the competition since the day she arrived here. She killed Michael Syla, and she's already made moves against me and the Irish. Now that she's teamed up with Rose, who knows where that might lead, to what lengths they might go."

A cold-blooded femme fatale and a blood-thirsty Colombian cartel head combining powers isn't good for any of us on the outside of it. Even Rose's own brother doesn't trust him, and I can't say I blame Felipe in that regard.

We need answers.

I need answers.

Dmitri nods. "I had the same thought."

"But Galen implied it could be me."

My first in command since Syla slaughtered Oleg pauses at the door and turns back to me. "What do you mean?"

I release a heavy sigh. "He suggested it was somebody trying to set up Kat, and given our close connections with that area of the world, it might be easy for us to be the ones behind it. They were using Soviet weapons at the church..."

Dmitri narrows his eyes on me. "Was it you?"

Is he fucking serious with this question?

"*Poshol na khuy*. Dmitri. Do you really think I would make a move like that without telling you?"

He offers a shrug again. "I don't know. Times are changing. It's hard to trust anyone, right?"

"That it is."

He closes the door behind him, and I stare at the shiny black wood of my desk, drumming my fingers, considering all the ways life has gone to hell lately. One solitary good thing has occupied my thoughts and haunted my dreams at night.

Julia...

My gaze drifts over to the couch, and I can almost taste her release on my tongue again, remembering her little moans. I flip on my computer and click on the file for the video surveillance from when Julia arrived only a few days ago.

The alley camera shows her standing, staring at the outer door for a while, shifting uneasily in the too-high-for-her heels, hesitant to come in, before she squares her shoulders and steps up to it.

I was right; she was scared.

But she also has balls.

She made the decision to enter and never looked back.

I focus on the next camera, watching her approach the check-in area and her interaction with Connie. The way she responds to the other woman draws a chuckle from deep in my chest.

Julia wanted in and wouldn't be deterred by Connie's icy demeanor.

She steps into the club, and even from this camera angle and darkened room, the change in her body language the second she sees the people at play is readily apparent. Julia is more than interested in what goes on here. It isn't an act or a pretense. She climbs onto the stool at the bar, and my interaction with her unfolds like I'm watching a movie in my memory.

Heading back to my office past the playrooms...

Me pouring the drinks...

Me slipping my hand up her skirt...

Her head tipped back with her cries and gasps...

My cock swells watching the replay, and the taste of her release dances on my tongue again.

Blyad!

I press the button on the phone on my desk to buzz Dmitri.

"Yeah, *pakhan.*"

"Send Sasha in here right away."

I unzip my pants and free my aching cock, stroking it slowly as the door to the office swings open. Sasha enters with a sultry smile, closing the door behind her and throwing the lock. I push back from my desk and motion for her to come to me.

She approaches me seductively, her hips swaying in the miniskirt that barely covers her pussy and ass, red hair tumbling down over her shoulders and brushing the tops of her almost fully exposed breasts.

Of all the girls who work here at the club and make themselves available to our clientele, she's one of my favorites. Always willing to please and a fucking expert at sucking cock.

She rounds the desk and immediately drops to her knees between mine to wrap her mouth around my length. I groan at the wet heat engulfing me and drop my head back against the head-rest, burying my fingers in her lush waves.

Only it isn't her I'm picturing but a petite bleach-bottle blonde with tan skin and the sweetest cunt I've ever tasted.

SIX

VALERIAN

"Where did you find him?" I stare at Genti tied up in the chair at the center of the warehouse.

Blood trickles from a gash at his temple, his left eye already swelling from whatever my men did to get Kat's right-hand man into this position.

"It isn't like him to let down his guard."

Dmitri glances over at me. "We followed him leaving Kat's Cradle and managed to grab him when he got out of his car outside a smoke shop."

"Did anyone see you?"

He shakes his head. "No, the place doesn't have any security cameras, and we were careful following him."

"So, Kat has no idea we have him?"

Dmitri offers a shrug. "I don't know how she could, *pakhan*."

"Excellent."

That gives me some time to try to get answers from the one man who may have them.

Genti lifts his head and sneers at me, spitting blood onto the concrete floor. "She's going to fucking kill you when she finds out."

Chuckling, I approach and squat in front of him, putting myself at his level. "Your boss is already in a very precarious position, Genti. I don't think she's going to be doing anything of the sort."

"What the hell do you think you're going to accomplish with this?"

I pull my knife out of my boot and use the blade to pick at my cuticle. "I'm hoping I can get some answers about what the fuck has been going on around here."

Going after one of Kat's men seemed like the most obvious move to try to get to the bottom of her potential involvement in the recent attacks. Though, I never anticipated Dmitri would be able to pull off capturing Genti—the one who has her ear and is privy to the innermost workings of the mind of the woman who seems intent on destroying the families.

"You think I'm going to tell you anything?"

I grin at him. "I do, Genti...because you're a smart man. And you know the kind of pain I can inflict on you if you don't cooperate. I want to know everything about the men who came over from Albania. Are they working on Kat's behalf?"

Genti's lips twist as if he's tasted something bitter. "If they were, do you think I'd fucking tell you?"

I scowl at him and shake my head. "Already not being very cooperative. This would go a lot faster and be a lot less painful if you were."

"I have no desire to get sliced and diced today, Valerian, so I'll tell you what I can. It isn't much. Kat doesn't know anything about those guys and didn't send them. I would know if she did."

"She's never made a move behind your back without your knowledge?" I raise a brow at him. "I find that hard to believe."

Given how secretive Kat is and the way she betrayed his former boss—during a very *intimate* moment—I know the answer to that question before he even opens his mouth.

"Never something important. If you're trying to stop a war, kidnapping me and threatening me isn't the way to do it, Valerian."

Anger races through my blood, and I tighten my hand on the knife. "Oh, now you're giving me advice on how to run my business?"

"Seems like you might need it."

I push to my feet. "The only current threat to me is your bitch boss and her Colombian boy toy. Ever since she appeared in Chicago, everything's been one clusterfuck after another, yet you stand by her, ever loyal. Even when she linked up with Rose. Why is that?"

Anyone with eyes who has seen the two of them together would know why he's so loyal—he's in love with her—but given her relationship with Rose, he'll never have her.

"She killed your former boss, betrayed him. The man who trusted her and brought her into his fold. Now you're willing to put down your life for her. How do you know she isn't doing the same to you? To all of us?"

He tries to shrug, but the restraints on his arms make the movement almost imperceptible. "I guess I don't. But one thing I do know is that Kat isn't stupid. She was in that church and got shot. She was hunted at Felipe's condo with everyone. She's not going to let herself get caught in the crossfire intentionally. And certainly not *twice*."

"Unless she's trying to draw attention away from herself and remove suspicion."

It would be a smart play. And it has worked. Galen's voiced distrust of me only arose because Kat managed to make everyone believe she might be innocent.

Genti shakes his head. "This isn't that, Valerian. Something else is going on here. There's another player. I'm positive of it."

I walk around behind him, sliding the knife under his throat. "I'd love to hear your theory, Genti. And I hope, for your sake, it's one that explains all this. I tire of this game we play. Perhaps slitting your throat and going after Kat, guns blazing, is the only possible course of action."

He swallows, the motion pressing the blade against his skin enough to send a trickle of blood down the front of his shirt. "We all know the Berishas and the Dragushas tried to take out Kat when she was last in Albania because they weren't happy about her taking their girls."

I nod slowly. "Yes, I did hear something about that."

"So, who is to say they haven't decided to make an even stronger move here?"

"The Dragushas and Berishas never struck me as the types with enough manpower or enough balls to come across the ocean and try to supplant us."

"Normally, I would agree, but there have been rumblings."

"Ah, so you *do* know something."

He shakes his head. "Rumors, supposition."

"Do tell."

His eyes dart up to meet mine as much as the position allows. "Might be a little easier if you lowered the knife."

I lean in and press my mouth against his ear. "What fun would that be?" More blood trickles from the wound at his neck. "Tell me everything you know."

He tightens his jaw. "There's been more violence, more unrest and uncertainty ever since the Sylas and the Gashis left Albania and the Dragushas and Berishas stepped up. They've eliminated many of the smaller groups. Either decimating them completely or welcoming them into the fold if they bend the knee."

"And you think they're ambitious enough to come here to stage something like this?"

"I don't know. But that's the point, isn't it? We don't know *anything*."

As much as I hate to admit it, he's right. We don't know anything. Except that there are some very angry people with guns, shooting at anything that moves.

Pulling his head back, I press the knife to his jugular. "If you're lying or holding anything back from me, I'll slit your throat right now."

His stony eyes meet mine—no fear in them. "Do it. Do it and you'll create your worst enemy in Kat. If you think what she's done so far is bad, you can't imagine the lengths she will go to if you hurt me."

I slowly press the blade against the skin hard enough to send more rivulets of blood down his neck. "I don't trust you. I don't trust anyone. But on this, I don't think you're lying. You just better pray I don't find out that I'm wrong about that."

A phone dings somewhere in the warehouse, and I jerk my head up and watch Dmitri glance at his.

"*Pakhan?*"

"What is it?"

This isn't the time to be interrupting me, and Dmitri knows that. Which means whatever is going on is serious.

"There's a visitor trying to enter the club."

"You know what I said—no visitors until all of this is resolved. Members only."

He inclines his head. "It's the blonde."

Almost instantly, my cock stirs, and I can't fight the grin that pulls at my lips. "Tell them to let her in and to bring her to playroom one to wait for me."

"Yes, *pakhan.*" Dmitri texts whoever contacted him from the club.

I release my hold on our captive and walk around to face him again. "It's men like you and me who prevent wars, Genti. We are the ones who understand that there are some lines we don't cross. There are rules that aren't broken. Your boss needs to learn that. If she doesn't, she's going to be the one who ends up regretting it." I force a tight smile. "You make sure she understands that, or the next time we meet, it won't be on such pleasant terms."

Having to restrain myself from lashing out at Genti with my rage against Kat takes every ounce of willpower I have, but it wouldn't solve anything. He's right—if I kill him, Kat will only come at me harder.

I stalk toward the exit of the warehouse and pause next to Dmitri.

He peers over his shoulder at our captive. "What do you want me to do with him?"

I glance back to where Genti still sits restrained, fury flashing in his eyes. "Let him go, but see if you can slip a tracker and a mic on him somewhere. A coat pocket, perhaps. I want to know everything Kat and Rose are doing, and since we don't have anyone on the inside, we need to find a way to get out of the dark on all this."

He nods. "I'll see what I can do."

"I'm heading back to the club and will be otherwise engaged for the rest of the evening. Don't interrupt me for anything."

SEVEN

JULIA

THE GIANT WOODEN *X* next to the wall directly across from me appears inconspicuous enough to someone who doesn't know, just a polished piece of black wood. Nothing anyone should be afraid of...until I let my eyes drift to the manacles at the top and bottom of it—a St. Andrew's Cross.

I've never seen one in person before, but staring it down sends a flutter of fear and excitement through me that matches what I felt with Valerian the other night in his office.

Coming back was a calculated risk I had to take.

Either Valerian didn't recognize me, or he did and let me go for some ulterior purpose. If he doesn't know who I am, it's only a matter of time before he will figure it out, and then, he'll want to know why I'm actually here.

That doesn't bode well for my future.

For the third time since I was escorted in here, I push to my feet from the red leather bench and make my way over to the door to try it.

Still locked.

I don't know why I thought it wouldn't be. Nothing has changed in the time I've been sitting here other than my anxiety ramping up.

Where the hell is Valerian?

Footsteps sound in the hallway, barely audible over the music from the main club. The walls in here are almost soundproof, likely designed that way so that whatever goes on in here remains absolutely private. Which, if my guess is correct, is precisely why Valerian had me put here.

He doesn't want anyone to know what he's about to do.

My skin breaks out in a cold sweat, and I retreat to the bench as the footsteps stop just outside the door. The sound of a key in the lock makes me tense, then the door swings open slowly.

Valerian steps in, and his icy-blue gaze lands on me immediately. The hint of warmth that was there the last time I saw him appears to have dissipated in the interim.

He doesn't say anything, just slowly closes the door behind him and walks past me to the other side of the room. With his back to me, he removes his suit coat. The bulky muscles of his broad shoulders bunch and flex with the movement, his physique barely contained in the crisp white dress shirt underneath. Laying the coat across a stool, he turns toward me and begins to unbutton his shirt, exposing smooth skin stretched over a hard, lean, chiseled chest.

My mouth waters, and my fingers itch to reach out and touch him. But I don't dare move, not when I don't have a clue what's happening right now, when I have no idea what I should be doing or saying.

The silence lingering between us is my friend in that regard, but it also makes me squirm under his assessing gaze. It rakes over me from head to toe, the red leather miniskirt and tank top barely containing my breasts, leaving very little to the imagination.

Valerian stops in front of me and squats. "You came back."

I give a sharp nod.

One corner of his lip twitches. "I thought I might have scared you off."

I fight a grin. "I don't scare that easily."

If I did, after everything I've been through, I'd be a sobbing mess in the fetal position in a padded room instead of in *this* one with *this* man.

"I can see that, but I haven't done anything yet, *kotyonok*." His gaze drifts down to the green band on my wrist, and his dark eyebrows rise. "You've been approved?"

"Yes."

"Is that why you came back? You want to play?"

I hesitate this time—the word *yes* just as likely to come out as *no*.

Over the last few years, I've learned everything there is to know about this man, made it my job to ensure I did. It was essential. *Know your enemies better than they know themselves.* I know his favorite food, the cigars he can't live without, the only brand of vodka he'll drink; still, he's a complete stranger who holds my life in his hands in more ways than one. A man I absolutely, positively should never trust.

Yet, he gave me an incredible orgasm I can still feel to this day and let me walk away. If he had wanted to hurt me, he easily could have during our last encounter. That *should* earn him a modicum of trust.

He reaches out and brushes his thumb across my lips. "Well, Julia?"

"Yes..."

The word comes out breathy, barely a whisper, but it draws a grin from the dangerous man in front of me.

"Excellent." He motions over his shoulder. "Do you know what that is?"

I struggle to swallow through my suddenly dry throat. "A St. Andrew's Cross."

His dark brow rises. "Do you know what it's for?"

"Torture."

He barks out a laugh that echoes around the room and shakes his head. "No, that's for what we talked about the other night. Pleasure. Freedom. Release. Will you let me give it to you?"

A shudder rolls through me, and I nod. "Yes."

It's all I've ever wanted—release from the life I've been forced into, the box I've been stuffed in.

Valerian slowly climbs to his feet. "Strip."

It's a single word that holds a heavy weight.

If I say no, if I deny him, whatever *this* is will be over, but if I comply, if I leave myself bare and open to him, it could expose me in the way I've been dreading. The way that could end up with me in a shallow grave or at the bottom of the Chicago River.

Leave. Run. Now.

The little voice inside my head that has been my only confidante and companion my entire life screams at me, begging to be heard, but I shove it aside and push myself up from the bench on shaky legs, my heels only making it harder for me to find my balance.

Or maybe it's the nerves.

Acid churns in my stomach as I reach behind me to the zipper of my skirt and slowly tug it down. His eyes never leave me, watching every move keenly, like he's searching for something he isn't sure if he's seeing or not. With shaking hands, I grasp the hem of my tank top and tug it up and over my head, freeing my breasts to the slightly cool air. My nipples pebble immediately, both from the chill and from his assessment.

It already feels like this man stripped me bare the other night, but now, as I nudge down my skirt, I truly am exposed.

His brow furrows as he takes in my body and the pink, puckered scars crisscrossing my abdomen before his gaze darts up to meet mine again. "Who did this to you?"

I shake my head, forcing myself not to tell the truth. "Car accident. Years ago..."

He steps forward and grazes a finger across one of the scars, making my body tense. "This doesn't look old. Don't lie to me."

The warning is there in his words, and I meet his gaze.

"Car accident...what *feels* like a long time ago."

If he knows I'm lying, he doesn't call me out on it. Instead, he takes a step back, pulling my hand into his. He tugs me across the room and over to the cross, pushing my back against the wood with a strong palm to my chest.

A tiny gasp slips from my lips, and he raises an eyebrow at me.

"Do you know how this works, Julia?"

I nod. "I think so."

"You will give me a safe word. A word you only use if you want me to stop, and I will. So only use it if you really mean it."

Only one word comes to mind while staring into the fathomless depths of his blue eyes. "Mercy."

Something tells me he won't give it to me.

He leans in, his lips feathering against my ear. "There will be times you'll beg me to stop, but you won't really want me to. I need to know the difference."

Fucking hell...

I clench my thighs together against the throb of my clit, and his gaze slowly lowers to that spot. "Spread your legs."

Heat pools there at his command, and I step my heeled feet out, air hitting the moisture already forming at the apex of my thighs.

Valerian steps back and bends down to secure the restraints at the bottom of the cross, then he rises and grips both my wrists, jerking them up and out across the top to fasten them there.

The light clink of each one falling into place makes me flinch slightly.

This is such a bad idea.

You don't trust him.

Not really.

You shouldn't.

Not with what you know.

Not with who he is or what he will do to you when he finds out why you're here.

But I also can't say no to him when so much depends on what happens tonight, on where this might lead.

He retreats slightly and examines me spread out in front of him, a glint of something in his eye sucking all the heat from the room and replacing it with an icy coolness that raises goosebumps over my skin.

"You look stunning, Julia, and now, I have you right where I want you."

EIGHT

JULIA

His words sound more like a threat than a promise, and the ice they send through my veins almost makes me yell the word that will end all this before it even starts. Yet I bite it back—not only because my body is screaming for it, but also because I need something from him, something more, and this may be the only way to get it.

Valerian walks over to a black cabinet against the wall and opens it, then steps back, holding a red leather flogger. My body tenses, the restraints suddenly feeling tighter, even more restrictive, and I try to shift but am unable to move.

I'm completely powerless to this man who has killed dozens and likely ordered the deaths of hundreds. A man who would, undoubtedly, add me to that list if he discovers my true intent.

He glances over his shoulder at me with a smirk, then reaches in to grab something else, which he slips into his back pocket as he turns to face me so I can't see what it is. "Since this is your first time, I should go easy on you. *Should* being the operative word, but after our conversation the other night, I don't think that's what you want, is it, Julia? You don't want easy, do you?"

"I don't know what I want."

Valerian stops in front of me and grips my chin between his fingers harshly, forcing my gaze to meet his. "I appreciate the honesty, *kotyonok*. That's the only way this works, you know—complete honesty."

It's almost like he's calling me out, giving me an opening to come clean. I suck in a heavy breath and nod even though I haven't been honest with him about hardly anything since I walked in here the first time.

Nothing really...

Except for when we were sitting on the couch. I was honest then, and now, the truth sits heavy in my throat, threatening to choke me.

I swallow it back.

It's too soon.

Things are too uncertain.

I have to ensure other things are firmly cemented before I can make the final move.

A devious grin grows on his face. "I like that look of fear in your eyes."

¡Qué chimbada!

He takes a step back, and his hand whips out, the tails of the flogger striking against my inner thigh. I jerk against the bindings, the sting sizzling across my skin and making my core clench. But spread open like this, I can't press my legs together.

There's no relief.

No way to ease it.

My need or the bite from the flogger.

He watches my reaction, enjoys seeing me squirm, and shifts, only instead of striking me again, he drops to his knees and drags his tongue across the red mark on my thigh.

So close to where I want him.

Where I *need* him.

Arousal pools between my legs, my entire body heating with each stroke of his tongue against my sensitive flesh.

He lifts his head and looks up at me, something sinister dancing in his gaze. "You're at my mercy like this, Julia. I have so many ideas, so many things I long to do to you."

Somehow, I manage to find words despite the way the heat of his breath against my wet pussy is making me almost mindless. "Like what?"

"If I told you, that would ruin the fun."

He dips his head and glides his tongue through my core, making me gasp and tug against the restraints. But all too soon, he's gone, rising to his feet, leaving me wanting more, needing more.

Exactly his intent.

Without warning, he strikes again, the flogger hitting the inside of the other thigh and making me jerk again.

"That doesn't hurt, does it, Julia?"

I take a deep breath and shake my head. "No, not really."

The burn of the strike isn't exactly painful. It's more like a spark threatening to ignite an inferno than anything bad.

He drops to his knees again and licks the spot, one strong hand squeezing my thigh while the other takes the flogger's handle and drags the tip of it through my slit.

"¡Dios mío!"

The words tumble from my lips and earn a soft chuckle against my skin, and he pulls the flogger back, my arousal glistening on it under the warm, sensual lighting. He swirls his tongue across it, a low, contented moan rumbling in his chest before he pushes to his feet again.

His third strike lands on my abdomen, just above my crotch, and I groan this time, the sting a little harsher against the damaged nerve endings of the scars there.

He presses his hand to it to help ease the bite, and his fingers almost reverently stroke over the raised pinkish-red flesh. "I won't let anything like this happen to you again. Do you understand?"

I nod sharply, though I really don't understand what he means.

He won't let pain happen to me again?

He won't let a car accident happen to me again?

He won't let another man touch me like this again?

The words can be taken so many different ways. Each of them more concerning than the last.

He skates the handle of the flogger up my inner thigh and pushes it inside me. My mouth falls open with a groan, and I squeeze my eyes closed, my body tightening and heating in a way I've never experienced before. It's only *just* inside me, barely an inch, but I clasp around it, needing more.

His lips ghost over my cheek and reach my ear. "Tell me what you want, Julia, and not the answer you gave me the other night. Tell me what you want in this exact moment. Right here. Right now."

"You. Your..."

"Say it!" He nudges the handle inside me a little farther. "Open your eyes and look at me when you say it."

I let my eyelids flicker open to meet his lustful gaze. "Your cock inside me."

A dark grin tilts his lips, and he reaches down, only he doesn't unbutton his pants, doesn't free his hard cock I can see pressing against the front of them. Instead, he goes to his back pocket and brings up a small silver cylinder. He twists his fingers on it, and the vibrations begin.

My breath catches. "No. Please...I don't know if I can—"

He presses it against my clit, and my mouth falls open on a silent gasp as my body jerks, the orgasm hitting me immediately—so fast and so hard that the entire room around us disappears in a flash of bright light.

The restraints at my hands and feet keep me upright as convulsions roll through me while he uses his other hand to pump the end of the goddamn flogger inside me.

My pussy clamps and ripples around the tiny bit he's inserted, seeking more.

"Oh, God. Oh, God..."

He keeps the vibrator pressed to my clit, ensuring the orgasm drags on and on—almost endlessly—until I'm so sensitive it hurts.

"Stop, God. Stop! I can't take—I can't—"

"You can."

He nips at my ear and alters the angle of the buzzing device against me, bringing on another orgasm—this one so deep inside me it feels like it's tearing me apart from the inside out.

"Fu—"

My ability to speak disappears, washed away on a flood of ecstasy. He kisses my cheek, then pulls the flogger from inside me while my body still twists and contorts with the vibrator pressed to it.

A second later, the harsh, fast rustle of fabric is quickly followed by the head of his cock dragging through my release. I mewl at the tease, and he withdraws the vibrator and shoves up into me in one harsh thrust.

"Fucking Christ!" My body seizes at the sensation, struggling to accept his size and the abrupt intrusion, my head dropping back against the wood behind me.

He growls low, his hot chest pressed to mine, and drags back his hips to plunge into me again.

"*U tebya takaya tugaya kiska.*" He cups my face in his calloused palm, jerking my face to his. "You're fucking exquisite, Julia."

Every drag of his hips and grind of his pelvis against my hypersensitive clit sends my body spiraling in a new direction, sensations I never even knew existed before cascading through me, threatening to destroy me. He thrusts into me like the madman everyone knows he is, desperately searching for his release as my body struggles against another one coming.

"I can't...Oh, God, I can't...Stop."

"You don't want me to stop."

I don't. I do.

I—

"No, I don't." I shake my head back and forth, thrashing against the bindings as he redoubles his efforts, driving up into me, pushing me toward another orgasm. "Come for me, *kotyonok*. You can."

Trust after thrust, he forces me toward that ultimate cataclysm until it finally happens and my breath is ripped from my lungs on a scream so loud they can probably hear it in the club despite the soundproofing and the music.

Valerian roars and empties himself into me, my clenching pussy dragging hot spurts of cum from his cock. His motions become erratic, and he sags slightly against my heated, twitching body, then pulls his head back, lifting my chin.

"Open your eyes, Julia."

I do, and he locks his gaze with mine, holding it in an unwavering stare that's made of a thousand questions. He doesn't say a word, just eventually takes a step back, letting his cock slip from inside me.

He glances down at the blood and jerks his head back up to meet my gaze. "Are you a virgin?"

I'm so exhausted that I can't even answer him. I just let my eyes drift closed, and my body finally gives in to the sleep it wants so badly.

NINE

VALERIAN

I TAKE a puff of my cigar, letting the smoke fill my lungs and the nicotine race through my blood, then slowly release it. It curls up toward the ceiling of my office, and I allow my gaze to follow it—the first time I've dragged my eyes off the woman passed out on my couch since I cleaned her up and brought her in here an hour ago.

Aside from the steady rise and fall of her chest, she's barely moved, but after *that*, it doesn't surprise me she's passed out so hard.

She was a fucking virgin.

I shake my head. Here I thought we were just toying with the word, making a joke of the fact that it was her first time here at *Gluttony* and partaking in this type of play. I never thought she actually *meant* it.

If I had known, I never would have touched her.

Never.

There is gluttony and then there is *gluttony.* Sinking my cock into a young woman who has been saving herself for someone, for *something* special how I did is certainly the latter.

She deserved better—than this. Than me.

I let my gaze drift over her soft features—perfect pink bow lips slightly parted, flawless, lightly tanned skin covering high cheekbones, the dyed blond hair falling over her forehead.

Fucking hell.

So young.

So innocent.

And I defiled her.

My cock stirs to life again remembering being inside her, how tight and hot her cunt was clasping around me so greedily.

Blyad!

A good man would feel some guilt about what happened, but no one has ever accused me of being one of those. Instead, pride blooms in my chest at knowing I was her first, that no one else ever touched her like that, ever gave her that release. Knowing I was the one who helped her get what she said she wanted the other night only makes my cock harder.

I take a sip of my vodka and lean back in my chair, watching her sleep.

Peaceful.

Relaxed.

Content.

I can't even remember the last time I slept like that—maybe not ever. Certainly not in the last few years with all the unrest. And given the uncertainty still lingering, a good night's sleep doesn't seem like it will come anytime soon.

And if I leave Julia on the couch all night, she'll wake up even more sore than she already will be. I need to get her back home—wherever that is.

I down the rest of my drink, snuff out my cigar, and push to my feet. Even after already coming so hard inside her, my body craves more. Being with this woman was the first time I've felt any sort of relief from the tension and stress that's weighed down on me recently. And I want more of it. More of her. No matter how dangerous it might be to get involved with her right now.

Dangerous.

Stupid.

Self-destructive.

All those and then some.

I slowly walk over to the couch and squat next to it, brushing her blond locks back from her face. The soft, silky texture juxtaposed with my rough fingers is a strong reminder of how different we are, of how *wrong* this is.

Chto ya delayu?

Being a selfish bastard...

I refuse to let her go. She won't walk away like she did the other night. Not now. Not ever. Not again.

A soft knock comes from the door, and Dmitri pushes in. His eyes dart from her curled up on the couch to me.

"I told you I wasn't to be interrupted."

He raises his hand in apology. "I'm sorry, *pakhan*, but we need to talk."

This better be fucking good.

Reluctantly, I follow him into the hallway lined with the variously themed private playrooms, pulling the door to my office closed behind me so we don't disrupt the beautiful woman passed out on my couch.

He glances up and down it to ensure we're alone. "One of Galen's shipments was just hit again."

"What?"

"A caravan of trucks coming from the docks."

"Was he with it?"

Dmitri shakes his head. "No, but it seems like it was a bit of a bloodbath. And they took two trucks worth of weapons. He called, looking for you, but I told them you were indisposed."

He glances toward the office, and I scrub a hand over my face, the smell of her cunt still on my skin, making my cock twitch again.

"Did he say who it was?"

"No." Dmitri shakes his head. "He's not certain, but he thinks it was the Luna Cartel. It was their M.O."

"How the fuck can it be Luna? They don't have anyone left after what we did in that warehouse."

Dmitri shrugs. "Perhaps more men came up from Mexico? We're still trying to figure out where the bomb came from, could be one of their guys south of the border. If it was their leader who got away that night, they might be rebuilding to seek revenge for the warehouse attack."

Revenge.

"Then they'll be coming for us, too."

Just what I fucking need.

Genti will have run straight back to Kat to tell her what we did to him, which means she's going to have a stick up her ass even *more* and want to come at me. Coupled with the hit squad running around town, that's enough of a threat. The Luna Cartel after me because I helped Galen means fighting on three fronts at the same time.

Splitting resources and trying to keep our eyes in so many different directions means things could slip through the cracks, things that could very well be deadly to me and anyone close to me.

Including the woman in my office.

"Okay." I scrub my hands over my face again and sigh. "Make sure she gets home safely. I have to talk to Galen in person so we can try to formulate a plan." I start to walk away, then turn back. "But leave a man on her."

"*Pakhan?*" He raises an eyebrow in question. "Why?"

I stare at the closed door in my office. "She's a target now. I want someone on her twenty-four-seven, and I need to know *everything* about that woman. Where she goes. Who she talks to. What she eats. Where she shops. Everything she does." I lock my gaze with his. "I don't want eyes off her for even a moment, do you understand?"

He nods sharply. "*Da, pakhan.*"

"And make sure she doesn't know she's being watched."

After what I just did to her, I'm the last person she's going to want to see, and if she finds out I have someone assigned to keep tabs on her, she isn't the type of girl to appreciate it.

I have to deal with this Galen situation and get my head screwed back on properly because that woman has thrown me completely off my game.

A fucking virgin...

This isn't the time to have my mind wrapped up in that woman and what I did. If I'm not focused, I'll pay for it—likely painfully.

TEN

JULIA

EVEN TWO DAYS LATER, my body still aches from my night at the club with Valerian. My mind keeps dragging me back there, too—to that time, that space, to his touch, the feel of his lips and hands on me, his cock driving into me relentlessly.

I clench my legs together against the throb I've had to self-relieve so many times already that it's almost embarrassing. The lingering hints of pain and the red welts still on my body can't deter me from wanting more, from wanting it again, from wanting *him* despite all the reasons it's a horrible idea to ever go back, to have ever gone there in the first place.

But I've never felt that like, never acted like that—so needy, so wanton. It felt...powerful knowing that even though I was restrained, I was also in control and could stop him at any time.

Maybe that was his intent all along when he said he was giving me what I said I wanted. He saw I had no control over my life, and he gave it to me where I could have it.

It would have been perfect had I not let him see all of me, even the scars that no one else ever has—the ones I've kept well hidden. They didn't scare him away, didn't send him running. They only seemed to draw him closer, make him more possessive, more determined.

And now, after everything that happened that night, I have to watch my back even more. I have to be sure I'm always aware because this is when things get really dangerous. The time is coming when there will be no more hiding behind fake names and dyed hair, when all the cards will be on the table and the past will rear its ugly head to potentially destroy everything I've worked for.

That can't happen.

I slip into the black jeans and off-the-shoulder sweater and glance at my watch. If I'm going to make my meeting, I need to leave now. I hustle through the living room, grab my purse off the counter, and step out of the condo, throwing the lock behind me.

This place has never felt like home; it's a temporary answer to a problem. A place for me to rest my head even though I barely sleep anymore. The nightmares and the visions of everything I still need to accomplish constantly combine to make me restless. The other night only exacerbated my nerves. Too many pieces are in play, too many things can go wrong. But despite this not being my home, every time I leave it, a knot forms in my stomach. It might not be home, but it provides some modicum of safety.

No matter how false it might be.

Out here, in this city, in this *world*, anything can happen.

It's a harsh lesson I learned at a very young age. Something that has served me well to remember every day of the life that has become so complicated that I don't know what direction it's going.

I certainly never expected it to lead me to a place where I'd be in the arms of Valerian Kamenev. Where I'd be facing down danger in a man built like a linebacker who fucks like a god.

Or at least, I think he did.

Without anything to compare it to, I don't really have a frame of reference. I just know it definitely wasn't how I saw my first time being when I imagined it over the years. He wasn't the kind of man I saw giving myself to. And not like *that*. This life wasn't anything I ever could have created in my own head.

Until that day changed everything...

Until I woke up in that hospital bed, torn apart, in agony.

Until all the uncertainties and lies ripped me in two.

Until I had to become something else.

And this meeting is just another necessary step to bring my plans to fruition.

I make my way down the stairs and out the front door onto the street. The crisp fall air the city is named for whirls around me, sending my hair flying in my face.

Tires squeal on the road to my left, and I turn toward the sound, brushing the blond strands out of my eyes as a set of strong arms grabs me and drags me backward across the sidewalk.

No. No. No!

I try to kick at the man's shins and scratch at any exposed skin, anything to get the assailant off me, but he wrestles me easily into the back of the vehicle waiting at the curb. He pushes me against the leather seat, pinning me down, keeping me prone as we tear away from the curb with more squealing tires that seem to be sealing my fate.

This is what they warned me about, what they always tried to keep me insulated from. I've become a target, and now, our enemies have found what they've been searching for—a bargaining chip.

They'll take me and use me any way they can to get what they want.

Over my dead fucking body.

I've worked too hard for too long and suffered too much to be used as a pawn in the game these people play. I refuse to lose control again. The weight on me makes it almost impossible to move, but I twist until one of my eyes sees flesh. I shift my head and bite down as hard as I can.

"Fuck."

The familiar voice fills the space, and I freeze as he jerks his hand back. I lift my head and shove the hair from my eyes again. Valerian's gaze meets mine. Ice cold. He shakes his hand out, my teeth marks still in the fleshy part of his palm. But despite the pain I must have caused him, a smirk slowly spreads across his face. A look of amusement breaking that ice-cold gaze.

"Very good, Julia." He inclines his head toward me. "Though, letting yourself get dragged into a vehicle wasn't very smart."

I lash out at him with my foot, landing the kick squarely against his shin.

"Fuck." He curses and rubs at it. "That hurt, *kotyonok*."

My chest heaves with my anger, my fists at my sides, ready to lash out at him again. "What the hell are you thinking? Snatching me off the street like that?"

He releases a heavy sigh and leans back across the plush leather seats, any discomfort I may have caused him easily forgotten. "I didn't think you would come if I invited you."

"You're probably right. Especially after a move like that."

I huff and cross my arms over my chest, but it only earns a grin from him.

His tongue darts out across his lower lip. "I'm going to quite enjoy this."

"Enjoy what? Having me kick you in the balls the next time?"

His eyes heat, the ice melting away instantly. The flame of lust that matches what was there the other night taking over. "Taking you out to dinner and then back to my place."

I scoff and shake my head. "You think I'm going to go to dinner with you or let you touch me again after you just kidnapped me off the street?"

His grin only spreads. "You think you have any choice?"

ELEVEN

VALERIAN

JULIA GLARES at me from across the table as the waitress sets our meals in front of us.

I smile at the redheaded woman who has served me for years and incline my head. "Thank you."

She returns my smile and glances between Julia and me, her gaze lingering on my date a bit longer than is comfortable. It's rare that I'm here with anyone other than Dmitri or one of the other guys, so her interest in my companion is warranted.

"Is there anything else I can get you?"

"We're good." I shake my head. "Just some privacy, please."

With a little half-bow, she backs away, understanding exactly what I mean. That's the entire reason I requested this table in the back corner of *Kachka*, one of my favorite restaurants in my territory. No one questions me here, and they know to keep their mouths shut about anything they see or hear.

I return my focus to Julia, who hasn't spoken a word since we arrived. "Are you going to give me the silent treatment all evening?"

Julia's lips twist slightly as she looks down at her plate.

"I ordered pelmeni for you since you didn't want to make your own choice. I think you'll enjoy it. Kind of like Russian ravioli."

She leans forward and sniffs at the bowl doubtfully, unwilling to wipe the scowl from her beautiful lips.

"You know, your anger isn't going to deter me, *kotyonok*." I lean slightly closer to her and drop my voice. "It's only going to get my cock even harder."

A pink flush quickly spreads across her cheeks, and she shifts uneasily in her seat, glancing around us to ensure no one can hear me.

"It's quite private back here, Julia. I assure you—we can speak freely."

"You want me to speak freely?" Her eyebrows rise. "Because I don't think you're going to like what I have to say."

I chuckle and take a bite of my shashlik. *Kachka* has the best marinade, and the flavors practically dance in my mouth, bringing memories of home I usually struggle to keep buried. Swallowing, I wash it down with a sip of wine. "I very much would love to know what goes on in that head of yours, Julia. So, please, fill me in."

She gives me a tight smile. "I think you're used to getting everything you want and don't care how you get it. You could have just, oh, I don't know, *asked* me out to dinner. But instead, you snatched me off the street like a common criminal."

My barked laugh draws the attention of the waitress near the kitchen door, but I wave her off as she tries to approach and lean against the table, resting my elbow. "I have a surprise for you, Julia. In case you haven't noticed, I *am* a criminal."

Annoyance flashes in her bourbon eyes, and she presses her lips together in a firm line. "Well, yes, of course, you are, but—"

"But what?"

"But you didn't have to do *that*."

I take another sip of my wine and turn the glass in my fingers, watching the liquid spin inside as I consider her words. "I was worried that after the other night, you wouldn't want to see me again."

At her silence, I chance a glance up at her, to find her staring at me with wide eyes.

"Why?"

"Because of how I treated you."

"How you *treated* me?" Her brow furrows. "I'm not quite following you."

It appears she's going to make me *say* it, spell it out for her in words that leave no room for misunderstandings, no matter how uncomfortable the topic may be.

"If I had known you were..." I don't finish the sentence—the word feeling almost sacrilegious to speak under the circumstances. "I wouldn't have done what I did."

Her flush darkens even more. She squirms again, the topic of conversation as unpleasant for her as it is for me. "I'm an adult, Valerian. Not a child you have to try to protect."

"You're partially right. You're certainly not a child. *Definitely* all woman." The memory of her cunt clasping around my cock, her gasps and moans of pleasure, the way she begged for it, all fill my head. "But you're young and naïve. And you believe you're invincible. That nothing and no one can harm you. You couldn't be more wrong, *kotyonok*."

She considers my words and the several layers of meaning within them. Then, instead of responding, she takes her first bite from the meal I ordered for her.

Her eyes widen slightly, and her little moan of approval makes my cock harden. "This is good."

"I told you I would never do anything that isn't good for you."

She snorts, the sound so un-lady-like that it makes me grin. "I can tell you right now that snatching me off the street isn't good for me."

"Did you have somewhere else to be? Another date, perhaps?"

Even saying the words makes my hand fist around the knife I had raised to cut my next bite. This type of possessiveness has never overtaken me before. I've never cared about the women I've fucked, never given a shit who or what else they do when we aren't together, but it's different with the young woman sitting across from me.

It has been from the first second she stepped into *Gluttony*.

Her gaze zeroes in on my grip on the knife. "No. Nothing like that. Just an appointment I needed to keep."

"Well..." I relax slightly, cutting a piece of meat with a little more force than necessary. "My apologies. I'm happy to pay for any fee you incur due to my actions."

She drums her nails on the table, and my eyes drift to her exposed shoulder blade peeking out from the loose gray sweater.

"Did I tell you that you look beautiful tonight?"

"No, you didn't."

"*Takoy zhenshchine kak ty nuzhno keazhdyy den' govorit' kak ona prekrasna.*"

Her lips twist in confusion. "What does that mean?"

I grin at her. "If I told you, that would ruin the fun."

She offers me a saccharine sweet fake smile. "*Tienes razón. Eso arruinaría la diversión. Cómo yo podría decirte que eres un imbécil arrogante y tú ni lo sabrías.*"

"Touché, *kotyonok*."

We both dig into our meals, Julia clearly enjoying what I've chosen for her.

"I grew up on those, you know. Ate them almost every day."

"Really?" Her eyebrows rise. "Did you grow up in Russia?"

Her question takes me slightly off guard, my back stiffening. It isn't something I talk about with anyone. And I hadn't expected her to ask anything so personal, especially after the fury she's thrown at me since I pulled her into the car.

I take another bite as I consider my answer and how to keep her from prying any deeper. "I was born there. But my father died when I was quite young, a casualty of the business. I have seven brothers and sisters, and my mother couldn't care for all of us properly on her own. So, she sent me to live with her brother, my uncle, here in Chicago."

She stops eating and watches me closely. "How old were you?"

"Seven."

A look of sympathy flashes in her bourbon eyes. "That must have been very difficult for you. A bit of culture shock?"

"No." I shrug nonchalantly, trying not to get lost in the bad memories of what it was like back home before I left or what it was like here when I first arrived. There isn't any time to get drawn into those emotions, and she's the last person I want to expose them to. "I was surrounded by my uncle and his family, his men, his crew. The bratva accepted me into their fold. It almost felt like living in Russia at times."

"But it wasn't home..."

"It wasn't, and it still isn't."

"Would you ever go back?"

I grin at her question. "And give up all this?" I drop my utensils and spread my hands wide. "I've worked far too hard to ever leave."

She nods slowly and takes another bite, considering my words. "What if you were forced out?"

My knife stills on my plate, and I lift my gaze to meet hers again. "Quite the odd question to ask, *kotyonok*. Do you know something I don't?"

Fear darkens her eyes for a moment, but she quickly smiles and shakes her head. "No. I just know you have a very dangerous business that you love and wouldn't willingly walk away from."

Nice recovery.

"That I do. Which is why I intend to keep you safe from it."

I don't want to elaborate because something tells me if she knew my intent, I'd have to drag her out of here kicking and screaming instead of walking out hand in hand and ravishing her in the limo on the way back to her place like I had planned.

Sometimes, it's better if people are left in the dark.

The truth can hurt.

The truth can ruin everything.

TWELVE

VALERIAN

Dᴍɪᴛʀɪ ʙᴜʀsᴛs through my office door, a grin on his face and a stack of papers in his hand. "We have something."

"What do you mean?"

"Cutter's guy came through."

I scowl at him, and he holds up a hand before I can interject my annoyance.

"I know. I'm still trying to find somebody to handle this type of shit for us who we can trust, but in the meantime, we need to work with what we have, right?"

It isn't completely his fault that he's having trouble locating someone who can do this kind of work for us. The last guy I had failed so miserably that I took him out in a way that would send a message. Apparently, it was one everyone got since no one wants to come work for me.

I release a heavy sigh. "What do you have?"

He approaches the desk and slaps down the papers. "IDs, real names of all the men on that flight out of Vlorë."

"Seriously?"

He nods. "Cutter's guy ran them through facial rec software and did some other...I don't know... techie shit...and came up with these files on all the guys."

Finally.

Something we can go off of.

"Good, then we should be able to figure out who they're working for."

Dmitri's smile falters, and he shifts awkwardly on his feet on the other side of my desk. "That question isn't as easy as who they are."

"Why the fuck not?"

He shakes his head. "Because, like Genti told us, things have been in flux over there. Especially after Kat made her little visit and Berisha and Dragusha ended up full of bullet holes. They've kept a low profile since then. There were even rumors they died, but their crews certainly haven't slowed down at all. They've been busy expanding their reach and diversifying their businesses."

"So Genti was right. It could be them?"

"As much as it could be Kat. Turn to page fifteen."

I flip through the stack and stare at a photograph of one of the men who attacked the church— *Aron Kadare. Affiliation—Gashi.*

Dmitri inclines his head toward the page. "We know he was one of Aleksander's men. But that was years ago, before The Dragon came to Chicago to take over after Konstandin Morina killed Saban here. He could be working for anyone now."

"Including that cunt Kat." I shove the papers off my desk and watch them flutter to the floor. "Fucking useless. All of this is useless. If we can't get what we need from here, then we need someone on the ground over there. Someone who can get us some real information. Who do we have who might be close?"

"Roan is in Odesa. He could get there quickly with a few men we can rely on."

"Do it...and tell him to be quiet about it. The last thing we need is any of the other families getting wind that we're sending people in to investigate locally."

Galen already suggested I could be involved with all this, and finding out my men are running around Albania would only reinforce that belief.

Heavy footsteps sound behind Dmitri in the hall, and Aleksei rushes into the office, out of breath, eyes wide. "*Pakhan*, we have a problem."

My chest tightens, and I grit my teeth. "What now?"

"We had Ilya on Julia today, and she went into a shop down the street from her house..."

"And?"

He rubs at the back of his neck, averting his gaze from me. "And he lost her."

"What do you mean he *lost* her?"

How the fuck does one lose *someone? Especially a tiny woman like that...*

"Well, a minute or two after she went in, he went in after her, and she wasn't inside."

"Shit. So, she ditched him?"

"It gets worse."

"How could it possibly get worse?"

Aleksei glances away again. "After he searched the place for her, he stepped out onto the street to call us, and someone managed to knock him to the ground and pin him down with a knee on his neck and an armbar."

Dmitri's eyes widen. "What the fuck?"

He winces. "It was Julia."

Holy hell.

"She demanded to know why he was following her and who he was working for. And it wasn't very pretty when he told her the answer. He came back bloody."

"Shit."

Aleksei offers a tight smile that holds no humor. "She's here."

I raise a brow at him. "Now?"

He nods.

"Fucking hell." This isn't something I can ignore or put off until later. Julia won't wait, and expecting her to will only allow her anger to grow. It's best if I address this head-on and explain to her why it was necessary. "Both of you go and let her in."

One of Aleksei's dark eyebrows rises. "Are you sure, *pakhan?* She looks pretty fucking pissed."

I scowl at him. "You think keeping her out there is going to relieve any of that? Send her in."

Dmitri offers me one final sympathetic look, then leaves with Aleksei at his side, pulling the door closed behind him.

This is definitely not how I wanted any of this to go. The guys are usually so good at remaining inconspicuous. It couldn't have come at a worse time. Things were tense at dinner, but she had finally started to thaw by the time I dropped her off at her place last night. I knew she wouldn't let me touch her in the car, and I respected her boundaries on that. But now, any progress I made getting her to open up to me has been wiped away because Ilya was a fucking idiot and couldn't remain hidden.

I sit back and brace myself for Hurricane Julia to enter.

It doesn't take long to feel her energy approaching.

The door flies open, slamming against the wall, and she storms in, her eyes blazing with rage. Her sweet lips, the ones I've been dying to taste but have somehow restrained myself from taking thus far, twist with her rage. "You have some fucking nerve, Valerian."

"It's nice to see you, too, *kotyonok*." I smile at her. "I trust you slept well?"

She strides toward the desk and slams her palms down on it. "You *asshole*! Why were you having me followed?"

"Because being with me makes you a target, whether you want to be or not."

Her brow furrows. "Who says I'm *with* you?"

Feisty as always.

This kitten has some bite.

"Before our dinner last night, I wasn't so sure. But I am now. Just like I told you the other night, I won't let anything bad happen to you. And that requires me to know what you're doing every moment of every day."

She points a finger at me. "First, I don't belong to anyone. No one fucking *owns* me. Second, I don't need your protection, as I just proved when I took down that moron you had following me and smashed his face into the sidewalk. Third, if you *ever* pull shit like this again, you're going to pay the price for it."

I can't fight the grin that pulls up my lips as I rise from my chair and slowly make my way around the desk toward her. Her chest rises and falls rapidly at my approach. Her anger and her fear darken her eyes and tighten her fists at her sides.

Stopping just in front of her, I reach up and rub the strands of her blond hair between my fingers. "I like you like this, *kotyonok*." I release her hair and take her face between my palms. "So feisty with your claws out."

She scowls at me again, trying unsuccessfully to pull away from my hold. "You're not going to like it when you get cut by them."

"Oh, I will." Leaning closer, I feather my lips against her cheek. "A little pain always makes the pleasure better."

A shudder rolls through her body—no doubt the memory of being together the other night flickering through her head the same way it does mine.

"That's something I'm more than ready to show you more of, *kotyonok*."

"*Pakhan?*" Dmitri's voice is like a bucket of ice-cold water being thrown over me.

"Oh, for the love of fucking Christ." I turn toward the open door and find Dmitri standing there with a phone in his hand. "*What?*"

"It's Galen. He says it's an emergency."

Fuck.

I point toward him. "Give me a second."

Dmitri nods and moves down the hallway, far enough away that he can't hear us anymore.

Julia continues to gaze up at me, her anger not fully quelled but somehow subdued. "That sounds like it's important."

"Not as important as you are." I tighten my grip on her. "I need you to understand that everything I do is to protect you, to ensure your safety, because I can't be distracted, worrying about you with everything else I have going on."

She considers me for a moment, eyes softening before she tilts her head and presses her lips to my palm. "Okay.

The vise around my chest loosens slightly. "We're good?"

Some of the rage she carried in here seems to have evaporated, either with my words or my touch. "We're good."

I drop my head and press my lips to hers for the first time.

Our first real kiss.

My first taste of her mouth.

Something I've been holding off doing for so long that it feels like an eternity has passed since I first saw these lips pressed to that glass at the bar, downing a double shot of tequila.

She issues a little mewl and clutches at my shirt, dragging me even closer. I sweep my tongue across her lips, and she opens for me, tangling her own with mine as our bodies mold against each other, my cock pinned between us.

"Hhmhm." Dmitri clears his throat in the hall.
I pull back reluctantly, staring into her lust-soaked eyes. "I'll be right back."
As quickly as possible because I have plans.
Big ones.

THIRTEEN

JULIA

VALERIAN TAKES the phone from Dmitri and disappears into one of the playrooms down the hall while his right-hand man steps back into the main club, leaving me alone in Valerian's office.

My heart thunders against my chest, my breaths coming short and fast—though I don't know whether it's because I just threatened him like that, because of the kiss, or because of what he promised. Maybe all three.

Regardless, I don't have time to wonder and think about it because this might be the only chance I'll have to get what I need. I hustle around the desk, slide into Valerian's chair, and fire up his computer. My fingers fly over the keyboard as I keep my eye on the door for any signs of someone approaching.

This isn't how I imagined this going down, but I have to take advantage of any opportunity I can get when it comes to Valerian Kamenev.

Accessing his computer has proven harder than I ever imagined. The man is smart enough not to connect it to the internet so it can't be hacked, which means *this* is the only way to get inside—to physically sit at his desk, in his office, deep within *his* club, with him only a dozen yards down the hall.

Sweat breaks out across my forehead as I easily get past his password screen and into his files. No real security here. And why would he have or need any when he's never leave anyone he doesn't trust alone in his office...

I slip the tiny flash drive from my pocket and slide it into a USB port to start duplicating his hard drive as I scroll through the files, trying to locate what I need. One folder name makes me freeze, and I quickly click on it. My eyes dart across the individual file names until they land on one that makes bile climb up to the back of my throat.

Oh, hell...

A door closes in the hallway, and I jerk back and quickly exit out of all the screens, but the files aren't done downloading yet.

¡Ay hijueputa!

I shift some papers from the desk over the drive to try to conceal it and rest my hand near it, ready to pull it from the computer as soon as I have what I need.

Footsteps approach, and Valerian comes into view, his eyes narrowed on me. "What are you doing, *kotyonok?*" He enters his office and pushes the door close behind him with a deafening click. "Need something?"

I offer him a sweet smile and pull my hand away from his computer. "Just waiting for you. I was going to check my email."

His dark brows slowly rise. "Check your email?"

"Yeah." I nod. "That meeting I missed last night...they were supposed to email me to reschedule."

He casually strolls around the desk and toward me, silent and deadly like a predator stalking his unsuspecting prey.

Feigning concern, I press my hand over my chest. "Is everything okay...with your phone call?"

Valerian nods as he casually leans against the desk, right next to where I sit in his chair. "For the moment, yes." He offers me a gentle smile. "Again, I'm very sorry you missed your important appointment last night."

¡Mierda!

I should stop bringing it up, so he'll stop asking about it. The last thing he needs to know is where I was going.

"It's okay." I spin the chair to face him. "Nothing urgent at all."

Certainly not more urgent than convincing Valerian I wasn't doing anything I wasn't supposed to in here while he was on the phone. I reach out and run my fingers across the top of his hand, where it's flattened against the desktop.

Heat crackles between us where our skin touches, that same spark that combusted into an inferno in the playroom.

As angry as I was with him last night, a huge part of me regretted the way we left things. I almost *wanted* him to bring me back here, to do to me what he did the other night. My body craved it even through my anger at what he had done. Or maybe *because* of my anger.

His hard gaze locks with mine. "What about *now*...any urgent, pressing business to attend to, *kotyonok?*"

I pull my bottom lip between my teeth and shake my head. "No."

His cock begins to swell against the black fabric of his pants, and my pussy clenches at the way his blue eyes darken to almost black. I reach out with my free hand and rub over the bulge, feeling his length stiffen even more under my palm.

He issues a little grunt, takes my other hand in his, and tugs me from the chair, then pushes me down to my knees in front of him. "Good, because I do have something pressing and urgent for you to take care of, *kotyonok.*"

I fight the desire to glance over at the computer where the tiny drive still sticks out, just barely visible from under the papers I tried to shove over it. If he looks over there, he'll know what I was doing. I'll be busted, and then, all this will be over.

Not just my plans but also *this.*

Whatever *this* is with Valerian.

Unexpected. Dangerous. Frantic.

I never expected to end up like this with him, but now that I'm here, I don't want it to end.

It can't.

I unbuckle his belt and slowly lower the zipper, keeping my eyes on his. Lust burns across the blue, igniting a fire deep in my belly for all the things I shouldn't want.

My mouth waters at the thought of what I'm about to do, and I free his cock, pulling his pants down to his mid-thighs. It juts out from his body—thick, heavy, a drop of pre-cum already beading at the tip.

I flick my tongue over it, the salty flavor making me moan in approval as he buries his hands in my hair.

"Fuck, *kotyonok*..."

Swirling my tongue around the head several times, I revel in the way his body stiffens. I inhale a deep breath and take him in my mouth, suctioning around his hot flesh.

I don't have a fucking clue what I'm doing. Watching a video is the closest I've ever come to doing this before, but given how tense his body is, his thighs rock hard, muscles straining, I must be doing something right.

That knowledge spurs me on, encourages me to keep going even when I feel like a bumbling idiot on my knees with this man who has no doubt had his cock sucked by women far more talented than I am.

Determination to be the best, to get him to lose control, overtakes me, and I suck him back as far as I can until I have to fight the reflex to gag. Something rumbles in his chest, and his grip on my hair tightens.

He tugs on it slightly to get me to look at him. "Have you ever done this before, *kotyonok*?"

I shake my head, his cock still buried in my throat, and something dark flashes in his eyes.

"Fucking hell..." He pushes his hips forward, driving himself even deeper. "Breathe through your nose, *kotyonok*."

Taking his advice, I inhale through my nose as he pushes more, the head of his cock hitting the back of my throat. I angle my head up more, allowing him to ease even farther down, and swallow.

"Jesus, fuck!"

He jerks on my hair and grits his jaw, then slowly pulls his hips back, drawing his cock from my mouth, glistening with my saliva. I swallow a few times, taking several deep breathes, and he presses his thumb across my lips.

"I'm going to come down your throat, and you're gonna swallow all of it. Understand?"

I nod.

"Good. Open."

He pushes his dick past my lips, and I glide my tongue along the underside of his length, swirling it as I go. A little choking sound falls from his mouth, and his hips begin to move, thrusting and forcing himself down my throat as I work him over with my tongue.

His movements become erratic, his hips bucking, the head of his cock hitting that soft spot deep down.

Heat pools between my legs even as I fight my gag reflex, not wanting to fail at this, not wanting to fail him. I swallow, letting my throat close around him, and suck as hard as I can until he finally barks out something in Russian and hot spurts of cum hit the back of my throat.

I swallow the best I can.

Salty yet sweet.

A flavor I didn't know I could love so much.

Finally, his hips still, and I open my eyes and look up at Valerian Kamenev. His cheeks slightly flushed. His chest moving up and down rapidly. He pulls one hand from my hair and reaches to his waistband for something.

The gun comes into my line of vision, his lips starting to curl into a smirk. "That was fucking magnificent, *kotyonok*." He points the barrel at my forehead, his cock still buried down my throat, my lips stretched around him. "What would your brothers think if they could see you now, Sofia Rose?"

CONSUMING GLUTTONY

Gluttony is an emotional escape, a sign something is eating us.

- Peter De Vries

ONE

VALERIAN

SOFIA STARES UP AT ME, the fear darkening her eyes and hardening my cock even more in her mouth. She swallows thickly around me. The rippling of her throat against my throbbing flesh and the tightening of her lips around me makes me bite back a groan even as I clench the grip on my gun with my right hand.

"Scared, *kotyonok*?"

She doesn't answer, but a single tear sneaks from the corner of her eye.

I brush it away with my thumb and grin at her. "You *should* be." Leaning down slightly, I bring my face and the gun closer to her. "Did you really think I wouldn't recognize you?" Twisting a strand of her blond hair around my finger, I tug on it sharply, making her lips tighten on my length abruptly. "Did you think this dye job and all the makeup would conceal your identity?"

The moment she appeared outside the club that night, standing in too-high heels in the middle of the alley, debating with herself whether she should attempt to come in or not, I recognized her on the surveillance camera. Even after almost dying with Galen, my heart still pounding in my chest, knowing the bomb that could have killed us rested in the backroom of the club, the heavy eyeliner, thick mascara, and hair color couldn't conceal the woman beneath it all—the *girl*, really.

Because even though she's an adult and was raised by two men who are just as ruthless and cold as I am, her innocence shines in her terrified gaze.

I slowly pull my hard cock from her throat so she can answer me. "As much as I truly enjoy the feeling of your mouth on me, *kotyonok*, it's time you spoke up and offered me an explanation for what the *fuck* you're doing here."

Given her prowess with computers, there isn't a doubt in my mind she was trying to get to something stored in mine that she couldn't retrieve from the outside. It was likely the very reason she came here in the first place.

I use the gun to nudge the pile of papers to the side, revealing a small, black drive plugged into the USB port.

Sofia's glassy eyes dart over to the damning item, and the swollen lips that just wrapped around my cock quiver. Her hands pressed against my bare thighs curl until her nails dig into my skin. "I didn't think you'd recognize me."

I smirk at her and use the barrel of my gun to brush the hair off her cheek. "I could never forget this face..."

"But..." Her mouth opens and closes a few times like she's trying to choose her words carefully. "But we never even *met*."

Rose never would have let their baby sister close enough to me for that to happen, and even though it was only a few moments from across the meeting space packed with the heads of all the major players in Chicago, my eyes immediately went to her the moment she entered with Cutter's group.

I shake my head. "Not formally, no, but believe me, *kotyonok*, I noticed you the moment you walked into that room. Even surrounded by all the animosity of the five families and their crews, I couldn't take my eyes off you." I glide my fingertips across her soft cheek. "You were so pure, so soft, while everyone else in that room was so hardened by the lives we live. I could see why Rose kept you locked away and hidden from all of us for so long."

Something flashes in her eyes, an anger the depth of which I haven't seen before from the young woman who has remained so in control of her emotions around me. "My brothers never wanted me to be part of this life. They never wanted me to have *any* life."

She said as much the other night—that they sheltered her and kept her wrapped in the veil of the church where Felipe hid. Given who her brothers are and how she must have grown up, it certainly makes sense that they'd do anything to keep her protected in a way that would seem crushing to Sofia, a woman who clearly has wants, needs, desires, and goals.

Grazing my thumb softly over her quivering lips, my cock twitches. "When you said that the other night, I knew exactly what you needed."

What happened in the playroom proved I was right.

Sofia has never been in control of her own life, has always had her brothers running it and making demands of her. When she disappeared after Cutter's raid on Rose's compound, everyone assumed she was hiding until she thought it was safe to return, but that wasn't the case at all.

She was hiding *from* them.

The only question is why.

What is your end game, Sofia?

I glance at the computer and motion toward the drive with the thing that could end her life with the simple twitch of my finger against the trigger. "Tell me, Sofia, why are you here? I can guess, but I'd rather hear it out of your sweet mouth."

She shifts on her knees in front of me, and her eyes dart to my weapon and the evidence of her attempted espionage. "I can't tell you that."

Even staring down death at the hands of one of her family's enemies, Sofia has more sass than is good for her.

I nudge her lips with the barrel of my gun. "It's cute that you think you have a choice in the matter, Sofia, but the moment you stepped into *Gluttony*, you entered my world. I'm in control here unless we're in one of the playrooms and your safe word means something. If you think for one moment that I'm going to let you walk out of here without finding out what you're up to, then you're far more naïve than I thought."

Confusion furrows her soft brow. "If you've known who I was this whole time, why didn't you just kill me? Why don't you just kill me now?"

I lean down and press my lips to the top of her head, into the silky dyed hair that couldn't conceal her identity. The light flowery scent that always seems to hang around her invades my breath. "Because playing with you is so much more fun—"

The door to the office flies open, and Sofia and I both whip our heads in that direction.

Dmitri's gaze darts between me and Sofia on her knees in front of me, my pants down and my hard cock still poised near her mouth. "I'm sorry, *pakhan*. We have a problem."

"Fucking handle it." The words said through my clenched jaw carry all the malice I hold for him in this moment. "Close the door, and don't interrupt me again."

My men can't know who Sofia is. They'll never understand why I let her walk in here and pretend to be someone else. Why I've given her access to the club and me.

They don't *need* to know.

They just need to obey orders—like the one I gave them to stay the fuck *out* of my office when I'm with her.

Dmitri shifts uneasily, glancing over his shoulder down the hallway back to the main club. "This needs your *personal* attention."

"The world better be fucking burning down."

"It kind of is, *pakhan*."

"Shit." I set my gun on the desk, tuck my cock back into my pants, and take Sofia's face between my palms. "Don't fucking move an inch while I'm gone."

It will be painful for her to remain on her knees on the hard concrete floor, but it's exactly what she needs to understand the magnitude of her situation.

I grab my gun, slip it back into the holster at my hip, and approach Dmitri at the door.

He glances over at Sofia kneeling behind the desk. "You're just going to leave her there like that?"

"Trust me, she's getting off easy."

There's a reason she lied about who she is, a reason she's here, and something tells me it's more than just breaking into my computer for information. As soon as I deal with whatever fire I need to put out, I'm going to find out what that reason is.

Pausing next to Dmitri, I glance over my shoulder at her before locking eyes with him. "Get Ivan to stand at the door and keep an eye on her. I don't want her to move a fucking inch."

Dmitri swallows thickly. "I would if I could."

"What do you mean?"

"Ivan is currently occupied."

"Doing what?"

His gaze darts toward Sofia again, and then he leans closer to me so she can't hear him. "Cutter Jackson has a gun to Ivan's forehead through the slot in the front door of the club."

"Fucking hell." I take one last look at the woman who could be the key to unraveling all of this. "We'll continue our conversation when I return, *kotyonok*."

If I don't end up pumped full of lead first.

TWO

VALERIAN

STORMING through the still and empty club, I make my way past Connie's hostess stand to where Yuri, Nikon, and Grigory wait near the door that leads out to the alley. Ivan stands with the barrel of what appears to be a Glock pressed against the middle of his forehead. Its barrel juts through the slit in the heavy metal that's supposed to protect us and prevent incidents like this from ever happening.

Fucking Cutter...

Ilya stands directly behind Ivan, gun drawn and pointed at the small hole where Ivan's life hangs in the balance. He glances my way as I approach.

I incline my head behind me. "Go back to my office and keep an eye on Julia."

His eyes widen slightly, and his mouth opens, perhaps about to argue over leaving his friend while he has a gun pressed to his head or maybe because the woman on her knees bested him—the evidence of which still mars his face. I lock my gaze with his, silently warning him against argument, and without complaint, he whirls and hustles past the other men and Dmitri and toward my office.

He and I will have a talk later about how easily he was taken down by a woman less than half his size, but there are more important issues to deal with right now.

I squeeze Ivan's shoulder and slowly urge him back from the threat. "Well, Mr. Jackson"—I push Ivan off to the side fully, putting my own forehead into the spot Ivan's once occupied, the barrel pushed to the skin—"it seems you've come to make a statement." I raise an eyebrow at him, staring at the reflective sunglasses he wears in an attempt to conceal the gnarly scars that mar the entire right side of his face. "But all you had to do is call if you wanted to chat."

He scowls at me, the scar across his cheek twisting down with his lips, making him appear even more deadly, and leans forward slightly, pressing the gun against me even harder. "You never would have let me in."

I smirk at him, unmoved by his unnecessary show of force. "Likely true but putting a gun to my man's head isn't the way to build any sort of goodwill with me, either."

Cutter issues a low growl, likely meant as some type of warning. "Open the fucking door."

Chuckling, I shake my head, the gun moving with it. "Why should I, Mr. Jackson? As it stands now, you can get off one shot before Dmitri pushes my body out of the way and slides this thing closed, ensuring the safety of the rest of my men. One death instead of what will undoubtedly be far more should I let you and *your* men *in*."

He takes a half step closer until his chest is almost pressed against the door. "You would sacrifice yourself for your men?"

"You wouldn't?"

Cutter mutters a curse under his breath and glances behind him in the alley. Someone dressed in dark clothing moves next to him, and Valentina Marconi pushes him aside, knocking his hand and the gun down from the window.

As far as I'm aware, it's the first time the Donna of the Italian family has been seen by anyone since she gave birth to Cutter's child. If she's here personally, instead of only speaking through her boyfriend, the guard dog, something big is going down.

"*Smettila*, Cutter." She glares at him in reproach, her reproach evident even in the dim lighting of the alley. "We need to speak with him without spitting venom."

He mumbles something back at her in Italian, holsters his weapon, and steps back, crossing his arms over his barrel chest with an annoyed huff. Cutter Jackson doesn't like being told what to do or having to answer to the woman he loves and comply with her commands when his nature begs him to take control.

Valentina squares her slender shoulders, locking her amber gaze with mine through the slit in the metal door. "We need to talk, Valerian. It's important."

Undoubtedly.

I would have taken a bullet from Cutter's gun to ensure the rest of my men stay safe because I don't trust that man not to come in here, shooting indiscriminately, just to prove whatever point he thinks he needs to, but Valentina is a different story.

She's the reason and the restraint in their Bonnie and Clyde relationship—the only thing keeping him from completely eliminating every one of the Marconi rivals in a very bloody way.

And everyone in this city knows it.

If she wants a conversation, I need to let her have it.

I offer her a friendly smile. "All you had to do was ask, Valentina." As I flip the lock with a loud clank and drag the heavy metal door open to permit them entry, Dmitri offers me a concerned look. "Do come in."

Valentina moves to step inside, but Cutter pushes her out of the way to enter first, his shoulders tense, chest puffed out in a completely obvious display.

He leans toward me, those nasty scars bright pink and twisted near my face. "You even think of fucking touching her and I'll kill you in the most painful way I can devise."

I hold up my hands, palms out, and shake my head. "I'm not the one putting a gun to people's heads."

Valentina steps in, her heels clicking on concrete floors, and pats Cutter on the shoulder. "I think he got the message, *amore mio*." She turns toward me. "Is there somewhere we can talk"—she glances toward Dmitri, Aleksei, and my other men now standing behind me—"privately."

Normally, I would bring her into my office, but given who waits there for me, that would be incredibly unwise at the moment. Cutter's men have worked with Sofia in the past, and he would recognize her in an instant. The ensuing drama would be best avoided at all costs—especially because I don't have the answer to the ultimate question of why she's here yet.

"Of course." I swing out my arm to indicate they should walk forward and slowly fall in line next to her and behind Cutter. "Let's go to the bar."

Once we enter the main club, I hold up a hand to stop Dmitri and the rest of the men from following. "*Podozhdi, stoy toot*, Dmitri."

Concern flashes in Dmitri's eyes, but I shake my head.

This isn't the time for a power struggle.

All eyes remain locked on Valentina and Cutter, who make their way across the empty room and stop in front of the central hub of the club. I follow slowly, watching the unusual couple's body language in an attempt to determine the motivation behind this impromptu meeting, and move behind the bar, motioning to the long line of liquor bottles.

"A drink?"

Cutter sneers. "It's 11:30 in the morning."

I raise a brow at him. "Your point?'

Valentina offers a half smile. "We'll politely decline."

"Your loss." I shrug and grab a bottle of vodka for myself, pouring a double into a crystal tumbler. "So, Ms. Marconi, to what do I owe the pleasure of this *friendly* visit?" Their timing couldn't have been worse—both for my cock and my attempts to gain the information I seek from Sofia. "You haven't been around very much lately. You've been missing all the fun."

Her lips harden into a thin line. "I've heard plenty about the *fun* everyone's been experiencing, and that's precisely why we're here to talk."

"Dmitri already provided me the information your friend, Preacher, found"—I glance at Cutter —"and it appears as though there are more unanswered questions. So, what is there to talk about?"

Cutter stiffens next to her, taking a second to turn and focus on my men before replying.

Valentina leans forward slightly, lowering her voice. "The information I *didn't* send you. The information that might help us unravel this entire mystery."

THREE

VALERIAN

I TAKE a sip of my vodka and examine the woman standing at the bar in front of me. Her swift rise to power and removal of her cousin from his position threw everyone for a loop, but she filled her father's shoes well.

Il Patrone was harsh but fair. Deadly but measured. A man of his word. Not a friend nor ally, yet somehow, not an enemy, either. Someone I could count on to enforce the status quo. A man who understood the necessity of maintaining peace along the borders we hold with each other. A man who saw the ramifications of letting violence spiral out of control in the city.

One can only hope Valentina is here because she knows the same.

But they've been withholding things from me, undoubtedly from *everyone*. "What information would that be?"

Valentina slides onto one of the stools, and Cutter does the same beside her, resting his forearms on the bar top, appearing anything but casual as he continues to surreptitiously check the status of my men, who have spaced themselves out around us and the bar—out of earshot but definitely close enough to hit their marks should it be necessary.

He drums his fingers against the wood ominously. "We know at least some of the men came from Vlorë, and at least one worked for Aleksander Gashi—"

I incline my head toward him. "Which points the finger at his widow, our dear friend, Kat."

Cutter nods slowly. "So it would seem..."

"Seem?"

He glances around to ensure my men can't eavesdrop. "There has been some suggestion by others that perhaps you are behind setting it up to make it appear as if Kat was the one who betrayed us all. We know some of your guys arrived there recently. That does nothing to help dispel that concern."

I tighten my hand on the glass and fist the other on the bar, forcing back the desire to chuck my drink at his already-marred face. "I'm not defending my actions to you. Either you accuse me of something, tell me why you're here, or you get the fuck out."

This dance has gone on long enough. It's time to lay our cards on the table, or we'll all end up dead. I thought we had learned that after the attack on the church, but apparently, I'm the only one.

Cutter snarls at me, the tension between us palpable enough that Dmitri takes a step forward. "We're here because Preacher found something else."

I raise a brow. "Which *was*?"

They've been dangling this additional information in front of me but not giving it, and I've lost my patience. I have Sofia on her knees, waiting for me, and plans for her I don't want to put off any longer.

Cutter huffs. "The false identities these men were flying under, the ones they use to get into the States in the first place...they weren't just random names."

His words make me freeze with my glass at my lips, and I slowly take a sip before lowering it. "What names were they?"

Cutter leans forward slightly. "The names of men killed by the Gashis and the Sylas over twenty years ago."

Fucking hell.

The Albanian families have always been a complication even when they stayed in their own country, but once they made their way here and set up in Chicago, their clashes have boiled over into our businesses far too much.

"That *is* intriguing. And perhaps another piece of evidence against Kat—using the Gashi names on behalf of her late husband's family's lost men and the Syla ones as a statement against the man she killed so violently in revenge for her love's death. It's a nod to the war that was started when Aleksander began his vendetta against everyone involved with Saban's death—starting with Konstandin Morina."

Valentina nods slowly. "My contacts in the region have indicated there has been activity in some of the older, retired groups. Men who left the life or at least have stepped away from it."

"You don't think Kat is trying to rebuild *there* and take over everything *here* at the same time?" I snort and shake my head at the mere thought. "There's no possible way she could control a territory in Albania and Chicago, let alone move in on *ours* here."

Cutter gives a stiff nod. "Those were our thoughts, as well. It doesn't make sense. Kat is too damn smart and would know she could never hold down two major territories on opposite sides of the world. It's almost as if someone has gone one step too far in trying to set her up and shown themselves by making her too..." He scans the club and smirks. "*Gluttonous* for control over everything."

Smirking at his choice of words, I take another drink and sigh. "Agreed."

Valentina locks her amber eyes with me and coolly straightens her shoulders. "Is it you?" She continues before I have a chance to respond to her question. "You and I are the ones with the most contacts in the area, the ones who would have the most to gain from making a move against the Berishas and Dragushas in Albania and leveraging it here."

She isn't wrong about that, and the accusation equally annoys me and flatters me in a way that draws a grin across my lips.

I shake my head. "It's quite flattering you think me capable of such a convoluted scheme to put a target squarely on Kat. And as much as I would love to see that back-stabbing cunt with a bullet in her head, alas, I must inform you that none of this is my doing."

The deadly couple watches me skeptically, and even from behind Cutter's reflective aviators, I can feel his disdain and disbelief of my denial.

"I would have preferred to avoid being shot at in that church and targeted by a death squad at Felipe's penthouse. If I were behind this, I would have figured out a way to ensure my own safety before I did any of those things."

Valentina shifts in her seat, the first sign of any uneasiness on her part. "And so would every one of us"—a sigh slips from her red lips—"which means there's another player."

"That's precisely the same conclusion I'd come to on my own and with Galen. None of us are stupid enough to put ourselves in the crossfire, even to maintain appearances or make everyone believe we're not involved. We're all smart enough to find a way to do it without being there or drawing suspicion. So, who does that leave if it's none of the five families?"

They share a furtive glance, and Valentina locks her gaze with mine again.

"We thought perhaps you might be able to shed some insight on that given that your men now have feet on the ground and have been questioning people—quite ruthlessly, according to what we've heard."

I down the rest of my vodka. "Is there any other way to do it?"

Unfortunately, no amount of torture to any of the men in Vlorë has brought forth anything useful thus far, nothing more than I already learned from Genti when I managed to get my hands on him. No one is talking, or if they are, it's nothing that offers any answers.

"I do not have any information at this time that would shed light on the new foe we all face, but if you wish to stay updated on developments, I'd be happy to share them with you"—I cut my gaze to Cutter—"without having guns pressed to my head in order to get the information."

Cutter offers an indignant snort, and Valentina casts a dirty look toward him—her censure clear.

"My apologies for Cutter's behavior. Since the birth of our child, his protectiveness has become even stronger and his trigger finger has become even quicker."

I reach down and pull my gun from my holster to set it on the counter, barrel facing him, finger hovering over the trigger. "Recent events have made mine the same, but they have also made one thing clear."

One of Valentina's slender dark brows rises. "What's that?"

"Whoever is doing this is smart enough to know how to pit us against each other. You. Me. Galen. We've maintained a peace here for almost twenty years and for decades prior to that through my uncle, your father, and Galen's kin. Those long-term relationships are the only thing keeping us from taking each other out."

She nods, her long, dark hair swinging around her face. "Agreed."

"Whoever this new opponent is, they aren't going to just go away. Until we can find them, we all have to watch our backs—and fronts—very carefully."

Cutter pushes to his feet. "Preacher is still digging. If there's something to find, he *will* find it. In the meantime, have your men digging, too."

I grin at him. "If there are any bodies to be discovered, believe me, my men will locate them and ensure the graves are refilled quickly with new people."

Anyone who thinks they can betray me, that they can try to set us against each other, is in for a rude awakening when they discover that we are not so easily manipulated.

FOUR

SOFIA

Pain radiates from my knees up and down my legs, and I shift on them for the thousandth time since Valerian left the room. Everything in me wants to scream, "*MERCY*," at the top of my lungs, so it will reach him wherever he is in the club and force him to come back and release me from my misery.

But even more than that, I want to *not* cave.

He isn't the kind of man I can show any weakness to, and he's already proven he's more than a decent game player. He's a goddamn master.

The entire time...

Valerian knew *the entire time and strung me along...*

A shiver rolls down my spine at the realization that he probably lied about everything. If he could look me in the eye and pretend not to know me, not to know I surely have an ulterior motive for being here with him, he's capable of anything.

"*We'll continue our conversation when I return,* kotyonok."

His parting words echo in my ears, mingling with my own thoughts and the warnings screaming at me to flee while I can.

I glance over at the man by the door again, the same one whose face I ground into the pavement when he was following me. If I did it once, surely, I can do it again and find a way out of here with my life intact—at least for now.

Heavy footsteps sound down the hallway, and without even seeing him...I know who approaches.

Valerian...

My heart thunders against my ribcage, the blood rushing in my ears. The taste of his release lingers in my mouth. My entire body throbs in anticipation.

I shift again restlessly, still on my knees for the man who has called me out and left me in anticipation of the punishment coming for my lies and actions. Something tells me what he did to me that first night will be nothing compared to how he will "*continue our conversation*" now.

His ice-cold gaze meets mine, raising goosebumps over my skin. He leans in and says something to the man at the door, who casts a dirty look my way over his shoulder before ambling away down the hall and leaving me alone to face my fate and the man who holds it in his calloused capable hands.

He slowly makes his way around the desk toward me, stopping in front, just where he stood with his cock down my throat, what feels like hours ago. It likely hasn't been anywhere near that long, but the anticipation and nerves have left me trembling.

Harsh fingers grip my chin, tilting my head even more toward him. "You can get up now, *kotyonok*."

I slowly climb to my feet on legs so shaky that Valerian has to put a steadying hand at my hip to keep me from tumbling over. He squeezes me there, the heat of his palm radiating through my shirt and straight to the apex of my thighs.

How can I react to him like this when he's just as likely to kiss me as kill me?

It's the same question I've been asking since I walked into *Gluttony* the first time, and I still don't have the answer.

Before I have time to consider any further, Valerian lowers his shoulder and flips me over it. A surprised yelp slips from my lips as my face ends up squarely aligned with his firm ass in perfectly tailored pants. His broad, hard shoulder presses against my stomach, arm clamped around my thighs to hold me in place.

He stalks out of his office and down the hall, past the playroom with the St. Andrew's Cross where he took my virginity, and stops in front of the closed door just before the main club.

Oh, hell.

There's no telling what's behind each of these doors—every room different, designed to appeal to various kinks and desires. A place to play a special game each time.

Which does he have planned for me?

He faces the door, twists the knob, and pushes it open with determination. Flipped over like this, I can't see anything but the polished concrete floor, yet a million possibilities flash through my head—any number of torture devices and ways to get what he wants from me.

I hold my breath, and he finally stops walking and whips me off his shoulder with another yelp as I instinctively claw at him to keep myself upright. My body hits something soft and bounces, releasing my breath in a rush, and I push my hair from my face to try to gather my bearings.

The same black walls as the cross room surround us, but this one is mostly empty except for the massive bed I'm now in the center of and a long, leather bench at the foot of it beside where Valerian stands.

Thank God this is just a bed...

That thought dies when his gaze locks with mine, a mixture of lust and heated anger burning there.

"Valerian?" Breathy, his name falls from my lips, barely audible.

One side of his mouth twitches, like he's trying to withhold a smile threatening to break across his hard face, and he reaches for his waistband and pulls out his gun.

My entire body tenses, and I scramble backward until my shoulders hit the wooden, slatted headboard behind me. "Wh-what are you going to do?"

Eyes locked with mine, he sets it on the bench beside him, then slowly eases off his jacket and lays it beside the weapons. Slowly, he unbuttons his shirt, exposing the smooth skin of his chiseled chest and the rippling abs below it. My gaze tracks him as he removes the crisp white material and adds it on top of the coat. His hands move to his belt buckle, and he undoes it and snaps it between his hands, the sharp crack of the leather making me jump and press a palm against my chest over my racing heart.

"I'm not going to do anything you don't want me to, and you're going to tell me why you're really here, Sofia." He sets the belt on the bench, unbuttons his pants, and lowers the zipper at an agonizingly unhurried pace. His hard cock strains against the fabric, but he doesn't do anything to free it; he just watches me with a mix of amusement and determination. "Why has my little *kotyonok* been sneaking around and sticking her nose in places it doesn't belong?"

He grabs the belt, kicks off his shoes, and walks around the bed to the right, stopping next to me, close enough to strike me with the leather should he choose. I hold my breath, waiting for the sharp bite, but he climbs onto the bed and trails his fingers down my exposed arm almost affectionately, sending a shudder through me.

I swallow thickly as he takes my wrist and raises it above my head. My gaze follows his movements, and he pins my hand in place, then reaches for the other one and brings them together. He has them wrapped with the belt before I can even process what he's doing, and he straps it into place on the headboard, effectively cuffing me to it, unable to pull them free.

Fuck.

While I tug at the binding uselessly, Valerian issues a low chuckle and drops his head close to my face until his lips barely whisper over mine.

"The more you struggle, the more it will hurt, *kotyonok*."

"The more *what* will hurt?"

He smirks and straddles my legs at the knees, pinning me in place, his hands slowly shifting up the hem of my dress until it's gathered just above my hips. In one quick jerking motion, he tears away my thong and pulls the strip of fabric free, completely exposing me to his hungry gaze.

I wait for him to toss it off the side of the bed, but he closes his eyes, brings it to his nose, and inhales deeply. The low groan of appreciation rumbling from his chest makes me want to clench my legs together against the throb between them, but the solid man pinning me in place makes it impossible.

Fear and need simultaneously roar through my blood, and he opens his eyes and tucks the remnants of my thong into his pocket. He shifts back slightly, enough to force my legs open so he can lightly feather his fingertips over my now-wet lips.

"Getting the truth, Sofia. The more getting the *truth* will hurt."

"*Ay Dios, estoy jodida.*"

FIVE

VALERIAN

TRAILING my fingers over her bare legs, I relish the way the goosebumps follow in their wake and how she squirms under me.

She has no idea what I have in store for her.

I hadn't planned to push Sofia on what she's doing here yet, rather wanted to wait for her to approach me with whatever plan she has in that beautiful head of hers. But she's forced my hand in more ways than one. If she's going to be so bold as to try to hack into my computer while I'm in the damn building, she's going to pay the price.

That's something I can't ignore.

It's time to get the truth from the trembling woman under me.

"*Ti blya pozhaleesh, chto ne priznalas' mne, kotyonok.*"

Sofia shudders under me even though she doesn't understand my warning.

"Remember, you can always ask for *mercy*."

Her already big eyes widen even more, but instead of shrinking back or tugging against the restraints in a vain attempt to escape, her face hardens with a determination I am now set on breaking. "Never."

"Never is a very long time, *kotyonok*."

I shift back off her legs, which she immediately presses together like she desperately wants to protect what's between them. A slow grin pulls at my lips, and I climb from the bed and open the bench at the end of it.

Sofia lifts her head, trying to see over the top of it, but I deliberately hide the chosen implement of her demise.

There isn't any way she'll be able to withstand this—not with her inexperience. She'll crack faster than the ice on the Chicago River on a warm spring day.

And I'll get the answers I need.

I slowly close the lid, and her gaze narrows in on the device in my hands. The metal gleams ominously under the overhead lights, and Sofia gulps, darting her tongue across her lips.

"What's that?"

So innocent.

So naïve.

That grin tugs at my lips again as I climb back on the bed at her feet. "The thing that's going to ensure I find out what you're really up to, *kotyonok*."

I attach one of the fur-lined leather cuffs of the spreader bar to her right ankle, then grasp her left one before she can try to move it away, securing it in place.

She twists slightly, trying to force her legs together, but the realization that she won't be able to makes her bottom lip quiver. I narrow my focus on her glistening cunt, already wet and ready for me even though she's scared of what might be coming.

And she should be.

I slowly lower myself between her legs and blow against her flesh. She squirms and rocks her hips, but my shoulders keep her from moving, her body fully under my control. I trail a finger up her inner thigh, making her twitch and clench her eyes closed.

She's fighting it already, intent on winning this battle, but I've been at war for years and have never lost. I don't intend to now.

"I'm going to ask you again, Sofia...why has my little *kotyonok* been sneaking around and sticking her nose in places it doesn't belong?"

I snake out my tongue and flick it once over her clit, making her buck against my chest in a way that makes my hard cock ache where it's pressed against my pants and the mattress.

"B-because if I told you who I was..." Another soft blow against her mound makes her twist. "I-I never would have g-gotten in the door."

Her words draw a low chuckle from deep in my chest. "That's probably true, *kotyonok*." I drag my tongue across her wet lips, my groan of appreciation mingling with hers of frustration. "I would have assumed you were here at your brothers' behest, that you bore ill will, or were sent as a Trojan horse. But..."

I thrust my tongue inside her, and she bucks up on a gasp, tugging at the restraints on the headboard. The low creak of the wood blooms satisfaction in my chest. I've barely touched her, and she's already nearing her breaking point.

Slowly probing her cunt, I grip her thighs, digging my fingers into the flesh and holding her still from her desire to throw me off. She tugs at my belt, her eyes darting up to it, her brain trying to calculate a way to free herself.

"Don't even try, *kotyonok*." I lock my gaze with her frantic one. "The only escape you have from this is the truth." Dipping my head again, I glide my tongue across her thigh, up toward her core, then back down the other side, then blow across them again. "Or to ask for mercy."

She doesn't want to do either. That reality hardens her stare, and she sets her jaw.

If she's intent on remaining silent, then she'll pay for it.

Settling between her legs again, I set to work on her cunt, devouring her, pushing my tongue inside her the way I want to with my cock. It throbs to be enveloped in that wet heat, but if I do that, I won't get the answers I need. Instead, I lick at her—everywhere except where she really needs it.

Sofia has underestimated what I'm willing to do to get what I want. If it means leaving her hanging for a month, I'll do it.

She thrashes under my ministrations, and I slip two fingers inside her, earning me a strangled moan that fills the room and makes my cock twitch and seep pre-cum. Her pussy clenches around them, desperately seeking that which I refuse to give her.

"Tell me, now, Sofia, and this can be over." I curl into her G-spot and pulse there, my thumb lightly grazing her clit but not applying the pressure she needs. "Why are you here?"

Her eyes flutter open and meet mine, the frustration and anger there heating them to a molten bourbon. "Because I need you..."

I still my hand, my heart thudding against my ribcage loud enough that it almost drowns out her words. "You *need* me? Why, *kotyonok*? Why do you need me?"

She presses her lips into a thin line, her resolve to keep her secrets hidden back in place. But not for long. I feather the pad of my thumb across her clit again, and she winces and sucks in a breath of air, squeezing her cunt around my fingers and grasping at them.

"Tell me now."

Her head shifts back and forth against the pillows. "I-I can't..."

Another flutter of a touch to her most sensitive spot brings her hips flying up toward me. "Why not?"

"Be-because...it isn't time yet."

It isn't time yet?

I freeze and lean over her, pressing my chest to hers, my fingers still deep inside her, hand and cock pinned between us. Her eyes flicker open, and I brush my lips across hers. She lifts her head to meet me, seeking the kiss I refuse to give her as much as I refuse to give the orgasm she needs.

"I can make this end quickly, *kotyonok*, but you can't talk in riddles."

Whatever she's hiding darkens her eyes.

"Are you here for your brothers? Are they planning something? Are they behind everything that's been happening?"

She quickly shakes her head, her chest heaving against mine. "No. I haven't seen them or spoken to them since I left Andres' house when Cutter took him."

"Then explain what you mean, Sofia." I shift my hips, making my palm brush against her clit. "It isn't time for what?"

"It..." she gasps, trying to find her breath. "It isn't time to tell you."

I issue a chuckle and slip my tongue past her lips into her mouth to tangle with hers. She moans and arches against me, trying to grind her hips and find the friction she needs, but I pull back and shift between her legs again so she can't get what she seeks.

"It is time, Sofia. Tell me everything. This is your only chance before I really get going."

Fear flashes in her gaze.

"I always get what I want, *kotyonok*, and I will today, too, no matter how long it takes or how hard you might fight me."

I dip my head to eat at her again, groaning at the taste of her arousal filling my mouth. She's practically dripping now, the bedspread wet beneath her with the evidence of how close she is and how badly she wants it, but I don't relent for a moment.

Every flick of my tongue, every suck, every feather-light touch and relentless probing digit designed to drive her to madness so she'll come clean.

She writhes under me, twisting against the belt at the headboard and the metal bar pushing against my thighs that keeps her spread open for me. It's close—that cataclysm she seeks—but I won't give it to her.

I lift my head, and she finally releases a heavy breath of resignation, still twitching and rocking her hips against nothing. "I can't tell you until I'm sure you won't betray me."

Her statement freezes me in place. "Betray you?"

She nods slightly. "Yes. I need to know you will be on my side, and right now, I don't trust that."

I narrow my eyes on her. "On your side for what?"

"For the fight I'll likely get from my brothers when I try to get what they owe me."

"What do they owe you, *kotyonok*."

She swallows thickly. "The truth."

I raise a brow. "About what?"

"About what happened to our parents, about what they've done and tried to hide from me."

What the hell is she talking about?

"I don't understand, Sofia."

"You don't have to."

"I do." I lean in again and grind my pelvis against my hand still buried between her legs, earning a moan from her sweet lips. "I need to understand everything before I can stop this."

Her eyes clamped shut, she shifts under me and clenches her cunt around my fingers. "I-I know they've lied to me about a lot of things, used me to grow their business all based on a lie. I want the truth they would never give me."

I flutter my mouth over hers. "What does any of this have to do with me? Why did you come to *me*?"

She opens her eyes to meet mine. "Because I've wanted you since the moment I first saw you. I wanted *this*, and I needed to know you weren't in bed with them."

Hell...

I slide back from her, withdraw my hand, and set to work removing the spreader bar from her ankles.

Sofia lifts her head, her wide, confused gaze following my work. "What are you doing?"

It's a good question—one made even more complicated by what she just said.

"We're going home..."

SIX

SOFIA

THE SOFT PILLOW AND MATTRESS, silky sheets, and heavy, warm comforter try to hold me captive to sleep, but my brain slowly comes back online, one sense at a time. I shift slightly and wince as memories of last night flutter through my head and my clit throbs for the release Valerian never gave me.

El bastardo...

He knew exactly what he was doing and relished knowing he was going to leave me hanging and miserable. It was torture. A punishment designed to make a deadly point about lying to him and keeping things from him—that it will cost me.

And it certainly did last night.

It left me begging for relief—relief he wouldn't offer. When he removed the bar at my feet, I thought for sure he would drive his cock into me and finally give me what I craved so badly, but instead, he threw me over his shoulder and tossed me into his car to drive me here.

I spread out a hand over the empty side of the bed next to me where he slept last night—ever watchful to ensure I didn't violate the command he gave when he pulled his T-shirt over my head and placed me in this bed beside him.

"If you touch yourself, you'll have to answer for your actions."

¿En que putas me metí?

I squeeze my eyes closed and inhale a deep breath filled with the heady scent of leather and danger Valerian carries.

This is more than a sinister game; it's a deadly one for me, for Valerian, for all of us. But now that I've started, there isn't any way to go back. Once I made that first fateful step, I took my own life into my hands.

And I may lose it for thinking I can win.

I roll toward the side of the bed and slowly push back the covers. The chilly air of the room hits me, sending a shiver through my limbs as I finally take a moment to scan my surroundings. Last night, the furthest thing from my mind was what Valerian's bedroom looked like.

All I wanted was his touch. For him to bring me here, throw me on the massive bed, and give me what he so diabolically withheld. But he didn't even touch me all night. Not a hand at my hip, not a press of his lips, not even a brush of skin to skin.

He just lay beside me, his warm, hard body radiating heat toward me.

I was tempted so many times to slip my hand between my legs when I heard his steady, rhythmic breathing of sleep, yet each time, I stopped myself because he would know. I'm not sure *how* he would, but I'm confident my punishment for that would be far worse than how I'm suffering now.

Valerian Kamenev is a master—of his domain, of me, and of my body.

By walking into his club, I put myself in his crosshairs willingly, but even I couldn't have imagined how far this would go, that I would end up in his bed with my body craving him more than it does oxygen.

Heavy footsteps sound just outside the door before it clicks and swings open toward me. Valerian's icy-blue gaze meets mine, and he raises a heavy, dark eyebrow. "Going somewhere, *kotyonok*?"

I shake my head and drop my focus to the tray in his hands, unable to meet the eyes of the man who has me twisted up so badly. "No. I just woke up."

He smirks as he enters and nudges the door closed behind him with his bare foot. Dressed casually in black lounge pants and a dark T-shirt that pulls tightly across his broad, muscled chest, this version of Valerian doesn't appear nearly as threatening as when he's in his element in his office or one of the playrooms—but I am not dumb enough to lower my guard around him.

One thing growing up with Felipe and Andres has taught me is that no one is what they appear. Everyone has secrets and ulterior motives. And I still have no fucking clue what Valerian's are.

He's known who I am this whole time, yet he let me waltz in. He fucked me. He allowed me to get closer to him, said words that made something flutter in my chest. Even after catching me in his office on his computer, he took me to the playroom and then here rather than putting a bullet in my head.

Why?

This man will never show his cards, not until we're on the final hand and he's ready to win the game.

"I imagine you're hungry." He approaches a small round table against the far wall near a set of shuttered windows and sets the tray on it, then turns to me. "Come eat. You need your strength."

"Why?" I raise a brow at him. "Do you plan on torturing me?"

Valerian barks out a laugh and approaches slowly, like a predator stalking his prey, and stops just in front of me, close enough that my fingers itch to touch his warm skin.

He takes another step forward, nudging open my knees and grasping my chin in his firm grip, jerking my head up. "If you think that was torture, then I've greatly underestimated what your brothers have taught you over the years."

"My brothers kept me insulated from everything, *protected* me from the realities of life, and kept me naïve to what was really happening." It's impossible to keep my anger from the word Andres and Felipe always used to justify their actions. "Or, at least, they *tried*."

A grin tugs at the corner of Valerian's lips. "But you aren't naïve, Sofia, are you?" His icy gaze bores into mine. "They had no idea what was going on in that beautiful mind of yours."

I shake my head. "No, they didn't."

"I'm not so sure I do, either."

¡Mierda!

I stiffen at his words.

Does he know I lied to him last night?

Has he figured out that despite the way he toyed with me and had me frantic, I somehow managed to still keep the truth hidden?

He slowly grazes his thumb over my lips, then tips his head back toward the table. "Come."

I'd fucking love to.

My body is still wound so tightly that it feels like I might snap.

He reaches down and pulls my hand into his, tugging me up against his firm body. "I've had my chef prepare some Russian favorites. And perhaps, if you behave, when you're done, I'll eat *my* favorite thing for breakfast."

There isn't any point in trying to bite back the moan that climbs up my throat. His words make my entire body clench, my clit screaming for attention, but Valerian just smiles smugly and leads me over to the table, pulling out the chair for me like the perfect gentleman he's anything but.

The man who has twisted me in more ways than I could have possibly imagined motions for me to take a seat, and I lower myself to the chair as he removes the cloche covering the food on the tray.

An amazing plate of sausages, potatoes, and small pancakes makes my mouth water and my stomach growl.

"Please, enjoy, *kotyonok*."

Valerian takes a seat across from me casually and crosses his legs, watching me as I lift my fork and knife and shove a piece of sausage straight into my mouth.

Unfamiliar spices dance across my tongue, the flavor unique and unlike anything I've ever tasted. "What is this? It's delicious."

His lips twitched slightly. "*Kolbasa.* My mother used to make this family recipe."

"But you didn't make this?"

He barks out a laugh and shakes his head. "No, *kotyonok*. I don't have the time or the inclination to become an expert in the kitchen. I have far more important things to deal with."

"Was it always that way, though? Surely, you must have spent time in the kitchen as a child with your mother?"

Valerian stiffens but keeps a fake smile on his lips. "Back home, that isn't really a man's role— even at a young age. My sisters spent time in the kitchen while I spent time with my father doing..." He shifts slightly and reaches forward for one of the two cups of what appears to be tea on the tray. "He brought me along to many things. I saw a lot I shouldn't have at that age, but I was too young to really understand what he did. I never got a true grasp of it until I moved here to live with my uncle. He's the one who introduced me to the life."

"And you became the heir."

He nods slowly. "He didn't have any children. It's one of the reasons I came to live with him. I became his heir apparent, and he trained me to take over for him. When he was killed..."

Valerian shrugs and doesn't finish the sentence.

Killed is a nice way of putting it.

The man was brutally murdered in a dispute with a rival Russian family that was trying to step up their activities here. It was a move that ultimately failed, mostly because of the man sitting across from me and his ability to step into his uncle's shoes immediately and hunt down those responsible. He squashed any hope they had of moving into Chicago with a brutality that ensured no one would fuck with him again.

Just as the Blood Rose Cartel gained its name from what happened in that mansion that fateful day, Valerian earned his reputation from his acts of revenge.

And he's accomplished so much, maintained this territory and a thriving business through two decades. His experience so far outweighs my own that it brings back all the reservations I had when I set this plan into motion.

He's right; I'm not naïve. But I am still only twenty-one when the heads of the other families and Andres and Felipe have decades of experience living in this volatile world.

"You were still relatively young when that happened. When you took over?"

He nods again and takes a drink from his cup. "In my early twenties, but now that I have been the head of this family for two decades, I can confidently say he did an excellent job teaching me everything I would need to know."

I take another bite of sausage and consider his words.

Everything...

"Except how to survive an unknown opponent?"

He watches me over the lip of his cup as he takes a sip of his tea, then sets it down almost deliberately slowly. "You have a lot of questions this morning, *kotyonok*."

I freeze with a bite of potatoes poised in front of my lips and swallow thickly. "Is it wrong to want to know more about you?"

His barked laugh carries around the high ceiling of the room. "That depends on the purpose of your questions." He sets down the cup and fingers the handle absently. "Do you really think I believed what you told me last night, Sofia?"

I chew the potatoes, trying to hide my unease. "I would hope so. It's the truth."

This all comes down to alliances—who you can rely on and where people have loyalties. And when I saw Valerian for the first time at that meeting, before the world exploded around us, I sensed it immediately. Everything people say about him is true. He's a man of his word, something rare in this business. He's also powerful and driven, a man who can get things done and isn't afraid to leave blood spilled along the way.

He's exactly the kind of partner I need.

A slight smirk pulls at his lips. "Maybe a version of it, but you aren't a very good liar, *kotyonok*. Until I find out the *full* truth, you're staying here."

My hand tightens around my fork and knife. Sitting so close across the small table, it seems like it would be easy to lunge across it and jab it into the side of his neck. And part of me—the part that was always taught to fight, never to give in or give up, never to let anyone get the upper hand—wants to do that. But the rational part, the part that's been working this plan for so long, knows I can't.

"You're going to hold me hostage?"

"I know you're keeping things from me, and I won't let you go until you come clean." He pushes to his feet and approaches me slowly, then captures my cheek in his palm and tilts my head up until my eyes meet his. "Although, I may keep you as a bargaining chip with your brothers even once I finally get the truth..."

SEVEN

VALERIAN

FELIPE AND ANDRES sit huddled close together in the back corner booth of *Brasa Roja*—exactly where Dmitri and Aleksei said I could find them. It's a rare opportunity to meet with the Rose brothers without Kat attached to the hip of the man we know as Rose, and if we're going to have this conversation, it needs to happen without that bitch interfering.

I approach with a grin as two of their guards step in front of me, each holding up a hand to stop me while reaching for their guns. The brothers eye me warily, their hard, identical gazes assessing my intent, then share a glance.

Felipe motions for me forward. "Let him come."

With a satisfied grin, I step past the perturbed goons and ease into the round booth at one end across from them.

Rose scowls at me. "What the hell are you doing here?"

"I thought it was time the three of us have a little chat unfettered by your significant other's presence."

He sneers. "You really think I won't go home and tell Kat every word you say?"

"No doubt you will. But she won't be here to cloud your judgment while we have this conversation."

The corner of Felipe's lips twitches in amusement while he manages to suppress this full grin. He isn't Kat's biggest supporter, either, and something tells me he only tolerates her in order to maintain this tenuous truce with his brother. "Whatever you have to say must be important if you're willing to approach us like this."

I lean back in the booth and examine two of the men who have caused so much unrest since they arrived in town and equally with the woman back at my house. "It is important, not just to me but to all of us."

What Sofia said knocked me off my axis and left too many questions she hasn't answered fully yet. Her brothers did something bad enough to make her leave the safety and security they provided, something she wants them to answer for.

My mind immediately goes to the death squad after all of us, the one connected—at least on its face—to the woman Rose shares a bed with.

"Chicago has turned into a goddamn shooting gallery. Nobody knows where anyone stands anymore, and that makes things very dangerous for all of us." I pause for effect before continuing with what I came to say. "Valentina approached me..."

Their matching brows rise.

Rose sneers again. "My old friend..."

I can't say I blame him. After the way Kat threw him under the bus and handed him over to Valentina and Cutter, like a sacrificed pawn in a deadly game of chess, it's easy to understand his feelings toward her.

"Long before you two showed up here, Valentina, Galen, Saban Gashi, and I had an understanding. You two and Kat shattered the truce we had entered into long ago, that had been held in place by mutually assured destruction. And now there are even more players. The Luna Cartel that moved in on Galen's territory, this group from Albania that seems intent on destroying one or all of us. If we don't sort this all out soon, the Chicago River will flow red with the blood from all of us."

Felipe nods and takes a drink from a tumbler with amber liquid, tilting it toward me. "Would you like one?"

I incline my head, and he motions to the waiter, then takes a sip and leans back slightly in the booth.

The brother who managed to convince everyone he was a pious priest for so long considers me for a moment. "Everyone appears quite confident the Luna Cartel attacks are different than this other group. There's no way they're connected?"

Shaking my head, I accept the drink from the waiter and wait for him to depart before I respond. "Galen said the Luna Cartel seems to have only been targeting him, and while it's possible what happened at the church may have just been us getting caught in the crossfire of somebody after *him*, he says the groups operate differently."

Rose narrows his eyes. "How so?"

I offer a shrug. "The Luna Cartel is more...how do I phrase this? Disorganized. They clearly aren't trained the way the men who came at us in the church were."

Felipe twirls the drink in his glass. "But the question remains, who sent them and for what purpose?"

Rose stiffens and looks at his brother. "For the last time, it wasn't Kat. If it were her, I would know."

I snort a sardonic laugh at how insistent he is that his woman will always be truthful to him. "I'll ask you the same question I asked Genti. You don't think she's capable of keeping this from you?"

Even after leaving Sofia hanging last night, she still hasn't completely come clean with me, and Kat is far icier and stronger than Sofia. She's keeping things from everyone—even the man who fucks her—of that, I'm certain.

Rose scowls at me incredulously. "Kat and I don't keep things from each other. Not anymore. Not when the stakes are this high. And she wouldn't have risked her own life. Not now that she has her son here."

I nod slowly. Perhaps having a child has weakened her and made her more careful, but I'm not entirely convinced. "Do you buy it, Felipe? That Kat is innocent and has been set up."

He nods. "Based on all the evidence, I would say someone's done a fairly decent job of setting her up. But they've made enough mistakes that are showing."

"Valentina, Cutter, and I came to the same conclusion."

Rose's shoulders relax slightly at the confirmation that, ultimately, none of us believe Kat is behind it. It doesn't mean I trust her—or him—but it helps eliminate at least one potential source for the group of men causing so much trouble for all of us.

He takes a sip of his drink and glances between his brother and me. "So, where does that leave us?"

After what Sofia said last night, I'm starting to think it's the two sitting across from me...or at least *one* of them.

"Well, the Luna Cartel seems to purely be Galen's problem at this point, but they could very well become an issue for all of us if we don't take care of it soon."

Felipe's brow furrows. "It was my understanding that's what you and Galen did shortly after we all left my condo?"

"We thought so, too. But we didn't find their leader. He escaped, somehow managed to regroup, and perhaps brought in more men from Mexico—they attacked one of Galen's shipments again. As soon as anyone has any information that might be useful in putting them down for good, it needs to be shared. The same about these Albanian men and their death mission." I let my gaze drift over the brothers as I take a drink, trying to catch any signs of deception or unease on their part. "I have a man on the ground in Vlorë doing some questioning. Hopefully, he'll be able to shed light on the subject before they can accomplish the job they came here for, and I have everyone at my disposal scouring high and low for any other information."

I wait for them to offer something or interject, sipping slowly at my drink. Neither moves nor makes any effort to provide anything further. "I don't suppose there's any chance your sister has shown back up and can use some of her incredible computer skills to get us what we need?"

Their identical faces harden, and Felipe leans toward me across the table. "Sofia is still missing. Though, we have had people looking for her since the day Cutter's men raided Andres' compound, without any sign of where she might be." His hard gaze locks with mine. "I don't suppose you have any information in that regard?"

I smirk and take a sip of my drink. "What could I possibly know about your sister?"

EIGHT

VALERIAN

THAT LAST COMMENT should have gotten me killed since the Rose brothers are so volatile and protective when it comes to Sofia and have been losing their minds trying to find her. Yet, somehow, I step out of the restaurant unscathed and onto the bustling street where the cool wind coming off Lake Michigan whips around me.

I chuckle to myself and shake my head. They have no idea what they have in Sofia—or rather *had*. She's smart, determined, feisty. My cock swells just thinking about her, and even though I know she's keeping things from me, things that could very well come back to bite me in the worst way, my fingers still itch to touch her again. My tongue waters to taste her. And after her punishment last night, she deserves a little something special.

Something that will help her trust me with the truth. Something that will show her I won't betray her the way she seems to suggest her brothers have.

And I know the perfect thing.

I wave to Ivan parked in the SUV down the street, and he pulls to a stop in front of the restaurant, vigilantly scanning the street for any potential issues. Though, I don't expect any from Felipe or Andres. They'd be fools to make a move against me here with so many witnesses.

Besides, we need each other right now. Until all this gets sorted out, those who have always been adversaries must be viewed as allies—at least, at face value. We all know we have ulterior motives and lie as easily as we speak the truth. The real issue is figuring out who is doing what—before you get shot in the back. My first inclination when Sofia revealed her vendetta against her brothers was that they may be setting up Kat to get her out of the picture and absorb her territory into theirs, but after seeing how defensive Rose was and the tension still between them over her, that possibility can be checked off the list.

Which means Sofia was talking about something *else,* some other way they wronged her, something bad enough to send her looking for an ally in me.

I pull open the passenger door and slide into the welcome warmth.

Ivan glances at me. "Where to, *pakhan*?"

"Tiffany's."

His eyes widen. "Really?"

"Trust me, Ivan, when you have a woman like Julia, you want to go to places like Tiffany's."

He shrugs and peels away from the curb toward Michigan Avenue. Sofia will no doubt get more and more angry the longer I keep her at my place and refuse her requests to leave, but hopefully, what I bring home for her in the little blue box will appease some of the burn from the game we continue to play.

I settle back in my seat and tug out my phone to scroll through my messages.

Ivan glances at me as he turns the corner. "How did the meeting go?"

I shrug. "About as well as can be expected. They're in agreement that we must share information."

"Do you think they're hiding anything?"

"I think everyone's always hiding something. If you haven't figured that out after all these years working for me, then perhaps you're in the wrong profession."

His skin flushes, and he returns his attention to the road as my phone rings with Dmitri's name flashing across the screen.

"*Da?*"

"We have something on the bomb."

"Fucking finally!"

"Maksim tore the thing apart, examined every single piece of it for fingerprints, any signatures, anything that would lead to who might have built it, and he found the guy."

"Excellent."

"Don't get too excited."

I should have known it wouldn't be that simple.

"What's the problem?"

"The problem is it doesn't really help us decipher much of anything. The man who built it goes by Atom, and he's for hire by anyone with enough money who can find a way to get in touch with him. He's built explosive devices for numerous organizations over the years and doesn't give a shit about their ideologies or how they plan to use it. It doesn't help us locate who is behind this."

"Then we find Atom and make him tell us. Were we able to trace any of the pieces to a specific purchase location?"

"No, Atom's too good to leave a SKU number or any other way to track it. He only uses readily available commercial items where millions of them would be on the common marketplace."

Ivan takes a corner sharply, and I throw a glare at him. "So, it's a dead end on the bomb?"

"Yes. The box—no."

I sit up a little straighter. "The box?"

"When you asked me to have the bomb examined, I almost threw away the wooden box it was in, but then I realized there were remnants of a shipping sticker near one of the corners on the bottom."

"You're kidding?" A tiny glimmer of hope lights in my chest. "Anything we can do with that?"

"I had it scanned in so we could try to enhance it, but it's still unreadable. Someone with better technological knowledge than I have might be able to really figure it out."

I tighten my grip on the phone. "I know just who to ask."

It's almost like fate put Sofia in my grasp for this, to help us solve the problem plaguing Galen with the Luna Cartel...and she just might be who we need to discover the truth of who is behind this Albanian mess. I had asked the question of her brothers more to see their reaction and gauge whether there was any potential they knew I have her, but using her to solve this might help us all.

We pull up outside Tiffany's on Michigan Avenue, and I end the call and shove the phone into my pocket. "Stay here. I won't be long."

Ivan nods, and I step out on to the bustling sidewalk filled with tourists and locals, bags in their hands, phones to their ears, ignorant to who and what surrounds them, completely oblivious to the fact that the people who keep the violence contained in this town are on the verge of losing that battle.

This could very well devolve into a war like the one in the thirties when blood literally ran through the streets. None of us should want that. No matter how ambitious we may be, we're also realists. We all must understand that attacking each other constantly will only lead to losses on both sides and the police and FBI breathing down our necks.

Chicago is too big to be controlled by any one family. Many have tried and failed over the years. Kat made moves thinking she could eventually get to that point, and so did the Rose brothers, and they all paid the price for it. But I won't. I'm not stupid enough to try to take anything by force. My plan has always been less aggressive and more tactful—keep your friends close and enemies closer. Once Kat and the Blood Rose Cartel showed up, stirring the pot, I knew what I needed to do.

These interlopers are interfering with that plan, but it doesn't mean I'm about to quit. Hopefully, Sofia can help me track them down before things go too far. I've worked too hard for this, waited too long to have everything, to just walk away and accept the status quo. It's right there, almost within reach. The last few weeks have proven it. But these wild gunmen are throwing everything into question.

I take two steps toward the door of Tiffany's, dodge a brunette hustling down the sidewalk on her phone who almost walks right into me, and the first crack of gunfire sounds as the searing pain hits me.

NINE

SOFIA

Frantic shouting and hurried footsteps up and down the hallway outside Valerian's bedroom draw me from the bathroom after my shower and toward the closed door.

I didn't see Valerian lock it when he left or hear the click of something moving into place that would prevent me from leaving, but his words certainly implied that even if I attempted it, there is no way I'm free to simply walk away.

His men will have been told as much and will stop me from trying, but something is clearly happening on the other side of that wood panel.

Something big.

I hurry over to it, turn the handle, and pull it open to a frenzied scene. Dmitri and several other men rush down the hallway from one end to the other, carrying various items and yelling to each other in Russian.

Dmitri passes again, and I fall into step with him. "What's going on? Where's Valerian?"

His hard eyes flash with something—concern, anger, perhaps a hint of irritation at my presence and question—before he answers. "Valerian's been shot."

A vise instantly tightens around my chest, squeezing the air from my lungs and making the edges of my vision blur. My steps falter, and I freeze in the hallway. "Wh-what?"

Dmitri stops and turns toward me, his gaze flaming with heated annoyance. "He was shot on Michigan Avenue."

"Oh, my God. Is-is he…"

I can't even voice the word. It lodges in my throat like a solid rock, making it impossible for me to even swallow. Dropping my head slightly, I squeeze my eyes closed and try to regain control of whatever is happening to my body.

"He's alive…for now. Ivan managed to get him back into the SUV, and he's headed here now."

I whip my head up and focus on Dmitri again. "Here? Shouldn't he be going to the hospital?"

Dmitri starts walking again, and I fall in behind him. We step out into a large, open living room and kitchen space decorated in dark grays with splashes of red and white. I barely glanced at it when we came in last night, but now, the red seems sinister, like a premonition or warning of what was to come.

"Hospitals mean cops. There's a chance no one ID'd him as the victim of the shooting, so we may be able to avoid any police contacts, but if we bring him to a hospital, we'll have the last people we want digging into our affairs buried balls deep in them."

"But what if he needs—"

He whirls toward me, stopping me abruptly in my tracks, his large, wide chest directly in my face. "We know how to take care of our own, Julia. Go back to the bedroom."

He must be joking.

Squaring my shoulders, I do my best to hide what a fucking mess I am right now internally. "I'm not going anywhere. I can help."

His mouth twists into a sneer. "You'll just get in the way, *kukolka.*"

I haven't the slightest clue what he just called me, but the look he's giving me leaves no doubt it wasn't kind. "If you want me back in that bedroom, you'll have to throw me over your shoulder and carry me back kicking and screaming."

The tiniest twitch at the corner of his lips tells me I've won this battle but not the war. He doesn't want me around Valerian, doesn't trust me. And he shouldn't...

He shoves the box in his hands into my stomach. "If you're staying, make yourself useful."

I glance down at the various medical supplies that seem woefully inadequate for what might come through the door. "This is all we have?"

Another one of Valerian's men glances toward me from where he stands at one of the large windows overlooking the street, likely watching for them to arrive. "We have a call into the doctor we use, too. He's coming, but it might be a while. He's on the other side of town."

¡Mierda!

In all the years I lived with Felipe and then Andres, I never had to personally deal with anyone coming in with a gunshot wound. Felipe kept me locked away in the rectory of whatever church he was at, and once Andres was released from prison, he whisked me away to his estate, where none of that ever touched me.

I knew it happened, understood what he did, but it wasn't until Kat set that bomb that blew up the meeting of the five families that I was introduced to the true violence of this world.

It left me permanently scarred and even more determined to complete the plan I had set in motion years ago. One that now relies on the man whose life hangs in the balance.

If Valerian dies, everything I've worked for might crumble to the ground around me.

No.

I shake off that thought because even allowing it to enter my head somehow seems like a bad omen, and the last thing I need right now is anything dark hovering around this place.

Valerian's man at the window drops the blinds back into place and turns to where Dmitri and one other man wait. "They're here!"

Dmitri throws opens a door in the kitchen and dashes out into what must be a garage attached to the house while I hold my breath, waiting to see how bad the damage really is.

Every second that passes tightens that vise around my ribcage until I can barely stand still and have to fight the urge to run out there myself. I tighten my grip on the box instead and wait for them to bring Valerian inside.

Muffled, indecipherable Russian words float to me through the open door, and I crane my neck to try to see out into the garage. Dmitri comes into view through the frame, his arm wrapped around Valerian, with Ivan on the other side, helping hold him upright.

Red fills my vision—both the blood soaking his white shirt under his suitcoat and the rage filling me toward whoever did this.

I shouldn't care. Valerian was only supposed to be a means to an end. A stop on the way to my ultimate goal. A necessary piece to the puzzle I need to put into place in order to get what I want. Yet, somehow, he's become so much more than that. From that first moment I saw him, and now, after getting so close to him, I'm not certain I can separate my feelings for him from what needs to happen.

"Valerian..."

His name tumbles from my lips on a gasp, and I set the box on the end table beside the black leather sofa to rush toward them as they struggle to get him up the single step from the garage into the kitchen. His massive, solid frame makes it nearly impossible for them to accomplish the task without turning him sideways and jostling him in a way that makes a wince overtake his already-pained face.

"*Kotyonok?*" His voice breaks the same way his body so obviously is.

Ivan forces me out of the way, and he and Dmitri maneuver Valerian down the hallway toward his bedroom. I snatch the box of medical supplies off the end table, snag a stack of towels someone set on another table, and rush after them, my eyes catching the drops of blood in a trail on the wood floors.

Acid churns in my stomach, but I can't lose my shit now. Valerian's life is at stake, and with him, the future of this city.

"*Ne pooskayte eyo!*" Valerian's words come out clipped and harsh.

I stop just inside the door, watching them turn to try to get his back to the bed. "What did he say?"

Dmitri glares at me. "He doesn't want you here. Go out to the living room."

"What?" I rush forward in front of them, where they stand at the side of the bed we shared last night, shove the box and towels on the nightstand, and squat down so my gaze can meet Valerian's. "If you think I'm leaving you like this, *estas putamente loco.*"

He mutters something under his breath and winces again as drops of blood start to pool under where he's held erect by Ivan and Dmitri. They both glance down at it, then share a concerned look before finagling him onto the bed with a lot of grunts and Valerian gritting his jaw so tightly it looks like it might break.

Ivan digs through the box of supplies and pulls out a pair of scissors, immediately setting to work on cutting open the shirt and exposing Valerian's blood-soaked torso.

Dios mio!

Dmitri grabs a towel and wipes at the blood, looking for the source. "Where is he hit?"

"*Mudak!*" The muscles in Valerian's neck strain against the pain wracking his body, his hand clenching at the comforter beneath him. "Could you make it hurt more?"

Something tells me it's going to.

A lot.

We need to control this bleeding until the doctor they called arrives and can actually treat him —hopefully treat him. If there is any internal damage and Valerian needs surgery, there's no way we're doing it here, and he's not in any shape to be moved again with as much blood as he's losing.

Ivan leans over Valerian and rolls his body to the right side, earning another angry litany of curses from the man bleeding on the bed. "It looks like it went through his left side."

I round the bed to climb onto the mattress next to Valerian. He opens his eyes and glares at me like he wants to argue again about my being in here, but I grab his hand in mine and squeeze. For a split second, it looks like he might push away the touch, but instead, he squeezes back before inhaling a deep, unsteady breath while Ivan and Dmitri poke and prod at him.

With their large bodies and hands all over Valerian, I can't see much. "How bad is it?"

Dmitri shakes his head. "Hard to say if there's any internal damage, but he's bleeding a lot, so it may have hit an artery."

"Shit." I tighten my grip on Valerian's hand, swallowing back that acid rising in my throat. "When is the doctor getting here?"

Ivan glances at his watch while applying pressure to the wound at Valerian's back with a towel, while Dmitri does the same from the front. "Maybe not soon enough."

TEN

VALERIAN

DOCTOR VOLKOV ZIPS UP his bag and offers me one more look of reproach. "You're very lucky you weren't dead by the time I got here. If I hadn't been able to repair that artery, you'd be dead right now."

"But he'll be okay?"

Sofia's soft voice drags my attention away from the doctor to where she sits beside me on the other side of the bed with her hands clasped together and brow furrowed.

Doc casts a glance her way before zeroing in on the bandage covering my abdomen. "As long as the bullet didn't nick his intestines or any other vital organs, he should recover fine." He locks his gaze with mine. "But without opening him up fully or doing a CT scan, I can't know that for certain. If he develops a fever, call me right away." He motions toward the bottle on the nightstand. "I gave him IV antibiotics and left oral ones to continue. He lost a lot of blood and will be weak for a few days. Stay in bed as much as possible, stay hydrated, and try to avoid stress."

Avoid stress?

I chuckle and immediately regret it when pain slices through me the same way his scalpel did when he had to cut me open slightly to try to control the bleeding. Whatever he gave me in the IV dulled the pain and left me in a cloudy fog, but it wasn't enough to completely eliminate the feeling of someone inside me. Passing out was a blessing, but coming to was an agonizing slap of reality only soothed by focusing on Sofia's soft hands at my face and whispered words in my ear.

She climbs from the bed and walks the doctor to the door. "Thank you, Doctor."

Leaning in, she says something else to him, and he quickly glances my way before shaking his head and ducking out of the room. Whatever she asked him, she didn't appear to like the answer.

Her entire body stiff, she closes the door behind him and pauses for a moment, staring at the wood. Slowly, she turns back toward me and makes her way over to stand at the side of the bed, staring down at me like I'm something broken and useless.

The worst position for a man like me, for anyone who relies on their power to control an empire. I never wanted her to see me like this. It's the very reason I didn't want her in here. Uncle Boris always said to show no weakness, and I've managed not to until now.

"Stop looking at me like that, *kotyonok.*"

Her gaze softens with concern, and she brushes her fingers over my exposed arm near where the IV was. "The doctor said you're likely still in a lot of pain. Are you okay? Is there anything you need?"

"To be left alone."

The corners of her lips twitch. "Well, that's not going to happen. So, you're just going have to learn to put up with me."

I raise an eyebrow. "Only this morning, you were so eager to leave, so angry at my insistence that you stay, but now, you want to? This is your chance, your opportunity to try to escape while I'm down for the count."

She sits on the side of the mattress next to me and releases a heavy sigh. "I was mad because you were trying to keep me here as a hostage, to use me against my brothers. Staying because I want to is totally different..."

Something warm blooms in my chest. Something I can't ever remember feeling before this moment. Something I didn't think could exist for a man like me—who has lied, stolen, and killed to get what he wants—could ever have.

"Why do you want to stay, Sofia?"

Her words in the playroom about how she *wanted* me from the first time she saw me return to my thoughts. Something about it has nagged at the back of my mind since. She may have said she wanted me, but she never said *why*. This woman now seems capable of so much more than I expected. She could have wanted me to let down my guard for any number of reasons, making her words true but hiding their real meaning.

"Why *do* you want to stay? To watch me suffer?"

Sofia gently spreads her hand over my exposed chest, the light touch sending a shiver through me that makes me wince. "Sorry."

"Don't apologize for that." The thought of her touch seems to be the only thing keeping me here, connected with this world, when the pain and darkness want to drag me away with it.

"Despite what you may think, Valerian, I don't want to see you in hurt. I don't want to see you suffer or die."

"Would you care if I did?"

I shouldn't have asked because if she gives an answer I don't like, I'll have to live with the consequences of knowing.

She pauses for a moment before answering, scanning my face for something, sharp nails curling into the skin on my pec. "I would very much care if you died."

"Because you need me for your plan—whatever it is?"

Whatever Sofia has been hiding, her true intention for coming to the club and getting involved with me, isn't yet clear, but it's only a matter of time before I uncover her real motivations.

Her almost-affectionate gaze sweeps over me, and she presses her hand tightly over my chest. "Yes, I need you..." She releases a resigned sigh. "And maybe because I actually care more than I thought I would."

I reach out and brush a strand of dyed-blond hair away from her face. She leans into my hand slightly, and my heart thuds loudly in my ears, the very blood that was so freely flowing from me only hours ago now pushing life through my body.

"I never thought I'd hear you say that, *kotyonok*." And I want to believe she means it for one very real reason. "I never thought I would want to hear it."

It's as close to a proclamation of feelings she'll ever get from me, and she seems to recognize it, swallowing thickly and pressing a kiss to my palm before lowering my hand to my side.

"Do you want to tell me what happened?"

I had already told Ivan and Dmitri everything while she stepped out of the room to help the doctor in the bathroom. I hadn't intended on discussing it with her, especially not with this pain medication induced fog enveloping my brain.

"Why were you on Michigan Avenue?"

"I was getting something for you."

Her eyebrows rise. "For me?"

I nod. "To apologize for having to hold you here against your will."

That draws a smile across her face that warms my body for the first time since the bullet slammed into me.

"I guess I'll have to go back for it because I never made it inside."

She offers a tight smile. "What happened?"

There really isn't any reason not to tell her at this point. Not when she's in so deep already. If I expect her to come clean with me, I need to reveal certain things to her, too. She isn't some random woman being dragged into this world by my advances; Sofia has been part of it her entire life, even if her brothers tried to keep her clear of it.

In reality, she may be the only one who can truly understand any of it.

"I got out of the car and was going into a store when I was shot on the sidewalk."

"Did you see who shot you?"

I shake my head, blurry flashes of the memory flickering in my mind. "No, no face, but I saw *something*?"

"What?"

"A familiar tattoo."

She narrows her eyes. "A tattoo?"

After disappearing for so long, there's no way to know how much of what has happened Sofia is really aware of. "A tattoo that belongs to a group that has been stirring up trouble called The Luna Cartel..."

Her entire body stiffens, her eyes widening. "Are you sure?"

I nod, trying to assess her reaction.

She pulls her bottom lip between her teeth. "But why would they come after you in such a targeted attack? I thought their issue was with Galen?"

Something she shouldn't know if she's been in hiding this whole time.

"I've tied myself to Galen, and I helped him take out one of their primary warehouses and most of their men. They have already brought in more and retaliated against him, attacking one of his shipments. My guess is this was their retaliation against me for the same action."

Sofia purses her lips and drums her fingers on her knee. "What about the group that attacked the church? Couldn't it have been them, maybe trying to draw away suspicion by using the obvious tattoo?"

"You've kept abreast of all the goings on while you were away, haven't you?"

She stills and clears her throat, darting her eyes away from mine. "Just because I wasn't living with my brothers doesn't mean I wasn't keeping an eye on what was happening as much as I could. In order to stay hidden, I had to limit what I was doing so they couldn't track me, but I still have eyes and ears and ways to get information."

And secrets.

My conversation with her brothers comes back to me. "Do *you* know who was behind the group that attacked us in the church?"

"No." She swallows thickly and shakes her head. "And I also don't think this attack was Luna Cartel."

"Why not? I saw the tattoo they all bear. It couldn't have been anyone else."

She stiffens slightly. "They've been focused on Galen. Even if you helped him, I don't think they'd expose themselves like this, attack you out in the open if they didn't have to. There were plenty of other places they could have come at you. They didn't have to do it there."

"They chased after Galen, shot at his car in a populated suburban area, and were ready to blow a bomb to eliminate him that could have injured anyone near that building when it blew. They don't seem concerned with doing things discreetly."

"Maybe not." She purses her lips together and stares at a spot on the wall. "I don't know what's going on, but I can find out." Her eyes finally meet mine again. "You get me access to a computer, and I will do some digging. I'm sure I can find out a lot you haven't managed to about the Luna Cartel and maybe even who was behind these other attacks."

"Won't that require exposing yourself?"

She tightens her jaw, a look of determination set in her gaze. "I'm not going to hide anymore."

"Worried about your brothers?"

"No." She shakes her head. "They've made their beds to lie in."

I brush my fingers across the top of her hand. "Does that mean you're worried about me?"

The tiniest of smiles graces her lips. "Don't let your head swell too big."

It isn't my head that's swelling at the thought that she actually gives a shit and this might not just be all a game.

"I'll get you the computer. Find out anything you can help us solve this mystery and end the threats."

ELEVEN

VALERIAN

GALEN SMIRKS, looking immaculate in his perfectly tailored gray suit and dark tie. His eyes sweep over me, from my bare feet, up the silk pajama pants over my legs, over the loose black T-shirt that hides the wrappings around the hole in my side, and to my face, that no doubt holds the evidence of just how shitty the last forty-eight hours have been. "You look like shit, my friend."

I offer a grunt of acknowledgment, press my hand against the wound, and shuffle farther into the living room to Galen waiting in front of the fireplace, where Ivan left him after he let him in a few minutes ago.

His green gaze narrows on my face. "Should you even be out of bed?"

Not if Sofia had her way.

The only reason I was able to sneak away from the bedroom was that she was in the shower. If she hadn't been, she would have ensured I didn't move from the bed, just like she has since the moment the doctor left. Other than getting up to use the bathroom, that woman hasn't let me move a muscle. I would say it's romantic, but it's more like being a child again and being cared for by my mother. And thinking of Sofia like my *mother* is the absolute last thing I ever want.

Casting a glare his way, I wave him off with my free hand. "It's been two days. I can't spend another minute flat on my back without feeling like I'm dead."

Or a helpless baby.

Galen barks out a laugh and shakes his head, sliding his hands into his pockets casually. "I've been there. I understand completely what you mean. But at least I had Nicki nursing me back to health."

I snort and grin at him. "Yes, the touch of a beautiful woman helps, doesn't it?"

He narrows his eyes on me again. "Something you want to tell me?"

Hell no.

If Galen discovered that Sofia Rose is here, there would be far too many questions I can't answer. Either because it would unravel my plans or because I don't know them.

When it comes to that woman in my bedroom, the longer she's around, the more I start to wonder if I truly know anything anymore.

The room spins slightly around me, and I shake my head and motion toward the couch. Perhaps being on my feet wasn't such a good idea. "Let's sit before I collapse."

Galen obliges with a smirk and lowers himself into one of the leather chairs facing the couch as I grit my teeth and take my seat across from him with a little groan.

He eyes me warily, his concern over my condition evident. And since I'm his only ally, I can see why. "Dmitri called to say you thought it was the Luna Cartel."

"It was a woman, and she had a tattoo on her neck, behind her ear. I saw it as she moved away from me after firing."

"The same one we found on the rest of the members?"

I nod.

Galen leans back in the chair and crosses his ankle over his knee. "That doesn't really leave any question, then, does it, other than when they added women to their crew?"

"No."

"Retaliation for what we did?"

"That's my assumption." The only one I can make, given everything that's happened and what little memory of the event I still have. "I was clearly targeted."

He drums his fingers on the arm of the chair. "Bold to do it in the middle of Michigan Avenue with all the people around."

"It is..." I lock my gaze with his. "And it makes me concerned for what they might do next."

When they first arrived in Chicago and started pushing in on Galen's territory, they seemed a minor complication. Not unlike any of the other smaller groups who have tried—and failed—to stake some sort of claim on something that wasn't theirs to take. None of the families have ever fallen to these interlopers, and aside from the occasional loss of a few men's lives, everyone has walked away relatively unscathed.

Until the Luna Cartel...whatever their issue is with Galen, it's marrow-deep, and they seem almost obsessed with finding a way to take his territory.

He shakes his head. "What can we do? We all but wiped them out, and they came back like a cockroach infestation."

Deadly cockroaches—ones who apparently aren't afraid to take aim in the middle of a crowded sidewalk in broad daylight.

"I have someone doing some digging. If we can locate whoever's running their entire operation, we might be able to get the upper hand."

"But we have nothing to go on. I have been up against them for months and it took me *that* long to find the warehouse."

"Yes, but we found something on the bomb."

One of his brows rises over the scar bisecting his eye. "And you didn't think to tell me?"

I glare at him. "I've been a little busy. There was a shipping label on the box. We scanned it into our computers to try to enhance it. If we can decipher any of the words on it or even a location stamp, it might give us information we didn't have before. Like I've said before, if we take off the head of the snake, we can kill the entire thing."

He nods slowly. "That would eliminate one threat but leave another looming that's just as large if not larger."

"Everyone is working on that problem, too."

Valentina and Cutter, along with their source, Preacher, the Roses, and now Sofia. Someone is bound to find *something*. It just needs to happen before more bullets fly.

A long, slow sigh slips from his lips. "They just keep coming for us, though, don't they?"

"Maybe if you weren't pissing them off, they wouldn't be trying to kill you."

We both jerk our heads toward where Sofia stands at the end of the hallway, arms crossed over her chest defiantly, wearing one of the simple black dresses I had Ilya buy her with a *V* low enough to show her cleavage.

What the hell is she doing?

If I was able to recognize her so easily, despite the blond hair, there's a good chance Galen will, as well. This could get very ugly very fast. Knowing him as well as I do—and given the fact that he's already accused me of keeping things from him and even being behind the death squad from Albania—he won't take too kindly to my harboring the woman the Roses have been breaking their backs scouring the Earth for. One who has a skill set that could bring down just about any government—or *group*—she sets her sights on.

Galen's shrewd gaze zeroes in on her. "Who the fuck are you?"

Sofia takes a step closer, her eyes locked on Galen, not even acknowledging I'm in the damn room.

What the hell is she thinking, engaging him like this?

I try to push to my feet, but the agony that engulfs my body and the immediate dizziness that overwhelms my head drop me back with gritted teeth. "Julia..." The name comes out on a wheezed breath. "What are you doing out here?"

She finally breaks her stare-down with Galen and looks my way. "Sorry, I couldn't help but over-hear and offer my view as an outsider to your world." A fake smile curls her lips, and she flashes it at Galen. "I meant no offense. I was just observing that it seems as though a lot of the problems stem from one person doing something to piss off the other. If everyone just *stopped*, all the trouble would disappear, would it not?"

Her shrug may appear nonchalant, but it isn't.

What she just said gnaws at my gut and makes acid crawl up my throat.

It almost sounded like a *threat*.

TWELVE

VALERIAN

Steeling my expression, I raise my hand and beckon Sofia over to me. "Julia, come here."

She approaches cautiously and glances at Galen before stepping between my spread legs and leaning down to me on the couch. I wrap one hand around her wrist and tug her even closer, brushing my lips against her and taking her face in my other palm.

"I don't know what the fuck you're doing, *kotyonok,* but stop and get the hell back in the bedroom before he pulls a gun or something worse."

Galen is on edge right now—as he should be. And her comment isn't going to help ease that.

She presses a kiss to my cheek and smiles at me sweetly. "Whatever you want, *sabrosito.*"

Sabrosito?

I don't know what the fuck that means, and at the moment, I don't care. I just need her to get the fuck out of here before the shit hits the fan in a way that can't be undone.

Tightening my hand around her wrist until I'm sure it hurts, I issue a low growl of warning under my breath. "Watch yourself."

She straightens and inclines her head toward Galen before she saunters off casually down the hallway.

Galen turns toward me, brows raised, his jaw tight. "Who. The fuck. Is that?"

I wave a dismissive hand as if I couldn't care less about the woman who just came in here and rattled me more than I want to admit, without a thought that Galen might recognize her. "Nobody. A girl from the club named Julia."

He glances toward the hallway she just disappeared down. "A girl from the club?" Narrowing his eyes on me, he shakes his head. "She didn't seem like one of your club girls, Valerian. Since when do you bring them home?"

I smirk at him. "Julia has many talents..."

"Including caring for gunshots?"

And destroying my sanity.

I shrug as much as I can, biting back the groan at the little stab of pain, then climb to my feet. "I can't complain about that, but she needs to learn to keep her nose out of my business if she's going to stay around."

That dismissive comment is meant to show Galen my reproach of her intruding and that I will deal with her in private, but he still watches me cautiously, as if he isn't sure he buys what I just said.

"She has a much gentler touch than Dmitri, so I'd like to keep her for a bit." Offering him a smirk, I incline my head toward the hallway. "I'll make sure she has something in her mouth so she can't speak out of line again."

Galen issues a deep chuckle and climbs to his feet, still watching me with suspicion. "You do that. And you'll keep me apprised of any developments on any of these issues?"

"Of course."

He glances toward the hall again before he steps to the door. "Hey, try not to die, okay. It's hard enough around here without you to help watch my back."

I nod and shuffle to the door behind him to throw the lock. The movement makes my entire body ache, but I push away the exhaustion and move to the window to watch him drive off. Once he's safely out of sight, I return my focus to the problem waiting in my bedroom, clench my jaw, and turn toward the hallway to go deal with Sofia.

She sits on the bed, typing away on the laptop I got her, completely engrossed in whatever she's doing—which over the last two days *hasn't* included finding anything useful in our search for our enemies.

When she doesn't acknowledge me, I kick the door closed with my foot. The slam makes her jump, and her head jerks up, her eyes meeting mine in question.

I approach her slowly, giving her all the time in the world to anticipate what I might say or do, then slowly lower myself to the edge of the bed to sit beside her. "What. The. Fuck. Was. That?"

One of her brows rises. "What was *what*?"

Grasping her wrist again, I knock the laptop onto the bed beside her. "What the hell was that move you just pulled with Galen? Are you trying to get caught or get me killed?"

She narrows her eyes on me. "I told you I was done hiding."

"In *that* world!" I point toward the computer. "The *digital* one. This is the *real* world, where people carry guns and want to exploit you to get to your brothers."

Her lips twist slightly. "People like you?"

"Oh no..." I shake my head. "We're not doing that right now. You know as well as I do that if you really *wanted* to leave, I would have let you go days ago. In fact, I *told* you to. And I've done nothing to your brothers except try to find out what they know—something *you're* supposed to be helping me with."

She leans back slightly against the headboard. "What do you think I've been doing the last two days?"

"Treating me like a fucking child who can't take care of himself."

"You *can't*." Her words come out angrier than I've ever heard from her. "All you've managed to do is fuck up everything and almost get yourself killed."

Moving with speed she certainly doesn't anticipate, given my condition, I climb onto the bed and wrap my hand around her throat, pushing her head back against the wall, ignoring the pain in my body screaming at me to stop. "What is your game, *kotyonok*? Tell me now."

Sofia swallows against my hand and has the nerve to snake her tongue out over her lips like she's enjoying having it there rather than fearing what I might do. "What's yours?"

She asks it coolly, not a hint of emotion in her voice, as if she's asking me the time of day or discussing the weather. My cock hardens almost instantly, jutting against the thin silk pants that can do nothing to restrain it. It pushes against her, an undeniable sign that this woman still controls parts of me I wish she couldn't. Sofia has too much power over me, over my body, over things that are even more important and could leave me vulnerable.

"Really, Valerian...you don't really expect me to believe that you haven't been working on something behind the scenes and you haven't been planning something of your own that will affect all these people you pretend to be friends with?"

I snarl at her. "I don't have friends. I have people I tolerate. People I work with because it's necessary. But make no mistake, I do *not* have friends."

"You and Galen looked very friendly out there."

"Galen and I are old school. We respect old alliances, and we don't allow people like your brothers to come in and rattle us."

"Really?" She slowly raises an eyebrow. "Because you appear pretty fucking rattled right now."

I growl and lower my head, anger flaring for the woman for the first time since she set foot in the club. "I've enjoyed our little dance, Sofia, truly I have, but the time has come to end this, and—"

"And what?" She shifts forward, forcing her neck tighter against my palm, until her lips feather over mine. "If I don't spill all my secrets, you'll kill me?"

She presses her hands to my chest and shoves, and in my state, it's enough to set me off balance and make the room tilt slightly around me. I rock back on my heels, my hand falling from her throat as I squeeze my eyes closed.

Sofia nudges my shoulder until I tilt sideways and my back hits the mattress, spreading me out across it while things still spin around me. She shifts and straddles my waist, placing her cunt directly over my hard silk-covered cock.

The heat of her core sears me through the material, and she rolls her hips, making me bite back a groan as my body heats and responds to the friction against my dick.

I open my eyes to her face hovering over me, and she leans down, bracing herself on her elbows on either side of my face, and runs her fingers through my hair almost lovingly.

"I'll tell you what, *sabrosito*. I'll tell you the truth. All of it." She flutters her lips against mine. "But you may not like what you're going to hear."

THIRTEEN

SOFIA

IT WAS INEVITABLE.

This confrontation.

Having to come clean.

I couldn't hide behind Julia forever, and things are coming to a head.

It would have been nice to spend a bit more time like this with Valerian—locked away from the tension and bloodshed, from the uncertainty. But Galen showing up just pushed my buttons in a way that made it impossible for me to keep my mouth shut and impossible for Valerian to keep waiting when he knows I'm withholding from him.

I grind down on his cock, rocking my hips forward and back, the pressure and friction in exactly the right place for both of us. He releases a strangled groan against my lips, and I deepen our kiss, twining my tongue with his and then sucking it into my mouth the way I did his cock the other night and have wanted to again so many times since then.

The man tastes every bit as good as he looks, and after having his hand at my throat like that, my body craves him in a way I never thought I would.

He lifts his hand and cups my cheek in his rough palm, brushing his thumb across my lips. "Tell me, *kotyonok*. Even if it's going to hurt."

Oh, it will hurt...

The truth always does, especially when you've been keeping it from someone close to you. It can throw their world into chaos, change the color of the sky, alter the reality they've been living in their entire lives.

It's what happened to me, and it will to Valerian...and everyone else, too.

"I'll try to make sure it doesn't." I sit back and reach between us to free his cock, dragging the head through my wetness before sinking down on it slowly. "Fuuuuck..."

Bracing my hands on his thighs, I rise up and lower myself back onto him, a gasp tumbling from my lips. He's so big this way, spreading me open and filling me like he's always meant to be there.

He groans, and his hands tighten on my hips almost painfully. "*Kotyonok*..."

I suck in a deep breath, trying to force my brain to process words while I keep moving on him. "What I told you the other night was true...that day, at the meeting, when I saw you...it changed everything."

Rolling my hips, I grind down on him, pushing my clit against his pelvis and digging my nails into his thighs.

He grunts and shifts slightly, slipping impossibly deeper inside me. "How, *kotyonok*?"

So much has happened.

So much time has passed since I learned the shocking truth.

So many things have changed and shifted—alliances, feelings, the world in which we all operate.

I've grown from that scared teenager into a woman, one who has desires and needs. One who is capable of so much more than anyone ever believed I was.

Yet, somehow, explaining all this to Valerian is far harder than I imagined. I hadn't anticipated caring, wanting him for more than what he could do for my plans, *needing* him.

With his cock buried deep inside me, the head dragging across just the right spot each time I lift up and sink back down on him, my mind doesn't want to relive all those traumas, doesn't want the agony of the betrayal to influence the pleasure of what's happening now.

Valerian slips his hand to where our bodies connect and finds my clit with the pad of his thumb. He rolls it across my sensitive nub expertly while I move over him, seeking the release I desire as much as he does the words I can't seem to get out.

"I'll stop, kotyonok"—his voice comes husky, even lower than normal, heavy with the strain of holding himself back and the pain he undoubtedly feels doing this—"if you don't keep talking."

I swallow thickly and increase my pace. "I-I had already discovered something about my brothers, something they had been hiding from me from the beginning...it had made me—"

Valerian thrusts up, and I gasp, struggling to inhale again as pleasure courses through my body. "Angry. I knew I couldn't trust them..."

"What did you do, Sofia?"

"I...I...I formed a plan."

His fingers dig into my hips. "A plan for what?"

"To destroy them..."

He drives up into me again, and I groan and fall forward, bracing my hands on his broad shoulders, trying not to put any pressure on his abdomen. The change in position pins his hand between us, but he pinches my clit between his fingers and twists.

An orgasm slams into me as my hips buck wildly. "Fuck!"

The word tumbles from my lips, and he lifts his head and captures it with a soul-bruising kiss that steals all the breath from my lungs.

I pull away, gasping, every limb tingling and pulsing with ecstasy. He pushes into me again, rolling his hips, keeping my pleasure going in what feels like a never-ending wave designed to drown us both. I clench around him as he fucks me relentlessly, chasing his own cataclysm until he finally groans my name and empties himself inside me.

He kisses me again, and my eyes drift closed, wanting to get lost in this feeling forever and ignore the world around us. But Valerian pulls away abruptly, clasping my face between his hands harshly. "How were you going to destroy them, kotyonok?"

Pushing away the fog enveloping my brain, I open my eyes to meet his. They have gone arctic cold, like he switched off that part that allows him to care about anything the moment he came, the minute our game ended.

I stare down at the man who became the core of my plan, the only way I could see to reach my ultimate goal, and something tightens around my ribcage. "By doing the one thing they never can."

He releases a heavy breath. "What's that?"

"Remain completely detached. Not care about anyone or anything except making them pay and getting what I am owed."

His cock twitches inside me, and he drags his fingers across my cheek. "That may be the sexiest thing I've ever heard you say."

I can't stop the grin pulling at my lips. "That's pretty fucked up."

"Aren't we?" He feathers kisses down my neck and across my exposed cleavage while I try to find my breath again.

"True..." I sigh and shift slightly, the motion making me clench around his still-hard cock.

He groans again, and his eyes reignite with the same desire I've seen there since our gazes met at the club that night.

"I used my hacking skills to my benefit. Set myself up to win and them to fail."

"You haven't been able to track down anything on the Luna Cartel or this group that's after us." His hard gaze locks with mine, and he grins. "Maybe you're not as good as you think you are."

I smirk at the audacity of his statement and how insanely wrong he is, how naïve the head of the bratva truly is about what I can do with a single computer and the internet, and I dart my tongue across my lips. "Oh, I am good. Better than any of you even knows." I motion absently with my hand at the air. "I'm everywhere and nowhere. Everything and nothing. I can be anything and anyone I want."

His brow furrows, like something is finally clicking in his head, and he grips my chin firmly, true fear finally settling into his icy gaze. He doesn't even need to voice the question because I know what he's thinking, what he's managed to piece together after all this time, what I've managed to hide so well for so long.

Nodding slowly, I lean in and press what might be our final kiss to his lips. "I'm the head of the Luna Cartel..."

INDULGING GLUTTONY

Gluttony kills more than the sword.

- Proverb

ONE

VALERIAN

"I am the head of the Luna Cartel..."

"But—" I open and close my mouth as my brain struggles to process her confession and line it up with everything that's happened.

She's only been missing since Cutter and Valentina took Rose from his compound months ago. What the Luna Cartel has done—the attacks on Galen and pushing their way into his territory and that of others here has been going on long before that, when she was still living with Rose and working for him.

"How is that possible? You're..."

Sofia slowly raises an eyebrow at me, a smug tilt to her petal-soft pink lips. "A *child*? Is that what you were going to say?" She squeezes her cunt around my cock still embedded in her to make her point, then rolls her hips and glides up and down my length, grinding down at my pelvis as a final exclamation point of emphasis. "Because I think I've proven to you that I'm not."

"*Bylad!*"

This can't be real.

It must be some sort of hallucination brought on by the strain my body has been through and overexertion.

She can't possibly be serious...

I scrub my hands over my face and push her off me, using every bit of energy left in my body. My wet cock slips from inside her heat, and a low groan rumbles from my lips at the sudden loss of the feeling of being cocooned in her pussy.

But it's necessary.

It's physically impossible to think with this woman riding me.

She rolls to the side and shifts back to the headboard as I lie prone and panting, staring at the ceiling, trying to wrap my head around all this.

If she's the head of the Luna Cartel, then that means she's responsible for the bullet that almost killed me.

I glance over at her, searching for any signs of deception on her part. "Luna Cartel shot me."

Some of that day remains fuzzy, lost in a haze of pain, but I *saw* that tattoo. I know I did. And it's the calling card of the group she claims she's controlling.

Her bourbon eyes meet mine, but there isn't any denial in them, rather, something softer, perhaps an apology, guilt, or both. "They did, but it wasn't at *my* command." She shakes her head slightly. "No one had heard from me, and I missed another meeting while you had me on my knees in your office. Only one person knew where I was and what I was doing...and she knew I was at the club. She thought you were holding me against my will. She thought by taking you out that it would allow me to escape. I *never* would have ordered them to hurt you. I *didn't* order it. I swear."

"Jesus Christ..." I grit my teeth against the inevitable discomfort and climb off the side of the bed, unable to lie there so exposed after this bombshell. Tucking my semi-hard cock back into the silk pajama pants, I turn to her. "You're going to have to fill in some holes here, Sofia, because I don't understand a fucking thing about what's going on."

Whether it's the lust-induced haze still hanging around or the lingering pain meds, I can't seem to line up what she's saying with what's happened.

Sofia sighs and casually smooths her dress back down over her thighs, like my cum isn't dripping from her pussy right now and she hasn't just flipped the entire world upside down. "I told you I wanted to get back at my brothers because they lied to me about something."

"Yes."

But starting a rival cartel seems like a bit of an overreaction.

"Well..." She locks her gaze with mine, pain flashing in it. "That something is bigger than you could ever have imagined."

Clenching my fists at my sides, I growl at her, frustration over her riddles and games making it nearly impossible to hold back my rage. "Don't leave me hanging, Sofia. You're already on some pretty fucking thin ice."

And I'm on the verge of punching through it and drowning her in the frigid waters.

No matter how my body may react to her.

No matter how badly I want to pin her to the bed and fuck the truth out of her.

No matter how much my hands shake, trying to restrain myself from doing *unspeakable* things to her.

At this moment, she's the enemy.

She's just admitted to that.

And I'm *this* close to letting loose and getting answers my own way.

Yet Sofia barely reacts to my veiled threat. She just crosses her legs at the bare ankle and folds her arms across her chest. In a split-second, she's morphed into someone who might be able actually be able to run a cartel, not the young, sheltered woman I once believed her to be.

How could I have missed it?

A smug smile spreads her lips. "I've basically been running their empire since I was fourteen. That's when I started making my moves and preparing my revenge against them."

"For *what*? What could they *possibly* have done to you that was so bad? They seem to love you, to care about you—obsessively even. They've been scouring the goddamn planet for you for months."

She nods slowly. "Because they *need* me. Because I'm the only one they've ever been able to trust who can actually handle everything that keeps our organization successful entails." A perturbed huff slips from her lips. "You think Andres or Felipe are organizing shipments, booking cargo ships, making sure the men get paid?" She raises a brow. "You think they have any idea how to track down information on any of their potential adversaries? Or know how to take them down from the inside by using that information?"

Annoyance hardens her face as I pace at the foot of the bed.

"I've done it *all*, Valerian. Everything." She slams her fists into the mattress at her sides. "*I've* built the Blood Rose Cartel into what it is today, starting from the day I first realized how good I really was with a damn computer. And they let me do it because they wanted to keep themselves insulated. They didn't want to bring in any outsiders. They thought it kept them protected, that their secrets would remain buried, and as long as only *family* was involved, there was no chance of betrayal. They never expected I would find out the *truth* about what they did."

The Blood Rose Cartel has done a *lot* of horrific shit over the years, starting in Colombia, then expanding into other areas, and ultimately, moving in here. There are so many things Sofia could be referring to, yet nothing jumps out at me as warranting this kind of vitriol toward her brothers.

"What the *fuck* could they have done to deserve this?"

Even after all these years of being separated from them, if any of my brothers or sisters ever needed *anything*, I would ensure they had it, even at my own expense—monetarily or emotionally. The bond that flows through blood is hard to ignore, impossible at times, even. And what fills Sofia's veins has been poisoned by something powerful.

I slowly approach her side of the bed and tilt her chin until her eyes meet mine. "What did they do, Sofia? What hardened your heart and turned you against your own blood?"

Her bottom lip trembles slightly, the first real emotion besides anger I've seen since she made her confession. "The man you know as Father Felipe...he murdered our parents, and Andres helped him cover it up."

It takes a moment for her words to sink in, for their depth and meaning to fully settle on my chest like the lead weight they must be for her. "Felipe...*killed* your parents?"

A single tear trickles from the corner of her eye, and she offers a stiff nod against my grip on her chin. "Yes, when I was only a year or so old."

She closes her eyes for a moment and inhales a deep breath. "I don't even remember them. I was simply told one of the cartels in the area wanted their land and killed them for it, taking me to raise in their sinister world until my brother rescued me, but that isn't the truth." Her lids flutter open, her tear-soaked eyes meeting mine. "Felipe did it—ostensibly to save them from torture at the hands of the cartel who would have done it in a worse way—and when Andres discovered our parents dead and me missing, he went and killed the head of the cartel who he believed had murdered our parents."

I let my grip fall away from her chin and scrub my hands over my face. "Holy hell..."

"It gets worse."

TWO

VALERIAN

"HOW CAN IT *POSSIBLY* BE WORSE?"

Sofia offers a hard smile devoid of any real humor. "With my brothers, you never really know. One had already developed a name for himself on the streets—"

"Felipe?"

She shakes her head. "No, not Felipe. Felipe was the one who was the perfect altar boy and son. *Andres* was the one everyone assumed committed the murders that created the blood bath that earned our cartel its name in revenge for our parents. But it wasn't Andres. So, in order to protect Felipe, who was soft and weak and not at all violent before that day, they swapped identities when he went to prison."

"What?" I settle onto the edge of the bed, trying to picture the brothers and how this all could have gone down.

The story behind the cartel's name is legendary—how Rose annihilated one of the most powerful men in Colombia and took out his top men...even his *wife*...before stepping up to take over their territory. Sofia's story puts a whole new sinister spin on what we all thought we knew.

"How is that even possible?"

Her shoulders rise and fall nonchalantly. "They're identical twins, and there is only one way to tell them apart. Something no one would ever know if they didn't dig in their medical records. Andres had a tiny scar on his lower left back from a piece of farming equipment that sliced him as a child."

"How did you find out what happened and that they had switched places?"

"For the first ten years of my life, I lived with who I believed was Felipe, the proud, pious priest who moved from church to church on different missions, helping the poor of our country. He ensured I was educated and insulated, that I knew nothing about the family business. I truly believed he was what he appeared to be and had nothing to do with the violence *Andres* had perpetrated. But then the man I believed to be Andres escaped from prison, and he showed up insisting Felipe turn me over and let him raise me. They had an argument..." She shakes her head. "I only caught bits and pieces of it, but it was enough to know that Andres didn't trust Felipe, which I couldn't quite understand..."

I can.

Those two don't just look alike; they're both rotten to the core. Something that seems easy to see now, but Felipe managed to convince a lot of people for a very long time that he had no involvement in his brother's business when he was really the one pulling all the strings.

If he could deceive the entire world, it isn't that far-fetched that he could dupe his own sister, especially at such a young age.

"You aren't to blame for not seeing the truth, Sofia. No one could have."

Sofia nods slowly, her eyes focused somewhere on the dark comforter rather than at me. "Eventually, Felipe relented, probably fearing the truth would be revealed if he didn't, and Andres shuttled me off to his estate in the mountains. He had tutors come—one who worked with me on computers who discovered my aptitude for it. But it wasn't until I was fourteen that I learned the real truth."

"What happened to you at fourteen?"

She drums her fingers on her leg nervously. "I got into a fight with Andres about something stupid, stole one of his cars, and drove about twenty miles away to the church where Felipe was the pastor."

I smirk, picturing her as a hormonal, destructive teenager with too much spunk to contain—not that different than the woman in front of me now. "I bet that went over well."

A sardonic smile curls her lips, and she glances up at me. "I entered the rectory, and I saw something I shouldn't have—my brother, the priest, having sex with one of the young nuns...and it looked like he knew what he was doing. Saying things that..."—she shakes her head—"a priest definitely shouldn't have been saying."

"Damn!"

"I caught a glimpse of a scar on his back. At the time, I didn't realize what it meant. I didn't fully comprehend what had happened, just that something was very wrong. I went back to Andres, apologized for our tiff, and I started digging for anything that would explain Felipe's behavior... including looking into old medical records. That's where I found the answer—stitches *Andres* had received, not Felipe."

"And you never confronted them about this?"

If she had, surely, the charade would have stopped long ago. There wouldn't have been any reason to continue to lie to her if she knew the truth.

"No." She shakes her head sadly. "I played the role of young, naïve little sister very well."

"How do you know Felipe...or Andres...whoever the fuck he is...killed your parents?"

Her face hardens. "Because my brother, the one you know as *Rose*, talks in his sleep." She gives me a sad smile. "I set up microphones everywhere around the house so I would record anything he said to anyone, any time of day. I didn't want to miss a single word. I wanted to know everything about the business, everything they didn't tell me. I knew they had switched places, but I didn't know *why*. Not until he had a nightmare one night and the truth came out."

Fucking hell...

I pace away from her, no longer able to stand still when everything she's revealed races through my head at a million miles an hour. It explains so much—the animosity between the brothers, her desire to get back at them...

Sofia watches me carefully, assessing my reaction. "That's when I started plotting my revenge. When I knew I would do whatever it took to make them pay for their sins and their deception. That's when I created the Luna Cartel."

"But I don't understand how?"

She waves toward the computer still resting on the other side of the bed. "With *that*. It gives me the power to be anyone, anywhere. Save for one woman—one I trust almost as much as I do myself —none of my crew have ever seen me in person. I'm not who they believed me to be."

The image of the car racing away from the warehouse that night with Galen when the bomb almost destroyed us flashes through my head. "Was that you? At the warehouse the other night?"

Shaking her head, she shoves her hands back through her hair. "No. My first in command, the woman who gives all the orders when I'm not available." Her eyes meet mine, an apology in them. "For the record, that bomb was intended for Galen, not you. I would never let them hurt you."

"What's your deal with Galen? Why go after him? Why target him with the Luna Cartel when they showed up in Chicago?"

A slow grin spreads across her face. "Because I knew who Rowan was. I discovered her while researching materials on all the families here and tracked her down. I knew if Felipe was with her, it would create a tie between Galen and my brothers. He won't pull the trigger and kill the man his sister loves and risk losing her forever. That might force him to side with them...instead of with us."

"*Us?*" I raise a brow at her. "Why me? Why partner with anyone? Why not enact your revenge on a broad scale and take out all the other families and control Chicago yourself?"

"Because I'm not stupid enough to believe any *one* person can control all this."

"What is it you want, then, Sofia?" I wave a hand around. "What is all *this* about?"

She slams her palms against the mattress, anger tightening her shoulders. "I want everything I have built. They haven't done shit. I've been doing all the work for years while they've reaped all the rewards. I've been kept locked in an ivory tower. No more."

Her anger is warranted, given everything that's happened, but one question lingers. One that needs an answer before this goes any further.

"Why do you need me?"

"My brothers and Galen need to disappear. Kat along with them. That leaves you and Valentina..."

Bylad!

"And Cutter's sister is with Galen..."

She nods slowly. "Which means the Italians will *never* agree to help take him out." Pushing up on her knees, she presses her palms against my chest. "I wasn't lying when I said I wanted you from the moment I saw you." She feathers her lips over mine. "You were the first man I ever laid eyes on who made something flutter in my belly, who brought a heat between my legs with just one look."

I grasp her chin harshly, jerking her head up until her gaze meets mine. "You expect me to believe a word you say after revealing all this?"

Sofia doesn't flinch. "Look into my eyes and tell me you don't."

Staring into the molten bourbon pools, I don't find deception. Far from it. A lust burns there, ignited by both her desire for me and for revenge against those who wronged her most.

But I learned a long time ago not to always trust what you see.

Lies come in all forms, sometimes as simple as a look.

"I don't believe you, Sofia. You need help from one of the original families. Someone with an organization that's been around for a long time—one with relationships, supply lines, friends, and a crew you can use in your favor. One who knows Galen, Valentina, and Cutter better than anyone. You *need* me"—I squeeze her even tighter, my fingers digging into the soft skin of her jaw as I brush my lips against hers—"and not just to fill your greedy cunt with my cum."

She whimpers softly, kissing me back until I jerk her away.

For a moment, we stare at each other, both of us heated by the exchange, her chest rising and falling rapidly.

Her nails curl into my pecs, and she offers a slow nod. "That's all true, and it may have been how it started out—that I needed your help to get rid of my brothers, Kat, and Galen, and to smooth out things with the Italians. But the moment you touched me in your office that first night, my plans changed. I want you to do this *with* me, Valerian. I want you to help me take back what's rightfully mine, what I've earned. I want you to help me take Chicago."

THREE

SOFIA

"HELP *YOU*?" Valerian scoffs, and his hand slips from my chin down around my throat to tighten there ominously. "You have it backward, *kotyonok*. I'm the one with the power here—not you. All you have is a ragtag band of men you clearly can't even control. Galen and I have observed how sloppy the Luna Cartel is and how it acts recklessly. You're so caught up in your desire for revenge that you aren't doing things carefully. You aren't doing things *smartly*."

His reproach stings more than I should let it. I shouldn't care at all what he thinks of my business or what I've done. I've tried to harden myself against caring what *anyone* thinks, but still, I flinch. Deep down, I wanted Valerian to be in awe of everything I've accomplished without anyone the wiser. I wanted him to be *proud* of what I've done.

The last few years of my life have been spent trying to climb out from under Andres and Felipe's lies and shadows to establish something that's only for *me*. It isn't perfect. My men may not be as polished as the goons any of the other families have, and controlling them by proxy is far from easy, but they get the job done—spilling an awful lot of blood along the way from those who deserve it.

I've already turned the Luna Cartel into a multi-billion-dollar business that has taken over territories in several major cities, moving drugs and guns easily as if we've always been there, stomping out the competition.

But all he sees is our weaknesses. *My* failures.

I struggle to swallow against his hand, refusing to let the tears welling in my eyes fall. "Then *help* me." Pressing my hands against his chest, I lean in until we're sharing breath. "If we team up, we will be unstoppable. With what I know about my brothers and their business, what I know about Kat, what I know and can find out about anyone else with that computer, combined with your organization and what I know you have in the pipeline, we can control Chicago and beyond—"

"What *I* have in the pipeline?" He raises a dark brow at me and presses his thumb against where my blood races through the artery in my neck, making my head spin slightly at the lack of oxygen reaching my brain. "What the fuck do you know about what I have in the pipeline?"

This isn't how I wanted to have this conversation, not how I intended any of this to go down, but now, I have no choice. It's time to call him out on what I know he's been doing behind the scenes, the secrets he's kept so close to the chest that his own men likely don't even know them.

I square my shoulders and press my hands harder against his chest. Valerian Kamenev is a wall of a man, a beast bred for exactly this—to take and destroy and dominate. He's exactly what I need.

"I told you I've been watching everything, Valerian. Very little gets by me, and I know what you've been doing, even if everyone else remains in the dark."

A flicker of fear dances across his blue eyes, and he leans in, his hot breath on my face. "And what the hell is that, *kotyonok*?"

I knew it wouldn't be easy to call him out, that looking him in the eye and accusing him of *this* would be difficult, but with his grip on my throat, it's more than that—it could be deadly.

Still, I have to do it if I want any chance of achieving my goal and getting him on board. What he's been doing affects my plans, too.

"You've been working for years to step up and control more of Chicago. You've been making moves carefully, quietly, hoping no one will notice, and you've managed to conceal who your partner is...until now." I motion backward toward the computer. "You can't hide it from me."

Valerian's lips curl into a sneer. "That's what you were doing on my computer at the office, trying to get confirmation of whatever it is you *think* is going on."

I grin at him. "I don't *think* it's going on. I *know* it. You may have been able to prevent me from getting into your records, but your counterparts aren't so smart. Once you gave me that laptop and I decided to come out of hiding, you gave me access to everything they have. I was free to use *all* my skills and resources. And I did."

It was almost *too* easy to get into their systems and unravel their entire businesses to follow the trails back here to Valerian. All it did was confirm what I had long suspected—one of the reasons I came to him in the first place.

His gaze hardens. "I don't believe you."

I smirk at him. "You don't? I'll prove it by giving you one word...proof that I know everything."

He freezes and squeezes tightly at my neck. "Then do it, *kotyonok*. Expose whatever you think you know."

Leaning forward into his hand, I whisper the word against his lips. "Vlorë."

The word barely leaves my lips before the crack of gunfire erupts somewhere in the house. We both whip our heads toward the sound and the closed door that offers the only protection from whatever lies outside.

Valerian releases his grip on me to dive for the nightstand, where he keeps a weapon. He jerks open the drawer, pulls out a Makarov, and tugs me off the bed with his free hand.

I jerk my gaze between him and the sounds of all-out war coming from the house. "What the hell is going on?"

He issues a low growl. "I don't know. No one should know about this place. Unless..." He turns to me and narrows his eyes, his lips twisting in a snarl as he drags me against him. "Unless you used that computer to tell your people where to find me."

"What?" I shake my head. "No, I didn't. I swear. I sent them a message to let them know I was all right, specifically so they *wouldn't* try to come after you again."

"I'm just supposed to believe you? Take you at your word?"

Valerian releases a sardonic laugh, and another burst of gunfire sounds—this time closer to the bedroom door. He shoves me into the bathroom behind us, eyes on a thin piece of wood keeping whatever's out there from us in here. He steps in behind me and closes the door partially so he can still peek out and see into the room, gun at the ready.

"I swear, it isn't my guys, Valerian. They have no way of knowing where you are. If it were them, I would go out there and tell them to back down because you're on our side."

He glances over his shoulder at me. "That's a pretty bold assumption. You don't know as much as you think you know, *kotyonok*." Valerian returns his focus to the gap in the door and the gunfire from outside. "I'll tell you right now, whoever's out there shooting is going to come in here if my men can't stop them. If it's whoever the fuck this group is that has been coming after everyone, then they're going to kill you, too." He freezes and narrows his eyes on me. "Unless that's been your doing all along, too..."

The shots sound immediately outside the bedroom door, and more garbled yelling and bangs reach us.

I shake my head. "No, it wasn't me. And I heard what you told Galen about it not being Kat, and you're right. It isn't. Be careful, *sabrosito*. Your allies may not be who you think they are."

He snarls at me, gun poised and his finger already on the trigger. "What the hell is that supposed to mean? If you're referring to Galen, you need to back off him. I need him. He's with Nicki, which means Valentina and Cutter will never act against him—"

"Does Valentina know what you've been doing?"

The door to the bedroom bangs open, and bullets tear into the bathroom, several coming through the wood mere inches from where Valerian stands. He fires out, rapidly shooting at an unseen enemy as he backs toward the far wall where I wait.

More gunfire and shouting come from somewhere in the house, and Valerian inclines his head toward the window. "Open it."

I scramble to do what I'm told, unlocking and throwing up the window to stare down at the ground two stories below us. "We're jumping?"

"Do you have a better idea? My men haven't called for me and someone made it into the bedroom, which means many, or all of them, are likely dead." He hustles to the window. "You go first, and I'll cover you."

"You don't want to throw me to the wolves?"

He scowls. "You have useful skills, but I'm not saying I won't kill you myself later."

I grin at him. "It's nice to know you care, but you're going first." I nudge him toward the window. "And I'll cover *your* back. It's more important to get you out of here. They won't even know who I am."

His gaze locks with mine, hard and determined. "You're coming with me."

"I didn't say I wasn't. Now go!" I shove his shoulder to get him moving, and he slips his silk-pants-covered legs through the window, resting his ass on the ledge before he jumps.

I lean out, watch him hit the ground, and roll to the side. Muttered curses in Russian break the silence of the night, along with more gunfire.

Additional shots come from the bedroom behind me and into the bathroom, striking the marble counter and floors and shattering the glass mirror. Shards pelt the side of my face as I fire back through the still-closed, now-Swiss-cheese-like door, but only two bullets remain in the gun I just took from Valerian. It looks empty, and the bathroom door finally flies open.

FOUR

VALERIAN

AGONY RADIATES through my entire body as I roll to the side and force myself up from the cold, light snow-covered ground. I glance up at the window, watching through fuzzy vision and waiting for Sofia to follow.

The crack of more shots and her cry of pain hit my ears.

Bylad!

Footsteps from around the front of the house make me tense, and I whirl toward whoever approaches without any weapon but my bare hands and my wits to defend myself. If it's one of the people shooting in the house, I'm as good as dead at this point.

Aleksei appears out of breath, gun in one hand and the other pressed over a wound on his arm, blood seeping from between his fingers. "*Pakhan...*"

I rush toward him, take the gun, and turn back toward the window with it. The pain from the fall still fogging my head, I almost yell out for Sofia without thinking of the potential consequences. A figure appears at the window and fires down at us, and I manage to make it through my pain and confusion long enough to unleash on him and push Aleksei toward the back of the house.

"We need to get out of here." I pause with my back to the house for a second to catch my breath. "What the fuck happened?"

We push away from the brick and rush toward the car we leave parked two blocks over for just these kinds of emergencies, glancing back to ensure we aren't being followed.

Aleksei stumbles but catches himself before he faceplants someone's lawn, barely keeping pace. "Four gunmen. They came in hot and heavy. Shot the damn locks right off the door to get in."

"Why wasn't anyone watching the goddamn surveillance cameras?"

The car comes into view, and we slow, still scanning the area for threats or cops. Those shots will have drawn the type of attention we can't afford right now.

He shakes his head as I climb into the driver's seat, and he slides into the passenger side and slams the door closed behind him. "Yes, but they must have looped the feed so we didn't see any movement as they approached. By the time we knew, it was too late."

Mudaks!

"Who was inside and got hit?"

Pressing his hand against the wound on his arm, he clenches his jaw. "They got Yuri, Ilya, and Ivan. Dmitri was out. We need to call him and let him know what happened."

"*Bylad!*" I grab the hidden key from under the seat, start the car, throw it in drive, and peel away from the curb. "We can't go back..."

Aleksei watches over his shoulder in the direction of the house. "Where are we going?"

"The safe house on Leavitt. We can't go to the club. If they found us here, they've either already been there or will hit the club next. Call Dmitri and update him..." I suck in a heavy breath as we speed down the residential street, which is thankfully empty this time of night. "And call Cutter."

He pauses with the phone in his bloody hand. "Why?"

"I'm going to need his help with figuring out who the fuck this was and who has Julia."

"How do you know they didn't just kill her?"

I glance over at him. "Because they didn't. She's too beautiful. And I got away. They're going take her and try to use her either as bait or to get information."

"Does she know anything?"

Fucking hell...

I stare at the road in front of me, hands tightly gripped to the wheel and her words from earlier flitting through my head.

I told you I've been watching everything, Valerian. Very little gets by me, and I know what you've been doing, even if everyone else remains in the dark.

"She knows everything."

One word was all it took to convince me of that—Vlorë. And if the truth gets out, it could be more dangerous than whoever just came at us.

Aleksei dials Dmitri and gives him the quick rundown of the attack while how badly things have been fucked up occupies my mind, along with keeping the damn car on the road.

How could those idiots be stupid enough to leave their systems open to a hacker?

After all this time, all the years working together, building and fighting, meeting in the shadows to keep our connections hidden, *this* is how we get exposed by a *girl*—barely a woman in so many senses—and a damn laptop.

I tear through the city on my way to the safe house, and Aleksei ends his call with Dmitri and calls Cutter.

Aleksei glances over at me. "Cutter, I have Valerian for you."

Tightening my grip on the wheel, I peer over at him quickly. "Put it on speakerphone."

He presses the button and holds out the phone, clamping his other hand over the wound again, though it seems to be doing little to stop the bleeding, judging by the pool forming under him.

I clear my throat, trying to dislodge the discomfort at what I'm going to have to say. "My house was just hit."

"What?" The phone jostles slightly as I take a turn. "Who was it?"

"I don't know. I'm assuming our mystery gang of thugs."

"Fuck, are you hit?"

"No."

"I heard you weren't so lucky a few days ago."

I glance at Aleksei, who gives me a look but doesn't say anything. "Yes, that was unfortunate, but I'm fine."

"Why are you calling me, Valerian? Shouldn't you be phoning your best buddy, Galen, for help?"

Swallowing thickly, I cast another quick look toward Aleksei before I take another turn and have to stop at a red light. Tension tightens my shoulders as I scan around the car and watch in the rearview for any threats coming after us.

The city seems quiet, almost peaceful, at the moment, but we all know how swiftly that can change for the worse. What I'm about to do could be the catalyst for that change, or it could be the salvation I need.

Here it goes.

The moment of truth.

I can't go to Galen. Not with this information. Not about Sofia. *Not yet.* But Valentina and Cutter will see how important it is to get her back, how essential she could be in the future of shaping this city if we have her on our side. Which was the only thing keeping me from lashing out at her when she revealed the truth.

"I need you to have Valentina on the line, too."

Cutter may pull the trigger, but Valentina makes the decisions. She's the one who needs to hear this and ultimately determine my fate.

"Who the fuck are you to give me any orders?" Cutter's anger vibrates through the line. "If there's something she needs to know, I'll tell her."

"Get. Her. On. The. Line." I growl the words as the light changes to green. Then I make a left-hand turn to pull onto the street where one of our safe houses sits, a modicum finally hitting me, knowing we're so close.

After some muttered cursing and jostling of the phone, Valentina clears her throat. "Cutter filled me in. Why did you need to talk to me?"

To confess. At least some things...

"Whoever just hit my place took a woman who is very important to me."

A momentary pause lingers while I wait for her to say something.

"I'm very sorry to hear that, Valerian. I wasn't aware you were with anyone."

With anyone...

Those words somehow seem inadequate to describe whatever is happening between Sofia and me, but I can't let the Marconis know that. It would expose a major weakness they will leverage against me.

"I'm not." The lie burns like acid on my tongue. "She's important in another way. A way that's important to you, too."

I pull down the alley behind the safe house and throw the car into park beside the dilapidated garage. Aleksei furrows his brows at me in confusion.

I'm going to have some serious explaining to do after tonight.

"The night Galen and I took out the Luna Cartel's warehouse, a woman showed up at my club. She and I have grown...friendly over the last couple of weeks, and she could be a major asset to both of us if we want to return this city to what it once was."

"I don't know what you're talking about, Valerian."

You're about to.

"It's Sofia Rose."

"What?" The phone jostles again. Cutter growls. "Did I just fucking hear you right? You've been harboring Sofia rose this entire time?"

"No. I never knew where she was. She showed up unannounced with a false name and under false pretenses."

"Where the hell has she been? What has she been doing?"

"That's not for me to tell, but suffice it to say, I need her. *We* need her. She has information no one else in the world does against people who have made our lives Hell, and now, she was just taken by whoever attacked my house. I need your help finding her and getting her back—before her brothers realize what's going on."

Cutter offers a scoff. "Jesus Christ, Valerian, you really know how to put us in a fucked-up position, don't you?"

Valentina whispers something to Cutter in Italian. "I'm not sure we can assist you, Valerian. If the Roses get wind that we knew where she was and think we knew the whole time—"

"I know, but I'm telling you, they don't suspect a thing. They won't know unless whoever took her approaches them directly before we can find her." I shut off the engine and scrub a hand over my face. "We can cut this off at the pass and ensure she remains an asset to us and not a pawn in her brothers' games."

"Fuck"—Cutter growls again—"give us a second."

The line goes silent for a moment as Aleksei scowls at me.

He finally shakes his head incredulously. "Julia is Sofia, the Roses' sister?"

I give him a sharp nod and open the car door, snatching the phone from his hand and putting it to my ear. He climbs from the car and slams the door, following me up the rear stairs. With a trem-

bling hand that I do my best to hide, I manage to punch in the code on the lock and step inside. Aleksei closes the door behind us and throws the deadbolt back into place.

Valentina clears her throat again. "I'll help you...under one condition."

"What's that?"

"When we get her back, Sofia comes with me, not you."

I freeze midway through the living room of the old brownstone that's still under renovation. "You expect me to let you take her? Over my fucking dead body."

"It sounds like that's likely happening soon, anyway, Valerian. Someone wants you dead, and you're the one who called us, remember? Those are my terms."

Bylad!

My closest and most trusted men have been killed. My house was destroyed. My body is already in shambles. And the woman I am in love with has been taken.

What other choice do I have?

FIVE

VALERIAN

MY BULLET STRIKES the oblivious man squarely in the chest, and his lifeless body crumbles to the ground outside the inconspicuous dilapidated warehouse. It was the perfect shot, but there isn't any time to celebrate that small victory. The man standing guard beside him whirls toward me, ready to return fire, but I get off four more rounds before he can. They slam into him center mass, and he drops beside his *comrade* before he even has a chance to see who was shooting at him.

Cutter glances over at me from my left side, his weapon ready but unfired. "You said you needed my help."

I offer him an incredulous snort as we advance toward the door that will get us inside now that it isn't "protected" by these two. Moving fast and being deadly accurate is the only way we have any chance of finding Sofia alive and unscathed.

Too much time has passed since they took her.

Anything could have happened in the hours since then.

I can't even allow myself to consider the possibilities. If I do, it will only cloud my judgment and prevent me from doing what's important right now—killing all these fuckers and getting her back.

"I *do* need your help." I continue to scan the area around the outside of the building to ensure no one else poses a threat—not that those two really did. They never saw us coming, likely thought no one would ever find them here since they've managed to hide well the last few months. "I never would have found her if it weren't for you."

Not a chance in hell.

This is the last place I would have looked for a well-trained group like the ones who have been coming after us. Only technology and skills I'll never have made this possible.

Cutter's friend, Preacher, really is a miracle worker. In less than an hour after my call to them, he had hacked the traffic light cameras around my house and was able to follow the vehicle that left my place and brought the attackers—and Sofia—*here*. Their apparent headquarters, though, whether they've been here the entire time they've been wreaking havoc on Chicago or have kept moving to avoid detection, remains to be seen.

And while Cutter's computer guru uses what he's found to dig more, Aleksei, Dmitri, Cutter, and a few men in his crew have come with me to do the dirty work.

It doesn't matter that my body aches and is on the verge of giving out completely or that we haphazardly sewed Aleksei's wound before we got the call from Cutter and came.

In these situations, time is of the essence. The longer they have Sofia, the greater chance she says something that will get me—and her—killed. If she reveals what she knows and it comes out, Cutter, Aleksei, and Dmitri will likely turn their guns on me before I ever have a chance to explain.

My long-term, well-thought-out plan may end up putting me in an early grave, which is exactly what I had hoped to avoid by doing it in the first place.

Cutter motions for me to fall in line behind him as we approach the main entry door that the two men were not protecting very well. Aleksei, Dmitri, and two of Cutter's guys follow closely, prepared to split off from us once we're inside to cover the entire warehouse. We don't know how many men might be inside or how well-armed they are, so we have to be ready for anything they could possibly throw at us.

The attacks they've executed have proven they're worthy adversaries, meaning this fight could get very dirty.

Cutter places a small charge on the door and steps back, raising his hand for everyone to hold while he alerts Preacher to cut the power and counts down to the detonation. The lights go out on the exterior of the building, and the sharp crack of the explosion echoes through the night. If the shots didn't alert anyone inside to what's happening, that sure did.

We enter through the lingering smoke and advance down a short hallway toward a barely visible *T* intersection of halls ahead of us. Heavy, rushed footsteps echo somewhere in the space, and we hit the end of the hallway, where it branches off in two different directions. Cutter motions for me to follow him, along with Dmitri, while Aleksei and two of his men split off the other way.

Everyone knows the plan—find the girl, kill everyone else on sight.

No matter how badly we want to take a prisoner for questioning, it can't be at the risk of Sofia— Julia to everyone except Cutter and Aleksei, who are the only ones privy to the truth in this group. But if we can manage to get one of these fuckers alive, we certainly aren't going to pass up the chance to potentially find out who's really behind all of this.

It's gone on long enough and interfered with my plans, and now these fuckers think they can take what's mine. They'll pay for it in blood.

A barrage of bullets flies at us the moment we turn the corner, and we return fire and press against the wall—our only cover for whatever lies dead ahead of us. The old building plans Preacher found likely aren't accurate anymore, so we're going in partially blind against an unknown enemy.

The shots stop, and we move forward again, stepping over the bodies of three men dressed in black sprawled across the floor. It seems our aim is better than theirs—or luck is on our side tonight.

It certainly isn't God.

With all the sins we've committed, there won't be any help from Him anytime soon.

We've already taken out five, but we have no idea how many more there might or how much resistance we'll meet. Given how aggressively they've come on in their previous attacks, there's every reason to believe they'll go down fighting if we try to take their only bargaining chip—and that's *without* them knowing who they really hold.

If they discover she's Sofia Rose, all bets are off.

There's no way I'll get her back...

My chest tightens painfully, and I force myself to shake off that thought. If I let it linger, it will cloud my judgment and slow my reactions. That would spell certain death against these opponents.

We approach the end of the hallway, where it seems to open up to the main warehouse area. Cutter holds up his hand to stop us and scans around the corner, signaling there are two more men just on the other side. He motions for me to take the guy on the left and he'll take the one on the right.

I suck in a deep breath, then we move around the corner and step into the open space, immediately firing shots at our intended targets. Mine hit their mark, as do his. The two men drop, leaving the warehouse empty but for a few chairs and tables set up on one side next to a closed door that must lead to some sort of office.

This can't be where they've been operating from the whole time. There isn't anything here. It's just a temporary holding location for their prize, somewhere to interrogate her and do whatever else they want to the beautiful woman who has twisted me up and made me forget all the reasons why getting involved with her, knowing who she was, was such a horrible idea.

Cutter signals to the other men to hang back and secure the room while we approach the unknown on the other side of the dilapidated wood. A million scenarios of what we might be walking into flash through my head, each worse than the last.

Pausing just outside, we listen for signs of any movement, and Cutter indicates he's going in first. He turns and kicks open the door. The old material gives easily, shattering inward to the small room.

My breath catches in my throat.

Kotyonok!

Sofia stands at the center of it, blood streaking down one side of her face and over her arm. A gun is pressed to her temple by a dark-haired man behind her, using her as a shield.

Rage boils through my blood, heating my body and making my hand tighten on the gun grip. I'm a good shot, but I'm not good enough to risk trying to take him out with that gun on Sofia.

Cutter is another story. The man has the kind of skills and accuracy I could only dream of, and he has his weapon trained on them like he's ready to shoot. But something twists in my gut, a feeling that something is about to go very wrong if I let him take the shot.

Without even thinking, I step up and put myself slightly in front of him, directly in his line of fire and in the sightline of the man holding Sofia hostage. It takes a second for my brain to process his face.

Bylad!

Fury surges through my veins.

I never forget a face, and I know exactly where I saw his—which makes this standoff even more dangerous. Even without Sofia, he knows things he shouldn't, things that could destroy me.

He presses the muzzle of the gun more tightly into her temple that's already bloodied from a gash. She was either grazed by a bullet or pistol-whipped. Likely what caused the cry of pain I heard from the ground below the window back at the house.

His lips curl into a sneer. "I'm impressed you found us, but it won't matter in the end. All of you will be dead."

Cutter sidesteps me and offers a sardonic snort-laugh, his gun zeroed in on the man. "If I were going to let you live, I would have you tell whoever you're working for to go fuck themselves if they think any of us will go down that easily."

A sinister grin spreads across his lips. "There are a lot of things you don't know. I wouldn't be so confident." His gaze darts over to me. "Right, Valerian? Why don't you tell—"

I pull the trigger before he can utter another word.

SIX

VALERIAN

MY BULLET HITS him between the temples, and the back of his head explodes against the dingy, dirty wall behind them—the only place I could aim without hitting Sofia. If she had moved even slightly, she would have been the one taking the lead in the face, but I couldn't risk him saying anything else that might put me in hot water with the scarred mercenary next to me.

He isn't the type who would offer me any chance to explain if anything else has been said, if my secret had been exposed...

The gunman collapses, his weapon tumbling to the ground beside his body as Sofia sags to her knees on the concrete floor, her legs incapable of supporting her anymore.

I holster my gun and rush forward, pulling her into my arms. She trembles against my chest, her body practically vibrating, but she isn't crying.

Not a sob.

Not a tear.

Nothing but silence.

Slowly, I pull back and take her face between my palms, looking into her bourbon eyes. "Are you okay?"

Pure rage stares back at me—the kind of anger that burns down entire cities with a single word. The kind of fury that set her on this path in the first place. *This* is the Sofia who wants revenge, the one willing to do anything to get it, the one who swallowed her fear and came into *Gluttony* to find a partner.

Squaring her shoulders, she swallows and nods. "I will be"—her rock-hard gaze flashes briefly to where her captor's body lies—"when all these fuckers are gone."

"What the hell was that, Valerian?" Cutter approaches, his marred face hard and lips twisted into a sneer. "We could have questioned him and tried to find out who they're working for."

I shake my head. "He wouldn't have told us. He was going to kill her, anyway, because he knew you were going to kill him."

"Bullshit. I could have gotten something out of him—something *useful*."

That was exactly my concern...

I help Sofia to unsteady feet, and she turns to face Cutter, undeterred by his wrath.

"He wouldn't have told you. They were too careful about what they said in front of me to have ever revealed anything. He would have shot himself before letting you take him to torture and question."

Cutter scowls at Sofia. "I'd say it's a pleasure to see you again, Sofia, but under the circumstances..." He takes a step forward. "We'll have time catch up later. Now, you're coming with me."

He takes another step and freezes when Dmitri nestles the muzzle of his gun against the back of Cutter's head.

I shift to place myself firmly between him and Sofia. "You're not going to be taking her anywhere, Cutter."

Even from behind the sunglasses he wears, the hatred with which he looks at me sends heat radiating from him. "What the fuck are you doing, Valerian? This wasn't our deal."

Cutter glances behind him to where Dmitri stands and beyond to where Aleksei holds Cutter's two men at gunpoint, too. There isn't any way out of this for them—at least, not alive or with Sofia.

I incline my head toward him in acknowledgment. "You were an idiot for believing I would ever let you take her."

With my arm wrapped around Sofia, I guide her past him and to the door, but his growl stops me in my tracks just outside in the hallway.

"You're gonna pay for this, Valerian." His jaw tightens, and Aleksei pushes the gun against him harder. "Valentina doesn't take kindly to betrayal."

No one does.

And that's exactly why I have to do this.

I need a plan—quickly. Both Sofia and apparently our adversary know something that could get me killed. And seeing him, I may finally understand what's been going on.

There has to be a way to do damage control. Something I need to figure out before Cutter comes after us...

I don't respond to his warning, just keep moving. Dmitri and Aleksei slowly back away after us, keeping their weapons trained on Cutter and his men until we're clear of the small room, the warehouse, and have dashed down the hallway and around the corner to the exit.

Climbing over the remnants of the destroyed door, I scoop Sofia up in my arms and rush toward the SUV parked down the street.

Dmitri opens the back door, and I slide in as Aleksei starts the engine and peels away before Dmitri even has his door closed. Sofia shifts in my hold to try to move onto the bench seat next to me, but I tighten my grip on her and brush my lips against her ear.

"If you think I'm letting you out of my arms for one second, *kotyonok*, you're far crazier than I imagined."

She turns her head slightly toward me. "What was that all about with Cutter? What did he mean when he said I was going with him?"

Sofia isn't going to like what I had to do to secure Cutter's assistance, but I did what was necessary at the time—without any intention of ever handing her over.

"I made a deal with Valentina to secure his help getting your freedom."

Her bourbon eyes narrow on me with concern. "Did you tell her who I am?"

I brush her disheveled, dyed-blond hair behind her ear. "I had to in order to assure her cooperation. She had to know how important you were if I was going to get her help."

Sofia swallows thickly. "Did you tell her..."

She trails off, but I know what she's asking—if I told Valentina that I'm fucking her.

"No." I shake my head, cupping her soft cheek in one palm. "The last thing I want is Valentina Marconi knowing *our* secrets."

"She's going to come after you now."

Don't I know it.

My only hope is to redirect her anger where it really belongs. And now, I have an idea where that is; it's just the last place I expected the danger to be coming from.

Everything has been a lie.

Allies have become enemies.

Friends have become traitors.

My plans that took years to build have disintegrated in an instant, and now, Valentina is putting a target squarely on my back.

"Perhaps." I nod slowly and lightly feather my thumb across Sofia's lips, trying desperately not to think about what it felt like to have my cock buried between them. "Which is why I have to get ahead of it."

"How the hell are you going to do that?"

By stepping into the fire.

"I'm calling a meeting of the five families."

With everyone gathered together, I can explain what I've discovered and hopefully ensure we're all on the same page with who our real enemy is instead of pointing fingers and weapons at each other.

"Do you think they'll actually show up, given what happened the last time?"

No.

Having the five families together in one spot is a recipe for disaster.

First, a bomb, then the attack at the church, and the attempted one at Felipe's condo...

No one will be eager to jump at the invitation, which means I need to make them an offer they can't refuse.

"Yes"—I brush my lips across hers—"because I might know who's behind all this."

She raises an eyebrow. "How?"

"I recognized the man in that room."

Her lips press together into a tense, thin line. "Who was he?"

I clench my jaw, biting back the reality still rattling around in my head. "Someone who could stir up a lot of trouble for me if I don't get in front of it. I'm taking you back to our safe house. I'll have the doctor come look at you...and then, I'm calling the meeting."

She releases an exasperated sigh and tries to slip out of my hold again. "I'm fine, Valerian. I don't need a doctor."

"Really?" I squeeze her tighter, ensuring she can't get away, and motion to the gash on the side of her head. "What happened here?"

"One of their shots hit the mirror in the bathroom and shattered it. I got hit by flying glass. It stunned me for a moment, and they came in and pistol-whipped me. Knocked me out cold. I came to and was already in that place. They started questioning me but didn't get very far before you came storming in."

My grip on her tenses, and I carefully pull the blood-matted hair away from her temple. "You could have a concussion."

She shakes her head. "I don't think so. I think I'm okay." Her determined gaze locks with mine. "I'm coming with you to the meeting."

It isn't a question or request for permission, and my cock stirs under her ass at the look she gives me.

So much strength in such a little package.

So much fire contained in the woman kept restrained for too long.

She wants to let it all out, to finally unleash all that is Sofia Rose onto the world, but I'm not about to put her in the crossfire that's about to happen.

"Fuck no. That's the last place you need to go." I take her face in my hands again. "Until all of this gets sorted out, no one can see you. Your brothers can't see you. Kat can't see you. Galen can't see you. No one. *Anyone* finding out you've been with me will be catastrophic on top of an already tenuous situation."

Her eyes harden slightly like she's getting ready to argue, but the SUV pulls to a stop outside the safehouse. "Fine. I won't go, but we *are* going to finish our conversation before you do." She leans in and grazes her lips against my ear. "And you're going to tell me exactly who is behind all of this."

SEVEN

SOFIA

THE BEDROOM DOOR SWINGS OPEN, and Valerian enters, closing it behind him and instantly zeroing his assessing gaze on me on the bed.

"Stop looking at me like that."

One of his dark brows wings up. "Like what, *kotyonok?*"

"Like I'm broken and need to be fixed."

He barks out a laugh and approaches slowly, humor and concern mixing in the blue of his eyes. "Not broken, *kotyonok*, just a little bruised."

"The doctor said I don't have a concussion and I'm completely fine."

Valerian settles on the side of the bed and tucks a strand of hair behind my ear. "I don't care what the doctor says. You were pistol-whipped." He raises a hand to gently brush over the bandage at my temple that covers the few stitches I needed there. "You need to relax and rest."

"I'm pretty sure I told you the same thing after you were *shot* and you told me to fuck off."

A low growl rumbles in his chest as he leans even closer, his lips just short of mine. "I did, *kotyonok*, but you are not me. And I am not going to let you do anything but sleep and relax."

Sitting up straighter, I press my chest against his. "First, who are *you* to tell *me* what I can or can't do? Second, I am *not* going to relax when I know that as soon as you leave here, you're going to walk into a potential firestorm with the other families. When you tell them everything, they're—"

He silences me with a kiss that steals the words and my breath, burying his hands in my hair to draw me even closer to him. His lips move over mine slowly, almost reverently, so unlike the way he's kissed me before—always so desperate and needy.

This feels different, like he's trying to tell me something he can't in words.

Something he's afraid to say.

But Valerian Kamenev isn't a man ruled by fear. Far from it. He's the man who stands it down, stares it straight in the face, and keeps advancing.

So, whatever it is he's feeling must truly terrify him.

I drag my face back from his, looking into the depths of blue that can flash from icy cold to warm and inviting so quickly. "What's wrong, *sabrosito?*"

He swallows thickly, his jaw hardening like he's struggling to bite back something he wants to say. "I almost lost you tonight, and..."

"And before the shots started, you were ready to kill me yourself."

"No." He shakes his head, tightening his hold on me. "I was angry...reeling from what you revealed. I was questioning everything, and I didn't know what to make of all of it. But when it came down to it, I never could have hurt you, not like this."

His fingertips feather over my temple, where the dull throb of the wound seems to be vanishing the longer I'm in his arms. The sincerity of his declaration makes my heart ache, and I lean into his touch while considering all the things the man is capable of.

"You would have hurt me in other ways."

He presses his lips to my forehead. "But I would have made it better eventually...like I want to now."

Heat spreads between my legs at the promise in his words as my stomach twists at what it might mean. A war between what my body wants and the complication I've created with the man I was supposed to only use as a means to an end.

Whatever this is between us was never supposed to happen. No matter how attracted to him I was from the first time I saw him, I was never supposed to *care*. I was supposed to use him and his resources to destroy Felipe, Andres, Kat, and Galen...then toss him away the way he does those who are useless to him.

Instead, I find myself needing the comfort and warmth of his touch, especially now, knowing what those men would have done to me had he not come, knowing what might happen to him when he tells the families the truth about what he's been doing and who is really behind this.

I wrap my arms around his neck, delving my fingers into the thick, dark hair at his nape, and press my lips to his. His tongue darts out along mine, seeking entrance, and I comply, moaning into his mouth and scoring my nails across his skin.

He groans and lowers me onto my back on the bed, suspending himself over me carefully with his arm braced at my side, ensuring he isn't hurting me, yet staying as close as humanly possible without being inside me.

My body yearns for just that, and my hips roll against his, seeking that which I'm not sure he will give me now. Not when he's so worried about me being hurt, wanting to treat me like I'm made of porcelain and might shatter with one wrong move.

Far from it.

Those men taking me, threatening me, it was only fuel on the fire already raging inside me, the determination to succeed in getting the revenge I've always craved and finally take ownership of everything I deserve for all my hard work and suffering.

And I deserve to feel good before everything goes to shit.

To feel this man's body molded to mine, him moving inside me, to reach that pinnacle of ecstasy only he can bring me to.

His lips move across my cheek to my ear, then down my neck, each press of them against my heated skin sending a blazing zing of electricity between my legs. I roll my hips against his, grinding his hard cock against my core, trying to find the friction I need for release.

But he reaches a hand down and stops me, pinning my pelvis down, and slips it between my legs to cup it possessively.

"You don't get to come by rubbing against me like a cat in heat, *kotyonok*." He kisses the exposed skin between the *V* of my shirt, sending goosebumps skittering across my body. "Your pleasure is mine to give. Mine to own. I want all of it because I am a glutton for all the little mewls and gasps and groans that tumble from your lips when you climax." His kiss drifts lower, and he drags my shirt down under my breasts along with the cups of my bra, exposing my taut nipples to the cool air of the room. "I revel in knowing I am doing that to you. I *live* for it. *Ya nye magoo byez tyebye zhyt', kotyonok*."

I've never wished I spoke Russian as much as I do in this moment because whatever he said simultaneously tightens my core and twists my stomach. The heaviness of the words, even though I don't know what they mean, weighs down on me as much as his large body does.

He shifts his hand to the waistband of the yoga pants I changed into after I got back and showered and easily shoves them down my hips so he can cup my bare pussy. "Already so wet, *kotyonok*."

A rumble of satisfaction in his chest vibrates through me, and I groan and arch into his touch, willing him to give me what I seek without words. His lips find one nipple, and he sucks it into his mouth, drawing a gasp from my throat. I squeeze my thighs around his hand, the only thing I can do in the moment to tell him what I need.

But he already knows.

He always seems to know.

To anticipate my needs and desires.

To be ready and willing to give them to me.

He uses his free hand to unbuckle his belt and shove his pants down far enough to free his cock. It strains between us, hard and ready, a bead of pre-cum glistening at the tip.

My mouth waters to taste him again, to swallow him down and watch him unravel as I work him over, but my body wants him more. He shifts his hand and slips two fingers inside me. I clasp around him greedily, demanding more. His thumb slides up across my clit, and he presses it down firmly.

"*Ty moy.*"

EIGHT

SOFIA

"Yes!"

The word falls from my lips on a heavy exhale before I can bite it back. Without even knowing what he said, I could feel the intent of the word. The passion and power and command in it.

I'd agree to anything right now. Anything to find my release, to free myself of the pain and the worry and the ominous cloud of tension and turmoil swirling around us.

As soon as he walks out that door, he might not be coming back, and this may be the last time I ever get to experience this with him. I need it almost as much as I need oxygen in my lungs. Somehow, this man has become the air I breathe and what I need to keep moving forward, to keep pushing for what I want. What *we* want.

No matter what he's done in the past—to others or to me—I can't handle the thought of walking away, of him saying *no* or ever turning his back on me and what we could accomplish together.

And whatever he just said confirmed he feels the same way.

He pulls his hand from between my legs and quickly replaces it with his cock, brushing the broad head through my wetness and across my clit.

"Fuck! Yes—"

His lips capture my cry, and he eases into me in a long, slow thrust that lets me feel every inch until I'm completely filled with him. Surrounded by his hard, wide, strong body, he cocoons me in his strength, in his unrelenting drive to succeed and to take what he wants.

We share that desire, and we both want the same thing—in this bed and in this city. It's the perfect union. One built on gluttony and aspiration. One sealed in blood and unspoken oaths.

He stills inside me, buried deep into my core, to the very center of my being. His eyes bore into mine, blue pools I can get lost swimming in forever, but he doesn't move, just brushes my hair back from my face and presses a kiss to my lips so filled with pain and worship it makes a tear leak out of the corner of my eye.

Tearing my mouth away from his, I gasp for breath, struggling to keep my head clear while he holds me, hanging between flying with the angels and burning with the demons we both hold so close to our hearts.

I scratch my nails down the back of his neck and clench around him, arching my hips as much as I can pressed below him to urge him to go, to give us both what we want.

"*Ya tebya nikomu ne otdam, kotyonok.*"

He knows I don't understand, but he does it intentionally, so I can't fight him or argue against what he's saying. And he does it like this, embedded deep inside me, while I'm right on the edge of exploding. His lips move over mine, demanding I comply and let him do what he will with me.

There's one word that will stop all this, that will end everything.

I've never dared utter it, could never fathom a situation where I would give in and admit defeat, but this is it. I can't take any more of his games or his whispered confessions in a language I don't speak. Not when so much is on the line, so much is at risk.

"*Mercy!*"

He freezes, his entire body going stock still, and slowly drags his head back until our eyes meet again. "What did you say, *kotyonok?*"

I suck in a deep breath and let it out in a rush. "Mercy."

Valerian reaches up and flutters his fingers across my lips he just ravaged. "You want me to stop, Sofia?"

"Yes!" I shake my head and squeeze my eyes closed. "No. I mean...fuck!"

My pussy involuntarily squeezes around him, and he clenches his jaw, his eyes darkening like the deepest part of the ocean, almost black. "You shouldn't say that word unless you really mean it, *kotyonok.*"

Do I really mean it?

I don't know anymore.

I can't know what's real and what's all a game. Not with my brothers. Not with the other families. Certainly not with this man.

His entire life has been built on lies and violence. He lives and breathes it. Yet when he's with me, I see flickers of someone else, of *something* else. Perhaps what he might have been if he hadn't been born into this world.

Something he only shows me.

Something that terrifies me.

I've become his weakness.

If he goes into that meeting and shows it, they'll devour him the way he does my soul, and we'll never have any chance of succeeding in conquering this city. Valentina will never relent and will always share it with us, but ridding ourselves of the other competition is the ultimate goal. One we won't be able to achieve if we give in to whatever feelings are consuming us now.

Lust.

That's all it is.

That's what I'll keep telling myself.

Because though it's one of the deadliest sins, it's less dangerous than love.

"I do mean it, Valerian." I hold his gaze, trying my damnedest not to cry. "You have to stop doing this to me; stop invading my heart the way you do. We won't survive this if you think or say what we're both feeling."

He leans closer until we're sharing breath and rolls his hips, driving himself impossibly deeper. "I won't survive if I lose you. That's the truth, *kotyonok.* Whether you want to accept it or not, you're mine now. You wanted my help, to become my partner. Well, you've got me, and you won't run away or push me away to protect yourself from needing me. I won't allow it."

The slow drag of the head of his cock as he retreats ignites a burn deep in my core that threatens to fully consume me.

"Please..." My plea comes on a thready breath, my head spinning too wildly with his words and his touch to make sense of anything.

"Tell me again, Sofia." He grinds his pelvis down, applying pressure straight onto my clit, sending that same heat out through my limbs. "Do you really want me to stop?"

"No." I thrash my head from side to side, fighting to need to move while being pinned beneath him, with him completely in control of my body and heart. "God, no. Don't stop."

I know what I'm doing.

I'm giving Valerian permission to destroy me and becoming the thing that could destroy him.

But I'm too far gone to care.

He lowers his head until his lips brush against my ear. "I love you, *kotyonok.* You are mine."

"Yes. Yours..."

It's the only permission he needs to unleash the monster he's been restraining. He pulls his hips back and plunges into me, and I drop my head back on a gasp at the pleasure coursing through me.

Every drive forward and retreat pulls me closer to the release he promised me. He hammers into me like a madman intent on claiming what's his and making it clear who I belong to, and when he sinks his teeth into my collarbone, I cry out with the crashing wave of my orgasm rushing over me.

He rams into me again and again. Dragging it out. Forcing me to keep coming, to keep accepting the ecstasy he's giving me.

Enemies are forgotten. Reality disappears on the cloud of lust. The only thing that can hurt us now is this feeling. The only thing that can bring us down is the fact that we care.

It could kill us.

But sometimes, pain is the price for sin.

And we just might pay it.

NINE

VALERIAN

Bylad!

And I thought the last time we all got together was tense...

Scanning the long table, not a single friendly face stares back. They only offer hard glares and twisted expressions of barely restrained rage. Especially from Valentina and Cutter...

If looks could kill.

I thought I understood that saying, but this gives it a whole new meaning. Though she has every reason to be angry with me after my betrayal, she's somehow managed to keep Cutter leashed enough that he hasn't attacked me.

Yet...

There's no telling what he might—and more than likely *will*—do when this is over. When I tell them everything, when I reveal my deception and the moves I've been making behind their backs, it will unleash a torrent of wrath unlike anything we've ever seen, and it may not be stoppable, even with what I am going to propose.

My only hope is that they give me a chance to explain myself and refocus everyone's ire where it truly belongs—our common enemy.

It might be easier with Sofia at my side, her strength united with mine, but the time hasn't come for that. Not when wounds are fresh and bleeding with Valentina and Cutter, the closest things I had to allies besides Galen. And even he appears annoyed. His green eyes hold trepidation as he watches all the people here carefully, especially me.

He didn't fully buy my explanation when he came to see me and Sofia appeared. That much was readily evident. But he didn't push the issue at the time, likely giving me a chance to either come clean on my own terms or to hang myself in a noose of my own making.

What I'm about to do may be the latter.

Given what happened the last time we all sat around a table like this, everyone had their people scan the entire private room at the abandoned restaurant to ensure there wouldn't be any "surprises" like the explosion that rocked us before and left Sofia with her scars.

I called this meeting to try to cut off our enemy at the knees before another massive attack happens that no one can survive, but the tension in here doesn't bode well for the potential of the five families working together on this—or them giving me a chance to give an explanation that will keep their guns from being trained on me.

Still, I have to try.

There isn't any other way to do this.

Rising to my feet at the head of the table, I clear my throat, letting my eyes meet those of each head of family before finally getting to the point. "Thank you, everyone, for coming." I button my suit coat and square my shoulders, preparing to absorb the onslaught from the people who could destroy me so easily. "I know no one wants to be here, but it's important we all meet together instead of everyone talking behind each other's backs. We need to share information and get to the bottom of what's been happening in this city, and we need to do it *now*."

Kat's blue gaze cuts through me like ice. As much as I despise the woman and want to see her buried six feet under along with the Rose brothers, that's a battle for another day—one that will be fought with Sofia at my side. Today is about addressing our shared adversary and ensuring we don't *all* go down. Losing the five families would decimate this city, sending it spiraling into a lawlessness it hasn't ever seen the likes of before.

No one wants that. We've all worked too hard, built up our territories, our empires, to let them be destroyed by an outside opponent.

"I want to start by saying…"

Everyone tenses, Kat's gaze narrowing on me.

"I have confirmed Kat isn't involved with the hit squad we've been facing."

She releases a heavy breath, her shoulders relaxing slightly, and Rose shifts in the seat next to her, resting his forearms on the table. Now knowing what I do about the brothers, it's hard to look at either the same way.

One killed his own parents while the other single-handedly wiped out a major cartel at the age of fifteen, and both allowed the world to believe they were something else, something and someone they are not.

They've both become formidable enemies, though. Neither to be crossed. Which is precisely why I had to keep Sofia away from this meeting.

Beside him, Felipe raises a suspicious brow. "How was this confirmed?"

His brother and Kat both offer him a dirty look, and Valentina and Cutter assess me coolly. Galen leans back in his chair, arms crossed over his chest, clearly perturbed he wasn't the first one to hear whatever it is I have to say—privately.

I press my palms flat on the table and lean forward slightly. "We've all had people attempting to track this group, attempting to figure out who is behind all this mayhem. And our assailants did a good job of trying to make it look like it was Kat, but one of my trusted sources has confirmed that at least one of the men who is part of the crew is a loyal member of the Dragusha *fis*."

"The Dragushas?" Kat sits forward slightly. "We don't even know if Kreshnik Dragusha survived the shootout I had with him on that tarmac, yet you're claiming he has the power to organize something like this?" She shakes her head. "I don't buy it. Even if he were healthy and had the power, he doesn't have the *balls*."

Valentina glances at Cutter before turning her attention back to us. "It would explain what we've heard rumblings about—activity with some of the older crew members, like someone is trying to rebuild using former Syla and Morina men."

Cutter stares at me from behind the shades. "Who is your source, Valerian?"

"Someone I *trust*."

One of his eyebrows rises over the frame. "You don't trust anyone but yourself."

Bylad!

I knew Cutter caught on to what happened last night, that I fired that shot not just to get her back but to silence the man holding her before he could keep talking. If he reveals anything about Sofia, any chance I have of walking out of here alive will disappear.

Leveling my gaze on him, I nod. "You're right. I *am* the only person I trust, and that's why I know this information is accurate. I personally *saw* this man with Dragusha in the past, and while I didn't initially recognize him in the photos on the documents they used to fly that Cutter's man found for us, I had my own people do some digging and locate additional photos confirming his identity and affiliation."

Cutter's jaw hardens. "And how was it you *personally* saw this man with Dragusha?"

Bylad!

This is where things get dangerous, but sometimes, it's necessary to step into the lion's den rather than be chased by them and mauled in the open.

I stand to my full height, squaring my shoulders to absorb the coming wrath and locking gazes with Cutter when I respond to his question. "I know this man works for Dragusha because I have been working with the Dragushas and the Berishas for years."

Kat slams her fists on the tables and leaps to her heeled feet. "What the hell? You've been working with them? They tried to kill me!"

I meet her icy-cold blue glare. "I know. I'm the one who told them you were coming to Albania so they could meet you at the airport. After we grabbed Rose and Genti, I had one of my men trying to track your plane. Eventually, he found it and realized where you were headed. I just gave my friends a little warning of what was coming their way."

"You motherfucker!"

She lurches around the table, reaching for what is undoubtedly a weapon in the purse at her side, but Genti steps forward and presses a hand to her chest, stopping her in her tracks.

He turns his head toward me, giving me a look that says he didn't stop her for my benefit but to help stop an all-out gun battle in here that no one would walk away from. It's precisely what we discussed when I took him—the second time—that cooler heads need to prevail.

Valentina twists her lips, her annoyance evident, too. "I flat out asked you if you were behind this, if you were working with them, and you said no."

I shake my head. "Because I'm *not* behind these attacks. My agreement with the Dragushas and Berishas began when they started making waves in Albania a few years back. That part of the world is very important to my business, and Vlorë is an important port. I had to ensure I maintained access to it. But I never discussed any sort of moves being made *here*."

At least, not yet.

The plan had always been to have my Albanian friends take out Kat and—if I was lucky—Rose since they were attached at the hip. But that was before we knew there were *two* of them to contend with. Discovering Felipe and Andres' deception complicated things, and that's when all hell broke loose.

"I never authorized or had any knowledge of their intent to send men to Chicago to come after anyone. If I had known, I sure as hell wouldn't have been in that church that night. I haven't been able to speak with Dragusha or Berisha for weeks. They are either dead, and their men are coming after us for it, or they've gone into hiding and are operating somewhere I can't find them."

The Rose brothers maintain stoic expressions, concealing their anger behind impassive masks that hide true fury—especially from Rose. Considering I tortured him and Genti and tried to kill his woman, I can understand his fury.

Galen sits ominously still, jaw locked, body tense. He's on the verge of letting loose, and it will all be directed at me when he does. "You expect any of us to believe anything you say?"

"You don't have a choice, *comrade*. These men are determined to take us out, and now that we have some idea who is pulling the strings, we can cut them and hopefully save ourselves from another attack."

Cutter issues a low growl, stepping forward aggressively until Valentina places a hand on his abdomen and stops him in his tracks. "I should fucking kill you right here and now. You—"

The shrill ring of my phone cuts him off, and I reach to my inside coat pocket to grab it. Anyone who would be calling me is here—the men all wait outside except for Aleksei, who I left with Sofia.

An unknown number flashes on the screen, and bile climbs my throat as I swipe to accept the call.

"Hello?"

"Get out of there. Now. All of you. They're coming."

TEN

SOFIA

PACING the worn floorboards of the safehouse, I keep glancing toward the door, clenching the phone so tightly in my hand that it almost hurts. Aleksei watches out the front window, periodically pulling back the drapes to check for any sign of Valerian and the rest of the men.

"Where the hell are they?"

My question goes unanswered for the hundredth time because he doesn't know, either.

I peek at the phone and try dialing him again, but I know what the result will be—nothing. He hasn't answered a single call or text from Aleksei or me. None of the men have since they left.

Anything could have happened at that meeting.

They could all be dead—

No.

I refuse to even think that. If something had happened, I would know. I return to the computer on the coffee table and check the screen again.

Still nothing on the police scanners.

It should be a relief, but instead, my stomach tightens and I swallow back the urge to throw up all over the device that is the only thing keeping me connected to the outside world at this moment.

Aleksei glances over at me. "Anything on the police scanners?"

I shake my head. "No."

He releases a heavy breath and checks the street again. "Wait...there's the SUV."

My heart finally starts beating again. I jump to my feet and race over to him to see for myself. "Thank God."

The vehicle pulls into the alley that runs behind the house, and I rush toward the back door and throw it open just as Valerian climbs from the passenger side.

His cool gaze locks with mine and warms instantly. He hurries up the steps, apparently unscathed, his men following closely behind, scanning the area for any threats.

He wraps his arm around me and drags me against him, clutching me to his warm, hard body as Dmitri fills in Aleksei on what happened.

Aleksei's gaze darts to Valerian. "You were working with the Albanians?"

Valerian stiffens and pulls away from me, keeping one hand possessively around me. "We'll discuss that later." He pulls his phone from his pocket and tosses it to him. "See if you can find out where the last call on that came from. It was an unknown number."

That should be easy for me, and I start to offer to do it, "I can track that down—"

"No." Valerian cuts me off instantly, shaking his head. "You and I need to talk privately first."

Without another word to his men, he leads me to the bedroom with a firm hand on my lower back. He closes and locks the door behind him, then grabs me and spins us to press me against the solid wood. His mouth hits mine before I can question him, and his demanding kiss robs me of any ability to speak.

He devours my mouth like a man who hasn't eaten in years, frantic hands working at his waist to free his hard cock and then shoving down my pants with an aggression that instantly makes heat pool at my core.

I manage to kick off my pants as he continues to kiss me with reckless abandon. Whatever happened at that meeting got him worked up, pent up, on the verge of snapping. He's always been so in control with me, taking what he wants—demanding it. But this is different. This is a wild animal unleashed, and I am helpless to save myself from being savaged by him.

Valerian lifts me easily, pinning me to the door, and I wrap my legs around his waist. Frantic fingers pull my thong to the side, and he shoves into me in one powerful thrust.

A gasp falls from my open mouth, and my eyes drift closed at the feeling of suddenly being full. Complete. Grounded and locked to this moment.

He pumps into me harshly. His strokes unrelenting. His rhythm as severe and ruthless as the man himself.

With the door behind me and Valerian's hard body keeping me pinned in place, I'm helpless against him. He takes what he needs and what I'm more than willing to give him.

He takes everything.

All of me.

Releasing whatever built up and was threatening to tear him to shreds while we were apart.

Each thrust grinds the base of his cock against my clit, sending flashes of heat and pulses of pleasure reverberating through me until I finally come on a strangled moan that he captures in his mouth in another searing kiss.

He pounds into me again and again. His fingers dig into my hips hard enough to bruise, but he's already marked me, already ensured everyone will know I'm his—including me.

His orgasm stiffens his body, his cock growing impossibly harder inside me for a brief moment before he comes and releases a long, low groan, pressing his face against my neck.

We stay like this for a moment, hung between the two worlds—one of chaos and death, the other of ignorance and bliss.

When he finally lifts his head and meets my gaze, a fog lays over the blue in his eyes.

I take his face in my palms and kiss him softly. "What happened at the meeting?"

He shakes his head as if to clear it and grits his teeth. "I told them the truth, and they likely would have torn me apart for it, but we were interrupted."

"Interrupted? By who?"

His grip tightens on me. "That's just it...I don't know. Whoever called me warned us all to get out, but I have no idea who it was."

"You didn't recognize the voice?"

Valerian shakes his head again. "No, and I can't figure out who the hell would *warn* us. Who would want to *protect* the five families from an outside threat? It doesn't make any sense."

I run my fingers through his dark, unruly hair. "No, it doesn't. But it sounds like you have a guardian angel out there somewhere."

He barks out a humorless laugh. "I'm more likely to have demons than angels, *kotyonok*."

"That's true of all of us, isn't it?"

For a moment, he remains still, considering my words before he nods. "Da, *kotyonok*. We all have demons and have committed the worst of sins. And it feels like we are all finally being punished for it."

I squeeze my cunt around his semi-hard cock still buried inside me. "But you're still alive. And as long as you breathe and your heart beats"—I press my hand against his chest, to where his heart thunders rapidly—"then there's hope that we will still succeed."

His dark brows rise. "You still want to move forward when we have so many unknowns?"

"Isn't now the time to strike? When my brothers and Kat and Galen are off their game? When they're looking elsewhere for threats?"

He narrows his gaze on me. "I told you—I won't hurt Galen. The Irish, Italians, and Russians have controlled this city long before the Albanians and your brothers move into it. That's the way it's always been, the way it should remain. We need to get back to the old ways, when the families respected each other. Galen understands that and will fall in line."

"You believe that even after your confession at the meeting?"

"He was angry, but when we reveal our true plan to him, I do believe he will be on board."

"Even if his sister doesn't forgive him for allowing Felipe to be removed?"

His grip tightens on me, and he leans in, feathering his lips across mine as his cock fully hardens inside me again. "The only person I care about is you, *kotyonok*. Galen can deal with the fallout in his own way. Once we've regained the city fully, he'll understand why we had to make sacrifices."

"What are you sacrificing, Valerian?"

He pulls his hips back and rams into me harshly. "My heart—to you."

The knock on the door behind me breaks the spell Valerian has cast over me, and he growls low. "What is it?"

"You need to get out here, *pakhan*. Now."

¡Mierda!

The concern in Dmitri's voice doesn't sound good.

I squeeze around his cock again in a last-ditch effort to get him to ignore whatever is happening on the other side of that door, and he issues a low groan as he pulls out. My body instantly weeps at the loss, and he releases my hips, letting me slide down the door until my feet hit the floor.

He nudges me to the side so I'm hidden and opens the door as he tucks his dick back into his pants and redoes his belt. "What the fuck is going on?"

"We have armed visitors outside."

"*Blyad!*" Valerian glances over at me as I pull my pants back on. "You stay here."

Like hell.

He steps out into the hall and hustles after Dmitri while I race to the nightstand to grab the gun Valerian keeps there. I pause at the door and wait for them to get far enough away not to notice I'm following, then slip out of the room and hustle to the end of the corridor. Reaching the end, I press my back against the wall so I can hear, but no one can see me from the living room.

Valerian's unwavering voice floats to me clearly. "Felipe, Andres, to what do I owe this unexpected, surprise visit?"

How the hell did they find us here?

"Let's drop the pretenses, Valerian." Felipe's voice comes cold enough to send a shiver down my spine. "You know why we're here."

He isn't playing. He came here for something and isn't leaving without it.

Heavy footsteps sound in the living room, and I peek around the corner to try to ascertain what's happening.

Felipe and Andres stand just inside the door with two men behind them, guns drawn, pointed squarely at Valerian, who stands with Dmitri, Aleksei, and two others, equally armed.

Valerian offers a cool smile. "I'm not sure what you mean, Felipe, unless you're here with your brother to enact some sort of revenge on me for what I did to Kat"—his gaze flicks over to Andres—"which was one hundred percent earned on her part, Rose. And you know it."

Andres issues a low snarl and looks ready to shoot Valerian, but Felipe nudges his arm down.

"If we wanted him dead immediately, we would have come in shooting instead of knocking, *hermano*." Felipe turns to Valerian. "We want our sister, and once we're sure she's safe and out of the way of any stray bullets, then I'll allow my brother to draw the blood he feels is warranted."

ELEVEN

SOFIA

This is so bad.

How does he know I'm here?

Valerian just grins at Felipe, unconcerned with the overt threat and promise in his words. "And my men will stop you."

A slow smile spreads across Felipe's face as he opens his hands wide. "Then, it seems we're at an impasse."

I step out from the hallway, my free hand tightening to a fist at my sides at the dick-swinging going on while I raise the gun and point it at Felipe and Andres with the other. "No, we aren't. *All* of you are going to put the weapons away."

All eyes turn toward me—a smug smirk on Valerian's lips and shocked looks from Felipe, Andres, and their men.

Felipe holsters his weapon and approaches me, arms open, while Andres' gaze darts from me to Valerian suspiciously. "Sofia, you're all right, *mija?*"

I hold up my free hand to stop his advance, centering the muzzle at his chest. "Don't come at me like that."

His dark brows fly up. "Like what, *mija?* I'm so happy to see you're okay and just wanted to embrace my sister."

Acid churns in my stomach, rising in my throat. For years, I managed to hide my disdain for them, to keep it buried deep below the sweet smiles and soft demeanor I maintained while growing *their* empire. I allowed them to believe I am someone I am not. But it's time for them to understand who and what I really am.

I square my shoulders and shake my head. "I don't want your embrace or your rescue. All I want is what I'm owed."

Andres finally lowers his weapon from Valerian and approaches. "What are you talking about, *mjia?*" He shakes his head, glancing over his shoulder at Valerian and the men still in the tense standoff. "What you're *owed?*"

That fact that they can stand in front of me, oblivious to the fact that they've been caught in their lies, that their betrayal has finally caught up to them, makes me bark out a laugh.

They exchange a look that makes me wonder if the twin-telepathy thing really does exist.

Felipe settles his hard gaze on me. "*Mi querido hermano,* I think we have misjudged this situation." He peers over his shoulder at Valerian. "Sofia is here of her own free will, and we've greatly underestimated her."

Andres' lips twist into a sneer. "Is this where you've been this entire time? Cutter's friend Preacher let us know that you'd recently resurfaced on the web, and he tracked you here. We assumed you were in trouble. That—"

"I'm not the one in trouble, *mis querido hermanos.*"

But damn Preacher for finding me.

I knew once I started truly deep diving and trying to help Valerian sort out this threat that there was a chance someone would find me. Covering my tracks from most people is easy. Hiding from a master hacker like Preacher isn't. He's even better than I remembered.

Valerian chuckles and makes his way to stand beside me, bringing with him both his men and those belonging to my brothers, who all still hold their weapons ready to fire should anyone cross that invisible line we all walk the edge of so dangerously.

He eyes my brothers, that smug smirk coming back and earning him a death glare from Andres. "You two have no idea what you're up against in your sister. My little *kotyonok* has claws."

I finally lower my gun and step into Valerian's hold, wrapping an arm around him possessively as he pulls me snugly to his side. "I know *everything, mis hermanos*. And not just what you *think* I do. I know it all, every bloody, backstabbing, merciless, unforgiveable detail, going *all* the way back." I let my gaze drift to their men standing behind him as a warning. "And if you want your secrets kept that way, I suggest you listen very carefully to what I have to say."

Any humor drains from Felipe's face, and Andres' knuckles whiten around the grip of his gun.

A warm smile at knowing I've won—at least temporarily—grows on my lips. "Valerian and I are together. In *every* sense of the word. We share everything. Now, he knows your dirty laundry, too. And unless you want me to spill every single bit of it to the world, all the evil deeds you've done and people you've fucked over, all the things that will land you in prison for the rest of your life or worse, you will give me what I have worked so hard for."

Andres shakes his head, still confused about what's really happening here. "What is it you want, Sofia?"

Felipe glances at him before smiling at me. "Don't you see, *hermano*? She wants the Blood Rose Cartel."

"What?" His eyes widen. "But she can't possibly—"

I step out from Valerian's arms, prepared to do battle with the men who were supposed to love me, care for me, and protect me from everything vile in this world instead of dragging me right into it. My hand holding the gun remains steady as I raise it to them again. "I can't possibly run the business? What the hell do you think I've been doing for the two of *you* for the last seven years?" I snort and shake my head. "You are both clueless. Blinded by your own ambitions and lies."

"Oh, I see you quite clearly, *mija*." Felipe takes a half-step toward me, hand up in surrender. "You've been planning this for some time, haven't you?"

The hint of respect in his words and eyes makes my chest tighten for a moment, but I breathe through it and nod. "Yes, but I was forced into action early when you came to Chicago. I knew you and Andres would end up at war, and I had hoped you might eliminate each other and make it easy for me to step in. But you never make anything easy, do you, *hermano*?"

He offers a genuine smile. "What fun would that be?"

"It would have made things simpler, far less work for my men and me."

Andres raises a brow. "Your *men*? What *men*?"

Valerian chuckles and steps up beside me. "Haven't you two heard? Your sister runs the Luna Cartel."

For some reason, hearing Valerian say it with such authority and pride makes all the hurt that has brought me to this moment worth it. All the tears, the hours and hours at my computer working, the feelings of betrayal at what they did to me.

My brothers stand speechless, unable to process his words, unable to believe I am capable of it.

"Don't look so shocked, *mis hermanos*. I've run ours since I was fourteen, too. And now, it's my time. I'm giving you *one* chance to step down, to go back to Colombia or wherever else you want to, to disappear with Kat and Rowan and never show your faces again, never interfere with *my* business again. It's time to retire."

Felipe keeps his hard eyes on me, and looking at him now, it's hard to imagine anyone ever believed he was the pious priest he portrayed himself as for so long. "Or *what, mija*?"

This man who shares my blood, who shares our *real* last name, who should have stood up for our family, is the one who killed the people who brought us into the world and handed me over to a cartel like I was some commodity to be traded. "Or..." I move the barrel of my gun up to point between his eyes. "I'll do what you did to our parents."

All the air sucks from the room in an instant, both of them going stock still and tense.

"When I said I know everything, I *mean*...I know *every*thing."

I look to Andres, the one born Felipe, the one destined to be a priest who ended up in prison and became that which he always hated so much. He, of the two, deserves the *least* of my ire. But he was still complicit in the plot to lie to me, to keep me insulated from the truth, to keep me locked away in an ivory tower where he believed I belonged.

"I would say I'm sorry it's come to this brothers, but that would be a lie. The Blood Rose Cartel no longer belongs to you. It will absorb the Luna Cartel and continue doing business under my *sole* leadership with my allies at my side."

Valerian inclines his head toward the door. "I suggest you both take her suggestion to heart and disappear. She's offering you mercy when I would not in her shoes."

His use of my safe word makes warmth bloom in my chest, a reminder that he's truly at my side in every sense, that he will defend me and what is mine with his men, his hand, his life, his blood.

Andres shakes his head, his mouth opening and closing a few times, as if he can't believe any of this is happening. "This isn't you, Sofia. This isn't who we raised you to be. You shouldn't be part of this world."

The laugh bubbles up my throat and bursts out into the room, making Andres and Felipe flinch. "It's a little late for that. You used my skills for the last almost decade to advance your goals. You pretended he wasn't involved"—I motion to Felipe with the gun—"and maintained the ruse. You lied about everything important, even who you *are,* while I kept the business running and handled *everything* behind the scenes. *You* two brought me into this world just as our dear parents did before they were so cruelly killed. Don't tell me I don't belong. That this isn't me. I am Sofia Rose. I *am* the Blood Rose Cartel."

Valerian motions toward the door. "Leave here. Leave Chicago. Take your women with you. Disappear now. If you don't, you know the consequences."

Andres snorts a sardonic laugh. "We're all dead anyway if we can't stop this group after everyone. You say it's the Albanians, but for all we know, it's you two."

His gaze darts accusingly between us, and Felipe nods his agreement.

"The timing of the 'confession' from Valerian at the meeting is quite suspect given this new revelation."

Valerian shakes his head. "It isn't us. What I said about my limited involvement with Berisha and Dragusha was true. But perhaps if you flee now, you can escape that threat and your sister's, too. Dodging two bullets." He grins. "Sounds like a wise course of action."

Felipe considers me for a moment, his lips tilting slightly into a sad smile. "I'm sorry it has come to this, Sofia. Truly..."

He takes a step forward, and Valerian shifts to put himself between us, but I nudge him to the side, too interested in what Felipe has to say to worry about an ulterior motive on his part.

"One last embrace, sister?" He opens his arms wide. "It's been far too long."

For a split second, I see him again as the priest in vestments, the man who used to play with me in the churchyard, who read to me and nurtured me all those years until Andres finally came and took me away.

But it was all a lie.

I shake my head. "No, brother. That time has passed. Now, go and hope you never see me again because next time, I won't hesitate to fire and rid this world of two more sinners."

TWELVE

VALERIAN

SOFIA EMERGES FROM THE BEDROOM, hair disheveled, eyes red and glossy, arching her back and stretching her arms above her head, but the grin on her face makes me push to my feet from the table where I've been eating with Dmitri and Aleksei.

It's the first time I've seen her smile since her brothers left almost two days ago.

"What's that look for?"

She approaches and steps into my embrace, glancing at Dmitri and Aleksei. "Because I finally found something that might actually help us."

Hope fills my chest. Sofia wouldn't say something like that lightly.

"What did you find?"

She slips out of my arms and goes into the half-renovated kitchen to pour herself a cup of coffee. "Well, you know how Valentina and Cutter said they had information that some of the older men who used to work for the Syla and Morina groups have suddenly resurfaced?"

I nod and lean against the counter. "Yes, and Roan confirmed that since he's been in Vlorë."

"And the group that's here now who have been attacking the five families traveled under names of Syla and Morina men who were killed years ago. Everyone thought it was just someone trying to set up Kat and make it appear she was behind it. But that wasn't the only reason."

"What other reason could there possibly be?" I glance back at Dmitri and Aleksei, who appear just as confused as I feel at this moment.

She takes a sip of her coffee. "I found some chatter that someone connected to the Morinas or Sylas is the one behind gathering the older members together, and it seems like the person is also behind the group we're dodging bullets from."

"Someone connected to the Morinas or Sylas?" I rub the back of my neck. "But there isn't anyone *left*. Michael was the last Syla, and Kat took care of him. As far as the Morinas go, we know Konstandin is still alive, but he made it clear that he's *out*."

Dmitri barks out a laugh. "That doesn't mean anything. He could be back."

Sofia takes another drink and shakes her head. "I don't think it's him. There hasn't been *any* mention of him or Rea in anything I've found. If he were back and building a new army to stage some sort of massive coup, I would have found *some* indication of it."

Aleksei throws up his hands. "Then who?"

Offering a shrug, Sofia downs the rest of her coffee. "That...I don't know yet, but I have somewhere we can start. A building was purchased *here* two months ago, using the name of Konstandin and Tarek Morina's aunt...who died in Philadelphia two years ago."

I raise a brow at her. "How do you know that?"

She pushes up on her tiptoes to kiss me on the cheek, leaning into me and ensuring her body brushes against my crotch. "Because I am *that* good. I ran every name I could find tied to *any* of the Albanian families."

Bylad!

Sofia *is* good.

I glance back at Dmitri and Aleksei. "Get as many men as you can. We're going now."

Dmitri pushes to his feet. "Should we call Cutter or Galen?"

Going in with more bodies and guns might be the safer move, but I'm likely on both of their hit lists right now. If this place really is where the rest of this crew and potentially whoever is behind this has been hiding out, then time is of the essence—and I can't risk having to watch my back for Cutter and Galen while I'm taking out the larger threat.

"No. We go alone."

Sofia squeezes her arms around my waist. "I'm going with you."

"Like fucking hell you are, *kotyonok*."

Her face hardens, and she leans up to put her lips to my ear. "I'm not going to embarrass you in front of your men, but you know there's no way I'm letting you stop me from coming along. There will be no more benching me."

Bylad!

Ever since her brothers walked out that door the other night, I've been anticipating this moment when Sofia fully takes on her role as the head of the Blood Rose Cartel and stops letting me control things. We are equals in every sense of the word, and she won't allow anyone to treat her otherwise—especially me.

I pull her firmly against me to ensure she can feel my hard cock and turn my head toward her, pressing a kiss to her cheek. "I like this side of you, *kotyonok*. You come, but I want you to listen to me to ensure you stay safe."

She may be a master at pulling strings from behind a computer screen, but she isn't trained the way my men are, and I can't risk anything happening to her.

Things are already so tenuous with her brothers. We're still waiting for them to make their move—either to leave Chicago as she commanded or to step up and fight. But Sofia has already set things in motion to cripple them—cutting off their access to their bank accounts, burning bridges with their contacts to establish her own direct ones, spreading the word in any way she can that she's now in control. If they do choose to fight, it will be against a much stronger enemy in Sofia than the one they saw here only a few nights ago.

Sofia brushes a hand over my cock and squeezes, then presses her lips to mine. "Okay, *sabrosito*. I'll give you that."

I peer over at Dmitri and Aleksei, who have the good sense to try to appear that they aren't trying to eavesdrop on us. "Move. Now."

They rush from the table, pulling out their phones to make the necessary calls to assemble the men we'll need for this mission. Sofia attempts to slip from my hold, but I drag her back and crush my lips to hers, a groan of frustration slipping from my mouth to hers at not being able to fuck her one more time before we go.

"We'll make this quick. Then, we'll go to the club and celebrate after it's finally done."

Her dark eyes flicker with a scalding heat that threatens to make me combust instantly. "I like that plan."

I finally release her, and we gather our weapons and hustle out to Dmitri and Aleksei waiting in one of the SUVs. We slide into the back, close our doors, and settle in for the ride to the other side of the city.

Dmitri turns from the driver's seat. "We have Grigory, Nikon, Kirill, Leonid, and Sasha meeting us at the address."

"Good. Let's go."

He backs out and hits the street away from the safehouse and toward what could end up being the final battle in this war we've been embroiled in against the unknown enemy for what feels like forever.

Sofia reaches across the bench seat and slips her hand into mine, squeezing it gently. "Why do you look so worried?"

I stare out at the city that became my home at such a young age. When I first arrived, it was so different from Russia, so much bigger, brighter, louder. It was everything my life there had not been. But it was also cold, sterile. Uncle Boris wasn't one to offer any sort of affection or comfort, and I was a small boy who missed his mother.

Now, this city has become like my new mother. Her arms have welcomed me, drawn me in and held me. She has given me a new life, watched me grow and step up to become the head of this family. She's seen my gluttony for the good things in life and the sins this way of living relies upon.

She's been witness to it all.

And now, we're so close to the end. The ultimate goal is within reach—a city in which Sofia and I can rule our combined territory in peace without worry about intrusion from Valentina, who has never had aspirations for expanding her control.

It may take a bit to smooth things over with Galen—but it *will* happen. He will see the light at the end of the tunnel. A Chicago controlled by those who are smart enough not to try to take the whole damn thing by keeping our weapons trained solely on true enemies, not each other.

I squeeze her hand back and turn to look at her. "I was just thinking that tonight could be the end of one chapter and the beginning of another."

"Not the end of our story, though."

"Definitely not."

She leans across the small space between us and kisses me softly. "Good, because I like where it's going."

"Me too, *kotyonok.*"

Aleksei turns from the passenger seat and clears his throat. "Sorry to interrupt, *pakhan*, but we've arrived."

Sofia and I both pull away and turn our focus to the building rising near the end of the street in front of the vehicle. Red brick and four stories, it looks like it's been here for a hundred years—a survivor of so much change standing tall—just like we will be at end of all of this.

We pull to the curb just down the street and climb from the SUV into the chilly winter Chicago air. Dark clouds fill the night sky above, a storm threatening to dump massive amounts of snow on us.

Another dark SUV pulls up behind ours, and the rest of my men hustle from it, all armed to the teeth and prepared for battle. Sofia's gaze locks on me for a moment, and I take a deep breath of the cold air and nod.

Our group advances on the building in the dark, the poorly lit street offering plenty of shadows to keep to in an effort to avoid detection should anyone be watching the exterior. All remains quiet, though, and with Sofia at my back and Aleksei and Grigory behind her, I can concentrate on the uneasy feeling settling over me instead of worrying about her safety.

Something's wrong.

Dmitri leads us to the side of the building to a door already knocked off its hinges. He pauses just outside it and glances back at me, brows raised.

My gut tells me to retreat and regroup to get more information, but if they're still here, this might be our only chance at finding whoever is behind the attacks.

I incline my head for him to go, and our group moves through the jamb and into the main floor of what appears to be an old retail space—the cases now void of glass and covered in dust and cobwebs.

Each step we advance farther raises the hairs on the back of my neck. Muffled voices float to us from deeper in the building—rushed, angry, the kind we should be moving *away* from, not toward.

But there isn't any way we can turn back now.

Dmitri moves toward the back of the building, and just as he's about to step into what appears to be a storage area, I recognize one of the voices.

Hell...

I reach out to grab his shoulder and stop him, but it's too late. He walks into the room, and I have no choice but to follow.

THIRTEEN

SOFIA

VALERIAN FREEZES in front of me, coming to an abrupt halt. "What the hell is going on?"

The fear in his voice stops me in my tracks just inside a large room with a high ceiling and suspended catwalk that must have once been used to store whatever was sold in this place before it fell into disrepair.

I step to the side of his massive frame to see around him and almost choke on my own breath. *¡Mierda!*

Valentina, Cutter, and his armed men face down Galen and his men to one side, with Felipe, Andres, Kat, Genti, and a few of her men at the other. Our group occupies the fourth corner of this deadly stand-off.

There's only one explanation for why everyone would be in the same place at once: we've walked into some sort of trap intended to ensnare all of us.

All eyes turn our way, with several guns now trained on us while others remain pointed at various other enemies.

Cutter mutters something unintelligible under his breath. "Now, how the fuck did *you* end up here?"

Valerian scans the faces of everyone in the room slowly before focusing his attention on Valentina's guard dog. "We found information concerning the attack squad that led us here..."

Valentina glances at the other heads of families. "So did we."

Felipe nods. "We received information from one of Kat's sources."

Galen releases a litany of what must be curses in Irish. "As did I."

Valerian advances another few steps from me. "It seems someone wanted all of us in one room and knew we wouldn't voluntarily do it. I fear we just made ourselves easy targets for our common unknown enemy."

"You would be *correct*, Mr. Kamenev."

The new accented voice draws everyone's attention toward a door on the opposite side of the room, and a petite woman enters through it with three men, and another group of armed assailants comes from behind us, pushing the rest of our men inside.

We're surrounded now, and they have all the exits I can see blocked. It's possible we could get off a few shots and take out some of these guys—and the woman, whoever she is—but many of us would die in the storm of bullets.

There isn't any way this ends without blood splattered on these old brick walls.

Slowly, something that should have been obvious dawns on me, and I lean forward slightly toward Valerian. "Today is Valentine's Day."

He peers over his shoulder at me with a brow raised. "Is now really the time to complain about me not getting back to Tiffany's for your fucking gift?"

"No, *idiota*." I motion to the room. "Does this scenario remind you of anything?"

It takes a second before his eyes widen, then he winces and turns back to the mystery woman who is apparently behind all the havoc occurring recently. Valerian and Cutter managed to take out several men at the warehouse where they took me, but we all knew there were more, and it seems they've found us—and hold ill intent.

The St. Valentine's Day Massacre...

We should have seen it coming—the building tension and violence, the date, how we *suddenly* located the information we needed—but all of us were too interested in ending the threat to see the true one.

A beautiful woman who could have walked past any of us on the street at any time and none of us would have been the wiser. She steps farther into the room, an icy grin on her crimson-red lips, long, shiny dark hair cascading over her shoulders. Her golden eyes meet those of everyone in the room and finally land on me. Her lips twitch into an almost genuine smile for a split second before her impassive mask returns.

She spreads her hands out wide. "I'm so glad everyone could join me. You'll all drop your weapons now."

Everyone examines the others in the room, trying to gauge if anyone is actually going to follow through on her orders, but no one moves to lower their guns and give up the only defense we have.

"*Tsk. Tsk.*" She shakes her head. "I warned you."

The gunfire erupts before anyone can react, and almost simultaneously, the men with Cutter and Valentina drop along with those behind Kat, except Genti. Dmitri, Aleksei, and the others with us fall at my back and jerk away from the spray of blood in horror.

What the fuck?

Her men have very good aim and knew who their targets were. They could have taken out everyone in an instant, but they chose their victims to leave the heads of the families untouched—at least for now.

It was a clear show of strength, and slowly, all of us squat to lower our weapons onto the cracked concrete beneath us. We're completely exposed now. It would only take one look or word from her to have her men slaughter all of us.

Who the hell is she?

After all this time, I thought I knew everyone involved in this world, anyone who might stir up trouble for us. This woman does look vaguely familiar, and the accent in her voice suggests the right area of the world to have been gathering this crew together, but my brain can't connect the dots fast enough.

"Who the fuck are you?" Cutter's voice finally rings out in the open space, asking the question we've all been wanting to since she appeared. "The least you could do is give us an introduction, unless one of you recognizes her?"

No one speaks up, and the woman offers a mirthless chuckle and clasps her hands together in front of her long black peacoat.

"That's an interesting question—who are you?" An almost wistful sigh slips from her mouth. "Once, I was a young girl who lived oblivious to the world you all occupy. I had no idea it was in my blood or that it would end up being the thing that destroyed everything I love."

Pain weighs heavy in her final words, and she offers a tight smile while she seems to consider what she will say next. She paces forward slightly, making sure to keep close to her men and away from the reach of any of us.

"None of you would know me. I was a pawn in this game long before any of you came in as players. My father used me to infiltrate his enemy, gave me away easily with his sights set on his ultimate goal. And he succeeded. He got the power he wanted—at my expense. By the time I was finally free, I was nothing but a shell of the girl I had been when she sent me off to a man five times my age."

Her words spark a memory.

A name flickers somewhere deep in the recesses of my mind—one that I've seen during my research on the families.

It's right there, just out of reach.

She chuckles again and releases a heavy sigh. "Unlike you all, I tried to escape my name. As soon as I was free of my husband, I fled, became someone else, took a new name, built a new life with a wonderful man, and had children who became my entire world." Tears shimmer in her eyes, but she blinks them away, anger tightening her jaw. "Until they were taken from me by this one."

Oh no...

My gut twists, and a newspaper article I located a few days ago flashes before my eyes.

A family slaughtered in Albania.

The wife missing—presumed taken by the assailants.

No suspects identified but the authorities believed it to be mob related—though there was no apparent connection to organized crime for the couple and their children living in the small, remote village.

Who the hell is she?

Valerian shakes his head. "I don't know who the hell you are, lady, but I don't harm innocent people, and certainly not children, so whatever it is you think—"

"Lies!" The woman *roars* the word so loud that it echoes around us like a wild animal crying out in pain. She points a finger directly at Valerian. "You worked with Dragusha and Berisha. You helped them grow in their power. *You* have my children's blood on your hands as much as the men they sent to destroy my life."

Kat steps forward, her face twisting viciously. "*Valerian* was your target all along? Why drag any of us into this? We would have gladly handed him over to you to end these attacks."

Our captor whirls to face Kat, fury flashing in her golden eyes. "Don't pretend you're innocent, Brynn Katherine Gashi. You prey on women seeking to flee bad situations by convincing them to sell their bodies to sleazy men. You are the one who got Kreshnik Dragusha and Afrim Berisha all riled up by taking their supply. *You're* the one who sent them after me."

Kat shakes her head. "Why would they come after you?"

A man steps out onto a catwalk above us, half-hidden in the shadows created by the sparse bulbs hanging high overhead, his footsteps heavy on the old metal. "Because they wanted *me* and thought they could use her to get me to come out of hiding."

¡Mierda!

Even in the dim lighting, I'd recognize that face anywhere and that of the woman who follows him out.

Konstandin Morina...

And Rea Dragusha...

FOURTEEN

SOFIA

ALL EYES FOLLOW them as they slowly make their way across the rickety metal structure and down a set of stairs in the corner.

Konstandin reaches the concrete floor and approaches the woman with a not-unkind, sad smile. "*Motra*, it's good to see you after all the time, though I wish it were under different circumstances."

Valerian's gaze darts from them to me. "Sister?"

I nod as the name finally clicks in my head, the rush of information I've seen on the Albanian families over the years racing in my brain. "The Morinas had a sister. Agron, I think. Her father married her to Michael and Lorenc Syla's grandfather when she was a teenager."

His face hardens—but I can't tell whether it's because of his anger over our current situation or the one she was placed in so young.

Both would warrant it.

I take a cautious step closer to him, then another, 'til we're standing side by side, watching the unhappy reunion in front of us. Konstandin's clear affection for her radiates in his gaze, but hers seems clouded by the rage she must feel to have done all this in the first place.

Agron offers Konstandin a tight smile. "I haven't been Agron for a long time. I prefer Adelina."

He nods slowly. "I know, but tonight it appears Agron is here with us. Adelina was a peaceful woman who lived a quiet life. That is none of these things." His dark eyes with hints of gold scan everyone before settling back on her. "You don't want to do this, *motra*."

Behind Konstandin, Cutter surreptitiously slides Valentina to the side of him, closer to the exit and away from the nearest man with a gun. If he thinks he's getting her out of here without anyone noticing, he's insane.

Agron clenches her fists at her sides, her anger heating her cheeks pink even in the cold Chicago air permeating the old building. "Yes, I do. These people"—she swings an arm out—"this *world*. It destroyed everything. It destroyed *me*."

Konstandin sighs and shakes his head. "This won't solve anything. Rea and I have been trying to catch up with you for weeks to tell you just that."

Rea moves closer to Agron tentatively, her blazing-red hair pulled back from her face set with determination. "He's right. You and I never got to meet, but I've been where you were. My father sold me to your brother in a greedy bid to build his empire with Tarek's support. I was used and abused and only escaped because of Konstandin. We thought we were free, but no one is ever really free of this life. You can't outrun the sins you commit, and trying to only leads to a lot more death and destruction."

Her green eyes shift to Kat, who stands stock still, chest heaving with her barely restrained fury.

It's common knowledge that Konstandin killed Aleksander Gashi and left Kat a widow, but the way the two women are looking at each other, it appears there may be more to the story than we all know.

Rea takes a small step toward Kat, holding up her hands in surrender, and Andres wraps his arm around Kat—either to hold her back or offer her comfort.

The beautiful redhead motions toward Konstandin. "Konstandin killed Saban for assisting

Tarek, and *I* killed Aleksander to protect our son from his wrath over his brother's death. That set Kat down her path, which set off a series of events that affected *all* of us and brought us all here today."

Seeing everyone all together now, knowing the history the families have together, how one bad deed has spawned another and another, it's laid out before me like a massive chess board. Only instead of just two players, there are half a dozen—each making moves that affect another. Each digging their own graves even deeper by creating more and more enemies and committing more and more unforgivable sins.

I don't see any way for this to end well—for any of us.

Konstandin approaches Kat and inclines his head toward her. "Kat and I attempted to end this. We came to a truce to protect our children, to try to keep them from living the kind of anguish you're going through now, Agron. But even then, I got pulled back into it because Rea's father would never let what I did to Tarek, did with his daughter, go unpunished."

After all these years, Rea's father just couldn't let it go. He couldn't forgive what Rea and Konstandin did for love, and instead, he was willing to destroy Agron and her family to find the man he held responsible.

That's a heavy weight for Konstandin to bear, one I wouldn't wish on anyone—even one of my enemies in this room.

Felipe moves away from one of the armed men and closer to Agron. "When the Lord said, 'An eye for an eye and a tooth for a tooth,' it was not to encourage or justify vengeance but rather to limit it."

Galen laughs, the first interjection he's made since Agron's arrival. "That's rich, coming from you, *Father* Felipe."

I can't fight my own smirk at Galen's response because it's true. The irony of my brother quoting the Bible about vengeance isn't lost on anyone.

Perhaps Galen isn't so bad after all.

If we survive this and Valerian can get him to forgive me for what I did to him through the Luna Cartel, there may be room for him in our new Chicago.

But right now, that's a very big *if.*

Konstandin ignores Felipe and Galen's comments, turns to his sister, and grasps her shoulders. "You can't do this and walk away, Agron. There will always be *someone* else to step up. *Someone* who will come after you for what you've done. Your past will always be there, no matter how hard you try to forget it or how much time passes. Killing them won't bring your husband and children back. All it will do is stain your hands with blood you'll never be able to clean from them that will taint everything you touch."

Tears stream down her face now, her lips quivering—the façade of strength she wore when she entered crumbling in the arms of her brother. "I have to do *something. Someone* has to pay for what they did to me."

Konstandin presses a delicate kiss to her forehead. "You've already managed to kill the men responsible. Rea's father and his partner are dead. The rest"—he scans us—"the rest is in God's hands. It is not for you to judge them for their sins. Let Him do it whenever their day comes."

His words make my chest tighten, and I swallow through the lump in my throat, surveying all the people in the room, each now facing the reality of what their actions have caused—even indirectly—though, I doubt many care.

Each of us has plans, goals, desires, wants, and needs, and no one is afraid to remove any obstacles to those.

It's made for a very violent few years in this city.

Slowly, Rea steps up and takes Konstandin's place, embracing Agron while he turns to look us each in the eye.

"I have no quarrel with any of you. I tried to stop all this when I called and warned Valerian that your last meeting was about to have visitors. What's done is done. And these men"—he makes eye contact with each of the men Agron brought with her—"will *not* hurt you because they know if they do, they will have to answer to *me*."

The chilling effect of his words rings clear as the men slowly lower their weapons. They may have assisted Agron out of some loyalty to the Morinas or because they knew her when she was married to the elder Syla, but they know Konstandin's reputation and won't dare do anything to cross the deadly man.

Wise choice on their part.

But everyone here still has beef with someone else in the sinister circle.

Me with my brothers and Kat.

Galen with Valerian for betraying him by working with the Albanians and Kat for her assault on his business—and me if he finds out I'm behind Luna.

Valentina and Cutter with Valerian for him stabbing them in the back to take me.

Kat with basically everyone, dragging Andres along with her in her hate and desire to control everything.

The only ones who don't are Konstandin and Rea. They've been battered and bruised, lost everything more than once, had their lives destroyed by the sins of those around this room and those outside it, too, yet they both stand here as the voice of reason, begging Agron to see it.

Everyone here has blood on their hands, has committed sins we will have to pay for eventually; I don't want that to be today. Konstandin and Rea may have stopped his sister for the time being, but the five families have been at each other's throats since the day the Blood Rose Cartel moved into Chicago.

This will never stop unless someone does something about it.

FIFTEEN

SOFIA

OUR BUSINESSES WILL ONLY SURVIVE if we respect each other's territories and admit that no one family will ever be powerful enough to control all of Chicago.

We have to co-exist as peacefully as possible, or it's mutually assured destruction. That fact has been proven over and over again by everyone in this room.

I move to step around Valerian to argue just that, but he wraps a strong arm around me and drags me back against his hard body, dropping his mouth to my ear from behind me.

"I don't know where you think you're going, *kotyonok*, but you're not leaving my side."

Twisting my head, I look up at him. "Someone has to do something, say something. Otherwise, this will keep happening even if Konstandin has stopped Agron."

Valerian considers me for a moment. "You're wise beyond your years, *kotyonok*, but I should do the talking."

I open my mouth to argue with him, but he leans down again and tightens his grip on me.

"I wouldn't argue with me, not unless you want to pay for it later."

A zing of anticipation shoots through me despite the tense surroundings, but our debate gets interrupted by Valentina finally taking a half-step away from Cutter in her heels.

Her amber eyes assess everyone carefully. "It appears our mutual enemy has been handled, but that still leaves many of us at a stalemate. We must decide the future of this city if we hope to have anything left of it. Despite the many wrongs done to me, I have tried to remain neutral in the squabbles of others, and I am willing to move forward with a clean slate to avoid any more bloodshed."

Her eyes lock on Valerian. At least Valentina is thinking about it, too, and realizes we're all screwed if we keep going like this. She will find a way to make him pay for what he did to her, but it won't be today and it won't be anything we can anticipate. Cutter's smug grin from behind her confirms that.

Felipe turns to her. "And what do you suggest, Ms. Marconi? I don't think any of us are willing to back down from our businesses—"

I pull free of Valerian's hold and approach Felipe. "You don't have a choice, *hermano*. I made myself clear the other night. You and Andres are no longer in control of the Blood Rose Cartel, and you need to leave Chicago." I let my gaze drift over to Kat. "And take her with you."

Galen's eyes widen as he takes in the scene, then his gaze flicks to Valerian. "What the *fuck* is going on?"

Valerian inclines his head toward his friend. "I apologize for not properly introducing you. This is Sofia, Felipe and Andres' sister. She runs the Luna Cartel and is the new head of the Blood Rose Cartel."

Galen's scarred face twists in rage as he lungs toward me, but Valerian stops him from advancing with a strong hand at his chest.

"I understand your anger, *comrade*. But I assure you, we will make amends once this is over."

The green in Galen's eyes darkens as he glares at me, lips curled into a sneer. He points a finger at me. "You and I will have a talk after this, Sofia Rose."

His veiled threat sends a shiver down my spine, but I'm confident Valerian and I can iron things out with him in the future. Once he sees our plan—to return Chicago to what it once was—he won't be able to resist. But in order to achieve that, we need to deal with my brothers and Kat. And it's out there now—my challenge to them, done in front of the other families.

This is the kind of insult Felipe can't let go unanswered, but a smile spreads across his face and he issues a low chuckle. "*Mija*, it is so hard to be angry with you when I'm so full of pride."

Andres approaches, his face impassive despite the fact that I'm in the middle of tearing them down. "We've discussed the situation, and Felipe, Kat, and I have decided it is best for us to leave Chicago."

A rumbling of excited chatter from the room fills my ears as I process his words. "You'll go?"

Felipe nods. "Chicago has become..."—his eyes flicker across everyone— "crowded. We feel there are other places more suitable for us to expand our business. Valentina, Galen, and Valerian's groups have a long history here and will remain respected. We'll leave the *Chicago* branch of the Blood Rose Cartel to Sofia and allow her to do with it what she will."

It isn't what I asked for—what I demanded, really. They aren't backing down on the control of the business, just offering to share it with me, but it still feels like a win. When it came down to it, I'm not confident I could have ordered my men to take them out, let alone pulled the trigger myself.

Despite everything they've done, there were good times, good feelings. They did what they thought was best for me—even if it was wrong.

Konstandin nods. "I'm happy to see you reached an amicable agreement on this. Blood spilled between blood is the greatest of sins."

He would know.

Kat's heels click as she approaches us, her eyes narrowed on me in accusation. "But before we go and leave Chicago to you, I need to know something."

This can't be good.

I prepare myself for whatever she might want—or a shot from the gun she undoubtedly has concealed in her purse. "What?"

"Were you the one who took down my plane and almost killed me and Andres?"

I can't stop the grin spreading across my face as I shake my head. "I wish I could take credit for that. Truth be told, I considered it, but I didn't have enough time to prepare and get things lined up. It wasn't me."

Kat turns to Cutter. "You?"

He smirks and shakes his head. "I wish, but no."

Her accusatory gaze hits Valerian and Galen. "You two?"

They both shake their heads, and she finally settles on Agron, dark brows raised.

"Was it you, then?"

Agron pulls out of Rea's arms and swipes at her tears, her golden eyes darting to Genti where Kat just stood beside him.

¡Dios mío!

If Genti has been working with Agron, it would certainly explain how she's been able to keep her crew on the five families so easily, finding them at each

Kat catches the look between them, and her jaw hardens as she approaches her most loyal man, the one who has always been at her side since she took over from Syla. "Were you *helping* her this whole time?"

Genti's hands fist at his sides, his lips curling into a snarl. "I was loyal to Michael, and you killed him like he was a cockroach under your shoe. Then, I devoted myself to *you*, only to have you throw yourself into *his* arms." He points at Andres in disgust. "I helped her because I could never have what I wanted—*you!* And if I couldn't have you, at least I could have your territory in Chicago once you were six feet under with Rose."

He's so busy raging at his boss that he doesn't even notice her reach into her purse and pull out her gun.

Everyone remains silent, watching to see what she will do with the man who has stood by her side since the day she sought her revenge against Michael Syla for her husband's death.

Just as Valerian and I have made it clear where we stand, so has Valentina. Galen is a wild card, but one I hope Valerian can manage. The only thing left standing in the way of me taking what I deserve and ruling it with Valerian at my side is for Kat to make her final statement.

This will be her final act as the head of the Albanian *fis* here in Chicago before she hightails it out of town with her son and my brothers. Knowing Kat, it will be one that leaves an impression.

She raises it with a steady hand and points it at his face. "I trusted you, Genti—with my business, my life, with my son's life. You've committed the ultimate betrayal. These people...everything I've done to them and them to me was just business. None of it was personal. But what you've done, it is unthinkable. The ultimate knife in the back. The greatest of sins. And you know what they say...sin kills."

Bang.

I HOPE YOU ENJOYED THE DEADLIEST SIN SERIES. KEEP READING FOR A NOTE FROM GWYN about the series, and enjoy the Inland Seas Series which features some familiar characters and overlaps the Deadliest Sin Series.

The series is complete and available now, starting with *Squall Line*!

SQUALL LINE: books2read.com/SquallLine

A NOTE FROM THE AUTHOR

Hello, Readers!

I have thoroughly enjoyed writing the Deadliest Sin Series over the last few years. The five families are near and dear to my heart. Finally saying goodbye to them is hard, but I am comforted by knowing things will go on in Chicago, with Valentina and Cutter, Sofia and Valerian, and Galen at the heads of their families while Kat, Rose, and Felipe start a new adventure in another city that will soon be in their tight grasps.

These characters live so deeply in my brain that I have several other series that overlap this one where familiar faces appear - The Inland Seas Series and The Scarred Heroes Series. They are both complete and available now!

Start the Inland Seas Series here with Squall Line —> books2read.com/SquallLine

Start the Scarred Heroes Series here with Dead Reckoning —> books2read.com/DeadReckoningGM

And watch for more appearances from the Deadliest Sin families in future books! Thank you for reading!

Gwyn

ABOUT GWYN MCNAMEE

Gwyn McNamee is an attorney, writer, wife, and mother (to one human baby and two fur babies). Originally from the Midwest, Gwyn relocated to her husband's home town of Las Vegas in 2015 and is enjoying her respite from the cold and snow. Gwyn has been writing down her crazy stories and ideas for years and finally decided to share them with the world. She loves to write stories with a bit of suspense and action mingled with romance and heat.

When she isn't either writing or voraciously devouring any books she can get her hands on, Gwyn is busy adding to her tattoo collection, golfing, and stirring up trouble with her perfect mix of sweetness and sarcasm (usually while wearing heels). Gwyn loves to hear from her readers. Here is where you can find her:

Website: http://www.gwynmcnamee.com/
Facebook: https://www.facebook.com/AuthorGwynMcNamee/
FB Reader Group: https://www.facebook.com/groups/1667380963540655/
Newsletter: www.gwynmcnamee.com/newsletter
Tiktok: https://www.tiktok.com/@authorgwynmcnamee
Instagram: https://www.instagram.com/gwynmcnamee
Bookbub: https://www.bookbub.com/authors/gwynmcnamee

Printed in the USA
CPSIA information can be obtained
at www.ICGtesting.com
CBHW051110091023
1278CB00003B/6